HENRY JAMES

NOVELS
1903-1911

THE AMBASSADORS

THE GOLDEN BOWL

THE OUTCRY

I0669511

HERITAGE ILLUSTRATED
PUBLISHING

All text and images in this edition are in the public domain
First published by Heritage Illustrated Publishing © 2014

Contents

The Ambassadors

PREFACE

Nothing is more easy than to state the subject of "The Ambassadors," which first appeared in twelve numbers of *The North American Review* (1903) and was published as a whole the same year. The situation involved is gathered up betimes, that is in the second chapter of Book Fifth, for the reader's benefit, into as few words as possible—planted or "sunk," stiffly and saliently, in the centre of the current, almost perhaps to the obstruction of traffic. Never can a composition of this sort have sprung straighter from a dropped grain of suggestion, and never can that grain, developed, overgrown and smothered, have yet lurked more in the mass as an independent particle. The whole case, in fine, is in Lambert Strether's irrepressible outbreak to little Bilham on the Sunday afternoon in Gloriani's garden, the candour with which he yields, for his young friend's enlightenment, to the charming admonition of that crisis. The idea of the tale resides indeed in the very fact that an hour of such unprecedented ease should have been felt by him AS a crisis, and he is at pains to express it for us as neatly as we could desire. The remarks to which he thus gives utterance contain the essence of "The Ambassadors," his fingers close, before he has done, round the stem of the full-blown flower; which, after that fashion, he continues officiously to present to us. "Live all you can; it's a mistake not to. It doesn't so much matter what you do in particular so long as you have your life. If you haven't had that what HAVE you had? I'm too old—too old at any rate for what I see. What one loses one loses; make no mistake about that. Still, we have the illusion of freedom; therefore don't, like me to-day, be without the memory of that illusion. I was either, at the right time, too stupid or too intelligent to have it, and now I'm a case of reaction against the mistake. Do what you like so long as you don't make it. For it WAS a mistake. Live, live!" Such is the gist of Strether's appeal to the impressed youth, whom he likes and whom he desires to befriend; the word "mistake" occurs several times, it will be seen, in the course of his remarks—which gives the measure of the signal warning he feels attached to his case. He has accordingly missed too much, though perhaps after all constitutionally qualified for a better part, and he wakes up to it in conditions that press the spring of a terrible question. WOULD there yet perhaps be time for reparation?—reparation, that is, for the injury done his character; for the affront, he is quite ready to say, so stupidly put upon it and in which he has even himself had so clumsy a hand? The answer to which is that he now at all events SEES; so that the business of my tale and the march of my action, not to say the precious moral of everything, is just my demonstration of this process of vision.

Nothing can exceed the closeness with which the whole fits again into its germ. That had been given me bodily, as usual, by the spoken word, for I was to take the image over exactly as I happened to have met it. A friend had repeated to me, with great appreciation, a thing or two said to him by a man of distinction, much his senior, and to which a sense akin to that of Strether's melancholy eloquence might be imputed—said as chance would have, and so easily might, in Paris, and in a charming old garden attached to a house of art, and on a Sunday afternoon of summer, many persons of great interest being present. The observation there listened to and gathered up had contained part of the "note" that I was to recognise on the spot as to my purpose—had contained in fact the greater part; the rest was in the place and the time and the scene they sketched: these constituents clustered and combined to give me further support; to give me what I may call the note absolute. There it stands, accordingly, full in the tideway; driven in, with hard taps, like some strong stake for the noose of a cable, the swirl of the current roundabout it. What amplified the hint to more than the bulk of hints in general was the gift with it of the old Paris garden, for in that token were sealed up values infinitely precious. There was of course the seal to break and each item of the packet to count over and handle and estimate; but somehow, in the light of the hint, all the elements of a situation of the sort most to my taste were there. I could even remember no occasion on which, so confronted, I had found it of a livelier interest to take stock, in this fashion, of suggested wealth. For I think, verily, that there are degrees of merit in subjects—in spite of the fact that to treat even one of the most ambiguous with due decency we must for the time, for the feverish and prejudiced hour, at least figure its merit and its dignity as POSSIBLY absolute. What it comes to, doubtless, is that even among the supremely good—since with such alone is it one's theory of one's honour to be concerned—there is an ideal BEAUTY of goodness the invoked action of which is to raise the artistic faith to its maximum. Then truly, I hold, one's theme may be said to shine, and that of "The Ambassadors," I confess, wore this glow for me from beginning to end. Fortunately thus I am able to estimate this as, frankly, quite the best, "all round," of all my productions; any failure of that justification would have made such an extreme of complacency publicly fatuous.

I recall then in this connexion no moment of subjective intermittence, never one of those alarms as for a suspected hollow beneath one's feet, a felt ingratitude in the scheme adopted, under which confidence fails and opportunity seems but to mock. If the motive of "The Wings of the Dove," as I have noted, was to worry me at moments by a sealing-up of its face—though without prejudice to its again, of a sudden, fairly grimacing with expression—so in this other business I had absolute conviction and constant clearness to deal with; it had been a frank proposition, the whole bunch of data, installed on my premises like a monotony of fine weather. (The order of composition, in these things, I may mention, was reversed by the order of publication; the earlier written of the two books having appeared as the later.) Even under the weight of my hero's years I could feel my postulate firm; even under the strain of the difference between those of Madame de Vionnet and those of Chad Newsome, a difference liable to be denounced as shocking, I could still feel it serene. Nothing resisted, nothing betrayed, I seem to make out, in this full and sound sense of the matter; it shed from any side I could turn it to the same golden glow. I rejoiced in the promise of a hero so mature, who would give me thereby the more to bite into—since it's only into thickened motive and accumulated character, I think, that the painter of life bites more than a little. My poor friend should have accumulated character, certainly; or rather would be quite naturally and handsomely possessed of it, in the sense that he would have, and would always have felt he had, imagination galore, and that this yet wouldn't have wrecked him. It was immeasurable, the opportunity to "do" a man of imagination, for if THERE mightn't be a chance to "bite," where in the world might it be? This personage of course, so enriched, wouldn't give me, for his type, imagination in PREDOMINANCE or as his prime faculty, nor should I, in view of other matters, have found that convenient. So particular a luxury—some occasion, that is, for study of the high gift in SUPREME command of a case or of a career—would still doubtless come on the day I should be ready to pay for it; and till then might, as from far back, remain hung up well in view and just out of reach. The comparative case meanwhile would serve—it was only on the minor scale that I had treated myself even to comparative cases.

I was to hasten to add however that, happy stopgaps as the minor scale had thus yielded, the instance in hand should enjoy the advantage of the full range of the major; since most immediately to the point was the question of that SUPPLEMENT of situation logically involved in our gentleman's impulse to deliver himself in the Paris garden on the Sunday afternoon—or if not involved by strict logic then all ideally and enchantingly implied in it. (I say "ideally," because I need scarce mention that for development, for expression of its maximum, my glimmering story was, at the earliest stage, to have nipped the thread of connexion with the possibilities of the actual reported speaker. HE remains but the happiest of accidents; his actualities, all too definite, precluded any range of possibilities; it had only been his charming office to project upon that wide field of the artist's vision—which hangs there ever in place like the white sheet suspended for the figures of a child's magic-lantern—a more fantastic and more moveable shadow.) No privilege of the teller of tales and the handler of puppets is more delightful, or has more of the suspense and the thrill of a game of difficulty breathlessly played, than just this business of looking for the unseen and the occult, in a scheme half-grasped, by the light or, so to speak, by the clinging scent, of the gage already in hand. No dreadful old pursuit of the hidden slave with bloodhounds and the rag of association can ever, for "excitement," I judge, have bettered it at its best. For the dramatist always, by the very law of his genius, believes not only in a possible right issue from the rightly-conceived tight place; he does much more than this—he believes, irresistibly, in the necessary, the precious "tightness" of the place (whatever the issue) on the strength of any respectable hint. It being thus the respectable hint that I had with such avidity picked up, what would be the story to which it would most inevitably form the centre? It is part of the charm attendant on such questions that the "story," with the omens true, as I say, puts on from this stage the authenticity of concrete existence. It then is, essentially—it begins to be, though it may more or less obscurely lurk, so that the point is not in the least what to make of it, but only, very delightfully and very damnably, where to put one's hand on it.

In which truth resides surely much of the interest of that admirable mixture for salutary application which we know as art. Art deals with what we see, it must first contribute full-handed that ingredient; it plucks its material, otherwise expressed, in the garden of life—which material elsewhere grown is stale and uneatable. But it has no sooner done this than it has to take account of a PROCESS—from which only when it's the basest of the servants of man, incurring ignominious dismissal with no "character," does it, and whether under some muddled pretext of morality or on any other, pusillanimously edge away. The process, that of the expression, the literal squeezing-out, of value is another affair— with which the happy luck of mere finding has little to do. The joys of finding, at this stage, are pretty well over; that quest of the subject as a whole by "matching," as the ladies say at the shops, the big piece with the snippet, having ended, we assume, with a capture. The subject is found, and if the problem is then transferred to the ground of what to do with it the field opens out for any amount of doing. This is precisely the infusion that, as I submit, completes the strong mixture. It is on the other hand that the part of the business that can least be likened to the chase with horn and hound. It's all a sedentary part—involves as much ciphering, of sorts, as would merit the highest salary paid to a chief accountant. Not, however, that the chief accountant hasn't HIS gleams of bliss; for the felicity, or at least the equilibrium of the artist's state dwells less, surely, in the further delightful complications he can smuggle in than in those he succeeds in keeping out. He sows his seed at the risk of too thick a crop; wherefore yet again, like the gentlemen who audit ledgers, he must keep his head at any price. In consequence of all which, for the interest of the matter, I might seem here to have my choice of narrating my "hunt" for Lambert Strether, of describing the capture of the shadow projected by my friend's anecdote, or of reporting on the occurrences subsequent to that triumph. But I had probably best attempt a little to glance in each direction; since it comes to me again and again, over this licentious record, that one's bag of adventures, conceived or conceivable, has been only half-emptied by the mere telling of one's story. It depends so on what one means by that equivocal quantity. There is the story of one's hero, and then, thanks to the intimate connexion of things, the story of one's story itself. I blush to confess it, but if one's a dramatist one's a dramatist, and the latter imbroglio is liable on occasion to strike me as really the more objective of the two.

The philosophy imputed to him in that beautiful outbreak, the hour there, amid such happy provision, striking for him, would have been then, on behalf of my man of imagination, to be logically and, as the artless craft of comedy has it, "led up" to; the probable course to such a goal, the goal of so conscious a predicament, would have in short to be finely calculated. Where has he come from and why has he come, what is he doing (as we Anglo-Saxons, and we only, say, in our foredoomed clutch of exotic aids to expression) in that galere? To answer these questions plausibly, to answer them as under cross-examination in the witness-box by counsel for the prosecution, in other words satisfactorily to account for Strether and for his "peculiar tone," was to possess myself of the entire fabric. At the same time the question of his whereabouts would lie in a certain principle of probability: he wouldn't have indulged in his peculiar tone without a reason; it would take a felt predicament or a false position to give him so ironic an accent. One hadn't been noting "tones" all one's life without recognising when one heard it the voice of the false position. The dear man in the Paris garden was then admirably and unmistakeably IN one—which was no small point gained; what next accordingly concerned us was the determination of THIS identity. One could only go by probabilities, but there was the advantage that the most general of the probabilities were virtual certainties. Possessed of our friend's nationality, to start with, there was a general probability in his narrower localism; which, for that matter, one had really but to keep under the lens for an hour to see it give up its secrets. He would have issued, our rueful worthy, from the very heart of New England—at the heels of which matter of course a perfect train of secrets tumbled for me into the light. They had to be sifted and sorted, and I shall not reproduce the detail of that process; but unmistakeably they were all there, and it was but a question, auspiciously, of picking among them. What the "position" would infallibly be, and why, on his hands, it had turned "false"—these inductive steps could only be as rapid as they were distinct. I accounted for everything—and "everything" had by this time become the most promising quantity—by the view that he had come to Paris in some state of mind which was literally undergoing, as a result of new and unexpected assaults and infusions, a change almost from hour to hour. He had come with a view that might have been figured by a clear green liquid, say, in a neat glass phial; and the liquid, once poured into the open cup of APPLICATION, once exposed to the action of another air, had begun to turn from green to red, or whatever, and might, for all he knew, be on its way to purple, to black, to yellow. At the still wilder extremes represented perhaps, for all he could say to the contrary, by a variability so violent, he would at first, naturally, but have gazed in surprise and alarm; whereby the SITUATION clearly would spring from the play of wildness and the development of extremes. I saw in a moment that, should this development proceed both with force and logic, my "story" would leave nothing to be desired. There is always, of course, for the story-teller, the irresistible determinant and the incalculable advantage of his interest in the story AS SUCH; it is ever, obviously, overwhelmingly, the prime and precious thing (as other than this I have never been able to see it); as to which what makes for it, with whatever headlong energy, may be said to pale before the energy with which it simply makes for itself. It rejoices, none the less, at its best, to seem to offer itself in a light, to seem to know, and with the very last knowledge, what it's about—liable as it yet is at moments to be caught by us with its tongue in its cheek and absolutely no warrant but its splendid impudence. Let us grant then that the impudence is always there—there, so to speak, for grace and effect and ALLURE; there, above all, because the Story is just the spoiled child of art, and because, as we are always disappointed when the pampered don't "play up," we like it, to that extent, to look all its character. It probably does so, in truth, even when we most flatter ourselves that we negotiate with it by treaty.

All of which, again, is but to say that the STEPS, for my fable, placed themselves with a prompt and, as it were, functional assurance—an air quite as of readiness to have dispensed with logic had I been in fact too stupid for my clue. Never, positively, none the less, as the links multiplied, had I felt less stupid than for the determination of poor Strether's errand and for the apprehension of his issue. These things continued to fall together, as by the neat action of their own weight and form, even while their commentator scratched his head about them; he easily sees now that they were always well in advance of him. As the case completed itself he had in fact, from a good way behind, to catch up with them, breathless and a little flurried, as he best could. THE false position, for our belated man of the world—belated because he had endeavoured so long to escape being one, and now at last had really to face his doom—the false position for him, I say, was obviously to have presented himself at the gate of that boundless menagerie primed with a moral scheme of the most approved pattern which was yet framed to break down on any approach to vivid facts; that is to any at all liberal appreciation of them. There would have been of course the case of the Strether prepared, wherever presenting himself, only to judge and to feel meanly; but HE would have moved for me, I confess, enveloped in no legend whatever. The actual man's note, from the first of our seeing it struck, is the note of discrimination, just as his drama is to become, under stress, the drama of discrimination. It would have been his blest imagination, we have seen, that had already helped him to discriminate; the element that was for so much of the pleasure of my cutting thick, as I have intimated, into his intellectual, into his moral substance. Yet here it was, at the same time, just here, that a shade for a moment fell across the scene.

There was the dreadful little old tradition, one of the platitudes of the human comedy, that people's moral scheme DOES break down in Paris; that nothing is more frequently observed; that hundreds of thousands of more or less hypocritical or more or less cynical persons annually visit the place for the sake of the probable catastrophe, and that I came late in the day to work myself up about it. There was in fine the TRIVIAL association, one of the vulgarest in the world; but which give me pause no longer, I think, simply because its vulgarity is so advertised. The revolution performed by Strether under the influence of the most interesting of great cities was to have nothing to do with any betise of the imputably "tempted" state; he was to be thrown forward, rather, thrown quite with violence, upon his lifelong trick of intense reflexion: which friendly test indeed was to bring him out, through winding passages, through alternations of darkness and light, very much IN Paris, but with the surrounding scene itself a minor matter, a mere symbol for more things than had been dreamt of in the philosophy of Woollett. Another surrounding scene would have done as well for our show could it have represented a place in which Strether's errand was likely to lie and his crisis to await him. The LIKELY place had the great merit of sparing me preparations; there would have been too many involved—not at all impossibilities, only rather worrying and delaying difficulties—in positing elsewhere Chad Newsome's interesting relation, his so interesting complexity of relations. Strether's appointed stage, in fine, could be but Chad's most luckily selected one. The young man had gone in, as they say, for circumjacent charm; and where he would have found it, by the turn of his mind, most "authentic," was where his earnest friend's analysis would most find HIM; as well as where, for that matter, the former's whole analytic faculty would be led such a wonderful dance.

"The Ambassadors" had been, all conveniently, "arranged for"; its first appearance was from month to month, in the *North American Review* during 1903, and I had been open from far back to any pleasant provocation for ingenuity that might reside in one's actively adopting—so as to make it, in its way, a small compositional law—recurrent breaks and resumptions. I had made up my mind here regularly to exploit and enjoy these often rather rude jolts—having found, as I believed an admirable way to it; yet every question of form and pressure, I easily remember, paled in the light of the major propriety, recognised as soon as really weighed; that of employing but one centre and keeping it all within my hero's compass. The thing was to be so much this worthy's intimate adventure that even the projection of his consciousness upon it from beginning to end without intermission or deviation would probably still leave a part of its value for him, and a fortiori for ourselves, unexpressed. I might, however, express every grain of it that there would be room for—on condition of contriving a splendid particular economy. Other persons in no small number were to people the scene, and each with his or her axe to grind, his or her situation to treat, his or her coherency not to fail of, his or her relation to my leading motive, in a word, to establish and carry on. But Strether's sense of these things, and Strether's only, should avail me for showing them; I should know them but through his more or less groping knowledge of them, since his very gropings would figure among his most interesting motions, and a full observance of the rich rigour I speak of would give me more of the effect I should be most "after" than all other possible observances together. It would give me a large unity, and that in turn would crown me with the grace to which the enlightened story-teller will at any time, for his interest, sacrifice if need be all other graces whatever. I refer of course to the grace of intensity, which there are ways of signally achieving and ways of signally missing—as we see it, all round us, helplessly and woefully missed. Not that it isn't, on the other hand, a virtue eminently subject to appreciation—there being no strict, no absolute measure of it; so that one may hear it acclaimed where it has quite escaped one's perception, and see it unnoticed where one has gratefully hailed it. After all of which I am not sure, either, that the immense amusement of the whole cluster of difficulties so arrayed may not operate, for the fond fabulist, when judicious not less than fond, as his best of determinants. That charming principle is always there, at all events, to keep interest fresh: it is a principle, we remember, essentially ravenous, without scruple and without mercy, appeased with no cheap nor easy nourishment. It enjoys the costly sacrifice and rejoices thereby in the very odour of difficulty—even as ogres, with their "Fee-faw-fum!" rejoice in the smell of the blood of Englishmen.

Thus it was, at all events, that the ultimate, though after all so speedy, definition of my gentleman's job—his coming out, all solemnly appointed and deputed, to "save" Chad, and his then finding the young man so disobligingly and, at first, so bewilderingly not lost that a new issue altogether, in the connexion, prodigiously faces them, which has to be dealt with in a new light—promised as many calls on ingenuity and on the higher branches of the compositional art as one could possibly desire. Again and yet again, as, from book to book, I proceed with my survey, I find no source of interest equal to this verification after the fact, as I may call it, and the more in detail the better, of the scheme of consistency "gone in" for. As always—since the charm never fails—the retracing of the process from point to point brings back the old illusion. The old intentions bloom again and flower—in spite of all the blossoms they were to have dropped by the way. This is the charm, as I say, of adventure TRANSPOSED—the thrilling ups and downs, the intricate ins and outs of the compositional problem, made after such a fashion admirably objective, becoming the question at issue and keeping the author's heart in his mouth. Such an element, for instance, as his intention that Mrs. Newsome, away off with her finger on the pulse of Massachusetts, should yet be no less intensely than circuitously present through the whole thing, should be no less felt as to be reckoned with than the most direct exhibition, the finest portrayal at first hand could make her, such a sign of artistic good faith, I say, once it's unmistakeably there, takes on again an actuality not too much impaired by the comparative dimness of the particular success. Cherished intention too inevitably acts and operates, in the book, about fifty times as little as I had fondly dreamt it might; but that scarce spoils for me the pleasure of recognising the fifty ways in which I had sought to provide for it. The mere charm of seeing such an idea constituent, in its degree; the fineness of the measures taken—a real extension, if successful, of the very terms and possibilities of representation and figuration—such things alone were, after this fashion, inspiring, such things alone were a gage of the probable success of that dissimulated calculation with which the whole effort was to square. But oh the cares begotten, none the less, of that same "judicious" sacrifice to a particular form of interest! One's work should have composition, because composition alone is positive beauty; but all the while—apart from one's inevitable consciousness too of the dire paucity of readers ever recognising or ever missing positive beauty—how, as to the cheap and easy, at every turn, how, as to immediacy and facility, and even as to the commoner vivacity, positive beauty might have to be sweated for and paid for! Once achieved and installed it may always be trusted to make the poor seeker feel he would have blushed to the roots of his hair for failing of it; yet, how, as its virtue can be essentially but the virtue of the whole, the wayside traps set in the interest of muddlement and pleading but the cause of the moment, of the particular bit in itself, have to be kicked out of the path! All the sophistications in life, for example, might have appeared to muster on behalf of the menace—the menace to a bright variety—involved in Strether's having all the subjective "say," as it were, to himself.

Had I, meanwhile, made him at once hero and historian, endowed him with the romantic privilege of the "first person"—the darkest abyss of romance this, inveterately, when enjoyed on the grand scale—variety, and many other queer matters as well, might have been smuggled in by a back door. Suffice it, to be brief, that the first person, in the long piece, is a form foredoomed to looseness and that looseness, never much my affair, had never been so little so as on this particular occasion. All of which reflexions flocked to the standard from the moment—a very early one—the question of how to keep my form amusing while sticking so close to my central figure and constantly taking its pattern from him had to be faced. He arrives (arrives at Chester) as for the dreadful purpose of giving his creator "no end" to tell about him—before which rigorous mission the serenest of creators might well have quailed. I was far from the serenest; I was more than agitated enough to reflect that, grimly deprived of one alternative or one substitute for "telling," I must address myself tooth and nail to another. I couldn't, save by implication, make other persons tell EACH OTHER about him—blest resource, blest necessity, of the drama, which reaches its effects of unity, all remarkably, by paths absolutely opposite to the paths of the novel: with other persons, save as they were primarily HIS persons (not he primarily but one of theirs), I had simply nothing to do. I had relations for him none the less, by the mercy of Providence, quite as much as if my exhibition was to be a muddle; if I could only by implication and a show of consequence make other persons tell each other about him, I could at least make him tell THEM whatever in the world he must; and could so, by the same token—which was a further luxury thrown in—see straight into the deep differences between what that could do for me, or at all events for HIM, and the large ease of "autobiography." It may be asked why, if one so keeps to one's hero, one shouldn't make a single mouthful of "method," shouldn't throw the reins on his neck and, letting them flap there as free as in "Gil Blas" or in "David Copperfield," equip him with the double privilege of subject and object—a course that has at least the merit of brushing away questions at a sweep. The answer to which is, I think, that one makes that surrender only if one is prepared NOT to make certain precious discriminations.

The "first person" then, so employed, is addressed by the author directly to ourselves, his possible readers, whom he has to reckon with, at the best, by our English tradition, so loosely and vaguely after all, so little respectfully, on so scant a presumption of exposure to criticism. Strether, on the other hand, encaged and provided for as "The Ambassadors" encages and provides, has to keep in view proprieties much stiffer and more salutary than any our straight and credulous gape are likely to bring home to him, has exhibitional conditions to meet, in a word, that forbid the terrible FLUIDITY of self-revelation. I may seem not to better the case for my discrimination if I say that, for my first care, I had thus inevitably to set him up a confidant or two, to wave away with energy the custom of the seated mass of explanation after the fact, the inserted block of merely referential narrative, which flourishes so, to the shame of the modern impatience, on the serried page of Balzac, but which seems simply to appal our actual, our general weaker, digestion. "Harking back to make up" took at any rate more doing, as the phrase is, not only than the reader of to-day demands, but than he will tolerate at any price any call upon him either to understand or remotely to measure; and for the beauty of the thing when done the current editorial mind in particular appears wholly without sense. It is not, however, primarily for either of these reasons, whatever their weight, that Strether's friend Waymarsh is so keenly clutched at, on the threshold of the book, or that no less a pounce is made on Maria Gostrey—without even the pretext, either, of HER being, in essence, Strether's friend. She is the reader's friend much rather—in consequence of dispositions that make him so eminently require one; and she acts in that capacity, and REALLY in that capacity alone, with exemplary devotion from beginning to and of the book. She is an enrolled, a direct, aid to lucidity; she is in fine, to tear off her mask, the most unmitigated and abandoned of ficelles. Half the dramatist's art, as we well know—since if we don't it's not the fault of the proofs that lie scattered about us—is in the use of ficelles; by which I mean in a deep dissimulation of his dependence on them. Waymarsh only to a slighter degree belongs, in the whole business, less to my subject than to my treatment of it; the interesting proof, in these connexions, being that one has but to take one's subject for the stuff of drama to interweave with enthusiasm as many Gostreys as need be.

The material of "The Ambassadors," conforming in this respect exactly to that of "The Wings of the Dove," published just before it, is taken absolutely for the stuff of drama; so that, availing myself of the opportunity given me by this edition for some prefatory remarks on the latter work, I had mainly to make on its behalf the point of its scenic consistency. It disguises that virtue, in the oddest way in the world, by just LOOKING, as we turn its pages, as little scenic as possible; but it sharply divides itself, just as the composition before us does, into the parts that prepare, that tend in fact to over-prepare, for scenes, and the parts, or otherwise into the scenes, that justify and crown the preparation. It may definitely be said, I think, that everything in it that is not scene (not, I of course mean, complete and functional scene, treating ALL the submitted matter, as by logical start, logical turn, and logical finish) is discriminated preparation, is the fusion and synthesis of picture. These alternations propose themselves all recogniseably, I think, from an early stage, as the very form and figure of "The Ambassadors"; so that, to repeat, such an agent as Miss Gostrey pre-engaged at a high salary, but waits in the draughty wing with her shawl and her smelling-salts. Her function speaks at once for itself, and by the time she has dined with Strether in London and gone to a play with him her intervention as a ficelle is, I hold, expertly justified. Thanks to it we have treated scenically, and scenically alone, the whole lumpish question of Strether's "past," which has seen us more happily on the way than anything else could have done; we have strained to a high lucidity and vivacity (or at least we hope we have) certain indispensable facts; we have seen our two or three immediate friends all conveniently and profitably in "action"; to say nothing of our beginning to descry others, of a remoter intensity, getting into motion, even if a bit vaguely as yet, for our further enrichment. Let my first point be here that the scene in question, that in which the whole situation at Woollett and the complex forces that have propelled my hero to where this lively extractor of his value and distiller of his essence awaits him, is normal and entire, is really an excellent STANDARD scene; copious, comprehensive, and accordingly never short, but with its office as definite as that of the hammer on the gong of the clock, the office of expressing ALL THAT IS IN the hour.

The "ficelle" character of the subordinate party is as artfully dissimulated, throughout, as may be, and to that extent that, with the seams or joints of Maria Gostrey's ostensible connectedness taken particular care of, duly smoothed over, that is, and anxiously kept from showing as "pieced on;" this figure doubtless achieves, after a fashion, something of the dignity of a prime idea: which circumstance but shows us afresh how many quite incalculable but none the less clear sources of enjoyment for the infatuated artist, how many copious springs of our never-to-be-slighted "fun" for the reader and critic susceptible of contagion, may sound their incidental plash as soon as an artistic process begins to enjoy free development. Exquisite—in illustration of this—the mere interest and amusement of such at once "creative" and critical questions as how and where and why to make Miss Gostrey's false connexion carry itself, under a due high polish, as a real one. Nowhere is it more of an artful expedient for mere consistency of form, to mention a case, than in the last "scene" of the book, where its function is to give or to add nothing whatever, but only to express as vividly as possible certain things quite other than itself and that are of the already fixed and appointed measure. Since, however, all art is EXPRESSION, and is thereby vividness, one was to find the door open here to any amount of delightful dissimulation. These verily are the refinements and ecstasies of method—amid which, or certainly under the influence of any exhilarated demonstration of which, one must keep one's head and not lose one's way. To cultivate an adequate intelligence for them and to make that sense operative is positively to find a charm in any produced ambiguity of appearance that is not by the same stroke, and all helplessly, an ambiguity of sense. To project imaginatively, for my hero, a relation that has nothing to do with the matter (the matter of my subject) but has everything to do with the manner (the manner of my presentation of the same) and yet to treat it, at close quarters and for fully economic expression's possible sake, as if it were important and essential—to do that sort of thing and yet muddle nothing may easily become, as one goes, a signally attaching proposition; even though it all remains but part and parcel, I hasten to recognise, of the merely general and related question of expressional curiosity and expressional decency.

I am moved to add after so much insistence on the scenic side of my labour that I have found the steps of re-perusal almost as much waylaid here by quite another style of effort in the same signal interest—or have in other words not failed to note how, even so associated and so discriminated, the finest proprieties and charms of the non-scenic may, under the right hand for them, still keep their intelligibility and assert their office. Infinitely suggestive such an observation as this last on the whole delightful head, where representation is concerned, of possible variety, of effective expressional change and contrast. One would like, at such an hour as this, for critical licence, to go into the matter of the noted inevitable deviation (from too fond an original vision) that the exquisite treachery even of the straightest execution may ever be trusted to inflict even on the most mature plan—the case being that, though one's last reconsidered production always seems to bristle with that particular evidence, "The Ambassadors" would place a flood of such light at my service. I must attach to my final remark here a different import; noting in the other connexion I just glanced at that such passages as that of my hero's first encounter with Chad Newsome, absolute attestations of the non-scenic form though they be, yet lay the firmest hand too—so far at least as intention goes—on representational effect. To report at all closely and completely of what "passes" on a given occasion is inevitably to become more or less scenic; and yet in the instance I allude to, WITH the conveyance, expressional curiosity and expressional decency are sought and arrived at under quite another law. The true inwardness of this may be at bottom but that one of the suffered treacheries has consisted precisely, for Chad's whole figure and presence, of a direct presentability diminished and compromised—despoiled, that is, of its PROPORTIONAL advantage; so that, in a word, the whole economy of his author's relation to him has at important points to be redetermined. The book, however, critically viewed, is touchingly full of these disguised and repaired losses, these insidious recoveries, these intensely redemptive consistencies. The pages in which Mamie Pocock gives her appointed and, I can't but think, duly felt lift to the whole action by the so inscrutably-applied side-stroke or short-cut of our just watching and as quite at an angle of vision as yet untried, her single hour of suspense in the hotel salon, in our partaking of her concentrated study of the sense of matters bearing on her own case, all the bright warm Paris afternoon, from the balcony that overlooks the Tuileries garden—these are as marked an example of the representational virtue that insists here and there on being, for the charm of opposition and renewal, other than the scenic. It wouldn't take much to make me further argue that from an equal play of such oppositions the book gathers an intensity that fairly adds to the dramatic—though the latter is supposed to be the sum of all intensities; or that has at any rate nothing to fear from juxtaposition with it. I consciously fail to shrink in fact from that extravagance—I risk it rather, for the sake of the moral involved; which is not that the particular production before us exhausts the interesting questions it raises, but that the Novel remains still, under the right persuasion, the most independent, most elastic, most prodigious of literary forms.

HENRY JAMES.

The Ambassadors

Volume I

Book First

CHAPTER I

Ship docking at Liverpool (c.1910) by J. S Mann (1879-1930)

Strether's first question, when he reached the hotel, was about his friend; yet on his learning that Waymarsh was apparently not to arrive till evening he was not wholly disconcerted. A telegram from him bespeaking a room "only if not noisy," reply paid, was produced for the enquirer at the office, so that the understanding they should meet at Chester rather than at Liverpool remained to that extent sound. The same secret principle, however, that had prompted Strether not absolutely to desire Waymarsh's presence at the dock, that had led him thus to postpone for a few hours his enjoyment of it, now operated to make him feel he could still wait without disappointment. They would dine together at the worst, and, with all respect to dear old Waymarsh—if not even, for that matter, to himself—there was little fear that in the sequel they shouldn't see enough of each other. The principle I have just mentioned as operating had been, with the most newly disembarked of the two men, wholly instinctive—the fruit of a sharp sense that, delightful as it would be to find himself looking, after so much separation, into his comrade's face, his business would be a trifle bungled should he simply arrange for this countenance to present itself to the nearing steamer as the first "note," of Europe. Mixed with everything was the apprehension, already, on Strether's part, that it would, at best, throughout, prove the note of Europe in quite a sufficient degree.

That note had been meanwhile—since the previous afternoon, thanks to this happier device—such a consciousness of personal freedom as he hadn't known for years; such a deep taste of change and of having above all for the moment nobody and nothing to consider, as promised already, if headlong hope were not too foolish, to colour his adventure with cool success. There were people on the ship with whom he had easily consorted—so far as ease could up to now be imputed to him—and who for the most part plunged straight into the current that set from the landing-stage to London; there were others who had invited him to a tryst at the inn and had even invoked his aid for a "look round" at the beauties of Liverpool; but he had stolen away from every one alike, had kept no appointment and renewed no acquaintance, had been indifferently aware of the number of persons who esteemed themselves fortunate in being, unlike himself, "met," and had even independently, unsociably, alone, without encounter or relapse and by mere quiet evasion, given his afternoon and evening to the immediate and the sensible. They formed a qualified draught of Europe, an afternoon and an evening on the banks of the Mersey, but such as it was he took his potion at least undiluted. He winced a little, truly, at the thought that Waymarsh might be already at Chester; he reflected that, should he have to describe himself there as having "got in" so early, it would be difficult to make the interval look particularly eager; but he was like a man who, elatedly finding in his pocket more money than usual, handles it a while and idly and pleasantly chinks it before addressing himself to the business of spending. That he was prepared to be vague to Waymarsh about the hour of the ship's touching, and that he both wanted extremely to see him and enjoyed extremely the duration of delay—these things, it is to be conceived, were early signs in him that his relation to his actual errand might prove none of the simplest. He was burdened, poor Strether—it had better be confessed at the outset—with the oddity of a double consciousness. There was detachment in his zeal and curiosity in his indifference.

After the young woman in the glass cage had held up to him across her counter the pale-pink leaflet bearing his friend's name, which she neatly pronounced, he turned away to find himself, in the hall, facing a lady who met his eyes as with an intention suddenly determined, and whose features—not freshly young, not markedly fine, but on happy terms with each other—came back to him as from a recent vision. For a moment they stood confronted; then the moment placed her: he had noticed her the day before, noticed her at his previous inn, where—again in the hall—she had been briefly engaged with some people of his own ship's company. Nothing had actually passed between them, and he would as little have been able to say what had been the sign of her face for him on the first occasion as to name the ground of his present recognition. Recognition at any rate appeared to prevail on her own side as well—which would only have added to the mystery. All she now began by saying to him nevertheless was that, having chanced to catch his enquiry, she was moved to ask, by his leave, if it were possibly a question of Mr. Waymarsh of Milrose Connecticut—Mr. Waymarsh the American lawyer.

"Oh yes," he replied, "my very well-known friend. He's to meet me here, coming up from Malvern, and I supposed he'd already have arrived. But he doesn't come till later, and I'm relieved not to have kept him. Do you know him?" Strether wound up.

It wasn't till after he had spoken that he became aware of how much there had been in him of response; when the tone of her own rejoinder, as well as the play of something more in her face—something more, that is, than its apparently usual restless light—seemed to notify him. "I've met him at Milrose—where I used sometimes, a good while ago, to stay; I had friends there who were friends of his, and I've been at his house. I won't answer for it that he would know me," Strether's new acquaintance pursued; "but I should be delighted to see him. Perhaps," she added, "I shall—for I'm staying over." She paused while our friend took in these things, and it was as if a good deal of talk had already passed. They even vaguely smiled at it, and Strether presently observed that Mr. Waymarsh would, no doubt, be easily to be seen. This, however, appeared to affect the lady as if she might have advanced too far. She appeared to have no reserves about anything. "Oh," she said, "he won't care!"—and she immediately thereupon remarked that she believed Strether knew the Munsters; the Munsters being the people he had seen her with at Liverpool.

But he didn't, it happened, know the Munsters well enough to give the case much of a lift; so that they were left together as if over the mere laid table of conversation. Her qualification of the mentioned connexion had rather removed than placed a dish, and there seemed nothing else to serve. Their attitude remained, none the less, that of not forsaking the board; and the effect of this in turn was to give them the appearance of having accepted each other with an absence of preliminaries practically complete. They moved along the hall together, and Strether's companion threw off that the hotel had the advantage of a garden. He was aware by this time of his strange inconsequence: he had shirked the intimacies of the steamer and had muffled the shock of Waymarsh only to find himself forsaken, in this sudden case, both of avoidance and of caution. He passed, under this unsought protection and before he had so much as gone up to his room, into the garden of the hotel, and at the end of ten minutes had agreed to meet there again, as soon as he should have made himself tidy, the dispenser of such good assurances. He wanted to look at the town, and they would forthwith look together. It was almost as if she had been in possession and received him as a guest. Her acquaintance with the place presented her in a manner as a hostess, and Strether had a rueful glance for the lady in the glass cage. It was as if this personage had seen herself instantly superseded.

When in a quarter of an hour he came down, what his hostess saw, what she might have taken in with a vision kindly adjusted, was the lean, the slightly loose figure of a man of the middle height and something more perhaps than the middle age—a man of five-and-fifty, whose most immediate signs were a marked bloodless brownness of face, a thick dark moustache, of characteristically American cut, growing strong and falling low, a head of hair still abundant but irregularly streaked with grey, and a nose of bold free prominence, the even line, the high finish, as it might have been called, of which, had a certain effect of mitigation. A perpetual pair of glasses astride of this fine ridge, and a line, unusually deep and drawn, the prolonged pen-stroke of time, accompanying the curve of the moustache from nostril to chin, did something to complete the facial furniture that an attentive observer would have seen catalogued, on the spot, in the vision of the other party to Strether's appointment. She waited for him in the garden, the other party, drawing on a pair of singularly fresh soft and elastic light gloves and presenting herself with a superficial readiness which, as he approached her over the small smooth lawn and in the watery English sunshine, he might, with his rougher preparation, have marked as the model for such an occasion. She had, this lady, a perfect plain propriety, an expensive subdued suitability, that her companion was not free to analyse, but that struck him, so that his consciousness of it was instantly acute, as a quality quite new to him. Before reaching her he stopped on the grass and went through the form of feeling for something, possibly forgotten, in the light overcoat he carried on his arm; yet the essence of the act was no more than the impulse to gain time. Nothing could have been odder than Strether's sense of himself as at that moment launched in something of which the sense would be quite disconnected from the sense of his past and which was literally beginning there and then. It had begun in fact already upstairs and before the dressing glass that struck him as blocking further, so strangely, the dimness of the window of his dull bedroom; begun with a sharper survey of the elements of Appearance than he had for a long time been moved to make. He had during those moments felt these elements to be not so much to his hand as he should have liked, and then had fallen back on the thought that they were precisely a matter as to which help was supposed to come from what he was about to do. He was about to go up to London, so that hat and necktie might wait. What had come as straight to him as a ball in a well-played game—and caught moreover not less neatly—was just the air, in the person of his friend, of having seen and chosen, the air of achieved possession of those vague qualities and quantities that collectively figured to him as the advantage snatched from lucky chances. Without pomp or circumstance, certainly, as her original address to him, equally with his own response, had been, he would have sketched to himself his impression of her as: "Well, she's more thoroughly civilized—!" If "More thoroughly than WHOM?" would not have been for him a sequel to this remark, that was just by reason of his deep consciousness of the bearing of his comparison.

The amusement, at all events, of a civilisation intenser was what—familiar compatriot as she was, with the full tone of the compatriot and the rattling link not with mystery but only with dear dyspeptic Waymarsh—she appeared distinctly to promise. His pause while he felt in his overcoat was positively the pause of confidence, and it enabled his eyes to make out as much of a case for her, in proportion, as her own made out for himself. She affected him as almost insolently young; but an easily carried five-and-thirty could still do that. She was, however, like himself marked and wan; only it naturally couldn't have been known to him how much a spectator looking from one to the other might have discerned that they had in common. It wouldn't for such a spectator have been altogether insupposable that, each so finely brown and so sharply spare, each confessing so to dents of surface and aids to sight, to a disproportionate nose and a head delicately or grossly grizzled, they might have been brother and sister. On this ground indeed there would have been a residuum of difference; such a sister having surely known in respect to such a brother the extremity of separation, and such a brother now feeling in respect to such a sister the extremity of surprise. Surprise, it was true, was not on the other hand what the eyes of Strether's friend most showed him while she gave him, stroking her gloves smoother, the time he appreciated. They had taken hold of him straightway measuring him up and down as if they knew how; as if he were human material they had already in some sort handled. Their possessor was in truth, it may be communicated, the mistress of a hundred cases or categories, receptacles of the mind, subdivisions for convenience, in which, from a full experience, she pigeon-holed her fellow mortals with a hand as free as that of a compositor scattering type. She was as equipped in this particular as Strether was the reverse, and it made an opposition between them which he might well have shrunk from submitting to if he had fully suspected it. So far as he did suspect it he was on the contrary, after a short shake of his consciousness, as pleasantly passive as might be. He really had a sort of sense of what she knew. He had quite the sense that she knew things he didn't, and though this was a concession that in general he found not easy to make to women, he made it now as good-humouredly as if it lifted a burden. His eyes were so quiet behind his eternal nippers that they might almost have been absent without changing his face, which took its expression mainly, and not least its stamp of sensibility, from other sources, surface and grain and form. He joined his guide in an instant, and then felt she had profited still better than he by his having been for the moments just mentioned, so at the disposal of her intelligence. She knew even intimate things about him that he hadn't yet told her and perhaps never would. He wasn't unaware that he had told her rather remarkably many for the time, but these were not the real ones. Some of the real ones, however, precisely, were what she knew.

They were to pass again through the hall of the inn to get into the street, and it was here she presently checked him with a question. "Have you looked up my name?"

He could only stop with a laugh. "Have you looked up mine?"

"Oh dear, yes—as soon as you left me. I went to the office and asked. Hadn't YOU better do the same?"

He wondered. "Find out who you are?—after the uplifted young woman there has seen us thus scrape acquaintance!"

She laughed on her side now at the shade of alarm in his amusement. "Isn't it a reason the more? If what you're afraid of is the injury for me—my being seen to walk off with a gentleman who has to ask who I am—I assure you I don't in the least mind. Here, however," she continued, "is my card, and as I find there's something else again I have to say at the office, you can just study it during the moment I leave you."

She left him after he had taken from her the small pasteboard she had extracted from her pocket-book, and he had extracted another from his own, to exchange with it, before she came back. He read thus the simple designation "Maria Gostrey," to which was attached, in a corner of the card, with a number, the name of a street, presumably in Paris, without other appreciable identity than its foreignness. He put the card into his waistcoat pocket, keeping his own meanwhile in evidence; and as he leaned against the door-post he met with the smile of a straying thought what the expanse before the hotel offered to his view. It was positively droll to him that he should already have Maria Gostrey, whoever she was—of which he hadn't really the least idea—in a place of safe keeping. He had somehow an assurance that he should carefully preserve the little token he had just tucked in. He gazed with unseeing lingering eyes as he followed some of the implications of his act, asking himself if he really felt admonished to qualify it as disloyal. It was prompt, it was possibly even premature, and there was little doubt of the expression of face the sight of it would have produced in a certain person. But if it was "wrong"—why then he had better not have come out at all. At this, poor man, had he already—and even before meeting Waymarsh—arrived. He had believed he had a limit, but the limit had been transcended within thirty-six hours. By how long a space on the plane of manners or even of morals, moreover, he felt still more sharply after Maria Gostrey had come back to him and with a gay decisive "So now—!" led him forth into the world. This counted, it struck him as he walked beside her with his overcoat on an arm, his umbrella under another and his personal pasteboard a little stiffly retained between forefinger and thumb, this struck him as really, in comparison his introduction to things. It hadn't been "Europe" at Liverpool no—not even in the dreadful delightful impressive streets the night before—to the extent his present companion made it so. She hadn't yet done that so much as when, after their walk had lasted a few minutes and he had had time to wonder if a couple of sidelong glances from her meant that he had best have put on gloves she almost pulled him up with an amused challenge. "But why—fondly as it's so easy to imagine your clinging to it—don't you put it away? Or if it's an inconvenience to you to carry it, one's often glad to have one's card back. The fortune one spends in them!"

Then he saw both that his way of marching with his own prepared tribute had affected her as a deviation in one of those directions he couldn't yet measure, and that she supposed this emblem to be still the one he had received from her. He accordingly handed her the card as if in restitution, but as soon as she had it she felt the difference, and, with her eyes on it, stopped short for apology. "I like," she observed, "your name."

"Oh," he answered, "you won't have heard of it!" Yet he had his reasons for not being sure but that she perhaps might.

Ah it was but too visible! She read it over again as one who had never seen it. "'Mr. Lewis Lambert Strether'"—she sounded it almost as freely as for any stranger. She repeated however that she liked it—"particularly the Lewis Lambert. It's the name of a novel of Balzac's."

"Oh I know that!" said Strether.

"But the novel's an awfully bad one."

"I know that too," Strether smiled. To which he added with an irrelevance that was only superficial: "I come from Woollett Massachusetts." It made her for some reason—the irrelevance or whatever—laugh. Balzac had described many cities, but hadn't described Woollett Massachusetts. "You say that," she returned, "as if you wanted one immediately to know the worst."

"Oh I think it's a thing," he said, "that you must already have made out. I feel it so that I certainly must look it, speak it, and, as people say there, 'act' it. It sticks out of me, and you knew surely for yourself as soon as you looked at me."

"The worst, you mean?"

"Well, the fact of where I come from. There at any rate it IS; so that you won't be able, if anything happens, to say I've not been straight with you."

"I see"—and Miss Gostrey looked really interested in the point he had made. "But what do you think of as happening?"

Though he wasn't shy—which was rather anomalous—Strether gazed about without meeting her eyes; a motion that was frequent with him in talk, yet of which his words often seemed not at all the effect. "Why that you should find me too hopeless." With which they walked on again together while she answered, as they went, that the most "hopeless" of her countryfolk were in general precisely those she liked best. All sorts of other pleasant small things-small things that were yet large for him—flowered in the air of the occasion, but the bearing of the occasion itself on matters still remote concerns us too closely to permit us to multiply our illustrations. Two or three, however, in truth, we should perhaps regret to lose. The tortuous wall—girdle, long since snapped, of the little swollen city, half held in place by careful civic hands—wanders in narrow file between parapets smoothed by peaceful generations, pausing here and there for a dismantled gate or a bridged gap, with rises and drops, steps up and steps down, queer twists, queer contacts, peeps into homely streets and under the brows of gables, views of cathedral tower and waterside fields, of huddled English town and ordered English country. Too deep almost for words was the delight of these things to Strether; yet as deeply mixed with it were certain images of his inward picture. He had trod this walks in the far-off time, at twenty-five; but that, instead of spoiling it, only enriched it for present feeling and marked his renewal as a thing substantial enough to share. It was with Waymarsh he should have shared it, and he was now accordingly taking from him something that was his due. He looked repeatedly at his watch, and when he had done so for the fifth time Miss Gostrey took him up.

"You're doing something that you think not right."

It so touched the place that he quite changed colour and his laugh grew almost awkward. "Am I enjoying it as much as THAT?"

"You're not enjoying it, I think, so much as you ought."

"I see"—he appeared thoughtfully to agree. "Great is my privilege."

"Oh it's not your privilege! It has nothing to do with me. It has to do with yourself. Your failure's general."

"Ah there you are!" he laughed. "It's the failure of Woollett. THAT'S general."

"The failure to enjoy," Miss Gostrey explained, "is what I mean."

"Precisely. Woollett isn't sure it ought to enjoy. If it were it would. But it hasn't, poor thing," Strether continued, "any one to show it how. It's not like me. I have somebody."

They had stopped, in the afternoon sunshine—constantly pausing, in their stroll, for the sharper sense of what they saw—and Strether rested on one of the high sides of the old stony groove of the little rampart. He leaned back on this support with his face to the tower of the cathedral, now admirably commanded by their station, the high red-brown mass, square and subordinately spired and crocketed, retouched and restored, but charming to his long-sealed eyes and with the first swallows of the year weaving their flight all round it. Miss Gostrey lingered near him, full of an air, to which she more and more justified her right, of understanding the effect of things. She quite concurred. "You've indeed somebody." And she added: "I wish you WOULD let me show you how!"

"Oh I'm afraid of you!" he cheerfully pleaded.

She kept on him a moment, through her glasses and through his own, a certain pleasant pointedness. "Ah no, you're not! You're not in the least, thank goodness! If you had been we shouldn't so soon have found ourselves here together. I think," she comfortably concluded, "you trust me."

"I think I do!—but that's exactly what I'm afraid of. I shouldn't mind if I didn't. It's falling thus in twenty minutes so utterly into your hands. I dare say," Strether continued, "it's a sort of thing you're thoroughly familiar with; but nothing more extraordinary has ever happened to me."

She watched him with all her kindness. "That means simply that you've recognised me—which IS rather beautiful and rare. You see what I am." As on this, however, he protested, with a good-humoured headshake, a resignation of any such claim, she had a moment of explanation. "If you'll only come on further as you HAVE come you'll at any rate make out. My own fate has been too many for me, and I've succumbed to it. I'm a general guide—to 'Europe,' don't you know? I wait for people—I put them through. I pick them up—I set them down. I'm a sort of superior 'courier-maid.' I'm a companion at large. I take people, as I've told you, about. I never sought it—it has come to me. It has been my fate, and one's fate one accepts. It's a dreadful thing to have to say, in so wicked a world, but I verily believe that, such as you see me, there's nothing I don't know. I know all the shops and the prices—but I know worse things still. I bear on my back the huge load of our national consciousness, or, in other words—for it comes to that—of our nation itself. Of what is our nation composed but of the men and women individually on my shoulders? I don't do it, you know, for any particular advantage. I don't do it, for instance—some people do, you know—for money."

Strether could only listen and wonder and weigh his chance. "And yet, affected as you are then to so many of your clients, you can scarcely be said to do it for love." He waited a moment. "How do we reward you?"

She had her own hesitation, but "You don't!" she finally returned, setting him again in motion. They went on, but in a few minutes, though while still thinking over what she had said, he once more took out his watch; mechanically, unconsciously and as if made nervous by the mere exhilaration of what struck him as her strange and cynical wit. He looked at the hour without seeing it, and then, on something again said by his companion, had another pause. "You're really in terror of him."

He smiled a smile that he almost felt to be sickly. "Now you can see why I'm afraid of you."

"Because I've such illuminations? Why they're all for your help! It's what I told you," she added, "just now. You feel as if this were wrong."

He fell back once more, settling himself against the parapet as if to hear more about it. "Then get me out!"

Her face fairly brightened for the joy of the appeal, but, as if it were a question of immediate action, she visibly considered. "Out of waiting for him?—of seeing him at all?"

"Oh no—not that," said poor Strether, looking grave. "I've got to wait for him—and I want very much to see him. But out of the terror. You did put your finger on it a few minutes ago. It's general, but it avails itself of particular occasions. That's what it's doing for me now. I'm always considering something else; something else, I mean, than the thing of the moment. The obsession of the other thing is the terror. I'm considering at present for instance something else than YOU."

She listened with charming earnestness. "Oh you oughtn't to do that!"

"It's what I admit. Make it then impossible."

She continued to think. "Is it really an 'order' from you?—that I shall take the job? WILL you give yourself up?"

Poor Strether heaved his sigh. "If I only could! But that's the deuce of it—that I never can. No—I can't."

She wasn't, however, discouraged. "But you want to at least?"

"Oh unspeakably!"

"Ah then, if you'll try!"—and she took over the job, as she had called it, on the spot. "Trust me!" she exclaimed, and the action of this, as they retraced their steps, was presently to make him pass his hand into her arm in the manner of a benign dependent paternal old person who wishes to be "nice" to a younger one. If he drew it out again indeed as they approached the inn this may have been because, after more talk had passed between them, the relation of age, or at least of experience—which, for that matter, had already played to and fro with some freedom—affected him as incurring a readjustment. It was at all events perhaps lucky that they arrived in sufficiently separate fashion within range of the hotel-door. The young lady they had left in the glass cage watched as if she had come to await them on the threshold. At her side stood a person equally interested, by his attitude, in their return, and the effect of the sight of whom was instantly to determine for Strether another of those responsive arrests that we have had so repeatedly to note. He left it to Miss Gostrey to name, with the fine full bravado as it almost struck him, of her "Mr. Waymarsh!" what was to have been, what—he more than ever felt as his short stare of suspended welcome took things in—would have been, but for herself, his doom. It was already upon him even at that distance—Mr. Waymarsh was for HIS part joyless.

II

He had none the less to confess to this friend that evening that he knew almost nothing about her, and it was a deficiency that Waymarsh, even with his memory refreshed by contact, by her own prompt and lucid allusions and enquiries, by their having publicly partaken of dinner in her company, and by another stroll, to which she was not a stranger, out into the town to look at the cathedral by moonlight—it was a blank that the resident of Milrose, though admitting acquaintance with the Munsters, professed himself unable to fill. He had no recollection of Miss Gostrey, and two or three questions that she put to him about those members of his circle had, to Strether's observation, the same effect he himself had already more directly felt—the effect of appearing to place all knowledge, for the time, on this original woman's side. It interested him indeed to mark the limits of any such relation for her with his friend as there could possibly be a question of, and it particularly struck him that they were to be marked altogether in Waymarsh's quarter. This added to his own sense of having gone far with her-gave him an early illustration of a much shorter course. There was a certitude he immediately grasped—a conviction that Waymarsh would quite fail, as it were, and on whatever degree of acquaintance to profit by her.

There had been after the first interchange among the three a talk of some five minutes in the hall, and then the two men had adjourned to the garden, Miss Gostrey for the time disappearing. Strether in due course accompanied his friend to the room he had bespoken and had, before going out, scrupulously visited; where at the end of another half-hour he had no less discreetly left him. On leaving him he repaired straight to his own room, but with the prompt effect of feeling the compass of that chamber resented by his condition. There he enjoyed at once the first consequence of their reunion. A place was too small for him after it that had seemed large enough before. He had awaited it with something he would have been sorry, have been almost ashamed not to recognise as emotion, yet with a tacit assumption at the same time that emotion would in the event find itself relieved. The actual oddity was that he was only more excited; and his excitement-to which indeed he would have found it difficult instantly to give a name—brought him once more downstairs and caused him for some minutes vaguely to wander. He went once more to the garden; he looked into the public room, found Miss Gostrey writing letters and backed out; he roamed, fidgeted and wasted time; but he was to have his more intimate session with his friend before the evening closed.

It was late—not till Strether had spent an hour upstairs with him—that this subject consented to betake himself to doubtful rest. Dinner and the subsequent stroll by moonlight—a dream, on Strether's part, of romantic effects rather prosaically merged in a mere missing of thicker coats—had measurably intervened, and this midnight conference was the result of Waymarsh's having (when they were free, as he put it, of their fashionable friend) found the smoking-room not quite what he wanted, and yet bed what he wanted less. His most frequent form of words was that he knew himself, and they were applied on this occasion to his certainty of not sleeping. He knew himself well enough to know that he should have a night of prowling unless he should succeed, as a preliminary, in getting prodigiously tired. If the effort directed to this end involved till a late hour the presence of Strether—consisted, that is, in the detention of the latter for full discourse—there was yet an impression of minor discipline involved for our friend in the picture Waymarsh made as he sat in trousers and shirt on the edge of his couch. With his long legs extended and his large back much bent, he nursed alternately, for an almost incredible time, his elbows and his beard. He struck his visitor as extremely, as almost wilfully uncomfortable; yet what had this been for Strether, from that first glimpse of him disconcerted in the porch of the hotel, but the predominant notes. The discomfort was in a manner contagious, as well as also in a manner inconsequent and unfounded; the visitor felt that unless he should get used to it—or unless Waymarsh himself should—it would constitute a menace for his own prepared, his own already confirmed, consciousness of the agreeable. On their first going up together to the room Strether had selected for him Waymarsh had looked it over in silence and with a sigh that represented for his companion, if not the habit of disapprobation, at least the despair of felicity; and this look had recurred to Strether as the key of much he had since observed. "Europe," he had begun to gather from these things, had up to now rather failed of its message to him; he hadn't got into tune with it and had at the end of three months almost renounced any such expectation.

He really appeared at present to insist on that by just perching there with the gas in his eyes. This of itself somehow conveyed the futility of single rectifications in a multiform failure. He had a large handsome head and a large sallow seamed face—a striking significant physiognomic total, the upper range of which, the great political brow, the thick loose hair, the dark fuliginous eyes, recalled even to a generation whose standard had dreadfully deviated the impressive image, familiar by engravings and busts, of some great national worthy of the earlier part of the mid-century. He was of the personal type—and it was an element in the power and promise that in their early time Strether had found in him—of the American statesman, the statesman trained in "Congressional halls," of an elder day. The legend had been in later years that as the lower part of his face, which was weak, and slightly crooked, spoiled the likeness, this was the real reason for the growth of his beard, which might have seemed to spoil it for those not in the secret. He shook his mane; he fixed, with his admirable eyes, his auditor or his observer; he wore no glasses and had a way, partly formidable, yet also partly encouraging, as from a representative to a constituent, of looking very hard at those who approached him. He met you as if you had knocked and he had bidden you enter. Strether, who hadn't seen him for so long an interval, apprehended him now with a freshness of taste, and had perhaps never done him such ideal justice. The head was bigger, the eyes finer, than they need have been for the career; but that only meant, after all, that the career was itself expressive. What it expressed at midnight in the gas-glaring bedroom at Chester was that the subject of it had, at the end of years, barely escaped, by flight in time, a general nervous collapse. But this very proof of the full life, as the full life was understood at Milrose, would have made to Strether's imagination an element in which Waymarsh could have floated easily had he only consented to float. Alas nothing so little resembled floating as the rigour with which, on the edge of his bed, he hugged his posture of prolonged impermanence. It suggested to his comrade something that always, when kept up, worried him—a person established in a railway-coach with a forward inclination. It represented the angle at which poor Waymarsh was to sit through the ordeal of Europe.

Thanks to the stress of occupation, the strain of professions, the absorption and embarrassment of each, they had not, at home, during years before this sudden brief and almost bewildering reign of comparative ease, found so much as a day for a meeting; a fact that was in some degree an explanation of the sharpness with which most of his friend's features stood out to Strether. Those he had lost sight of since the early time came back to him; others that it was never possible to forget struck him now as sitting, clustered and expectant, like a somewhat defiant family-group, on the doorstep of their residence. The room was narrow for its length, and the occupant of the bed thrust so far a pair of slippered feet that the visitor had almost to step over them in his recurrent rebounds from his chair to fidget back and forth. There were marks the friends made on things to talk about, and on things not to, and one of the latter in particular fell like the tap of chalk on the blackboard. Married at thirty, Waymarsh had not lived with his wife for fifteen years, and it came up vividly between them in the glare of the gas that Strether wasn't to ask about her. He knew they were still separate and that she lived at hotels, travelled in Europe, painted her face and wrote her husband abusive letters, of not one of which, to a certainty, that sufferer spared himself the perusal; but he respected without difficulty the cold twilight that had settled on this side of his companion's life. It was a province in which mystery reigned and as to which Waymarsh had never spoken the informing word. Strether, who wanted to do him the highest justice wherever he COULD do it, singularly admired him for the dignity of this reserve, and even counted it as one of the grounds—grounds all handled and numbered—for ranking him, in the range of their acquaintance, as a success. He WAS a success, Waymarsh, in spite of overwork, or prostration, of sensible shrinkage, of his wife's letters and of his not liking Europe. Strether would have reckoned his own career less futile had he been able to put into it anything so handsome as so much fine silence. One might one's self easily have left Mrs. Waymarsh; and one would assuredly have paid one's tribute to the ideal in covering with that attitude the derision of having been left by her. Her husband had held his tongue and had made a large income; and these were in especial the achievements as to which Strether envied him. Our friend had had indeed on his side too a subject for silence, which he fully appreciated; but it was a matter of a different sort, and the figure of the income he had arrived at had never been high enough to look any one in the face.

"I don't know as I quite see what you require it for. You don't appear sick to speak of." It was of Europe Waymarsh thus finally spoke.

"Well," said Strether, who fell as much as possible into step, "I guess I don't FEEL sick now that I've started. But I had pretty well run down before I did start."

Waymarsh raised his melancholy look. "Ain't you about up to your usual average?"

It was not quite failed to pointedly sceptical, but it seemed somehow a plea for the purest veracity, and it thereby affected our friend as the very voice of Milrose. He had long since made a mental distinction—though never in truth daring to betray it—between the voice of Milrose and the voice even of Woollett. It was the former he felt, that was most in the real tradition. There had been occasions in his past when the sound of it had reduced him to temporary confusion, and the present, for some reason, suddenly became such another. It was nevertheless no light matter that the very effect of his confusion should be to make him again prevaricate. "That description hardly does justice to a man to whom it has done such a lot of good to see YOU."

Waymarsh fixed on his washing-stand the silent detached stare with which Milrose in person, as it were, might have marked the unexpectedness of a compliment from Woollett, and Strether for his part, felt once more like Woollett in person. "I mean," his friend presently continued, "that your appearance isn't as bad as I've seen it: it compares favourably with what it was when I last noticed it." On this appearance Waymarsh's eyes almost as if they obeyed an instinct of propriety, and the effect was still stronger when, always considering the basin and jug, he added: "You've filled out some since then."

"I'm afraid I have," Strether laughed: "one does fill out some with all one takes in, and I've taken in, I dare say, more than I've natural room for. I was dog-tired when I sailed." It had the oddest sound of cheerfulness.

"I was dog-tired," his companion returned, "when I arrived, and it's this wild hunt for rest that takes all the life out of me. The fact is, Strether—and it's a comfort to have you here at last to say it to; though I don't know, after all, that I've really waited; I've told it to people I've met in the cars—the fact is, such a country as this ain't my KIND of country anyway. There ain't a country I've seen over here that DOES seem my kind. Oh I don't say but what there are plenty of pretty places and remarkable old things; but the trouble is that I don't seem to feel anywhere in tune. That's one of the reasons why I suppose I've gained so little. I haven't had the first sign of that lift I was led to expect." With this he broke out more earnestly. "Look here—I want to go back."

His eyes were all attached to Strether's now, for he was one of the men who fully face you when they talk of themselves. This enabled his friend to look at him hard and immediately to appear to the highest advantage in his eyes by doing so. "That's a genial thing to say to a fellow who has come out on purpose to meet you!"

Nothing could have been finer, on this, than Waymarsh's sombre glow. "HAVE you come out on purpose?"

"Well—very largely."

"I thought from the way you wrote there was something back of it."

Strether hesitated. "Back of my desire to be with you?"

"Back of your prostration."

Strether, with a smile made more dim by a certain consciousness, shook his head. "There are all the causes of it!"

"And no particular cause that seemed most to drive you?"

Our friend could at last conscientiously answer. "Yes. One. There IS a matter that has had much to do with my coming out."

Waymarsh waited a little. "Too private to mention?"

"No, not too private—for YOU. Only rather complicated."

"Well," said Waymarsh, who had waited again, "I MAY lose my mind over here, but I don't know as I've done so yet."

"Oh you shall have the whole thing. But not tonight."

Waymarsh seemed to sit stiffer and to hold his elbows tighter. "Why not—if I can't sleep?"

"Because, my dear man, I CAN!"

"Then where's your prostration?"

"Just in that—that I can put in eight hours." And Strether brought it out that if Waymarsh didn't "gain" it was because he didn't go to bed: the result of which was, in its order, that, to do the latter justice, he permitted his friend to insist on his really getting settled. Strether, with a kind coercive hand for it, assisted him to this consummation, and again found his own part in their relation auspiciously enlarged by the smaller touches of lowering the lamp and seeing to a sufficiency of blanket. It somehow ministered for him to indulgence to feel Waymarsh, who looked unnaturally big and black in bed, as much tucked in as a patient in a hospital, and with his covering up to his chin, as much simplified by it He hovered in vague pity, to be brief, while his companion challenged him out of the bedclothes; "Is she really after you? Is that what's behind?"

Strether felt an uneasiness at the direction taken by his companion's insight, but he played a little at uncertainty. "Behind my coming out?"

"Behind your prostration or whatever. It's generally felt, you know, that she follows you up pretty close."

Strether's candour was never very far off. "Oh it has occurred to you that I'm literally running away from Mrs. Newsome?"

"Well, I haven't KNOWN but what you are. You're a very attractive man, Strether. You've seen for yourself," said Waymarsh "what that lady downstairs makes of it. Unless indeed," he rambled on with an effect between the ironic and the anxious, "it's you who are after HER. IS Mrs. Newsome OVER here?" He spoke as with a droll dread of her.

It made his friend—though rather dimly—smile. "Dear no she's safe, thank goodness—as I think I more and more feel—at home. She thought of coming, but she gave it up. I've come in a manner instead of her; and come to that extent—for you're right in your inference—on her business. So you see there IS plenty of connexion."

Waymarsh continued to see at least all there was. "Involving accordingly the particular one I've referred to?"

Strether took another turn about the room, giving a twitch to his companion's blanket and finally gaining the door. His feeling was that of a nurse who had earned personal rest by having made everything straight. "Involving more things than I can think of breaking ground on now. But don't be afraid—you shall have them from me: you'll probably find yourself having quite as much of them as you can do with. I shall—if we keep together—very much depend on your impression of some of them."

Waymarsh's acknowledgement of this tribute was characteristically indirect. "You mean to say you don't believe we WILL keep together?"

"I only glance at the danger," Strether paternally said, "because when I hear you wail to go back I seem to see you open up such possibilities of folly."

Waymarsh took it—silent a little—like a large snubbed child "What are you going to do with me?"

It was the very question Strether himself had put to Miss Gostrey, and he wondered if he had sounded like that. But HE at least could be more definite. "I'm going to take you right down to London."

"Oh I've been down to London!" Waymarsh more softly moaned. "I've no use, Strether, for anything down there."

"Well," said Strether, good-humouredly, "I guess you've some use for me."

"So I've got to go?"

"Oh you've got to go further yet."

"Well," Waymarsh sighed, "do your damnedest! Only you WILL tell me before you lead me on all the way—?"

Our friend had again so lost himself, both for amusement and for contrition, in the wonder of whether he had made, in his own challenge that afternoon, such another figure, that he for an instant missed the thread. "Tell you—?"

"Why what you've got on hand."

Strether hesitated. "Why it's such a matter as that even if I positively wanted I shouldn't be able to keep it from you."

Waymarsh gloomily gazed. "What does that mean then but that your trip is just FOR her?"

"For Mrs. Newsome? Oh it certainly is, as I say. Very much."

"Then why do you also say it's for me?"

Strether, in impatience, violently played with his latch. "It's simple enough. It's for both of you."

Waymarsh at last turned over with a groan. "Well, I won't marry you!"

"Neither, when it comes to that—!" But the visitor had already laughed and escaped.

III

He had told Miss Gostrey he should probably take, for departure with Waymarsh, some afternoon train, and it thereupon in the morning appeared that this lady had made her own plan for an earlier one. She had breakfasted when Strether came into the coffee-room; but, Waymarsh not having yet emerged, he was in time to recall her to the terms of their understanding and to pronounce her discretion overdone. She was surely not to break away at the very moment she had created a want. He had met her as she rose from her little table in a window, where, with the morning papers beside her, she reminded him, as he let her know, of Major Pendennis breakfasting at his club—a compliment of which she professed a deep appreciation; and he detained her as pleadingly as if he had already—and notably under pressure of the visions of the night—learned to be unable to do without her. She must teach him at all events, before she went, to order breakfast as breakfast was ordered in Europe, and she must especially sustain him in the problem of ordering for Waymarsh. The latter had laid upon his friend, by desperate sounds through the door of his room, dreadful divined responsibilities in respect to beefsteak and oranges—responsibilities which Miss Gostrey took over with an alertness of action that matched her quick intelligence. She had before this weaned the expatriated from traditions compared with which the matutinal beefsteak was but the creature of an hour, and it was not for her, with some of her memories, to falter in the path though she freely enough declared, on reflexion, that there was always in such cases a choice of opposed policies. "There are times when to give them their head, you know—!"

They had gone to wait together in the garden for the dressing of the meal, and Strether found her more suggestive than ever "Well, what?"

"Is to bring about for them such a complexity of relations-unless indeed we call it a simplicity!—that the situation HAS to wind itself up. They want to go back."

"And you want them to go!" Strether gaily concluded.

"I always want them to go, and I send them as fast as I can."

"Oh I know—you take them to Liverpool."

"Any port will serve in a storm. I'm—with all my other functions—an agent for repatriation. I want to re-people our stricken country. What will become of it else? I want to discourage others."

The ordered English garden, in the freshness of the day, was delightful to Strether, who liked the sound, under his feet, of the tight fine gravel, packed with the chronic damp, and who had the idlest eye for the deep smoothness of turf and the clean curves of paths. "Other people?"

"Other countries. Other people—yes. I want to encourage our own."

Strether wondered. "Not to come? Why then do you 'meet' them—since it doesn't appear to be to stop them?"

"Oh that they shouldn't come is as yet too much to ask. What I attend to is that they come quickly and return still more so. I meet them to help it to be over as soon as possible, and though I don't stop them I've my way of putting them through. That's my little system; and, if you want to know," said Maria Gostrey, "it's my real secret, my innermost mission and use. I only seem, you see, to beguile and approve; but I've thought it all out and I'm working all the while underground. I can't perhaps quite give you my formula, but I think that practically I succeed. I send you back spent. So you stay back. Passed through my hands—"

"We don't turn up again?" The further she went the further he always saw himself able to follow. "I don't want your formula—I feel quite enough, as I hinted yesterday, your abysses. Spent!" he echoed. "If that's how you're arranging so subtly to send me I thank you for the warning."

For a minute, amid the pleasantness—poetry in tariffed items, but all the more, for guests already convicted, a challenge to consumption—they smiled at each other in confirmed fellowship. "Do you call it subtly? It's a plain poor tale. Besides, you're a special case."

"Oh special cases—that's weak!" She was weak enough, further still, to defer her journey and agree to accompany the gentlemen on their own, might a separate carriage mark her independence; though it was in spite of this to befall after luncheon that she went off alone and that, with a tryst taken for a day of her company in London, they lingered another night. She had, during the morning—spent in a way that he was to remember later on as the very climax of his foretaste, as warm with presentiments, with what he would have called collapses—had all sorts of things out with Strether; and among them the fact that though there was never a moment of her life when she wasn't "due" somewhere, there was yet scarce a perfidy to others of which she wasn't capable for his sake. She explained moreover that wherever she happened to be she found a dropped thread to pick up, a ragged edge to repair, some familiar appetite in ambush, jumping out as she approached, yet appeasable with a temporary biscuit. It became, on her taking the risk of the deviation imposed on him by her insidious arrangement of his morning meal, a point of honour for her not to fail with Waymarsh of the larger success too; and her subsequent boast to Strether was that she had made their friend fare—and quite without his knowing what was the matter—as Major Pendennis would have fared at the Megatherium. She had made him breakfast like a gentleman, and it was nothing, she forcibly asserted, to what she would yet make him do. She made him participate in the slow reiterated ramble with which, for Strether, the new day amply filled itself; and it was by her art that he somehow had the air, on the ramparts and in the Rows, of carrying a point of his own.

The three strolled and stared and gossiped, or at least the two did; the case really yielding for their comrade, if analysed, but the element of stricken silence. This element indeed affected Strether as charged with audible rumblings, but he was conscious of the care of taking it explicitly as a sign of pleasant peace. He wouldn't appeal too much, for that provoked stiffness; yet he wouldn't be too freely tacit, for that suggested giving up. Waymarsh himself adhered to an ambiguous dumbness that might have represented either the growth of a perception or the despair of one; and at times and in places—where the low-browed galleries were darkest, the opposite gables queerest, the solicitations of every kind densest—the others caught him fixing hard some object of minor interest, fixing even at moments nothing discernible, as if he were indulging it with a truce. When he met Strether's eye on such occasions he looked guilty and furtive, fell the next minute into some attitude of retraction. Our friend couldn't show him the right things for fear of provoking some total renouncement, and was tempted even to show him the wrong in order to make him differ with triumph. There were moments when he himself felt shy of professing the full sweetness of the taste of leisure, and there were others when he found himself feeling as if his passages of interchange with the lady at his side might fall upon the third member of their party very much as Mr. Burchell, at Dr. Primrose's fireside, was influenced by the high flights of the visitors from London. The smallest things so arrested and amused him that he repeatedly apologised—brought up afresh in explanation his plea of a previous grind. He was aware at the same time that his grind had been as nothing to Waymarsh's, and he repeatedly confessed that, to cover his frivolity, he was doing his best for his previous virtue. Do what he might, in any case, his previous virtue was still there, and it seemed fairly to stare at him out of the windows of shops that were not as the shops of Woollett, fairly to make him want things that he shouldn't know what to do with. It was by the oddest, the least admissible of laws demoralising him now; and the way it boldly took was to make him want more wants. These first walks in Europe were in fact a kind of finely lurid intimation of what one might find at the end of that process. Had he come back after long years, in something already so like the evening of life, only to be exposed to it? It was at all events over the shop-windows that he made, with Waymarsh, most free; though it would have been easier had not the latter most sensibly yielded to the appeal of the merely useful trades. He pierced with his sombre detachment the plate-glass of ironmongers and saddlers, while Strether flaunted an affinity with the dealers in stamped letter-paper and in smart neckties. Strether was in fact recurrently shameless in the presence of the tailors, though it was just over the heads of the tailors that his countryman most loftily looked. This gave Miss Gostrey a grasped opportunity to back up Waymarsh at his expense. The weary lawyer—it was unmistakeable—had a conception of dress; but that, in view of some of the features of the effect produced, was just what made the danger of insistence on it. Strether wondered if he by this time thought Miss Gostrey less fashionable or Lambert Strether more so; and it appeared probable that most of the remarks exchanged between this latter pair about passers, figures, faces, personal types, exemplified in their degree the disposition to talk as "society" talked.

Was what was happening to himself then, was what already HAD happened, really that a woman of fashion was floating him into society and that an old friend deserted on the brink was watching the force of the current? When the woman of fashion permitted Strether—as she permitted him at the most—the purchase of a pair of gloves, the terms she made about it, the prohibition of neckties and other items till she should be able to guide him through the Burlington Arcade, were such as to fall upon a sensitive ear as a challenge to just imputations. Miss Gostrey was such a woman of fashion as could make without a symptom of vulgar blinking an appointment for the Burlington Arcade. Mere discriminations about a pair of gloves could thus at any rate represent—always for such sensitive ears as were in question—possibilities of something that Strether could make a mark against only as the peril of apparent wantonness. He had quite the consciousness of his new friend, for their companion, that he might have had of a Jesuit in petticoats, a representative of the recruiting interests of the Catholic Church. The Catholic Church, for Waymarsh-that was to say the enemy, the monster of bulging eyes and far-reaching quivering groping tentacles—was exactly society, exactly the multiplication of shibboleths, exactly the discrimination of types and tones, exactly the wicked old Rows of Chester, rank with feudalism; exactly in short Europe.

There was light for observation, however, in an incident that occurred just before they turned back to luncheon. Waymarsh had been for a quarter of an hour exceptionally mute and distant, and something, or other—Strether was never to make out exactly what—proved, as it were, too much for him after his comrades had stood for three minutes taking in, while they leaned on an old balustrade that guarded the edge of the Row, a particularly crooked and huddled street-view. "He thinks us sophisticated, he thinks us worldly, he thinks us wicked, he thinks us all sorts of queer things," Strether reflected; for wondrous were the vague quantities our friend had within a couple of short days acquired the habit of conveniently and conclusively lumping together. There seemed moreover a direct connexion between some such inference and a sudden grim dash taken by Waymarsh to the opposite side. This movement was startlingly sudden, and his companions at first supposed him to have espied, to be pursuing, the glimpse of an acquaintance. They next made out, however, that an open door had instantly received him, and they then recognised him as engulfed in the establishment of a jeweller, behind whose glittering front he was lost to view. The fact had somehow the note of a demonstration, and it left each of the others to show a face almost of fear. But Miss Gostrey broke into a laugh. "What's the matter with him?"

"Well," said Strether, "he can't stand it."

"But can't stand what?"

"Anything. Europe."

"Then how will that jeweller help him?"

Strether seemed to make it out, from their position, between the interstices of arrayed watches, of close-hung dangling gewgaws. "You'll see."

"Ah that's just what—if he buys anything—I'm afraid of: that I shall see something rather dreadful."

Strether studied the finer appearances. "He may buy everything."

"Then don't you think we ought to follow him?"

"Not for worlds. Besides we can't. We're paralysed. We exchange a long scared look, we publicly tremble. The thing is, you see, we 'realise.' He has struck for freedom."

She wondered but she laughed. "Ah what a price to pay! And I was preparing some for him so cheap."

"No, no," Strether went on, frankly amused now; "don't call it that: the kind of freedom you deal in is dear." Then as to justify himself: "Am I not in MY way trying it? It's this."

"Being here, you mean, with me?"

"Yes, and talking to you as I do. I've known you a few hours, and I've known HIM all my life; so that if the ease I thus take with you about him isn't magnificent"—and the thought of it held him a moment—"why it's rather base."

"It's magnificent!" said Miss Gostrey to make an end of it. "And you should hear," she added, "the ease I take—and I above all intend to take—with Mr. Waymarsh."

Strether thought. "About ME? Ah that's no equivalent. The equivalent would be Waymarsh's himself serving me up—his remorseless analysis of me. And he'll never do that"—he was sadly clear. "He'll never remorselessly analyse me." He quite held her with the authority of this. "He'll never say a word to you about me."

She took it in; she did it justice; yet after an instant her reason, her restless irony, disposed of it. "Of course he won't. For what do you take people, that they're able to say words about anything, able remorselessly to analyse? There are not many like you and me. It will be only because he's too stupid."

It stirred in her friend a sceptical echo which was at the same time the protest of the faith of years. "Waymarsh stupid?"

"Compared with you."

Strether had still his eyes on the jeweller's front, and he waited a moment to answer. "He's a success of a kind that I haven't approached."

"Do you mean he has made money?"

"He makes it—to my belief. And I," said Strether, "though with a back quite as bent, have never made anything. I'm a perfectly equipped failure."

He feared an instant she'd ask him if he meant he was poor; and he was glad she didn't, for he really didn't know to what the truth on this unpleasant point mightn't have prompted her. She only, however, confirmed his assertion. "Thank goodness you're a failure—it's why I so distinguish you! Anything else to-day is too hideous. Look about you—look at the successes. Would you BE one, on your honour? Look, moreover," she continued, "at me."

For a little accordingly their eyes met. "I see," Strether returned. "You too are out of it."

"The superiority you discern in me," she concurred, "announces my futility. If you knew," she sighed, "the dreams of my youth! But our realities are what has brought us together. We're beaten brothers in arms."

He smiled at her kindly enough, but he shook his head. "It doesn't alter the fact that you're expensive. You've cost me already—!"

But he had hung fire. "Cost you what?"

"Well, my past—in one great lump. But no matter," he laughed: "I'll pay with my last penny."

Her attention had unfortunately now been engaged by their comrade's return, for Waymarsh met their view as he came out of his shop. "I hope he hasn't paid," she said, "with HIS last; though I'm convinced he has been splendid, and has been so for you."

"Ah no—not that!"

"Then for me?"

"Quite as little." Waymarsh was by this time near enough to show signs his friend could read, though he seemed to look almost carefully at nothing in particular.

"Then for himself?"

"For nobody. For nothing. For freedom."

"But what has freedom to do with it?"

Strether's answer was indirect. "To be as good as you and me. But different."

She had had time to take in their companion's face; and with it, as such things were easy for her, she took in all. "Different—yes. But better!"

If Waymarsh was sombre he was also indeed almost sublime. He told them nothing, left his absence unexplained, and though they were convinced he had made some extraordinary purchase they were never to learn its nature. He only glowered grandly at the tops of the old gables. "It's the sacred rage," Strether had had further time to say; and this sacred rage was to become between them, for convenient comprehension, the description of one of his periodical necessities. It was Strether who eventually contended that it did make him better than they. But by that time Miss Gostrey was convinced that she didn't want to be better than Strether.

Book Second

I

London theatre (1818) by Robert Biemmell Schnebbelie (c.1800-1847)

Those occasions on which Strether was, in association with the exile from Milrose, to see the sacred rage glimmer through would doubtless have their due periodicity; but our friend had meanwhile to find names for many other matters. On no evening of his life perhaps, as he reflected, had he had to supply so many as on the third of his short stay in London; an evening spent by Miss Gostrey's side at one of the theatres, to which he had found himself transported, without his own hand raised, on the mere expression of a conscientious wonder. She knew her theatre, she knew her play, as she had triumphantly known, three days running, everything else, and the moment filled to the brim, for her companion, that apprehension of the interesting which, whether or no the interesting happened to filter through his guide, strained now to its limits his brief opportunity. Waymarsh hadn't come with them; he had seen plays enough, he signified, before Strether had joined him—an affirmation that had its full force when his friend ascertained by questions that he had seen two and a circus. Questions as to what he had seen had on him indeed an effect only less favourable than questions as to what he hadn't. He liked the former to be discriminated; but how could it be done, Strether asked of their constant counsellor, without discriminating the latter?

Miss Gostrey had dined with him at his hotel, face to face over a small table on which the lighted candles had rose-coloured shades; and the rose-coloured shades and the small table and the soft fragrance of the lady—had anything to his mere sense ever been so soft?—were so many touches in he scarce knew what positive high picture. He had been to the theatre, even to the opera, in Boston, with Mrs. Newsome, more than once acting as her only escort; but there had been no little confronted dinner, no pink lights, no whiff of vague sweetness, as a preliminary: one of the results of which was that at present, mildly rueful, though with a sharpish accent, he actually asked himself WHY there hadn't. There was much the same difference in his impression of the noticed state of his companion, whose dress was "cut down," as he believed the term to be, in respect to shoulders and bosom, in a manner quite other than Mrs. Newsome's, and who wore round her throat a broad red velvet band with an antique jewel—he was rather complacently sure it was antique—attached to it in front. Mrs. Newsome's dress was never in any degree "cut down," and she never wore round her throat a broad red velvet band: if she had, moreover, would it ever have served so to carry on and complicate, as he now almost felt, his vision?

It would have been absurd of him to trace into ramifications the effect of the ribbon from which Miss Gostrey's trinket depended, had he not for the hour, at the best, been so given over to uncontrolled perceptions. What was it but an uncontrolled perception that his friend's velvet band somehow added, in her appearance, to the value of every other item—to that of her smile and of the way she carried her head, to that of her complexion, of her lips, her teeth, her eyes, her hair? What, certainly, had a man conscious of a man's work in the world to do with red velvet bands? He wouldn't for anything have so exposed himself as to tell Miss Gostrey how much he liked hers, yet he HAD none the less not only caught himself in the act—frivolous, no doubt, idiotic, and above all unexpected—of liking it: he had in addition taken it as a starting-point for fresh backward, fresh forward, fresh lateral flights. The manner in which Mrs. Newsome's throat WAS encircled suddenly represented for him, in an alien order, almost as many things as the manner in which Miss Gostrey's was. Mrs. Newsome wore, at operatic hours, a black silk dress—very handsome, he knew it was "handsome"—and an ornament that his memory was able further to identify as a ruche. He had his association indeed with the ruche, but it was rather imperfectly romantic. He had once said to the wearer—and it was as "free" a remark as he had ever made to her—that she looked, with her ruff and other matters, like Queen Elizabeth; and it had after this in truth been his fancy that, as a consequence of that tenderness and an acceptance of the idea, the form of this special tribute to the "frill" had grown slightly more marked. The connexion, as he sat there and let his imagination roam, was to strike him as vaguely pathetic; but there it all was, and pathetic was doubtless in the conditions the best thing it could possibly be. It had assuredly existed at any rate; for it seemed now to come over him that no gentleman of his age at Woollett could ever, to a lady of Mrs. Newsome's, which was not much less than his, have embarked on such a simile.

All sorts of things in fact now seemed to come over him, comparatively few of which his chronicler can hope for space to mention. It came over him for instance that Miss Gostrey looked perhaps like Mary Stuart: Lambert Strether had a candour of fancy which could rest for an instant gratified in such an antithesis. It came over him that never before—no, literally never—had a lady dined with him at a public place before going to the play. The publicity of the place was just, in the matter, for Strether, the rare strange thing; it affected him almost as the achievement of privacy might have affected a man of a different experience. He had married, in the far-away years, so young as to have missed the time natural in Boston for taking girls to the Museum; and it was absolutely true of hint that—even after the close of the period of conscious detachment occupying the centre of his life, the grey middle desert of the two deaths, that of his wife and that, ten years later, of his boy—he had never taken any one anywhere. It came over him in especial—though the monition had, as happened, already sounded, in other forms—that the business he had come out on hadn't yet been so brought home to him as by the sight of the people about him. She gave him the impression, his friend, at first, more straight than he got it for himself—gave it simply by saying with off-hand illumination: "Oh yes, they're types!"—but after he had taken it he made to the full his own use of it; both while he kept silence for the four acts and while he talked in the intervals. It was an evening, it was a world of types, and this was a connexion above all in which the figures and faces in the stalls were interchangeable with those on the stage.

He felt as if the play itself penetrated him with the naked elbow of his neighbour, a great stripped handsome red-haired lady who conversed with a gentleman on her other side in stray dissyllables which had for his ear, in the oddest way in the world, so much sound that he wondered they hadn't more sense; and he recognised by the same law, beyond the footlights, what he was pleased to take for the very flush of English life. He had distracted drops in which he couldn't have said if it were actors or auditors who were most true, and the upshot of which, each time, was the consciousness of new contacts. However he viewed his job it was "types" he should have to tackle. Those before him and around him were not as the types of Woollett, where, for that matter, it had begun to seem to him that there must only have been the male and the female. These made two exactly, even with the individual varieties. Here, on the other hand, apart from the personal and the sexual range—which might be greater or less—a series of strong stamps had been applied, as it were, from without; stamps that his observation played with as, before a glass case on a table, it might have passed from medal to medal and from copper to gold. It befell that in the drama precisely there was a bad woman in a yellow frock who made a pleasant weak good-looking young man in perpetual evening dress do the most dreadful things. Strether felt himself on the whole not afraid of the yellow frock, but he was vaguely anxious over a certain kindness into which he found himself drifting for its victim. He hadn't come out, he reminded himself, to be too kind, or indeed to be kind at all, to Chadwick Newsome. Would Chad also be in perpetual evening dress? He somehow rather hoped it—it seemed so to add to THIS young man's general amenability; though he wondered too if, to fight him with his own weapons, he himself (a thought almost startling) would have likewise to be. This young man furthermore would have been much more easy to handle—at least for HIM—than appeared probable in respect to Chad.

It came up for him with Miss Gostrey that there were things of which she would really perhaps after all have heard, and she admitted when a little pressed that she was never quite sure of what she heard as distinguished from things such as, on occasions like the present, she only extravagantly guessed. "I seem with this freedom, you see, to have guessed Mr. Chad. He's a young man on whose head high hopes are placed at Woollett; a young man a wicked woman has got hold of and whom his family over there have sent you out to rescue. You've accepted the mission of separating him from the wicked woman. Are you quite sure she's very bad for him?"

Something in his manner showed it as quite pulling him up. "Of course we are. Wouldn't YOU be?"

"Oh I don't know. One never does—does one?—beforehand. One can only judge on the facts. Yours are quite new to me; I'm really not in the least, as you see, in possession of them: so it will be awfully interesting to have them from you. If you're satisfied, that's all that's required. I mean if you're sure you ARE sure: sure it won't do."

"That he should lead such a life? Rather!"

"Oh but I don't know, you see, about his life; you've not told me about his life. She may be charming—his life!"

"Charming?"—Strether stared before him. "She's base, venal—out of the streets."

"I see. And HE—?"

"Chad, wretched boy?"

"Of what type and temper is he?" she went on as Strether had lapsed.

"Well—the obstinate." It was as if for a moment he had been going to say more and had then controlled himself.

That was scarce what she wished. "Do you like him?"

This time he was prompt. "No. How CAN I?"

"Do you mean because of your being so saddled with him?"

"I'm thinking of his mother," said Strether after a moment. "He has darkened her admirable life." He spoke with austerity. "He has worried her half to death."

"Oh that's of course odious." She had a pause as if for renewed emphasis of this truth, but it ended on another note. "Is her life very admirable?"

"Extraordinarily."

There was so much in the tone that Miss Gostrey had to devote another pause to the appreciation of it. "And has he only HER? I don't mean the bad woman in Paris," she quickly added—"for I assure you I shouldn't even at the best be disposed to allow him more than one. But has he only his mother?"

"He has also a sister, older than himself and married; and they're both remarkably fine women."

"Very handsome, you mean?"

This promptitude—almost, as he might have thought, this precipitation, gave him a brief drop; but he came up again. "Mrs. Newsome,

I think, is handsome, though she's not of course, with a son of twenty-eight and a daughter of thirty, in her very first youth. She married, however, extremely young."

"And is wonderful," Miss Gostrey asked, "for her age?"

Strether seemed to feel with a certain disquiet the pressure of it. "I don't say she's wonderful. Or rather," he went on the next moment, "I do say it. It's exactly what she IS—wonderful. But I wasn't thinking of her appearance," he explained—"striking as that doubtless is. I was thinking—well, of many other things." He seemed to look at these as if to mention some of them; then took, pulling himself up, another turn. "About Mrs. Pocock people may differ."

"Is that the daughter's name—'Pocock'?"

"That's the daughter's name," Strether sturdily confessed.

"And people may differ, you mean, about HER beauty?"

"About everything."

"But YOU admire her?"

He gave his friend a glance as to show how he could bear this "I'm perhaps a little afraid of her."

"Oh," said Miss Gostrey, "I see her from here! You may say then I see very fast and very far, but I've already shown you I do. The young man and the two ladies," she went on, "are at any rate all the family?"

"Quite all. His father has been dead ten years, and there's no brother, nor any other sister. They'd do," said Strether, "anything in the world for him."

"And you'd do anything in the world for THEM?"

He shifted again; she had made it perhaps just a shade too affirmative for his nerves. "Oh I don't know!"

"You'd do at any rate this, and the 'anything' they'd do is represented by their MAKING you do it."

"Ah they couldn't have come—either of them. They're very busy people and Mrs. Newsome in particular has a large full life. She's moreover highly nervous—and not at all strong."

"You mean she's an American invalid?"

He carefully distinguished. "There's nothing she likes less than to be called one, but she would consent to be one of those things, I think," he laughed, "if it were the only way to be the other."

"Consent to be an American in order to be an invalid?"

"No," said Strether, "the other way round. She's at any rate delicate sensitive high-strung. She puts so much of herself into everything—"

Ah Maria knew these things! "That she has nothing left for anything else? Of course she hasn't. To whom do you say it? High-strung? Don't I spend my life, for them, jamming down the pedal? I see moreover how it has told on you."

Strether took this more lightly. "Oh I jam down the pedal too!"

"Well," she lucidly returned, "we must from this moment bear on it together with all our might." And she forged ahead. "Have they money?"

But it was as if, while her energetic image still held him, her enquiry fell short. "Mrs. Newsome," he wished further to explain, "hasn't moreover your courage on the question of contact. If she had come it would have been to see the person herself."

"The woman? Ah but that's courage."

"No—it's exaltation, which is a very different thing. Courage," he, however, accommodatingly threw out, "is what YOU have."

She shook her head. "You say that only to patch me up—to cover the nudity of my want of exaltation. I've neither the one nor the other. I've mere battered indifference. I see that what you mean," Miss Gostrey pursued, "is that if your friend HAD come she would take great views, and the great views, to put it simply, would be too much for her."

Strether looked amused at her notion of the simple, but he adopted her formula. "Everything's too much for her."

"Ah then such a service as this of yours—"

"Is more for her than anything else? Yes—far more. But so long as it isn't too much for ME—!"

"Her condition doesn't matter? Surely not; we leave her condition out; we take it, that is, for granted. I see it, her condition, as behind and beneath you; yet at the same time I see it as bearing you up."

"Oh it does bear me up!" Strether laughed.

"Well then as yours bears ME nothing more's needed." With which she put again her question. "Has Mrs. Newsome money?"

This time he heeded. "Oh plenty. That's the root of the evil. There's money, to very large amounts, in the concern. Chad has had the free use of a great deal. But if he'll pull himself together and come home, all the same, he'll find his account in it."

She had listened with all her interest. "And I hope to goodness you'll find yours!"

"He'll take up his definite material reward," said Strether without acknowledgement of this. "He's at the parting of the ways. He can come into the business now—he can't come later."

"Is there a business?"

"Lord, yes—a big brave bouncing business. A roaring trade."

"A great shop?"

"Yes—a workshop; a great production, a great industry. The concern's a manufacture—and a manufacture that, if it's only properly looked after, may well be on the way to become a monopoly. It's a little thing they make—make better, it appears, than other people can, or than other people, at any rate, do. Mr. Newsome, being a man of ideas, at least in that particular line," Strether explained, "put them on it with great effect, and gave the place altogether, in his time, an immense lift."

"It's a place in itself?"

"Well, quite a number of buildings; almost a little industrial colony. But above all it's a thing. The article produced."

"And what IS the article produced?"

Strether looked about him as in slight reluctance to say; then the curtain, which he saw about to rise, came to his aid. "I'll tell you next time." But when the next time came he only said he'd tell her later on—after they should have left the theatre; for she had immediately reverted to their topic, and even for himself the picture of the stage was now overlaid with another image. His postponements, however, made her wonder—wonder if the article referred to were anything bad. And she explained that she meant improper or ridiculous or wrong. But Strether, so far as that went, could satisfy her. "Unmentionable? Oh no, we constantly talk of it; we are quite familiar and brazen about it. Only, as a small, trivial, rather ridiculous object of the commonest domestic use, it's just wanting in-what shall I say? Well, dignity, or the least approach to distinction. Right here therefore, with everything about us so grand—!" In short he shrank.

"It's a false note?"

"Sadly. It's vulgar."

"But surely not vulgarer than this." Then on his wondering as she herself had done: "Than everything about us." She seemed a trifle irritated. "What do you take this for?"

"Why for—comparatively—divine!"

"This dreadful London theatre? It's impossible, if you really want to know."

"Oh then," laughed Strether, "I DON'T really want to know!"

It made between them a pause, which she, however, still fascinated by the mystery of the production at Woollett, presently broke. "'Rather ridiculous'? Clothes-pins? Saleratus? Shoe-polish?"

It brought him round. "No—you don't even 'burn.' I don't think, you know, you'll guess it."

"How then can I judge how vulgar it is?"

"You'll judge when I do tell you"—and he persuaded her to patience. But it may even now frankly be mentioned that he in the sequel never WAS to tell her. He actually never did so, and it moreover oddly occurred that by the law, within her, of the incalculable, her desire for the information dropped and her attitude to the question converted itself into a positive cultivation of ignorance. In ignorance she could humour her fancy, and that proved a useful freedom. She could treat the little nameless object as indeed unnameable—she could make their abstention enormously definite. There might indeed have been for Strether the portent of this in what she next said.

"Is it perhaps then because it's so bad—because your industry as you call it, IS so vulgar—that Mr. Chad won't come back? Does he feel the taint? Is he staying away not to be mixed up in it?"

"Oh," Strether laughed, "it wouldn't appear—would it?—that he feels 'taints'! He's glad enough of the money from it, and the money's his whole basis. There's appreciation in that—I mean as to the allowance his mother has hitherto made him. She has of course the resource of cutting this allowance off; but even then he has unfortunately, and on no small scale, his independent supply—money left him by his grandfather, her own father."

"Wouldn't the fact you mention then," Miss Gostrey asked, "make it just more easy for him to be particular? Isn't he conceivable as fastidious about the source—the apparent and public source—of his income?"

Strether was able quite good-humouredly to entertain the proposition. "The source of his grandfather's wealth—and thereby of his own share in it—was not particularly noble."

"And what source was it?"

Strether cast about. "Well—practices."

"In business? Infamies? He was an old swindler?"

"Oh," he said with more emphasis than spirit, "I shan't describe HIM nor narrate his exploits."

"Lord, what abysses! And the late Mr. Newsome then?"

"Well, what about him?"

"Was he like the grandfather?"

"No—he was on the other side of the house. And he was different."

Miss Gostrey kept it up. "Better?"

Her friend for a moment hung fire. "No."

Her comment on his hesitation was scarce the less marked for being mute. "Thank you. NOW don't you see," she went on, "why the boy doesn't come home? He's drowning his shame."

"His shame? What shame?"

"What shame? Comment donc? THE shame."

"But where and when," Strether asked, "is 'THE shame'—where is any shame—to-day? The men I speak of—they did as every one does; and (besides being ancient history) it was all a matter of appreciation."

She showed how she understood. "Mrs. Newsome has appreciated?"

"Ah I can't speak for HER!"

"In the midst of such doings—and, as I understand you, profiting by them, she at least has remained exquisite?"

"Oh I can't talk of her!" Strether said.

"I thought she was just what you COULD talk of. You DON'T trust me," Miss Gostrey after a moment declared.

It had its effect. "Well, her money is spent, her life conceived and carried on with a large beneficence—"

"That's a kind of expiation of wrongs? Gracious," she added before he could speak, "how intensely you make me see her!"

"If you see her," Strether dropped, "it's all that's necessary."

She really seemed to have her. "I feel that. She IS, in spite of everything, handsome."

This at least enlivened him. "What do you mean by everything?"

"Well, I mean YOU." With which she had one of her swift changes of ground. "You say the concern needs looking after; but doesn't Mrs. Newsome look after it?"

"So far as possible. She's wonderfully able, but it's not her affair, and her life's a good deal overcharged. She has many, many things."

"And you also?"

"Oh yes—I've many too, if you will."

"I see. But what I mean is," Miss Gostrey amended, "do you also look after the business?"

"Oh no, I don't touch the business."

"Only everything else?"

"Well, yes—some things."

"As for instance—?"

Strether obligingly thought. "Well, the Review."

"The Review?—you have a Review?"

"Certainly. Woollett has a Review—which Mrs. Newsome, for the most part, magnificently pays for and which I, not at all magnificently, edit. My name's on the cover," Strether pursued, "and I'm really rather disappointed and hurt that you seem never to have heard of it."

She neglected for a moment this grievance. "And what kind of a Review is it?"

His serenity was now completely restored. "Well, it's green."

"Do you mean in political colour as they say here—in thought?"

"No; I mean the cover's green—of the most lovely shade."

Henry James

"And with Mrs. Newsome's name on it too?"

He waited a little. "Oh as for that you must judge if she peeps out. She's behind the whole thing; but she's of a delicacy and a discretion—!"

Miss Gostrey took it all. "I'm sure. She WOULD be. I don't underrate her. She must be rather a swell."

"Oh yes, she's rather a swell!"

"A Woollett swell—bon! I like the idea of a Woollett swell. And you must be rather one too, to be so mixed up with her."

"Ah no," said Strether, "that's not the way it works."

But she had already taken him up. "The way it works—you needn't tell me!—is of course that you efface yourself."

"With my name on the cover?" he lucidly objected.

"Ah but you don't put it on for yourself."

"I beg your pardon—that's exactly what I do put it on for. It's exactly the thing that I'm reduced to doing for myself. It seems to rescue a little, you see, from the wreck of hopes and ambitions, the refuse-heap of disappointments and failures, my one presentable little scrap of an identity."

On this she looked at him as to say many things, but what she at last simply said was: "She likes to see it there. You're the bigger swell of the two," she immediately continued, "because you think you're not one. She thinks she IS one. However," Miss Gostrey added, "she thinks you're one too. You're at all events the biggest she can get hold of." She embroidered, she abounded. "I don't say it to interfere between you, but on the day she gets hold of a bigger one—!" Strether had thrown back his head as in silent mirth over something that struck him in her audacity or felicity, and her flight meanwhile was already higher. "Therefore close with her—!"

"Close with her?" he asked as she seemed to hang poised.

"Before you lose your chance."

Their eyes met over it. "What do you mean by closing?"

"And what do I mean by your chance? I'll tell you when you tell me all the things YOU don't. Is it her GREATEST fad?" she briskly pursued.

"The Review?" He seemed to wonder how he could best describe it. This resulted however but in a sketch. "It's her tribute to the ideal."

"I see. You go in for tremendous things."

"We go in for the unpopular side—that is so far as we dare."

"And how far DO you dare?"

"Well, she very far. I much less. I don't begin to have her faith. She provides," said Strether, "three fourths of that. And she provides, as I've confided to you, ALL the money."

It evoked somehow a vision of gold that held for a little Miss Gostrey's eyes, and she looked as if she heard the bright dollars shovelled in. "I hope then you make a good thing—"

"I NEVER made a good thing!" he at once returned.

She just waited. "Don't you call it a good thing to be loved?"

"Oh we're not loved. We're not even hated. We're only just sweetly ignored."

She had another pause. "You don't trust me!" she once more repeated.

"Don't I when I lift the last veil?—tell you the very secret of the prison-house?"

Again she met his eyes, but to the result that after an instant her own turned away with impatience. "You don't sell? Oh I'm glad of THAT!" After which however, and before he could protest, she was off again. "She's just a MORAL swell."

He accepted gaily enough the definition. "Yes—I really think that describes her."

But it had for his friend the oddest connexion. "How does she do her hair?"

He laughed out. "Beautifully!"

"Ah that doesn't tell me. However, it doesn't matter—I know. It's tremendously neat—a real reproach; quite remarkably thick and without, as yet, a single strand of white. There!"

He blushed for her realism, but gaped at her truth. "You're the very deuce."

"What else SHOULD I be? It was as the very deuce I pounced on you. But don't let it trouble you, for everything but the very deuce—at our age—is a bore and a delusion, and even he himself, after all, but half a joy." With which, on a single sweep of her wing, she resumed. "You assist her to expiate—which is rather hard when you've yourself not sinned."

"It's she who hasn't sinned," Strether replied. "I've sinned the most."

"Ah," Miss Gostrey cynically laughed, "what a picture of HER! Have you robbed the widow and the orphan?"

"I've sinned enough," said Strether.

"Enough for whom? Enough for what?"

"Well, to be where I am."

"Thank you!" They were disturbed at this moment by the passage between their knees and the back of the seats before them of a gentleman who had been absent during a part of the performance and who now returned for the close; but the interruption left Miss Gostrey time, before the subsequent hush, to express as a sharp finality her sense of the moral of all their talk. "I knew you had something up your sleeve!" This finality, however, left them in its turn, at the end of the play, as disposed to hang back as if they had still much to say; so that they easily agreed to let every one go before them—they found an interest in waiting. They made out from the lobby that the night had turned to rain; yet Miss Gostrey let her friend know that he wasn't to see her home. He was simply to put her, by herself, into a four-wheeler; she liked so in London, of wet nights after wild pleasures, thinking things over, on the return, in lonely four-wheelers. This was her great time, she intimated, for pulling herself together. The delays caused by the weather, the struggle for vehicles at the door, gave them occasion to subside on a divan at the back of the vestibule and just beyond the reach of the fresh damp gusts from the street. Here Strether's comrade resumed that free handling of the subject to which his own imagination of it already owed so much. "Does your young friend in Paris like you?"

It had almost, after the interval, startled him. "Oh I hope not! Why SHOULD he?"

"Why shouldn't he?" Miss Gostrey asked. "That you're coming down on him need have nothing to do with it."

"You see more in it," he presently returned, "than I."

"Of course I see you in it."

"Well then you see more in 'me'!"

"Than you see in yourself? Very likely. That's always one's right. What I was thinking of," she explained, "is the possible particular effect on him of his milieu."

"Oh his milieu—!" Strether really felt he could imagine it better now than three hours before.

"Do you mean it can only have been so lowering?"

"Why that's my very starting-point."

"Yes, but you start so far back. What do his letters say?"

"Nothing. He practically ignores us—or spares us. He doesn't write."

"I see. But there are all the same," she went on, "two quite distinct things that—given the wonderful place he's in—may have happened to him. One is that he may have got brutalised. The other is that he may have got refined."

Strether stared—this WAS a novelty. "Refined?"

"Oh," she said quietly, "there ARE refinements."

The way of it made him, after looking at her, break into a laugh. "YOU have them!"

"As one of the signs," she continued in the same tone, "they constitute perhaps the worst."

He thought it over and his gravity returned. "Is it a refinement not to answer his mother's letters?"

She appeared to have a scruple, but she brought it out. "Oh I should say the greatest of all."

"Well," said Strether, "I'M quite content to let it, as one of the signs, pass for the worst that I know he believes he can do what he likes with me."

This appeared to strike her. "How do you know it?"

"Oh I'm sure of it. I feel it in my bones."

"Feel he CAN do it?"

"Feel that he believes he can. It may come to the same thing!" Strether laughed.

She wouldn't, however, have this. "Nothing for you will ever come to the same thing as anything else." And she understood what she meant, it seemed, sufficiently to go straight on. "You say that if he does break he'll come in for things at home?"

"Quite positively. He'll come in for a particular chance—a chance that any properly constituted young man would jump at. The business has so developed that an opening scarcely apparent three years ago, but which his father's will took account of as in certain conditions possible and which, under that will, attaches to Chad's availing himself of it a large contingent advantage—this opening, the conditions having come about, now simply awaits him. His mother has kept it for him, holding out against strong pressure, till the last possible moment. It requires, naturally, as it carries with it a handsome 'part,' a large share in profits, his being on the spot and making a big effort for a big result. That's what I mean by his chance. If he misses it he comes in, as you say, for nothing. And to see that he doesn't miss it is, in a word, what I've come out for."

She let it all sink in. "What you've come out for then is simply to render him an immense service."

Well, poor Strether was willing to take it so. "Ah if you like."

"He stands, as they say, if you succeed with him, to gain—"

"Oh a lot of advantages." Strether had them clearly at his fingers' ends.

"By which you mean of course a lot of money."

"Well, not only. I'm acting with a sense for him of other things too. Consideration and comfort and security—the general safety of being anchored by a strong chain. He wants, as I see him, to be protected. Protected I mean from life."

"Ah voila!"—her thought fitted with a click. "From life. What you REALLY want to get him home for is to marry him."

"Well, that's about the size of it."

"Of course," she said, "it's rudimentary. But to any one in particular?"

He smiled at this, looking a little more conscious. "You get everything out."

For a moment again their eyes met. "You put everything in!"

He acknowledged the tribute by telling her. "To Mamie Pocock."

She wondered; then gravely, even exquisitely, as if to make the oddity also fit: "His own niece?"

"Oh you must yourself find a name for the relation. His brother-in-law's sister. Mrs. Jim's sister-in-law."

It seemed to have on Miss Gostrey a certain hardening effect. "And who in the world's Mrs. Jim?"

"Chad's sister—who was Sarah Newsome. She's married—didn't I mention it?—to Jim Pocock."

"Ah yes," she tacitly replied; but he had mentioned things—! Then, however, with all the sound it could have, "Who in the world's Jim Pocock?" she asked.

"Why Sally's husband. That's the only way we distinguish people at Woollett," he good-humoredly explained.

"And is it a great distinction—being Sally's husband?"

He considered. "I think there can be scarcely a greater—unless it may become one, in the future, to be Chad's wife."

"Then how do they distinguish YOU?"

"They DON'T—except, as I've told you, by the green cover."

Once more their eyes met on it, and she held him an instant. "The green cover won't—nor will ANY cover—avail you with ME. You're of a depth of duplicity!" Still, she could in her own large grasp of the real condone it. "Is Mamie a great parti?"

"Oh the greatest we have—our prettiest brightest girl."

Miss Gostrey seemed to fix the poor child. "I know what they CAN be. And with money?"

"Not perhaps with a great deal of that—but with so much of everything else that we don't miss it. We DON'T miss money much, you know," Strether added, "in general, in America, in pretty girls."

"No," she conceded; "but I know also what you do sometimes miss. And do you," she asked, "yourself admire her?"

It was a question, he indicated, that there might be several ways of taking; but he decided after an instant for the humorous. "Haven't I sufficiently showed you how I admire ANY pretty girl?"

Her interest in his problem was by this time such that it scarce left her freedom, and she kept close to the facts. "I supposed that at Woollett you wanted them—what shall I call it?—blameless. I mean your young men for your pretty girls."

"So did I!" Strether confessed. "But you strike there a curious fact—the fact that Woollett too accommodates itself to the spirit of the age and the increasing mildness of manners. Everything changes, and I hold that our situation precisely marks a date. We SHOULD prefer them blameless, but we have to make the best of them as we find them. Since the spirit of the age and the increasing mildness send them so much more to Paris—"

"You've to take them back as they come. When they DO come. Bon!" Once more she embraced it all, but she had a moment of thought. "Poor Chad!"

"Ah," said Strether cheerfully "Mamie will save him!"

She was looking away, still in her vision, and she spoke with impatience and almost as if he hadn't understood her. "YOU'LL save him. That's who'll save him."

"Oh but with Mamie's aid. Unless indeed you mean," he added, "that I shall effect so much more with yours!"

It made her at last again look at him. "You'll do more—as you're so much better—than all of us put together."

"I think I'm only better since I've known YOU!" Strether bravely returned.

The depletion of the place, the shrinkage of the crowd and now comparatively quiet withdrawal of its last elements had already brought them nearer the door and put them in relation with a messenger of whom he bespoke Miss Gostrey's cab. But this left them a few minutes more, which she was clearly in no mood not to use. "You've spoken to me of what—by your success—Mr. Chad stands to gain. But you've not spoken to me of what you do."

"Oh I've nothing more to gain," said Strether very simply.

She took it as even quite too simple. "You mean you've got it all 'down'? You've been paid in advance?"

"Ah don't talk about payment!" he groaned.

Something in the tone of it pulled her up, but as their messenger still delayed she had another chance and she put it in another way. "What—by failure—do you stand to lose?"

He still, however, wouldn't have it. "Nothing!" he exclaimed, and on the messenger's at this instant reappearing he was able to sink the subject in their responsive advance. When, a few steps up the street, under a lamp, he had put her into her four-wheeler and she asked him if the man had called for him no second conveyance, he replied before the door was closed. "You won't take me with you?"

"Not for the world."

"Then I shall walk."

"In the rain?"

"I like the rain," said Strether. "Good-night!"

She kept him a moment, while his hand was on the door, by not answering; after which she answered by repeating her question. "What do you stand to lose?"

Why the question now affected him as other he couldn't have said; he could only this time meet it otherwise. "Everything."

"So I thought. Then you shall succeed. And to that end I'm yours—"

"Ah, dear lady!" he kindly breathed.

"Till death!" said Maria Gostrey. "Good-night."

II

Strether called, his second morning in Paris, on the bankers of the Rue Scribe to whom his letter of credit was addressed, and he made this visit attended by Waymarsh, in whose company he had crossed from London two days before. They had hastened to the Rue Scribe on the morrow of their arrival, but Strether had not then found the letters the hope of which prompted this errand. He had had as yet none at all; hadn't expected them in London, but had counted on several in Paris, and, disconcerted now, had presently strolled back to the Boulevard with a sense of injury that he felt himself taking for as good a start as any other. It would serve, this spur to his spirit, he reflected, as, pausing at the top of the street, he looked up and down the great foreign avenue, it would serve to begin business with. His idea was to begin business immediately, and it did much for him the rest of his day that the beginning of business awaited him. He did little else till night but ask himself what he should do if he hadn't fortunately had so much to do; but he put himself the question in many different situations and connexions. What carried him hither and yon was an admirable theory that nothing he could do wouldn't be in some manner related to what he fundamentally had on hand, or WOULD be—should he happen to have a scruple—wasted for it. He did happen to have a scruple—a scruple about taking no definite step till he should get letters; but this reasoning carried it off. A single day to feel his feet—he had felt them as yet only at Chester and in London—was he could consider, none too much; and having, as he had often privately expressed it, Paris to reckon with, he threw these hours of freshness consciously into the reckoning. They made it continually greater, but that was what it had best be if it was to be anything at all, and he gave himself up till far into the evening, at the theatre and on the return, after the theatre, along the bright congested Boulevard, to feeling it grow. Waymarsh had accompanied him this time to the play, and the two men had walked together, as a first stage, from the Gymnase to the Cafe Riche, into the crowded "terrace" of which establishment—the night, or rather the morning, for midnight had struck, being bland and populous—they had wedged themselves for refreshment. Waymarsh, as a result of some discussion with his friend, had made a marked virtue of his having now let himself go; and there had been elements of impression in their half-hour over their watered beer-glasses that gave him his occasion for conveying that he held this compromise with his stiffer self to have become extreme. He conveyed it—for it was still, after all, his stiffer self who gloomed out of the glare of the terrace—in solemn silence; and there was indeed a great deal of critical silence, every way, between the companions, even till they gained the Place de l'Opera, as to the character of their nocturnal progress.

This morning there WERE letters—letters which had reached London, apparently all together, the day of Strether's journey, and had taken their time to follow him; so that, after a controlled impulse to go into them in the reception-room of the bank, which, reminding him of the post-office at Woollett, affected him as the abutment of some transatlantic bridge, he slipped them into the pocket of his loose grey overcoat with a sense of the felicity of carrying them off. Waymarsh, who had had letters yesterday, had had them again to-day, and Waymarsh suggested in this particular no controlled impulses. The last one he was at all events likely to be observed to struggle with was clearly that of bringing to a premature close any visit to the Rue Scribe. Strether had left him there yesterday; he wanted to see the papers, and he had spent, by what his friend could make out, a succession of hours with the papers. He spoke of the establishment, with emphasis, as a post of superior observation; just as he spoke generally of his actual damnable doom as a device for hiding from him what was going on. Europe was best described, to his mind, as an elaborate engine for dissociating the confined American from that indispensable knowledge, and was accordingly only rendered bearable by these occasional stations of relief, traps for the arrest of wandering western airs. Strether, on his side, set himself to walk again—he had his relief in his pocket; and indeed, much as he had desired his budget, the growth of restlessness might have been marked in him from the moment he had assured himself of the superscription of most of the missives it contained. This restlessness became therefore his temporary law; he knew he should recognise as soon as see it the best place of all for settling down with his chief correspondent. He had for the next hour an accidental air of looking for it in the windows of shops; he came down the Rue de la Paix in the sun, and, passing across the Tuileries and the river, indulged more than once—as if on finding himself determined—in a sudden pause before the book-stalls of the opposite quay. In the garden of the Tuileries he had lingered, on two or three spots, to look; it was as if the wonderful Paris spring had stayed him as he roamed. The prompt Paris morning struck its cheerful notes—in a soft breeze and a sprinkled smell, in the light flit, over the garden-floor, of bareheaded girls with the buckled strap of oblong boxes, in the type of ancient thrifty persons basking betimes where terrace-walls were warm, in the blue-frocked brass-labelled officialism of humble rakers and scrapers, in the deep references of a straight-pacing priest or the sharp ones of a white-gaitered red-legged soldier. He watched little brisk figures, figures whose movement was as the tick of the great Paris clock, take their smooth diagonal from point to point; the air had a taste as of something mixed with art, something that presented nature as a white-capped master-chef. The palace was gone, Strether remembered the palace; and when he gazed into the irremediable void of its site the historic sense in him might have been freely at play—the play under which in Paris indeed it so often winces like a touched nerve. He filled out spaces with dim symbols of scenes; he caught the gleam of white statues at the base of which, with his letters out, he could tilt back a straw-bottomed chair. But his drift was, for reasons, to the other side, and it floated him unspent up the Rue de Seine and as far as the Luxembourg. In the Luxembourg Gardens he pulled up; here at last he found his nook, and here, on a penny chair from which terraces, alleys, vistas, fountains, little trees in green tubs, little women in white caps and shrill little girls at play all sunnily "composed" together, he passed an hour in which the cup of his impressions seemed truly to overflow. But a week had elapsed since he quitted the ship, and there were more things in his mind than so few days could account for. More than once, during the time, he had regarded himself as admonished; but the admonition this morning was formidably sharp. It took as it hadn't done yet the form of a question—the question of what he was doing with such an extraordinary sense of escape. This sense was sharpest after he had read his letters, but that was also precisely why the question pressed. Four of the letters were from Mrs. Newsome and none of them short; she had lost no time, had followed on his heels while he moved, so expressing herself that he now could measure the probable frequency with which he should hear. They would arrive, it would seem, her communications, at the rate of several a week; he should be able to count, it might even prove, on more than one by each mail. If he had begun yesterday with a small grievance he had therefore an opportunity to begin to-day with its opposite. He read the letters successively and slowly, putting others back into his pocket but keeping these for a long time afterwards gathered in his lap. He held them there, lost in thought, as if to prolong the presence of what they gave him; or as if at the least to assure them their part in the constitution of some lucidity. His friend wrote admirably, and her tone was even more in her style than in her voice—he might almost, for the hour, have had to come this distance to get its full carrying quality; yet the plenitude of his consciousness of difference consorted perfectly with the deepened intensity of the connexion. It was the difference, the difference of being just where he was and AS he was, that formed the escape—this difference was so much greater than he had dreamed it would be; and what he finally sat there turning over was the strange logic of his finding himself so free. He felt it in a manner his duty to think out his state, to approve the process, and when he came in fact to trace the steps and add up the items they sufficiently accounted for the sum. He had never expected—that was the truth of it—again to find himself young, and all the years and other things it had taken to make him so were exactly his present arithmetic. He had to make sure of them to put his scruple to rest.

It all sprang at bottom from the beauty of Mrs. Newsome's desire that he should be worried with nothing that was not of the essence of his task; by insisting that he should thoroughly intermit and break she had so provided for his freedom that she would, as it were, have only herself to thank. Strether could not at this point indeed have completed his thought by the image of what she might have to thank herself FOR: the image, at best, of his own likeness-poor Lambert Strether washed up on the sunny strand by the waves of a single day, poor Lambert Strether thankful for breathing-time and stiffening himself while he gasped. There he was, and with nothing in his aspect or his posture to scandalise: it was only true that if he had seen Mrs. Newsome coming he would instinctively have jumped up to walk away a little. He would have come round and back to her bravely, but he would have had first to pull himself together. She abounded in news of the situation at home, proved to him how perfectly she was arranging for his absence, told him who would take up this and who take up that exactly where he had left it, gave him in fact chapter and verse for the moral that nothing would suffer. It filled for him, this tone of hers, all the air; yet it struck him at the same time as the hum of vain things. This latter effect was what he tried to justify—and with the success that, grave though the appearance, he at last lighted on a form that was happy. He arrived at it by the inevitable recognition of his having been a fortnight before one of the weariest of men. If ever a man had come off tired Lambert Strether was that man; and hadn't it been distinctly on the ground of his fatigue that his wonderful friend at home had so felt for him and so contrived? It seemed to him somehow at these instants that, could he only maintain with sufficient firmness his grasp of that truth, it might become in a manner his compass and his helm. What he wanted most was some idea that would simplify, and nothing would do this so much as the fact that he was done for and finished. If it had been in such a light that he had just detected in his cup the dregs of youth, that was a mere flaw of the surface of his scheme. He was so distinctly fagged-out that it must serve precisely as his convenience, and if he could but consistently be good for little enough he might do everything he wanted.

Everything he wanted was comprised moreover in a single boon—the common unattainable art of taking things as they came. He appeared to himself to have spent his best years in so active an appreciation of the way they didn't come; but perhaps—as they would seemingly here be things quite other—this long ache might at last drop to rest. He could easily see that from the moment he should accept the notion of his foredoomed collapse the last thing he would lack would be reasons and memories. Oh if he SHOULD do the sum no slate would hold the figures! The fact that he had failed, as he considered, in everything, in each relation and in half a dozen trades, as he liked luxuriously to put it, might have made, might still make, for an empty present; but it stood solidly for a crowded past. It had not been, so much achievement missed, a light yoke nor a short load. It was at present as if the backward picture had hung there, the long crooked course, grey in the shadow of his solitude. It had been a dreadful cheerful sociable solitude, a solitude of life or choice, of community; but though there had been people enough all round it there had been but three or four persons IN it. Waymarsh was one of these, and the fact struck him just now as marking the record. Mrs. Newsome was another, and Miss Gostrey had of a sudden shown signs of becoming a third. Beyond, behind them was the pale figure of his real youth, which held against its breast the two presences paler than itself—the young wife he had lost, and the young son he had stupidly sacrificed. He had again and again made out for himself that he might have kept his little boy, his little dull boy who had died at school of rapid diphtheria, if he had not in those years so insanely given himself to merely missing the mother. It was the soreness of his remorse that the child had in all likelihood not really been dull—had been dull, as he had been banished and neglected, mainly because the father had been unwittingly selfish. This was doubtless but the secret habit of sorrow, which had slowly given way to time; yet there remained an ache sharp enough to make the spirit, at the sight now and again of some fair young man just growing up, wince with the thought of an opportunity lost. Had ever a man, he had finally fallen into the way of asking himself, lost so much and even done so much for so little? There had been particular reasons why all yesterday, beyond other days, he should have had in one ear this cold enquiry. His name on the green cover, where he had put it for Mrs. Newsome, expressed him doubtless just enough to make the world—the world as distinguished, both for more and for less, from Woollett—ask who he was. He had incurred the ridicule of having to have his explanation explained. He was Lambert Strether because he was on the cover, whereas it should have been, for anything like glory, that he was on the cover because he was Lambert Strether. He would have done anything for Mrs. Newsome, have been still more ridiculous—as he might, for that matter, have occasion to be yet; which came to saying that his acceptance of fate was all he had to show at fifty-five.

He judged the quantity as small because it WAS small, and all the more egregiously since it couldn't, as he saw the case, so much as thinkably have been larger. He hadn't had the gift of making the most of what he tried, and if he had tried and tried again—no one but himself knew how often—it appeared to have been that he might demonstrate what else, in default of that, COULD be made. Old ghosts of experiments came back to him, old drudgeries and delusions, and disgusts, old recoveries with their relapses, old fevers with their chills, broken moments of good faith, others of still better doubt; adventures, for the most part, of the sort qualified as lessons. The special spring that had constantly played for him the day before was the recognition—frequent enough to surprise him—of the promises to himself that he had after his other visit never kept. The reminiscence to-day most quickened for him was that of the vow taken in the course of the pilgrimage that, newly-married, with the War just over, and helplessly young in spite of it, he had recklessly made with the creature who was so much younger still. It had been a bold dash, for which they had taken money set apart for necessities, but kept sacred at the moment in a hundred ways, and in none more so than by this private pledge of his own to treat the occasion as a relation formed with the higher culture and see that, as they said at Woollett, it should bear a good harvest. He had believed, sailing home again, that he had gained something great, and his theory—with an elaborate innocent plan of reading, digesting, coming back even, every few years—had then been to preserve, cherish and extend it. As such plans as these had come to nothing, however, in respect to acquisitions still more precious, it was doubtless little enough of a marvel that he should have lost account of that handful of seed. Buried for long years in dark corners at any rate these few germs had sprouted again under forty-eight hours of Paris. The process of yesterday had really been the process of feeling the general stirred life of connexions long since individually dropped. Strether had become acquainted even on this ground with short gusts of speculation—sudden flights of fancy in Louvre galleries, hungry gazes through clear plates behind which lemon-coloured volumes were as fresh as fruit on the tree.

There were instants at which he could ask whether, since there had been fundamentally so little question of his keeping anything, the fate after all decreed for him hadn't been only to BE kept. Kept for something, in that event, that he didn't pretend, didn't possibly dare as yet to divine; something that made him hover and wonder and laugh and sigh, made him advance and retreat, feeling half ashamed of his impulse to plunge and more than half afraid of his impulse to wait. He remembered for instance how he had gone back in the sixties with lemon-coloured volumes in general on the brain as well as with a dozen—selected for his wife too—in his trunk; and nothing had at the moment shown more confidence than this invocation of the finer taste. They were still somewhere at home, the dozen—stale and soiled and never sent to the binder; but what had become of the sharp initiation they represented? They represented now the mere sallow paint on the door of the temple of taste that he had dreamed of raising up—a structure he had practically never carried further. Strether's present highest flights were perhaps those in which this particular lapse figured to him as a symbol, a symbol of his long grind and his want of odd moments, his want moreover of money, of opportunity, of positive dignity. That the memory of the vow of his youth should, in order to throb again, have had to wait for this last, as he felt it, of all his accidents—that was surely proof enough of how his conscience had been encumbered. If any further proof were needed it would have been to be found in the fact that, as he perfectly now saw, he had ceased even to measure his meagreness, a meagreness that sprawled, in this retrospect, vague and comprehensive, stretching back like some unmapped Hinterland from a rough coast-settlement. His conscience had been amusing itself for the forty-eight hours by forbidding him the purchase of a book; he held off from that, held off from everything; from the moment he didn't yet call on Chad he wouldn't for the world have taken any other step. On this evidence, however, of the way they actually affected him he glared at the lemon-coloured covers in confession of the subconsciousness that, all the same, in the great desert of the years, he must have had of them. The green covers at home comprised, by the law of their purpose, no tribute to letters; it was of a mere rich kernel of economics, politics, ethics that, glazed and, as Mrs. Newsome maintained rather against HIS view, pre-eminently pleasant to touch, they formed the specious shell. Without therefore any needed instinctive knowledge of what was coming out, in Paris, on the bright highway, he struck himself at present as having more than once flushed with a suspicion: he couldn't otherwise at present be feeling so many fears confirmed. There were "movements" he was too late for: weren't they, with the fun of them, already spent? There were sequences he had missed and great gaps in the procession: he might have been watching it all recede in a golden cloud of dust. If the playhouse wasn't closed his seat had at least fallen to somebody else. He had an uneasy feeling the night before that if he was at the theatre at all—though he indeed justified the theatre, in the specific sense, and with a grotesqueness to which his imagination did all honour, as something he owed poor Waymarsh—he should have been there with, and as might have been said, FOR Chad.

This suggested the question of whether he could properly have taken him to such a play, and what effect—it was a point that suddenly rose—his peculiar responsibility might be held in general to have on his choice of entertainment. It had literally been present to him at the Gymnase—where one was held moreover comparatively safe—that having his young friend at his side would have been an odd feature of the work of redemption; and this quite in spite of the fact that the picture presented might well, confronted with Chad's own private stage, have seemed the pattern of propriety. He clearly hadn't come out in the name of propriety but to visit unattended equivocal performances; yet still less had he done so to undermine his authority by sharing them with the graceless youth. Was he to renounce all amusement for the sweet sake of that authority? and WOULD such renouncement give him for Chad a moral glamour? The little problem bristled the more by reason of poor Strether's fairly open sense of the irony of things. Were there then sides on which his predicament threatened to look rather droll to him? Should he have to pretend to believe—either to himself or the wretched boy—that there was anything that could make the latter worse? Wasn't some such pretence on the other hand involved in the assumption of possible processes that would make him better? His greatest uneasiness seemed to peep at him out of the imminent impression that almost any acceptance of Paris might give one's authority away. It hung before him this morning, the vast bright Babylon, like some huge iridescent object, a jewel brilliant and hard, in which parts were not to be discriminated nor differences comfortably marked. It twinkled and trembled and melted together, and what seemed all surface one moment seemed all depth the next. It was a place of which, unmistakeably, Chad was fond; wherefore if he, Strether, should like it too much, what on earth, with such a bond, would become of either of them? It all depended of course—which was a gleam of light—on how the "too much" was measured; though indeed our friend fairly felt, while he prolonged the meditation I describe, that for himself even already a certain measure had been reached. It will have been sufficiently seen that he was not a man to neglect any good chance for reflexion. Was it at all possible for instance to like Paris enough without liking it too much? He luckily however hadn't promised Mrs. Newsome not to like it at all. He was ready to recognise at this stage that such an engagement WOULD have tied his hands. The Luxembourg Gardens were incontestably just so adorable at this hour by reason—in addition to their intrinsic charm—of his not having taken it. The only engagement he had taken, when he looked the thing in the face, was to do what he reasonably could.

It upset him a little none the less and after a while to find himself at last remembering on what current of association he had been floated so far. Old imaginations of the Latin Quarter had played their part for him, and he had duly recalled its having been with this scene of rather ominous legend that, like so many young men in fiction as well as in fact, Chad had begun. He was now quite out of it, with his "home," as Strether figured the place, in the Boulevard Malesherbes; which was perhaps why, repairing, not to fail of justice either, to the elder neighbourhood, our friend had felt he could allow for the element of the usual, the immemorial, without courting perturbation. He was not at least in danger of seeing the youth and the particular Person flaunt by together; and yet he was in the very air of which—just to feel what the early natural note must have been—he wished most to take counsel. It became at once vivid to him that he had originally had, for a few days, an almost envious vision of the boy's romantic privilege. Melancholy Murger, with Francine and Musette and Rodolphe, at home, in the company of the tattered, one—if he not in his single self two or three—of the unbound, the paper-covered dozen on the shelf; and when Chad had written, five years ago, after a sojourn then already prolonged to six months, that he had decided to go in for economy and the real thing, Strether's fancy had quite fondly accompanied him in this migration, which was to convey him, as they somewhat confusedly learned at Woollett, across the bridges and up the Montagne Sainte-Geneviève. This was the region—Chad had been quite distinct about it—in which the best French, and many other things, were to be learned at least cost, and in which all sorts of clever fellows, compatriots there for a purpose, formed an awfully pleasant set. The clever fellows, the friendly countrymen were mainly young painters, sculptors, architects, medical students; but they were, Chad sagely opined, a much more profitable lot to be with—even on the footing of not being quite one of them—than the "terrible toughs" (Strether remembered the edifying discrimination) of the American bars and banks roundabout the Opera. Chad had thrown out, in the communications following this one—for at that time he did once in a while communicate—that several members of a band of earnest workers under one of the great artists had taken him right in, making him dine every night, almost for nothing, at their place, and even pressing him not to neglect the hypothesis of there being as much "in him" as in any of them. There had been literally a moment at which it appeared there might be something in him; there had been at any rate a moment at which he had written that he didn't know but what a month or two more might see him enrolled in some atelier. The season had been one at which Mrs. Newsome was moved to gratitude for small mercies; it had broken on them all as a blessing that their absentee HAD perhaps a conscience—that he was sated in fine with idleness, was ambitious of variety. The exhibition was doubtless as yet not brilliant, but Strether had been comparatively innocent, even by that time much enlisted and immersed, had determined, on the part of the two ladies, a temperate approval and in fact, as he now recollected, a certain austere enthusiasm.

But the very next thing that happened had been a dark drop of the curtain. The son and brother had not browsed long on the Montagne Sainte-Genevieve—his effective little use of the name of which, like his allusion to the best French, appeared to have been but one of the notes of his rough cunning. The light refreshment of these vain appearances had not accordingly carried any of them very far. On the other hand it had gained Chad time; it had given him a chance, unchecked, to strike his roots, had paved the way for initiations more direct and more deep. It was Strether's belief that he had been comparatively innocent before this first migration, and even that the first effects of the migration would not have been, without some particular bad accident, to have been deplored. There had been three months—he had sufficiently figured it out—in which Chad had wanted to try. He HAD tried, though not very hard—he had had his little hour of good faith. The weakness of this principle in him was that almost any accident attestedly bad enough was stronger. Such had at any rate markedly been the case for the precipitation of a special series of impressions. They had proved, successively, these impressions—all of Musette and Francine, but Musette and Francine vulgarised by the larger evolution of the type—irresistibly sharp: he had "taken up," by what was at the time to be shrinkingly gathered, as it was scantly mentioned, with one ferociously "interested" little person after another. Strether had read somewhere of a Latin motto, a description of the hours, observed on a clock by a traveller in Spain; and he had been led to apply it in thought to Chad's number one, number two, number three. Omnes vulnerant, ultima necat—they had all morally wounded, the last had morally killed. The last had been longest in possession—in possession, that is, of whatever was left of the poor boy's finer mortality. And it hadn't been she, it had been one of her early predecessors, who had determined the second migration, the expensive return and relapse, the exchange again, as was fairly to be presumed, of the vaunted best French for some special variety of the worst.

He pulled himself then at last together for his own progress back; not with the feeling that he had taken his walk in vain. He prolonged it a little, in the immediate neighbourhood, after he had quitted his chair; and the upshot of the whole morning for him was that his campaign had begun. He had wanted to put himself in relation, and he would be hanged if he were NOT in relation. He was that at no moment so much as while, under the old arches of the Odeon, he lingered before the charming open-air array of literature classic and casual. He found the effect of tone and tint, in the long charged tables and shelves, delicate and appetising; the impression—substituting one kind of low-priced consummation for another—might have been that of one of the pleasant cafes that overlapped, under an awning, to the pavement; but he edged along, grazing the tables, with his hands firmly behind him. He wasn't there to dip, to consume—he was there to reconstruct. He wasn't there for his own profit—not, that is, the direct; he was there on some chance of feeling the brush of the wing of the stray spirit of youth. He felt it in fact, he had it beside him; the old arcade indeed, as his inner sense listened, gave out the faint sound, as from far off, of the wild waving of wings. They were folded now over the breasts of buried generations; but a flutter or two lived again in the turned page of shock-headed slouch-hatted loiterers whose young intensity of type, in the direction of pale acuteness, deepened his vision, and even his appreciation, of racial differences, and whose manipulation of the uncut volume was too often, however, but a listening at closed doors. He reconstructed a possible groping Chad of three or four years before, a Chad who had, after all, simply—for that was the only way to see it—been too vulgar for his privilege. Surely it WAS a privilege to have been young and happy just there. Well, the best thing Strether knew of him was that he had had such a dream.

But his own actual business half an hour later was with a third floor on the Boulevard Malesherbes—so much as that was definite; and the fact of the enjoyment by the third-floor windows of a continuous balcony, to which he was helped by this knowledge, had perhaps something to do with his lingering for five minutes on the opposite side of the street. There were points as to which he had quite made up his mind, and one of these bore precisely on the wisdom of the abruptness to which events had finally committed him, a policy that he was pleased to find not at all shaken as he now looked at his watch and wondered. He HAD announced himself—six months before; had written out at least that Chad wasn't to be surprised should he see him some day turn up. Chad had thereupon, in a few words of rather carefully colourless answer, offered him a general welcome; and Strether, ruefully reflecting that he might have understood the warning as a hint to hospitality, a bid for an invitation, had fallen back upon silence as the corrective most to his own taste. He had asked Mrs. Newsome moreover not to announce him again; he had so distinct an opinion on his attacking his job, should he attack it at all, in his own way. Not the least of this lady's high merits for him was that he could absolutely rest on her word. She was the only woman he had known, even at Woollett, as to whom his conviction was positive that to lie was beyond her art. Sarah Pocock, for instance, her own daughter, though with social ideals, as they said, in some respects different—Sarah who WAS, in her way, aesthetic, had never refused to human commerce that mitigation of rigour; there were occasions when he had distinctly seen her apply it. Since, accordingly, at all events, he had had it from Mrs. Newsome that she had, at whatever cost to her more strenuous view, conformed, in the matter of preparing Chad, wholly to his restrictions, he now looked up at the fine continuous balcony with a safe sense that if the case had been bungled the mistake was at least his property. Was there perhaps just a suspicion of that in his present pause on the edge of the Boulevard and well in the pleasant light?

Many things came over him here, and one of them was that he should doubtless presently know whether he had been shallow or sharp. Another was that the balcony in question didn't somehow show as a convenience easy to surrender. Poor Strether had at this very moment to recognise the truth that wherever one paused in Paris the imagination reacted before one could stop it. This perpetual reaction put a price, if one would, on pauses; but it piled up consequences till there was scarce room to pick one's steps among them. What call had he, at such a juncture, for example, to like Chad's very house? High broad clear—he was expert enough to make out in a moment that it was admirably built—it fairly embarrassed our friend by the quality that, as he would have said, it "sprang" on him. He had struck off the fancy that it might, as a preliminary, be of service to him to be seen, by a happy accident, from the third-story windows, which took all the March sun, but of what service was it to find himself making out after a moment that the quality "sprang," the quality produced by measure and balance, the fine relation of part to part and space to space, was probably—aided by the presence of ornament as positive as it was discreet, and by the complexion of the stone, a cold fair grey, warmed and polished a little by life—neither more nor less than a case of distinction, such a case as he could only feel unexpectedly as a sort of delivered challenge? Meanwhile, however, the chance he had allowed for—the chance of being seen in time from the balcony—had become a fact. Two or three of the windows stood open to the violet air; and, before Strether had cut the knot by crossing, a young man had come out and looked about him, had lighted a cigarette and tossed the match over, and then, resting on the rail, had given himself up to watching the life below while he smoked. His arrival contributed, in its order, to keeping Strether in position; the result of which in turn was that Strether soon felt himself noticed. The young man began to look at him as in acknowledgement of his being himself in observation.

This was interesting so far as it went, but the interest was affected by the young man's not being Chad. Strether wondered at first if he were perhaps Chad altered, and then saw that this was asking too much of alteration. The young man was light bright and alert—with an air too pleasant to have been arrived at by patching. Strether had conceived Chad as patched, but not beyond recognition. He was in presence, he felt, of amendments enough as they stood; it was a sufficient amendment that the gentleman up there should be Chad's friend. He was young too then, the gentleman up there—he was very young; young enough apparently to be amused at an elderly watcher, to be curious even to see what the elderly watcher would do on finding himself watched. There was youth in that, there was youth in the surrender to the balcony, there was youth for Strether at this moment in everything but his own business; and Chad's thus pronounced association with youth had given the next instant an extraordinary quick lift to the issue. The balcony, the distinguished front, testified suddenly, for Strether's fancy, to something that was up and up; they placed the whole case materially, and as by an admirable image, on a level that he found himself at the end of another moment rejoicing to think he might reach. The young man looked at him still, he looked at the young man; and the issue, by a rapid process, was that this knowledge of a perched privacy appeared to him the last of luxuries. To him too the perched privacy was open, and he saw it now but in one light—that of the only domicile, the only fireside, in the great ironic city, on which he had the shadow of a claim. Miss Gostrey had a fireside; she had told him of it, and it was something that doubtless awaited him; but Miss Gostrey hadn't yet arrived—she mightn't arrive for days; and the sole attenuation of his excluded state was his vision of the small, the admittedly secondary hotel in the bye-street from the Rue de la Paix, in which her solicitude for his purse had placed him, which affected him somehow as all indoor chill, glass-roofed court and slippery staircase, and which, by the same token, expressed the presence of Waymarsh even at times when Waymarsh might have been certain to be round at the bank. It came to pass before he moved that Waymarsh, and Waymarsh alone, Waymarsh not only undiluted but positively strengthened, struck him as the present alternative to the young man in the balcony. When he did move it was fairly to escape that alternative. Taking his way over the street at last and passing through the porte-cochere of the house was like consciously leaving Waymarsh out. However, he would tell him all about it.

Book Third

I

The Little Restaurant (1894) by Edouard Vuillard (1868-1940)

Strether told Waymarsh all about it that very evening, on their dining together at the hotel; which needn't have happened, he was all the while aware, hadn't he chosen to sacrifice to this occasion a rarer opportunity. The mention to his companion of the sacrifice was moreover exactly what introduced his recital—or, as he would have called it with more confidence in his interlocutor, his confession. His confession was that he had been captured and that one of the features of the affair had just failed to be his engaging himself on the spot to dinner. As by such a freedom Waymarsh would have lost him he had obeyed his scruple; and he had likewise obeyed another scruple—which bore on the question of his himself bringing a guest.

Waymarsh looked gravely ardent, over the finished soup, at this array of scruples; Strether hadn't yet got quite used to being so unprepared for the consequences of the impression he produced. It was comparatively easy to explain, however, that he hadn't felt sure his guest would please. The person was a young man whose acquaintance he had made but that afternoon in the course of rather a hindered enquiry for another person—an enquiry his new friend had just prevented in fact from being vain. "Oh," said Strether, "I've all sorts of things to tell you!"—and he put it in a way that was a virtual hint to Waymarsh to help him to enjoy the telling. He waited for his fish, he drank of his wine, he wiped his long moustache, he leaned back in his chair, he took in the two English ladies who had just creaked past them and whom he would even have articulately greeted if they hadn't rather chilled the impulse; so that all he could do was—by way of doing something—to say "Merci, Francois!" out quite loud when his fish was brought. Everything was there that he wanted, everything that could make the moment an occasion, that would do beautifully—everything but what Waymarsh might give. The little waxed salle-a-manger was sallow and sociable; Francois, dancing over it, all smiles, was a man and a brother; the high-shouldered patronne, with her high-held, much-rubbed hands, seemed always assenting exuberantly to something unsaid; the Paris evening in short was, for Strether, in the very taste of the soup, in the goodness, as he was innocently pleased to think it, of the wine, in the pleasant coarse texture of the napkin and the crunch of the thick-crusted bread. These all were things congruous with his confession, and his confession was that he HAD—it would come out properly just there if Waymarsh would only take it properly—agreed to breakfast out, at twelve literally, the next day. He didn't quite know where; the delicacy of the case came straight up in the remembrance of his new friend's "We'll see; I'll take you somewhere!"—for it had required little more than that, after all, to let him right in. He was affected after a minute, face to face with his actual comrade, by the impulse to overcolour. There had already been things in respect to which he knew himself tempted by this perversity. If Waymarsh thought them bad he should at least have his reason for his discomfort; so Strether showed them as worse. Still, he was now, in his way, sincerely perplexed.

Chad had been absent from the Boulevard Malesherbes—was absent from Paris altogether; he had learned that from the concierge, but had nevertheless gone up, and gone up—there were no two ways about it—from an uncontrollable, a really, if one would, depraved curiosity. The concierge had mentioned to him that a friend of the tenant of the troisieme was for the time in possession; and this had been Strether's pretext for a further enquiry, an experiment carried on, under Chad's roof, without his knowledge. "I found his friend in fact there keeping the place warm, as he called it, for him; Chad himself being, as appears, in the south. He went a month ago to Cannes and though his return begins to be looked for it can't be for some days. I might, you see, perfectly have waited a week; might have beaten a retreat as soon as I got this essential knowledge. But I beat no retreat; I did the opposite; I stayed, I dawdled, I trifled; above all I looked round. I saw, in fine; and—I don't know what to call it—I sniffed. It's a detail, but it's as if there were something—something very good—TO sniff."

Waymarsh's face had shown his friend an attention apparently so remote that the latter was slightly surprised to find it at this point abreast with him. "Do you mean a smell? What of?"

"A charming scent. But I don't know."

Waymarsh gave an inferential grunt. "Does he live there with a woman?"

"I don't know."

Waymarsh waited an instant for more, then resumed. "Has he taken her off with him?"

"And will he bring her back?"—Strether fell into the enquiry. But he wound it up as before. "I don't know."

The way he wound it up, accompanied as this was with another drop back, another degustation of the Leoville, another wipe of his moustache and another good word for Francois, seemed to produce in his companion a slight irritation. "Then what the devil DO you know?"

"Well," said Strether almost gaily, "I guess I don't know anything!" His gaiety might have been a tribute to the fact that the state he had been reduced to did for him again what had been done by his talk of the matter with Miss Gostrey at the London theatre. It was somehow enlarging; and the air of that amplitude was now doubtless more or less—and all for Waymarsh to feel—in his further response. "That's what I found out from the young man."

"But I thought you said you found out nothing."

"Nothing but that—that I don't know anything."

"And what good does that do you?"

"It's just," said Strether, "what I've come to you to help me to discover. I mean anything about anything over here. I FELT that, up there. It regularly rose before me in its might. The young man moreover—Chad's friend—as good as told me so."

"As good as told you you know nothing about anything?" Waymarsh appeared to look at some one who might have as good as told HIM. "How old is he?"

"Well, I guess not thirty."

"Yet you had to take that from him?"

"Oh I took a good deal more—since, as I tell you, I took an invitation to dejeuner."

"And are you GOING to that unholy meal?"

"If you'll come with me. He wants you too, you know. I told him about you. He gave me his card," Strether pursued, "and his name's rather funny. It's John Little Bilham, and he says his two surnames are, on account of his being small, inevitably used together."

"Well," Waymarsh asked with due detachment from these details, "what's he doing up there?"

"His account of himself is that he's 'only a little artist-man.' That seemed to me perfectly to describe him. But he's yet in the phase of study; this, you know, is the great art-school—to pass a certain number of years in which he came over. And he's a great friend of Chad's, and occupying Chad's rooms just now because they're so pleasant. HE'S very pleasant and curious too," Strether added—"though he's not from Boston."

Waymarsh looked already rather sick of him. "Where is he from?"

Strether thought. "I don't know that, either. But he's 'notoriously,' as he put it himself, not from Boston."

"Well," Waymarsh moralised from dry depths, "every one can't notoriously be from Boston. Why," he continued, "is he curious?"

"Perhaps just for THAT—for one thing! But really," Strether added, "for everything. When you meet him you'll see."

"Oh I don't want to meet him," Waymarsh impatiently growled. "Why don't he go home?"

Strether hesitated. "Well, because he likes it over here."

This appeared in particular more than Waymarsh could bear. "He ought then to be ashamed of himself, and, as you admit that you think so too, why drag him in?"

Strether's reply again took time. "Perhaps I do think so myself—though I don't quite yet admit it. I'm not a bit sure—it's again one of the things I want to find out. I liked him, and CAN you like people—? But no matter." He pulled himself up. "There's no doubt I want you to come down on me and squash me."

Waymarsh helped himself to the next course, which, however proving not the dish he had just noted as supplied to the English ladies, had the effect of causing his imagination temporarily to wander. But it presently broke out at a softer spot. "Have they got a handsome place up there?"

"Oh a charming place; full of beautiful and valuable things. I never saw such a place"—and Strether's thought went back to it. "For a little artist-man—!" He could in fact scarce express it.

But his companion, who appeared now to have a view, insisted. "Well?"

"Well, life can hold nothing better. Besides, they're things of which he's in charge."

"So that he does doorkeeper for your precious pair? Can life," Waymarsh enquired, "hold nothing better than THAT?" Then as Strether, silent, seemed even yet to wonder, "Doesn't he know what SHE is?" he went on.

"I don't know. I didn't ask him. I couldn't. It was impossible. You wouldn't either. Besides I didn't want to. No more would you." Strether in short explained it at a stroke. "You can't make out over here what people do know."

"Then what did you come over for?"

"Well, I suppose exactly to see for myself—without their aid."

"Then what do you want mine for?"

"Oh," Strether laughed, "you're not one of THEM! I do know what you know."

As, however, this last assertion caused Waymarsh again to look at him hard—such being the latter's doubt of its implications—he felt his justification lame. Which was still more the case when Waymarsh presently said: "Look here, Strether. Quit this."

Our friend smiled with a doubt of his own. "Do you mean my tone?"

"No—damn your tone. I mean your nosing round. Quit the whole job. Let them stew in their juice. You're being used for a thing you ain't fit for. People don't take a fine-tooth comb to groom a horse."

"Am I a fine-tooth comb?" Strether laughed. "It's something I never called myself!"

"It's what you are, all the same. You ain't so young as you were, but you've kept your teeth."

He acknowledged his friend's humour. "Take care I don't get them into YOU! You'd like them, my friends at home, Waymarsh," he declared; "you'd really particularly like them. And I know"—it was slightly irrelevant, but he gave it sudden and singular force—"I know they'd like you!"

"Oh don't work them off on ME!" Waymarsh groaned.

Yet Strether still lingered with his hands in his pockets. "It's really quite as indispensable as I say that Chad should be got back."

"Indispensable to whom? To you?"

"Yes," Strether presently said.

"Because if you get him you also get Mrs. Newsome?"

Strether faced it. "Yes."

"And if you don't get him you don't get her?"

It might be merciless, but he continued not to flinch. "I think it might have some effect on our personal understanding. Chad's of real importance—or can easily become so if he will—to the business."

"And the business is of real importance to his mother's husband?"

"Well, I naturally want what my future wife wants. And the thing will be much better if we have our own man in it."

"If you have your own man in it, in other words," Waymarsh said, "you'll marry—you personally—more money. She's already rich, as I understand you, but she'll be richer still if the business can be made to boom on certain lines that you've laid down."

"I haven't laid them down," Strether promptly returned. "Mr. Newsome—who knew extraordinarily well what he was about—laid them down ten years ago."

Oh well, Waymarsh seemed to indicate with a shake of his mane, THAT didn't matter! "You're fierce for the boom anyway."

His friend weighed a moment in silence the justice of the charge. "I can scarcely be called fierce, I think, when I so freely take my chance of the possibility, the danger, of being influenced in a sense counter to Mrs. Newsome's own feelings."

Waymarsh gave this proposition a long hard look. "I see. You're afraid yourself of being squared. But you're a humbug," he added, "all the same."

"Oh!" Strether quickly protested.

"Yes, you ask me for protection—which makes you very interesting; and then you won't take it. You say you want to be squashed—"

"Ah but not so easily! Don't you see," Strether demanded "where my interest, as already shown you, lies? It lies in my not being squared. If I'm squared where's my marriage? If I miss my errand I miss that; and if I miss that I miss everything—I'm nowhere."

Waymarsh—but all relentlessly—took this in. "What do I care where you are if you're spoiled?"

Their eyes met on it an instant. "Thank you awfully," Strether at last said. "But don't you think HER judgement of that—?"

"Ought to content me? No."

It kept them again face to face, and the end of this was that Strether again laughed. "You do her injustice. You really MUST know her. Good-night."

He breakfasted with Mr. Bilham on the morrow, and, as inconsequently befell, with Waymarsh massively of the party. The latter announced, at the eleventh hour and much to his friend's surprise, that, damn it, he would as soon join him as do anything else; on which they proceeded together, strolling in a state of detachment practically luxurious for them to the Boulevard Malesherbes, a couple engaged that day with the sharp spell of Paris as confessedly, it might have been seen, as any couple among the daily thousands so compromised. They walked, wandered, wondered and, a little, lost themselves; Strether hadn't had for years so rich a consciousness of time—a bag of gold into which he constantly dipped for a handful. It was present to him that when the little business with Mr. Bilham should be over he would still have shining hours to use absolutely as he liked. There was no great pulse of haste yet in this process of saving Chad; nor was that effect a bit more marked as he sat, half an hour later, with his legs under Chad's mahogany, with Mr. Bilham on one side, with a friend of Mr. Bilham's on the other, with Waymarsh stupendously opposite, and with the great hum of Paris coming up in softness, vagueness-for Strether himself indeed already positive sweetness—through the sunny windows toward which, the day before, his curiosity had raised its wings from below. The feeling strongest with him at that moment had borne fruit almost faster than he could taste it, and Strether literally felt at the present hour that there was a precipitation in his fate. He had known nothing and nobody as he stood in the street; but hadn't his view now taken a bound in the direction of every one and of every thing?

"What's he up to, what's he up to?"—something like that was at the back of his head all the while in respect to little Bilham; but meanwhile, till he should make out, every one and every thing were as good as represented for him by the combination of his host and the lady on his left. The lady on his left, the lady thus promptly and ingeniously invited to "meet" Mr. Strether and Mr. Waymarsh—it was the way she herself expressed her case—was a very marked person, a person who had much to do with our friend's asking himself if the occasion weren't in its essence the most baited, the most gilded of traps. Baited it could properly be called when the repast was of so wise a savour, and gilded surrounding objects seemed inevitably to need to be when Miss Barrace—which was the lady's name—looked at them with convex Parisian eyes and through a glass with a remarkably long tortoise-shell handle. Why Miss Barrace, mature meagre erect and eminently gay, highly adorned, perfectly familiar, freely contradictions and reminding him of some last-century portrait of a clever head without powder—why Miss Barrace should have been in particular the note of a "trap" Strether couldn't on the spot have explained; he blinked in the light of a conviction that he should know later on, and know well—as it came over him, for that matter, with force, that he should need to. He wondered what he was to think exactly of either of his new friends; since the young man, Chad's intimate and deputy, had, in thus constituting the scene, practised so much more subtly than he had been prepared for, and since in especial Miss Barrace, surrounded clearly by every consideration, hadn't scrupled to figure as a familiar object. It was interesting to him to feel that he was in the presence of new measures, other standards, a different scale of relations, and that evidently here were a happy pair who didn't think of things at all as he and Waymarsh thought. Nothing was less to have been calculated in the business than that it should now be for him as if he and Waymarsh were comparatively quite at one.

The latter was magnificent—this at least was an assurance privately given him by Miss Barrace. "Oh your friend's a type, the grand old American—what shall one call it? The Hebrew prophet, Ezekiel, Jeremiah, who used when I was a little girl in the Rue Montaigne to come to see my father and who was usually the American Minister to the Tuileries or some other court. I haven't seen one these ever so many years; the sight of it warms my poor old chilled heart; this specimen is wonderful; in the right quarter, you know, he'll have a succes fou." Strether hadn't failed to ask what the right quarter might be, much as he required his presence of mind to meet such a change in their scheme. "Oh the artist-quarter and that kind of thing; HERE already, for instance, as you see." He had been on the point of echoing "'Here'?—is THIS the artist-quarter?" but she had already disposed of the question with a wave of all her tortoise-shell and an easy "Bring him to ME!" He knew on the spot how little he should be able to bring him, for the very air was by this time, to his sense, thick and hot with poor Waymarsh's judgement of it. He was in the trap still more than his companion and, unlike his companion, not making the best of it; which was precisely what doubtless gave him his admirable sombre glow. Little did Miss Barrace know that what was behind it was his grave estimate of her own laxity. The general assumption with which our two friends had arrived had been that of finding Mr. Bilham ready to conduct them to one or other of those resorts of the earnest, the aesthetic fraternity which were shown among the sights of Paris. In this character it would have justified them in a proper insistence on discharging their score. Waymarsh's only proviso at the last had been that nobody should pay for him; but he found himself, as the occasion developed, paid for on a scale as to which Strether privately made out that he already nursed retribution. Strether was conscious across the table of what worked in him, conscious when they passed back to the small salon to which, the previous evening, he himself had made so rich a reference; conscious most of all as they stepped out to the balcony in which one would have had to be an ogre not to recognise the perfect place for easy aftertastes. These things were enhanced for Miss Barrace by a succession of excellent cigarettes—acknowledged, acclaimed, as a part of the wonderful supply left behind him by Chad—in an almost equal absorption of which Strether found himself blindly, almost wildly pushing forward. He might perish by the sword as well as by famine, and he knew that his having abetted the lady by an excess that was rare with him would count for little in the sum—as Waymarsh might so easily add it up—of her licence. Waymarsh had smoked of old, smoked hugely; but Waymarsh did nothing now, and that gave him his advantage over people who took things up lightly just when others had laid them heavily down. Strether had never smoked, and he felt as if he flaunted at his friend that this had been only because of a reason. The reason, it now began to appear even to himself, was that he had never had a lady to smoke with.

It was this lady's being there at all, however, that was the strange free thing; perhaps, since she WAS there, her smoking was the least of her freedoms. If Strether had been sure at each juncture of what—with Bilham in especial—she talked about, he might have traced others and winced at them and felt Waymarsh wince; but he was in fact so often at sea that his sense of the range of reference was merely general and that he on several different occasions guessed and interpreted only to doubt. He wondered what they meant, but there were things he scarce thought they could be supposed to mean, and "Oh no—not THAT!" was at the end of most of his ventures. This was the very beginning with him of a condition as to which, later on, it will be seen, he found cause to pull himself up; and he was to remember the moment duly as the first step in a process. The central fact of the place was neither more nor less, when analysed—and a pressure superficial sufficed—than the fundamental impropriety of Chad's situation, round about which they thus seemed cynically clustered. Accordingly, since they took it for granted, they took for granted all that was in connexion with it taken for granted at Woollett—matters as to which, verily, he had been reduced with Mrs. Newsome to the last intensity of silence. That was the consequence of their being too bad to be talked about, and was the accompaniment, by the same token, of a deep conception of their badness. It befell therefore that when poor Strether put it to himself that their badness was ultimately, or perhaps even insolently, what such a scene as the one before him was, so to speak, built upon, he could scarce shirk the dilemma of reading a roundabout echo of them into almost anything that came up. This, he was well aware, was a dreadful necessity; but such was the stern logic, he could only gather, of a relation to the irregular life.

It was the way the irregular life sat upon Bilham and Miss Barrace that was the insidious, the delicate marvel. He was eager to concede that their relation to it was all indirect, for anything else in him would have shown the grossness of bad manners; but the indirectness was none the less consonant—THAT was striking-with a grateful enjoyment of everything that was Chad's. They spoke of him repeatedly, invoking his good name and good nature, and the worst confusion of mind for Strether was that all their mention of him was of a kind to do him honour. They commended his munificence and approved his taste, and in doing so sat down, as it seemed to Strether, in the very soil out of which these things flowered. Our friend's final predicament was that he himself was sitting down, for the time, WITH them, and there was a supreme moment at which, compared with his collapse, Waymarsh's erectness affected him as really high. One thing was certain—he saw he must make up his mind. He must approach Chad, must wait for him, deal with him, master him, but he mustn't dispossess himself of the faculty of seeing things as they were. He must bring him to HIM—not go himself, as it were, so much of the way. He must at any rate be clearer as to what—should he continue to do that for convenience—he was still condoning. It was on the detail of this quantity—and what could the fact be but mystifying?-that Bilham and Miss Barrace threw so little light. So there they were.

II

When Miss Gostrey arrived, at the end of a week, she made him a sign; he went immediately to see her, and it wasn't till then that he could again close his grasp on the idea of a corrective. This idea however was luckily all before him again from the moment he crossed the threshold of the little entresol of the Quartier Marboeuf into which she had gathered, as she said, picking them up in a thousand flights and funny little passionate pounces, the makings of a final nest. He recognised in an instant that there really, there only, he should find the boon with the vision of which he had first mounted Chad's stairs. He might have been a little scared at the picture of how much more, in this place, he should know himself "in" hadn't his friend been on the spot to measure the amount to his appetite. Her compact and crowded little chambers, almost dusky, as they at first struck him, with accumulations, represented a supreme general adjustment to opportunities and conditions. Wherever he looked he saw an old ivory or an old brocade, and he scarce knew where to sit for fear of a misappliance. The life of the occupant struck him of a sudden as more charged with possession even than Chad's or than Miss Barrace's; wide as his glimpse had lately become of the empire of "things," what was before him still enlarged it; the lust of the eyes and the pride of life had indeed thus their temple. It was the innermost nook of the shrine—as brown as a pirate's cave. In the brownness were glints of gold; patches of purple were in the gloom; objects all that caught, through the muslin, with their high rarity, the light of the low windows. Nothing was clear about them but that they were precious, and they brushed his ignorance with their contempt as a flower, in a liberty taken with him, might have been whisked under his nose. But after a full look at his hostess he knew none the less what most concerned him. The circle in which they stood together was warm with life, and every question between them would live there as nowhere else. A question came up as soon as they had spoken, for his answer, with a laugh, was quickly: "Well, they've got hold of me!" Much of their talk on this first occasion was his development of that truth. He was extraordinarily glad to see her, expressing to her frankly what she most showed him, that one might live for years without a blessing unsuspected, but that to know it at last for no more than three days was to need it or miss it for ever. She was the blessing that had now become his need, and what could prove it better than that without her he had lost himself?

"What do you mean?" she asked with an absence of alarm that, correcting him as if he had mistaken the "period" of one of her pieces, gave him afresh a sense of her easy movement through the maze he had but begun to tread. "What in the name of all the Pococks have you managed to do?"

"Why exactly the wrong thing. I've made a frantic friend of little Bilham."

"Ah that sort of thing was of the essence of your case and to have been allowed for from the first." And it was only after this that, quite as a minor matter, she asked who in the world little Bilham might be. When she learned that he was a friend of Chad's and living for the time in Chad's rooms in Chad's absence, quite as if acting in Chad's spirit and serving Chad's cause, she showed, however, more interest. "Should you mind my seeing him? Only once, you know," she added.

"Oh the oftener the better: he's amusing—he's original."

"He doesn't shock you?" Miss Gostrey threw out.

"Never in the world! We escape that with a perfection—! I feel it to be largely, no doubt, because I don't half-understand him; but our modus vivendi isn't spoiled even by that. You must dine with me to meet him," Strether went on. "Then you'll see.'

"Are you giving dinners?"

"Yes—there I am. That's what I mean."

All her kindness wondered. "That you're spending too much money?"

"Dear no—they seem to cost so little. But that I do it to THEM. I ought to hold off."

She thought again—she laughed. "The money you must be spending to think it cheap! But I must be out of it—to the naked eye." He looked for a moment as if she were really failing him. "Then you won't meet them?" It was almost as if she had developed an unexpected personal prudence.

She hesitated. "Who are they—first?"

"Why little Bilham to begin with." He kept back for the moment Miss Barrace. "And Chad—when he comes—you must absolutely see."

"When then does he come?"

"When Bilham has had time to write him, and hear from him about me. Bilham, however," he pursued, "will report favourably—favourably for Chad. That will make him not afraid to come. I want you the more therefore, you see, for my bluff."

"Oh you'll do yourself for your bluff." She was perfectly easy. "At the rate you've gone I'm quiet."

"Ah but I haven't," said Strether, "made one protest."

She turned it over. "Haven't you been seeing what there's to protest about?"

He let her, with this, however ruefully, have the whole truth. "I haven't yet found a single thing."

"Isn't there any one WITH him then?"

"Of the sort I came out about?" Strether took a moment. "How do I know? And what do I care?"

"Oh oh!"—and her laughter spread. He was struck in fact by the effect on her of his joke. He saw now how he meant it as a joke. SHE saw, however, still other things, though in an instant she had hidden them. "You've got at no facts at all?"

He tried to muster them. "Well, he has a lovely home."

"Ah that, in Paris," she quickly returned, "proves nothing. That is rather it DISproves nothing. They may very well, you see, the people your mission is concerned with, have done it FOR him."

"Exactly. And it was on the scene of their doings then that Waymarsh and I sat guzzling."

"Oh if you forbore to guzzle here on scenes of doings," she replied, "you might easily die of starvation." With which she smiled at him. "You've worse before you."

"Ah I've EVERYTHING before me. But on our hypothesis, you know, they must be wonderful."

"They ARE!" said Miss Gostrey. "You're not therefore, you see," she added, "wholly without facts. They've BEEN, in effect, wonderful."

To have got at something comparatively definite appeared at last a little to help—a wave by which moreover, the next moment, recollection was washed. "My young man does admit furthermore that they're our friend's great interest."

"Is that the expression he uses?"

Strether more exactly recalled. "No—not quite."

"Something more vivid? Less?"

He had bent, with neared glasses, over a group of articles on a small stand; and at this he came up. "It was a mere allusion, but, on the lookout as I was, it struck me. 'Awful, you know, as Chad is'—those were Bilham's words."

"'Awful, you know'—? Oh!"—and Miss Gostrey turned them over. She seemed, however, satisfied. "Well, what more do you want?"

He glanced once more at a bibelot or two, and everything sent him back. "But it is all the same as if they wished to let me have it between the eyes."

She wondered. "Quoi donc?"

"Why what I speak of. The amenity. They can stun you with that as well as with anything else."

"Oh," she answered, "you'll come round! I must see them each," she went on, "for myself. I mean Mr. Bilham and Mr. Newsome—Mr. Bilham naturally first. Once only—once for each; that will do. But face to face—for half an hour. What's Mr. Chad," she immediately pursued, "doing at Cannes with the—well, with the kind of ladies you mean."

"Don't they?" Strether asked with an interest in decent men that amused her.

"No, elsewhere, but not to Cannes. Cannes is different. Cannes is better. Cannes is best. I mean it's all people you know—when you do know them. And if HE does, why that's different too. He must have gone alone. She can't be with him."

"I haven't," Strether confessed in his weakness, "the least idea." There seemed much in what she said, but he was able after a little to help her to a nearer impression. The meeting with little Bilham took place, by easy arrangement, in the great gallery of the Louvre; and when, standing with his fellow visitor before one of the splendid Titians—the overwhelming portrait of the young man with the strangely-shaped glove and the blue-grey eyes—he turned to see the third member of their party advance from the end of the waxed and gilded vista, he had a sense of having at last taken hold. He had agreed with Miss Gostrey—it dated even from Chester—for a morning at the Louvre, and he had embraced independently the same idea as thrown out by little Bilham, whom he had already accompanied to the museum of the Luxembourg. The fusion of these schemes presented no difficulty, and it was to strike him again that in little Bilham's company contrarieties in general dropped.

"Oh he's all right—he's one of US!" Miss Gostrey, after the first exchange, soon found a chance to murmur to her companion; and Strether, as they proceeded and paused and while a quick unanimity between the two appeared to have phrased itself in half a dozen remarks—Strether knew that he knew almost immediately what she meant, and took it as still another sign that he had got his job in hand. This was the more grateful to him that he could think of the intelligence now serving him as an acquisition positively new. He wouldn't have known even the day before what she meant—that is if she meant, what he assumed, that they were intense Americans together. He had just worked round—and with a sharper turn of the screw than any yet—to the conception of an American intense as little Bilham was intense. The young man was his first specimen; the specimen had profoundly perplexed him; at present however there was light. It was by little Bilham's amazing serenity that he had at first been affected, but he had inevitably, in his circumspection, felt it as the trail of the serpent, the corruption, as he might conveniently have said, of Europe; whereas the promptness with which it came up for Miss Gostrey but as a special little form of the oldest thing they knew justified it at once to his own vision as well. He wanted to be able to like his specimen with a clear good conscience, and this fully permitted it. What had muddled him was precisely the small artist-man's way—it was so complete—of being more American than anybody. But it now for the time put Strether vastly at his ease to have this view of a new way.

The amiable youth then looked out, as it had first struck Strether, at a world in respect to which he hadn't a prejudice. The one our friend most instantly missed was the usual one in favour of an occupation accepted. Little Bilham had an occupation, but it was only an occupation declined; and it was by his general exemption from alarm, anxiety or remorse on this score that the impression of his serenity was made. He had come out to Paris to paint—to fathom, that is, at large, that mystery; but study had been fatal to him so far as anything COULD be fatal, and his productive power faltered in proportion as his knowledge grew. Strether had gathered from him that at the moment of his finding him in Chad's rooms he hadn't saved from his shipwreck a scrap of anything but his beautiful intelligence and his confirmed habit of Paris. He referred to these things with an equal fond familiarity, and it was sufficiently clear that, as an outfit, they still served him. They were charming to Strether through the hour spent at the Louvre, where indeed they figured for him as an unseparated part of the charged iridescent air, the glamour of the name, the splendour of the space, the colour of the masters. Yet they were present too wherever the young man led, and the day after the visit to the Louvre they hung, in a different walk, about the steps of our party. He had invited his companions to cross the river with him, offering to show them his own poor place; and his own poor place, which was very poor, gave to his idiosyncrasies, for Strether—the small sublime indifference and independences that had struck the latter as fresh—an odd and engaging dignity. He lived at the end of an alley that went out of an old short cobbled street, a street that went in turn out of a new long smooth avenue—street and avenue and alley having, however, in common a sort of social shabbiness; and he introduced them to the rather cold and blank little studio which he had lent to a comrade for the term of his elegant absence. The comrade was another ingenuous compatriot, to whom he had wired that tea was to await them "regardless," and this reckless repast, and the second ingenuous compatriot, and the faraway makeshift life, with its jokes and its gaps, its delicate daubs and its three or four chairs, its overflow of taste and conviction and its lack of nearly all else—these things wove round the occasion a spell to which our hero unreservedly surrendered.

He liked the ingenuous compatriots—for two or three others soon gathered; he liked the delicate daubs and the free discriminations—involving references indeed, involving enthusiasms and execrations that made him, as they said, sit up; he liked above all the legend of good-humoured poverty, of mutual accommodation fairly raised to the romantic, that he soon read into the scene. The ingenuous compatriots showed a candour, he thought, surpassing even the candour of Woollett; they were red-haired and long-legged, they were quaint and queer and dear and droll; they made the place resound with the vernacular, which he had never known so marked as when figuring for the chosen language, he must suppose, of contemporary art. They twanged with a vengeance the aesthetic lyre—they drew from it wonderful airs. This aspect of their life had an admirable innocence; and he looked on occasion at Maria Gostrey to see to what extent that element reached her. She gave him however for the hour, as she had given him the previous day, no further sign to show how she dealt with boys; meeting them with the air of old Parisian practice that she had for every one, for everything, in turn. Wonderful about the delicate daubs, masterful about the way to make tea, trustful about the legs of chairs and familiarly reminiscent of those, in the other time, the named, the numbered or the caricatured, who had flourished or failed, disappeared or arrived, she had accepted with the best grace her second course of little Bilham, and had said to Strether, the previous afternoon on his leaving them, that, since her impression was to be renewed, she would reserve judgement till after the new evidence.

The new evidence was to come, as it proved, in a day or two. He soon had from Maria a message to the effect that an excellent box at the Francais had been lent her for the following night; it seeming on such occasions not the least of her merits that she was subject to such approaches. The sense of how she was always paying for something in advance was equalled on Strether's part only by the sense of how she was always being paid; all of which made for his consciousness, in the larger air, of a lively bustling traffic, the exchange of such values as were not for him to handle. She hated, he knew, at the French play, anything but a box—just as she hated at the English anything but a stall; and a box was what he was already in this phase girding himself to press upon her. But she had for that matter her community with little Bilham: she too always, on the great issues, showed as having known in time. It made her constantly beforehand with him and gave him mainly the chance to ask himself how on the day of their settlement their account would stand. He endeavoured even now to keep it a little straight by arranging that if he accepted her invitation she should dine with him first; but the upshot of this scruple was that at eight o'clock on the morrow he awaited her with Waymarsh under the pillared portico. She hadn't dined with him, and it was characteristic of their relation that she had made him embrace her refusal without in the least understanding it. She ever caused her rearrangements to affect him as her tenderest touches. It was on that principle for instance that, giving him the opportunity to be amiable again to little Bilham, she had suggested his offering the young man a seat in their box. Strether had dispatched for this purpose a small blue missive to the Boulevard Malesherbes, but up to the moment of their passing into the theatre he had received no response to his message. He held, however, even after they had been for some time conveniently seated, that their friend, who knew his way about, would come in at his own right moment. His temporary absence moreover seemed, as never yet, to make the right moment for Miss Gostrey. Strether had been waiting till tonight to get back from her in some mirrored form her impressions and conclusions. She had elected, as they said, to see little Bilham once; but now she had seen him twice and had nevertheless not said more than a word.

Waymarsh meanwhile sat opposite him with their hostess between; and Miss Gostrey spoke of herself as an instructor of youth introducing her little charges to a work that was one of the glories of literature. The glory was happily unobjectionable, and the little charges were candid; for herself she had travelled that road and she merely waited on their innocence. But she referred in due time to their absent friend, whom it was clear they should have to give up. "He either won't have got your note," she said, "or you won't have got his: he has had some kind of hindrance, and, of course, for that matter, you know, a man never writes about coming to a box." She spoke as if, with her look, it might have been Waymarsh who had written to the youth, and the latter's face showed a mixture of austerity and anguish. She went on however as if to meet this. "He's far and away, you know, the best of them."

"The best of whom, ma'am?"

"Why of all the long procession—the boys, the girls, or the old men and old women as they sometimes really are; the hope, as one may say, of our country. They've all passed, year after year; but there has been no one in particular I've ever wanted to stop. I feel—don't YOU?—that I want to stop little Bilham; he's so exactly right as he is." She continued to talk to Waymarsh. "He's too delightful. If he'll only not spoil it! But they always WILL; they always do; they always have."

"I don't think Waymarsh knows," Strether said after a moment, "quite what it's open to Bilham to spoil."

"It can't be a good American," Waymarsh lucidly enough replied; "for it didn't strike me the young man had developed much in THAT shape."

"Ah," Miss Gostrey sighed, "the name of the good American is as easily given as taken away! What IS it, to begin with, to BE one, and what's the extraordinary hurry? Surely nothing that's so pressing was ever so little defined. It's such an order, really, that before we cook you the dish we must at least have your receipt. Besides the poor chicks have time! What I've seen so often spoiled," she pursued, "is the happy attitude itself, the state of faith and—what shall I call it?—the sense of beauty. You're right about him"—she now took in Strether; "little Bilham has them to a charm, we must keep little Bilham along." Then she was all again for Waymarsh. "The others have all wanted so dreadfully to do something, and they've gone and done it in too many cases indeed. It leaves them never the same afterwards; the charm's always somehow broken. Now HE, I think, you know, really won't. He won't do the least dreadful little thing. We shall continue to enjoy him just as he is. No—he's quite beautiful. He isn't a bit ashamed. He has every scrap of the courage of it that one could ask. Only think what he MIGHT do. One wants really—for fear of some accident—to keep him in view. At this very moment perhaps what mayn't he be up to? I've had my disappointments—the poor things are never really safe; or only at least when you have them under your eye. One can never completely trust them. One's uneasy, and I think that's why I most miss him now."

She had wound up with a laugh of enjoyment over her embroidery of her idea—an enjoyment that her face communicated to Strether, who almost wished none the less at this moment that she would let poor Waymarsh alone. HE knew more or less what she meant; but the fact wasn't a reason for her not pretending to Waymarsh that he didn't. It was craven of him perhaps, but he would, for the high amenity of the occasion, have liked Waymarsh not to be so sure of his wit. Her recognition of it gave him away and, before she had done with him or with that article, would give him worse. What was he, all the same, to do? He looked across the box at his friend; their eyes met; something queer and stiff, something that bore on the situation but that it was better not to touch, passed in silence between them. Well, the effect of it for Strether was an abrupt reaction, a final impatience of his own tendency to temporise. Where was that taking him anyway? It was one of the quiet instants that sometimes settle more matters than the outbreaks dear to the historic muse. The only qualification of the quietness was the synthetic "Oh hang it!" into which Strether's share of the silence soundlessly flowered. It represented, this mute ejaculation, a final impulse to burn his ships. These ships, to the historic muse, may seem of course mere cockles, but when he presently spoke to Miss Gostrey it was with the sense at least of applying the torch. "Is it then a conspiracy?"

"Between the two young men? Well, I don't pretend to be a seer or a prophetess," she presently replied; "but if I'm simply a woman of sense he's working for you to-night. I don't quite know how—but it's in my bones." And she looked at him at last as if, little material as she yet gave him, he'd really understand. "For an opinion THAT'S my opinion. He makes you out too well not to."

"Not to work for me to-night?" Strether wondered. "Then I hope he isn't doing anything very bad."

"They've got you," she portentously answered.

"Do you mean he IS—?"

"They've got you," she merely repeated. Though she disclaimed the prophetic vision she was at this instant the nearest approach he had ever met to the priestess of the oracle. The light was in her eyes. "You must face it now."

He faced it on the spot. "They HAD arranged—?"

"Every move in the game. And they've been arranging ever since. He has had every day his little telegram from Cannes."

It made Strether open his eyes. "Do you KNOW that?"

"I do better. I see it. This was, before I met him, what I wondered whether I WAS to see. But as soon as I met him I ceased to wonder, and our second meeting made me sure. I took him all in. He was acting—he is still—on his daily instructions."

"So that Chad has done the whole thing?"

"Oh no—not the whole. WE'VE done some of it. You and I and 'Europe.'"

"Europe—yes," Strether mused.

"Dear old Paris," she seemed to explain. But there was more, and, with one of her turns, she risked it. "And dear old Waymarsh. You," she declared, "have been a good bit of it."

He sat massive. "A good bit of what, ma'am?"

"Why of the wonderful consciousness of our friend here. You've helped too in your way to float him to where he is."

"And where the devil IS he?"

She passed it on with a laugh. "Where the devil, Strether, are you?"

He spoke as if he had just been thinking it out. "Well, quite already in Chad's hands, it would seem." And he had had with this another thought. "Will that be—just all through Bilham—the way he's going to work it? It would be, for him, you know, an idea. And Chad with an idea—!"

"Well?" she asked while the image held him.

"Well, is Chad—what shall I say?—monstrous?"

"Oh as much as you like! But the idea you speak of," she said, "won't have been his best. He'll have a better. It won't be all through little Bilham that he'll work it."

This already sounded almost like a hope destroyed. "Through whom else then?"

"That's what we shall see!" But quite as she spoke she turned, and Strether turned; for the door of the box had opened, with the click of the ouvreuse, from the lobby, and a gentleman, a stranger to them, had come in with a quick step. The door closed behind him, and, though their faces showed him his mistake, his air, which was striking, was all good confidence. The curtain had just again arisen, and, in the hush of the general attention, Strether's challenge was tacit, as was also the greeting, with a quickly deprecating hand and smile, of the unannounced visitor. He discreetly signed that he would wait, would stand, and these things and his face, one look from which she had caught, had suddenly worked for Miss Gostrey. She fitted to them all an answer for Strether's last question. The solid stranger was simply the answer—as she now, turning to her friend, indicated. She brought it straight out for him—it presented the intruder. "Why, through this gentleman!" The gentleman indeed, at the same time, though sounding for Strether a very short name, did practically as much to explain. Strether gasped the name back—then only had he seen Miss Gostrey had said more than she knew. They were in presence of Chad himself.

Our friend was to go over it afterwards again and again—he was going over it much of the time that they were together, and they were together constantly for three or four days: the note had been so strongly struck during that first half-hour that everything happening since was comparatively a minor development. The fact was that his perception of the young man's identity—so absolutely checked for a minute—had been quite one of the sensations that count in life; he certainly had never known one that had acted, as he might have said, with more of a crowded rush. And the rush though both vague and multitudinous, had lasted a long time, protected, as it were, yet at the same time aggravated, by the circumstance of its coinciding with a stretch of decorous silence. They couldn't talk without disturbing the spectators in the part of the balcony just below them; and it, for that matter, came to Strether—being a thing of the sort that did come to him—that these were the accidents of a high civilisation; the imposed tribute to propriety, the frequent exposure to conditions, usually brilliant, in which relief has to await its time. Relief was never quite near at hand for kings, queens, comedians and other such people, and though you might be yourself not exactly one of those, you could yet, in leading the life of high pressure, guess a little how they sometimes felt. It was truly the life of high pressure that Strether had seemed to feel himself lead while he sat there, close to Chad, during the long tension of the act. He was in presence of a fact that occupied his whole mind, that occupied for the half-hour his senses themselves all together; but he couldn't without inconvenience show anything—which moreover might count really as luck. What he might have shown, had he shown at all, was exactly the kind of emotion—the emotion of bewilderment—that he had proposed to himself from the first, whatever should occur, to show least. The phenomenon that had suddenly sat down there with him was a phenomenon of change so complete that his imagination, which had worked so beforehand, felt itself, in the connexion, without margin or allowance. It had faced every contingency but that Chad should not BE Chad, and this was what it now had to face with a mere strained smile and an uncomfortable flush.

He asked himself if, by any chance, before he should have in some way to commit himself, he might feel his mind settled to the new vision, might habituate it, so to speak, to the remarkable truth. But oh it was too remarkable, the truth; for what could be more remarkable than this sharp rupture of an identity? You could deal with a man as himself—you couldn't deal with him as somebody else. It was a small source of peace moreover to be reduced to wondering how little he might know in such an event what a sum he was setting you. He couldn't absolutely not know, for you couldn't absolutely not let him. It was a CASE then simply, a strong case, as people nowadays called such things,' a case of transformation unsurpassed, and the hope was but in the general law that strong cases were liable to control from without. Perhaps he, Strether himself, was the only person after all aware of it. Even Miss Gostrey, with all her science, wouldn't be, would she?—and he had never seen any one less aware of anything than Waymarsh as he glowered at Chad. The social sightlessness of his old friend's survey marked for him afresh, and almost in an humiliating way, the inevitable limits of direct aid from this source. He was not certain, however, of not drawing a shade of compensation from the privilege, as yet untasted, of knowing more about something in particular than Miss Gostrey did. His situation too was a case, for that matter, and he was now so interested, quite so privately agog, about it, that he had already an eye to the fun it would be to open up to her afterwards. He derived during his half-hour no assistance from her, and just this fact of her not meeting his eyes played a little, it must be confessed, into his predicament.

He had introduced Chad, in the first minutes, under his breath, and there was never the primness in her of the person unacquainted; but she had none the less betrayed at first no vision but of the stage, where she occasionally found a pretext for an appreciative moment that she invited Waymarsh to share. The latter's faculty of participation had never had, all round, such an assault to meet; the pressure on him being the sharper for this chosen attitude in her, as Strether judged it, of isolating, for their natural intercourse, Chad and himself. This intercourse was meanwhile restricted to a frank friendly look from the young man, something markedly like a smile, but falling far short of a grin, and to the vivacity of Strether's private speculation as to whether HE carried himself like a fool. He didn't quite see how he could so feel as one without somehow showing as one. The worst of that question moreover was that he knew it as a symptom the sense of which annoyed him. "If I'm going to be so odiously conscious of how I may strike the fellow," he reflected, "it was so little what I came out for that I may as well stop before I begin." This sage consideration too, distinctly, seemed to leave untouched the fact that he WAS going to be conscious. He was conscious of everything but of what would have served him.

He was to know afterwards, in the watches of the night, that nothing would have been more open to him than after a minute or two to propose to Chad to seek with him the refuge of the lobby. He hadn't only not proposed it, but had lacked even the presence of mind to see it as possible. He had stuck there like a schoolboy wishing not to miss a minute of the show; though for that portion of the show then presented he hadn't had an instant's real attention. He couldn't when the curtain fell have given the slightest account of what had happened. He had therefore, further, not at that moment acknowledged the amenity added by this acceptance of his awkwardness to Chad's general patience. Hadn't he none the less known at the very time—known it stupidly and without reaction—that the boy was accepting something? He was modestly benevolent, the boy—that was at least what he had been capable of the superiority of making out his chance to be; and one had one's self literally not had the gumption to get in ahead of him. If we should go into all that occupied our friend in the watches of the night we should have to mend our pen; but an instance or two may mark for us the vividness with which he could remember. He remembered the two absurdities that, if his presence of mind HAD failed, were the things that had had most to do with it. He had never in his life seen a young man come into a box at ten o'clock at night, and would, if challenged on the question in advance, have scarce been ready to pronounce as to different ways of doing so. But it was in spite of this definite to him that Chad had had a way that was wonderful: a fact carrying with it an implication that, as one might imagine it, he knew, he had learned, how.

Here already then were abounding results; he had on the spot and without the least trouble of intention taught Strether that even in so small a thing as that there were different ways. He had done in the same line still more than this; had by a mere shake or two of the head made his old friend observe that the change in him was perhaps more than anything else, for the eye, a matter of the marked streaks of grey, extraordinary at his age, in his thick black hair; as well as that this new feature was curiously becoming to him, did something for him, as characterisation, also even—of all things in the world—as refinement, that had been a good deal wanted. Strether felt, however, he would have had to confess, that it wouldn't have been easy just now, on this and other counts, in the presence of what had been supplied, to be quite clear as to what had been missed. A reflexion a candid critic might have made of old, for instance, was that it would have been happier for the son to look more like the mother; but this was a reflexion that at present would never occur. The ground had quite fallen away from it, yet no resemblance whatever to the mother had supervened. It would have been hard for a young man's face and air to disconnect themselves more completely than Chad's at this juncture from any discerned, from any imaginable aspect of a New England female parent. That of course was no more than had been on the cards; but it produced in Strether none the less one of those frequent phenomena of mental reference with which all judgement in him was actually beset.

Again and again as the days passed he had had a sense of the pertinence of communicating quickly with Woollett—communicating with a quickness with which telegraphy alone would rhyme; the fruit really of a fine fancy in him for keeping things straight, for the happy forestalment of error. No one could explain better when needful, nor put more conscience into an account or a report; which burden of conscience is perhaps exactly the reason why his heart always sank when the clouds of explanation gathered. His highest ingenuity was in keeping the sky of life clear of them. Whether or no he had a grand idea of the lucid, he held that nothing ever was in fact—for any one else—explained. One went through the vain motions, but it was mostly a waste of life. A personal relation was a relation only so long as people either perfectly understood or, better still, didn't care if they didn't. From the moment they cared if they didn't it was living by the sweat of one's brow; and the sweat of one's brow was just what one might buy one's self off from by keeping the ground free of the wild weed of delusion. It easily grew too fast, and the Atlantic cable now alone could race with it. That agency would each day have testified for him to something that was not what Woollett had argued. He was not at this moment absolutely sure that the effect of the morrow's—or rather of the night's—appreciation of the crisis wouldn't be to determine some brief missive. "Have at last seen him, but oh dear!"—some temporary relief of that sort seemed to hover before him. It hovered somehow as preparing them all—yet preparing them for what? If he might do so more luminously and cheaply he would tick out in four words: "Awfully old—grey hair." To this particular item in Chad's appearance he constantly, during their mute half-hour, reverted; as if so very much more than he could have said had been involved in it. The most he could have said would have been: "If he's going to make me feel young—!" which indeed, however, carried with it quite enough. If Strether was to feel young, that is, it would be because Chad was to feel old; and an aged and hoary sinner had been no part of the scheme.

The question of Chadwick's true time of life was, doubtless, what came up quickest after the adjournment of the two, when the play was over, to a cafe in the Avenue de l'Opera. Miss Gostrey had in due course been perfect for such a step; she had known exactly what they wanted—to go straight somewhere and talk; and Strether had even felt she had known what he wished to say and that he was arranging immediately to begin. She hadn't pretended this, as she HAD pretended on the other hand, to have divined Waymarsh's wish to extend to her an independent protection homeward; but Strether nevertheless found how, after he had Chad opposite to him at a small table in the brilliant halls that his companion straightway selected, sharply and easily discriminated from others, it was quite, to his mind, as if she heard him speak; as if, sitting up, a mile away, in the little apartment he knew, she would listen hard enough to catch. He found too that he liked that idea, and he wished that, by the same token, Mrs. Newsome might have caught as well. For what had above all been determined in him as a necessity of the first order was not to lose another hour, nor a fraction of one; was to advance, to overwhelm, with a rush. This was how he would anticipate—by a night-attack, as might be—any forced maturity that a crammed consciousness of Paris was likely to take upon itself to assert on behalf of the boy. He knew to the full, on what he had just extracted from Miss Gostrey, Chad's marks of alertness; but they were a reason the more for not dawdling. If he was himself moreover to be treated as young he wouldn't at all events be so treated before he should have struck out at least once. His arms might be pinioned afterwards, but it would have been left on record that he was fifty. The importance of this he had indeed begun to feel before they left the theatre; it had become a wild unrest, urging him to seize his chance. He could scarcely wait for it as they went; he was on the verge of the indecency of bringing up the question in the street; he fairly caught himself going on—so he afterwards invidiously named it—as if there would be for him no second chance should the present be lost. Not till, on the purple divan before the perfunctory bock, he had brought out the words themselves, was he sure, for that matter, that the present would be saved.

Book Fourth

I

Writing by Angelica Kauffman (1741-1807)

"I've come, you know, to make you break with everything, neither more nor less, and take you straight home; so you'll be so good as immediately and favourably to consider it!"—Strether, face to face with Chad after the play, had sounded these words almost breathlessly, and with an effect at first positively disconcerting to himself alone. For Chad's receptive attitude was that of a person who had been gracefully quiet while the messenger at last reaching him has run a mile through the dust. During some seconds after he had spoken Strether felt as if HE had made some such exertion; he was not even certain that the perspiration wasn't on his brow. It was the kind of consciousness for which he had to thank the look that, while the strain lasted, the young man's eyes gave him. They reflected—and the deuce of the thing was that they reflected really with a sort of shyness of kindness—his momentarily disordered state; which fact brought on in its turn for our friend the dawn of a fear that Chad might simply "take it out"—take everything out—in being sorry for him. Such a fear, any fear, was unpleasant. But everything was unpleasant; it was odd how everything had suddenly turned so. This however was no reason for letting the least thing go. Strether had the next minute proceeded as roundly as if with an advantage to follow up. "Of course I'm a busybody, if you want to fight the case to the death; but after all mainly in the sense of having known you and having given you such attention as you kindly permitted when you were in jackets and knickerbockers. Yes—it was knickerbockers, I'm busybody enough to remember that; and that you had, for your age—I speak of the first far-away time—tremendously stout legs. Well, we want you to break. Your mother's heart's passionately set upon it, but she has above and beyond that excellent arguments and reasons. I've not put them into her head—I needn't remind you how little she's a person who needs that. But they exist—you must take it from me as a friend both of hers and yours—for myself as well. I didn't invent them, I didn't originally work them out; but I understand them, I think I can explain them—by which I mean make you actively do them justice; and that's why you see me here. You had better know the worst at once. It's a question of an immediate rupture and an immediate return. I've been conceited enough to dream I can sugar that pill. I take at any rate the greatest interest in the question. I took it already before I left home, and I don't mind telling you that, altered as you are, I take it still more now that I've seen you. You're older and—I don't know what to call it!—more of a handful; but you're by so much the more, I seem to make out, to our purpose."

"Do I strike you as improved?" Strether was to recall that Chad had at this point enquired.

He was likewise to recall—and it had to count for some time as his greatest comfort—that it had been "given" him, as they said at Woollett, to reply with some presence of mind: "I haven't the least idea." He was really for a while to like thinking he had been positively hard. On the point of conceding that Chad had improved in appearance, but that to the question of appearance the remark must be confined, he checked even that compromise and left his reservation bare. Not only his moral, but also, as it were, his aesthetic sense had a little to pay for this, Chad being unmistakeably—and wasn't it a matter of the confounded grey hair again?—handsomer than he had ever promised. That however fell in perfectly with what Strether had said. They had no desire to keep down his proper expansion, and he wouldn't be less to their purpose for not looking, as he had too often done of old, only bold and wild. There was indeed a signal particular in which he would distinctly be more so. Strether didn't, as he talked, absolutely follow himself; he only knew he was clutching his thread and that he held it from moment to moment a little tighter; his mere uninterruptedness during the few minutes helped him to do that. He had frequently for a month, turned over what he should say on this very occasion, and he seemed at last to have said nothing he had thought of—everything was so totally different.

But in spite of all he had put the flag at the window. This was what he had done, and there was a minute during which he affected himself as having shaken it hard, flapped it with a mighty flutter, straight in front of his companion's nose. It gave him really almost the sense of having already acted his part. The momentary relief—as if from the knowledge that nothing of THAT at least could be undone—sprang from a particular cause, the cause that had flashed into operation, in Miss Gostrey's box, with direct apprehension, with amazed recognition, and that had been concerned since then in every throb of his consciousness. What it came to was that with an absolutely new quantity to deal with one simply couldn't know. The new quantity was represented by the fact that Chad had been made over. That was all; whatever it was it was everything. Strether had never seen the thing so done before—it was perhaps a speciality of Paris. If one had been present at the process one might little by little have mastered the result; but he was face to face, as matters stood, with the finished business. It had freely been noted for him that he might be received as a dog among skittles, but that was on the basis of the old quantity. He had originally thought of lines and tones as things to be taken, but these possibilities had now quite melted away. There was no computing at all what the young man before him would think or feel or say on any subject whatever. This intelligence Strether had afterwards, to account for his nervousness, reconstituted as he might, just as he had also reconstituted the promptness with which Chad had corrected his uncertainty. An extraordinarily short time had been required for the correction, and there had ceased to be anything negative in his companion's face and air as soon as it was made. "Your engagement to my mother has become then what they call here a fait accompli?"—it had consisted, the determinant touch, in nothing more than that.

Well, that was enough, Strether had felt while his answer hung fire. He had felt at the same time, however, that nothing could less become him than that it should hang fire too long. "Yes," he said brightly, "it was on the happy settlement of the question that I started. You see therefore to what tune I'm in your family. Moreover," he added, "I've been supposing you'd suppose it."

"Oh I've been supposing it for a long time, and what you tell me helps me to understand that you should want to do something. To do something, I mean," said Chad, "to commemorate an event so—what do they call it?—so auspicious. I see you make out, and not unnaturally," he continued, "that bringing me home in triumph as a sort of wedding-present to Mother would commemorate it better than anything else. You want to make a bonfire in fact," he laughed, "and you pitch me on. Thank you, thank you!" he laughed again.

He was altogether easy about it, and this made Strether now see how at bottom, and in spite of the shade of shyness that really cost him nothing, he had from the first moment been easy about everything. The shade of shyness was mere good taste. People with manners formed could apparently have, as one of their best cards, the shade of shyness too. He had leaned a little forward to speak; his elbows were on the table; and the inscrutable new face that he had got somewhere and somehow was brought by the movement nearer to his critics There was a fascination for that critic in its not being, this ripe physiognomy, the face that, under observation at least, he had originally carried away from Woollett. Strether found a certain freedom on his own side in defining it as that of a man of the world—a formula that indeed seemed to come now in some degree to his relief; that of a man to whom things had happened and were variously known. In gleams, in glances, the past did perhaps peep out of it; but such lights were faint and instantly merged. Chad was brown and thick and strong, and of old Chad had been rough. Was all the difference therefore that he was actually smooth? Possibly; for that he WAS smooth was as marked as in the taste of a sauce or in the rub of a hand. The effect of it was general—it had retouched his features, drawn them with a cleaner line. It had cleared his eyes and settled his colour and polished his fine square teeth—the main ornament of his face; and at the same time that it had given him a form and a surface, almost a design, it had toned his voice, established his accent, encouraged his smile to more play and his other motions to less. He had formerly, with a great deal of action, expressed very little; and he now expressed whatever was necessary with almost none at all. It was as if in short he had really, copious perhaps but shapeless, been put into a firm mould and turned successfully out. The phenomenon—Strether kept eyeing it as a phenomenon, an eminent case—was marked enough to be touched by the finger. He finally put his hand across the table and laid it on Chad's arm. "If you'll promise me—here on the spot and giving me your word of honour—to break straight off, you'll make the future the real right thing for all of us alike. You'll ease off the strain of this decent but none the less acute suspense in which I've for so many days been waiting for you, and let me turn in to rest. I shall leave you with my blessing and go to bed in peace."

Chad again fell back at this and, his hands pocketed, settled himself a little; in which posture he looked, though he rather anxiously smiled, only the more earnest. Then Strether seemed to see that he was really nervous, and he took that as what he would have called a wholesome sign. The only mark of it hitherto had been his more than once taking off and putting on his wide-brimmed crush hat. He had at this moment went the motion again to remove it, then had only pushed it back, so that it hung informally on his strong young grizzled crop. It was a touch that gave the note of the familiar—the intimate and the belated—to their quiet colloquy; and it was indeed by some such trivial aid that Strether became aware at the same moment of something else. The observation was at any rate determined in him by some light too fine to distinguish from so many others, but it was none the less sharply determined. Chad looked unmistakeably during these instants—well, as Strether put it to himself, all he was worth. Our friend had a sudden apprehension of what that would on certain sides be. He saw him in a flash as the young man marked out by women; and for a concentrated minute the dignity, the comparative austerity, as he funnily fancied it, of this character affected him almost with awe. There was an experience on his interlocutor's part that looked out at him from under the displaced hat, and that looked out moreover by a force of its own, the deep fact of its quantity and quality, and not through Chad's intending bravado or swagger. That was then the way men marked out by women WERE—and also the men by whom the women were doubtless in turn sufficiently distinguished. It affected Strether for thirty seconds as a relevant truth, a truth which, however, the next minute, had fallen into its relation. "Can't you imagine there being some questions," Chad asked, "that a fellow—however much impressed by your charming way of stating things—would like to put to you first?"

"Oh yes—easily. I'm here to answer everything. I think I can even tell you things, of the greatest interest to you, that you won't know enough to ask me. We'll take as many days to it as you like. But I want," Strether wound up, "to go to bed now."

"Really?"

Chad had spoken in such surprise that he was amused. "Can't you believe it?—with what you put me through?"

The young man seemed to consider. "Oh I haven't put you through much—yet."

"Do you mean there's so much more to come?" Strether laughed. "All the more reason then that I should gird myself." And as if to mark what he felt he could by this time count on he was already on his feet.

Chad, still seated, stayed him, with a hand against him, as he passed between their table and the next. "Oh we shall get on!"

The tone was, as who should say, everything Strether could have desired; and quite as good the expression of face with which the speaker had looked up at him and kindly held him. All these things lacked was their not showing quite so much as the fruit of experience. Yes, experience was what Chad did play on him, if he didn't play any grossness of defiance. Of course experience was in a manner defiance; but it wasn't, at any rate—rather indeed quite the contrary!—grossness; which was so much gained. He fairly grew older, Strether thought, while he himself so reasoned. Then with his mature pat of his visitor's arm he also got up; and there had been enough of it all by this time to make the visitor feel that something WAS settled. Wasn't it settled that he had at least the testimony of Chad's own belief in a settlement? Strether found himself treating Chad's profession that they would get on as a sufficient basis for going to bed. He hadn't nevertheless after this gone to bed directly; for when they had again passed out together into the mild bright night a check had virtually sprung from nothing more than a small circumstance which might have acted only as confirming quiescence. There were people, expressive sound, projected light, still abroad, and after they had taken in for a moment, through everything, the great clear architectural street, they turned off in tacit union to the quarter of Strether's hotel. "Of course," Chad here abruptly began, "of course Mother's making things out with you about me has been natural—and of course also you've had a good deal to go upon. Still, you must have filled out."

He had stopped, leaving his friend to wonder a little what point he wished to make; and this it was that enabled Strether meanwhile to make one. "Oh we've never pretended to go into detail. We weren't in the least bound to THAT. It was 'filling out' enough to miss you as we did."

But Chad rather oddly insisted, though under the high lamp at their corner, where they paused, he had at first looked as if touched by Strether's allusion to the long sense, at home, of his absence. "What I mean is you must have imagined."

"Imagined what?"

"Well—horrors."

It affected Strether: horrors were so little—superficially at least—in this robust and reasoning image. But he was none the less there to be veracious. "Yes, I dare say we HAVE imagined horrors. But where's the harm if we haven't been wrong?"

Chad raised his face to the lamp, and it was one of the moments at which he had, in his extraordinary way, most his air of designedly showing himself. It was as if at these instants he just presented himself, his identity so rounded off, his palpable presence and his massive young manhood, as such a link in the chain as might practically amount to a kind of demonstration. It was as if—and how but anomalously?—he couldn't after all help thinking sufficiently well of these things to let them go for what they were worth. What could there be in this for Strether but the hint of some self-respect, some sense of power, oddly perverted; something latent and beyond access, ominous and perhaps enviable? The intimation had the next thing, in a flash, taken on a name—a name on which our friend seized as he asked himself if he weren't perhaps really dealing with an irreducible young Pagan. This description—he quite jumped at it—had a sound that gratified his mental ear, so that of a sudden he had already adopted it. Pagan—yes, that was, wasn't it? what Chad WOULD logically be. It was what he must be. It was what he was. The idea was a clue and, instead of darkening the prospect, projected a certain clearness. Strether made out in this quick ray that a Pagan was perhaps, at the pass they had come to, the thing most wanted at Woollett. They'd be able to do with one—a good one; he'd find an opening—yes; and Strether's imagination even now prefigured and accompanied the first appearance there of the rousing personage. He had only the slight discomfort of feeling, as the young man turned away from the lamp, that his thought had in the momentary silence possibly been guessed. "Well, I've no doubt," said Chad, "you've come near enough. The details, as you say, don't matter. It HAS been generally the case that I've let myself go. But I'm coming round—I'm not so bad now." With which they walked on again to Strether's hotel.

"Do you mean," the latter asked as they approached the door, "that there isn't any woman with you now?"

"But pray what has that to do with it?"

"Why it's the whole question."

"Of my going home?" Chad was clearly surprised. "Oh not much! Do you think that when I want to go any one will have any power—"

"To keep you"—Strether took him straight up—"from carrying out your wish? Well, our idea has been that somebody has hitherto—or a good many persons perhaps—kept you pretty well from 'wanting.' That's what—if you're in anybody's hands—may again happen. You don't answer my question"—he kept it up; "but if you aren't in anybody's hands so much the better. There's nothing then but what makes for your going."

Chad turned this over. "I don't answer your question?" He spoke quite without resenting it. "Well, such questions have always a rather exaggerated side. One doesn't know quite what you mean by being in women's 'hands.' It's all so vague. One is when one isn't. One isn't when one is. And then one can't quite give people away." He seemed kindly to explain. "I've NEVER got stuck—so very hard; and, as against anything at any time really better, I don't think I've ever been afraid." There was something in it that held Strether to wonder, and this gave him time to go on. He broke out as with a more helpful thought. "Don't you know how I like Paris itself?"

The upshot was indeed to make our friend marvel. "Oh if THAT'S all that's the matter with you—!" It was HE who almost showed resentment.

Chad's smile of a truth more than met it. "But isn't that enough?"

Strether hesitated, but it came out. "Not enough for your mother!" Spoken, however, it sounded a trifle odd—the effect of which was that Chad broke into a laugh. Strether, at this, succumbed as well, though with extreme brevity. "Permit us to have still our theory. But if you ARE so free and so strong you're inexcusable. I'll write in the morning," he added with decision. "I'll say I've got you."

This appeared to open for Chad a new interest. "How often do you write?"

"Oh perpetually."

"And at great length?"

Strether had become a little impatient. "I hope it's not found too great."

"Oh I'm sure not. And you hear as often?"

Again Strether paused. "As often as I deserve."

"Mother writes," said Chad, "a lovely letter."

Strether, before the closed porte-cochère, fixed him a moment. "It's more, my boy, than YOU do! But our suppositions don't matter," he added, "if you're actually not entangled."

Chad's pride seemed none the less a little touched. "I never WAS that—let me insist. I always had my own way." With which he pursued: "And I have it at present."

"Then what are you here for? What has kept you," Strether asked, "if you HAVE been able to leave?"

It made Chad, after a stare, throw himself back. "Do you think one's kept only by women?" His surprise and his verbal emphasis rang out so clear in the still street that Strether winced till he remembered the safety of their English speech. "Is that," the young man demanded, "what they think at Woollett?" At the good faith in the question Strether had changed colour, feeling that, as he would have said, he had put his foot in it. He had appeared stupidly to misrepresent what they thought at Woollett; but before he had time to rectify Chad again was upon him. "I must say then you show a low mind!"

It so fell in, unhappily for Strether, with that reflexion of his own prompted in him by the pleasant air of the Boulevard Malesherbes, that its disconcerting force was rather unfairly great. It was a dig that, administered by himself—and administered even to poor Mrs. Newsome— was no more than salutary; but administered by Chad—and quite logically—it came nearer drawing blood. They HADn't a low mind—nor any approach to one; yet incontestably they had worked, and with a certain smugness, on a basis that might be turned against them. Chad had at any rate pulled his visitor up; he had even pulled up his admirable mother; he had absolutely, by a turn of the wrist and a jerk of the far-flung noose, pulled up, in a bunch, Woollett browsing in its pride. There was no doubt Woollett HAD insisted on its coarseness; and what he at present stood there for in the sleeping street was, by his manner of striking the other note, to make of such insistence a preoccupation compromising to the insisters. It was exactly as if they had imputed to him a vulgarity that he had by a mere gesture caused to fall from him. The devil of the case was that Strether felt it, by the same stroke, as falling straight upon himself. He had been wondering a minute ago if the boy weren't a Pagan, and he found himself wondering now if he weren't by chance a gentleman. It didn't in the least, on the spot, spring up helpfully for him that a person couldn't at the same time be both. There was nothing at this moment in the air to challenge the combination; there was everything to give it on the contrary something of a flourish. It struck Strether into the bargain as doing something to meet the most difficult of the questions; though perhaps indeed only by substituting another. Wouldn't it be precisely by having learned to be a gentleman that he had mastered the consequent trick of looking so well that one could scarce speak to him straight? But what in the world was the clue to such a prime producing cause? There were too many clues then that Strether still lacked, and these clues to clues were among them. What it accordingly amounted to for him was that he had to take full in the face a fresh attribution of ignorance. He had grown used by this time to reminders, especially from his own lips, of what he didn't know; but he had borne them because in the first place they were private and because in the second they practically conveyed a tribute. He didn't know what was bad, and—as others didn't know how little he knew it—he could put up with his state. But if he didn't know, in so important a particular, what was good, Chad at least was now aware he didn't; and that, for some reason, affected our friend as curiously public. It was in fact an exposed condition that the young man left him in long enough for him to feel its chill—till he saw fit, in a word, generously again to cover him. This last was in truth what Chad quite gracefully did. But he did it as with a simple thought that met the whole of the case. "Oh I'm all right!" It was what Strether had rather bewilderedly to go to bed on.

II

It really looked true moreover from the way Chad was to behave after this. He was full of attentions to his mother's ambassador; in spite of which, all the while, the latter's other relations rather remarkably contrived to assert themselves. Strether's sittings pen in hand with Mrs. Newsome up in his own room were broken, yet they were richer; and they were more than ever interspersed with the hours in which he reported himself, in a different fashion, but with scarce less earnestness and fulness, to Maria Gostrey. Now that, as he would have expressed it, he had really something to talk about he found himself, in respect to any oddity that might reside for him in the double connexion, at once more aware and more indifferent. He had been fine to Mrs. Newsome about his useful friend, but it had begun to haunt his imagination that Chad, taking up again for her benefit a pen too long disused, might possibly be finer. It wouldn't at all do, he saw, that anything should come up for him at Chad's hand but what specifically was to have come; the greatest divergence from which would be precisely the element of any lubrication of their intercourse by levity It was accordingly to forestall such an accident that he frankly put before the young man the several facts, just as they had occurred, of his funny alliance. He spoke of these facts, pleasantly and obligingly, as "the whole story," and felt that he might qualify the alliance as funny if he remained sufficiently grave about it. He flattered himself that he even exaggerated the wild freedom of his original encounter with the wonderful lady; he was scrupulously definite about the absurd conditions in which they had made acquaintance—their having picked each other up almost in the street; and he had (finest inspiration of all!) a conception of carrying the war into the enemy's country by showing surprise at the enemy's ignorance.

He had always had a notion that this last was the grand style of fighting; the greater therefore the reason for it, as he couldn't remember that he had ever before fought in the grand style. Every one, according to this, knew Miss Gostrey: how came it Chad didn't know her? The difficulty, the impossibility, was really to escape it; Strether put on him, by what he took for granted, the burden of proof of the contrary. This tone was so far successful as that Chad quite appeared to recognise her as a person whose fame had reached him, but against his acquaintance with whom much mischance had worked. He made the point at the same time that his social relations, such as they could be called, were perhaps not to the extent Strether supposed with the rising flood of their compatriots. He hinted at his having more and more given way to a different principle of selection; the moral of which seemed to be that he went about little in the "colony." For the moment certainly he had quite another interest. It was deep, what he understood, and Strether, for himself, could only so observe it. He couldn't see as yet how deep. Might he not all too soon? For there was really too much of their question that Chad had already committed himself to liking. He liked, to begin with, his prospective stepfather; which was distinctly what had not been on the cards. His hating him was the untowardness for which Strether had been best prepared; he hadn't expected the boy's actual form to give him more to do than he imputed. It gave him more through suggesting that he must somehow make up to himself for not being sure he was sufficiently disagreeable. That had really been present to him as his only way to be sure he was sufficiently thorough. The point was that if Chad's tolerance of his thoroughness were insincere, were but the best of devices for gaining time, it none the less did treat everything as tacitly concluded.

That seemed at the end of ten days the upshot of the abundant, the recurrent talk through which Strether poured into him all it concerned him to know, put him in full possession of facts and figures. Never cutting these colloquies short by a minute, Chad behaved, looked and spoke as if he were rather heavily, perhaps even a trifle gloomily, but none the less fundamentally and comfortably free. He made no crude profession of eagerness to yield, but he asked the most intelligent questions, probed, at moments, abruptly, even deeper than his friend's layer of information, justified by these touches the native estimate of his latent stuff, and had in every way the air of trying to live, reflectively, into the square bright picture. He walked up and down in front of this production, sociably took Strether's arm at the points at which he stopped, surveyed it repeatedly from the right and from the left, inclined a critical head to either quarter, and, while he puffed a still more critical cigarette, animadverted to his companion on this passage and that. Strether sought relief—there were hours when he required it—in repeating himself; it was in truth not to be blinked that Chad had a way. The main question as yet was of what it was a way TO. It made vulgar questions no more easy; but that was unimportant when all questions save those of his own asking had dropped. That he was free was answer enough, and it wasn't quite ridiculous that this freedom should end by presenting itself as what was difficult to move. His changed state, his lovely home, his beautiful things, his easy talk, his very appetite for Strether, insatiable and, when all was said, flattering—what were such marked matters all but the notes of his freedom? He had the effect of making a sacrifice of it just in these handsome forms to his visitor; which was mainly the reason the visitor was privately, for the time, a little out of countenance. Strether was at this period again and again thrown back on a felt need to remodel somehow his plan. He fairly caught himself shooting rueful glances, shy looks of pursuit, toward the embodied influence, the definite adversary, who had by a stroke of her own failed him and on a fond theory of whose palpable presence he had, under Mrs. Newsome's inspiration, altogether proceeded. He had once or twice, in secret, literally expressed the irritated wish that SHE would come out and find her.

He couldn't quite yet force it upon Woollett that such a career, such a perverted young life, showed after all a certain plausible side, DID in the case before them flaunt something like an impunity for the social man; but he could at least treat himself to the statement that would prepare him for the sharpest echo. This echo—as distinct over there in the dry thin air as some shrill "heading" above a column of print—seemed to reach him even as he wrote. "He says there's no woman," he could hear Mrs. Newsome report, in capitals almost of newspaper size, to Mrs. Pocock; and he could focus in Mrs. Pocock the response of the reader of the journal. He could see in the younger lady's face the earnestness of her attention and catch the full scepticism of her but slightly delayed "What is there then?" Just so he could again as little miss the mother's clear decision: "There's plenty of disposition, no doubt, to pretend there isn't." Strether had, after posting his letter, the whole scene out; and it was a scene during which, coming and going, as befell, he kept his eye not least upon the daughter. He had his fine sense of the conviction Mrs. Pocock would take occasion to reaffirm—a conviction bearing, as he had from the first deeply divined it to bear, on Mr. Strether's essential inaptitude. She had looked him in his conscious eyes even before he sailed, and that she didn't believe HE would find the woman had been written in her book. Hadn't she at the best but a scant faith in his ability to find women? It wasn't even as if he had found her mother—so much more, to her discrimination, had her mother performed the finding. Her mother had, in a case her private judgement of which remained educative of Mrs. Pocock's critical sense, found the man. The man owed his unchallenged state, in general, to the fact that Mrs. Newsome's discoveries were accepted at Woollett; but he knew in his bones, our friend did, how almost irresistibly Mrs. Pocock would now be moved to show what she thought of his own. Give HER a free hand, would be the moral, and the woman would soon be found.

His impression of Miss Gostrey after her introduction to Chad was meanwhile an impression of a person almost unnaturally on her guard. He struck himself as at first unable to extract from her what he wished; though indeed OF what he wished at this special juncture he would doubtless have contrived to make but a crude statement. It sifted and settled nothing to put to her, tout betement, as she often said, "Do you like him, eh?"—thanks to his feeling it actually the least of his needs to heap up the evidence in the young man's favour. He repeatedly knocked at her door to let her have it afresh that Chad's case—whatever else of minor interest it might yield—was first and foremost a miracle almost monstrous. It was the alteration of the entire man, and was so signal an instance that nothing else, for the intelligent observer, could—COULD it?—signify. "It's a plot," he declared—"there's more in it than meets the eye." He gave the rein to his fancy. "It's a plant!"

His fancy seemed to please her. "Whose then?"

"Well, the party responsible is, I suppose, the fate that waits for one, the dark doom that rides. What I mean is that with such elements one can't count. I've but my poor individual, my modest human means. It isn't playing the game to turn on the uncanny. All one's energy goes to facing it, to tracking it. One wants, confound it, don't you see?" he confessed with a queer face—"one wants to enjoy anything so rare. Call it then life"—he puzzled it out—"call it poor dear old life simply that springs the surprise. Nothing alters the fact that the surprise is paralysing, or at any rate engrossing—all, practically, hang it, that one sees, that one CAN see."

Her silences were never barren, nor even dull. "Is that what you've written home?"

He tossed it off. "Oh dear, yes!"

She had another pause while, across her carpets, he had another walk. "If you don't look out you'll have them straight over."

"Oh but I've said he'll go back."

"And WILL he?" Miss Gostrey asked.

The special tone of it made him, pulling up, look at her long. "What's that but just the question I've spent treasures of patience and ingenuity in giving you, by the sight of him—after everything had led up—every facility to answer? What is it but just the thing I came here to-day to get out of you? Will he?"

"No—he won't," she said at last. "He's not free."

The air of it held him. "Then you've all the while known—?"

"I've known nothing but what I've seen; and I wonder," she declared with some impatience, "that you didn't see as much. It was enough to be with him there—"

"In the box? Yes," he rather blankly urged.

"Well—to feel sure."

"Sure of what?"

She got up from her chair, at this, with a nearer approach than she had ever yet shown to dismay at his dimness. She even, fairly pausing for it, spoke with a shade of pity. "Guess!"

It was a shade, fairly, that brought a flush into his face; so that for a moment, as they waited together, their difference was between them. "You mean that just your hour with him told you so much of his story? Very good; I'm not such a fool, on my side, as that I don't understand you, or as that I didn't in some degree understand HIM. That he has done what he liked most isn't, among any of us, a matter the least in dispute. There's equally little question at this time of day of what it is he does like most. But I'm not talking," he reasonably explained, "of any mere wretch he may still pick up. I'm talking of some person who in his present situation may have held her own, may really have counted."

"That's exactly what I am!" said Miss Gostrey. But she as quickly made her point. "I thought you thought—or that they think at Woollett—that that's what mere wretches necessarily do. Mere wretches necessarily DON'T!" she declared with spirit. "There must, behind every appearance to the contrary, still be somebody—somebody who's not a mere wretch, since we accept the miracle. What else but such a somebody can such a miracle be?"

He took it in. "Because the fact itself IS the woman?"

"A woman. Some woman or other. It's one of the things that HAVE to be."

"But you mean then at least a good one."

"A good woman?" She threw up her arms with a laugh. "I should call her excellent!"

"Then why does he deny her?"

Miss Gostrey thought a moment. "Because she's too good to admit! Don't you see," she went on, "how she accounts for him?"

Strether clearly, more and more, did see; yet it made him also see other things. "But isn't what we want that he shall account for HER?"

"Well, he does. What you have before you is his way. You must forgive him if it isn't quite outspoken. In Paris such debts are tacit."

Strether could imagine; but still—! "Even when the woman's good?"

Again she laughed out. "Yes, and even when the man is! There's always a caution in such cases," she more seriously explained—"for what it may seem to show. There's nothing that's taken as showing so much here as sudden unnatural goodness."

"Ah then you're speaking now," Strether said, "of people who are NOT nice."

"I delight," she replied, "in your classifications. But do you want me," she asked, "to give you in the matter, on this ground, the wisest advice I'm capable of? Don't consider her, don't judge her at all in herself. Consider her and judge her only in Chad."

He had the courage at least of his companion's logic. "Because then I shall like her?" He almost looked, with his quick imagination as if he already did, though seeing at once also the full extent of how little it would suit his book. "But is that what I came out for?"

She had to confess indeed that it wasn't. But there was something else. "Don't make up your mind. There are all sorts of things. You haven't seen him all."

This on his side Strether recognised; but his acuteness none the less showed him the danger. "Yes, but if the more I see the better he seems?"

Well, she found something. "That may be—but his disavowal of her isn't, all the same, pure consideration. There's a hitch." She made it out. "It's the effort to sink her."

Strether winced at the image. "To 'sink'—?"

"Well, I mean there's a struggle, and a part of it is just what he hides. Take time—that's the only way not to make some mistake that you'll regret. Then you'll see. He does really want to shake her off."

Our friend had by this time so got into the vision that he almost gasped. "After all she has done for him?"

Miss Gostrey gave him a look which broke the next moment into a wonderful smile. "He's not so good as you think!"

They remained with him, these words, promising him, in their character of warning, considerable help; but the support he tried to draw from them found itself on each renewal of contact with Chad defeated by something else. What could it be, this disconcerting force, he asked himself, but the sense, constantly renewed, that Chad WAS—quite in fact insisted on being—as good as he thought? It seemed somehow as if he couldn't BUT be as good from the moment he wasn't as bad. There was a succession of days at all events when contact with him—and in its immediate effect, as if it could produce no other—elbowed out of Strether's consciousness everything but itself. Little Bilham once more pervaded the scene, but little Bilham became even in a higher degree than he had originally been one of the numerous forms of the inclusive relation; a consequence promoted, to our friend's sense, by two or three incidents with which we have yet to make acquaintance. Waymarsh himself, for the occasion, was drawn into the eddy; it absolutely, though but temporarily, swallowed him down, and there were days when Strether seemed to bump against him as a sinking swimmer might brush a submarine object. The fathomless medium held them—Chad's manner was the fathomless medium; and our friend felt as if they passed each other, in their deep immersion, with the round impersonal eye of silent fish. It was practically produced between them that Waymarsh was giving him his chance; and the shade of discomfort that Strether drew from the allowance resembled not a little the embarrassment he had known at school, as a boy, when members of his family had been present at exhibitions. He could perform before strangers, but relatives were fatal, and it was now as if, comparatively, Waymarsh were a relative. He seemed to hear him say "Strike up then!" and to enjoy a foretaste of conscientious domestic criticism. He HAD struck up, so far as he actually could; Chad knew by this time in profusion what he wanted; and what vulgar violence did his fellow pilgrim expect of him when he had really emptied his mind? It went somehow to and fro that what poor Waymarsh meant was "I told you so—that you'd lose your immortal soul!" but it was also fairly explicit that Strether had his own challenge and that, since they must go to the bottom of things, he wasted no more virtue in watching Chad than Chad wasted in watching him. His dip for duty's sake—where was it worse than Waymarsh's own? For HE needn't have stopped resisting and refusing, needn't have parleyed, at that rate, with the foe.

The strolls over Paris to see something or call somewhere were accordingly inevitable and natural, and the late sessions in the wondrous troisieme, the lovely home, when men dropped in and the picture composed more suggestively through the haze of tobacco, of music more or less good and of talk more or less polyglot, were on a principle not to be distinguished from that of the mornings and the afternoons. Nothing, Strether had to recognise as he leaned back and smoked, could well less resemble a scene of violence than even the liveliest of these occasions. They were occasions of discussion, none the less, and Strether had never in his life heard so many opinions on so many subjects. There were opinions at Woollett, but only on three or four. The differences were there to match; if they were doubtless deep, though few, they were quiet—they were, as might be said, almost as shy as if people had been ashamed of them. People showed little diffidence about such things, on the other hand, in the Boulevard Malesherbes, and were so far from being ashamed of them—or indeed of anything else—that they often seemed to have invented them to avert those agreements that destroy the taste of talk. No one had ever done that at Woollett, though Strether could remember times when he himself had been tempted to it without quite knowing why. He saw why at present—he had but wanted to promote intercourse.

These, however, were but parenthetic memories, and the turn taken by his affair on the whole was positively that if his nerves were on the stretch it was because he missed violence. When he asked himself if none would then, in connexion with it, ever come at all, he might almost have passed as wondering how to provoke it. It would be too absurd if such a vision as THAT should have to be invoked for relief; it was already marked enough as absurd that he should actually have begun with flutters and dignities on the score of a single accepted meal. What sort of a brute had he expected Chad to be, anyway?—Strether had occasion to make the enquiry but was careful to make it in private. He could himself, comparatively recent as it was—it was truly but the fact of a few days since—focus his primal crudity; but he would on the approach of an observer, as if handling an illicit possession, have slipped the reminiscence out of sight. There were echoes of it still in Mrs. Newsome's letters, and there were moments when these echoes made him exclaim on her want of tact. He blushed of course, at once, still more for the explanation than for the ground of it: it came to him in time to save his manners that she couldn't at the best become tactful as quickly as he. Her tact had to reckon with the Atlantic Ocean, the General Post-Office and the extravagant curve of the globe. Chad had one day offered tea at the Boulevard Malesherbes to a chosen few, a group again including the unobscured Miss Barrace; and Strether had on coming out walked away with the acquaintance whom in his letters to Mrs. Newsome he always spoke of as the little artist-man. He had had full occasion to mention him as the other party, so oddly, to the only close personal alliance observation had as yet detected in Chad's existence. Little Bilham's way this afternoon was not Strether's, but he had none the less kindly come with him, and it was somehow a part of his kindness that as it had sadly begun to rain they suddenly found themselves seated for conversation at a cafe in which they had taken refuge. He had passed no more crowded hour in Chad's society than the one just ended; he had talked with Miss Barrace, who had reproached him with not having come to see her, and he had above all hit on a happy thought for causing Waymarsh's tension to relax. Something might possibly be extracted for the latter from the idea of his success with that lady, whose quick apprehension of what might amuse her had given Strether a free hand. What had she meant if not to ask whether she couldn't help him with his splendid encumbrance, and mightn't the sacred rage at any rate be kept a little in abeyance by thus creating for his comrade's mind even in a world of irrelevance the possibility of a relation? What was it but a relation to be regarded as so decorative and, in especial, on the strength of it, to be whirled away, amid flounces and feathers, in a coupe lined, by what Strether could make out, with dark blue brocade? He himself had never been whirled away—never at least in a coupe and behind a footman; he had driven with Miss Gostrey in cabs, with Mrs. Pocock, a few times, in an open buggy, with Mrs. Newsome in a four-seated cart and, occasionally up at the mountains, on a buckboard; but his friend's actual adventure transcended his personal experience. He now showed his companion soon enough indeed how inadequate, as a general monitor, this last queer quantity could once more feel itself.

"What game under the sun is he playing?" He signified the next moment that his allusion was not to the fat gentleman immersed in dominoes on whom his eyes had begun by resting, but to their host of the previous hour, as to whom, there on the velvet bench, with a final collapse of all consistency, he treated himself to the comfort of indiscretion. "Where do you see him come out?"

Little Bilham, in meditation, looked at him with a kindness almost paternal. "Don't you like it over here?"

Strether laughed out—for the tone was indeed droll; he let himself go. "What has that to do with it? The only thing I've any business to like is to feel that I'm moving him. That's why I ask you whether you believe I AM? Is the creature"—and he did his best to show that he simply wished to ascertain—"honest?"

His companion looked responsible, but looked it through a small dim smile. "What creature do you mean?"

It was on this that they did have for a little a mute interchange. "Is it untrue that he's free? How then," Strether asked wondering "does he arrange his life?"

"Is the creature you mean Chad himself?" little Bilham said.

Strether here, with a rising hope, just thought, "We must take one of them at a time." But his coherence lapsed. "IS there some woman? Of whom he's really afraid of course I mean—or who does with him what she likes."

"It's awfully charming of you," Bilham presently remarked, "not to have asked me that before."

"Oh I'm not fit for my job!"

The exclamation had escaped our friend, but it made little Bilham more deliberate. "Chad's a rare case!" he luminously observed. "He's awfully changed," he added.

"Then you see it too?"

"The way he has improved? Oh yes—I think every one must see it. But I'm not sure," said little Bilham, "that I didn't like him about as well in his other state."

"Then this IS really a new state altogether?"

"Well," the young man after a moment returned, "I'm not sure he was really meant by nature to be quite so good. It's like the new edition of an old book that one has been fond of—revised and amended, brought up to date, but not quite the thing one knew and loved. However that may be at all events," he pursued, "I don't think, you know, that he's really playing, as you call it, any game. I believe he really wants to go back and take up a career. He's capable of one, you know, that will improve and enlarge him still more. He won't then," little Bilham continued to remark, "be my pleasant well-rubbed old-fashioned volume at all. But of course I'm beastly immoral. I'm afraid it would be a funny world altogether—a world with things the way I like them. I ought, I dare say, to go home and go into business myself. Only I'd simply rather die—simply. And I've not the least difficulty in making up my mind not to, and in knowing exactly why, and in defending my ground against all comers. All the same," he wound up, "I assure you I don't say a word against it—for himself, I mean—to Chad. I seem to see it as much the best thing for him. You see he's not happy."

"DO I?"—Strether stared. "I've been supposing I see just the opposite—an extraordinary case of the equilibrium arrived at and assured."

"Oh there's a lot behind it."

"Ah there you are!" Strether exclaimed. "That's just what I want to get at. You speak of your familiar volume altered out of recognition. Well, who's the editor?"

Little Bilham looked before him a minute in silence. "He ought to get married. THAT would do it. And he wants to."

"Wants to marry her?"

Again little Bilham waited, and, with a sense that he had information, Strether scarce knew what was coming. "He wants to be free. He isn't used, you see," the young man explained in his lucid way, "to being so good."

Strether hesitated. "Then I may take it from you that he IS good?"

His companion matched his pause, but making it up with a quiet fulness. "DO take it from me."

"Well then why isn't he free? He swears to me he is, but meanwhile does nothing—except of course that he's so kind to me—to prove it; and couldn't really act much otherwise if he weren't. My question to you just now was exactly on this queer impression of his diplomacy: as if instead of really giving ground his line were to keep me on here and set me a bad example."

As the half-hour meanwhile had ebbed Strether paid his score, and the waiter was presently in the act of counting out change. Our friend pushed back to him a fraction of it, with which, after an emphatic recognition, the personage in question retreated. "You give too much," little Bilham permitted himself benevolently to observe.

"Oh I always give too much!" Strether helplessly sighed. "But you don't," he went on as if to get quickly away from the contemplation of that doom, "answer my question. Why isn't he free?"

Little Bilham had got up as if the transaction with the waiter had been a signal, and had already edged out between the table and the divan. The effect of this was that a minute later they had quitted the place, the gratified waiter alert again at the open door. Strether found himself deferring to his companion's abruptness as to a hint that he should be answered as soon as they were more isolated. This happened when after a few steps in the outer air they had turned the next corner. There our friend had kept it up. "Why isn't he free if he's good?"

Little Bilham looked him full in the face. "Because it's a virtuous attachment."

This had settled the question so effectually for the time—that is for the next few days—that it had given Strether almost a new lease of life. It must be added however that, thanks to his constant habit of shaking the bottle in which life handed him the wine of experience, he presently found the taste of the lees rising as usual into his draught. His imagination had in other words already dealt with his young friend's assertion; of which it had made something that sufficiently came out on the very next occasion of his seeing Maria Gostrey. This occasion moreover had been determined promptly by a new circumstance—a circumstance he was the last man to leave her for a day in ignorance of. "When I said to him last night," he immediately began, "that without some definite word from him now that will enable me to speak to them over there of our sailing—or at least of mine, giving them some sort of date—my responsibility becomes uncomfortable and my situation awkward; when I said that to him what do you think was his reply?" And then as she this time gave it up: "Why that he has two particular friends, two ladies, mother and daughter, about to arrive in Paris—coming back from an absence; and that he wants me so furiously to meet them, know them and like them, that I shall oblige him by kindly not bringing our business to a crisis till he has had a chance to see them again himself. Is that," Strether enquired, "the way he's going to try to get off? These are the people," he explained, "that he must have gone down to see before I arrived. They're the best friends he has in the world, and they take more interest than any one else in what concerns him. As I'm his next best he sees a

46

thousand reasons why we should comfortably meet. He hasn't broached the question sooner because their return was uncertain—seemed in fact for the present impossible. But he more than intimates that—if you can believe it—their desire to make my acquaintance has had to do with their surmounting difficulties."

"They're dying to see you?" Miss Gostrey asked.

"Dying. Of course," said Strether, "they're the virtuous attachment." He had already told her about that—had seen her the day after his talk with little Bilham; and they had then threshed out together the bearing of the revelation. She had helped him to put into it the logic in which little Bilham had left it slightly deficient Strether hadn't pressed him as to the object of the preference so unexpectedly described; feeling in the presence of it, with one of his irrepressible scruples, a delicacy from which he had in the quest of the quite other article worked sufficiently free. He had held off, as on a small principle of pride, from permitting his young friend to mention a name; wishing to make with this the great point that Chad's virtuous attachments were none of his business. He had wanted from the first not to think too much of his dignity, but that was no reason for not allowing it any little benefit that might turn up. He had often enough wondered to what degree his interference might pass for interested; so that there was no want of luxury in letting it be seen whenever he could that he didn't interfere. That had of course at the same time not deprived him of the further luxury of much private astonishment; which however he had reduced to some order before communicating his knowledge. When he had done this at last it was with the remark that, surprised as Miss Gostrey might, like himself, at first be, she would probably agree with him on reflexion that such an account of the matter did after all fit the confirmed appearances. Nothing certainly, on all the indications, could have been a greater change for him than a virtuous attachment, and since they had been in search of the "word" as the French called it, of that change, little Bilham's announcement—though so long and so oddly delayed—would serve as well as another. She had assured Strether in fact after a pause that the more she thought of it the more it did serve; and yet her assurance hadn't so weighed with him as that before they parted he hadn't ventured to challenge her sincerity. Didn't she believe the attachment was virtuous?—he had made sure of her again with the aid of that question. The tidings he brought her on this second occasion were moreover such as would help him to make surer still.

She showed at first none the less as only amused. "You say there are two? An attachment to them both then would, I suppose, almost necessarily be innocent."

Our friend took the point, but he had his clue. "Mayn't he be still in the stage of not quite knowing which of them, mother or daughter, he likes best?"

She gave it more thought. "Oh it must be the daughter—at his age."

"Possibly. Yet what do we know," Strether asked, "about hers? She may be old enough."

"Old enough for what?"

"Why to marry Chad. That may be, you know, what they want. And if Chad wants it too, and little Bilham wants it, and even we, at a pinch, could do with it—that is if she doesn't prevent repatriation—why it may be plain sailing yet."

It was always the case for him in these counsels that each of his remarks, as it came, seemed to drop into a deeper well. He had at all events to wait a moment to hear the slight splash of this one. "I don't see why if Mr. Newsome wants to marry the young lady he hasn't already done it or hasn't been prepared with some statement to you about it. And if he both wants to marry her and is on good terms with them why isn't he 'free'?"

Strether, responsively, wondered indeed. "Perhaps the girl herself doesn't like him."

"Then why does he speak of them to you as he does?"

Strether's mind echoed the question, but also again met it. "Perhaps it's with the mother he's on good terms."

"As against the daughter?"

"Well, if she's trying to persuade the daughter to consent to him, what could make him like the mother more? Only," Strether threw out, "why shouldn't the daughter consent to him?"

"Oh," said Miss Gostrey, "mayn't it be that every one else isn't quite so struck with him as you?"

"Doesn't regard him you mean as such an 'eligible' young man? Is that what I've come to?" he audibly and rather gravely sought to know. "However," he went on, "his marriage is what his mother most desires—that is if it will help. And oughtn't ANY marriage to help? They must want him"—he had already worked it out—"to be better off. Almost any girl he may marry will have a direct interest in his taking up his chances. It won't suit HER at least that he shall miss them."

Miss Gostrey cast about. "No—you reason well! But of course on the other hand there's always dear old Woollett itself."

"Oh yes," he mused—"there's always dear old Woollett itself."

She waited a moment. "The young lady mayn't find herself able to swallow THAT quantity. She may think it's paying too much; she may weigh one thing against another."

Strether, ever restless in such debates, took a vague turn "It will all depend on who she is. That of course—the proved ability to deal with dear old Woollett, since I'm sure she does deal with it—is what makes so strongly for Mamie."

"Mamie?"

He stopped short, at her tone, before her; then, though seeing that it represented not vagueness, but a momentary embarrassed fulness, let his exclamation come. "You surely haven't forgotten about Mamie!"

"No, I haven't forgotten about Mamie," she smiled. "There's no doubt whatever that there's ever so much to be said for her. Mamie's MY girl!" she roundly declared.

Strether resumed for a minute his walk. "She's really perfectly lovely, you know. Far prettier than any girl I've seen over here yet."

"That's precisely on what I perhaps most build." And she mused a moment in her friend's way. "I should positively like to take her in hand!"

He humoured the fancy, though indeed finally to deprecate it. "Oh but don't, in your zeal, go over to her! I need you most and can't, you know, be left."

But she kept it up. "I wish they'd send her out to me!"

"If they knew you," he returned, "they would."

"Ah but don't they?—after all that, as I've understood you you've told them about me?"

He had paused before her again, but he continued his course "They WILL—before, as you say, I've done." Then he came out with the point he had wished after all most to make. "It seems to give away now his game. This is what he has been doing—keeping me along for it. He has been waiting for them."

Miss Gostrey drew in her lips. "You see a good deal in it!"

"I doubt if I see as much as you. Do you pretend," he went on, "that you don't see—?"

"Well, what?"—she pressed him as he paused.

"Why that there must be a lot between them—and that it has been going on from the first; even from before I came."

She took a minute to answer. "Who are they then—if it's so grave?"

"It mayn't be grave—it may be gay. But at any rate it's marked. Only I don't know," Strether had to confess, "anything about them. Their name for instance was a thing that, after little Bilham's information, I found it a kind of refreshment not to feel obliged to follow up."

"Oh," she returned, "if you think you've got off—!"

Her laugh produced in him a momentary gloom. "I don't think I've got off. I only think I'm breathing for about five minutes. I dare say I SHALL have, at the best, still to get on." A look, over it all, passed between them, and the next minute he had come back to good humour. "I don't meanwhile take the smallest interest in their name."

"Nor in their nationality?—American, French, English, Polish?"

"I don't care the least little 'hang,'" he smiled, "for their nationality. It would be nice if they're Polish!" he almost immediately added.

"Very nice indeed." The transition kept up her spirits. "So you see you do care."

He did this contention a modified justice. "I think I should if they WERE Polish. Yes," he thought—"there might be joy in THAT."

"Let us then hope for it." But she came after this nearer to the question. "If the girl's of the right age of course the mother can't be. I mean for the virtuous attachment. If the girl's twenty—and she can't be less—the mother must be at least forty. So it puts the mother out. SHE'S too old for him."

Strether, arrested again, considered and demurred. "Do you think so? Do you think any one would be too old for him? I'M eighty, and I'm too young. But perhaps the girl," he continued, "ISn't twenty. Perhaps she's only ten—but such a little dear that Chad finds himself counting her in as an attraction of the acquaintance. Perhaps she's only five. Perhaps the mother's but five-and-twenty—a charming young widow."

Miss Gostrey entertained the suggestion. "She IS a widow then?"

"I haven't the least idea!" They once more, in spite of this vagueness, exchanged a look—a look that was perhaps the longest yet. It seemed in fact, the next thing, to require to explain itself; which it did as it could. "I only feel what I've told you—that he has some reason."

Miss Gostrey's imagination had taken its own flight. "Perhaps she's NOT a widow."

Strether seemed to accept the possibility with reserve. Still he accepted it. "Then that's why the attachment—if it's to her—is virtuous."

But she looked as if she scarce followed. "Why is it virtuous if—since she's free—there's nothing to impose on it any condition?"

He laughed at her question. "Oh I perhaps don't mean as virtuous as THAT! Your idea is that it can be virtuous—in any sense worthy of the name—only if she's NOT free? But what does it become then," he asked, "for HER?"

"Ah that's another matter." He said nothing for a moment, and she soon went on. "I dare say you're right, at any rate, about Mr. Newsome's little plan. He HAS been trying you—has been reporting on you to these friends."

Strether meanwhile had had time to think more. "Then where's his straightness?"

"Well, as we say, it's struggling up, breaking out, asserting itself as it can. We can be on the side, you see, of his straightness. We can help him. But he has made out," said Miss Gostrey, "that you'll do."

"Do for what?"

"Why, for THEM—for ces dames. He has watched you, studied you, liked you—and recognised that THEY must. It's a great compliment to you, my dear man; for I'm sure they're particular. You came out for a success. Well," she gaily declared, "you're having it!"

He took it from her with momentary patience and then turned abruptly away. It was always convenient to him that there were so many fine things in her room to look at. But the examination of two or three of them appeared soon to have determined a speech that had little to do with them. "You don't believe in it!"

"In what?"

"In the character of the attachment. In its innocence."

But she defended herself. "I don't pretend to know anything about it. Everything's possible. We must see."

"See?" he echoed with a groan. "Haven't we seen enough?"

"I haven't," she smiled.

"But do you suppose then little Bilham has lied?"

"You must find out."

It made him almost turn pale. "Find out any MORE?"

He had dropped on a sofa for dismay; but she seemed, as she stood over him, to have the last word. "Wasn't what you came out for to find out ALL?"

Book Fifth

I

Sculptor at work (1883) by José Malhoa (1855-1933)

The Sunday of the next week was a wonderful day, and Chad Newsome had let his friend know in advance that he had provided for it. There had already been a question of his taking him to see the great Gloriani, who was at home on Sunday afternoons and at whose house, for the most part, fewer bores were to be met than elsewhere; but the project, through some accident, had not had instant effect, and now revived in happier conditions. Chad had made the point that the celebrated sculptor had a queer old garden, for which the weather—spring at last frank and fair—was propitious; and two or three of his other allusions had confirmed for Strether the expectation of something special. He had by this time, for all introductions and adventures, let himself recklessly go, cherishing the sense that whatever the young man showed him he was showing at least himself. He could have wished indeed, so far as this went, that Chad were less of a mere cicerone; for he was not without the impression—now that the vision of his game, his plan, his deep diplomacy, did recurrently assert itself—of his taking refuge from the realities of their intercourse in profusely dispensing, as our friend mentally phrased et panem et circenses. Our friend continued to feel rather smothered in flowers, though he made in his other moments the almost angry inference that this was only because of his odious ascetic suspicion of any form of beauty. He periodically assured himself—for his reactions were sharp—that he shouldn't reach the truth of anything till he had at least got rid of that.

He had known beforehand that Madame de Vionnet and her daughter would probably be on view, an intimation to that effect having constituted the only reference again made by Chad to his good friends from the south. The effect of Strether's talk about them with Miss Gostrey had been quite to consecrate his reluctance to pry; something in the very air of Chad's silence—judged in the light of that talk—offered it to him as a reserve he could markedly match. It shrouded them about with he scarce knew what, a consideration, a distinction; he was in presence at any rate—so far as it placed him there—of ladies; and the one thing that was definite for him was that they themselves should be, to the extent of his responsibility, in presence of a gentleman. Was it because they were very beautiful, very clever, or even very good—was it for one of these reasons that Chad was, so to speak, nursing his effect? Did he wish to spring them, in the Woollett phrase, with a fuller force—to confound his critic, slight though as yet the criticism, with some form of merit exquisitely incalculable? The most the critic had at all events asked was whether the persons in question were French; and that enquiry had been but a proper comment on the sound of their name. "Yes. That is no!" had been Chad's reply; but he had immediately added that their English was the most charming in the world, so that if Strether were wanting an excuse for not getting on with them he wouldn't in the least find one. Never in fact had Strether—in the mood into which the place had quickly launched him—felt, for himself, less the need of an excuse. Those he might have found would have been, at the worst, all for the others, the people before him, in whose liberty to be as they were he was aware that he positively rejoiced. His fellow guests were multiplying, and these things, their liberty, their intensity, their variety, their conditions at large, were in fusion in the admirable medium of the scene.

The place itself was a great impression—a small pavilion, clear-faced and sequestered, an effect of polished parquet, of fine white panel and spare sallow gilt, of decoration delicate and rare, in the heart of the Faubourg Saint-Germain and on the edge of a cluster of gardens attached to old noble houses. Far back from streets and unsuspected by crowds, reached by a long passage and a quiet court, it was as striking to the unprepared mind, he immediately saw, as a treasure dug up; giving him too, more than anything yet, the note of the range of the immeasurable town and sweeping away, as by a last brave brush, his usual landmarks and terms. It was in the garden, a spacious cherished remnant, out of which a dozen persons had already passed, that Chad's host presently met them while the tall bird-haunted trees, all of a twitter with the spring and the weather, and the high party-walls, on the other side of which grave hotels stood off for privacy, spoke of survival, transmission, association, a strong indifferent persistent order. The day was so soft that the little party had practically adjourned to the open air but the open air was in such conditions all a chamber of state. Strether had presently the sense of a great convent, a convent of missions, famous for he scarce knew what, a nursery of young priests, of scattered shade, of straight alleys and chapel-bells, that spread its mass in one quarter; he had the sense of names in the air, of ghosts at the windows, of signs and tokens, a whole range of expression, all about him, too thick for prompt discrimination.

This assault of images became for a moment, in the address of the distinguished sculptor, almost formidable: Gloriani showed him, in such perfect confidence, on Chad's introduction of him, a fine worn handsome face, a face that was like an open letter in a foreign tongue. With his genius in his eyes, his manners on his lips, his long career behind him and his honours and rewards all round, the great artist, in the course of a single sustained look and a few words of delight at receiving him, affected our friend as a dazzling prodigy of type. Strether had seen in museums—in the Luxembourg as well as, more reverently, later on, in the New York of the billionaires—the work of his hand; knowing too that after an earlier time in his native Rome he had migrated, in mid-career, to Paris, where, with a personal lustre almost violent, he shone in a constellation: all of which was more than enough to crown him, for his guest, with the light, with the romance, of glory. Strether, in contact with that element as he had never yet so intimately been, had the consciousness of opening to it, for the happy instant, all the windows of his mind, of letting this rather grey interior drink in for once the sun of a clime not marked in his old geography. He was to remember again repeatedly the medal-like Italian face, in which every line was an artist's own, in which time told only as tone and consecration; and he was to recall in especial, as the penetrating radiance, as the communication of the illustrious spirit itself, the manner in which, while they stood briefly, in welcome and response, face to face, he was held by the sculptor's eyes. He wasn't soon to forget them, was to think of them, all unconscious, unintending, preoccupied though they were, as the source of the deepest intellectual sounding to which he had ever been exposed. He was in fact quite to cherish his vision of it, to play with it in idle hours; only speaking of it to no one and quite aware he couldn't have spoken without appearing to talk nonsense. Was it what it had told him or what it had asked him the greater of the mysteries? Was it the most special flare, unequalled, supreme, of the aesthetic torch, lighting that wondrous world for ever, or was it above all the long straight shaft sunk by a personal acuteness that life had seasoned to steel? Nothing on earth could have been stranger and no one doubtless more surprised than the artist himself, but it was for all the world to Strether just then as if in the matter of his accepted duty he had positively been on trial. The deep human expertness in Gloriani's charming smile—oh the terrible life behind it!—was flashed upon him as a test of his stuff.

Chad meanwhile, after having easily named his companion, had more easily turned away and was already greeting other persons present. He was as easy, clever Chad, with the great artist as with his obscure compatriot, and as easy with every one else as with either: this fell into its place for Strether and made almost a new light, giving him, as a concatenation, something more he could enjoy. He liked Gloriani, but should never see him again; of that he was sufficiently sure. Chad accordingly, who was wonderful with both of them, was a kind of link for hopeless fancy, an implication of possibilities—oh if everything had been different! Strether noted at all events that he was thus on terms with illustrious spirits, and also that—yes, distinctly—he hadn't in the least swaggered about it. Our friend hadn't come there only for this figure of Abel Newsome's son, but that presence threatened to affect the observant mind as positively central. Gloriani indeed, remembering something and excusing himself, pursued Chad to speak to him, and Strether was left musing on many things. One of them was the question of whether, since he had been tested, he had passed. Did the artist drop him from having made out that he wouldn't do? He really felt just to-day that he might do better than usual. Hadn't he done well enough, so far as that went, in being exactly so dazzled? and in not having too, as he almost believed, wholly hidden from his host that he felt the latter's plummet? Suddenly, across the garden, he saw little Bilham approach, and it was a part of the fit that was on him that as their eyes met he guessed also HIS knowledge. If he had said to him on the instant what was uppermost he would have said: "HAVE I passed?—for of course I know one has to pass here." Little Bilham would have reassured him, have told him that he exaggerated, and have adduced happily enough the argument of little Bilham's own very presence; which, in truth, he could see, was as easy a one as Gloriani's own or as Chad's. He himself would perhaps then after a while cease to be frightened, would get the point of view for some of the faces—types tremendously alien, alien to Woollett—that he had already begun to take in. Who were they all, the dispersed groups and couples, the ladies even more unlike those of Woollett than the gentlemen?—this was the enquiry that, when his young friend had greeted him, he did find himself making.

"Oh they're every one—all sorts and sizes; of course I mean within limits, though limits down perhaps rather more than limits up. There are always artists—he's beautiful and inimitable to the cher confrere; and then gros bonnets of many kinds—ambassadors, cabinet ministers, bankers, generals, what do I know? even Jews. Above all always some awfully nice women—and not too many; sometimes an actress, an artist, a great performer—but only when they're not monsters; and in particular the right femmes du monde. You can fancy his history on that side—I believe it's fabulous: they NEVER give him up. Yet he keeps them down: no one knows how he manages; it's too beautiful and bland.

Never too many—and a mighty good thing too; just a perfect choice. But there are not in any way many bores; it has always been so; he has some secret. It's extraordinary. And you don't find it out. He's the same to every one. He doesn't ask questions.'

"Ah doesn't he?" Strether laughed.

Bilham met it with all his candour. "How then should I be here?

"Oh for what you tell me. You're part of the perfect choice."

Well, the young man took in the scene. "It seems rather good to-day."

Strether followed the direction of his eyes. "Are they all, this time, femmes du monde?"

Little Bilham showed his competence. "Pretty well."

This was a category our friend had a feeling for; a light, romantic and mysterious, on the feminine element, in which he enjoyed for a little watching it. "Are there any Poles?"

His companion considered. "I think I make out a 'Portuguee.' But I've seen Turks."

Strether wondered, desiring justice. "They seem—all the women—very harmonious."

"Oh in closer quarters they come out!" And then, while Strether was aware of fearing closer quarters, though giving himself again to the harmonies, "Well," little Bilham went on, "it IS at the worst rather good, you know. If you like it, you feel it, this way, that shows you're not in the least out But you always know things," he handsomely added, "immediately."

Strether liked it and felt it only too much; so "I say, don't lay traps for me!" he rather helplessly murmured.

"Well," his companion returned, "he's wonderfully kind to us."

"To us Americans you mean?"

"Oh no—he doesn't know anything about THAT. That's half the battle here—that you can never hear politics. We don't talk them. I mean to poor young wretches of all sorts. And yet it's always as charming as this; it's as if, by something in the air, our squalor didn't show. It puts us all back—into the last century."

"I'm afraid," Strether said, amused, "that it puts me rather forward: oh ever so far!"

"Into the next? But isn't that only," little Bilham asked, "because you're really of the century before?"

"The century before the last? Thank you!" Strether laughed. "If I ask you about some of the ladies it can't be then that I may hope, as such a specimen of the rococo, to please them."

"On the contrary they adore—we all adore here—the rococo, and where is there a better setting for it than the whole thing, the pavilion and the garden, together? There are lots of people with collections," little Bilham smiled as he glanced round. "You'll be secured!"

It made Strether for a moment give himself again to contemplation. There were faces he scarce knew what to make of. Were they charming or were they only strange? He mightn't talk politics, yet he suspected a Pole or two. The upshot was the question at the back of his head from the moment his friend had joined him. "Have Madame de Vionnet and her daughter arrived?"

"I haven't seen them yet, but Miss Gostrey has come. She's in the pavilion looking at objects. One can see SHE'S a collector," little Bilham added without offence.

"Oh yes, she's a collector, and I knew she was to come. Is Madame de Vionnet a collector?" Strether went on.

"Rather, I believe; almost celebrated." The young man met, on it, a little, his friend's eyes. "I happen to know—from Chad, whom I saw last night—that they've come back; but only yesterday. He wasn't sure—up to the last. This, accordingly," little Bilham went on, "will be—if they ARE here—their first appearance after their return."

Strether, very quickly, turned these things over. "Chad told you last night? To me, on our way here, he said nothing about it."

"But did you ask him?"

Strether did him the justice. "I dare say not."

"Well," said little Bilham, "you're not a person to whom it's easy to tell things you don't want to know. Though it is easy, I admit—it's quite beautiful," he benevolently added, "when you do want to."

Strether looked at him with an indulgence that matched his intelligence. "Is that the deep reasoning on which—about these ladies—you've been yourself so silent?"

Little Bilham considered the depth of his reasoning. "I haven't been silent. I spoke of them to you the other day, the day we sat together after Chad's tea-party."

Strether came round to it. "They then are the virtuous attachment?"

"I can only tell you that it's what they pass for. But isn't that enough? What more than a vain appearance does the wisest of us know? I commend you," the young man declared with a pleasant emphasis, "the vain appearance."

Strether looked more widely round, and what he saw, from face to face, deepened the effect of his young friend's words. "Is it so good?"

"Magnificent."

Strether had a pause. "The husband's dead?"

"Dear no. Alive."

"Oh!" said Strether. After which, as his companion laughed: "How then can it be so good?"

"You'll see for yourself. One does see."

"Chad's in love with the daughter?"

"That's what I mean."

Strether wondered. "Then where's the difficulty?"

"Why, aren't you and I—with our grander bolder ideas?"

"Oh mine—!" Strether said rather strangely. But then as if to attenuate: "You mean they won't hear of Woollett?"

Little Bilham smiled. "Isn't that just what you must see about?"

It had brought them, as she caught the last words, into relation with Miss Barrace, whom Strether had already observed—as he had never before seen a lady at a party—moving about alone. Coming within sound of them she had already spoken, and she took again, through her long-handled glass, all her amused and amusing possession. "How much, poor Mr. Strether, you seem to have to see about! But you can't say," she gaily declared, "that I don't do what I can to help you. Mr. Waymarsh is placed. I've left him in the house with Miss Gostrey."

"The way," little Bilham exclaimed, "Mr. Strether gets the ladies to work for him! He's just preparing to draw in another; to pounce—don't you see him?—on Madame de Vionnet."

"Madame de Vionnet? Oh, oh, oh!" Miss Barrace cried in a wonderful crescendo. There was more in it, our friend made out, than met the ear. Was it after all a joke that he should be serious about anything? He envied Miss Barrace at any rate her power of not being. She seemed, with little cries and protests and quick recognitions, movements like the darts of some fine high-feathered free-pecking bird, to stand before life as before some full shop-window. You could fairly hear, as she selected and pointed, the tap of her tortoise-shell against the glass. "It's certain that we do need seeing about; only I'm glad it's not I who have to do it. One does, no doubt, begin that way; then suddenly one finds that one has given it up. It's too much, it's too difficult. You're wonderful, you people," she continued to Strether, "for not feeling those things—by which I mean impossibilities. You never feel them. You face them with a fortitude that makes it a lesson to watch you."

"Ah but"—little Bilham put it with discouragement—"what do we achieve after all? We see about you and report—when we even go so far as reporting. But nothing's done."

"Oh you, Mr. Bilham," she replied as with an impatient rap on the glass, "you're not worth sixpence! You come over to convert the savages—for I know you verily did, I remember you—and the savages simply convert YOU."

"Not even!" the young man woefully confessed: "they haven't gone through that form. They've simply—the cannibals!—eaten me; converted me if you like, but converted me into food. I'm but the bleached bones of a Christian."

"Well then there we are! Only"—and Miss Barrace appealed again to Strether—"don't let it discourage you. You'll break down soon enough, but you'll meanwhile have had your moments. Il faut en avoir. I always like to see you while you last. And I'll tell you who WILL last."

"Waymarsh?"—he had already taken her up.

She laughed out as at the alarm of it. "He'll resist even Miss Gostrey: so grand is it not to understand. He's wonderful."

"He is indeed," Strether conceded. "He wouldn't tell me of this affair—only said he had an engagement; but with such a gloom, you must let me insist, as if it had been an engagement to be hanged. Then silently and secretly he turns up here with you. Do you call THAT 'lasting'?"

"Oh I hope it's lasting!" Miss Barrace said. "But he only, at the best, bears with me. He doesn't understand—not one little scrap. He's delightful. He's wonderful," she repeated.

"Michelangelesque!"—little Bilham completed her meaning. "He IS a success. Moses, on the ceiling, brought down to the floor; overwhelming, colossal, but somehow portable."

"Certainly, if you mean by portable," she returned, "looking so well in one's carriage. He's too funny beside me in his corner; he looks like somebody, somebody foreign and famous, en exil; so that people wonder—it's very amusing—whom I'm taking about. I show him Paris, show him everything, and he never turns a hair. He's like the Indian chief one reads about, who, when he comes up to Washington to see the Great Father, stands wrapt in his blanket and gives no sign. I might be the Great Father—from the way he takes everything." She was delighted at this hit of her identity with that personage—it fitted so her character; she declared it was the title she meant henceforth to adopt. "And the way he sits, too, in the corner of my room, only looking at my visitors very hard and as if he wanted to start something! They wonder what he does want to start. But he's wonderful," Miss Barrace once more insisted. "He has never started anything yet."

It presented him none the less, in truth, for her actual friends, who looked at each other in intelligence, with frank amusement on Bilham's part and a shade of sadness on Strether's. Strether's sadness sprang—for the image had its grandeur—from his thinking how little he himself was wrapt in his blanket, how little, in marble halls, all too oblivious of the Great Father, he resembled a really majestic aboriginal. But he had also another reflexion. "You've all of you here so much visual sense that you've somehow all 'run' to it. There are moments when it strikes one that you haven't any other."

"Any moral," little Bilham explained, watching serenely, across the garden, the several femmes du monde. "But Miss Barrace has a moral distinction," he kindly continued; speaking as if for Strether's benefit not less than for her own.

"HAVE you?" Strether, scarce knowing what he was about, asked of her almost eagerly.

"Oh not a distinction"—she was mightily amused at his tone—"Mr. Bilham's too good. But I think I may say a sufficiency. Yes, a sufficiency. Have you supposed strange things of me?"—and she fixed him again, through all her tortoise-shell, with the droll interest of it. "You ARE all indeed wonderful. I should awfully disappoint you. I do take my stand on my sufficiency. But I know, I confess," she went on, "strange people. I don't know how it happens; I don't do it on purpose; it seems to be my doom—as if I were always one of their habits: it's wonderful! I dare say moreover," she pursued with an interested gravity, "that I do, that we all do here, run too much to mere eye. But how can it be helped? We're all looking at each other—and in the light of Paris one sees what things resemble. That's what the light of Paris seems always to show. It's the fault of the light of Paris—dear old light!"

"Dear old Paris!" little Bilham echoed.

"Everything, every one shows," Miss Barrace went on.

"But for what they really are?" Strether asked.

"Oh I like your Boston 'reallys'! But sometimes—yes."

"Dear old Paris then!" Strether resignedly sighed while for a moment they looked at each other. Then he broke out: "Does Madame de Vionnet do that? I mean really show for what she is?"

Her answer was prompt. "She's charming. She's perfect."

"Then why did you a minute ago say 'Oh, oh, oh!' at her name?"

She easily remembered. "Why just because—! She's wonderful."

"Ah she too?"—Strether had almost a groan.

But Miss Barrace had meanwhile perceived relief. "Why not put your question straight to the person who can answer it best?"

"No," said little Bilham; "don't put any question; wait, rather—it will be much more fun—to judge for yourself. He has come to take you to her."

II

On which Strether saw that Chad was again at hand, and he afterwards scarce knew, absurd as it may seem, what had then quickly occurred. The moment concerned him, he felt, more deeply than he could have explained, and he had a subsequent passage of speculation as to whether, on walking off with Chad, he hadn't looked either pale or red. The only thing he was clear about was that, luckily, nothing indiscreet had in fact been said and that Chad himself was more than ever, in Miss Barrace's great sense, wonderful. It was one of the connexions—though really why it should be, after all, was none so apparent—in which the whole change in him came out as most striking. Strether recalled as they approached the house that he had impressed him that first night as knowing how to enter a box. Well, he impressed him scarce less now as knowing how to make a presentation. It did something for Strether's own quality—marked it as estimated; so that our poor friend, conscious and passive, really seemed to feel himself quite handed over and delivered; absolutely, as he would have said, made a present of, given away. As they reached the house a young woman, about to come forth, appeared, unaccompanied, on the steps; at the exchange with whom of a word on Chad's part Strether immediately perceived that, obligingly, kindly, she was there to meet them. Chad had left her in the house, but she had afterwards come halfway and then the next moment had joined them in the garden. Her air of youth, for Strether, was at first almost disconcerting, while his second impression was, not less sharply, a degree of relief at there not having just been, with the others, any freedom used about her. It was upon him at a touch that she was no subject for that, and meanwhile, in Miss Barrace's introducing him, she had spoken to him, very simply and gently, in an English clearly of the easiest to her, yet unlike any other he had ever heard. It wasn't as if she tried; nothing, he could see after they had been a few minutes together, was as if she tried; but her speech, charming correct and odd, was like a precaution against her passing for a Pole. There were precautions, he seemed indeed to see, only when there were really dangers.

Later on he was to feel many more of them, but by that time he was to feel other things besides. She was dressed in black, but in black that struck him as light and transparent; she was exceedingly fair, and, though she was as markedly slim, her face had a roundness, with eyes far apart and a little strange. Her smile was natural and dim; her hat not extravagant; he had only perhaps a sense of the clink, beneath her fine black sleeves, of more gold bracelets and bangles than he had ever seen a lady wear. Chad was excellently free and light about their encounter; it was one of the occasions on which Strether most wished he himself might have arrived at such ease and such humour: "Here you are then, face to face at last; you're made for each other—vous allez voir; and I bless your union." It was indeed, after he had gone off, as if he had been partly serious too. This latter motion had been determined by an enquiry from him about "Jeanne"; to which her mother had replied that she was probably still in the house with Miss Gostrey, to whom she had lately committed her. "Ah but you know," the young man had rejoined, "he must see her"; with which, while Strether pricked up his ears, he had started as if to bring her, leaving the other objects of his interest together. Strether wondered to find Miss Gostrey already involved, feeling that he missed a link; but feeling also, with small delay, how much he should like to talk with her of Madame de Vionnet on this basis of evidence.

The evidence as yet in truth was meagre; which, for that matter, was perhaps a little why his expectation had had a drop. There was somehow not quite a wealth in her; and a wealth was all that, in his simplicity, he had definitely prefigured. Still, it was too much to be sure already that there was but a poverty. They moved away from the house, and, with eyes on a bench at some distance, he proposed that they should sit down. "I've heard a great deal about you," she said as they went; but he had an answer to it that made her stop short. "Well, about YOU, Madame de Vionnet, I've heard, I'm bound to say, almost nothing"—those struck him as the only words he himself could utter with any lucidity; conscious as he was, and as with more reason, of the determination to be in respect to the rest of his business perfectly plain and go perfectly straight. It hadn't at any rate been in the least his idea to spy on Chad's proper freedom. It was possibly, however, at this very instant and under the impression of Madame de Vionnet's pause, that going straight began to announce itself as a matter for care. She had only after all to smile at him ever so gently in order to make him ask himself if he weren't already going crooked. It might be going crooked to find it of a sudden just only clear that she intended very definitely to be what he would have called nice to him. This was what passed between them while, for another instant, they stood still; he couldn't at least remember afterwards what else it might have been. The thing indeed really unmistakeable was its rolling over him as a wave that he had been, in conditions incalculable and unimaginable, a subject of discussion. He had been, on some ground that concerned her, answered for; which gave her an advantage he should never be able to match.

"Hasn't Miss Gostrey," she asked, "said a good word for me?"

What had struck him first was the way he was bracketed with that lady; and he wondered what account Chad would have given of their acquaintance. Something not as yet traceable, at all events, had obviously happened. "I didn't even know of her knowing you."

"Well, now she'll tell you all. I'm so glad you're in relation with her."

This was one of the things—the "all" Miss Gostrey would now tell him—that, with every deference to present preoccupation, was uppermost for Strether after they had taken their seat. One of the others was, at the end of five minutes, that she—oh incontestably, yes— DIFFERED less; differed, that is, scarcely at all—well, superficially speaking, from Mrs. Newsome or even from Mrs. Pocock. She was ever so much younger than the one and not so young as the other; but what WAS there in her, if anything, that would have made it impossible he should meet her at Woollett? And wherein was her talk during their moments on the bench together not the same as would have been found adequate for a Woollett garden-party?—unless perhaps truly in not being quite so bright. She observed to him that Mr. Newsome had, to her knowledge, taken extraordinary pleasure in his visit; but there was no good lady at Woollett who wouldn't have been at least up to that. Was there in Chad, by chance, after all, deep down, a principle of aboriginal loyalty that had made him, for sentimental ends, attach himself to elements, happily encountered, that would remind him most of the old air and the old soil? Why accordingly be in a flutter—Strether could even put it that way— about this unfamiliar phenomenon of the femme du monde? On these terms Mrs. Newsome herself was as much of one. Little Bilham verily had testified that they came out, the ladies of the type, in close quarters; but it was just in these quarters—now comparatively close—that he felt Madame de Vionnet's common humanity. She did come out, and certainly to his relief, but she came out as the usual thing. There might be motives behind, but so could there often be at Woollett. The only thing was that if she showed him she wished to like him—as the motives behind might conceivably prompt—it would possibly have been more thrilling for him that she should have shown as more vividly alien. Ah she was neither Turk nor Pole!—which would be indeed flat once more for Mrs. Newsome and Mrs. Pocock. A lady and two gentlemen had meanwhile, however, approached their bench, and this accident stayed for the time further developments.

They presently addressed his companion, the brilliant strangers; she rose to speak to them, and Strether noted how the escorted lady, though mature and by no means beautiful, had more of the bold high look, the range of expensive reference, that he had, as might have been said, made his plans for. Madame de Vionnet greeted her as "Duchesse" and was greeted in turn, while talk started in French, as "Ma toute-belle"; little facts that had their due, their vivid interest for Strether. Madame de Vionnet didn't, none the less, introduce him—a note he was conscious of as false to the Woollett scale and the Woollett humanity; though it didn't prevent the Duchess, who struck him as confident and free, very much what he had obscurely supposed duchesses, from looking at him as straight and as hard—for it WAS hard—as if she would have liked, all the same, to know him. "Oh yes, my dear, it's all right, it's ME; and who are YOU, with your interesting wrinkles and your most effective (is it the handsomest, is it the ugliest?) of noses?"—some such loose handful of bright flowers she seemed, fragrantly enough, to fling at him. Strether almost wondered—at such a pace was he going—if some divination of the influence of either party were what determined Madame de Vionnet's abstention. One of the gentlemen, in any case, succeeded in placing himself in close relation with our friend's companion; a gentleman rather stout and importantly short, in a hat with a wonderful wide curl to its brim and a frock coat buttoned with an effect of superlative decision. His French had quickly turned to equal English, and it occurred to Strether that he might well be one of the ambassadors. His design was evidently to assert a claim to Madame de Vionnet's undivided countenance, and he made it good in the course of a minute—led her away with a trick of three words; a trick played with a social art of which Strether, looking after them as the four, whose backs were now all turned, moved off, felt himself no master.

He sank again upon his bench and, while his eyes followed the party, reflected, as he had done before, on Chad's strange communities. He sat there alone for five minutes, with plenty to think of; above all with his sense of having suddenly been dropped by a charming woman overlaid now by other impressions and in fact quite cleared and indifferent. He hadn't yet had so quiet a surrender; he didn't in the least care if nobody spoke to him more. He might have been, by his attitude, in for something of a march so broad that the want of ceremony with which he had just been used could fall into its place as but a minor incident of the procession. Besides, there would be incidents enough, as he felt when this term of contemplation was closed by the reappearance of little Bilham, who stood before him a moment with a suggestive "Well?" in which he saw himself reflected as disorganised, as possibly floored. He replied with a "Well!" intended to show that he wasn't floored in the least. No indeed; he gave it out, as the young man sat down beside him, that if, at the worst, he had been overturned at all, he had been overturned into the upper air, the sublimer element with which he had an affinity and in which he might be trusted a while to float. It wasn't a descent to earth to say after an instant and in sustained response to the reference: "You're quite sure her husband's living?"

"Oh dear, yes."

"Ah then—!"

"Ah then what?"

Strether had after all to think. "Well, I'm sorry for them." But it didn't for the moment matter more than that. He assured his young friend he was quite content. They wouldn't stir; were all right as they were. He didn't want to be introduced; had been introduced already about as far as he could go. He had seen moreover an immensity; liked Gloriani, who, as Miss Barrace kept saying, was wonderful; had made out, he was sure, the half-dozen other 'men who were distinguished, the artists, the critics and oh the great dramatist—HIM it was easy to spot; but wanted—no, thanks, really—to talk with none of them; having nothing at all to say and finding it would do beautifully as it was; do beautifully because what it was—well, was just simply too late. And when after this little Bilham, submissive and responsive, but with an eye to the consolation nearest, easily threw off some "Better late than never!" all he got in return for it was a sharp "Better early than late!" This note indeed the next thing overflowed for Strether into a quiet stream of demonstration that as soon as he had let himself go he felt as the real relief. It had consciously gathered to a head, but the reservoir had filled sooner than he knew, and his companion's touch was to make the waters spread. There were some things that had to come in time if they were to come at all. If they didn't come in time they were lost for ever. It was the general sense of them that had overwhelmed him with its long slow rush.

"It's not too late for YOU, on any side, and you don't strike me as in danger of missing the train; besides which people can be in general pretty well trusted, of course—with the clock of their freedom ticking as loud as it seems to do here—to keep an eye on the fleeting hour. All the same don't forget that you're young—blessedly young; be glad of it on the contrary and live up to it. Live all you can; it's a mistake not to. It doesn't so much matter what you do in particular, so long as you have your life. If you haven't had that what HAVE you had? This place and these impressions—mild as you may find them to wind a man up so; all my impressions of Chad and of people I've seen at HIS place—well, have had their abundant message for me, have just dropped THAT into my mind. I see it now. I haven't done so enough before—and now I'm old; too old at any rate for what I see. Oh I DO see, at least; and more than you'd believe or I can express. It's too late. And it's as if the train had fairly waited at the station for me without my having had the gumption to know it was there. Now I hear its faint receding whistle miles and miles down the line. What one loses one loses; make no mistake about that. The affair—I mean the affair of life—couldn't, no doubt, have been different for me; for it's at the best a tin mould, either fluted and embossed, with ornamental excrescences, or else smooth and dreadfully plain, into which, a helpless jelly, one's consciousness is poured—so that one 'takes' the form as the great cook says, and is more or less compactly held by it: one lives in fine as one can. Still, one has the illusion of freedom; therefore don't be, like me, without the memory of that illusion. I was either, at the right time, too stupid or too intelligent to have it; I don't quite know which. Of course at present I'm a case of reaction against the mistake; and the voice of reaction should, no doubt, always be taken with an allowance. But that doesn't affect the point that the right time is now yours. The right time is ANY time that one is still so lucky as to have. You've plenty; that's the great thing; you're, as I say, damn you, so happily and hatefully young. Don't at any rate miss things out of stupidity. Of course I don't take you for a fool, or I shouldn't be addressing you thus awfully. Do what you like so long as you don't make MY mistake. For it was a mistake. Live!" ... Slowly and sociably, with full pauses and straight dashes, Strether had so delivered himself, holding little Bilham from step to step deeply and gravely attentive. The end of all was that the young man had turned quite solemn, and that this was a contradiction of the innocent gaiety the speaker had wished to promote. He watched for a moment the consequence of his words, and then, laying a hand on his listener's knee and as if to end with the proper joke: "And now for the eye I shall keep on you!"

"Oh but I don't know that I want to be, at your age, too different from you!"

"Ah prepare while you're about it," said Strether, "to be more amusing."

Little Bilham continued to think, but at last had a smile. "Well, you ARE amusing—to ME."

"Impayable, as you say, no doubt. But what am I to myself?" Strether had risen with this, giving his attention now to an encounter that, in the middle of the garden, was in the act of taking place between their host and the lady at whose side Madame de Vionnet had quitted him. This lady, who appeared within a few minutes to have left her friends, awaited Gloriani's eager approach with words on her lips that Strether couldn't catch, but of which her interesting witty face seemed to give him the echo. He was sure she was prompt and fine, but also that she had met her match, and he liked—in the light of what he was quite sure was the Duchess's latent insolence—the good humour with which the great artist asserted equal resources. Were they, this pair, of the "great world"?—and was he himself, for the moment and thus related to them by his observation, IN it? Then there was something in the great world covertly tigerish, which came to him across the lawn and in the charming air as a waft from the jungle. Yet it made him admire most of the two, made him envy, the glossy male tiger, magnificently marked. These absurdities of the stirred sense, fruits of suggestion ripening on the instant, were all reflected in his next words to little Bilham. "I know—if we talk of that—whom I should enjoy being like!"

Little Bilham followed his eyes; but then as with a shade of knowing surprise: "Gloriani?"

Our friend had in fact already hesitated, though not on the hint of his companion's doubt, in which there were depths of critical reserve. He had just made out, in the now full picture, something and somebody else; another impression had been superimposed. A young girl in a white dress and a softly plumed white hat had suddenly come into view, and what was presently clear was that her course was toward them. What was clearer still was that the handsome young man at her side was Chad Newsome, and what was clearest of all was that she was therefore Mademoiselle de Vionnet, that she was unmistakeably pretty—bright gentle shy happy wonderful—and that Chad now, with a consummate calculation of effect, was about to present her to his old friend's vision. What was clearest of all indeed was something much more than this, something at the single stroke of which—and wasn't it simply juxtaposition?—all vagueness vanished. It was the click of a spring—he saw the truth. He had by this time also met Chad's look; there was more of it in that; and the truth, accordingly, so far as Bilham's enquiry was concerned, had thrust in the answer. "Oh Chad!"—it was that rare youth he should have enjoyed being "like." The virtuous attachment would be all there before him; the virtuous attachment would be in the very act of appeal for his blessing; Jeanne de Vionnet, this charming creature, would be exquisitely, intensely now—the object of it. Chad brought her straight up to him, and Chad was, oh yes, at this moment—for the glory of Woollett or whatever—better still even than Gloriani. He had plucked this blossom; he had kept it over-night in water; and at last as he held it up to wonder he did enjoy his effect. That was why Strether had met Chad's look—and why moreover, as he now knew, his look at the girl would be, for the young man, a sign of the latter's success. What young man had ever paraded about that way, without a reason, a maiden in her flower? And there was nothing in his reason at present obscure. Her type sufficiently told of it—they wouldn't, they couldn't, want her to go to Woollett. Poor Woollett, and what it might miss!—though brave Chad indeed too, and what it might gain! Brave Chad however had just excellently spoken. "This is a good little friend of mine who knows all about you and has moreover a message for you. And this, my dear"—he had turned to the child herself—"is the best man in the world, who has it in his power to do a great deal for us and whom I want you to like and revere as nearly as possible as much as I do."

She stood there quite pink, a little frightened, prettier and prettier and not a bit like her mother. There was in this last particular no resemblance but that of youth to youth; and here was in fact suddenly Strether's sharpest impression. It went wondering, dazed, embarrassed, back to the woman he had just been talking with; it was a revelation in the light of which he already saw she would become more interesting. So slim and fresh and fair, she had yet put forth this perfection; so that for really believing it of her, for seeing her to any such developed degree as a mother, comparison would be urgent. Well, what was it now but fairly thrust upon him? "Mamma wishes me to tell you before we go," the girl said, "that she hopes very much you'll come to see us very soon. She has something important to say to you."

"She quite reproaches herself," Chad helpfully explained: "you were interesting her so much when she accidentally suffered you to be interrupted."

"Ah don't mention it!" Strether murmured, looking kindly from one to the other and wondering at many things.

"And I'm to ask you for myself," Jeanne continued with her hands clasped together as if in some small learnt prayer—"I'm to ask you for myself if you won't positively come."

"Leave it to me, dear—I'll take care of it!" Chad genially declared in answer to this, while Strether himself almost held his breath. What was in the girl was indeed too soft, too unknown for direct dealing; so that one could only gaze at it as at a picture, quite staying one's own hand. But with Chad he was now on ground—Chad he could meet; so pleasant a confidence in that and in everything did the young man freely exhale. There was the whole of a story in his tone to his companion, and he spoke indeed as if already of the family. It made Strether guess the more quickly what it might be about which Madame de Vionnet was so urgent. Having seen him then she had found him easy; she wished to have it out with him that some way for the young people must be discovered, some way that would not impose as a condition the transplantation of her daughter. He already saw himself discussing with this lady the attractions of Woollett as a residence for Chad's companion. Was that youth going now to trust her with the affair—so that it would be after all with one of his "lady-friends" that his mother's missionary should be condemned to deal? It was quite as if for an instant the two men looked at each other on this question. But there was no mistaking at last Chad's pride in the display of such a connexion. This was what had made him so carry himself while, three minutes before, he was bringing it into view; what had caused his friend, first catching sight of him, to be so struck with his air. It was, in a word, just when he thus finally felt Chad putting things straight off on him that he envied him, as he had mentioned to little Bilham, most. The whole exhibition however was but a matter of three or four minutes, and the author of it had soon explained that, as Madame de Vionnet was immediately going "on," this could be for Jeanne but a snatch. They would all meet again soon, and Strether was meanwhile to stay and amuse himself—"I'll pick you up again in plenty of time." He took the girl off as he had brought her, and Strether, with the faint sweet foreignness of her "Au revoir, monsieur!" in his ears as a note almost unprecedented, watched them recede side by side and felt how, once more, her companion's relation to her got an accent from it. They disappeared among the others and apparently into the house; whereupon our friend turned round to give out to little Bilham the conviction of which he was full. But there was no little Bilham any more; little Bilham had within the few moments, for reasons of his own, proceeded further: a circumstance by which, in its order, Strether was also sensibly affected.

III

Chad was not in fact on this occasion to keep his promise of coming back; but Miss Gostrey had soon presented herself with an explanation of his failure. There had been reasons at the last for his going off with ces dames; and he had asked her with much instance to come out and take charge of their friend. She did so, Strether felt as she took her place beside him, in a manner that left nothing to desire. He had dropped back on his bench, alone again for a time, and the more conscious for little Bilham's defection of his unexpressed thought; in respect to which however this next converser was a still more capacious vessel. "It's the child!" he had exclaimed to her almost as soon as she appeared; and though her direct response was for some time delayed he could feel in her meanwhile the working of this truth. It might have been simply, as she waited, that they were now in presence altogether of truth spreading like a flood and not for the moment to be offered her in the mere cupful; inasmuch as who should ces dames prove to be but persons about whom—once thus face to face with them—she found she might from the first have told him almost everything? This would have freely come had he taken the simple precaution of giving her their name. There could be no better example—and she appeared to note it with high amusement—than the way, making things out already so much for himself, he was at last throwing precautions to the winds. They were neither more nor less, she and the child's mother, than old school-friends—friends who had scarcely met for years but whom this unlooked-for chance had brought together with a rush. It was a relief, Miss Gostrey hinted, to feel herself no longer groping; she was unaccustomed to grope and as a general thing, he might well have seen, made straight enough for her clue. With the one she had now picked up in her hands there need be at least no waste of wonder. "She's coming to see me—that's for YOU," Strether's counsellor continued; "but I don't require it to know where I am."

The waste of wonder might be proscribed; but Strether, characteristically, was even by this time in the immensity of space. "By which you mean that you know where SHE is?"

She just hesitated. "I mean that if she comes to see me I shall—now that I've pulled myself round a bit after the shock—not be at home."

Strether hung poised. "You call it—your recognition—a shock?"

She gave one of her rare flickers of impatience. "It was a surprise, an emotion. Don't be so literal. I wash my hands of her."

Poor Strether's face lengthened. "She's impossible—?"

"She's even more charming than I remembered her."

"Then what's the matter?"

She had to think how to put it. "Well, I'M impossible. It's impossible. Everything's impossible."

He looked at her an instant. "I see where you're coming out. Everything's possible." Their eyes had on it in fact an exchange of some duration; after which he pursued: "Isn't it that beautiful child?" Then as she still said nothing: "Why don't you mean to receive her?"

Her answer in an instant rang clear. "Because I wish to keep out of the business."

It provoked in him a weak wail. "You're going to abandon me NOW?"

"No, I'm only going to abandon HER. She'll want me to help her with you. And I won't."

"You'll only help me with her? Well then—!" Most of the persons previously gathered had, in the interest of tea, passed into the house, and they had the gardens mainly to themselves. The shadows were long, the last call of the birds, who had made a home of their own in the noble interspaced quarter, sounded from the high trees in the other gardens as well, those of the old convent and of the old hotels; it was as if our friends had waited for the full charm to come out. Strether's impressions were still present; it was as if something had happened that "nailed" them, made them more intense; but he was to ask himself soon afterwards, that evening, what really HAD happened—conscious as he could after all remain that for a gentleman taken, and taken the first time, into the "great world," the world of ambassadors and duchesses, the items made a meagre total. It was nothing new to him, however, as we know, that a man might have—at all events such a man as he—an amount of experience out of any proportion to his adventures; so that, though it was doubtless no great adventure to sit on there with Miss Gostrey and hear about Madame de Vionnet, the hour, the picture, the immediate, the recent, the possible—as well as the communication itself, not a note of which failed to reverberate—only gave the moments more of the taste of history.

It was history, to begin with, that Jeanne's mother had been three-and-twenty years before, at Geneva, schoolmate and good girlfriend to Maria Gostrey, who had moreover enjoyed since then, though interruptedly and above all with a long recent drop, other glimpses of her. Twenty-three years had put them both on, no doubt; and Madame de Vionnet—though she had married straight after school—couldn't be today an hour less than thirty-eight. This made her ten years older than Chad—though ten years, also, if Strether liked, older than she looked; the least, at any rate, that a prospective mother-in-law could be expected to do with. She would be of all mothers-in-law the most charming; unless indeed, · through some perversity as yet insupposeable, she should utterly belie herself in that relation. There was none surely in which, as Maria remembered her, she mustn't be charming; and this frankly in spite of the stigma of failure in the tie where failure always most showed. It was no test there—when indeed WAS it a test there?—for Monsieur de Vionnet had been a brute. She had lived for years apart from him—which was of course always a horrid position; but Miss Gostrey's impression of the matter had been that she could scarce have made a better thing of it had she done it on purpose to show she was amiable. She was so amiable that nobody had had a word to say; which was luckily not the case for her husband. He was so impossible that she had the advantage of all her merits.

It was still history for Strether that the Comte de Vionnet—it being also history that the lady in question was a Countess—should now, under Miss Gostrey's sharp touch, rise before him as a high distinguished polished impertinent reprobate, the product of a mysterious order; it was history, further, that the charming girl so freely sketched by his companion should have been married out of hand by a mother, another figure of striking outline, full of dark personal motive; it was perhaps history most of all that this company was, as a matter of course, governed by such considerations as put divorce out of the question. "Ces gens-la don't divorce, you know, any more than they emigrate or abjure—they think it impious and vulgar"; a fact in the light of which they seemed but the more richly special. It was all special; it was all, for Strether's imagination, more or less rich. The girl at the Genevese school, an isolated interesting attaching creature, then both sensitive and violent, audacious but always forgiven, was the daughter of a French father and an English mother who, early left a widow, had married again—tried afresh with a foreigner; in her career with whom she had apparently given her child no example of comfort. All these people—the people of the English mother's side—had been of condition more or less eminent; yet with oddities and disparities that had often since made Maria, thinking them over, wonder what they really quite rhymed to. It was in any case her belief that the mother, interested and prone to adventure, had been without conscience, had only thought of ridding herself most quickly of a possible, an actual encumbrance. The father, by her impression, a Frenchman with a name one knew, had been a different matter, leaving his child, she clearly recalled, a memory all fondness, as well as an assured little fortune which was unluckily to make her more or less of a prey later on. She had been in particular, at school, dazzlingly, though quite booklessly, clever; as polyglot as a little Jewess (which she wasn't, oh no!) and chattering French, English, German, Italian, anything one would, in a way that made a clean sweep, if not of prizes and parchments, at least of every "part," whether memorised or improvised, in the curtained costumed school repertory, and in especial of all mysteries of race and vagueness of reference, all swagger about "home," among their variegated mates.

It would doubtless be difficult to-day, as between French and English, to name her and place her; she would certainly show, on knowledge, Miss Gostrey felt, as one of those convenient types who don't keep you explaining—minds with doors as numerous as the many-tongued cluster of confessionals at Saint Peter's. You might confess to her with confidence in Roumelian, and even Roumelian sins. Therefore—! But Strether's narrator covered her implication with a laugh; a laugh by which his betrayal of a sense of the lurid in the picture was also perhaps sufficiently protected. He had a moment of wondering, while his friend went on, what sins might be especially Roumelian. She went on at all events to the mention of her having met the young thing—again by some Swiss lake—in her first married state, which had appeared for the few intermediate years not at least violently disturbed. She had been lovely at that moment, delightful to HER, full of responsive emotion, of amused recognitions and amusing reminders, and then once more, much later, after a long interval, equally but differently charming—touching and rather mystifying for the five minutes of an encounter at a railway-station en province, during which it had come out that her life was all changed. Miss Gostrey had understood enough to see, essentially, what had happened, and yet had beautifully dreamed that she was herself faultless. There were doubtless depths in her, but she was all right; Strether would see if she wasn't. She was another person however—that had been promptly marked—from the small child of nature at the Geneva school, a little person quite made over (as foreign women WERE, compared with American) by marriage. Her situation too had evidently cleared itself up; there would have been—all that was possible—a judicial separation. She had settled in Paris, brought up her daughter, steered her boat. It was no very pleasant boat—especially there—to be in; but Marie de Vionnet would have headed straight. She would have friends, certainly—and very good ones. There she was at all events—and it was very interesting. Her knowing Mr. Chad didn't in the least prove she hadn't friends; what it proved was what good ones HE had. "I saw that," said Miss Gostrey, "that night at the Francais; it came out for me in three minutes. I saw HER—or somebody like her. And so," she immediately added, "did you."

"Oh no—not anybody like her!" Strether laughed. "But you mean," he as promptly went on, "that she has had such an influence on him?"

Miss Gostrey was on her feet; it was time for them to go. "She has brought him up for her daughter."

Their eyes, as so often, in candid conference, through their settled glasses, met over it long; after which Strether's again took in the whole place. They were quite alone there now. "Mustn't she rather—in the time then—have rushed it?"

"Ah she won't of course have lost an hour. But that's just the good mother—the good French one. You must remember that of her—that as a mother she's French, and that for them there's a special providence. It precisely however—that she mayn't have been able to begin as far back as she'd have liked—makes her grateful for aid."

Strether took this in as they slowly moved to the house on their way out. "She counts on me then to put the thing through?"

"Yes—she counts on you. Oh and first of all of course," Miss Gostrey added, "on her—well, convincing you."

"Ah," her friend returned, "she caught Chad young!"

"Yes, but there are women who are for all your 'times of life.' They're the most wonderful sort."

She had laughed the words out, but they brought her companion, the next thing, to a stand. "Is what you mean that she'll try to make a fool of me?"

"Well, I'm wondering what she WILL—with an opportunity—make."

"What do you call," Strether asked, "an opportunity? My going to see her?"

"Ah you must go to see her"—Miss Gostrey was a trifle evasive. "You can't not do that. You'd have gone to see the other woman. I mean if there had been one—a different sort. It's what you came out for."

It might be; but Strether distinguished. "I didn't come out to see THIS sort."

She had a wonderful look at him now. "Are you disappointed she isn't worse?"

He for a moment entertained the question, then found for it the frankest of answers. "Yes. If she were worse she'd be better for our purpose. It would be simpler."

"Perhaps," she admitted. "But won't this be pleasanter?"

"Ah you know," he promptly replied, "I didn't come out—wasn't that just what you originally reproached me with?—for the pleasant."

"Precisely. Therefore I say again what I said at first. You must take things as they come. Besides," Miss Gostrey added, "I'm not afraid for myself."

"For yourself—?"

"Of your seeing her. I trust her. There's nothing she'll say about me. In fact there's nothing she CAN."

Strether wondered—little as he had thought of this. Then he broke out. "Oh you women!"

There was something in it at which she flushed. "Yes—there we are. We're abysses." At last she smiled. "But I risk her!"

He gave himself a shake. "Well then so do I!" But he added as they passed into the house that he would see Chad the first thing in the morning.

This was the next day the more easily effected that the young man, as it happened, even before he was down, turned up at his hotel. Strether took his coffee, by habit; in the public room; but on his descending for this purpose Chad instantly proposed an adjournment to what he called greater privacy. He had himself as yet had nothing—they would sit down somewhere together; and when after a few steps and a turn into the Boulevard they had, for their greater privacy, sat down among twenty others, our friend saw in his companion's move a fear of the advent of Waymarsh. It was the first time Chad had to that extent given this personage "away"; and Strether found himself wondering of what it was symptomatic. He made out in a moment that the youth was in earnest as he hadn't yet seen him; which in its turn threw a ray perhaps a trifle startling on what they had each up to that time been treating as earnestness. It was sufficiently flattering however that the real thing—if this WAS at last the real thing—should have been determined, as appeared, precisely by an accretion of Strether's importance. For this was what it quickly enough came to—that Chad, rising with the lark, had rushed down to let him know while his morning consciousness was yet young that he had literally made the afternoon before a tremendous impression. Madame de Vionnet wouldn't, couldn't rest till she should have some assurance from him that he WOULD consent again to see her. The announcement was made, across their marble-topped table, while the foam of the hot milk was in their cups and its plash still in the air, with the smile of Chad's easiest urbanity; and this expression of his face caused our friend's doubts to gather on the spot into a challenge of the lips. "See here"—that was all; he only for the moment said again "See here." Chad met it with all his air of straight intelligence, while Strether remembered again that fancy of the first impression of him, the happy young Pagan, handsome and hard but oddly indulgent, whose mysterious measure he had under the street-lamp tried mentally to take. The young Pagan, while a long look passed between them, sufficiently understood. Strether scarce needed at last to say the rest—"I want to know where I am." But he said it, adding before any answer something more. "Are you engaged to be married—is that your secret?—to the young lady?"

Chad shook his head with the slow amenity that was one of his ways of conveying that there was time for everything. "I have no secret—though I may have secrets! I haven't at any rate that one. We're not engaged. No."

"Then where's the hitch?"

"Do you mean why I haven't already started with you?" Chad, beginning his coffee and buttering his roll, was quite ready to explain. "Nothing would have induced me—nothing will still induce me—not to try to keep you here as long as you can be made to stay. It's too visibly good for you." Strether had himself plenty to say about this, but it was amusing also to measure the march of Chad's tone. He had never been more a man of the world, and it was always in his company present to our friend that one was seeing in successive connexions a man of the world acquitted himself. Chad kept it up beautifully. "My idea—voyons!—is simply that you should let Madame de Vionnet know you, simply that you should consent to know HER. I don't in the least mind telling you that, clever and charming as she is, she's ever so much in my confidence. All I ask of you is to let her talk to you. You've asked me about what you call my hitch, and so far as it goes she'll explain it to you. She's herself my hitch, hang it—if you must really have it all out. But in a sense," he hastened in the most wonderful manner to add, "that you'll quite make out for yourself. She's too good a friend, confound her. Too good, I mean, for me to leave without—without—" It was his first hesitation.

"Without what?"

"Well, without my arranging somehow or other the damnable terms of my sacrifice."

"It WILL be a sacrifice then?"

"It will be the greatest loss I ever suffered. I owe her so much."

It was beautiful, the way Chad said these things, and his plea was now confessedly—oh quite flagrantly and publicly—interesting. The moment really took on for Strether an intensity. Chad owed Madame de Vionnet so much? What DID that do then but clear up the whole mystery? He was indebted for alterations, and she was thereby in a position to have sent in her bill for expenses incurred in reconstruction. What was this at bottom but what had been to be arrived at? Strether sat there arriving at it while he munched toast and stirred his second cup. To do this with the aid of Chad's pleasant earnest face was also to do more besides. No, never before had he been so ready to take him as he was. What was it that had suddenly so cleared up? It was just everybody's character; that is everybody's but—in a measure—his own. Strether felt HIS character receive for the instant a smutch from all the wrong things he had suspected or believed. The person to whom Chad owed it that he could positively turn out such a comfort to other persons—such a person was sufficiently raised above any "breath" by the nature of her work and the young man's steady light. All of which was vivid enough to come and go quickly; though indeed in the midst of it Strether could utter a question. "Have I your word of honour that if I surrender myself to Madame de Vionnet you'll surrender yourself to me?"

Chad laid his hand firmly on his friend's. "My dear man, you have it."

There was finally something in his felicity almost embarrassing and oppressive—Strether had begun to fidget under it for the open air and the erect posture. He had signed to the waiter that he wished to pay, and this transaction took some moments, during which he thoroughly felt, while he put down money and pretended—it was quite hollow—to estimate change, that Chad's higher spirit, his youth, his practice, his paganism, his felicity, his assurance, his impudence, whatever it might be, had consciously scored a success. Well, that was all right so far as it went; his sense of the thing in question covered our friend for a minute like a veil through which—as if he had been muffled—he heard his interlocutor ask him if he mightn't take him over about five. "Over" was over the river, and over the river was where Madame de Vionnet lived, and five was that very afternoon. They got at last out of the place—got out before he answered. He lighted, in the street, a cigarette, which again gave him more time. But it was already sharp for him that there was no use in time. "What does she propose to do to me?" he had presently demanded.

Chad had no delays. "Are you afraid of her?"

"Oh immensely. Don't you see it?"

"Well," said Chad, "she won't do anything worse to you than make you like her."

"It's just of that I'm afraid."

"Then it's not fair to me."

Strether cast about. "It's fair to your mother."

"Oh," said Chad, "are you afraid of HER?"

"Scarcely less. Or perhaps even more. But is this lady against your interests at home?" Strether went on.

"Not directly, no doubt; but she's greatly in favour of them here."

"And what—'here'—does she consider them to be?"

"Well, good relations!"

"With herself?"

"With herself."

"And what is it that makes them so good?"

"What? Well, that's exactly what you'll make out if you'll only go, as I'm supplicating you, to see her."

Strether stared at him with a little of the wanness, no doubt, that the vision of more to "make out" could scarce help producing. "I mean HOW good are they?"

"Oh awfully good."

Again Strether had faltered, but it was brief. It was all very well, but there was nothing now he wouldn't risk. "Excuse me, but I must really—as I began by telling you—know where I am. Is she bad?"

"'Bad'?"—Chad echoed it, but without a shock. "Is that what's implied—?"

"When relations are good?" Strether felt a little silly, and was even conscious of a foolish laugh, at having it imposed on him to have appeared to speak so. What indeed was he talking about? His stare had relaxed; he looked now all round him. But something in him brought him back, though he still didn't know quite how to turn it. The two or three ways he thought of, and one of them in particular, were, even with scruples dismissed, too ugly. He none the less at last found something. "Is her life without reproach?"

It struck him, directly he had found it, as pompous and priggish; so much so that he was thankful to Chad for taking it only in the right spirit. The young man spoke so immensely to the point that the effect was practically of positive blandness. "Absolutely without reproach. A beautiful life. Allez donc voir!"

These last words were, in the liberality of their confidence, so imperative that Strether went through no form of assent; but before they separated it had been confirmed that he should be picked up at a quarter to five.

Book Sixth

I

Paris (c.1880) by Jean Béraud (1849-1935)

It was quite by half-past five—after the two men had been together in Madame de Vionnet's drawing-room not more than a dozen minutes—that Chad, with a look at his watch and then another at their hostess, said genially, gaily: "I've an engagement, and I know you won't complain if I leave him with you. He'll interest you immensely; and as for her," he declared to Strether, "I assure you, if you're at all nervous, she's perfectly safe."

He had left them to be embarrassed or not by this guarantee, as they could best manage, and embarrassment was a thing that Strether wasn't at first sure Madame de Vionnet escaped. He escaped it himself, to his surprise; but he had grown used by this time to thinking of himself as brazen. She occupied, his hostess, in the Rue de Bellechasse, the first floor of an old house to which our visitors had had access from an old clean court. The court was large and open, full of revelations, for our friend, of the habit of privacy, the peace of intervals, the dignity of distances and approaches; the house, to his restless sense, was in the high homely style of an elder day, and the ancient Paris that he was always looking for—sometimes intensely felt, sometimes more acutely missed—was in the immemorial polish of the wide waxed staircase and in the fine boiseries, the medallions, mouldings, mirrors, great clear spaces, of the greyish-white salon into which he had been shown. He seemed at the very outset to see her in the midst of possessions not vulgarly numerous, but hereditary cherished charming. While his eyes turned after a little from those of his hostess and Chad freely talked—not in the least about HIM, but about other people, people he didn't know, and quite as if he did know them—he found himself making out, as a background of the occupant, some glory, some prosperity of the First Empire, some Napoleonic glamour, some dim lustre of the great legend; elements clinging still to all the consular chairs and mythological brasses and sphinxes' heads and faded surfaces of satin striped with alternate silk.

The place itself went further back—that he guessed, and how old Paris continued in a manner to echo there; but the post-revolutionary period, the world he vaguely thought of as the world of Chateaubriand, of Madame de Stael, even of the young Lamartine, had left its stamp of harps and urns and torches, a stamp impressed on sundry small objects, ornaments and relics. He had never before, to his knowledge, had present to him relics, of any special dignity, of a private order—little old miniatures, medallions, pictures, books; books in leather bindings, pinkish and greenish, with gilt garlands on the back, ranged, together with other promiscuous properties, under the glass of brass-mounted cabinets. His attention took them all tenderly into account. They were among the matters that marked Madame de Vionnet's apartment as something quite different from Miss Gostrey's little museum of bargains and from Chad's lovely home; he recognised it as founded much more on old accumulations that had possibly from time to time shrunken than on any contemporary method of acquisition or form of curiosity. Chad and Miss Gostrey had rummaged and purchased and picked up and exchanged, sifting, selecting, comparing; whereas the mistress of the scene before him, beautifully passive under the spell of transmission—transmission from her father's line, he quite made up his mind—had only received, accepted and been quiet. When she hadn't been quiet she had been moved at the most to some occult charity for some fallen fortune. There had been objects she or her predecessors might even conceivably have parted with under need, but Strether couldn't suspect them of having sold old pieces to get "better" ones. They would have felt no difference as to better or worse. He could but imagine their having felt—perhaps in emigration, in proscription, for his sketch was slight and confused—the pressure of want or the obligation of sacrifice.

The pressure of want—whatever might be the case with the other force—was, however, presumably not active now, for the tokens of a chastened ease still abounded after all, many marks of a taste whose discriminations might perhaps have been called eccentric. He guessed at intense little preferences and sharp little exclusions, a deep suspicion of the vulgar and a personal view of the right. The general result of this was something for which he had no name on the spot quite ready, but something he would have come nearest to naming in speaking of it as the air of supreme respectability, the consciousness, small, still, reserved, but none the less distinct and diffused, of private honour. The air of supreme respectability—that was a strange blank wall for his adventure to have brought him to break his nose against. It had in fact, as he was now aware, filled all the approaches, hovered in the court as he passed, hung on the staircase as he mounted, sounded in the grave rumble of the old bell, as little electric as possible, of which Chad, at the door, had pulled the ancient but neatly-kept tassel; it formed in short the clearest medium of its particular kind that he had ever breathed. He would have answered for it at the end of a quarter of an hour that some of the glass cases contained swords and epaulettes of ancient colonels and generals; medals and orders once pinned over hearts that had long since ceased to beat; snuff-boxes bestowed on ministers and envoys; copies of works presented, with inscriptions, by authors now classic. At bottom of it all for him was the sense of her rare unlikeness to the women he had known. This sense had grown, since the day before, the more he recalled her, and had been above all singularly fed by his talk with Chad in the morning. Everything in fine made her immeasurably new, and nothing so new as the old house and the old objects. There were books, two or three, on a small table near his chair, but they hadn't the lemon-coloured covers with which his eye had begun to dally from the hour of his arrival and to the opportunity of a further acquaintance with which he had for a fortnight now altogether succumbed. On another table, across the room, he made out the great *Revue*; but even that familiar face, conspicuous in Mrs. Newsome's parlours, scarce counted here as a modern note. He was sure on the spot—and he afterwards knew he was right—that this was a touch of Chad's own hand. What would Mrs. Newsome say to the circumstance that Chad's interested "influence" kept her paper-knife in the *Revue*? The interested influence at any rate had, as we say, gone straight to the point—had in fact soon left it quite behind.

She was seated, near the fire, on a small stuffed and fringed chair one of the few modern articles in the room, and she leaned back in it with her hands clasped in her lap and no movement, in all her person, but the fine prompt play of her deep young face. The fire, under the low white marble, undraped and academic, had burnt down to the silver ashes of light wood, one of the windows, at a distance, stood open to the mildness and stillness, out of which, in the short pauses, came the faint sound, pleasant and homely, almost rustic, of a plash and a clatter of sabots from some coach-house on the other side of the court. Madame de Vionnet, while Strether sat there, wasn't to shift her posture by an inch. "I don't think you seriously believe in what you're doing," she said; "but all the same, you know, I'm going to treat you quite as if I did."

"By which you mean," Strether directly replied, "quite as if you didn't! I assure you it won't make the least difference with me how you treat me."

"Well," she said, taking that menace bravely and philosophically enough, "the only thing that really matters is that you shall get on with me."

"Ah but I don't!" he immediately returned.

It gave her another pause; which, however, she happily enough shook off. "Will you consent to go on with me a little—provisionally—as if you did?"

Then it was that he saw how she had decidedly come all the way; and there accompanied it an extraordinary sense of her raising from somewhere below him her beautiful suppliant eyes. He might have been perched at his door-step or at his window and she standing in the road. For a moment he let her stand and couldn't moreover have spoken. It had been sad, of a sudden, with a sadness that was like a cold breath in his face. "What can I do," he finally asked, "but listen to you as I promised Chadwick?"

"Ah but what I'm asking you," she quickly said, "isn't what Mr. Newsome had in mind." She spoke at present, he saw, as if to take courageously ALL her risk. "This is my own idea and a different thing."

It gave poor Strether in truth—uneasy as it made him too—something of the thrill of a bold perception justified. "Well," he answered kindly enough, "I was sure a moment since that some idea of your own had come to you."

She seemed still to look up at him, but now more serenely. "I made out you were sure—and that helped it to come. So you see," she continued, "we do get on."

"Oh but it appears to me I don't at all meet your request. How can I when I don't understand it?"

"It isn't at all necessary you should understand; it will do quite well enough if you simply remember it. Only feel I trust you—and for nothing so tremendous after all. Just," she said with a wonderful smile, "for common sympathy."

Strether had a long pause while they sat again face to face, as they had sat, scarce less conscious, before the poor lady had crossed the stream. She was the poor lady for Strether now because clearly she had some trouble, and her appeal to him could only mean that her trouble was deep. He couldn't help it; it wasn't his fault; he had done nothing; but by a turn of the hand she had somehow made their encounter a relation. And the relation profited by a mass of things that were not strictly in it or of it; by the very air in which they sat, by the high cold delicate room, by the world outside and the little plash in the court, by the First Empire and the relics in the stiff cabinets, by matters as far off as those and by others as near as the unbroken clasp of her hands in her lap and the look her expression had of being most natural when her eyes were most fixed. "You count upon me of course for something really much greater than it sounds."

"Oh it sounds great enough too!" she laughed at this.

He found himself in time on the point of telling her that she was, as Miss Barrace called it, wonderful; but, catching himself up, he said something else instead. "What was it Chad's idea then that you should say to me?"

"Ah his idea was simply what a man's idea always is—to put every effort off on the woman."

"The 'woman'—?" Strether slowly echoed.

"The woman he likes—and just in proportion as he likes her. In proportion too—for shifting the trouble—as she likes HIM."

Strether followed it; then with an abruptness of his own: "How much do you like Chad?"

"Just as much as THAT—to take all, with you, on myself." But she got at once again away from this. "I've been trembling as if we were to stand or fall by what you may think of me; and I'm even now," she went on wonderfully, "drawing a long breath—and, yes, truly taking a great courage—from the hope that I don't in fact strike you as impossible."

"That's at all events, clearly," he observed after an instant, "the way I don't strike YOU."

"Well," she so far assented, "as you haven't yet said you WON'T have the little patience with me I ask for—"

"You draw splendid conclusions? Perfectly. But I don't understand them," Strether pursued. "You seem to me to ask for much more than you need. What, at the worst for you, what at the best for myself, can I after all do? I can use no pressure that I haven't used. You come really late with your request. I've already done all that for myself the case admits of. I've said my say, and here I am."

"Yes, here you are, fortunately!" Madame de Vionnet laughed. "Mrs. Newsome," she added in another tone, "didn't think you can do so little."

He had an hesitation, but he brought the words out. "Well, she thinks so now."

"Do you mean by that—?" But she also hung fire.

"Do I mean what?"

She still rather faltered. "Pardon me if I touch on it, but if I'm saying extraordinary things, why, perhaps, mayn't I? Besides, doesn't it properly concern us to know?"

"To know what?" he insisted as after thus beating about the bush she had again dropped.

She made the effort. "Has she given you up?"

He was amazed afterwards to think how simply and quietly he had met it. "Not yet." It was almost as if he were a trifle disappointed—had expected still more of her freedom. But he went straight on. "Is that what Chad has told you will happen to me?"

She was evidently charmed with the way he took it. "If you mean if we've talked of it—most certainly. And the question's not what has had least to do with my wishing to see you."

"To judge if I'm the sort of man a woman CAN—?"

"Precisely," she exclaimed—"you wonderful gentleman! I do judge—I HAVE judged. A woman can't. You're safe—with every right to be. You'd be much happier if you'd only believe it."

Strether was silent a little; then he found himself speaking with a cynicism of confidence of which even at the moment the sources were strange to him. "I try to believe it. But it's a marvel," he exclaimed, "how YOU already get at it!"

Oh she was able to say. "Remember how much I was on the way to it through Mr. Newsome—before I saw you. He thinks everything of your strength."

"Well, I can bear almost anything!" our friend briskly interrupted. Deep and beautiful on this her smile came back, and with the effect of making him hear what he had said just as she had heard it. He easily enough felt that it gave him away, but what in truth had everything done but that? It had been all very well to think at moments that he was holding her nose down and that he had coerced her: what had he by this time done but let her practically see that he accepted their relation? What was their relation moreover—though light and brief enough in form as yet—but whatever she might choose to make it? Nothing could prevent her—certainly he couldn't—from making it pleasant. At the back of his head, behind everything, was the sense that she was—there, before him, close to him, in vivid imperative form—one of the rare women he had so often heard of, read of, thought of, but never met, whose very presence, look, voice, the mere contemporaneous FACT of whom, from the moment it was at all presented, made a relation of mere recognition. That was not the kind of woman he had ever found Mrs. Newsome, a contemporaneous fact who had been distinctly slow to establish herself; and at present, confronted with Madame de Vionnet, he felt the simplicity of his original impression of Miss Gostrey. She certainly had been a fact of rapid growth; but the world was wide, each day was more and more a new lesson. There were at any rate even among the stranger ones relations and relations. "Of course I suit Chad's grand way," he quickly added. "He hasn't had much difficulty in working me in."

She seemed to deny a little, on the young man's behalf, by the rise of her eyebrows, an intention of any process at all inconsiderate. "You must know how grieved he'd be if you were to lose anything. He believes you can keep his mother patient."

Strether wondered with his eyes on her. "I see. THAT'S then what you really want of me. And how am I to do it? Perhaps you'll tell me that."

"Simply tell her the truth."

"And what do you call the truth?"

"Well, any truth—about us all—that you see yourself. I leave it to you."

"Thank you very much. I like," Strether laughed with a slight harshness, "the way you leave things!"

But she insisted kindly, gently, as if it wasn't so bad. "Be perfectly honest. Tell her all."

"All?" he oddly echoed.

"Tell her the simple truth," Madame de Vionnet again pleaded.

"But what is the simple truth? The simple truth is exactly what I'm trying to discover."

She looked about a while, but presently she came back to him. "Tell her, fully and clearly, about US."

Strether meanwhile had been staring. "You and your daughter?"

"Yes—little Jeanne and me. Tell her," she just slightly quavered, "you like us."

"And what good will that do me? Or rather"—he caught himself up—"what good will it do YOU?"

She looked graver. "None, you believe, really?"

Strether debated. "She didn't send me out to 'like' you."

"Oh," she charmingly contended, "she sent you out to face the facts."

He admitted after an instant that there was something in that. "But how can I face them till I know what they are? Do you want him," he then braced himself to ask, "to marry your daughter?"

She gave a headshake as noble as it was prompt. "No—not that."

"And he really doesn't want to himself?"

She repeated the movement, but now with a strange light in her face. "He likes her too much."

Strether wondered. "To be willing to consider, you mean, the question of taking her to America?"

"To be willing to do anything with her but be immensely kind and nice—really tender of her. We watch over her, and you must help us. You must see her again."

Strether felt awkward. "Ah with pleasure—she's so remarkably attractive."

The mother's eagerness with which Madame de Vionnet jumped at this was to come back to him later as beautiful in its grace. "The dear thing DID please you?" Then as he met it with the largest "Oh!" of enthusiasm: "She's perfect. She's my joy."

"Well, I'm sure that—if one were near her and saw more of her—she'd be mine."

"Then," said Madame de Vionnet, "tell Mrs. Newsome that!"

He wondered the more. "What good will that do you?" As she appeared unable at once to say, however, he brought out something else. "Is your daughter in love with our friend?"

"Ah," she rather startlingly answered, "I wish you'd find out!"

He showed his surprise. "I? A stranger?"

"Oh you won't be a stranger—presently. You shall see her quite, I assure you, as if you weren't."

It remained for him none the less an extraordinary notion. "It seems to me surely that if her mother can't—"

"Ah little girls and their mothers to-day!" she rather inconsequently broke in. But she checked herself with something she seemed to give out as after all more to the point. "Tell her I've been good for him. Don't you think I have?"

It had its effect on him—more than at the moment he quite measured. Yet he was consciously enough touched. "Oh if it's all you—!"

"Well, it may not be 'all,'" she interrupted, "but it's to a great extent. Really and truly," she added in a tone that was to take its place with him among things remembered.

"Then it's very wonderful." He smiled at her from a face that he felt as strained, and her own face for a moment kept him so. At last she also got up. "Well, don't you think that for that—"

"I ought to save you?" So it was that the way to meet her—and the way, as well, in a manner, to get off—came over him. He heard himself use the exorbitant word, the very sound of which helped to determine his flight. "I'll save you if I can."

II

In Chad's lovely home, however, one evening ten days later, he felt himself present at the collapse of the question of Jeanne de Vionnet's shy secret. He had been dining there in the company of that young lady and her mother, as well as of other persons, and he had gone into the petit salon, at Chad's request, on purpose to talk with her. The young man had put this to him as a favour—"I should like so awfully to know what you think of her. It will really be a chance for you," he had said, "to see the jeune fille—I mean the type—as she actually is, and I don't think that, as an observer of manners, it's a thing you ought to miss. It will be an impression that—whatever else you take—you can carry home with you, where you'll find again so much to compare it with."

Strether knew well enough with what Chad wished him to compare it, and though he entirely assented he hadn't yet somehow been so deeply reminded that he was being, as he constantly though mutely expressed it, used. He was as far as ever from making out exactly to what end; but he was none the less constantly accompanied by a sense of the service he rendered. He conceived only that this service was highly agreeable to those who profited by it; and he was indeed still waiting for the moment at which he should catch it in the act of proving disagreeable, proving in some degree intolerable, to himself. He failed quite to see how his situation could clear up at all logically except by some turn of events that would give him the pretext of disgust. He was building from day to day on the possibility of disgust, but each day brought forth meanwhile a new and more engaging bend of the road. That possibility was now ever so much further from sight than on the eve of his arrival, and he perfectly felt that, should it come at all, it would have to be at best inconsequent and violent. He struck himself as a little nearer to it only when he asked himself what service, in such a life of utility, he was after all rendering Mrs. Newsome. When he wished to help himself to believe that he was still all right he reflected—and in fact with wonder—on the unimpaired frequency of their correspondence; in relation to which what was after all more natural than that it should become more frequent just in proportion as their problem became more complicated?

Certain it is at any rate that he now often brought himself balm by the question, with the rich consciousness of yesterday's letter, "Well, what can I do more than that—what can I do more than tell her everything?" To persuade himself that he did tell her, had told her, everything, he used to try to think of particular things he hadn't told her. When at rare moments and in the watches of the night he pounced on one it generally showed itself to be—to a deeper scrutiny—not quite truly of the essence. When anything new struck him as coming up, or anything already noted as reappearing, he always immediately wrote, as if for fear that if he didn't he would miss something; and also that he might be able to say to himself from time to time "She knows it NOW—even while I worry." It was a great comfort to him in general not to have left past things to be dragged to light and explained; not to have to produce at so late a stage anything not produced, or anything even veiled and attenuated, at the moment. She knew it now: that was what he said to himself to-night in relation to the fresh fact of Chad's acquaintance with the two ladies—not to speak of the fresher one of his own. Mrs. Newsome knew in other words that very night at Woollett that he himself knew Madame de Vionnet and that he had conscientiously been to see her; also that he had found her remarkably attractive and that there would probably be a good deal more to tell. But she further knew, or would know very soon, that, again conscientiously, he hadn't repeated his visit; and that when Chad had asked him on the Countess's behalf—Strether made her out vividly, with a thought at the back of his head, a Countess—if he wouldn't name a day for dining with her, he had replied lucidly: "Thank you very much—impossible." He had begged the young man would present his excuses and had trusted him to understand that it couldn't really strike one as quite the straight thing. He hadn't reported to Mrs. Newsome that he had promised to "save" Madame de Vionnet; but, so far as he was concerned with that reminiscence, he hadn't at any rate promised to haunt her house. What Chad had understood could only, in truth, be inferred from Chad's behaviour, which had been in this connexion as easy as in every other. He was easy, always, when he understood; he was easier still, if possible, when he didn't; he had replied that he would make it all right; and he had proceeded to do this by substituting the present occasion—as he was ready to substitute others—for any, for every occasion as to which his old friend should have a funny scruple.

"Oh but I'm not a little foreign girl; I'm just as English as I can be," Jeanne de Vionnet had said to him as soon as, in the petit salon, he sank, shyly enough on his own side, into the place near her vacated by Madame Gloriani at his approach. Madame Gloriani, who was in black velvet, with white lace and powdered hair, and whose somewhat massive majesty melted, at his contact, into the graciousness of some incomprehensible tongue, moved away to make room for the vague gentleman, after benevolent greetings to him which embodied, as he believed, in baffling accents, some recognition of his face from a couple of Sundays before. Then he had remarked—making the most of the advantage of his years—that it frightened him quite enough to find himself dedicated to the entertainment of a little foreign girl. There were girls he wasn't afraid of—he was quite bold with little Americans. Thus it was that she had defended herself to the end—"Oh but I'm almost American too. That's what mamma has wanted me to be—I mean LIKE that; for she has wanted me to have lots of freedom. She has known such good results from it."

She was fairly beautiful to him—a faint pastel in an oval frame: he thought of her already as of some lurking image in a long gallery, the portrait of a small old-time princess of whom nothing was known but that she had died young. Little Jeanne wasn't, doubtless, to die young, but one couldn't, all the same, bear on her lightly enough. It was bearing hard, it was bearing as HE, in any case, wouldn't bear, to concern himself, in relation to her, with the question of a young man. Odious really the question of a young man; one didn't treat such a person as a maid-servant suspected of a "follower." And then young men, young men—well, the thing was their business simply, or was at all events hers. She was fluttered, fairly fevered—to the point of a little glitter that came and went in her eyes and a pair of pink spots that stayed in her cheeks—with the great adventure of dining out and with the greater one still, possibly, of finding a gentleman whom she must think of as very, very old, a gentleman with eye-glasses, wrinkles, a long grizzled moustache. She spoke the prettiest English, our friend thought, that he had ever heard spoken, just as he believed her a few minutes before to be speaking the prettiest French. He wondered almost wistfully if such a sweep of the lyre didn't react on the spirit itself; and his fancy had in fact, before he knew it, begun so to stray and embroider that he finally found himself, absent and extravagant, sitting with the child in a friendly silence. Only by this time he felt her flutter to have fortunately dropped and that she was more at her ease. She trusted him, liked him, and it was to come back to him afterwards that she had told him things. She had dipped into the waiting medium at last and found neither surge nor chill—nothing but the small splash she could herself make in the pleasant warmth, nothing but the safety of dipping and dipping again. At the end of the ten minutes he was to spend with her his impression—with all it had thrown off and all it had taken in—was complete. She had been free, as she knew freedom, partly to show him that, unlike other little persons she knew, she had imbibed that ideal. She was delightfully quaint about herself, but the vision of what she had imbibed was what most held him. It really consisted, he was soon enough to feel, in just one great little matter, the fact that, whatever her nature, she was thoroughly—he had to cast about for the word, but it came—bred. He couldn't of course on so short an acquaintance speak for her nature, but the idea of breeding was what she had meanwhile dropped into his mind. He had never yet known it so sharply presented. Her mother gave it, no doubt; but her mother, to make that less sensible, gave so much else besides, and on neither of the two previous occasions, extraordinary woman, Strether felt, anything like what she was giving tonight. Little Jeanne was a case, an exquisite case of education; whereas the Countess, whom it so amused him to think of by that denomination, was a case, also exquisite, of—well, he didn't know what.

"He has wonderful taste, notre jeune homme": this was what Gloriani said to him on turning away from the inspection of a small picture suspended near the door of the room. The high celebrity in question had just come in, apparently in search of Mademoiselle de Vionnet, but while Strether had got up from beside her their fellow guest, with his eye sharply caught, had paused for a long look. The thing was a landscape, of no size, but of the French school, as our friend was glad to feel he knew, and also of a quality—which he liked to think he should also have guessed; its frame was large out of proportion to the canvas, and he had never seen a person look at anything, he thought, just as Gloriani, with his nose very near and quick movements of the head from side to side and bottom to top, examined this feature of Chad's collection. The artist used that word the next moment smiling courteously, wiping his nippers and looking round him further—paying the place in short by the very manner of his presence and by something Strether fancied he could make out in this particular glance, such a tribute as, to the latter's sense, settled many things once for all. Strether was conscious at this instant, for that matter, as he hadn't yet been, of how, round about him, quite without him, they WERE consistently settled. Gloriani's smile, deeply Italian, he considered, and finely inscrutable, had had for him, during dinner, at which they were not neighbours, an indefinite greeting; but the quality in it was one that had appeared on the other occasion to turn him inside out; it was as if even the momentary link supplied by the doubt between them had snapped. He was conscious now of the final reality, which was that there wasn't so much a doubt as a difference altogether; all the more that over the difference the famous sculptor seemed to signal almost condolingly, yet oh how vacantly! as across some great flat sheet of water. He threw out the bridge of a charming hollow civility on which Strether wouldn't have trusted his own full weight a moment. That idea, even though but transient and perhaps belated, had performed the office of putting Strether more at his ease, and the blurred picture had already dropped—dropped with the sound of something else said and with his becoming aware, by another quick turn, that Gloriani was now on the sofa talking with Jeanne, while he himself had in his ears again the familiar friendliness and the elusive meaning of the "Oh, oh, oh!" that had made him, a fortnight before, challenge Miss Barrace in vain. She had always the air, this picturesque and original lady, who struck him, so oddly, as both antique and modern—she had always the air of taking up some joke that one had already had out with her. The point itself, no doubt, was what was antique, and the use she made of it what was modern. He felt just now that her good-natured irony did bear on something, and it troubled him a little that she wouldn't be more explicit only assuring him, with the pleasure of observation so visible in her, that she wouldn't tell him more for the world. He could take refuge but in asking her what she had done with Waymarsh, though it must be added that he felt himself a little on the way to a clue after she had answered that this personage was, in the other room, engaged in conversation with Madame de Vionnet. He stared a moment at the image of such a conjunction; then, for Miss Barrace's benefit, he wondered. "Is she too then under the charm—?"

"No, not a bit"—Miss Barrace was prompt. "She makes nothing of him. She's bored. She won't help you with him."

"Oh," Strether laughed, "she can't do everything."

"Of course not—wonderful as she is. Besides, he makes nothing of HER. She won't take him from me—though she wouldn't, no doubt, having other affairs in hand, even if she could. I've never," said Miss Barrace, "seen her fail with any one before. And to-night, when she's so magnificent, it would seem to her strange—if she minded. So at any rate I have her all. Je suis tranquille!"

Strether understood, so far as that went; but he was feeling for his clue. "She strikes you to-night as particularly magnificent?"

"Surely. Almost as I've never seen her. Doesn't she you? Why it's FOR you."

He persisted in his candour. "'For' me—?"

"Oh, oh, oh!" cried Miss Barrace, who persisted in the opposite of that quality.

"Well," he acutely admitted, "she IS different. She's gay."

"She's gay!" Miss Barrace laughed. "And she has beautiful shoulders—though there's nothing different in that."

"No," said Strether, "one was sure of her shoulders. It isn't her shoulders."

His companion, with renewed mirth and the finest sense, between the puffs of her cigarette, of the drollery of things, appeared to find their conversation highly delightful. "Yes, it isn't her shoulders ."

"What then is it?" Strether earnestly enquired.

"Why, it's SHE—simply. It's her mood. It's her charm."

"Of course it's her charm, but we're speaking of the difference." "Well," Miss Barrace explained, "she's just brilliant, as we used to say. That's all. She's various. She's fifty women."

"Ah but only one"—Strether kept it clear—"at a time."

"Perhaps. But in fifty times—!"

"Oh we shan't come to that," our friend declared; and the next moment he had moved in another direction. "Will you answer me a plain question? Will she ever divorce?"

Miss Barrace looked at him through all her tortoise-shell. "Why should she?"

It wasn't what he had asked for, he signified; but he met it well enough. "To marry Chad."

"Why should she marry Chad?"

"Because I'm convinced she's very fond of him. She has done wonders for him."

"Well then, how could she do more? Marrying a man, or woman either," Miss Barrace sagely went on, "is never the wonder for any Jack and Jill can bring THAT off. The wonder is their doing such things without marrying."

Strether considered a moment this proposition. "You mean it's so beautiful for our friends simply to go on so?"

But whatever he said made her laugh. "Beautiful."

He nevertheless insisted. "And THAT because it's disinterested?"

She was now, however, suddenly tired of the question. "Yes then—call it that. Besides, she'll never divorce. Don't, moreover," she added, "believe everything you hear about her husband."

"He's not then," Strether asked, "a wretch?"

"Oh yes. But charming."

"Do you know him?"

"I've met him. He's bien aimable."

"To every one but his wife?"

"Oh for all I know, to her too—to any, to every woman. I hope you at any rate," she pursued with a quick change, "appreciate the care I take of Mr. Waymarsh."

"Oh immensely." But Strether was not yet in line. "At all events," he roundly brought out, "the attachment's an innocent one."

"Mine and his? Ah," she laughed, "don't rob it of ALL interest!"

"I mean our friend's here—to the lady we've been speaking of." That was what he had settled to as an indirect but none the less closely involved consequence of his impression of Jeanne. That was where he meant to stay. "It's innocent," he repeated—"I see the whole thing."

Mystified by his abrupt declaration, she had glanced over at Gloriani as at the unnamed subject of his allusion, but the next moment she had understood; though indeed not before Strether had noticed her momentary mistake and wondered what might possibly be behind that too. He already knew that the sculptor admired Madame de Vionnet; but did this admiration also represent an attachment of which the innocence was discussable? He was moving verily in a strange air and on ground not of the firmest. He looked hard for an instant at Miss Barrace, but she had already gone on. "All right with Mr. Newsome? Why of course she is!"—and she got gaily back to the question of her own good friend. "I dare say you're surprised that I'm not worn out with all I see—it being so much!—of Sitting Bull. But I'm not, you know—I don't mind him; I bear up, and we get on beautifully. I'm very strange; I'm like that; and often I can't explain. There are people who are supposed interesting or remarkable or whatever, and who bore me to death; and then there are others as to whom nobody can understand what anybody sees in them—in whom I see no end of things." Then after she had smoked a moment, "He's touching, you know," she said.

"'Know'?" Strether echoed—"don't I, indeed? We must move you almost to tears."

"Oh but I don't mean YOU!" she laughed.

"You ought to then, for the worst sign of all—as I must have it for you—is that you can't help me. That's when a woman pities."

"Ah but I do help you!" she cheerfully insisted.

Again he looked at her hard, and then after a pause: "No you don't!"

Her tortoise-shell, on its long chain, rattled down. "I help you with Sitting Bull. That's a good deal."

"Oh that, yes." But Strether hesitated. "Do you mean he talks of me?"

"So that I have to defend you? No, never.'

"I see," Strether mused. "It's too deep."

"That's his only fault," she returned—"that everything, with him, is too deep. He has depths of silence—which he breaks only at the longest intervals by a remark. And when the remark comes it's always something he has seen or felt for himself—never a bit banal THAT would be what one might have feared and what would kill me But never." She smoked again as she thus, with amused complacency, appreciated her acquisition. "And never about you. We keep clear of you. We're wonderful. But I'll tell you what he does do," she continued: "he tries to make me presents."

"Presents?" poor Strether echoed, conscious with a pang that HE hadn't yet tried that in any quarter.

"Why you see," she explained, "he's as fine as ever in the victoria; so that when I leave him, as I often do almost for hours—he likes it so—at the doors of shops, the sight of him there helps me, when I come out, to know my carriage away off in the rank. But sometimes, for a change, he goes with me into the shops, and then I've all I can do to prevent his buying me things."

"He wants to 'treat' you?" Strether almost gasped at all he himself hadn't thought of. He had a sense of admiration. "Oh he's much more in the real tradition than I. Yes," he mused, "it's the sacred rage."

"The sacred rage, exactly!"—and Miss Barrace, who hadn't before heard this term applied, recognised its bearing with a clap of her gemmed hands. "Now I do know why he's not banal. But I do prevent him all the same—and if you saw what he sometimes selects—from buying. I save him hundreds and hundreds. I only take flowers."

"Flowers?" Strether echoed again with a rueful reflexion. How many nosegays had her present converser sent?

"Innocent flowers," she pursued, "as much as he likes. And he sends me splendours; he knows all the best places—he has found them for himself; he's wonderful."

"He hasn't told them to me," her friend smiled, "he has a life of his own." But Strether had swung back to the consciousness that for himself after all it never would have done. Waymarsh hadn't Mrs. Waymarsh in the least to consider, whereas Lambert Strether had constantly, in the inmost honour of his thoughts, to consider Mrs. Newsome. He liked moreover to feel how much his friend was in the real tradition. Yet he had his conclusion. "WHAT a rage it is!" He had worked it out. "It's an opposition."

She followed, but at a distance. "That's what I feel. Yet to what?"

"Well, he thinks, you know, that I'VE a life of my own. And I haven't!"

"You haven't?" She showed doubt, and her laugh confirmed it. "Oh, oh, oh!"

"No—not for myself. I seem to have a life only for other people."

"Ah for them and WITH them! Just now for instance with—"

"Well, with whom?" he asked before she had had time to say.

His tone had the effect of making her hesitate and even, as he guessed, speak with a difference. "Say with Miss Gostrey. What do you do for HER?" It really made him wonder. "Nothing at all!"

III

Madame de Vionnet, having meanwhile come in, was at present close to them, and Miss Barrace hereupon, instead of risking a rejoinder, became again with a look that measured her from top to toe all mere long-handled appreciative tortoise-shell. She had struck our friend, from the first of her appearing, as dressed for a great occasion, and she met still more than on either of the others the conception reawakened in him at their garden-party, the idea of the femme du monde in her habit as she lived. Her bare shoulders and arms were white and beautiful; the materials of her dress, a mixture, as he supposed, of silk and crape, were of a silvery grey so artfully composed as to give an impression of warm splendour; and round her neck she wore a collar of large old emeralds, the green note of which was more dimly repeated, at other points of her apparel, in embroidery, in enamel, in satin, in substances and textures vaguely rich. Her head, extremely fair and exquisitely festal, was like a happy fancy, a notion of the antique, on an old precious medal, some silver coin of the Renaissance; while her slim lightness and brightness, her gaiety, her expression, her decision, contributed to an effect that might have been felt by a poet as half mythological and half conventional. He could have compared her to a goddess still partly engaged in a morning cloud, or to a sea-nymph waist-high in the summer surge. Above all she suggested to him the reflexion that the femme du monde—in these finest developments of the type—was, like Cleopatra in the play, indeed various and multifold. She had aspects, characters, days, nights—or had them at least, showed them by a mysterious law of her own, when in addition to everything she happened also to be a woman of genius. She was an obscure person, a muffled person one day, and a showy person, an uncovered person the next. He thought of Madame de Vionnet to-night as showy and uncovered, though he felt the formula rough, because, thanks to one of the short-cuts of genius she had taken all his categories by surprise. Twice during dinner he had met Chad's eyes in a longish look; but these communications had in truth only stirred up again old ambiguities—so little was it clear from them whether they were an appeal or an admonition. "You see how I'm fixed," was what they appeared to convey; yet how he was fixed was exactly what Strether didn't see. However, perhaps he should see now.

"Are you capable of the very great kindness of going to relieve Newsome, for a few minutes, of the rather crushing responsibility of Madame Gloriani, while I say a word, if he'll allow me, to Mr. Strether, of whom I've a question to ask? Our host ought to talk a bit to those other ladies, and I'll come back in a minute to your rescue." She made this proposal to Miss Barrace as if her consciousness of a special duty had just flickered-up, but that lady's recognition of Strether's little start at it—as at a betrayal on the speaker's part of a domesticated state—was as mute as his own comment; and after an instant, when their fellow guest had good-naturedly left them, he had been given something else to think of. "Why has Maria so suddenly gone? Do you know?" That was the question Madame de Vionnet had brought with her.

"I'm afraid I've no reason to give you but the simple reason I've had from her in a note—the sudden obligation to join in the south a sick friend who has got worse."

"Ah then she has been writing you?"

"Not since she went—I had only a brief explanatory word before she started. I went to see her," Strether explained—"it was the day after I called on you—but she was already on her way, and her concierge told me that in case of my coming I was to be informed she had written to me. I found her note when I got home."

Madame de Vionnet listened with interest and with her eyes on Strether's face; then her delicately decorated head had a small melancholy motion. "She didn't write to ME. I went to see her," she added, "almost immediately after I had seen you, and as I assured her I would do when I met her at Gloriani's. She hadn't then told me she was to be absent, and I felt at her door as if I understood. She's absent—with all respect to her sick friend, though I know indeed she has plenty—so that I may not see her. She doesn't want to meet me again. Well," she continued with a beautiful conscious mildness, "I liked and admired her beyond every one in the old time, and she knew it—perhaps that's precisely what has made her go—and I dare say I haven't lost her for ever." Strether still said nothing; he had a horror, as he now thought of himself, of being in question between women—was in fact already quite enough on his way to that, and there was moreover, as it came to him, perceptibly, something behind these allusions and professions that, should he take it in, would square but ill with his present resolve to simplify. It was as if, for him, all the same, her softness and sadness were sincere. He felt that not less when she soon went on: "I'm extremely glad of her happiness." But it also left him mute—sharp and fine though the imputation it conveyed. What it conveyed was that HE was Maria Gostrey's happiness, and for the least little instant he had the impulse to challenge the thought. He could have done so however only by saying "What then do you suppose to be between us?" and he was wonderfully glad a moment later not to have spoken. He would rather seem stupid any day than fatuous, and he drew back as well, with a smothered inward shudder, from the consideration of what women—of highly-developed type in particular—might think of each other. Whatever he had come out for he hadn't come to go into that; so that he absolutely took up nothing his interlocutress had now let drop. Yet, though he had kept away from her for days, had laid wholly on herself the burden of their meeting again, she hadn't a gleam of irritation to show him. "Well, about Jeanne now?" she smiled—it had the gaiety with which she had originally come in. He felt it on the instant to represent her motive and real errand. But he had been schooling her of a truth to say much in proportion to his little. "Do you make out that she has a sentiment? I mean for Mr. Newsome."

Almost resentful, Strether could at last be prompt. "How can I make out such things?"

She remained perfectly good-natured. "Ah but they're beautiful little things, and you make out—don't pretend—everything in the world. Haven't you," she asked, "been talking with her?"

"Yes, but not about Chad. At least not much."

"Oh you don't require 'much'!" she reassuringly declared. But she immediately changed her ground. "I hope you remember your promise of the other day."

"To 'save' you, as you called it?"

"I call it so still. You WILL?" she insisted. "You haven't repented?"

He wondered. "No—but I've been thinking what I meant."

She kept it up. "And not, a little, what I did?"

"No—that's not necessary. It will be enough if I know what I meant myself."

"And don't you know," she asked, "by this time?"

Again he had a pause. "I think you ought to leave it to me. But how long," he added, "do you give me?"

"It seems to me much more a question of how long you give ME. Doesn't our friend here himself, at any rate," she went on, "perpetually make me present to you?"

"Not," Strether replied, "by ever speaking of you to me."

"He never does that?"

"Never."

She considered, and, if the fact was disconcerting to her, effactually concealed it. The next minute indeed she had recovered. "No, he wouldn't. But do you NEED that?"

65

Her emphasis was wonderful, and though his eyes had been wandering he looked at her longer now. "I see what you mean."

"Of course you see what I mean."

Her triumph was gentle, and she really had tones to make justice weep. "I've before me what he owes you."

"Admit then that that's something," she said, yet still with the same discretion in her pride.

He took in this note but went straight on. "You've made of him what I see, but what I don't see is how in the world you've done it."

"Ah that's another question!" she smiled. "The point is of what use is your declining to know me when to know Mr. Newsome—as you do me the honour to find him—IS just to know me."

"I see," he mused, still with his eyes on her. "I shouldn't have met you to-night."

She raised and dropped her linked hands. "It doesn't matter. If I trust you why can't you a little trust me too? And why can't you also," she asked in another tone, "trust yourself?" But she gave him no time to reply. "Oh I shall be so easy for you! And I'm glad at any rate you've seen my child."

"I'm glad too," he said; "but she does you no good."

"No good?"—Madame de Vionnet had a clear stare. "Why she's an angel of light."

"That's precisely the reason. Leave her alone. Don't try to find out. I mean," he explained, "about what you spoke to me of—the way she feels."

His companion wondered. "Because one really won't?"

"Well, because I ask you, as a favour to myself, not to. She's the most charming creature I've ever seen. Therefore don't touch her. Don't know—don't want to know. And moreover—yes—you won't."

It was an appeal, of a sudden, and she took it in. "As a favour to you?"

"Well—since you ask me."

"Anything, everything you ask," she smiled. "I shan't know then—never. Thank you," she added with peculiar gentleness as she turned away.

The sound of it lingered with him, making him fairly feel as if he had been tripped up and had a fall. In the very act of arranging with her for his independence he had, under pressure from a particular perception, inconsistently, quite stupidly, committed himself, and, with her subtlety sensitive on the spot to an advantage, she had driven in by a single word a little golden nail, the sharp intention of which he signally felt. He hadn't detached, he had more closely connected himself, and his eyes, as he considered with some intensity this circumstance, met another pair which had just come within their range and which struck him as reflecting his sense of what he had done. He recognised them at the same moment as those of little Bilham, who had apparently drawn near on purpose to speak to him, and little Bilham wasn't, in the conditions, the person to whom his heart would be most closed. They were seated together a minute later at the angle of the room obliquely opposite the corner in which Gloriani was still engaged with Jeanne de Vionnet, to whom at first and in silence their attention had been benevolently given. "I can't see for my life," Strether had then observed, "how a young fellow of any spirit—such a one as you for instance—can be admitted to the sight of that young lady without being hard hit. Why don't you go in, little Bilham?" He remembered the tone into which he had been betrayed on the garden-bench at the sculptor's reception, and this might make up for that by being much more the right sort of thing to say to a young man worthy of any advice at all. "There WOULD be some reason."

"Some reason for what?"

"Why for hanging on here."

"To offer my hand and fortune to Mademoiselle de Vionnet?"

"Well," Strether asked, "to what lovelier apparition COULD you offer them? She's the sweetest little thing I've ever seen."

"She's certainly immense. I mean she's the real thing. I believe the pale pink petals are folded up there for some wondrous efflorescence in time; to open, that is, to some great golden sun. I'M unfortunately but a small farthing candle. What chance in such a field for a poor little painter-man?"

"Oh you're good enough," Strether threw out.

"Certainly I'm good enough. We're good enough, I consider, nous autres, for anything. But she's TOO good. There's the difference. They wouldn't look at me."

Strether, lounging on his divan and still charmed by the young girl, whose eyes had consciously strayed to him, he fancied, with a vague smile—Strether, enjoying the whole occasion as with dormant pulses at last awake and in spite of new material thrust upon him, thought over his companion's words. "Whom do you mean by 'they'? She and her mother?"

"She and her mother. And she has a father too, who, whatever else he may be, certainly can't be indifferent to the possibilities she represents. Besides, there's Chad."

Strether was silent a little. "Ah but he doesn't care for her—not, I mean, it appears, after all, in the sense I'm speaking of. He's NOT in love with her."

"No—but he's her best friend; after her mother. He's very fond of her. He has his ideas about what can be done for her."

"Well, it's very strange!" Strether presently remarked with a sighing sense of fulness.

"Very strange indeed. That's just the beauty of it. Isn't it very much the kind of beauty you had in mind," little Bilham went on, "when you were so wonderful and so inspiring to me the other day? Didn't you adjure me, in accents I shall never forget, to see, while I've a chance, everything I can?—and REALLY to see, for it must have been that only you meant. Well, you did me no end of good, and I'm doing my best. I DO make it out a situation."

"So do I!" Strether went on after a moment. But he had the next minute an inconsequent question. "How comes Chad so mixed up, anyway?"

"Ah, ah, ah!"—and little Bilham fell back on his cushions.

It reminded our friend of Miss Barrace, and he felt again the brush of his sense of moving in a maze of mystic closed allusions. Yet he kept hold of his thread. "Of course I understand really; only the general transformation makes me occasionally gasp. Chad with such a voice in the settlement of the future of a little countess—no," he declared, "it takes more time! You say moreover," he resumed, "that we're inevitably, people like you and me, out of the running. The curious fact remains that Chad himself isn't. The situation doesn't make for it, but in a different one he could have her if he would."

"Yes, but that's only because he's rich and because there's a possibility of his being richer. They won't think of anything but a great name or a great fortune."

"Well," said Strether, "he'll have no great fortune on THESE lines. He must stir his stumps."

"Is that," little Bilham enquired, "what you were saying to Madame de Vionnet?"

"No—I don't say much to her. Of course, however," Strether continued, "he can make sacrifices if he likes."

Little Bilham had a pause. "Oh he's not keen for sacrifices; or thinks, that is, possibly, that he has made enough."

"Well, it IS virtuous," his companion observed with some decision.

"That's exactly," the young man dropped after a moment, "what I mean."

It kept Strether himself silent a little. "I've made it out for myself," he then went on; "I've really, within the last half-hour, got hold of it. I understand it in short at last; which at first—when you originally spoke to me—I didn't. Nor when Chad originally spoke to me either."

"Oh," said little Bilham, "I don't think that at that time you believed me."

"Yes—I did; and I believed Chad too. It would have been odious and unmannerly—as well as quite perverse—if I hadn't. What interest have you in deceiving me?"

The young man cast about. "What interest have I?"

"Yes. Chad MIGHT have. But you?"

"Ah, ah, ah!" little Bilham exclaimed.

It might, on repetition, as a mystification, have irritated our friend a little, but he knew, once more, as we have seen, where he was, and his being proof against everything was only another attestation that he meant to stay there. "I couldn't, without my own impression, realise. She's a tremendously clever brilliant capable woman, and with an extraordinary charm on top of it all—the charm we surely all of us this evening know what to think of. It isn't every clever brilliant capable woman that has it. In fact it's rare with any woman. So there you are," Strether proceeded as if not for little Bilham's benefit alone. "I understand what a relation with such a woman—what such a high fine friendship—may be. It can't be vulgar or coarse, anyway—and that's the point."

"Yes, that's the point," said little Bilham. "It can't be vulgar or coarse. And, bless us and save us, it ISn't! It's, upon my word, the very finest thing I ever saw in my life, and the most distinguished."

Strether, from beside him and leaning back with him as he leaned, dropped on him a momentary look which filled a short interval and of which he took no notice. He only gazed before him with intent participation. "Of course what it has done for him," Strether at all events presently pursued, "of course what it has done for him—that is as to HOW it has so wonderfully worked—isn't a thing I pretend to understand. I've to take it as I find it. There he is."

"There he is!" little Bilham echoed. "And it's really and truly she. I don't understand either, even with my longer and closer opportunity. But I'm like you," he added; "I can admire and rejoice even when I'm a little in the dark. You see I've watched it for some three years, and especially for this last. He wasn't so bad before it as I seem to have made out that you think—"

"Oh I don't think anything now!" Strether impatiently broke in: "that is but what I DO think! I mean that originally, for her to have cared for him—"

"There must have been stuff in him? Oh yes, there was stuff indeed, and much more of it than ever showed, I dare say, at home. Still, you know," the young man in all fairness developed, "there was room for her, and that's where she came in. She saw her chance and took it. That's what strikes me as having been so fine. But of course," he wound up, "he liked her first."

"Naturally," said Strether.

"I mean that they first met somehow and somewhere—I believe in some American house—and she, without in the least then intending it, made her impression. Then with time and opportunity he made his; and after THAT she was as bad as he."

Strether vaguely took it up. "As 'bad'?"

"She began, that is, to care—to care very much. Alone, and in her horrid position, she found it, when once she had started, an interest. It was, it is, an interest, and it did—it continues to do—a lot for herself as well. So she still cares. She cares in fact," said little Bilham thoughtfully "more."

Strether's theory that it was none of his business was somehow not damaged by the way he took this. "More, you mean, than he?" On which his companion looked round at him, and now for an instant their eyes met. "More than he?" he repeated.

Little Bilham, for as long, hung fire. "Will you never tell any one?"

Strether thought. "Whom should I tell?"

"Why I supposed you reported regularly—"

"To people at home?"—Strether took him up. "Well, I won't tell them this."

The young man at last looked away. "Then she does now care more than he."

"Oh!" Strether oddly exclaimed.

But his companion immediately met it. "Haven't you after all had your impression of it? That's how you've got hold of him."

"Ah but I haven't got hold of him!"

"Oh I say!" But it was all little Bilham said.

"It's at any rate none of my business. I mean," Strether explained, "nothing else than getting hold of him is." It appeared, however, to strike him as his business to add: "The fact remains nevertheless that she has saved him."

Little Bilham just waited. "I thought that was what you were to do."

But Strether had his answer ready. "I'm speaking—in connexion with her—of his manners and morals, his character and life. I'm speaking of him as a person to deal with and talk with and live with—speaking of him as a social animal."

"And isn't it as a social animal that you also want him?"

"Certainly; so that it's as if she had saved him FOR us."

"It strikes you accordingly then," the young man threw out, "as for you all to save HER?"

"Oh for us 'all'—!" Strether could but laugh at that. It brought him back, however, to the point he had really wished to make. "They've accepted their situation—hard as it is. They're not free—at least she's not; but they take what's left to them. It's a friendship, of a beautiful sort; and that's what makes them so strong. They're straight, they feel; and they keep each other up. It's doubtless she, however, who, as you yourself have hinted, feels it most."

Little Bilham appeared to wonder what he had hinted. "Feels most that they're straight?"

"Well, feels that SHE is, and the strength that comes from it. She keeps HIM up—she keeps the whole thing up. When people are able to it's fine. She's wonderful, wonderful, as Miss Barrace says; and he is, in his way, too; however, as a mere man, he may sometimes rebel and not feel that he finds his account in it. She has simply given him an immense moral lift, and what that can explain is prodigious. That's why I speak of it as a situation. It IS one, if there ever was." And Strether, with his head back and his eyes on the ceiling, seemed to lose himself in the vision of it.

His companion attended deeply. "You state it much better than I could." "Oh you see it doesn't concern you."

Little Bilham considered. "I thought you said just now that it doesn't concern you either."

"Well, it doesn't a bit as Madame de Vionnet's affair. But as we were again saying just now, what did I come out for but to save him?"

"Yes—to remove him."

"To save him by removal; to win him over to HIMSELF thinking it best he shall take up business—thinking he must immediately do therefore what's necessary to that end."

"Well," said little Bilham after a moment, "you HAVE won him over. He does think it best. He has within a day or two again said to me as much."

"And that," Strether asked, "is why you consider that he cares less than she?"

"Cares less for her than she for him? Yes, that's one of the reasons. But other things too have given me the impression. A man, don't you think?" little Bilham presently pursued, "CAN'T, in such conditions, care so much as a woman. It takes different conditions to make him, and then perhaps he cares more. Chad," he wound up, "has his possible future before him."

"Are you speaking of his business future?"

"No—on the contrary; of the other, the future of what you so justly call their situation. M. de Vionnet may live for ever."

"So that they can't marry?"

The young man waited a moment. "Not being able to marry is all they've with any confidence to look forward to. A woman—a particular woman—may stand that strain. But can a man?" he propounded.

Strether's answer was as prompt as if he had already, for himself, worked it out. "Not without a very high ideal of conduct. But that's just what we're attributing to Chad. And how, for that matter," he mused, "does his going to America diminish the particular strain? Wouldn't it rather seem to add to it?"

"Out of sight out of mind!" his companion laughed. Then more bravely: "Wouldn't distance lessen the torment?" But before Strether could reply, "The thing is, you see, Chad ought to marry!" he wound up.

Strether, for a little, appeared to think of it. "If you talk of torments you don't diminish mine!" he then broke out. The next moment he was on his feet with a question. "He ought to marry whom?"

Little Bilham rose more slowly. "Well, some one he CAN—some thoroughly nice girl."

Strether's eyes, as they stood together, turned again to Jeanne. "Do you mean HER?"

His friend made a sudden strange face. "After being in love with her mother? No."

"But isn't it exactly your idea that he ISn't in love with her mother?"

His friend once more had a pause. "Well, he isn't at any rate in love with Jeanne."

"I dare say not."

"How CAN he be with any other woman?"

"Oh that I admit. But being in love isn't, you know, here"—little Bilham spoke in friendly reminder—"thought necessary, in strictness, for marriage."

"And what torment—to call a torment—can there ever possibly be with a woman like that?" As if from the interest of his own question Strether had gone on without hearing. "Is it for her to have turned a man out so wonderfully, too, only for somebody else?" He appeared to make a point of this, and little Bilham looked at him now. "When it's for each other that people give things up they don't miss them." Then he threw off as with an extravagance of which he was conscious: "Let them face the future together!"

Little Bilham looked at him indeed. "You mean that after all he shouldn't go back?"

"I mean that if he gives her up—!"

"Yes?"

"Well, he ought to be ashamed of himself." But Strether spoke with a sound that might have passed for a laugh.

Volume II

Book Seventh

I

Church interior by Emanuel de Witte (1617-1692)

It wasn't the first time Strether had sat alone in the great dim church—still less was it the first of his giving himself up, so far as conditions permitted, to its beneficent action on his nerves. He had been to Notre Dame with Waymarsh, he had been there with Miss Gostrey, he had been there with Chad Newsome, and had found the place, even in company, such a refuge from the obsession of his problem that, with renewed pressure from that source, he had not unnaturally recurred to a remedy meeting the case, for the moment, so indirectly, no doubt, but so relievingly. He was conscious enough that it was only for the moment, but good moments—if he could call them good—still had their value for a man who by this time struck himself as living almost disgracefully from hand to mouth. Having so well learnt the way, he had lately made the pilgrimage more than once by himself—had quite stolen off, taking an unnoticed chance and making no point of speaking of the adventure when restored to his friends.

His great friend, for that matter, was still absent, as well as remarkably silent; even at the end of three weeks Miss Gostrey hadn't come back. She wrote to him from Mentone, admitting that he must judge her grossly inconsequent—perhaps in fact for the time odiously faithless; but asking for patience, for a deferred sentence, throwing herself in short on his generosity. For her too, she could assure him, life was complicated—more complicated than he could have guessed; she had moreover made certain of him—certain of not wholly missing him on her return—before her disappearance. If furthermore she didn't burden him with letters it was frankly because of her sense of the other great commerce he had to carry on. He himself, at the end of a fortnight, had written twice, to show how his generosity could be trusted; but he reminded himself in each case of Mrs. Newsome's epistolary manner at the times when Mrs. Newsome kept off delicate ground. He sank his problem, he talked of Waymarsh and Miss Barrace, of little Bilham and the set over the river, with whom he had again had tea, and he was easy, for convenience, about Chad and Madame de Vionnet and Jeanne. He admitted that he continued to see them, he was decidedly so confirmed a haunter of Chad's premises and that young man's practical intimacy with them was so undeniably great; but he had his reason for not attempting to render for Miss Gostrey's benefit the impression of these last days. That would be to tell her too much about himself—it being at present just from himself he was trying to escape.

This small struggle sprang not a little, in its way, from the same impulse that had now carried him across to Notre Dame; the impulse to let things be, to give them time to justify themselves or at least to pass. He was aware of having no errand in such a place but the desire not to be, for the hour, in certain other places; a sense of safety, of simplification, which each time he yielded to it he amused himself by thinking of as a private concession to cowardice. The great church had no altar for his worship, no direct voice for his soul; but it was none the less soothing even to sanctity; for he could feel while there what he couldn't elsewhere, that he was a plain tired man taking the holiday he had earned. He was tired, but he wasn't plain—that was the pity and the trouble of it; he was able, however, to drop his problem at the door very much as if it had been the copper piece that he deposited, on the threshold, in the receptacle of the inveterate blind beggar. He trod the long dim nave, sat in the splendid choir, paused before the cluttered chapels of the east end, and the mighty monument laid upon him its spell. He might have been a student under the charm of a museum—which was exactly what, in a foreign town, in the afternoon of life, he would have liked to be free to be. This form of sacrifice did at any rate for the occasion as well as another; it made him quite sufficiently understand how, within the precinct, for the real refugee, the things of the world could fall into abeyance. That was the cowardice, probably—to dodge them, to beg the question, not to deal with it in the hard outer light; but his own oblivions were too brief, too vain, to hurt any one but himself, and he had a vague and fanciful kindness for certain persons whom he met, figures of mystery and anxiety, and whom, with observation for his pastime, he ranked as those who were fleeing from justice. Justice was outside, in the hard light, and injustice too; but one was as absent as the other from the air of the long aisles and the brightness of the many altars.

Thus it was at all events that, one morning some dozen days after the dinner in the Boulevard Malesherbes at which Madame de Vionnet had been present with her daughter, he was called upon to play his part in an encounter that deeply stirred his imagination. He had the habit, in these contemplations, of watching a fellow visitant, here and there, from a respectable distance, remarking some note of behaviour, of penitence, of prostration, of the absolved, relieved state; this was the manner in which his vague tenderness took its course, the degree of demonstration to which it naturally had to confine itself. It hadn't indeed so felt its responsibility as when on this occasion he suddenly measured the suggestive effect of a lady whose supreme stillness, in the shade of one of the chapels, he had two or three times noticed as he made, and made once more, his slow circuit. She wasn't prostrate—not in any degree bowed, but she was strangely fixed, and her prolonged immobility showed her, while he passed and paused, as wholly given up to the need, whatever it was, that had brought her there. She only sat and gazed before her, as he himself often sat; but she had placed herself, as he never did, within the focus of the shrine, and she had lost herself, he could easily see, as he would only have liked to do. She was not a wandering alien, keeping back more than she gave, but one of the familiar, the intimate, the fortunate, for whom these dealings had a method and a meaning. She reminded our friend—since it was the way of nine tenths of his current impressions to act as recalls of things imagined—of some fine firm concentrated heroine of an old story, something he had heard, read, something that, had he had a hand for drama, he might himself have written, renewing her courage, renewing her clearness, in splendidly-protected meditation. Her back, as she sat, was turned to him, but his impression absolutely required that she should be young and interesting, and she carried her head moreover, even in the sacred shade, with a discernible faith in herself, a kind of implied conviction of consistency, security, impunity. But what had such a woman come for if she hadn't come to pray? Strether's reading of such matters was, it must be owned, confused; but he wondered if her attitude were some congruous fruit of absolution, of "indulgence." He knew but dimly what indulgence, in such a place, might mean; yet he had, as with a soft sweep, a vision of how it might indeed add to the zest of active rites. All this was a good deal to have been denoted by a mere lurking figure who was nothing to him; but, the last thing before leaving the church, he had the surprise of a still deeper quickening.

He had dropped upon a seat halfway down the nave and, again in the museum mood, was trying with head thrown back and eyes aloft, to reconstitute a past, to reduce it in fact to the convenient terms of Victor Hugo, whom, a few days before, giving the rein for once in a way to the joy of life, he had purchased in seventy bound volumes, a miracle of cheapness, parted with, he was assured by the shopman, at the price of the red-and-gold alone. He looked, doubtless, while he played his eternal nippers over Gothic glooms, sufficiently rapt in reverence; but what his thought really bumped against was the question of where, among packed accumulations, so multiform a wedge would be able to enter. Were seventy volumes in red-and-gold to be perhaps what he should most substantially have to show at Woollett as the fruit of his mission? It was a possibility that held him a minute—held him till he happened to feel that some one, unnoticed, had approached him and paused. Turning, he saw that a lady stood there as for a greeting, and he sprang up as he next took her, securely, for Madame de Vionnet, who appeared to have recognised him as she passed near him on her way to the door. She checked, quickly and gaily, a certain confusion in him, came to meet it, turned it back, by an art of her own; the confusion having threatened him as he knew her for the person he had lately been observing. She was the lurking figure of the dim chapel; she had occupied him more than she guessed; but it came to him in time, luckily, that he needn't tell her and that no harm, after all, had been done. She herself, for that matter, straightway showing she felt their encounter as the happiest of accidents, had for him a "You come here too?" that despoiled surprise of every awkwardness.

"I come often," she said. "I love this place, but I'm terrible, in general, for churches. The old women who live in them all know me; in fact I'm already myself one of the old women. It's like that, at all events, that I foresee I shall end." Looking about for a chair, so that he instantly pulled one nearer, she sat down with him again to the sound of an "Oh, I like so much your also being fond—!"

He confessed the extent of his feeling, though she left the object vague; and he was struck with the tact, the taste of her vagueness, which simply took for granted in him a sense of beautiful things. He was conscious of how much it was affected, this sense, by something subdued and discreet in the way she had arranged herself for her special object and her morning walk—he believed her to have come on foot; the way her slightly thicker veil was drawn—a mere touch, but everything; the composed gravity of her dress, in which, here and there, a dull wine-colour seemed to gleam faintly through black; the charming discretion of her small compact head; the quiet note, as she sat, of her folded, grey-gloved hands. It was, to Strether's mind, as if she sat on her own ground, the light honours of which, at an open gate, she thus easily did him, while all the vastness and mystery of the domain stretched off behind. When people were so completely in possession they could be extraordinarily civil; and our friend had indeed at this hour a kind of revelation of her heritage. She was romantic for him far beyond what she could have guessed, and again he found his small comfort in the conviction that, subtle though she was, his impression must remain a secret from her. The thing that, once more, made him uneasy for secrets in general was this particular patience she could have with his own want of colour; albeit that on the other hand his uneasiness pretty well dropped after he had been for ten minutes as colourless as possible and at the same time as responsive.

The moments had already, for that matter, drawn their deepest tinge from the special interest excited in him by his vision of his companion's identity with the person whose attitude before the glimmering altar had so impressed him. This attitude fitted admirably into the stand he had privately taken about her connexion with Chad on the last occasion of his seeing them together. It helped him to stick fast at the point he had then reached; it was there he had resolved that he WOULD stick, and at no moment since had it seemed as easy to do so. Unassailably innocent was a relation that could make one of the parties to it so carry herself. If it wasn't innocent why did she haunt the churches?—into which, given the woman he could believe he made out, she would never have come to flaunt an insolence of guilt. She haunted them for continued help, for strength, for peace—sublime support which, if one were able to look at it so, she found from day to day. They talked, in low easy tones and with lifted lingering looks, about the great monument and its history and its beauty—all of which, Madame de Vionnet professed, came to her most in the other, the outer view. "We'll presently, after we go," she said, "walk round it again if you like. I'm not in a particular hurry, and it will be pleasant to look at it well with you." He had spoken of the great romancer and the great romance, and of what, to his imagination, they had done for the whole, mentioning to her moreover the exorbitance of his purchase, the seventy blazing volumes that were so out of proportion.

"Out of proportion to what?"

"Well, to any other plunge." Yet he felt even as he spoke how at that instant he was plunging. He had made up his mind and was impatient to get into the air; for his purpose was a purpose to be uttered outside, and he had a fear that it might with delay still slip away from him. She however took her time; she drew out their quiet gossip as if she had wished to profit by their meeting, and this confirmed precisely an interpretation of her manner, of her mystery. While she rose, as he would have called it, to the question of Victor Hugo, her voice itself, the light low quaver of her deference to the solemnity about them, seemed to make her words mean something that they didn't mean openly. Help, strength, peace, a sublime support—she hadn't found so much of these things as that the amount wouldn't be sensibly greater for any scrap his appearance of faith in her might enable her to feel in her hand. Every little, in a long strain, helped, and if he happened to affect her as a firm object she could hold on by, he wouldn't jerk himself out of her reach. People in difficulties held on by what was nearest, and he was perhaps after all not further off than sources of comfort more abstract. It was as to this he had made up his mind; he had made it up, that is, to give her a sign. The sign would be that—though it was her own affair—he understood; the sign would be that—though it was her own affair—she was free to clutch. Since she took him for a firm object—much as he might to his own sense appear at times to rock—he would do his best to BE one.

The end of it was that half an hour later they were seated together for an early luncheon at a wonderful, a delightful house of entertainment on the left bank—a place of pilgrimage for the knowing, they were both aware, the knowing who came, for its great renown, the homage of restless days, from the other end of the town. Strether had already been there three times—first with Miss Gostrey, then with Chad, then with Chad again and with Waymarsh and little Bilham, all of whom he had himself sagaciously entertained; and his pleasure was deep now on learning that Madame de Vionnet hadn't yet been initiated. When he had said as they strolled round the church, by the river, acting at last on what, within, he had made up his mind to, "Will you, if you have time, come to dejeuner with me somewhere? For instance, if you know it, over there on the other side, which is so easy a walk"—and then had named the place; when he had done this she stopped short as for quick intensity, and yet deep difficulty, of response. She took in the proposal as if it were almost too charming to be true; and there had perhaps never yet been for her companion so unexpected a moment of pride—so fine, so odd a case, at any rate, as his finding himself thus able to offer to a person in such universal possession a new, a rare amusement. She had heard of the happy spot, but she asked him in reply to a further question how in the world he could suppose her to have been there. He supposed himself to have supposed that Chad might have taken her, and she guessed this the next moment to his no small discomfort.

"Ah, let me explain," she smiled, "that I don't go about with him in public; I never have such chances—not having them otherwise—and it's just the sort of thing that, as a quiet creature living in my hole, I adore." It was more than kind of him to have thought of it—though, frankly, if he asked whether she had time she hadn't a single minute. That however made no difference—she'd throw everything over. Every duty at home, domestic, maternal, social, awaited her; but it was a case for a high line. Her affairs would go to smash, but hadn't one a right to one's snatch of scandal when one was prepared to pay? It was on this pleasant basis of costly disorder, consequently, that they eventually seated themselves, on either side of a small table, at a window adjusted to the busy quay and the shining barge-burdened Seine; where, for an hour, in the matter of letting himself go, of diving deep, Strether was to feel he had touched bottom. He was to feel many things on this occasion, and one of the first of them was that he had travelled far since that evening in London, before the theatre, when his dinner with Maria Gostrey, between the pink-shaded candles, had struck him as requiring so many explanations. He had at that time gathered them in, the explanations—he had stored them up; but it was at present as if he had either soared above or sunk below them—he couldn't tell which; he could somehow think of none that didn't seem to leave the appearance of collapse and cynicism easier for him than lucidity. How could he wish it to be lucid for others, for any one, that he, for the hour, saw reasons enough in the mere way the bright clean ordered water-side life came in at the open window?—the mere way Madame de Vionnet, opposite him over their intensely white table-linen, their omelette aux tomates, their bottle of straw-coloured Chablis, thanked him for everything almost with the smile of a child, while her grey eyes moved in and out of their talk, back to the quarter of the warm spring air, in which early summer had already begun to throb, and then back again to his face and their human questions.

Their human questions became many before they had done—many more, as one after the other came up, than our friend's free fancy had at all foreseen. The sense he had had before, the sense he had had repeatedly, the sense that the situation was running away with him, had never been so sharp as now; and all the more that he could perfectly put his finger on the moment it had taken the bit in its teeth. That accident had definitely occurred, the other evening, after Chad's dinner; it had occurred, as he fully knew, at the moment when he interposed between this lady and her child, when he suffered himself to discuss with her a matter closely concerning them that her own subtlety, marked by its significant "Thank you!" instantly sealed the occasion in her favour. Again he had held off for ten days, but the situation had continued out of hand in spite of that; the fact that it was running so fast being indeed just WHY he had held off. What had come over him as he recognised her in the nave of the church was that holding off could be but a losing game from the instant she was worked for not only by her subtlety, but by the hand of fate itself. If all the accidents were to fight on her side—and by the actual showing they loomed large—he could only give himself up. This was what he had done in privately deciding then and there to propose she should breakfast with him. What did the success of his proposal in fact resemble but the smash in which a regular runaway properly ends? The smash was their walk, their dejeuner, their omelette, the Chablis, the place, the view, their present talk and his present pleasure in it—to say nothing, wonder of wonders, of her own. To this tune and nothing less, accordingly, was his surrender made good. It sufficiently lighted up at least the folly of holding off. Ancient proverbs sounded, for his memory, in the tone of their words and the clink of their glasses, in the hum of the town and the plash of the river. It WAS clearly better to suffer as a sheep than as a lamb. One might as well perish by the sword as by famine.

"Maria's still away?"—that was the first thing she had asked him; and when he had found the frankness to be cheerful about it in spite of the meaning he knew her to attach to Miss Gostrey's absence, she had gone on to enquire if he didn't tremendously miss her. There were reasons that made him by no means sure, yet he nevertheless answered "Tremendously"; which she took in as if it were all she had wished to prove. Then, "A man in trouble MUST be possessed somehow of a woman," she said; "if she doesn't come in one way she comes in another."

"Why do you call me a man in trouble?"

"Ah because that's the way you strike me." She spoke ever so gently and as if with all fear of wounding him while she sat partaking of his bounty. "AREn't you in trouble?"

He felt himself colour at the question, and then hated that—hated to pass for anything so idiotic as woundable. Woundable by Chad's lady, in respect to whom he had come out with such a fund of indifference—was he already at that point? Perversely, none the less, his pause gave a strange air of truth to her supposition; and what was he in fact but disconcerted at having struck her just in the way he had most dreamed of not doing? "I'm not in trouble yet," he at last smiled. "I'm not in trouble now."

"Well, I'm always so. But that you sufficiently know." She was a woman who, between courses, could be graceful with her elbows on the table. It was a posture unknown to Mrs. Newsome, but it was easy for a femme du monde. "Yes—I am 'now'!"

"There was a question you put to me," he presently returned, "the night of Chad's dinner. I didn't answer it then, and it has been very handsome of you not to have sought an occasion for pressing me about it since."

She was instantly all there. "Of course I know what you allude to. I asked you what you had meant by saying, the day you came to see me, just before you left me, that you'd save me. And you then said—at our friend's—that you'd have really to wait to see, for yourself, what you did mean."

"Yes, I asked for time," said Strether. "And it sounds now, as you put it, like a very ridiculous speech."

"Oh!" she murmured—she was full of attenuation. But she had another thought. "If it does sound ridiculous why do you deny that you're in trouble?"

"Ah if I were," he replied, "it wouldn't be the trouble of fearing ridicule. I don't fear it."

"What then do you?"

"Nothing—now." And he leaned back in his chair.

"I like your 'now'!" she laughed across at him.

"Well, it's precisely that it fully comes to me at present that I've kept you long enough. I know by this time, at any rate, what I meant by my speech; and I really knew it the night of Chad's dinner."

"Then why didn't you tell me?"

"Because it was difficult at the moment. I had already at that moment done something for you, in the sense of what I had said the day I went to see you; but I wasn't then sure of the importance I might represent this as having."

She was all eagerness. "And you're sure now?"

"Yes; I see that, practically, I've done for you—had done for you when you put me your question—all that it's as yet possible to me to do. I feel now," he went on, "that it may go further than I thought. What I did after my visit to you," he explained, "was to write straight off to Mrs. Newsome about you, and I'm at last, from one day to the other, expecting her answer. It's this answer that will represent, as I believe, the consequences."

Patient and beautiful was her interest. "I see—the consequences of your speaking for me." And she waited as if not to hustle him.

He acknowledged it by immediately going on. "The question, you understand, was HOW I should save you. Well, I'm trying it by thus letting her know that I consider you worth saving."

"I see—I see." Her eagerness broke through.

"How can I thank you enough?" He couldn't tell her that, however, and she quickly pursued. "You do really, for yourself, consider it?" His only answer at first was to help her to the dish that had been freshly put before them. "I've written to her again since then—I've left her in no doubt of what I think. I've told her all about you."

"Thanks—not so much. 'All about' me," she went on—"yes."

"All it seems to me you've done for him."

"Ah and you might have added all it seems to ME!" She laughed again, while she took up her knife and fork, as in the cheer of these assurances. "But you're not sure how she'll take it."

"No, I'll not pretend I'm sure."

"Voila." And she waited a moment. "I wish you'd tell me about her."

"Oh," said Strether with a slightly strained smile, "all that need concern you about her is that she's really a grand person."

Madame de Vionnet seemed to demur. "Is that all that need concern me about her?"

But Strether neglected the question. "Hasn't Chad talked to you?"

"Of his mother? Yes, a great deal—immensely. But not from your point of view."

"He can't," our friend returned, "have said any ill of her."

"Not the least bit. He has given me, like you, the assurance that she's really grand. But her being really grand is somehow just what hasn't seemed to simplify our case. Nothing," she continued, "is further from me than to wish to say a word against her; but of course I feel how little she can like being told of her owing me anything. No woman ever enjoys such an obligation to another woman."

This was a proposition Strether couldn't contradict. "And yet what other way could I have expressed to her what I felt? It's what there was most to say about you."

"Do you mean then that she WILL be good to me?"

"It's what I'm waiting to see. But I've little doubt she would," he added, "if she could comfortably see you."

It seemed to strike her as a happy, a beneficent thought. "Oh then couldn't that be managed? Wouldn't she come out? Wouldn't she if you so put it to her? DID you by any possibility?" she faintly quavered.

"Oh no"—he was prompt. "Not that. It would be, much more, to give an account of you that—since there's no question of YOUR paying the visit—I should go home first."

It instantly made her graver. "And are you thinking of that?"

"Oh all the while, naturally."

"Stay with us—stay with us!" she exclaimed on this. "That's your only way to make sure."

"To make sure of what?"

"Why that he doesn't break up. You didn't come out to do that to him."

"Doesn't it depend," Strether returned after a moment, "on what you mean by breaking up?"

"Oh you know well enough what I mean!"

His silence seemed again for a little to denote an understanding. "You take for granted remarkable things."

"Yes, I do—to the extent that I don't take for granted vulgar ones. You're perfectly capable of seeing that what you came out for wasn't really at all to do what you'd now have to do."

"Ah it's perfectly simple," Strether good-humouredly pleaded. "I've had but one thing to do—to put our case before him. To put it as it could only be put here on the spot—by personal pressure. My dear lady," he lucidly pursued, "my work, you see, is really done, and my reasons for staying on even another day are none of the best. Chad's in possession of our case and professes to do it full justice. What remains is with himself. I've had my rest, my amusement and refreshment; I've had, as we say at Woollett, a lovely time. Nothing in it has been more lovely than this happy meeting with you—in these fantastic conditions to which you've so delightfully consented. I've a sense of success. It's what I wanted. My getting all this good is what Chad has waited for, and I gather that if I'm ready to go he's the same."

She shook her head with a finer deeper wisdom. "You're not ready. If you're ready why did you write to Mrs. Newsome in the sense you've mentioned to me?"

Strether considered. "I shan't go before I hear from her. You're too much afraid of her," he added.

It produced between them a long look from which neither shrank. "I don't think you believe that—believe I've not really reason to fear her."

"She's capable of great generosity," Strether presently stated.

"Well then let her trust me a little. That's all I ask. Let her recognise in spite of everything what I've done."

"Ah remember," our friend replied, "that she can't effectually recognise it without seeing it for herself. Let Chad go over and show her what you've done, and let him plead with her there for it and, as it were, for YOU."

She measured the depth of this suggestion. "Do you give me your word of honour that if she once has him there she won't do her best to marry him?"

It made her companion, this enquiry, look again a while out at the view; after which he spoke without sharpness. "When she sees for herself what he is—"

But she had already broken in. "It's when she sees for herself what he is that she'll want to marry him most."

Strether's attitude, that of due deference to what she said, permitted him to attend for a minute to his luncheon. "I doubt if that will come off. It won't be easy to make it."

"It will be easy if he remains there—and he'll remain for the money. The money appears to be, as a probability, so hideously much."

"Well," Strether presently concluded, "nothing COULD really hurt you but his marrying."

She gave a strange light laugh. "Putting aside what may really hurt HIM."

But her friend looked at her as if he had thought of that too. "The question will come up, of course, of the future that you yourself offer him."

She was leaning back now, but she fully faced him. "Well, let it come up!"

"The point is that it's for Chad to make of it what he can. His being proof against marriage will show what he does make."

"If he IS proof, yes"—she accepted the proposition. "But for myself," she added, "the question is what YOU make."

"Ah I make nothing. It's not my affair."

"I beg your pardon. It's just there that, since you've taken it up and are committed to it, it most intensely becomes yours. You're not saving me, I take it, for your interest in myself, but for your interest in our friend. The one's at any rate wholly dependent on the other. You can't in honour not see me through," she wound up, "because you can't in honour not see HIM."

Strange and beautiful to him was her quiet soft acuteness. The thing that most moved him was really that she was so deeply serious. She had none of the portentous forms of it, but he had never come in contact, it struck him, with a force brought to so fine a head. Mrs. Newsome, goodness knew, was serious; but it was nothing to this. He took it all in, he saw it all together. "No," he mused, "I can't in honour not see him."

Her face affected him as with an exquisite light. "You WILL then?"

"I will."

At this she pushed back her chair and was the next moment on her feet. "Thank you!" she said with her hand held out to him across the table and with no less a meaning in the words than her lips had so particularly given them after Chad's dinner. The golden nail she had then driven in pierced a good inch deeper. Yet he reflected that he himself had only meanwhile done what he had made up his mind to on the same occasion. So far as the essence of the matter went he had simply stood fast on the spot on which he had then planted his feet.

II

He received three days after this a communication from America, in the form of a scrap of blue paper folded and gummed, not reaching him through his bankers, but delivered at his hotel by a small boy in uniform, who, under instructions from the concierge, approached him as he slowly paced the little court. It was the evening hour, but daylight was long now and Paris more than ever penetrating. The scent of flowers was in the streets, he had the whiff of violets perpetually in his nose; and he had attached himself to sounds and suggestions, vibrations of the air, human and dramatic, he imagined, as they were not in other places, that came out for him more and more as the mild afternoons deepened—a far-off hum, a sharp near click on the asphalt, a voice calling, replying, somewhere and as full of tone as an actor's in a play. He was to dine at home, as usual, with Waymarsh—they had settled to that for thrift and simplicity; and he now hung about before his friend came down.

He read his telegram in the court, standing still a long time where he had opened it and giving five minutes afterwards to the renewed study of it. At last, quickly, he crumpled it up as if to get it out of the way; in spite of which, however, he kept it there—still kept it when, at the end of another turn, he had dropped into a chair placed near a small table. Here, with his scrap of paper compressed in his fist and further concealed by his folding his arms tight, he sat for some time in thought, gazed before him so straight that Waymarsh appeared and approached him without catching his eye. The latter in fact, struck with his appearance, looked at him hard for a single instant and then, as if determined to that course by some special vividness in it, dropped back into the salon de lecture without addressing him. But the pilgrim from Milrose permitted himself still to observe the scene from behind the clear glass plate of that retreat. Strether ended, as he sat, by a fresh scrutiny of his compressed missive, which he smoothed out carefully again as he placed it on his table. There it remained for some minutes, until, at last looking up, he saw Waymarsh watching him from within. It was on this that their eyes met—met for a moment during which neither moved. But Strether then got up, folding his telegram more carefully and putting it into his waistcoat pocket.

A few minutes later the friends were seated together at dinner; but Strether had meanwhile said nothing about it, and they eventually parted, after coffee in the court, with nothing said on either side. Our friend had moreover the consciousness that even less than usual was on this occasion said between them, so that it was almost as if each had been waiting for something from the other. Waymarsh had always more or less the air of sitting at the door of his tent, and silence, after so many weeks, had come to play its part in their concert. This note indeed, to Strether's sense, had lately taken a fuller tone, and it was his fancy to-night that they had never quite so drawn it out. Yet it befell, none the less that he closed the door to confidence when his companion finally asked him if there were anything particular the matter with him. "Nothing," he replied, "more than usual."

On the morrow, however, at an early hour, he found occasion to give an answer more in consonance with the facts. What was the matter had continued to be so all the previous evening, the first hours of which, after dinner, in his room, he had devoted to the copious composition of a letter. He had quitted Waymarsh for this purpose, leaving him to his own resources with less ceremony than their wont, but finally coming down again with his letter unconcluded and going forth into the streets without enquiry for his comrade. He had taken a long vague walk, and one o'clock had struck before his return and his re-ascent to his room by the aid of the glimmering candle-end left for him on the shelf outside the porter's lodge. He had possessed himself, on closing his door, of the numerous loose sheets of his unfinished composition, and then, without reading them over, had torn them into small pieces. He had thereupon slept—as if it had been in some measure thanks to that sacrifice—the sleep of the just, and had prolonged his rest considerably beyond his custom. Thus it was that when, between nine and ten, the tap of the knob of a walking-stick sounded on his door, he had not yet made himself altogether presentable. Chad Newsome's bright deep voice determined quickly enough none the less the admission of the visitor. The little blue paper of the evening before, plainly an object the more precious for its escape from premature destruction, now lay on the sill of the open window, smoothed out afresh and kept from blowing away by the superincumbent weight of his watch. Chad, looking about with careless and competent criticism, as he looked about immediately espied it and permitted himself to fix it for a moment rather hard. After which he turned his eyes to his host. "It has come then at last?"

Strether paused in the act of pinning his necktie. "Then you know—? You've had one too?"

"No, I've had nothing, and I only know what I see. I see that thing and I guess. Well," he added, "it comes as pat as in a play, for I've precisely turned up this morning—as I would have done yesterday, but it was impossible—to take you."

"To take me?" Strether had turned again to his glass.

"Back, at last, as I promised. I'm ready—I've really been ready this month. I've only been waiting for you—as was perfectly right. But you're better now; you're safe—I see that for myself; you've got all your good. You're looking, this morning, as fit as a flea."

Strether, at his glass, finished dressing; consulting that witness moreover on this last opinion. WAS he looking preternaturally fit? There was something in it perhaps for Chad's wonderful eye, but he had felt himself for hours rather in pieces. Such a judgement, however, was after all but a contribution to his resolve; it testified unwittingly to his wisdom. He was still firmer, apparently—since it shone in him as a light—than he had flattered himself. His firmness indeed was slightly compromised, as he faced about to his friend, by the way this very personage looked—though the case would of course have been worse hadn't the secret of personal magnificence been at every hour Chad's unfailing possession. There he was in all the pleasant morning freshness of it—strong and sleek and gay, easy and fragrant and fathomless, with happy health in his colour, and pleasant silver in his thick young hair, and the right word for everything on the lips that his clear brownness caused to show as red. He had never struck Strether as personally such a success; it was as if now, for his definite surrender, he had gathered himself vividly together. This, sharply and rather strangely, was the form in which he was to be presented to Woollett. Our friend took him in again—he was always taking him in and yet finding that parts of him still remained out; though even thus his image showed through a mist of other things. "I've had a cable," Strether said, "from your mother."

"I dare say, my dear man. I hope she's well."

Strether hesitated. "No—she's not well, I'm sorry to have to tell you."

"Ah," said Chad, "I must have had the instinct of it. All the more reason then that we should start straight off."

Strether had now got together hat, gloves and stick, but Chad had dropped on the sofa as if to show where he wished to make his point. He kept observing his companion's things; he might have been judging how quickly they could be packed. He might even have wished to hint that he'd send his own servant to assist. "What do you mean," Strether enquired, "by 'straight off'?"

"Oh by one of next week's boats. Everything at this season goes out so light that berths will be easy anywhere."

Strether had in his hand his telegram, which he had kept there after attaching his watch, and he now offered it to Chad, who, however, with an odd movement, declined to take it. "Thanks, I'd rather not. Your correspondence with Mother's your own affair. I'm only WITH you both on it, whatever it is." Strether, at this, while their eyes met, slowly folded the missive and put it in his pocket; after which, before he had spoken again, Chad broke fresh ground. "Has Miss Gostrey come back?"

But when Strether presently spoke it wasn't in answer. "It's not, I gather, that your mother's physically ill; her health, on the whole, this spring, seems to have been better than usual. But she's worried, she's anxious, and it appears to have risen within the last few days to a climax. We've tired out, between us, her patience."

"Oh it isn't YOU!" Chad generously protested.

"I beg your pardon—it IS me." Strether was mild and melancholy, but firm. He saw it far away and over his companion's head. "It's very particularly me."

"Well then all the more reason. Marchons, marchons!" said the young man gaily. His host, however, at this, but continued to stand agaze; and he had the next thing repeated his question of a moment before. "Has Miss Gostrey come back?"

"Yes, two days ago."

"Then you've seen her?"

"No—I'm to see her to-day." But Strether wouldn't linger now on Miss Gostrey. "Your mother sends me an ultimatum. If I can't bring you I'm to leave you; I'm to come at any rate myself."

"Ah but you CAN bring me now," Chad, from his sofa, reassuringly replied.

Strether had a pause. "I don't think I understand you. Why was it that, more than a month ago, you put it to me so urgently to let Madame de Vionnet speak for you?"

"'Why'?" Chad considered, but he had it at his fingers' ends. "Why but because I knew how well she'd do it? It was the way to keep you quiet and, to that extent, do you good. Besides," he happily and comfortably explained, "I wanted you really to know her and to get the impression of her—and you see the good that HAS done you."

"Well," said Strether, "the way she has spoken for you, all the same—so far as I've given her a chance—has only made me feel how much she wishes to keep you. If you make nothing of that I don't see why you wanted me to listen to her."

"Why my dear man," Chad exclaimed, "I make everything of it! How can you doubt—?"

"I doubt only because you come to me this morning with your signal to start."

Chad stared, then gave a laugh. "And isn't my signal to start just what you've been waiting for?"

Strether debated; he took another turn. "This last month I've been awaiting, I think, more than anything else, the message I have here."

"You mean you've been afraid of it?"

"Well, I was doing my business in my own way. And I suppose your present announcement," Strether went on, "isn't merely the result of your sense of what I've expected. Otherwise you wouldn't have put me in relation—" But he paused, pulling up.

At this Chad rose. "Ah HER wanting me not to go has nothing to do with it! It's only because she's afraid—afraid of the way that, over there, I may get caught. But her fear's groundless."

He had met again his companion's sufficiently searching look. "Are you tired of her?"

Chad gave him in reply to this, with a movement of the head, the strangest slow smile he had ever had from him. "Never."

It had immediately, on Strether's imagination, so deep and soft an effect that our friend could only for the moment keep it before him. "Never?"

"Never," Chad obligingly and serenely repeated.

It made his companion take several more steps. "Then YOU'RE not afraid."

"Afraid to go?"

Strether pulled up again. "Afraid to stay."

The young man looked brightly amazed. "You want me now to 'stay'?"

"If I don't immediately sail the Pococks will immediately come out. That's what I mean," said Strether, "by your mother's ultimatum ."

Chad showed a still livelier, but not an alarmed interest. "She has turned on Sarah and Jim?"

Strether joined him for an instant in the vision. "Oh and you may be sure Mamie. THAT'S whom she's turning on."

This also Chad saw—he laughed out. "Mamie—to corrupt me?"

"Ah," said Strether, "she's very charming."

"So you've already more than once told me. I should like to see her."

Something happy and easy, something above all unconscious, in the way he said this, brought home again to his companion the facility of his attitude and the enviability of his state. "See her then by all means. And consider too," Strether went on, "that you really give your sister a lift in letting her come to you. You give her a couple of months of Paris, which she hasn't seen, if I'm not mistaken, since just after she was married, and which I'm sure she wants but the pretext to visit."

Chad listened, but with all his own knowledge of the world. "She has had it, the pretext, these several years, yet she has never taken it."

"Do you mean YOU?" Strether after an instant enquired.

"Certainly—the lone exile. And whom do you mean?" said Chad.

"Oh I mean ME. I'm her pretext. That is—for it comes to the same thing—I'm your mother's."

"Then why," Chad asked, "doesn't Mother come herself?"

His friend gave him a long look. "Should you like her to?" And as he for the moment said nothing: "It's perfectly open to you to cable for her."

Chad continued to think. "Will she come if I do?"

"Quite possibly. But try, and you'll see."

"Why don't YOU try?" Chad after a moment asked.

"Because I don't want to."

Chad thought. "Don't desire her presence here?"

Strether faced the question, and his answer was the more emphatic. "Don't put it off, my dear boy, on ME!"

"Well—I see what you mean. I'm sure you'd behave beautifully but you DON'T want to see her. So I won't play you that trick.'

"Ah," Strether declared, "I shouldn't call it a trick. You've a perfect right, and it would be perfectly straight of you." Then he added in a different tone: "You'd have moreover, in the person of Madame de Vionnet, a very interesting relation prepared for her."

Their eyes, on this proposition, continued to meet, but Chad's pleasant and bold, never flinched for a moment. He got up at last and he said something with which Strether was struck. "She wouldn't understand her, but that makes no difference. Madame de Vionnet would like to see her. She'd like to be charming to her. She believes she could work it."

Strether thought a moment, affected by this, but finally turning away. "She couldn't!"

"You're quite sure?" Chad asked.

"Well, risk it if you like!"

Strether, who uttered this with serenity, had urged a plea for their now getting into the air; but the young man still waited. "Have you sent your answer?"

"No, I've done nothing yet."

"Were you waiting to see me?"

"No, not that."

"Only waiting"—and Chad, with this, had a smile for him—"to see Miss Gostrey?"

"No—not even Miss Gostrey. I wasn't waiting to see any one. I had only waited, till now, to make up my mind—in complete solitude; and, since I of course absolutely owe you the information, was on the point of going out with it quite made up. Have therefore a little more patience with me. Remember," Strether went on, "that that's what you originally asked ME to have. I've had it, you see, and you see what has come of it. Stay on with me."

Chad looked grave. "How much longer?"

"Well, till I make you a sign. I can't myself, you know, at the best, or at the worst, stay for ever. Let the Pococks come," Strether repeated.

"Because it gains you time?"

"Yes—it gains me time."

Chad, as if it still puzzled him, waited a minute. "You don't want to get back to Mother?"

"Not just yet. I'm not ready."

"You feel," Chad asked in a tone of his own, "the charm of life over here?"

"Immensely." Strether faced it. "You've helped me so feel it that that surely needn't surprise you."

"No, it doesn't surprise me, and I'm delighted. But what, my dear man," Chad went on with conscious queerness, "does it all lead to for you?"

The change of position and of relation, for each, was so oddly betrayed in the question that Chad laughed out as soon as he had uttered it—which made Strether also laugh. "Well, to my having a certitude that has been tested—that has passed through the fire. But oh," he couldn't help breaking out, "if within my first month here you had been willing to move with me—!"

"Well?" said Chad, while he broke down as for weight of thought.

"Well, we should have been over there by now."

"Ah but you wouldn't have had your fun!"

"I should have had a month of it; and I'm having now, if you want to know," Strether continued, "enough to last me for the rest of my days."

Chad looked amused and interested, yet still somewhat in the dark; partly perhaps because Strether's estimate of fun had required of him from the first a good deal of elucidation. "It wouldn't do if I left you—?"

"Left me?"—Strether remained blank.

"Only for a month or two—time to go and come. Madame de Vionnet," Chad smiled, "would look after you in the interval."

"To go back by yourself, I remaining here?" Again for an instant their eyes had the question out; after which Strether said: "Grotesque!"

"But I want to see Mother," Chad presently returned. "Remember how long it is since I've seen Mother."

"Long indeed; and that's exactly why I was originally so keen for moving you. Hadn't you shown us enough how beautifully you could do without it?"

"Oh but," said Chad wonderfully, "I'm better now."

There was an easy triumph in it that made his friend laugh out again. "Oh if you were worse I SHOULD know what to do with you. In that case I believe I'd have you gagged and strapped down, carried on board resisting, kicking. How MUCH," Strether asked, "do you want to see Mother?"

"How much?"—Chad seemed to find it in fact difficult to say.

"How much."

"Why as much as you've made me. I'd give anything to see her. And you've left me," Chad went on, "in little enough doubt as to how much SHE wants it."

Strether thought a minute. "Well then if those things are really your motive catch the French steamer and sail to-morrow. Of course, when it comes to that, you're absolutely free to do as you choose. From the moment you can't hold yourself I can only accept your flight."

"I'll fly in a minute then," said Chad, "if you'll stay here."

"I'll stay here till the next steamer—then I'll follow you."

"And do you call that," Chad asked, "accepting my flight?"

"Certainly—it's the only thing to call it. The only way to keep me here, accordingly," Strether explained, "is by staying yourself."

Chad took it in. "All the more that I've really dished you, eh?"

"Dished me?" Strether echoed as inexpressively as possible.

"Why if she sends out the Pococks it will be that she doesn't trust you, and if she doesn't trust you, that bears upon—well, you know what."

Strether decided after a moment that he did know what, and in consonance with this he spoke. "You see then all the more what you owe me."

"Well, if I do see, how can I pay?"

"By not deserting me. By standing by me."

"Oh I say—!" But Chad, as they went downstairs, clapped a firm hand, in the manner of a pledge, upon his shoulder. They descended slowly together and had, in the court of the hotel, some further talk, of which the upshot was that they presently separated. Chad Newsome departed, and Strether, left alone, looked about, superficially, for Waymarsh. But Waymarsh hadn't yet, it appeared, come down, and our friend finally went forth without sight of him.

III

At four o'clock that afternoon he had still not seen him, but he was then, as to make up for this, engaged in talk about him with Miss Gostrey. Strether had kept away from home all day, given himself up to the town and to his thoughts, wandered and mused, been at once restless and absorbed—and all with the present climax of a rich little welcome in the Quartier Marboeuf. "Waymarsh has been, 'unbeknown' to me, I'm convinced"—for Miss Gostrey had enquired—"in communication with Woollett: the consequence of which was, last night, the loudest possible call for me."

"Do you mean a letter to bring you home?"

"No—a cable, which I have at this moment in my pocket: a 'Come back by the first ship.'"

Strether's hostess, it might have been made out, just escaped changing colour. Reflexion arrived but in time and established a provisional serenity. It was perhaps exactly this that enabled her to say with duplicity: "And you're going—?"

"You almost deserve it when you abandon me so."

She shook her head as if this were not worth taking up. "My absence has helped you—as I've only to look at you to see. It was my calculation, and I'm justified. You're not where you were. And the thing," she smiled, "was for me not to be there either. You can go of yourself."

"Oh but I feel to-day," he comfortably declared, "that I shall want you yet."

She took him all in again. "Well, I promise you not again to leave you, but it will only be to follow you. You've got your momentum and can toddle alone."

He intelligently accepted it. "Yes—I suppose I can toddle. It's the sight of that in fact that has upset Waymarsh. He can bear it—the way I strike him as going—no longer. That's only the climax of his original feeling. He wants me to quit; and he must have written to Woollett that I'm in peril of perdition."

"Ah good!" she murmured. "But is it only your supposition?"

"I make it out—it explains."

"Then he denies?—or you haven't asked him?"

"I've not had time," Strether said; "I made it out but last night, putting various things together, and I've not been since then face to face with him."

She wondered. "Because you're too disgusted? You can't trust yourself?"

He settled his glasses on his nose. "Do I look in a great rage?"

"You look divine!"

"There's nothing," he went on, "to be angry about. He has done me on the contrary a service."

She made it out. "By bringing things to a head?"

"How well you understand!" he almost groaned. "Waymarsh won't in the least, at any rate, when I have it out with him, deny or extenuate. He has acted from the deepest conviction, with the best conscience and after wakeful nights. He'll recognise that he's fully responsible, and will consider that he has been highly successful; so that any discussion we may have will bring us quite together again—bridge the dark stream that has kept us so thoroughly apart. We shall have at last, in the consequences of his act, something we can definitely talk about."

She was silent a little. "How wonderfully you take it! But you're always wonderful."

He had a pause that matched her own; then he had, with an adequate spirit, a complete admission. "It's quite true. I'm extremely wonderful just now. I dare say in fact I'm quite fantastic, and I shouldn't be at all surprised if I were mad."

"Then tell me!" she earnestly pressed. As he, however, for the time answered nothing, only returning the look with which she watched him, she presented herself where it was easier to meet her. "What will Mr. Waymarsh exactly have done?"

"Simply have written a letter. One will have been quite enough. He has told them I want looking after."

"And DO you?"—she was all interest.

"Immensely. And I shall get it."

"By which you mean you don't budge?"

"I don't budge."

"You've cabled?"

"No—I've made Chad do it."

"That you decline to come?"

"That HE declines. We had it out this morning and I brought him round. He had come in, before I was down, to tell me he was ready—ready, I mean, to return. And he went off, after ten minutes with me, to say he wouldn't."

Miss Gostrey followed with intensity. "Then you've STOPPED him?"

Strether settled himself afresh in his chair. "I've stopped him. That is for the time. That"—he gave it to her more vividly—"is where I am."

"I see, I see. But where's Mr. Newsome? He was ready," she asked, "to go?"

"All ready."

"And sincerely—believing YOU'D be?"

"Perfectly, I think; so that he was amazed to find the hand I had laid on him to pull him over suddenly converted into an engine for keeping him still."

It was an account of the matter Miss Gostrey could weigh. "Does he think the conversion sudden?"

"Well," said Strether, "I'm not altogether sure what he thinks. I'm not sure of anything that concerns him, except that the more I've seen of him the less I've found him what I originally expected. He's obscure, and that's why I'm waiting."

She wondered. "But for what in particular?"

"For the answer to his cable."

"And what was his cable?"

"I don't know," Strether replied; "it was to be, when he left me, according to his own taste. I simply said to him: 'I want to stay, and the only way for me to do so is for you to.' That I wanted to stay seemed to interest him, and he acted on that."

Miss Gostrey turned it over. "He wants then himself to stay."

"He half wants it. That is he half wants to go. My original appeal has to that extent worked in him. Nevertheless," Strether pursued, "he won't go. Not, at least, so long as I'm here."

"But you can't," his companion suggested, "stay here always. I wish you could."

"By no means. Still, I want to see him a little further. He's not in the least the case I supposed, he's quite another case. And it's as such that he interests me." It was almost as if for his own intelligence that, deliberate and lucid, our friend thus expressed the matter. "I don't want to give him up."

Miss Gostrey but desired to help his lucidity. She had however to be light and tactful. "Up, you mean—a—to his mother?"

"Well, I'm not thinking of his mother now. I'm thinking of the plan of which I was the mouthpiece, which, as soon as we met, I put before him as persuasively as I knew how, and which was drawn up, as it were, in complete ignorance of all that, in this last long period, has been happening to him. It took no account whatever of the impression I was here on the spot immediately to begin to receive from him—impressions of which I feel sure I'm far from having had the last."

Miss Gostrey had a smile of the most genial criticism. "So your idea is—more or less—to stay out of curiosity?"

"Call it what you like! I don't care what it's called—"

"So long as you do stay? Certainly not then. I call it, all the same, immense fun," Maria Gostrey declared; "and to see you work it out will be one of the sensations of my life. It IS clear you can toddle alone!"

He received this tribute without elation. "I shan't be alone when the Pococks have come."

Her eyebrows went up. "The Pococks are coming?"

"That, I mean, is what will happen—and happen as quickly as possible—in consequence of Chad's cable. They'll simply embark. Sarah will come to speak for her mother—with an effect different from MY muddle."

Miss Gostrey more gravely wondered. "SHE then will take him back?"

"Very possibly—and we shall see. She must at any rate have the chance, and she may be trusted to do all she can."

"And do you WANT that?"

"Of course," said Strether, "I want it. I want to play fair."

But she had lost for a moment the thread. "If it devolves on the Pococks why do you stay?"

"Just to see that I DO play fair—and a little also, no doubt, that they do." Strether was luminous as he had never been. "I came out to find myself in presence of new facts—facts that have kept striking me as less and less met by our old reasons. The matter's perfectly simple. New reasons—reasons as new as the facts themselves—are wanted; and of this our friends at Woollett—Chad's and mine—were at the earliest moment definitely notified. If any are producible Mrs. Pocock will produce them; she'll bring over the whole collection. They'll be," he added with a pensive smile "a part of the 'fun' you speak of."

She was quite in the current now and floating by his side. "It's Mamie—so far as I've had it from you—who'll be their great card." And then as his contemplative silence wasn't a denial she significantly added: "I think I'm sorry for her."

"I think I am!"—and Strether sprang up, moving about a little as her eyes followed him. "But it can't be helped."

"You mean her coming out can't be?"

He explained after another turn what he meant. "The only way for her not to come is for me to go home—as I believe that on the spot I could prevent it. But the difficulty as to that is that if I do go home—"

"I see, I see"—she had easily understood. "Mr. Newsome will do the same, and that's not"—she laughed out now—"to be thought of."

Strether had no laugh; he had only a quiet comparatively placid look that might have shown him as proof against ridicule. "Strange, isn't it?"

They had, in the matter that so much interested them, come so far as this without sounding another name—to which however their present momentary silence was full of a conscious reference. Strether's question was a sufficient implication of the weight it had gained with him during the absence of his hostess; and just for that reason a single gesture from her could pass for him as a vivid answer. Yet he was answered still better when she said in a moment: "Will Mr. Newsome introduce his sister—?"

"To Madame de Vionnet?" Strether spoke the name at last. "I shall be greatly surprised if he doesn't."

She seemed to gaze at the possibility. "You mean you've thought of it and you're prepared."

"I've thought of it and I'm prepared."

It was to her visitor now that she applied her consideration. "Bon! You ARE magnificent!"

"Well," he answered after a pause and a little wearily, but still standing there before her—"well, that's what, just once in all my dull days, I think I shall like to have been!"

Two days later he had news from Chad of a communication from Woollett in response to their determinant telegram, this missive being addressed to Chad himself and announcing the immediate departure for France of Sarah and Jim and Mamie. Strether had meanwhile on his own side cabled; he had but delayed that act till after his visit to Miss Gostrey, an interview by which, as so often before, he felt his sense of things cleared up and settled. His message to Mrs. Newsome, in answer to her own, had consisted of the words: "Judge best to take another month, but with full appreciation of all re-enforcements." He had added that he was writing, but he was of course always writing; it was a practice that continued, oddly enough, to relieve him, to make him come nearer than anything else to the consciousness of doing something: so that he often wondered if he hadn't really, under his recent stress, acquired some hollow trick, one of the specious arts of make-believe. Wouldn't the pages he still so freely dispatched by the American post have been worthy of a showy journalist, some master of the great new science of beating the sense out of words? Wasn't he writing against time, and mainly to show he was kind?—since it had become quite his habit not to like to read himself over. On those lines he could still be liberal, yet it was at best a sort of whistling in the dark. It was unmistakeable moreover that the sense of being in the dark now pressed on him more sharply—creating thereby the need for a louder and livelier whistle. He whistled long and hard after sending his message; he whistled again and again in celebration of Chad's news; there was an interval of a fortnight in which this exercise helped him. He had no great notion of what, on the spot, Sarah Pocock would have to say, though he had indeed confused premonitions; but it shouldn't be in her power to say—it shouldn't be in any one's anywhere to say—that he was neglecting his mother. He might have written before more freely, but he had never written more copiously; and he frankly gave for a reason at Woollett that he wished to fill the void created there by Sarah's departure.

The increase of his darkness, however, and the quickening, as I have called it, of his tune, resided in the fact that he was hearing almost nothing. He had for some time been aware that he was hearing less than before, and he was now clearly following a process by which Mrs. Newsome's letters could but logically stop. He hadn't had a line for many days, and he needed no proof—though he was, in time, to have plenty—that she wouldn't have put pen to paper after receiving the hint that had determined her telegram. She wouldn't write till Sarah should have seen him and reported on him. It was strange, though it might well be less so than his own behaviour appeared at Woollett. It was at any rate significant, and what WAS remarkable was the way his friend's nature and manner put on for him, through this very drop of demonstration, a greater intensity. It struck him really that he had never so lived with her as during this period of her silence; the silence was a sacred hush, a finer clearer medium, in which her idiosyncrasies showed. He walked about with her, sat with her, drove with her and dined face-to-face with her—a rare treat "in his life," as he could perhaps have scarce escaped phrasing it; and if he had never seen her so soundless he had never, on the other hand, felt her so highly, so almost austerely, herself: pure and by the vulgar estimate "cold," but deep devoted delicate sensitive noble. Her vividness in these respects became for him, in the special conditions, almost an obsession; and though the obsession sharpened his pulses, adding really to the excitement of life, there were hours at which, to be less on the stretch, he directly sought forgetfulness. He knew it for the queerest of adventures—a circumstance capable of playing such a part only for Lambert Strether—that in Paris itself, of all places, he should find this ghost of the lady of Woollett more importunate than any other presence.

When he went back to Maria Gostrey it was for the change to something else. And yet after all the change scarcely operated for he talked to her of Mrs. Newsome in these days as he had never talked before. He had hitherto observed in that particular a discretion and a law; considerations that at present broke down quite as if relations had altered. They hadn't REALLY altered, he said to himself, so much as that came to; for if what had occurred was of course that Mrs. Newsome had ceased to trust him, there was nothing on the other hand to prove that he shouldn't win back her confidence. It was quite his present theory that he would leave no stone unturned to do so; and in fact if he now told Maria things about her that he had never told before this was largely because it kept before him the idea of the honour of such a woman's esteem. His relation with Maria as well was, strangely enough, no longer quite the same; this truth—though not too disconcertingly—had come up between them on the renewal of their meetings. It was all contained in what she had then almost immediately said to him; it was represented by the remark she had needed but ten minutes to make and that he hadn't been disposed to gainsay. He could toddle alone, and the difference that showed was extraordinary. The turn taken by their talk had promptly confirmed this difference; his larger confidence on the score of Mrs. Newsome did the rest; and the time seemed already far off when he had held out his small thirsty cup to the spout of her pail. Her pail was scarce touched now, and other fountains had flowed for him; she fell into her place as but one of his tributaries; and there was a strange sweetness—a melancholy mildness that touched him—in her acceptance of the altered order.

It marked for himself the flight of time, or at any rate what he was pleased to think of with irony and pity as the rush of experience; it having been but the day before yesterday that he sat at her feet and held on by her garment and was fed by her hand. It was the proportions that were changed, and the proportions were at all times, he philosophised, the very conditions of perception, the terms of thought. It was as if, with her effective little entresol and and her wide acquaintance, her activities, varieties, promiscuities, the duties and devotions that took up nine tenths of her time and of which he got, guardedly, but the side-wind—it was as if she had shrunk to a secondary element and had consented to the shrinkage with the perfection of tact. This perfection had never failed her; it had originally been greater than his prime measure for it; it had kept him quite apart, kept him out of the shop, as she called her huge general acquaintance, made their commerce as quiet, as much a thing of the home alone—the opposite of the shop—as if she had never another customer. She had been wonderful to him at first, with the memory of her little entresol, the image to which, on most mornings at that time, his eyes directly opened; but now she mainly figured for him as but part of the bristling total—though of course always as a person to whom he should never cease to be indebted. It would never be given to him certainly to inspire a greater kindness. She had decked him out for others, and he saw at this point at least nothing she would ever ask for. She only wondered and questioned and listened, rendering him the homage of a wistful speculation. She expressed it repeatedly; he was already far beyond her, and she must prepare herself to lose him. There was but one little chance for her.

Often as she had said it he met it—for it was a touch he liked—each time the same way. "My coming to grief?"

"Yes—then I might patch you up."

"Oh for my real smash, if it takes place, there will be no patching."

"But you surely don't mean it will kill you."

"No—worse. It will make me old."

"Ah nothing can do that! The wonderful and special thing about you is that you ARE, at this time of day, youth." Then she always made, further, one of those remarks that she had completely ceased to adorn with hesitations or apologies, and that had, by the same token, in spite of their extreme straightness, ceased to produce in Strether the least embarrassment. She made him believe them, and they became thereby as impersonal as truth itself. "It's just your particular charm."

His answer too was always the same. "Of course I'm youth—youth for the trip to Europe. I began to be young, or at least to get the benefit of it, the moment I met you at Chester, and that's what has been taking place ever since. I never had the benefit at the proper time—which comes to saying that I never had the thing itself. I'm having the benefit at this moment; I had it the other day when I said to Chad 'Wait'; I shall have it still again when Sarah Pocock arrives. It's a benefit that would make a poor show for many people; and I don't know who else but you and I, frankly, could begin to see in it what I feel. I don't get drunk; I don't pursue the ladies; I don't spend money; I don't even write sonnets. But nevertheless I'm making up late for what I didn't have early. I cultivate my little benefit in my own little way. It amuses me more than anything that has happened to me in all my life. They may say what they like—it's my surrender, it's my tribute, to youth. One puts that in where one can— it has to come in somewhere, if only out of the lives, the conditions, the feelings of other persons. Chad gives me the sense of it, for all his grey hairs, which merely make it solid in him and safe and serene; and SHE does the same, for all her being older than he, for all her marriageable daughter, her separated husband, her agitated history. Though they're young enough, my pair, I don't say they're, in the freshest way, their own absolutely prime adolescence; for that has nothing to do with it. The point is that they're mine. Yes, they're my youth; since somehow at the right time nothing else ever was. What I meant just now therefore is that it would all go—go before doing its work—if they were to fail me."

On which, just here, Miss Gostrey inveterately questioned. "What do you, in particular, call its work?"

"Well, to see me through."

"But through what?"—she liked to get it all out of him.

"Why through this experience." That was all that would come.

It regularly gave her none the less the last word. "Don't you remember how in those first days of our meeting it was I who was to see you through?"

"Remember? Tenderly, deeply"—he always rose to it. "You're just doing your part in letting me maunder to you thus."

"Ah don't speak as if my part were small; since whatever else fails you—"

"YOU won't, ever, ever, ever?"—he thus took her up. "Oh I beg your pardon; you necessarily, you inevitably WILL. Your conditions—that's what I mean—won't allow me anything to do for you."

"Let alone—I see what you mean—that I'm drearily dreadfully old. I AM, but there's a service—possible for you to render—that I know, all the same, I shall think of."

"And what will it be?"

This, in fine, however, she would never tell him. "You shall hear only if your smash takes place. As that's really out of the question, I won't expose myself"—a point at which, for reasons of his own, Strether ceased to press.

He came round, for publicity—it was the easiest thing—to the idea that his smash WAS out of the question, and this rendered idle the discussion of what might follow it. He attached an added importance, as the days elapsed, to the arrival of the Pococks; he had even a shameful sense of waiting for it insincerely and incorrectly. He accused himself of making believe to his own mind that Sarah's presence, her impression, her judgement would simplify and harmonise, he accused himself of being so afraid of what they MIGHT do that he sought refuge, to beg the whole question, in a vain fury. He had abundantly seen at home what they were in the habit of doing, and he had not at present the smallest ground. His clearest vision was when he made out that what he most desired was an account more full and free of Mrs. Newsome's state of mind than any he felt he could even now expect from herself; that calculation at least went hand in hand with the sharp consciousness of wishing to prove to himself that he was not afraid to look his behaviour in the face. If he was by an inexorable logic to pay for it he was literally impatient to know the cost, and he held himself ready to pay in instalments. The first instalment would be precisely this entertainment of Sarah; as a consequence of which moreover, he should know vastly better how he stood.

Book Eighth

I

Paris street by David Cox (1783-1859)

Strether rambled alone during these few days, the effect of the incident of the previous week having been to simplify in a marked fashion his mixed relations with Waymarsh. Nothing had passed between them in reference to Mrs. Newsome's summons but that our friend had mentioned to his own the departure of the deputation actually at sea—giving him thus an opportunity to confess to the occult intervention he imputed to him. Waymarsh however in the event confessed to nothing; and though this falsified in some degree Strether's forecast the latter amusedly saw in it the same depth of good conscience out of which the dear man's impertinence had originally sprung. He was patient with the dear man now and delighted to observe how unmistakeably he had put on flesh; he felt his own holiday so successfully large and free that he was full of allowances and charities in respect to those cabined and confined' his instinct toward a spirit so strapped down as Waymarsh's was to walk round it on tiptoe for fear of waking it up to a sense of losses by this time irretrievable. It was all very funny he knew, and but the difference, as he often said to himself, of tweedledum and tweedledee—an emancipation so purely comparative that it was like the advance of the door-mat on the scraper; yet the present crisis was happily to profit by it and the pilgrim from Milrose to know himself more than ever in the right.

Strether felt that when he heard of the approach of the Pococks the impulse of pity quite sprang up in him beside the impulse of triumph. That was exactly why Waymarsh had looked at him with eyes in which the heat of justice was measured and shaded. He had looked very hard, as if affectionately sorry for the friend—the friend of fifty-five—whose frivolity had had thus to be recorded; becoming, however, but obscurely sententious and leaving his companion to formulate a charge. It was in this general attitude that he had of late altogether taken refuge; with the drop of discussion they were solemnly sadly superficial; Strether recognised in him the mere portentous rumination to which Miss Barrace had so good-humouredly described herself as assigning a corner of her salon. It was quite as if he knew his surreptitious step had been divined, and it was also as if he missed the chance to explain the purity of his motive; but this privation of relief should be precisely his small penance: it was not amiss for Strether that he should find himself to that degree uneasy. If he had been challenged or accused, rebuked for meddling or otherwise pulled up, he would probably have shown, on his own system, all the height of his consistency, all the depth of his good faith. Explicit resentment of his course would have made him take the floor, and the thump of his fist on the table would have affirmed him as consciously incorruptible. Had what now really prevailed with Strether been but a dread of that thump—a dread of wincing a little painfully at what it might invidiously demonstrate? However this might be, at any rate, one of the marks of the crisis was a visible, a studied lapse, in Waymarsh, of betrayed concern. As if to make up to his comrade for the stroke by which he had played providence he now conspicuously ignored his movements, withdrew himself from the pretension to share them, stiffened up his sensibility to neglect, and, clasping his large empty hands and swinging his large restless foot, clearly looked to another quarter for justice.

This made for independence on Strether's part, and he had in truth at no moment of his stay been so free to go and come. The early summer brushed the picture over and blurred everything but the near; it made a vast warm fragrant medium in which the elements floated together on the best of terms, in which rewards were immediate and reckonings postponed. Chad was out of town again, for the first time since his visitor's first view of him; he had explained this necessity—without detail, yet also without embarrassment, the circumstance was one of those which, in the young man's life, testified to the variety of his ties. Strether wasn't otherwise concerned with it than for its so testifying—a pleasant multitudinous image in which he took comfort. He took comfort, by the same stroke, in the swing of Chad's pendulum back from that other swing, the sharp jerk towards Woollett, so stayed by his own hand. He had the entertainment of thinking that if he had for that moment stopped the clock it was to promote the next minute this still livelier motion. He himself did what he hadn't done before; he took two or three times whole days off—irrespective of others, of two or three taken with Miss Gostrey, two or three taken with little Bilham: he went to Chartres and cultivated, before the front of the cathedral, a general easy beatitude; he went to Fontainebleau and imagined himself on the way to Italy; he went to Rouen with a little handbag and inordinately spent the night.

One afternoon he did something quite different; finding himself in the neighbourhood of a fine old house across the river, he passed under the great arch of its doorway and asked at the porter's lodge for Madame de Vionnet. He had already hovered more than once about that possibility, been aware of it, in the course of ostensible strolls, as lurking but round the corner. Only it had perversely happened, after his morning at Notre Dame, that his consistency, as he considered and intended it, had come back to him; whereby he had reflected that the encounter in question had been none of his making; clinging again intensely to the strength of his position, which was precisely that there was nothing in it for himself. From the moment he actively pursued the charming associate of his adventure, from that moment his position weakened, for he was then acting in an interested way. It was only within a few days that he had fixed himself a limit: he promised himself his consistency should end with Sarah's arrival. It was arguing correctly to feel the title to a free hand conferred on him by this event. If he wasn't to be let alone he should be merely a dupe to act with delicacy. If he wasn't to be trusted he could at least take his ease. If he was to be placed under control he gained leave to try what his position MIGHT agreeably give him. An ideal rigour would perhaps postpone the trial till after the Pococks had shown their spirit; and it was to an ideal rigour that he had quite promised himself to conform.

Suddenly, however, on this particular day, he felt a particular fear under which everything collapsed. He knew abruptly that he was afraid of himself—and yet not in relation to the effect on his sensibilities of another hour of Madame de Vionnet. What he dreaded was the effect of a single hour of Sarah Pocock, as to whom he was visited, in troubled nights, with fantastic waking dreams. She loomed at him larger than life; she increased in volume as she drew nearer; she so met his eyes that, his imagination taking, after the first step, all, and more than all, the strides, he already felt her come down on him, already burned, under her reprobation, with the blush of guilt, already consented, by way of penance, to the instant forfeiture of everything. He saw himself, under her direction, recommitted to Woollett as juvenile offenders are committed to reformatories. It wasn't of course that Woollett was really a place of discipline; but he knew in advance that Sarah's salon at the hotel would be. His danger, at any rate, in such moods of alarm, was some concession, on this ground, that would involve a sharp rupture with the actual; therefore if he waited to take leave of that actual he might wholly miss his chance. It was represented with supreme vividness by Madame de Vionnet, and that is why, in a word, he waited no longer. He had seen in a flash that he must anticipate Mrs. Pocock. He was accordingly much disappointed on now learning from the portress that the lady of his quest was not in Paris. She had gone for some days to the country. There was nothing in this accident but what was natural; yet it produced for poor Strether a drop of all confidence. It was suddenly as if he should never see her again, and as if moreover he had brought it on himself by not having been quite kind to her.

It was the advantage of his having let his fancy lose itself for a little in the gloom that, as by reaction, the prospect began really to brighten from the moment the deputation from Woollett alighted on the platform of the station. They had come straight from Havre, having sailed from New York to that port, and having also, thanks to a happy voyage, made land with a promptitude that left Chad Newsome, who had meant to meet them at the dock, belated. He had received their telegram, with the announcement of their immediate further advance, just as he was taking the train for Havre, so that nothing had remained for him but to await them in Paris. He hastily picked up Strether, at the hotel, for this purpose, and he even, with easy pleasantry, suggested the attendance of Waymarsh as well—Waymarsh, at the moment his cab rattled up, being engaged, under Strether's contemplative range, in a grave perambulation of the familiar court. Waymarsh had learned from his companion, who had already had a note, delivered by hand, from Chad, that the Pococks were due, and had ambiguously, though, as always, impressively, glowered at him over the circumstance; carrying himself in a manner in which Strether was now expert enough to recognise his uncertainty, in the premises, as to the best tone. The only tone he aimed at with confidence was a full tone—which was necessarily difficult in the absence of a full knowledge. The Pococks were a quantity as yet unmeasured, and, as he had practically brought them over, so this witness had to that extent exposed himself. He wanted to feel right about it, but could only, at the best, for the time, feel vague. "I shall look to you, you know, immensely," our friend had said, "to help me with them," and he had been quite conscious of the effect of the remark, and of others of the same sort, on his comrade's sombre sensibility. He had insisted on the fact that Waymarsh would quite like Mrs. Pocock—one could be certain he would: he would be with her about everything, and she would be with HIM, and Miss Barrace's nose, in short, would find itself out of joint.

Strether had woven this web of cheerfulness while they waited in the court for Chad; he had sat smoking cigarettes to keep himself quiet while, caged and leonine, his fellow traveller paced and turned before him. Chad Newsome was doubtless to be struck, when he arrived, with the sharpness of their opposition at this particular hour; he was, as a part of it, how Waymarsh came with him and left Strether to the street and stood there with a face half-wistful and half-rueful. They talked of him, the two others, as they drove, and Strether put Chad in possession of much of his own strained sense of things. He had already, a few days before, named to him the wire he was convinced their friend had pulled—a confidence that had made on the young man's part quite hugely for curiosity and diversion. The action of the matter, moreover, Strether could see, was to penetrate; he saw that is, how Chad judged a system of influence in which Waymarsh had served as a determinant—an impression just now quickened again; with the whole bearing of such a fact on the youth's view of his relatives. As it came up between them that they might now take their friend for a feature of the control of these latter now sought to be exerted from Woollett, Strether felt indeed how it would be stamped all over him, half an hour later for Sarah Pocock's eyes, that he was as much on Chad's "side" as Waymarsh probably described him. He was letting himself at present, go; there was no denying it; it might be desperation, it might be confidence; he should offer himself to the arriving travellers bristling with all the lucidity he had cultivated.

He repeated to Chad what he had been saying in the court to Waymarsh; how there was no doubt whatever that his sister would find the latter a kindred spirit, no doubt of the alliance, based on an exchange of views, that the pair would successfully strike up. They would become as thick as thieves—which moreover was but a development of what Strether remembered to have said in one of his first discussions with his mate, struck as he had then already been with the elements of affinity between that personage and Mrs. Newsome herself. "I told him, one day, when he had questioned me on your mother, that she was a person who, when he should know her, would rouse in him, I was sure, a special enthusiasm; and that hangs together with the conviction we now feel—this certitude that Mrs. Pocock will take him into her boat. For it's your mother's own boat that she's pulling."

"Ah," said Chad, "Mother's worth fifty of Sally!"

"A thousand; but when you presently meet her, all the same you'll be meeting your mother's representative—just as I shall. I feel like the outgoing ambassador," said Strether, "doing honour to his appointed successor." A moment after speaking as he had just done he felt he had inadvertently rather cheapened Mrs. Newsome to her son; an impression audibly reflected, as at first seen, in Chad's prompt protest. He had recently rather failed of apprehension of the young man's attitude and temper—remaining principally conscious of how little worry, at the worst, he wasted, and he studied him at this critical hour with renewed interest. Chad had done exactly what he had promised him a fortnight previous— had accepted without another question his plea for delay. He was waiting cheerfully and handsomely, but also inscrutably and with a slight increase perhaps of the hardness originally involved in his acquired high polish. He was neither excited nor depressed; was easy and acute and deliberate—unhurried unflurried unworried, only at most a little less amused than usual. Strether felt him more than ever a justification of the extraordinary process of which his own absurd spirit had been the arena; he knew as their cab rolled along, knew as he hadn't even yet known, that nothing else than what Chad had done and had been would have led to his present showing. They had made him, these things, what he was, and the business hadn't been easy; it had taken time and trouble, it had cost, above all, a price. The result at any rate was now to be offered to Sally; which Strether, so far as that was concerned, was glad to be there to witness. Would she in the least make it out or take it in, the result, or would she in the least care for it if she did? He scratched his chin as he asked himself by what name, when challenged—as he was sure he should be—he could call it for her. Oh those were determinations she must herself arrive at; since she wanted so much to see, let her see then and welcome. She had come out in the pride of her competence, yet it hummed in Strether's inner sense that she practically wouldn't see.

That this was moreover what Chad shrewdly suspected was clear from a word that next dropped from him. "They're children; they play at life!"—and the exclamation was significant and reassuring. It implied that he hadn't then, for his companion's sensibility, appeared to give Mrs. Newsome away; and it facilitated our friend's presently asking him if it were his idea that Mrs. Pocock and Madame de Vionnet should become acquainted. Strether was still more sharply struck, hereupon, with Chad's lucidity. "Why, isn't that exactly—to get a sight of the company I keep—what she has come out for?"

"Yes—I'm afraid it is," Strether unguardedly replied.

Chad's quick rejoinder lighted his precipitation. "Why do you say you're afraid?"

"Well, because I feel a certain responsibility. It's my testimony, I imagine, that will have been at the bottom of Mrs. Pocock's curiosity. My letters, as I've supposed you to understand from the beginning, have spoken freely. I've certainly said my little say about Madame de Vionnet."

All that, for Chad, was beautifully obvious. "Yes, but you've only spoken handsomely."

"Never more handsomely of any woman. But it's just that tone—!"

"That tone," said Chad, "that has fetched her? I dare say; but I've no quarrel with you about it. And no more has Madame de Vionnet. Don't you know by this time how she likes you?"

"Oh!"—and Strether had, with his groan, a real pang of melancholy. "For all I've done for her!"

"Ah you've done a great deal."

Chad's urbanity fairly shamed him, and he was at this moment absolutely impatient to see the face Sarah Pocock would present to a sort of thing, as he synthetically phrased it to himself, with no adequate forecast of which, despite his admonitions, she would certainly arrive. "I've done THIS!"

"Well, this is all right. She likes," Chad comfortably remarked, "to be liked."

It gave his companion a moment's thought. "And she's sure Mrs. Pocock WILL—?"

"No, I say that for you. She likes your liking her; it's so much, as it were," Chad laughed, "to the good. However, she doesn't despair of Sarah either, and is prepared, on her own side, to go all lengths."

"In the way of appreciation?"

"Yes, and of everything else. In the way of general amiability, hospitality and welcome. She's under arms," Chad laughed again; "she's prepared."

Strether took it in; then as if an echo of Miss Barrace were in the air: "She's wonderful."

"You don't begin to know HOW wonderful!"

There was a depth in it, to Strether's ear, of confirmed luxury—almost a kind of unconscious insolence of proprietorship; but the effect of the glimpse was not at this moment to foster speculation: there was something so conclusive in so much graceful and generous assurance. It was in fact a fresh evocation; and the evocation had before many minutes another consequence. "Well, I shall see her oftener now. I shall see her as much as I like—by your leave; which is what I hitherto haven't done."

"It has been," said Chad, but without reproach, "only your own fault. I tried to bring you together, and SHE, my dear fellow—I never saw her more charming to any man. But you've got your extraordinary ideas."

"Well, I DID have," Strether murmured, while he felt both how they had possessed him and how they had now lost their authority. He couldn't have traced the sequence to the end, but it was all because of Mrs. Pocock. Mrs. Pocock might be because of Mrs. Newsome, but that was still to be proved. What came over him was the sense of having stupidly failed to profit where profit would have been precious. It had been open to him to see so much more of her, and he had but let the good days pass. Fierce in him almost was the resolve to lose no more of them, and he whimsically reflected, while at Chad's side he drew nearer to his destination, that it was after all Sarah who would have quickened his chance. What her visit of inquisition might achieve in other directions was as yet all obscure—only not obscure that it would do supremely much to bring two earnest persons together. He had but to listen to Chad at this moment to feel it; for Chad was in the act of remarking to him that they of course both counted on him—he himself and the other earnest person—for cheer and support. It was brave to Strether to hear him talk as if the line of wisdom they had struck out was to make things ravishing to the Pococks. No, if Madame de Vionnet compassed THAT, compassed the ravishment of the Pococks, Madame de Vionnet would be prodigious. It would be a beautiful plan if it succeeded, and it all came to the question of Sarah's being really bribeable. The precedent of his own case helped Strether perhaps but little to consider she might prove so; it being distinct that her character would rather make for every possible difference. This idea of his own bribeability set him apart for himself; with the further mark in fact that his case was absolutely proved. He liked always, where Lambert Strether was concerned, to know the worst, and what he now seemed to know was not only that he was bribeable, but that he had been effectually bribed. The only difficulty was that he couldn't quite have said with what. It was as if he had sold himself, but hadn't somehow got the cash. That, however, was what, characteristically, WOULD happen to him. It would naturally be his kind of traffic. While he thought of these things he reminded Chad of the truth they mustn't lose sight of—the truth that, with all deference to her susceptibility to new interests, Sarah would have come out with a high firm definite purpose. "She hasn't come out, you know, to be bamboozled. We may all be ravishing—nothing perhaps can be more easy for us; but she hasn't come out to be ravished. She has come out just simply to take you home."

"Oh well, with HER I'll go," said Chad good-humouredly. "I suppose you'll allow THAT." And then as for a minute Strether said nothing: "Or is your idea that when I've seen her I shan't want to go?" As this question, however, again left his friend silent he presently went on: "My own idea at any rate is that they shall have while they're here the best sort of time."

It was at this that Strether spoke. "Ah there you are! I think if you really wanted to go—!"

"Well?" said Chad to bring it out.

"Well, you wouldn't trouble about our good time. You wouldn't care what sort of a time we have."

Chad could always take in the easiest way in the world any ingenious suggestion. "I see. But can I help it? I'm too decent."

"Yes, you're too decent!" Strether heavily sighed. And he felt for the moment as if it were the preposterous end of his mission.

It ministered for the time to this temporary effect that Chad made no rejoinder. But he spoke again as they came in sight of the station. "Do you mean to introduce her to Miss Gostrey?"

As to this Strether was ready. "No."

"But haven't you told me they know about her?"

"I think I've told you your mother knows."

"And won't she have told Sally?"

"That's one of the things I want to see."

"And if you find she HAS—?"

"Will I then, you mean, bring them together?"

"Yes," said Chad with his pleasant promptness: "to show her there's nothing in it."

Strether hesitated. "I don't know that I care very much what she may think there's in it."

"Not if it represents what Mother thinks?"

"Ah what DOES your mother think?" There was in this some sound of bewilderment.

But they were just driving up, and help, of a sort, might after all be quite at hand. "Isn't that, my dear man, what we're both just going to make out?"

II

Strether quitted the station half an hour later in different company. Chad had taken charge, for the journey to the hotel, of Sarah, Mamie, the maid and the luggage, all spaciously installed and conveyed; and it was only after the four had rolled away that his companion got into a cab with Jim. A strange new feeling had come over Strether, in consequence of which his spirits had risen; it was as if what had occurred on the alighting of his critics had been something other than his fear, though his fear had vet not been of an instant scene of violence. His impression had been nothing but what was inevitable—he said that to himself; yet relief and reassurance had softly dropped upon him. Nothing could be so odd as to be indebted for these things to the look of faces and the sound of voices that had been with him to satiety, as he might have said, for years; but he now knew, all the same, how uneasy he had felt; that was brought home to him by his present sense of a respite. It had come moreover in the flash of an eye, it had come in the smile with which Sarah, whom, at the window of their compartment, they had effusively greeted from the platform, rustled down to them a moment later, fresh and handsome from her cool June progress through the charming land. It was only a sign, but enough: she was going to be gracious and unallusive, she was going to play the larger game—which was still more apparent, after she had emerged from Chad's arms, in her direct greeting to the valued friend of her family.

Strether WAS then as much as ever the valued friend of her family, it was something he could at all events go on with; and the manner of his response to it expressed even for himself how little he had enjoyed the prospect of ceasing to figure in that likeness. He had always seen Sarah gracious—had in fact rarely seen her shy or dry, her marked thin-lipped smile, intense without brightness and as prompt to act as the scrape of a safety-match; the protrusion of her rather remarkably long chin, which in her case represented invitation and urbanity, and not, as in most others, pugnacity and defiance; the penetration of her voice to a distance, the general encouragement and approval of her manner, were all elements with which intercourse had made him familiar, but which he noted today almost as if she had been a new acquaintance. This first glimpse of her had given a brief but vivid accent to her resemblance to her mother; he could have taken her for Mrs. Newsome while she met his eyes as the train rolled into the station. It was an impression that quickly dropped; Mrs. Newsome was much handsomer, and while Sarah inclined to the massive her mother had, at an age, still the girdle of a maid; also the latter's chin was rather short, than long, and her smile, by good fortune, much more, oh ever so much more, mercifully vague. Strether had seen Mrs. Newsome reserved; he had literally heard her silent, though he had never known her unpleasant. It was the case with Mrs. Pocock that he had known HER unpleasant, even though he had never known her not affable. She had forms of affability that were in a high degree assertive; nothing for instance had ever been more striking than that she was affable to Jim.

What had told in any case at the window of the train was her high clear forehead, that forehead which her friends, for some reason, always thought of as a "brow"; the long reach of her eyes—it came out at this juncture in such a manner as to remind him, oddly enough, also of that of Waymarsh's; and the unusual gloss of her dark hair, dressed and hatted, after her mother's refined example, with such an avoidance of extremes that it was always spoken of at Woollett as "their own." Though this analogy dropped as soon as she was on the platform it had lasted long enough to make him feel all the advantage, as it were, of his relief. The woman at home, the woman to whom he was attached, had been before him just long enough to give him again the measure of the wretchedness, in fact really of the shame, of their having to recognise the formation, between them, of a "split." He had taken this measure in solitude and meditation: but the catastrophe, as Sarah steamed up, looked for its seconds unprecedentedly dreadful—or proved, more exactly, altogether unthinkable; so that his finding something free and familiar to respond to brought with it an instant renewal of his loyalty. He had suddenly sounded the whole depth, had gasped at what he might have lost.

Well, he could now, for the quarter of an hour of their detention hover about the travellers as soothingly as if their direct message to him was that he had lost nothing. He wasn't going to have Sarah write to her mother that night that he was in any way altered or strange. There had been times enough for a month when it had seemed to him that he was strange, that he was altered, in every way; but that was a matter for himself; he knew at least whose business it was not; it was not at all events such a circumstance as Sarah's own unaided lights would help her to. Even if she had come out to flash those lights more than yet appeared she wouldn't make much headway against mere pleasantness. He counted on being able to be merely pleasant to the end, and if only from incapacity moreover to formulate anything different. He couldn't even formulate to himself his being changed and queer; it had taken place, the process, somewhere deep down; Maria Gostrey had caught glimpses of it; but how was he to fish it up, even if he desired, for Mrs. Pocock? This was then the spirit in which he hovered, and with the easier throb in it much indebted furthermore to the impression of high and established adequacy as a pretty girl promptly produced in him by Mamie. He had wondered vaguely—turning over many things in the fidget of his thoughts—if Mamie WERE as pretty as Woollett published her; as to which issue seeing her now again was to be so swept away by Woollett's opinion that this consequence really let loose for the imagination an avalanche of others.

There were positively five minutes in which the last word seemed of necessity to abide with a Woollett represented by a Mamie. This was the sort of truth the place itself would feel; it would send her forth in confidence; it would point to her with triumph; it would take its stand on her with assurance; it would be conscious of no requirements she didn't meet, of no question she couldn't answer.

Well, it was right, Strether slipped smoothly enough into the cheerfulness of saying: granted that a community MIGHT be best represented by a young lady of twenty-two, Mamie perfectly played the part, played it as if she were used to it, and looked and spoke and dressed the character. He wondered if she mightn't, in the high light of Paris, a cool full studio-light, becoming yet treacherous, show as too conscious of these matters; but the next moment he felt satisfied that her consciousness was after all empty for its size, rather too simple than too mixed, and that the kind way with her would be not to take many things out of it, but to put as many as possible in. She was robust and conveniently tall; just a trifle too bloodlessly fair perhaps, but with a pleasant public familiar radiance that affirmed her vitality. She might have been "receiving" for Woollett, wherever she found herself, and there was something in her manner, her tone, her motion, her pretty blue eyes, her pretty perfect teeth and her very small, too small, nose, that immediately placed her, to the fancy, between the windows of a hot bright room in which voices were high—up at that end to which people were brought to be "presented." They were there to congratulate, these images, and Strether's renewed vision, on this hint, completed the idea. What Mamie was like was the happy bride, the bride after the church and just before going away. She wasn't the mere maiden, and yet was only as much married as that quantity came to. She was in the brilliant acclaimed festal stage. Well, might it last her long!

Strether rejoiced in these things for Chad, who was all genial attention to the needs of his friends, besides having arranged that his servant should reinforce him; the ladies were certainly pleasant to see, and Mamie would be at any time and anywhere pleasant to exhibit. She would look extraordinarily like his young wife—the wife of a honeymoon, should he go about with her; but that was his own affair—or perhaps it was hers; it was at any rate something she couldn't help. Strether remembered how he had seen him come up with Jeanne de Vionnet in Gloriani's garden, and the fancy he had had about that—the fancy obscured now, thickly overlaid with others; the recollection was during these minutes his only note of trouble. He had often, in spite of himself, wondered if Chad but too probably were not with Jeanne the object of a still and shaded flame. It was on the cards that the child MIGHT be tremulously in love, and this conviction now flickered up not a bit the less for his disliking to think of it, for its being, in a complicated situation, a complication the more, and for something indescribable in Mamie, something at all events straightway lent her by his own mind, something that gave her value, gave her intensity and purpose, as the symbol of an opposition. Little Jeanne wasn't really at all in question—how COULD she be?—yet from the moment Miss Pocock had shaken her skirts on the platform, touched up the immense bows of her hat and settled properly over her shoulder the strap of her morocco-and-gilt travelling-satchel, from that moment little Jeanne was opposed.

It was in the cab with Jim that impressions really crowded on Strether, giving him the strangest sense of length of absence from people among whom he had lived for years. Having them thus come out to him was as if he had returned to find them: and the droll promptitude of Jim's mental reaction threw his own initiation far back into the past. Whoever might or mightn't be suited by what was going on among them, Jim, for one, would certainly be: his instant recognition—frank and whimsical—of what the affair was for HIM gave Strether a glow of pleasure. "I say, you know, this IS about my shape, and if it hadn't been for YOU—!" so he broke out as the charming streets met his healthy appetite; and he wound up, after an expressive nudge, with a clap of his companion's knee and an "Oh you, you—you ARE doing it!" that was charged with rich meaning. Strether felt in it the intention of homage, but, with a curiosity otherwise occupied, postponed taking it up. What he was asking himself for the time was how Sarah Pocock, in the opportunity already given her, had judged her brother—from whom he himself, as they finally, at the station, separated for their different conveyances, had had a look into which he could read more than one message. However Sarah was judging her brother, Chad's conclusion about his sister, and about her husband and her husband's sister, was at the least on the way not to fail of confidence. Strether felt the confidence, and that, as the look between them was an exchange, what he himself gave back was relatively vague. This comparison of notes however could wait; everything struck him as depending on the effect produced by Chad. Neither Sarah nor Mamie had in any way, at the station—where they had had after all ample time—broken out about it; which, to make up for this, was what our friend had expected of Jim as soon as they should find themselves together.

It was queer to him that he had that noiseless brush with Chad; an ironic intelligence with this youth on the subject of his relatives, an intelligence carried on under their nose and, as might be said, at their expense—such a matter marked again for him strongly the number of stages he had come; albeit that if the number seemed great the time taken for the final one was but the turn of a hand. He had before this had many moments of wondering if he himself weren't perhaps changed even as Chad was changed. Only what in Chad was conspicuous improvement—well, he had no name ready for the working, in his own organism, of his own more timid dose. He should have to see first what this action would amount to. And for his occult passage with the young man, after all, the directness of it had no greater oddity than the fact that the young man's way with the three travellers should have been so happy a manifestation. Strether liked him for it, on the spot, as he hadn't yet liked him; it affected him while it lasted as he might have been affected by some light pleasant perfect work of art: to that degree that he wondered if they were really worthy of it, took it in and did it justice; to that degree that it would have been scarce a miracle if, there in the luggage-room, while they waited for their things, Sarah had pulled his sleeve and drawn him aside. "You're right; we haven't quite known what you mean, Mother and I, but now we see. Chad's magnificent; what can one want more? If THIS is the kind of thing—!" On which they might, as it were, have embraced and begun to work together.

Ah how much, as it was, for all her bridling brightness—which was merely general and noticed nothing—WOULD they work together? Strether knew he was unreasonable; he set it down to his being nervous: people couldn't notice everything and speak of everything in a quarter of an hour. Possibly, no doubt, also, he made too much of Chad's display. Yet, none the less, when, at the end of five minutes, in the cab, Jim Pocock had said nothing either—hadn't said, that is, what Strether wanted, though he had said much else—it all suddenly bounced back to their being either stupid or wilful. It was more probably on the whole the former; so that that would be the drawback of the bridling brightness. Yes, they would bridle and be bright; they would make the best of what was before them, but their observation would fail; it would be beyond them; they simply wouldn't understand. Of what use would it be then that they had come?—if they weren't to be intelligent up to THAT point: unless indeed he himself were utterly deluded and extravagant? Was he, on this question of Chad's improvement, fantastic and away from the truth? Did he live in a false world, a world that had grown simply to suit him, and was his present slight irritation—in the face now of Jim's silence in particular—but the alarm of the vain thing menaced by the touch of the real? Was this contribution of the real possibly the mission of the Pococks?—had they come to make the work of observation, as HE had practised observation, crack and crumble, and to reduce Chad to the plain terms in which honest minds could deal with him? Had they come in short to be sane where Strether was destined to feel that he himself had only been silly?

He glanced at such a contingency, but it failed to hold him long when once he had reflected that he would have been silly, in this case, with Maria Gostrey and little Bilham, with Madame de Vionnet and little Jeanne, with Lambert Strether, in fine, and above all with Chad Newsome himself. Wouldn't it be found to have made more for reality to be silly with these persons than sane with Sarah and Jim? Jim in fact, he presently made up his mind, was individually out of it; Jim didn't care; Jim hadn't come out either for Chad or for him; Jim in short left the moral side to Sally and indeed simply availed himself now, for the sense of recreation, of the fact that he left almost everything to Sally. He was nothing compared to Sally, and not so much by reason of Sally's temper and will as by that of her more developed type and greater acquaintance with the world. He quite frankly and serenely confessed, as he sat there with Strether, that he felt his type hang far in the rear of his wife's and still further, if possible, in the rear of his sister's. Their types, he well knew, were recognised and acclaimed; whereas the most a leading Woollett business-man could hope to achieve socially, and for that matter industrially, was a certain freedom to play into this general glamour.

The impression he made on our friend was another of the things that marked our friend's road. It was a strange impression, especially as so soon produced; Strether had received it, he judged, all in the twenty minutes; it struck him at least as but in a minor degree the work of the long Woollett years. Pocock was normally and consentingly though not quite wittingly out of the question. It was despite his being normal; it was despite his being cheerful; it was despite his being a leading Woollett business-man; and the determination of his fate left him thus perfectly usual—as everything else about it was clearly, to his sense, not less so. He seemed to say that there was a whole side of life on which the perfectly usual WAS for leading Woollett business-men to be out of the question. He made no more of it than that, and Strether, so far as Jim was concerned, desired to make no more. Only Strether's imagination, as always, worked, and he asked himself if this side of life were not somehow connected, for those who figured on it with the fact of marriage. Would HIS relation to it, had he married ten years before, have become now the same as Pocock's? Might it even become the same should he marry in a few months? Should he ever know himself as much out of the question for Mrs. Newsome as Jim knew himself—in a dim way—for Mrs. Jim?

To turn his eyes in that direction was to be personally reassured; he was different from Pocock; he had affirmed himself differently and was held after all in higher esteem. What none the less came home to him, however, at this hour, was that the society over there, that of which Sarah and Mamie—and, in a more eminent way, Mrs. Newsome herself—were specimens, was essentially a society of women, and that poor Jim wasn't in it. He himself Lambert Strether, WAS as yet in some degree—which was an odd situation for a man; but it kept coming back to him in a whimsical way that he should perhaps find his marriage had cost him his place. This occasion indeed, whatever that fancy represented, was not a time of sensible exclusion for Jim, who was in a state of manifest response to the charm of his adventure. Small and fat and constantly facetious, straw-coloured and destitute of marks, he would have been practically indistinguishable hadn't his constant preference for light-grey clothes, for white hats, for very big cigars and very little stories, done what it could for his identity. There were signs in him, though none of them plaintive, of always paying for others; and the principal one perhaps was just this failure of type. It was with this that he paid, rather than with fatigue or waste; and also doubtless a little with the effort of humour—never irrelevant to the conditions, to the relations, with which he was acquainted.

He gurgled his joy as they rolled through the happy streets; he declared that his trip was a regular windfall, and that he wasn't there, he was eager to remark, to hang back from anything: he didn't know quite what Sally had come for, but HE had come for a good time. Strether indulged him even while wondering if what Sally wanted her brother to go back for was to become like her husband. He trusted that a good time was to be, out and out, the programme for all of them; and he assented liberally to Jim's proposal that, disencumbered and irresponsible—his things were in the omnibus with those of the others—they should take a further turn round before going to the hotel. It wasn't for HIM to tackle Chad—it was Sally's job; and as it would be like her, he felt, to open fire on the spot, it wouldn't be amiss of them to hold off and give her time. Strether, on his side, only asked to give her time; so he jogged with his companion along boulevards and avenues, trying to extract from meagre material some forecast of his catastrophe. He was quick enough to see that Jim Pocock declined judgement, had hovered quite round the outer edge of discussion and anxiety, leaving all analysis of their question to the ladies alone and now only feeling his way toward some small droll cynicism. It broke out afresh, the cynicism—it had already shown a flicker—in a but slightly deferred: "Well, hanged if I would if I were he!"

"You mean you wouldn't in Chad's place—?"

"Give up this to go back and boss the advertising!" Poor Jim, with his arms folded and his little legs out in the open fiacre, drank in the sparkling Paris noon and carried his eyes from one side of their vista to the other. "Why I want to come right out and live here myself. And I want to live while I AM here too. I feel with YOU—oh you've been grand, old man, and I've twigged—that it ain't right to worry Chad. I don't mean to persecute him; I couldn't in conscience. It's thanks to you at any rate that I'm here, and I'm sure I'm much obliged. You're a lovely pair."

There were things in this speech that Strether let pass for the time. "Don't you then think it important the advertising should be thoroughly taken in hand? Chad WILL be, so far as capacity is concerned," he went on, "the man to do it."

"Where did he get his capacity," Jim asked, "over here?"

"He didn't get it over here, and the wonderful thing is that over here he hasn't inevitably lost it. He has a natural turn for business, an extraordinary head. He comes by that," Strether explained, "honestly enough. He's in that respect his father's son, and also—for she's wonderful in her way too—his mother's. He has other tastes and other tendencies; but Mrs. Newsome and your wife are quite right about his having that. He's very remarkable."

"Well, I guess he is!" Jim Pocock comfortably sighed. "But if you've believed so in his making us hum, why have you so prolonged the discussion? Don't you know we've been quite anxious about you?"

These questions were not informed with earnestness, but Strether saw he must none the less make a choice and take a line. "Because, you see, I've greatly liked it. I've liked my Paris, I dare say I've liked it too much."

"Oh you old wretch!" Jim gaily exclaimed.

"But nothing's concluded," Strether went on. "The case is more complex than it looks from Woollett."

"Oh well, it looks bad enough from Woollett!" Jim declared.

"Even after all I've written?"

Jim bethought himself. "Isn't it what you've written that has made Mrs. Newsome pack us off? That at least and Chad's not turning up?"

Strether made a reflexion of his own. "I see. That she should do something was, no doubt, inevitable, and your wife has therefore of course come out to act."

"Oh yes," Jim concurred—"to act. But Sally comes out to act, you know," he lucidly added, "every time she leaves the house. She never comes out but she DOES act. She's acting moreover now for her mother, and that fixes the scale." Then he wound up, opening all his senses to it, with a renewed embrace of pleasant Paris. "We haven't all the same at Woollett got anything like this."

Strether continued to consider. "I'm bound to say for you all that you strike me as having arrived in a very mild and reasonable frame of mind. You don't show your claws. I felt just now in Mrs. Pocock no symptom of that. She isn't fierce," he went on. "I'm such a nervous idiot that I thought she might be."

"Oh don't you know her well enough," Pocock asked, "to have noticed that she never gives herself away, any more than her mother ever does? They ain't fierce, either of 'em; they let you come quite close. They wear their fur the smooth side out—the warm side in. Do you know what they are?" Jim pursued as he looked about him, giving the question, as Strether felt, but half his care—"do you know what they are? They're about as intense as they can live."

"Yes"—and Strether's concurrence had a positive precipitation; "they're about as intense as they can live."

"They don't lash about and shake the cage," said Jim, who seemed pleased with his analogy; "and it's at feeding-time that they're quietest. But they always get there."

"They do indeed—they always get there!" Strether replied with a laugh that justified his confession of nervousness. He disliked to be talking sincerely of Mrs. Newsome with Pocock; he could have talked insincerely. But there was something he wanted to know, a need created in him by her recent intermission, by his having given from the first so much, as now more than ever appeared to him, and got so little. It was as if a queer truth in his companion's metaphor had rolled over him with a rush. She HAD been quiet at feeding-time; she had fed, and Sarah had fed with her, out of the big bowl of all his recent free communication, his vividness and pleasantness, his ingenuity and even his eloquence, while the current of her response had steadily run thin. Jim meanwhile however, it was true, slipped characteristically into shallowness from the moment he ceased to speak out of the experience of a husband.

"But of course Chad has now the advantage of being there before her. If he doesn't work that for all it's worth—!" He sighed with contingent pity at his brother-in-law's possible want of resource. "He has worked it on YOU, pretty well, eh?" and he asked the next moment if there were anything new at the Varieties, which he pronounced in the American manner. They talked about the Varieties—Strether confessing to a knowledge which produced again on Pocock's part a play of innuendo as vague as a nursery-rhyme, yet as aggressive as an elbow in his side; and they finished their drive under the protection of easy themes. Strether waited to the end, but still in vain, for any show that Jim had seen Chad as different; and he could scarce have explained the discouragement he drew from the absence of this testimony. It was what he had taken his own stand on, so far as he had taken a stand; and if they were all only going to see nothing he had only wasted his time. He gave his friend till the very last moment, till they had come into sight of the hotel; and when poor Pocock only continued cheerful and envious and funny he fairly grew to dislike him, to feel him extravagantly common. If they were ALL going to see nothing!—Strether knew, as this came back to him, that he was also letting Pocock represent for him what Mrs. Newsome wouldn't see. He went on disliking, in the light of Jim's commonness, to talk to him about that lady; yet just before the cab pulled up he knew the extent of his desire for the real word from Woollett.

"Has Mrs. Newsome at all given way—?"

"Given way'?"—Jim echoed it with the practical derision of his sense of a long past.

"Under the strain, I mean, of hope deferred, of disappointment repeated and thereby intensified."

"Oh is she prostrate, you mean?"—he had his categories in hand. "Why yes, she's prostrate—just as Sally is. But they're never so lively, you know, as when they're prostrate."

"Ah Sarah's prostrate?" Strether vaguely murmured.

"It's when they're prostrate that they most sit up."

"And Mrs. Newsome's sitting up?"

"All night, my boy—for YOU!" And Jim fetched him, with a vulgar little guffaw, a thrust that gave relief to the picture. But he had got what he wanted. He felt on the spot that this WAS the real word from Woollett. "So don't you go home!" Jim added while he alighted and while his friend, letting him profusely pay the cabman, sat on in a momentary muse. Strether wondered if that were the real word too.

III

As the door of Mrs. Pocock's salon was pushed open for him, the next day, well before noon, he was reached by a voice with a charming sound that made him just falter before crossing the threshold. Madame de Vionnet was already on the field, and this gave the drama a quicker pace than he felt it as yet—though his suspense had increased—in the power of any act of his own to do. He had spent the previous evening with all his old friends together yet he would still have described himself as quite in the dark in respect to a forecast of their influence on his situation. It was strange now, none the less, that in the light of this unexpected note of her presence he felt Madame de Vionnet a part of that situation as she hadn't even yet been. She was alone, he found himself assuming, with Sarah, and there was a bearing in that—somehow beyond his control—on his personal fate. Yet she was only saying something quite easy and independent—the thing she had come, as a good friend of Chad's, on purpose to say. "There isn't anything at all—? I should be so delighted."

It was clear enough, when they were there before him, how she had been received. He saw this, as Sarah got up to greet him, from something fairly hectic in Sarah's face. He saw furthermore that they weren't, as had first come to him, alone together; he was at no loss as to the identity of the broad high back presented to him in the embrasure of the window furthest from the door. Waymarsh, whom he had to-day not yet seen, whom he only knew to have left the hotel before him, and who had taken part, the night previous, on Mrs. Pocock's kind invitation, conveyed by Chad, in the entertainment, informal but cordial, promptly offered by that lady—Waymarsh had anticipated even as Madame de Vionnet had done, and, with his hands in his pockets and his attitude unaffected by Strether's entrance, was looking out, in marked detachment, at the Rue de Rivoli. The latter felt it in the air—it was immense how Waymarsh could mark things—that he had remained deeply dissociated from the overture to their hostess made we have recorded on Madame de Vionnet's side. He had, conspicuously, tact, besides a stiff general view; and this was why he had left Mrs. Pocock to struggle alone. He would outstay the visitor; he would unmistakeably wait; to what had he been doomed for months past but waiting? Therefore she was to feel that she had him in reserve. What support she drew from this was still to be seen, for, although Sarah was vividly bright, she had given herself up for the moment to an ambiguous flushed formalism. She had had to reckon more quickly than she expected; but it concerned her first of all to signify that she was not to be taken unawares. Strether arrived precisely in time for her showing it. "Oh you're too good; but I don't think I feel quite helpless. I have my brother—and these American friends. And then you know I've been to Paris. I KNOW Paris," said Sally Pocock in a tone that breathed a certain chill on Strether's heart.

"Ah but a woman, in this tiresome place where everything's always changing, a woman of good will," Madame de Vionnet threw off, "can always help a woman. I'm sure you 'know'—but we know perhaps different things." She too, visibly, wished to make no mistake; but it was a fear of a different order and more kept out of sight. She smiled in welcome at Strether; she greeted him more familiarly than Mrs. Pocock; she put out her hand to him without moving from her place; and it came to him in the course of a minute and in the oddest way that—yes, positively—she was giving him over to ruin. She was all kindness and ease, but she couldn't help so giving him; she was exquisite, and her being just as she was poured for Sarah a sudden rush of meaning into his own equivocations. How could she know how she was hurting him? She wanted to show as simple and humble—in the degree compatible with operative charm; but it was just this that seemed to put him on her side. She struck him as dressed, as arranged, as prepared infinitely to conciliate—with the very poetry of good taste in her view of the conditions of her early call. She was ready to advise about dressmakers and shops; she held herself wholly at the disposition of Chad's family. Strether noticed her card on the table—her coronet and her "Comtesse"—and the imagination was sharp in him of certain private adjustments in Sarah's mind. She had never, he was sure, sat with a "Comtesse" before, and such was the specimen of that class he had been keeping to play on her. She had crossed the sea very particularly for a look at her; but he read in Madame de Vionnet's own eyes that this curiosity hadn't been so successfully met as that she herself wouldn't now have more than ever need of him. She looked much as she had looked to him that morning at Notre Dame; he noted in fact the suggestive sameness of her discreet and delicate dress. It seemed to speak—perhaps a little prematurely or too finely—of the sense in which she would help Mrs. Pocock with the shops. The way that lady took her in, moreover, added depth to his impression of what Miss Gostrey, by their common wisdom, had escaped. He winced as he saw himself but for that timely prudence ushering in Maria as a guide and an example. There was however a touch of relief for him in his glimpse, so far as he had got it, of Sarah's line. She "knew Paris." Madame de Vionnet had, for that matter, lightly taken this up. "Ah then you've a turn for that, an affinity that belongs to your family. Your brother, though his long experience makes a difference, I admit, has become one of us in a marvellous way." And she appealed to Strether in the manner of a woman who could always glide off with smoothness into another subject. Wasn't HE struck with the way Mr. Newsome had made the place his own, and hadn't he been in a position to profit by his friend's wondrous expertness?

Strether felt the bravery, at the least, of her presenting herself so promptly to sound that note, and yet asked himself what other note, after all, she COULD strike from the moment she presented herself at all. She could meet Mrs. Pocock only on the ground of the obvious, and what feature of Chad's situation was more eminent than the fact that he had created for himself a new set of circumstances? Unless she hid herself altogether she could show but as one of these, an illustration of his domiciled and indeed of his confirmed condition. And the consciousness of all this in her charming eyes was so clear and fine that as she thus publicly drew him into her boat she produced in him such a silent agitation as he was not to fail afterwards to denounce as pusillanimous. "Ah don't be so charming to me!—for it makes us intimate, and after all what IS between us when I've been so tremendously on my guard and have seen you but half a dozen times?" He recognised once more the perverse law that so inveterately governed his poor personal aspects: it would be exactly LIKE the way things always turned out for him that he should affect Mrs. Pocock and Waymarsh as launched in a relation in which he had really never been launched at all. They were at this very moment—they could only be—attributing to him the full licence of it, and all by the operation of her own tone with him; whereas his sole licence had been to cling with intensity to the brink, not to dip so much as a toe into the flood. But the flicker of his fear on this occasion was not, as may be added, to repeat itself; it sprang up, for its moment, only to die down and then go out for ever. To meet his fellow visitor's invocation and, with Sarah's brilliant eyes on him, answer, WAS quite sufficiently to step into her boat. During the rest of the time her visit lasted he felt himself proceed to each of the proper offices, successively, for helping to keep the adventurous skiff afloat. It rocked beneath him, but he settled himself in his place. He took up an oar and, since he was to have the credit of pulling, pulled.

"That will make it all the pleasanter if it so happens that we DO meet," Madame de Vionnet had further observed in reference to Mrs. Pocock's mention of her initiated state; and she had immediately added that, after all, her hostess couldn't be in need with the good offices of Mr. Strether so close at hand. "It's he, I gather, who has learnt to know his Paris, and to love it, better than any one ever before in so short a time; so that between him and your brother, when it comes to the point, how can you possibly want for good guidance? The great thing, Mr. Strether will show you," she smiled, "is just to let one's self go."

"Oh I've not let myself go very far," Strether answered, feeling quite as if he had been called upon to hint to Mrs. Pocock how Parisians could talk. "I'm only afraid of showing I haven't let myself go enough. I've taken a good deal of time, but I must quite have had the air of not budging from one spot." He looked at Sarah in a manner that he thought she might take as engaging, and he made, under Madame de Vionnet's protection, as it were, his first personal point. "What has really happened has been that, all the while, I've done what I came out for."

Yet it only at first gave Madame de Vionnet a chance immediately to take him up. "You've renewed acquaintance with your friend—you've learnt to know him again." She spoke with such cheerful helpfulness that they might, in a common cause, have been calling together and pledged to mutual aid.

Waymarsh, at this, as if he had been in question, straightway turned from the window. "Oh yes, Countess—he has renewed acquaintance with ME, and he HAS, I guess, learnt something about me, though I don't know how much he has liked it. It's for Strether himself to say whether he has felt it justifies his course."

"Oh but YOU," said the Countess gaily, "are not in the least what he came out for—is he really, Strether? and I hadn't you at all in my mind. I was thinking of Mr. Newsome, of whom we think so much and with whom, precisely, Mrs. Pocock has given herself the opportunity to take up threads. What a pleasure for you both!" Madame de Vionnet, with her eyes on Sarah, bravely continued.

Mrs. Pocock met her handsomely, but Strether quickly saw she meant to accept no version of her movements or plans from any other lips. She required no patronage and no support, which were but other names for a false position; she would show in her own way what she chose to show, and this she expressed with a dry glitter that recalled to him a fine Woollett winter morning. "I've never wanted for opportunities to see my brother. We've many things to think of at home, and great responsibilities and occupations, and our home's not an impossible place. We've plenty of reasons," Sarah continued a little piercingly, "for everything we do"—and in short she wouldn't give herself the least little scrap away. But she added as one who was always bland and who could afford a concession: "I've come because—well, because we do come."

"Ah then fortunately!"—Madame de Vionnet breathed it to the air. Five minutes later they were on their feet for her to take leave, standing together in an affability that had succeeded in surviving a further exchange of remarks; only with the emphasised appearance on Waymarsh's part of a tendency to revert, in a ruminating manner and as with an instinctive or a precautionary lightening of his tread, to an open window and his point of vantage. The glazed and gilded room, all red damask, ormolu, mirrors, clocks, looked south, and the shutters were bowed upon the summer morning; but the Tuileries garden and what was beyond it, over which the whole place hung, were things visible through gaps; so that the far-spreading presence of Paris came up in coolness, dimness and invitation, in the twinkle of gilt-tipped palings, the crunch of gravel, the click of hoofs, the crack of whips, things that suggested some parade of the circus. "I think it probable," said Mrs. Pocock, "that I shall have the opportunity of going to my brother's I've no doubt it's very pleasant indeed." She spoke as to Strether, but her face was turned with an intensity of brightness to Madame de Vionnet, and there was a moment during which, while she thus fronted her, our friend expected to hear her add: "I'm much obliged to you, I'm sure, for inviting me there." He guessed that for five seconds these words were on the point of coming; he heard them as clearly as if they had been spoken; but he presently knew they had just failed—knew it by a glance, quick and fine, from Madame de Vionnet, which told him that she too had felt them in the air, but that the point had luckily not been made in any manner requiring notice. This left her free to reply only to what had been said.

"That the Boulevard Malesherbes may be common ground for us offers me the best prospect I see for the pleasure of meeting you again."

"Oh I shall come to see you, since you've been so good": and Mrs. Pocock looked her invader well in the eyes. The flush in Sarah's cheeks had by this time settled to a small definite crimson spot that was not without its own bravery; she held her head a good deal up, and it came to Strether that of the two, at this moment, she was the one who most carried out the idea of a Countess. He quite took in, however, that she would really return her visitor's civility: she wouldn't report again at Woollett without at least so much producible history as that in her pocket.

"I want extremely to be able to show you my little daughter." Madame de Vionnet went on; "and I should have brought her with me if

I hadn't wished first to ask your leave. I was in hopes I should perhaps find Miss Pocock, of whose being with you I've heard from Mr. Newsome and whose acquaintance I should so much like my child to make. If I have the pleasure of seeing her and you do permit it I shall venture to ask her to be kind to Jeanne. Mr. Strether will tell you"—she beautifully kept it up—"that my poor girl is gentle and good and rather lonely. They've made friends, he and she, ever so happily, and he doesn't, I believe, think ill of her. As for Jeanne herself he has had the same success with her that I know he has had here wherever he has turned." She seemed to ask him for permission to say these things, or seemed rather to take it, softly and happily, with the ease of intimacy, for granted, and he had quite the consciousness now that not to meet her at any point more than halfway would be odiously, basely to abandon her. Yes, he was WITH her, and, opposed even in this covert, this semi-safe fashion to those who were not, he felt, strangely and confusedly, but excitedly, inspiringly, how much and how far. It was as if he had positively waited in suspense for something from her that would let him in deeper, so that he might show her how he could take it. And what did in fact come as she drew out a little her farewell served sufficiently the purpose. "As his success is a matter that I'm sure he'll never mention for himself, I feel, you see, the less scruple; which it's very good of me to say, you know, by the way," she added as she addressed herself to him; "considering how little direct advantage I've gained from your triumphs with ME. When does one ever see you? I wait at home and I languish. You'll have rendered me the service, Mrs. Pocock, at least," she wound up, "of giving me one of my much-too-rare glimpses of this gentleman."

"I certainly should be sorry to deprive you of anything that seems as much, as you describe it, your natural due. Mr. Strether and I are very old friends," Sarah allowed, "but the privilege of his society isn't a thing I shall quarrel about with any one."

"And yet, dear Sarah," he freely broke in, "I feel, when I hear you say that, that you don't quite do justice to the important truth of the extent to which—as you're also mine—I'm your natural due. I should like much better," he laughed, "to see you fight for me."

She met him, Mrs. Pocock, on this, with an arrest of speech—with a certain breathlessness, as he immediately fancied, on the score of a freedom for which she wasn't quite prepared. It had flared up—for all the harm he had intended by it—because, confoundedly, he didn't want any more to be afraid about her than he wanted to be afraid about Madame de Vionnet. He had never, naturally, called her anything but Sarah at home, and though he had perhaps never quite so markedly invoked her as his "dear," that was somehow partly because no occasion had hitherto laid so effective a trap for it. But something admonished him now that it was too late—unless indeed it were possibly too early; and that he at any rate shouldn't have pleased Mrs. Pocock the more by it. "Well, Mr. Strether—!" she murmured with vagueness, yet with sharpness, while her crimson spot burned a trifle brighter and he was aware that this must be for the present the limit of her response. Madame de Vionnet had already, however, come to his aid, and Waymarsh, as if for further participation, moved again back to them. It was true that the aid rendered by Madame de Vionnet was questionable; it was a sign that, for all one might confess to with her, and for all she might complain of not enjoying, she could still insidiously show how much of the material of conversation had accumulated between them.

"The real truth is, you know, that you sacrifice one without mercy to dear old Maria. She leaves no room in your life for anybody else. Do you know," she enquired of Mrs. Pocock, "about dear old Maria? The worst is that Miss Gostrey is really a wonderful woman."

"Oh yes indeed," Strether answered for her, "Mrs. Pocock knows about Miss Gostrey. Your mother, Sarah, must have told you about her; your mother knows everything," he sturdily pursued. "And I cordially admit," he added with his conscious gaiety of courage, "that she's as wonderful a woman as you like."

"Ah it isn't I who 'like,' dear Mr. Strether, anything to do with the matter!" Sarah Pocock promptly protested; "and I'm by no means sure I have—from my mother or from any one else—a notion of whom you're talking about."

"Well, he won't let you see her, you know," Madame de Vionnet sympathetically threw in. "He never lets me—old friends as we are: I mean as I am with Maria. He reserves her for his best hours; keeps her consummately to himself; only gives us others the crumbs of the feast."

"Well, Countess, I'VE had some of the crumbs," Waymarsh observed with weight and covering her with his large look; which led her to break in before he could go on.

"Comment donc, he shares her with YOU?" she exclaimed in droll stupefaction. "Take care you don't have, before you go much further, rather more of all ces dames than you may know what to do with!"

But he only continued in his massive way. "I can post you about the lady, Mrs. Pocock, so far as you may care to hear. I've seen her quite a number of times, and I was practically present when they made acquaintance. I've kept my eye on her right along, but I don't know as there's any real harm in her."

"'Harm'?" Madame de Vionnet quickly echoed. "Why she's the dearest and cleverest of all the clever and dear."

"Well, you run her pretty close, Countess," Waymarsh returned with spirit; "though there's no doubt she's pretty well up in things. She knows her way round Europe. Above all there's no doubt she does love Strether."

"Ah but we all do that—we all love Strether: it isn't a merit!" their fellow visitor laughed, keeping to her idea with a good conscience at which our friend was aware that he marvelled, though he trusted also for it, as he met her exquisitely expressive eyes, to some later light.

The prime effect of her tone, however—and it was a truth which his own eyes gave back to her in sad ironic play—could only be to make him feel that, to say such things to a man in public, a woman must practically think of him as ninety years old. He had turned awkwardly, responsively red, he knew, at her mention of Maria Gostrey; Sarah Pocock's presence—the particular quality of it—had made this inevitable; and then he had grown still redder in proportion as he hated to have shown anything at all. He felt indeed that he was showing much, as, uncomfortably and almost in pain, he offered up his redness to Waymarsh, who, strangely enough, seemed now to be looking at him with a certain explanatory yearning. Something deep—something built on their old old relation—passed, in this complexity, between them; he got the side-wind of a loyalty that stood behind all actual queer questions. Waymarsh's dry bare humour—as it gave itself to be taken—gloomed out to demand justice. "Well, if you talk of Miss Barrace I've MY chance too," it appeared stiffly to nod, and it granted that it was giving him away, but struggled to add that it did so only to save him. The sombre glow stared it at him till it fairly sounded out—"to save you, poor old man, to save you; to save you in spite of yourself." Yet it was somehow just this communication that showed him to himself as more than ever lost. Still another result of it was to put before him as never yet that between this comrade and the interest represented by Sarah there was already a basis. Beyond all question now, yes: Waymarsh had been in occult relation with Mrs. Newsome—out, out it all came in the very effort of his face. "Yes, you're feeling my hand"—he as good as proclaimed it; "but only because this is at least I SHALL have got out of the damned Old World: that I shall have picked up the pieces into which it has caused you to crumble." It was as if in short, after an instant, Strether had not only had it from him, but had recognised that so far as this went the instant had cleared the air. Our friend understood and approved; he had the sense that they wouldn't otherwise speak of it. This would be all, and it would amount to himself a kind of intelligent generosity. It was with grim Sarah then—Sarah grim for all her grace—that Waymarsh had begun at ten o'clock in the morning to save him. Well—if he COULD, poor dear man, with his big bleak kindness! The upshot of which crowded perception was that Strether, on his own side, still showed no more than he absolutely had to. He showed the least possible by saying to Mrs. Pocock after an interval much briefer than our glance at the picture reflected in him: "Oh it's as true as they please!—There's no Miss Gostrey for any one but me—not the least little peep. I keep her to myself."

"Well, it's very good of you to notify me," Sarah replied without looking at him and thrown for a moment by this discrimination, as the direction of her eyes showed, upon a dimly desperate little community with Madame de Vionnet. "But I hope I shan't miss her too much."

Madame de Vionnet instantly rallied. "And you know—though it might occur to one—it isn't in the least that he's ashamed of her. She's really—in a way—extremely good-looking."

"Ah but extremely!" Strether laughed while he wondered at the odd part he found thus imposed on him.

It continued to be so by every touch from Madame de Vionnet. "Well, as I say, you know, I wish you would keep ME a little more to yourself. Couldn't you name some day for me, some hour—and better soon than late? I'll be at home whenever it best suits you. There—I can't say fairer."

Strether thought a moment while Waymarsh and Mrs. Pocock affected him as standing attentive. "I did lately call on you. Last week—while Chad was out of town."

"Yes—and I was away, as it happened, too. You choose your moments well. But don't wait for my next absence, for I shan't make another," Madame de Vionnet declared, "while Mrs. Pocock's here."

"That vow needn't keep you long, fortunately," Sarah observed with reasserted suavity. "I shall be at present but a short time in Paris. I have my plans for other countries. I meet a number of charming friends"—and her voice seemed to caress that description of these persons.

"Ah then," her visitor cheerfully replied, "all the more reason! To-morrow, for instance, or next day?" she continued to Strether. "Tuesday would do for me beautifully."

"Tuesday then with pleasure."

"And at half-past five?—or at six?"

It was ridiculous, but Mrs. Pocock and Waymarsh struck him as fairly waiting for his answer. It was indeed as if they were arranged, gathered for a performance, the performance of "Europe" by his confederate and himself. Well, the performance could only go on. "Say five forty-five."

"Five forty-five—good." And now at last Madame de Vionnet must leave them, though it carried, for herself, the performance a little further. "I DID hope so much also to see Miss Pocock. Mayn't I still?"

Sarah hesitated, but she rose equal. "She'll return your visit with me. She's at present out with Mr. Pocock and my brother."

"I see—of course Mr. Newsome has everything to show them. He has told me so much about her. My great desire's to give my daughter the opportunity of making her acquaintance. I'm always on the lookout for such chances for her. If I didn't bring her to-day it was only to make sure first that you'd let me." After which the charming woman risked a more intense appeal. "It wouldn't suit you also to mention some near time, so that we shall be sure not to lose you?" Strether on his side waited, for Sarah likewise had, after all, to perform; and it occupied him to have been thus reminded that she had stayed at home—and on her first morning of Paris—while Chad led the others forth. Oh she was up to her eyes; if she had stayed at home she had stayed by an understanding, arrived at the evening before, that Waymarsh would come and find her alone. This was beginning well—for a first day in Paris; and the thing might be amusing yet. But Madame de Vionnet's earnestness was meanwhile beautiful. "You may think me indiscreet, but I've SUCH a desire my Jeanne shall know an American girl of the really delightful kind. You see I throw myself for it on your charity."

The manner of this speech gave Strether such a sense of depths below it and behind it as he hadn't yet had—ministered in a way that almost frightened him to his dim divinations of reasons; but if Sarah still, in spite of it, faltered, this was why he had time for a sign of sympathy with her petitioner. "Let me say then, dear lady, to back your plea, that Miss Mamie is of the most delightful kind of all—is charming among the charming."

Even Waymarsh, though with more to produce on the subject, could get into motion in time. "Yes, Countess, the American girl's a thing that your country must at least allow ours the privilege to say we CAN show you. But her full beauty is only for those who know how to make use of her."

"Ah then," smiled Madame de Vionnet, "that's exactly what I want to do. I'm sure she has much to teach us."

It was wonderful, but what was scarce less so was that Strether found himself, by the quick effect of it, moved another way. "Oh that may be! But don't speak of your own exquisite daughter, you know, as if she weren't pure perfection. I at least won't take that from you. Mademoiselle de Vionnet," he explained, in considerable form, to Mrs. Pocock, "IS pure perfection. Mademoiselle de Vionnet IS exquisite."

It had been perhaps a little portentous, but "Ah?" Sarah simply glittered.

Waymarsh himself, for that matter, apparently recognised, in respect to the facts, the need of a larger justice, and he had with it an inclination to Sarah. "Miss Jane's strikingly handsome—in the regular French style."

It somehow made both Strether and Madame de Vionnet laugh out, though at the very moment he caught in Sarah's eyes, as glancing at the speaker, a vague but unmistakeable "You too?" It made Waymarsh in fact look consciously over her head. Madame de Vionnet meanwhile, however, made her point in her own way. "I wish indeed I could offer you my poor child as a dazzling attraction: it would make one's position simple enough! She's as good as she can be, but of course she's different, and the question is now—in the light of the way things seem to go—if she isn't after all TOO different: too different I mean from the splendid type every one is so agreed that your wonderful country produces. On the other hand of course Mr. Newsome, who knows it so well, has, as a good friend, dear kind man that he is, done everything he can—to keep us from fatal benightedness—for my small shy creature. Well," she wound up after Mrs. Pocock had signified, in a murmur still a little stiff, that she would speak to her own young charge on the question—"well, we shall sit, my child and I, and wait and wait and wait for you." But her last fine turn was for Strether. "Do speak of us in such a way—!"

"As that something can't but come of it? Oh something SHALL come of it! I take a great interest!" he further declared; and in proof of it, the next moment, he had gone with her down to her carriage.

Book Ninth

I

"The difficulty is," Strether said to Madame de Vionnet a couple of days later, "that I can't surprise them into the smallest sign of his not being the same old Chad they've been for the last three years glowering at across the sea. They simply won't give any, and as a policy, you know—what you call a parti pris, a deep game—that's positively remarkable."

It was so remarkable that our friend had pulled up before his hostess with the vision of it; he had risen from his chair at the end of ten minutes and begun, as a help not to worry, to move about before her quite as he moved before Maria. He had kept his appointment with her to the minute and had been intensely impatient, though divided in truth between the sense of having everything to tell her and the sense of having nothing at all. The short interval had, in the face of their complication, multiplied his impressions—it being meanwhile to be noted, moreover, that he already frankly, already almost publicly, viewed the complication as common to them. If Madame de Vionnet, under Sarah's eyes, had pulled him into her boat, there was by this time no doubt whatever that he had remained in it and that what he had really most been conscious of for many hours together was the movement of the vessel itself. They were in it together as they hadn't yet been, and he hadn't at present uttered the least of the words of alarm or remonstrance that had died on his lips at the hotel. He had other things to say to her than that she had put him in a position; so quickly had his position grown to affect him as quite excitingly, altogether richly, inevitable. That the outlook, however—given the point of exposure—hadn't cleared up half so much as he had reckoned was the first warning she received from him on his arrival. She had replied with indulgence that he was in too great a hurry, and had remarked soothingly that if she knew how to be patient surely HE might be. He felt her presence, on the spot, he felt her tone and everything about her, as an aid to that effort; and it was perhaps one of the proofs of her success with him that he seemed so much to take his ease while they talked. By the time he had explained to her why his impressions, though multiplied, still baffled him, it was as if he had been familiarly talking for hours. They baffled him because Sarah—well, Sarah was deep, deeper than she had ever yet had a chance to show herself. He didn't say that this was partly the effect of her opening so straight down, as it were, into her mother, and that, given Mrs. Newsome's profundity, the shaft thus sunk might well have a reach; but he wasn't without a resigned apprehension that, at such a rate of confidence between the two women, he was likely soon to be moved to show how already, at moments, it had been for him as if he were dealing directly with Mrs. Newsome. Sarah, to a certainty, would have begun herself to feel it in him—and this naturally put it in her power to torment him the more. From the moment she knew she COULD be tormented—!

"But WHY can you be?"—his companion was surprised at his use of the word.

"Because I'm made so—I think of everything."

"Ah one must never do that," she smiled. "One must think of as few things as possible."

"Then," he answered, "one must pick them out right. But all I mean is—for I express myself with violence—that she's in a position to watch me. There's an element of suspense for me, and she can see me wriggle. But my wriggling doesn't matter," he pursued. "I can bear it. Besides, I shall wriggle out."

The picture at any rate stirred in her an appreciation that he felt to be sincere. "I don't see how a man can be kinder to a woman than you are to me."

Well, kind was what he wanted to be; yet even while her charming eyes rested on him with the truth of this he none the less had his humour of honesty. "When I say suspense I mean, you know," he laughed, "suspense about my own case too!"

"Oh yes—about your own case too!" It diminished his magnanimity, but she only looked at him the more tenderly.

"Not, however," he went on, "that I want to talk to you about that. It's my own little affair, and I mentioned it simply as part of Mrs. Pocock's advantage." No, no; though there was a queer present temptation in it, and his suspense was so real that to fidget was a relief, he wouldn't talk to her about Mrs. Newsome, wouldn't work off on her the anxiety produced in him by Sarah's calculated omissions of reference. The effect she produced of representing her mother had been produced—and that was just the immense, the uncanny part of it—without her having so much as mentioned that lady. She had brought no message, had alluded to no question, had only answered his enquiries with hopeless limited propriety. She had invented a way of meeting them—as if he had been a polite perfunctory poor relation, of distant degree—that made them almost ridiculous in him. He couldn't moreover on his own side ask much without appearing to publish how he had lately lacked news; a circumstance of which it was Sarah's profound policy not to betray a suspicion. These things, all the same, he wouldn't breathe to Madame de Vionnet—much as they might make him walk up and down. And what he didn't say—as well as what SHE didn't, for she had also her high decencies—enhanced the effect of his being there with her at the end of ten minutes more intimately on the basis of saving her than he had yet had occasion to be. It ended in fact by being quite beautiful between them, the number of things they had a manifest consciousness of not saying. He would have liked to turn her, critically, to the subject of Mrs. Pocock, but he so stuck to the line he felt to be the point of honour and of delicacy that he scarce even asked her what her personal impression had been. He knew it, for that matter, without putting her to trouble: that she wondered how, with such elements, Sarah could still have no charm, was one of the principal things she held her tongue about. Strether would have been interested in her estimate of the elements—indubitably there, some of them, and to be appraised according to taste—but he denied himself even the luxury of this diversion. The way Madame de Vionnet affected him to-day was in itself a kind of demonstration of the happy employment of gifts. How could a woman think Sarah had charm who struck one as having arrived at it herself by such different roads? On the other hand of course Sarah wasn't obliged to have it. He felt as if somehow Madame de Vionnet WAS. The great question meanwhile was what Chad thought of his sister; which was naturally ushered in by that of Sarah's apprehension of Chad. THAT they could talk of, and with a freedom purchased by their discretion in other senses. The difficulty however was that they were reduced as yet to conjecture. He had given them in the day or two as little of a lead as Sarah, and Madame de Vionnet mentioned that she hadn't seen him since his sister's arrival.

"And does that strike you as such an age?"

She met it in all honesty. "Oh I won't pretend I don't miss him. Sometimes I see him every day. Our friendship's like that. Make what you will of it!" she whimsically smiled; a little flicker of the kind, occasional in her, that had more than once moved him to wonder what he might best make of HER. "But he's perfectly right," she hastened to add, "and I wouldn't have him fail in any way at present for the world. I'd sooner not see him for three months. I begged him to be beautiful to them, and he fully feels it for himself."

Strether turned away under his quick perception; she was so odd a mixture of lucidity and mystery. She fell in at moments with the theory about her he most cherished, and she seemed at others to blow it into air. She spoke now as if her art were all an innocence, and then again as if her innocence were all an art. "Oh he's giving himself up, and he'll do so to the end. How can he but want, now that it's within reach, his full impression?—which is much more important, you know, than either yours or mine. But he's just soaking," Strether said as he came back; "he's going in conscientiously for a saturation. I'm bound to say he IS very good."

"Ah," she quietly replied, "to whom do you say it?" And then more quietly still: "He's capable of anything."

Strether more than reaffirmed—"Oh he's excellent. I more and more like," he insisted, "to see him with them;" though the oddity of this tone between them grew sharper for him even while they spoke. It placed the young man so before them as the result of her interest and the product of her genius, acknowledged so her part in the phenomenon and made the phenomenon so rare, that more than ever yet he might have been on the very point of asking her for some more detailed account of the whole business than he had yet received from her. The occasion almost forced upon him some question as to how she had managed and as to the appearance such miracles presented from her own singularly close place of survey. The moment in fact however passed, giving way to more present history, and he continued simply to mark his appreciation of the happy truth. "It's a tremendous comfort to feel how one can trust him." And then again while for a little she said nothing—as if after all to HER trust there might be a special limit: "I mean for making a good show to them."

"Yes," she thoughtfully returned—"but if they shut their eyes to it!"

Strether for an instant had his own thought. "Well perhaps that won't matter!"

"You mean because he probably—do what they will—won't like them?"

"Oh 'do what they will'—! They won't do much; especially if Sarah hasn't more—well, more than one has yet made out—to give."

Madame de Vionnet weighed it. "Ah she has all her grace!" It was a statement over which, for a little, they could look at each other sufficiently straight, and though it produced no protest from Strether the effect was somehow as if he had treated it as a joke. "She may be persuasive and caressing with him; she may be eloquent beyond words. She may get hold of him," she wound up—"well, as neither you nor I have."

"Yes, she MAY"—and now Strether smiled. "But he has spent all his time each day with Jim. He's still showing Jim round."

She visibly wondered. "Then how about Jim?"

Strether took a turn before he answered. "Hasn't he given you Jim? Hasn't he before this 'done' him for you?" He was a little at a loss. "Doesn't he tell you things?"

She hesitated. "No"—and their eyes once more gave and took. "Not as you do. You somehow make me see them—or at least feel them. And I haven't asked too much," she added; "I've of late wanted so not to worry him."

"Ah for that, so have I," he said with encouraging assent; so that—as if she had answered everything—they were briefly sociable on it. It threw him back on his other thought, with which he took another turn; stopping again, however, presently with something of a glow. "You see Jim's really immense. I think it will be Jim who'll do it."

She wondered. "Get hold of him?"

"No—just the other thing. Counteract Sarah's spell." And he showed now, our friend, how far he had worked it out. "Jim's intensely cynical."

"Oh dear Jim!" Madame de Vionnet vaguely smiled.

"Yes, literally—dear Jim! He's awful. What HE wants, heaven forgive him, is to help us."

"You mean"—she was eager—"help ME?"

"Well, Chad and me in the first place. But he throws you in too, though without as yet seeing you much. Only, so far as he does see you—if you don't mind—he sees you as awful."

"Awful?"—she wanted it all.

"A regular bad one—though of course of a tremendously superior kind. Dreadful, delightful, irresistible."

"Ah dear Jim! I should like to know him. I MUST."

"Yes, naturally. But will it do? You may, you know," Strether suggested, "disappoint him."

She was droll and humble about it. "I can but try. But my wickedness then," she went on, "is my recommendation for him?"

"Your wickedness and the charms with which, in such a degree as yours, he associates it. He understands, you see, that Chad and I have above all wanted to have a good time, and his view is simple and sharp. Nothing will persuade him—in the light, that is, of my behaviour—that I really didn't, quite as much as Chad, come over to have one before it was too late. He wouldn't have expected it of me; but men of my age, at Woollett—and especially the least likely ones—have been noted as liable to strange outbreaks, belated uncanny clutches at the unusual, the ideal. It's an effect that a lifetime of Woollett has quite been observed as having; and I thus give it to you, in Jim's view, for what it's worth. Now his wife and his mother-in-law," Strether continued to explain, "have, as in honour bound, no patience with such phenomena, late or early—which puts Jim, as against his relatives, on the other side. Besides," he added, "I don't think he really wants Chad back. If Chad doesn't come—"

"He'll have"—Madame de Vionnet quite apprehended—"more of the free hand?"

"Well, Chad's the bigger man."

"So he'll work now, en dessous, to keep him quiet?"

"No—he won't 'work' at all, and he won't do anything en dessous. He's very decent and won't be a traitor in the camp. But he'll be amused with his own little view of our duplicity, he'll sniff up what he supposes to be Paris from morning till night, and he'll be, as to the rest, for Chad—well, just what he is."

She thought it over. "A warning?"

He met it almost with glee. "You ARE as wonderful as everybody says!" And then to explain all he meant: "I drove him about for his first hour, and do you know what—all beautifully unconscious—he most put before me? Why that something like THAT is at bottom, as an improvement to his present state, as in fact the real redemption of it, what they think it may not be too late to make of our friend." With which, as, taking it in, she seemed, in her recurrent alarm, bravely to gaze at the possibility, he completed his statement. "But it IS too late. Thanks to you!"

It drew from her again one of her indefinite reflexions. "Oh 'me'—after all!"

He stood before her so exhilarated by his demonstration that he could fairly be jocular. "Everything's comparative. You're better than THAT."

"You"—she could but answer him—"are better than anything." But she had another thought. "WILL Mrs. Pocock come to me?"

"Oh yes—she'll do that. As soon, that is, as my friend Waymarsh—HER friend now—leaves her leisure."

She showed an interest. "Is he so much her friend as that?"

"Why, didn't you see it all at the hotel?"

"Oh"—she was amused—"'all' is a good deal to say. I don't know—I forget. I lost myself in HER."

"You were splendid," Strether returned—"but 'all' isn't a good deal to say: it's only a little. Yet it's charming so far as it goes. She wants a man to herself."

"And hasn't she got you?"

"Do you think she looked at me—or even at you—as if she had?" Strether easily dismissed that irony. "Every one, you see, must strike her as having somebody. You've got Chad—and Chad has got you."

"I see"—she made of it what she could. "And you've got Maria."

Well, he on his side accepted that. "I've got Maria. And Maria has got me. So it goes."

"But Mr. Jim—whom has he got?"

"Oh he has got—or it's as IF he had—the whole place."

"But for Mr. Waymarsh"—she recalled—"isn't Miss Barrace before any one else?"

He shook his head. "Miss Barrace is a raffinee, and her amusement won't lose by Mrs. Pocock. It will gain rather—especially if Sarah triumphs and she comes in for a view of it."

"How well you know us!" Madame de Vionnet, at this, frankly sighed.

"No—it seems to me it's we that I know. I know Sarah—it's perhaps on that ground only that my feet are firm. Waymarsh will take her round while Chad takes Jim—and I shall be, I assure you delighted for both of them. Sarah will have had what she requires—she will have paid her tribute to the ideal; and he will have done about the same. In Paris it's in the air—so what can one do less? If there's a point that, beyond any other, Sarah wants to make, it's that she didn't come out to be narrow. We shall feel at least that."

"Oh," she sighed, "the quantity we seem likely to 'feel'! But what becomes, in these conditions, of the girl?"

"Of Mamie—if we're all provided? Ah for that," said Strether, "you can trust Chad."

"To be, you mean, all right to her?"

"To pay her every attention as soon as he has polished off Jim. He wants what Jim can give him—and what Jim really won't—though he has had it all, and more than all, from me. He wants in short his own personal impression, and he'll get it—strong. But as soon as he has got it Mamie won't suffer."

"Oh Mamie mustn't SUFFER!" Madame de Vionnet soothingly emphasised.

But Strether could reassure her. "Don't fear. As soon as he has done with Jim, Jim will fall to me. And then you'll see."

It was as if in a moment she saw already; yet she still waited. Then "Is she really quite charming?" she asked.

He had got up with his last words and gathered in his hat and gloves. "I don't know; I'm watching. I'm studying the case, as it were—and I dare say I shall be able to tell you."

She wondered. "Is it a case?"

"Yes—I think so. At any rate I shall see.'

"But haven't you known her before?"

"Yes," he smiled—"but somehow at home she wasn't a case. She has become one since." It was as if he made it out for himself. "She has become one here."

"So very very soon?"

He measured it, laughing. "Not sooner than I did."

"And you became one—?"

"Very very soon. The day I arrived."

Her intelligent eyes showed her thought of it. "Ah but the day you arrived you met Maria. Whom has Miss Pocock met?"

He paused again, but he brought it out. "Hasn't she met Chad?"

"Certainly—but not for the first time. He's an old friend." At which Strether had a slow amused significant headshake that made her go on: "You mean that for HER at least he's a new person—that she sees him as different?"

"She sees him as different."

"And how does she see him?"

Strether gave it up. "How can one tell how a deep little girl sees a deep young man?"

"Is every one so deep? Is she too?"

"So it strikes me deeper than I thought. But wait a little—between us we'll make it out. You'll judge for that matter yourself."

Madame de Vionnet looked for the moment fairly bent on the chance. "Then she WILL come with her?—I mean Mamie with Mrs. Pocock?"

"Certainly. Her curiosity, if nothing else, will in any case work that. But leave it all to Chad."

"Ah," wailed Madame de Vionnet, turning away a little wearily, "the things I leave to Chad!"

The tone of it made him look at her with a kindness that showed his vision of her suspense. But he fell back on his confidence. "Oh well—trust him. Trust him all the way." He had indeed no sooner so spoken than the queer displacement of his point of view appeared again to come up for him in the very sound, which drew from him a short laugh, immediately checked. He became still more advisory. "When they do come give them plenty of Miss Jeanne. Let Mamie see her well."

She looked for a moment as if she placed them face to face. "For Mamie to hate her?"

He had another of his corrective headshakes. "Mamie won't. Trust THEM."

She looked at him hard, and then as if it were what she must always come back to: "It's you I trust. But I was sincere," she said, "at the hotel. I did, I do, want my child—"

"Well?"—Strether waited with deference while she appeared to hesitate as to how to put it.

"Well, to do what she can for me."

Strether for a little met her eyes on it; after which something that might have been unexpected to her came from him. "Poor little duck!"

Not more expected for himself indeed might well have been her echo of it. "Poor little duck! But she immensely wants herself," she said, "to see our friend's cousin."

"Is that what she thinks her?"

"It's what we call the young lady."

He thought again; then with a laugh: "Well, your daughter will help you."

And now at last he took leave of her, as he had been intending for five minutes. But she went part of the way with him, accompanying him out of the room and into the next and the next. Her noble old apartment offered a succession of three, the first two of which indeed, on entering, smaller than the last, but each with its faded and formal air, enlarged the office of the antechamber and enriched the sense of approach. Strether fancied them, liked them, and, passing through them with her more slowly now, met a sharp renewal of his original impression. He stopped, he looked back; the whole thing made a vista, which he found high melancholy and sweet—full, once more, of dim historic shades, of the faint faraway cannon-roar of the great Empire. It was doubtless half the projection of his mind, but his mind was a thing that, among old waxed parquets, pale shades of pink and green, pseudo-classic candelabra, he had always needfully to reckon with. They could easily make him irrelevant. The oddity, the originality, the poetry—he didn't know what to call it—of Chad's connexion reaffirmed for him its romantic side. "They ought to see this, you know. They MUST."

"The Pococks?"—she looked about in deprecation; she seemed to see gaps he didn't.

"Mamie and Sarah—Mamie in particular."

"My shabby old place? But THEIR things—!"

"Oh their things! You were talking of what will do something for you—"

"So that it strikes you," she broke in, "that my poor place may? Oh," she ruefully mused, "that WOULD be desperate!"

"Do you know what I wish?" he went on. "I wish Mrs. Newsome could have a look."

She stared, missing a little his logic. "It would make a difference?"

Her tone was so earnest that as he continued to look about he laughed. "It might!"

"But you've told her, you tell me—"

"All about you? Yes, a wonderful story. But there's all the indescribable—what one gets only on the spot."

"Thank you!" she charmingly and sadly smiled.

"It's all about me here," he freely continued. "Mrs. Newsome feels things."

But she seemed doomed always to come back to doubt. "No one feels so much as YOU. No—not any one."

"So much the worse then for every one. It's very easy."

They were by this time in the antechamber, still alone together, as she hadn't rung for a servant. The antechamber was high and square, grave and suggestive too, a little cold and slippery even in summer, and with a few old prints that were precious, Strether divined, on the walls. He stood in the middle, slightly lingering, vaguely directing his glasses, while, leaning against the door-post of the room, she gently pressed her cheek to the side of the recess. "YOU would have been a friend."

"I?"—it startled him a little.

"For the reason you say. You're not stupid." And then abruptly, as if bringing it out were somehow founded on that fact: "We're marrying Jeanne."

It affected him on the spot as a move in a game, and he was even then not without the sense that that wasn't the way Jeanne should be married. But he quickly showed his interest, though—as quickly afterwards struck him—with an absurd confusion of mind. "'You'? You and—a—not Chad?" Of course it was the child's father who made the 'we,' but to the child's father it would have cost him an effort to allude. Yet didn't it seem the next minute that Monsieur de Vionnet was after all not in question?—since she had gone on to say that it was indeed to Chad she referred and that he had been in the whole matter kindness itself.

"If I must tell you all, it is he himself who has put us in the way. I mean in the way of an opportunity that, so far as I can yet see, is all I could possibly have dreamed of. For all the trouble Monsieur de Vionnet will ever take!" It was the first time she had spoken to him of her husband, and he couldn't have expressed how much more intimate with her it suddenly made him feel. It wasn't much, in truth—there were other things in what she was saying that were far more; but it was as if, while they stood there together so easily in these cold chambers of the past, the single touch had shown the reach of her confidence. "But our friend," she asked, "hasn't then told you?"

"He has told me nothing."

"Well, it has come with rather a rush—all in a very few days; and hasn't moreover yet taken a form that permits an announcement. It's only for you—absolutely you alone—that I speak; I so want you to know." The sense he had so often had, since the first hour of his disembarkment, of being further and further "in," treated him again at this moment to another twinge; but in this wonderful way of her putting him in there continued to be something exquisitely remorseless. "Monsieur de Vionnet will accept what he MUST accept. He has proposed half a dozen things—each one more impossible than the other; and he wouldn't have found this if he lives to a hundred. Chad found it," she continued with her lighted, faintly flushed, her conscious confidential face, "in the quietest way in the world. Or rather it found HIM—for everything finds him; I mean finds him right. You'll think we do such things strangely—but at my age," she smiled, "one has to accept one's conditions. Our young man's people had seen her; one of his sisters, a charming woman—we know all about them—had observed her somewhere with me. She had spoken to her brother—turned him on; and we were again observed, poor Jeanne and I, without our in the least knowing it. It was at the beginning of the winter; it went on for some time; it outlasted our absence; it began again on our return; and it luckily seems all right. The young man had met Chad, and he got a friend to approach him—as having a decent interest in us. Mr. Newsome looked well before he leaped; he kept beautifully quiet and satisfied himself fully; then only he spoke. It's what has for some time past occupied us. It seems as if it were what would do; really, really all one could wish. There are only two or three points to be settled—they depend on her father. But this time I think we're safe."

Strether, consciously gaping a little, had fairly hung upon her lips. "I hope so with all my heart." And then he permitted himself: "Does nothing depend on HER?"

"Ah naturally; everything did. But she's pleased comme tout. She has been perfectly free; and he—our young friend—is really a combination. I quite adore him."

Strether just made sure. "You mean your future son-in-law?"

"Future if we all bring it off."

"Ah well," said Strether decorously, "I heartily hope you may." There seemed little else for him to say, though her communication had the oddest effect on him. Vaguely and confusedly he was troubled by it; feeling as if he had even himself been concerned in something deep and dim. He had allowed for depths, but these were greater: and it was as if, oppressively—indeed absurdly—he was responsible for what they had now thrown up to the surface. It was—through something ancient and cold in it—what he would have called the real thing. In short his hostess's news, though he couldn't have explained why, was a sensible shock, and his oppression a weight he felt he must somehow or other immediately get rid of. There were too many connexions missing to make it tolerable he should do anything else. He was prepared to suffer—before his own inner tribunal—for Chad; he was prepared to suffer even for Madame de Vionnet. But he wasn't prepared to suffer for the little girl. So now having said the proper thing, he wanted to get away. She held him an instant, however, with another appeal.

"Do I seem to you very awful?"

"Awful? Why so?" But he called it to himself, even as he spoke, his biggest insincerity yet.

"Our arrangements are so different from yours."

"Mine?" Oh he could dismiss that too! "I haven't any arrangements."

"Then you must accept mine; all the more that they're excellent. They're founded on a vieille sagesse. There will be much more, if all goes well, for you to hear and to know, and everything, believe me, for you to like. Don't be afraid; you'll be satisfied." Thus she could talk to him of what, of her innermost life—for that was what it came to—he must "accept"; thus she could extraordinarily speak as if in such an affair his being satisfied had an importance. It was all a wonder and made the whole case larger. He had struck himself at the hotel, before Sarah and Waymarsh, as being in her boat; but where on earth was he now? This question was in the air till her own lips quenched it with another. "And do you suppose HE—who loves her so—would do anything reckless or cruel?"

He wondered what he supposed. "Do you mean your young man—?"

"I mean yours. I mean Mr. Newsome." It flashed for Strether the next moment a finer light, and the light deepened as she went on. "He takes, thank God, the truest tenderest interest in her."

It deepened indeed. "Oh I'm sure of that!"

"You were talking," she said, "about one's trusting him. You see then how I do."

He waited a moment—it all came. "I see—I see." He felt he really did see.

"He wouldn't hurt her for the world, nor—assuming she marries at all—risk anything that might make against her happiness. And—willingly, at least—he would never hurt ME."

Her face, with what he had by this time grasped, told him more than her words; whether something had come into it, or whether he only read clearer, her whole story—what at least he then took for such—reached out to him from it. With the initiative she now attributed to Chad it all made a sense, and this sense—a light, a lead, was what had abruptly risen before him. He wanted, once more, to get off with these things; which was at last made easy, a servant having, for his assistance, on hearing voices in the hall, just come forward. All that Strether had made out was, while the man opened the door and impersonally waited, summed up in his last word. "I don't think, you know, Chad will tell me anything."

"No—perhaps not yet."

"And I won't as yet speak to him."

"Ah that's as you'll think best. You must judge."

She had finally given him her hand, which he held a moment. "How MUCH I have to judge!"

"Everything," said Madame de Vionnet: a remark that was indeed—with the refined disguised suppressed passion of her face—what he most carried away.

II

So far as a direct approach was concerned Sarah had neglected him, for the week now about to end, with a civil consistency of chill that, giving him a higher idea of her social resource, threw him back on the general reflexion that a woman could always be amazing. It indeed helped a little to console him that he felt sure she had for the same period also left Chad's curiosity hanging; though on the other hand, for his personal relief, Chad could at least go through the various motions—and he made them extraordinarily numerous—of seeing she had a good time. There wasn't a motion on which, in her presence, poor Strether could so much as venture, and all he could do when he was out of it was to walk over for a talk with Maria. He walked over of course much less than usual, but he found a special compensation in a certain half-hour during which, toward the close of a crowded expensive day, his several companions seemed to him so disposed of as to give his forms and usages a rest. He had been with them in the morning and had nevertheless called on the Pococks in the afternoon; but their whole group, he then found, had dispersed after a fashion which it would amuse Miss Gostrey to hear. He was sorry again, gratefully sorry she was so out of it—she who had really put him in; but she had fortunately always her appetite for news. The pure flame of the disinterested burned in her cave of treasures as a lamp in a Byzantine vault. It was just now, as happened, that for so fine a sense as hers a near view would have begun to pay. Within three days, precisely, the situation on which he was to report had shown signs of an equilibrium; the effect of his look in at the hotel was to confirm this appearance. If the equilibrium might only prevail! Sarah was out with Waymarsh, Mamie was out with Chad, and Jim was out alone. Later on indeed he himself was booked to Jim, was to take him that evening to the Varieties—which Strether was careful to pronounce as Jim pronounced them.

Miss Gostrey drank it in. "What then to-night do the others do?"

"Well, it has been arranged. Waymarsh takes Sarah to dine at Bignons."

She wondered. "And what do they do after? They can't come straight home."

"No, they can't come straight home—at least Sarah can't. It's their secret, but I think I've guessed it." Then as she waited: "The circus."

It made her stare a moment longer, then laugh almost to extravagance. "There's no one like you!"

"Like ME?"—he only wanted to understand.

"Like all of you together—like all of us: Woollett, Milrose and their products. We're abysmal—but may we never be less so! Mr. Newsome," she continued, "meanwhile takes Miss Pocock—?"

"Precisely—to the Francais: to see what you took Waymarsh and me to, a family-bill."

"Ah then may Mr. Chad enjoy it as I did!" But she saw so much in things. "Do they spend their evenings, your young people, like that, alone together?"

"Well, they're young people—but they're old friends."

"I see, I see. And do THEY dine—for a difference—at Brebant's?"

"Oh where they dine is their secret too. But I've my idea that it will be, very quietly, at Chad's own place."

"She'll come to him there alone?"

They looked at each other a moment. "He has known her from a child. Besides," said Strether with emphasis, "Mamie's remarkable. She's splendid."

She wondered. "Do you mean she expects to bring it off?"

"Getting hold of him? No—I think not."

"She doesn't want him enough?—or doesn't believe in her power?" On which as he said nothing she continued: "She finds she doesn't care for him?"

"No—I think she finds she does. But that's what I mean by so describing her. It's IF she does that she's splendid. But we'll see," he wound up, "where she comes out."

"You seem to show me sufficiently," Miss Gostrey laughed, "where she goes in! But is her childhood's friend," she asked, "permitting himself recklessly to flirt with her?"

"No—not that. Chad's also splendid. They're ALL splendid!" he declared with a sudden strange sound of wistfulness and envy. "They're at least HAPPY."

"Happy?"—it appeared, with their various difficulties, to surprise her.

"Well—I seem to myself among them the only one who isn't."

She demurred. "With your constant tribute to the ideal?"

He had a laugh at his tribute to the ideal, but he explained after a moment his impression. "I mean they're living. They're rushing about. I've already had my rushing. I'm waiting."

"But aren't you," she asked by way of cheer, "waiting with ME?"

He looked at her in all kindness. "Yes—if it weren't for that!"

"And you help me to wait," she said. "However," she went on, "I've really something for you that will help you to wait and which you shall have in a minute. Only there's something more I want from you first. I revel in Sarah."

"So do I. If it weren't," he again amusedly sighed, "for THAT—!"

"Well, you owe more to women than any man I ever saw. We do seem to keep you going. Yet Sarah, as I see her, must be great."

"She IS" Strether fully assented: "great! Whatever happens, she won't, with these unforgettable days, have lived in vain."

Miss Gostrey had a pause. "You mean she has fallen in love?"

"I mean she wonders if she hasn't—and it serves all her purpose."

"It has indeed," Maria laughed, "served women's purposes before!"

"Yes—for giving in. But I doubt if the idea—as an idea—has ever up to now answered so well for holding out. That's HER tribute to the ideal—we each have our own. It's her romance—and it seems to me better on the whole than mine. To have it in Paris too," he explained—"on this classic ground, in this charged infectious air, with so sudden an intensity: well, it's more than she expected. She has had in short to recognise the breaking out for her of a real affinity—and with everything to enhance the drama."

Miss Gostrey followed. "Jim for instance?"

"Jim. Jim hugely enhances. Jim was made to enhance. And then Mr. Waymarsh. It's the crowning touch—it supplies the colour. He's positively separated."

"And she herself unfortunately isn't—that supplies the colour too." Miss Gostrey was all there. But somehow—! "Is HE in love?"

Strether looked at her a long time; then looked all about the room; then came a little nearer. "Will you never tell any one in the world as long as ever you live?"

"Never." It was charming.

"He thinks Sarah really is. But he has no fear," Strether hastened to add.

"Of her being affected by it?"

"Of HIS being. He likes it, but he knows she can hold out. He's helping her, he's floating her over, by kindness."

Maria rather funnily considered it. "Floating her over in champagne? The kindness of dining her, nose to nose, at the hour when all Paris is crowding to profane delights, and in the—well, in the great temple, as one hears of it, of pleasure?"

"That's just IT, for both of them," Strether insisted—"and all of a supreme innocence. The Parisian place, the feverish hour, the putting before her of a hundred francs' worth of food and drink, which they'll scarcely touch—all that's the dear man's own romance; the expensive kind, expensive in francs and centimes, in which he abounds. And the circus afterwards—which is cheaper, but which he'll find some means of making as dear as possible—that's also HIS tribute to the ideal. It does for him. He'll see her through. They won't talk of anything worse than you and me."

"Well, we're bad enough perhaps, thank heaven," she laughed, "to upset them! Mr. Waymarsh at any rate is a hideous old coquette." And the next moment she had dropped everything for a different pursuit. "What you don't appear to know is that Jeanne de Vionnet has become engaged. She's to marry—it has been definitely arranged—young Monsieur de Montbron."

He fairly blushed. "Then—if you know it—it's 'out'?"

"Don't I often know things that are NOT out? However," she said, "this will be out to-morrow. But I see I've counted too much on your possible ignorance. You've been before me, and I don't make you jump as I hoped."

He gave a gasp at her insight. "You never fail! I've HAD my jump. I had it when I first heard."

"Then if you knew why didn't you tell me as soon as you came in?"

"Because I had it from her as a thing not yet to be spoken of."

Miss Gostrey wondered. "From Madame de Vionnet herself?"

"As a probability—not quite a certainty: a good cause in which Chad has been working. So I've waited."

"You need wait no longer," she returned. "It reached me yesterday—roundabout and accidental, but by a person who had had it from one of the young man's own people—as a thing quite settled. I was only keeping it for you."

"You thought Chad wouldn't have told me?"

She hesitated. "Well, if he hasn't—"

"He hasn't. And yet the thing appears to have been practically his doing. So there we are."

"There we are!" Maria candidly echoed.

"That's why I jumped. I jumped," he continued to explain, "because it means, this disposition of the daughter, that there's now nothing else: nothing else but him and the mother."

"Still—it simplifies."

"It simplifies"—he fully concurred. "But that's precisely where we are. It marks a stage in his relation. The act is his answer to Mrs. Newsome's demonstration."

"It tells," Maria asked, "the worst?"

"The worst."

"But is the worst what he wants Sarah to know?"

"He doesn't care for Sarah."

At which Miss Gostrey's eyebrows went up. "You mean she has already dished herself?"

Strether took a turn about; he had thought it out again and again before this, to the end; but the vista seemed each time longer. "He wants his good friend to know the best. I mean the measure of his attachment. She asked for a sign, and he thought of that one. There it is."

"A concession to her jealousy?"

Strether pulled up. "Yes—call it that. Make it lurid—for that makes my problem richer."

"Certainly, let us have it lurid—for I quite agree with you that we want none of our problems poor. But let us also have it clear. Can he, in the midst of such a preoccupation, or on the heels of it, have seriously cared for Jeanne?—cared, I mean, as a young man at liberty would have cared?"

Well, Strether had mastered it. "I think he can have thought it would be charming if he COULD care. It would be nicer."

"Nicer than being tied up to Marie?"

"Yes—than the discomfort of an attachment to a person he can never hope, short of a catastrophe, to marry. And he was quite right," said Strether. "It would certainly have been nicer. Even when a thing's already nice there mostly is some other thing that would have been nicer— or as to which we wonder if it wouldn't. But his question was all the same a dream. He COULDn't care in that way. He IS tied up to Marie. The relation is too special and has gone too far. It's the very basis, and his recent lively contribution toward establishing Jeanne in life has been his definite and final acknowledgement to Madame de Vionnet that he has ceased squirming. I doubt meanwhile," he went on, "if Sarah has at all directly attacked him."

His companion brooded. "But won't he wish for his own satisfaction to make his ground good to her?"

"No—he'll leave it to me, he'll leave everything to me. I 'sort of feel'"—he worked it out—"that the whole thing will come upon me. Yes, I shall have every inch and every ounce of it. I shall be USED for it—!" And Strether lost himself in the prospect. Then he fancifully expressed the issue. "To the last drop of my blood."

Maria, however, roundly protested. "Ah you'll please keep a drop for ME. I shall have a use for it!"—which she didn't however follow up. She had come back the next moment to another matter. "Mrs. Pocock, with her brother, is trusting only to her general charm?"

"So it would seem."

"And the charm's not working?"

Well, Strether put it otherwise, "She's sounding the note of home—which is the very best thing she can do."

"The best for Madame de Vionnet?"

"The best for home itself. The natural one; the right one."

"Right," Maria asked, "when it fails?"

Strether had a pause. "The difficulty's Jim. Jim's the note of home."

She debated. "Ah surely not the note of Mrs. Newsome."

But he had it all. "The note of the home for which Mrs. Newsome wants him—the home of the business. Jim stands, with his little legs apart, at the door of THAT tent; and Jim is, frankly speaking, extremely awful."

Maria stared. "And you in, you poor thing, for your evening with him?"

"Oh he's all right for ME!" Strether laughed. "Any one's good enough for ME. But Sarah shouldn't, all the same, have brought him. She doesn't appreciate him."

His friend was amused with this statement of it. "Doesn't know, you mean, how bad he is?"

Strether shook his head with decision. "Not really."

She wondered. "Then doesn't Mrs. Newsome?"

It made him frankly do the same. "Well, no—since you ask me."

Maria rubbed it in. "Not really either?"

"Not at all. She rates him rather high." With which indeed, immediately, he took himself up. "Well, he IS good too, in his way. It depends on what you want him for."

Miss Gostrey, however, wouldn't let it depend on anything—wouldn't have it, and wouldn't want him, at any price. "It suits my book," she said, "that he should be impossible; and it suits it still better," she more imaginatively added, "that Mrs. Newsome doesn't know he is."

Strether, in consequence, had to take it from her, but he fell back on something else. "I'll tell you who does really know."

"Mr. Waymarsh! Never!"

"Never indeed. I'm not ALWAYS thinking of Mr. Waymarsh; in fact I find now I never am." Then he mentioned the person as if there were a good deal in it. "Mamie."

"His own sister?" Oddly enough it but let her down. "What good will that do?"

"None perhaps. But there—as usual—we are!"

III

There they were yet again, accordingly, for two days more; when Strether, on being, at Mrs. Pocock's hotel, ushered into that lady's salon, found himself at first assuming a mistake on the part of the servant who had introduced him and retired. The occupants hadn't come in, for the room looked empty as only a room can look in Paris, of a fine afternoon when the faint murmur of the huge collective life, carried on out of doors, strays among scattered objects even as a summer air idles in a lonely garden. Our friend looked about and hesitated; observed, on the evidence of a table charged with purchases and other matters, that Sarah had become possessed—by no aid from HIM—of the last number of the salmon-coloured Revue; noted further that Mamie appeared to have received a present of Fromentin's "Maitres d'Autrefois" from Chad, who had written her name on the cover; and pulled up at the sight of a heavy letter addressed in a hand he knew. This letter, forwarded by a banker and arriving in Mrs. Pocock's absence, had been placed in evidence, and it drew from the fact of its being unopened a sudden queer power to intensify the reach of its author. It brought home to him the scale on which Mrs. Newsome—for she had been copious indeed this time—was writing to her daughter while she kept HIM in durance; and it had altogether such an effect upon him as made him for a few minutes stand still and breathe low. In his own room, at his own hotel, he had dozens of well-filled envelopes superscribed in that character; and there was actually something in the renewal of his interrupted vision of the character that played straight into the so frequent question of whether he weren't already disinherited beyond appeal. It was such an assurance as the sharp downstrokes of her pen hadn't yet had occasion to give him; but they somehow at the present crisis stood for a probable absoluteness in any decree of the writer. He looked at Sarah's name and address, in short, as if he had been looking hard into her mother's face, and then turned from it as if the face had declined to relax. But since it was in a manner as if Mrs. Newsome were thereby all the more, instead of the less, in the room, and were conscious, sharply and sorely conscious, of himself, so he felt both held and hushed, summoned to stay at least and take his punishment. By staying, accordingly, he took it—creeping softly and vaguely about and waiting for Sarah to come in. She WOULD come in if he stayed long enough, and he had now more than ever the sense of her success in leaving him a prey to anxiety. It wasn't to be denied that she had had a happy instinct, from the point of view of Woollett, in placing him thus at the mercy of her own initiative. It was very well to try to say he didn't care—that she might break ground when she would, might never break it at all if she wouldn't, and that he had no confession whatever to wait upon her with: he breathed from day to day an air that damnably required clearing, and there were moments when he quite ached to precipitate that process. He couldn't doubt that, should she only oblige him by surprising him just as he then was, a clarifying scene of some sort would result from the concussion.

He humbly circulated in this spirit till he suddenly had a fresh arrest. Both the windows of the room stood open to the balcony, but it was only now that, in the glass of the leaf of one of them, folded back, he caught a reflexion quickly recognised as the colour of a lady's dress. Somebody had been then all the while on the balcony, and the person, whoever it might be, was so placed between the windows as to be hidden from him; while on the other hand the many sounds of the street had covered her own entrance and movements. If the person were Sarah he might on the spot therefore be served to his taste. He might lead her by a move or two up to the remedy for his vain tension; as to which, should he get nothing else from it, he would at least have the relief of pulling down the roof on their heads. There was fortunately no one at hand to observe—in respect to his valour—that even on this completed reasoning he still hung fire. He had been waiting for Mrs. Pocock—the sound of the oracle; but he had to gird himself afresh—which he did in the embrasure of the window, neither advancing nor retreating—before provoking the revelation. It was apparently for Sarah to come more into view; he was in that case there at her service. She did however, as meanwhile happened, come more into view; only she luckily came at the last minute as a contradiction of Sarah. The occupant of the balcony was after all quite another person, a person presented, on a second look, by a charming back and a slight shift of her position, as beautiful brilliant unconscious Mamie—Mamie alone at home, Mamie passing her time in her own innocent way, Mamie in short rather shabbily used, but Mamie absorbed interested and interesting. With her arms on the balustrade and her attention dropped to the street she allowed Strether to watch her, to consider several things, without her turning round.

But the oddity was that when he HAD so watched and considered he simply stepped back into the room without following up his advantage. He revolved there again for several minutes, quite as with something new to think of and as if the bearings of the possibility of Sarah had been superseded. For frankly, yes, it HAD bearings thus to find the girl in solitary possession. There was something in it that touched him to a point not to have been reckoned beforehand, something that softly but quite pressingly spoke to him, and that spoke the more each time he paused again at the edge of the balcony and found her still unaware. His companions were plainly scattered; Sarah would be off somewhere with Waymarsh and Chad off somewhere with Jim. Strether didn't at all mentally impute to Chad that he was with his "good friend"; he gave him the benefit of supposing him involved in appearances that, had he had to describe them—for instance to Maria—he would have conveniently qualified as more subtle. It came to him indeed the next thing that there was perhaps almost an excess of refinement in having left Mamie in such weather up there alone; however she might in fact have extemporised, under the charm of the Rue de Rivoli, a little makeshift Paris of wonder arid fancy. Our friend in any case now recognised—and it was as if at the recognition Mrs. Newsome's fixed intensity had suddenly, with a deep audible gasp, grown thin and vague—that day after day he had been conscious in respect to his young lady of something odd and ambiguous, yet something into which he could at last read a meaning. It had been at the most, this mystery, an obsession—oh an obsession agreeable; and it had just now fallen into its place as at the touch of a spring. It had represented the possibility between them of some communication baffled by accident and delay—the possibility even of some relation as yet unacknowledged.

There was always their old relation, the fruit of the Woollett years; but that—and it was what was strangest—had nothing whatever in common with what was now in the air. As a child, as a "bud," and then again as a flower of expansion, Mamie had bloomed for him, freely, in the almost incessantly open doorways of home; where he remembered her as first very forward, as then very backward—for he had carried on at one period, in Mrs. Newsome's parlours (oh Mrs. Newsome's phases and his own!) a course of English Literature re-enforced by exams and teas—and once more, finally, as very much in advance. But he had kept no great sense of points of contact; it not being in the nature of things at Woollett that the freshest of the buds should find herself in the same basket with the most withered of the winter apples. The child had given sharpness, above all, to his sense of the flight of time; it was but the day before yesterday that he had tripped up on her hoop, yet his experience of remarkable women—destined, it would seem, remarkably to grow—felt itself ready this afternoon, quite braced itself, to include her. She had in fine more to say to him than he had ever dreamed the pretty girl of the moment COULD have; and the proof of the circumstance was that, visibly, unmistakeably, she had been able to say it to no one else. It was something she could mention neither to her brother, to her sister-in-law nor to Chad; though he could just imagine that had she still been at home she might have brought it out, as a supreme tribute to age, authority and attitude, for Mrs. Newsome. It was moreover something in which they all took an interest; the strength of their interest was in truth just the reason of her prudence. All this then, for five minutes, was vivid to Strether, and it put before him that, poor child, she had now but her prudence to amuse her. That, for a pretty girl in Paris, struck him, with a rush, as a sorry state; so that under the impression he went out to her with a step as hypocritically alert, he was well aware, as if he had just come into the room. She turned with a start at his voice; preoccupied with him though she might be, she was just a scrap disappointed. "Oh I thought you were Mr. Bilham!"

The remark had been at first surprising and our friend's private thought, under the influence of it, temporarily blighted; yet we are able to add that he presently recovered his inward tone and that many a fresh flower of fancy was to bloom in the same air. Little Bilham—since little Bilham was, somewhat incongruously, expected—appeared behindhand; a circumstance by which Strether was to profit. They came back into the room together after a little, the couple on the balcony, and amid its crimson-and-gold elegance, with the others still absent, Strether passed forty minutes that he appraised even at the time as far, in the whole queer connexion, from his idlest. Yes indeed, since he had the other day so agreed with Maria about the inspiration of the lurid, here was something for his problem that surely didn't make it shrink and that was floated in upon him as part of a sudden flood. He was doubtless not to know till afterwards, on turning them over in thought, of how many elements his impression was composed; but he none the less felt, as he sat with the charming girl, the signal growth of a confidence. For she WAS charming, when all was said—and none the less so for the visible habit and practice of freedom and fluency. She was charming, he was aware, in spite of the fact that if he hadn't found her so he would have found her something he should have been in peril of expressing as "funny." Yes, she was funny, wonderful Mamie, and without dreaming it; she was bland, she was bridal—with never, that he could make out as yet, a bridegroom to support it; she was handsome and portly and easy and chatty, soft and sweet and almost disconcertingly reassuring. She was dressed, if we might so far discriminate, less as a young lady than as an old one—had an old one been supposable to Strether as so committed to vanity; the complexities of her hair missed moreover also the looseness of youth; and she had a mature manner of bending a little, as to encourage and reward, while she held neatly together in front of her a pair of strikingly polished hands: the combination of all of which kept up about her the glamour of her "receiving," placed her again perpetually between the windows and within sound of the ice-cream plates, suggested the enumeration of all the names, all the Mr. Brookses and Mr. Snookses, gregarious specimens of a single type, she was happy to "meet." But if all this was where she was funny, and if what was funnier than the rest was the contrast between her beautiful benevolent patronage—such a hint of the polysyllabic as might make her something of a bore toward middle age—and her rather flat little voice, the voice, naturally, unaffectedly yet, of a girl of fifteen; so Strether, none the less, at the end of ten minutes, felt in her a quiet dignity that pulled things bravely together. If quiet dignity, almost more than matronly, with voluminous, too voluminous clothes, was the effect she proposed to produce, that was an ideal one could like in her when once one had got into relation. The great thing now for her visitor was that this was exactly what he had done; it made so extraordinary a mixture of the brief and crowded hour. It was the mark of a relation that he had begun so quickly to find himself sure she was, of all people, as might have been said, on the side and of the party of Mrs. Newsome's original ambassador. She was in HIS interest and not in Sarah's, and some sign of that was precisely what he had been feeling in her, these last days, as imminent. Finally placed, in Paris, in immediate presence of the situation and of the hero of it—by whom Strether was incapable of meaning any one but Chad—she had accomplished, and really in a manner all unexpected to herself, a change of base; deep still things had come to pass within her, and by the time she had grown sure of them Strether had become aware of the little drama. When she knew where she was, in short, he had made it out; and he made it out at present still better; though with never a direct word passing between them all the while on the subject of his own predicament. There had been at first, as he sat there with her, a moment during which he wondered if she meant to break ground in respect to his prime undertaking. That door stood so strangely ajar that he was half-prepared to be conscious, at any juncture, of her having, of any one's having, quite bounced in. But, friendly, familiar, light of touch and happy of tact, she exquisitely stayed out; so that it was for all the world as if to show she could deal with him without being reduced to—well, scarcely anything.

It fully came up for them then, by means of their talking of everything BUT Chad, that Mamie, unlike Sarah, unlike Jim, knew perfectly what had become of him. It fully came up that she had taken to the last fraction of an inch the measure of the change in him, and that she wanted Strether to know what a secret being proposed to make of it. They talked most conveniently—as if they had had no chance ever—about Woollett; and that had virtually the effect of their keeping the secret more close. The hour took on for Strether, little by little, a queer sad sweetness of quality, he had such a revulsion in Mamie's favour and on behalf of her social value as might have come from remorse at some early injustice. She made him, as under the breath of some vague western whiff, homesick and freshly restless; he could really for the time have fancied himself stranded with her on a far shore, during an ominous calm, in a quaint community of shipwreck. Their little interview was like a picnic on a coral strand; they passed each other, with melancholy smiles and looks sufficiently allusive, such cupfuls of water as they had saved. Especially sharp in Strether meanwhile was the conviction that his companion really knew, as we have hinted, where she had come out. It was at a very particular place—only THAT she would never tell him; it would be above all what he should have to puzzle for himself. This was what he hoped for, because his interest in the girl wouldn't be complete without it. No more would the appreciation to which she was entitled—so assured was he that the more he saw of her process the more he should see of her pride. She saw, herself, everything; but she knew what she didn't want, and that it was that had helped her. What didn't she want?—there was a pleasure lost for her old friend in not yet knowing, as there would doubtless be a thrill in getting a glimpse. Gently and sociably she kept that dark to him, and it was as if she soothed and beguiled him in other ways to make up for it. She came out with her impression of Madame de Vionnet—of whom she had "heard so much"; she came out with her impression of Jeanne, whom she had been "dying to see": she brought it out with a blandness by which her auditor was really stirred that she had been with Sarah early that very afternoon, and after dreadful delays caused by all sorts of things, mainly, eternally, by the purchase of clothes—clothes that unfortunately wouldn't be themselves eternal—to call in the Rue de Bellechasse.

At the sound of these names Strether almost blushed to feel that he couldn't have sounded them first—and yet couldn't either have justified his squeamishness. Mamie made them easy as he couldn't have begun to do, and yet it could only have cost her more than he should ever have had to spend. It was as friends of Chad's, friends special, distinguished, desirable, enviable, that she spoke of them, and she beautifully carried it off that much as she had heard of them—though she didn't say how or where, which was a touch of her own—she had found them beyond her supposition. She abounded in praise of them, and after the manner of Woollett—which made the manner of Woollett a loveable thing again to Strether. He had never so felt the true inwardness of it as when his blooming companion pronounced the elder of the ladies of the Rue de Bellechasse too fascinating for words and declared of the younger that she was perfectly ideal, a real little monster of charm. "Nothing," she said of Jeanne, "ought ever to happen to her—she's so awfully right as she is. Another touch will spoil her—so she oughtn't to BE touched."

"Ah but things, here in Paris," Strether observed, "do happen to little girls." And then for the joke's and the occasion's sake: "Haven't you found that yourself?"

"That things happen—? Oh I'm not a little girl. I'm a big battered blowsy one. I don't care," Mamie laughed, "WHAT happens."

Strether had a pause while he wondered if it mightn't happen that he should give her the pleasure of learning that he found her nicer than he had really dreamed—a pause that ended when he had said to himself that, so far as it at all mattered for her, she had in fact perhaps already made this out. He risked accordingly a different question—though conscious, as soon as he had spoken, that he seemed to place it in relation to her last speech. "But that Mademoiselle de Vionnet is to be married—I suppose you've heard of THAT." For all, he then found, he need fear! "Dear, yes; the gentleman was there: Monsieur de Montbron, whom Madame de Vionnet presented to us."

"And was he nice?"

Mamie bloomed and bridled with her best reception manner. "Any man's nice when he's in love."

It made Strether laugh. "But is Monsieur de Montbron in love—already—with YOU?"

"Oh that's not necessary—it's so much better he should be so with HER: which, thank goodness, I lost no time in discovering for myself. He's perfectly gone—and I couldn't have borne it for her if he hadn't been. She's just too sweet."

Strether hesitated. "And through being in love too?"

On which with a smile that struck him as wonderful Mamie had a wonderful answer. "She doesn't know if she is or not."

It made him again laugh out. "Oh but YOU do!"

She was willing to take it that way. "Oh yes, I know everything." And as she sat there rubbing her polished hands and making the best of it—only holding her elbows perhaps a little too much out—the momentary effect for Strether was that every one else, in all their affair, seemed stupid.

"Know that poor little Jeanne doesn't know what's the matter with her?"

It was as near as they came to saying that she was probably in love with Chad; but it was quite near enough for what Strether wanted; which was to be confirmed in his certitude that, whether in love or not, she appealed to something large and easy in the girl before him. Mamie would be fat, too fat, at thirty; but she would always be the person who, at the present sharp hour, had been disinterestedly tender. "If I see a little more of her, as I hope I shall, I think she'll like me enough—for she seemed to like me to-day—to want me to tell her."

"And SHALL you?"

"Perfectly. I shall tell her the matter with her is that she wants only too much to do right. To do right for her, naturally," said Mamie, "is to please."

"Her mother, do you mean?"

"Her mother first."

Strether waited. "And then?"

"Well, 'then'—Mr. Newsome."

There was something really grand for him in the serenity of this reference. "And last only Monsieur de Montbron?"

"Last only"—she good-humouredly kept it up.

Strether considered. "So that every one after all then will be suited?"

She had one of her few hesitations, but it was a question only of a moment; and it was her nearest approach to being explicit with him about what was between them. "I think I can speak for myself. I shall be."

It said indeed so much, told such a story of her being ready to help him, so committed to him that truth, in short, for such use as he might make of it toward those ends of his own with which, patiently and trustfully, she had nothing to do—it so fully achieved all this that he appeared to himself simply to meet it in its own spirit by the last frankness of admiration. Admiration was of itself almost accusatory, but nothing less would serve to show her how nearly he understood. He put out his hand for good-bye with a "Splendid, splendid, splendid!" And he left her, in her splendour, still waiting for little Bilham.

Book Tenth

I

Strether occupied beside little Bilham, three evenings after his interview with Mamie Pocock, the same deep divan they had enjoyed together on the first occasion of our friend's meeting Madame de Vionnet and her daughter in the apartment of the Boulevard Malesherbes, where his position affirmed itself again as ministering to an easy exchange of impressions. The present evening had a different stamp; if the company was much more numerous, so, inevitably, were the ideas set in motion. It was on the other hand, however, now strongly marked that the talkers moved, in respect to such matters, round an inner, a protected circle. They knew at any rate what really concerned them to-night, and Strether had begun by keeping his companion close to it. Only a few of Chad's guests had dined—that is fifteen or twenty, a few compared with the large concourse offered to sight by eleven o'clock; but number and mass, quantity and quality, light, fragrance, sound, the overflow of hospitality meeting the high tide of response, had all from the first pressed upon Strether's consciousness, and he felt himself somehow part and parcel of the most festive scene, as the term was, in which he had ever in his life been engaged. He had perhaps seen, on Fourths of July and on dear old domestic Commencements, more people assembled, but he had never seen so many in proportion to the space, or had at all events never known so great a promiscuity to show so markedly as picked. Numerous as was the company, it had still been made so by selection, and what was above all rare for Strether was that, by no fault of his own, he was in the secret of the principle that had worked. He hadn't enquired, he had averted his head, but Chad had put him a pair of questions that themselves smoothed the ground. He hadn't answered the questions, he had replied that they were the young man's own affair; and he had then seen perfectly that the latter's direction was already settled.

Chad had applied for counsel only by way of intimating that he knew what to do; and he had clearly never known it better than in now presenting to his sister the whole circle of his society. This was all in the sense and the spirit of the note struck by him on that lady's arrival; he had taken at the station itself a line that led him without a break, and that enabled him to lead the Pococks—though dazed a little, no doubt, breathless, no doubt, and bewildered—to the uttermost end of the passage accepted by them perforce as pleasant. He had made it for them violently pleasant and mercilessly full; the upshot of which was, to Strether's vision, that they had come all the way without discovering it to be really no passage at all. It was a brave blind alley, where to pass was impossible and where, unless they stuck fast, they would have—which was always awkward—publicly to back out. They were touching bottom assuredly tonight; the whole scene represented the terminus of the cul-de-sac. So could things go when there was a hand to keep them consistent—a hand that pulled the wire with a skill at which the elder man more and more marvelled. The elder man felt responsible, but he also felt successful, since what had taken place was simply the issue of his own contention, six weeks before, that they properly should wait to see what their friends would have really to say. He had determined Chad to wait, he had determined him to see; he was therefore not to quarrel with the time given up to the business. As much as ever, accordingly, now that a fortnight had elapsed, the situation created for Sarah, and against which she had raised no protest, was that of her having accommodated herself to her adventure as to a pleasure-party surrendered perhaps even somewhat in excess to bustle and to "pace." If her brother had been at any point the least bit open to criticism it might have been on the ground of his spicing the draught too highly and pouring the cup too full. Frankly treating the whole occasion of the presence of his relatives as an opportunity for amusement, he left it, no doubt, but scant margin as an opportunity for anything else. He suggested, invented, abounded—yet all the while with the loosest easiest rein. Strether, during his own weeks, had gained a sense of knowing Paris; but he saw it afresh, and with fresh emotion, in the form of the knowledge offered to his colleague.

A thousand unuttered thoughts hummed for him in the air of these observations; not the least frequent of which was that Sarah might well of a truth not quite know whither she was drifting. She was in no position not to appear to expect that Chad should treat her handsomely; yet she struck our friend as privately stiffening a little each time she missed the chance of marking the great nuance. The great nuance was in brief that of course her brother must treat her handsomely—she should like to see him not; but that treating her handsomely, none the less, wasn't all in all—treating her handsomely buttered no parsnips; and that in fine there were moments when she felt the fixed eyes of their admirable absent mother fairly screw into the flat of her back. Strether, watching, after his habit, and overscoring with thought, positively had moments of his own in which he found himself sorry for her—occasions on which she affected him as a person seated in a runaway vehicle and turning over the question of a possible jump. WOULD she jump, could she, would THAT be a safe placed—this question, at such instants, sat for him in her lapse into pallor, her tight lips, her conscious eyes. It came back to the main point at issue: would she be, after all, to be squared? He believed on the whole she would jump; yet his alternations on this subject were the more especial stuff of his suspense. One thing remained well before him—a conviction that was in fact to gain sharpness from the impressions of this evening: that if she SHOULD gather in her skirts, close her eyes and quit the carriage while in motion, he would promptly enough become aware. She would alight from her headlong course more or less directly upon him; it would be appointed to him, unquestionably, to receive her entire weight. Signs and portents of the experience thus in reserve for him had as it happened, multiplied even through the dazzle of Chad's party. It was partly under the nervous consciousness of such a prospect that, leaving almost every one in the two other rooms, leaving those of the guests already known to him as well as a mass of brilliant strangers of both sexes and of several varieties of speech, he had desired five quiet minutes with little Bilham, whom he always found soothing and even a little inspiring, and to whom he had actually moreover something distinct and important to say.

He had felt of old—for it already seemed long ago—rather humiliated at discovering he could learn in talk with a personage so much his junior the lesson of a certain moral ease; but he had now got used to that—whether or no the mixture of the fact with other humiliations had made it indistinct, whether or no directly from little Bilham's example, the example of his being contentedly just the obscure and acute little Bilham he was. It worked so for him, Strether seemed to see; and our friend had at private hours a wan smile over the fact that he himself, after so many more years, was still in search of something that would work. However, as we have said, it worked just now for them equally to have found a corner a little apart. What particularly kept it apart was the circumstance that the music in the salon was admirable, with two or three such singers as it was a privilege to hear in private. Their presence gave a distinction to Chad's entertainment, and the interest of calculating their effect on Sarah was actually so sharp as to be almost painful. Unmistakeably, in her single person, the motive of the composition and dressed in a splendour of crimson which affected Strether as the sound of a fall through a skylight, she would now be in the forefront of the listening circle and committed to it up to her eyes. Those eyes during the wonderful dinner itself he hadn't once met; having confessedly—perhaps a little pusillanimously—arranged with Chad that he should be on the same side of the table. But there was no use in having arrived now with little Bilham at an unprecedented point of intimacy unless he could pitch everything into the pot. "You who sat where you could see her, what does she make of it all? By which I mean on what terms does she take it?"

"Oh she takes it, I judge, as proving that the claim of his family is more than ever justified."

"She isn't then pleased with what he has to show?"

"On the contrary; she's pleased with it as with his capacity to do this kind of thing—more than she has been pleased with anything for a long time. But she wants him to show it THERE. He has no right to waste it on the likes of us."

Strether wondered. "She wants him to move the whole thing over?"

"The whole thing—with an important exception. Everything he has 'picked up'—and the way he knows how. She sees no difficulty in that. She'd run the show herself, and she'll make the handsome concession that Woollett would be on the whole in some ways the better for it. Not that it wouldn't be also in some ways the better for Woollett. The people there are just as good."

"Just as good as you and these others? Ah that may be. But such an occasion as this, whether or no," Strether said, "isn't the people. It's what has made the people possible."

"Well then," his friend replied, "there you are; I give you my impression for what it's worth. Mrs. Pocock has SEEN, and that's to-night how she sits there. If you were to have a glimpse of her face you'd understand me. She has made up her mind—to the sound of expensive music."

Strether took it freely in. "Ah then I shall have news of her."

"I don't want to frighten you, but I think that likely. However," little Bilham continued, "if I'm of the least use to you to hold on by—!"

"You're of the least!"—and Strether laid an appreciative hand on him to say it. "No one's of the least." With which, to mark how gaily he could take it, he patted his companion's knee. "I must meet my fate alone, and I SHALL—oh you'll see! And yet," he pursued the next moment, "you CAN help me too. You once said to me"—he followed this further—"that you held Chad should marry. I didn't see then so well as I know now that you meant he should marry Miss Pocock. Do you still consider that he should? Because if you do"—he kept it up—"I want you immediately to change your mind. You can help me that way."

"Help you by thinking he should NOT marry?"

"Not marry at all events Mamie."

"And who then?"

"Ah," Strether returned, "that I'm not obliged to say. But Madame de Vionnet—I suggest—when he can.'

"Oh!" said little Bilham with some sharpness.

"Oh precisely! But he needn't marry at all—I'm at any rate not obliged to provide for it. Whereas in your case I rather feel that I AM."

Little Bilham was amused. "Obliged to provide for my marrying?"

"Yes—after all I've done to you!"

The young man weighed it. "Have you done as much as that?"

"Well," said Strether, thus challenged, "of course I must remember what you've also done to ME. We may perhaps call it square. But all the same," he went on, "I wish awfully you'd marry Mamie Pocock yourself."

Little Bilham laughed out. "Why it was only the other night, in this very place, that you were proposing to me a different union altogether."

"Mademoiselle de Vionnet?" Well, Strether easily confessed it. "That, I admit, was a vain image. THIS is practical politics. I want to do something good for both of you—I wish you each so well; and you can see in a moment the trouble it will save me to polish you off by the same stroke. She likes you, you know. You console her. And she's splendid."

Little Bilham stared as a delicate appetite stares at an overheaped plate. "What do I console her for?"

It just made his friend impatient. "Oh come, you knows"

"And what proves for you that she likes me?"

"Why the fact that I found her three days ago stopping at home alone all the golden afternoon on the mere chance that you'd come to her, and hanging over her balcony on that of seeing your cab drive up. I don't know what you want more."

Little Bilham after a moment found it. "Only just to know what proves to you that I like HER."

"Oh if what I've just mentioned isn't enough to make you do it, you're a stony-hearted little fiend. Besides"—Strether encouraged his fancy's flight—"you showed your inclination in the way you kept her waiting, kept her on purpose to see if she cared enough for you."

His companion paid his ingenuity the deference of a pause. "I didn't keep her waiting. I came at the hour. I wouldn't have kept her waiting for the world," the young man honourably declared.

"Better still—then there you are!" And Strether, charmed, held him the faster. "Even if you didn't do her justice, moreover," he continued, "I should insist on your immediately coming round to it. I want awfully to have worked it. I want"—and our friend spoke now with a yearning that was really earnest—"at least to have done THAT."

"To have married me off—without a penny?"

"Well, I shan't live long; and I give you my word, now and here, that I'll leave you every penny of my own. I haven't many, unfortunately, but you shall have them all. And Miss Pocock, I think, has a few. I want," Strether went on, "to have been at least to that extent constructive even expiatory. I've been sacrificing so to strange gods that I feel I want to put on record, somehow, my fidelity—fundamentally unchanged after all—to our own. I feel as if my hands were embrued with the blood of monstrous alien altars—of another faith altogether. There it is—it's done." And then he further explained. "It took hold of me because the idea of getting her quite out of the way for Chad helps to clear my ground."

The young man, at this, bounced about, and it brought them face to face in admitted amusement. "You want me to marry as a convenience to Chad?"

"No," Strether debated—"HE doesn't care whether you marry or not. It's as a convenience simply to my own plan FOR him."

"'Simply'!"—and little Bilham's concurrence was in itself a lively comment. "Thank you. But I thought," he continued, "you had exactly NO plan 'for' him."

"Well then call it my plan for myself—which may be well, as you say, to have none. His situation, don't you see? is reduced now to the bare facts one has to recognise. Mamie doesn't want him, and he doesn't want Mamie: so much as that these days have made clear. It's a thread we can wind up and tuck in."

But little Bilham still questioned. "YOU can—since you seem so much to want to. But why should I?"

Poor Strether thought it over, but was obliged of course to admit that his demonstration did superficially fail. "Seriously, there is no reason. It's my affair—I must do it alone. I've only my fantastic need of making my dose stiff."

Little Bilham wondered. "What do you call your dose?"

"Why what I have to swallow. I want my conditions unmitigated."

He had spoken in the tone of talk for talk's sake, and yet with an obscure truth lurking in the loose folds; a circumstance presently not without its effect on his young friend. Little Bilham's eyes rested on him a moment with some intensity; then suddenly, as if everything had cleared up, he gave a happy laugh. It seemed to say that if pretending, or even trying, or still even hoping, to be able to care for Mamie would be of use, he was all there for the job. "I'll do anything in the world for you!"

"Well," Strether smiled, "anything in the world is all I want. I don't know anything that pleased me in her more," he went on, "than the way that, on my finding her up there all alone, coming on her unawares and feeling greatly for her being so out of it, she knocked down my tall house of cards with her instant and cheerful allusion to the next young man. It was somehow so the note I needed—her staying at home to receive him."

"It was Chad of course," said little Bilham, "who asked the next young man—I like your name for me!—to call."

"So I supposed—all of which, thank God, is in our innocent and natural manners. But do you know," Strether asked, "if Chad knows—?" And then as this interlocutor seemed at a loss: "Why where she has come out."

Little Bilham, at this, met his face with a conscious look—it was as if, more than anything yet, the allusion had penetrated. "Do you know yourself?"

Strether lightly shook his head. "There I stop. Oh, odd as it may appear to you, there ARE things I don't know. I only got the sense from her of something very sharp, and very deep down, that she was keeping all to herself. That is I had begun with the belief that she HAD kept it to herself; but face to face with her there I soon made out that there was a person with whom she would have shared it. I had thought she possibly might with ME—but I saw then that I was only half in her confidence. When, turning to me to greet me—for she was on the balcony and I had come in without her knowing it—she showed me she had been expecting YOU and was proportionately disappointed, I got hold of the tail of my conviction. Half an hour later I was in possession of all the rest of it. You know what has happened." He looked at his young friend hard—then he felt sure. "For all you say, you're up to your eyes. So there you are."

Little Bilham after an instant pulled half round. "I assure you she hasn't told me anything."

"Of course she hasn't. For what do you suggest that I suppose her to take you? But you've been with her every day, you've seen her freely, you've liked her greatly—I stick to that—and you've made your profit of it. You know what she has been through as well as you know that she has dined here to-night—which must have put her, by the way, through a good deal more."

The young man faced this blast; after which he pulled round the rest of the way. "I haven't in the least said she hasn't been nice to me. But she's proud."

"And quite properly. But not too proud for that."

"It's just her pride that has made her. Chad," little Bilham loyally went on, "has really been as kind to her as possible. It's awkward for a man when a girl's in love with him."

"Ah but she isn't—now."

Little Bilham sat staring before him; then he sprang up as if his friend's penetration, recurrent and insistent, made him really after all too nervous. "No—she isn't now. It isn't in the least," he went on, "Chad's fault. He's really all right. I mean he would have been willing. But she came over with ideas. Those she had got at home. They had been her motive and support in joining her brother and his wife. She was to SAVE our friend."

"Ah like me, poor thing?" Strether also got to his feet.

"Exactly—she had a bad moment. It was very soon distinct to her, to pull her up, to let her down, that, alas, he was, he IS, saved. There's nothing left for her to do."

"Not even to love him?"

"She would have loved him better as she originally believed him."

Strether wondered "Of course one asks one's self what notion a little girl forms, where a young man's in question, of such a history and such a state."

"Well, this little girl saw them, no doubt, as obscure, but she saw them practically as wrong. The wrong for her WAS the obscure. Chad turns out at any rate right and good and disconcerting, while what she was all prepared for, primed and girded and wound up for, was to deal with him as the general opposite."

"Yet wasn't her whole point"—Strether weighed it—"that he was to be, that he COULD be, made better, redeemed?"

Little Bilham fixed it all a moment, and then with a small headshake that diffused a tenderness: "She's too late. Too late for the miracle."

"Yes"—his companion saw enough. "Still, if the worst fault of his condition is that it may be all there for her to profit by—?"

"Oh she doesn't want to 'profit,' in that flat way. She doesn't want to profit by another woman's work—she wants the miracle to have been her own miracle. THAT'S what she's too late for."

Strether quite felt how it all fitted, yet there seemed one loose piece. "I'm bound to say, you know, that she strikes one, on these lines, as fastidious—what you call here difficile."

Little Bilham tossed up his chin. "Of course she's difficile—on any lines! What else in the world ARE our Mamies—the real, the right ones?"

"I see, I see," our friend repeated, charmed by the responsive wisdom he had ended by so richly extracting. "Mamie is one of the real and the right."

"The very thing itself."

"And what it comes to then," Strether went on, "is that poor awful Chad is simply too good for her."

"Ah too good was what he was after all to be; but it was she herself, and she herself only, who was to have made him so."

It hung beautifully together, but with still a loose end. "Wouldn't he do for her even if he should after all break—"

"With his actual influence?" Oh little Bilham had for this enquiry the sharpest of all his controls. "How can he 'do'—on any terms whatever—when he's flagrantly spoiled?"

Strether could only meet the question with his passive, his receptive pleasure. "Well, thank goodness, YOU'RE not! You remain for her to save, and I come back, on so beautiful and full a demonstration, to my contention of just now—that of your showing distinct signs of her having already begun."

The most he could further say to himself—as his young friend turned away—was that the charge encountered for the moment no renewed denial. Little Bilham, taking his course back to the music, only shook his good-natured ears an instant, in the manner of a terrier who has got wet; while Strether relapsed into the sense—which had for him in these days most of comfort—that he was free to believe in anything that from hour to hour kept him going. He had positively motions and flutters of this conscious hour-to-hour kind, temporary surrenders to irony, to fancy, frequent instinctive snatches at the growing rose of observation, constantly stronger for him, as he felt, in scent and colour, and in which he could bury his nose even to wantonness. This last resource was offered him, for that matter, in the very form of his next clear perception—the vision of a prompt meeting, in the doorway of the room, between little Bilham and brilliant Miss Barrace, who was entering as Bilham withdrew. She had apparently put him a question, to which he had replied by turning to indicate his late interlocutor; toward whom, after an interrogation further aided by a resort to that optical machinery which seemed, like her other ornaments, curious and archaic, the genial lady, suggesting more than ever for her fellow guest the old French print, the historic portrait, directed herself with an intention that Strether instantly met. He knew in advance the first note she would sound, and took in as she approached all her need of sounding it. Nothing yet had been so "wonderful" between them as the present occasion; and it was her special sense of this quality in occasions that she was there, as she was in most places, to feed. That sense had already been so well fed by the situation about them that she had quitted the other room, forsaken the music, dropped out of the play, abandoned, in a word, the stage itself, that she might stand a minute behind the scenes with Strether and so perhaps figure as one of the famous augurs replying, behind the oracle, to the wink of the other. Seated near him presently where little Bilham had sat, she replied in truth to many things; beginning as soon as he had said to her—what he hoped he said without fatuity—"All you ladies are extraordinarily kind to me."

She played her long handle, which shifted her observation; she saw in an instant all the absences that left them free. "How can we be anything else? But isn't that exactly your plight? 'We ladies'—oh we're nice, and you must be having enough of us! As one of us, you know, I don't pretend I'm crazy about us. But Miss Gostrey at least to-night has left you alone, hasn't she?" With which she again looked about as if Maria might still lurk.

"Oh yes," said Strether; "she's only sitting up for me at home." And then as this elicited from his companion her gay "Oh, oh, oh!" he explained that he meant sitting up in suspense and prayer. "We thought it on the whole better she shouldn't be present; and either way of course it's a terrible worry for her." He abounded in the sense of his appeal to the ladies, and they might take their choice of his doing so from humility or from pride. "Yet she inclines to believe I shall come out."

"Oh I incline to believe too you'll come out!"—Miss Barrace, with her laugh, was not to be behind. "Only the question's about WHERE, isn't it? However," she happily continued, "if it's anywhere at all it must be very far on, mustn't it? To do us justice, I think, you know," she laughed, "we do, among us all, want you rather far on. Yes, yes," she repeated in her quick droll way; "we want you very, VERY far on!" After which she wished to know why he had thought it better Maria shouldn't be present.

"Oh," he replied, "it was really her own idea. I should have wished it. But she dreads responsibility."

"And isn't that a new thing for her?"

"To dread it? No doubt—no doubt. But her nerve has given way."

Miss Barrace looked at him a moment. "She has too much at stake." Then less gravely: "Mine, luckily for me, holds out."

"Luckily for me too"—Strether came back to that. "My own isn't so firm, MY appetite for responsibility isn't so sharp, as that I haven't felt the very principle of this occasion to be 'the more the merrier.' If we ARE so merry it's because Chad has understood so well."

"He has understood amazingly," said Miss Barrace.

"It's wonderful—Strether anticipated for her.

"It's wonderful!" she, to meet it, intensified; so that, face to face over it, they largely and recklessly laughed. But she presently added: "Oh I see the principle. If one didn't one would be lost. But when once one has got hold of it—"

"It's as simple as twice two! From the moment he had to do something—"

"A crowd"—she took him straight up—"was the only thing? Rather, rather: a rumpus of sound," she laughed, "or nothing. Mrs. Pocock's built in, or built out—whichever you call it; she's packed so tight she can't move. She's in splendid isolation"—Miss Barrace embroidered the theme.

Strether followed, but scrupulous of justice. "Yet with every one in the place successively introduced to her."

"Wonderfully—but just so that it does build her out. She's bricked up, she's buried alive!"

Strether seemed for a moment to look at it; but it brought him to a sigh. "Oh but she's not dead! It will take more than this to kill her." His companion had a pause that might have been for pity. "No, I can't pretend I think she's finished—or that it's for more than to-night." She remained pensive as if with the same compunction. "It's only up to her chin." Then again for the fun of it: "She can breathe."

"She can breathe!"—he echoed it in the same spirit. "And do you know," he went on, "what's really all this time happening to me?—through the beauty of music, the gaiety of voices, the uproar in short of our revel and the felicity of your wit? The sound of Mrs. Pocock's respiration drowns for me, I assure you, every other. It's literally all I hear."

She focussed him with her clink of chains. "Well—!" she breathed ever so kindly.

"Well, what?"

"She IS free from her chin up," she mused; "and that WILL be enough for her."

"It will be enough for me!" Strether ruefully laughed. "Waymarsh has really," he then asked, "brought her to see you?"

"Yes—but that's the worst of it. I could do you no good. And yet I tried hard."

Strether wondered. "And how did you try?"

"Why I didn't speak of you."

"I see. That was better."

"Then what would have been worse? For speaking or silent," she lightly wailed, "I somehow 'compromise.' And it has never been any one but you."

"That shows"—he was magnanimous—"that it's something not in you, but in one's self. It's MY fault."

She was silent a little. "No, it's Mr. Waymarsh's. It's the fault of his having brought her."

"Ah then," said Strether good-naturedly, "why DID he bring her?"

"He couldn't afford not to."

"Oh you were a trophy—one of the spoils of conquest? But why in that case, since you do 'compromise'—"

"Don't I compromise HIM as well? I do compromise him as well," Miss Barrace smiled. "I compromise him as hard as I can. But for Mr. Waymarsh it isn't fatal. It's—so far as his wonderful relation with Mrs. Pocock is concerned—favourable." And then, as he still seemed slightly at sea: "The man who had succeeded with ME, don't you see? For her to get him from me was such an added incentive."

Strether saw, but as if his path was still strewn with surprises. "It's 'from' you then that she has got him?"

She was amused at his momentary muddle. "You can fancy my fight! She believes in her triumph. I think it has been part of her joy."

"Oh her joy!" Strether sceptically murmured.

"Well, she thinks she has had her own way. And what's to-night for her but a kind of apotheosis? Her frock's really good."

"Good enough to go to heaven in? For after a real apotheosis," Strether went on, "there's nothing BUT heaven. For Sarah there's only to-morrow."

"And you mean that she won't find to-morrow heavenly?"

"Well, I mean that I somehow feel to-night—on her behalf—too good to be true. She has had her cake; that is she's in the act now of having it, of swallowing the largest and sweetest piece. There won't be another left for her. Certainly I haven't one. It can only, at the best, be Chad." He continued to make it out as for their common entertainment. "He may have one, as it were, up his sleeve; yet it's borne in upon me that if he had—"

"He wouldn't"—she quite understood—"have taken all THIS trouble? I dare say not, and, if I may be quite free and dreadful, I very much hope he won't take any more. Of course I won't pretend now," she added, "not to know what it's a question of."

"Oh every one must know now," poor Strether thoughtfully admitted; "and it's strange enough and funny enough that one should feel everybody here at this very moment to be knowing and watching and waiting."

"Yes—isn't it indeed funny?" Miss Barrace quite rose to it. "That's the way we ARE in Paris." She was always pleased with a new contribution to that queerness. "It's wonderful! But, you know," she declared, "it all depends on you. I don't want to turn the knife in your vitals, but that's naturally what you just now meant by our all being on top of you. We know you as the hero of the drama, and we're gathered to see what you'll do."

Strether looked at her a moment with a light perhaps slightly obscured. "I think that must be why the hero has taken refuge in this corner. He's scared at his heroism—he shrinks from his part."

"Ah but we nevertheless believe he'll play it. That's why," Miss Barrace kindly went on, "we take such an interest in you. We feel you'll come up to the scratch." And then as he seemed perhaps not quite to take fire: "Don't let him do it."

"Don't let Chad go?"

"Yes, keep hold of him. With all this"—and she indicated the general tribute—"he has done enough. We love him here—he's charming."

"It's beautiful," said Strether, "the way you all can simplify when you will."

But she gave it to him back. "It's nothing to the way you will when you must."

He winced at it as at the very voice of prophecy, and it kept him a moment quiet. He detained her, however, on her appearing about to leave him alone in the rather cold clearance their talk had made. "There positively isn't a sign of a hero to-night; the hero's dodging and shirking, the hero's ashamed. Therefore, you know, I think, what you must all REALLY be occupied with is the heroine."

Miss Barrace took a minute. "The heroine?"

"The heroine. I've treated her," said Strether, "not a bit like a hero. Oh," he sighed, "I don't do it well!"

She eased him off. "You do it as you can." And then after another hesitation: "I think she's satisfied."

But he remained compunctious. "I haven't been near her. I haven't looked at her."

"Ah then you've lost a good deal!"

He showed he knew it. "She's more wonderful than ever?"

"Than ever. With Mr. Pocock."

Strether wondered. "Madame de Vionnet—with Jim?"

"Madame de Vionnet—with 'Jim.'" Miss Barrace was historic.

"And what's she doing with him?"

"Ah you must ask HIM!"

Strether's face lighted again at the prospect. "It WILL be amusing to do so." Yet he continued to wonder. "But she must have some idea."

"Of course she has—she has twenty ideas. She has in the first place," said Miss Barrace, swinging a little her tortoise-shell, "that of doing her part. Her part is to help YOU."

It came out as nothing had come yet; links were missing and connexions unnamed, but it was suddenly as if they were at the heart of their subject. "Yes; how much more she does it," Strether gravely reflected, "than I help HER!" It all came over him as with the near presence of the beauty, the grace, the intense, dissimulated spirit with which he had, as he said, been putting off contact. "SHE has courage."

"Ah she has courage!" Miss Barrace quite agreed; and it was as if for a moment they saw the quantity in each other's face.

But indeed the whole thing was present. "How much she must care!"

"Ah there it is. She does care. But it isn't, is it," Miss Barrace considerately added, "as if you had ever had any doubt of that?"

Strether seemed suddenly to like to feel that he really never had. "Why of course it's the whole point."

"Voila!" Miss Barrace smiled.

"It's why one came out," Strether went on. "And it's why one has stayed so long. And it's also"—he abounded—"why one's going home. It's why, it's why—"

"It's why everything!" she concurred. "It's why she might be to-night—for all she looks and shows, and for all your friend 'Jim' does—about twenty years old. That's another of her ideas; to be for him, and to be quite easily and charmingly, as young as a little girl."

Strether assisted at his distance. "For him'? For Chad—?"

"For Chad, in a manner, naturally, always. But in particular to-night for Mr. Pocock." And then as her friend still stared: "Yes, it IS of a bravery But that's what she has: her high sense of duty." It was more than sufficiently before them. "When Mr. Newsome has his hands so embarrassed with his sister—"

"It's quite the least"—Strether filled it out—"that she should take his sister's husband? Certainly—quite the least. So she has taken him."

"She has taken him." It was all Miss Barrace had meant.

Still it remained enough. "It must be funny."

"Oh it IS funny." That of course essentially went with it.

But it brought them back. "How indeed then she must care!" In answer to which Strether's entertainer dropped a comprehensive "Ah!" expressive perhaps of some impatience for the time he took to get used to it. She herself had got used to it long before.

II

When one morning within the week he perceived the whole thing to be really at last upon him Strether's immediate feeling was all relief. He had known this morning that something was about to happen—known it, in a moment, by Waymarsh's manner when Waymarsh appeared before him during his brief consumption of coffee and a roll in the small slippery salle-a-manger so associated with rich rumination. Strether had taken there of late various lonely and absent-minded meals; he communed there, even at the end of June, with a suspected chill, the air of old shivers mixed with old savours, the air in which so many of his impressions had perversely matured; the place meanwhile renewing its message to him by the very circumstance of his single state. He now sat there, for the most part, to sigh softly, while he vaguely tilted his carafe, over the vision of how much better Waymarsh was occupied. That was really his success by the common measure—to have led this companion so on and on. He remembered how at first there had been scarce a squatting-place he could beguile him into passing; the actual outcome of which at last was that there was scarce one that could arrest him in his rush. His rush—as Strether vividly and amusedly figured it—continued to be all with Sarah, and contained perhaps moreover the word of the whole enigma, whipping up in its fine full-flavoured froth the very principle, for good or for ill, of his own, of Strether's destiny. It might after all, to the end, only be that they had united to save him, and indeed, so far as Waymarsh was concerned, that HAD to be the spring of action. Strether was glad at all events, in connexion with the case, that the saving he required was not more scant; so constituted a luxury was it in certain lights just to lurk there out of the full glare. He had moments of quite seriously wondering whether Waymarsh wouldn't in fact, thanks to old friendship and a conceivable indulgence, make about as good terms for him as he might make for himself. They wouldn't be the same terms of course; but they might have the advantage that he himself probably should be able to make none at all.

He was never in the morning very late, but Waymarsh had already been out, and, after a peep into the dim refectory, he presented himself with much less than usual of his large looseness. He had made sure, through the expanse of glass exposed to the court, that they would be alone; and there was now in fact that about him that pretty well took up the room. He was dressed in the garments of summer; and save that his white waistcoat was redundant and bulging these things favoured, they determined, his expression. He wore a straw hat such as his friend hadn't yet seen in Paris, and he showed a buttonhole freshly adorned with a magnificent rose. Strether read on the instant his story—how, astir for the previous hour, the sprinkled newness of the day, so pleasant at that season in Paris, he was fairly panting with the pulse of adventure and had been with Mrs. Pocock, unmistakeably, to the Marche aux Fleurs. Strether really knew in this vision of him a joy that was akin to envy; so reversed as he stood there did their old positions seem; so comparatively doleful now showed, by the sharp turn of the wheel, the posture of the pilgrim from Woollett. He wondered, this pilgrim, if he had originally looked to Waymarsh so brave and well, so remarkably launched, as it was at present the latter's privilege to appear. He recalled that his friend had remarked to him even at Chester that his aspect belied his plea of prostration; but there certainly couldn't have been, for an issue, an aspect less concerned than Waymarsh's with the menace of decay. Strether had at any rate never resembled a Southern planter of the great days—which was the image picturesquely suggested by the happy relation between the fuliginous face and the wide panama of his visitor. This type, it further amused him to guess, had been, on Waymarsh's part, the object of Sarah's care; he was convinced that her taste had not been a stranger to the conception and purchase of the hat, any more than her fine fingers had been guiltless of the bestowal of the rose. It came to him in the current of thought, as things so oddly did come, that HE had never risen with the lark to attend a brilliant woman to the Marche aux Fleurs; this could be fastened on him in connexion neither with Miss Gostrey nor with Madame de Vionnet; the practice of getting up early for adventures could indeed in no manner be fastened on him. It came to him in fact that just here was his usual case: he was for ever missing things through his general genius for missing them, while others were for ever picking them up through a contrary bent. And it was others who looked abstemious and he who looked greedy; it was somehow who finally paid, and it was others who mainly partook. Yes, he should go to the scaffold yet for he wouldn't know quite whom. He almost, for that matter, felt on the scaffold now and really quite enjoying it. It worked out as BECAUSE he was anxious there—it worked out as for this reason that Waymarsh was so blooming—it was HIS trip for health, for a change, that proved the success—which was just what Strether, planning and exerting himself, had desired it should be. That truth already sat full-blown on his companion's lips; benevolence breathed from them as with the warmth of active exercise, and also a little as with the bustle of haste.

"Mrs. Pocock, whom I left a quarter of an hour ago at her hotel, has asked me to mention to you that she would like to find you at home here in about another hour. She wants to see you; she has something to say—or considers, I believe, that you may have: so that I asked her myself why she shouldn't come right round. She hasn't BEEN round yet—to see our place; and I took upon myself to say that I was sure you'd be glad to have her. The thing's therefore, you see, to keep right here till she comes."

The announcement was sociably, even though, after Waymarsh's wont, somewhat solemnly made; but Strether quickly felt other things in it than these light features. It was the first approach, from that quarter, to admitted consciousness; it quickened his pulse; it simply meant at last that he should have but himself to thank if he didn't know where he was. He had finished his breakfast; he pushed it away and was on his feet. There were plenty of elements of surprise, but only one of doubt. "The thing's for YOU to keep here too?" Waymarsh had been slightly ambiguous.

He wasn't ambiguous, however, after this enquiry; and Strether's understanding had probably never before opened so wide and effective a mouth as it was to open during the next five minutes. It was no part of his friend's wish, as appeared, to help to receive Mrs. Pocock; he quite understood the spirit in which she was to present herself, but his connexion with her visit was limited to his having—well, as he might say—perhaps a little promoted it. He had thought, and had let her know it, that Strether possibly would think she might have been round before. At any rate, as turned out, she had been wanting herself, quite a while, to come. "I told her," said Waymarsh, "that it would have been a bright idea if she had only carried it out before."

Strether pronounced it so bright as to be almost dazzling. "But why HASn't she carried it out before? She has seen me every day—she had only to name her hour. I've been waiting and waiting."

"Well, I told her you had. And she has been waiting too." It was, in the oddest way in the world, on the showing of this tone, a genial new pressing coaxing Waymarsh; a Waymarsh conscious with a different consciousness from any he had yet betrayed, and actually rendered by it almost insinuating. He lacked only time for full persuasion, and Strether was to see in a moment why. Meantime, however, our friend perceived, he was announcing a step of some magnanimity on Mrs. Pocock's part, so that he could deprecate a sharp question. It was his own high purpose in fact to have smoothed sharp questions to rest. He looked his old comrade very straight in the eyes, and he had never conveyed to him in so mute a manner so much kind confidence and so much good advice. Everything that was between them was again in his face, but matured and shelved and finally disposed of. "At any rate," he added, "she's coming now."

Considering how many pieces had to fit themselves, it all fell, in Strether's brain, into a close rapid order. He saw on the spot what had happened, and what probably would not yet; and it was all funny enough. It was perhaps just this freedom of appreciation that wound him up to his flare of high spirits. "What is she coming FOR?—to kill me?"

"She's coming to be very VERY kind to you, and you must let me say that I greatly hope you'll not be less so to herself."

This was spoken by Waymarsh with much gravity of admonition, and as Strether stood there he knew he had but to make a movement to take the attitude of a man gracefully receiving a present. The present was that of the opportunity dear old Waymarsh had flattered himself he had divined in him the slight soreness of not having yet thoroughly enjoyed; so he had brought it to him thus, as on a little silver breakfast-tray, familiarly though delicately—without oppressive pomp; and he was to bend and smile and acknowledge, was to take and use and be grateful. He was not—that was the beauty of it—to be asked to deflect too much from his dignity. No wonder the old boy bloomed in this bland air of his own distillation. Strether felt for a moment as if Sarah were actually walking up and down outside. Wasn't she hanging about the porte-cochere while her friend thus summarily opened a way? Strether would meet her but to take it, and everything would be for the best in the best of possible worlds. He had never so much known what any one meant as, in the light of this demonstration, he knew what Mrs. Newsome did. It had reached Waymarsh from Sarah, but it had reached Sarah from her mother, and there was no break in the chain by which it reached HIM. "Has anything particular happened," he asked after a minute—"so suddenly to determine her? Has she heard anything unexpected from home?"

Waymarsh, on this, it seemed to him, looked at him harder than ever. "'Unexpected'?" He had a brief hesitation; then, however, he was firm. "We're leaving Paris."

"Leaving? That IS sudden."

Waymarsh showed a different opinion. "Less so than it may seem. The purpose of Mrs. Pocock's visit is to explain to you in fact that it's NOT."

Strether didn't at all know if he had really an advantage—anything that would practically count as one; but he enjoyed for the moment—as for the first time in his life—the sense of so carrying it off. He wondered—it was amusing—if he felt as the impudent feel. "I shall take great pleasure, I assure you, in any explanation. I shall be delighted to receive Sarah."

The sombre glow just darkened in his comrade's eyes; but he was struck with the way it died out again. It was too mixed with another consciousness—it was too smothered, as might be said, in flowers. He really for the time regretted it—poor dear old sombre glow! Something straight and simple, something heavy and empty, had been eclipsed in its company; something by which he had best known his friend. Waymarsh wouldn't BE his friend, somehow, without the occasional ornament of the sacred rage, and the right to the sacred rage—inestimably precious for Strether's charity—he also seemed in a manner, and at Mrs. Pocock's elbow, to have forfeited. Strether remembered the occasion early in their stay when on that very spot he had come out with his earnest, his ominous "Quit it!"—and, so remembering, felt it hang by a hair that he didn't himself now utter the same note. Waymarsh was having a good time—this was the truth that was embarrassing for him, and he was having it then and there, he was having it in Europe, he was having it under the very protection of circumstances of which he didn't in the least approve; all of which placed him in a false position, with no issue possible—none at least by the grand manner. It was practically in the manner of any one—it was all but in poor Strether's own—that instead of taking anything up he merely made the most of having to be himself explanatory. "I'm not leaving for the United States direct. Mr. and Mrs. Pocock and Miss Mamie are thinking of a little trip before their own return, and we've been talking for some days past of our joining forces. We've settled it that we do join and that we sail together the end of next month. But we start to-morrow for Switzerland. Mrs. Pocock wants some scenery. She hasn't had much yet."

He was brave in his way too, keeping nothing back, confessing all there was, and only leaving Strether to make certain connexions. "Is what Mrs. Newsome had called her daughter an injunction to break off short?"

The grand manner indeed at this just raised its head a little. "I know nothing about Mrs. Newsome's cables."

Their eyes met on it with some intensity—during the few seconds of which something happened quite out of proportion to the time. It happened that Strether, looking thus at his friend, didn't take his answer for truth—and that something more again occurred in consequence of THAT. Yes—Waymarsh just DID know about Mrs. Newsome's cables: to what other end than that had they dined together at Bignon's? Strether almost felt for the instant that it was to Mrs. Newsome herself the dinner had been given; and, for that matter, quite felt how she must have known about it and, as he might think, protected and consecrated it. He had a quick blurred view of daily cables, questions, answers, signals: clear enough was his vision of the expense that, when so wound up, the lady at home was prepared to incur. Vivid not less was his memory of what, during his long observation of her, some of her attainments of that high pitch had cost her. Distinctly she was at the highest now, and Waymarsh, who imagined himself an independent performer, was really, forcing his fine old natural voice, an overstrained accompanist. The whole reference of his errand seemed to mark her for Strether as by this time consentingly familiar to him, and nothing yet had so despoiled her of a special shade of consideration. "You don't know," he asked, "whether Sarah has been directed from home to try me on the matter of my also going to Switzerland?"

"I know," said Waymarsh as manfully as possible, "nothing whatever about her private affairs; though I believe her to be acting in conformity with things that have my highest respect." It was as manful as possible, but it was still the false note—as it had to be to convey so sorry a statement. He knew everything, Strether more and more felt, that he thus disclaimed, and his little punishment was just in this doom to a second fib. What falser position—given the man—could the most vindictive mind impose? He ended by squeezing through a passage in which three months before he would certainly have stuck fast. "Mrs Pocock will probably be ready herself to answer any enquiry you may put to her. But," he continued, "BUT—!" He faltered on it.

"But what? Don't put her too many?"

Waymarsh looked large, but the harm was done; he couldn't, do what he would, help looking rosy. "Don't do anything you'll be sorry for."

It was an attenuation, Strether guessed, of something else that had been on his lips; it was a sudden drop to directness, and was thereby the voice of sincerity. He had fallen to the supplicating note, and that immediately, for our friend, made a difference and reinstated him. They were in communication as they had been, that first morning, in Sarah's salon and in her presence and Madame de Vionnet's; and the same recognition of a great good will was again thus alive, after all, possible. Only the amount of response Waymarsh had then taken for granted was doubled, decupled now. This came out when he presently said: "Of course I needn't assure you I hope you'll come with us." Then it was that his implications and expectations loomed up for Strether as almost pathetically gross.

The latter patted his shoulder while he thanked him, giving the go-by to the question of joining the Pococks; he expressed the joy he felt at seeing him go forth again so brave and free, and he in fact almost took leave of him on the spot. "I shall see you again of course before you go; but I'm meanwhile much obliged to you for arranging so conveniently for what you've told me. I shall walk up and down in the court there— dear little old court which we've each bepaced so, this last couple of months, to the tune of our flights and our drops, our hesitations and our plunges: I shall hang about there, all impatience and excitement, please let Sarah know, till she graciously presents herself. Leave me with her without fear," he laughed; "I assure you I shan't hurt her. I don't think either she'll hurt ME: I'm in a situation in which damage was some time ago discounted. Besides, THAT isn't what worries you—but don't, don't explain! We're all right as we are: which was the degree of success our adventure was pledged to for each of us. We weren't, it seemed, all right as we were before; and we've got over the ground, all things considered, quickly. I hope you'll have a lovely time in the Alps."

Waymarsh fairly looked up at him as from the foot of them. "I don't know as I OUGHT really to go."

It was the conscience of Milrose in the very voice of Milrose, but, oh it was feeble and flat! Strether suddenly felt quite ashamed for him; he breathed a greater boldness. "LET yourself, on the contrary, go—in all agreeable directions. These are precious hours—at our age they mayn't recur. Don't have it to say to yourself at Milrose, next winter, that you hadn't courage for them." And then as his comrade queerly stared: "Live up to Mrs. Pocock."

"Live up to her?"

"You're a great help to her."

Waymarsh looked at it as at one of the uncomfortable things that were certainly true and that it was yet ironical to say. "It's more then than you are."

"That's exactly your own chance and advantage. Besides," said Strether, "I do in my way contribute. I know what I'm about."

Waymarsh had kept on his great panama, and, as he now stood nearer the door, his last look beneath the shade of it had turned again to darkness and warning. "So do I! See here, Strether."

"I know what you're going to say. 'Quit this'?"

"Quit this!" But it lacked its old intensity; nothing of it remained; it went out of the room with him.

III

Almost the first thing, strangely enough, that, about an hour later, Strether found himself doing in Sarah's presence was to remark articulately on this failure, in their friend, of what had been superficially his great distinction. It was as if—he alluded of course to the grand manner—the dear man had sacrificed it to some other advantage; which would be of course only for himself to measure. It might be simply that he was physically so much more sound than on his first coming out; this was all prosaic, comparatively cheerful and vulgar. And fortunately, if one came to that, his improvement in health was really itself grander than any manner it could be conceived as having cost him. "You yourself alone, dear Sarah"—Strether took the plunge—"have done him, it strikes me, in these three weeks, as much good as all the rest of his time together."

It was a plunge because somehow the range of reference was, in the conditions, "funny," and made funnier still by Sarah's attitude, by the turn the occasion had, with her appearance, so sensibly taken. Her appearance was really indeed funnier than anything else—the spirit in which he felt her to be there as soon as she was there, the shade of obscurity that cleared up for him as soon as he was seated with her in the small salon de lecture that had, for the most part, in all the weeks, witnessed the wane of his early vivacity of discussion with Waymarsh. It was an immense thing, quite a tremendous thing, for her to have come: this truth opened out to him in spite of his having already arrived for himself at a fairly vivid view of it. He had done exactly what he had given Waymarsh his word for—had walked and re-walked the court while he awaited her advent; acquiring in this exercise an amount of light that affected him at the time as flooding the scene. She had decided upon the step in order to give him the benefit of a doubt, in order to be able to say to her mother that she had, even to abjectness, smoothed the way for him. The doubt had been as to whether he mightn't take her as not having smoothed it—and the admonition had possibly come from Waymarsh's more detached spirit. Waymarsh had at any rate, certainly, thrown his weight into the scale—he had pointed to the importance of depriving her friend of a grievance. She had done justice to the plea, and it was to set herself right with a high ideal that she actually sat there in her state. Her calculation was sharp in the immobility with which she held her tall parasol-stick upright and at arm's length, quite as if she had struck the place to plant her flag; in the separate precautions she took not to show as nervous; in the aggressive repose in which she did quite nothing but wait for him. Doubt ceased to be possible from the moment he had taken in that she had arrived with no proposal whatever; that her concern was simply to show what she had come to receive. She had come to receive his submission, and Waymarsh was to have made it plain to him that she would expect nothing less. He saw fifty things, her host, at this convenient stage; but one of those he most saw was that her anxious friend hadn't quite had the hand required of him. Waymarsh HAD, however, uttered the request that she might find him mild, and while hanging about the court before her arrival he had turned over with zeal the different ways in which he could be so. The difficulty was that if he was mild he wasn't, for her purpose, conscious. If she wished him conscious—as everything about her cried aloud that she did—she must accordingly be at costs to make him so. Conscious he was, for himself—but only of too many things; so she must choose the one she required.

Practically, however, it at last got itself named, and when once that had happened they were quite at the centre of their situation. One thing had really done as well as another; when Strether had spoken of Waymarsh's leaving him, and that had necessarily brought on a reference to Mrs. Pocock's similar intention, the jump was but short to supreme lucidity. Light became indeed after that so intense that Strether would doubtless have but half made out, in the prodigious glare, by which of the two the issue had been in fact precipitated. It was, in their contracted quarters, as much there between them as if it had been something suddenly spilled with a crash and a splash on the floor. The form of his submission was to be an engagement to acquit himself within the twenty-four hours. "He'll go in a moment if you give him the word—he assures me on his honour he'll do that": this came in its order, out of its order, in respect to Chad, after the crash had occurred. It came repeatedly during the time taken by Strether to feel that he was even more fixed in his rigour than he had supposed—the time he was not above adding to a little by telling her that such a way of putting it on her brother's part left him sufficiently surprised. She wasn't at all funny at last—she was really fine; and he felt easily where she was strong—strong for herself. It hadn't yet so come home to him that she was nobly and appointedly officious. She was acting in interests grander and clearer than that of her poor little personal, poor little Parisian equilibrium, and all his consciousness of her mother's moral pressure profited by this proof of its sustaining force. She would be held up; she would be strengthened; he needn't in the least be anxious for her. What would once more have been distinct to him had he tried to make it so was that, as Mrs. Newsome was essentially all moral pressure, the presence of this element was almost identical with her own presence. It wasn't perhaps that he felt he was dealing with her straight, but it was certainly as if she had been dealing straight with HIM. She was reaching him somehow by the lengthened arm of the spirit, and he was having to that extent to take her into account; but he wasn't reaching her in turn, not making her take HIM; he was only reaching Sarah, who appeared to take so little of him. "Something has clearly passed between you and Chad," he presently said, "that I think I ought to know something more about. Does he put it all," he smiled, "on me?"

"Did you come out," she asked, "to put it all on HIM?"

But he replied to this no further than, after an instant, by saying: "Oh it's all right. Chad I mean's all right in having said to you—well anything he may have said. I'll TAKE it all—what he does put on me. Only I must see him before I see you again."

She hesitated, but she brought it out. "Is it absolutely necessary you should see me again?"

"Certainly, if I'm to give you any definite word about anything."

"Is it your idea then," she returned, "that I shall keep on meeting you only to be exposed to fresh humiliation?"

He fixed her a longer time. "Are your instructions from Mrs. Newsome that you shall, even at the worst, absolutely and irretrievably break with me?"

"My instructions from Mrs. Newsome are, if you please, my affair. You know perfectly what your own were, and you can judge for yourself of what it can do for you to have made what you have of them. You can perfectly see, at any rate, I'll go so far as to say, that if I wish not to expose myself I must wish still less to expose HER." She had already said more than she had quite expected; but, though she had also pulled up, the colour in her face showed him he should from one moment to the other have it all. He now indeed felt the high importance of his having it. "What is your conduct," she broke out as if to explain—"what is your conduct but an outrage to women like US? I mean your acting as if there can be a doubt—as between us and such another—of his duty?"

He thought a moment. It was rather much to deal with at once; not only the question itself, but the sore abysses it revealed. "Of course they're totally different kinds of duty."

"And do you pretend that he has any at all—to such another?"

"Do you mean to Madame de Vionnet?" He uttered the name not to affront her, but yet again to gain time—time that he needed for taking in something still other and larger than her demand of a moment before. It wasn't at once that he could see all that was in her actual challenge; but when he did he found himself just checking a low vague sound, a sound which was perhaps the nearest approach his vocal chords had ever known to a growl. Everything Mrs. Pocock had failed to give a sign of recognising in Chad as a particular part of a transformation—everything that had lent intention to this particular failure—affected him as gathered into a large loose bundle and thrown, in her words, into his face. The missile made him to that extent catch his breath; which however he presently recovered. "Why when a woman's at once so charming and so beneficent—"

"You can sacrifice mothers and sisters to her without a blush and can make them cross the ocean on purpose to feel the more and take from you the straighter, HOW you do it?"

Yes, she had taken him up as short and as sharply as that, but he tried not to flounder in her grasp. "I don't think there's anything I've done in any such calculated way as you describe. Everything has come as a sort of indistinguishable part of everything else. Your coming out belonged closely to my having come before you, and my having come was a result of our general state of mind. Our general state of mind had proceeded, on its side, from our queer ignorance, our queer misconceptions and confusions—from which, since then, an inexorable tide of light seems to have floated us into our perhaps still queerer knowledge. Don't you LIKE your brother as he is," he went on, "and haven't you given your mother an intelligible account of all that that comes to?"

It put to her also, doubtless, his own tone, so many things, this at least would have been the case hadn't his final challenge directly helped her. Everything, at the stage they had reached, directly helped her, because everything betrayed in him such a basis of intention. He saw—the odd way things came out!—that he would have been held less monstrous had he only been a little wilder. What exposed him was just his poor old trick of quiet inwardness, what exposed him was his THINKING such offence. He hadn't in the least however the desire to irritate that Sarah imputed to him, and he could only at last temporise, for the moment, with her indignant view. She was altogether more inflamed than he had expected, and he would probably understand this better when he should learn what had occurred for her with Chad. Till then her view of his particular blackness, her clear surprise at his not clutching the pole she held out, must pass as extravagant. "I leave you to flatter yourself," she returned, "that what you speak of is what YOU'VE beautifully done. When a thing has been already described in such a lovely way—!" But she caught herself up, and her comment on his description rang out sufficiently loud. "Do you consider her even an apology for a decent woman?"

Ah there it was at last! She put the matter more crudely than, for his own mixed purposes, he had yet had to do; but essentially it was all one matter. It was so much—so much; and she treated it, poor lady, as so little. He grew conscious, as he was now apt to do, of a strange smile, and the next moment he found himself talking like Miss Barrace. "She has struck me from the first as wonderful. I've been thinking too moreover that, after all, she would probably have represented even for yourself something rather new and rather good."

He was to have given Mrs. Pocock with this, however, but her best opportunity for a sound of derision. "Rather new? I hope so with all my heart!"

"I mean," he explained, "that she might have affected you by her exquisite amiability—a real revelation, it has seemed to myself; her high rarity, her distinction of every sort."

He had been, with these words, consciously a little "precious"; but he had had to be—he couldn't give her the truth of the case without them; and it seemed to him moreover now that he didn't care. He had at all events not served his cause, for she sprang at its exposed side. "A 'revelation'—to ME: I've come to such a woman for a revelation? You talk to me about 'distinction'—YOU, you who've had your privilege?—when the most distinguished woman we shall either of us have seen in this world sits there insulted, in her loneliness, by your incredible comparison!"

Strether forbore, with an effort, from straying; but he looked all about him. "Does your mother herself make the point that she sits insulted?"

Sarah's answer came so straight, so "pat," as might have been said, that he felt on the instant its origin. "She has confided to my judgement and my tenderness the expression of her personal sense of everything, and the assertion of her personal dignity."

They were the very words of the lady of Woollett—he would have known them in a thousand; her parting charge to her child. Mrs. Pocock accordingly spoke to this extent by book, and the fact immensely moved him. "If she does really feel as you say it's of course very very dreadful. I've given sufficient proof, one would have thought," he added, "of my deep admiration for Mrs. Newsome."

"And pray what proof would one have thought you'd CALL sufficient? That of thinking this person here so far superior to her?"

He wondered again; he waited. "Ah dear Sarah, you must LEAVE me this person here!"

In his desire to avoid all vulgar retorts, to show how, even perversely, he clung to his rag of reason, he had softly almost wailed this plea. Yet he knew it to be perhaps the most positive declaration he had ever made in his life, and his visitor's reception of it virtually gave it that importance. "That's exactly what I'm delighted to do. God knows WE don't want her! You take good care not to meet," she observed in a still higher key, "my question about their life. If you do consider it a thing one can even SPEAK of, I congratulate you on your taste!"

The life she alluded to was of course Chad's and Madame de Vionnet's, which she thus bracketed together in a way that made him wince a little; there being nothing for him but to take home her full intention. It was none the less his inconsequence that while he had himself been enjoying for weeks the view of the brilliant woman's specific action, he just suffered from any characterisation of it by other lips. "I think tremendously well of her, at the same time that I seem to feel her 'life' to be really none of my business. It's my business, that is, only so far as Chad's own life is affected by it; and what has happened, don't you see? is that Chad's has been affected so beautifully. The proof of the pudding's in the eating"—he tried, with no great success, to help it out with a touch of pleasantry, while she let him go on as if to sink and sink. He went on however well enough, as well as he could do without fresh counsel; he indeed shouldn't stand quite firm, he felt, till he should have re-established his communications with Chad. Still, he could always speak for the woman he had so definitely promised to "save." This wasn't quite for her the air of salvation; but as that chill fairly deepened what did it become but a reminder that one might at the worst perish WITH her? And it was simple enough—it was rudimentary: not, not to give her away. "I find in her more merits than you would probably have patience with my counting over. And do you know," he enquired, "the effect you produce on me by alluding to her in such terms? It's as if you had some motive in not recognising all she has done for your brother, and so shut your eyes to each side of the matter, in order, whichever side comes up, to get rid of the other. I don't, you must allow me to say, see how you can with any pretence to candour get rid of the side nearest you."

"Near me—THAT sort of thing?" And Sarah gave a jerk back of her head that well might have nullified any active proximity.

It kept her friend himself at his distance, and he respected for a moment the interval. Then with a last persuasive effort he bridged it. "You don't, on your honour, appreciate Chad's fortunate development?"

"Fortunate?" she echoed again. And indeed she was prepared. "I call it hideous."

Her departure had been for some minutes marked as imminent, and she was already at the door that stood open to the court, from the threshold of which she delivered herself of this judgement. It rang out so loud as to produce for the time the hush of everything else. Strether quite, as an effect of it, breathed less bravely; he could acknowledge it, but simply enough. "Oh if you think THAT—!"

"Then all's at an end? So much the better. I do think that!" She passed out as she spoke and took her way straight across the court, beyond which, separated from them by the deep arch of the porte-cochere the low victoria that had conveyed her from her own hotel was drawn up. She made for it with decision, and the manner of her break, the sharp shaft of her rejoinder, had an intensity by which Strether was at first kept in arrest. She had let fly at him as from a stretched cord, and it took him a minute to recover from the sense of being pierced. It was not the penetration of surprise; it was that, much more, of certainty; his case being put for him as he had as yet only put it to himself. She was away at any rate; she had distanced him—with rather a grand spring, an effect of pride and ease, after all; she had got into her carriage before he could overtake her, and the vehicle was already in motion. He stopped halfway; he stood there in the court only seeing her go and noting that she gave him no other look. The way he had put it to himself was that all quite MIGHT be at an end. Each of her movements, in this resolute rupture, reaffirmed, re-enforced that idea. Sarah passed out of sight in the sunny street while, planted there in the centre of the comparatively grey court, he continued merely to look before him. It probably WAS all at an end.

Book Eleventh

I

Paris boulevard by night (1897) by Camille Pissarro (1830-1903)

He went late that evening to the Boulevard Malesherbes, having his impression that it would be vain to go early, and having also, more than once in the course of the day, made enquiries of the concierge. Chad hadn't come in and had left no intimation; he had affairs, apparently, at this juncture—as it occurred to Strether he so well might have—that kept him long abroad. Our friend asked once for him at the hotel in the Rue de Rivoli, but the only contribution offered there was the fact that every one was out. It was with the idea that he would have to come home to sleep that Strether went up to his rooms, from which however he was still absent, though, from the balcony, a few moments later, his visitor heard eleven o'clock strike. Chad's servant had by this time answered for his reappearance; he HAD, the visitor learned, come quickly in to dress for dinner and vanish again. Strether spent an hour in waiting for him—an hour full of strange suggestions, persuasions, recognitions; one of those that he was to recall, at the end of his adventure, as the particular handful that most had counted. The mellowest lamplight and the easiest chair had been placed at his disposal by Baptiste, subtlest of servants; the novel half-uncut, the novel lemon-coloured and tender, with the ivory knife athwart it like the dagger in a contadina's hair, had been pushed within the soft circle—a circle which, for some reason, affected Strether as softer still after the same Baptiste had remarked that in the absence of a further need of anything by Monsieur he would betake himself to bed. The night was hot and heavy and the single lamp sufficient; the great flare of the lighted city, rising high, spending itself afar, played up from the Boulevard and, through the vague vista of the successive rooms, brought objects into view and added to their dignity. Strether found himself in possession as he never yet had been; he had been there alone, had turned over books and prints, had invoked, in Chad's absence, the spirit of the place, but never at the witching hour and never with a relish quite so like a pang.

He spent a long time on the balcony; he hung over it as he had seen little Bilham hang the day of his first approach, as he had seen Mamie hang over her own the day little Bilham himself might have seen her from below; he passed back into the rooms, the three that occupied the front and that communicated by wide doors; and, while he circulated and rested, tried to recover the impression that they had made on him three months before, to catch again the voice in which they had seemed then to speak to him. That voice, he had to note, failed audibly to sound; which he took as the proof of all the change in himself. He had heard, of old, only what he COULD then hear; what he could do now was to think of three months ago as a point in the far past. All voices had grown thicker and meant more things; they crowded on him as he moved about—it was the way they sounded together that wouldn't let him be still. He felt, strangely, as sad as if he had come for some wrong, and yet as excited as if he had come for some freedom. But the freedom was what was most in the place and the hour, it was the freedom that most brought him round again to the youth of his own that he had long ago missed. He could have explained little enough to-day either why he had missed it or why, after years and years, he should care that he had; the main truth of the actual appeal of everything was none the less that everything represented the substance of his loss put it within reach, within touch, made it, to a degree it had never been, an affair of the senses. That was what it became for him at this singular time, the youth he had long ago missed—a queer concrete presence, full of mystery, yet full of reality, which he could handle, taste, smell, the deep breathing of which he could positively hear. It was in the outside air as well as within; it was in the long watch, from the balcony, in the summer night, of the wide late life of Paris, the unceasing soft quick rumble, below, of the little lighted carriages that, in the press, always suggested the gamblers he had seen of old at Monte Carlo pushing up to the tables. This image was before him when he at last became aware that Chad was behind.

"She tells me you put it all on ME"—he had arrived after this promptly enough at that information; which expressed the case however quite as the young man appeared willing for the moment to leave it. Other things, with this advantage of their virtually having the night before them, came up for them, and had, as well, the odd effect of making the occasion, instead of hurried and feverish, one of the largest, loosest and easiest to which Strether's whole adventure was to have treated him. He had been pursuing Chad from an early hour and had overtaken him only now; but now the delay was repaired by their being so exceptionally confronted. They had foregathered enough of course in all the various times; they had again and again, since that first night at the theatre, been face to face over their question; but they had never been so alone together as they were actually alone—their talk hadn't yet been so supremely for themselves. And if many things moreover passed before them, none passed more distinctly for Strether than that striking truth about Chad of which he had been so often moved to take note: the truth that everything came happily back with him to his knowing how to live. It had been seated in his pleased smile—a smile that pleased exactly in the right degree—as his visitor turned round, on the balcony, to greet his advent; his visitor in fact felt on the spot that there was nothing their meeting would so much do as bear witness to that facility. He surrendered himself accordingly to so approved a gift; for what was the meaning of the facility but that others DID surrender themselves? He didn't want, luckily, to prevent Chad from living; but he was quite aware that even if he had he would himself have thoroughly gone to pieces. It was in truth essentially by bringing down his personal life to a function all subsidiary to the young man's own that he held together. And the great point, above all, the sign of how completely Chad possessed the knowledge in question, was that one thus became, not only with a proper cheerfulness, but with wild native impulses, the feeder of his stream. Their talk had accordingly not lasted three minutes without Strether's feeling basis enough for the excitement in which he had waited. This overflow fairly deepened, wastefully abounded, as he observed the smallness of anything corresponding to it on the part of his friend. That was exactly this friend's happy case; he "put out" his excitement, or whatever other emotion the matter involved, as he put out his washing; than which no arrangement could make more for domestic order. It was quite for Strether himself in short to feel a personal analogy with the laundress bringing home the triumphs of the mangle.

When he had reported on Sarah's visit, which he did very fully, Chad answered his question with perfect candour. "I positively referred her to you—told her she must absolutely see you. This was last night, and it all took place in ten minutes. It was our first free talk—really the first time she had tackled me. She knew I also knew what her line had been with yourself; knew moreover how little you had been doing to make anything difficult for her. So I spoke for you frankly—assured her you were all at her service. I assured her I was too," the young man continued; "and I pointed out how she could perfectly, at any time, have got at me. Her difficulty has been simply her not finding the moment she fancied."

"Her difficulty," Strether returned, "has been simply that she finds she's afraid of you. She's not afraid of ME, Sarah, one little scrap; and it was just because she has seen how I can fidget when I give my mind to it that she has felt her best chance, rightly enough to be in making me as uneasy as possible. I think she's at bottom as pleased to HAVE you put it on me as you yourself can possibly be to put it."

"But what in the world, my dear man," Chad enquired in objection to this luminosity, "have I done to make Sally afraid?"

"You've been 'wonderful, wonderful,' as we say—we poor people who watch the play from the pit; and that's what has, admirably, made her. Made her all the more effectually that she could see you didn't set about it on purpose—I mean set about affecting her as with fear."

Chad cast a pleasant backward glance over his possibilities of motive. "I've only wanted to be kind and friendly, to be decent and attentive—and I still only want to be."

Strether smiled at his comfortable clearness. "Well, there can certainly be no way for it better than by my taking the onus. It reduces your personal friction and your personal offence to almost nothing."

Ah but Chad, with his completer conception of the friendly, wouldn't quite have this! They had remained on the balcony, where, after their day of great and premature heat, the midnight air was delicious; and they leaned back in turn against the balustrade, all in harmony with the chairs and the flower-pots, the cigarettes and the starlight. "The onus isn't REALLY yours—after our agreeing so to wait together and judge together. That was all my answer to Sally," Chad pursued—"that we have been, that we are, just judging together."

"I'm not afraid of the burden," Strether explained; "I haven't come in the least that you should take it off me. I've come very much, it seems to me, to double up my fore legs in the manner of the camel when he gets down on his knees to make his back convenient. But I've supposed you all this while to have been doing a lot of special and private judging—about which I haven't troubled you; and I've only wished to have your conclusion first from you. I don't ask more than that; I'm quite ready to take it as it has come."

Chad turned up his face to the sky with a slow puff of his smoke. "Well, I've seen."

Strether waited a little. "I've left you wholly alone; haven't I, I think I may say, since the first hour or two—when I merely preached patience—so much as breathed on you."

"Oh you've been awfully good!"

"We've both been good then—we've played the game. We've given them the most liberal conditions."

"Ah," said Chad, "splendid conditions! It was open to them, open to them"—he seemed to make it out, as he smoked, with his eyes still on the stars. He might in quiet sport have been reading their horoscope. Strether wondered meanwhile what had been open to them, and he finally let him have it. "It was open to them simply to let me alone; to have made up their minds, on really seeing me for themselves, that I could go on well enough as I was."

Strether assented to this proposition with full lucidity, his companion's plural pronoun, which stood all for Mrs. Newsome and her daughter, having no ambiguity for him. There was nothing, apparently, to stand for Mamie and Jim; and this added to our friend's sense of Chad's knowing what he thought. "But they've made up their minds to the opposite—that you CAN'T go on as you are."

"No," Chad continued in the same way; "they won't have it for a minute."

Strether on his side also reflectively smoked. It was as if their high place really represented some moral elevation from which they could look down on their recent past. "There never was the smallest chance, do you know, that they WOULD have it for a moment."

"Of course not—no real chance. But if they were willing to think there was—!"

"They weren't willing." Strether had worked it all out. "It wasn't for you they came out, but for me. It wasn't to see for themselves what you're doing, but what I'm doing. The first branch of their curiosity was inevitably destined, under my culpable delay, to give way to the second; and it's on the second that, if I may use the expression and you don't mind my marking the invidious fact, they've been of late exclusively perched. When Sarah sailed it was me, in other words, they were after."

Chad took it in both with intelligence and with indulgence. "It IS rather a business then—what I've let you in for!"

Strether had again a brief pause; which ended in a reply that seemed to dispose once for all of this element of compunction. Chad was to treat it, at any rate, so far as they were again together, as having done so. "I was 'in' when you found me."

"Ah but it was you," the young man laughed, "who found ME."

"I only found you out. It was you who found me in. It was all in the day's work for them, at all events, that they should come. And they've greatly enjoyed it," Strether declared.

"Well, I've tried to make them," said Chad.

His companion did himself presently the same justice. "So have I. I tried even this very morning—while Mrs. Pocock was with me. She enjoys for instance, almost as much as anything else, not being, as I've said, afraid of me; and I think I gave her help in that."

Chad took a deeper interest. "Was she very very nasty?"

Strether debated. "Well, she was the most important thing—she was definite. She was—at last—crystalline. And I felt no remorse. I saw that they must have come."

"Oh I wanted to see them for myself; so that if it were only for THAT—!" Chad's own remorse was as small.

This appeared almost all Strether wanted. "Isn't your having seen them for yourself then THE thing, beyond all others, that has come of their visit?"

Chad looked as if he thought it nice of his old friend to put it so. "Don't you count it as anything that you're dished—if you ARE dished? Are you, my dear man, dished?"

It sounded as if he were asking if he had caught cold or hurt his foot, and Strether for a minute but smoked and smoked. "I want to see her again. I must see her."

"Of course you must." Then Chad hesitated. "Do you mean—a—Mother herself?"

"Oh your mother—that will depend."

It was as if Mrs. Newsome had somehow been placed by the words very far off. Chad however endeavoured in spite of this to reach the place. "What do you mean it will depend on?"

Strether, for all answer, gave him a longish look. "I was speaking of Sarah. I must positively—though she quite cast me off—see HER again. I can't part with her that way."

"Then she was awfully unpleasant?"

Again Strether exhaled. "She was what she had to be. I mean that from the moment they're not delighted they can only be—well what I admit she was. We gave them," he went on, "their chance to be delighted, and they've walked up to it, and looked all round it, and not taken it."

"You can bring a horse to water—!" Chad suggested.

"Precisely. And the tune to which this morning Sarah wasn't delighted—the tune to which, to adopt your metaphor, she refused to drink—leaves us on that side nothing more to hope."

Chad had a pause, and then as if consolingly: "It was never of course really the least on the cards that they would be 'delighted.'"

"Well, I don't know, after all," Strether mused. "I've had to come as far round. However"—he shook it off—"it's doubtless MY performance that's absurd."

"There are certainly moments," said Chad, "when you seem to me too good to be true. Yet if you are true," he added, "that seems to be all that need concern me."

"I'm true, but I'm incredible. I'm fantastic and ridiculous—I don't explain myself even TO myself. How can they then," Strether asked, "understand me? So I don't quarrel with them."

"I see. They quarrel," said Chad rather comfortably, "with US." Strether noted once more the comfort, but his young friend had already gone on. "I should feel greatly ashamed, all the same, if I didn't put it before you again that you ought to think, after all, tremendously well. I mean before giving up beyond recall—" With which insistence, as from a certain delicacy, dropped.

Ah but Strether wanted it. "Say it all, say it all."

"Well, at your age, and with what—when all's said and done—Mother might do for you and be for you."

Chad had said it all, from his natural scruple, only to that extent; so that Strether after an instant himself took a hand. "My absence of an assured future. The little I have to show toward the power to take care of myself. The way, the wonderful way, she would certainly take care of me. Her fortune, her kindness, and the constant miracle of her having been disposed to go even so far. Of course, of course"—he summed it up. "There are those sharp facts."

Chad had meanwhile thought of another still. "And don't you really care—?"

His friend slowly turned round to him. "Will you go?"

"I'll go if you'll say you now consider I should. You know," he went on, "I was ready six weeks ago."

"Ah," said Strether, "that was when you didn't know I wasn't! You're ready at present because you do know it."

"That may be," Chad returned; "but all the same I'm sincere. You talk about taking the whole thing on your shoulders, but in what light do you regard me that you think me capable of letting you pay?" Strether patted his arm, as they stood together against the parapet, reassuringly—seeming to wish to contend that he HAD the wherewithal; but it was again round this question of purchase and price that the young man's sense of fairness continued to hover. "What it literally comes to for you, if you'll pardon my putting it so, is that you give up money. Possibly a good deal of money."

"Oh," Strether laughed, "if it were only just enough you'd still be justified in putting it so! But I've on my side to remind you too that YOU give up money; and more than 'possibly'—quite certainly, as I should suppose—a good deal."

"True enough; but I've got a certain quantity," Chad returned after a moment. "Whereas you, my dear man, you—"

"I can't be at all said"—Strether took him up—"to have a 'quantity' certain or uncertain? Very true. Still, I shan't starve."

"Oh you mustn't STARVE!" Chad pacifically emphasised; and so, in the pleasant conditions, they continued to talk; though there was, for that matter, a pause in which the younger companion might have been taken as weighing again the delicacy of his then and there promising the elder some provision against the possibility just mentioned. This, however, he presumably thought best not to do, for at the end of another minute they had moved in quite a different direction. Strether had broken in by returning to the subject of Chad's passage with Sarah and enquiring if they had arrived, in the event, at anything in the nature of a "scene." To this Chad replied that they had on the contrary kept tremendously polite; adding moreover that Sally was after all not the woman to have made the mistake of not being. "Her hands are a good deal tied, you see. I got so, from the first," he sagaciously observed, "the start of her."

"You mean she has taken so much from you?"

"Well, I couldn't of course in common decency give less: only she hadn't expected, I think, that I'd give her nearly so much. And she began to take it before she knew it."

"And she began to like it," said Strether, "as soon as she began to take it!"

"Yes, she has liked it—also more than she expected." After which Chad observed: "But she doesn't like ME. In fact she hates me."

Strether's interest grew. "Then why does she want you at home?"

"Because when you hate you want to triumph, and if she should get me neatly stuck there she WOULD triumph."

Strether followed afresh, but looking as he went. "Certainly—in a manner. But it would scarce be a triumph worth having if, once entangled, feeling her dislike and possibly conscious in time of a certain quantity of your own, you should on the spot make yourself unpleasant to her."

"Ah," said Chad, "she can bear ME—could bear me at least at home. It's my being there that would be her triumph. She hates me in Paris."

"She hates in other words—"

"Yes, THAT'S it!"—Chad had quickly understood this understanding; which formed on the part of each as near an approach as they had yet made to naming Madame de Vionnet. The limitations of their distinctness didn't, however, prevent its fairly lingering in the air that it was this lady Mrs. Pocock hated. It added one more touch moreover to their established recognition of the rare intimacy of Chad's association with her. He had never yet more twitched away the last light veil from this phenomenon than in presenting himself as confounded and submerged in the feeling she had created at Woollett. "And I'll tell you who hates me too," he immediately went on.

Strether knew as immediately whom he meant, but with as prompt a protest. "Ah no! Mamie doesn't hate—well," he caught himself in time—"anybody at all. Mamie's beautiful."

Chad shook his head. "That's just why I mind it. She certainly doesn't like me."

"How much do you mind it? What would you do for her?"

"Well, I'd like her if she'd like me. Really, really," Chad declared.

It gave his companion a moment's pause. "You asked me just now if I don't, as you said, 'care' about a certain person. You rather tempt me therefore to put the question in my turn. Don't YOU care about a certain other person?"

Chad looked at him hard in the lamplight of the window. "The difference is that I don't want to."

Strether wondered. "'Don't want' to?"

"I try not to—that is I HAVE tried. I've done my best. You can't be surprised," the young man easily went on, "when you yourself set me on it. I was indeed," he added, "already on it a little; but you set me harder. It was six weeks ago that I thought I had come out."

Strether took it well in. "But you haven't come out!"

"I don't know—it's what I WANT to know," said Chad. "And if I could have sufficiently wanted—by myself—to go back, I think I might have found out."

"Possibly"—Strether considered. "But all you were able to achieve was to want to want to! And even then," he pursued, "only till our friends there came. Do you want to want to still?" As with a sound half-dolorous, half-droll and all vague and equivocal, Chad buried his face for a little in his hands, rubbing it in a whimsical way that amounted to an evasion, he brought it out more sharply: "DO you?"

Chad kept for a time his attitude, but at last he looked up, and then abruptly, "Jim IS a damned dose!" he declared.

"Oh I don't ask you to abuse or describe or in any way pronounce on your relatives; I simply put it to you once more whether you're NOW ready. You say you've 'seen.' Is what you've seen that you can't resist?"

Chad gave him a strange smile—the nearest approach he had ever shown to a troubled one. "Can't you make me NOT resist?"

"What it comes to," Strether went on very gravely now and as if he hadn't heard him, "what it comes to is that more has been done for you, I think, than I've ever seen done—attempted perhaps, but never so successfully done—by one human being for another."

"Oh an immense deal certainly"—Chad did it full justice. "And you yourself are adding to it."

It was without heeding this either that his visitor continued. "And our friends there won't have it."

"No, they simply won't."

"They demand you on the basis, as it were, of repudiation and ingratitude; and what has been the matter with me," Strether went on, "is that I haven't seen my way to working with you for repudiation."

Chad appreciated this. "Then as you haven't seen yours you naturally haven't seen mine. There it is." After which he proceeded, with a certain abruptness, to a sharp interrogation. "NOW do you say she doesn't hate me?"

Strether hesitated. "'She'—?"

"Yes—Mother. We called it Sarah, but it comes to the same thing."

"Ah," Strether objected, "not to the same thing as her hating YOU."

On which—though as if for an instant it had hung fire—Chad remarkably replied: "Well, if they hate my good friend, THAT comes to the same thing." It had a note of inevitable truth that made Strether take it as enough, feel he wanted nothing more. The young man spoke in it for his "good friend" more than he had ever yet directly spoken, confessed to such deep identities between them as he might play with the idea of working free from, but which at a given moment could still draw him down like a whirlpool. And meanwhile he had gone on. "Their hating you too moreover—that also comes to a good deal."

"Ah," said Strether, "your mother doesn't."

Chad, however, loyally stuck to it—loyally, that is, to Strether. "She will if you don't look out."

"Well, I do look out. I am, after all, looking out. That's just why," our friend explained, "I want to see her again."

It drew from Chad again the same question. "To see Mother?"

"To see—for the present—Sarah."

"Ah then there you are! And what I don't for the life of me make out," Chad pursued with resigned perplexity, "is what you GAIN by it."

Oh it would have taken his companion too long to say! "That's because you have, I verily believe, no imagination. You've other qualities. But no imagination, don't you see? at all."

"I dare say. I do see." It was an idea in which Chad showed interest. "But haven't you yourself rather too much?"

"Oh RATHER—!" So that after an instant, under this reproach and as if it were at last a fact really to escape from, Strether made his move for departure.

II

One of the features of the restless afternoon passed by him after Mrs. Pocock's visit was an hour spent, shortly before dinner, with Maria Gostrey, whom of late, in spite of so sustained a call on his attention from other quarters, he had by no means neglected. And that he was still not neglecting her will appear from the fact that he was with her again at the same hour on the very morrow—with no less fine a consciousness moreover of being able to hold her ear. It continued inveterately to occur, for that matter, that whenever he had taken one of his greater turns he came back to where she so faithfully awaited him. None of these excursions had on the whole been livelier than the pair of incidents—the fruit of the short interval since his previous visit—on which he had now to report to her. He had seen Chad Newsome late the night before, and he had had that morning, as a sequel to this conversation, a second interview with Sarah. "But they're all off," he said, "at last."

It puzzled her a moment. "All?—Mr. Newsome with them?"

"Ah not yet! Sarah and Jim and Mamie. But Waymarsh with them—for Sarah. It's too beautiful," Strether continued; "I find I don't get over that—it's always a fresh joy. But it's a fresh joy too," he added, "that—well, what do you think? Little Bilham also goes. But he of course goes for Mamie."

Miss Gostrey wondered. "'For' her? Do you mean they're already engaged?"

"Well," said Strether, "say then for ME. He'll do anything for me; just as I will, for that matter—anything I can—for him. Or for Mamie either. SHE'LL do anything for me."

Miss Gostrey gave a comprehensive sigh. "The way you reduce people to subjection!"

"It's certainly, on one side, wonderful. But it's quite equalled, on another, by the way I don't. I haven't reduced Sarah, since yesterday; though I've succeeded in seeing her again, as I'll presently tell you. The others however are really all right. Mamie, by that blessed law of ours, absolutely must have a young man."

"But what must poor Mr. Bilham have? Do you mean they'll MARRY for you?"

"I mean that, by the same blessed law, it won't matter a grain if they don't—I shan't have in the least to worry."

She saw as usual what he meant. "And Mr. Jim?—who goes for him?"

"Oh," Strether had to admit, "I couldn't manage THAT. He's thrown, as usual, on the world; the world which, after all, by his account—for he has prodigious adventures—seems very good to him. He fortunately—'over here,' as he says—finds the world everywhere; and his most prodigious adventure of all," he went on, "has been of course of the last few days."

Miss Gostrey, already knowing, instantly made the connexion. "He has seen Marie de Vionnet again?"

"He went, all by himself, the day after Chad's party—didn't I tell you?—to tea with her. By her invitation—all alone."

"Quite like yourself!" Maria smiled.

"Oh but he's more wonderful about her than I am!" And then as his friend showed how she could believe it, filling it out, fitting it on to old memories of the wonderful woman: "What I should have liked to manage would have been HER going."

"To Switzerland with the party?"

"For Jim—and for symmetry. If it had been workable moreover for a fortnight she'd have gone. She's ready"—he followed up his renewed vision of her—"for anything."

Miss Gostrey went with him a minute. "She's too perfect!"

"She WILL, I think," he pursued, "go to-night to the station."

"To see him off?"

"With Chad—marvellously—as part of their general attention. And she does it"—it kept before him—"with a light, light grace, a free, free gaiety, that may well softly bewilder Mr. Pocock."

It kept her so before him that his companion had after an instant a friendly comment. "As in short it has softly bewildered a saner man. Are you really in love with her?" Maria threw off.

"It's of no importance I should know," he replied. "It matters so little—has nothing to do, practically, with either of us."

"All the same"—Maria continued to smile—"they go, the five, as I understand you, and you and Madame de Vionnet stay."

"Oh and Chad." To which Strether added: "And you."

"Ah 'me'!"—she gave a small impatient wail again, in which something of the unreconciled seemed suddenly to break out. "I don't stay, it somehow seems to me, much to my advantage. In the presence of all you cause to pass before me I've a tremendous sense of privation."

Strether hesitated. "But your privation, your keeping out of everything, has been—hasn't it?—by your own choice."

"Oh yes; it has been necessary—that is it has been better for you. What I mean is only that I seem to have ceased to serve you."

"How can you tell that?" he asked. "You don't know how you serve me. When you cease—"

"Well?" she said as he dropped.

"Well, I'll LET you know. Be quiet till then."

She thought a moment. "Then you positively like me to stay?"

"Don't I treat you as if I did?"

"You're certainly very kind to me. But that," said Maria, "is for myself. It's getting late, as you see, and Paris turning rather hot and dusty. People are scattering, and some of them, in other places want me. But if you want me here—!"

She had spoken as resigned to his word, but he had of a sudden a still sharper sense than he would have expected of desiring not to lose her. "I want you here."

She took it as if the words were all she had wished; as if they brought her, gave her something that was the compensation of her case. "Thank you," she simply answered. And then as he looked at her a little harder, "Thank you very much," she repeated.

It had broken as with a slight arrest into the current of their talk, and it held him a moment longer. "Why, two months, or whatever the time was, ago, did you so suddenly dash off? The reason you afterwards gave me for having kept away three weeks wasn't the real one."

She recalled. "I never supposed you believed it was. Yet," she continued, "if you didn't guess it was just what helped you."

He looked away from her on this; he indulged, so far as space permitted, in one of his slow absences. "I've often thought of it, but never to feel that I could guess it. And you see the consideration with which I've treated you in never asking till now."

"Now then why DO you ask?"

"To show you how I miss you when you're not here, and what it does for me."

"It doesn't seem to have done," she laughed, "all it might! However," she added, "if you've really never guessed the truth I'll tell it you."

"I've never guessed it," Strether declared.

"Never?"

"Never."

"Well then I dashed off, as you say, so as not to have the confusion of being there if Marie de Vionnet should tell you anything to my detriment."

He looked as if he considerably doubted. "You even then would have had to face it on your return."

"Oh if I had found reason to believe it something very bad I'd have left you altogether."

"So then," he continued, "it was only on guessing she had been on the whole merciful that you ventured back?"

Maria kept it together. "I owe her thanks. Whatever her temptation she didn't separate us. That's one of my reasons," she went on "for admiring her so."

"Let it pass then," said Strether, "for one of mine as well. But what would have been her temptation?"

"What are ever the temptations of women?"

He thought—but hadn't, naturally, to think too long. "Men?"

"She would have had you, with it, more for herself. But she saw she could have you without it."

"Oh 'have' me!" Strether a trifle ambiguously sighed. "YOU," he handsomely declared, "would have had me at any rate WITH it."

"Oh 'have' you!"—she echoed it as he had done. "I do have you, however," she less ironically said, "from the moment you express a wish."

He stopped before her, full of the disposition. "I'll express fifty."

Which indeed begot in her, with a certain inconsequence, a return of her small wail. "Ah there you are!"

There, if it were so, he continued for the rest of the time to be, and it was as if to show her how she could still serve him that, coming back to the departure of the Pococks, he gave her the view, vivid with a hundred more touches than we can reproduce, of what had happened for him that morning. He had had ten minutes with Sarah at her hotel, ten minutes reconquered, by irresistible pressure, from the time over which he had already described her to Miss Gostrey as having, at the end of their interview on his own premises, passed the great sponge of the future. He had caught her by not announcing himself, had found her in her sitting-room with a dressmaker and a lingere whose accounts she appeared to have been more or less ingenuously settling and who soon withdrew. Then he had explained to her how he had succeeded, late the night before, in keeping his promise of seeing Chad. "I told her I'd take it all."

"You'd 'take' it?"

"Why if he doesn't go."

Maria waited. "And who takes it if he does?" she enquired with a certain grimness of gaiety.

"Well," said Strether, "I think I take, in any event, everything."

"By which I suppose you mean," his companion brought out after a moment, "that you definitely understand you now lose everything."

He stood before her again. "It does come perhaps to the same thing. But Chad, now that he has seen, doesn't really want it."

She could believe that, but she made as always, for clearness. "Still, what, after all, HAS he seen?"

"What they want of him. And it's enough."

"It contrasts so unfavourably with what Madame de Vionnet wants?"

"It contrasts—just so; all round, and tremendously."

"Therefore, perhaps, most of all with what YOU want?"

"Oh," said Strether, "what I want is a thing I've ceased to measure or even to understand."

But his friend none the less went on. "Do you want Mrs. Newsome—after such a way of treating you?"

It was a straighter mode of dealing with this lady than they had as yet—such was their high form—permitted themselves; but it seemed not wholly for this that he delayed a moment. "I dare say it has been, after all, the only way she could have imagined."

"And does that make you want her any more?"

"I've tremendously disappointed her," Strether thought it worth while to mention.

"Of course you have. That's rudimentary; that was plain to us long ago. But isn't it almost as plain," Maria went on, "that you've even yet your straight remedy? Really drag him away, as I believe you still can, and you'd cease to have to count with her disappointment."

"Ah then," he laughed, "I should have to count with yours!"

But this barely struck her now. "What, in that case, should you call counting? You haven't come out where you are, I think, to please ME."

"Oh," he insisted, "that too, you know, has been part of it. I can't separate—it's all one; and that's perhaps why, as I say, I don't understand." But he was ready to declare again that this didn't in the least matter; all the more that, as he affirmed, he HADn't really as yet "come out." "She gives me after all, on its coming to the pinch, a last mercy, another chance. They don't sail, you see, for five or six weeks more, and they haven't—she admits that—expected Chad would take part in their tour. It's still open to him to join them, at the last, at Liverpool."

Miss Gostrey considered. "How in the world is it 'open' unless you open it? How can he join them at Liverpool if he but sinks deeper into his situation here?"

"He has given her—as I explained to you that she let me know yesterday—his word of honour to do as I say."

Maria stared. "But if you say nothing!"

Well, he, as usual walked about on it. "I did say something this morning. I gave her my answer—the word I had promised her after hearing from himself what HE had promised. What she demanded of me yesterday, you'll remember, was the engagement then and there to make him take up his vow."

"Well then," Miss Gostrey enquired, "was the purpose of your visit to her only to decline?"

"No; it was to ask, odd as that may seem to you, for another delay."

"Ah that's weak!"

"Precisely!" She had spoken with impatience, but, so far as that at least, he knew where he was. "If I AM weak I want to find it out. If I don't find it out I shall have the comfort, the little glory, of thinking I'm strong."

"It's all the comfort, I judge," she returned, "that you WILL have!"

"At any rate," he said, "it will have been a month more. Paris may grow, from day to day, hot and dusty, as you say; but there are other things that are hotter and dustier. I'm not afraid to stay on; the summer here must be amusing in a wild—if it isn't a tame—way of its own; the place at no time more picturesque. I think I shall like it. And then," he benevolently smiled for her, "there will be always you."

"Oh," she objected, "it won't be as a part of the picturesqueness that I shall stay, for I shall be the plainest thing about you. You may, you see, at any rate," she pursued, "have nobody else. Madame de Vionnet may very well be going off, mayn't she?—and Mr. Newsome by the same stroke: unless indeed you've had an assurance from them to the contrary. So that if your idea's to stay for them"—it was her duty to suggest it—"you may be left in the lurch. Of course if they do stay"—she kept it up—"they would be part of the picturesqueness. Or else indeed you might join them somewhere."

Strether seemed to face it as if it were a happy thought; but the next moment he spoke more critically. "Do you mean that they'll probably go off together?"

She just considered. "I think it will be treating you quite without ceremony if they do; though after all," she added, "it would be difficult to see now quite what degree of ceremony properly meets your case."

"Of course," Strether conceded, "my attitude toward them is extraordinary."

"Just so; so that one may ask one's self what style of proceeding on their own part can altogether match it. The attitude of their own that won't pale in its light they've doubtless still to work out. The really handsome thing perhaps," she presently threw off, "WOULD be for them to withdraw into more secluded conditions, offering at the same time to share them with you." He looked at her, on this, as if some generous irritation—all in his interest—had suddenly again flickered in her; and what she next said indeed half-explained it. "Don't really be afraid to tell me if what now holds you IS the pleasant prospect of the empty town, with plenty of seats in the shade, cool drinks, deserted museums, drives to the Bois in the evening, and our wonderful woman all to yourself." And she kept it up still more. "The handsomest thing of ALL, when one makes it out, would, I dare say, be that Mr. Chad should for a while go off by himself. It's a pity, from that point of view," she wound up, "that he doesn't pay his mother a visit. It would at least occupy your interval." The thought in fact held her a moment. "Why doesn't he pay his mother a visit? Even a week, at this good moment, would do."

"My dear lady," Strether replied—and he had it even to himself surprisingly ready—"my dear lady, his mother has paid HIM a visit. Mrs. Newsome has been with him, this month, with an intensity that I'm sure he has thoroughly felt; he has lavishly entertained her, and she has let him have her thanks. Do you suggest he shall go back for more of them?"

Well, she succeeded after a little in shaking it off. "I see. It's what you don't suggest—what you haven't suggested. And you know."

"So would you, my dear," he kindly said, "if you had so much as seen her."

"As seen Mrs. Newsome?"

"No, Sarah—which, both for Chad and for myself, has served all the purpose."

"And served it in a manner," she responsively mused, "so extraordinary!"

"Well, you see," he partly explained, "what it comes to is that she's all cold thought—which Sarah could serve to us cold without its really losing anything. So it is that we know what she thinks of us."

Maria had followed, but she had an arrest. "What I've never made out, if you come to that, is what you think—I mean you personally—of HER. Don't you so much, when all's said, as care a little?"

"That," he answered with no loss of promptness, "is what even Chad himself asked me last night. He asked me if I don't mind the loss—well, the loss of an opulent future. Which moreover," he hastened to add, "was a perfectly natural question."

"I call your attention, all the same," said Miss Gostrey, "to the fact that I don't ask it. What I venture to ask is whether it's to Mrs. Newsome herself that you're indifferent."

"I haven't been so"—he spoke with all assurance. "I've been the very opposite. I've been, from the first moment, preoccupied with the impression everything might be making on her—quite oppressed, haunted, tormented by it. I've been interested ONLY in her seeing what I've seen. And I've been as disappointed in her refusal to see it as she has been in what has appeared to her the perversity of my insistence."

"Do you mean that she has shocked you as you've shocked her?"

Strether weighed it. "I'm probably not so shockable. But on the other hand I've gone much further to meet her. She, on her side, hasn't budged an inch."

"So that you're now at last"—Maria pointed the moral—"in the sad stage of recriminations."

"No—it's only to you I speak. I've been like a lamb to Sarah. I've only put my back to the wall. It's to THAT one naturally staggers when one has been violently pushed there."

She watched him a moment. "Thrown over?"

"Well, as I feel I've landed somewhere I think I must have been thrown."

She turned it over, but as hoping to clarify much rather than to harmonise. "The thing is that I suppose you've been disappointing—"

"Quite from the very first of my arrival? I dare say. I admit I was surprising even to myself."

"And then of course," Maria went on, "I had much to do with it."

"With my being surprising—?"

"That will do," she laughed, "if you're too delicate to call it MY being! Naturally," she added, "you came over more or less for surprises."

"Naturally!"—he valued the reminder.

"But they were to have been all for you"—she continued to piece it out—"and none of them for HER."

Once more he stopped before her as if she had touched the point. "That's just her difficulty—that she doesn't admit surprises. It's a fact that, I think, describes and represents her; and it falls in with what I tell you—that she's all, as I've called it, fine cold thought. She had, to her own mind, worked the whole thing out in advance, and worked it out for me as well as for herself. Whenever she has done that, you see, there's no room left; no margin, as it were, for any alteration. She's filled as full, packed as tight, as she'll hold and if you wish to get anything more or different either out or in—"

"You've got to make over altogether the woman herself?"

"What it comes to," said Strether, "is that you've got morally and intellectually to get rid of her."

"Which would appear," Maria returned, "to be practically what you've done."

But her friend threw back his head. "I haven't touched her. She won't BE touched. I see it now as I've never done; and she hangs together with a perfection of her own," he went on, "that does suggest a kind of wrong in ANY change of her composition. It was at any rate," he wound up, "the woman herself, as you call her the whole moral and intellectual being or block, that Sarah brought me over to take or to leave."

It turned Miss Gostrey to deeper thought. "Fancy having to take at the point of the bayonet a whole moral and intellectual being or block!"

"It was in fact," said Strether, "what, at home, I HAD done. But somehow over there I didn't quite know it."

"One never does, I suppose," Miss Gostrey concurred, "realise in advance, in such a case, the size, as you may say, of the block. Little by little it looms up. It has been looming for you more and more till at last you see it all."

"I see it all," he absently echoed, while his eyes might have been fixing some particularly large iceberg in a cool blue northern sea. "It's magnificent!" he then rather oddly exclaimed.

But his friend, who was used to this kind of inconsequence in him, kept the thread. "There's nothing so magnificent—for making others feel you—as to have no imagination."

It brought him straight round. "Ah there you are! It's what I said last night to Chad. That he himself, I mean, has none."

"Then it would appear," Maria suggested, "that he has, after all, something in common with his mother."

"He has in common that he makes one, as you say, 'feel' him. And yet," he added, as if the question were interesting, "one feels others too, even when they have plenty."

Miss Gostrey continued suggestive. "Madame de Vionnet?"

"SHE has plenty."

"Certainly—she had quantities of old. But there are different ways of making one's self felt."

"Yes, it comes, no doubt, to that. You now—"

He was benevolently going on, but she wouldn't have it. "Oh I DON'T make myself felt; so my quantity needn't be settled. Yours, you know," she said, "is monstrous. No one has ever had so much."

It struck him for a moment. "That's what Chad also thinks."

"There YOU are then—though it isn't for him to complain of it!"

"Oh he doesn't complain of it," said Strether.

"That's all that would be wanting! But apropos of what," Maria went on, "did the question come up?"

"Well, of his asking me what it is I gain."

She had a pause. "Then as I've asked you too it settles my case. Oh you HAVE," she repeated, "treasures of imagination."

But he had been for an instant thinking away from this, and he came up in another place. "And yet Mrs. Newsome—it's a thing to remember—HAS imagined, did, that is, imagine, and apparently still does, horrors about what I should have found. I was booked, by her vision—extraordinarily intense, after all—to find them; and that I didn't, that I couldn't, that, as she evidently felt, I wouldn't—this evidently didn't at all, as they say, 'suit' her book. It was more than she could bear. That was her disappointment."

"You mean you were to have found Chad himself horrible?"

"I was to have found the woman."

"Horrible?"

"Found her as she imagined her." And Strether paused as if for his own expression of it he could add no touch to that picture.

His companion had meanwhile thought. "She imagined stupidly—so it comes to the same thing."

"Stupidly? Oh!" said Strether.

But she insisted. "She imagined meanly."

He had it, however, better. "It couldn't but be ignorantly."

"Well, intensity with ignorance—what do you want worse?"

This question might have held him, but he let it pass. "Sarah isn't ignorant—now; she keeps up the theory of the horrible."

"Ah but she's intense—and that by itself will do sometimes as well. If it doesn't do, in this case, at any rate, to deny that Marie's charming, it will do at least to deny that she's good."

"What I claim is that she's good for Chad."

"You don't claim"—she seemed to like it clear—"that she's good for YOU."

But he continued without heeding. "That's what I wanted them to come out for—to see for themselves if she's bad for him."

"And now that they've done so they won't admit that she's good even for anything?"

"They do think," Strether presently admitted, "that she's on the whole about as bad for me. But they're consistent of course, inasmuch as they've their clear view of what's good for both of us."

"For you, to begin with"—Maria, all responsive, confined the question for the moment—"to eliminate from your existence and if possible even from your memory the dreadful creature that I must gruesomely shadow forth for them, even more than to eliminate the distincter evil—thereby a little less portentous—of the person whose confederate you've suffered yourself to become. However, that's comparatively simple. You can easily, at the worst, after all, give me up."

"I can easily at the worst, after all, give you up." The irony was so obvious that it needed no care. "I can easily at the worst, after all, even forget you."

"Call that then workable. But Mr. Newsome has much more to forget. How can HE do it?"

"Ah there again we are! That's just what I was to have made him do; just where I was to have worked with him and helped."

She took it in silence and without attenuation—as if perhaps from very familiarity with the facts; and her thought made a connexion without showing the links. "Do you remember how we used to talk at Chester and in London about my seeing you through?" She spoke as of far-off things and as if they had spent weeks at the places she named.

"It's just what you ARE doing."

"Ah but the worst—since you've left such a margin—may be still to come. You may yet break down."

"Yes, I may yet break down. But will you take me—?"

He had hesitated, and she waited. "Take you?"

"For as long as I can bear it."

She also debated "Mr. Newsome and Madame de Vionnet may, as we were saying, leave town. How long do you think you can bear it without them?"

Strether's reply to this was at first another question. "Do you mean in order to get away from me?"

Her answer had an abruptness. "Don't find me rude if I say I should think they'd want to!"

He looked at her hard again—seemed even for an instant to have an intensity of thought under which his colour changed. But he smiled. "You mean after what they've done to me?"

"After what SHE has."

At this, however, with a laugh, he was all right again. "Ah but she hasn't done it yet!"

III

He had taken the train a few days after this from a station—as well as to a station—selected almost at random; such days, whatever should happen, were numbered, and he had gone forth under the impulse—artless enough, no doubt—to give the whole of one of them to that French ruralism, with its cool special green, into which he had hitherto looked only through the little oblong window of the picture-frame. It had been as yet for the most part but a land of fancy for him—the background of fiction, the medium of art, the nursery of letters; practically as distant as Greece, but practically also well-nigh as consecrated. Romance could weave itself, for Strether's sense, out of elements mild enough; and even after what he had, as he felt, lately "been through," he could thrill a little at the chance of seeing something somewhere that would remind him of a certain small Lambinet that had charmed him, long years before, at a Boston dealer's and that he had quite absurdly never forgotten. It had been offered, he remembered, at a price he had been instructed to believe the lowest ever named for a Lambinet, a price he had never felt so poor as on having to recognise, all the same, as beyond a dream of possibility. He had dreamed—had turned and twisted possibilities for an hour: it had been the only adventure of his life in connexion with the purchase of a work of art. The adventure, it will be perceived, was modest; but the memory, beyond all reason and by some accident of association, was sweet. The little Lambinet abode with him as the picture he WOULD have bought—the particular production that had made him for the moment overstep the modesty of nature. He was quite aware that if he were to see it again he should perhaps have a drop or a shock, and he never found himself wishing that the wheel of time would turn it up again, just as he had seen it in the maroon-coloured, sky-lighted inner shrine of Tremont Street. It would be a different thing, however, to see the remembered mixture resolved back into its elements—to assist at the restoration to nature of the whole far-away hour: the dusty day in Boston, the background of the Fitchburg Depot, of the maroon-coloured sanctum, the special-green vision, the ridiculous price, the poplars, the willows, the rushes, the river, the sunny silvery sky, the shady woody horizon.

He observed in respect to his train almost no condition save that it should stop a few times after getting out of the banlieue; he threw himself on the general amiability of the day for the hint of where to alight. His theory of his excursion was that he could alight anywhere—not nearer Paris than an hour's run—on catching a suggestion of the particular note required. It made its sign, the suggestion—weather, air, light, colour and his mood all favouring—at the end of some eighty minutes; the train pulled up just at the right spot, and he found himself getting out as securely as if to keep an appointment. It will be felt of him that he could amuse himself, at his age, with very small things if it be again noted that his appointment was only with a superseded Boston fashion. He hadn't gone far without the quick confidence that it would be quite sufficiently kept. The oblong gilt frame disposed its enclosing lines; the poplars and willows, the reeds and river—a river of which he didn't know, and didn't want to know, the name—fell into a composition, full of felicity, within them; the sky was silver and turquoise and varnish; the village on the left was white and the church on the right was grey; it was all there, in short—it was what he wanted: it was Tremont Street, it was France, it was Lambinet. Moreover he was freely walking about in it. He did this last, for an hour, to his heart's content, making for the shady woody horizon and boring so deep into his impression and his idleness that he might fairly have got through them again and reached the maroon-coloured wall. It was a wonder, no doubt, that the taste of idleness for him shouldn't need more time to sweeten; but it had in fact taken the few previous days; it had been sweetening in truth ever since the retreat of the Pococks. He walked and walked as if to show himself how little he had now to do; he had nothing to do but turn off to some hillside where he might stretch himself and hear the poplars rustle, and whence—in the course of an afternoon so spent, an afternoon richly suffused too with the sense of a book in his pocket—he should sufficiently command the scene to be able to pick out just the right little rustic inn for an experiment in respect to dinner. There was a train back to Paris at 9.20, and he saw himself partaking, at the close of the day, with the enhancements of a coarse white cloth and a sanded door, of something fried and felicitous, washed down with authentic wine; after which he might, as he liked, either stroll back to his station in the gloaming or propose for the local carriole and converse with its driver, a driver who naturally wouldn't fail of a stiff clean blouse, of a knitted nightcap and of the genius of response—who, in fine, would sit on the shafts, tell him what the French people were thinking, and remind him, as indeed the whole episode would incidentally do, of Maupassant. Strether heard his lips, for the first time in French air, as this vision assumed consistency, emit sounds of expressive intention without fear of his company. He had been afraid of Chad and of Maria and of Madame de Vionnet; he had been most of all afraid of Waymarsh, in whose presence, so far as they had mixed together in the light of the town, he had never without somehow paying for it aired either his vocabulary or his accent. He usually paid for it by meeting immediately afterwards Waymarsh's eye.

Such were the liberties with which his fancy played after he had turned off to the hillside that did really and truly, as well as most amiably, await him beneath the poplars, the hillside that made him feel, for a murmurous couple of hours, how happy had been his thought. He had the sense of success, of a finer harmony in things; nothing but what had turned out as yet according to his plan. It most of all came home to him, as he lay on his back on the grass, that Sarah had really gone, that his tension was really relaxed; the peace diffused in these ideas might be delusive, but it hung about him none the less for the time. It fairly, for half an hour, sent him to sleep; he pulled his straw hat over his eyes—he had bought it the day before with a reminiscence of Waymarsh's—and lost himself anew in Lambinet. It was as if he had found out he was tired—tired not from his walk, but from that inward exercise which had known, on the whole, for three months, so little intermission. That was it—when once they were off he had dropped; this moreover was what he had dropped to, and now he was touching bottom. He was kept luxuriously quiet, soothed and amused by the consciousness of what he had found at the end of his descent. It was very much what he had told Maria Gostrey he should like to stay on for, the hugely-distributed Paris of summer, alternately dazzling and dusky, with a weight lifted for him off its columns and cornices and with shade and air in the flutter of awnings as wide as avenues. It was present to him without attenuation that, reaching out, the day after making the remark, for some proof of his freedom, he had gone that very afternoon to see Madame de Vionnet. He had gone again the next day but one, and the effect of the two visits, the after-sense of the couple of hours spent with her, was almost that of fulness and frequency. The brave intention of frequency, so great with him from the moment of his finding himself unjustly suspected at Woollett, had remained rather theoretic, and one of the things he could muse about under his poplars was the source of the special shyness that had still made him careful. He had surely got rid of it now, this special shyness; what had become of it if it hadn't precisely, within the week, rubbed off?

It struck him now in fact as sufficiently plain that if he had still been careful he had been so for a reason. He had really feared, in his behaviour, a lapse from good faith; if there was a danger of one's liking such a woman too much one's best safety in waiting at least till one had the right to do so. In the light of the last few days the danger was fairly vivid; so that it was proportionately fortunate that the right was likewise established. It seemed to our friend that he had on each occasion profited to the utmost by the latter: how could he have done so more, he at all events asked himself, than in having immediately let her know that, if it was all the same to her, he preferred not to talk about anything tiresome? He had never in his life so sacrificed an armful of high interests as in that remark; he had never so prepared the way for the comparatively frivolous as in addressing it to Madame de Vionnet's intelligence. It hadn't been till later that he quite recalled how in conjuring away everything but the pleasant he had conjured away almost all they had hitherto talked about; it was not till later even that he remembered how, with their new tone, they hadn't so much as mentioned the name of Chad himself. One of the things that most lingered with him on his hillside was this delightful facility, with such a woman, of arriving at a new tone; he thought, as he lay on his back, of all the tones she might make possible if one were to try her, and at any rate of the probability that one could trust her to fit them to occasions. He had wanted her to feel that, as he was disinterested now, so she herself should be, and she had showed she felt it, and he had showed he was grateful, and it had been for all the world as if he were calling for the first time. They had had other, but irrelevant, meetings; it was quite as if, had they sooner known how much they REALLY had in common, there were quantities of comparatively dull matters they might have skipped. Well, they were skipping them now, even to graceful gratitude, even to handsome "Don't mention it!"—and it was amazing what could still come up without reference to what had been going on between them. It might have been, on analysis, nothing more than Shakespeare and the musical glasses; but it had served all the purpose of his appearing to have said to her: "Don't like me, if it's a question of liking me, for anything obvious and clumsy that I've, as they call it, 'done' for you: like me—well, like me, hang it, for anything else you choose. So, by the same propriety, don't be for me simply the person I've come to know through my awkward connexion with Chad—was ever anything, by the way, MORE awkward? Be for me, please, with all your admirable tact and trust, just whatever I may show you it's a present pleasure to me to think you." It had been a large indication to meet; but if she hadn't met it what HAD she done, and how had their time together slipped along so smoothly, mild but not slow, and melting, liquefying, into his happy illusion of idleness? He could recognise on the other hand that he had probably not been without reason, in his prior, his restricted state, for keeping an eye on his liability to lapse from good faith.

He really continued in the picture—that being for himself his situation—all the rest of this rambling day; so that the charm was still, was indeed more than ever upon him when, toward six o'clock he found himself amicably engaged with a stout white-capped deep-voiced woman at the door of the auberge of the biggest village, a village that affected him as a thing of whiteness, blueness and crookedness, set in coppery green, and that had the river flowing behind or before it—one couldn't say which; at the bottom, in particular, of the inn-garden. He had had other adventures before this; had kept along the height, after shaking off slumber; had admired, had almost coveted, another small old church, all steep roof and dim slate-colour without and all whitewash and paper flowers within; had lost his way and had found it again; had conversed with rustics who struck him perhaps a little more as men of the world than he had expected; had acquired at a bound a fearless facility in French; had had, as the afternoon waned, a watery bock, all pale and Parisian, in the cafe of the furthest village, which was not the biggest; and had meanwhile not once overstepped the oblong gilt frame. The frame had drawn itself out for him, as much as you please; but that was just his luck. He had finally come down again to the valley, to keep within touch of stations and trains, turning his face to the quarter from which he had started; and thus it was that he had at last pulled up before the hostess of the Cheval Blanc, who met him, with a rough readiness that was like the clatter of sabots over stones, on their common ground of a cotelette de veau a l'oseille and a subsequent lift. He had walked many miles and didn't know he was tired; but he still knew he was amused, and even that, though he had been alone all day, he had never yet so struck himself as engaged with others and in midstream of his drama. It might have passed for finished his drama, with its catastrophe all but reached: it had, however, none the less been vivid again for him as he thus gave it its fuller chance. He had only had to be at last well out of it to feel it, oddly enough, still going on.

For this had been all day at bottom the spell of the picture—that it was essentially more than anything else a scene and a stage, that the very air of the play was in the rustle of the willows and the tone of the sky. The play and the characters had, without his knowing it till now, peopled all his space for him, and it seemed somehow quite happy that they should offer themselves, in the conditions so supplied, with a kind of inevitability. It was as if the conditions made them not only inevitable, but so much more nearly natural and right as that they were at least easier, pleasanter, to put up with. The conditions had nowhere so asserted their difference from those of Woollett as they appeared to him to assert it in the little court of the Cheval Blanc while he arranged with his hostess for a comfortable climax. They were few and simple, scant and humble, but they were THE THING, as he would have called it, even to a greater degree than Madame de Vionnet's old high salon where the ghost of the Empire walked. "The" thing was the thing that implied the greatest number of other things of the sort he had had to tackle; and it was queer of course, but so it was—the implication here was complete. Not a single one of his observations but somehow fell into a place in it; not a breath of the cooler evening that wasn't somehow a syllable of the text. The text was simply, when condensed, that in THESE places such things were, and that if it was in them one elected to move about one had to make one's account with what one lighted on. Meanwhile at all events it was enough that they did affect one—so far as the village aspect was concerned—as whiteness, crookedness and blueness set in coppery green; there being positively, for that matter, an outer wall of the White Horse that was painted the most improbable shade. That was part of the amusement—as if to show that the fun was harmless; just as it was enough, further, that the picture and the play seemed supremely to melt together in the good woman's broad sketch of what she could do for her visitor's appetite. He felt in short a confidence, and it was general, and it was all he wanted to feel. It suffered no shock even on her mentioning that she had in fact just laid the cloth for two persons who, unlike Monsieur, had arrived by the river—in a boat of their own; who had asked her, half an hour before, what she could do for them, and had then paddled away to look at something a little further up—from which promenade they would presently return. Monsieur might meanwhile, if he liked, pass into the garden, such as it was, where she would serve him, should he wish it—for there were tables and benches in plenty—a "bitter" before his repast. Here she would also report to him on the possibility of a conveyance to his station, and here at any rate he would have the agrement of the river.

It may be mentioned without delay that Monsieur had the agrement of everything, and in particular, for the next twenty minutes, of a small and primitive pavilion that, at the garden's edge, almost overhung the water, testifying, in its somewhat battered state, to much fond frequentation. It consisted of little more than a platform, slightly raised, with a couple of benches and a table, a protecting rail and a projecting roof; but it raked the full grey-blue stream, which, taking a turn a short distance above, passed out of sight to reappear much higher up; and it was clearly in esteemed requisition for Sundays and other feasts. Strether sat there and, though hungry, felt at peace; the confidence that had so gathered for him deepened with the lap of the water, the ripple of the surface, the rustle of the reeds on the opposite bank, the faint diffused coolness and the slight rock of a couple of small boats attached to a rough landing-place hard by. The valley on the further side was all coppery-green level and glazed pearly sky, a sky hatched across with screens of trimmed trees, which looked flat, like espaliers; and though the rest of the village straggled away in the near quarter the view had an emptiness that made one of the boats suggestive. Such a river set one afloat almost before one could take up the oars—the idle play of which would be moreover the aid to the full impression. This perception went so far as to bring him to his feet; but that movement, in turn, made him feel afresh that he was tired, and while he leaned against a post and continued to look out he saw something that gave him a sharper arrest.

IV

What he saw was exactly the right thing—a boat advancing round the bend and containing a man who held the paddles and a lady, at the stern, with a pink parasol. It was suddenly as if these figures, or something like them, had been wanted in the picture, had been wanted more or less all day, and had now drifted into sight, with the slow current, on purpose to fill up the measure. They came slowly, floating down, evidently directed to the landing-place near their spectator and presenting themselves to him not less clearly as the two persons for whom his hostess was already preparing a meal. For two very happy persons he found himself straightway taking them—a young man in shirt-sleeves, a young woman easy and fair, who had pulled pleasantly up from some other place and, being acquainted with the neighbourhood, had known what this particular retreat could offer them. The air quite thickened, at their approach, with further intimations; the intimation that they were expert, familiar, frequent—that this wouldn't at all events be the first time. They knew how to do it, he vaguely felt—and it made them but the more idyllic, though at the very moment of the impression, as happened, their boat seemed to have begun to drift wide, the oarsman letting it go. It had by this time none the less come much nearer—near enough for Strether to dream the lady in the stern had for some reason taken account of his being there to watch them. She had remarked on it sharply, yet her companion hadn't turned round; it was in fact almost as if our friend had felt her bid him keep still. She had taken in something as a result of which their course had wavered, and it continued to waver while they just stood off. This little effect was sudden and rapid, so rapid that Strether's sense of it was separate only for an instant from a sharp start of his own. He too had within the minute taken in something, taken in that he knew the lady whose parasol, shifting as if to hide her face, made so fine a pink point in the shining scene. It was too prodigious, a chance in a million, but, if he knew the lady, the gentleman, who still presented his back and kept off, the gentleman, the coatless hero of the idyll, who had responded to her start, was, to match the marvel, none other than Chad.

Chad and Madame de Vionnet were then like himself taking a day in the country—though it was as queer as fiction, that farce, that their country could happen to be exactly his; and she had been the first at recognition, the first to feel, across the water, the shock—for it appeared to come to that—of their wonderful accident. Strether became aware, with this, of what was taking place—that her recognition had been even stranger for the pair in the boat, that her immediate impulse had been to control it, and that she was quickly and intensely debating with Chad the risk of betrayal. He saw they would show nothing if they could feel sure he hadn't made them out; so that he had before him for a few seconds his own hesitation. It was a sharp fantastic crisis that had popped up as if in a dream, and it had had only to last the few seconds to make him feel it as quite horrible. They were thus, on either side, TRYING the other side, and all for some reason that broke the stillness like some unprovoked harsh note. It seemed to him again, within the limit, that he had but one thing to do—to settle their common question by some sign of surprise and joy. He hereupon gave large play to these things, agitating his hat and his stick and loudly calling out—a demonstration that brought him relief as soon as he had seen it answered. The boat, in mid-stream, still went a little wild—which seemed natural, however, while Chad turned round, half springing up; and his good friend, after blankness and wonder, began gaily to wave her parasol. Chad dropped afresh to his paddles and the boat headed round, amazement and pleasantry filling the air meanwhile, and relief, as Strether continued to fancy, superseding mere violence. Our friend went down to the water under this odd impression as of violence averted—the violence of their having "cut" him, out there in the eye of nature, on the assumption that he wouldn't know it. He awaited them with a face from which he was conscious of not being able quite to banish this idea that they would have gone on, not seeing and not knowing, missing their dinner and disappointing their hostess, had he himself taken a line to match. That at least was what darkened his vision for the moment. Afterwards, after they had bumped at the landing-place and he had assisted their getting ashore, everything found itself sponged over by the mere miracle of the encounter.

They could so much better at last, on either side, treat it as a wild extravagance of hazard, that the situation was made elastic by the amount of explanation called into play. Why indeed—apart from oddity—the situation should have been really stiff was a question naturally not practical at the moment, and in fact, so far as we are concerned, a question tackled, later on and in private, only by Strether himself. He was to reflect later on and in private that it was mainly HE who had explained—as he had moreover comparatively little difficulty in doing. He was to have at all events meanwhile the worrying thought of their perhaps secretly suspecting him of having plotted this coincidence, taking such pains as might be to give it the semblance of an accident. That possibility—as their imputation—didn't of course bear looking into for an instant; yet the whole incident was so manifestly, arrange it as they would, an awkward one, that he could scarce keep disclaimers in respect to his own presence from rising to his lips. Disclaimers of intention would have been as tactless as his presence was practically gross; and the narrowest escape they either of them had was his lucky escape, in the event, from making any. Nothing of the sort, so far as surface and sound were involved, was even in question; surface and sound all made for their common ridiculous good fortune, for the general invraisemblance of the occasion, for the charming chance that they had, the others, in passing, ordered some food to be ready, the charming chance that he had himself not eaten, the charming chance, even more, that their little plans, their hours, their train, in short, from la-bas, would all match for their return together to Paris. The chance that was most charming of all, the chance that drew from Madame de Vionnet her clearest, gayest "Comme cela se trouve!" was the announcement made to Strether after they were seated at table, the word given him by their hostess in respect to his carriage for the station, on which he might now count. It settled the matter for his friends as well; the conveyance—it WAS all too lucky!—would serve for them; and nothing was more delightful than his being in a position to make the train so definite. It might have been, for themselves—to hear Madame de Vionnet—almost unnaturally vague, a detail left to be fixed; though Strether indeed was afterwards to remember that Chad had promptly enough intervened to forestall this appearance, laughing at his companion's flightiness and making the point that he had after all, in spite of the bedazzlement of a day with her, known what he was about.

Strether was to remember afterwards further that this had for him the effect of forming Chad's almost sole intervention; and indeed he was to remember further still, in subsequent meditation, many things that, as it were, fitted together. Another of them was for instance that the wonderful woman's overflow of surprise and amusement was wholly into French, which she struck him as speaking with an unprecedented command of idiomatic turns, but in which she got, as he might have said, somewhat away from him, taking all at once little brilliant jumps that he could but lamely match. The question of his own French had never come up for them; it was the one thing she wouldn't have permitted—it belonged, for a person who had been through much, to mere boredom; but the present result was odd, fairly veiling her identity, shifting her back into a mere voluble class or race to the intense audibility of which he was by this time inured. When she spoke the charming slightly strange English he best knew her by he seemed to feel her as a creature, among all the millions, with a language quite to herself, the real monopoly of a special shade of speech, beautifully easy for her, yet of a colour and a cadence that were both inimitable and matters of accident. She came back to these things after they had shaken down in the inn-parlour and knew, as it were, what was to become of them; it was inevitable that loud ejaculation over the prodigy of their convergence should at last wear itself out. Then it was that his impression took fuller form—the impression, destined only to deepen, to complete itself, that they had something to put a face upon, to carry off and make the best of, and that it was she who, admirably on the whole, was doing it. It was familiar to him of course that they had something to put a face upon; their friendship, their connexion, took any amount of explaining—that would have been made familiar by his twenty minutes with Mrs. Pocock if it hadn't already been so. Yet his theory, as we know, had bountifully been that the facts were specifically none of his business, and were, over and above, so far as one had to do with them, intrinsically beautiful; and this might have prepared him for anything, as well as rendered him proof against mystification. When he reached home that night, however, he knew he had been, at bottom, neither prepared nor proof; and since we have spoken of what he was, after his return, to recall and interpret, it may as well immediately be said that his real experience of these few hours put on, in that belated vision—for he scarce went to bed till morning—the aspect that is most to our purpose.

He then knew more or less how he had been affected—he but half knew at the time. There had been plenty to affect him even after, as has been said, they had shaken down; for his consciousness, though muffled, had its sharpest moments during this passage, a marked drop into innocent friendly Bohemia. They then had put their elbows on the table, deploring the premature end of their two or three dishes; which they had tried to make up with another bottle while Chad joked a little spasmodically, perhaps even a little irrelevantly, with the hostess. What it all came to had been that fiction and fable WERE, inevitably, in the air, and not as a simple term of comparison, but as a result of things said; also that they were blinking it, all round, and that they yet needn't, so much as that, have blinked it—though indeed if they hadn't Strether didn't quite see what else they could have done. Strether didn't quite see THAT even at an hour or two past midnight, even when he had, at his hotel, for a long time, without a light and without undressing, sat back on his bedroom sofa and stared straight before him. He was, at that point of vantage, in full possession, to make of it all what he could. He kept making of it that there had been simply a LIE in the charming affair—a lie on which one could now, detached and deliberate, perfectly put one's finger. It was with the lie that they had eaten and drunk and talked and laughed, that they had waited for their carriole rather impatiently, and had then got into the vehicle and, sensibly subsiding, driven their three or four miles through the darkening summer night. The eating and drinking, which had been a resource, had had the effect of having served its turn; the talk and laughter had done as much; and it was during their somewhat tedious progress to the station, during the waits there, the further delays, their submission to fatigue, their silences in the dim compartment of the much-stopping train, that he prepared himself for reflexions to come. It had been a performance, Madame de Vionnet's manner, and though it had to that degree faltered toward the end, as through her ceasing to believe in it, as if she had asked herself, or Chad had found a moment surreptitiously to ask her, what after all was the use, a performance it had none the less quite handsomely remained, with the final fact about it that it was on the whole easier to keep up than to abandon.

From the point of view of presence of mind it had been very wonderful indeed, wonderful for readiness, for beautiful assurance, for the way her decision was taken on the spot, without time to confer with Chad, without time for anything. Their only conference could have been the brief instants in the boat before they confessed to recognising the spectator on the bank, for they hadn't been alone together a moment since and must have communicated all in silence. It was a part of the deep impression for Strether, and not the least of the deep interest, that they COULD so communicate—that Chad in particular could let her know he left it to her. He habitually left things to others, as Strether was so well aware, and it in fact came over our friend in these meditations that there had been as yet no such vivid illustration of his famous knowing how to live. It was as if he had humoured her to the extent of letting her lie without correction—almost as if, really, he would be coming round in the morning to set the matter, as between Strether and himself, right. Of course he couldn't quite come; it was a case in which a man was obliged to accept the woman's version, even when fantastic; if she had, with more flurry than she cared to show, elected, as the phrase was, to represent that they had left Paris that morning, and with no design but of getting back within the day—if she had so sized-up, in the Woollett phrase, their necessity, she knew best her own measure. There were things, all the same, it was impossible to blink and which made this measure an odd one—the too evident fact for instance that she hadn't started out for the day dressed and hatted and shod, and even, for that matter, pink parasol'd, as she had been in the boat. From what did the drop in her assurance proceed as the tension increased—from what did this slightly baffled ingenuity spring but from her consciousness of not presenting, as night closed in, with not so much as a shawl to wrap her round, an appearance that matched her story? She admitted that she was cold, but only to blame her imprudence which Chad suffered her to give such account of as she might. Her shawl and Chad's overcoat and her other garments, and his, those they had each worn the day before, were at the place, best known to themselves—a quiet retreat enough, no doubt—at which they had been spending the twenty-four hours, to which they had fully meant to return that evening, from which they had so remarkably swum into Strether's ken, and the tacit repudiation of which had been thus the essence of her comedy. Strether saw how she had perceived in a flash that they couldn't quite look to going back there under his nose; though, honestly, as he gouged deeper into the matter, he was somewhat surprised, as Chad likewise had perhaps been, at the uprising of this scruple. He seemed even to divine that she had entertained it rather for Chad than for herself, and that, as the young man had lacked the chance to enlighten her, she had had to go on with it, he meanwhile mistaking her motive.

He was rather glad, none the less, that they had in point of fact not parted at the Cheval Blanc, that he hadn't been reduced to giving them his blessing for an idyllic retreat down the river. He had had in the actual case to make-believe more than he liked, but this was nothing, it struck him, to what the other event would have required. Could he, literally, quite have faced the other event? Would he have been capable of making the best of it with them? This was what he was trying to do now; but with the advantage of his being able to give more time to it a good deal counteracted by his sense of what, over and above the central fact itself, he had to swallow. It was the quantity of make-believe involved and so vividly exemplified that most disagreed with his spiritual stomach. He moved, however, from the consideration of that quantity—to say nothing of the consciousness of that organ—back to the other feature of the show, the deep, deep truth of the intimacy revealed. That was what, in his vain vigil, he oftenest reverted to: intimacy, at such a point, was LIKE that—and what in the world else would one have wished it to be like? It was all very well for him to feel the pity of its being so much like lying; he almost blushed, in the dark, for the way he had dressed the possibility in vagueness, as a little girl might have dressed her doll. He had made them—and by no fault of their own—momentarily pull it for him, the possibility, out of this vagueness; and must he not therefore take it now as they had had simply, with whatever thin attenuations, to give it to him? The very question, it may be added, made him feel lonely and cold. There was the element of the awkward all round, but Chad and Madame de Vionnet had at least the comfort that they could talk it over together. With whom could HE talk of such things?—unless indeed always, at almost any stage, with Maria? He foresaw that Miss Gostrey would come again into requisition on the morrow; though it wasn't to be denied that he was already a little afraid of her "What on earth—that's what I want to know now—had you then supposed?" He recognised at last that he had really been trying all along to suppose nothing. Verily, verily, his labour had been lost. He found himself supposing innumerable and wonderful things.

Book Twelfth

I

Strether couldn't have said he had during the previous hours definitely expected it; yet when, later on, that morning—though no later indeed than for his coming forth at ten o'clock—he saw the concierge produce, on his approach, a petit bleu delivered since his letters had been sent up, he recognised the appearance as the first symptom of a sequel. He then knew he had been thinking of some early sign from Chad as more likely, after all, than not; and this would be precisely the early sign. He took it so for granted that he opened the petit bleu just where he had stopped, in the pleasant cool draught of the porte-cochere—only curious to see where the young man would, at such a juncture, break out. His curiosity, however, was more than gratified; the small missive, whose gummed edge he had detached without attention to the address, not being from the young man at all, but from the person whom the case gave him on the spot as still more worth while. Worth while or not, he went round to the nearest telegraph-office, the big one on the Boulevard, with a directness that almost confessed to a fear of the danger of delay. He might have been thinking that if he didn't go before he could think he wouldn't perhaps go at all. He at any rate kept, in the lower side-pocket of his morning coat, a very deliberate hand on his blue missive, crumpling it up rather tenderly than harshly. He wrote a reply, on the Boulevard, also in the form of a petit bleu—which was quickly done, under pressure of the place, inasmuch as, like Madame de Vionnet's own communication, it consisted of the fewest words. She had asked him if he could do her the very great kindness of coming to see her that evening at half-past nine, and he answered, as if nothing were easier, that he would present himself at the hour she named. She had added a line of postscript, to the effect that she would come to him elsewhere and at his own hour if he preferred; but he took no notice of this, feeling that if he saw her at all half the value of it would be in seeing her where he had already seen her best. He mightn't see her at all; that was one of the reflexions he made after writing and before he dropped his closed card into the box; he mightn't see any one at all any more at all; he might make an end as well now as ever, leaving things as they were, since he was doubtless not to leave them better, and taking his way home so far as should appear that a home remained to him. This alternative was for a few minutes so sharp that if he at last did deposit his missive it was perhaps because the pressure of the place had an effect.

There was none other, however, than the common and constant pressure, familiar to our friend under the rubric of Postes et Telegraphes—the something in the air of these establishments; the vibration of the vast strange life of the town, the influence of the types, the performers concocting their messages; the little prompt Paris women, arranging, pretexting goodness knew what, driving the dreadful needle-pointed public pen at the dreadful sand-strewn public table: implements that symbolised for Strether's too interpretative innocence something more acute in manners, more sinister in morals, more fierce in the national life. After he had put in his paper he had ranged himself, he was really amused to think, on the side of the fierce, the sinister, the acute. He was carrying on a correspondence, across the great city, quite in the key of the Postes et Telegraphes in general; and it was fairly as if the acceptance of that fact had come from something in his state that sorted with the occupation of his neighbours. He was mixed up with the typical tale of Paris, and so were they, poor things—how could they all together help being? They were no worse than he, in short, and he no worse than they—if, queerly enough, no better; and at all events he had settled his hash, so that he went out to begin, from that moment, his day of waiting. The great settlement was, as he felt, in his preference for seeing his correspondent in her own best conditions. THAT was part of the typical tale, the part most significant in respect to himself. He liked the place she lived in, the picture that each time squared itself, large and high and clear, around her: every occasion of seeing it was a pleasure of a different shade. Yet what precisely was he doing with shades of pleasure now, and why hadn't he properly and logically compelled her to commit herself to whatever of disadvantage and penalty the situation might throw up? He might have proposed, as for Sarah Pocock, the cold hospitality of his own salon de lecture, in which the chill of Sarah's visit seemed still to abide and shades of pleasure were dim; he might have suggested a stone bench in the dusty Tuileries or a penny chair at the back part of the Champs Elysees. These things would have been a trifle stern, and sternness alone now wouldn't be sinister. An instinct in him cast about for some form of discipline in which they might meet—some awkwardness they would suffer from, some danger, or at least some grave inconvenience, they would incur. This would give a sense—which the spirit required, rather ached and sighed in the absence of—that somebody was paying something somewhere and somehow, that they were at least not all floating together on the silver stream of impunity. Just instead of that to go and see her late in the evening, as if, for all the world—well, as if he were as much in the swim as anybody else: this had as little as possible in common with the penal form.

Even when he had felt that objection melt away, however, the practical difference was small; the long stretch of his interval took the colour it would, and if he lived on thus with the sinister from hour to hour it proved an easier thing than one might have supposed in advance. He reverted in thought to his old tradition, the one he had been brought up on and which even so many years of life had but little worn away; the notion that the state of the wrongdoer, or at least this person's happiness, presented some special difficulty. What struck him now rather was the ease of it—for nothing in truth appeared easier. It was an ease he himself fairly tasted of for the rest of the day; giving himself quite up; not so much as trying to dress it out, in any particular whatever, as a difficulty; not after all going to see Maria—which would have been in a manner a result of such dressing; only idling, lounging, smoking, sitting in the shade, drinking lemonade and consuming ices. The day had turned to heat and eventual thunder, and he now and again went back to his hotel to find that Chad hadn't been there. He hadn't yet struck himself, since leaving Woollett, so much as a loafer, though there had been times when he believed himself touching bottom. This was a deeper depth than any, and with no foresight, scarcely with a care, as to what he should bring up. He almost wondered if he didn't LOOK demoralised and disreputable; he had the fanciful vision, as he sat and smoked, of some accidental, some motived, return of the Pococks, who would be passing along the Boulevard and would catch this view of him. They would have distinctly, on his appearance, every ground for scandal. But fate failed to administer even that sternness; the Pococks never passed and Chad made no sign. Strether meanwhile continued to hold off from Miss Gostrey, keeping her till to-morrow; so that by evening his irresponsibility, his impunity, his luxury, had become—there was no other word for them—immense.

Between nine and ten, at last, in the high clear picture—he was moving in these days, as in a gallery, from clever canvas to clever canvas—he drew a long breath: it was so presented to him from the first that the spell of his luxury wouldn't be broken. He wouldn't have, that is, to become responsible—this was admirably in the air: she had sent for him precisely to let him feel it, so that he might go on with the comfort (comfort already established, hadn't it been?) of regarding his ordeal, the ordeal of the weeks of Sarah's stay and of their climax, as safely traversed and left behind him. Didn't she just wish to assure him that SHE now took it all and so kept it; that he was absolutely not to worry any more, was only to rest on his laurels and continue generously to help her? The light in her beautiful formal room was dim, though it would do, as everything would always do; the hot night had kept out lamps, but there was a pair of clusters of candles that glimmered over the chimney-piece like the tall tapers of an altar. The windows were all open, their redundant hangings swaying a little, and he heard once more, from the empty court, the small plash of the fountain. From beyond this, and as from a great distance—beyond the court, beyond the corps de logis forming the front—came, as if excited and exciting, the vague voice of Paris. Strether had all along been subject to sudden gusts of fancy in connexion with such matters as these—odd starts of the historic sense, suppositions and divinations with no warrant but their intensity. Thus and so, on the eve of the great recorded dates, the days and nights of revolution, the sounds had come in, the omens, the beginnings broken out. They were the smell of revolution, the smell of the public temper—or perhaps simply the smell of blood.

It was at present queer beyond words, "subtle," he would have risked saying, that such suggestions should keep crossing the scene; but it was doubtless the effect of the thunder in the air, which had hung about all day without release. His hostess was dressed as for thunderous times, and it fell in with the kind of imagination we have just attributed to him that she should be in simplest coolest white, of a character so old-fashioned, if he were not mistaken, that Madame Roland must on the scaffold have worn something like it. This effect was enhanced by a small black fichu or scarf, of crape or gauze, disposed quaintly round her bosom and now completing as by a mystic touch the pathetic, the noble analogy. Poor Strether in fact scarce knew what analogy was evoked for him as the charming woman, receiving him and making him, as she could do such things, at once familiarly and gravely welcome, moved over her great room with her image almost repeated in its polished floor, which had been fully bared for summer. The associations of the place, all felt again; the gleam here and there, in the subdued light, of glass and gilt and parquet, with the quietness of her own note as the centre—these things were at first as delicate as if they had been ghostly, and he was sure in a moment that, whatever he should find he had come for, it wouldn't be for an impression that had previously failed him. That conviction held him from the outset, and, seeming singularly to simplify, certified to him that the objects about would help him, would really help them both. No, he might never see them again—this was only too probably the last time; and he should certainly see nothing in the least degree like them. He should soon be going to where such things were not, and it would be a small mercy for memory, for fancy, to have, in that stress, a loaf on the shelf. He knew in advance he should look back on the perception actually sharpest with him as on the view of something old, old, old, the oldest thing he had ever personally touched; and he also knew, even while he took his companion in as the feature among features, that memory and fancy couldn't help being enlisted for her. She might intend what she would, but this was beyond anything she could intend, with things from far back—tyrannies of history, facts of type, values, as the painters said, of expression—all working for her and giving her the supreme chance, the chance of the happy, the really luxurious few, the chance, on a great occasion, to be natural and simple. She had never, with him, been more so; or if it was the perfection of art it would never—and that came to the same thing—be proved against her.

What was truly wonderful was her way of differing so from time to time without detriment to her simplicity. Caprices, he was sure she felt, were before anything else bad manners, and that judgement in her was by itself a thing making more for safety of intercourse than anything that in his various own past intercourses he had had to reckon on. If therefore her presence was now quite other than the one she had shown him the night before, there was nothing of violence in the change—it was all harmony and reason. It gave him a mild deep person, whereas he had had on the occasion to which their interview was a direct reference a person committed to movement and surface and abounding in them; but she was in either character more remarkable for nothing than for her bridging of intervals, and this now fell in with what he understood he was to leave to her. The only thing was that, if he was to leave it ALL to her, why exactly had she sent for him? He had had, vaguely, in advance, his explanation, his view of the probability of her wishing to set something right, to deal in some way with the fraud so lately practised on his presumed credulity. Would she attempt to carry it further or would she blot it out? Would she throw over it some more or less happy colour; or would she do nothing about it at all? He perceived soon enough at least that, however reasonable she might be, she wasn't vulgarly confused, and it herewith pressed upon him that their eminent "lie," Chad's and hers, was simply after all such an inevitable tribute to good taste as he couldn't have wished them not to render. Away from them, during his vigil, he had seemed to wince at the amount of comedy involved; whereas in his present posture he could only ask himself how he should enjoy any attempt from her to take the comedy back. He shouldn't enjoy it at all; but, once more and yet once more, he could trust her. That is he could trust her to make deception right. As she presented things the ugliness—goodness knew why—went out of them; none the less too that she could present them, with an art of her own, by not so much as touching them. She let the matter, at all events, lie where it was—where the previous twenty-four hours had placed it; appearing merely to circle about it respectfully, tenderly, almost piously, while she took up another question.

She knew she hadn't really thrown dust in his eyes; this, the previous night, before they separated, had practically passed between them; and, as she had sent for him to see what the difference thus made for him might amount to, so he was conscious at the end of five minutes that he had been tried and tested. She had settled with Chad after he left them that she would, for her satisfaction, assure herself of this quantity, and Chad had, as usual, let her have her way. Chad was always letting people have their way when he felt that it would somehow turn his wheel for him; it somehow always did turn his wheel. Strether felt, oddly enough, before these facts, freshly and consentingly passive; they again so rubbed it into him that the couple thus fixing his attention were intimate, that his intervention had absolutely aided and intensified their intimacy, and that in fine he must accept the consequence of that. He had absolutely become, himself, with his perceptions and his mistakes, his concessions and his reserves, the droll mixture, as it must seem to them, of his braveries and his fears, the general spectacle of his art and his innocence, almost an added link and certainly a common priceless ground for them to meet upon. It was as if he had been hearing their very tone when she brought out a reference that was comparatively straight. "The last twice that you've been here, you know, I never asked you," she said with an abrupt transition—they had been pretending before this to talk simply of the charm of yesterday and of the interest of the country they had seen. The effort was confessedly vain; not for such talk had she invited him; and her impatient reminder was of their having done for it all the needful on his coming to her after Sarah's flight. What she hadn't asked him then was to state to her where and how he stood for her; she had been resting on Chad's report of their midnight hour together in the Boulevard Malesherbes. The thing therefore she at present desired was ushered in by this recall of the two occasions on which, disinterested and merciful, she hadn't worried him. To-night truly she WOULD worry him, and this was her appeal to him to let her risk it. He wasn't to mind if she bored him a little: she had behaved, after all—hadn't she?—so awfully, awfully well.

II

"Oh, you're all right, you're all right," he almost impatiently declared; his impatience being moreover not for her pressure, but for her scruple. More and more distinct to him was the tune to which she would have had the matter out with Chad: more and more vivid for him the idea that she had been nervous as to what he might be able to "stand." Yes, it had been a question if he had "stood" what the scene on the river had given him, and, though the young man had doubtless opined in favour of his recuperation, her own last word must have been that she should feel easier in seeing for herself. That was it, unmistakeably; she WAS seeing for herself. What he could stand was thus, in these moments, in the balance for Strether, who reflected, as he became fully aware of it, that he must properly brace himself. He wanted fully to appear to stand all he might; and there was a certain command of the situation for him in this very wish not to look too much at sea. She was ready with everything, but so, sufficiently, was he; that is he was at one point the more prepared of the two, inasmuch as, for all her cleverness, she couldn't produce on the spot—and it was surprising—an account of the motive of her note. He had the advantage that his pronouncing her "all right" gave him for an enquiry. "May I ask, delighted as I've been to come, if you've wished to say something special?" He spoke as if she might have seen he had been waiting for it—not indeed with discomfort, but with natural interest. Then he saw that she was a little taken aback, was even surprised herself at the detail she had neglected—the only one ever yet; having somehow assumed he would know, would recognise, would leave some things not to be said. She looked at him, however, an instant as if to convey that if he wanted them ALL—!

"Selfish and vulgar—that's what I must seem to you. You've done everything for me, and here I am as if I were asking for more. But it isn't," she went on, "because I'm afraid—though I AM of course afraid, as a woman in my position always is. I mean it isn't because one lives in terror—it isn't because of that one is selfish, for I'm ready to give you my word to-night that I don't care; don't care what still may happen and what I may lose. I don't ask you to raise your little finger for me again, nor do I wish so much as to mention to you what we've talked of before, either my danger or my safety, or his mother, or his sister, or the girl he may marry, or the fortune he may make or miss, or the right or the wrong, of any kind, he may do. If after the help one has had from you one can't either take care of one's self or simply hold one's tongue, one must renounce all claim to be an object of interest. It's in the name of what I DO care about that I've tried still to keep hold of you. How can I be indifferent," she asked, "to how I appear to you?" And as he found himself unable to say immediately to say: "Why, if you're going, NEED you, after all? Is it impossible you should stay on—so that one mayn't lose you?"

"Impossible I should live with you here instead of going home?"

"Not 'with' us, if you object to that, but near enough to us, somewhere, for us to see you—well," she beautifully brought out, "when we feel we MUST. How shall we not sometimes feel it? I've wanted to see you often when I couldn't," she pursued, "all these last weeks. How shan't I then miss you now, with the sense of your being gone forever?" Then as if the straightness of this appeal, taking him unprepared, had visibly left him wondering: "Where IS your 'home' moreover now—what has become of it? I've made a change in your life, I know I have; I've upset everything in your mind as well; in your sense of—what shall I call it?—all the decencies and possibilities. It gives me a kind of detestation—" She pulled up short.

Oh but he wanted to hear. "Detestation of what?"

"Of everything—of life."

"Ah that's too much," he laughed—"or too little!"

"Too little, precisely"—she was eager. "What I hate is myself—when I think that one has to take so much, to be happy, out of the lives of others, and that one isn't happy even then. One does it to cheat one's self and to stop one's mouth—but that's only at the best for a little. The wretched self is always there, always making one somehow a fresh anxiety. What it comes to is that it's not, that it's never, a happiness, any happiness at all, to TAKE. The only safe thing is to give. It's what plays you least false." Interesting, touching, strikingly sincere as she let these things come from her, she yet puzzled and troubled him—so fine was the quaver of her quietness. He felt what he had felt before with her, that there was always more behind what she showed, and more and more again behind that. "You know so, at least," she added, "where you are!"

"YOU ought to know it indeed then; for isn't what you've been giving exactly what has brought us together this way? You've been making, as I've so fully let you know I've felt," Strether said, "the most precious present I've ever seen made, and if you can't sit down peacefully on that performance you ARE, no doubt, born to torment yourself. But you ought," he wound up, "to be easy."

"And not trouble you any more, no doubt—not thrust on you even the wonder and the beauty of what I've done; only let you regard our business as over, and well over, and see you depart in a peace that matches my own? No doubt, no doubt, no doubt," she nervously repeated—"all the more that I don't really pretend I believe you couldn't, for yourself, NOT have done what you have. I don't pretend you feel yourself victimised, for this evidently is the way you live, and it's what—we're agreed—is the best way. Yes, as you say," she continued after a moment, "I ought to be easy and rest on my work. Well then here am I doing so. I AM easy. You'll have it for your last impression. When is it you say you go?" she asked with a quick change.

He took some time to reply—his last impression was more and more so mixed a one. It produced in him a vague disappointment, a drop that was deeper even than the fall of his elation the previous night. The good of what he had done, if he had done so much, wasn't there to enliven him quite to the point that would have been ideal for a grand gay finale. Women were thus endlessly absorbent, and to deal with them was to walk on water. What was at bottom the matter with her, embroider as she might and disclaim as she might—what was at bottom the matter with her was simply Chad himself. It was of Chad she was after all renewedly afraid; the strange strength of her passion was the very strength of her fear; she clung to HIM, Lambert Strether, as to a source of safety she had tested, and, generous graceful truthful as she might try to be, exquisite as she was, she dreaded the term of his being within reach. With this sharpest perception yet, it was like a chill in the air to him, it was almost appalling, that a creature so fine could be, by mysterious forces, a creature so exploited. For at the end of all things they WERE mysterious: she had but made Chad what he was—so why could she think she had made him infinite? She had made him better, she had made him best, she had made him anything one would; but it came to our friend with supreme queerness that he was none the less only Chad. Strether had the sense that HE, a little, had made him too; his high appreciation had as it were, consecrated her work. The work, however admirable, was nevertheless of the strict human order, and in short it was marvellous that the companion of mere earthly joys, of comforts, aberrations (however one classed them) within the common experience should be so transcendently prized. It might have made Strether hot or shy, as such secrets of others brought home sometimes do make us; but he was held there by something so hard that it was fairly grim. This was not the discomposure of last night; that had quite passed—such discomposures were a detail; the real coercion was to see a man ineffably adored. There it was again—it took women, it took women; if to deal with them was to walk on water what wonder that the water rose? And it had never surely risen higher than round this woman. He presently found himself taking a long look from her, and the next thing he knew he had uttered all his thought. "You're afraid for your life!"

It drew out her long look, and he soon enough saw why. A spasm came into her face, the tears she had already been unable to hide overflowed at first in silence, and then, as the sound suddenly comes from a child, quickened to gasps, to sobs. She sat and covered her face with her hands, giving up all attempt at a manner. "It's how you see me, it's how you see me"—she caught her breath with it—"and it's as I AM, and as I must take myself, and of course it's no matter." Her emotion was at first so incoherent that he could only stand there at a loss, stand with his sense of having upset her, though of having done it by the truth. He had to listen to her in a silence that he made no immediate effort to attenuate, feeling her doubly woeful amid all her dim diffused elegance; consenting to it as he had consented to the rest, and even conscious of some vague inward irony in the presence of such a fine free range of bliss and bale. He couldn't say it was NOT no matter; for he was serving her to the end, he now knew, anyway—quite as if what he thought of her had nothing to do with it. It was actually moreover as if he didn't think of her at all, as if he could think of nothing but the passion, mature, abysmal, pitiful, she represented, and the possibilities she betrayed. She was older for him to-night, visibly less exempt from the touch of time; but she was as much as ever the finest and subtlest creature, the happiest apparition, it had been given him, in all his years, to meet; and yet he could see her there as vulgarly troubled, in very truth, as a maidservant crying for her young man. The only thing was that she judged herself as the maidservant wouldn't; the weakness of which wisdom too, the dishonour of which judgement, seemed but to sink her lower. Her collapse, however, no doubt, was briefer and she had in a manner recovered herself before he intervened. "Of course I'm afraid for my life. But that's nothing. It isn't that."

He was silent a little longer, as if thinking what it might be. "There's something I have in mind that I can still do."

But she threw off at last, with a sharp sad headshake, drying her eyes, what he could still do. "I don't care for that. Of course, as I've said, you're acting, in your wonderful way, for yourself; and what's for yourself is no more my business—though I may reach out unholy hands so clumsily to touch it—than if it were something in Timbuctoo. It's only that you don't snub me, as you've had fifty chances to do—it's only your beautiful patience that makes one forget one's manners. In spite of your patience, all the same," she went on, "you'd do anything rather than be with us here, even if that were possible. You'd do everything for us but be mixed up with us—which is a statement you can easily answer to the advantage of your own manners. You can say 'What's the use of talking of things that at the best are impossible?' What IS of course the use? It's only my little madness. You'd talk if you were tormented. And I don't mean now about HIM. Oh for him—!" Positively, strangely, bitterly, as it seemed to Strether, she gave "him," for the moment, away. "You don't care what I think of you; but I happen to care what you think of me. And what you MIGHT," she added. "What you perhaps even did."

He gained time. "What I did—?"

"Did think before. Before this. DIDn't you think—?"

But he had already stopped her. "I didn't think anything. I never think a step further than I'm obliged to."

"That's perfectly false, I believe," she returned—"except that you may, no doubt, often pull up when things become TOO ugly; or even, I'll say, to save you a protest, too beautiful. At any rate, even so far as it's true, we've thrust on you appearances that you've had to take in and that have therefore made your obligation. Ugly or beautiful—it doesn't matter what we call them—you were getting on without them, and that's where we're detestable. We bore you—that's where we are. And we may well—for what we've cost you. All you can do NOW is not to think at all. And I who should have liked to seem to you—well, sublime!"

He could only after a moment re-echo Miss Barrace. "You're wonderful!"

"I'm old and abject and hideous"—she went on as without hearing him. "Abject above all. Or old above all. It's when one's old that it's worst. I don't care what becomes of it—let what WILL; there it is. It's a doom—I know it; you can't see it more than I do myself. Things have to happen as they will." With which she came back again to what, face to face with him, had so quite broken down. "Of course you wouldn't, even if possible, and no matter what may happen to you, be near us. But think of me, think of me—!" She exhaled it into air.

He took refuge in repeating something he had already said and that she had made nothing of. "There's something I believe I can still do." And he put his hand out for good-bye.

She again made nothing of it; she went on with her insistence. "That won't help you. There's nothing to help you."

"Well, it may help YOU," he said.

She shook her head. "There's not a grain of certainty in my future—for the only certainty is that I shall be the loser in the end."

She hadn't taken his hand, but she moved with him to the door. "That's cheerful," he laughed, "for your benefactor!"

"What's cheerful for ME," she replied, "is that we might, you and I, have been friends. That's it—that's it. You see how, as I say, I want everything. I've wanted you too."

"Ah but you've HAD me!" he declared, at the door, with an emphasis that made an end.

III

His purpose had been to see Chad the next day, and he had prefigured seeing him by an early call; having in general never stood on ceremony in respect to visits at the Boulevard Malesherbes. It had been more often natural for him to go there than for Chad to come to the small hotel, the attractions of which were scant; yet it nevertheless, just now, at the eleventh hour, did suggest itself to Strether to begin by giving the young man a chance. It struck him that, in the inevitable course, Chad would be "round," as Waymarsh used to say—Waymarsh who already, somehow, seemed long ago. He hadn't come the day before, because it had been arranged between them that Madame de Vionnet should see their friend first; but now that this passage had taken place he would present himself, and their friend wouldn't have long to wait. Strether assumed, he became aware, on this reasoning, that the interesting parties to the arrangement would have met betimes, and that the more interesting of the two—as she was after all—would have communicated to the other the issue of her appeal. Chad would know without delay that his mother's messenger had been with her, and, though it was perhaps not quite easy to see how she could qualify what had occurred, he would at least have been sufficiently advised to feel he could go on. The day, however, brought, early or late, no word from him, and Strether felt, as a result of this, that a change had practically come over their intercourse. It was perhaps a premature judgement; or it only meant perhaps—how could he tell?—that the wonderful pair he protected had taken up again together the excursion he had accidentally checked. They might have gone back to the country, and gone back but with a long breath drawn; that indeed would best mark Chad's sense that reprobation hadn't rewarded Madame de Vionnet's request for an interview. At the end of the twenty-four hours, at the end of the forty-eight, there was still no overture; so that Strether filled up the time, as he had so often filled it before, by going to see Miss Gostrey.

He proposed amusements to her; he felt expert now in proposing amusements; and he had thus, for several days, an odd sense of leading her about Paris, of driving her in the Bois, of showing her the penny steamboats—those from which the breeze of the Seine was to be best enjoyed—that might have belonged to a kindly uncle doing the honours of the capital to an Intelligent niece from the country. He found means even to take her to shops she didn't know, or that she pretended she didn't; while she, on her side, was, like the country maiden, all passive modest and grateful—going in fact so far as to emulate rusticity in occasional fatigues and bewilderments. Strether described these vague proceedings to himself, described them even to her, as a happy interlude; the sign of which was that the companions said for the time no further word about the matter they had talked of to satiety. He proclaimed satiety at the outset, and she quickly took the hint; as docile both in this and in everything else as the intelligent obedient niece. He told her as yet nothing of his late adventure—for as an adventure it now ranked with him; he pushed the whole business temporarily aside and found his interest in the fact of her beautiful assent. She left questions unasked—she who for so long had been all questions; she gave herself up to him with an understanding of which mere mute gentleness might have seemed the sufficient expression. She knew his sense of his situation had taken still another step—of that he was quite aware; but she conveyed that, whatever had thus happened for him, it was thrown into the shade by what was happening for herself. This—though it mightn't to a detached spirit have seemed much—was the major interest, and she met it with a new directness of response, measuring it from hour to hour with her grave hush of acceptance. Touched as he had so often been by her before, he was, for his part too, touched afresh; all the more that though he could be duly aware of the principle of his own mood he couldn't be equally so of the principle of hers. He knew, that is, in a manner—knew roughly and resignedly—what he himself was hatching; whereas he had to take the chance of what he called to himself Maria's calculations. It was all he needed that she liked him enough for what they were doing, and even should they do a good deal more would still like him enough for that; the essential freshness of a relation so simple was a cool bath to the soreness produced by other relations. These others appeared to him now horribly complex; they bristled with fine points, points all unimaginable beforehand, points that pricked and drew blood; a fact that gave to an hour with his present friend on a bateau-mouche, or in the afternoon shade of the Champs Elysees, something of the innocent pleasure of handling rounded ivory. His relation with Chad personally—from the moment he had got his point of view—had been of the simplest; yet this also struck him as bristling, after a third and a fourth blank day had passed. It was as if at last however his care for such indications had dropped; there came a fifth blank day and he ceased to enquire or to heed.

They now took on to his fancy, Miss Gostrey and he, the image of the Babes in the Wood; they could trust the merciful elements to let them continue at peace. He had been great already, as he knew, at postponements; but he had only to get afresh into the rhythm of one to feel its fine attraction. It amused him to say to himself that he might for all the world have been going to die—die resignedly; the scene was filled for him with so deep a death-bed hush, so melancholy a charm. That meant the postponement of everything else—which made so for the quiet lapse of life; and the postponement in especial of the reckoning to come—unless indeed the reckoning to come were to be one and the same thing with extinction. It faced him, the reckoning, over the shoulder of much interposing experience—which also faced him; and one would float to it doubtless duly through these caverns of Kubla Khan. It was really behind everything; it hadn't merged in what he had done; his final appreciation of what he had done—his appreciation on the spot—would provide it with its main sharpness. The spot so focussed was of course Woollett, and he was to see, at the best, what Woollett would be with everything there changed for him. Wouldn't THAT revelation practically amount to the wind-up of his career? Well, the summer's end would show; his suspense had meanwhile exactly the sweetness of vain delay; and he had with it, we should mention, other pastimes than Maria's company—plenty of separate musings in which his luxury failed him but at one point. He was well in port, the outer sea behind him, and it was only a matter of getting ashore. There was a question that came and went for him, however, as he rested against the side of his ship, and it was a little to get rid of the obsession that he prolonged his hours with Miss Gostrey. It was a question about himself, but it could only be settled by seeing Chad again; it was indeed his principal reason for wanting to see Chad. After that it wouldn't signify—it was a ghost that certain words would easily lay to rest. Only the young man must be there to take the words. Once they were taken he wouldn't have a question left; none, that is, in connexion with this particular affair. It wouldn't then matter even to himself that he might now have been guilty of speaking BECAUSE of what he had forfeited. That was the refinement of his supreme scruple—he wished so to leave what he had forfeited out of account. He wished not to do anything because he had missed something else, because he was sore or sorry or impoverished, because he was maltreated or desperate; he wished to do everything because he was lucid and quiet, just the same for himself on all essential points as he had ever been. Thus it was that while he virtually hung about for Chad he kept mutely putting it: "You've been chucked, old boy; but what has that to do with it?" It would have sickened him to feel vindictive.

These tints of feeling indeed were doubtless but the iridescence of his idleness, and they were presently lost in a new light from Maria. She had a fresh fact for him before the week was out, and she practically met him with it on his appearing one night. He hadn't on this day seen her, but had planned presenting himself in due course to ask her to dine with him somewhere out of doors, on one of the terraces, in one of the gardens, of which the Paris of summer was profuse. It had then come on to rain, so that, disconcerted, he changed his mind; dining alone at home, a little stuffily and stupidly, and waiting on her afterwards to make up his loss. He was sure within a minute that something had happened; it was so in the air of the rich little room that he had scarcely to name his thought. Softly lighted, the whole colour of the place, with its vague values, was in cool fusion—an effect that made the visitor stand for a little agaze. It was as if in doing so now he had felt a recent presence—his recognition of the passage of which his hostess in turn divined. She had scarcely to say it—"Yes, she has been here, and this time I received her." It wasn't till a minute later that she added: "There being, as I understand you, no reason NOW—!"

"None for your refusing?"

"No—if you've done what you've had to do."

"I've certainly so far done it," Strether said, "as that you needn't fear the effect, or the appearance of coming between us. There's nothing between us now but what we ourselves have put there, and not an inch of room for anything else whatever. Therefore you're only beautifully WITH us as always—though doubtless now, if she has talked to you, rather more with us than less. Of course if she came," he added, "it was to talk to you."

"It was to talk to me," Maria returned; on which he was further sure that she was practically in possession of what he himself hadn't yet told her. He was even sure she was in possession of things he himself couldn't have told; for the consciousness of them was now all in her face and accompanied there with a shade of sadness that marked in her the close of all uncertainties. It came out for him more than ever yet that she had had from the first a knowledge she believed him not to have had, a knowledge the sharp acquisition of which might be destined to make a difference for him. The difference for him might not inconceivably be an arrest of his independence and a change in his attitude—in other words a revulsion in favour of the principles of Woollett. She had really prefigured the possibility of a shock that would send him swinging back to Mrs. Newsome. He hadn't, it was true, week after week, shown signs of receiving it, but the possibility had been none the less in the air. What Maria accordingly had had now to take in was that the shock had descended and that he hadn't, all the same, swung back. He had grown clear, in a flash, on a point long since settled for herself; but no reapproximation to Mrs. Newsome had occurred in consequence. Madame de Vionnet had by her visit held up the torch to these truths, and what now lingered in poor Maria's face was the somewhat smoky light of the scene between them. If the light however wasn't, as we have hinted, the glow of joy, the reasons for this also were perhaps discernible to Strether even through the blur cast over them by his natural modesty. She had held herself for months with a firm hand; she hadn't interfered on any chance—and chances were specious enough—that she might interfere to her profit. She had turned her back on the dream that Mrs. Newsome's rupture, their friend's forfeiture—the engagement the relation itself, broken beyond all mending—might furnish forth her advantage; and, to stay her hand from promoting these things, she had on private, difficult, but rigid, lines, played strictly fair. She couldn't therefore but feel that, though, as the end of all, the facts in question had been stoutly confirmed, her ground for personal, for what might have been called interested, elation remained rather vague. Strether might easily have made out that she had been asking herself, in the hours she had just sat through, if there were still for her, or were only not, a fair shade of uncertainty. Let us hasten to add, however, that what he at first made out on this occasion he also at first kept to himself. He only asked what in particular Madame de Vionnet had come for, and as to this his companion was ready.

"She wants tidings of Mr. Newsome, whom she appears not to have seen for some days."

"Then she hasn't been away with him again?"

"She seemed to think," Maria answered, "that he might have gone away with YOU."

"And did you tell her I know nothing of him?"

She had her indulgent headshake. "I've known nothing of what you know. I could only tell her I'd ask you."

"Then I've not seen him for a week—and of course I've wondered." His wonderment showed at this moment as sharper, but he presently went on. "Still, I dare say I can put my hand on him. Did she strike you," he asked, "as anxious?"

"She's always anxious."

"After all I've done for her?" And he had one of the last flickers of his occasional mild mirth. "To think that was just what I came out to prevent!"

She took it up but to reply. "You don't regard him then as safe?"

"I was just going to ask you how in that respect you regard Madame de Vionnet."

She looked at him a little. "What woman was EVER safe? She told me," she added—and it was as if at the touch of the connexion—"of your extraordinary meeting in the country. After that a quoi se fier?"

"It was, as an accident, in all the possible or impossible chapter," Strether conceded, "amazing enough. But still, but still—!"

"But still she didn't mind?"

"She doesn't mind anything."

"Well, then, as you don't either, we may all sink to rest!"

He appeared to agree with her, but he had his reservation. "I do mind Chad's disappearance."

"Oh you'll get him back. But now you know," she said, "why I went to Mentone." He had sufficiently let her see that he had by this time gathered things together, but there was nature in her wish to make them clearer still. "I didn't want you to put it to me."

"To put it to you—?"

"The question of what you were at last—a week ago—to see for yourself. I didn't want to have to lie for her. I felt that to be too much for me. A man of course is always expected to do it—to do it, I mean, for a woman; but not a woman for another woman; unless perhaps on the tit-for-tat principle, as an indirect way of protecting herself. I don't need protection, so that I was free to 'funk' you—simply to dodge your test. The responsibility was too much for me. I gained time, and when I came back the need of a test had blown over."

Strether thought of it serenely. "Yes; when you came back little Bilham had shown me what's expected of a gentleman. Little Bilham had lied like one."

"And like what you believed him?"

"Well," said Strether, "it was but a technical lie—he classed the attachment as virtuous. That was a view for which there was much to be said—and the virtue came out for me hugely There was of course a great deal of it. I got it full in the face, and I haven't, you see, done with it yet."

"What I see, what I saw," Maria returned, "is that you dressed up even the virtue. You were wonderful—you were beautiful, as I've had the honour of telling you before; but, if you wish really to know," she sadly confessed, "I never quite knew WHERE you were. There were moments," she explained, "when you struck me as grandly cynical; there were others when you struck me as grandly vague."

Her friend considered. "I had phases. I had flights."

"Yes, but things must have a basis."

"A basis seemed to me just what her beauty supplied."

"Her beauty of person?"

"Well, her beauty of everything. The impression she makes. She has such variety and yet such harmony."

She considered him with one of her deep returns of indulgence—returns out of all proportion to the irritations they flooded over. "You're complete."

"You're always too personal," he good-humouredly said; "but that's precisely how I wondered and wandered."

"If you mean," she went on, "that she was from the first for you the most charming woman in the world, nothing's more simple. Only that was an odd foundation."

"For what I reared on it?"

"For what you didn't!"

"Well, it was all not a fixed quantity. And it had for me—it has still—such elements of strangeness. Her greater age than his, her different world, traditions, association; her other opportunities, liabilities, standards."

His friend listened with respect to his enumeration of these disparities; then she disposed of them at a stroke. "Those things are nothing when a woman's hit. It's very awful. She was hit."

Strether, on his side, did justice to that plea. "Oh of course I saw she was hit. That she was hit was what we were busy with; that she was hit was our great affair. But somehow I couldn't think of her as down in the dust. And as put there by OUR little Chad!"

"Yet wasn't 'your' little Chad just your miracle?"

Strether admitted it. "Of course I moved among miracles. It was all phantasmagoric. But the great fact was that so much of it was none of my business—as I saw my business. It isn't even now."

His companion turned away on this, and it might well have been yet again with the sharpness of a fear of how little his philosophy could bring her personally. "I wish SHE could hear you!"

"Mrs. Newsome?"

"No—not Mrs. Newsome; since I understand you that it doesn't matter now what Mrs. Newsome hears. Hasn't she heard everything?"

"Practically—yes." He had thought a moment, but he went on. "You wish Madame de Vionnet could hear me?"

"Madame de Vionnet." She had come back to him. "She thinks just the contrary of what you say. That you distinctly judge her."

He turned over the scene as the two women thus placed together for him seemed to give it. "She might have known—!"

"Might have known you don't?" Miss Gostrey asked as he let it drop. "She was sure of it at first," she pursued as he said nothing; "she took it for granted, at least, as any woman in her position would. But after that she changed her mind; she believed you believed—"

"Well?"—he was curious.

"Why in her sublimity. And that belief had remained with her, I make out, till the accident of the other day opened your eyes. For that it did," said Maria, "open them—"

"She can't help"—he had taken it up—"being aware? No," he mused; "I suppose she thinks of that even yet."

"Then they WERE closed? There you are! However, if you see her as the most charming woman in the world it comes to the same thing. And if you'd like me to tell her that you do still so see her—!" Miss Gostrey, in short, offered herself for service to the end.

It was an offer he could temporarily entertain; but he decided. "She knows perfectly how I see her."

"Not favourably enough, she mentioned to me, to wish ever to see her again. She told me you had taken a final leave of her. She says you've done with her."

"So I have."

Maria had a pause; then she spoke as if for conscience. "She wouldn't have done with YOU. She feels she has lost you—yet that she might have been better for you."

"Oh she has been quite good enough!" Strether laughed.

"She thinks you and she might at any rate have been friends."

"We might certainly. That's just"—he continued to laugh—"why I'm going."

It was as if Maria could feel with this then at last that she had done her best for each. But she had still an idea. "Shall I tell her that?"

"No. Tell her nothing."

"Very well then." To which in the next breath Miss Gostrey added: "Poor dear thing!"

Her friend wondered; then with raised eyebrows: "Me?"

"Oh no. Marie de Vionnet."

He accepted the correction, but he wondered still. "Are you so sorry for her as that?"

It made her think a moment—made her even speak with a smile. But she didn't really retract. "I'm sorry for us all!"

IV

He was to delay no longer to re-establish communication with Chad, and we have just seen that he had spoken to Miss Gostrey of this intention on hearing from her of the young man's absence. It was not moreover only the assurance so given that prompted him; it was the need of causing his conduct to square with another profession still—the motive he had described to her as his sharpest for now getting away. If he was to get away because of some of the relations involved in staying, the cold attitude toward them might look pedantic in the light of lingering on. He must do both things; he must see Chad, but he must go. The more he thought of the former of these duties the more he felt himself make a subject of insistence of the latter. They were alike intensely present to him as he sat in front of a quiet little cafe into which he had dropped on quitting Maria's entresol. The rain that had spoiled his evening with her was over; for it was still to him as if his evening HAD been spoiled—though it mightn't have been wholly the rain. It was late when he left the cafe, yet not too late; he couldn't in any case go straight to bed, and he would walk round by the Boulevard Malesherbes—rather far round—on his way home. Present enough always was the small circumstance that had originally pressed for him the spring of so big a difference—the accident of little Bilham's appearance on the balcony of the mystic troisieme at the moment of his first visit, and the effect of it on his sense of what was then before him. He recalled his watch, his wait, and the recognition that had proceeded from the young stranger, that had played frankly into the air and had presently brought him up—things smoothing the way for his first straight step. He had since had occasion, a few times, to pass the house without going in; but he had never passed it without again feeling how it had then spoken to him. He stopped short to-night on coming to sight of it: it was as if his last day were oddly copying his first. The windows of Chad's apartment were open to the balcony—a pair of them lighted; and a figure that had come out and taken up little Bilham's attitude, a figure whose cigarette-spark he could see leaned on the rail and looked down at him. It denoted however no reappearance of his younger friend; it quickly defined itself in the tempered darkness as Chad's more solid shape; so that Chad's was the attention that after he had stepped forward into the street and signalled, he easily engaged; Chad's was the voice that, sounding into the night with promptness and seemingly with joy, greeted him and called him up.

That the young man had been visible there just in this position expressed somehow for Strether that, as Maria Gostrey had reported, he had been absent and silent; and our friend drew breath on each landing—the lift, at that hour, having ceased to work—before the implications of the fact. He had been for a week intensely away, away to a distance and alone; but he was more back than ever, and the attitude in which Strether had surprised him was something more than a return—it was clearly a conscious surrender. He had arrived but an hour before, from London, from Lucerne, from Homburg, from no matter where—though the visitor's fancy, on the staircase, liked to fill it out; and after a bath, a talk with Baptiste and a supper of light cold clever French things, which one could see the remains of there in the circle of the lamp, pretty and ultra-Parisian, he had come into the air again for a smoke, was occupied at the moment of Strether's approach in what might have been called taking up his life afresh. His life, his life!—Strether paused anew, on the last flight, at this final rather breathless sense of what Chad's life was doing with Chad's mother's emissary. It was dragging him, at strange hours, up the staircases of the rich; it was keeping him out of bed at the end of long hot days; it was transforming beyond recognition the simple, subtle, conveniently uniform thing that had anciently passed with him for a life of his own. Why should it concern him that Chad was to be fortified in the pleasant practice of smoking on balconies, of supping on salads, of feeling his special conditions agreeably reaffirm themselves, of finding reassurance in comparisons and contrasts? There was no answer to such a question but that he was still practically committed—he had perhaps never yet so much known it. It made him feel old, and he could buy his railway-ticket—feeling, no doubt, older—the next day; but he had meanwhile come up four flights, counting the entresol, at midnight and without a lift, for Chad's life. The young man, hearing him by this time, and with Baptiste sent to rest, was already at the door; so that Strether had before him in full visibility the cause in which he was labouring and even, with the troisieme fairly gained, panting a little.

Chad offered him, as always, a welcome in which the cordial and the formal—so far as the formal was the respectful—handsomely met; and after he had expressed a hope that he would let him put him up for the night Strether was in full possession of the key, as it might have been called, to what had lately happened. If he had just thought of himself as old Chad at sight of him thinking of him as older: he wanted to put him up for the night just because he was ancient and weary. It could never be said the tenant of these quarters wasn't nice to him; a tenant who, if he might indeed now keep him, was probably prepared to work it all still more thoroughly. Our friend had in fact the impression that with the minimum of encouragement Chad would propose to keep him indefinitely; an impression in the lap of which one of his own possibilities seemed to sit. Madame de Vionnet had wished him to stay—so why didn't that happily fit? He could enshrine himself for the rest of his days in his young host's chambre d'ami and draw out these days at his young host's expense: there could scarce be greater logical expression of the countenance he had been moved to give. There was literally a minute—it was strange enough—during which he grasped the idea that as he WAS acting, as he could only act, he was inconsistent. The sign that the inward forces he had obeyed really hung together would be that—in default always of another career—he should promote the good cause by mounting guard on it. These things, during his first minutes, came and went; but they were after all practically disposed of as soon as he had mentioned his errand. He had come to say good-bye—yet that was only a part; so that from the moment Chad accepted his farewell the question of a more ideal affirmation gave way to something else. He proceeded with the rest of his business. "You'll be a brute, you know—you'll be guilty of the last infamy—if you ever forsake her."

That, uttered there at the solemn hour, uttered in the place that was full of her influence, was the rest of his business; and when once he had heard himself say it he felt that his message had never before been spoken. It placed his present call immediately on solid ground, and the effect of it was to enable him quite to play with what we have called the key. Chad showed no shade of embarrassment, but had none the less been troubled for him after their meeting in the country; had had fears and doubts on the subject of his comfort. He was disturbed, as it were, only FOR him, and had positively gone away to ease him off, to let him down—if it wasn't indeed rather to screw him up—the more gently. Seeing him now fairly jaded he had come, with characteristic good humour, all the way to meet him, and what Strether thereupon supremely made out was that he would abound for him to the end in conscientious assurances. This was what was between them while the visitor remained; so far from having to go over old ground he found his entertainer keen to agree to everything. It couldn't be put too strongly for him that he'd be a brute. "Oh rather!—if I should do anything of THAT sort. I hope you believe I really feel it."

"I want it," said Strether, "to be my last word of all to you. I can't say more, you know; and I don't see how I can do more, in every way, than I've done."

Chad took this, almost artlessly, as a direct allusion. "You've seen her?"

"Oh yes—to say good-bye. And if I had doubted the truth of what I tell you—"

"She'd have cleared up your doubt?" Chad understood—"rather"—again! It even kept him briefly silent. But he made that up. "She must have been wonderful."

"She WAS," Strether candidly admitted—all of which practically told as a reference to the conditions created by the accident of the previous week.

They appeared for a little to be looking back at it; and that came out still more in what Chad next said. "I don't know what you've really thought, all along; I never did know—for anything, with you, seemed to be possible. But of course—of course—" Without confusion, quite with nothing but indulgence, he broke down, he pulled up. "After all, you understand. I spoke to you originally only as I HAD to speak. There's only one way—isn't there?—about such things. However," he smiled with a final philosophy, "I see it's all right."

Strether met his eyes with a sense of multiplying thoughts. What was it that made him at present, late at night and after journeys, so renewedly, so substantially young? Strether saw in a moment what it was—it was that he was younger again than Madame de Vionnet. He himself said immediately none of the things that he was thinking; he said something quite different. "You HAVE really been to a distance?"

"I've been to England." Chad spoke cheerfully and promptly, but gave no further account of it than to say: "One must sometimes get off."

Strether wanted no more facts—he only wanted to justify, as it were, his question. "Of course you do as you're free to do. But I hope, this time, that you didn't go for ME."

"For very shame at bothering you really too much? My dear man," Chad laughed, "what WOULDn't I do for you?"

Strether's easy answer for this was that it was a disposition he had exactly come to profit by. "Even at the risk of being in your way I've waited on, you know, for a definite reason."

Chad took it in. "Oh yes—for us to make if possible a still better impression." And he stood there happily exhaling his full general consciousness. "I'm delighted to gather that you feel we've made it."

There was a pleasant irony in the words, which his guest, preoccupied and keeping to the point, didn't take up. "If I had my sense of wanting the rest of the time—the time of their being still on this side," he continued to explain—"I know now why I wanted it."

He was as grave, as distinct, as a demonstrator before a blackboard, and Chad continued to face him like an intelligent pupil. "You wanted to have been put through the whole thing."

Strether again, for a moment, said nothing; he turned his eyes away, and they lost themselves, through the open window, in the dusky outer air. "I shall learn from the Bank here where they're now having their letters, and my last word, which I shall write in the morning and which they're expecting as my ultimatum, will so immediately reach them." The light of his plural pronoun was sufficiently reflected in his companion's face as he again met it; and he completed his demonstration. He pursued indeed as if for himself. "Of course I've first to justify what I shall do."

"You're justifying it beautifully!" Chad declared.

"It's not a question of advising you not to go," Strether said, "but of absolutely preventing you, if possible, from so much as thinking of it. Let me accordingly appeal to you by all you hold sacred."

Chad showed a surprise. "What makes you think me capable—?"

"You'd not only be, as I say, a brute; you'd be," his companion went on in the same way, "a criminal of the deepest dye."

Chad gave a sharper look, as if to gauge a possible suspicion. "I don't know what should make you think I'm tired of her."

Strether didn't quite know either, and such impressions, for the imaginative mind, were always too fine, too floating, to produce on the spot their warrant. There was none the less for him, in the very manner of his host's allusion to satiety as a thinkable motive, a slight breath of the ominous. "I feel how much more she can do for you. She hasn't done it all yet. Stay with her at least till she has."

"And leave her THEN?"

Chad had kept smiling, but its effect in Strether was a shade of dryness. "Don't leave her BEFORE. When you've got all that can be got—I don't say," he added a trifle grimly. "That will be the proper time. But as, for you, from such a woman, there will always be something to be got, my remark's not a wrong to her." Chad let him go on, showing every decent deference, showing perhaps also a candid curiosity for this sharper accent. "I remember you, you know, as you were."

"An awful ass, wasn't I?"

The response was as prompt as if he had pressed a spring; it had a ready abundance at which he even winced; so that he took a moment to meet it. "You certainly then wouldn't have seemed worth all you've let me in for. You've defined yourself better. Your value has quintupled."

"Well then, wouldn't that be enough—?"

Chad had risked it jocosely, but Strether remained blank. "Enough?"

"If one SHOULD wish to live on one's accumulations?" After which, however, as his friend appeared cold to the joke, the young man as easily dropped it. "Of course I really never forget, night or day, what I owe her. I owe her everything. I give you my word of honour," he frankly rang out, "that I'm not a bit tired of her." Strether at this only gave him a stare: the way youth could express itself was again and again a wonder. He meant no harm, though he might after all be capable of much; yet he spoke of being "tired" of her almost as he might have spoken of being tired of roast mutton for dinner. "She has never for a moment yet bored me—never been wanting, as the cleverest women sometimes are, in tact. She has never talked about her tact—as even they too sometimes talk; but she has always had it. She has never had it more"—he handsomely made the point—"than just lately." And he scrupulously went further. "She has never been anything I could call a burden."

Strether for a moment said nothing; then he spoke gravely, with his shade of dryness deepened. "Oh if you didn't do her justice—!"

"I SHOULD be a beast, eh?"

Strether devoted no time to saying what he would be; THAT, visibly, would take them far. If there was nothing for it but to repeat, however, repetition was no mistake. "You owe her everything—very much more than she can ever owe you. You've in other words duties to her, of the most positive sort; and I don't see what other duties—as the others are presented to you—can be held to go before them."

Chad looked at him with a smile. "And you know of course about the others, eh?—since it's you yourself who have done the presenting."

"Much of it—yes—and to the best of my ability. But not all—from the moment your sister took my place."

"She didn't," Chad returned. "Sally took a place, certainly; but it was never, I saw from the first moment, to be yours. No one—with us—will ever take yours. It wouldn't be possible."

"Ah of course," sighed Strether, "I knew it. I believe you're right. No one in the world, I imagine, was ever so portentously solemn. There I am," he added with another sigh, as if weary enough, on occasion, of this truth. "I was made so."

Chad appeared for a little to consider the way he was made; he might for this purpose have measured him up and down. His conclusion favoured the fact. "YOU have never needed any one to make you better. There has never been any one good enough. They couldn't," the young man declared.

His friend hesitated. "I beg your pardon. They HAVE."

Chad showed, not without amusement, his doubt. "Who then?"

Strether—though a little dimly—smiled at him. "Women—too."

"'Two'?"—Chad stared and laughed. "Oh I don't believe, for such work, in any more than one! So you're proving too much. And what IS beastly, at all events," he added, "is losing you."

Strether had set himself in motion for departure, but at this he paused. "Are you afraid?"

"Afraid—?"

"Of doing wrong. I mean away from my eye." Before Chad could speak, however, he had taken himself up. "I AM, certainly," he laughed, "prodigious."

"Yes, you spoil us for all the stupid—!" This might have been, on Chad's part, in its extreme emphasis, almost too freely extravagant; but it was full, plainly enough, of the intention of comfort, it carried with it a protest against doubt and a promise, positively, of performance. Picking up a hat in the vestibule he came out with his friend, came downstairs, took his arm, affectionately, as to help and guide him, treating him if not exactly as aged and infirm, yet as a noble eccentric who appealed to tenderness, and keeping on with him, while they walked, to the next corner and the next. "You needn't tell me, you needn't tell me!"—this again as they proceeded, he wished to make Strether feel. What he needn't tell him was now at last, in the geniality of separation, anything at all concerned him to know. He knew, up to the hilt—that really came over Chad; he understood, felt, recorded his vow; and they lingered on it as they had lingered in their walk to Strether's hotel the night of their first meeting. The latter took, at this hour, all he could get; he had given all he had had to give; he was as depleted as if he had spent his last sou. But there was just one thing for which, before they broke off, Chad seemed disposed slightly to bargain. His companion needn't, as he said, tell him, but he might himself mention that he had been getting some news of the art of advertisement. He came out quite suddenly with this announcement while Strether wondered if his revived interest were what had taken him, with strange inconsequence, over to London. He appeared at all events to have been looking into the question and had encountered a revelation. Advertising scientifically worked presented itself thus as the great new force. "It really does the thing, you know."

They were face to face under the street-lamp as they had been the first night, and Strether, no doubt, looked blank. "Affects, you mean, the sale of the object advertised?"

"Yes—but affects it extraordinarily; really beyond what one had supposed. I mean of course when it's done as one makes out that in our roaring age, it CAN be done. I've been finding out a little, though it doubtless doesn't amount to much more than what you originally, so awfully vividly—and all, very nearly, that first night—put before me. It's an art like another, and infinite like all the arts." He went on as if for the joke of it—almost as if his friend's face amused him. "In the hands, naturally, of a master. The right man must take hold. With the right man to work it c'est un monde."

Strether had watched him quite as if, there on the pavement without a pretext, he had begun to dance a fancy step. "Is what you're thinking of that you yourself, in the case you have in mind, would be the right man?"

Chad had thrown back his light coat and thrust each of his thumbs into an armhole of his waistcoat; in which position his fingers played up and down. "Why, what is but what you yourself, as I say, took me for when you first came out?"

Strether felt a little faint, but he coerced his attention. "Oh yes, and there's no doubt that, with your natural parts, you'd have much in common with him. Advertising is clearly at this time of day the secret of trade. It's quite possible it will be open to you—giving the whole of your mind to it—to make the whole place hum with you. Your mother's appeal is to the whole of your mind, and that's exactly the strength of her case."

Chad's fingers continued to twiddle, but he had something of a drop. "Ah we've been through my mother's case!"

"So I thought. Why then do you speak of the matter?"

"Only because it was part of our original discussion. To wind up where we began, my interest's purely platonic. There at any rate the fact is—the fact of the possible. I mean the money in it."

"Oh damn the money in it!" said Strether. And then as the young man's fixed smile seemed to shine out more strange: "Shall you give your friend up for the money in it?"

Chad preserved his handsome grimace as well as the rest of his attitude. "You're not altogether—in your so great 'solemnity'—kind. Haven't I been drinking you in—showing you all I feel you're worth to me? What have I done, what am I doing, but cleave to her to the death? The only thing is," he good-humouredly explained, "that one can't but have it before one, in the cleaving—the point where the death comes in. Don't be afraid for THAT. It's pleasant to a fellow's feelings," he developed, "to 'size-up' the bribe he applies his foot to."

"Oh then if all you want's a kickable surface the bribe's enormous."

"Good. Then there it goes!" Chad administered his kick with fantastic force and sent an imaginary object flying. It was accordingly as if they were once more rid of the question and could come back to what really concerned him. "Of course I shall see you tomorrow."

But Strether scarce heeded the plan proposed for this; he had still the impression—not the slighter for the simulated kick—of an irrelevant hornpipe or jig. "You're restless."

"Ah," returned Chad as they parted, "you're exciting."

V

He had, however, within two days, another separation to face. He had sent Maria Gostrey a word early, by hand, to ask if he might come to breakfast; in consequence of which, at noon, she awaited him in the cool shade of her little Dutch-looking dining-room. This retreat was at the back of the house, with a view of a scrap of old garden that had been saved from modern ravage; and though he had on more than one other occasion had his legs under its small and peculiarly polished table of hospitality, the place had never before struck him as so sacred to pleasant knowledge, to intimate charm, to antique order, to a neatness that was almost august. To sit there was, as he had told his hostess before, to see life reflected for the time in ideally kept pewter; which was somehow becoming, improving to life, so that one's eyes were held and comforted. Strether's were comforted at all events now—and the more that it was the last time—with the charming effect, on the board bare of a cloth and proud of its perfect surface, of the small old crockery and old silver, matched by the more substantial pieces happily disposed about the room. The specimens of vivid Delf, in particular had the dignity of family portraits; and it was in the midst of them that our friend resignedly expressed himself. He spoke even with a certain philosophic humour. "There's nothing more to wait for; I seem to have done a good day's work. I've let them have it all round. I've seen Chad, who has been to London and come back. He tells me I'm 'exciting,' and I seem indeed pretty well to have upset every one. I've at any rate excited HIM. He's distinctly restless."

"You've excited ME," Miss Gostrey smiled. "I'M distinctly restless."

"Oh you were that when I found you. It seems to me I've rather got you out of it. What's this," he asked as he looked about him, "but a haunt of ancient peace?"

"I wish with all my heart," she presently replied, "I could make you treat it as a haven of rest." On which they fronted each other, across the table, as if things unuttered were in the air.

Strether seemed, in his way, when he next spoke, to take some of them up. "It wouldn't give me—that would be the trouble—what it will, no doubt, still give you. I'm not," he explained, leaning back in his chair, but with his eyes on a small ripe round melon—"in real harmony with what surrounds me. You ARE. I take it too hard. You DON'T. It makes—that's what it comes to in the end—a fool of me." Then at a tangent, "What has he been doing in London?" he demanded.

"Ah one may go to London," Maria laughed. "You know I did."

Yes—he took the reminder. "And you brought ME back." He brooded there opposite to her, but without gloom. "Whom has Chad brought? He's full of ideas. And I wrote to Sarah," he added, "the first thing this morning. So I'm square. I'm ready for them."

She neglected certain parts of this speech in the interest of others. "Marie said to me the other day that she felt him to have the makings of an immense man of business."

"There it is. He's the son of his father!"

"But SUCH a father!"

"Ah just the right one from that point of view! But it isn't his father in him," Strether added, "that troubles me."

"What is it then?" He came back to his breakfast; he partook presently of the charming melon, which she liberally cut for him; and it was only after this that he met her question. Then moreover it was but to remark that he'd answer her presently. She waited, she watched, she served him and amused him, and it was perhaps with this last idea that she soon reminded him of his having never even yet named to her the article produced at Woollett. "Do you remember our talking of it in London—that night at the play?" Before he could say yes, however, she had put it to him for other matters. Did he remember, did he remember—this and that of their first days? He remembered everything, bringing up with humour even things of which she professed no recollection, things she vehemently denied; and falling back above all on the great interest of their early time, the curiosity felt by both of them as to where he would "come out." They had so assumed it was to be in some wonderful place—they had thought of it as so very MUCH out. Well, that was doubtless what it had been—since he had come out just there. He was out, in truth, as far as it was possible to be, and must now rather bethink himself of getting in again. He found on the spot the image of his recent history; he was like one of the figures of the old clock at Berne. THEY came out, on one side, at their hour, jigged along their little course in the public eye, and went in on the other side. He too had jigged his little course—him too a modest retreat awaited. He offered now, should she really like to know, to name the great product of Woollett. It would be a great commentary on everything. At this she stopped him off; she not only had no wish to know, but she wouldn't know for the world. She had done with the products of Woollett—for all the good she had got from them. She desired no further news of them, and she mentioned that Madame de Vionnet herself had, to her knowledge, lived exempt from the information he was ready to supply. She had never consented to receive it, though she would have taken it, under stress, from Mrs. Pocock. But it was a matter about which Mrs. Pocock appeared to have had little to say—never sounding the word—and it didn't signify now. There was nothing clearly for Maria Gostrey that signified now—save one sharp point, that is, to which she came in time. "I don't know whether it's before you as a possibility that, left to himself, Mr. Chad may after all go back. I judge that it IS more or less so before you, from what you just now said of him."

Her guest had his eyes on her, kindly but attentively, as if foreseeing what was to follow this. "I don't think it will be for the money." And then as she seemed uncertain: "I mean I don't believe it will be for that he'll give her up."

"Then he WILL give her up?"

Strether waited a moment, rather slow and deliberate now, drawing out a little this last soft stage, pleading with her in various suggestive and unspoken ways for patience and understanding. "What were you just about to ask me?"

"Is there anything he can do that would make you patch it up?"

"With Mrs. Newsome?"

Her assent, as if she had had a delicacy about sounding the name, was only in her face; but she added with it: "Or is there anything he can do that would make HER try it?"

"To patch it up with me?" His answer came at last in a conclusive headshake. "There's nothing any one can do. It's over. Over for both of us."

Maria wondered, seemed a little to doubt. "Are you so sure for her?"

"Oh yes—sure now. Too much has happened. I'm different for her."

She took it in then, drawing a deeper breath. "I see. So that as she's different for YOU—"

"Ah but," he interrupted, "she's not." And as Miss Gostrey wondered again: "She's the same. She's more than ever the same. But I do what I didn't before—I SEE her."

He spoke gravely and as if responsibly—since he had to pronounce; and the effect of it was slightly solemn, so that she simply exclaimed "Oh!" Satisfied and grateful, however, she showed in her own next words an acceptance of his statement. "What then do you go home to?"

He had pushed his plate a little away, occupied with another side of the matter; taking refuge verily in that side and feeling so moved that he soon found himself on his feet. He was affected in advance by what he believed might come from her, and he would have liked to forestall it and deal with it tenderly; yet in the presence of it he wished still more to be—though as smoothly as possible—deterrent and conclusive. He put her question by for the moment; he told her more about Chad. "It would have been impossible to meet me more than he did last night on the question of the infamy of not sticking to her."

"Is that what you called it for him—'infamy'?"

"Oh rather! I described to him in detail the base creature he'd be, and he quite agrees with me about it."

"So that it's really as if you had nailed him?"

"Quite really as if—! I told him I should curse him."

"Oh," she smiled, "you HAVE done it." And then having thought again: "You CAN'T after that propose—!" Yet she scanned his face. "Propose again to Mrs. Newsome?"

She hesitated afresh, but she brought it out. "I've never believed, you know, that you did propose. I always believed it was really she— and, so far as that goes, I can understand it. What I mean is," she explained, "that with such a spirit—the spirit of curses!—your breach is past mending. She has only to know what you've done to him never again to raise a finger."

"I've done," said Strether, "what I could—one can't do more. He protests his devotion and his horror. But I'm not sure I've saved him. He protests too much. He asks how one can dream of his being tired. But he has all life before him."

Maria saw what he meant. "He's formed to please."

"And it's our friend who has formed him." Strether felt in it the strange irony.

"So it's scarcely his fault!"

"It's at any rate his danger. I mean," said Strether, "it's hers. But she knows it."

"Yes, she knows it. And is your idea," Miss Gostrey asked, "that there was some other woman in London?"

"Yes. No. That is I HAVE no ideas. I'm afraid of them. I've done with them." And he put out his hand to her. "Good-bye."

It brought her back to her unanswered question. "To what do you go home?"

"I don't know. There will always be something."

"To a great difference," she said as she kept his hand.

"A great difference—no doubt. Yet I shall see what I can make of it."

"Shall you make anything so good—?" But, as if remembering what Mrs. Newsome had done, it was as far as she went.

He had sufficiently understood. "So good as this place at this moment? So good as what YOU make of everything you touch?" He took a moment to say, for, really and truly, what stood about him there in her offer—which was as the offer of exquisite service, of lightened care, for the rest of his days—might well have tempted. It built him softly round, it roofed him warmly over, it rested, all so firm, on selection. And what ruled selection was beauty and knowledge. It was awkward, it was almost stupid, not to seem to prize such things; yet, none the less, so far as they made his opportunity they made it only for a moment. She'd moreover understand—she always understood.

That indeed might be, but meanwhile she was going on. "There's nothing, you know, I wouldn't do for you."

"Oh yes—I know."

"There's nothing," she repeated, "in all the world."

"I know. I know. But all the same I must go." He had got it at last. "To be right."

"To be right?"

She had echoed it in vague deprecation, but he felt it already clear for her. "That, you see, is my only logic. Not, out of the whole affair, to have got anything for myself."

She thought. "But with your wonderful impressions you'll have got a great deal."

"A great deal"—he agreed. "But nothing like YOU. It's you who would make me wrong!"

Honest and fine, she couldn't greatly pretend she didn't see it. Still she could pretend just a little. "But why should you be so dreadfully right?"

"That's the way that—if I must go—you yourself would be the first to want me. And I can't do anything else."

So then she had to take it, though still with her defeated protest. "It isn't so much your BEING 'right'—it's your horrible sharp eye for what makes you so."

"Oh but you're just as bad yourself. You can't resist me when I point that out."

She sighed it at last all comically, all tragically, away. "I can't indeed resist you."

"Then there we are!" said Strether.

The End.

The Golden Bowl

BOOK FIRST: THE PRINCE

PART FIRST

The Thames (c.1876) by James Tissot (1836–1902)

1

The Prince had always liked his London, when it had come to him; he was one of the modern Romans who find by the Thames a more convincing image of the truth of the ancient state than any they have left by the Tiber. Brought up on the legend of the City to which the world paid tribute, he recognised in the present London much more than in contemporary Rome the real dimensions of such a case. If it was a question of an Imperium, he said to himself, and if one wished, as a Roman, to recover a little the sense of that, the place to do so was on London Bridge, or even, on a fine afternoon in May, at Hyde Park Corner. It was not indeed to either of those places that these grounds of his predilection, after all sufficiently vague, had, at the moment we are concerned with him, guided his steps; he had strayed, simply enough, into Bond Street, where his imagination, working at comparatively short range, caused him now and then to stop before a window in which objects massive and lumpish, in silver and gold, in the forms to which precious stones contribute, or in leather, steel, brass, applied to a hundred uses and abuses, were as tumbled together as if, in the insolence of the Empire, they had been the loot of far-off victories. The young man's movements, however, betrayed no consistency of attention—not even, for that matter, when one of his arrests had proceeded from possibilities in faces shaded, as they passed him on the pavement, by huge beribboned hats, or more delicately tinted still under the tense silk of parasols held at perverse angles in waiting victorias. And the Prince's undirected thought was not a little symptomatic, since, though the turn of the season had come and the flush of the streets begun to fade, the possibilities of faces, on the August afternoon, were still one of the notes of the scene. He was too restless—that was the fact—for any concentration, and the last idea that would just now have occurred to him in any connection was the idea of pursuit.

He had been pursuing for six months as never in his life before, and what had actually unsteadied him, as we join him, was the sense of how he had been justified. Capture had crowned the pursuit—or success, as he would otherwise have put it, had rewarded virtue; whereby the consciousness of these things made him, for the hour, rather serious than gay. A sobriety that might have consorted with failure sat in his handsome face, constructively regular and grave, yet at the same time oddly and, as might be, functionally almost radiant, with its dark blue eyes, its dark brown moustache and its expression no more sharply "foreign" to an English view than to have caused it sometimes to be observed of him with a shallow felicity that he looked like a "refined" Irishman. What had happened was that shortly before, at three o'clock, his fate had practically been sealed, and that even when one pretended to no quarrel with it the moment had something of the grimness of a crunched key in the strongest lock that could be made. There was nothing to do as yet, further, but feel what one had done, and our personage felt it while he aimlessly wandered. It was already as if he were married, so definitely had the solicitors, at three o'clock, enabled the date to be fixed, and by so few days was that date now distant. He was to dine at half-past eight o'clock with the young lady on whose behalf, and on whose father's, the London lawyers had reached an inspired harmony with his own man of business, poor Calderoni, fresh from Rome and now apparently in the wondrous situation of being "shown London," before promptly leaving it again, by Mr. Verver himself, Mr. Verver whose easy way with his millions had taxed to such small purpose, in the arrangements, the principle of reciprocity. The reciprocity with which the Prince was during these minutes most struck was that of Calderoni's bestowal of his company for a view of the lions. If there was one thing in the world the young man, at this juncture, clearly intended, it was to be much more decent as a son-in-law than lots of fellows he could think of had shown themselves in that character. He thought of these fellows, from whom he was so to differ, in English; he used, mentally, the English term to describe his difference, for, familiar with the tongue from his earliest years, so that no note of strangeness remained with him either for lip or for ear, he found it convenient, in life, for the greatest number of relations. He found it convenient, oddly, even for his relation with himself—though not unmindful that there might still, as time went on, be others, including a more intimate degree of that one, that would seek, possibly with violence, the larger or the finer issue—which was it?—of the vernacular. Miss Verver had told him he spoke English too well—it was his only fault, and he had not been able to speak worse even to oblige her. "When I speak worse, you see, I speak French," he had said; intimating thus that there were discriminations, doubtless of the invidious kind, for which that language was the most apt. The girl had taken this, she let him know, as a reflection on her own French, which she had always so dreamed of making good, of making better; to say nothing of his evident feeling that the idiom supposed a cleverness she was not a person to rise to. The Prince's answer to such remarks—genial, charming, like every answer the parties to his new arrangement had yet had from him—was that he was practising his American in order to converse properly, on equal terms as it were, with Mr. Verver. His prospective father-in-law had a command of it, he said, that put him at a disadvantage in any discussion; besides which—well, besides which he had made to the girl the observation that positively, of all his observations yet, had most finely touched her.

"You know I think he's a REAL galantuomo—'and no mistake.' There are plenty of sham ones about. He seems to me simply the best man I've ever seen in my life."

"Well, my dear, why shouldn't he be?" the girl had gaily inquired.

It was this, precisely, that had set the Prince to think. The things, or many of them, that had made Mr. Verver what he was seemed practically to bring a charge of waste against the other things that, with the other people known to the young man, had failed of such a result. "Why, his 'form,'" he had returned, "might have made one doubt."

"Father's form?" She hadn't seen it. "It strikes me he hasn't got any."

"He hasn't got mine—he hasn't even got yours."

"Thank you for 'even'!" the girl had laughed at him. "Oh, yours, my dear, is tremendous. But your father has his own. I've made that out. So don't doubt it. It's where it has brought him out—that's the point."

"It's his goodness that has brought him out," our young woman had, at this, objected.

"Ah, darling, goodness, I think, never brought anyone out. Goodness, when it's real, precisely, rather keeps people in." He had been interested in his discrimination, which amused him. "No, it's his WAY. It belongs to him."

But she had wondered still. "It's the American way. That's all."

"Exactly—it's all. It's all, I say! It fits him—so it must be good for something."

"Do you think it would be good for you?" Maggie Verver had smilingly asked.

To which his reply had been just of the happiest. "I don't feel, my dear, if you really want to know, that anything much can now either hurt me or help me. Such as I am—but you'll see for yourself. Say, however, I am a galantuomo—which I devoutly hope: I'm like a chicken, at best, chopped up and smothered in sauce; cooked down as a creme de volaille, with half the parts left out. Your father's the natural fowl running about the bassecour. His feathers, movements, his sounds—those are the parts that, with me, are left out."

"All, as a matter of course—since you can't eat a chicken alive!"

The Prince had not been annoyed at this, but he had been positive. "Well, I'm eating your father alive—which is the only way to taste him. I want to continue, and as it's when he talks American that he is most alive, so I must also cultivate it, to get my pleasure. He couldn't make one like him so much in any other language."

It mattered little that the girl had continued to demur—it was the mere play of her joy. "I think I could make you like him in Chinese."

"It would be an unnecessary trouble. What I mean is that he's a kind of result of his inevitable tone. My liking is accordingly FOR the tone—which has made him possible."

"Oh, you'll hear enough of it," she laughed, "before you've done with us."

Only this, in truth, had made him frown a little.

"What do you mean, please, by my having 'done' with you?"

"Why, found out about us all there is to find."

He had been able to take it indeed easily as a joke. "Ah, love, I began with that. I know enough, I feel, never to be surprised. It's you yourselves meanwhile," he continued, "who really know nothing. There are two parts of me"—yes, he had been moved to go on. "One is made up of the history, the doings, the marriages, the crimes, the follies, the boundless betises of other people—especially of their infamous waste of money that might have come to me. Those things are written—literally in rows of volumes, in libraries; are as public as they're abominable. Everybody can get at them, and you've, both of you, wonderfully, looked them in the face. But there's another part, very much smaller doubtless, which, such as it is, represents my single self, the unknown, unimportant, unimportant—unimportant save to YOU—personal quantity. About this you've found out nothing."

"Luckily, my dear," the girl had bravely said; "for what then would become, please, of the promised occupation of my future?"

The young man remembered even now how extraordinarily CLEAR—he couldn't call it anything else—she had looked, in her prettiness, as she had said it. He also remembered what he had been moved to reply. "The happiest reigns, we are taught, you know, are the reigns without any history."

"Oh, I'm not afraid of history!" She had been sure of that. "Call it the bad part, if you like—yours certainly sticks out of you. What was it else," Maggie Verver had also said, "that made me originally think of you? It wasn't—as I should suppose you must have seen—what you call your unknown quantity, your particular self. It was the generations behind you, the follies and the crimes, the plunder and the waste—the wicked Pope, the monster most of all, whom so many of the volumes in your family library are all about. If I've read but two or three yet, I shall give myself up but the more—as soon as I have time—to the rest. Where, therefore"—she had put it to him again—"without your archives, annals, infamies, would you have been?"

He recalled what, to this, he had gravely returned. "I might have been in a somewhat better pecuniary situation." But his actual situation under the head in question positively so little mattered to them that, having by that time lived deep into the sense of his advantage, he had kept no impression of the girl's rejoinder. It had but sweetened the waters in which he now floated, tinted them as by the action of some essence, poured from a gold-topped phial, for making one's bath aromatic. No one before him, never—not even the infamous Pope—had so sat up to his neck in such a bath. It showed, for that matter, how little one of his race could escape, after all, from history. What was it but history, and of THEIR kind very much, to have the assurance of the enjoyment of more money than the palace-builder himself could have dreamed of? This was the element that bore him up and into which Maggie scattered, on occasion, her exquisite colouring drops. They were of the colour—of what on earth? of what but the extraordinary American good faith? They were of the colour of her innocence, and yet at the same time of her imagination, with which their relation, his and these people's, was all suffused. What he had further said on the occasion of which we thus represent him as catching the echoes from his own thoughts while he loitered—what he had further said came back to him, for it had been the voice itself of his luck, the soothing sound that was always with him. "You Americans are almost incredibly romantic."

"Of course we are. That's just what makes everything so nice for us."

"Everything?" He had wondered.

"Well, everything that's nice at all. The world, the beautiful, world—or everything in it that is beautiful. I mean we see so much."

He had looked at her a moment—and he well knew how she had struck him, in respect to the beautiful world, as one of the beautiful, the most beautiful things. But what he had answered was: "You see too much—that's what may sometimes make you difficulties. When you don't, at least," he had amended with a further thought, "see too little." But he had quite granted that he knew what she meant, and his warning perhaps was needless.

He had seen the follies of the romantic disposition, but there seemed somehow no follies in theirs—nothing, one was obliged to recognise, but innocent pleasures, pleasures without penalties. Their enjoyment was a tribute to others without being a loss to themselves. Only the funny thing, he had respectfully submitted, was that her father, though older and wiser, and a man into the bargain, was as bad—that is as good—as herself.

"Oh, he's better," the girl had freely declared "that is he's worse. His relation to the things he cares for—and I think it beautiful—is absolutely romantic. So is his whole life over here—it's the most romantic thing I know."

"You mean his idea for his native place?"

"Yes—the collection, the Museum with which he wishes to endow it, and of which he thinks more, as you know, than of anything in the world. It's the work of his life and the motive of everything he does."

The young man, in his actual mood, could have smiled again—smiled delicately, as he had then smiled at her. "Has it been his motive in letting me have you?"

"Yes, my dear, positively—or in a manner," she had said.

"American City isn't, by the way, his native town, for, though he's not old, it's a young thing compared with him—a younger one. He started there, he has a feeling about it, and the place has grown, as he says, like the programme of a charity performance. You're at any rate a part of his collection," she had explained—"one of the things that can only be got over here. You're a rarity, an object of beauty, an object of price. You're not perhaps absolutely unique, but you're so curious and eminent that there are very few others like you—you belong to a class about which everything is known. You're what they call a morceau de musee."

"I see. I have the great sign of it," he had risked—"that I cost a lot of money."

"I haven't the least idea," she had gravely answered, "what you cost"—and he had quite adored, for the moment, her way of saying it. He had felt even, for the moment, vulgar. But he had made the best of that. "Wouldn't you find out if it were a question of parting with me? My value would in that case be estimated."

Portrait by Alexandre Cabanel (1823–1889)

She had looked at him with her charming eyes, as if his value were well before her. "Yes, if you mean that I'd pay rather than lose you."

And then there came again what this had made him say. "Don't talk about ME—it's you who are not of this age. You're a creature of a braver and finer one, and the cinquecento, at its most golden hour, wouldn't have been ashamed of you. It would of me, and if I didn't know some of the pieces your father has acquired, I should rather fear, for American City, the criticism of experts. Would it at all events be your idea," he had then just ruefully asked, "to send me there for safety?"

"Well, we may have to come to it."

"I'll go anywhere you want."

"We must see first—it will be only if we have to come to it. There are things," she had gone on, "that father puts away—the bigger and more cumbrous of course, which he stores, has already stored in masses, here and in Paris, in Italy, in Spain, in warehouses, vaults, banks, safes, wonderful secret places. We've been like a pair of pirates—positively stage pirates, the sort who wink at each other and say 'Ha-ha!' when they come to where their treasure is buried. Ours is buried pretty well everywhere—except what we like to see, what we travel with and have about us. These, the smaller pieces, are the things we take out and arrange as we can, to make the hotels we stay at and the houses we hire a little less ugly. Of course it's a danger, and we have to keep watch. But father loves a fine piece, loves, as he says, the good of it, and it's for the company of some of his things that he's willing to run his risks. And we've had extraordinary luck"—Maggie had made that point; "we've never lost anything yet. And the finest objects are often the smallest. Values, in lots of cases, you must know, have nothing to do with size. But there's nothing, however tiny," she had wound up, "that we've missed."

"I like the class," he had laughed for this, "in which you place me! I shall be one of the little pieces that you unpack at the hotels, or at the worst in the hired houses, like this wonderful one, and put out with the family photographs and the new magazines. But it's something not to be so big that I have to be buried."

"Oh," she had returned, "you shall not be buried, my dear, till you're dead. Unless indeed you call it burial to go to American City."

"Before I pronounce I should like to see my tomb." So he had had, after his fashion, the last word in their interchange, save for the result of an observation that had risen to his lips at the beginning, which he had then checked, and which now came back to him. "Good, bad or indifferent, I hope there's one thing you believe about me."

He had sounded solemn, even to himself, but she had taken it gaily. "Ah, don't fix me down to 'one'! I believe things enough about you, my dear, to have a few left if most of them, even, go to smash. I've taken care of THAT. I've divided my faith into water-tight compartments. We must manage not to sink."

"You do believe I'm not a hypocrite? You recognise that I don't lie or dissemble or deceive? Is THAT water-tight?"

The question, to which he had given a certain intensity, had made her, he remembered, stare an instant, her colour rising as if it had sounded to her still stranger than he had intended. He had perceived on the spot that any SERIOUS discussion of veracity, of loyalty, or rather of the want of them, practically took her unprepared, as if it were quite new to her. He had noticed it before: it was the English, the American sign that duplicity, like "love," had to be joked about. It couldn't be "gone into." So the note of his inquiry was—well, to call it nothing else—premature; a mistake worth making, however, for the almost overdone drollery in which her answer instinctively sought refuge.

"Water-tight—the biggest compartment of all? Why, it's the best cabin and the main deck and the engine-room and the steward's pantry! It's the ship itself—it's the whole line. It's the captain's table and all one's luggage—one's reading for the trip." She had images, like that, that were drawn from steamers and trains, from a familiarity with "lines," a command of "own" cars, from an experience of continents and seas, that he was unable as yet to emulate; from vast modern machineries and facilities whose acquaintance he had still to make, but as to which it was part of the interest of his situation as it stood that he could, quite without wincing, feel his future likely to bristle with them.

It was in fact, content as he was with his engagement and charming as he thought his affianced bride, his view of THAT furniture that mainly constituted our young man's "romance"—and to an extent that made of his inward state a contrast that he was intelligent enough to feel. He was intelligent enough to feel quite humble, to wish not to be in the least hard or voracious, not to insist on his own side of the bargain, to warn himself in short against arrogance and greed. Odd enough, of a truth, was his sense of this last danger—which may illustrate moreover his general attitude toward dangers from within. Personally, he considered, he hadn't the vices in question—and that was so much to the good. His race, on the other hand, had had them handsomely enough, and he was somehow full of his race. Its presence in him was like the consciousness of some inexpugnable scent in which his clothes, his whole person, his hands and the hair of his head, might have been steeped as in some chemical bath: the effect was nowhere in particular, yet he constantly felt himself at the mercy of the cause. He knew his antenatal history, knew it in every detail, and it was a thing to keep causes well before him. What was his frank judgment of so much of its ugliness, he asked himself, but a part of the cultivation of humility? What was this so important step he had just taken but the desire for some new history that should, so far as possible, contradict, and even if need be flatly dishonour, the old? If what had come to him wouldn't do he must MAKE something different. He perfectly recognised—always in his humility—that the material for the making had to be Mr. Verver's millions. There was nothing else for him on earth to make it with; he had tried before—had had to look about and see the truth. Humble as he was, at the same time, he was not so humble as if he had known himself frivolous or stupid. He had an idea—which may amuse his historian—that when you were stupid enough to be mistaken about such a matter you did know it. Therefore he wasn't mistaken—his future might be MIGHT be scientific. There was nothing in himself, at all events, to prevent it. He was allying himself to science, for what was science but the absence of prejudice backed by the presence of money? His life would be full of machinery, which was the antidote to superstition, which was in its turn, too much, the consequence, or at least the exhalation, of archives. He thought of these—of his not being at all events futile, and of his absolute acceptance of the developments of the coming age to redress the balance of his being so differently considered. The moments when he most winced were those at which he found himself believing that, really, futility would have been forgiven him. Even WITH it, in that absurd view, he would have been good enough. Such was the laxity, in the Ververs, of the romantic spirit. They didn't, indeed, poor dears, know what, in that line—the line of futility—the real thing meant. He did—having seen it, having tried it, having taken its measure. This was a memory in fact simply to screen out—much as, just in front of him while he walked, the iron shutter of a shop, closing early to the stale summer day, rattled down at the turn of some crank. There was machinery again, just as the plate glass, all about him, was money, was power, the power of the rich peoples. Well, he was OF them now, of the rich peoples; he was on their side—if it wasn't rather the pleasanter way of putting it that they were on his.

Something of this sort was in any case the moral and the murmur of his walk. It would have been ridiculous—such a moral from such a source—if it hadn't all somehow fitted to the gravity of the hour, that gravity the oppression of which I began by recording. Another feature was the immediate nearness of the arrival of the contingent from home. He was to meet them at Charing Cross on the morrow: his younger brother, who had married before him, but whose wife, of Hebrew race, with a portion that had gilded the pill, was not in a condition to travel; his sister and her husband, the most anglicised of Milanesi, his maternal uncle, the most shelved of diplomatists, and his Roman cousin, Don Ottavio, the most disponible of ex-deputies and of relatives—a scant handful of the consanguineous who, in spite of Maggie's plea for hymeneal reserve, were to accompany him to the altar. It was no great array, yet it was apparently to be a more numerous muster than any possible to the bride herself, having no wealth of kinship to choose from and making it up, on the other hand, by loose invitations. He had been interested in the girl's attitude on the matter and had wholly deferred to it, giving him, as it did, a glimpse, distinctly pleasing, of the kind of ruminations she would in general be governed by—which were quite such as fell in with his own taste. They hadn't natural relations, she and her father, she had explained; so they wouldn't try to supply the place by artificial, by make-believe ones, by any searching of highways and hedges. Oh yes, they had acquaintances enough—but a marriage was an intimate thing. You asked acquaintances when you HAD your kith and kin—you asked them over and above. But you didn't ask them alone, to cover your nudity and look like what they weren't. She knew what she meant and what she liked, and he was all ready to take from her, finding a good omen in both of the facts. He expected her, desired her, to have character; his wife SHOULD have it, and he wasn't afraid of her having much. He had had, in his earlier time, to deal with plenty of people who had had it; notably with the three four ecclesiastics, his great-uncle, the Cardinal, above all, who had taken a hand and played a part in his education: the effect of all of which had never been to upset him. He was thus fairly on the look-out for the characteristic in this most intimate, as she was to come, of his associates. He encouraged it when it appeared.

He felt therefore, just at present, as if his papers were in order, as if his accounts so balanced as they had never done in his life before and he might close the portfolio with a snap. It would open again, doubtless, of itself, with the arrival of the Romans; it would even perhaps open with his dining to-night in Portland Place, where Mr. Verver had pitched a tent suggesting that of Alexander furnished with the spoils of Darius. But what meanwhile marked his crisis, as I have said, was his sense of the immediate two or three hours. He paused on corners, at crossings; there kept rising for him, in waves, that consciousness, sharp as to its source while vague as to its end, which I began by speaking of—the consciousness of an appeal to do something or other, before it was too late, for himself. By any friend to whom he might have mentioned it the appeal could have been turned to frank derision. For what, for whom indeed but himself and the high advantages attached, was he about to marry an extraordinarily charming girl, whose "prospects," of the solid sort, were as guaranteed as her amiability? He wasn't to do it, assuredly, all for her. The Prince, as happened, however, was so free to feel and yet not to formulate that there rose before him after a little, definitely, the image of a friend whom he had often found ironic. He withheld the tribute of attention from passing faces only to let his impulse accumulate. Youth and beauty made him scarcely turn, but the image of Mrs. Assingham made him presently stop a hansom. HER youth, her beauty were things more or less of the past, but to find her at home, as he possibly might, would be "doing" what he still had time for, would put something of a reason into his restlessness and thereby probably soothe it. To recognise the propriety of this particular pilgrimage—she lived far enough off, in long Cadogan Place—was already in fact to work it off a little. A perception of the propriety of formally thanking her, and of timing the act just as he happened to be doing—this, he made out as he went, was obviously all that had been the matter with him. It was true that he had mistaken the mood of the moment, misread it rather, superficially, as an impulse to look the other way—the other way from where his pledges had accumulated. Mrs. Assingham, precisely, represented, embodied his pledges—was, in her pleasant person, the force that had set them successively in motion. She had MADE his marriage, quite as truly as his papal ancestor had made his family—though he could scarce see what she had made it for unless because she too was perversely romantic. He had neither bribed nor persuaded her, had given her nothing—scarce even till now articulate thanks; so that her profit-to think of it vulgarly—must have all had to come from the Ververs.

Yet he was far, he could still remind himself, from supposing that she had been grossly remunerated. He was wholly sure she hadn't; for if there were people who took presents and people who didn't she would be quite on the right side and of the proud class. Only then, on the other hand, her disinterestedness was rather awful—it implied, that is, such abysses of confidence. She was admirably attached to Maggie—whose possession of such a friend might moreover quite rank as one of her "assets"; but the great proof of her affection had been in bringing them, with her design, together. Meeting him during a winter in Rome, meeting him afterwards in Paris, and "liking" him, as she had in time frankly let him know from the first, she had marked him for her young friend's own and had then, unmistakably, presented him in a light. But the interest in Maggie—that was the point—would have achieved but little without her interest in HIM. On what did that sentiment, unsolicited and unrecompensed, rest? what good, again—for it was much like his question about Mr. Verver—should he ever have done her? The Prince's notion of a recompense to women—similar in this to his notion of an appeal—was more or less to make love to them. Now he hadn't, as he believed, made love the least little bit to Mrs. Assingham—nor did he think she had for a moment supposed it. He liked in these days, to mark them off, the women to whom he hadn't made love: it represented— and that was what pleased him in it—a different stage of existence from the time at which he liked to mark off the women to whom he had. Neither, with all this, had Mrs. Assingham herself been either aggressive or resentful. On what occasion, ever, had she appeared to find him wanting? These things, the motives of such people, were obscure—a little alarmingly so; they contributed to that element of the impenetrable which alone slightly qualified his sense of his good fortune. He remembered to have read, as a boy, a wonderful tale by Allan Poe, his prospective wife's countryman-which was a thing to show, by the way, what imagination Americans COULD have: the story of the shipwrecked Gordon Pym, who, drifting in a small boat further toward the North Pole—or was it the South?—than anyone had ever done, found at a given moment before him a thickness of white air that was like a dazzling curtain of light, concealing as darkness conceals, yet of the colour of milk or of snow. There were moments when he felt his own boat move upon some such mystery. The state of mind of his new friends, including Mrs. Assingham herself, had resemblances to a great white curtain. He had never known curtains but as purple even to blackness—but as producing where they hung a darkness intended and ominous. When they were so disposed as to shelter surprises the surprises were apt to be shocks.

Shocks, however, from these quite different depths, were not what he saw reason to apprehend; what he rather seemed to himself not yet to have measured was something that, seeking a name for it, he would have called the quantity of confidence reposed in him. He had stood still, at many a moment of the previous month, with the thought, freshly determined or renewed, of the general expectation—to define it roughly—of which he was the subject. What was singular was that it seemed not so much an expectation of anything in particular as a large, bland, blank assumption of merits almost beyond notation, of essential quality and value. It was as if he had been some old embossed coin, of a purity of gold no longer used, stamped with glorious arms, mediaeval, wonderful, of which the "worth" in mere modern change, sovereigns and half crowns, would be great enough, but as to which, since there were finer ways of using it, such taking to pieces was superfluous. That was the image for the security in which it was open to him to rest; he was to constitute a possession, yet was to escape being reduced to his component parts. What would this mean but that, practically, he was never to be tried or tested? What would it mean but that, if they didn't "change" him, they really wouldn't know—he wouldn't know himself—how many pounds, shillings and pence he had to give? These at any rate, for the present, were unanswerable questions; all that was before him was that he was invested with attributes. He was taken seriously. Lost there in the white mist was the seriousness in them that made them so take him. It was even in Mrs. Assingham, in spite of her having, as she had frequently shown, a more mocking spirit. All he could say as yet was that he had done nothing, so far as to break any charm. What should he do if he were to ask her frankly this afternoon what he was, morally speaking, behind their veil. It would come to asking what they expected him to do. She would answer him probably: "Oh, you know, it's what we expect you to be!" on which he would have no resource but to deny his knowledge. Would that break the spell, his saying he had no idea? What idea in fact could he have? He also took himself seriously—made a point of it; but it wasn't simply a question of fancy and pretension. His own estimate he saw ways, at one time and another, of dealing with: but theirs, sooner or later, say what they might, would put him to the practical proof. As the practical proof, accordingly, would naturally be proportionate to the cluster of his attributes, one arrived at a scale that he was not, honestly, the man to calculate. Who but a billionaire could say what was fair exchange for a billion? That measure was the shrouded object, but he felt really, as his cab stopped in Cadogan Place, a little nearer the shroud. He promised himself, virtually, to give the latter a twitch.

II

"They're not good days, you know," he had said to Fanny Assingham after declaring himself grateful for finding her, and then, with his cup of tea, putting her in possession of the latest news—the documents signed an hour ago, de part et d'autre, and the telegram from his backers, who had reached Paris the morning before, and who, pausing there a little, poor dears, seemed to think the whole thing a tremendous lark. "We're very simple folk, mere country cousins compared with you," he had also observed, "and Paris, for my sister and her husband, is the end of the world. London therefore will be more or less another planet. It has always been, as with so many of us, quite their Mecca, but this is their first real caravan; they've mainly known 'old England' as a shop for articles in india-rubber and leather, in which they've dressed themselves as much as possible. Which all means, however, that you'll see them, all of them, wreathed in smiles. We must be very easy with them. Maggie's too wonderful—her preparations are on a scale! She insists on taking in the sposi and my uncle. The others will come to me. I've been engaging their rooms at the hotel, and, with all those solemn signatures of an hour ago, that brings the case home to me."

"Do you mean you're afraid?" his hostess had amusedly asked.

"Terribly afraid. I've now but to wait to see the monster come. They're not good days; they're neither one thing nor the other. I've really got nothing, yet I've everything to lose. One doesn't know what still may happen."

The way she laughed at him for was for an instant almost irritating; it came out, for his fancy, from behind the white curtain. It was a sign, that is, of her deep serenity, which worried instead of soothing him. And to be soothed, after all, to be tided over, in his mystic impatience, to be told what he could understand and believe—that was what he had come for. "Marriage then," said Mrs. Assingham, "is what you call the monster? I admit it's a fearful thing at the best; but, for heaven's sake, if that's what you're thinking of, don't run away from it."

"Ah, to run away from it would be to run away from you," the Prince replied; "and I've already told you often enough how I depend on you to see me through." He so liked the way she took this, from the corner of her sofa, that he gave his sincerity—for it WAS sincerity—fuller expression. "I'm starting on the great voyage—across the unknown sea; my ship's all rigged and appointed, the cargo's stowed away and the company complete. But what seems the matter with me is that I can't sail alone; my ship must be one of a pair, must have, in the waste of waters, a—what do you call it?—a consort. I don't ask you to stay on board with me, but I must keep your sail in sight for orientation. I don't in the least myself know, I assure you, the points of the compass. But with a lead I can perfectly follow. You MUST be my lead."

"How can you be sure," she asked, "where I should take you?"

"Why, from your having brought me safely thus far. I should never have got here without you. You've provided the ship itself, and, if you've not quite seen me aboard, you've attended me, ever so kindly, to the dock. Your own vessel is, all conveniently, in the next berth, and you can't desert me now."

She showed him again her amusement, which struck him even as excessive, as if, to his surprise, he made her also a little nervous; she treated him in fine as if he were not uttering truths, but making pretty figures for her diversion. "My vessel, dear Prince?" she smiled. "What vessel, in the world, have I? This little house is all our ship, Bob's and mine—and thankful we are, now, to have it. We've wandered far, living, as you may say, from hand to mouth, without rest for the soles of our feet. But the time has come for us at last to draw in."

He made at this, the young man, an indignant protest. "You talk about rest—it's too selfish!—when you're just launching me on adventures?"

She shook her head with her kind lucidity. "Not adventures—heaven forbid! You've had yours—as I've had mine; and my idea has been, all along, that we should neither of us begin again. My own last, precisely, has been doing for you all you so prettily mention. But it consists simply in having conducted you to rest. You talk about ships, but they're not the comparison. Your tossings are over—you're practically IN port. The port," she concluded, "of the Golden Isles."

He looked about, to put himself more in relation with the place; then, after an hesitation, seemed to speak certain words instead of certain others. "Oh, I know where I AM—! I do decline to be left, but what I came for, of course, was to thank you. If to-day has seemed, for the first time, the end of preliminaries, I feel how little there would have been any at all without you. The first were wholly yours."

"Well," said Mrs. Assingham, "they were remarkably easy. I've seen them, I've HAD them," she smiled, "more difficult. Everything, you must feel, went of itself. So, you must feel, everything still goes."

The Prince quickly agreed. "Oh, beautifully! But you had the conception."

"Ah, Prince, so had you!"

He looked at her harder a moment. "You had it first. You had it most."

She returned his look as if it had made her wonder. "I LIKED it, if that's what you mean. But you liked it surely yourself. I protest, that I had easy work with you. I had only at last—when I thought it was time—to speak for you."

"All that is quite true. But you're leaving me, all the same, you're leaving me—you're washing your hands of me," he went on. "However, that won't be easy; I won't BE left." And he had turned his eyes about again, taking in the pretty room that she had just described as her final refuge, the place of peace for a world-worn couple, to which she had lately retired with "Bob." "I shall keep this spot in sight. Say what you will, I shall need you. I'm not, you know," he declared, "going to give you up for anybody."

"If you're afraid—which of course you're not—are you trying to make me the same?" she asked after a moment.

He waited a minute too, then answered her with a question. "You say you 'liked' it, your undertaking to make my engagement possible. It remains beautiful for me that you did; it's charming and unforgettable. But, still more, it's mysterious and wonderful. WHY, you dear delightful woman, did you like it?"

"I scarce know what to make," she said, "of such an inquiry. If you haven't by this time found out yourself, what meaning can anything I say have for you? Don't you really after all feel," she added while nothing came from him—"aren't you conscious every minute, of the perfection of the creature of whom I've put you into possession?"

"Every minute—gratefully conscious. But that's exactly the ground of my question. It wasn't only a matter of your handing me over—it was a matter of your handing her. It was a matter of HER fate still more than of mine. You thought all the good of her that one woman can think of another, and yet, by your account, you enjoyed assisting at her risk."

She had kept her eyes on him while he spoke, and this was what, visibly, determined a repetition for her. "Are you trying to frighten me?"

"Ah, that's a foolish view—I should be too vulgar. You apparently can't understand either my good faith or my humility. I'm awfully humble," the young man insisted; "that's the way I've been feeling to-day, with everything so finished and ready. And you won't take me for serious."

She continued to face him as if he really troubled her a little. "Oh, you deep old Italians!"

"There you are," he returned—"it's what I wanted you to come to. That's the responsible note."

"Yes," she went on—"if you're 'humble' you MUST be dangerous."

She had a pause while she only smiled; then she said: "I don't in the least want to lose sight of you. But even if I did I shouldn't think it right."

"Thank you for that—it's what I needed of you. I'm sure, after all, that the more you're with me the more I shall understand. It's the only thing in the world I want. I'm excellent, I really think, all round—except that I'm stupid. I can do pretty well anything I SEE. But I've got to see it first." And he pursued his demonstration. "I don't in the least mind its having to be shown me—in fact I like that better. Therefore it is that I want, that I shall always want, your eyes. Through THEM I wish to look—even at any risk of their showing me what I mayn't like. For then," he wound up, "I shall know. And of that I shall never be afraid."

She might quite have been waiting to see what he would come to, but she spoke with a certain impatience. "What on earth are you talking about?"

But he could perfectly say: "Of my real, honest fear of being 'off' some day, of being wrong, WITHOUT knowing it. That's what I shall always trust you for—to tell me when I am. No—with you people it's a sense. We haven't got it—not as you have. Therefore—!" But he had said enough. "Ecco!" he simply smiled.

It was not to be concealed that he worked upon her, but of course she always liked him. "I should be interested," she presently remarked, "to see some sense you don't possess."

Well, he produced one on the spot. "The moral, dear Mrs. Assingham. I mean, always, as you others consider it. I've of course something that in our poor dear backward old Rome sufficiently passes for it. But it's no more like yours than the tortuous stone staircase—half-ruined into the bargain!—in some castle of our quattrocento is like the `lightning elevator' in one of Mr. Verver's fifteen-storey buildings. Your moral sense works by steam—it sends you up like a rocket. Ours is slow and steep and unlighted, with so many of the steps missing that—well, that it's as short, in almost any case, to turn round and come down again."

"Trusting," Mrs. Assingham smiled, "to get up some other way?"

"Yes—or not to have to get up at all. However," he added, "I told you that at the beginning."

"Machiavelli!" she simply exclaimed.

"You do me too much honour. I wish indeed I had his genius. However, if you really believe I have his perversity you wouldn't say it. But it's all right," he gaily enough concluded; "I shall always have you to come to."

On this, for a little, they sat face to face; after which, without comment, she asked him if he would have more tea. All she would give him, he promptly signified; and he developed, making her laugh, his idea that the tea of the English race was somehow their morality, "made," with boiling water, in a little pot, so that the more of it one drank the more moral one would become. His drollery served as a transition, and she put to him several questions about his sister and the others, questions as to what Bob, in particular, Colonel Assingham, her husband, could do for the arriving gentlemen, whom, by the Prince's leave, he would immediately go to see. He was funny, while they talked, about his own people too, whom he described, with anecdotes of their habits, imitations of their manners and prophecies of their conduct, as more rococo than anything Cadogan Place would ever have known. This, Mrs. Assingham professed, was exactly what would endear them to her, and that, in turn, drew from her visitor a fresh declaration of all the comfort of his being able so to depend on her. He had been with her, at this point, some twenty minutes; but he had paid her much longer visits, and he stayed now as if to make his attitude prove his appreciation. He stayed moreover—THAT was really the sign of the hour—in spite of the nervous unrest that had brought him and that had in truth much rather fed on the scepticism by which she had apparently meant to soothe it. She had not soothed him, and there arrived, remarkably, a moment when the cause of her failure gleamed out. He had not frightened her, as she called it—he felt that; yet she was herself not at ease. She had been nervous, though trying to disguise it; the sight of him, following on the announcement of his name, had shown her as disconcerted. This conviction, for the young man, deepened and sharpened; yet with the effect, too, of making him glad in spite of it. It was as if, in calling, he had done even better than he intended. For it was somehow IMPORTANT—that was what it was—that there should be at this hour something the matter with Mrs. Assingham, with whom, in all their acquaintance, so considerable now, there had never been the least little thing the matter. To wait thus and watch for it was to know, of a truth, that there was something the matter with HIM; since strangely, with so little to go upon—his heart had positively begun to beat to the tune of suspense. It fairly befell at last, for a climax, that they almost ceased to pretend—to pretend, that is, to cheat each other with forms. The unspoken had come up, and there was a crisis—neither could have said how long it lasted—during which they were reduced, for all interchange, to looking at each other on quite an inordinate scale. They might at this moment, in their positively portentous stillness, have been keeping it up for a wager, sitting for their photograph or even enacting a tableau-vivant.

The spectator of whom they would thus well have been worthy might have read meanings of his own into the intensity of their communion—or indeed, even without meanings, have found his account, aesthetically, in some gratified play of our modern sense of type, so scantly to be distinguished from our modern sense of beauty. Type was there, at the worst, in Mrs. Assingham's dark, neat head, on which the crisp black hair made waves so fine and so numerous that she looked even more in the fashion of the hour than she desired. Full of discriminations against the obvious, she had yet to accept a flagrant appearance and to make the best of misleading signs. Her richness of hue, her generous nose, her eyebrows marked like those of an actress—these things, with an added amplitude of person on which middle age had set its seal, seemed to present her insistently as a daughter of the south, or still more of the east, a creature formed by hammocks and divans, fed upon sherbets and waited upon by slaves. She looked as if her most active effort might be to take up, as she lay back, her mandolin, or to share a sugared fruit with a pet gazelle. She was in fact, however, neither a pampered Jewess nor a lazy Creole; New York had been, recordedly, her birthplace and "Europe" punctually her discipline. She wore yellow and purple because she thought it better, as she said, while one was about it, to look like the Queen of Sheba than like a revendeuse; she put pearls in her hair and crimson and gold in her tea-gown for the same reason: it was her theory that nature itself had overdressed her and that her only course was to drown, as it was hopeless to try to chasten, the overdressing. So she was covered and surrounded with "things," which were frankly toys and shams, a part of the amusement with which she rejoiced to supply her friends. These friends were in the game that of playing with the disparity between her aspect and her character. Her character was attested by the second movement of her face, which convinced the beholder that her vision of the humours of the world was not supine, not passive. She enjoyed, she needed the warm air of friendship, but the eyes of the American city looked out, somehow, for the opportunity of it, from under the lids of Jerusalem. With her false indolence, in short, her false leisure, her false pearls and palms and courts and fountains, she was a person for whom life was multitudinous detail, detail that left her, as it at any moment found her, unappalled and unwearied.

"Sophisticated as I may appear"—it was her frequent phrase—she had found sympathy her best resource. It gave her plenty to do; it made her, as she also said, sit up. She had in her life two great holes to fill, and she described herself as dropping social scraps into them as she had known old ladies, in her early American time, drop morsels of silk into the baskets in which they collected the material for some eventual patchwork quilt.

One of these gaps in Mrs. Assingham's completeness was her want of children; the other was her want of wealth. It was wonderful how little either, in the fulness of time, came to show; sympathy and curiosity could render their objects practically filial, just as an English husband who in his military years had "run" everything in his regiment could make economy blossom like the rose. Colonel Bob had, a few years after his marriage, left the army, which had clearly, by that time, done its laudable all for the enrichment of his personal experience, and he could thus give his whole time to the gardening in question. There reigned among the younger friends of this couple a legend, almost too venerable for historical criticism, that the marriage itself, the happiest of its class, dated from the far twilight of the age, a primitive period when such things—such things as American girls accepted as "good enough"—had not begun to be;—so that the pleasant pair had been, as to the risk taken on either side, bold and original, honourably marked, for the evening of life, as discoverers of a kind of hymeneal Northwest Passage. Mrs. Assingham knew better, knew there had been no historic hour, from that of Pocahontas down, when some young Englishman hadn't precipitately believed and some American girl hadn't, with a few more gradations, availed herself to the full of her incapacity to doubt; but she accepted resignedly the laurel of the founder, since she was in fact pretty well the doyenne, above ground, of her transplanted tribe, and since, above all, she HAD invented combinations, though she had not invented Bob's own. It was he who had done that, absolutely puzzled it out, by himself, from his first odd glimmer-resting upon it moreover, through the years to come, as proof enough, in him, by itself, of the higher cleverness. If she kept her own cleverness up it was largely that he should have full credit. There were moments in truth when she privately felt how little—striking out as he had done—he could have afforded that she should show the common limits. But Mrs. Assingham's cleverness was in truth tested when her present visitor at last said to her: "I don't think, you know, that you're treating me quite right. You've something on your mind that you don't tell me."

It was positive too that her smile, in reply, was a trifle dim. "Am I obliged to tell you everything I have on my mind?"

"It isn't a question of everything, but it's a question of anything that may particularly concern me. Then you shouldn't keep it back. You know with what care I desire to proceed, taking everything into account and making no mistake that may possibly injure HER."

Mrs. Assingham, at this, had after an instant an odd interrogation. "'Her'?"

"Her and him. Both our friends. Either Maggie or her father."

"I have something on my mind," Mrs. Assingham presently returned; "something has happened for which I hadn't been prepared. But it isn't anything that properly concerns you."

The Prince, with immediate gaiety, threw back his head. "What do you mean by 'properly'? I somehow see volumes in it. It's the way people put a thing when they put it—well, wrong. I put things right. What is it that has happened for me?"

His hostess, the next moment, had drawn spirit from his tone.

"Oh, I shall be delighted if you'll take your share of it. Charlotte Stant is in London. She has just been here."

"Miss Stant? Oh really?" The Prince expressed clear surprise—a transparency through which his eyes met his friend's with a certain hardness of concussion. "She has arrived from America?" he then quickly asked.

"She appears to have arrived this noon—coming up from Southampton; at an hotel. She dropped upon me after luncheon and was here for more than an hour."

The young man heard with interest, though not with an interest too great for his gaiety. "You think then I've a share in it? What IS my share?"

"Why, any you like—the one you seemed just now eager to take. It was you yourself who insisted."

He looked at her on this with conscious inconsistency, and she could now see that he had changed colour. But he was always easy. "I didn't know then what the matter was."

"You didn't think it could be so bad?"

"Do you call it very bad?" the young man asked. "Only," she smiled, "because that's the way it seems to affect YOU."

He hesitated, still with the trace of his quickened colour, still looking at her, still adjusting his manner. "But you allowed you were upset."

"To the extent—yes—of not having in the least looked for her. Any more," said Mrs. Assingham, "than I judge Maggie to have done." The Prince thought; then as if glad to be able to say something very natural and true: "No—quite right. Maggie hasn't looked for her. But I'm sure," he added, "she'll be delighted to see her."

"That, certainly"—and his hostess spoke with a different shade of gravity.

"She'll be quite overjoyed," the Prince went on. "Has Miss Stant now gone to her?"

"She has gone back to her hotel, to bring her things here. I can't have her," said Mrs. Assingham, "alone at an hotel."

"No; I see."

"If she's here at all she must stay with me." He quite took it in. "So she's coming now?"

"I expect her at any moment. If you wait you'll see her."

"Oh," he promptly declared—"charming!" But this word came out as if, a little, in sudden substitution for some other. It sounded accidental, whereas he wished to be firm. That accordingly was what he next showed himself. "If it wasn't for what's going on these next days Maggie would certainly want to have her. In fact," he lucidly continued, "isn't what's happening just a reason to MAKE her want to?" Mrs. Assingham, for answer, only looked at him, and this, the next instant, had apparently had more effect than if she had spoken. For he asked a question that seemed incongruous. "What has she come for!"

It made his companion laugh. "Why, for just what you say. For your marriage."

"Mine?"—he wondered.

"Maggie's—it's the same thing. It's 'for' your great event. And then," said Mrs. Assingham, "she's so lonely."

"Has she given you that as a reason?"

"I scarcely remember—she gave me so many. She abounds, poor dear, in reasons. But there's one that, whatever she does, I always remember for myself."

"And which is that?" He looked as if he ought to guess but couldn't.

"Why, the fact that she has no home—absolutely none whatever. She's extraordinarily alone."

Again he took it in. "And also has no great means."

"Very small ones. Which is not, however, with the expense of railways and hotels, a reason for her running to and fro."

"On the contrary. But she doesn't like her country."

"Hers, my dear man?—it's little enough 'hers.'" The attribution, for the moment, amused his hostess. "She has rebounded now—but she has had little enough else to do with it."

"Oh, I say hers," the Prince pleasantly explained, "very much as, at this time of day, I might say mine. I quite feel, I assure you, as if the great place already more or less belonged to ME."

"That's your good fortune and your point of view. You own—or you soon practically WILL own—so much of it. Charlotte owns almost nothing in the world, she tells me, but two colossal trunks-only one of which I have given her leave to introduce into this house. She'll depreciate to you," Mrs. Assingham added, "your property."

He thought of these things, he thought of every thing; but he had always his resource at hand of turning all to the easy. "Has she come with designs upon me?" And then in a moment, as if even this were almost too grave, he sounded the note that had least to do with himself. "Est-elle toujours aussi belle?" That was the furthest point, somehow, to which Charlotte Stant could be relegated.

Mrs. Assingham treated it freely. "Just the same. The person in the world, to my sense, whose looks are most subject to appreciation. It's all in the way she affects you. One admires her if one doesn't happen not to. So, as well, one criticises her."

"Ah, that's not fair!" said the Prince.

"To criticise her? Then there you are! You've answered."

"I'm answered." He took it, humorously, as his lesson—sank his previous self-consciousness, with excellent effect, in grateful docility. "I only meant that there are perhaps better things to be done with Miss Stant than to criticise her. When once you begin THAT, with anyone—!" He was vague and kind.

"I quite agree that it's better to keep out of it as long as one can. But when one MUST do it—"

"Yes?" he asked as she paused. "Then know what you mean."

"I see. Perhaps," he smiled, "I don't know what I mean."

"Well, it's what, just now, in all ways, you particularly should know." Mrs. Assingham, however, made no more of this, having, before anything else, apparently, a scruple about the tone she had just used. "I quite understand, of course, that, given her great friendship with Maggie, she should have wanted to be present. She has acted impulsively—but she has acted generously."

"She has acted beautifully," said the Prince.

"I say 'generously' because I mean she hasn't, in any way, counted the cost. She'll have it to count, in a manner, now," his hostess continued. "But that doesn't matter."

He could see how little. "You'll look after her."

"I'll look after her."

"So it's all right."

"It's all right," said Mrs. Assingham. "Then why are you troubled?"

It pulled her up—but only for a minute. "I'm not—any more than you."

The Prince's dark blue eyes were of the finest, and, on occasion, precisely, resembled nothing so much as the high windows of a Roman palace, of an historic front by one of the great old designers, thrown open on a feast-day to the golden air. His look itself, at such times, suggested an image—that of some very noble personage who, expected, acclaimed by the crowd in the street and with old precious stuffs falling over the sill for his support, had gaily and gallantly come to show himself: always moreover less in his own interest than in that of spectators and subjects whose need to admire, even to gape, was periodically to be considered. The young man's expression became, after this fashion, something vivid and concrete—a beautiful personal presence, that of a prince in very truth, a ruler, warrior, patron, lighting up brave architecture and diffusing the sense of a function. It had been happily said of his face that the figure thus appearing in the great frame was the ghost of some proudest ancestor. Whoever the ancestor now, at all events, the Prince was, for Mrs. Assingham's benefit, in view of the people. He seemed, leaning on crimson damask, to take in the bright day. He looked younger than his years; he was beautiful, innocent, vague.

"Oh, well, I'M not!" he rang out clear.

"I should like to SEE you, sir!" she said. "For you wouldn't have a shadow of excuse." He showed how he agreed that he would have been at a loss for one, and the fact of their serenity was thus made as important as if some danger of its opposite had directly menaced them. The only thing was that if the evidence of their cheer was so established Mrs. Assingham had a little to explain her original manner, and she came to this before they dropped the question. "My first impulse is always to behave, about everything, as if I feared complications. But I don't fear them—I really like them. They're quite my element."

He deferred, for her, to this account of herself. "But still," he said, "if we're not in the presence of a complication."

She hesitated. "A handsome, clever, odd girl staying with one is always a complication."

The young man weighed it almost as if the question were new to him. "And will she stay very long?"

His friend gave a laugh. "How in the world can I know? I've scarcely asked her."

"Ah yes. You can't."

But something in the tone of it amused her afresh. "Do you think you could?"

"I?" he wondered.

"Do you think you could get it out of her for me—the probable length of her stay?"

He rose bravely enough to the occasion and the challenge. "I daresay, if you were to give me the chance."

"Here it is then for you," she answered; for she had heard, within the minute, the stop of a cab at her door. "She's back."

III

It had been said as a joke, but as, after this, they awaited their friend in silence, the effect of the silence was to turn the time to gravity—a gravity not dissipated even when the Prince next spoke. He had been thinking the case over and making up his mind. A handsome, clever, odd girl staying with one was a complication. Mrs. Assingham, so far, was right. But there were the facts—the good relations, from schooldays, of the two young women, and the clear confidence with which one of them had arrived. "She can come, you know, at any time, to US."

Mrs. Assingham took it up with an irony beyond laughter. "You'd like her for your honeymoon?"

"Oh no, you must keep her for that. But why not after?"

She had looked at him a minute; then, at the sound of a voice in the corridor, they had got up. "Why not? You're splendid!" Charlotte Stant, the next minute, was with them, ushered in as she had alighted from her cab, and prepared for not finding Mrs. Assingham alone—this would have been to be noticed—by the butler's answer, on the stairs, to a question put to him. She could have looked at her hostess with such straightness and brightness only from knowing that the Prince was also there—the discrimination of but a moment, yet which let him take her in still better than if she had instantly faced him. He availed himself of the chance thus given him, for he was like a lamp she was holding aloft for his benefit and for his pleasure. It showed him everything—above all her presence in the world, so closely, so irretrievably contemporaneous with his own: a sharp, sharp fact, sharper during these instants than any other at all, even than that of his marriage, but accompanied, in a subordinate and controlled way, with those others, facial, physiognomic, that Mrs. Assingham had been speaking of as subject to appreciation. So they were, these others, as he met them again, and that was the connection they instantly established with her. If they had to be interpreted, this made at least for intimacy. There was but one way certainly for HIM—to interpret them in the sense of the already known.

Making use then of clumsy terms of excess, the face was too narrow and too long, the eyes not large, and the mouth, on the other hand, by no means small, with substance in its lips and a slight, the very slightest, tendency to protrusion in the solid teeth, otherwise indeed well arrayed and flashingly white. But it was, strangely, as a cluster of possessions of his own that these things, in Charlotte Stant, now affected him; items in a full list, items recognised, each of them, as if, for the long interval, they had been "stored" wrapped up, numbered, put away in a cabinet. While she faced Mrs. Assingham the door of the cabinet had opened of itself; he took the relics out, one by one, and it was more and more, each instant, as if she were giving him time. He saw again that her thick hair was, vulgarly speaking, brown, but that there was a shade of tawny autumn leaf in it, for "appreciation"—a colour indescribable and of which he had known no other case, something that gave her at moments the sylvan head of a huntress. He saw the sleeves of her jacket drawn to her wrists, but he again made out the free arms within them to be of the completely rounded, the polished slimness that Florentine sculptors, in the great time, had loved, and of which the apparent firmness is expressed in their old silver and old bronze. He knew her narrow hands, he knew her long fingers and the shape and colour of her finger-nails, he knew her special beauty of movement and line when she turned her back, and the perfect working of all her main attachments, that of some wonderful finished instrument, something intently made for exhibition, for a prize. He knew above all the extraordinary fineness of her flexible waist, the stem of an expanded flower, which gave her a likeness also to some long, loose silk purse, well filled with gold pieces, but having been passed, empty, through a finger-ring that held it together. It was as if, before she turned to him, he had weighed the whole thing in his open palm and even heard a little the chink of the metal. When she did turn to him it was to recognise with her eyes what he might have been doing. She made no circumstance of thus coming upon him, save so far as the intelligence in her face could at any moment make a circumstance of almost anything. If when she moved off she looked like a huntress, she looked when she came nearer like his notion, perhaps not wholly correct, of a muse. But what she said was simply: "You see you're not rid of me. How is dear Maggie?"

It was to come soon enough by the quite unforced operation of chance, the young man's opportunity to ask her the question suggested by Mrs. Assingham shortly before her entrance. The license, had he chosen to embrace it, was within a few minutes all there—the license given him literally to inquire of this young lady how long she was likely to be with them. For a matter of the mere domestic order had quickly determined, on Mrs. Assingham's part, a withdrawal, of a few moments, which had the effect of leaving her visitors free. "Mrs. Betterman's there?" she had said to Charlotte in allusion to some member of the household who was to have received her and seen her belongings settled; to which Charlotte had replied that she had encountered only the butler, who had been quite charming. She had deprecated any action taken on behalf of her effects; but her hostess, rebounding from accumulated cushions, evidently saw more in Mrs. Betterman's non-appearance than could meet the casual eye. What she saw, in short, demanded her intervention, in spite of an earnest "Let ME go!" from the girl, and a prolonged smiling wail over the trouble she was giving. The Prince was quite aware, at this moment, that departure, for himself, was indicated; the question of Miss Stant's installation didn't demand his presence; it was a case for one to go away—if one hadn't a reason for staying. He had a reason, however—of that he was equally aware; and he had not for a good while done anything more conscious and intentional than not, quickly, to take leave. His visible insistence—for it came to that—even demanded of him a certain disagreeable effort, the sort of effort he had mostly associated with acting for an idea. His idea was there, his idea was to find out something, something he wanted much to know, and to find it out now tomorrow, not at some future time, not in short with waiting and wondering, but if possible before quitting the place. This particular curiosity, moreover, confounded itself a little with the occasion offered him to satisfy Mrs. Assingham's own; he wouldn't have admitted that he was staying to ask a rude question—there was distinctly nothing rude in his having his reasons. It would be rude, for that matter, to turn one's back, without a word or two, on an old friend.

Well, as it came to pass, he got the word or two, for Mrs. Assingham's preoccupation was practically simplifying. The little crisis was of shorter duration than our account of it; duration, naturally, would have forced him to take up his hat. He was somehow glad, on finding himself alone with Charlotte, that he had not been guilty of that inconsequence. Not to be flurried was the kind of consistency he wanted, just as consistency was the kind of dignity. And why couldn't he have dignity when he had so much of the good conscience, as it were, on which such advantages rested? He had done nothing he oughtn't—he had in fact done nothing at all. Once more, as a man conscious of having known many women, he could assist, as he would have called it, at the recurrent, the predestined phenomenon, the thing always as certain as sunrise or the coming round of Saints' days, the doing by the woman of the thing that gave her away. She did it, ever, inevitably, infallibly—she couldn't possibly not do it. It was her nature, it was her life, and the man could always expect it without lifting a finger. This was HIS, the man's, any man's, position and strength—that he had necessarily the advantage, that he only had to wait, with a decent patience, to be placed, in spite of himself, it might really be said, in the right. Just so the punctuality of performance on the part of the other creature was her weakness and her deep misfortune—not less, no doubt, than her beauty. It produced for the man that extraordinary mixture of pity and profit in which his relation with her, when he was not a mere brute, mainly consisted; and gave him in fact his most pertinent ground of being always nice to her, nice about her, nice FOR her. She always dressed her act up, of course, she muffled and disguised and arranged it, showing in fact in these dissimulations a cleverness equal to but one thing in the world, equal to her abjection: she would let it be known for anything, for everything, but the truth of which it was made. That was what, precisely, Charlotte Stant would be doing now; that was the present motive and support, to a certainty, of each of her looks and motions. She was the twentieth woman, she was possessed by her doom, but her doom was also to arrange appearances, and what now concerned him was to learn how she proposed. He would help her, would arrange WITH her to any point in reason; the only thing was to know what appearance could be produced and best be preserved. Produced and preserved on her part of course; since on his own there had been luckily no folly to cover up, nothing but a perfect accord between conduct and obligation.

They stood there together, at all events, when the door had closed behind their friend, with a conscious, strained smile and very much as if each waited for the other to strike the note or give the pitch. The young man held himself, in his silent suspense—only not more afraid because he felt her own fear. She was afraid of herself, however; whereas, to his gain of lucidity, he was afraid only of her. Would she throw herself into his arms, or would she be otherwise wonderful? She would see what he would do—so their queer minute without words told him; and she would act accordingly. But what could he do but just let her see that he would make anything, everything, for her, as honourably easy as possible? Even if she should throw herself into his arms he would make that easy—easy, that is, to overlook, to ignore, not to remember, and not, by the same token, either, to regret. This was not what in fact happened, though it was also not at a single touch, but by the finest gradations, that his tension subsided. "It's too delightful to be back!" she said at last; and it was all she definitely gave him—being moreover nothing but what anyone else might have said. Yet with two or three other things that, on his response, followed it, it quite pointed the path, while the tone of it, and her whole attitude, were as far removed as need have been from the truth of her situation. The abjection that was present to him as of the essence quite failed to peep out, and he soon enough saw that if she was arranging she could be trusted to arrange. Good—it was all he asked; and all the more that he could admire and like her for it.

The particular appearance she would, as they said, go in for was that of having no account whatever to give him—it would be in fact that of having none to give anybody—of reasons or of motives, of comings or of goings. She was a charming young woman who had met him before, but she was also a charming young woman with a life of her own. She would take it high—up, up, up, ever so high. Well then, he would do the same; no height would be too great for them, not even the dizziest conceivable to a young person so subtle. The dizziest seemed indeed attained when, after another moment, she came as near as she was to come to an apology for her abruptness.

"I've been thinking of Maggie, and at last I yearned for her. I wanted to see her happy—and it doesn't strike me I find you too shy to tell me I SHALL."

"Of course she's happy, thank God! Only it's almost terrible, you know, the happiness of young, good, generous creatures. It rather frightens one. But the Blessed Virgin and all the Saints," said the Prince, "have her in their keeping."

"Certainly they have. She's the dearest of the dear. But I needn't tell you," the girl added.

"Ah," he returned with gravity, "I feel that I've still much to learn about her." To which he subjoined "She'll rejoice awfully in your being with us."

"Oh, you don't need me!" Charlotte smiled. "It's her hour. It's a great hour. One has seen often enough, with girls, what it is. But that," she said, "is exactly why. Why I've wanted, I mean, not to miss it."

He bent on her a kind, comprehending face. "You mustn't miss anything." He had got it, the pitch, and he could keep it now, for all he had needed was to have it given him. The pitch was the happiness of his wife that was to be—the sight of that happiness as a joy for an old friend. It was, yes, magnificent, and not the less so for its coming to him, suddenly, as sincere, as nobly exalted. Something in Charlotte's eyes seemed to tell him this, seemed to plead with him in advance as to what he was to find in it. He was eager—and he tried to show her that too—to find what she liked; mindful as he easily could be of what the friendship had been for Maggie. It had been armed with the wings of young imagination, young generosity; it had been, he believed—always counting out her intense devotion to her father—the liveliest emotion she had known before the dawn of the sentiment inspired by himself. She had not, to his knowledge, invited the object of it to their wedding, had not thought of proposing to her, for a matter of a couple of hours, an arduous and expensive journey. But she had kept her connected and informed, from week to week, in spite of preparations and absorptions. "Oh, I've been writing to Charlotte—I wish you knew her better:" he could still hear, from recent weeks, this record of the fact, just as he could still be conscious, not otherwise than queerly, of the gratuitous element in Maggie's wish, which he had failed as yet to indicate to her. Older and perhaps more intelligent, at any rate, why shouldn't Charlotte respond—and be quite FREE to respond—to such fidelities with something more than mere formal good manners? The relations of women with each other were of the strangest, it was true, and he probably wouldn't have trusted here a young person of his own race. He was proceeding throughout on the ground of the immense difference—difficult indeed as it might have been to disembroil in this young person HER race-quality. Nothing in her definitely placed her; she was a rare, a special product. Her singleness, her solitude, her want of means, that is her want of ramifications and other advantages, contributed to enrich her somehow with an odd, precious neutrality, to constitute for her, so detached yet so aware, a sort of small social capital. It was the only one she had—it was the only one a lonely, gregarious girl COULD have, since few, surely, had in anything like the same degree arrived at it, and since this one indeed had compassed it but through the play of some gift of nature to which you could scarce give a definite name.

It wasn't a question of her strange sense for tongues, with which she juggled as a conjuror at a show juggled with balls or hoops or lighted brands—it wasn't at least entirely that, for he had known people almost as polyglot whom their accomplishment had quite failed to make interesting. He was polyglot himself, for that matter—as was the case too with so many of his friends and relations; for none of whom, more than for himself, was it anything but a common convenience. The point was that in this young woman it was a beauty in itself, and almost a mystery: so, certainly, he had more than once felt in noting, on her lips, that rarest, among the Barbarians, of all civil graces, a perfect felicity in the use of Italian. He had known strangers—a few, and mostly men—who spoke his own language agreeably; but he had known neither man nor woman who showed for it Charlotte's almost mystifying instinct. He remembered how, from the first of their acquaintance, she had made no display of it, quite as if English, between them, his English so matching with hers, were their inevitable medium. He had perceived all by accident—by hearing her talk before him to somebody else that they had an alternative as good; an alternative in fact as much better as the amusement for him was greater in watching her for the slips that never came. Her account of the mystery didn't suffice: her recall of her birth in Florence and Florentine childhood; her parents, from the great country, but themselves already of a corrupt generation, demoralised, falsified, polyglot well before her, with the Tuscan balia who was her first remembrance; the servants of the villa, the dear contadini of the poder, the little girls and the other peasants of the next podere, all the rather shabby but still ever so pretty human furniture of her early time, including the good sisters of the poor convent of the Tuscan hills, the convent shabbier than almost anything else, but prettier too, in which she had been kept at school till the subsequent phase, the phase of the much grander institution in Paris at which Maggie was to arrive, terribly frightened, and as a smaller girl, three years before her own ending of her period of five. Such reminiscences, naturally, gave a ground, but they had not prevented him from insisting that some strictly civil ancestor—generations back, and from the Tuscan hills if she would-made himself felt, ineffaceably, in her blood and in her tone. She knew nothing of the ancestor, but she had taken his theory from him, gracefully enough, as one of the little presents that make friendship flourish. These matters, however, all melted together now, though a sense of them was doubtless concerned, not unnaturally, in the next thing, of the nature of a surmise, that his discretion let him articulate. "You haven't, I rather gather, particularly liked your country?" They would stick, for the time, to their English.

"It doesn't, I fear, seem particularly mine. And it doesn't in the least matter, over there, whether one likes it or not—that is to anyone but one's self. But I didn't like it," said Charlotte Stant.

"That's not encouraging then to me, is it?" the Prince went on.

"Do you mean because you're going?"

"Oh yes, of course we're going. I've wanted immensely to go." She hesitated. "But now?—immediately?"

"In a month or two—it seems to be the new idea." On which there was something in her face—as he imagined—that made him say: "Didn't Maggie write to you?"

"Not of your going at once. But of course you must go. And of course you must stay"—Charlotte was easily clear—"as long as possible."

"Is that what you did?" he laughed. "You stayed as long as possible?"

"Well, it seemed to me so—but I hadn't 'interests.' You'll have them—on a great scale. It's the country for interests," said Charlotte. "If I had only had a few I doubtless wouldn't have left it."

He waited an instant; they were still on their feet. "Yours then are rather here?"

"Oh, mine!"—the girl smiled. "They take up little room, wherever they are."

It determined in him, the way this came from her and what it somehow did for her-it determined in him a speech that would have seemed a few minutes before precarious and in questionable taste. The lead she had given him made the difference, and he felt it as really a lift on finding an honest and natural word rise, by its license, to his lips. Nothing surely could be, for both of them, more in the note of a high bravery. "I've been thinking it all the while so probable, you know, that you would have seen your way to marrying."

She looked at him an instant, and, just for these seconds, he feared for what he might have spoiled. "To marrying whom?"

"Why, some good, kind, clever, rich American."

Again his security hung in the balance—then she was, as he felt, admirable.

"I tried everyone I came across. I did my best. I showed I had come, quite publicly, FOR that. Perhaps I showed it too much. At any rate it was no use. I had to recognise it. No one would have me." Then she seemed to show so sorry for his having to hear of her anything so disconcerting. She pitied his feeling about it; if he was disappointed she would cheer him up. "Existence, you know, all the same, doesn't depend on that. I mean," she smiled, "on having caught a husband."

"Oh—existence!" the Prince vaguely commented. "You think I ought to argue for more than mere existence?" she asked. "I don't see why MY existence—even reduced as much as you like to being merely mine—should be so impossible. There are things, of sorts, I should be able to have—things I should be able to be. The position of a single woman to-day is very favourable, you know."

"Favourable to what?"

"Why, just TO existence—which may contain, after all, in one way and another, so much. It may contain, at the worst, even affections; affections in fact quite particularly; fixed, that is, on one's friends. I'm extremely fond of Maggie, for instance—I quite adore her. How could I adore her more if I were married to one of the people you speak of?"

The Prince gave a laugh. "You might adore HIM more—!"

"Ah, but it isn't, is it?" she asked, "a question of that."

"My dear friend," he returned, "it's always a question of doing the best for one's self one can—without injury to others." He felt by this time that they were indeed on an excellent basis; so he went on again, as if to show frankly his sense of its firmness. "I venture therefore to repeat my hope that you'll marry some capital fellow; and also to repeat my belief that such a marriage will be more favourable to you, as you call it, than even the spirit of the age."

She looked at him at first only for answer, and would have appeared to take it with meekness had she not perhaps appeared a little more to take it with gaiety. "Thank you very much," she simply said; but at that moment their friend was with them again. It was undeniable that, as she came in, Mrs. Assingham looked, with a certain smiling sharpness, from one of them to the other; the perception of which was perhaps what led Charlotte, for reassurance, to pass the question on. "The Prince hopes so much I shall still marry some good person."

Whether it worked for Mrs. Assingham or not, the Prince was himself, at this, more than ever reassured. He was SAFE, in a word—that was what it all meant; and he had required to be safe. He was really safe enough for almost any joke. "It's only," he explained to their hostess, "because of what Miss Stant has been telling me. Don't we want to keep up her courage?" If the joke was broad he had at least not begun it—not, that is, AS a joke; which was what his companion's address to their friend made of it. "She has been trying in America, she says, but hasn't brought it off."

The tone was somehow not what Mrs. Assingham had expected, but she made the best of it. "Well then," she replied to the young man, "if you take such an interest you must bring it off."

"And you must help, dear," Charlotte said unperturbed—"as you've helped, so beautifully, in such things before." With which, before Mrs. Assingham could meet the appeal, she had addressed herself to the Prince on a matter much nearer to him. "YOUR marriage is on Friday?—on Saturday?"

"Oh, on Friday, no! For what do you take us? There's not a vulgar omen we're neglecting. On Saturday, please, at the Oratory, at three o'clock—before twelve assistants exactly."

"Twelve including ME?"

It struck him—he laughed. "You'll make the thirteenth. It won't do!"

"Not," said Charlotte, "if you're going in for 'omens.' Should you like me to stay away?"

"Dear no—we'll manage. We'll make the round number—we'll have in some old woman. They must keep them there for that, don't they?"

Mrs. Assingham's return had at last indicated for him his departure; he had possessed himself again of his hat and approached her to take leave. But he had another word for Charlotte. "I dine to-night with Mr. Verver. Have you any message?"

The girl seemed to wonder a little. "For Mr. Verver?"

"For Maggie—about her seeing you early. That, I know, is what she'll like."

"Then I'll come early—thanks."

"I daresay," he went on, "she'll send for you. I mean send a carriage."

"Oh, I don't require that, thanks. I can go, for a penny, can't I?" she asked of Mrs. Assingham, "in an omnibus."

"Oh, I say!" said the Prince while Mrs. Assingham looked at her blandly.

"Yes, love—and I'll give you the penny. She shall get there," the good lady added to their friend.

But Charlotte, as the latter took leave of her, thought of something else. "There's a great favour, Prince, that I want to ask of you. I want, between this and Saturday, to make Maggie a marriage-present."

"Oh, I say!" the young man again soothingly exclaimed.

"Ah, but I MUST," she went on. "It's really almost for that I came back. It was impossible to get in America what I wanted."

Mrs. Assingham showed anxiety. "What is it then, dear, you want?"

But the girl looked only at their companion. "That's what the Prince, if he'll be so good, must help me to decide."

"Can't I," Mrs. Assingham asked, "help you to decide?"

"Certainly, darling, we must talk it well over." And she kept her eyes on the Prince. "But I want him, if he kindly will, to go with me to look. I want him to judge with me and choose. That, if you can spare the hour," she said, "is the great favour I mean."

He raised his eyebrows at her—he wonderfully smiled. "What you came back from America to ask? Ah, certainly then, I must find the hour!" He wonderfully smiled, but it was rather more, after all, than he had been reckoning with. It went somehow so little with the rest that, directly, for him, it wasn't the note of safety; it preserved this character, at the best, but by being the note of publicity. Quickly, quickly, however, the note of publicity struck him as better than any other. In another moment even it seemed positively what he wanted; for what so much as publicity put their relation on the right footing? By this appeal to Mrs. Assingham it was established as right, and she immediately showed that such was her own understanding.

"Certainly, Prince," she laughed, "you must find the hour!" And it was really so express a license from her, as representing friendly judgment, public opinion, the moral law, the margin allowed a husband about to be, or whatever, that, after observing to Charlotte that, should she come to Portland Place in the morning, he would make a point of being there to see her and so, easily, arrange with her about a time, he took his departure with the absolutely confirmed impression of knowing, as he put it to himself, where he was. Which was what he had prolonged his visit for. He was where he could stay.

IV

"I don't quite see, my dear," Colonel Assingham said to his wife the night of Charlotte's arrival, "I don't quite see, I'm bound to say, why you take it, even at the worst, so ferociously hard. It isn't your fault, after all, is it? I'll be hanged, at any rate, if it's mine."

The hour was late, and the young lady who had disembarked at Southampton that morning to come up by the "steamer special," and who had then settled herself at an hotel only to re-settle herself a couple of hours later at a private house, was by this time, they might hope, peacefully resting from her exploits. There had been two men at dinner, rather battered brothers-in-arms, of his own period, casually picked up by her host the day before, and when the gentlemen, after the meal, rejoined the ladies in the drawing-room, Charlotte, pleading fatigue, had already excused herself. The beguiled warriors, however, had stayed till after eleven—Mrs. Assingham, though finally quite without illusions, as she said, about the military character, was always beguiling to old soldiers; and as the Colonel had come in, before dinner, only in time to dress, he had not till this moment really been summoned to meet his companion over the situation that, as he was now to learn, their visitor's advent had created for them. It was actually more than midnight, the servants had been sent to bed, the rattle of the wheels had ceased to come in through a window still open to the August air, and Robert Assingham had been steadily learning, all the while, what it thus behoved him to know. But the words just quoted from him presented themselves, for the moment, as the essence of his spirit and his attitude. He disengaged, he would be damned if he didn't—they were both phrases he repeatedly used—his responsibility. The simplest, the sanest, the most obliging of men, he habitually indulged in extravagant language. His wife had once told him, in relation to his violence of speech; that such excesses, on his part, made her think of a retired General whom she had once seen playing with toy soldiers, fighting and winning battles, carrying on sieges and annihilating enemies with little fortresses of wood and little armies of tin. Her husband's exaggerated emphasis was his box of toy soldiers, his military game. It harmlessly gratified in him, for his declining years, the military instinct; bad words, when sufficiently numerous and arrayed in their might, could represent battalions, squadrons, tremendous cannonades and glorious charges of cavalry. It was natural, it was delightful—the romance, and for her as well, of camp life and of the perpetual booming of guns. It was fighting to the end, to the death, but no one was ever killed.

Less fortunate than she, nevertheless, in spite of his wealth of expression, he had not yet found the image that described her favourite game; all he could do was practically to leave it to her, emulating her own philosophy. He had again and again sat up late to discuss those situations in which her finer consciousness abounded, but he had never failed to deny that anything in life, anything of hers, could be a situation for himself. She might be in fifty at once if she liked—and it was what women did like, at their ease, after all; there always being, when they had too much of any, some man, as they were well aware, to get them out. He wouldn't at any price, have one, of any sort whatever, of his own, or even be in one along with her. He watched her, accordingly, in her favourite element, very much as he had sometimes watched, at the Aquarium, the celebrated lady who, in a slight, though tight, bathing-suit, turned somersaults and did tricks in the tank of water which looked so cold and uncomfortable to the non-amphibious. He listened to his companion to-night, while he smoked his last pipe, he watched her through her demonstration, quite as if he had paid a shilling. But it was true that, this being the case, he desired the value of his money. What was it, in the name of wonder, that she was so bent on being responsible FOR? What did she pretend was going to happen, and what, at the worst, could the poor girl do, even granting she wanted to do anything? What, at the worst, for that matter, could she be conceived to have in her head?

"If she had told me the moment she got here," Mrs. Assingham replied, "I shouldn't have my difficulty in finding out. But she wasn't so obliging, and I see no sign at all of her becoming so. What's certain is that she didn't come for nothing. She wants"—she worked it out at her leisure—"to see the Prince again. THAT isn't what troubles me. I mean that such a fact, as a fact, isn't. But what I ask myself is, What does she want it FOR?"

"What's the good of asking yourself if you know you don't know?" The Colonel sat back at his own ease, with an ankle resting on the other knee and his eyes attentive to the good appearance of an extremely slender foot which he kept jerking in its neat integument of fine-spun black silk and patent leather. It seemed to confess, this member, to consciousness of military discipline, everything about it being as polished and perfect, as straight and tight and trim, as a soldier on parade. It went so far as to imply that someone or other would have "got" something or other, confinement to barracks or suppression of pay, if it hadn't been just as it was. Bob Assingham was distinguished altogether by a leanness of person, a leanness quite distinct from physical laxity, which might have been determined, on the part of superior powers, by views of transport and accommodation, and which in fact verged on the abnormal. He "did" himself as well as his friends mostly knew, yet remained hungrily thin, with facial, with abdominal cavities quite grim in their effect, and with a consequent looseness of apparel that, combined with a choice of queer light shades and of strange straw-like textures, of the aspect of Chinese mats, provocative of wonder at his sources of supply, suggested the habit of tropic islands, a continual cane-bottomed chair, a governorship exercised on wide verandahs. His smooth round head, with the particular shade of its white hair, was like a silver pot reversed; his cheekbones and the bristle of his moustache were worthy of Attila the Hun. The hollows of his eyes were deep and darksome, but the eyes within them, were like little blue flowers plucked that morning. He knew everything that could be known about life, which he regarded as, for far the greater part, a matter of pecuniary arrangement. His wife accused him of a want, alike, of moral and of intellectual reaction, or rather indeed of a complete incapacity for either. He never went even so far as to understand what she meant, and it didn't at all matter, since he could be in spite of the limitation a perfectly social creature. The infirmities, the predicaments of men neither surprised nor shocked him, and indeed—which was perhaps his only real loss in a thrifty career—scarce even amused; he took them for granted without horror, classifying them after their kind and calculating results and chances. He might, in old bewildering climates, in old campaigns of cruelty and license, have had such revelations and known such amazements that he had nothing more to learn. But he was wholly content, in spite of his fondness, in domestic discussion, for the superlative degree; and his kindness, in the oddest way, seemed to have nothing to do with his experience. He could deal with things perfectly, for all his needs, without getting near them.

This was the way he dealt with his wife, a large proportion of whose meanings he knew he could neglect. He edited, for their general economy, the play of her mind, just as he edited, savingly, with the stump of a pencil, her redundant telegrams. The thing in the world that was least of a mystery to him was his Club, which he was accepted as perhaps too completely managing, and which he managed on lines of perfect penetration. His connection with it was really a master-piece of editing. This was in fact, to come back, very much the process he might have been proposing to apply to Mrs. Assingham's view of what was now before them; that is to their connection with Charlotte Stant's possibilities. They wouldn't lavish on them all their little fortune of curiosity and alarm; certainly they wouldn't spend their cherished savings so early in the day. He liked Charlotte, moreover, who was a smooth and compact inmate, and whom he felt as, with her instincts that made against waste, much more of his own sort than his wife. He could talk with her about Fanny almost better than he could talk with Fanny about Charlotte. However, he made at present the best of the latter necessity, even to the pressing of the question he has been noted as having last uttered. "If you can't think what to be afraid of, wait till you can think. Then you'll do it much better. Or otherwise, if that's waiting too long, find out from HER. Don't try to find out from ME. Ask her herself."

Mrs. Assingham denied, as we know, that her husband had a play of mind; so that she could, on her side, treat these remarks only as if they had been senseless physical gestures or nervous facial movements. She overlooked them as from habit and kindness; yet there was no one to whom she talked so persistently of such intimate things. "It's her friendship with Maggie that's the immense complication. Because THAT," she audibly mused, "is so natural."

"Then why can't she have come out for it?"

"She came out," Mrs. Assingham continued to meditate, "because she hates America. There was no place for her there—she didn't fit in. She wasn't in sympathy—no more were the people she saw. Then it's hideously dear; she can't, on her means, begin to live there. Not at all as she can, in a way, here."

"In the way, you mean, of living with US?"

"Of living with anyone. She can't live by visits alone—and she doesn't want to. She's too good for it even if she could. But she will—she MUST, sooner or later—stay with THEM. Maggie will want her—Maggie will make her. Besides, she'll want to herself."

"Then why won't that do," the Colonel asked, "for you to think it's what she has come for?"

"How will it do, HOW?"—she went on as without hearing him.

"That's what one keeps feeling."

"Why shouldn't it do beautifully?"

"That anything of the past," she brooded, "should come back NOW? How will it do, how will it do?"

"It will do, I daresay, without your wringing your hands over it. When, my dear," the Colonel pursued as he smoked, "have you ever seen anything of yours—anything that you've done—NOT do?"

"Ah, I didn't do this!" It brought her answer straight. "I didn't bring her back."

"Did you expect her to stay over there all her days to oblige you?"

"Not a bit—for I shouldn't have minded her coming after their marriage. It's her coming, this way, before." To which she added with inconsequence: "I'm too sorry for her—of course she can't enjoy it. But I don't see what perversity rides her. She needn't have looked it all so in the face—as she doesn't do it, I suppose, simply for discipline. It's almost—that's the bore of it—discipline to ME."

"Perhaps then," said Bob Assingham, "that's what has been her idea. Take it, for God's sake, as discipline to you and have done with it. It will do," he added, "for discipline to me as well."

She was far, however, from having done with it; it was a situation with such different sides, as she said, and to none of which one could, in justice, be blind. "It isn't in the least, you know, for instance, that I believe she's bad. Never, never," Mrs. Assingham declared. "I don't think that of her."

"Then why isn't that enough?"

Nothing was enough, Mrs. Assingham signified, but that she should develop her thought. "She doesn't deliberately intend, she doesn't consciously wish, the least complication. "I'm too sorry for her—of course she can't enjoy it—as who doesn't? She's incapable of any PLAN to hurt a hair of her head. Yet here she is—and there THEY are," she wound up.

Her husband again, for a little, smoked in silence. "What in the world, between them, ever took place?"

"Between Charlotte and the Prince? Why, nothing—except their having to recognise that nothing COULD. That was their little romance—it was even their little tragedy."

"But what the deuce did they DO?"

"Do? They fell in love with each other—but, seeing it wasn't possible, gave each other up."

"Then where was the romance?"

"Why, in their frustration, in their having the courage to look the facts in the face."

"What facts?" the Colonel went on.

"Well, to begin with, that of their neither of them having the means to marry. If she had had even a little—a little, I mean, for two—I believe he would bravely have done it." After which, as her husband but emitted an odd vague sound, she corrected herself. "I mean if he himself had had only a little—or a little more than a little, a little for a prince. They would have done what they could"—she did them justice—"if there had been a way. But there wasn't a way, and Charlotte, quite to her honour, I consider, understood it. He HAD to have money—it was a question of life and death. It wouldn't have been a bit amusing, either, to marry him as a pauper—I mean leaving him one. That was what she had—as HE had—the reason to see."

"And their reason is what you call their romance?"

She looked at him a moment. "What do you want more?"

"Didn't HE," the Colonel inquired, "want anything more? Or didn't, for that matter, poor Charlotte herself?"

She kept her eyes on him; there was a manner in it that half answered. "They were thoroughly in love. She might have been his—" She checked herself; she even for a minute lost herself. "She might have been anything she liked—except his wife."

"But she wasn't," said the Colonel very smokingly.

"She wasn't," Mrs. Assingham echoed.

The echo, not loud but deep, filled for a little the room. He seemed to listen to it die away; then he began again. "How are you sure?"

She waited before saying, but when she spoke it was definite. "There wasn't time."

He had a small laugh for her reason; he might have expected some other. "Does it take so much time?"

She herself, however, remained serious. "It takes more than they had."

He was detached, but he wondered. "What was the matter with their time?" After which, as, remembering it all, living it over and piecing it together, she only considered, "You mean that you came in with your idea?" he demanded.

It brought her quickly to the point, and as if also in a measure to answer herself. "Not a bit of it—THEN. But you surely recall," she went on, "the way, a year ago, everything took place. They had parted before he had ever heard of Maggie."

"Why hadn't he heard of her from Charlotte herself?"

"Because she had never spoken of her."

"Is that also," the Colonel inquired, "what she has told you?"

"I'm not speaking," his wife returned, "of what she has told me. That's one thing. I'm speaking of what I know by myself. That's another."

"You feel, in other words, that she lies to you?" Bob Assingham more sociably asked.

She neglected the question, treating it as gross. "She never so much, at the time, as named Maggie."

It was so positive that it appeared to strike him. "It's he then who has told you?"

She after a moment admitted it. "It's he."

"And he doesn't lie?"

"No—to do him justice. I believe he absolutely doesn't. If I hadn't believed it," Mrs. Assingham declared, for her general justification, "I would have had nothing to do with him—that is in this connection. He's a gentleman—I mean ALL as much of one as he ought to be. And he had nothing to gain. That helps," she added, "even a gentleman. It was I who named Maggie to him—a year from last May. He had never heard of her before."

"Then it's grave," said the Colonel.

She hesitated. "Do you mean grave for me?"

"Oh, that everything's grave for 'you' is what we take for granted and are fundamentally talking about. It's grave—it WAS—for Charlotte. And it's grave for Maggie. That is it WAS—when he did see her. Or when she did see HIM."

"You don't torment me as much as you would like," she presently went on, "because you think of nothing that I haven't a thousand times thought of, and because I think of everything that you never will. It would all," she recognised, "have been grave if it hadn't all been right.

You can't make out," she contended, "that we got to Rome before the end of February."

He more than agreed. "There's nothing in life, my dear, that I CAN make out."

Well, there was nothing in life, apparently, that she, at real need, couldn't. "Charlotte, who had been there, that year, from early, quite from November, left suddenly, you'll quite remember, about the 10th of April. She was to have stayed on—she was to have stayed, naturally, more or less, for us; and she was to have stayed all the more that the Ververs, due all winter, but delayed, week after week, in Paris, were at last really coming. They were coming—that is Maggie was—largely to see her, and above all to be with her THERE. It was all altered—by Charlotte's going to Florence. She went from one day to the other—you forget everything. She gave her reasons, but I thought it odd, at the time; I had a sense that something must have happened. The difficulty was that, though I knew a little, I didn't know enough. I didn't know her relation with him had been, as you say, a 'near' thing—that is I didn't know HOW near. The poor girl's departure was a flight—she went to save herself."

He had listened more than he showed—as came out in his tone. "To save herself?"

"Well, also, really, I think, to save HIM too. I saw it afterwards—I see it all now. He would have been sorry—he didn't want to hurt her."

"Oh, I daresay," the Colonel laughed. "They generally don't!"

"At all events," his wife pursued, "she escaped—they both did; for they had had simply to face it. Their marriage couldn't be, and, if that was so, the sooner they put the Apennines between them the better. It had taken them, it is true, some time to feel this and to find it out. They had met constantly, and not always publicly, all that winter; they had met more than was known—though it was a good deal known. More, certainly," she said, "than I then imagined—though I don't know what difference it would make afterwards. I liked him, I thought him charming, from the first of our knowing him; and now, after more than a year, he has done nothing to spoil it. And there are things he might have done—things that many men easily would. Therefore I believe in him, and I was right, at first, in knowing I was going to. So I haven't"—and she stated it as she might have quoted from a slate, after adding up the items, the sum of a column of figures—"so I haven't, I say to myself, been a fool."

"Well, are you trying to make out that I've said you have? All their case wants, at any rate," Bob Assingham declared, "is that you should leave it well alone. It's theirs now; they've bought it, over the counter, and paid for it. It has ceased to be yours."

"Of which case," she asked, "are you speaking?"

He smoked a minute: then with a groan: "Lord, are there so many?"

"There's Maggie's and the Prince's, and there's the Prince's and Charlotte's."

"Oh yes; and then," the Colonel scoffed, "there's Charlotte's and the Prince's."

"There's Maggie's and Charlotte's," she went on—"and there's also Maggie's and mine. I think too that there's Charlotte's and mine. Yes," she mused, "Charlotte's and mine is certainly a case. In short, you see, there are plenty. But I mean," she said, "to keep my head."

"Are we to settle them all," he inquired, "to-night?"

"I should lose it if things had happened otherwise—if I had acted with any folly." She had gone on in her earnestness, unheeding of his question. "I shouldn't be able to bear that now. But my good conscience is my strength; no one can accuse me. The Ververs came to Rome alone—Charlotte, after their days with her in Florence, had decided about America. Maggie, I daresay, had helped her; she must have made her a present, and a handsome one, so that many things were easy. Charlotte left them, came to England, 'joined' somebody or other, sailed for New York. I have still her letter from Milan, telling me; I didn't know at the moment all that was behind it, but I felt in it nevertheless the undertaking of a new life. Certainly, in any case, it cleared THAT air—I mean the dear old Roman, in which we were steeped. It left the field free—it gave me a free hand. There was no question for me of anybody else when I brought the two others together. More than that, there was no question for them. So you see," she concluded, "where that puts me." She got up, on the words, very much as if they were the blue daylight towards which, through a darksome tunnel, she had been pushing her way, and the elation in her voice, combined with her recovered alertness, might have signified the sharp whistle of the train that shoots at last into the open. She turned about the room; she looked out a moment into the August night; she stopped, here and there, before the flowers in bowls and vases. Yes, it was distinctly as if she had proved what was needing proof, as if the issue of her operation had been, almost unexpectedly, a success. Old arithmetic had perhaps been fallacious, but she now settled the question. Her husband, oddly, however, kept his place without apparently measuring these results. As he had been amused at her intensity, so he was not uplifted by her relief; his interest might in fact have been more enlisted than he allowed. "Do you mean," he presently asked, "that he had already forgot about Charlotte?"

She faced round as if he had touched a spring. "He WANTED to, naturally—and it was much the best thing he could do." She was in possession of the main case, as it truly seemed; she had it all now. "He was capable of the effort, and he took the best way. Remember too what Maggie then seemed to us."

"She's very nice; but she always seems to me, more than anything else, the young woman who has a million a year. If you mean that that's what she especially seemed to him, you of course place the thing in your light. The effort to forget Charlotte couldn't, I grant you, have been so difficult."

This pulled her up but for an instant. "I never said he didn't from the first—I never said that he doesn't more and more—like Maggie's money."

"I never said I shouldn't have liked it myself," Bob Assingham returned. He made no movement; he smoked another minute. "How much did Maggie know?"

"How much?" She seemed to consider—as if it were between quarts and gallons—how best to express the quantity. "She knew what Charlotte, in Florence, had told her."

"And what had Charlotte told her?"

"Very little."

"What makes you so sure?"

"Why, this—that she couldn't tell her." And she explained a little what she meant. "There are things, my dear—haven't you felt it yourself, coarse as you are?—that no one could tell Maggie. There are things that, upon my word, I shouldn't care to attempt to tell her now."

The Colonel smoked on it. "She'd be so scandalised?"

"She'd be so frightened. She'd be, in her strange little way, so hurt. She wasn't born to know evil. She must never know it." Bob Assingham had a queer grim laugh; the sound of which, in fact, fixed his wife before him. "We're taking grand ways to prevent it."

But she stood there to protest. "We're not taking any ways. The ways are all taken; they were taken from the moment he came up to our carriage that day in Villa Borghese—the second or third of her days in Rome, when, as you remember, you went off somewhere with Mr. Verver, and the Prince, who had got into the carriage with us, came home with us to tea. They had met; they had seen each other well; they were in relation: the rest was to come of itself and as it could. It began, practically, I recollect, in our drive. Maggie happened to learn, by some other man's greeting of him, in the bright Roman way, from a streetcorner as we passed, that one of the Prince's baptismal names, the one always used for him among his relations, was Amerigo: which (as you probably don't know, however, even after a lifetime of ME), was the name, four hundred years ago, or whenever, of the pushing man who followed, across the sea, in the wake of Columbus and succeeded, where Columbus had failed, in becoming godfather, or name-father, to the new Continent; so that the thought of any connection with him can even now thrill our artless breasts."

The Colonel's grim placidity could always quite adequately meet his wife's not infrequent imputation of ignorances, on the score of the land of her birth, unperturbed and unashamed; and these dark depths were even at the present moment not directly lighted by an inquiry that managed to be curious without being apologetic. "But where does the connection come in?"

His wife was prompt. "By the women—that is by some obliging woman, of old, who was a descendant of the pushing man, the make-believe discoverer, and whom the Prince is therefore luckily able to refer to as an ancestress. A branch of the other family had become great—great enough, at least, to marry into his; and the name of the navigator, crowned with glory, was, very naturally, to become so the fashion among them that some son, of every generation, was appointed to wear it. My point is, at any rate, that I recall noticing at the time how the Prince was, from the start, helped with the dear Ververs by his wearing it. The connection became romantic for Maggie the moment she took it in; she filled out, in a flash, every link that might be vague. 'By that sign,' I quite said to myself, 'he'll conquer'—with his good fortune, of course, of having the other necessary signs too. It really," said Mrs. Assingham, "was, practically, the fine side of the wedge. Which struck me as also," she wound up, "a lovely note for the candour of the Ververs."

The Colonel took in the tale, but his comment was prosaic. "He knew, Amerigo, what he was about. And I don't mean the OLD one."

"I know what you mean!" his wife bravely threw off.

"The old one"—he pointed his effect "isn't the only discoverer in the family."

"Oh, as much as you like! If he discovered America—or got himself honoured as if he had—his successors were, in due time, to discover the Americans. And it was one of them in particular, doubtless, who was to discover how patriotic we are."

"Wouldn't this be the same one," the Colonel asked, "who really discovered what you call the connection?"

She gave him a look. "The connection's a true thing—the connection's perfectly historic, Your insinuations recoil upon your cynical mind. Don't you understand," she asked, "that the history of such people is known, root and branch, at every moment of its course?"

"Oh, it's all right," said Bob Assingham.

"Go to the British Museum," his companion continued with spirit.

"And what am I to do there?"

"There's a whole immense room, or recess, or department, or whatever, filled with books written about his family alone. You can see for yourself."

"Have you seen for YOUR self?"

She faltered but an instant. "Certainly—I went one day with Maggie. We looked him up, so to say. They were most civil." And she fell again into the current her husband had slightly ruffled. "The effect was produced, the charm began to work, at all events, in Rome, from that hour of the Prince's drive with us. My only course, afterwards, had to be to make the best of it. It was certainly good enough for that," Mrs. Assingham hastened to add, "and I didn't in the least see my duty in making the worst. In the same situation, to-day; I wouldn't act differently. I entered into the case as it then appeared to me—and as, for the matter of that, it still does. I LIKED it, I thought all sorts of good of it, and nothing can even now," she said with some intensity, "make me think anything else."

"Nothing can ever make you think anything you don't want to," the Colonel, still in his chair, remarked over his pipe. "You've got a precious power of thinking whatever you do want. You want also, from moment to moment, to think such desperately different things. What happened," he went on, "was that you fell violently in love with the Prince yourself, and that as you couldn't get me out of the way you had to take some roundabout course. You couldn't marry him, any more than Charlotte could—that is not to yourself. But you could to somebody else—it was always the Prince, it was always marriage. You could to your little friend, to whom there were no objections."

"Not only there were no objections, but there were reasons, positive ones—and all excellent, all charming." She spoke with an absence of all repudiation of his exposure of the spring of her conduct; and this abstention, clearly and effectively conscious, evidently cost her nothing. "It IS always the Prince; and it IS always, thank heaven, marriage. And these are the things, God grant, that it will always be. That I could help, a year ago, most assuredly made me happy, and it continues to make me happy."

"Then why aren't you quiet?"

"I AM quiet," said Fanny Assingham.

He looked at her, with his colourless candour, still in his place; she moved about again, a little, emphasising by her unrest her declaration of her tranquillity. He was as silent, at first, as if he had taken her answer, but he was not to keep it long. "What do you make of it that, by your own show, Charlotte couldn't tell her all? What do you make of it that the Prince didn't tell her anything? Say one understands that there are things she can't be told—since, as you put it, she is so easily scared and shocked." He produced these objections slowly, giving her time, by his pauses, to stop roaming and come back to him. But she was roaming still when he concluded his inquiry. "If there hadn't been anything there shouldn't have been between the pair before Charlotte bolted—in order, precisely, as you say, that there SHOULDN'T be: why in the world was what there HAD been too bad to be spoken of?"

Mrs. Assingham, after this question, continued still to circulate—not directly meeting it even when at last she stopped.

"I thought you wanted me to be quiet."

"So I do—and I'm trying to make you so much so that you won't worry more. Can't you be quiet on THAT?"

She thought a moment—then seemed to try. "To relate that she had to 'bolt' for the reasons we speak of, even though the bolting had done for her what she wished—THAT I can perfectly feel Charlotte's not wanting to do."

"Ah then, if it HAS done for her what she wished—!" But the Colonel's conclusion hung by the "if" which his wife didn't take up. So it hung but the longer when he presently spoke again. "All one wonders, in that case, is why then she has come back to him."

"Say she hasn't come back to him. Not really to HIM."

"I'll say anything you like. But that won't do me the same good as your saying it."

"Nothing, my dear, will do you good," Mrs. Assingham returned. "You don't care for anything in itself; you care for nothing but to be grossly amused because I don't keep washing my hands—!"

"I thought your whole argument was that everything is so right that this is precisely what you do."

But his wife, as it was a point she had often made, could go on as she had gone on before. "You're perfectly indifferent, really; you're perfectly immoral. You've taken part in the sack of cities, and I'm sure you've done dreadful things yourself. But I DON'T trouble my head, if you like. 'So now there!'" she laughed.

He accepted her laugh, but he kept his way. "Well, I back poor Charlotte."

"'Back' her?"

"To know what she wants."

"Ah then, so do I. She does know what she wants." And Mrs. Assingham produced this quantity, at last, on the girl's behalf, as the ripe result of her late wanderings and musings. She had groped through their talk, for the thread, and now she had got it. "She wants to be magnificent."

"She is," said the Colonel almost cynically.

"She wants"—his wife now had it fast "to be thoroughly superior, and she's capable of that."

"Of wanting to?"

"Of carrying out her idea."

"And what IS her idea?"

"To see Maggie through."

Bob Assingham wondered. "Through what?"

"Through everything. She KNOWS the Prince."

"And Maggie doesn't. No, dear thing"—Mrs. Assingham had to recognise it—"she doesn't."

"So that Charlotte has come out to give her lessons?"

She continued, Fanny Assingham, to work out her thought. "She has done this great thing for him. That is, a year ago, she practically did it. She practically, at any rate, helped him to do it himself—and helped me to help him. She kept off, she stayed away, she left him free; and what, moreover, were her silences to Maggie but a direct aid to him? If she had spoken in Florence; if she had told her own poor story; if she had, come back at any time—till within a few weeks ago; if she hadn't gone to New York and hadn't held out there: if she hadn't done these things all that has happened since would certainly have been different. Therefore she's in a position to be consistent now. She knows the Prince," Mrs. Assingham repeated. It involved even again her former recognition. "And Maggie, dear thing, doesn't."

She was high, she was lucid, she was almost inspired; and it was but the deeper drop therefore to her husband's flat common sense. "In other words Maggie is, by her ignorance, in danger? Then if she's in danger, there IS danger."

"There WON'T be—with Charlotte's understanding of it. That's where she has had her conception of being able to be heroic, of being able in fact to be sublime. She is, she will be"—the good lady by this time glowed. "So she sees it—to become, for her best friend, an element of POSITIVE safety."

Bob Assingham looked at it hard. "Which of them do you call her best friend?"

She gave a toss of impatience. "I'll leave you to discover!" But the grand truth thus made out she had now completely adopted. "It's for US, therefore, to be hers."

"'Hers'?"

"You and I. It's for us to be Charlotte's. It's for us, on our side, to see HER through."

"Through her sublimity?"

"Through her noble, lonely life. Only—that's essential—it mustn't be lonely. It will be all right if she marries."

"So we're to marry her?"

"We're to marry her. It will be," Mrs. Assingham continued, "the great thing I can do." She made it out more and more. "It will make up."

"Make up for what?" As she said nothing, however, his desire for lucidity renewed itself. "If everything's so all right what is there to make up for?"

"Why, if I did do either of them, by any chance, a wrong. If I made a mistake."

"You'll make up for it by making another?" And then as she again took her time: "I thought your whole point is just that you're sure."

"One can never be ideally sure of anything. There are always possibilities."

"Then, if we can but strike so wild, why keep meddling?"

It made her again look at him. "Where would you have been, my dear, if I hadn't meddled with YOU?"

"Ah, that wasn't meddling—I was your own. I was your own," said the Colonel, "from the moment I didn't object."

"Well, these people won't object. They are my own too—in the sense that I'm awfully fond of them. Also in the sense," she continued, "that I think they're not so very much less fond of me. Our relation, all round, exists—it's a reality, and a very good one; we're mixed up, so to speak, and it's too late to change it. We must live IN it and with it. Therefore to see that Charlotte gets a good husband as soon as possible—that, as I say, will be one of my ways of living. It will cover," she said with conviction, "all the ground." And then as his own conviction appeared to continue as little to match: "The ground, I mean, of any nervousness I may ever feel. It will be in fact my duty and I shan't rest till my duty's performed." She had arrived by this time at something like exaltation. "I shall give, for the next year or two if necessary, my life to it. I shall have done in that case what I can."

He took it at last as it came. "You hold there's no limit to what you 'can'?"

"I don't say there's no limit, or anything of the sort. I say there are good chances—enough of them for hope. Why shouldn't there be when a girl is, after all, all that she is?"

"By after 'all' you mean after she's in love with somebody else?"

The Colonel put his question with a quietude doubtless designed to be fatal; but it scarcely pulled her up. "She's not too much in love not herself to want to marry. She would now particularly like to."

"Has she told you so?"

"Not yet. It's too soon. But she will. Meanwhile, however, I don't require the information. Her marrying will prove the truth."

"And what truth?"

"The truth of everything I say."

"Prove it to whom?"

"Well, to myself, to begin with. That will be enough for me—to work for her. What it will prove," Mrs. Assingham presently went on, "will be that she's cured. That she accepts the situation."

He paid this tribute of a long pull at his pipe. "The situation of doing the one thing she can that will really seem to cover her tracks?"

His wife looked at him, the good dry man, as if now at last he were merely vulgar. "The one thing she can do that will really make new tracks altogether. The thing that, before any other, will be wise and right. The thing that will best give her her chance to be magnificent."

He slowly emitted his smoke. "And best give you, by the same token, yours to be magnificent with her?"

"I shall be as magnificent, at least, as I can."

Bob Assingham got up. "And you call ME immoral?"

She hesitated. "I'll call you stupid if you prefer. But stupidity pushed to a certain point IS, you know, immorality. Just so what is morality but high intelligence?" This he was unable to tell her; which left her more definitely to conclude. "Besides, it's all, at the worst, great fun."

"Oh, if you simply put it at THAT—!"

His implication was that in this case they had a common ground; yet even thus he couldn't catch her by it. "Oh, I don't mean," she said from the threshold, "the fun that you mean. Good-night." In answer to which, as he turned out the electric light, he gave an odd, short groan, almost a grunt. He HAD apparently meant some particular kind.

V

"Well, now I must tell you, for I want to be absolutely honest." So Charlotte spoke, a little ominously, after they had got into the Park. "I don't want to pretend, and I can't pretend a moment longer. You may think of me what you will, but I don't care. I knew I shouldn't and I find now how little. I came back for this. Not really for anything else. For this," she repeated as, under the influence of her tone, the Prince had already come to a pause.

"For 'this'?" He spoke as if the particular thing she indicated were vague to him—or were, rather, a quantity that couldn't, at the most, be much.

It would be as much, however, as she should be able to make it. "To have one hour alone with you." It had rained heavily in the night, and though the pavements were now dry, thanks to a cleansing breeze, the August morning, with its hovering, thick-drifting clouds and freshened air, was cool and grey. The multitudinous green of the Park had been deepened, and a wholesome smell of irrigation, purging the place of dust and of odours less acceptable, rose from the earth. Charlotte had looked about her, with expression, from the first of their coming in, quite as if for a deep greeting, for general recognition: the day was, even in the heart of London, of a rich, low-browed, weatherwashed English type. It was as if it had been waiting for her, as if she knew it, placed it, loved it, as if it were in fact a part of what she had come back for. So far as this was the case the impression of course could only be lost on a mere vague Italian; it was one of those for which you had to be, blessedly, an American—as indeed you had to be, blessedly, an American for all sorts of things: so long as you hadn't, blessedly or not, to remain in America. The Prince had, by half-past ten—as also by definite appointment—called in Cadogan Place for Mrs. Assingham's visitor, and then, after brief delay, the two had walked together up Sloane Street and got straight into the Park from Knightsbridge. The understanding to this end had taken its place, after a couple of days, as inevitably consequent on the appeal made by the girl during those first moments in Mrs. Assingham's drawing-room. It was an appeal the couple of days had done nothing to invalidate—everything, much rather, to place in a light, and as to which, obviously, it wouldn't have fitted that anyone should raise an objection. Who was there, for that matter, to raise one, from the moment Mrs. Assingham, informed and apparently not disapproving, didn't intervene? This the young man had asked himself—with a very sufficient sense of what would have made him ridiculous. He wasn't going to begin—that at least was certain—by showing a fear. Even had fear at first been sharp in him, moreover, it would already, not a little, have dropped; so happy, all round, so propitious, he quite might have called it, had been the effect of this rapid interval.

The time had been taken up largely by his active reception of his own wedding-guests and by Maggie's scarce less absorbed entertainment of her friend, whom she had kept for hours together in Portland Place; whom she had not, as wouldn't have been convenient, invited altogether as yet to migrate, but who had been present, with other persons, his contingent, at luncheon, at tea, at dinner, at perpetual repasts—he had never in his life, it struck him, had to reckon with so much eating—whenever he had looked in. If he had not again, till this hour, save for a minute, seen Charlotte alone, so, positively, all the while, he had not seen even Maggie; and if, therefore, he had not seen even Maggie, nothing was more natural than that he shouldn't have seen Charlotte. The exceptional minute, a mere snatch, at the tail of the others, on the huge Portland Place staircase had sufficiently enabled the girl to remind him—so ready she assumed him to be—of what they were to do. Time pressed if they were to do it at all. Everyone had brought gifts; his relations had brought wonders—how did they still find, where did they still find, such treasures? She only had brought nothing, and she was ashamed; yet even by the sight of the rest of the tribute she wouldn't be put off. She would do what she could, and he was, unknown to Maggie, he must remember, to give her his aid. He had prolonged the minute so far as to take time to hesitate, for a reason, and then to risk bringing his reason out. The risk was because he might hurt her—hurt her pride, if she had that particular sort. But she might as well be hurt one way as another; and, besides, that particular sort of pride was just what she hadn't. So his slight resistance, while they lingered, had been just easy enough not to be impossible.

"I hate to encourage you—and for such a purpose, after all—to spend your money."

She had stood a stair or two below him; where, while she looked up at him beneath the high, domed light of the hall, she rubbed with her palm the polished mahogany of the balustrade, which was mounted on fine ironwork, eighteenth-century English. "Because you think I must have so little? I've enough, at any rate—enough for us to take our hour. Enough," she had smiled, "is as good as a feast! And then," she had said, "it isn't of course a question of anything expensive, gorged with treasure as Maggie is; it isn't a question of competing or outshining. What, naturally, in the way of the priceless, hasn't she got? Mine is to be the offering of the poor—something, precisely, that—no rich person COULD ever give her, and that, being herself too rich ever to buy it, she would therefore never have." Charlotte had spoken as if after so much thought. "Only, as it can't be fine, it ought to be funny—and that's the sort of thing to hunt for. Hunting in London, besides, is amusing in itself."

He recalled even how he had been struck with her word. "'Funny'?" "Oh, I don't mean a comic toy—I mean some little thing with a charm. But absolutely RIGHT, in its comparative cheapness. That's what I call funny," she had explained. "You used," she had also added, "to help me to get things cheap in Rome. You were splendid for beating down. I have them all still, I needn't say—the little bargains I there owed you. There are bargains in London in August."

"Ah, but I don't understand your English buying, and I confess I find it dull." So much as that, while they turned to go up together, he had objected. "I understood my poor dear Romans."

"It was they who understood you—that was your pull," she had laughed. "Our amusement here is just that they don't understand us. We can make it amusing. You'll see."

If he had hesitated again it was because the point permitted. "The amusement surely will be to find our present."

"Certainly—as I say."

"Well, if they don't come down—?"

"Then we'll come up. There's always something to be done. Besides, Prince," she had gone on, "I'm not, if you come to that, absolutely a pauper. I'm too poor for some things," she had said—yet, strange as she was, lightly enough; "but I'm not too poor for others." And she had paused again at the top. "I've been saving up."

He had really challenged it. "In America?"

"Yes, even there—with my motive. And we oughtn't, you know," she had wound up, "to leave it beyond to-morrow."

That, definitely, with ten words more, was what had passed—he feeling all the while how any sort of begging-off would only magnify it. He might get on with things as they were, but he must do anything rather than magnify. Besides which it was pitiful to make her beg of him. He WAS making her—she had begged; and this, for a special sensibility in him, didn't at all do. That was accordingly, in fine, how they had come to where they were: he was engaged, as hard as possible, in the policy of not magnifying. He had kept this up even on her making a point—and as if it were almost the whole point—that Maggie of course was not to have an idea. Half the interest of the thing at least would be that she shouldn't suspect; therefore he was completely to keep it from her—as Charlotte on her side would—that they had been anywhere at all together or had so much as seen each other for five minutes alone. The absolute secrecy of their little excursion was in short of the essence; she appealed to his kindness to let her feel that he didn't betray her. There had been something, frankly, a little disconcerting in such an appeal at such an hour, on the very eve of his nuptials: it was one thing to have met the girl casually at Mrs. Assingham's, and another to arrange with her thus for a morning practically as private as their old mornings in Rome and practically not less intimate. He had immediately told Maggie, the same evening, of the minutes that had passed between them in Cadogan Place—though not mentioning those of Mrs. Assingham's absence any more than he mentioned the fact of what their friend had then, with such small delay, proposed. But what had briefly checked his assent to any present, to any positive making of mystery—what had made him, while they stood at the top of the stairs, demur just long enough for her to notice it—was the sense of the resemblance of the little plan before him to occasions, of the past, from which he was quite disconnected, from which he could only desire to be. This was like beginning something over, which was the last thing he wanted. The strength, the beauty of his actual position was in its being wholly a fresh start, was that what it began would be new altogether. These items of his consciousness had clustered so quickly that by the time Charlotte read them in his face he was in presence of what they amounted to. She had challenged them as soon as read them, had met them with a "Do you want then to go and tell her?" that had somehow made them ridiculous. It had made him, promptly, fall back on minimizing it—that is on minimizing "fuss." Apparent scruples were, obviously, fuss, and he had on the spot clutched, in the light of this truth, at the happy principle that would meet every case.

This principle was simply to be, with the girl, always simple—and with the very last simplicity. That would cover everything. It had covered, then and there, certainly, his immediate submission to the sight of what was clearest. This was, really, that what she asked was little compared to what she gave. What she gave touched him, as she faced him, for it was the full tune of her renouncing. She really renounced—renounced everything, and without even insisting now on what it had all been for her. Her only insistence was her insistence on the small matter of their keeping their appointment to themselves. That, in exchange for "everything," everything she gave up, was verily but a trifle. He let himself accordingly be guided; he so soon assented, for enlightened indulgence, to any particular turn she might wish the occasion to take, that the stamp of her preference had been well applied to it even while they were still in the Park. The application in fact presently required that they should sit down a little, really to see where they were; in obedience to which propriety they had some ten minutes, of a quality quite distinct, in a couple of penny-chairs under one of the larger trees. They had taken, for their walk, to the cropped, rain-freshened grass, after finding it already dry; and the chairs, turned away from the broad alley, the main drive and the aspect of Park Lane, looked across the wide reaches of green which seemed in a manner to refine upon their freedom. They helped Charlotte thus to make her position—her temporary position—still more clear, and it was for this purpose, obviously, that, abruptly, on seeing her opportunity, she sat down. He stood for a little before her, as if to mark the importance of not wasting time, the importance she herself had previously insisted on; but after she had said a few words it was impossible for him not to resort again to good-nature. He marked as he could, by this concession, that if he had finally met her first proposal for what would be "amusing" in it, so any idea she might have would contribute to that effect. He had consequently—in all consistency—to treat it as amusing that she reaffirmed, and reaffirmed again, the truth that was HER truth.

"I don't care what you make of it, and I don't ask anything whatever of you—anything but this. I want to have said it—that's all; I want not to have failed to say it. To see you once and be with you, to be as we are now and as we used to be, for one small hour—or say for two—that's what I have had for weeks in my head. I mean, of course, to get it BEFORE—before what you're going to do. So, all the while, you see," she went on with her eyes on him, "it was a question for me if I should be able to manage it in time. If I couldn't have come now I probably shouldn't have come at all—perhaps even ever. Now that I'm here I shall stay, but there were moments, over there, when I despaired. It wasn't easy—there were reasons; but it was either this or nothing. So I didn't struggle, you see, in vain. AFTER—oh, I didn't want that! I don't mean," she smiled, "that it wouldn't have been delightful to see you even then—to see you at any time; but I would never have come for it. This is different. This is what I wanted. This is what I've got. This is what I shall always have. This is what I should have missed, of course," she pursued, "if you had chosen to make me miss it. If you had thought me horrid, had refused to come, I should, naturally, have been immensely 'sold.' I had to take the risk. Well, you're all I could have hoped. That's what I was to have said. I didn't want simply to get my time with you, but I wanted you to know. I wanted you"—she kept it up, slowly, softly, with a small tremor of voice, but without the least failure of sense or sequence—"I wanted you to understand. I wanted you, that is, to hear. I don't care, I think, whether you understand or not. If I ask nothing of you I don't—I mayn't—ask even so much as that. What you may think of me—that doesn't in the least matter. What I want is that it shall always be with you—so that you'll never be able quite to get rid of it—that I DID. I won't say that you did—you may make as little of that as you like. But that I was here with you where we are and as we are—I just saying this. Giving myself, in other words, away—and perfectly willing to do it for nothing. That's all."

She paused as if her demonstration was complete—yet, for the moment, without moving; as if in fact to give it a few minutes to sink in; into the listening air, into the watching face, into the conscious hospitality of nature, so far as nature was, all Londonised, all vulgarised, with them there; or even, for that matter, into her own open ears, rather than into the attention of her passive and prudent friend. His attention had done all that attention could do; his handsome, slightly anxious, yet still more definitely "amused" face sufficiently played its part. He clutched, however, at what he could best clutch at—the fact that she let him off, definitely let him off. She let him off, it seemed, even from so much as answering; so that while he smiled back at her in return for her information he felt his lips remain closed to the successive vaguenesses of rejoinder, of objection, that rose for him from within. Charlotte herself spoke again at last—"You may want to know what I get by it. But that's my own affair." He really didn't want to know even this—or continued, for the safest plan, quite to behave as if he didn't; which prolonged the mere dumbness of diversion in which he had taken refuge. He was glad when, finally—the point she had wished to make seeming established to her satisfaction—they brought to what might pass for a close the moment of his life at which he had had least to say. Movement and progress, after this, with more impersonal talk, were naturally a relief; so that he was not again, during their excursion, at a loss for the right word. The air had been, as it were, cleared; they had their errand itself to discuss, and the opportunities of London, the sense of the wonderful place, the pleasures of prowling there, the question of shops, of possibilities, of particular objects, noticed by each in previous prowls. Each professed surprise at the extent of the other's knowledge; the Prince in especial wondered at his friend's possession of her London. He had rather prized his own possession, the guidance he could really often give a cabman; it was a whim of his own, a part of his Anglomania, and congruous with that feature, which had, after all, so much more surface than depth. When his companion, with the memory of other visits and other rambles, spoke of places he hadn't seen and things he didn't know, he actually felt again—as half the effect—just a shade humiliated. He might even have felt a trifle annoyed—if it hadn't been, on this spot, for his being, even more, interested. It was a fresh light on Charlotte and on her curious world-quality, of which, in Rome, he had had his due sense, but which clearly would show larger on the big London stage. Rome was, in comparison, a village, a family-party, a little old-world spinnet for the fingers of one hand. By the time they reached the Marble Arch it was almost as if she were showing him a new side, and that, in fact, gave amusement a new and a firmer basis. The right tone would be easy for putting himself in her hands. Should they disagree a little—frankly and fairly—about directions and chances, values and authenticities, the situation would be quite gloriously saved. They were none the less, as happened, much of one mind on the article of their keeping clear of resorts with which Maggie would be acquainted. Charlotte recalled it as a matter of course, named it in time as a condition—they would keep away from any place to which he had already been with Maggie.

This made indeed a scant difference, for though he had during the last month done few things so much as attend his future wife on her making of purchases, the antiquarii, as he called them with Charlotte, had not been the great affair. Except in Bond Street, really, Maggie had had no use for them: her situation indeed, in connection with that order of traffic, was full of consequences produced by her father's. Mr. Verver, one of the great collectors of the world, hadn't left his daughter to prowl for herself; he had little to do with shops, and was mostly, as a purchaser, approached privately and from afar. Great people, all over Europe, sought introductions to him; high personages, incredibly high, and more of them than would ever be known, solemnly sworn as everyone was, in such cases, to discretion, high personages made up to him as the one man on the short authentic list likely to give the price. It had therefore been easy to settle, as they walked, that the tracks of the Ververs, daughter's as well as father's, were to be avoided; the importance only was that their talk about it led for a moment to the first words they had as yet exchanged on the subject of Maggie. Charlotte, still in the Park, proceeded to them—for it was she who began—with a serenity of appreciation that was odd, certainly, as a sequel to her words of ten minutes before. This was another note on her—what he would have called another light—for her companion, who, though without giving a sign, admired, for what it was, the simplicity of her transition, a transition that took no trouble either to trace or to explain itself. She paused again an instant, on the grass, to make it; she stopped before him with a sudden "Anything of course, dear as she is, will do for her. I mean if I were to give her a pin-cushion from the Baker-Street Bazaar."

"That's exactly what *I* meant"—the Prince laughed out this allusion to their snatch of talk in Portland Place. "It's just what I suggested."

She took, however, no notice of the reminder; she went on in her own way. "But it isn't a reason. In that case one would never do anything for her. I mean," Charlotte explained, "if one took advantage of her character."

"Of her character?"

"We mustn't take advantage of her character," the girl, again unheeding, pursued. "One mustn't, if not for HER, at least for one's self. She saves one such trouble."

She had spoken thoughtfully, with her eyes on her friend's; she might have been talking, preoccupied and practical, of someone with whom he was comparatively unconnected. "She certainly GIVES one no trouble," said the Prince. And then as if this were perhaps ambiguous or inadequate: "She's not selfish—God forgive her!—enough."

"That's what I mean," Charlotte instantly said. "She's not selfish enough. There's nothing, absolutely, that one NEED do for her. She's so modest," she developed—"she doesn't miss things. I mean if you love her—or, rather, I should say, if she loves you. She lets it go."

The Prince frowned a little—as a tribute, after all, to seriousness. "She lets what—?"

"Anything—anything that you might do and that you don't. She lets everything go but her own disposition to be kind to you. It's of herself that she asks efforts—so far as she ever HAS to ask them. She hasn't, much. She does everything herself. And that's terrible."

The Prince had listened; but, always with propriety, he didn't commit himself. "Terrible?"

"Well, unless one is almost as good as she. It makes too easy terms for one. It takes stuff, within one, so far as one's decency is concerned, to stand it. And nobody," Charlotte continued in the same manner, "is decent enough, good enough, to stand it—not without help from religion, or something of that kind. Not without prayer and fasting—that is without taking great care. Certainly," she said, "such people as you and I are not."

The Prince, obligingly, thought an instant. "Not good enough to stand it?"

"Well, not good enough not rather to feel the strain. We happen each, I think, to be of the kind that are easily spoiled."

Her friend, again, for propriety, followed the argument. "Oh, I don't know. May not one's affection for her do something more for one's decency, as you call it, than her own generosity—her own affection, HER 'decency'—has the unfortunate virtue to undo?"

"Ah, of course it must be all in that."

But she had made her question, all the same, interesting to him. "What it comes to—one can see what you mean—is the way she believes in one. That is if she believes at all."

"Yes, that's what it comes to," said Charlotte Stant.

"And why," he asked, almost soothingly, "should it be terrible?" He couldn't, at the worst, see that.

"Because it's always so—the idea of having to pity people."

"Not when there's also, with it, the idea of helping them."

"Yes, but if we can't help them?"

"We CAN—we always can. That is," he competently added, "if we care for them. And that's what we're talking about."

"Yes"—she on the whole assented. "It comes back then to our absolutely refusing to be spoiled."

"Certainly. But everything," the Prince laughed as they went on—"all your 'decency,' I mean—comes back to that."

She walked beside him a moment. "It's just what *I* meant," she then reasonably said.

VI

The man in the little shop in which, well after this, they lingered longest, the small but interesting dealer in the Bloomsbury street who was remarkable for an insistence not importunate, inasmuch as it was mainly mute, but singularly, intensely coercive—this personage fixed on his visitors an extraordinary pair of eyes and looked from one to the other while they considered the object with which he appeared mainly to hope to tempt them. They had come to him last, for their time was nearly up; an hour of it at least, from the moment of their getting into a hansom at the Marble Arch, having yielded no better result than the amusement invoked from the first. The amusement, of course, was to have consisted in seeking, but it had also involved the idea of finding; which latter necessity would have been obtrusive only if they had found too soon. The question at present was if they were finding, and they put it to each other, in the Bloomsbury shop, while they enjoyed the undiverted attention of the shopman. He was clearly the master, and devoted to his business—the essence of which, in his conception, might precisely have been this particular secret that he possessed for worrying the customer so little that it fairly made for their relations a sort of solemnity. He had not many things, none of the redundancy of "rot" they had elsewhere seen, and our friends had, on entering, even had the sense of a muster so scant that, as high values obviously wouldn't reign, the effect might be almost pitiful. Then their impression had changed; for, though the show was of small pieces, several taken from the little window and others extracted from a cupboard behind the counter—dusky, in the rather low-browed place, despite its glass doors—each bid for their attention spoke, however modestly, for itself, and the pitch of their entertainer's pretensions was promptly enough given. His array was heterogeneous and not at all imposing; still, it differed agreeably from what they had hitherto seen.

Charlotte, after the incident, was to be full of impressions, of several of which, later on, she gave her companion—always in the interest of their amusement—the benefit; and one of the impressions had been that the man himself was the greatest curiosity they had looked at. The Prince was to reply to this that he himself hadn't looked at him; as, precisely, in the general connection, Charlotte had more than once, from other days, noted, for his advantage, her consciousness of how, below a certain social plane, he never SAW. One kind of shopman was just like another to him—which was oddly inconsequent on the part of a mind that, where it did notice, noticed so much. He took throughout, always, the meaner sort for granted—the night of their meanness, or whatever name one might give it for him, made all his cats grey. He didn't, no doubt, want to hurt them, but he imaged them no more than if his eyes acted only for the level of his own high head. Her own vision acted for every relation—this he had seen for himself: she remarked beggars, she remembered servants, she recognised cabmen; she had often distinguished beauty, when out with him, in dirty children; she had admired "type" in faces at hucksters' stalls. Therefore, on this occasion, she had found their antiquario interesting; partly because he cared so for his things, and partly because he cared—well, so for them. "He likes his things—he loves them," she was to say; "and it isn't only—it isn't perhaps even at all—that he loves to sell them. I think he would love to keep them if he could; and he prefers, at any rate, to sell them to right people. We, clearly, were right people—he knows them when he sees them; and that's why, as I say, you could make out, or at least *I* could, that he cared for us. Didn't you see"—she was to ask it with an insistence—"the way he looked at us and took us in? I doubt if either of us have ever been so well looked at before. Yes, he'll remember us"—she was to profess herself convinced of that almost to uneasiness. "But it was after all"—this was perhaps reassuring—"because, given his taste, since he HAS taste, he was pleased with us, he was struck—he had ideas about us. Well, I should think people might; we're beautiful—aren't we?—and he knows. Then, also, he has his way; for that way of saying nothing with his lips when he's all the while pressing you so with his face, which shows how he knows you feel it—that is a regular way."

Of decent old gold, old silver, old bronze, of old chased and jewelled artistry, were the objects that, successively produced, had ended by numerously dotting the counter, where the shopman's slim, light fingers, with neat nails, touched them at moments, briefly, nervously, tenderly, as those of a chess-player rest, a few seconds, over the board, on a figure he thinks he may move and then may not: small florid ancientries, ornaments, pendants, lockets, brooches, buckles, pretexts for dim brilliants, bloodless rubies, pearls either too large or too opaque for value; miniatures mounted with diamonds that had ceased to dazzle; snuffboxes presented to—or by—the too-questionable great; cups, trays, taper-stands, suggestive of pawn-tickets, archaic and brown, that would themselves, if preserved, have been prized curiosities. A few commemorative medals, of neat outline but dull reference; a classic monument or two, things of the first years of the century; things consular, Napoleonic, temples, obelisks, arches, tinily re-embodied, completed the discreet cluster; in which, however, even after tentative reinforcement from several quaint rings, intaglios, amethysts, carbuncles, each of which had found a home in the ancient sallow satin of some weakly-snapping little box, there was, in spite of the due proportion of faint poetry, no great force of persuasion. They looked, the visitors, they touched, they vaguely pretended to consider, but with scepticism, so far as courtesy permitted, in the quality of their attention. It was impossible they shouldn't, after a little, tacitly agree as to the absurdity of carrying to Maggie a token from such a stock. It would be—that was the difficulty—pretentious without being "good"; too usual, as a treasure, to have been an inspiration of the giver, and yet too primitive to be taken as tribute welcome on any terms. They had been out more than two hours and, evidently, had found nothing. It forced from Charlotte a kind of admission.

"It ought, really, if it should be a thing of this sort, to take its little value from having belonged to one's self."

"Ecco!" said the Prince—just triumphantly enough. "There you are."

Behind the dealer were sundry small cupboards in the wall. Two or three of these Charlotte had seen him open, so that her eyes found themselves resting on those he had not visited. But she completed her admission. "There's nothing here she could wear."

It was only after a moment that her companion rejoined. "Is there anything—do you think—that you could?"

It made her just start. She didn't, at all events, look at the objects; she but looked for an instant very directly at him. "No."

"Ah!" the Prince quietly exclaimed.

"Would it be," Charlotte asked, "your idea to offer me something?"

"Well, why not—as a small ricordo."

"But a ricordo of what?"

"Why, of 'this'—as you yourself say. Of this little hunt."

"Oh, I say it—but hasn't my whole point been that I don't ask you? Therefore," she demanded—but smiling at him now—"where's the logic?"

"Oh, the logic—!" he laughed.

"But logic's everything. That, at least, is how I feel it. A ricordo from you—from you to me—is a ricordo of nothing. It has no reference."

"Ah, my dear!" he vaguely protested. Their entertainer, meanwhile, stood there with his eyes on them, and the girl, though at this minute more interested in her passage with her friend than in anything else, again met his gaze. It was a comfort to her that their foreign tongue covered what they said—and they might have appeared of course, as the Prince now had one of the snuffboxes in his hand, to be discussing a purchase.

"You don't refer," she went on to her companion. "*I* refer."

He had lifted the lid of his little box and he looked into it hard. "Do you mean by that then that you would be free—?"

"'Free'—?"

"To offer me something?"

This gave her a longer pause, and when she spoke again she might have seemed, oddly, to be addressing the dealer. "Would you allow me—?"

"No," said the Prince into his little box.

"You wouldn't accept it from me?"

"No," he repeated in the same way.

She exhaled a long breath that was like a guarded sigh. "But you've touched an idea that HAS been mine. It's what I've wanted." Then she added: "It was what I hoped."

He put down his box—this had drawn his eyes. He made nothing, clearly, of the little man's attention. "It's what you brought me out for?"

"Well, that's, at any rate," she returned, "my own affair. But it won't do?"

"It won't do, cara mia."

"It's impossible?"

"It's impossible." And he took up one of the brooches.

She had another pause, while the shopman only waited. "If I were to accept from you one of these charming little ornaments as you suggest, what should I do with it?"

He was perhaps at last a little irritated; he even—as if HE might understand—looked vaguely across at their host. "Wear it, per Bacco!"

"Where then, please? Under my clothes?"

"Wherever you like. But it isn't then, if you will," he added, "worth talking about."

"It's only worth talking about, mio caro," she smiled, "from your having begun it. My question is only reasonable—so that your idea may stand or fall by your answer to it. If I should pin one of these things on for you would it be, to your mind, that I might go home and show it to Maggie as your present?"

They had had between them often in talk the refrain, jocosely, descriptively applied, of "old Roman." It had been, as a pleasantry, in the other time, his explanation to her of everything; but nothing, truly, had even seemed so old-Roman as the shrug in which he now indulged. "Why in the world not?"

"Because—on our basis—it would be impossible to give her an account of the pretext."

"The pretext—?" He wondered.

"The occasion. This ramble that we shall have had together and that we're not to speak of."

"Oh yes," he said after a moment "I remember we're not to speak of it."

"That of course you're pledged to. And the one thing, you see, goes with the other. So you don't insist."

He had again, at random, laid back his trinket; with which he quite turned to her, a little wearily at last—even a little impatiently. "I don't insist."

It disposed for the time of the question, but what was next apparent was that it had seen them no further. The shopman, who had not stirred, stood there in his patience—which, his mute intensity helping, had almost the effect of an ironic comment. The Prince moved to the glass door and, his back to the others, as with nothing more to contribute, looked—though not less patiently—into the street. Then the shopman, for Charlotte, momentously broke silence. "You've seen, disgraziatamente, signora principessa," he sadly said, "too much"—and it made the Prince face about. For the effect of the momentous came, if not from the sense, from the sound of his words; which was that of the suddenest, sharpest Italian. Charlotte exchanged with her friend a glance that matched it, and just for the minute they were held in check. But their glance had, after all, by that time, said more than one thing; had both exclaimed on the apprehension, by the wretch, of their intimate conversation, let alone of her possible, her impossible, title, and remarked, for mutual reassurance, that it didn't, all the same, matter. The Prince remained by the door, but immediately addressing the speaker from where he stood.

"You're Italian then, are you?"

But the reply came in English. "Oh dear no."

"You're English?"

To which the answer was this time, with a smile, in briefest Italian. "Che!" The dealer waived the question—he practically disposed of it by turning straightway toward a receptacle to which he had not yet resorted and from which, after unlocking it, he extracted a square box, of some twenty inches in height, covered with worn-looking leather. He placed the box on the counter, pushed back a pair of small hooks, lifted the lid and removed from its nest a drinking-vessel larger than a common cup, yet not of exorbitant size, and formed, to appearance, either of old fine gold or of some material once richly gilt. He handled it with tenderness, with ceremony, making a place for it on a small satin mat. "My Golden Bowl," he observed—and it sounded, on his lips, as if it said everything. He left the important object—for as "important" it did somehow present itself—to produce its certain effect. Simple, but singularly elegant, it stood on a circular foot, a short pedestal with a slightly spreading base, and, though not of signal depth, justified its title by the charm of its shape as well as by the tone of its surface. It might have been a large goblet diminished, to the enhancement of its happy curve, by half its original height. As formed of solid gold it was impressive; it seemed indeed to warn off the prudent admirer. Charlotte, with care, immediately took it up, while the Prince, who had after a minute shifted his position again, regarded it from a distance.

It was heavier than Charlotte had thought. "Gold, really gold?" she asked of their companion.

He hesitated. "Look a little, and perhaps you'll make out."

She looked, holding it up in both her fine hands, turning it to the light. "It may be cheap for what it is, but it will be dear, I'm afraid, for me."

"Well," said the man, "I can part with it for less than its value. I got it, you see, for less."

"For how much then?"

Again he waited, always with his serene stare. "Do you like it then?"

Charlotte turned to her friend. "Do YOU like it?" He came no nearer; he looked at their companion. "Cos'e?"

"Well, signori miei, if you must know, it's just a perfect crystal."

"Of course we must know, per Dio!" said the Prince. But he turned away again—he went back to his glass door.

Charlotte set down the bowl; she was evidently taken. "Do you mean it's cut out of a single crystal?"

"If it isn't I think I can promise you that you'll never find any joint or any piecing."

She wondered. "Even if I were to scrape off the gold?"

He showed, though with due respect, that she amused him. "You couldn't scrape it off—it has been too well put on; put on I don't know when and I don't know how. But by some very fine old worker and by some beautiful old process."

Charlotte, frankly charmed with the cup, smiled back at him now. "A lost art?"

"Call it a lost art,"

"But of what time then is the whole thing?"

"Well, say also of a lost time."

The girl considered. "Then if it's so precious, how comes it to be cheap?"

Her interlocutor once more hung fire, but by this time the Prince had lost patience. "I'll wait for you out in the air," he said to his companion, and, though he spoke without irritation, he pointed his remark by passing immediately into the street, where, during the next minutes, the others saw him, his back to the shopwindow, philosophically enough hover and light a fresh cigarette. Charlotte even took, a little, her time; she was aware of his funny Italian taste for London street-life.

Her host meanwhile, at any rate, answered her question. "Ah, I've had it a long time without selling it. I think I must have been keeping it, madam, for you."

"You've kept it for me because you've thought I mightn't see what's the matter with it?"

He only continued to face her—he only continued to appear to follow the play of her mind. "What IS the matter with it?"

"Oh, it's not for me to say; it's for you honestly to tell me. Of course I know something must be."

"But if it's something you can't find out, isn't it as good as if it were nothing?"

"I probably SHOULD find out as soon as I had paid for it."

"Not," her host lucidly insisted, "if you hadn't paid too much."

"What do you call," she asked, "little enough?"

"Well, what should you say to fifteen pounds?"

"I should say," said Charlotte with the utmost promptitude, "that it's altogether too much."

The dealer shook his head slowly and sadly, but firmly. "It's my price, madam—and if you admire the thing I think it really might be yours. It's not too much. It's too little. It's almost nothing. I can't go lower."

Charlotte, wondering, but resisting, bent over the bowl again. "Then it's impossible. It's more than I can afford."

"Ah," the man returned, "one can sometimes afford for a present more than one can afford for one's self." He said it so coaxingly that she found herself going on without, as might be said, putting him in his place. "Oh, of course it would be only for a present—!"

"Then it would be a lovely one."

"Does one make a present," she asked, "of an object that contains, to one's knowledge, a flaw?"

"Well, if one knows of it one has only to mention it. The good faith," the man smiled, "is always there."

"And leave the person to whom one gives the thing, you mean, to discover it?"

"He wouldn't discover it—if you're speaking of a gentleman."

"I'm not speaking of anyone in particular," Charlotte said.

"Well, whoever it might be. He might know—and he might try. But he wouldn't find."

She kept her eyes on him as if, though unsatisfied, mystified, she yet had a fancy for the bowl. "Not even if the thing should come to pieces?" And then as he was silent: "Not even if he should have to say to me 'The Golden Bowl is broken'?"

He was still silent; after which he had his strangest smile. "Ah, if anyone should WANT to smash it—!"

She laughed; she almost admired the little man's expression. "You mean one could smash it with a hammer?"

"Yes; if nothing else would do. Or perhaps even by dashing it with violence—say upon a marble floor."

"Oh, marble floors!" But she might have been thinking—for they were a connection, marble floors; a connection with many things: with her old Rome, and with his; with the palaces of his past, and, a little, of hers; with the possibilities of his future, with the sumptuosities of his marriage, with the wealth of the Ververs. All the same, however, there were other things; and they all together held for a moment her fancy. "Does crystal then break—when it IS crystal? I thought its beauty was its hardness."

Her friend, in his way, discriminated. "Its beauty is its BEING crystal. But its hardness is certainly, its safety. It doesn't break," he went on, "like vile glass. It splits—if there is a split."

"Ah!"—Charlotte breathed with interest. "If there is a split." And she looked down again at the bowl. "There IS a split, eh? Crystal does split, eh?"

"On lines and by laws of its own."

"You mean if there's a weak place?"

For all answer, after an hesitation, he took the bowl up again, holding it aloft and tapping it with a key. It rang with the finest, sweetest sound. "Where is the weak place?"

She then did the question justice. "Well, for ME, only the price. I'm poor, you see—very poor. But I thank you and I'll think." The Prince, on the other side of the shop-window, had finally faced about and, as to see if she hadn't done, was trying to reach, with his eyes, the comparatively dim interior. "I like it," she said—"I want it. But I must decide what I can do."

The man, not ungraciously, resigned himself. "Well, I'll keep it for you."

The small quarter-of-an-hour had had its marked oddity—this she felt even by the time the open air and the Bloomsbury aspects had again, in their protest against the truth of her gathered impression, made her more or less their own. Yet the oddity might have been registered as small as compared to the other effect that, before they had gone much further, she had, with her companion, to take account of. This latter was simply the effect of their having, by some tacit logic, some queer inevitability, quite dropped the idea of a continued pursuit. They didn't say so, but it was on the line of giving up Maggie's present that they practically proceeded—the line of giving it up without more reference to it. The Prince's first reference was in fact quite independently made. "I hope you satisfied yourself, before you had done, of what was the matter with that bowl."

"No indeed, I satisfied myself of nothing. Of nothing at least but that the more I looked at it the more I liked it, and that if you weren't so unaccommodating this would be just the occasion for your giving me the pleasure of accepting it."

He looked graver for her, at this, than he had looked all the morning. "Do you propose it seriously—without wishing to play me a trick?"

She wondered. "What trick would it be?"

He looked at her harder. "You mean you really don't know?"

"But know what?"

"Why, what's the matter with it. You didn't see, all the while?"

She only continued, however, to stare. "How could you see—out in the street?"

"I saw before I went out. It was because I saw that I did go out. I didn't want to have another scene with you, before that rascal, and I judged you would presently guess for yourself."

"Is he a rascal?" Charlotte asked. "His price is so moderate." She waited but a moment. "Five pounds. Really so little."

"Five pounds?"

He continued to look at her. "Five pounds."

He might have been doubting her word, but he was only, it appeared, gathering emphasis. "It would be dear—to make a gift of—at five shillings. If it had cost you even but five pence I wouldn't take it from you."

"Then," she asked, "what IS the matter?"

"Why, it has a crack."

It sounded, on his lips, so sharp, it had such an authority, that she almost started, while her colour, at the word, rose. It was as if he had been right, though his assurance was wonderful. "You answer for it without having looked?"

"I did look. I saw the object itself. It told its story. No wonder it's cheap."

"But it's exquisite," Charlotte, as if with an interest in it now made even tenderer and stranger, found herself moved to insist.

"Of course it's exquisite. That's the danger." Then a light visibly came to her—a light in which her friend suddenly and intensely showed. The reflection of it, as she smiled at him, was in her own face. "The danger—I see—is because you're superstitious."

"Per Dio, I'm superstitious! A crack is a crack—and an omen's an omen."

"You'd be afraid—?"

"Per Bacco!"

"For your happiness?"

"For my happiness."

"For your safety?"

"For my safety."

She just paused. "For your marriage?"

"For my marriage. For everything."

She thought again. "Thank goodness then that if there BE a crack we know it! But if we may perish by cracks in things that we don't know—!" And she smiled with the sadness of it. "We can never then give each other anything."

He considered, but he met it. "Ah, but one does know. *I* do, at least—and by instinct. I don't fail. That will always protect me."

It was funny, the way he said such things; yet she liked him, really, the more for it. They fell in for her with a general, or rather with a special, vision. But she spoke with a mild despair.

"What then will protect ME?"

"Where I'm concerned *I* will. From me at least you've nothing to fear," he now quite amiably responded. "Anything you consent to accept from me—" But he paused.

"Well?"

"Well, shall be perfect."

"That's very fine," she presently answered. "It's vain, after all, for you to talk of my accepting things when you'll accept nothing from me."

Ah, THERE, better still, he could meet her. "You attach an impossible condition. That, I mean, of my keeping your gift so to myself."

Well, she looked, before him there, at the condition—then, abruptly, with a gesture, she gave it up. She had a headshake of disenchantment—so far as the idea had appealed to her. It all appeared too difficult. "Oh, my 'condition'—I don't hold to it. You may cry it on the housetops—anything I ever do."

"Ah well, then—!" This made, he laughed, all the difference.

But it was too late. "Oh, I don't care now! I SHOULD have liked the Bowl. But if that won't do there's nothing."

He considered this; he took it in, looking graver again; but after a moment he qualified. "Yet I shall want some day to give you something."

She wondered at him. "What day?"

"The day you marry. For you WILL marry. You must—SERIOUSLY—marry."

She took it from him, but it determined in her the only words she was to have uttered, all the morning, that came out as if a spring had been pressed. "To make you feel better?"

"Well," he replied frankly, wonderfully—"it will. But here," he added, "is your hansom."

He had signalled—the cab was charging. She put out no hand for their separation, but she prepared to get in. Before she did so, however, she said what had been gathering while she waited. "Well, I would marry, I think, to have something from you in all freedom."

PART SECOND

Autumn scene (c.1909) by Edward Middleton Manigault (1887–1922)

VII

Adam Verver, at Fawns, that autumn Sunday, might have been observed to open the door of the billiard-room with a certain freedom—might have been observed, that is, had there been a spectator in the field. The justification of the push he had applied, however, and of the push, equally sharp, that, to shut himself in, he again applied—the ground of this energy was precisely that he might here, however briefly, find himself alone, alone with the handful of letters, newspapers and other unopened missives, to which, during and since breakfast, he had lacked opportunity to give an eye. The vast, square, clean apartment was empty, and its large clear windows looked out into spaces of terrace and garden, of park and woodland and shining artificial lake, of richly-condensed horizon, all dark blue upland and church-towered village and strong cloudshadow, which were, together, a thing to create the sense, with everyone else at church, of one's having the world to one's self. We share this world, none the less, for the hour, with Mr. Verver; the very fact of his striking, as he would have said, for solitude, the fact of his quiet flight, almost on tiptoe, through tortuous corridors, investing him with an interest that makes our attention—tender indeed almost to compassion—qualify his achieved isolation. For it may immediately be mentioned that this amiable man bethought himself of his personal advantage, in general, only when it might appear to him that other advantages, those of other persons, had successfully put in their claim. It may be mentioned also that he always figured other persons—such was the law of his nature—as a numerous array, and that, though conscious of but a single near tie, one affection, one duty deepest-rooted in his life, it had never, for many minutes together, been his portion not to feel himself surrounded and committed, never quite been his refreshment to make out where the many-coloured human appeal, represented by gradations of tint, diminishing concentric zones of intensity, of importunity, really faded to the blessed impersonal whiteness for which his vision sometimes ached. It shaded off, the appeal—he would have admitted that; but he had as yet noted no point at which it positively stopped.

Thus had grown in him a little habit—his innermost secret, not confided even to Maggie, though he felt she understood it, as she understood, to his view, everything—thus had shaped itself the innocent trick of occasionally making believe that he had no conscience, or at least that blankness, in the field of duty, did reign for an hour; a small game to which the few persons near enough to have caught him playing it, and of whom Mrs. Assingham, for instance, was one, attached indulgently that idea of quaintness, quite in fact that charm of the pathetic, involved in the preservation by an adult of one of childhood's toys. When he took a rare moment "off," he did so with the touching, confessing eyes of a man of forty-seven caught in the act of handling a relic of infancy—sticking on the head of a broken soldier or trying the lock of a wooden gun. It was essentially, in him, the IMITATION of depravity—which, for amusement, as might have been, he practised "keeping up." In spite of practice he was still imperfect, for these so artlessly-artful interludes were condemned, by the nature of the case, to brevity. He had fatally stamped himself—it was his own fault—a man who could be interrupted with impunity. The greatest of wonders, moreover, was exactly in this, that so interrupted a man should ever have got, as the phrase was, should above all have got so early, to where he was. It argued a special genius; he was clearly a case of that. The spark of fire, the point of light, sat somewhere in his inward vagueness as a lamp before a shrine twinkles in the dark perspective of a church; and while youth and early middle-age, while the stiff American breeze of example and opportunity were blowing upon it hard, had made of the chamber of his brain a strange workshop of fortune. This establishment, mysterious and almost anonymous, the windows of which, at hours of highest pressure, never seemed, for starers and wonderers, perceptibly to glow, must in fact have been during certain years the scene of an unprecedented, a miraculous white-heat, the receipt for producing which it was practically felt that the master of the forge could not have communicated even with the best intentions.

The essential pulse of the flame, the very action of the cerebral temperature, brought to the highest point, yet extraordinarily contained—these facts themselves were the immensity of the result; they were one with perfection of machinery, they had constituted the kind of acquisitive power engendered and applied, the necessary triumph of all operations. A dim explanation of phenomena once vivid must at all events for the moment suffice us; it being obviously no account of the matter to throw on our friend's amiability alone the weight of the demonstration of his economic history. Amiability, of a truth, is an aid to success; it has even been known to be the principle of large accumulations; but the link, for the mind, is none the less fatally missing between proof, on such a scale, of continuity, if of nothing more insolent, in one field, and accessibility to distraction in every other. Variety of imagination—what is that but fatal, in the world of affairs, unless so disciplined as not to be distinguished from monotony? Mr. Verver then, for a fresh, full period, a period betraying, extraordinarily, no wasted year, had been inscrutably monotonous behind an iridescent cloud. The cloud was his native envelope—the soft looseness, so to say, of his temper and tone, not directly expressive enough, no doubt, to figure an amplitude of folds, but of a quality unmistakable for sensitive feelers. He was still reduced, in fine, to getting his rare moments with himself by feigning a cynicism. His real inability to maintain the pretence, however, had perhaps not often been better instanced than by his acceptance of the inevitable to-day—his acceptance of it on the arrival, at the end of a quarter-of-an-hour, of that element of obligation with which he had all the while known he must reckon. A quarter-of-an-hour of egoism was about as much as he, taking one situation with another, usually got. Mrs. Rance opened the door—more tentatively indeed than he himself had just done; but on the other hand, as if to make up for this, she pushed forward even more briskly on seeing then than he had been moved to do on seeing nobody. Then, with force, it came home to him that he had, definitely, a week before, established a precedent. He did her at least that justice—it was a kind of justice he was always doing someone. He had on the previous Sunday liked to stop at home, and he had exposed himself thereby to be caught in the act. To make this possible, that is, Mrs. Rance had only had to like to do the same—the trick was so easily played. It had not occurred to him to plan in any way for her absence—which would have destroyed, somehow, in principle, the propriety of his own presence. If persons under his roof hadn't a right not to go to church, what became, for a fair mind, of his own right? His subtlest manoeuvre had been simply to change from the library to the billiard-room, it being in the library that his guest, or his daughter's, or the guest of the Miss Lutches—he scarce knew in which light to regard her—had then, and not unnaturally, of course, joined him. It was urged on him by his memory of the duration of the visit she had that time, as it were, paid him, that the law of recurrence would already have got itself enacted. She had spent the whole morning with him, was still there, in the library, when the others came back—thanks to her having been tepid about their taking, Mr. Verver and she, a turn outside. It had been as if she looked on that as a kind of subterfuge—almost as a form of disloyalty. Yet what was it she had in mind, what did she wish to make of him beyond what she had already made, a patient, punctilious host, mindful that she had originally arrived much as a stranger, arrived not at all deliberately or yearningly invited?—so that one positively had her possible susceptibilities the MORE on one's conscience. The Miss Lutches, the sisters from the middle West, were there as friends of Maggie's, friends of the earlier time; but Mrs. Rance was there—or at least had primarily appeared—only as a friend of the Miss Lutches.

This lady herself was not of the middle West—she rather insisted on it—but of New Jersey, Rhode Island or Delaware, one of the smallest and most intimate States: he couldn't remember which, though she insisted too on that. It was not in him—we may say it for him—to go so far as to wonder if their group were next to be recruited by some friend of her own; and this partly because she had struck him, verily, rather as wanting to get the Miss Lutches themselves away than to extend the actual circle, and partly, as well as more essentially, because such connection as he enjoyed with the ironic question in general resided substantially less in a personal use of it than in the habit of seeing it as easy to others. He was so framed by nature as to be able to keep his inconveniences separate from his resentments; though indeed if the sum of these latter had at the most always been small, that was doubtless in some degree a consequence of the fewness of the former. His greatest inconvenience, he would have admitted, had he analyzed, was in finding it so taken for granted that, as he had money, he had force. It pressed upon him hard, and all round, assuredly, this attribution of power. Everyone had need of one's power, whereas one's own need, at the best, would have seemed to be but some trick for not communicating it. The effect of a reserve so merely, so meanly defensive would in most cases, beyond question, sufficiently discredit the cause; wherefore, though it was complicating to be perpetually treated as an infinite agent, the outrage was not the greatest of which a brave man might complain. Complaint, besides, was a luxury, and he dreaded the imputation of greed. The other, the constant imputation, that of being able to "do," would have no ground if he hadn't been, to start with—this was the point—provably luxurious. His lips, somehow, were closed—and by a spring connected moreover with the action of his eyes themselves. The latter showed him what he had done, showed him where he had come out; quite at the top of his hill of difficulty, the tall sharp spiral round which he had begun to wind his ascent at the age of twenty, and the apex of which was a platform looking down, if one would, on the kingdoms of the earth and with standing-room for but half-a-dozen others.

His eyes, in any case, now saw Mrs. Rance approach with an instant failure to attach to the fact any grossness of avidity of Mrs. Rance's own—or at least to descry any triumphant use even for the luridest impression of her intensity. What was virtually supreme would be her vision of his having attempted, by his desertion of the library, to mislead her—which in point of fact barely escaped being what he had designed. It was not easy for him, in spite of accumulations fondly and funnily regarded as of systematic practice, not now to be ashamed; the one thing comparatively easy would be to gloss over his course. The billiard-room was NOT, at the particular crisis, either a natural or a graceful place for the nominally main occupant of so large a house to retire to—and this without prejudice, either, to the fact that his visitor wouldn't, as he

158

apprehended, explicitly make him a scene. Should she frankly denounce him for a sneak he would simply go to pieces; but he was, after an instant, not afraid of that. Wouldn't she rather, as emphasising their communion, accept and in a manner exploit the anomaly, treat it perhaps as romantic or possibly even as comic?—show at least that they needn't mind even though the vast table, draped in brown holland, thrust itself between them as an expanse of desert sand. She couldn't cross the desert, but she could, and did, beautifully get round it; so that for him to convert it into an obstacle he would have had to cause himself, as in some childish game or unbecoming romp, to be pursued, to be genially hunted. This last was a turn he was well aware the occasion should on no account take; and there loomed before him—for the mere moment—the prospect of her fairly proposing that they should knock about the balls. That danger certainly, it struck him, he should manage in some way to deal with. Why too, for that matter, had he need of defences, material or other?—how was it a question of dangers really to be called such? The deep danger, the only one that made him, as an idea, positively turn cold, would have been the possibility of her seeking him in marriage, of her bringing up between them that terrible issue. Here, fortunately, she was powerless, it being apparently so provable against her that she had a husband in undiminished existence.

She had him, it was true, only in America, only in Texas, in Nebraska, in Arizona or somewhere—somewhere that, at old Fawns House, in the county of Kent, scarcely counted as a definite place at all; it showed somehow, from afar, as so lost, so indistinct and illusory, in the great alkali desert of cheap Divorce. She had him even in bondage, poor man, had him in contempt, had him in remembrance so imperfect as barely to assert itself, but she had him, none the less, in existence unimpeached: the Miss Lutches had seen him in the flesh—as they had appeared eager to mention; though when they were separately questioned their descriptions failed to tally. He would be at the worst, should it come to the worst, Mrs. Rance's difficulty, and he served therefore quite enough as the stout bulwark of anyone else. This was in truth logic without a flaw, yet it gave Mr. Verver less comfort than it ought. He feared not only danger—he feared the idea of danger, or in other words feared, hauntedly, himself. It was above all as a symbol that Mrs. Rance actually rose before him—a symbol of the supreme effort that he should have sooner or later, as he felt, to make. This effort would be to say No—he lived in terror of having to. He should be proposed to at a given moment—it was only a question of time—and then he should have to do a thing that would be extremely disagreeable. He almost wished, on occasion, that he wasn't so sure he WOULD do it. He knew himself, however, well enough not to doubt: he knew coldly, quite bleakly, where he would, at the crisis, draw the line. It was Maggie's marriage and Maggie's finer happiness—happy as he had supposed her before—that had made the difference; he hadn't in the other time, it now seemed to him, had to think of such things. They hadn't come up for him, and it was as if she, positively, had herself kept them down. She had only been his child—which she was indeed as much as ever; but there were sides on which she had protected him as if she were more than a daughter. She had done for him more than he knew—much, and blissfully, as he always HAD known. If she did at present more than ever, through having what she called the change in his life to make up to him for, his situation still, all the same, kept pace with her activity—his situation being simply that there was more than ever to be done.

There had not yet been quite so much, on all the showing, as since their return from their twenty months in America, as since their settlement again in England, experimental though it was, and the consequent sense, now quite established for him, of a domestic air that had cleared and lightened, producing the effect, for their common personal life, of wider perspectives and large waiting spaces. It was as if his son-in-law's presence, even from before his becoming his son-in-law, had somehow filled the scene and blocked the future—very richly and handsomely, when all was said, not at all inconveniently or in ways not to have been desired: inasmuch as though the Prince, his measure now practically taken, was still pretty much the same "big fact," the sky had lifted, the horizon receded, the very foreground itself expanded, quite to match him, quite to keep everything in comfortable scale. At first, certainly, their decent little old-time union, Maggie's and his own, had resembled a good deal some pleasant public square, in the heart of an old city, into which a great Palladian church, say—something with a grand architectural front—had suddenly been dropped; so that the rest of the place, the space in front, the way round, outside, to the east end, the margin of street and passage, the quantity of over-arching heaven, had been temporarily compromised. Not even then, of a truth, in a manner disconcerting—given, that is, for the critical, or at least the intelligent, eye, the great style of the facade and its high place in its class. The phenomenon that had since occurred, whether originally to have been pronounced calculable or not, had not, naturally, been the miracle of a night, but had taken place so gradually, quietly, easily, that from this vantage of wide, wooded Fawns, with its eighty rooms, as they said, with its spreading park, with its acres and acres of garden and its majesty of artificial lake—though that, for a person so familiar with the "great" ones, might be rather ridiculous—no visibility of transition showed, no violence of adjustment, in retrospect, emerged. The Palladian church was always there, but the piazza took care of itself. The sun stared down in his fulness, the air circulated, and the public not less; the limit stood off, the way round was easy, the east end was as fine, in its fashion, as the west, and there were also side doors for entrance, between the two—large, monumental, ornamental, in their style—as for all proper great churches. By some such process, in fine, had the Prince, for his father-in-law, while remaining solidly a feature, ceased to be, at all ominously, a block.

Mr. Verver, it may further be mentioned, had taken at no moment sufficient alarm to have kept in detail the record of his reassurance; but he would none the less not have been unable, not really have been indisposed, to impart in confidence to the right person his notion of the history of the matter. The right person—it is equally distinct—had not, for this illumination, been wanting, but had been encountered in the form of Fanny Assingham, who for the first time indeed admitted to his counsels, and who would have doubtless consented at present, in any case, from plenitude of interest and with equal guarantees, repeated his secret. It all came then, the great clearance, from the one prime fact that the Prince, by good fortune, hadn't proved angular. He clung to that description of his daughter's husband as he often did to terms and phrases, in the human, the social connection, that he had found for himself: it was his way to have times of using them constantly, as if they just then lighted the world, or his own path in it, for him—even when for some of his interlocutors they covered less ground. It was true that with Mrs. Assingham he never felt quite sure of the ground anything covered; she disputed with him so little, agreed with him so much, surrounded him with such systematic consideration, such predetermined tenderness, that it was almost—which he had once told her in irritation as if she were nursing a sick baby. He had accused her of not taking him seriously, and she had replied—as from her it couldn't frighten him—that she took him religiously, adoringly. She had laughed again, as she had laughed before, on his producing for her that good right word about the happy issue of his connection with the Prince—with an effect the more odd perhaps as she had not contested its value. She couldn't of course, however, be, at the best, as much in love with his discovery as he was himself. He was so much so that he fairly worked it—to his own comfort; came in fact sometimes near publicly pointing the moral of what might have occurred if friction, so to speak, had occurred. He pointed it frankly one day to the personage in question, mentioned to the Prince the particular justice he did him, was even explicit as to the danger that, in their remarkable relation, they had thus escaped. Oh, if he HAD been angular!—who could say what might THEN have happened? He spoke—and it was the way he had spoken to Mrs. Assingham too—as if he grasped the facts, without exception, for which angularity stood.

It figured for him, clearly, as a final idea, a conception of the last vividness. He might have been signifying by it the sharp corners and hard edges, all the stony pointedness, the grand right geometry of his spreading Palladian church. Just so, he was insensible to no feature of the felicity of a contact that, beguilingly, almost confoundingly, was a contact but with practically yielding lines and curved surfaces. "You're round, my boy," he had said—"you're ALL, you're variously and inexhaustibly round, when you might, by all the chances, have been abominably square. I'm not sure, for that matter," he had added, "that you're not square in the general mass—whether abominably or not. The abomination isn't a question, for you're inveterately round—that's what I mean—in the detail. It's the sort of thing, in you, that one feels—or at least I do—with one's hand. Say you had been formed, all over, in a lot of little pyramidal lozenges like that wonderful side of the Ducal Palace in Venice—so lovely in a building, but so damnable, for rubbing against, in a man, and especially in a near relation. I can see them all from here—each of them sticking out by itself—all the architectural cut diamonds that would have scratched one's softer sides. One would have been scratched by diamonds—doubtless the neatest way if one was to be scratched at all—but one would have been more or less reduced to a hash. As it is, for living with, you're a pure and perfect crystal. I give you my idea—I think you ought to have it—just as it has come to me." The Prince had taken the idea, in his way, for he was well accustomed, by this time, to taking; and nothing perhaps even could more have confirmed Mr. Verver's account of his surface than the manner in which these golden drops evenly flowed over it. They caught in no interstice, they gathered in no concavity; the uniform smoothness betrayed the dew but by showing for the moment a richer tone. The young man, in other words, unconfusedly smiled—though indeed as if assenting, from principle and habit, to more than he understood. He liked all signs that things were well, but he cared rather less WHY they were.

In regard to the people among whom he had since his marriage been living, the reasons they so frequently gave—so much oftener than he had ever heard reasons given before—remained on the whole the element by which he most differed from them; and his father-in-law and his wife were, after all, only first among the people among whom he had been living. He was never even yet sure of how, at this, that or the other point, he would strike them; they felt remarkably, so often, things he hadn't meant, and missed not less remarkably, and not less often, things he had. He had fallen back on his general explanation—"We haven't the same values;" by which he understood the same measure of importance. His "curves" apparently were important because they had been unexpected, or, still more, unconceived; whereas when one had always, as in his relegated old world, taken curves, and in much greater quantities too, for granted, one was no more surprised at the resulting feasibility of intercourse than one was surprised at being upstairs in a house that had a staircase. He had in fact on this occasion disposed alertly enough of the subject of Mr. Verver's approbation. The promptitude of his answer, we may in fact well surmise, had sprung not a little from a particular kindled remembrance; this had given his acknowledgment its easiest turn. "Oh, if I'm a crystal I'm delighted that I'm a perfect one, for I believe that they sometimes have cracks and flaws—in which case they're to be had very cheap!" He had stopped short of the emphasis it would have given his joke to add that there had been certainly no having HIM cheap; and it was doubtless a mark of the good taste practically reigning between them that Mr. Verver had not, on his side either, taken up the opportunity. It is the latter's relation to such aspects, however, that now most concerns us, and the bearing of his pleased view of this absence of friction upon Amerigo's character as a representative precious object. Representative precious objects, great ancient pictures and other works of art, fine eminent "pieces" in gold, in silver, in enamel, majolica, ivory, bronze, had for a number of years so multiplied themselves round him and, as a general challenge to acquisition and appreciation, so engaged all the faculties of his mind, that the instinct, the particular sharpened appetite of the collector, had fairly served as a basis for his acceptance of the Prince's suit.

Over and above the signal fact of the impression made on Maggie herself, the aspirant to his daughter's hand showed somehow the great marks and signs, stood before him with the high authenticities, that he had learned to look for in pieces of the first order. Adam Verver knew, by this time, knew thoroughly; no man in Europe or in America, he privately believed, was less capable, in such estimates, of vulgar mistakes. He had never spoken of himself as infallible—it was not his way; but, apart from the natural affections, he had acquainted himself with no greater joy, of the intimately personal type, than the joy of his originally coming to feel, and all so unexpectedly, that he had in him the spirit of the connoisseur. He had, like many other persons, in the course of his reading, been struck with Keats's sonnet about stout Cortez in the presence of the Pacific; but few persons, probably, had so devoutly fitted the poet's grand image to a fact of experience. It consorted so with Mr. Verver's consciousness of the way in which, at a given moment, he had stared at HIS Pacific, that a couple of perusals of the immortal lines had sufficed to stamp them in his memory. His "peak in Darien" was the sudden hour that had transformed his life, the hour of his perceiving with a mute inward gasp akin to the low moan of apprehensive passion, that a world was left him to conquer and that he might conquer it if he tried. It had been a turning of the page of the book of life—as if a leaf long inert had moved at a touch and, eagerly reversed, had made such a stir of the air as sent up into his face the very breath of the Golden Isles. To rifle the Golden Isles had, on the spot, become the business of his future, and with the sweetness of it—what was most wondrous of all—still more even in the thought than in the act. The thought was that of the affinity of Genius, or at least of Taste, with something in himself—with the dormant intelligence of which he had thus almost violently become aware and that affected him as changing by a mere revolution of the screw his whole intellectual plane. He was equal, somehow, with the great seers, the invokers and encouragers of beauty—and he didn't after all perhaps dangle so far below the great producers and creators. He had been nothing of that kind before-too decidedly, too dreadfully not; but now he saw why he had been what he had, why he had failed and fallen short even in huge success; now he read into his career, in one single magnificent night, the immense meaning it had waited for.

Father and daughter by François Gérard (1770–1837)

It was during his first visit to Europe after the death of his wife, when his daughter was ten years old, that the light, in his mind, had so broken—and he had even made out at that time why, on an earlier occasion, the journey of his honeymoon year, it had still been closely covered. He had "bought" then, so far as he had been able, but he had bought almost wholly for the frail, fluttered creature at his side, who had had her fancies, decidedly, but all for the art, then wonderful to both of them, of the Rue de la Paix, the costly authenticities of dressmakers and jewellers. Her flutter—pale disconcerted ghost as she actually was, a broken white flower tied round, almost grotesquely for his present sense, with a huge satin "bow" of the Boulevard—her flutter had been mainly that of ribbons, frills and fine fabrics; all funny, pathetic evidence, for memory, of the bewilderments overtaking them as a bridal pair confronted with opportunity. He could wince, fairly, still, as he remembered the sense in which the poor girl's pressure had, under his fond encouragement indeed, been exerted in favour of purchase and curiosity. These were wandering images, out of the earlier dusk, that threw her back, for his pity, into a past more remote than he liked their common past, their young affection, to appear. It would have had to be admitted, to an insistent criticism, that Maggie's mother, all too strangely, had not so much failed of faith as of the right application of it; since she had exercised it eagerly and restlessly, made it a pretext for innocent perversities in respect to which philosophic time was at, last to reduce all groans to gentleness. And they had loved each other so that his own intelligence, on the higher line, had temporarily paid for it. The futilities, the enormities, the depravities, of decoration and ingenuity, that, before his sense was unsealed, she had made him think lovely! Musing, reconsidering little man that he was, and addicted to silent pleasures—as he was accessible to silent pains—he even sometimes wondered what would have become of his intelligence, in the sphere in which it was to learn more and more exclusively to play, if his wife's influence upon it had not been, in the strange scheme of things, so promptly removed. Would she have led him altogether, attached as he was to her, into the wilderness of mere mistakes? Would she have prevented him from ever scaling his vertiginous Peak?—or would she, otherwise, have been able to accompany him to that eminence, where he might have pointed out to her, as Cortez to HIS companions, the revelation vouchsafed? No companion of Cortez had presumably been a real lady: Mr. Verver allowed that historic fact to determine his inference.

VIII

What was at all events not permanently hidden from him was a truth much less invidious about his years of darkness. It was the strange scheme of things again: the years of darkness had been needed to render possible the years of light. A wiser hand than he at first knew had kept him hard at acquisition of one sort as a perfect preliminary to acquisition of another, and the preliminary would have been weak and wanting if the good faith of it had been less. His comparative blindness had made the good faith, which in its turn had made the soil propitious for the flower of the supreme idea. He had had to LIKE forging and sweating, he had had to like polishing and piling up his arms. They were things at least he had had to believe he liked, just as he had believed he liked transcendent calculation and imaginative gambling all for themselves, the creation of "interests" that were the extinction of other interests, the livid vulgarity, even, of getting in, or getting out, first. That had of course been so far from really the case—with the supreme idea, all the while, growing and striking deep, under everything, in the warm, rich earth. He had stood unknowing, he had walked and worked where it was buried, and the fact itself, the fact of his fortune, would have been a barren fact enough if the first sharp tender shoot had never struggled into day. There on one side was the ugliness his middle time had been spared; there on the other, from all the portents, was the beauty with which his age might still be crowned. He was happier, doubtless, than he deserved; but

THAT, when one was happy at all, it was easy to be. He had wrought by devious ways, but he had reached the place, and what would ever have been straighter, in any man's life, than his way, now, of occupying it? It hadn't merely, his plan, all the sanctions of civilization; it was positively civilization condensed, concrete, consummate, set down by his hands as a house on a rock—a house from whose open doors and windows, open to grateful, to thirsty millions, the higher, the highest knowledge would shine out to bless the land. In this house, designed as a gift, primarily, to the people of his adoptive city and native State, the urgency of whose release from the bondage of ugliness he was in a position to measure—in this museum of museums, a palace of art which was to show for compact as a Greek temple was compact, a receptacle of treasures sifted to positive sanctity, his spirit to-day almost altogether lived, making up, as he would have said, for lost time and haunting the portico in anticipation of the final rites.

These would be the "opening exercises," the august dedication of the place. His imagination, he was well aware, got over the ground faster than his judgment; there was much still to do for the production of his first effect. Foundations were laid and walls were rising, the structure of the shell all determined; but raw haste was forbidden him in a connection so intimate with the highest effects of patience and piety; he should belie himself by completing without a touch at least of the majesty of delay a monument to the religion he wished to propagate, the exemplary passion, the passion for perfection at any price. He was far from knowing as yet where he would end, but he was admirably definite as to where he wouldn't begin. He wouldn't begin with a small show—he would begin with a great, and he could scarce have indicated, even had he wished to try, the line of division he had drawn. He had taken no trouble to indicate it to his fellow-citizens, purveyors and consumers, in his own and the circumjacent commonwealths, of comic matter in large lettering, diurnally "set up," printed, published, folded and delivered, at the expense of his presumptuous emulation of the snail. The snail had become for him, under this ironic suggestion, the loveliest beast in nature, and his return to England, of which we are present witnesses, had not been unconnected with the appreciation so determined. It marked what he liked to mark, that he needed, on the matter in question, instruction from no one on earth. A couple of years of Europe again, of renewed nearness to changes and chances, refreshed sensibility to the currents of the market, would fall in with the consistency of wisdom, the particular shade of enlightened conviction, that he wished to observe. It didn't look like much for a whole family to hang about waiting-they being now, since the birth of his grandson, a whole family; and there was henceforth only one ground in all the world, he felt, on which the question of appearance would ever really again count for him. He cared that a work of art of price should "look like" the master to whom it might perhaps be deceitfully attributed; but he had ceased on the whole to know any matter of the rest of life by its looks.

He took life in general higher up the stream; so far as he was not actually taking it as a collector, he was taking it, decidedly, as a grandfather. In the way of precious small pieces he had handled nothing so precious as the Principino, his daughter's first-born, whose Italian designation endlessly amused him and whom he could manipulate and dandle, already almost toss and catch again, as he couldn't a correspondingly rare morsel of an earlier pate tendre. He could take the small clutching child from his nurse's arms with an iteration grimly discountenanced, in respect to its contents, by the glass doors of high cabinets. Something clearly beatific in this new relation had, moreover, without doubt, confirmed for him the sense that none of his silent answers to public detraction, to local vulgarity, had ever been so legitimately straight as the mere element of attitude—reduce it, he said, to that—in his easy weeks at Fawns. The element of attitude was all he wanted of these weeks, and he was enjoying it on the spot, even more than he had hoped: enjoying it in spite of Mrs. Rance and the Miss Lutches; in spite of the small worry of his belief that Fanny Assingham had really something for him that she was keeping back; in spite of his full consciousness, overflowing the cup like a wine too generously poured, that if he had consented to marry his daughter, and thereby to make, as it were, the difference, what surrounded him now was, exactly, consent vivified, marriage demonstrated, the difference, in fine, definitely made. He could call back his prior, his own wedded consciousness—it was not yet out of range of vague reflection. He had supposed himself, above all he had supposed his wife, as married as anyone could be, and yet he wondered if their state had deserved the name, or their union worn the beauty, in the degree to which the couple now before him carried the matter. In especial since the birth of their boy, in New York—the grand climax of their recent American period, brought to so right an issue—the happy pair struck him as having carried it higher, deeper, further; to where it ceased to concern his imagination, at any rate, to follow them. Extraordinary, beyond question, was one branch of his characteristic mute wonderment—it characterised above all, with its subject before it, his modesty: the strange dim doubt, waking up for him at the end of the years, of whether Maggie's mother had, after all, been capable of the maximum. The maximum of tenderness he meant—as the terms existed for him; the maximum of immersion in the fact of being married. Maggie herself was capable; Maggie herself at this season, was, exquisitely, divinely, the maximum: such was the impression that, positively holding off a little for the practical, the tactful consideration it inspired in him, a respect for the beauty and sanctity of it almost amounting to awe—such was the impression he daily received from her. She was her mother, oh yes—but her mother and something more; it becoming thus a new light for him, and in such a curious way too, that anything more than her mother should prove at this time of day possible.

He could live over again at almost any quiet moment the long process of his introduction to his present interests—an introduction that had depended all on himself, like the "cheek" of the young man who approaches a boss without credentials or picks up an acquaintance, makes even a real friend, by speaking to a passer in the street. HIS real friend, in all the business, was to have been his own mind, with which nobody had put him in relation. He had knocked at the door of that essentially private house, and it, in truth, had not been immediately answered; so that when, after waiting and coming back, he had at last got in, it was, twirling his hat, as an embarrassed stranger, or, trying his keys, as a thief at night. He had gained confidence only with time, but when he had taken real possession of the place it had been never again to come away. All of which success represented, it must be allowed, his one principle of pride. Pride in the mere original spring, pride in his money, would have been pride in something that had come, in comparison, so easily. The right ground for elation was difficulty mastered, and his difficulty—thanks to his modesty—had been to believe in his facility. THIS was the problem he had worked out to its solution—the solution that was now doing more than all else to make his feet settle and his days flush; and when he wished to feel "good," as they said at American City, he had but to retrace his immense development. That was what the whole thing came back to—that the development had not been somebody's else passing falsely, accepted too ignobly, for his. To think how servile he might have been was absolutely to respect himself, was in fact, as much as he liked, to admire himself, as free. The very finest spring that ever responded to his touch was always there to press—the memory of his freedom as dawning upon him, like a sunrise all pink and silver, during a winter divided between Florence, Rome and Naples some three years after his wife's death. It was the hushed daybreak of the Roman revelation in particular that he could usually best recover, with the way that there, above all, where the princes and Popes had been before him, his divination of his faculty most went to his head. He was a plain American citizen, staying at an hotel where, sometimes, for days together, there were twenty others like him; but no Pope, no prince of them all had read a richer meaning, he believed, into the character of the Patron of Art. He was ashamed of them really, if he wasn't afraid, and he had on the whole never so climbed to the tip-top as in judging, over a perusal of Hermann Grimm, where Julius II and Leo X were "placed" by their treatment of Michael Angelo. Far below the plain American citizen—in the case at least in which this personage happened not to be too plain to be Adam Verver. Going to our friend's head, moreover, some of the results of such comparisons may doubtless be described as having stayed there. His freedom to see—of which the comparisons were part—what could it do but steadily grow and grow?

It came perhaps even too much to stand to him for ALL freedom—since, for example, it was as much there as ever at the very time of

Mrs. Rance's conspiring against him, at Fawns, with the billiard-room and the Sunday morning, on the occasion round which we have perhaps drawn our circle too wide. Mrs. Rance at least controlled practically each other license of the present and the near future: the license to pass the hour as he would have found convenient; the license to stop remembering, for a little, that, though if proposed to—and not only by this aspirant but by any other—he wouldn't prove foolish, the proof of wisdom was none the less, in such a fashion, rather cruelly conditioned; the license in especial to proceed from his letters to his journals and insulate, orientate, himself afresh by the sound, over his gained interval, of the many-mouthed monster the exercise of whose lungs he so constantly stimulated. Mrs. Rance remained with him till the others came back from church, and it was by that time clearer than ever that his ordeal, when it should arrive, would be really most unpleasant. His impression—this was the point—took somehow the form not so much of her wanting to press home her own advantage as of her building better than she knew; that is of her symbolising, with virtual unconsciousness, his own special deficiency, his unfortunate lack of a wife to whom applications could be referred. The applications, the contingencies with which Mrs. Rance struck him as potentially bristling, were not of a sort, really, to be met by one's self. And the possibility of them, when his visitor said, or as good as said, "I'm restrained, you see, because of Mr. Rance, and also because I'm proud and refined; but if it WASN'T for Mr. Rance and for my refinement and my pride!"—the possibility of them, I say, turned to a great murmurous rustle, of a volume to fill the future; a rustle of petticoats, of scented, many-paged letters, of voices as to which, distinguish themselves as they might from each other, it mattered little in what part of the resounding country they had learned to make themselves prevail. The Assinghams and the Miss Lutches had taken the walk, through the park, to the little old church, "on the property," that our friend had often found himself wishing he were able to transport, as it stood, for its simple sweetness, in a glass case, to one of his exhibitory halls; while Maggie had induced her husband, not inveterate in such practices, to make with her, by carriage, the somewhat longer pilgrimage to the nearest altar, modest though it happened to be, of the faith—her own as it had been her mother's, and as Mr. Verver himself had been loosely willing, always, to let it be taken for his—without the solid ease of which, making the stage firm and smooth, the drama of her marriage might not have been acted out.

What at last appeared to have happened, however, was that the divided parties, coming back at the same moment, had met outside and then drifted together, from empty room to room, yet not in mere aimless quest of the pair of companions they had left at home. The quest had carried them to the door of the billiard-room, and their appearance, as it opened to admit them, determined for Adam Verver, in the oddest way in the world, a new and sharp perception. It was really remarkable: this perception expanded, on the spot, as a flower, one of the strangest, might, at a breath, have suddenly opened. The breath, for that matter, was more than anything else, the look in his daughter's eyes—the look with which he SAW her take in exactly what had occurred in her absence: Mrs. Rance's pursuit of him to this remote locality, the spirit and the very form, perfectly characteristic, of his acceptance of the complication—the seal set, in short, unmistakably, on one of Maggie's anxieties. The anxiety, it was true, would have been, even though not imparted, separately shared; for Fanny Assingham's face was, by the same stroke, not at all thickly veiled for him, and a queer light, of a colour quite to match, fairly glittered in the four fine eyes of the Miss Lutches. Each of these persons—counting out, that is, the Prince and the Colonel, who didn't care, and who didn't even see that the others did—knew something, or had at any rate had her idea; the idea, precisely, that this was what Mrs. Rance, artfully biding her time, WOULD do. The special shade of apprehension on the part of the Miss Lutches might indeed have suggested the vision of an energy supremely asserted. It was droll, in truth, if one came to that, the position of the Miss Lutches: they had themselves brought, they had guilelessly introduced Mrs. Rance, strong in the fact of Mr. Rance's having been literally beheld of them; and it was now for them, positively, as if their handful of flowers—since Mrs. Rance was a handful!—had been but the vehicle of a dangerous snake. Mr. Verver fairly felt in the air the Miss Lutches' imputation—in the intensity of which, really, his own propriety might have been involved.

That, none the less, was but a flicker; what made the real difference, as I have hinted, was his mute passage with Maggie. His daughter's anxiety alone had depths, and it opened out for him the wider that it was altogether new. When, in their common past, when till this moment, had she shown a fear, however dumbly, for his individual life? They had had fears together, just as they had had joys, but all of hers, at least, had been for what equally concerned them. Here of a sudden was a question that concerned him alone, and the soundless explosion of it somehow marked a date. He was on her mind, he was even in a manner on her hands—as a distinct thing, that is, from being, where he had always been, merely deep in her heart and in her life; too deep down, as it were, to be disengaged, contrasted or opposed, in short objectively presented. But time itself had done it; their relation was altered: he SAW, again, the difference lighted for her. This marked it to himself—and it wasn't a question simply of a Mrs. Rance the more or the less. For Maggie too, at a stroke, almost beneficently, their visitor had, from being an inconvenience, become a sign. They had made vacant, by their marriage, his immediate foreground, his personal precinct—they being the Princess and the Prince. They had made room in it for others—so others had become aware. He became aware himself, for that matter, during the minute Maggie stood there before speaking; and with the sense, moreover, of what he saw her see, he had the sense of what she saw HIM. This last, it may be added, would have been his intensest perception had there not, the next instant, been more for him in Fanny Assingham. Her face couldn't keep it from him; she had seen, on top of everything, in her quick way, what they both were seeing.

IX

So much mute communication was doubtless, all this time, marvellous, and we may confess to having perhaps read into the scene, prematurely, a critical character that took longer to develop. Yet the quiet hour of reunion enjoyed that afternoon by the father and the daughter did really little else than deal with the elements definitely presented to each in the vibration produced by the return of the church-goers. Nothing allusive, nothing at all insistent, passed between them either before or immediately after luncheon—except indeed so far as their failure soon again to meet might be itself an accident charged with reference. The hour or two after luncheon—and on Sundays with especial rigour, for one of the domestic reasons of which it belonged to Maggie quite multitudinously to take account—were habitually spent by the Princess with her little boy, in whose apartment she either frequently found her father already established or was sooner or later joined by him. His visit to his grandson, at some hour or other, held its place, in his day, against all interventions, and this without counting his grandson's visits to HIM, scarcely less ordered and timed, and the odd bits, as he called them, that they picked up together when they could—communions snatched, for the most part, on the terrace, in the gardens or the park, while the Principino, with much pomp and circumstance of perambulator, parasol, fine lace over-veiling and incorruptible female attendance, took the air. In the private apartments, which, occupying in the great house the larger part of a wing of their own, were not much more easily accessible than if the place had been a royal palace and the small child an heir-apparent—in the nursery of nurseries the talk, at these instituted times, was always so prevailingly with or about the master of the scene that other interests and other topics had fairly learned to avoid the slighting and inadequate notice there taken of them. They came in, at the best, but as involved in the little boy's future, his past, or his comprehensive present, never getting so much as a chance to plead their own merits or to complain of being neglected. Nothing perhaps, in truth, had done more than this united participation to confirm in the elder parties that sense of a life not only uninterrupted but more deeply associated, more largely combined, of which, on Adam Verver's behalf, we have made some mention. It was of course an old story and a familiar idea that a beautiful baby could take its place as a new link between a wife and a husband, but Maggie and her father had, with every ingenuity, converted the precious creature into a link between a mamma and a grandpapa. The Principino, for a chance spectator of this process, might have become, by an untoward stroke, a hapless half-orphan, with the place of immediate male parent swept bare and open to the next nearest sympathy.

They had no occasion thus, the conjoined worshippers, to talk of what the Prince might be or might do for his son—the sum of service, in his absence, so completely filled itself out. It was not in the least, moreover, that there was doubt of him, for he was conspicuously addicted to the manipulation of the child, in the frank Italian way, at such moments as he judged discreet in respect to other claims: conspicuously, indeed, that is, for Maggie, who had more occasion, on the whole, to speak to her husband of the extravagance of her father than to speak to her father of the extravagance of her husband. Adam Verver had, all round, in this connection, his own serenity. He was sure of his son-in-law's auxiliary admiration—admiration, he meant, of his grand-son; since, to begin with, what else had been at work but the instinct—or it might fairly have been the tradition—of the latter's making the child so solidly beautiful as to HAVE to be admired? What contributed most to harmony in this play of relations, however, was the way the young man seemed to leave it to be gathered that, tradition for tradition, the grandpapa's own was not, in any estimate, to go for nothing. A tradition, or whatever it was, that had flowered prelusively in the Princess herself—well, Amerigo's very discretions were his way of taking account of it. His discriminations in respect to his heir were, in fine, not more angular than any others to be observed in him; and Mr. Verver received perhaps from no source so distinct an impression of being for him an odd and important phenomenon as he received from this impunity of appropriation, these unchallenged nursery hours. It was as if the grandpapa's special show of the character were but another side for the observer to study, another item for him to note. It came back, this latter personage knew, to his own previous perception—that of the Prince's inability, in any matter in which he was concerned, to CONCLUDE. The idiosyncrasy, for him, at each stage, had to be demonstrated—on which, however, he admirably accepted it. This last was, after all, the point; he really worked, poor young man, for acceptance, since he worked so constantly for comprehension. And how, when you came to that, COULD you know that a horse wouldn't shy at a brass-band, in a country road, because it didn't shy at a traction-engine? It might have been brought up to traction-engines without having been brought up to brass-bands. Little by little, thus, from month to month, the Prince was learning what his wife's father had been brought up to; and now it could be checked off—he had been brought, up to the romantic view of principini. Who would have thought it, and where would it all stop? The only fear somewhat sharp for Mr. Verver was a fear of disappointing him for strangeness. He felt that the evidence he offered, thus viewed, was too much on the positive side. He didn't know—he was learning, and it was funny for him—to how many things he HAD been brought up. If the Prince could only strike something to which he hadn't! This wouldn't, it seemed to him, ruffle the smoothness, and yet MIGHT, a little, add to the interest.

What was now clear, at all events, for the father and the daughter, was their simply knowing they wanted, for the time, to be together—at any cost, as it were; and their necessity so worked in them as to bear them out of the house, in a quarter hidden from that in which their friends were gathered, and cause them to wander, unseen, unfollowed, along a covered walk in the "old" garden, as it was called, old with an antiquity of formal things, high box and shaped yew and expanses of brick wall that had turned at once to purple and to pink. They went out of a door in the wall, a door that had a slab with a date set above it, 1713, but in the old multiplied lettering, and then had before them a small white gate, intensely white and clean amid all the greenness, through which they gradually passed to where some of the grandest trees spaciously clustered and where they would find one of the quietest places. A bench had been placed, long ago, beneath a great oak that helped to crown a mild eminence, and the ground sank away below it, to rise again, opposite, at a distance sufficient to enclose the solitude and figure a bosky horizon. Summer, blissfully, was with them yet, and the low sun made a splash of light where it pierced the looser shade; Maggie, coming down to go out, had brought a parasol, which, as, over her charming bare head, she now handled it, gave, with the big straw hat that her father in these days always wore a good deal tipped back, definite intention to their walk. They knew the bench; it was "sequestered"—they had praised it for that together, before, and liked the word; and after they had begun to linger there they could have smiled (if they hadn't been really too serious, and if the question hadn't so soon ceased to matter), over the probable wonder of the others as to what would have become of them.

The extent to which they enjoyed their indifference to any judgment of their want of ceremony, what did that of itself speak but for the way that, as a rule, they almost equally had others on their mind? They each knew that both were full of the superstition of not "hurting," but might precisely have been asking themselves, asking in fact each other, at this moment, whether that was to be, after all, the last word of their conscientious development. Certain it was, at all events, that, in addition to the Assinghams and the Lutches and Mrs. Rance, the attendance at tea, just in the right place on the west terrace, might perfectly comprise the four or five persons—among them the very pretty, the typically Irish Miss Maddock, vaunted, announced and now brought—from the couple of other houses near enough, one of these the minor residence Of their proprietor, established, thriftily, while he hired out his ancestral home, within sight and sense of his profit. It was not less certain, either, that, for once in a way, the group in question must all take the case as they found it. Fanny Assingham, at any time, for that matter, might perfectly be trusted to see Mr. Verver and his daughter, to see their reputation for a decent friendliness, through any momentary danger; might be trusted even to carry off their absence for Amerigo, for Amerigo's possible funny Italian anxiety; Amerigo always being, as the Princess was well aware, conveniently amenable to this friend's explanations, beguilements, reassurances, and perhaps in fact rather more than less dependent on them as his new life—since that was his own name for it—opened out. It was no secret to Maggie—it was indeed positively a public joke for her—that she couldn't explain as Mrs. Assingham did, and that, the Prince liking explanations, liking them almost as if he collected them, in the manner of book-plates or postage-stamps, for themselves, his requisition of this luxury had to be met. He didn't seem to want them as yet for use—rather for ornament and amusement, innocent amusement of the kind he most fancied and that was so characteristic of his blessed, beautiful, general, slightly indolent lack of more dissipated, or even just of more sophisticated, tastes.

However that might be, the dear woman had come to be frankly and gaily recognised—and not least by herself—as filling in the intimate little circle an office that was not always a sinecure. It was almost as if she had taken, with her kind, melancholy Colonel at her heels, a responsible engagement; to be within call, as it were, for all those appeals that sprang out of talk, that sprang not a little, doubtless too, out of leisure. It naturally led her position in the household, as, she called it, to considerable frequency of presence, to visits, from the good couple, freely repeated and prolonged, and not so much as under form of protest. She was there to keep him quiet—it was Amerigo's own description of her influence; and it would only have needed a more visible disposition to unrest in him to make the account perfectly fit. Fanny herself limited indeed, she minimised, her office; you didn't need a jailor, she contended, for a domesticated lamb tied up with pink ribbon. This was not an animal to be controlled—it was an animal to be, at the most, educated. She admitted accordingly that she was educative—which Maggie was so aware that she herself, inevitably, wasn't; so it came round to being true that what she was most in charge of was his mere intelligence. This left, goodness knew, plenty of different calls for Maggie to meet—in a case in which so much pink ribbon, as it might be symbolically named, was lavished on the creature. What it all amounted to, at any rate, was that Mrs. Assingham would be keeping him quiet now, while his wife and his father-in-law carried out their own little frugal picnic; quite moreover, doubtless, not much less neededly in respect to the members of the circle that were with them than in respect to the pair they were missing almost for the first time. It was present to Maggie that the Prince could bear, when he was with his wife, almost any queerness on the part of people, strange English types, who bored him, beyond convenience, by being so little as he himself was; for this was one of the ways in which a wife was practically sustaining. But she was as positively aware that she hadn't yet learned to see him as meeting such exposure in her absence. How did he move and talk, how above all did he, or how WOULD he, look—he who, with his so nobly handsome face, could look such wonderful things—in case of being left alone with some of the subjects of his wonder? There were subjects for wonder among these very neighbours; only Maggie herself had her own odd way—which didn't moreover the least irritate him—of really liking them in proportion as they could strike her as strange. It came out in her by heredity, he amused himself with declaring, this love of chinoiseries; but she actually this evening didn't mind—he might deal with her Chinese as he could.

Maggie indeed would always have had for such moments, had they oftener occurred, the impression made on her by a word of Mrs. Assingham's, a word referring precisely to that appetite in Amerigo for the explanatory which we have just found in our path. It wasn't that the Princess could be indebted to another person, even to so clever a one as this friend, for seeing anything in her husband that she mightn't see unaided; but she had ever, hitherto, been of a nature to accept with modest gratitude any better description of a felt truth than her little limits— terribly marked, she knew, in the direction of saying the right things—enabled her to make. Thus it was, at any rate, that she was able to live more or less in the light of the fact expressed so lucidly by their common comforter—the fact that the Prince was saving up, for some very mysterious but very fine eventual purpose, all the wisdom, all the answers to his questions, all the impressions and generalisations, he gathered; putting them away and packing them down because he wanted his great gun to be loaded to the brim on the day he should decide to let it off. He wanted first to make sure of the whole of the subject that was unrolling itself before him; after which the innumerable facts he had collected would find their use. He knew what he was about—trust him at last therefore to make, and to some effect, his big noise. And Mrs. Assingham had repeated that he knew what he was about. It was the happy form of this assurance that had remained with Maggie; it could always come in for her that Amerigo knew what he was about. He might at moments seem vague, seem absent, seem even bored: this when, away from her father, with whom it was impossible for him to appear anything but respectfully occupied, he let his native gaiety go in outbreaks of song, or even of quite whimsical senseless sound, either expressive of intimate relaxation or else fantastically plaintive. He might at times reflect with the frankest lucidity on the circumstance that the case was for a good while yet absolutely settled in regard to what he still had left, at home, of his very own; in regard to the main seat of his affection, the house in Rome, the big black palace, the Palazzo Nero, as he was fond of naming it, and also on the question of the villa in the Sabine hills, which she had, at the time of their engagement, seen and yearned over, and the Castello proper, described by him always as the "perched" place, that had, as she knew, formerly stood up, on the pedestal of its mountain-slope, showing beautifully blue from afar, as the head and front of the princedom. He might rejoice in certain moods over the so long-estranged state of these properties, not indeed all irreclaimably alienated, but encumbered with unending leases and charges, with obstinate occupants, with impossibilities of use—all without counting the cloud of mortgages that had, from far back, buried them beneath the ashes of rage and remorse, a shroud as thick as the layer once resting on the towns at the foot of Vesuvius, and actually making of any present restorative effort a process much akin to slow excavation. Just so he might with another turn of his humour almost wail for these brightest spots of his lost paradise, declaring that he was an idiot not to be able to bring himself to face the sacrifices—sacrifices resting, if definitely anywhere, with Mr. Verver—necessary for winning them back.

One of the most comfortable things between the husband and the wife meanwhile—one of those easy certitudes they could be merely gay about—was that she never admired him so much, or so found him heartbreakingly handsome, clever, irresistible, in the very degree in which he had originally and fatally dawned upon her, as when she saw other women reduced to the same passive pulp that had then begun, once for all, to constitute HER substance. There was really nothing they had talked of together with more intimate and familiar pleasantry than of the license and privilege, the boundless happy margin, thus established for each: she going so far as to put it that, even should he some day get drunk and beat her, the spectacle of him with hated rivals would, after no matter what extremity, always, for the sovereign charm of it, charm of it in itself and as the exhibition of him that most deeply moved her, suffice to bring her round. What would therefore be more open to him than to keep her in love with him? He agreed, with all his heart, at these light moments, that his course wouldn't then be difficult, inasmuch as, so simply constituted as he was on all the precious question—and why should he be ashamed of it?—he knew but one way with the fair. They had to be fair—and he was fastidious and particular, his standard was high; but when once this was the case what relation with them was conceivable, what relation was decent, rudimentary, properly human, but that of a plain interest in the fairness? His interest, she always answered, happened not to be "plain," and plainness, all round, had little to do with the matter, which was marked, on the contrary, by the richest variety of colour; but the working basis, at all events, had been settled—the Miss Maddocks of life been assured of their importance for him. How conveniently assured Maggie—to take him too into the joke—had more than once gone so far as to mention to her father; since it fell in easily with the tenderness of her disposition to remember she might occasionally make him happy by an intimate confidence. This was one of her rules-full as she was of little rules, considerations, provisions. There were things she of course couldn't tell him, in so many words, about Amerigo and herself, and about their happiness and their union and their deepest depths—and there were other things she needn't; but there were also those that were both true and amusing, both communicable and real, and of these, with her so conscious, so delicately cultivated scheme of conduct as a daughter, she could make her profit at will. A pleasant hush, for that matter, had fallen on most of the elements while she lingered apart with her companion; it involved, this serenity, innumerable complete assumptions: since so ordered and so splendid a rest, all the tokens, spreading about them, of confidence solidly supported, might have suggested for persons of poorer pitch the very insolence of facility. Still, they weren't insolent—THEY weren't, our pair could reflect; they were only blissful and grateful and personally modest, not ashamed of knowing, with competence, when great things were great, when good things were good, and when safe things were safe, and not, therefore, placed below their fortune by timidity which would have been as bad as being below it by impudence. Worthy of it as they were, and as each appears, under our last possible analysis, to have wished to make the other feel that they were, what they most finally exhaled into the evening air as their eyes mildly met may well have been a kind of helplessness in their felicity. Their rightness, the justification of everything—something they so felt the pulse of—sat there with them; but they might have been asking themselves a little blankly to what further use they could put anything so perfect. They had created and nursed and established it; they had housed it here in dignity and crowned it with comfort; but mightn't the moment possibly count for them—or count at least for us while we watch them with their fate all before them—as the dawn of the discovery that it doesn't always meet ALL contingencies to be right? Otherwise why should Maggie have found a word of definite doubt—the expression of the fine pang determined in her a few hours before—rise after a time to her lips? She took so for granted moreover her companion's intelligence of her doubt that the mere vagueness of her question could say it all. "What is it, after all, that they want to do to you?" "They" were for the Princess too the hovering forces of which Mrs. Rance was the symbol, and her father, only smiling back now, at his ease, took no trouble to appear not to know what she meant. What she meant—when once she had spoken—could come out well enough; though indeed it was nothing, after they had come to the point, that could serve as ground for a great defensive campaign. The waters of talk spread a little, and Maggie presently contributed an idea in saying: "What has really happened is that the proportions, for us, are altered." He accepted equally, for the time, this somewhat cryptic remark; he still failed to challenge her even when she added that it wouldn't so much matter if he hadn't been so terribly young. He uttered a sound of protest only when she went to declare that she ought as a daughter, in common decency, to have waited. Yet by that time she was already herself admitting that she should have had to wait long—if she waited, that is, till he was old. But there was a way. "Since you ARE an irresistible youth, we've got to face it. That, somehow, is what that woman has made me feel. There'll be others."

X

To talk of it thus appeared at last a positive relief to him. "Yes, there'll be others. But you'll see me through."

She hesitated. "Do you mean if you give in?"

"Oh no. Through my holding out."

Maggie waited again, but when she spoke it had an effect of abruptness. "Why SHOULD you hold out forever?"

He gave, none the less, no start—and this as from the habit of taking anything, taking everything, from her as harmonious. But it was quite written upon him too, for that matter, that holding out wouldn't be, so very completely, his natural, or at any rate his acquired, form. His appearance would have testified that he might have to do so a long time—for a man so greatly beset. This appearance, that is, spoke but little, as yet, of short remainders and simplified senses—and all in spite of his being a small, spare, slightly stale person, deprived of the general prerogative of presence. It was not by mass or weight or vulgar immediate quantity that he would in the future, any more than he had done in the past, insist or resist or prevail. There was even something in him that made his position, on any occasion, made his relation to any scene or to any group, a matter of the back of the stage, of an almost visibly conscious want of affinity with the footlights. He would have figured less than anything the stage-manager or the author of the play, who most occupy the foreground; he might be, at the best, the financial "backer," watching his interests from the wing, but in rather confessed ignorance of the mysteries of mimicry. Barely taller than his daughter, he pressed at no point on the presumed propriety of his greater stoutness. He had lost early in life much of his crisp, closely-curling hair, the fineness of which was repeated in a small neat beard, too compact to be called "full," though worn equally, as for a mark where other marks were wanting, on lip and cheek and chin. His neat, colourless face, provided with the merely indispensable features, suggested immediately, for a description, that it was CLEAR, and in this manner somewhat resembled a small decent room, clean-swept and unencumbered with furniture, but drawing a particular advantage, as might presently be noted, from the outlook of a pair of ample and uncurtained windows. There was something in Adam Verver's eyes that both admitted the morning and the evening in unusual quantities and gave the modest area the outward extension of a view that was "big" even when restricted to stars. Deeply and changeably blue, though not romantically large, they were yet youthfully, almost strangely beautiful, with their ambiguity of your scarce knowing if they most carried their possessor's vision out or most opened themselves to your own. Whatever you might feel, they stamped the place with their importance, as the house-agents say; so that, on one side or the other, you were never out of their range, were moving about, for possible community, opportunity, the sight of you scarce knew what, either before them or behind them. If other importances, not to extend the question, kept themselves down, they were in no direction less obtruded than in that of our friend's dress, adopted once for all as with a sort of sumptuary scruple. He wore every day of the year, whatever the occasion, the same little black "cut away" coat, of the fashion of his younger time; he wore the same cool-looking trousers, chequered in black and white—the proper harmony with which, he inveterately considered, was a sprigged blue satin necktie; and, over his concave little stomach, quaintly indifferent to climates and seasons, a white duck waistcoat. "Should you really," he now asked, "like me to marry?" He spoke as if, coming from his daughter herself, it MIGHT be an idea; which, for that matter, he would be ready to carry out should she definitely say so.

Definite, however, just yet, she was not prepared to be, though it seemed to come to her with force, as she thought, that there was a truth, in the connection, to utter. "What I feel is that there is something that used to be right and that I've made wrong. It used to be right that you hadn't married, and that you didn't seem to want to. It used also"—she continued to make out "to seem easy for the question not to come up. That's what I've made different. It does come up. It WILL come up."

"You don't think I can keep it down?" Mr. Verver's tone was cheerfully pensive.

"Well, I've given you, by MY move, all the trouble of having to."

He liked the tenderness of her idea, and it made him, as she sat near him, pass his arm about her. "I guess I don't feel as if you had 'moved' very far. You've only moved next door."

"Well," she continued, "I don't feel as if it were fair for me just to have given you a push and left you so. If I've made the difference for you, I must think of the difference."

"Then what, darling," he indulgently asked, "DO you think?"

"That's just what I don't yet know. But I must find out. We must think together—as we've always thought. What I mean," she went on after a moment, "is that it strikes me that I ought to at least offer you some alternative. I ought to have worked one out for you."

"An alternative to what?"

"Well, to your simply missing what you've lost—without anything being done about it."

"But what HAVE I lost?"

She thought a minute, as if it were difficult to say, yet as if she more and more saw it. "Well, whatever it was that, BEFORE, kept us from thinking, and kept you, really, as you might say, in the market. It was as if you couldn't be in the market when you were married to me. Or rather as if I kept people off, innocently, by being married to you. Now that I'm married to some one else you're, in consequence, married to nobody. Therefore you may be married to anybody, to everybody. People don't see why you shouldn't be married to THEM."

"Isn't it enough of a reason," he mildly inquired, "that I don't want to be?"

"It's enough of a reason, yes. But to BE enough of a reason it has to be too much of a trouble. I mean FOR you. It has to be too much of a fight. You ask me what you've lost," Maggie continued to explain. "The not having to take the trouble and to make the fight—that's what you've lost. The advantage, the happiness of being just as you were—because I was just as I was—that's what you miss."

"So that you think," her father presently said, "that I had better get married just in order to be as I was before?"

The detached tone of it—detached as if innocently to amuse her by showing his desire to accommodate—was so far successful as to draw from her gravity a short, light laugh. "Well, what I don't want you to feel is that if you were to I shouldn't understand. I SHOULD understand. That's all," said the Princess gently.

Her companion turned it pleasantly over. "You don't go so far as to wish me to take somebody I don't like?"

"Ah, father," she sighed, "you know how far I go—how far I COULD go. But I only wish that if you ever SHOULD like anybody, you may never doubt of my feeling how I've brought you to it. You'll always know that I know that it's my fault."

"You mean," he went on in his contemplative way, "that it will be you who'll take the consequences?"

Maggie just considered. "I'll leave you all the good ones, but I'll take the bad."

"Well, that's handsome." He emphasised his sense of it by drawing her closer and holding her more tenderly. "It's about all I could expect of you. So far as you've wronged me, therefore, we'll call it square. I'll let you know in time if I see a prospect of your having to take it up. But am I to understand meanwhile," he soon went on, "that, ready as you are to see me through my collapse, you're not ready, or not AS ready, to see me through my resistance? I've got to be a regular martyr before you'll be inspired?"

She demurred at his way of putting it. "Why, if you like it, you know, it won't BE a collapse."

"Then why talk about seeing me through at all? I shall only collapse if I do like it. But what I seem to feel is that I don't WANT to like it. That is," he amended, "unless I feel surer I do than appears very probable. I don't want to have to THINK I like it in a case when I really shan't. I've had to do that in some cases," he confessed—"when it has been a question of other things. I don't want," he wound up, "to be MADE to make a mistake."

"Ah, but it's too dreadful," she returned, "that you should even have to FEAR—or just nervously to dream—that you may be. What does that show, after all," she asked, "but that you do really, well within, feel a want? What does it show but that you're truly susceptible?"

"Well, it may show that"—he defended himself against nothing. "But it shows also, I think, that charming women are, in the kind of life we're leading now, numerous and formidable."

Maggie entertained for a moment the proposition; under cover of which, however, she passed quickly from the general to the particular. "Do you feel Mrs. Rance to be charming?"

"Well, I feel her to be formidable. When they cast a spell it comes to the same thing. I think she'd do anything."

"Oh well, I'd help you," the Princess said with decision, "as against HER—if that's all you require. It's too funny," she went on before he again spoke, "that Mrs. Rance should be here at all. But if you talk of the life we lead, much of it is, altogether, I'm bound to say, too funny. The thing is," Maggie developed under this impression, "that I don't think we lead, as regards other people, any life at all. We don't at any rate, it seems to me, lead half the life we might. And so it seems, I think, to Amerigo. So it seems also, I'm sure, to Fanny Assingham."

Mr. Verver-as if from due regard for these persons—considered a little. "What life would they like us to lead?"

"Oh, it's not a question, I think, on which they quite feel together. SHE thinks, dear Fanny, that we ought to be greater."

"Greater—?" He echoed it vaguely. "And Amerigo too, you say?"

"Ah yes"-her reply was prompt "but Amerigo doesn't mind. He doesn't care, I mean, what we do. It's for us, he considers, to see things exactly as we wish. Fanny herself," Maggie pursued, "thinks he's magnificent. Magnificent, I mean, for taking everything as it is, for accepting the 'social limitations' of our life, for not missing what we don't give him."

Mr. Verver attended. "Then if he doesn't miss his magnificence is easy."

"It IS easy-that's exactly what I think. If there were things he DID miss, and if in spite of them he were always sweet, then, no doubt, he would be a more or less unappreciated hero. He COULD be a Hero—he WILL be one if it's ever necessary. But it will be about something better than our dreariness. I know," the Princess declared, "where he's magnificent." And she rested a minute on that. She ended, however, as she had begun. "We're not, all the same, committed to anything stupid. If we ought to be grander, as Fanny thinks, we CAN be grander. There's nothing to prevent."

"Is it a strict moral obligation?" Adam Verver inquired.

"No—it's for the amusement."

"For whose? For Fanny's own?"

"For everyone's—though I dare say Fanny's would be a large part." She hesitated; she had now, it might have appeared, something more to bring out, which she finally produced. "For yours in particular, say—if you go into the question." She even bravely followed it up. "I haven't really, after all, had to think much to see that that much more can be done for you than is done."

Mr. Verver uttered an odd vague sound. "Don't you think a good deal is done when you come out and talk to me this way?"

"Ah," said his daughter, smiling at him, "we make too much of that!" And then to explain: "That's good, and it's natural—but it isn't great. We forget that we're as free as air."

"Well, THAT'S great," Mr. Verver pleaded. "Great if we act on it. Not if we don't."

She continued to smile, and he took her smile; wondering again a little by this time, however; struck more and more by an intensity in it that belied a light tone. "What do you want," he demanded, "to do to me?" And he added, as she didn't say: "You've got something in your mind." It had come to him within the minute that from the beginning of their session there she had been keeping something back, and that an impression of this had more than once, in spite of his general theoretic respect for her present right to personal reserves and mysteries, almost ceased to be vague in him. There had been from the first something in her anxious eyes, in the way she occasionally lost herself, that it would perfectly explain. He was therefore now quite sure. "You've got something up your sleeve."

She had a silence that made him right. "Well, when I tell you you'll understand. It's only up my sleeve in the sense of being in a letter I got this morning. All day, yes—it HAS been in my mind. I've been asking myself if it were quite the right moment, or in any way fair, to ask you if you could stand just now another woman."

It relieved him a little, yet the beautiful consideration of her manner made it in a degree portentous. "Stand one—?"

"Well, mind her coming."

He stared—then he laughed. "It depends on who she is."

"There—you see! I've at all events been thinking whether you'd take this particular person but as a worry the more. Whether, that is, you'd go so far with her in your notion of having to be kind."

He gave at this the quickest shake to his foot. How far would she go in HER notion of it.

"Well," his daughter returned, "you know how far, in a general way, Charlotte Stant goes."

"Charlotte? Is SHE coming?"

"She writes me, practically, that she'd like to if we're so good as to ask her."

Mr. Verver continued to gaze, but rather as if waiting for more. Then, as everything appeared to have come, his expression had a drop. If this was all it was simple. "Then why in the world not?"

Maggie's face lighted anew, but it was now another light. "It isn't a want of tact?"

"To ask her?"

"To propose it to you."

"That I should ask her?"

He put the question as an effect of his remnant of vagueness, but this had also its own effect. Maggie wondered an instant; after which, as with a flush of recognition, she took it up. "It would be too beautiful if you WOULD!"

This, clearly, had not been her first idea—the chance of his words had prompted it. "Do you mean write to her myself?"

"Yes—it would be kind. It would be quite beautiful of you. That is, of course," said Maggie, "if you sincerely CAN."

He appeared to wonder an instant why he sincerely shouldn't, and indeed, for that matter, where the question of sincerity came in. This virtue, between him and his daughter's friend, had surely been taken for granted. "My dear child," he returned, "I don't think I'm afraid of Charlotte."

"Well, that's just what it's lovely to have from you. From the moment you're NOT—the least little bit—I'll immediately invite her."

"But where in the world is she?" He spoke as if he had not thought of Charlotte, nor so much as heard her name pronounced, for a very long time. He quite in fact amicably, almost amusedly, woke up to her.

"She's in Brittany, at a little bathing-place, with some people I don't know. She's always with people, poor dear—she rather has to be; even when, as is sometimes the case; they're people she doesn't immensely like."

"Well, I guess she likes US," said Adam Verver. "Yes—fortunately she likes us. And if I wasn't afraid of spoiling it for you," Maggie added, "I'd even mention that you're not the one of our number she likes least."

"Why should that spoil it for me?"

"Oh, my dear, you know. What else have we been talking about? It costs you so much to be liked. That's why I hesitated to tell you of my letter."

He stared a moment—as if the subject had suddenly grown out of recognition. "But Charlotte—on other visits—never used to cost me anything."

"No—only her 'keep,'" Maggie smiled.

"Then I don't think I mind her keep—if that's all." The Princess, however, it was clear, wished to be thoroughly conscientious. "Well, it may not be quite all. If I think of its being pleasant to have her, it's because she WILL make a difference."

"Well, what's the harm in that if it's but a difference for the better?"

"Ah then—there you are!" And the Princess showed in her smile her small triumphant wisdom. "If you acknowledge a possible difference for the better we're not, after all, so tremendously right as we are. I mean we're not—as satisfied and amused. We do see there are ways of being grander."

"But will Charlotte Stant," her father asked with surprise, "make us grander?"

Maggie, on this, looking at him well, had a remarkable reply. "Yes, I think. Really grander."

He thought; for if this was a sudden opening he wished but the more to meet it. "Because she's so handsome?"

"No, father." And the Princess was almost solemn. "Because she's so great."

"Great—?"

"Great in nature, in character, in spirit. Great in life."

"So?" Mr. Verver echoed. "What has she done—in life?"

"Well, she has been brave and bright," said Maggie. "That mayn't sound like much, but she has been so in the face of things that might well have made it too difficult for many other girls. She hasn't a creature in the world really—that is nearly—belonging to her. Only acquaintances who, in all sorts of ways, make use of her, and distant relations who are so afraid she'll make use of THEM that they seldom let her look at them."

Mr. Verver was struck—and, as usual, to some purpose. "If we get her here to improve us don't we too then make use of her?"

It pulled the Princess up, however, but an instant. "We're old, old friends—we do her good too. I should always, even at the worst—speaking for myself—admire her still more than I used her."

"I see. That always does good."

Maggie hesitated. "Certainly—she knows it. She knows, I mean, how great I think her courage and her cleverness. She's not afraid—not of anything; and yet she no more ever takes a liberty with you than if she trembled for her life. And then she's INTERESTING—which plenty of other people with plenty of other merits never are a bit." In which fine flicker of vision the truth widened to the Princess's view "I myself of course don't take liberties, but then I do, always, by nature, tremble for my life. That's the way I live."

"Oh I say, love!" her father vaguely murmured.

"Yes, I live in terror," she insisted. "I'm a small creeping thing."

"You'll not persuade me that you're not as good as Charlotte Stant," he still placidly enough remarked.

"I may be as good, but I'm not so great—and that's what we're talking about. She has a great imagination. She has, in every way, a great attitude. She has above all a great conscience." More perhaps than ever in her life before Maggie addressed her father at this moment with a shade of the absolute in her tone. She had never come so near telling him what she should take it from her to believe. "She has only twopence in the world—but that has nothing to do with it. Or rather indeed"—she quickly corrected herself—"it has everything. For she doesn't care. I never saw her do anything but laugh at her poverty. Her life has been harder than anyone knows."

It was moreover as if, thus unprecedentedly positive, his child had an effect upon him that Mr. Verver really felt as a new thing. "Why then haven't you told me about her before?"

"Well, haven't we always known—?"

"I should have thought," he submitted, "that we had already pretty well sized her up."

"Certainly—we long ago quite took her for granted. But things change, with time, and I seem to know that, after this interval, I'm going to like her better than ever. I've lived more myself, I'm older, and one judges better. Yes, I'm going to see in Charlotte," said the Princess—and speaking now as with high and free expectation—"more than I've ever seen."

"Then I'll try to do so too. She WAS"—it came back to Mr. Verver more—"the one of your friends I thought the best for you."

His companion, however, was so launched in her permitted liberty of appreciation that she for the moment scarce heard him. She was lost in the case she made out, the vision of the different ways in which Charlotte had distinguished herself.

"She would have liked for instance—I'm sure she would have liked extremely—to marry; and nothing in general is more ridiculous, even when it has been pathetic, than a woman who has tried and has not been able."

It had all Mr. Verver's attention. "She has 'tried'—?"

"She has seen cases where she would have liked to."

"But she has not been able?"

"Well, there are more cases, in Europe, in which it doesn't come to girls who are poor than in which it does come to them. Especially," said Maggie with her continued competence, "when they're Americans."

Well, her father now met her, and met her cheerfully, on all sides. "Unless you mean," he suggested, "that when the girls are American there are more cases in which it comes to the rich than to the poor."

She looked at him good-humouredly. "That may be—but I'm not going to be smothered in MY case. It ought to make me—if I were in danger of being a fool—all the nicer to people like Charlotte. It's not hard for ME," she practically explained, "not to be ridiculous—unless in a very different way. I might easily be ridiculous, I suppose, by behaving as if I thought I had done a great thing. Charlotte, at any rate, has done nothing, and anyone can see it, and see also that it's rather strange; and yet no one—no one not awfully presumptuous or offensive would like, or would dare, to treat her, just as she is, as anything but quite RIGHT. That's what it is to have something about you that carries things off."

Mr. Verver's silence, on this, could only be a sign that she had caused her story to interest him; though the sign when he spoke was perhaps even sharper. "And is it also what you mean by Charlotte's being 'great'?"

"Well," said Maggie, "it's one of her ways. But she has many."

Again for a little her father considered. "And who is it she has tried to marry?"

Maggie, on her side as well, waited as if to bring it out with effect; but she after a minute either renounced or encountered an obstacle. "I'm afraid I'm not sure."

"Then how do you know?"

"Well, I don't KNOW"—and, qualifying again, she was earnestly emphatic. "I only make it out for myself."

"But you must make it out about someone in particular."

She had another pause. "I don't think I want even for myself to put names and times, to pull away any veil. I've an idea there has been, more than once, somebody I'm not acquainted with—and needn't be or want to be. In any case it's all over, and, beyond giving her credit for everything, it's none of my business."

Mr. Verver deferred, yet he discriminated. "I don't see how you can give credit without knowing the facts."

"Can't I give it—generally—for dignity? Dignity, I mean, in misfortune."

"You've got to postulate the misfortune first."

"Well," said Maggie, "I can do that. Isn't it always a misfortune to be—when you're so fine—so wasted? And yet," she went on, "not to wail about it, not to look even as if you knew it?"

Mr. Verver seemed at first to face this as a large question, and then, after a little, solicited by another view, to let the appeal drop. "Well, she mustn't be wasted. We won't at least have waste."

It produced in Maggie's face another gratitude. "Then, dear sir, that's all I want."

And it would apparently have settled their question and ended their talk if her father had not, after a little, shown the disposition to revert. "How many times are you supposing that she has tried?"

Once more, at this, and as if she hadn't been, couldn't be, hated to be, in such delicate matters, literal, she was moved to attenuate. "Oh, I don't say she absolutely ever TRIED—!"

He looked perplexed. "But if she has so absolutely failed, what then had she done?"

"She has suffered—she has done that." And the Princess added: "She has loved—and she has lost."

Mr. Verver, however, still wondered. "But how many times."

Maggie hesitated, but it cleared up. "Once is enough. Enough, that is, for one to be kind to her."

Her father listened, yet not challenging—only as with a need of some basis on which, under these new lights, his bounty could be firm. "But has she told you nothing?"

"Ah, thank goodness, no!"

He stared. "Then don't young women tell?"

"Because, you mean, it's just what they're supposed to do?" She looked at him, flushed again now; with which, after another hesitation, "Do young men tell?" she asked.

He gave a short laugh. "How do I know, my dear, what young men do?"

"Then how do I know, father, what vulgar girls do?"

"I see—I see," he quickly returned.

But she spoke the next moment as if she might, odiously, have been sharp. "What happens at least is that where there's a great deal of pride there's a great deal of silence. I don't know, I admit, what I should do if I were lonely and sore—for what sorrow, to speak of, have I ever had in my life? I don't know even if I'm proud—it seems to me the question has never come up for me."

"Oh, I guess you're proud, Mag," her father cheerfully interposed. "I mean I guess you're proud enough."

"Well then, I hope I'm humble enough too. I might, at all events, for all I know, be abject under a blow. How can I tell? Do you realise, father, that I've never had the least blow?"

He gave her a long, quiet look. "Who SHOULD realise if I don't?"

"Well, you'll realise when I HAVE one!" she exclaimed with a short laugh that resembled, as for good reasons, his own of a minute before. "I wouldn't in any case have let her tell me what would have been dreadful to me. For such wounds and shames are dreadful: at least," she added, catching herself up, "I suppose they are; for what, as I say, do I know of them? I don't WANT to know!"—she spoke quite with vehemence. "There are things that are sacred whether they're joys or pains. But one can always, for safety, be kind," she kept on; "one feels when that's right."

She had got up with these last words; she stood there before him with that particular suggestion in her aspect to which even the long habit of their life together had not closed his sense, kept sharp, year after year, by the collation of types and signs, the comparison of fine object with fine object, of one degree of finish, of one form of the exquisite with another—the appearance of some slight, slim draped "antique" of Vatican or Capitoline halls, late and refined, rare as a note and immortal as a link, set in motion by the miraculous infusion of a modern impulse and yet, for all the sudden freedom of folds and footsteps forsaken after centuries by their pedestal, keeping still the quality, the perfect felicity, of the statue; the blurred, absent eyes, the smoothed, elegant, nameless head, the impersonal flit of a creature lost in an alien age and passing as an image in worn relief round and round a precious vase. She had always had odd moments of striking him, daughter of his very own though she was, as, as a figure thus simplified, "generalised" in its grace, a figure with which his human connection was fairly interrupted by some vague analogy of turn and attitude, something shyly mythological and nymphlike. The trick, he was not uncomplacently aware, was mainly of his own mind; it came from his caring for precious vases only less than for precious daughters. And what was more to the point still, it often operated while he was quite at the same time conscious that Maggie had been described, even in her prettiness, as "prim"—Mrs. Rance herself had enthusiastically used the word of her; while he remembered that when once she had been told before him, familiarly, that she resembled a nun, she had replied that she was delighted to hear it and would certainly try to; while also, finally, it was present to him that, discreetly heedless, thanks to her long association with nobleness in art, to the leaps and bounds of fashion, she brought her hair down very straight and flat over her temples, in the constant manner of her mother, who had not been a bit mythological. Nymphs and nuns were certainly separate types, but Mr. Verver, when he really amused himself, let consistency go. The play of vision was at all events so rooted in him that he could receive impressions of sense even while positively thinking. He was positively thinking while Maggie stood there, and it led for him to yet another question—which in its turn led to others still. "Do you regard the condition as hers then that you spoke of a minute ago?"

"The condition—?"

"Why that of having loved so intensely that she's, as you say, 'beyond everything'?"

Maggie had scarcely to reflect—her answer was so prompt. "Oh no. She's beyond nothing. For she has had nothing."

"I see. You must have had things to be them. It's a kind of law of perspective."

Maggie didn't know about the law, but she continued definite. "She's not, for example, beyond help."

"Oh well then, she shall have all we can give her. I'll write to her," he said, "with pleasure."

"Angel!" she answered as she gaily and tenderly looked at him.

True as this might be, however, there was one thing more—he was an angel with a human curiosity. "Has she told you she likes me much?"

"Certainly she has told me—but I won't pamper you. Let it be enough for you it has always been one of my reasons for liking HER."

"Then she's indeed not beyond everything," Mr. Verver more or less humorously observed.

"Oh it isn't, thank goodness, that she's in love with you. It's not, as I told you at first, the sort of thing for you to fear."

He had spoken with cheer, but it appeared to drop before this reassurance, as if the latter overdid his alarm, and that should be corrected. "Oh, my dear, I've always thought of her as a little girl."

"Ah, she's not a little girl," said the Princess.

"Then I'll write to her as a brilliant woman."

"It's exactly what she is."

Mr. Verver had got up as he spoke, and for a little, before retracing their steps, they stood looking at each other as if they had really arranged something. They had come out together for themselves, but it had produced something more. What it had produced was in fact expressed by the words with which he met his companion's last emphasis. "Well, she has a famous friend in you, Princess."

Maggie took this in—it was too plain for a protest. "Do you know what I'm really thinking of?" she asked.

He wondered, with her eyes on him—eyes of contentment at her freedom now to talk; and he wasn't such a fool, he presently showed, as not, suddenly, to arrive at it. "Why, of your finding her at last yourself a husband."

"Good for YOU!" Maggie smiled. "But it will take," she added, "some looking."

"Then let me look right here with you," her father said as they walked on.

XI

Mrs. Assingham and the Colonel, quitting Fawns before the end of September, had come back later on; and now, a couple of weeks after, they were again interrupting their stay, but this time with the question of their return left to depend, on matters that were rather hinted at than importunately named. The Lutches and Mrs. Rance had also, by the action of Charlotte Stant's arrival, ceased to linger, though with hopes and theories, as to some promptitude of renewal, of which the lively expression, awakening the echoes of the great stone-paved, oak-panelled, galleried hall that was not the least interesting feature of the place, seemed still a property of the air. It was on this admirable spot that, before her October afternoon had waned, Fanny Assingham spent with her easy host a few moments which led to her announcing her own and her husband's final secession, at the same time as they tempted her to point the moral of all vain reverberations. The double door of the house stood open to an effect of hazy autumn sunshine, a wonderful, windless, waiting, golden hour, under the influence of which Adam Verver met his genial friend as she came to drop into the post-box with her own hand a thick sheaf of letters. They presently thereafter left the house together and drew out half-an-hour on the terrace in a manner they were to revert to in thought, later on, as that of persons who really had been taking leave of each other at a parting of the ways. He traced his impression, on coming to consider, back to a mere three words she had begun by using about Charlotte Stant. She simply "cleared them out"—those had been the three words, thrown off in reference to the general golden peace that the Kentish October had gradually ushered in, the "halcyon" days the full beauty of which had appeared to shine out for them after Charlotte's arrival. For it was during these days that Mrs. Rance and the Miss Lutches had been observed to be gathering themselves for departure, and it was with that difference made that the sense of the whole situation showed most fair—the sense of how right they had been to engage for so ample a residence, and of all the pleasure so fruity an autumn there could hold in its lap. This was what had occurred, that their lesson had been learned; and what Mrs. Assingham had dwelt upon was that without Charlotte it would have been learned but half. It would certainly not have been taught by Mrs. Rance and the Miss Lutches if these ladies had remained with them as long as at one time seemed probable. Charlotte's light intervention had thus become a cause, operating covertly but none the less actively, and Fanny Assingham's speech, which she had followed up a little, echoed within him, fairly to startle him, as the indication of something irresistible. He could see now how this superior force had worked, and he fairly liked to recover the sight—little harm as he dreamed of doing, little ill as he dreamed of wishing, the three ladies, whom he had after all entertained for a stiffish series of days. She had been so vague and quiet about it, wonderful Charlotte, that he hadn't known what was happening—happening, that is, as a result of her influence. "Their fires, as they felt her, turned to smoke," Mrs. Assingham remarked; which he was to reflect on indeed even while they strolled. He had retained, since his long talk with Maggie—the talk that had settled the matter of his own direct invitation to her friend—an odd little taste, as he would have described it, for hearing things said about this young woman, hearing, so to speak, what COULD be said about her: almost as if her portrait, by some eminent hand, were going on, so that he watched it grow under the multiplication of touches. Mrs. Assingham, it struck him, applied two or three of the finest in their discussion of their young friend—so different a figure now from that early playmate of Maggie's as to whom he could almost recall from of old the definite occasions of his having paternally lumped the two children together in the recommendation that they shouldn't make too much noise nor eat too much jam. His companion professed that in the light of Charlotte's prompt influence she had not been a stranger to a pang of pity for their recent visitors. "I felt in fact, privately, so sorry for them, that I kept my impression to myself while they were here—wishing not to put the rest of you on the scent; neither Maggie, nor the Prince, nor yourself, nor even Charlotte HERself, if you didn't happen to notice. Since you didn't, apparently, I perhaps now strike you as extravagant. But I'm not—I followed it all. One SAW the consciousness I speak of come over the poor things, very much as I suppose people at the court of the Borgias may have watched each other begin to look queer after having had the honour of taking wine with the heads of the family. My comparison's only a little awkward, for I don't in the least mean that Charlotte was consciously dropping poison into their cup. She was just herself their poison, in the sense of mortally disagreeing with them—but she didn't know it."

"Ah, she didn't know it?" Mr. Verver had asked with interest.

"Well, I THINK she didn't"—Mrs. Assingham had to admit that she hadn't pressingly sounded her. "I don't pretend to be sure, in every connection, of what Charlotte knows. She doesn't, certainly, like to make people suffer—not, in general, as is the case with so many of us, even other women: she likes much rather to put them at their ease with her. She likes, that is—as all pleasant people do—to be liked."

"Ah, she likes to be liked?" her companion had gone on.

"She did, at the same time, no doubt, want to help us—to put us at our ease. That is she wanted to put you—and to put Maggie about you. So far as that went she had a plan. But it was only AFTER—it was not before, I really believe—that she saw how effectively she could work."

Again, as Mr. Verver felt, he must have taken it up. "Ah, she wanted to help us?—wanted to help ME?"

"Why," Mrs. Assingham asked after an instant, "should it surprise you?"

He just thought. "Oh, it doesn't!"

"She saw, of course, as soon as she came, with her quickness, where we all were. She didn't need each of us to go, by appointment, to her room at night, or take her out into the fields, for our palpitating tale. No doubt even she was rather impatient."

"OF the poor things?" Mr. Verver had here inquired while he waited.

"Well, of your not yourselves being so—and of YOUR not in particular. I haven't the least doubt in the world, par exemple, that she thinks you too meek."

"Oh, she thinks me too meek?"

"And she had been sent for, on the very face of it, to work right in. All she had to do, after all, was to be nice to you."

"To—a—ME?" said Adam Verver.

He could remember now that his friend had positively had a laugh for his tone. "To you and to every one. She had only to be what she is—and to be it all round. If she's charming, how can she help it? So it was, and so only, that she 'acted'-as the Borgia wine used to act. One saw it come over them—the extent to which, in her particular way, a woman, a woman other, and SO other, than themselves, COULD be charming. One saw them understand and exchange looks, then one saw them lose heart and decide to move. For what they had to take home was that it's she who's the real thing."

"Ah, it's she who's the real thing?" As HE had not hitherto taken it home as completely as the Miss Lutches and Mrs. Rance, so, doubtless, he had now, a little, appeared to offer submission in his appeal. "I see, I see"—he could at least simply take it home now; yet as not without wanting, at the same time, to be sure of what the real thing was. "And what would it be—a—definitely that you understand by that?"

She had only for an instant not found it easy to say. "Why, exactly what those women themselves want to be, and what her effect on them is to make them recognise that they never will."

"Oh—of course never?"

It not only remained and abode with them, it positively developed and deepened, after this talk, that the luxurious side of his personal existence was now again furnished, socially speaking, with the thing classed and stamped as "real"—just as he had been able to think of it as not otherwise enriched in consequence of his daughter's marriage. The note of reality, in so much projected light, continued to have for him the charm and the importance of which the maximum had occasionally been reached in his great "finds"—continued, beyond any other, to keep him attentive and gratified. Nothing perhaps might affect us as queerer, had we time to look into it, than this application of the same measure of value to such different pieces of property as old Persian carpets, say, and new human acquisitions; all the more indeed that the amiable man was not without an inkling, on his own side, that he was, as a taster of life, economically constructed. He put into his one little glass everything he raised to his lips, and it was as if he had always carried in his pocket, like a tool of his trade, this receptacle, a little glass cut with a fineness of which the art had long since been lost, and kept in an old morocco case stamped in uneffaceable gilt with the arms of a deposed dynasty. As it had served him to satisfy himself, so to speak, both about Amerigo and about the Bernadino Luini he had happened to come to knowledge of at the time he was consenting to the announcement of his daughter's betrothal, so it served him at present to satisfy himself about Charlotte Stant and an extraordinary set of oriental tiles of which he had lately got wind, to which a provoking legend was attached, and as to which he had made out, contentedly, that further news was to be obtained from a certain Mr. Gutermann-Seuss of Brighton. It was all, at bottom, in him, the aesthetic principle, planted where it could burn with a cold, still flame; where it fed almost wholly on the material directly involved, on the idea (followed by appropriation) of plastic beauty, of the thing visibly perfect in its kind; where, in short, in spite of the general tendency of the "devouring element" to spread, the rest of his spiritual furniture, modest, scattered, and tended with unconscious care, escaped the consumption that in so many cases proceeds from the undue keeping-up of profane altar-fires. Adam Verver had in other words learnt the lesson of the senses, to the end of his own little book, without having, for a day, raised the smallest scandal in his economy at large; being in this particular not unlike those fortunate bachelors, or other gentlemen of pleasure, who so manage their entertainment of compromising company that even the austerest housekeeper, occupied and competent below-stairs, never feels obliged to give warning.

That figure has, however, a freedom that the occasion doubtless scarce demands, though we may retain it for its rough negative value. It was to come to pass, by a pressure applied to the situation wholly from within, that before the first ten days of November had elapsed he found himself practically alone at Fawns with his young friend; Amerigo and Maggie having, with a certain abruptness, invited his assent to their going abroad for a month, since his amusement was now scarce less happily assured than his security. An impulse eminently natural had stirred within the Prince; his life, as for some time established, was deliciously dull, and thereby, on the whole, what he best liked; but a small gust of yearning had swept over him, and Maggie repeated to her father, with infinite admiration, the pretty terms in which, after it had lasted a little, he had described to her this experience. He called it a "serenade," a low music that, outside one of the windows of the sleeping house, disturbed his rest at night. Timid as it was, and plaintive, he yet couldn't close his eyes for it, and when finally, rising on tiptoe, he had looked out, he had recognised in the figure below with a mandolin, all duskily draped in her grace, the raised appealing eyes and the one irresistible voice of the ever-to-be-loved Italy. Sooner or later, that way, one had to listen; it was a hovering, haunting ghost, as of a creature to whom one had done a wrong, a dim, pathetic shade crying out to be comforted. For this there was obviously but one way—as there were doubtless also many words for the simple fact that so prime a Roman had a fancy for again seeing Rome. They would accordingly—hadn't they better?—go for a little; Maggie meanwhile making the too-absurdly artful point with her father, so that he repeated it, in his amusement, to Charlotte Stant, to whom he was by this time conscious of addressing many remarks, that it was absolutely, when she came to think, the first thing Amerigo had ever asked of her. "She doesn't count of course his having asked of her to marry him"— this was Mr. Verver's indulgent criticism; but he found Charlotte, equally touched by the ingenuous Maggie, in easy agreement with him over the question. If the Prince had asked something of his wife every day in the year, this would be still no reason why the poor dear man should not, in a beautiful fit of homesickness, revisit, without reproach, his native country.

What his father-in-law frankly counselled was that the reasonable, the really too reasonable, pair should, while they were about it, take three or four weeks of Paris as well—Paris being always, for Mr. Verver, in any stress of sympathy, a suggestion that rose of itself to the lips. If they would only do that, on their way back, or however they preferred it, Charlotte and he would go over to join them there for a small look— though even then, assuredly, as he had it at heart to add, not in the least because they should have found themselves bored at being left together. The fate of this last proposal indeed was that it reeled, for the moment, under an assault of destructive analysis from Maggie, who—having, as she granted, to choose between being an unnatural daughter or an unnatural mother, and "electing" for the former—wanted to know what would become of the Principino if the house were cleared of everyone but the servants. Her question had fairly resounded, but it had afterwards, like many of her questions, dropped still more effectively than it had risen: the highest moral of the matter being, before the couple took their departure, that Mrs. Noble and Dr. Brady must mount unchallenged guard over the august little crib. If she hadn't supremely believed in the majestic value of the nurse, whose experience was in itself the amplest of pillows, just as her attention was a spreading canopy from which precedent and reminiscence dropped as thickly as parted curtains—if she hadn't been able to rest in this confidence she would fairly have sent her husband on his journey without her. In the same manner, if the sweetest—for it was so she qualified him—of little country doctors hadn't proved to her his wisdom by rendering irresistible, especially on rainy days and in direct proportion to the frequency of his calls, adapted to all weathers, that she should converse with him for hours over causes and consequences, over what he had found to answer with his little five at home, she would have drawn scant support from the presence of a mere grandfather and a mere brilliant friend. These persons, accordingly, her own predominance having thus, for the time, given way, could carry with a certain ease, and above all with mutual aid, their consciousness of a charge. So far as their office weighed they could help each other with it—which was in fact to become, as Mrs. Noble herself loomed larger for them, not a little of a relief and a diversion.

Mr. Verver met his young friend, at certain hours, in the day-nursery, very much as he had regularly met the child's fond mother—Charlotte having, as she clearly considered, given Maggie equal pledges and desiring never to fail of the last word for the daily letter she had promised to write. She wrote with high fidelity, she let her companion know, and the effect of it was, remarkably enough, that he himself didn't write. The reason of this was partly that Charlotte "told all about him"—which she also let him know she did—and partly that he enjoyed feeling, as a consequence, that he was generally, quite systematically, eased and, as they said, "done" for. Committed, as it were, to this charming and clever young woman, who, by becoming for him a domestic resource, had become for him practically a new person—and committed, especially, in his own house, which somehow made his sense of it a deeper thing—he took an interest in seeing how far the connection could carry him, could perhaps even lead him, and in thus putting to the test, for pleasant verification, what Fanny Assingham had said, at the last, about the difference such a girl could make. She was really making one now, in their simplified existence, and a very considerable one, though there was no one to compare her with, as there had been, so usefully, for Fanny—no Mrs. Rance, no Kitty, no Dotty Lutch, to help her to be felt, according to Fanny's diagnosis, as real. She was real, decidedly, from other causes, and Mr. Verver grew in time even a little amused at the amount of machinery Mrs. Assingham had seemed to see needed for pointing it. She was directly and immediately real, real on a pleasantly reduced and intimate scale, and at no moments more so than during those—at which we have just glanced—when Mrs. Noble made them both together feel that she, she alone, in the absence of the queen-mother, was regent of the realm and governess of the heir. Treated on such occasions as at best a pair of dangling and merely nominal court-functionaries, picturesque hereditary triflers entitled to the petites entrees but quite external to the State, which began and ended with the Nursery, they could only retire, in quickened sociability, to what was left them of the Palace, there to digest their gilded insignificance and cultivate, in regard to the true Executive, such snuff-taking ironies as might belong to rococo chamberlains moving among china lap-dogs.

Every evening, after dinner, Charlotte Stant played to him; seated at the piano and requiring no music, she went through his "favourite things"—and he had many favourites—with a facility that never failed, or that failed but just enough to pick itself up at a touch from his fitful voice. She could play anything, she could play everything—always shockingly, she of course insisted, but always, by his own vague measure, very much as if she might, slim, sinuous and strong, and with practised passion, have been playing lawn-tennis or endlessly and rhythmically waltzing. His love of music, unlike his other loves, owned to vaguenesses; but while, on his comparatively shaded sofa, and smoking, smoking, always smoking, in the great Fawns drawing-room as everywhere, the cigars of his youth, rank with associations—while, I say, he so listened to Charlotte's piano, where the score was ever absent but, between the lighted candles, the picture distinct, the vagueness spread itself about him like some boundless carpet, a surface delightfully soft to the pressure of his interest. It was a manner of passing the time that rather replaced conversation, but the air, at the end, none the less, before they separated, had a way of seeming full of the echoes of talk. They separated, in the hushed house, not quite easily, if not quite awkwardly either, with tapers that twinkled in the large dark spaces, and for the most part so late that the last solemn servant had been dismissed for the night.

Late as it was on a particular evening toward the end of October, there had been a full word or two dropped into the still-stirring sea of other voices—a word or two that affected our friend even at the moment, and rather oddly, as louder and rounder than any previous sound; and then he had lingered, under pretext of an opened window to be made secure, after taking leave of his companion in the hall and watching her glimmer away up the staircase. He had for himself another impulse than to go to bed; picking up a hat in the hall, slipping his arms into a sleeveless cape and lighting still another cigar, he turned out upon the terrace through one of the long drawing-room windows and moved to and fro there for an hour beneath the sharp autumn stars. It was where he had walked in the afternoon sun with Fanny Assingham, and the sense of that other hour, the sense of the suggestive woman herself, was before him again as, in spite of all the previous degustation we have hinted at, it had not yet been. He thought, in a loose, an almost agitated order, of many things; the power that was in them to agitate having been part of his conviction that he should not soon sleep. He truly felt for a while that he should never sleep again till something had come to him; some light, some idea, some mere happy word perhaps, that he had begun to want, but had been till now, and especially the last day or two, vainly groping for. "Can you really then come if we start early?"—that was practically all he had said to the girl as she took up her bedroom light. And "Why in the world not, when I've nothing else to do, and should, besides, so immensely like it?"—this had as definitely been, on her side, the limit of the little scene. There had in fact been nothing to call a scene, even of the littlest, at all—though he perhaps didn't quite know why something like the menace of one hadn't proceeded from her stopping half-way upstairs to turn and say, as she looked down on him, that she promised to content herself, for their journey, with a toothbrush and a sponge. There hovered about him, at all events, while he walked, appearances already familiar, as well as two or three that were new, and not the least vivid of the former connected itself with that sense of being treated with consideration which had become for him, as he have noted, one of the minor yet so far as there were any such, quite one of the compensatory, incidents of being a father-in-law. It had struck him, up to now, that this particular balm was a mixture of which Amerigo, as through some hereditary privilege, alone possessed the secret; so that he found himself wondering if it had come to Charlotte, who had unmistakably acquired it, through the young man's having amiably passed it on. She made use, for her so quietly grateful host, however this might be, of quite the same shades of attention and recognition, was mistress in an equal degree of the regulated, the developed art of placing him high in the scale of importance. That was even for his own thought a clumsy way of expressing the element of similarity in the agreeable effect they each produced on him, and it held him for a little only because this coincidence in their felicity caused him vaguely to connect or associate them in the matter of tradition, training, tact, or whatever else one might call it. It might almost have been—if such a link between them was to be imagined—that Amerigo had, a little, "coached" or incited their young friend, or perhaps rather that she had simply, as one of the signs of the general perfection Fanny Assingham commended in her, profited by observing, during her short opportunity before the start of the travellers, the pleasant application by the Prince of his personal system. He might wonder what exactly it was that they so resembled each other in treating him like—from what noble and propagated convention, in cases in which the exquisite "importance" was to be neither too grossly attributed nor too grossly denied, they had taken their specific lesson; but the difficulty was here of course that one could really never know—couldn't know without having been one's self a personage; whether a Pope, a King, a President, a Peer, a General, or just a beautiful Author.

Before such a question, as before several others when they recurred, he would come to a pause, leaning his arms on the old parapet and losing himself in a far excursion. He had as to so many of the matters in hand a divided view, and this was exactly what made him reach out, in his unrest, for some idea, lurking in the vast freshness of the night, at the breath of which disparities would submit to fusion, and so, spreading beneath him, make him feel that he floated. What he kept finding himself return to, disturbingly enough, was the reflection, deeper than anything else, that in forming a new and intimate tie he should in a manner abandon, or at the best signally relegate, his daughter. He should reduce to definite form the idea that he had lost her—as was indeed inevitable—by her own marriage; he should reduce to definite form the idea of his having incurred an injury, or at the best an inconvenience, that required some makeweight and deserved some amends. And he should do this the more, which was the great point, that he should appear to adopt, in doing it, the sentiment, in fact the very conviction, entertained, and quite sufficiently expressed, by Maggie herself, in her beautiful generosity, as to what he had suffered—putting it with extravagance—at her hands. If she put it with extravagance the extravagance was yet sincere, for it came—which she put with extravagance too—from her persistence, always, in thinking, feeling, talking about him, as young. He had had glimpses of moments when to hear her thus, in her absolutely unforced compunction, one would have supposed the special edge of the wrong she had done him to consist in his having still before him years and years to groan under it. She had sacrificed a parent, the pearl of parents, no older than herself: it wouldn't so much have mattered if he had been of common parental age. That he wasn't, that he was just her extraordinary equal and contemporary, this was what added to her act the long train of its effect. Light broke for him at last, indeed, quite as a consequence of the fear of breathing a chill upon this luxuriance of her spiritual garden. As at a turn of his labyrinth he saw his issue, which opened out so wide, for the minute, that he held his breath with wonder. He was afterwards to recall how, just then, the autumn night seemed to clear to a view in which the whole place, everything round him, the wide terrace where he stood, the others, with their steps, below, the gardens, the park, the lake, the circling woods, lay there as under some strange midnight sun. It all met him during these instants as a vast expanse of discovery, a world that looked, so lighted, extraordinarily like a loud, a spoken pretension to beauty, interest, importance, to he scarce knew what, gave them an inordinate quantity of character and, verily, an inordinate size. This hallucination, or whatever he might have called it, was brief, but it lasted long enough to leave him gasping. The gasp of admiration had by this time, however, lost itself in an intensity that quickly followed—the way the wonder of it, since wonder was in question, truly had been the strange DELAY of his vision. He had these several days groped and groped for an object that lay at his feet and as to which his blindness came from his stupidly looking beyond. It had sat all the while at his hearth-stone, whence it now gazed up in his face.

Once he had recognised it there everything became coherent. The sharp point to which all his light converged was that the whole call of his future to him, as a father, would be in his so managing that Maggie would less and less appear to herself to have forsaken him. And it not only wouldn't be decently humane, decently possible, not to make this relief easy to her—the idea shone upon him, more than that, as exciting, inspiring, uplifting. It fell in so beautifully with what might be otherwise possible; it stood there absolutely confronted with the material way in which it might be met. The way in which it might be met was by his putting his child at peace, and the way to put her at peace was to provide for his future—that is for hers—by marriage, by a marriage as good, speaking proportionately, as hers had been. As he fairly inhaled this measure of refreshment he tasted the meaning of recent agitations. He had seen that Charlotte could contribute—what he hadn't seen was what she could contribute TO. When it had all supremely cleared up and he had simply settled this service to his daughter well before him as the proper direction of his young friend's leisure, the cool darkness had again closed round him, but his moral lucidity was constituted. It wasn't only moreover that the word, with a click, so fitted the riddle, but that the riddle, in such perfection, fitted the word. He might have been equally in want and yet not have had his remedy. Oh, if Charlotte didn't accept him, of course the remedy would fail; but, as everything had fallen together, it was at least there to be tried. And success would be great—that was his last throb—if the measure of relief effected for Maggie should at all prove to have been given by his own actual sense of felicity. He really didn't know when in his life he had thought of anything happier. To think of it merely for himself would have been, even as he had but just lately felt, even doing all justice to that condition—yes, impossible. But there was a grand difference in thinking of it for his child.

XII

It was at Brighton, above all, that this difference came out; it was during the three wonderful days he spent there with Charlotte that he had acquainted himself further—though doubtless not even now quite completely—with the merits of his majestic scheme. And while, moreover, to begin with, he still but held his vision in place, steadying it fairly with his hands, as he had often steadied, for inspection, a precarious old pot or kept a glazed picture in its right relation to the light, the other, the outer presumptions in his favour, those independent of what he might himself contribute and that therefore, till he should "speak," remained necessarily vague—that quantity, I say, struck him as positively multiplying, as putting on, in the fresh Brighton air and on the sunny Brighton front, a kind of tempting palpability. He liked, in this preliminary stage, to feel that he should be able to "speak" and that he would; the word itself being romantic, pressing for him the spring of association with stories and plays where handsome and ardent young men, in uniforms, tights, cloaks, high-boots, had it, in soliloquies, ever on their lips; and the sense on the first day that he should probably have taken the great step before the second was over conduced already to make him say to his companion that they must spend more than their mere night or two. At his ease on the ground of what was before him he at all events definitely desired to be, and it was strongly his impression that he was proceeding step by step. He was acting—it kept coming back to that—not in the dark, but in the high golden morning; not in precipitation, flurry, fever, dangers these of the path of passion properly so called, but with the deliberation of a plan, a plan that might be a thing of less joy than a passion, but that probably would, in compensation for that loss, be found to have the essential property, to wear even the decent dignity, of reaching further and of providing for more contingencies. The season was, in local parlance, "on," the elements were assembled; the big windy hotel, the draughty social hall, swarmed with "types," in Charlotte's constant phrase, and resounded with a din in which the wild music of gilded and befrogged bands, Croatian, Dalmatian, Carpathian, violently exotic and nostalgic, was distinguished as struggling against the perpetual popping of corks. Much of this would decidedly have disconcerted our friends if it hadn't all happened, more preponderantly, to give them the brighter surprise. The noble privacy of Fawns had left them—had left Mr. Verver at least—with a little accumulated sum of tolerance to spend on the high pitch and high colour of the public sphere. Fawns, as it had been for him, and as Maggie and Fanny Assingham had both attested, was out of the world, whereas the scene actually about him, with the very sea a mere big booming medium for excursions and aquariums, affected him as so plump in the conscious centre that nothing could have been more complete for representing that pulse of life which they had come to unanimity at home on the subject of their advisedly not hereafter forgetting. The pulse of life was what Charlotte, in her way, at home, had lately reproduced, and there were positively current hours when it might have been open to her companion to feel himself again indebted to her for introductions. He had "brought" her, to put it crudely, but it was almost as if she were herself, in her greater gaiety, her livelier curiosity and intensity, her readier, happier irony, taking him about and showing him the place. No one, really, when he came to think, had ever taken him about before—it had always been he, of old, who took others and who in particular took Maggie. This quickly fell into its relation with him as part of an experience—marking for him, no doubt, what people call, considerately, a time of life; a new and pleasant order, a flattered passive state, that might become—why shouldn't it?— one of the comforts of the future.

Mr. Gutermann-Seuss proved, on the second day—our friend had waited till then—a remarkably genial, a positively lustrous young man occupying a small neat house in a quarter of the place remote from the front and living, as immediate and striking signs testified, in the bosom of his family. Our visitors found themselves introduced, by the operation of close contiguity, to a numerous group of ladies and gentlemen older and younger, and of children larger and smaller, who mostly affected them as scarce less anointed for hospitality and who produced at first the impression of a birthday party, of some anniversary gregariously and religiously kept, though they subsequently fell into their places as members of one quiet domestic circle, preponderantly and directly indebted for their being, in fact, to Mr. Gutermann-Seuss. To the casual eye a mere smart and shining youth of less than thirty summers, faultlessly appointed in every particular, he yet stood among his progeny—eleven in all, as he confessed without a sigh, eleven little brown clear faces, yet with such impersonal old eyes astride of such impersonal old noses—while he entertained the great American collector whom he had so long hoped he might meet, and whose charming companion, the handsome, frank, familiar young lady, presumably Mrs. Verver, noticed the graduated offspring, noticed the fat, ear-ringed aunts and the glossy, cockneyfied, familiar uncles, inimitable of accent and assumption, and of an attitude of cruder intention than that of the head of the firm; noticed the place in short, noticed the treasure produced, noticed everything, as from the habit of a person finding her account at any time, according to a wisdom well learned of life, in almost any "funny" impression. It really came home to her friend on the spot that this free range of observation in her, picking out the frequent funny with extraordinary promptness, would verily henceforth make a different thing for him of such experiences, of the customary hunt for the possible prize, the inquisitive play of his accepted monomania; which different thing could probably be a lighter and perhaps thereby a somewhat more boisterously refreshing form of sport. Such omens struck him as vivid, in any case, when Mr. Gutermann-Seuss, with a sharpness of discrimination he had at first scarce seemed to promise, invited his eminent couple into another room, before the threshold of which the rest of the tribe, unanimously faltering, dropped out of the scene. The treasure itself here, the objects on behalf of which Mr. Verver's interest had been booked, established quickly enough their claim to engage the latter's attention; yet at what point of his past did our friend's memory, looking back and back, catch him, in any such place, thinking so much less of wares artfully paraded than of some other and quite irrelevant presence? Such places were not strange to him when they took the form of bourgeois back-parlours, a trifle ominously grey and grim from their north light, at watering-places prevailingly homes of humbug, or even when they wore some aspect still less, if not perhaps still more, insidious. He had been everywhere, pried and prowled everywhere, going, on occasion, so far as to risk, he believed, life, health and the very bloom of honour; but where, while precious things, extracted one by one from thrice-locked yet often vulgar drawers and soft satchels of old oriental ilk, were impressively ranged before him, had he, till now, let himself, in consciousness, wander like one of the vague?

He didn't betray it—ah THAT he knew; but two recognitions took place for him at once, and one of them suffered a little in sweetness by the confusion. Mr. Gutermann-Seuss had truly, for the crisis, the putting down of his cards, a rare manner; he was perfect master of what not to say to such a personage as Mr. Verver while the particular importance that dispenses with chatter was diffused by his movements themselves, his repeated act of passage between a featureless mahogany meuble and a table so virtuously disinterested as to look fairly smug under a cotton cloth of faded maroon and indigo, all redolent of patriarchal teas. The Damascene tiles, successively, and oh so tenderly, unmuffled and revealed, lay there at last in their full harmony and their venerable splendour, but the tribute of appreciation and decision was, while the spectator considered, simplified to a point that but just failed of representing levity on the part of a man who had always acknowledged without shame, in such affairs, the intrinsic charm of what was called discussion. The infinitely ancient, the immemorial amethystine blue of the glaze, scarcely more meant to be breathed upon, it would seem, than the cheek of royalty—this property of the ordered and matched array had inevitably all its determination for him, but his submission was, perhaps for the first time in his life, of the quick mind alone, the process really itself, in its way, as fine as the perfection perceived and admired: every inch of the rest of him being given to the foreknowledge that an hour or two later he should have "spoken." The burning of his ships therefore waited too near to let him handle his opportunity with his usual firm and sentient fingers—waited somehow in the predominance of Charlotte's very person, in her being there exactly as she was, capable, as Mr. Gutermann-Seuss himself was capable, of the right felicity of silence, but with an embracing ease, through it all, that made deferred criticism as fragrant as some joy promised a lover by his mistress, or as a big bridal bouquet held patiently behind her. He couldn't otherwise have explained, surely, why he found himself thinking, to his enjoyment, of so many other matters than the felicity of his acquisition and the figure of his cheque, quite equally high; any more than why, later on, with their return to the room in which they had been received and the renewed encompassment of the tribe, he felt quite merged in the elated circle formed by the girl's free response to the collective caress of all the shining eyes, and by her genial acceptance of the heavy cake and port wine that, as she was afterwards to note, added to their transaction, for a finish, the touch of some mystic rite of old Jewry.

This characterisation came from her as they walked away—walked together, in the waning afternoon, back to the breezy sea and the bustling front, back to the nimble and the flutter and the shining shops that sharpened the grin of solicitation on the mask of night. They were walking thus, as he felt, nearer and nearer to where he should see his ships burn, and it was meanwhile for him quite as if this red glow would impart, at the harmonious hour, a lurid grandeur to his good faith. It was meanwhile too a sign of the kind of sensibility often playing up in him that—fabulous as this truth may sound—he found a sentimental link, an obligation of delicacy, or perhaps even one of the penalties of its opposite, in his having exposed her to the north light, the quite properly hard business-light, of the room in which they had been alone with the treasure and its master. She had listened to the name of the sum he was capable of looking in the face. Given the relation of intimacy with him she had already, beyond all retractation, accepted, the stir of the air produced at the other place by that high figure struck him as a thing that, from the moment she had exclaimed or protested as little as he himself had apologised, left him but one thing more to do. A man of decent feeling didn't thrust his money, a huge lump of it, in such a way, under a poor girl's nose—a girl whose poverty was, after a fashion, the very basis of her enjoyment of his hospitality—without seeing, logically, a responsibility attached. And this was to remain none the less true for the fact that twenty minutes later, after he had applied his torch, applied it with a sign or two of insistence, what might definitely result failed to be immediately clear. He had spoken—spoken as they sat together on the out-of-the-way bench observed during one of their walks and kept for the previous quarter of the present hour well in his memory's eye; the particular spot to which, between intense pauses and intenser advances, he had all the while consistently led her. Below the great consolidated cliff, well on to where the city of stucco sat most architecturally perched, with the rumbling beach and the rising tide and the freshening stars in front and above, the safe sense of the whole place yet prevailed in lamps and seats and flagged walks, hovering also overhead in the close neighbourhood of a great replete community about to assist anew at the removal of dish-covers.

"We've had, as it seems to me, such quite beautiful days together, that I hope it won't come to you too much as a shock when I ask if you think you could regard me with any satisfaction as a husband." As if he had known she wouldn't, she of course couldn't, at all gracefully, and whether or no, reply with a rush, he had said a little more—quite as he had felt he must in thinking it out in advance. He had put the question on which there was no going back and which represented thereby the sacrifice of his vessels, and what he further said was to stand for the redoubled thrust of flame that would make combustion sure. "This isn't sudden to me, and I've wondered at moments if you haven't felt me coming to it. I've been coming ever since we left Fawns—I really started while we were there." He spoke slowly, giving her, as he desired, time to think; all the more that it was making her look at him steadily, and making her also, in a remarkable degree, look "well" while she did so—a large and, so far, a happy, consequence. She wasn't at all events shocked—which he had glanced at but for a handsome humility—and he would give her as many minutes as she liked. "You mustn't think I'm forgetting that I'm not young."

"Oh, that isn't so. It's I that am old. You ARE young." This was what she had at first answered—and quite in the tone too of having taken her minutes. It had not been wholly to the point, but it had been kind—which was what he most wanted. And she kept, for her next words, to kindness, kept to her clear, lowered voice and unshrinking face. "To me too it thoroughly seems that these days have been beautiful. I shouldn't be grateful to them if I couldn't more or less have imagined their bringing us to this." She affected him somehow as if she had advanced a step to meet him and yet were at the same time standing still. It only meant, however, doubtless, that she was, gravely and reasonably, thinking—as he exactly desired to make her. If she would but think enough she would probably think to suit him. "It seems to me," she went on, "that it's for YOU to be sure."

"Ah, but I AM sure," said Adam Verver. "On matters of importance I never speak when I'm not. So if you can yourself FACE such a union you needn't in the least trouble."

She had another pause, and she might have been felt as facing it while, through lamplight and dusk, through the breath of the mild, slightly damp southwest, she met his eyes without evasion. Yet she had at the end of another minute debated only to the extent of saying: "I won't pretend I don't think it would be good for me to marry. Good for me, I mean," she pursued, "because I'm so awfully unattached. I should like to be a little less adrift. I should like to have a home. I should like to have an existence. I should like to have a motive for one thing more than another—a motive outside of myself. In fact," she said, so sincerely that it almost showed pain, yet so lucidly that it almost showed humour, "in fact, you know, I want to BE married. It's—well, it's the condition."

"The condition—?" He was just vague.

"It's the state, I mean. I don't like my own. 'Miss,' among us all, is too dreadful—except for a shopgirl. I don't want to be a horrible English old-maid."

"Oh, you want to be taken care of. Very well then, I'll do it."

"I dare say it's very much that. Only I don't see why, for what I speak of," she smiled—"for a mere escape from my state—I need do quite so MUCH."

"So much as marry me in particular?"

Her smile was as for true directness. "I might get what I want for less."

"You think it so much for you to do?"

"Yes," she presently said, "I think it's a great deal."

Then it was that, though she was so gentle, so quite perfect with him, and he felt he had come on far—then it was that of a sudden something seemed to fail and he didn't quite know where they were. There rose for him, with this, the fact, to be sure, of their disparity, deny it as mercifully and perversely as she would. He might have been her father. "Of course, yes—that's my disadvantage: I'm not the natural, I'm so far from being the ideal match to your youth and your beauty. I've the drawback that you've seen me always, so inevitably, in such another light."

But she gave a slow headshake that made contradiction soft—made it almost sad, in fact, as from having to be so complete; and he had already, before she spoke, the dim vision of some objection in her mind beside which the one he had named was light, and which therefore must be strangely deep. "You don't understand me. It's of all that it is for YOU to do—it's of that I'm thinking."

Oh, with this, for him, the thing was clearer! "Then you needn't think. I know enough what it is for me to do."

But she shook her head again. "I doubt if you know. I doubt if you CAN."

"And why not, please—when I've had you so before me? That I'm old has at least THAT fact about it to the good—that I've known you long and from far back."

"Do you think you've 'known' me?" asked Charlotte Stant. He hesitated—for the tone of it, and her look with it might have made him doubt. Just these things in themselves, however, with all the rest, with his fixed purpose now, his committed deed, the fine pink glow, projected forward, of his ships, behind him, definitely blazing and crackling—this quantity was to push him harder than any word of her own could warn him. All that she was herself, moreover, was so lighted, to its advantage, by the pink glow. He wasn't rabid, but he wasn't either, as a man of a proper spirit, to be frightened. "What is that then—if I accept it—but as strong a reason as I can want for just LEARNING to know you?"

She faced him always—kept it up as for honesty, and yet at the same time, in her odd way, as for mercy. "How can you tell whether if you did you would?"

It was ambiguous for an instant, as she showed she felt. "I mean when it's a question of learning, one learns sometimes too late."

"I think it's a question," he promptly enough made answer, "of liking you the more just for your saying these things. You should make something," he added, "of my liking you."

"I make everything. But are you sure of having exhausted all other ways?"

This, of a truth, enlarged his gaze. "But what other ways?"

"Why, you've more ways of being kind than anyone I ever knew."

"Take it then," he answered, "that I'm simply putting them all together for you." She looked at him, on this, long again—still as if it shouldn't be said she hadn't given him time or had withdrawn from his view, so to speak, a single inch of her surface. This at least she was fully to have exposed. It represented her as oddly conscientious, and he scarce knew in what sense it affected him. On the whole, however, with admiration. "You're very, very honourable."

"It's just what I want to be. I don't see," she added, "why you're not right, I don't see why you're not happy, as you are. I can not ask myself, I can not ask YOU," she went on, "if you're really as much at liberty as your universal generosity leads you to assume. Oughtn't we," she asked, "to think a little of others? Oughtn't I, at least, in loyalty—at any rate in delicacy—to think of Maggie?" With which, intensely gentle, so as not to appear too much to teach him his duty, she explained. "She's everything to you—she has always been. Are you so certain that there's room in your life—?"

"For another daughter?—is that what you mean?" She had not hung upon it long, but he had quickly taken her up.

He had not, however, disconcerted her. "For another young woman—very much of her age, and whose relation to her has always been so different from what our marrying would make it. For another companion," said Charlotte Stant.

"Can't a man be, all his life then," he almost fiercely asked, "anything but a father?" But he went on before she could answer. "You talk about differences, but they've been already made—as no one knows better than Maggie. She feels the one she made herself by her own marriage—made, I mean, for me. She constantly thinks of it—it allows her no rest. To put her at peace therefore," he explained, "what I'm trying, with you, to do. I can't do it alone, but I can do it with your help. You can make her," he said, "positively happy about me."

"About you?" she thoughtfully echoed. "But what can I make her about herself?"

"Oh, if she's at ease about me the rest will take care of itself. The case," he declared, "is in your hands. You'll effectually put out of her mind that I feel she has abandoned me."

Interest certainly now was what he had kindled in her face, but it was all the more honourable to her, as he had just called it that she should want to see each of the steps of his conviction. "If you've been driven to the 'likes' of me, mayn't it show that you've felt truly forsaken?"

"Well, I'm willing to suggest that, if I can show at the same time that I feel consoled."

"But HAVE you," she demanded, "really felt so?" He hesitated.

"Consoled?"

"Forsaken."

"No—I haven't. But if it's her idea—!" If it was her idea, in short, that was enough. This enunciation of motive, the next moment, however, sounded to him perhaps slightly thin, so that he gave it another touch. "That is if it's my idea. I happen, you see, to like my idea."

"Well, it's beautiful and wonderful. But isn't it, possibly," Charlotte asked, "not quite enough to marry me for?"

"Why so, my dear child? Isn't a man's idea usually what he does marry for?"

Charlotte, considering, looked as if this might perhaps be a large question, or at all events something of an extension of one they were immediately concerned with. "Doesn't that a good deal depend on the sort of thing it may be?" She suggested that, about marriage, ideas, as he called them, might differ; with which, however, giving no more time to it, she sounded another question. "Don't you appear rather to put it to me that I may accept your offer for Maggie's sake? Somehow"—she turned it over—"I don't so clearly SEE her quite so much finding reassurance, or even quite so much needing it."

"Do you then make nothing at all of her having been so ready to leave us?"

Ah, Charlotte on the contrary made much! "She was ready to leave us because she had to be. From the moment the Prince wanted it she could only go with him."

"Perfectly—so that, if you see your way, she will be able to 'go with him' in future as much as she likes."

Charlotte appeared to examine for a minute, in Maggie's interest, this privilege—the result of which was a limited concession. "You've certainly worked it out!"

"Of course I've worked it out—that's exactly what I HAVE done. She hadn't for a long time been so happy about anything as at your being there with me."

"I was to be with you," said Charlotte, "for her security."

"Well," Adam Verver rang out, "this IS her security. You've only, if you can't see it, to ask her."

"'Ask' her?"—the girl echoed it in wonder. "Certainly—in so many words. Telling her you don't believe me."

Still she debated. "Do you mean write it to her?"

"Quite so. Immediately. To-morrow."

"Oh, I don't think I can write it," said Charlotte Stant. "When I write to her"—and she looked amused for so different a shade—"it's about the Principino's appetite and Dr. Brady's visits."

"Very good then—put it to her face to face. We'll go straight to Paris to meet them."

Charlotte, at this, rose with a movement that was like a small cry; but her unspoken sense lost itself while she stood with her eyes on him—he keeping his seat as for the help it gave him, a little, to make his appeal go up. Presently, however, a new sense had come to her, and she covered him, kindly, with the expression of it. "I do think, you know, you must rather 'like' me."

"Thank you," said Adam Verver. "You WILL put it to her yourself then?"

She had another hesitation. "We go over, you say, to meet them?"

"As soon as we can get back to Fawns. And wait there for them, if necessary, till they come."

"Wait—a—at Fawns?"

"Wait in Paris. That will be charming in itself."

"You take me to pleasant places." She turned it over. "You propose to me beautiful things."

"It rests but with you to make them beautiful and pleasant. You've made Brighton—!"

"Ah!"—she almost tenderly protested. "With what I'm doing now?"

"You're promising me now what I want. Aren't you promising me," he pressed, getting up, "aren't you promising me to abide by what Maggie says?"

Oh, she wanted to be sure she was. "Do you mean she'll ASK it of me?"

It gave him indeed, as by communication, a sense of the propriety of being himself certain. Yet what was he but certain? "She'll speak to you. She'll speak to you FOR me."

This at last then seemed to satisfy her. "Very good. May we wait again to talk of it till she has done so?" He showed, with his hands down in his pockets and his shoulders expressively up, a certain disappointment. Soon enough, none the less, his gentleness was all back and his patience once more exemplary. "Of course I give you time. Especially," he smiled, "as it's time that I shall be spending with you. Our keeping on together will help you perhaps to see. To see, I mean, how I need you."

"I already see," said Charlotte, "how you've persuaded yourself you do." But she had to repeat it. "That isn't, unfortunately, all."

"Well then, how you'll make Maggie right."

"'Right'?" She echoed it as if the word went far. And "O—oh!" she still critically murmured as they moved together away.

XIII

He had talked to her of their waiting in Paris, a week later, but on the spot there this period of patience suffered no great strain. He had written to his daughter, not indeed from Brighton, but directly after their return to Fawns, where they spent only forty-eight hours before resuming their journey; and Maggie's reply to his news was a telegram from Rome, delivered to him at noon of their fourth day and which he brought out to Charlotte, who was seated at that moment in the court of the hotel, where they had agreed that he should join her for their proceeding together to the noontide meal. His letter, at Fawns—a letter of several pages and intended lucidly, unreservedly, in fact all but triumphantly, to inform—had proved, on his sitting down to it, and a little to his surprise, not quite so simple a document to frame as even his due consciousness of its weight of meaning had allowed him to assume: this doubtless, however, only for reasons naturally latent in the very wealth of that consciousness, which contributed to his message something of their own quality of impatience. The main result of their talk, for the time, had been a difference in his relation to his young friend, as well as a difference, equally sensible, in her relation to himself; and this in spite of his not having again renewed his undertaking to "speak" to her so far even as to tell her of the communication despatched to Rome. Delicacy, a delicacy more beautiful still, all the delicacy she should want, reigned between them—it being rudimentary, in their actual order, that she mustn't be further worried until Maggie should have put her at her ease.

It was just the delicacy, however, that in Paris—which, suggestively, was Brighton at a hundredfold higher pitch—made, between him and his companion, the tension, made the suspense, made what he would have consented perhaps to call the provisional peculiarity, of present conditions. These elements acted in a manner of their own, imposing and involving, under one head, many abstentions and precautions, twenty anxieties and reminders—things, verily, he would scarce have known how to express; and yet creating for them at every step an acceptance of their reality. He was hanging back, with Charlotte, till another person should intervene for their assistance, and yet they had, by what had already occurred, been carried on to something it was out of the power of other persons to make either less or greater. Common conventions—that was what was odd—had to be on this basis more thought of; those common conventions that, previous to the passage by the Brighton strand, he had so enjoyed the sense of their overlooking. The explanation would have been, he supposed—or would have figured it with less of unrest—that Paris had, in its way, deeper voices and warnings, so that if you went at all "far" there it laid bristling traps, as they might have been viewed, all smothered in flowers, for your going further still. There were strange appearances in the air, and before you knew it you might be unmistakably matching them. Since he wished therefore to match no appearance but that of a gentleman playing with perfect fairness any game in life he might be called to, he found himself, on the receipt of Maggie's missive, rejoicing with a certain inconsistency. The announcement made her from home had, in the act, cost some biting of his pen to sundry parts of him—his personal modesty, his imagination of her prepared state for so quick a jump, it didn't much matter which—and yet he was more eager than not for the drop of delay and for the quicker transitions promised by the arrival of the imminent pair. There was after all a hint of offence to a man of his age in being taken, as they said at the shops, on approval. Maggie, certainly, would have been as far as Charlotte herself from positively desiring this, and Charlotte, on her side, as far as Maggie from holding him light as a real value. She made him fidget thus, poor girl, but from generous rigour of conscience.

These allowances of his spirit were, all the same, consistent with a great gladness at the sight of the term of his ordeal; for it was the end of his seeming to agree that questions and doubts had a place. The more he had inwardly turned the matter over the more it had struck him that they had in truth only an ugliness. What he could have best borne, as he now believed, would have been Charlotte's simply saying to him that she didn't like him enough. This he wouldn't have enjoyed, but he would quite have understood it and been able ruefully to submit. She did like him enough—nothing to contradict that had come out for him; so that he was restless for her as well as for himself. She looked at him hard a moment when he handed her his telegram, and the look, for what he fancied a dim, shy fear in it, gave him perhaps his best moment of conviction that—as a man, so to speak—he properly pleased her. He said nothing—the words sufficiently did it for him, doing it again better still as Charlotte, who had left her chair at his approach, murmured them out. "We start to-night to bring you all our love and joy and sympathy." There they were, the words, and what did she want more? She didn't, however, as she gave him back the little unfolded leaf, say they were enough—though he saw, the next moment, that her silence was probably not disconnected from her having just visibly turned pale. Her extraordinarily fine eyes, as it was his present theory that he had always thought them, shone at him the more darkly out of this change of colour; and she had again, with it, her apparent way of subjecting herself, for explicit honesty and through her willingness to face him, to any view he might take, all at his ease, and even to wantonness, of the condition he produced in her. As soon as he perceived that emotion kept her soundless he knew himself deeply touched, since it proved that, little as she professed, she had been beautifully hoping. They stood there a minute while he took in from this sign that, yes then, certainly she liked him enough—liked him enough to make him, old as he was ready to brand himself, flush for the pleasure of it. The pleasure of it accordingly made him speak first. "Do you begin, a little, to be satisfied?"

Still, however, she had to think. "We've hurried them, you see. Why so breathless a start?"

"Because they want to congratulate us. They want," said Adam Verver, "to SEE our happiness."

She wondered again—and this time also, for him, as publicly as possible. "So much as that?"

"Do you think it's too much?"

She continued to think plainly. "They weren't to have started for another week."

"Well, what then? Isn't our situation worth the little sacrifice? We'll go back to Rome as soon as you like WITH them."

This seemed to hold her—as he had previously seen her held, just a trifle inscrutably, by his allusions to what they would do together on a certain contingency. "Worth it, the little sacrifice, for whom? For us, naturally—yes," she said. "We want to see them—for our reasons. That is," she rather dimly smiled, "YOU do."

"And you do, my dear, too!" he bravely declared. "Yes then—I do too," she after an instant ungrudging enough acknowledged. "For us, however, something depends on it."

"Rather! But does nothing depend on it for them?"

"What CAN—from the moment that, as appears, they don't want to nip us in the bud? I can imagine their rushing up to prevent us. But an enthusiasm for us that can wait so very little—such intense eagerness, I confess," she went on, "more than a little puzzles me. You may think me," she also added, "ungracious and suspicious, but the Prince can't at all want to come back so soon. He wanted quite too intensely to get away."

Mr. Verver considered. "Well, hasn't he been away?"

"Yes, just long enough to see how he likes it. Besides," said Charlotte, "he may not be able to join in the rosy view of our case that you impute to her. It can't in the least have appeared to him hitherto a matter of course that you should give his wife a bouncing stepmother."

Adam Verver, at this, looked grave. "I'm afraid then he'll just have to accept from us whatever his wife accepts; and accept it—if he can imagine no better reason—just because she does. That," he declared, "will have to do for him."

His tone made her for a moment meet his face; after which, "Let me," she abruptly said, "see it again"—taking from him the folded leaf that she had given back and he had kept in his hand. "Isn't the whole thing," she asked when she had read it over, "perhaps but a way like another for their gaining time?"

He again stood staring; but the next minute, with that upward spring of his shoulders and that downward pressure of his pockets which she had already, more than once, at disconcerted moments, determined in him, he turned sharply away and wandered from her in silence. He looked about in his small despair; he crossed the hotel court, which, overarched and glazed, muffled against loud sounds and guarded against crude sights, heated, gilded, draped, almost carpeted, with exotic trees in tubs, exotic ladies in chairs, the general exotic accent and presence suspended, as with wings folded or feebly fluttering, in the superior, the supreme, the inexorably enveloping Parisian medium, resembled some critical apartment of large capacity, some "dental," medical, surgical waiting-room, a scene of mixed anxiety and desire, preparatory, for gathered barbarians, to the due amputation or extraction of excrescences and redundancies of barbarism. He went as far as the porte-cochere, took counsel afresh of his usual optimism, sharpened even, somehow, just here, by the very air he tasted, and then came back smiling to Charlotte. "It is incredible to you that when a man is still as much in love as Amerigo his most natural impulse should be to feel what his wife feels, to believe what she believes, to want what she wants?—in the absence, that is, of special impediments to his so doing." The manner of it operated—she acknowledged with no great delay this natural possibility. "No—nothing is incredible to me of people immensely in love."

"Well, isn't Amerigo immensely in love?"

She hesitated but as for the right expression of her sense of the degree—but she after all adopted Mr. Verver's. "Immensely."

"Then there you are!"

She had another smile, however—she wasn't there quite yet. "That isn't all that's wanted."

"But what more?"

"Why that his wife shall have made him really believe that SHE really believes." With which Charlotte became still more lucidly logical. "The reality of his belief will depend in such a case on the reality of hers. The Prince may for instance now," she went on, "have made out to his satisfaction that Maggie may mainly desire to abound in your sense, whatever it is you do. He may remember that he has never seen her do anything else."

"Well," said Adam Verver, "what kind of a warning will he have found in that? To what catastrophe will he have observed such a disposition in her to lead?"

"Just to THIS one!" With which she struck him as rising straighter and clearer before him than she had done even yet.

"Our little question itself?" Her appearance had in fact, at the moment, such an effect on him that he could answer but in marvelling mildness. "Hadn't we better wait a while till we call it a catastrophe?"

Her rejoinder to this was to wait—though by no means as long as he meant. When at the end of her minute she spoke, however, it was mildly too. "What would you like, dear friend, to wait for?" It lingered between them in the air, this demand, and they exchanged for the time a look which might have made each of them seem to have been watching in the other the signs of its overt irony. These were indeed immediately so visible in Mr. Verver's face that, as if a little ashamed of having so markedly produced them—and as if also to bring out at last, under pressure, something she had all the while been keeping back—she took a jump to pure plain reason. "You haven't noticed for yourself, but I can't quite help noticing, that in spite of what you assume—WE assume, if you like—Maggie wires her joy only to you. She makes no sign of its overflow to me."

It was a point—and, staring a moment, he took account of it. But he had, as before, his presence of mind—to say nothing of his kindly humour. "Why, you complain of the very thing that's most charmingly conclusive! She treats us already as ONE."

Clearly now, for the girl, in spite of lucidity and logic, there was something in the way he said things—! She faced him in all her desire to please him, and then her word quite simply and definitely showed it. "I do like you, you know."

Well, what could this do but stimulate his humour? "I see what's the matter with you. You won't be quiet till you've heard from the Prince himself. I think," the happy man added, "that I'll go and secretly wire to him that you'd like, reply paid, a few words for yourself."

It could apparently but encourage her further to smile. "Reply paid for him, you mean—or for me?"

"Oh, I'll pay, with pleasure, anything back for you—as many words as you like." And he went on, to keep it up. "Not requiring either to see your message."

She could take it, visibly, as he meant it. "Should you require to see the Prince's?"

"Not a bit. You can keep that also to yourself."

On his speaking, however, as if his transmitting the hint were a real question, she appeared to consider—and almost as if for good taste—that the joke had gone far enough. "It doesn't matter. Unless he speaks of his own movement—! And why should it be," she asked, "a thing that WOULD occur to him?"

"I really think," Mr. Verver concurred, "that it naturally wouldn't. HE doesn't know you're morbid."

She just wondered—but she agreed. "No—he hasn't yet found it out. Perhaps he will, but he hasn't yet; and I'm willing to give him meanwhile the benefit of the doubt." So with this the situation, for her view, would appear to have cleared had she not too quickly had one of her restless relapses. "Maggie, however, does know I'm morbid. SHE hasn't the benefit."

"Well," said Adam Verver a little wearily at last, "I think I feel that you'll hear from her yet." It had even fairly come over him, under recurrent suggestion, that his daughter's omission WAS surprising. And Maggie had never in her life been wrong for more than three minutes.

"Oh, it isn't that I hold that I've a RIGHT to it," Charlotte the next instant rather oddly qualified—and the observation itself gave him a further push.

"Very well—I shall like it myself."

At this then, as if moved by his way of constantly—and more or less against his own contention—coming round to her, she showed how she could also always, and not less gently, come half way. "I speak of it only as the missing GRACE—the grace that's in everything that Maggie does. It isn't my due"—she kept it up—"but, taking from you that we may still expect it, it will have the touch. It will be beautiful."

"Then come out to breakfast." Mr. Verver had looked at his watch. "It will be here when we get back."

"If it isn't"—and Charlotte smiled as she looked about for a feather boa that she had laid down on descending from her room—"if it isn't it will have had but THAT slight fault."

He saw her boa on the arm of the chair from which she had moved to meet him, and, after he had fetched it, raising it to make its charming softness brush his face—for it was a wondrous product of Paris, purchased under his direct auspices the day before—he held it there a minute before giving it up. "Will you promise me then to be at peace?"

She looked, while she debated, at his admirable present. "I promise you."

"Quite for ever?"

"Quite for ever."

"Remember," he went on, to justify his demand, "remember that in wiring you she'll naturally speak even more for her husband than she has done in wiring me."

It was only at a word that Charlotte had a demur. "'Naturally'—?"

"Why, our marriage puts him for you, you see—or puts you for him—into a new relation, whereas it leaves his relation to me unchanged. It therefore gives him more to say to you about it."

"About its making me his stepmother-in-law—or whatever I SHOULD become?" Over which, for a little, she not undivertedly mused. "Yes, there may easily be enough for a gentleman to say to a young woman about that."

"Well, Amerigo can always be, according to the case, either as funny or as serious as you like; and whichever he may be for you, in sending you a message, he'll be it ALL." And then as the girl, with one of her so deeply and oddly, yet so tenderly, critical looks at him, failed to take up the remark, he found himself moved, as by a vague anxiety, to add a question. "Don't you think he's charming?"

"Oh, charming," said Charlotte Stant. "If he weren't I shouldn't mind."

"No more should I!" her friend harmoniously returned.

"Ah, but you DON'T mind. You don't have to. You don't have to, I mean, as I have. It's the last folly ever to care, in an anxious way, the least particle more than one is absolutely forced. If I were you," she went on—"if I had in my life, for happiness and power and peace, even a small fraction of what you have, it would take a great deal to make me waste my worry. I don't know," she said, "what in the world—that didn't touch my luck—I should trouble my head about."

"I quite understand you—yet doesn't it just depend," Mr. Verver asked, "on what you call one's luck? It's exactly my luck that I'm talking about. I shall be as sublime as you like when you've made me all right. It's only when one is right that one really has the things you speak of. It isn't they," he explained, "that make one so: it's the something else I want that makes THEM right. If you'll give me what I ask, you'll see."

She had taken her boa and thrown it over her shoulders, and her eyes, while she still delayed, had turned from him, engaged by another interest, though the court was by this time, the hour of dispersal for luncheon, so forsaken that they would have had it, for free talk, should they have been moved to loudness, quite to themselves. She was ready for their adjournment, but she was also aware of a pedestrian youth, in uniform, a visible emissary of the Postes et Telegraphes, who had approached, from the street, the small stronghold of the concierge and who presented there a missive taken from the little cartridge-box slung over his shoulder. The portress, meeting him on the threshold, met equally, across the court, Charlotte's marked attention to his visit, so that, within the minute, she had advanced to our friends with her cap-streamers flying and her smile of announcement as ample as her broad white apron. She raised aloft a telegraphic message and, as she delivered it, sociably discriminated. "Cette fois-ci pour madame!"—with which she as genially retreated, leaving Charlotte in possession. Charlotte, taking it, held it at first unopened. Her eyes had come back to her companion, who had immediately and triumphantly greeted it. "Ah, there you are!"

She broke the envelope then in silence, and for a minute, as with the message he himself had put before her, studied its contents without a sign. He watched her without a question, and at last she looked up. "I'll give you," she simply said, "what you ask."

The expression of her face was strange—but since when had a woman's at moments of supreme surrender not a right to be? He took it in with his own long look and his grateful silence—so that nothing more, for some instants, passed between them. Their understanding sealed itself—he already felt that she had made him right. But he was in presence too of the fact that Maggie had made HER so; and always, therefore, without Maggie, where, in fine, would he be? She united them, brought them together as with the click of a silver spring, and, on the spot, with the vision of it, his eyes filled, Charlotte facing him meanwhile with her expression made still stranger by the blur of his gratitude. Through it all, however, he smiled. "What my child does for me—!"

Through it all as well, that is still through the blur, he saw Charlotte, rather than heard her, reply. She held her paper wide open, but her eyes were all for his. "It isn't Maggie. It's the Prince."

"I SAY!"—he gaily rang out. "Then it's best of all."

"It's enough."

"Thank you for thinking so!" To which he added "It's enough for our question, but it isn't—is it? quite enough for our breakfast? Dejeunons."

She stood there, however, in spite of this appeal, her document always before them. "Don't you want to read it?"

He thought. "Not if it satisfies you. I don't require it."

But she gave him, as for her conscience, another chance. "You can if you like."

He hesitated afresh, but as for amiability, not for curiosity. "Is it funny?"

Thus, finally, she again dropped her eyes on it, drawing in her lips a little. "No—I call it grave."

"Ah, then, I don't want it."

"Very grave," said Charlotte Stant.

"Well, what did I tell you of him?" he asked, rejoicing, as they started: a question for all answer to which, before she took his arm, the girl thrust her paper, crumpled, into the pocket of her coat.

PART THIRD

Grand staircase by Hubert Robert (1733–1808)

XIV

Charlotte, half way up the "monumental" staircase, had begun by waiting alone—waiting to be rejoined by her companion, who had gone down all the way, as in common kindness bound, and who, his duty performed, would know where to find her. She was meanwhile, though extremely apparent, not perhaps absolutely advertised; but she would not have cared if she had been—so little was it, by this time, her first occasion of facing society with a consciousness materially, with a confidence quite splendidly, enriched. For a couple of years now she had known as never before what it was to look "well"—to look, that is, as well as she had always felt, from far back, that, in certain conditions, she might. On such an evening as this, that of a great official party in the full flush of the London spring-time, the conditions affected her, her nerves, her senses, her imagination, as all profusely present; so that perhaps at no moment yet had she been so justified of her faith as at the particular instant of our being again concerned with her, that of her chancing to glance higher up from where she stood and meeting in consequence the quiet eyes of Colonel Assingham, who had his elbows on the broad balustrade of the great gallery overhanging the staircase and who immediately exchanged with her one of his most artlessly familiar signals. This simplicity of his visual attention struck her, even with the other things she had to think about, as the quietest note in the whole high pitch—much, in fact, as if she had pressed a finger on a chord or a key and created, for the number of seconds, an arrest of vibration, a more muffled thump. The sight of him suggested indeed that Fanny would be there, though so far as opportunity went she had not seen her. This was about the limit of what it could suggest.

The air, however, had suggestions enough—it abounded in them, many of them precisely helping to constitute those conditions with which, for our young woman, the hour was brilliantly crowned. She was herself in truth crowned, and it all hung together, melted together, in light and colour and sound: the unsurpassed diamonds that her head so happily carried, the other jewels, the other perfections of aspect and arrangement that made her personal scheme a success, the PROVED private theory that materials to work with had been all she required and that there were none too precious for her to understand and use—to which might be added lastly, as the strong-scented flower of the total sweetness, an easy command, a high enjoyment, of her crisis. For a crisis she was ready to take it, and this ease it was, doubtless, that helped her, while she waited, to the right assurance, to the right indifference, to the right expression, and above all, as she felt, to the right view of her opportunity for happiness—unless indeed the opportunity itself, rather, were, in its mere strange amplitude, the producing, the precipitating cause. The ordered revellers, rustling and shining, with sweep of train and glitter of star and clink of sword, and yet, for all this, but so imperfectly articulate, so vaguely vocal—the double stream of the coming and the going, flowing together where she stood, passed her, brushed her, treated her to much crude contemplation and now and then to a spasm of speech, an offered hand, even in some cases to an unencouraged pause; but she missed no countenance and invited no protection: she fairly liked to be, so long as she might, just as she was—exposed a little to the public, no doubt, in her unaccompanied state, but, even if it were a bit brazen, careless of queer reflections on the dull polish of London faces, and exposed, since it was a question of exposure, to much more competent recognitions of her own. She hoped no one would stop—she was positively keeping herself; it was her idea to mark in a particular manner the importance of something that had just happened. She knew how she should mark it, and what she was doing there made already a beginning.

When presently, therefore, from her standpoint, she saw the Prince come back she had an impression of all the place as higher and wider and more appointed for great moments; with its dome of lustres lifted, its ascents and descents more majestic, its marble tiers more vividly overhung, its numerosity of royalties, foreign and domestic, more unprecedented, its symbolism of "State" hospitality both emphasised and refined. This was doubtless a large consequence of a fairly familiar cause, a considerable inward stir to spring from the mere vision, striking as that might be, of Amerigo in a crowd; but she had her reasons, she held them there, she carried them in fact, responsibly and overtly, as she carried her head, her high tiara, her folded fan, her indifferent, unattended eminence; and it was when he reached her and she could, taking his arm, show herself as placed in her relation, that she felt supremely justified. It was her notion of course that she gave a glimpse of but few of her grounds for this discrimination—indeed of the most evident alone; yet she would have been half willing it should be guessed how she drew inspiration, drew support, in quantity sufficient for almost anything, from the individual value that, through all the picture, her husband's son-in-law kept for the eye, deriving it from his fine unconscious way, in the swarming social sum, of outshining, overlooking and overtopping. It was as if in separation, even the shortest, she half forgot or disbelieved how he affected her sight, so that reappearance had, in him, each time, a virtue of its own—a kind of disproportionate intensity suggesting his connection with occult sources of renewal. What did he do when he was away from her that made him always come back only looking, as she would have called it, "more so?" Superior to any shade of cabotinage, he yet almost resembled an actor who, between his moments on the stage, revisits his dressing-room and, before the glass, pressed by his need of effect, retouches his make-up. The Prince was at present, for instance, though he had quitted her but ten minutes before, still more than then the person it pleased her to be left with—a truth that had all its force for her while he made her his care for their conspicuous return together to the upper rooms. Conspicuous beyond any wish they could entertain was what, poor wonderful man, he couldn't help making it; and when she raised her eyes again, on the ascent, to Bob Assingham, still aloft in his gallery and still looking down at her, she was aware that, in spite of hovering and warning inward voices, she even enjoyed the testimony rendered by his lonely vigil to the lustre she reflected.

Party (c.1903) by Gaston de La Touche (1854–1913)

He was always lonely at great parties, the dear Colonel—it wasn't in such places that the seed he sowed at home was ever reaped by him; but nobody could have seemed to mind it less, to brave it with more bronzed indifference; so markedly that he moved about less like one of the guests than like some quite presentable person in charge of the police arrangements or the electric light. To Mrs. Verver, as will be seen, he represented, with the perfect good faith of his apparent blankness, something definite enough; though her bravery was not thereby too blighted for her to feel herself calling him to witness that the only witchcraft her companion had used, within the few minutes, was that of attending Maggie, who had withdrawn from the scene, to her carriage. Notified, at all events, of Fanny's probable presence, Charlotte was, for a while after this, divided between the sense of it as a fact somehow to reckon with and deal with, which was a perception that made, in its degree, for the prudence, the pusillanimity of postponement, of avoidance—and a quite other feeling, an impatience that presently ended by prevailing, an eagerness, really, to BE suspected, sounded, veritably arraigned, if only that she might have the bad moment over, if only that she might prove to herself, let alone to Mrs. Assingham also, that she could convert it to good; if only, in short, to be "square," as they said, with her question. For herself indeed, particularly, it wasn't a question; but something in her bones told her that Fanny would treat it as one, and there was truly nothing that, from this friend, she was not bound in decency to take. She might hand things back with every tender precaution, with acknowledgments and assurances, but she owed it to them, in any case, and it to all Mrs. Assingham had done for her, not to get rid of them without having well unwrapped and turned them over.

To-night, as happened—and she recognised it more and more, with the ebbing minutes, as an influence of everything about her—to-night exactly, she would, no doubt, since she knew why, be as firm as she might at any near moment again hope to be for going through that process with the right temper and tone. She said, after a little, to the Prince, "Stay with me; let no one take you; for I want her, yes, I do want her to see us together, and the sooner the better"—said it to keep her hand on him through constant diversions, and made him, in fact, by saying it, profess a momentary vagueness. She had to explain to him that it was Fanny Assingham, she wanted to see—who clearly would be there, since the Colonel never either stirred without her or, once arrived, concerned himself for her fate; and she had, further, after Amerigo had met her with "See us together? why in the world? hasn't she often seen us together?" to inform him that what had elsewhere and otherwise happened didn't now matter and that she at any rate well knew, for the occasion, what she was about. "You're strange, cara mia," he consentingly enough dropped; but, for whatever strangeness, he kept her, as they circulated, from being waylaid, even remarking to her afresh as he had often done before, on the help rendered, in such situations, by the intrinsic oddity of the London "squash," a thing of vague, slow, senseless eddies, revolving as in fear of some menace of conversation suspended over it, the drop of which, with some consequent refreshing splash or spatter, yet never took place. Of course she was strange; this, as they went, Charlotte knew for herself: how could she be anything else when the situation holding her, and holding him, for that matter, just as much, had so the stamp of it? She had already accepted her consciousness, as we have already noted, that a crisis, for them all, was in the air; and when such hours were not depressing, which was the form indeed in which she had mainly known them, they were apparently in a high degree exhilarating.

Interior with sofa (1910) by Joaquin Sorolla (1863–1923)

Later on, in a corner to which, at sight of an empty sofa, Mrs. Assingham had, after a single attentive arrest, led her with a certain earnestness, this vision of the critical was much more sharpened than blurred. Fanny had taken it from her: yes, she was there with Amerigo alone, Maggie having come with them and then, within ten minutes, changed her mind, repented and departed. "So you're staying on together without her?" the elder woman had asked; and it was Charlotte's answer to this that had determined for them, quite indeed according to the latter's expectation, the need of some seclusion and her companion's pounce at the sofa. They were staying on together alone, and—oh distinctly!—it was alone that Maggie had driven away, her father, as usual, not having managed to come. "'As usual'—?" Mrs. Assingham had seemed to wonder; Mr. Verver's reluctances not having, she in fact quite intimated, hitherto struck her. Charlotte responded, at any rate, that his indisposition to go out had lately much increased—even though to-night, as she admitted, he had pleaded his not feeling well. Maggie had wished to stay with him—for the Prince and she, dining out, had afterwards called in Portland Place, whence, in the event, they had brought her, Charlotte, on. Maggie had come but to oblige her father—she had urged the two others to go without her; then she had yielded, for the time, to Mr. Verver's persuasion. But here, when they had, after the long wait in the carriage, fairly got in; here, once up the stairs, with the rooms before them, remorse had ended by seizing her: she had listened to no other remonstrance, and at present therefore, as Charlotte put it, the two were doubtless making together a little party at home. But it was all right—so Charlotte also put it: there was nothing in the world they liked better than these snatched felicities, little parties, long talks, with "I'll come to you to-morrow," and "No, I'll come to you," make-believe renewals of their old life. They were fairly, at times, the dear things, like children playing at paying visits, playing at "Mr. Thompson" and "Mrs. Fane," each hoping that the other would really stay to tea. Charlotte was sure she should find Maggie there on getting home—a remark in which Mrs. Verver's immediate response to her friend's inquiry had culminated. She had thus, on the spot, the sense of having given her plenty to think about, and that moreover of liking to see it even better than she had expected. She had plenty to think about herself, and there was already something in Fanny that made it seem still more.

"You say your husband's ill? He felt too ill to come?"

"No, my dear—I think not. If he had been too ill I wouldn't have left him."

"And yet Maggie was worried?" Mrs. Assingham asked.

"She worries, you know, easily. She's afraid of influenza—of which he has had, at different times, though never with the least gravity, several attacks."

"But you're not afraid of it?"

Charlotte had for a moment a pause; it had continued to come to her that really to have her case "out," as they said, with the person in the world to whom her most intimate difficulties had oftenest referred themselves, would help her, on the whole, more than hinder; and under that feeling all her opportunity, with nothing kept back; with a thing or two perhaps even thrust forward, seemed temptingly to open. Besides, didn't Fanny at bottom half expect, absolutely at the bottom half WANT, things?—so that she would be disappointed if, after what must just have occurred for her, she didn't get something to put between the teeth of her so restless rumination, that cultivation of the fear, of which our young woman had already had glimpses, that she might have "gone too far" in her irrepressible interest in other lives. What had just happened—it pieced itself together for Charlotte—was that the Assingham pair, drifting like everyone else, had had somewhere in the gallery, in the rooms, an accidental concussion; had had it after the Colonel, over his balustrade, had observed, in the favouring high light, her public junction with the Prince. His very dryness, in this encounter, had, as always, struck a spark from his wife's curiosity, and, familiar, on his side, with all that she saw in things, he had thrown her, as a fine little bone to pick, some report of the way one of her young friends was "going on" with another. He knew perfectly—such at least was Charlotte's liberal assumption—that she wasn't going on with anyone, but she also knew that, given the circumstances, she was inevitably to be sacrificed, in some form or another, to the humorous intercourse of the inimitable couple. The Prince meanwhile had also, under coercion, sacrificed her; the Ambassador had come up to him with a message from Royalty, to whom he was led away; after which she had talked for five minutes with Sir John Brinder, who had been of the Ambassador's company and who had rather artlessly remained with her. Fanny had then arrived in sight of them at the same moment as someone else she didn't know, someone who knew Mrs. Assingham and also knew Sir John. Charlotte had left it to her friend's competence to throw the two others immediately together and to find a way for entertaining her in closer quarters. This was the little history of the vision, in her, that was now rapidly helping her to recognise a precious chance, the chance that mightn't again soon be so good for the vivid making of a point. Her point was before her; it was sharp, bright, true; above all it was her own. She had reached it quite by herself; no one, not even Amerigo—Amerigo least of all, who would have nothing to do with it—had given her aid. To make it now with force for Fanny Assingham's benefit would see her further, in the direction in which the light had dawned, than any other spring she should, yet awhile, doubtless, be able to press. The direction was that of her greater freedom—which was all in the world she had in mind. Her opportunity had accordingly, after a few minutes of Mrs. Assingham's almost imprudently interested expression of face, positively acquired such a price for her that she may, for ourselves, while the intensity lasted, rather resemble a person holding out a small mirror at arm's length and consulting it with a special turn of the head. It was, in a word, with this value of her chance that she was intelligently playing when she said in answer to Fanny's last question: "Don't you remember what you told me, on the occasion of something or other, the other day? That you believe there's nothing I'm afraid of? So, my dear, don't ask me!"

"Mayn't I ask you," Mrs. Assingham returned, "how the case stands with your poor husband?"

"Certainly, dear. Only, when you ask me as if I mightn't perhaps know what to think, it seems to me best to let you see that I know perfectly what to think."

Mrs. Assingham hesitated; then, blinking a little, she took her risk. "You didn't think that if it was a question of anyone's returning to him, in his trouble, it would be better you yourself should have gone?"

Well, Charlotte's answer to this inquiry visibly shaped itself in the interest of the highest considerations. The highest considerations were good humour, candour, clearness and, obviously, the REAL truth. "If we couldn't be perfectly frank and dear with each other, it would be ever so much better, wouldn't it? that we shouldn't talk about anything at all; which, however, would be dreadful—and we certainly, at any rate, haven't yet come to it. You can ask me anything under the sun you like, because, don't you see? you can't upset me."

"I'm sure, my dear Charlotte," Fanny Assingham laughed, "I don't want to upset you."

"Indeed, love, you simply COULDN'T even if you thought it necessary—that's all I mean. Nobody could, for it belongs to my situation that I'm, by no merit of my own, just fixed—fixed as fast as a pin stuck, up to its head, in a cushion. I'm placed—I can't imagine anyone MORE placed. There I AM!"

Fanny had indeed never listened to emphasis more firmly applied, and it brought into her own eyes, though she had reasons for striving to keep them from betrayals, a sort of anxiety of intelligence. "I dare say—but your statement of your position, however you see it, isn't an answer to my inquiry. It seems to me, at the same time, I confess," Mrs. Assingham added, "to give but the more reason for it. You speak of our being 'frank.' How can we possibly be anything else? If Maggie has gone off through finding herself too distressed to stay, and if she's willing to leave you and her husband to show here without her, aren't the grounds of her preoccupation more or less discussable?"

"If they're not," Charlotte replied, "it's only from their being, in a way, too evident. They're not grounds for me—they weren't when I accepted Adam's preference that I should come to-night without him: just as I accept, absolutely, as a fixed rule, ALL his preferences. But that doesn't alter the fact, of course, that my husband's daughter, rather than his wife, should have felt SHE could, after all, be the one to stay with him, the one to make the sacrifice of this hour—seeing, especially, that the daughter has a husband of her own in the field." With which she produced, as it were, her explanation. "I've simply to see the truth of the matter—see that Maggie thinks more, on the whole, of fathers than of husbands. And my situation is such," she went on, "that this becomes immediately, don't you understand? a thing I have to count with."

Mrs. Assingham, vaguely heaving, panting a little but trying not to show it, turned about, from some inward spring, in her seat. "If you mean such a thing as that she doesn't adore the Prince—!"

"I don't say she doesn't adore him. What I say is that she doesn't think of him. One of those conditions doesn't always, at all stages, involve the other. This is just HOW she adores him," Charlotte said. "And what reason is there, in the world, after all, why he and I shouldn't, as you say, show together? We've shown together, my dear," she smiled, "before."

Her friend, for a little, only looked at her—speaking then with abruptness. "You ought to be absolutely happy. You live with such GOOD people."

The effect of it, as well, was an arrest for Charlotte; whose face, however, all of whose fine and slightly hard radiance, it had caused, the next instant, further to brighten. "Does one ever put into words anything so fatuously rash? It's a thing that must be said, in prudence, FOR one—by somebody who's so good as to take the responsibility: the more that it gives one always a chance to show one's best manners by not contradicting it. Certainly, you'll never have the distress, or whatever, of hearing me complain."

"Truly, my dear, I hope in all conscience not!" and the elder woman's spirit found relief in a laugh more resonant than was quite advised by their pursuit of privacy.

To this demonstration her friend gave no heed. "With all our absence after marriage, and with the separation from her produced in particular by our so many months in America, Maggie has still arrears, still losses to make up—still the need of showing how, for so long, she simply kept missing him. She missed his company—a large allowance of which is, in spite of everything else, of the first necessity to her. So she puts it in when she can—a little here, a little there, and it ends by making up a considerable amount. The fact of our distinct establishments—which has, all the same, everything in its favour," Charlotte hastened to declare, "makes her really see more of him than when they had the same house. To make sure she doesn't fail of it she's always arranging for it—which she didn't have to do while they lived together. But she likes to arrange," Charlotte steadily proceeded; "it peculiarly suits her; and the result of our separate households is really, for them, more contact and more intimacy. To-night, for instance, has been practically an arrangement. She likes him best alone. And it's the way," said our young woman, "in which he best likes HER. It's what I mean therefore by being 'placed.' And the great thing is, as they say, to 'know' one's place. Doesn't it all strike you," she wound up, "as rather placing the Prince too?"

Fanny Assingham had at this moment the sense as of a large heaped dish presented to her intelligence and inviting it to a feast—so thick were the notes of intention in this remarkable speech. But she also felt that to plunge at random, to help herself too freely, would—apart from there not being at such a moment time for it—tend to jostle the ministering hand, confound the array and, more vulgarly speaking, make a mess. So she picked out, after consideration, a solitary plum. "So placed that YOU have to arrange?"

"Certainly I have to arrange."

"And the Prince also—if the effect for him is the same?"

"Really, I think, not less."

"And does he arrange," Mrs. Assingham asked, "to make up HIS arrears?" The question had risen to her lips—it was as if another morsel, on the dish, had tempted her. The sound of it struck her own ear, immediately, as giving out more of her thought than she had as yet intended; but she quickly saw that she must follow it up, at any risk, with simplicity, and that what was simplest was the ease of boldness. "Make them up, I mean, by coming to see YOU?"

Charlotte replied, however, without, as her friend would have phrased it, turning a hair. She shook her head, but it was beautifully gentle. "He never comes."

"Oh!" said Fanny Assingham: with which she felt a little stupid. "There it is. He might as well, you know, otherwise."

"'Otherwise'?"—and Fanny was still vague.

It passed, this time, over her companion, whose eyes, wandering, to a distance, found themselves held. The Prince was at hand again; the Ambassador was still at his side; they were stopped a moment by a uniformed personage, a little old man, of apparently the highest military character, bristling with medals and orders. This gave Charlotte time to go on. "He has not been for three months." And then as with her friend's last word in her ear: "'Otherwise'—yes. He arranges otherwise. And in my position," she added, "I might too. It's too absurd we shouldn't meet."

"You've met, I gather," said Fanny Assingham, "to-night."

"Yes—as far as that goes. But what I mean is that I might—placed for it as we both are—go to see HIM."

"And do you?" Fanny asked with almost mistaken solemnity.

The perception of this excess made Charlotte, whether for gravity or for irony, hang fire a minute. "I HAVE been. But that's nothing," she said, "in itself, and I tell you of it only to show you how our situation works. It essentially becomes one, a situation, for both of us. The Prince's, however, is his own affair—I meant but to speak of mine."

"Your situation's perfect," Mrs. Assingham presently declared.

"I don't say it isn't. Taken, in fact, all round, I think it is. And I don't, as I tell you, complain of it. The only thing is that I have to act as it demands of me."

"To 'act'?" said Mrs. Assingham with an irrepressible quaver.

"Isn't it acting, my dear, to accept it? I do accept it. What do you want me to do less?"

"I want you to believe that you're a very fortunate person."

"Do you call that LESS?" Charlotte asked with a smile. "From the point of view of my freedom I call it more. Let it take, my position, any name you like."

"Don't let it, at any rate"—and Mrs. Assingham's impatience prevailed at last over her presence of mind—"don't let it make you think too much of your freedom."

"I don't know what you call too much—for how can I not see it as it is? You'd see your own quickly enough if the Colonel gave you the same liberty—and I haven't to tell you, with your so much greater knowledge of everything, what it is that gives such liberty most. For yourself personally of course," Charlotte went on, "you only know the state of neither needing it nor missing it. Your husband doesn't treat you as of less importance to him than some other woman."

"Ah, don't talk to me of other women!" Fanny now overtly panted. "Do you call Mr. Verver's perfectly natural interest in his daughter—?"

"The greatest affection of which he is capable?" Charlotte took it up in all readiness. "I do distinctly—and in spite of my having done all I could think of—to make him capable of a greater. I've done, earnestly, everything I could—I've made it, month after month, my study. But I haven't succeeded—it has been vividly brought home to me to-night. However," she pursued, "I've hoped against hope, for I recognise that, as I told you at the time, I was duly warned." And then as she met in her friend's face the absence of any such remembrance: "He did tell me that he wanted me just BECAUSE I could be useful about her." With which Charlotte broke into a wonderful smile. "So you see I AM!"

It was on Fanny Assingham's lips for the moment to reply that this was, on the contrary, exactly what she didn't see; she came in fact within an ace of saying: "You strike me as having quite failed to help his idea to work—since, by your account, Maggie has him not less, but so much more, on her mind. How in the world, with so much of a remedy, comes there to remain so much of what was to be obviated?" But she saved herself in time, conscious above all that she was in presence of still deeper things than she had yet dared to fear, that there was "more in it" than any admission she had made represented—and she had held herself familiar with admissions: so that, not to seem to understand where she couldn't accept, and not to seem to accept where she couldn't approve, and could still less, with precipitation, advise, she invoked the mere appearance of casting no weight whatever into the scales of her young friend's consistency. The only thing was that, as she was quickly enough to feel, she invoked it rather to excess. It brought her, her invocation, too abruptly to her feet. She brushed away everything. "I can't conceive, my dear, what you're talking about!"

Charlotte promptly rose then, as might be, to meet it, and her colour, for the first time, perceptibly heightened. She looked, for the minute, as her companion had looked—as if twenty protests, blocking each other's way, had surged up within her. But when Charlotte had to make a selection, her selection was always the most effective possible. It was happy now, above all, for being made not in anger but in sorrow. "You give me up then?"

"Give you up—?"

"You forsake me at the hour of my life when it seems to me I most deserve a friend's loyalty? If you do you're not just, Fanny; you're even, I think," she went on, "rather cruel; and it's least of all worthy of you to seem to wish to quarrel with me in order to cover your desertion." She spoke, at the same time, with the noblest moderation of tone, and the image of high, pale, lighted disappointment she meanwhile presented, as of a creature patient and lonely in her splendour, was an impression so firmly imposed that she could fill her measure to the brim and yet enjoy the last word, as it is called in such cases, with a perfection void of any vulgarity of triumph. She merely completed, for truth's sake, her demonstration. "What is a quarrel with me but a quarrel with my right to recognise the conditions of my bargain? But I can carry them out alone," she said as she turned away. She turned to meet the Ambassador and the Prince, who, their colloquy with their Field-Marshal ended, were now at hand and had already, between them, she was aware, addressed her a remark that failed to penetrate the golden glow in which her intelligence was temporarily bathed. She had made her point, the point she had foreseen she must make; she had made it thoroughly and once for all, so that no more making was required; and her success was reflected in the faces of the two men of distinction before her, unmistakably moved to admiration by her exceptional radiance. She at first but watched this reflection, taking no note of any less adequate form of it possibly presented by poor Fanny—poor Fanny left to stare at her incurred "score," chalked up in so few strokes on the wall; then she took in what the Ambassador was saying, in French, what he was apparently repeating to her.

"A desire for your presence, Madame, has been expressed en tres-haut lieu, and I've let myself in for the responsibility, to say nothing of the honour, of seeing, as the most respectful of your friends, that so august an impatience is not kept waiting." The greatest possible Personage had, in short, according to the odd formula of societies subject to the greatest personages possible, "sent for" her, and she asked, in her surprise, "What in the world does he want to do to me?" only to know, without looking, that Fanny's bewilderment was called to a still larger application, and to hear the Prince say with authority, indeed with a certain prompt dryness: "You must go immediately—it's a summons." The Ambassador, using authority as well, had already somehow possessed himself of her hand, which he drew into his arm, and she was further conscious as she went off with him that, though still speaking for her benefit, Amerigo had turned to Fanny Assingham. He would explain afterwards—besides which she would understand for herself. To Fanny, however, he had laughed—as a mark, apparently, that for this infallible friend no explanation at all would be necessary.

XV

It may be recorded none the less that the Prince was the next moment to see how little any such assumption was founded. Alone with him now Mrs. Assingham was incorruptible. "They send for Charlotte through YOU?"

"No, my dear; as you see, through the Ambassador."

"Ah, but the Ambassador and you, for the last quarter-of-an-hour, have been for them as one. He's YOUR ambassador." It may indeed be further mentioned that the more Fanny looked at it the more she saw in it. "They've connected her with you—she's treated as your appendage."

"Oh, my 'appendage,'" the Prince amusedly exclaimed—"cara mia, what a name! She's treated, rather, say, as my ornament and my glory. And it's so remarkable a case for a mother-in-law that you surely can't find fault with it."

"You've ornaments enough, it seems to me—as you've certainly glories enough—without her. And she's not the least little bit," Mrs. Assingham observed, "your mother-in-law. In such a matter a shade of difference is enormous. She's no relation to you whatever, and if she's known in high quarters but as going about with you, then—then—!" She failed, however, as from positive intensity of vision. "Then, then what?" he asked with perfect good-nature.

"She had better in such a case not be known at all."

"But I assure you I never, just now, so much as mentioned her. Do you suppose I asked them," said the young man, still amused, "if they didn't want to see her? You surely don't need to be shown that Charlotte speaks for herself—that she does so above all on such an occasion as this and looking as she does to-night. How, so looking, can she pass unnoticed? How can she not have 'success'? Besides," he added as she but watched his face, letting him say what he would, as if she wanted to see how he would say it, "besides, there IS always the fact that we're of the same connection, of—what's your word?—the same 'concern.' We're certainly not, with the relation of our respective sposi, simply formal acquaintances. We're in the same boat"—and the Prince smiled with a candour that added an accent to his emphasis.

Fanny Assingham was full of the special sense of his manner: it caused her to turn for a moment's refuge to a corner of her general consciousness in which she could say to herself that she was glad SHE wasn't in love with such a man. As with Charlotte just before, she was embarrassed by the difference between what she took in and what she could say, what she felt and what she could show. "It only appears to me of great importance that—now that you all seem more settled here—Charlotte should be known, for any presentation, any further circulation or introduction, as, in particular, her husband's wife; known in the least possible degree as anything else. I don't know what you mean by the 'same' boat. Charlotte is naturally in Mr. Verver's boat."

"And, pray, am I not in Mr. Verver's boat too? Why, but for Mr. Verver's boat, I should have been by this time"—and his quick Italian gesture, an expressive direction and motion of his forefinger, pointed to deepest depths—"away down, down, down." She knew of course what he meant—how it had taken his father-in-law's great fortune, and taken no small slice, to surround him with an element in which, all too fatally weighted as he had originally been, he could pecuniarily float; and with this reminder other things came to her—how strange it was that, with all allowance for their merit, it should befall some people to be so inordinately valued, quoted, as they said in the stock-market, so high, and how still stranger, perhaps, that there should be cases in which, for some reason, one didn't mind the so frequently marked absence in them of the purpose really to represent their price. She was thinking, feeling, at any rate, for herself; she was thinking that the pleasure SHE could take in this specimen of the class didn't suffer from his consent to be merely made buoyant: partly because it was one of those pleasures (he inspired them) that, by their nature, COULDN'T suffer, to whatever proof they were put; and partly because, besides, he after all visibly had on his conscience some sort of return for services rendered. He was a huge expense assuredly—but it had been up to now her conviction that his idea was to behave beautifully enough to make the beauty well nigh an equivalent. And that he had carried out his idea, carried it out by continuing to lead the life, to breathe the air, very nearly to think the thoughts, that best suited his wife and her father— this she had till lately enjoyed the comfort of so distinctly perceiving as to have even been moved more than once, to express to him the happiness it gave her. He had that in his favour as against other matters; yet it discouraged her too, and rather oddly, that he should so keep moving, and be able to show her that he moved, on the firm ground of the truth. His acknowledgment of obligation was far from unimportant, but she could find in his grasp of the real itself a kind of ominous intimation. The intimation appeared to peep at her even out of his next word, lightly as he produced it.

"Isn't it rather as if we had, Charlotte and I, for bringing us together, a benefactor in common?" And the effect, for his interlocutress, was still further to be deepened. "I somehow feel, half the time, as if he were her father-in-law too. It's as if he had saved us both—which is a fact in our lives, or at any rate in our hearts, to make of itself a link. Don't you remember"—he kept it up—"how, the day she suddenly turned up for you, just before my wedding, we so frankly and funnily talked, in her presence, of the advisability, for her, of some good marriage?" And then as his friend's face, in her extremity, quite again as with Charlotte, but continued to fly the black flag of general repudiation: "Well, we really began then, as it seems to me, the work of placing her where she is. We were wholly right—and so was she. That it was exactly the thing is shown by its success. We recommended a good marriage at almost any price, so to speak, and, taking us at our word, she has made the very best. That was really what we meant, wasn't it? Only—what she has got—something thoroughly good. It would be difficult, it seems to me, for her to have anything better—once you allow her the way it's to be taken. Of course if you don't allow her that the case is different. Her offset is a certain decent freedom— which, I judge, she'll be quite contented with. You may say that that will be very good of her, but she strikes me as perfectly humble about it. She proposes neither to claim it nor to use it with any sort of retentissement. She would enjoy it, I think, quite as quietly as it might be given. The 'boat,' you see"—the Prince explained it no less considerately and lucidly—"is a good deal tied up at the dock, or anchored, if you like, out in the stream. I have to jump out from time to time to stretch my legs, and you'll probably perceive, if you give it your attention, that Charlotte really can't help occasionally doing the same. It isn't even a question, sometimes, of one's getting to the dock—one has to take a header and splash about in the water. Call our having remained here together to-night, call the accident of my having put them, put our illustrious friends there, on my companion's track—for I grant you this as a practical result of our combination—call the whole thing one of the harmless little plunges off the deck, inevitable for each of us. Why not take them, when they occur, as inevitable—and, above all, as not endangering life or limb? We shan't drown, we shan't sink—at least I can answer for myself. Mrs. Verver too, moreover—do her the justice—visibly knows how to swim."

He could easily go on, for she didn't interrupt him; Fanny felt now that she wouldn't have interrupted him for the world. She found his eloquence precious; there was not a drop of it that she didn't, in a manner, catch, as it came, for immediate bottling, for future preservation. The crystal flask of her innermost attention really received it on the spot, and she had even already the vision of how, in the snug laboratory of her afterthought, she should be able chemically to analyse it. There were moments, positively, still beyond this, when, with the meeting of their eyes, something as yet unnamable came out for her in his look, when something strange and subtle and at variance with his words, something that GAVE THEM AWAY, glimmered deep down, as an appeal, almost an incredible one, to her finer comprehension. What, inconceivably, was it like? Wasn't it, however gross, such a rendering of anything so occult, fairly like a quintessential wink, a hint of the possibility of their REALLY treating their subject—of course on some better occasion—and thereby, as well, finding it much more interesting? If this far red spark, which might have been figured by her mind as the head-light of an approaching train seen through the length of a tunnel, was not, on her side, an ignis fatuus, a mere subjective phenomenon, it twinkled there at the direct expense of what the Prince was inviting her to understand. Meanwhile too, however, and unmistakably, the real treatment of their subject did, at a given moment, sound. This was when he proceeded, with just the same perfect possession of his thought—on the manner of which he couldn't have improved—to complete his successful simile by another, in fact by just the supreme touch, the touch for which it had till now been waiting. "For Mrs. Verver to be known to people so intensely and exclusively as her husband's wife, something is wanted that, you know, they haven't exactly got. He should manage to be known—or at least to be seen—a little more as his wife's husband. You surely must by this time have seen for yourself that he has his own habits and his own ways, and that he makes, more and more—as of course he has a perfect right to do—his own discriminations. He's so perfect, so ideal a father, and, doubtless largely by that very fact, a generous, a comfortable, an admirable father-in-law, that I should really feel it base to avail myself of any standpoint whatever to criticise him. To YOU, nevertheless, I may just put one remark; for you're not stupid—you always understand so blessedly what one means."

He paused an instant, as if even this one remark might be difficult for him should she give no sign of encouraging him to produce it. Nothing would have induced her, however, to encourage him; she was now conscious of having never in her life stood so still or sat, inwardly, as it were, so tight; she felt like the horse of the adage, brought—and brought by her own fault—to the water, but strong, for the occasion, in the one fact that she couldn't be forced to drink. Invited, in other words, to understand, she held her breath for fear of showing she did, and this for the excellent reason that she was at last fairly afraid to. It was sharp for her, at the same time, that she was certain, in advance, of his remark; that she heard it before it had sounded, that she already tasted, in fine, the bitterness it would have for her special sensibility. But her companion, from an inward and different need of his own, was presently not deterred by her silence. "What I really don't see is why, from his own point of view—given, that is, his conditions, so fortunate as they stood—he should have wished to marry at all." There it was then—exactly what she knew would come, and exactly, for reasons that seemed now to thump at her heart, as distressing to her. Yet she was resolved, meanwhile, not to suffer, as they used to say of the martyrs, then and there; not to suffer, odiously, helplessly, in public—which could be prevented but by her breaking off, with whatever inconsequence; by her treating their discussion as ended and getting away. She suddenly wanted to go home much as she had wanted, an hour or two before, to come. She wanted to leave well behind her both her question and the couple in whom it had, abruptly, taken such vivid form—but it was dreadful to have the appearance of disconcerted flight. Discussion had of itself, to her sense, become danger—such light, as from open crevices, it let in; and the overt recognition of danger was worse than anything else. The worst in fact came while she was thinking how she could retreat and still not overtly recognise. Her face had betrayed her trouble, and with that she was lost. "I'm afraid, however," the Prince said, "that I, for some reason, distress you—for which I beg your pardon. We've always talked so well together—it has been, from the beginning, the greatest pull for me." Nothing so much as such a tone could have quickened her collapse; she felt he had her now at his mercy, and he showed, as he went on, that he knew it. "We shall talk again, all the same, better than ever—I depend on it too much. Don't you remember what I told you, so definitely, one day before my marriage?—that, moving as I did in so many ways among new things, mysteries, conditions, expectations, assumptions different from any I had known, I looked to you, as my original sponsor, my fairy godmother, to see me through. I beg you to believe," he added, "that I look to you yet."

His very insistence had, fortunately, the next moment, affected her as bringing her help; with which, at least, she could hold up her head to speak. "Ah, you ARE through—you were through long ago. Or if you aren't you ought to be."

"Well then, if I ought to be it's all the more reason why you should continue to help me. Because, very distinctly, I assure you, I'm not. The new things or ever so many of them—are still for me new things; the mysteries and expectations and assumptions still contain an immense

186

element that I've failed to puzzle out. As we've happened, so luckily, to find ourselves again really taking hold together, you must let me, as soon as possible, come to see you; you must give me a good, kind hour. If you refuse it me"—and he addressed himself to her continued reserve—"I shall feel that you deny, with a stony stare, your responsibility."

At this, as from a sudden shake, her reserve proved an inadequate vessel. She could bear her own, her private reference to the weight on her mind, but the touch of another hand made it too horribly press. "Oh, I deny responsibility—to YOU. So far as I ever had it I've done with it."

He had been, all the while, beautifully smiling; but she made his look, now, penetrate her again more. "As to whom then do you confess it?"

"Ah, mio caro, that's—if to anyone—my own business!"

He continued to look at her hard. "You give me up then?"

It was what Charlotte had asked her ten minutes before, and its coming from him so much in the same way shook her in her place. She was on the point of replying "Do you and she agree together for what you'll say to me?"—but she was glad afterwards to have checked herself in time, little as her actual answer had perhaps bettered it. "I think I don't know what to make of you."

"You must receive me at least," he said.

"Oh, please, not till I'm ready for you!"—and, though she found a laugh for it, she had to turn away. She had never turned away from him before, and it was quite positively for her as if she were altogether afraid of him.

XVI

Later on, when their hired brougham had, with the long vociferation that tormented her impatience, been extricated from the endless rank, she rolled into the London night, beside her husband, as into a sheltering darkness where she could muffle herself and draw breath. She had stood for the previous half-hour in a merciless glare, beaten upon, stared out of countenance, it fairly seemed to her, by intimations of her mistake. For what she was most immediately feeling was that she had, in the past, been active, for these people, to ends that were now bearing fruit and that might yet bear a larger crop. She but brooded, at first, in her corner of the carriage: it was like burying her exposed face, a face too helplessly exposed, in the cool lap of the common indifference, of the dispeopled streets, of the closed shops and darkened houses seen through the window of the brougham, a world mercifully unconscious and unreproachful. It wouldn't, like the world she had just left, know sooner or later what she had done, or would know it, at least, only if the final consequence should be some quite overwhelming publicity. She fixed this possibility itself so hard, however, for a few moments, that the misery of her fear produced the next minute a reaction; and when the carriage happened, while it grazed a turn, to catch the straight shaft from the lamp of a policeman in the act of playing his inquisitive flash over an opposite house-front, she let herself wince at being thus incriminated only that she might protest, not less quickly, against mere blind terror. It had become, for the occasion, preposterously, terror—of which she must shake herself free before she could properly measure her ground. The perception of this necessity had in truth soon aided her; since she found, on trying, that, lurid as her prospect might hover there, she could none the less give it no name. The sense of seeing was strong in her, but she clutched at the comfort of not being sure of what she saw. Not to know what it would represent on a longer view was a help, in turn, to not making out that her hands were embrued; since if she had stood in the position of a producing cause she should surely be less vague about what she had produced. This, further, in its way, was a step toward reflecting that when one's connection with any matter was too indirect to be traced it might be described also as too slight to be deplored. By the time they were nearing Cadogan Place she had in fact recognised that she couldn't be as curious as she desired without arriving at some conviction of her being as innocent. But there had been a moment, in the dim desert of Eaton Square, when she broke into speech.

"It's only their defending themselves so much more than they need—it's only THAT that makes me wonder. It's their having so remarkably much to say for themselves."

Her husband had, as usual, lighted his cigar, remaining apparently as busy with it as she with her agitation. "You mean it makes you feel that you have nothing?" To which, as she made no answer, the Colonel added: "What in the world did you ever suppose was going to happen? The man's in a position in which he has nothing in life to do."

Her silence seemed to characterise this statement as superficial, and her thoughts, as always in her husband's company, pursued an independent course. He made her, when they were together, talk, but as if for some other person; who was in fact for the most part herself. Yet she addressed herself with him as she could never have done without him. "He has behaved beautifully—he did from the first. I've thought it, all along, wonderful of him; and I've more than once, when I've had a chance, told him so. Therefore, therefore—!" But it died away as she mused.

"Therefore he has a right, for a change, to kick up his heels?"

"It isn't a question, of course, however," she undivertedly went on, "of their behaving beautifully apart. It's a question of their doing as they should when together—which is another matter."

"And how do you think then," the Colonel asked with interest, "that, when together, they SHOULD do? The less they do, one would say, the better—if you see so much in it."

His wife, at this, appeared to hear him. "I don't see in it what YOU'D see. And don't, my dear," she further answered, "think it necessary to be horrid or low about them. They're the last people, really, to make anything of that sort come in right."

"I'm surely never horrid or low," he returned, "about anyone but my extravagant wife. I can do with all our friends—as I see them myself: what I can't do with is the figures you make of them. And when you take to adding your figures up—!" But he exhaled it again in smoke.

"My additions don't matter when you've not to pay the bill." With which her meditation again bore her through the air. "The great thing was that when it so suddenly came up for her he wasn't afraid. If he had been afraid he could perfectly have prevented it. And if I had seen he was—if I hadn't seen he wasn't—so," said Mrs. Assingham, "could I. So," she declared, "WOULD I. It's perfectly true," she went on—"it was too good a thing for her, such a chance in life, not to be accepted. And I LIKED his not keeping her out of it merely from a fear of his own nature. It was so wonderful it should come to her. The only thing would have been if Charlotte herself couldn't have faced it. Then, if SHE had not had confidence, we might have talked. But she had it to any amount."

"Did you ask her how much?" Bob Assingham patiently inquired.

He had put the question with no more than his usual modest hope of reward, but he had pressed, this time, the sharpest spring of response. "Never, never—it wasn't a time to 'ask.' Asking is suggesting—and it wasn't a time to suggest. One had to make up one's mind, as quietly as possible, by what one could judge. And I judge, as I say, that Charlotte felt she could face it. For which she struck me at the time as—for so proud a creature—almost touchingly grateful. The thing I should never forgive her for would be her forgetting to whom it is her thanks have remained most due."

"That is to Mrs. Assingham?"

She said nothing for a little—there were, after all, alternatives. "Maggie herself of course—astonishing little Maggie."

"Is Maggie then astonishing too?"—and he gloomed out of his window.

His wife, on her side now, as they rolled, projected the same look. "I'm not sure that I don't begin to see more in her than—dear little person as I've always thought—I ever supposed there was. I'm not sure that, putting a good many things together, I'm not beginning to make her out rather extraordinary."

"You certainly will if you can," the Colonel resignedly remarked.

Again his companion said nothing; then again she broke out. "In fact—I do begin to feel it—Maggie's the great comfort. I'm getting hold of it. It will be SHE who'll see us through. In fact she'll have to. And she'll be able."

Touch by touch her meditation had completed it, but with a cumulative effect for her husband's general sense of her method that caused him to overflow, whimsically enough, in his corner, into an ejaculation now frequent on his lips for the relief that, especially in communion like the present, it gave him, and that Fanny had critically traced to the quaint example, the aboriginal homeliness, still so delightful, of Mr. Verver. "Oh, Lordy, Lordy!"

"If she is, however," Mrs. Assingham continued, "she'll be extraordinary enough—and that's what I'm thinking of. But I'm not indeed so very sure," she added, "of the person to whom Charlotte ought in decency to be most grateful. I mean I'm not sure if that person is even almost the incredible little idealist who has made her his wife."

"I shouldn't think you would be, love," the Colonel with some promptness responded. "Charlotte as the wife of an incredible little idealist—!" His cigar, in short, once more, could alone express it.

"Yet what is that, when one thinks, but just what she struck one as more or less persuaded that she herself was really going to be?"—this memory, for the full view, Fanny found herself also invoking.

It made her companion, in truth, slightly gape. "An incredible little idealist—Charlotte herself?"

"And she was sincere," his wife simply proceeded "she was unmistakably sincere. The question is only how much is left of it."

"And that—I see—happens to be another of the questions you can't ask her. You have to do it all," said Bob Assingham, "as if you were playing some game with its rules drawn up—though who's to come down on you if you break them I don't quite see. Or must you do it in three guesses—like forfeits on Christmas eve?" To which, as his ribaldry but dropped from her, he further added: "How much of anything will have to be left for you to be able to go on with it?"

"I shall go on," Fanny Assingham a trifle grimly declared, "while there's a scrap as big as your nail. But we're not yet, luckily, reduced only to that." She had another pause, holding the while the thread of that larger perception into which her view of Mrs. Verver's obligation to Maggie had suddenly expanded. "Even if her debt was not to the others—even then it ought to be quite sufficiently to the Prince himself to keep her straight. For what, really, did the Prince do," she asked herself, "but generously trust her? What did he do but take it from her that if she felt herself willing it was because she felt herself strong? That creates for her, upon my word," Mrs. Assingham pursued, "a duty of considering him, of honourably repaying his trust, which—well, which she'll be really a fiend if she doesn't make the law of her conduct. I mean of course his trust that she wouldn't interfere with him—expressed by his holding himself quiet at the critical time."

The brougham was nearing home, and it was perhaps this sense of ebbing opportunity that caused the Colonel's next meditation to flower in a fashion almost surprising to his wife. They were united, for the most part, but by his exhausted patience; so that indulgent despair was generally, at the best, his note. He at present, however, actually compromised with his despair to the extent of practically admitting that he had followed her steps. He literally asked, in short, an intelligent, well nigh a sympathising, question. "Gratitude to the Prince for not having put a spoke in her wheel—that, you mean, should, taking it in the right way, be precisely the ballast of her boat?"

"Taking it in the right way." Fanny, catching at this gleam, emphasised the proviso.

"But doesn't it rather depend on what she may most feel to BE the right way?"

"No—it depends on nothing. Because there's only one way—for duty or delicacy."

"Oh—delicacy!" Bob Assingham rather crudely murmured.

"I mean the highest kind—moral. Charlotte's perfectly capable of appreciating that. By every dictate of moral delicacy she must let him alone."

"Then you've made up your mind it's all poor Charlotte?" he asked with an effect of abruptness.

The effect, whether intended or not, reached her—brought her face short round. It was a touch at which she again lost her balance, at which, somehow, the bottom dropped out of her recovered comfort. "Then you've made up yours differently? It really struck you that there IS something?"

The movement itself, apparently, made him once more stand off. He had felt on his nearer approach the high temperature of the question. "Perhaps that's just what she's doing: showing him how much she's letting him alone—pointing it out to him from day to day."

"Did she point it out by waiting for him to-night on the stair-case in the manner you described to me?"

"I really, my dear, described to you a manner?" the Colonel, clearly, from want of habit, scarce recognised himself in the imputation.

"Yes—for once in a way; in those few words you had after you had watched them come up you told me something of what you had seen. You didn't tell me very much—THAT you couldn't for your life; but I saw for myself that, strange to say, you had received your impression, and I felt therefore that there must indeed have been something out of the way for you so to betray it." She was fully upon him now, and she confronted him with his proved sensibility to the occasion—confronted him because of her own uneasy need to profit by it. It came over her still more than at the time, it came over her that he had been struck with something, even HE, poor dear man; and that for this to have occurred there must have been much to be struck with. She tried in fact to corner him, to pack him insistently down, in the truth of his plain vision, the very plainness of which was its value; for so recorded, she felt, none of it would escape—she should have it at hand for reference. "Come, my dear—you thought what you thought: in the presence of what you saw you couldn't resist thinking. I don't ask more of it than that. And your idea is worth, this time, quite as much as any of mine—so that you can't pretend, as usual, that mine has run away with me. I haven't caught up with you. I stay where I am. But I see," she concluded, "where you are, and I'm much obliged to you for letting me. You give me a point de repere outside myself—which is where I like it. Now I can work round you."

Their conveyance, as she spoke, stopped at their door, and it was, on the spot, another fact of value for her that her husband, though seated on the side by which they must alight, made no movement. They were in a high degree votaries of the latch-key, so that their household had gone to bed; and as they were unaccompanied by a footman the coachman waited in peace. It was so indeed that for a minute Bob Assingham waited—conscious of a reason for replying to this address otherwise than by the so obvious method of turning his back. He didn't turn his face, but he stared straight before him, and his wife had already perceived in the fact of his not moving all the proof she could desire— proof, that is, of her own contention. She knew he never cared what she said, and his neglect of his chance to show it was thereby the more eloquent. "Leave it," he at last remarked, "to THEM."

"'Leave' it—?" She wondered.

"Let them alone. They'll manage."

"They'll manage, you mean, to do everything they want? Ah, there then you are!"

"They'll manage in their own way," the Colonel almost cryptically repeated.

It had its effect for her: quite apart from its light on the familiar phenomenon of her husband's indurated conscience, it gave her, full in her face, the particular evocation of which she had made him guilty. It was wonderful truly, then, the evocation. "So cleverly—THAT'S your idea?—that no one will be the wiser? It's your idea that we shall have done all that's required of us if we simply protect them?"

The Colonel, still in his place, declined, however, to be drawn into a statement of his idea. Statements were too much like theories, in which one lost one's way; he only knew what he said, and what he said represented the limited vibration of which his confirmed old toughness had been capable. Still, none the less, he had his point to make—for which he took another instant. But he made it, for the third time, in the same fashion. "They'll manage in their own way." With which he got out.

Oh yes, at this, for his companion, it had indeed its effect, and while he mounted their steps she but stared, without following him, at his opening of their door. Their hall was lighted, and as he stood in the aperture looking back at her, his tall lean figure outlined in darkness and with his crush-hat, according to his wont, worn cavalierly, rather diabolically, askew, he seemed to prolong the sinister emphasis of his meaning. In general, on these returns, he came back for her when he had prepared their entrance; so that it was now as if he were ashamed to face her in closer quarters. He looked at her across the interval, and, still in her seat, weighing his charge, she felt her whole view of everything flare up. Wasn't it simply what had been written in the Prince's own face BENEATH what he was saying?—didn't it correspond with the mocking presence there that she had had her troubled glimpse of? Wasn't, in fine, the pledge that they would "manage in their own way" the thing he had been feeling for his chance to invite her to take from him? Her husband's tone somehow fitted Amerigo's look—the one that had, for her, so strangely, peeped, from behind, over the shoulder of the one in front. She had not then read it—but wasn't she reading it when she now saw in it his surmise that she was perhaps to be squared? She wasn't to be squared, and while she heard her companion call across to her "Well, what's the matter?" she also took time to remind herself that she had decided she couldn't be frightened. The "matter"?—why, it was sufficiently the matter, with all this, that she felt a little sick. For it was not the Prince that she had been prepared to regard as primarily the shaky one. Shakiness in Charlotte she had, at the most, perhaps postulated—it would be, she somehow felt, more easy to deal with. Therefore if HE had come so far it was a different pair of sleeves. There was nothing to choose between them. It made her so helpless that, as the time passed without her alighting, the Colonel came back and fairly drew her forth; after which, on the pavement, under the street-lamp, their very silence might have been the mark of something grave—their silence eked out for her by his giving her his arm and their then crawling up their steps quite mildly and unitedly together, like some old Darby and Joan who have had a disappointment. It almost resembled a return from a funeral—unless indeed it resembled more the hushed approach to a house of mourning. What indeed had she come home for but to bury, as decently as possible, her mistake?

XVII

It appeared thus that they might enjoy together extraordinary freedom, the two friends, from the moment they should understand their position aright. With the Prince himself, from an early stage, not unnaturally, Charlotte had made a great point of their so understanding it; she had found frequent occasion to describe to him this necessity, and, her resignation tempered, or her intelligence at least quickened, by irrepressible irony, she applied at different times different names to the propriety of their case. The wonderful thing was that her sense of propriety had been, from the first, especially alive about it. There were hours when she spoke of their taking refuge in what she called the commonest tact—as if this principle alone would suffice to light their way; there were others when it might have seemed, to listen to her, that their course would demand of them the most anxious study and the most independent, not to say original, interpretation of signs. She talked now as if it were indicated, at every turn, by finger-posts of almost ridiculous prominence; she talked again as if it lurked in devious ways and were to be tracked through bush and briar; and she even, on occasion, delivered herself in the sense that, as their situation was unprecedented, so their heaven was without stars. "'Do'?" she once had echoed to him as the upshot of passages covertly, though briefly, occurring between them on her return from the visit to America that had immediately succeeded her marriage, determined for her by this event as promptly as an excursion of the like strange order had been prescribed in his own case. "Isn't the immense, the really quite matchless beauty of our position that we have to 'do' nothing in life at all?—nothing except the usual, necessary, everyday thing which consists in one's not being more of a fool than one can help. That's all—but that's as true for one time as for another. There has been plenty of 'doing,' and there will doubtless be plenty still; but it's all theirs, every inch of it; it's all a matter of what they've done TO us." And she showed how the question had therefore been only of their taking everything as everything came, and all as quietly as might be. Nothing stranger surely had ever happened to a conscientious, a well-meaning, a perfectly passive pair: no more extraordinary decree had ever been launched against such victims than this of forcing them against their will into a relation of mutual close contact that they had done everything to avoid.

She was to remember not a little, meanwhile, the particular prolonged silent look with which the Prince had met her allusion to these primary efforts at escape. She was inwardly to dwell on the element of the unuttered that her tone had caused to play up into his irresistible eyes; and this because she considered with pride and joy that she had, on the spot, disposed of the doubt, the question, the challenge, or whatever else might have been, that such a look could convey. He had been sufficiently off his guard to show some little wonder as to their having plotted so very hard against their destiny, and she knew well enough, of course, what, in this connection, was at the bottom of his thought, and what would have sounded out more or less if he had not happily saved himself from words. All men were brutes enough to catch when they might at such chances for dissent—for all the good it really did them; but the Prince's distinction was in being one of the few who could check himself before acting on the impulse. This, obviously, was what counted in a man as delicacy. If her friend had blurted or bungled he would have said, in his simplicity, "Did we do 'everything to avoid' it when we faced your remarkable marriage?"—quite handsomely of course using the plural, taking his share of the case, by way of a tribute of memory to the telegram she had received from him in Paris after Mr. Verver had despatched to Rome the news of their engagement. That telegram, that acceptance of the prospect proposed to them—an acceptance quite other than perfunctory—she had never destroyed; though reserved for no eyes but her own it was still carefully reserved. She kept it in a safe place—from which, very privately, she sometimes took it out to read it over. "A la guerre comme a la guerre then"—it had been couched in the French tongue. "We must lead our lives as we see them; but I am charmed with your courage and almost surprised at my own." The message had remained ambiguous; she had read it in more lights than one; it might mean that even without her his career was up-hill work for him, a daily fighting-matter on behalf of a good appearance, and that thus, if they were to become neighbours again, the event would compel him to live still more under arms. It might mean on the other hand that he found he was happy enough, and that accordingly, so far as she might imagine herself a danger, she was to think of him as prepared in advance, as really seasoned and secure. On his arrival in Paris with his wife, none the less, she had asked for no explanation, just as he himself had not asked if the document were still in her possession. Such an inquiry, everything implied, was beneath him—just as it was beneath herself to mention to him, uninvited, that she had instantly offered, and in perfect honesty, to show the telegram to

Mr. Verver, and that if this companion had but said the word she would immediately have put it before him. She had thereby forborne to call his attention to her consciousness that such an exposure would, in all probability, straightway have dished her marriage; that all her future had in fact, for the moment, hung by the single hair of Mr. Verver's delicacy (as she supposed they must call it); and that her position, in the matter of responsibility, was therefore inattackably straight.

For the Prince himself, meanwhile, time, in its measured allowance, had originally much helped him—helped him in the sense of there not being enough of it to trip him up; in spite of which it was just this accessory element that seemed, at present, with wonders of patience, to lie in wait. Time had begotten at first, more than anything else, separations, delays and intervals; but it was troublesomely less of an aid from the moment it began so to abound that he had to meet the question of what to do with it. Less of it was required for the state of being married than he had, on the whole, expected; less, strangely, for the state of being married even as he was married. And there was a logic in the matter, he knew; a logic that but gave this truth a sort of solidity of evidence. Mr. Verver, decidedly, helped him with it—with his wedded condition; helped him really so much that it made all the difference. In the degree in which he rendered it the service on Mr. Verver's part was remarkable—as indeed what service, from the first of their meeting, had not been? He was living, he had been living these four or five years, on Mr. Verver's services: a truth scarcely less plain if he dealt with them, for appreciation, one by one, than if he poured them all together into the general pot of his gratitude and let the thing simmer to a nourishing broth. To the latter way with them he was undoubtedly most disposed; yet he would even thus, on occasion, pick out a piece to taste on its own merits. Wondrous at such hours could seem the savour of the particular "treat," at his father-in-law's expense, that he more and more struck himself as enjoying. He had needed months and months to arrive at a full appreciation—he couldn't originally have given offhand that a name to his deepest obligation; but by the time the name had flowered in his mind he was practically living at the ease guaranteed him. Mr. Verver then, in a word, took care of his relation to Maggie, as he took care, and apparently always would, of everything else. He relieved him of all anxiety about his married life in the same manner in which he relieved him on the score of his bank-account. And as he performed the latter office by communicating with the bankers, so the former sprang as directly from his good understanding with his daughter. This understanding had, wonderfully—THAT was in high evidence—the same deep intimacy as the commercial, the financial association founded, far down, on a community of interest. And the correspondence, for the Prince, carried itself out in identities of character the vision of which, fortunately, rather tended to amuse than to—as might have happened—irritate him. Those people—and his free synthesis lumped together capitalists and bankers, retired men of business, illustrious collectors, American fathers-in-law, American fathers, little American daughters, little American wives—those people were of the same large lucky group, as one might say; they were all, at least, of the same general species and had the same general instincts; they hung together, they passed each other the word, they spoke each other's language, they did each other "turns." In this last connection it of course came up for our young man at a given moment that Maggie's relation with HIM was also, on the perceived basis, taken care of. Which was in fact the real upshot of the matter. It was a "funny" situation—that is it was funny just as it stood. Their married life was in question, but the solution was, not less strikingly, before them. It was all right for himself, because Mr. Verver worked it so for Maggie's comfort; and it was all right for Maggie, because he worked it so for her husband's.

The fact that time, however, was not, as we have said, wholly on the Prince's side might have shown for particularly true one dark day on which, by an odd but not unprecedented chance, the reflections just noted offered themselves as his main recreation. They alone, it appeared, had been appointed to fill the hours for him, and even to fill the great square house in Portland Place, where the scale of one of the smaller saloons fitted them but loosely. He had looked into this room on the chance that he might find the Princess at tea; but though the fireside service of the repast was shiningly present the mistress of the table was not, and he had waited for her, if waiting it could be called, while he measured again and again the stretch of polished floor. He could have named to himself no pressing reason for seeing her at this moment, and her not coming in, as the half-hour elapsed, became in fact quite positively, however perversely, the circumstance that kept him on the spot. Just there, he might have been feeling, just there he could best take his note. This observation was certainly by itself meagre amusement for a dreary little crisis; but his walk to and fro, and in particular his repeated pause at one of the high front windows, gave each of the ebbing minutes, none the less, after a time, a little more of the quality of a quickened throb of the spirit. These throbs scarce expressed, however, the impatience of desire, any more than they stood for sharp disappointment: the series together resembled perhaps more than anything else those fine waves of clearness through which, for a watcher of the east, dawn at last trembles into rosy day. The illumination indeed was all for the mind, the prospect revealed by it a mere immensity of the world of thought; the material outlook was all the while a different matter. The March afternoon, judged at the window, had blundered back into autumn; it had been raining for hours, and the colour of the rain, the colour of the air, of the mud, of the opposite houses, of life altogether, in so grim a joke, so idiotic a masquerade, was an unutterable dirty brown. There was at first even, for the young man, no faint flush in the fact of the direction taken, while he happened to look out, by a slow-jogging four-wheeled cab which, awkwardly deflecting from the middle course, at the apparent instance of a person within, began to make for the left-hand pavement and so at last, under further instructions, floundered to a full stop before the Prince's windows. The person within, alighting with an easier motion, proved to be a lady who left the vehicle to wait and, putting up no umbrella, quickly crossed the wet interval that separated her from the house. She but flitted and disappeared; yet the Prince, from his standpoint, had had time to recognise her, and the recognition kept him for some minutes motionless.

Charlotte Stant, at such an hour, in a shabby four-wheeler and a waterproof, Charlotte Stant turning up for him at the very climax of his special inner vision, was an apparition charged with a congruity at which he stared almost as if it had been a violence. The effect of her coming to see him, him only, had, while he stood waiting, a singular intensity—though after some minutes had passed the certainty of this began to drop. Perhaps she had NOT come, or had come only for Maggie; perhaps, on learning below that the Princess had not returned, she was merely leaving a message, writing a word on a card. He could see, at any rate; and meanwhile, controlling himself, would do nothing. This thought of not interfering took on a sudden force for him; she would doubtless hear he was at home, but he would let her visit to him be all of her own choosing. And his view of a reason for leaving her free was the more remarkable that, though taking no step, he yet intensely hoped. The harmony of her breaking into sight while the superficial conditions were so against her was a harmony with conditions that were far from superficial and that gave, for his imagination, an extraordinary value to her presence. The value deepened strangely, moreover, with the rigour of his own attitude—with the fact too that, listening hard, he neither heard the house-door close again nor saw her go back to her cab; and it had risen to a climax by the time he had become aware, with his quickened sense, that she had followed the butler up to the landing from which his room opened. If anything could further then have added to it, the renewed pause outside, as if she had said to the man "Wait a moment!" would have constituted this touch. Yet when the man had shown her in, had advanced to the tea-table to light the lamp under the kettle and had then busied himself, all deliberately, with the fire, she made it easy for her host to drop straight from any height of tension and to meet her, provisionally, on the question of Maggie. While the butler remained it was Maggie that she had come to see and Maggie that—in spite of this attendant's high blankness on the subject of all possibilities on that lady's part—she would cheerfully, by the fire, wait for. As soon as they were alone together, however, she mounted, as with the whizz and the flash of a rocket, from the form to the fact, saying straight out, as she stood and looked at him: "What else, my dear, what in the world else can we do?"

It was as if he then knew, on the spot, why he had been feeling, for hours, as he had felt—as if he in fact knew, within the minute, things he had not known even while she was panting, as from the effect of the staircase, at the door of the room. He knew at the same time, none the less, that she knew still more than he—in the sense, that is, of all the signs and portents that might count for them; and his vision of alternative—she could scarce say what to call them, solutions, satisfactions—opened out, altogether, with this tangible truth of her attitude by the chimney-place, the way she looked at him as through the gained advantage of it; her right hand resting on the marble and her left keeping her skirt from the fire while she held out a foot to dry. He couldn't have told what particular links and gaps had at the end of a few minutes found themselves renewed and bridged; for he remembered no occasion, in Rome, from which the picture could have been so exactly copied. He remembered, that is, none of her coming to see him in the rain while a muddy four-wheeler waited, and while, though having left her waterproof downstairs, she was yet invested with the odd eloquence—the positive picturesqueness, yes, given all the rest of the matter—of a dull dress and a black Bowdlerised hat that seemed to make a point of insisting on their time of life and their moral mission, the hat's own, as well as on the irony of indifference to them practically playing in her so handsome rain-freshened face. The sense of the past revived for him nevertheless as it had not yet done: it made that other time somehow meet the future close, interlocking with it, before his watching eyes, as in a long embrace of arms and lips, and so handling and hustling the present that this poor quantity scarce retained substance enough, scarce remained sufficiently THERE, to be wounded or shocked.

What had happened, in short, was that Charlotte and he had, by a single turn of the wrist of fate—"led up" to indeed, no doubt, by steps and stages that conscious computation had missed—been placed face to face in a freedom that partook, extraordinarily, of ideal perfection, since the magic web had spun itself without their toil, almost without their touch. Above all, on this occasion, once more, there sounded through their safety, as an undertone, the very voice he had listened to on the eve of his marriage with such another sort of unrest. Dimly, again and again, from that period on, he had seemed to hear it tell him why it kept recurring; but it phrased the large music now in a way that filled the room. The reason was—into which he had lived, quite intimately, by the end of a quarter-of-an-hour—that just this truth of their safety offered it now a kind of unexampled receptacle, letting it spread and spread, but at the same time elastically enclosing it, banking it in, for softness, as with billows of eiderdown. On that morning; in the Park there had been, however dissimulated, doubt and danger, whereas the tale this afternoon was taken up with a highly emphasised confidence. The emphasis, for their general comfort, was what Charlotte had come to apply; inasmuch as, though it was not what she definitely began with, it had soon irrepressibly shaped itself. It was the meaning of the question she had put to him as soon as they were alone—even though indeed, as from not quite understanding, he had not then directly replied; it was the meaning of everything else, down to the conscious quaintness of her ricketty "growler" and the conscious humility of her dress. It had helped him a little, the question of these eccentricities, to let her immediate appeal pass without an answer. He could ask her instead what had become of her carriage and why, above all, she was not using it in such weather.

"It's just because of the weather," she explained. "It's my little idea. It makes me feel as I used to—when I could do as I liked."

XVIII

This came out so straight that he saw at once how much truth it expressed; yet it was truth that still a little puzzled him. "But did you ever like knocking about in such discomfort?"

"It seems to me now that I then liked everything. It's the charm, at any rate," she said from her place at the fire, "of trying again the old feelings. They come back—they come back. Everything," she went on, "comes back. Besides," she wound up, "you know for yourself."

He stood near her, his hands in his pockets; but not looking at her, looking hard at the tea-table. "Ah, I haven't your courage. Moreover," he laughed, "it seems to me that, so far as that goes, I do live in hansoms. But you must awfully want your tea," he quickly added; "so let me give you a good stiff cup."

He busied himself with this care, and she sat down, on his pushing up a low seat, where she had been standing; so that, while she talked, he could bring her what she further desired. He moved to and fro before her, he helped himself; and her visit, as the moments passed, had more and more the effect of a signal communication that she had come, all responsibly and deliberately, as on the clear show of the clock-face of their situation, to make. The whole demonstration, none the less, presented itself as taking place at a very high level of debate—in the cool upper air of the finer discrimination, the deeper sincerity, the larger philosophy. No matter what were the facts invoked and arrayed, it was only a question, as yet, of their seeing their way together: to which indeed, exactly, the present occasion appeared to have so much to contribute. "It's not that you haven't my courage," Charlotte said, "but that you haven't, I rather think, my imagination. Unless indeed it should turn out after all," she added, "that you haven't even my intelligence. However, I shall not be afraid of that till you've given me more proof." And she made again, but more clearly, her point of a moment before. "You knew, besides, you knew to-day, I would come. And if you knew that you know everything." So she pursued, and if he didn't meanwhile, if he didn't even at this, take her up, it might be that she was so positively fitting him again with the fair face of temporising kindness that he had given her, to keep her eyes on, at the other important juncture, and the sense of which she might ever since have been carrying about with her like a precious medal—not exactly blessed by the Pope suspended round her neck. She had come back, however this might be, to her immediate account of herself, and no mention of their great previous passage was to rise to the lips of either. "Above all," she said, "there has been the personal romance of it."

"Of tea with me over the fire? Ah, so far as that goes I don't think even my intelligence fails me."

"Oh, it's further than that goes; and if I've had a better day than you it's perhaps, when I come to think of it, that I AM braver. You bore yourself, you see. But I don't. I don't, I don't," she repeated.

"It's precisely boring one's self without relief," he protested, "that takes courage."

"Passive then—not active. My romance is that, if you want to know, I've been all day on the town. Literally on the town—isn't that what they call it? I know how it feels." After which, as if breaking off, "And you, have you never been out?" she asked.

He still stood there with his hands in his pockets. "What should I have gone out for?"

"Oh, what should people in our case do anything for? But you're wonderful, all of YOU—you know how to live. We're clumsy brutes, we other's, beside you—we must always be 'doing' something. However," Charlotte pursued, "if you had gone out you might have missed the chance of me—which I'm sure, though you won't confess it, was what you didn't want; and might have missed, above all, the satisfaction that, look blank about it as you will, I've come to congratulate you on. That's really what I can at last do. You can't not know at least, on such a day as this—you can't not know," she said, "where you are." She waited as for him either to grant that he knew or to pretend that he didn't; but he only drew a long deep breath which came out like a moan of impatience. It brushed aside the question of where he was or what he knew; it seemed to keep the ground clear for the question of his visitor herself, that of Charlotte Verver exactly as she sat there. So, for some moments, with their long look, they but treated the matter in silence; with the effect indeed, by the end of the time, of having considerably brought it on. This was sufficiently marked in what Charlotte next said. "There it all is—extraordinary beyond words. It makes such a relation for us as, I verily believe, was never before in the world thrust upon two well-meaning creatures. Haven't we therefore to take things as we find them?" She put the question still more directly than that of a moment before, but to this one, as well, he returned no immediate answer. Noticing only that she had finished her tea, he relieved her of her cup, carried it back to the table, asked her what more she would have; and then, on her "Nothing, thanks," returned to the fire and restored a displaced log to position by a small but almost too effectual kick. She had meanwhile got up again, and it was on her feet that she repeated the words she had first frankly spoken. "What else can we do, what in all the world else?"

He took them up, however, no more than at first. "Where then have you been?" he asked as from mere interest in her adventure.

"Everywhere I could think of—except to see people. I didn't want people—I wanted too much to think. But I've been back at intervals—three times; and then come away again. My cabman must think me crazy—it's very amusing; I shall owe him, when we come to settle, more money than he has ever seen. I've been, my dear," she went on, "to the British Museum—which, you know, I always adore. And I've been to the National Gallery, and to a dozen old booksellers', coming across treasures, and I've lunched, on some strange nastiness, at a cookshop in Holborn. I wanted to go to the Tower, but it was too far—my old man urged that; and I would have gone to the Zoo if it hadn't been too wet—which he also begged me to observe. But you wouldn't believe—I did put in St. Paul's. Such days," she wound up, "are expensive; for, besides the cab, I've bought quantities of books." She immediately passed, at any rate, to another point: "I can't help wondering when you must last have laid eyes on them." And then as it had apparently for her companion an effect of abruptness: "Maggie, I mean, and the child. For I suppose you know he's with her."

"Oh yes, I know he's with her. I saw them this morning."

"And did they then announce their programme?"

"She told me she was taking him, as usual, da nonno."

"And for the whole day?"

He hesitated, but it was as if his attitude had slowly shifted.

"She didn't say. And I didn't ask."

"Well," she went on, "it can't have been later than half-past ten—I mean when you saw them. They had got to Eaton Square before eleven. You know we don't formally breakfast, Adam and I; we have tea in our rooms—at least I have; but luncheon is early, and I saw my husband, this morning, by twelve; he was showing the child a picture-book. Maggie had been there with them, had left them settled together. Then she had gone out—taking the carriage for something she had been intending but that she offered to do instead."

The Prince appeared to confess, at this, to his interest. "Taking, you mean, YOUR carriage?"

"I don't know which, and it doesn't matter. It's not a question," she smiled, "of a carriage the more or the less. It's not a question even, if you come to that, of a cab. It's so beautiful," she said, "that it's not a question of anything vulgar or horrid." Which she gave him time to agree about; and though he was silent it was, rather remarkably, as if he fell in. "I went out—I wanted to. I had my idea. It seemed to me important. It has BEEN—it IS important. I know as I haven't known before the way they feel. I couldn't in any other way have made so sure of it."

"They feel a confidence," the Prince observed.

He had indeed said it for her. "They feel a confidence." And she proceeded, with lucidity, to the fuller illustration of it; speaking again of the three different moments that, in the course of her wild ramble, had witnessed her return—for curiosity, and even really a little from anxiety—to Eaton Square. She was possessed of a latch-key, rarely used: it had always irritated Adam—one of the few things that did—to find servants standing up so inhumanly straight when they came home, in the small hours, after parties. "So I had but to slip in, each time, with my cab at the door, and make out for myself, without their knowing it, that Maggie was still there. I came, I went—without their so much as dreaming. What do they really suppose," she asked, "becomes of one?—not so much sentimentally or morally, so to call it, and since that doesn't matter; but even just physically, materially, as a mere wandering woman: as a decent harmless wife, after all; as the best stepmother, after all, that really ever was; or at the least simply as a maitresse de maison not quite without a conscience. They must even in their odd way," she declared, "have SOME idea."

"Oh, they've a great deal of idea," said the Prince. And nothing was easier than to mention the quantity. "They think so much of us. They think in particular so much of you."

"Ah, don't put it all on 'me'!" she smiled.

But he was putting it now where she had admirably prepared the place. "It's a matter of your known character."

"Ah, thank you for 'known'!" she still smiled.

"It's a matter of your wonderful cleverness and wonderful charm. It's a matter of what those things have done for you in the world—I mean in THIS world and this place. You're a Personage for them—and Personages do go and come."

"Oh no, my dear; there you're quite wrong." And she laughed now in the happier light they had diffused. "That's exactly what Personages don't do: they live in state and under constant consideration; they haven't latch-keys, but drums and trumpets announce them; and when they go out in growlers it makes a greater noise still. It's you, caro mio," she said, "who, so far as that goes, are the Personage."

"Ah," he in turn protested, "don't put it all on me! What, at any rate, when you get home," he added, "shall you say that you've been doing?"

"I shall say, beautifully, that I've been here."

"All day?"

"Yes—all day. Keeping you company in your solitude. How can we understand anything," she went on, "without really seeing that this is what they must like to think I do for you?—just as, quite as comfortably, you do it for me. The thing is for us to learn to take them as they are."

He considered this a while, in his restless way, but with his eyes not turning from her; after which, rather disconnectedly, though very vehemently, he brought out: "How can I not feel more than anything else how they adore together my boy?" And then, further, as if, slightly disconcerted, she had nothing to meet this and he quickly perceived the effect: "They would have done the same for one of yours."

"Ah, if I could have had one—! I hoped and I believed," said Charlotte, "that that would happen. It would have been better. It would have made perhaps some difference. He thought so too, poor duck—that it might have been. I'm sure he hoped and intended so. It's not, at any rate," she went on, "my fault. There it is." She had uttered these statements, one by one, gravely, sadly and responsibly, owing it to her friend to be clear. She paused briefly, but, as if once for all, she made her clearness complete. "And now I'm too sure. It will never be."

He waited for a moment. "Never?"

"Never." They treated the matter not exactly with solemnity, but with a certain decency, even perhaps urgency, of distinctness. "It would probably have been better," Charlotte added. "But things turn out—! And it leaves us"—she made the point—"more alone."

He seemed to wonder. "It leaves you more alone."

"Oh," she again returned, "don't put it all on me! Maggie would have given herself to his child, I'm sure, scarcely less than he gives himself to yours. It would have taken more than any child of mine," she explained—"it would have taken more than ten children of mine, could I have had them—to keep our sposi apart." She smiled as for the breadth of the image, but, as he seemed to take it, in spite of this, for important, she then spoke gravely enough. "It's as strange as you like, but we're immensely alone." He kept vaguely moving, but there were moments when, again, with an awkward ease and his hands in his pockets, he was more directly before her. He stood there at these last words, which had the effect of making him for a little throw back his head and, as thinking something out, stare up at the ceiling. "What will you say," she meanwhile asked, "that you've been doing?" This brought his consciousness and his eyes back to her, and she pointed her question. "I mean when she comes in—for I suppose she WILL, some time, come in. It seems to me we must say the same thing."

Well, he thought again. "Yet I can scarce pretend to have had what I haven't."

"Ah, WHAT haven't you had?—what aren't you having?"

Her question rang out as they lingered face to face, and he still took it, before he answered, from her eyes. "We must at least then, not to be absurd together, do the same thing. We must act, it would really seem, in concert."

"It would really seem!" Her eyebrows, her shoulders went up, quite in gaiety, as for the relief this brought her. "It's all in the world I pretend. We must act in concert. Heaven knows," she said, "THEY do!"

So it was that he evidently saw and that, by his admission, the case, could fairly be put. But what he evidently saw appeared to come over him, at the same time, as too much for him, so that he fell back suddenly to ground where she was not awaiting him. "The difficulty is, and will always be, that I don't understand them. I didn't at first, but I thought I should learn to. That was what I hoped, and it appeared then that Fanny Assingham might help me."

"Oh, Fanny Assingham!" said Charlotte Verver.

He stared a moment at her tone. "She would do anything for us."

To which Charlotte at first said nothing—as if from the sense of too much. Then, indulgently enough, she shook her head. "We're beyond her."

He thought a moment—as of where this placed them. "She'd do anything then for THEM."

"Well, so would we—so that doesn't help us. She has broken down. She doesn't understand us. And really, my dear," Charlotte added, "Fanny Assingham doesn't matter."

He wondered again. "Unless as taking care of THEM."

"Ah," Charlotte instantly said, "isn't it for us, only, to do that?" She spoke as with a flare of pride for their privilege and their duty. "I think we want no one's aid."

She spoke indeed with a nobleness not the less effective for coming in so oddly; with a sincerity visible even through the complicated twist by which any effort to protect the father and the daughter seemed necessarily conditioned for them. It moved him, in any case, as if some spring of his own, a weaker one, had suddenly been broken by it. These things, all the while, the privilege, the duty, the opportunity, had been the substance of his own vision; they formed the note he had been keeping back to show her that he was not, in their so special situation, without a responsible view. A conception that he could name, and could act on, was something that now, at last, not to be too eminent a fool, he was required by all the graces to produce, and the luminous idea she had herself uttered would have been his expression of it. She had anticipated him, but, as her expression left, for positive beauty, nothing to be desired, he felt rather righted than wronged. A large response, as he looked at her, came into his face, a light of excited perception all his own, in the glory of which—as it almost might be called—what he gave her back had the value of what she had, given him. "They're extraordinarily happy."

Oh, Charlotte's measure of it was only too full. "Beatifically."

"That's the great thing," he went on; "so that it doesn't matter, really, that one doesn't understand. Besides, you do—enough."

"I understand my husband perhaps," she after an instant conceded. "I don't understand your wife."

"You're of the same race, at any rate—more or less; of the same general tradition and education, of the same moral paste. There are things you have in common with them. But I, on my side, as I've gone on trying to see if I haven't some of these things too—I, on my side, have more and more failed. There seem at last to be none worth mentioning. I can't help seeing it—I'm decidedly too different."

"Yet you're not"—Charlotte made the important point—"too different from ME."

"I don't know—as we're not married. That brings that out. Perhaps if we were," he said, "you WOULD find some abyss of divergence."

"Since it depends on that then," she smiled, "I'm safe—as you are anyhow. Moreover, as one has so often had occasion to feel, and even to remark, they're very, very simple. That makes," she added, "a difficulty for belief; but when once one has taken it in it makes less difficulty for action. I HAVE at last, for myself, I think, taken it in. I'm not afraid."

He wondered a moment. "Not afraid of what?"

"Well, generally, of some beastly mistake. Especially of any mistake founded on one's idea of their difference. For that idea," Charlotte developed, "positively makes one so tender."

"Ah, but rather!"

"Well then, there it is. I can't put myself into Maggie's skin—I can't, as I say. It's not my fit—I shouldn't be able, as I see it, to breathe in it. But I can feel that I'd do anything—to shield it from a bruise. Tender as I am for her too," she went on, "I think I'm still more so for my husband. HE'S in truth of a sweet simplicity—!"

The Prince turned over a while the sweet simplicity of Mr. Verver. "Well, I don't know that I can choose. At night all cats are grey. I only see how, for so many reasons, we ought to stand toward them—and how, to do ourselves justice, we do. It represents for us a conscious care—"

"Of every hour, literally," said Charlotte. She could rise to the highest measure of the facts. "And for which we must trust each other—!"

"Oh, as we trust the saints in glory. Fortunately," the Prince hastened to add, "we can." With which, as for the full assurance and the pledge it involved, their hands instinctively found their hands. "It's all too wonderful."

Firmly and gravely she kept his hand. "It's too beautiful."

And so for a minute they stood together, as strongly held and as closely confronted as any hour of their easier past even had seen them. They were silent at first, only facing and faced, only grasping and grasped, only meeting and met. "It's sacred," he said at last.

"It's sacred," she breathed back to him. They vowed it, gave it out and took it in, drawn, by their intensity, more closely together. Then of a sudden, through this tightened circle, as at the issue of a narrow strait into the sea beyond, everything broke up, broke down, gave way, melted and mingled. Their lips sought their lips, their pressure their response and their response their pressure; with a violence that had sighed itself the next moment to the longest and deepest of stillnesses they passionately sealed their pledge.

XIX

He had taken it from her, as we have seen, moreover, that Fanny Assingham didn't now matter—the "now" he had even himself supplied, as no more than fair to his sense of various earlier stages; and, though his assent remained scarce more than tacit, his behaviour, for the hour, so fell into line that, for many days, he kept postponing the visit he had promised his old friend on the occasion of their talk at the Foreign Office. With regret, none the less, would he have seen it quite extinguished, that theory of their relation as attached pupil and kind instructress in which they had from the first almost equally found a convenience. It had been he, no doubt, who had most put it forward, since his need of knowledge fairly exceeded her mild pretension; but he had again and again repeated to her that he should never, without her, have been where he was, and she had not successfully concealed the pleasure it might give her to believe it, even after the question of where he was had begun to show itself as rather more closed than open to interpretation. It had never indeed, before that evening, come up as during the passage at the official party, and he had for the first time at those moments, a little disappointedly, got the impression of a certain failure, on the dear woman's part, of something he was aware of having always rather freely taken for granted in her. Of what exactly the failure consisted he would still perhaps have felt it a little harsh to try to say; and if she had in fact, as by Charlotte's observation, "broken down," the details of the collapse would be comparatively unimportant. They came to the same thing, all such collapses—the failure of courage, the failure of friendship, or the failure just simply of tact; for didn't any one of them by itself amount really to the failure of wit?—which was the last thing he had expected of her and which would be but another name for the "triumph of stupidity." It had been Charlotte's remark that they were at last "beyond" her; whereas he had ever enjoyed believing that a certain easy imagination in her would keep up with him to the end. He shrank from affixing a label to Mrs. Assingham's want of faith; but when he thought, at his ease, of the way persons who were capable really entertained—or at least with any refinement—the passion of personal loyalty, he figured for them a play of fancy neither timorous nor scrupulous. So would his personal loyalty, if need be, have accepted the adventure for the good creature herself; to that definite degree that he had positively almost missed the luxury of some such call from her. That was what it all came back to again with these people among whom he was married—that one found one used one's imagination mainly for wondering how they contrived so little to appeal to it. He felt at moments as if there were never anything to do for them that was worthy—to call worthy—of the personal relation; never any charming charge to take of any confidence deeply reposed. He might vulgarly have put it that one had never to plot or to lie for them; he might humourously have put it that one had never, as by the higher conformity, to lie in wait with the dagger or to prepare, insidiously, the cup. These were the services that, by all romantic tradition, were consecrated to affection quite as much as to hate. But he could amuse himself with saying—so far as the amusement went—that they were what he had once for all turned his back on.

Fanny was meanwhile frequent, it appeared, in Eaton Square; so much he gathered from the visitor who was not infrequent, least of all at tea-time, during the same period, in Portland Place; though they had little need to talk of her after practically agreeing that they had outlived her. To the scene of these conversations and suppressions Mrs. Assingham herself made, actually, no approach; her latest view of her utility seeming to be that it had found in Eaton Square its most urgent field. It was finding there in fact everything and everyone but the Prince, who mostly, just now, kept away, or who, at all events, on the interspaced occasions of his calling, happened not to encounter the only person from whom he was a little estranged. It would have been all prodigious if he had not already, with Charlotte's aid, so very considerably lived into it—it would have been all indescribably remarkable, this fact that, with wonderful causes for it so operating on the surface, nobody else, as yet, in the combination, seemed estranged from anybody. If Mrs. Assingham delighted in Maggie she knew by this time how most easily to reach her, and if she was unhappy about Charlotte she knew, by the same reasoning, how most probably to miss that vision of her on which affliction would feed. It might feed of course on finding her so absent from her home—just as this particular phenomenon of her domestic detachment could be, by the anxious mind, best studied there. Fanny was, however, for her reasons, "shy" of Portland Place itself—this was appreciable; so that she might well, after all, have no great light on the question of whether Charlotte's appearances there were frequent or not, any more than on that of the account they might be keeping of the usual solitude (since it came to this) of the head of that house. There was always, to cover all ambiguities, to constitute a fund of explanation for the divisions of Mrs. Verver's day, the circumstance that, at the point they had all reached together, Mrs. Verver was definitely and by general acclamation in charge of the "social relations" of the family, literally of those of the two households; as to her genius for representing which in the great world and in the grand style vivid evidence had more and more accumulated. It had been established in the two households at an early stage, and with the highest good-humour, that Charlotte was a, was THE, "social success," whereas the Princess, though kind, though punctilious, though charming, though in fact the dearest little creature in the world and the Princess into the bargain, was distinctly not, would distinctly never be, and might as well, practically, give it up: whether through being above it or below it, too much outside of it or too much lost in it, too unequipped or too indisposed, didn't especially matter. What sufficed was that the whole thing, call it appetite or call it patience, the act of representation at large and the daily business of intercourse, fell in with Charlotte's tested facility and, not much less visibly, with her accommodating, her generous, view of her domestic use. She had come, frankly, into the connection, to do and to be what she could, "no questions asked," and she had taken over, accordingly, as it stood, and in the finest practical spirit, the burden of a visiting-list that Maggie, originally, left to herself, and left even more to the Principino, had suffered to get inordinately out of hand.

She had in a word not only mounted, cheerfully, the London treadmill—she had handsomely professed herself, for the further comfort of the three others, sustained in the effort by a "frivolous side," if that were not too harsh a name for a pleasant constitutional curiosity. There were possibilities of dulness, ponderosities of practice, arid social sands, the bad quarters-of-an-hour that turned up like false pieces in a debased currency, of which she made, on principle, very nearly as light as if she had not been clever enough to distinguish. The Prince had, on this score, paid her his compliment soon after her return from her wedding-tour in America, where, by all accounts, she had wondrously borne the brunt; facing brightly, at her husband's side, everything that came up—and what had come, often, was beyond words: just as, precisely, with her own interest only at stake, she had thrown up the game during the visit paid before her marriage. The discussion of the American world, the comparison of notes, impressions and adventures, had been all at hand, as a ground of meeting for Mrs. Verver and her husband's son-in-law, from the hour of the reunion of the two couples. Thus it had been, in short, that Charlotte could, for her friend's appreciation, so promptly make her point; even using expressions from which he let her see, at the hour, that he drew amusement of his own. "What could be more simple than one's going through with everything," she had asked, "when it's so plain a part of one's contract? I've got so much, by my marriage"—for she had never for a moment concealed from him how "much" she had felt it and was finding it "that I should deserve no charity if I stinted my return. Not to do that, to give back on the contrary all one can, are just one's decency and one's honour and one's virtue. These things, henceforth, if you're interested to know, are my rule of life, the absolute little gods of my worship, the holy images set up on the wall. Oh yes, since I'm not a brute," she had wound up, "you shall see me as I AM!" Which was therefore as he had seen her—dealing always, from month to month, from day to day and from one occasion to the other, with the duties of a remunerated office. Her perfect, her brilliant efficiency had doubtless, all the while, contributed immensely to the pleasant ease in which her husband and her husband's daughter were lapped. It had in fact probably done something more than this—it had given them a finer and sweeter view of the possible scope of that ease. They had brought her in—on the crudest expression of it—to do the "worldly" for them, and she had done it with such genius that they had themselves in consequence renounced it even more than they had originally intended. In proportion as she did it, moreover, was she to be relieved of other and humbler doings; which minor matters, by the properest logic, devolved therefore upon Maggie, in whose chords and whose province they more naturally lay. Not less naturally, by the same token, they included the repair, at the hands of the latter young woman, of every stitch conceivably dropped by Charlotte in Eaton Square. This was homely work, but that was just what made it Maggie's. Bearing in mind dear Amerigo, who was so much of her own great mundane feather, and whom the homeliness in question didn't, no doubt, quite equally provide for—that would be, to balance, just in a manner Charlotte's very most charming function, from the moment Charlotte could be got adequately to recognise it.

Well, that Charlotte might be appraised as at last not ineffectually recognising it, was a reflection that, during the days with which we are actually engaged, completed in the Prince's breast these others, these images and ruminations of his leisure, these gropings and fittings of his conscience and his experience, that we have attempted to set in order there. They bore him company, not insufficiently—considering, in especial, his fuller resources in that line—while he worked out—to the last lucidity the principle on which he forbore either to seek Fanny out in Cadogan Place or to perpetrate the error of too marked an assiduity in Eaton Square. This error would be his not availing himself to the utmost of the convenience of any artless theory of his constitution, or of Charlotte's, that might prevail there. That artless theories could and did prevail was a fact he had ended by accepting, under copious evidence, as definite and ultimate; and it consorted with common prudence, with the simplest economy of life, not to be wasteful of any odd gleaning. To haunt Eaton Square, in fine, would be to show that he had not, like his brilliant associate, a sufficiency of work in the world. It was just his having that sufficiency, it was just their having it together, that, so strangely and so blessedly, made, as they put it to each other, everything possible. What further propped up the case, moreover, was that the "world," by still another beautiful perversity of their chance, included Portland Place without including to anything like the same extent Eaton Square. The latter residence, at the same time, it must promptly be added, did, on occasion, wake up to opportunity and, as giving itself a frolic shake, send out a score of invitations—one of which fitful flights, precisely, had, before Easter, the effect of disturbing a little our young man's measure of his margin. Maggie, with a proper spirit, held that her father ought from time to time to give a really considered dinner, and Mr. Verver, who had as little idea as ever of not meeting expectation, was of the harmonious opinion that his wife ought. Charlotte's own judgment was, always, that they were ideally free—the proof of which would always be, she maintained, that everyone they feared they might most have alienated by neglect would arrive, wreathed with smiles, on the merest hint of a belated signal. Wreathed in smiles, all round, truly enough, these apologetic banquets struck Amerigo as being; they were, frankly, touching occasions to him, marked, in the great London bousculade, with a small, still grace of their own, an investing amenity and humanity. Everybody came, everybody rushed; but all succumbed to the soft influence, and the brutality of mere multitude, of curiosity without tenderness, was put off, at the foot of the fine staircase, with the overcoats and shawls. The entertainment offered a few evenings before Easter, and at which Maggie and he were inevitably present as guests, was a discharge of obligations not insistently incurred, and had thereby, possibly, all the more, the note of this almost Arcadian optimism: a large, bright, dull, murmurous, mild-eyed, middle-aged dinner, involving for the most part very bland, though very exalted, immensely announceable and hierarchically placeable couples, and followed, without the oppression of a later contingent, by a brief instrumental concert, over the preparation of which, the Prince knew, Maggie's anxiety had conferred with Charlotte's ingenuity and both had supremely revelled, as it were, in Mr. Verver's solvency.

The Assinghams were there, by prescription, though quite at the foot of the social ladder, and with the Colonel's wife, in spite of her humility of position, the Prince was more inwardly occupied than with any other person except Charlotte. He was occupied with Charlotte because, in the first place, she looked so inordinately handsome and held so high, where so much else was mature and sedate, the torch of responsive youth and the standard of passive grace; and because of the fact that, in the second, the occasion, so far as it referred itself with any confidence of emphasis to a hostess, seemed to refer itself preferentially, well-meaningly and perversely, to Maggie. It was not indistinguishable to him, when once they were all stationed, that his wife too had in perfection her own little character; but he wondered how it managed so visibly to simplify itself—and this, he knew, in spite of any desire she entertained—to the essential air of having overmuch on her mind the felicity, and indeed the very conduct and credit, of the feast. He knew, as well, the other things of which her appearance was at any time—and in Eaton Square especially—made up: her resemblance to her father, at times so vivid, and coming out, in the delicate warmth of occasions, like the quickened fragrance of a flower; her resemblance, as he had hit it off for her once in Rome, in the first flushed days, after their engagement, to a little dancing-girl at rest, ever so light of movement but most often panting gently, even a shade compunctiously, on a bench; her approximation, finally—for it was analogy, somehow, more than identity—to the transmitted images of rather neutral and negative propriety that made up, in his long line, the average of wifehood and motherhood. If the Roman matron had been, in sufficiency, first and last, the honour of that line, Maggie would no doubt, at fifty, have expanded, have solidified to some such dignity, even should she suggest a little but a Cornelia in miniature. A light, however, broke for him in season, and when once it had done so it made him more than ever aware of Mrs. Verver's vaguely, yet quite exquisitely, contingent participation—a mere hinted or tendered discretion; in short of Mrs. Verver's indescribable, unfathomable relation to the scene. Her placed condition, her natural seat and neighbourhood, her intenser presence, her quieter smile, her fewer jewels, were inevitably all as nothing compared with the preoccupation that burned in Maggie like a small flame and that had in fact kindled in each of her cheeks a little attesting, but fortunately by no means unbecoming, spot. The party was her father's party, and its greater or smaller success was a question having for her all the importance of his importance; so that sympathy created for her a sort of visible suspense, under pressure of which she bristled with filial reference, with little filial recalls of expression, movement, tone. It was all unmistakable, and as pretty as possible, if one would, and even as funny; but it put the pair so together, as undivided by the marriage of each, that the Princess il n'y avait pas a dire—might sit where she liked: she would still, always, in that house, be irremediably Maggie Verver. The Prince found himself on this occasion so beset with that perception that its natural complement for him would really have been to wonder if Mr. Verver had produced on people something of the same impression in the recorded cases of his having dined with his daughter.

This backward speculation, had it begun to play, however, would have been easily arrested; for it was at present to come over Amerigo as never before that his remarkable father-in-law was the man in the world least equipped with different appearances for different hours. He was simple, he was a revelation of simplicity, and that was the end of him so far as he consisted of an appearance at all—a question that might verily, for a weakness in it, have been argued. It amused our young man, who was taking his pleasure to-night, it will be seen, in sundry occult ways, it amused him to feel how everything else the master of the house consisted of, resources, possessions, facilities and amiabilities amplified by the social legend, depended, for conveying the effect of quantity, on no personal "equation," no mere measurable medium. Quantity was in the air for these good people, and Mr. Verver's estimable quality was almost wholly in that pervasion. He was meagre and modest and clearbrowed, and his eyes, if they wandered without fear, yet stayed without defiance; his shoulders were not broad, his chest was not high, his complexion was not fresh, and the crown of his head was not covered; in spite of all of which he looked, at the top of his table, so nearly like a little boy shyly entertaining in virtue of some imposed rank, that he COULD only be one of the powers, the representative of a force—quite as an infant king is the representative of a dynasty. In this generalised view of his father-in-law, intensified to-night but always operative, Amerigo had now for some time taken refuge. The refuge, after the reunion of the two households in England, had more and more offered itself as the substitute for communities, from man to man, that, by his original calculation, might have become possible, but that had not really ripened and flowered. He met the decent family eyes across the table, met them afterwards in the music-room, but only to read in them still what he had learned to read during his first months, the time of over-anxious initiation, a kind of apprehension in which the terms and conditions were finally fixed and absolute. This directed regard rested at its ease, but it neither lingered nor penetrated, and was, to the Prince's fancy, much of the same order as any glance directed, for due attention, from the same quarter, to the figure of a cheque received in the course of business and about to be enclosed to a banker. It made sure of the amount—and just so, from time to time, the amount of the Prince was made sure. He was being thus, in renewed instalments, perpetually paid in; he already reposed in the bank as a value, but subject, in this comfortable way, to repeated, to infinite endorsement. The net result of all of which, moreover, was that the young man had no wish to see his value diminish. He himself, after all, had not fixed it—the "figure" was a conception all of Mr. Verver's own. Certainly, however, everything must be kept up to it; never so much as to-night had the Prince felt this. He would have been uncomfortable, as these quiet expressions passed, had the case not been guaranteed for him by the intensity of his accord with Charlotte. It was impossible that he should not now and again meet Charlotte's eyes, as it was also visible that she too now and again met her husband's. For her as well, in all his pulses, he felt the conveyed impression. It put them, it kept them together, through the vain show of their separation, made the two other faces, made the whole lapse of the evening, the people, the lights, the flowers, the pretended talk, the exquisite music, a mystic golden bridge between them, strongly swaying and sometimes almost vertiginous, for that intimacy of which the sovereign law would be the vigilance of "care," would be never rashly to forget and never consciously to wound.

XX

The main interest of these hours for us, however, will have been in the way the Prince continued to know, during a particular succession of others, separated from the evening in Eaton Square by a short interval, a certain persistent aftertaste. This was the lingering savour of a cup presented to him by Fanny Assingham's hand after dinner, while the clustered quartette kept their ranged companions, in the music-room, moved if one would, but conveniently motionless. Mrs. Assingham contrived, after a couple of pieces, to convey to her friend that, for her part, she was moved—by the genius of Brahms—beyond what she could bear; so that, without apparent deliberation, she had presently floated away, at the young man's side, to such a distance as permitted them to converse without the effect of disdain. It was the twenty minutes enjoyed with her, during the rest of the concert, in the less associated electric glare of one of the empty rooms—it was their achieved and, as he would have said, successful, most pleasantly successful, talk on one of the sequestered sofas, it was this that was substantially to underlie his consciousness of the later occasion. The later occasion, then mere matter of discussion, had formed her ground for desiring—in a light undertone into which his quick ear read indeed some nervousness—these independent words with him: she had sounded, covertly but distinctly, by the time they were seated together, the great question of what it might involve. It had come out for him before anything else, and so abruptly that this almost needed an explanation. Then the abruptness itself had appeared to explain—which had introduced, in turn, a slight awkwardness. "Do you know that they're not, after all, going to Matcham; so that, if they don't—if, at least, Maggie doesn't—you won't, I suppose, go by yourself?" It was, as I say, at Matcham, where the event had placed him, it was at Matcham during the Easter days, that it most befell him, oddly enough, to live over, inwardly, for its wealth of special significance, this passage by which the event had been really a good deal determined. He had paid, first and last, many an English country visit; he had learned, even from of old, to do the English things, and to do them, all sufficiently, in the English way; if he didn't always enjoy them madly he enjoyed them at any rate as much, to an appearance, as the good people who had, in the night of time, unanimously invented them, and who still, in the prolonged afternoon of their good faith, unanimously, even if a trifle automatically, practised them; yet, with it all, he had never so much as during such sojourns the trick of a certain detached, the amusement of a certain inward critical, life; the determined need, which apparently all participant, of returning upon itself, of backing noiselessly in, far in again, and rejoining there, as it were, that part of his mind that was not engaged at the front. His body, very constantly, was engaged at the front—in shooting, in riding, in golfing, in walking, over the fine diagonals of meadow-paths or round the pocketed corners of billiard-tables; it sufficiently, on the whole, in fact, bore the brunt of bridge-playing, of breakfasting, lunching, tea-drinking, dining, and of the nightly climax over the bottigliera, as he called it, of the bristling tray; it met, finally, to the extent of the limited tax on lip, on gesture, on wit, most of the current demands of conversation and expression. Therefore something of him, he often felt at these times, was left out; it was much more when he was alone, or when he was with his own people—or when he was, say, with Mrs. Verver and nobody else—that he moved, that he talked, that he listened, that he felt, as a congruous whole.

"English society," as he would have said, cut him, accordingly, in two, and he reminded himself often, in his relations with it, of a man possessed of a shining star, a decoration, an order of some sort, something so ornamental as to make his identity not complete, ideally, without it, yet who, finding no other such object generally worn, should be perpetually, and the least bit ruefully, unpinning it from his breast to transfer it to his pocket. The Prince's shining star may, no doubt, having been nothing more precious than his private subtlety; but whatever the object he was he just now fingered it a good deal, out of sight—amounting as it mainly did for him to a restless play of memory and a fine embroidery of thought. Something had rather momentously occurred, in Eaton Square, during his enjoyed minutes with his old friend: his present perspective made definitely clear to him that she had plumped out for him her first little lie. That took on—and he could scarce have said why—a sharpness of importance: she had never lied to him before—if only because it had never come up for her, properly, intelligibly, morally, that she must. As soon as she had put to him the question of what he would do—by which she meant of what Charlotte would also do—in that event of Maggie's and Mr. Verver's not embracing the proposal they had appeared for a day or two resignedly to entertain; as soon as she had betrayed her curiosity as to the line the other pair, so left to themselves, might take, a desire to avoid the appearance of at all too directly prying had become marked in her. Betrayed by the solicitude of which she had, three weeks before, given him a view, she had been obliged, on a second thought, to name, intelligibly, a reason for her appeal; while the Prince, on his side, had had, not without mercy, his glimpse of her momentarily groping for one and yet remaining unprovided. Not without mercy because, absolutely, he had on the spot, in his friendliness, invented one for her use, presenting it to her with a look no more significant than if he had picked up, to hand back to her, a dropped flower. "You ask if I'm likely also to back out then, because it may make a difference in what you and the Colonel decide?"—he had gone as far as that for her, fairly inviting her to assent, though not having had his impression, from any indication offered him by Charlotte, that the Assinghams were really in question for the large Matcham party. The wonderful thing, after this, was that the active couple had, in the interval, managed to inscribe themselves on the golden roll; an exertion of a sort that, to do her justice, he had never before observed Fanny to make. This last passage of the chapter but proved, after all, with what success she could work when she would.

Once launched, himself, at any rate, as he had been directed by all the terms of the intercourse between Portland Place and Eaton Square, once steeped, at Matcham, in the enjoyment of a splendid hospitality, he found everything, for his interpretation, for his convenience, fall easily enough into place; and all the more that Mrs. Verver was at hand to exchange ideas and impressions with. The great house was full of people, of possible new combinations, of the quickened play of possible propinquity, and no appearance, of course, was less to be cultivated than that of his having sought an opportunity to foregather with his friend at a safe distance from their respective sposi. There was a happy boldness, at the best, in their mingling thus, each unaccompanied, in the same sustained sociability—just exactly a touch of that eccentricity of associated freedom which sat so lightly on the imagination of the relatives left behind. They were exposed as much as one would to its being pronounced funny that they should, at such a rate, go about together—though, on the other hand, this consideration drew relief from the fact that, in their high conditions and with the easy tradition, the almost inspiring allowances, of the house in question, no individual line, however freely marked, was pronounced anything more than funny. Both our friends felt afresh, as they had felt before, the convenience of a society so placed that it had only its own sensibility to consider—looking as it did well over the heads of all lower growths; and that moreover treated its own sensibility quite as the easiest, friendliest, most informal and domesticated party to the general alliance. What anyone "thought" of anyone else—above all of anyone else with anyone else—was a matter incurring in these lulls so little awkward formulation that hovering judgment, the spirit with the scales, might perfectly have been imaged there as some rather snubbed and subdued, but quite trained and tactful poor relation, of equal, of the properest, lineage, only of aspect a little dingy, doubtless from too limited a change of dress, for whose tacit and abstemious presence, never betrayed by a rattle of her rusty machine, a room in the attic and a plate at the side-table were decently usual. It was amusing, in such lightness of air, that the Prince should again present himself only to speak for the Princess, so unfortunately unable, again, to leave home; and that Mrs. Verver should as regularly figure as an embodied, a beautifully deprecating apology for her husband, who was all geniality and humility among his own treasures, but as to whom the legend had grown up that he couldn't bear, with the height of his standards and the tone of the company, in the way of sofas and cabinets, habitually kept by him, the irritation and depression to which promiscuous visiting, even at pompous houses, had been found to expose him. That was all right, the noted working harmony of the clever son-in-law and the charming stepmother, so long as the relation was, for the effect in question, maintained at the proper point between sufficiency and excess.

What with the noble fairness of the place, meanwhile, the generous mood of the sunny, gusty, lusty English April, all panting and heaving with impatience, or kicking and crying, even, at moments, like some infant Hercules who wouldn't be dressed; what with these things and the bravery of youth and beauty, the insolence of fortune and appetite so diffused among his fellow-guests that the poor Assinghams, in their comparatively marked maturity and their comparatively small splendour, were the only approach to a false note in the concert, the stir of the air was such, for going, in a degree, to one's head, that, as a mere matter of exposure, almost grotesque in its flagrancy, his situation resembled some elaborate practical joke carried out at his expense. Every voice in the great bright house was a call to the ingenuities and impunities of pleasure; every echo was a defiance of difficulty, doubt or danger; every aspect of the picture, a glowing plea for the immediate, and as with plenty more to come, was another phase of the spell. For a world so constituted was governed by a spell, that of the smile of the gods and the favour of the powers; the only handsome, the only gallant, in fact the only intelligent acceptance of which was a faith in its guarantees and a high spirit for its chances. Its demand—to that the thing came back—was above all for courage and good-humour; and the value of this as a general assurance—that is for seeing one through at the worst—had not even in the easiest hours of his old Roman life struck the Prince so convincingly. His old Roman life had had more poetry, no doubt, but as he looked back upon it now it seemed to hang in the air of mere iridescent horizons, to have been loose and vague and thin, with large languorous unaccountable blanks. The present order, as it spread about him, had somehow the ground under its feet, and a trumpet in its ears, and a bottomless bag of solid shining British sovereigns—which was much to the point—in its hand. Courage and good-humour therefore were the breath of the day; though for ourselves at least it would have been also much to the point that, with Amerigo, really, the innermost effect of all this perceptive ease was perhaps a strange final irritation. He compared the lucid result with the extraordinary substitute for perception that presided, in the bosom of his wife, at so contented a view of his conduct and course—a state of mind that was positively like a vicarious good conscience, cultivated ingeniously on his behalf, a perversity of pressure innocently persisted in; and this wonder of irony became on occasion too intense to be kept wholly to himself. It wasn't that, at Matcham, anything particular, anything monstrous, anything that had to be noticed permitted itself, as they said, to "happen"; there were only odd moments when the breath of the day, as it has been called, struck him so full in the face that he broke out with all the hilarity of "What indeed would THEY have made of it?" "They" were of course Maggie and her father, moping—so far as they ever consented to mope in monotonous Eaton Square, but placid too in the belief that they knew beautifully what their expert companions were in for. They knew, it might have appeared in these lights, absolutely nothing on earth worth speaking of—whether beautifully or cynically; and they would perhaps sometimes be a little less trying if they would only once for all peacefully admit that knowledge wasn't one of their needs and that they were in fact constitutionally inaccessible to it. They were good children, bless their hearts, and the children of good children; so that, verily, the Principino himself, as less consistently of that descent, might figure to the fancy as the ripest genius of the trio.

The difficulty was, for the nerves of daily intercourse with Maggie in particular, that her imagination was clearly never ruffled by the sense of any anomaly. The great anomaly would have been that her husband, or even that her father's wife, should prove to have been made, for the long run, after the pattern set from so far back by the Ververs. If one was so made one had certainly no business, on any terms, at Matcham; whereas if one wasn't one had no business there on the particular terms—terms of conformity with the principles of Eaton Square—under which one had been so absurdly dedicated. Deep at the heart of that resurgent unrest in our young man which we have had to content ourselves with calling his irritation—deep in the bosom of this falsity of position glowed the red spark of his inextinguishable sense of a higher and braver propriety. There were situations that were ridiculous, but that one couldn't yet help, as for instance when one's wife chose, in the most usual way, to make one so. Precisely here, however, was the difference; it had taken poor Maggie to invent a way so extremely unusual—yet to which, none the less, it would be too absurd that he should merely lend himself. Being thrust, systematically, with another woman, and a woman one happened, by the same token, exceedingly to like, and being so thrust that the theory of it seemed to publish one as idiotic or incapable—this WAS a predicament of which the dignity depended all on one's own handling. What was supremely grotesque, in fact, was the essential opposition of theories—as if a galantuomo, as HE at least constitutionally conceived galantuomini, could do anything BUT blush to "go about" at such a rate with such a person as Mrs. Verver in a state of childlike innocence, the state of our primitive parents before the Fall. The grotesque theory, as he would have called it, was perhaps an odd one to resent with violence, and he did it—also as a man of the world—all merciful justice; but, assuredly, none the less, there was but one way REALLY to mark, and for his companion as much as for himself, the commiseration in which they held it. Adequate comment on it could only be private, but it could also at least be active, and of rich and effectual comment Charlotte and he were fortunately alike capable. Wasn't this consensus literally their only way not to be ungracious? It was positively as if the measure of their escape from that danger were given by the growth between them, during their auspicious visit, of an exquisite sense of complicity.

XXI

He found himself therefore saying, with gaiety, even to Fanny Assingham, for their common, concerned glance at Eaton Square, the glance that was so markedly never, as it might have been, a glance at Portland Place: "What WOULD our cari sposi have made of it here? what would they, you know, really?"—which overflow would have been reckless if, already, and surprisingly perhaps even to himself, he had not got used to thinking of this friend as a person in whom the element of protest had of late been unmistakably allayed. He exposed himself of course to her replying: "Ah, if it would have been so bad for them, how can it be so good for you?"—but, quite apart from the small sense the question would have had at the best, she appeared already to unite with him in confidence and cheer. He had his view, as well—or at least a partial one—

of the inner spring of this present comparative humility, which was all consistent with the retraction he had practically seen her make after Mr. Verver's last dinner. Without diplomatising to do so, with no effort to square her, none to bribe her to an attitude for which he would have had no use in her if it were not sincere, he yet felt how he both held her and moved her by the felicity of his taking pity, all instinctively, on her just discernible depression. By just so much as he guessed that she felt herself, as the slang was, out of it, out of the crystal current and the expensive picture, by just so much had his friendship charmingly made up to her, from hour to hour, for the penalties, as they might have been grossly called, of her mistake. Her mistake had only been, after all, in her wanting to seem to him straight; she had let herself in for being—as she had made haste, for that matter, during the very first half-hour, at tea, to proclaim herself—the sole and single frump of the party. The scale of everything was so different that all her minor values, her quainter graces, her little local authority, her humour and her wardrobe alike, for which it was enough elsewhere, among her bons amis, that they were hers, dear Fanny Assingham's—these matters and others would be all, now, as nought: five minutes had sufficed to give her the fatal pitch. In Cadogan Place she could always, at the worst, be picturesque—for she habitually spoke of herself as "local" to Sloane Street whereas at Matcham she should never be anything but horrible. And it all would have come, the disaster, from the real refinement, in her, of the spirit of friendship. To prove to him that she wasn't really watching him—ground for which would have been too terribly grave—she had followed him in his pursuit of pleasure: SO she might, precisely, mark her detachment. This was handsome trouble for her to take—the Prince could see it all: it wasn't a shade of interference that a good-natured man would visit on her. So he didn't even say, when she told him how frumpy she knew herself, how frumpy her very maid, odiously going back on her, rubbed it into her, night and morning, with unsealed eyes and lips, that she now knew her—he didn't then say "Ah, see what you've done: isn't it rather your own fault?" He behaved differently altogether: eminently distinguished himself—for she told him she had never seen him so universally distinguished—he yet distinguished her in her obscurity, or in what was worse, her objective absurdity, and frankly invested her with her absolute value, surrounded her with all the importance of her wit. That wit, as discriminated from stature and complexion, a sense for "bridge" and a credit for pearls, could have importance was meanwhile but dimly perceived at Matcham; so that this "niceness" to her—she called it only niceness, but it brought tears into her eyes—had the greatness of a general as well as of a special demonstration.

"She understands," he said, as a comment on all this, to Mrs. Verver—"she understands all she needs to understand. She has taken her time, but she has at last made it out for herself: she sees how all we can desire is to give them the life they prefer, to surround them with the peace and quiet, and above all with the sense of security, most favourable to it. She can't of course very well put it to us that we have, so far as she is concerned, but to make the best of our circumstances; she can't say in so many words 'Don't think of me, for I too must make the best of mine: arrange as you can, only, and live as you must.' I don't get quite THAT from her, any more than I ask for it. But her tone and her whole manner mean nothing at all unless they mean that she trusts us to take as watchful, to take as artful, to take as tender care, in our way, as she so anxiously takes in hers. So that she's—well," the Prince wound up, "what you may call practically all right." Charlotte in fact, however, to help out his confidence, didn't call it anything; return as he might to the lucidity, the importance, or whatever it was, of this lesson, she gave him no aid toward reading it aloud. She let him, two or three times over, spell it out for himself; only on the eve of their visit's end was she, for once, clear or direct in response. They had found a minute together in the great hall of the house during the half-hour before dinner; this easiest of chances they had already, a couple of times, arrived at by waiting persistently till the last other loiterers had gone to dress, and by being prepared themselves to dress so expeditiously that they might, a little later on, be among the first to appear in festal array. The hall then was empty, before the army of rearranging, cushion-patting housemaids were marshalled in, and there was a place by the forsaken fire, at one end, where they might imitate, with art, the unpremeditated. Above all, here, for the snatched instants, they could breathe so near to each other that the interval was almost engulfed in it, and the intensity both of the union and the caution became a workable substitute for contact. They had prolongations of instants that counted as visions of bliss; they had slow approximations that counted as long caresses. The quality of these passages, in truth, made the spoken word, and especially the spoken word about other people, fall below them; so that our young woman's tone had even now a certain dryness. "It's very good of her, my dear, to trust us. But what else can she do?"

"Why, whatever people do when they don't trust. Let one see they don't."

"But let whom see?"

"Well, let ME, say, to begin with."

"And should you mind that?"

He had a slight show of surprise. "Shouldn't you?"

"Her letting you see? No," said Charlotte; "the only thing I can imagine myself minding is what you yourself, if you don't look out, may let HER see." To which she added: "You may let her see, you know, that you're afraid."

"I'm only afraid of you, a little, at moments," he presently returned. "But I shan't let Fanny see that."

It was clear, however, that neither the limits nor the extent of Mrs. Assingham's vision were now a real concern to her, and she gave expression to this as she had not even yet done. "What in the world can she do against us? There's not a word that she can breathe. She's helpless; she can't speak; she would be herself the first to be dished by it." And then as he seemed slow to follow: "It all comes back to her. It all began with her. Everything, from the first. She introduced you to Maggie. She made your marriage."

The Prince might have had his moment of demur, but at this, after a little, as with a smile dim but deep, he came on. "Mayn't she also be said, a good deal, to have made yours? That was intended, I think, wasn't it? for a kind of rectification."

Charlotte, on her side, for an instant, hesitated; then she was prompter still. "I don't mean there was anything to rectify; everything was as it had to be, and I'm not speaking of how she may have been concerned for you and me. I'm speaking of how she took, in her way, each time, THEIR lives in hand, and how, therefore, that ties her up to-day. She can't go to them and say 'It's very awkward of course, you poor dear things, but I was frivolously mistaken.'"

He took it in still, with his long look at her. "All the more that she wasn't. She was right. Everything's right," he went on, "and everything will stay so."

"Then that's all I say."

But he worked it out, for the deeper satisfaction, even to superfluous lucidity. "We're happy, and they're happy. What more does the position admit of? What more need Fanny Assingham want?"

"Ah, my dear," said Charlotte, "it's not I who say that she need want anything. I only say that she's FIXED, that she must stand exactly where everything has, by her own act, placed her. It's you who have seemed haunted with the possibility, for her, of some injurious alternative, something or other we must be prepared for." And she had, with her high reasoning, a strange cold smile. "We ARE prepared—for anything, for everything; and AS we are, practically, so she must take us. She's condemned to consistency; she's doomed, poor thing, to a genial optimism. That, luckily for her, however, is very much the law of her nature. She was born to soothe and to smooth. Now then, therefore," Mrs. Verver gently laughed, "she has the chance of her life!"

"So that her present professions may, even at the best, not be sincere?—may be but a mask for doubts and fears, and for gaining time?"

The Prince had looked, with the question, as if this, again, could trouble him, and it determined in his companion a slight impatience. "You keep talking about such things as if they were our affair at all. I feel, at any rate, that I've nothing to do with her doubts and fears, or with anything she may feel. She must arrange all that for herself. It's enough for me that she'll always be, of necessity, much more afraid for herself, REALLY, either to see or to speak, than we should be to have her do it even if we were the idiots and cowards we aren't." And Charlotte's face, with these words—to the mitigation of the slightly hard ring there might otherwise have been in them—fairly lightened, softened, shone out. It reflected as really never yet the rare felicity of their luck. It made her look for the moment as if she had actually pronounced that word of unpermitted presumption—so apt is the countenance, as with a finer consciousness than the tongue, to betray a sense of this particular lapse. She might indeed, the next instant, have seen her friend wince, in advance, at her use of a word that was already on her lips; for it was still unmistakable with him that there were things he could prize, forms of fortune he could cherish, without at all proportionately liking their names. Had all this, however, been even completely present to his companion, what other term could she have applied to the strongest and simplest of her ideas but the one that exactly fitted it? She applied it then, though her own instinct moved her, at the same time, to pay her tribute to the good taste from which they hadn't heretofore by a hair's breadth deviated. "If it didn't sound so vulgar I should say that we're—fatally, as it were—SAFE. Pardon the low expression—since it's what we happen to be. We're so because they are. And they're so because they can't be anything else, from the moment that, having originally intervened for them, she wouldn't now be able to bear herself if she didn't keep them so. That's the way she's inevitably WITH us," said Charlotte over her smile. "We hang, essentially, together."

Well, the Prince candidly allowed she did bring it home to him. Every way it worked out. "Yes, I see. We hang, essentially, together." His friend had a shrug—a shrug that had a grace. "Cosa volete?" The effect, beautifully, nobly, was more than Roman. "Ah, beyond doubt, it's a case."

He stood looking at her. "It's a case. There can't, he said, "have been many."

"Perhaps never, never, never any other. That," she smiled, "I confess I should like to think. Only ours."

"Only ours—most probably. Speriamo." To which, as after hushed connections, he presently added: "Poor Fanny!" But Charlotte had already, with a start and a warning hand, turned from a glance at the clock. She sailed away to dress, while he watched her reach the staircase. His eyes followed her till, with a simple swift look round at him, a simple swift look round at him, she vanished. Something in the sight, however, appeared to have renewed the spring of his last exclamation, which he breathed again upon the air. "Poor, poor Fanny!"

It was to prove, however, on the morrow, quite consistent with the spirit of these words that, the party at Matcham breaking up and multitudinously dispersing, he should be able to meet the question of the social side of the process of repatriation with due presence of mind. It was impossible, for reasons, that he should travel to town with the Assinghams; it was impossible, for the same reasons, that he should travel to town save in the conditions that he had for the last twenty-four hours been privately, and it might have been said profoundly, thinking out. The result of his thought was already precious to him, and this put at his service, he sufficiently believed, the right tone for disposing of his elder friend's suggestion, an assumption in fact equally full and mild, that he and Charlotte would conveniently take the same train and occupy the same compartment as the Colonel and herself. The extension of the idea to Mrs. Verver had been, precisely, a part of Mrs. Assingham's mildness, and nothing could better have characterised her sense for social shades than her easy perception that the gentleman from Portland Place and the lady from Eaton Square might now confess, quite without indiscretion, to simultaneity of movement. She had made, for the four days, no direct appeal to the latter personage, but the Prince was accidental witness of her taking a fresh start at the moment the company were about to scatter for the last night of their stay. There had been, at this climax, the usual preparatory talk about hours and combinations, in the midst of which poor Fanny gently approached Mrs. Verver. She said "You and the Prince, love,"—quite, apparently, without blinking; she took for granted their public withdrawal together; she remarked that she and Bob were alike ready, in the interest of sociability, to take any train that would make them all one party. "I feel really as if, all this time, I had seen nothing of you"—that gave an added grace to the candour of the dear thing's approach. But just then it was, on the other hand, that the young man found himself borrow most effectively the secret of the right tone for doing as he preferred. His preference had, during the evening, not failed of occasion to press him with mute insistences; practically without words, without any sort of straight telegraphy, it had arrived at a felt identity with Charlotte's own. She spoke all for their friend while she answered their friend's question, but she none the less signalled to him as definitely as if she had fluttered a white handkerchief from a window. "It's awfully sweet of you, darling—our going together would be charming. But you mustn't mind us—you must suit yourselves we've settled, Amerigo and I, to stay over till after luncheon."

Amerigo, with the chink of this gold in his ear, turned straight away, so as not to be instantly appealed to; and for the very emotion of the wonder, furthermore, of what divination may achieve when winged by a community of passion. Charlotte had uttered the exact plea that he had been keeping ready for the same foreseen necessity, and had uttered it simply as a consequence of their deepening unexpressed need of each other and without the passing between them of a word. He hadn't, God knew, to take it from her—he was too conscious of what he wanted; but the lesson for him was in the straight clear tone that Charlotte could thus distil, in the perfect felicity of her adding no explanation, no touch for plausibility, that she wasn't strictly obliged to add, and in the truly superior way in which women, so situated, express and distinguish themselves. She had answered Mrs. Assingham quite adequately; she had not spoiled it by a reason a scrap larger than the smallest that would serve, and she had, above all, thrown off, for his stretched but covered attention, an image that flashed like a mirror played at the face of the sun. The measure of EVERYTHING, to all his sense, at these moments, was in it—the measure especially of the thought that had been growing with him a positive obsession and that began to throb as never yet under this brush of her having, by perfect parity of imagination, the match for it. His whole consciousness had by this time begun almost to ache with a truth of an exquisite order, at the glow of which she too had, so unmistakably then, been warming herself—the truth that the occasion constituted by the last few days couldn't possibly, save by some poverty of their own, refuse them some still other and still greater beauty. It had already told them, with an hourly voice, that it had a meaning—a meaning that their associated sense was to drain even as thirsty lips, after the plough through the sands and the sight, afar, of the palm-cluster, might drink in at last the promised well in the desert. There had been beauty, day after day, and there had been, for the spiritual lips, something of the pervasive taste of it; yet it was all, none the less, as if their response had remained below their fortune. How to bring it, by some brave, free lift, up to the same height was the idea with which, behind and beneath everything, he was restlessly occupied, and in the exploration of which, as in that of the sun-chequered greenwood of romance, his spirit thus, at the opening of a vista, met hers. They were already, from that moment, so hand-in-hand in the place that he found himself making use, five minutes later, of exactly the same tone as Charlotte's for telling Mrs. Assingham that he was likewise, in the matter of the return to London, sorry for what mightn't be.

This had become, of a sudden, the simplest thing in the world—the sense of which moreover seemed really to amount to a portent that he should feel, forevermore, on the general head, conveniently at his ease with her. He went in fact a step further than Charlotte—put the latter forward as creating his necessity. She was staying over luncheon to oblige their hostess—as a consequence of which he must also stay to see her decently home. He must deliver her safe and sound, he felt, in Eaton Square. Regret as he might, too, the difference made by this obligation, he frankly didn't mind, inasmuch as, over and above the pleasure itself, his scruple would certainly gratify both Mr. Verver and Maggie. They never yet had absolutely and entirely learned, he even found deliberation to intimate, how little he really neglected the first—as it seemed nowadays quite to have become—of his domestic duties: therefore he still constantly felt how little he must remit his effort to make them remark it. To which he added with equal lucidity that they would return in time for dinner, and if he didn't, as a last word, subjoin that it would be "lovely" of Fanny to find, on her own return, a moment to go to Eaton Square and report them as struggling bravely on, this was not because the impulse, down to the very name for the amiable act, altogether failed to rise. His inward assurance, his general plan, had at moments, where she was concerned, its drops of continuity, and nothing would less have pleased him than that she should suspect in him, however tempted, any element of conscious "cheek." But he was always—that was really the upshot—cultivating thanklessly the considerate and the delicate: it was a long lesson, this unlearning, with people of English race, all the little superstitions that accompany friendship. Mrs. Assingham herself was the first to say that she would unfailingly "report"; she brought it out in fact, he thought, quite wonderfully—having attained the summit of the wonderful during the brief interval that had separated her appeal to Charlotte from this passage with himself. She had taken the five minutes, obviously, amid the rest of the talk and the movement, to retire into her tent for meditation—which showed, among several things, the impression Charlotte had made on her. It was from the tent she emerged, as with arms refurbished; though who indeed could say if the manner in which she now met him spoke most, really, of the glitter of battle or of the white waver of the flag of truce? The parley was short either way; the gallantry of her offer was all sufficient.

"I'll go to our friends then—I'll ask for luncheon. I'll tell them when to expect you."

"That will be charming. Say we're all right."

"All right—precisely. I can't say more," Mrs. Assingham smiled.

"No doubt." But he considered, as for the possible importance of it. "Neither can you, by what I seem to feel, say less."

"Oh, I WON'T say less!" Fanny laughed; with which, the next moment, she had turned away. But they had it again, not less bravely, on the morrow, after breakfast, in the thick of the advancing carriages and the exchange of farewells. "I think I'll send home my maid from Euston," she was then prepared to amend, "and go to Eaton Square straight. So you can be easy."

"Oh, I think we're easy," the Prince returned. "Be sure to say, at any rate, that we're bearing up."

"You're bearing up—good. And Charlotte returns to dinner?"

"To dinner. We're not likely, I think, to make another night away."

"Well then, I wish you at least a pleasant day,"

"Oh," he laughed as they separated, "we shall do our best for it!"—after which, in due course, with the announcement of their conveyance, the Assinghams rolled off.

XXII

It was quite, for the Prince, after this, as if the view had further cleared; so that the half-hour during which he strolled on the terrace and smoked—the day being lovely—overflowed with the plenitude of its particular quality. Its general brightness was composed, doubtless, of many elements, but what shone out of it as if the whole place and time had been a great picture, from the hand of genius, presented to him as a prime ornament for his collection and all varnished and framed to hang up—what marked it especially for the highest appreciation was his extraordinarily unchallenged, his absolutely appointed and enhanced possession of it. Poor Fanny Assingham's challenge amounted to nothing: one of the things he thought of while he leaned on the old marble balustrade—so like others that he knew in still more nobly-terraced Italy—was that she was squared, all-conveniently even to herself, and that, rumbling toward London with this contentment, she had become an image irrelevant to the scene. It further passed across him, as his imagination was, for reasons, during the time, unprecedentedly active,—that he had, after all, gained more from women than he had ever lost by them; there appeared so, more and more, on those mystic books that are kept, in connection with such commerce, even by men of the loosest business habits, a balance in his favour that he could pretty well, as a rule, take for granted. What were they doing at this very moment, wonderful creatures, but combine and conspire for his advantage?—from Maggie herself, most wonderful, in her way, of all, to his hostess of the present hour, into whose head it had so inevitably come to keep Charlotte on, for reasons of her own, and who had asked, in this benevolent spirit, why in the world, if not obliged, without plausibility, to hurry, her husband's son-in-law should not wait over in her company. He would at least see, Lady Castledean had said, that nothing dreadful should happen to her, either while still there or during the exposure of the run to town; and, for that matter, if they exceeded a little their license it would positively help them to have done so together. Each of them would, in this way, at home, have the other comfortably to blame. All of which, besides, in Lady Castledean as in Maggie, in Fanny Assingham as in Charlotte herself, was working; for him without provocation or pressure, by the mere play of some vague sense on their part—definite and conscious at the most only in Charlotte—that he was not, as a nature, as a character, as a gentleman, in fine, below his remarkable fortune.

But there were more things before him than even these; things that melted together, almost indistinguishably, to feed his sense of beauty. If the outlook was in every way spacious—and the towers of three cathedrals, in different counties, as had been pointed out to him, gleamed discernibly, like dim silver, in the rich sameness of tone—didn't he somehow the more feel it so because, precisely, Lady Castledean had kept over a man of her own, and that this offered a certain sweet intelligibility as the note of the day? It made everything fit; above all it diverted him to the extent of keeping up, while he lingered and waited, his meditative smile. She had detained Charlotte because she wished to detain Mr. Blint, and she couldn't detain Mr. Blint, disposed though he clearly was to oblige her, without spreading over the act some ampler drapery. Castledean had gone up to London; the place was all her own; she had had a fancy for a quiet morning with Mr. Blint, a sleek, civil, accomplished young man—distinctly younger than her ladyship—who played and sang delightfully (played even "bridge" and sang the English-comic as well as the French-tragic), and the presence—which really meant the absence—of a couple of other friends, if they were happily chosen, would make everything all right. The Prince had the sense, all good-humouredly, of being happily chosen, and it was not spoiled for him even by another sense that followed in its train and with which, during his life in England, he had more than once had reflectively to deal: the state of being reminded how, after all, as an outsider, a foreigner, and even as a mere representative husband and son-in-law, he was so irrelevant to the working of affairs that he could be bent on occasion to uses comparatively trivial. No other of her guests would have been thus convenient for their hostess; affairs, of whatever sorts, had claimed, by early trains, every active, easy, smoothly-working man, each in his way a lubricated item of the great social, political, administrative engrenage—claimed most of all Castledean himself, who was so very oddly, given the personage and the type, rather a large item. If he, on the other hand, had an affair, it was not of that order; it was of the order, verily, that he had been reduced to as a not quite glorious substitute.

It marked, however, the feeling of the hour with him that this vision of being "reduced" interfered not at all with the measure of his actual ease. It kept before him again, at moments, the so familiar fact of his sacrifices—down to the idea of the very relinquishment, for his wife's convenience, of his real situation in the world; with the consequence, thus, that he was, in the last analysis, among all these so often inferior people, practically held cheap and made light of. But though all this was sensible enough there was a spirit in him that could rise above it, a spirit that positively played with the facts, with all of them; from that of the droll ambiguity of English relations to that of his having in mind something quite beautiful and independent and harmonious, something wholly his own. He couldn't somehow take Mr. Blint seriously—he was much more an outsider, by the larger scale, even than a Roman prince who consented to be in abeyance. Yet it was past finding out, either, how such a woman as Lady Castledean could take him—since this question but sank for him again into the fathomless depths of English equivocation. He knew them all, as was said, "well"; he had lived with them, stayed with them, dined, hunted, shot and done various other things with them; but the number of questions about them he couldn't have answered had much rather grown than shrunken, so that experience struck him for the most part as having left in him but one residual impression. They didn't like les situations nettes—that was all he was very sure of. They wouldn't have them at any price; it had been their national genius and their national success to avoid them at every point. They called it themselves, with complacency, their wonderful spirit of compromise—the very influence of which actually so hung about him here, from moment to moment, that the earth and the air, the light and the colour, the fields and the hills and the sky, the blue-green counties and the cold cathedrals, owed it every accent of their tone. Verily, as one had to feel in presence of such a picture, it had succeeded; it had made, up to now, for that seated solidity, in the rich sea-mist, on which the garish, the supposedly envious, peoples have ever cooled their eyes. But it was at the same time precisely why even much initiation left one, at given moments, so puzzled as to the element of staleness in all the freshness and of freshness in all the staleness, of innocence in the guilt and of guilt in the innocence. There were other marble terraces, sweeping more purple prospects, on which he would have known what to think, and would have enjoyed thereby at least the small intellectual fillip of a discerned relation between a given appearance and a taken meaning. The inquiring mind, in these present conditions, might, it was true, be more sharply challenged; but the result of its attention and its ingenuity, it had unluckily learned to know, was too often to be confronted with a mere dead wall, a lapse of logic, a confirmed bewilderment. And moreover, above all, nothing mattered, in the relation of the enclosing scene to his own consciousness, but its very most direct bearings.

Lady Castledean's dream of Mr. Blint for the morning was doubtless already, with all the spacious harmonies re-established, taking the form of "going over" something with him, at the piano, in one of the numerous smaller rooms that were consecrated to the less gregarious uses; what she had wished had been effected—her convenience had been assured. This made him, however, wonder the more where Charlotte was—since he didn't at all suppose her to be making a tactless third, which would be to have accepted mere spectatorship, in the duet of their companions. The upshot of everything for him, alike of the less and of the more, was that the exquisite day bloomed there like a large fragrant flower that he had only to gather. But it was to Charlotte he wished to make the offering, and as he moved along the terrace, which rendered visible parts of two sides of the house, he looked up at all the windows that were open to the April morning, and wondered which of them would represent his friend's room. It befell thus that his question, after no long time, was answered; he saw Charlotte appear above as if she had been called by the pausing of his feet on the flags. She had come to the sill, on which she leaned to look down, and she remained there a minute smiling at him. He had been immediately struck with her wearing a hat and a jacket—which conduced to her appearance of readiness not so much to join him, with a beautiful uncovered head and a parasol, where he stood, as to take with him some larger step altogether. The larger step had been, since the evening before, intensely in his own mind, though he had not fully thought out, even yet, the slightly difficult detail of it; but he had had no chance, such as he needed, to speak the definite word to her, and the face she now showed affected him, accordingly, as a notice that she had wonderfully guessed it for herself. They had these identities of impulse—they had had them repeatedly before; and if such unarranged but unerring encounters gave the measure of the degree in which people were, in the common phrase, meant for each other, no union in the world had ever been more sweetened with rightness. What in fact most often happened was that her rightness went, as who should say, even further than his own; they were conscious of the same necessity at the same moment, only it was she, as a general thing, who most clearly saw her way to it. Something in her long look at him now out of the old grey window, something in the very poise of her hat, the colour of her necktie, the prolonged stillness of her smile, touched into sudden light for him all the wealth of the fact that he could count on her. He had his hand there, to pluck it, on the open bloom of the day; but what did the bright minute mean but that her answering hand was already intelligently out? So, therefore, while the minute lasted, it passed between them that their cup was full; which cup their very eyes, holding it fast, carried and steadied and began, as they tasted it, to praise. He broke, however, after a moment, the silence.

"It only wants a moon, a mandolin, and a little danger, to be a serenade."

"Ah, then," she lightly called down, "let it at least have THIS!" With which she detached a rich white rosebud from its company with another in the front of her dress and flung it down to him. He caught it in its fall, fixing her again after she had watched him place it in his buttonhole. "Come down quickly!" he said in an Italian not loud but deep.

"Vengo, vengo!" she as clearly, but more lightly, tossed out; and she had left him the next minute to wait for her.

He came along the terrace again, with pauses during which his eyes rested, as they had already often done, on the brave darker wash of far-away watercolour that represented the most distant of the cathedral towns. This place, with its great church and its high accessibility, its towers that distinguishably signalled, its English history, its appealing type, its acknowledged interest, this place had sounded its name to him half the night through, and its name had become but another name, the pronounceable and convenient one, for that supreme sense of things which now throbbed within him. He had kept saying to himself "Gloucester, Gloucester, Gloucester," quite as if the sharpest meaning of all the years just passed were intensely expressed in it. That meaning was really that his situation remained quite sublimely consistent with itself, and that they absolutely, he and Charlotte, stood there together in the very lustre of this truth. Every present circumstance helped to proclaim it; it was blown into their faces as by the lips of the morning. He knew why, from the first of his marriage, he had tried with such patience for such conformity; he knew why he had given up so much and bored himself so much; he knew why he, at any rate, had gone in, on the basis of all forms, on the basis of his having, in a manner, sold himself, for a situation nette. It had all been just in order that his—well, what on earth should he call it but his freedom?—should at present be as perfect and rounded and lustrous as some huge precious pearl. He hadn't struggled nor snatched; he was taking but what had been given him; the pearl dropped itself, with its exquisite quality and rarity, straight into his hand. Here, precisely, it was, incarnate; its size and its value grew as Mrs. Verver appeared, afar off, in one of the smaller doorways. She came toward him in silence, while he moved to meet her; the great scale of this particular front, at Matcham, multiplied thus, in the golden morning, the stages of their meeting and the successions of their consciousness. It wasn't till she had come quite close that he produced for her his "Gloucester, Gloucester, Gloucester," and his "Look at it over there!"

She knew just where to look. "Yes—isn't it one of the best? There are cloisters or towers or some thing." And her eyes, which, though her lips smiled, were almost grave with their depths of acceptance; came back to him. "Or the tomb of some old king."

"We must see the old king; we must 'do' the cathedral," he said; "we must know all about it. If we could but take," he exhaled, "the full opportunity!" And then while, for all they seemed to give him, he sounded again her eyes: "I feel the day like a great gold cup that we must somehow drain together."

"I feel it, as you always make me feel everything, just as you do; so that I know ten miles off how you feel! But do you remember," she asked, "apropos of great gold cups, the beautiful one, the real one, that I offered you so long ago and that you wouldn't have? Just before your marriage"—she brought it back to him: "the gilded crystal bowl in the little Bloomsbury shop."

"Oh yes!"—but it took, with a slight surprise on the 'Prince's part, some small recollecting. "The treacherous cracked thing you wanted to palm off on me, and the little swindling Jew who understood Italian and who backed you up! But I feel this an occasion," he immediately added, "and I hope you don't mean," he smiled, "that AS an occasion it's also cracked."

They spoke, naturally, more low than loud, overlooked as they were, though at a respectful distance, by tiers of windows; but it made each find in the other's voice a taste as of something slowly and deeply absorbed. "Don't you think too much of 'cracks,' and aren't you too afraid of them? I risk the cracks," said Charlotte, "and I've often recalled the bowl and the little swindling Jew, wondering if they've parted company. He made," she said, "a great impression on me."

"Well, you also, no doubt, made a great impression on him, and I dare say that if you were to go back to him you'd find he has been keeping that treasure for you. But as to cracks," the Prince went on—"what did you tell me the other day you prettily call them in English?-'rifts within the lute'?—risk them as much as you like for yourself, but don't risk them for me." He spoke it in all the gaiety of his just barely-tremulous serenity. "I go, as you know, by my superstitions. And that's why," he said, "I know where we are. They're every one, to-day, on our side."

Resting on the parapet; toward the great view, she was silent a little, and he saw the next moment that her eyes were closed. "I go but by one thing." Her hand was on the sun-warmed stone; so that, turned as they were away from the house, he put his own upon it and covered it. "I go by YOU," she said. "I go by you."

So they remained a moment, till he spoke again with a gesture that matched. "What is really our great necessity, you know, is to go by my watch. It's already eleven"—he had looked at the time; "so that if we stop here to luncheon what becomes of our afternoon?"

To this Charlotte's eyes opened straight. "There's not the slightest need of our stopping here to luncheon. Don't you see," she asked, "how I'm ready?" He had taken it in, but there was always more and more of her. "You mean you've arranged—?"

"It's easy to arrange. My maid goes up with my things. You've only to speak to your man about yours, and they can go together."

"You mean we can leave at once?"

She let him have it all. "One of the carriages, about which I spoke, will already have come back for us. If your superstitions are on our side," she smiled, "so my arrangements are, and I'll back my support against yours."

"Then you had thought," he wondered, "about Gloucester?"

She hesitated—but it was only her way. "I thought you would think. We have, thank goodness, these harmonies. They are food for superstition if you like. It's beautiful," she went on, "that it should be Gloucester; 'Glo'ster, Glo'ster,' as you say, making it sound like an old song. However, I'm sure Glo'ster, Glo'ster will be charming," she still added; "we shall be able easily to lunch there, and, with our luggage and our servants off our hands, we shall have at least three or four hours. We can wire," she wound up, "from there."

Ever so quietly she had brought it, as she had thought it, all out, and it had to be as covertly that he let his appreciation expand. "Then Lady Castledean—?"

"Doesn't dream of our staying."

He took it, but thinking yet. "Then what does she dream—?"

"Of Mr. Blint, poor dear; of Mr. Blint only." Her smile for him—for the Prince himself—was free. "Have I positively to tell you that she doesn't want us? She only wanted us for the others—to show she wasn't left alone with him. Now that that's done, and that they've all gone, she of course knows for herself—!"

"'Knows'?" the Prince vaguely echoed.

"Why, that we like cathedrals; that we inevitably stop to see them, or go round to take them in, whenever we've a chance; that it's what our respective families quite expect of us and would be disappointed for us to fail of. This, as forestieri," Mrs. Verver pursued, "would be our pull—if our pull weren't indeed already so great all round."

He could only keep his eyes on her. "And have you made out the very train—?"

"The very one. Paddington—the 6.50 'in.' That gives us oceans; we can dine, at the usual hour, at home; and as Maggie will of course be in Eaton Square I hereby invite you."

For a while he still but looked at her; it was a minute before he spoke. "Thank you very much. With pleasure." To which he in a moment added: "But the train for Gloucester?"

"A local one—11.22; with several stops, but doing it a good deal, I forget how much, within the hour. So that we've time. Only," she said, "we must employ our time."

He roused himself as from the mere momentary spell of her; he looked again at his watch while they moved back to the door through which she had advanced. But he had also again questions and stops—all as for the mystery and the charm. "You looked it up—without my having asked you?"

"Ah, my dear," she laughed, "I've seen you with Bradshaw! It takes Anglo-Saxon blood."

"'Blood'?" he echoed. "You've that of every race!" It kept her before him. "You're terrible."

Well, he could put it as he liked. "I know the name of the inn."

"What is it then?"

"There are two—you'll see. But I've chosen the right one. And I think I remember the tomb," she smiled.

"Oh, the tomb—!" Any tomb would do for him. "But I mean I had been keeping my idea so cleverly for you, while there you already were with it."

"You had been keeping it 'for' me as much as you like. But how do you make out," she asked, "that you were keeping it FROM me?"

"I don't—now. How shall I ever keep anything—some day when I shall wish to?"

"Ah, for things I mayn't want to know, I promise you shall find me stupid." They had reached their door, where she herself paused to explain. "These days, yesterday, last night, this morning, I've wanted everything."

Well, it was all right. "You shall have everything."

XXIII

Fanny, on her arrival in town, carried out her second idea, despatching the Colonel to his club for luncheon and packing her maid into a cab, for Cadogan Place, with the variety of their effects. The result of this for each of the pair was a state of occupation so unbroken that the day practically passed without fresh contact between them. They dined out together, but it was both in going to their dinner and in coming back that they appeared, on either side, to have least to communicate. Fanny was wrapped in her thoughts still more closely than in the lemon-coloured mantle that protected her bare shoulders, and her husband, with her silence to deal with, showed himself not less disposed than usual, when so challenged, to hold up, as he would have said, his end of it. They had, in general, in these days, longer pauses and more abrupt transitions; in one of which latter they found themselves, for a climax, launched at midnight. Mrs. Assingham, rather wearily housed again, ascended to the first floor, there to sink, overburdened, on the landing outside the drawing-room, into a great gilded Venetian chair—of which at first, however, she but made, with her brooding face, a sort of throne of meditation. She would thus have recalled a little, with her so free orientalism of type, the immemorially speechless Sphinx about at last to become articulate. The Colonel, not unlike, on his side, some old pilgrim of the desert camping at the foot of that monument, went, by way of reconnoissance, into the drawing-room. He visited, according to his wont, the windows and their fastenings; he cast round the place the eye, all at once, of the master and the manager, the commandant and the rate-payer; then he came back to his wife, before whom, for a moment, he stood waiting. But she herself, for a time, continued to wait, only looking up at him inscrutably. There was in these minor manoeuvres and conscious patiences something of a suspension of their old custom of divergent discussion, that intercourse by misunderstanding which had grown so clumsy now. This familiar pleasantry seemed to desire to show it could yield, on occasion, to any clear trouble; though it was also sensibly, just incoherently, in the air that no trouble was at present to be vulgarly recognised as clear.

There might, for that matter, even have been in Mr. Assingham's face a mild perception of some finer sense—a sense for his wife's situation, and the very situation she was, oddly enough, about to repudiate—that she had fairly caused to grow in him. But it was a flower to breathe upon gently, and this was very much what she finally did. She knew he needed no telling that she had given herself, all the afternoon, to her friends in Eaton Square, and that her doing so would have been but the prompt result of impressions gathered, in quantities, in brimming baskets, like the purple grapes of the vintage, at Matcham; a process surrounded by him, while it so unmistakably went on, with abstentions and discretions that might almost have counted as solemnities. The solemnities, at the same time, had committed him to nothing—to nothing beyond this confession itself of a consciousness of deep waters. She had been out on these waters, for him, visibly; and his tribute to the fact had been his keeping her, even if without a word, well in sight. He had not quitted for an hour, during her adventure, the shore of the mystic lake; he had on the contrary stationed himself where she could signal to him at need. Her need would have arisen if the planks of her bark had parted—THEN some sort of plunge would have become his immediate duty. His present position, clearly, was that of seeing her in the centre of her sheet of dark water, and of wondering if her actual mute gaze at him didn't perhaps mean that her planks WERE now parting. He held himself so ready that it was quite as if the inward man had pulled off coat and waistcoat. Before he had plunged, however—that is before he had uttered a question—he perceived, not without relief, that she was making for land. He watched her steadily, always a little nearer, and at last he felt her boat bump. The bump was distinct, and in fact she stepped ashore. "We were all wrong. There's nothing."

"Nothing—?" It was like giving her his hand up the bank.

"Between Charlotte Verver and the Prince. I was uneasy—but I'm satisfied now. I was in fact quite mistaken. There's nothing."

"But I thought," said Bob Assingham, "that that was just what you did persistently asseverate. You've guaranteed their straightness from the first."

"No—I've never till now guaranteed anything but my own disposition to worry. I've never till now," Fanny went on gravely from her chair, "had such a chance to see and to judge. I had it at that place—if I had, in my infatuation and my folly," she added with expression, "nothing else. So I did see—I HAVE seen. And now I know." Her emphasis, as she repeated the word, made her head, in her seat of infallibility, rise higher. "I know."

The Colonel took it—but took it at first in silence. "Do you mean they've TOLD you—?"

"No—I mean nothing so absurd. For in the first place I haven't asked them, and in the second their word in such a matter wouldn't count."

"Oh," said the Colonel with all his oddity, "they'd tell US."

It made her face him an instant as with her old impatience of his short cuts, always across her finest flower-beds; but she felt, none the less, that she kept her irony down. "Then when they've told you, you'll be perhaps so good as to let me know."

He jerked up his chin, testing the growth of his beard with the back of his hand while he fixed her with a single eye. "Ah, I don't say that they'd necessarily tell me that they ARE over the traces."

"They'll necessarily, whatever happens, hold their tongues, I hope, and I'm talking of them now as I take them for myself only. THAT'S enough for me—it's all I have to regard." With which, after an instant, "They're wonderful," said Fanny Assingham.

"Indeed," her husband concurred, "I really think they are."

"You'd think it still more if you knew. But you don't know—because you don't see. Their situation"—this was what he didn't see—"is too extraordinary."

"'Too'?" He was willing to try.

"Too extraordinary to be believed, I mean, if one didn't see. But just that, in a way, is what saves them. They take it seriously." He followed at his own pace. "Their situation?"

"The incredible side of it. They make it credible."

"Credible then—you do say—to YOU?"

She looked at him again for an interval. "They believe in it themselves. They take it for what it is. And that," she said, "saves them."

"But if what it 'is' is just their chance—?"

"It's their chance for what I told you when Charlotte first turned up. It's their chance for the idea that I was then sure she had."

The Colonel showed his effort to recall. "Oh, your idea, at different moments, of any one of THEIR ideas!" This dim procession, visibly, mustered before him, and, with the best will in the world, he could but watch its immensity. "Are you speaking now of something to which you can comfortably settle down?"

Again, for a little, she only glowered at him. "I've come back to my belief, and that I have done so—"

"Well?" he asked as she paused.

"Well, shows that I'm right—for I assure you I had wandered far. Now I'm at home again, and I mean," said Fanny Assingham, "to stay here. They're beautiful," she declared.

"The Prince and Charlotte?"

"The Prince and Charlotte. THAT'S how they're so remarkable. And the beauty," she explained, "is that they're afraid for them. Afraid, I mean, for the others."

"For Mr. Verver and Maggie?" It did take some following. "Afraid of what?"

"Afraid of themselves."

The Colonel wondered. "Of THEMSELVES? Of Mr. Verver's and Maggie's selves?"

Mrs. Assingham remained patient as well as lucid. "Yes—of SUCH blindness too. But most of all of their own danger."

He turned it over. "That danger BEING the blindness—?"

"That danger being their position. What their position contains—of all the elements—I needn't at this time of day attempt to tell you. It contains, luckily—for that's the mercy—everything BUT blindness: I mean on their part. The blindness," said Fanny, "is primarily her husband's."

He stood for a moment; he WOULD have it straight. "Whose husband's?"

"Mr. Verver's," she went on. "The blindness is most of all his. That they feel—that they see. But it's also his wife's."

"Whose wife's?" he asked as she continued to gloom at him in a manner at variance with the comparative cheer of her contention. And then as she only gloomed: "The Prince's?"

"Maggie's own—Maggie's very own," she pursued as for herself.

He had a pause. "Do you think Maggie so blind?"

"The question isn't of what I think. The question's of the conviction that guides the Prince and Charlotte—who have better opportunities than I for judging."

The Colonel again wondered. "Are you so very sure their opportunities are better?"

"Well," his wife asked, "what is their whole so extraordinary situation, their extraordinary relation, but an opportunity?"

"Ah, my dear, you have that opportunity—of their extraordinary situation and relation—as much as they."

"With the difference, darling," she returned with some spirit, "that neither of those matters are, if you please, mine. I see the boat they're in, but I'm not, thank God, in it myself. To-day, however," Mrs. Assingham added, "to-day in Eaton Square I did see."

"Well then, what?"

But she mused over it still. "Oh, many things. More, somehow, than ever before. It was as if, God help me, I was seeing FOR them—I mean for the others. It was as if something had happened—I don't know what, except some effect of these days with them at that place—that had either made things come out or had cleared my own eyes." These eyes indeed of the poor lady's rested on her companion's, meanwhile, with the lustre not so much of intenser insight as of a particular portent that he had at various other times had occasion to recognise. She desired, obviously, to reassure him, but it apparently took a couple of large, candid, gathering, glittering tears to emphasise the fact. They had immediately, for him, their usual direct action: she must reassure him, he was made to feel, absolutely in her own way. He would adopt it and conform to it as soon as he should be able to make it out. The only thing was that it took such incalculable twists and turns. The twist seemed remarkable for instance as she developed her indication of what had come out in the afternoon. "It was as if I knew better than ever what makes them—"

"What makes them?"—he pressed her as she fitfully dropped.

"Well, makes the Prince and Charlotte take it all as they do. It might well have been difficult to know HOW to take it; and they may even say for themselves that they were a long time trying to see. As I say, to-day," she went on, "it was as if I were suddenly, with a kind of horrible push, seeing through their eyes." On which, as to shake off her perversity, Fanny Assingham sprang up. But she remained there, under the dim illumination, and while the Colonel, with his high, dry, spare look of "type," to which a certain conformity to the whiteness of inaccessible snows in his necktie, shirt-front and waistcoat gave a rigour of accent, waited, watching her, they might, at the late hour and in the still house, have been a pair of specious worldly adventurers, driven for relief, under sudden stress, to some grim midnight reckoning in an odd corner. Her attention moved mechanically over the objects of ornament disposed too freely on the walls of staircase and landing, as to which recognition, for the time, had lost both fondness and compunction. "I can imagine the way it works," she said; "it's so easy to understand. Yet I don't want to be wrong," she the next moment broke out "I don't, I don't want to be wrong!"

"To make a mistake, you mean?"

Oh no, she meant nothing of the sort; she knew but too well what she meant. "I don't make mistakes. But I perpetrate—in thought— crimes." And she spoke with all intensity. "I'm a most dreadful person. There are times when I seem not to mind a bit what I've done, or what I think or imagine or fear or accept; when I feel that I'd do it again—feel that I'd do things myself."

"Ah, my dear!" the Colonel remarked in the coolness of debate.

"Yes, if you had driven me back on my 'nature.' Luckily for you you never have. You've done every thing else, but you've never done that. But what I really don't a bit want," she declared, "is to abet them or to protect them."

Her companion turned this over. "What is there to protect them from?—if, by your now so settled faith, they've done nothing that justly exposes them."

And it in fact half pulled her up. "Well, from a sudden scare. From the alarm, I mean, of what Maggie MAY think."

"Yet if your whole idea is that Maggie thinks nothing—?"

She waited again. "It isn't my 'whole' idea. Nothing is my 'whole' idea—for I felt to-day, as I tell you, that there's so much in the air."

"Oh, in the air—!" the Colonel dryly breathed.

"Well, what's in the air always HAS—hasn't it?—to come down to the earth. And Maggie," Mrs. Assingham continued, "is a very curious little person. Since I was 'in,' this afternoon, for seeing more than I had ever done—well, I felt THAT too, for some reason, as I hadn't yet felt it."

"For 'some' reason? For what reason?" And then, as his wife at first said nothing: "Did she give any sign? Was she in any way different?"

"She's always so different from anyone else in the world that it's hard to say when she's different from herself. But she has made me," said Fanny after an instant, "think of her differently. She drove me home."

"Home here?"

"First to Portland Place—on her leaving her father: since she does, once in a while, leave him. That was to keep me with her a little longer. But she kept the carriage and, after tea there, came with me herself back here. This was also for the same purpose. Then she went home, though I had brought her a message from the Prince that arranged their movements otherwise. He and Charlotte must have arrived—if they have arrived—expecting to drive together to Eaton Square and keep Maggie on to dinner there. She has everything there, you know—she has clothes."

The Colonel didn't in fact know, but he gave it his apprehension. "Oh, you mean a change?"

"Twenty changes, if you like—all sorts of things. She dresses, really, Maggie does, as much for her father—and she always did—as for her husband or for herself. She has her room in his house very much as she had it before she was married—and just as the boy has quite a second nursery there, in which Mrs. Noble, when she comes with him, makes herself, I assure you, at home. Si bien that if Charlotte, in her own house, so to speak, should wish a friend or two to stay with her, she really would be scarce able to put them up."

It was a picture into which, as a thrifty entertainer himself, Bob Assingham could more or less enter. "Maggie and the child spread so?"

"Maggie and the child spread so."

Well, he considered. "It IS rather rum."

"That's all I claim"—she seemed thankful for the word. "I don't say it's anything more—but it IS, distinctly, rum."

Which, after an instant, the Colonel took up. "'More'? What more COULD it be?"

"It could be that she's unhappy, and that she takes her funny little way of consoling herself. For if she were unhappy"—Mrs. Assingham had figured it out—"that's just the way, I'm convinced, she would take. But how can she be unhappy, since—as I'm also convinced—she, in the midst of everything, adores her husband as much as ever?"

The Colonel at this brooded for a little at large. "Then if she's so happy, please what's the matter?"

It made his wife almost spring at him. "You think then she's secretly wretched?"

But he threw up his arms in deprecation. "Ah, my dear, I give them up to YOU. I've nothing more to suggest."

"Then it's not sweet of you." She spoke at present as if he were frequently sweet. "You admit that it is 'rum.'"

And this indeed fixed again, for a moment, his intention. "Has Charlotte complained of the want of rooms for her friends?"

"Never, that I know of, a word. It isn't the sort of thing she does. And whom has she, after all," Mrs. Assingham added, "to complain to?"

"Hasn't she always you?"

"Oh, 'me'! Charlotte and I, nowadays—!" She spoke as of a chapter closed. "Yet see the justice I still do her. She strikes me, more and more, as extraordinary."

A deeper shade, at the renewal of the word, had come into the Colonel's face. "If they're each and all so extraordinary then, isn't that why one must just resign one's self to wash one's hands of them—to be lost?" Her face, however, so met the question as if it were but a flicker of the old tone that their trouble had now become too real for—her charged eyes so betrayed the condition of her nerves that he stepped back, alertly enough, to firmer ground. He had spoken before in this light of a plain man's vision, but he must be something more than a plain man now. "Hasn't she then, Charlotte, always her husband—?"

"To complain to? She'd rather die."

"Oh!"—and Bob Assingham's face, at the vision of such extremities, lengthened for very docility. "Hasn't she the Prince then?"

"For such matters? Oh, he doesn't count."

"I thought that was just what—as the basis of our agitation—he does do!"

Mrs. Assingham, however, had her distinction ready. "Not a bit as a person to bore with complaints. The ground of MY agitation is, exactly, that she never on any pretext bores him. Not Charlotte!" And in the imagination of Mrs. Verver's superiority to any such mistake she gave, characteristically, something like a toss of her head—as marked a tribute to that lady's general grace, in all the conditions, as the personage referred to doubtless had ever received.

"Ah, only Maggie!" With which the Colonel gave a short low gurgle. But it found his wife again prepared.

"No—not only Maggie. A great many people in London—and small wonder!—bore him."

"Maggie only bore him then?" But it was a question that he had promptly dropped at the returning brush of another, of which she had shortly before sown the seed. "You said just now that he would by this time be back with Charlotte 'if they HAVE arrived.' You think it then possible that they really won't have returned?"

His companion exhibited to view, for the idea, a sense of her responsibility; but this was insufficient, clearly, to keep her from entertaining it. "I think there's nothing they're not now capable of—in their so intense good faith."

"Good faith?"—he echoed the words, which had in fact something of an odd ring, critically.

"Their false position. It comes to the same thing." And she bore down, with her decision, the superficial lack of sequence. "They may very possibly, for a demonstration—as I see them—not have come back."

He wondered, visibly, at this, how she did see them. "May have bolted somewhere together?"

"May have stayed over at Matcham itself till tomorrow. May have wired home, each of them, since Maggie left me. May have done," Fanny Assingham continued, "God knows what!" She went on, suddenly, with more emotion—which, at the pressure of some spring of her inner vision, broke out in a wail of distress, imperfectly smothered. "Whatever they've done I shall never know. Never, never—because I don't want to, and because nothing will induce me. So they may do as they like. But I've worked for them ALL" She uttered this last with another irrepressible quaver, and the next moment her tears had come, though she had, with the explosion, quitted her husband as if to hide it from him. She passed into the dusky drawing-room, where, during his own prowl, shortly previous, he had drawn up a blind, so that the light of the street-lamps came in a little at the window. She made for this window, against which she leaned her head, while the Colonel, with his lengthened face, looked after her for a minute and hesitated. He might have been wondering what she had really done, to what extent, beyond his knowledge or his conception, in the affairs of these people, she COULD have committed herself. But to hear her cry, and yet try not to, was, quickly enough, too much for him; he had known her at other times quite not try not to, and that had not been so bad. He went to her and put his arm round her; he drew her head to his breast, where, while she gasped, he let her stay a little—all with a patience that presently stilled her. Yet the effect of this small crisis, oddly enough, was not to close their colloquy, with the natural result of sending them to bed: what was between them had opened out further, had somehow, through the sharp show of her feeling, taken a positive stride, had entered, as it were, without more words, the region of the understood, shutting the door after it and bringing them so still more nearly face to face. They remained for some minutes looking at it through the dim window which opened upon the world of human trouble in general and which let the vague light play here and there upon gilt and crystal and colour, the florid features, looming dimly, of Fanny's drawing-room. And the beauty of what thus passed between them, passed with her cry of pain, with her burst of tears, with his wonderment and his kindness and his comfort, with the moments of their silence, above all, which might have represented their sinking together, hand in hand, for a time, into the mystic lake where he had begun, as we have hinted, by seeing her paddle alone—the beauty of it was that they now could really talk better than before, because the basis had at last, once for all, defined itself. What was the basis, which Fanny absolutely exacted, but that Charlotte and the Prince must be saved—so far as consistently speaking of them as still safe might save them? It did save them, somehow, for Fanny's troubled mind—for that was the nature of the mind of women. He conveyed to her now, at all events, by refusing her no gentleness, that he had sufficiently got the tip, and that the tip was all he had wanted. This remained quite clear even when he presently reverted to what she had told him of her recent passage with Maggie. "I don't altogether see, you know, what you infer from it, or why you infer anything." When he so expressed himself it was quite as if in possession of what they had brought up from the depths.

XXIV

"I can't say more," this made his companion reply, "than that something in her face, her voice and her whole manner acted upon me as nothing in her had ever acted before; and just for the reason, above all, that I felt her trying her very best—and her very best, poor duck, is very good—to be quiet and natural. It's when one sees people who always ARE natural making little pale, pathetic, blinking efforts for it—then it is that one knows something's the matter. I can't describe my impression—you would have had it for yourself. And the only thing that ever CAN be the matter with Maggie is that. By 'that' I mean her beginning to doubt. To doubt, for the first time," Mrs. Assingham wound up, "of her wonderful little judgment of her wonderful little world."

It was impressive, Fanny's vision, and the Colonel, as if himself agitated by it, took another turn of prowling. "To doubt of fidelity—to doubt of friendship! Poor duck indeed! It will go hard with her. But she'll put it all," he concluded, "on Charlotte."

Mrs. Assingham, still darkly contemplative, denied this with a headshake. "She won't 'put' it anywhere. She won't do with it anything anyone else would. She'll take it all herself."

"You mean she'll make it out her own fault?"

"Yes—she'll find means, somehow, to arrive at that."

"Ah then," the Colonel dutifully declared, "she's indeed a little brick!"

"Oh," his wife returned, "you'll see, in one way or another, to what tune!" And she spoke, of a sudden, with an approach to elation—so that, as if immediately feeling his surprise, she turned round to him. "She'll see me somehow through!"

"See YOU—?"

"Yes, me. I'm the worst. For," said Fanny Assingham, now with a harder exaltation, "I did it all. I recognise that—I accept it. She won't cast it up at me—she won't cast up anything. So I throw myself upon her—she'll bear me up." She spoke almost volubly—she held him with her sudden sharpness. "She'll carry the whole weight of us."

There was still, nevertheless, wonder in it. "You mean she won't mind? I SAY, love—!" And he not unkindly stared. "Then where's the difficulty?"

"There isn't any!" Fanny declared with the same rich emphasis. It kept him indeed, as by the loss of the thread, looking at her longer. "Ah, you mean there isn't any for US!"

She met his look for a minute as if it perhaps a little too much imputed a selfishness, a concern, at any cost, for their own surface. Then she might have been deciding that their own surface was, after all, what they had most to consider. "Not," she said with dignity, "if we properly keep our heads." She appeared even to signify that they would begin by keeping them now. This was what it was to have at last a constituted basis. "Do you remember what you said to me that night of my first REAL anxiety—after the Foreign Office party?"

"In the carriage—as we came home? Yes—he could recall it. "Leave them to pull through?"

"Precisely. 'Trust their own wit,' you practically said, 'to save all appearances.' Well, I've trusted it. I HAVE left them to pull through." He hesitated. "And your point is that they're not doing so?"

"I've left them," she went on, "but now I see how and where. I've been leaving them all the while, without knowing it, to HER."

"To the Princess?"

"And that's what I mean," Mrs. Assingham pensively pursued. "That's what happened to me with her to-day," she continued to explain. "It came home to me that that's what I've really been doing."

"Oh, I see."

"I needn't torment myself. She has taken them over."

The Colonel declared that he "saw;" yet it was as if, at this, he a little sightlessly stared. "But what then has happened, from one day to the other, to HER? What has opened her eyes?"

"They were never really shut. She misses him."

"Then why hasn't she missed him before?"

Well, facing him there, among their domestic glooms and glints, Fanny worked it out. "She did—but she wouldn't let herself know it. She had her reason—she wore her blind. Now, at last, her situation has come to a head. To-day she does know it. And that's illuminating. It has been," Mrs. Assingham wound up, "illuminating to ME."

Her husband attended, but the momentary effect of his attention was vagueness again, and the refuge of his vagueness was a gasp. "Poor dear little girl!"

"Ah no—don't pity her!"

This did, however, pull him up. "We mayn't even be sorry for her?"

"Not now—or at least not yet. It's too soon—that is if it isn't very much too late. This will depend," Mrs. Assingham went on; "at any rate we shall see. We might have pitied her before—for all the good it would then have done her; we might have begun some time ago. Now, however, she has begun to live. And the way it comes to me, the way it comes to me—" But again she projected her vision.

"The way it comes to you can scarcely be that she'll like it!"

"The way it comes to me is that she will live. The way it comes to me is that she'll triumph."

She said this with so sudden a prophetic flare that it fairly cheered her husband. "Ah then, we must back her!"

"No—we mustn't touch her. We mayn't touch any of them. We must keep our hands off; we must go on tiptoe. We must simply watch and wait. And meanwhile," said Mrs. Assingham, "we must bear it as we can. That's where we are—and serves us right. We're in presence."

And so, moving about the room as in communion with shadowy portents, she left it till he questioned again. "In presence of what?"

"Well, of something possibly beautiful. Beautiful as it MAY come off."

She had paused there before him while he wondered. "You mean she'll get the Prince back?"

She raised her hand in quick impatience: the suggestion might have been almost abject. "It isn't a question of recovery. It won't be a question of any vulgar struggle. To 'get him back' she must have lost him, and to have lost him she must have had him." With which Fanny shook her head. "What I take her to be waking up to is the truth that all the while, she really HASN'T had him. Never."

"Ah, my dear—!" the poor Colonel panted.

"Never!" his wife repeated. And she went on without pity. "Do you remember what I said to you long ago—that evening, just before their marriage, when Charlotte had so suddenly turned up?"

The smile with which he met this appeal was not, it was to be feared, robust. "What haven't you, love, said in your time?"

"So many things, no doubt, that they make a chance for my having once or twice spoken the truth. I never spoke it more, at all events, than when I put it to you, that evening, that Maggie was the person in the world to whom a wrong thing could least be communicated. It was as if her imagination had been closed to it, her sense altogether sealed, That therefore," Fanny continued, "is what will now HAVE to happen. Her sense will have to open."

"I see." He nodded. "To the wrong." He nodded again, almost cheerfully—as if he had been keeping the peace with a baby or a lunatic. "To the very, very wrong."

But his wife's spirit, after its effort of wing, was able to remain higher. "To what's called Evil—with a very big E: for the first time in her life. To the discovery of it, to the knowledge of it, to the crude experience of it." And she gave, for the possibility, the largest measure. "To the harsh, bewildering brush, the daily chilling breath of it. Unless indeed"—and here Mrs. Assingham noted a limit "unless indeed, as yet (so far as she has come, and if she comes no further), simply to the suspicion and the dread. What we shall see is whether that mere dose of alarm will prove enough."

He considered. "But enough for what then, dear—if not enough to break her heart?"

"Enough to give her a shaking!" Mrs. Assingham rather oddly replied. "To give her, I mean, the right one. The right one won't break her heart. It will make her," she explained—"well, it will make her, by way of a change, understand one or two things in the world."

"But isn't it a pity," the Colonel asked, "that they should happen to be the one or two that will be the most disagreeable to her?"

"Oh, 'disagreeable'—? They'll have had to be disagreeable—to show her a little where she is. They'll have HAD to be disagreeable to make her sit up. They'll have had to be disagreeable to make her decide to live."

Bob Assingham was now at the window, while his companion slowly revolved; he had lighted a cigarette, for final patience, and he seemed vaguely to "time" her as she moved to and fro. He had at the same time to do justice to the lucidity she had at last attained, and it was doubtless by way of expression of this teachability that he let his eyes, for a minute, roll, as from the force of feeling, over the upper dusk of the room. He had thought of the response his wife's words ideally implied.

"Decide to live—ah yes!—for her child."

"Oh, bother her child!"—and he had never felt so snubbed, for an exemplary view, as when Fanny now stopped short. "To live, you poor dear, for her father—which is another pair of sleeves!"

And Mrs. Assingham's whole ample, ornamented person irradiated, with this, the truth that had begun, under so much handling, to glow. "Any idiot can do things for her child. She'll have a motive more original, and we shall see how it will work her. She'll have to save HIM."

"To 'save' him—?"

"To keep her father from his own knowledge. THAT"—and she seemed to see it, before her, in her husband's very eyes—"will be work cut out!" With which, as at the highest conceivable climax, she wound up their colloquy. "Good night!"

There was something in her manner, however—or in the effect, at least, of this supreme demonstration that had fairly, and by a single touch, lifted him to her side; so that, after she had turned her back to regain the landing and the staircase, he overtook her, before she had begun to mount, with the ring of excited perception. "Ah, but, you know, that's rather jolly!"

"Jolly'—?" she turned upon it, again, at the foot of the staircase.

"I mean it's rather charming."

"'Charming'—?" It had still to be their law, a little, that she was tragic when he was comic.

"I mean it's rather beautiful. You just said, yourself, it would be. Only," he pursued promptly, with the impetus of this idea, and as if it had suddenly touched with light for him connections hitherto dim—"only I don't quite see why that very care for him which has carried her to such other lengths, precisely, as affect one as so 'rum,' hasn't also, by the same stroke, made her notice a little more what has been going on."

"Ah, there you are! It's the question that I've all along been asking myself." She had rested her eyes on the carpet, but she raised them as she pursued—she let him have it straight. "And it's the question of an idiot."

"An idiot—?"

"Well, the idiot that I'VE been, in all sorts of ways—so often, of late, have I asked it. You're excusable, since you ask it but now. The answer, I saw to-day, has all the while been staring me in the face."

"Then what in the world is it?"

"Why, the very intensity of her conscience about him—the very passion of her brave little piety. That's the way it has worked," Mrs. Assingham explained "and I admit it to have been as 'rum' a way as possible. But it has been working from a rum start. From the moment the dear man married to ease his daughter off, and it then happened, by an extraordinary perversity, that the very opposite effect was produced—!" With the renewed vision of this fatality, however, she could give but a desperate shrug.

"I see," the Colonel sympathetically mused. "That WAS a rum start."

But his very response, as she again flung up her arms, seemed to make her sense, for a moment, intolerable. "Yes—there I am! I was really at the bottom of it," she declared; "I don't know what possessed me—but I planned for him, I goaded him on." With which, however, the next moment, she took herself up. "Or, rather, I DO know what possessed me—for wasn't he beset with ravening women, right and left, and didn't he, quite pathetically, appeal for protection, didn't he, quite charmingly, show one how he needed and desired it? Maggie," she thus lucidly continued, "couldn't, with a new life of her own, give herself up to doing for him in the future all she had done in the past—to fencing him in, to keeping him safe and keeping THEM off. One perceived this," she went on—"out of the abundance of one's affection and one's sympathy." It all blessedly came back to her—when it wasn't all, for the fiftieth time, obscured, in face of the present facts, by anxiety and compunction. "One was no doubt a meddlesome fool; one always IS, to think one sees people's lives for them better than they see them for themselves. But one's excuse here," she insisted, "was that these people clearly DIDN'T see them for themselves—didn't see them at all. It struck one for very pity—that they were making a mess of such charming material; that they were but wasting it and letting it go. They didn't know HOW to live—and somehow one couldn't, if one took an interest in them at all, simply stand and see it. That's what I pay for"—and the poor woman, in straighter communion with her companion's intelligence at this moment, she appeared to feel, than she had ever been before, let him have the whole of the burden of her consciousness. "I always pay for it, sooner or later, my sociable, my damnable, my unnecessary interest. Nothing of course would suit me but that it should fix itself also on Charlotte—Charlotte who was hovering there on the edge of our lives, when not beautifully, and a trifle mysteriously, flitting across them, and who was a piece of waste and a piece of threatened failure, just as, for any possible good to the WORLD, Mr. Verver and Maggie were. It began to come over me, in the watches of the night, that Charlotte was a person who COULD keep off ravening women—without being one herself, either, in the vulgar way of the others; and that this service to Mr. Verver would be a sweet employment for her future. There was something, of course, that might have stopped me: you know, you know what I mean—it looks at me," she veritably moaned, "out of your face! But all I can say is that it didn't; the reason largely being—once I had fallen in love with the beautiful symmetry of my plan—that I seemed to feel sure Maggie would accept Charlotte, whereas I didn't quite make out either what other woman, or what other KIND of woman, one could think of her accepting."

"I see—I see." She had paused, meeting all the while his listening look, and the fever of her retrospect had so risen with her talk that the desire was visibly strong in him to meet her, on his side, but with cooling breath. "One quite understands, my dear."

It only, however, kept her there sombre. "I naturally see, love, what you understand; which sits again, perfectly, in your eyes. You see that I saw that Maggie would accept her in helpless ignorance. Yes, dearest"—and the grimness of her dreariness suddenly once more possessed her: "you've only to tell me that that knowledge was my reason for what I did. How, when you do, can I stand up to you? You see," she said with an ineffable headshake, "that I don't stand up! I'm down, down, down," she declared; "yet" she as quickly added—"there's just one little thing that helps to save my life." And she kept him waiting but an instant. "They might easily—they would perhaps even certainly—have done something worse."

He thought. "Worse than that Charlotte—?"

"Ah, don't tell me," she cried, "that there COULD have been nothing worse. There might, as they were, have been many things. Charlotte, in her way, is extraordinary."

He was almost simultaneous. "Extraordinary!"

"She observes the forms," said Fanny Assingham.

He hesitated. "With the Prince—?"

"FOR the Prince. And with the others," she went on. "With Mr. Verver—wonderfully. But above all with Maggie. And the forms"—she had to do even THEM justice—"are two-thirds of conduct. Say he had married a woman who would have made a hash of them."

But he jerked back. "Ah, my dear, I wouldn't say it for the world!"

"Say," she none the less pursued, "he had married a woman the Prince would really have cared for."

"You mean then he doesn't care for Charlotte—?" This was still a new view to jump to, and the Colonel, perceptibly, wished to make sure of the necessity of the effort. For that, while he stared, his wife allowed him time; at the end of which she simply said: "No!"

"Then what on earth are they up to?" Still, however, she only looked at him; so that, standing there before her with his hands in his pockets, he had time, further, to risk, soothingly, another question. "Are the 'forms' you speak of—that are two-thirds of conduct—what will be keeping her now, by your hypothesis, from coming home with him till morning?"

"Yes—absolutely. THEIR forms."

"Theirs'—?"

"Maggie's and Mr. Verver's—those they IMPOSE on Charlotte and the Prince. Those," she developed, "that, so perversely, as I say, have succeeded in setting themselves up as the right ones."

He considered—but only now, at last, really to relapse into woe. "Your 'perversity,' my dear, is exactly what I don't understand. The state of things existing hasn't grown, like a field of mushrooms, in a night. Whatever they, all round, may be in for now is at least the consequence of what they've DONE. Are they mere helpless victims of fate?"

Well, Fanny at last had the courage of it, "Yes—they are. To be so abjectly innocent—that IS to be victims of fate."

"And Charlotte and the Prince are abjectly innocent—?"

It took her another minute, but she rose to the full height. "Yes. That is they WERE—as much so in their way as the others. There were beautiful intentions all round. The Prince's and Charlotte's were beautiful—of THAT I had my faith. They WERE—I'd go to the stake. Otherwise," she added, "I should have been a wretch. And I've not been a wretch. I've only been a double-dyed donkey."

"Ah then," he asked, "what does our muddle make THEM to have been?"

"Well, too much taken up with considering each other. You may call such a mistake as that by what ever name you please; it at any rate means, all round, their case. It illustrates the misfortune," said Mrs. Assingham gravely, "of being too, too charming."

This was another matter that took some following, but the Colonel again did his best. "Yes, but to whom?—doesn't it rather depend on that? To whom have the Prince and Charlotte then been too charming?"

"To each other, in the first place—obviously. And then both of them together to Maggie."

"To Maggie?" he wonderingly echoed.

"To Maggie." She was now crystalline. "By having accepted, from the first, so guilelessly—yes, so guilelessly, themselves—her guileless idea of still having her father, of keeping him fast, in her life."

"Then isn't one supposed, in common humanity, and if one hasn't quarrelled with him, and one has the means, and he, on his side, doesn't drink or kick up rows—isn't one supposed to keep one's aged parent in one's life?"

"Certainly—when there aren't particular reasons against it. That there may be others than his getting drunk is exactly the moral of what is before us. In the first place Mr. Verver isn't aged."

The Colonel just hung fire—but it came. "Then why the deuce does he—oh, poor dear man!—behave as if he were?"

She took a moment to meet it. "How do you know how he behaves?"

"Well, my own love, we see how Charlotte does!" Again, at this, she faltered; but again she rose. "Ah, isn't my whole point that he's charming to her?"

"Doesn't it depend a bit on what she regards as charming?"

She faced the question as if it were flippant, then with a headshake of dignity she brushed it away. "It's Mr. Verver who's really young—it's Charlotte who's really old. And what I was saying," she added, "isn't affected!"

"You were saying"—he did her the justice—"that they're all guileless."

"That they were. Guileless, all, at first—quite extraordinarily. It's what I mean by their failure to see that the more they took for granted they could work together the more they were really working apart. For I repeat," Fanny went on, "that I really believe Charlotte and the Prince honestly to have made up their minds, originally, that their very esteem for Mr. Verver—which was serious, as well it might be!—would save them."

"I see." The Colonel inclined himself. "And save HIM."

"It comes to the same thing!"

"Then save Maggie."

"That comes," said Mrs. Assingham, "to something a little different. For Maggie has done the most."

He wondered. "What do you call the most?"

"Well, she did it originally—she began the vicious circle. For that—though you make round eyes at my associating her with 'vice'—is simply what it has been. It's their mutual consideration, all round, that has made it the bottomless gulf; and they're really so embroiled but because, in their way, they've been so improbably GOOD."

"In their way—yes!" the Colonel grinned.

"Which was, above all, Maggie's way." No flicker of his ribaldry was anything to her now. "Maggie had in the first place to make up to her father for her having suffered herself to become—poor little dear, as she believed—so intensely married. Then she had to make up to her husband for taking so much of the time they might otherwise have spent together to make this reparation to Mr. Verver perfect. And her way to do this, precisely, was by allowing the Prince the use, the enjoyment, whatever you may call it, of Charlotte to cheer his path—by instalments, as it were—in proportion as she herself, making sure her father was all right, might be missed from his side. By so much, at the same time, however," Mrs. Assingham further explained, "by so much as she took her young stepmother, for this purpose, away from Mr. Verver, by just so much did this too strike her as something again to be made up for. It has saddled her, you will easily see, with a positively new obligation to her father, an obligation created and aggravated by her unfortunate, even if quite heroic, little sense of justice. She began with wanting to show him that his marriage could never, under whatever temptation of her own bliss with the Prince, become for her a pretext for deserting or neglecting HIM. Then that, in its order, entailed her wanting to show the Prince that she recognised how the other desire—this wish to remain, intensely, the same passionate little daughter she had always been—involved in some degree, and just for the present, so to speak, her neglecting and deserting him. I quite hold," Fanny with characteristic amplitude parenthesised, "that a person can mostly feel but one passion—one TENDER passion, that is—at a time. Only, that doesn't hold good for our primary and instinctive attachments, the 'voice of blood,' such as one's feeling for a parent or a brother. Those may be intense and yet not prevent other intensities—as you will recognise, my dear, when you remember how I continued, tout betement, to adore my mother, whom you didn't adore, for years after I had begun to adore you. Well, Maggie"—she kept it up—"is in the same situation as I was, PLUS complications from which I was, thank heaven, exempt: PLUS not having in the least begun with the sense for complications that I should have had. Before she knew it, at any rate, her little scruples and her little lucidities, which were really so divinely blind—her feverish little sense of justice, as I say—had brought the two others together as her grossest misconduct couldn't have done. And now she knows something or other has happened—yet hasn't heretofore known what. She has only piled up her remedy, poor child—something that she has earnestly but confusedly seen as her necessary policy; piled it on top of the policy, on top of the remedy, that she at first thought out for herself, and that would really have needed, since then, so much modification. Her only modification has been the growth of her necessity to prevent her father's wondering if all, in their life in common, MAY be so certainly for the best. She has now as never before to keep him unconscious that, peculiar, if he makes a point of it, as their situation is, there's anything in it all uncomfortable or disagreeable, anything morally the least out of the way. She has to keep touching it up to make it, each day, each month, look natural and normal to him; so that—God forgive me the comparison!—she's like an old woman who has taken to 'painting' and who has to lay it on thicker, to carry it off with a greater audacity, with a greater impudence even, the older she grows." And Fanny stood a moment captivated with the image she had thrown off. "I like the idea of Maggie audacious and impudent—learning to be so to gloss things over. She could—she even will, yet, I believe—learn it, for that sacred purpose, consummately, diabolically. For from the moment the dear man should see it's all rouge—!" She paused, staring at the vision.

It imparted itself even to Bob. "Then the fun would begin?" As it but made her look at him hard, however, he amended the form of his inquiry. "You mean that in that case she WILL, charming creature, be lost?"

She was silent a moment more. "As I've told you before, she won't be lost if her father's saved. She'll see that as salvation enough."

The Colonel took it in. "Then she's a little heroine."

"Rather—she's a little heroine. But it's his innocence, above all," Mrs. Assingham added, "that will pull them through."

Her companion, at this, focussed again Mr. Verver's innocence. "It's awfully quaint."

"Of course it's awfully quaint! That it's awfully quaint, that the pair are awfully quaint, quaint with all our dear old quaintness—by which I don't mean yours and mine, but that of my own sweet countrypeople, from whom I've so deplorably degenerated—that," Mrs. Assingham declared, "was originally the head and front of their appeal to me and of my interest in them. And of course I shall feel them quainter still," she rather ruefully subjoined, "before they've done with me!"

This might be, but it wasn't what most stood in the Colonel's way. "You believe so in Mr. Verver's innocence after two years of Charlotte?"

She stared. "But the whole point is just that two years of Charlotte are what he hasn't really—or what you may call undividedly—had."

"Any more than Maggie, by your theory, eh, has 'really or undividedly,' had four of the Prince? It takes all she hasn't had," the Colonel conceded, "to account for the innocence that in her, too, so leaves us in admiration."

So far as it might be ribald again she let this pass. "It takes a great many things to account for Maggie. What is definite, at all events, is that—strange though this be—her effort for her father has, up to now, sufficiently succeeded. She has made him, she makes him, accept the tolerably obvious oddity of their relation, all round, for part of the game. Behind her there, protected and amused and, as it were, consciously humbugged—the Principino, in whom he delights, always aiding—he has safely and serenely enough suffered the conditions of his life to pass for those he had sublimely projected. He hadn't worked them out in detail—any more than I had, heaven pity me!—and the queerness has been, exactly, in the detail. This, for him, is what it was to have married Charlotte. And they both," she neatly wound up, "'help.'"

"'Both'—?"

"I mean that if Maggie, always in the breach, makes it seem to him all so flourishingly to fit, Charlotte does her part not less. And her part is very large. Charlotte," Fanny declared, "works like a horse."

So there it all was, and her husband looked at her a minute across it. "And what does the Prince work like?"

She fixed him in return. "Like a Prince!" Whereupon, breaking short off, to ascend to her room, she presented her highly—decorated back—in which, in odd places, controlling the complications of its aspect, the ruby or the garnet, the turquoise and the topaz, gleamed like faint symbols of the wit that pinned together the satin patches of her argument.

He watched her as if she left him positively under the impression of her mastery of her subject; yes, as if the real upshot of the drama before them was but that he had, when it came to the tight places of life—as life had shrunk for him now—the most luminous of wives. He turned off, in this view of her majestic retreat, the comparatively faint little electric lamp which had presided over their talk; then he went up as immediately behind her as the billows of her amber train allowed, making out how all the clearness they had conquered was even for herself a relief—how at last the sense of the amplitude of her exposition sustained and floated her. Joining her, however, on the landing above, where she had already touched a metallic point into light, he found she had done perhaps even more to create than to extinguish in him the germ of a curiosity. He held her a minute longer—there was another plum in the pie. "What did you mean some minutes ago by his not caring for Charlotte?"

"The Prince's? By his not 'really' caring?" She recalled, after a little, benevolently enough. "I mean that men don't, when it has all been too easy. That's how, in nine cases out of ten, a woman is treated who has risked her life. You asked me just now how he works," she added; "but you might better perhaps have asked me how he plays."

Well, he made it up. "Like a Prince?"

"Like a Prince. He is, profoundly, a Prince. For that," she said with expression, "he's—beautifully—a case. They're far rarer, even in the 'highest circles,' than they pretend to be—and that's what makes so much of his value. He's perhaps one of the very last—the last of the real ones. So it is we must take him. We must take him all round."

The Colonel considered. "And how must Charlotte—if anything happens—take him?"

The question held her a minute, and while she waited, with her eyes on him, she put out a grasping hand to his arm, in the flesh of which he felt her answer distinctly enough registered. Thus she gave him, standing off a little, the firmest, longest, deepest injunction he had ever received from her. "Nothing—in spite of everything—WILL happen. Nothing HAS happened. Nothing IS happening."

He looked a trifle disappointed. "I see. For US."

"For us. For whom else?" And he was to feel indeed how she wished him to understand it. "We know nothing on earth—!" It was an undertaking he must sign.

So he wrote, as it were, his name. "We know nothing on earth." It was like the soldiers' watchword at night.

"We're as innocent," she went on in the same way, "as babes."

"Why not rather say," he asked, "as innocent as they themselves are?"

"Oh, for the best of reasons! Because we're much more so."

He wondered. "But how can we be more—?"

"For them? Oh, easily! We can be anything."

"Absolute idiots then?"

"Absolute idiots. And oh," Fanny breathed, "the way it will rest us!"

Well, he looked as if there were something in that. "But won't they know we're not?"

She barely hesitated. "Charlotte and the Prince think we are—which is so much gained. Mr. Verver believes in our intelligence—but he doesn't matter."

"And Maggie? Doesn't SHE know—?"

"That we see before our noses?" Yes, this indeed took longer. "Oh, so far as she may guess it she'll give no sign. So it comes to the same thing."

He raised his eyebrows. "Comes to our not being able to help her?"

"That's the way we SHALL help her."

"By looking like fools?"

She threw up her hands. "She only wants, herself, to look like a bigger! So there we are!" With which she brushed it away—his conformity was promised. Something, however, still held her; it broke, to her own vision, as a last wave of clearness. "Moreover NOW," she said, "I see! I mean," she added,—"what you were asking me: how I knew to-day, in Eaton Square, that Maggie's awake." And she had indeed visibly got it. "It was by seeing them together."

"Seeing her with her father?" He fell behind again. "But you've seen her often enough before."

"Never with my present eyes. For nothing like such a test—that of this length of the others' absence together—has hitherto occurred."

"Possibly! But if she and Mr. Verver insisted upon it—?"

"Why is it such a test? Because it has become one without their intending it. It has spoiled, so to speak, on their hands."

"It has soured, eh?" the Colonel said.

"The word's horrible—say rather it has 'changed.' Perhaps," Fanny went on, "she did wish to see how much she can bear. In that case she HAS seen. Only it was she alone who—about the visit—insisted. Her father insists on nothing. And she watches him do it."

Her husband looked impressed. "Watches him?"

"For the first faint sign. I mean of his noticing. It doesn't, as I tell you, come. But she's there for it to see. And I felt," she continued, "HOW she's there; I caught her, as it were, in the fact. She couldn't keep it from me—though she left her post on purpose—came home with me to throw dust in my eyes. I took it all—her dust; but it was what showed me." With which supreme lucidity she reached the door of her room. "Luckily it showed me also how she has succeeded. Nothing—from him—HAS come."

"You're so awfully sure?"

"Sure. Nothing WILL. Good-night," she said. "She'll die first."

BOOK SECOND: THE PRINCESS

PART FOURTH

Portrait (1864) by James Abbott McNeill Whistler (1834–1903)

XXV

       It was not till many days had passed that the Princess began to accept the idea of having done, a little, something she was not always doing, or indeed that of having listened to any inward voice that spoke in a new tone. Yet these instinctive postponements of reflection were the fruit, positively, of recognitions and perceptions already active; of the sense, above all, that she had made, at a particular hour, made by the mere touch of her hand, a difference in the situation so long present to her as practically unattackable. This situation had been occupying, for months and months, the very centre of the garden of her life, but it had reared itself there like some strange, tall tower of ivory, or perhaps rather some wonderful, beautiful, but outlandish pagoda, a structure plated with hard, bright porcelain, coloured and figured and adorned, at the overhanging eaves, with silver bells that tinkled, ever so charmingly, when stirred by chance airs. She had walked round and round it—that was what she felt; she had carried on her existence in the space left her for circulation, a space that sometimes seemed ample and sometimes narrow: looking up, all the while, at the fair structure that spread itself so amply and rose so high, but never quite making out, as yet, where she might have entered had she wished. She had not wished till now—such was the odd case; and what was doubtless equally odd, besides, was that, though her raised eyes seemed to distinguish places that must serve, from within, and especially far aloft, as apertures and outlooks, no door appeared to give access from her convenient garden level. The great decorated surface had remained consistently impenetrable and inscrutable. At present, however, to her considering mind, it was as if she had ceased merely to circle and to scan the elevation, ceased so vaguely, so quite helplessly to stare and wonder: she had caught herself distinctly in the act of pausing, then in that of lingering, and finally in that of stepping unprecedentedly near. The thing might have been, by the distance at which it kept her, a Mahometan mosque, with which no base heretic could take a liberty; there so hung about it the vision of one's putting off one's shoes to enter, and even, verily, of one's paying with one's life if found there as an interloper. She had not, certainly, arrived at the conception of paying with her life for anything she might do; but it was nevertheless quite as if she had sounded with a tap or two one of the rare porcelain plates. She had knocked, in short—though she could scarce have said whether for admission or for what; she had applied her hand to a cool smooth spot and had waited to see what would happen. Something had happened; it was as if a sound, at her touch, after a little, had come back to her from within; a sound sufficiently suggesting that her approach had been noted.

If this image, however, may represent our young woman's consciousness of a recent change in her life—a change now but a few days old—it must at the same time be observed that she both sought and found in renewed circulation, as I have called it, a measure of relief from the idea of having perhaps to answer for what she had done. The pagoda in her blooming garden figured the arrangement—how otherwise was it to be named?—by which, so strikingly, she had been able to marry without breaking, as she liked to put it, with the past. She had surrendered herself to her husband without the shadow of a reserve or a condition, and yet she had not, all the while, given up her father—the least little inch. She had compassed the high city of seeing the two men beautifully take to each other, and nothing in her marriage had marked it as more happy than this fact of its having practically given the elder, the lonelier, a new friend. What had moreover all the while enriched the whole aspect of success was that the latter's marriage had been no more meassurably paid for than her own. His having taken the same great step in the same free way had not in the least involved the relegation of his daughter. That it was remarkable they had been able at once so to separate and so to keep together had never for a moment, from however far back, been equivocal to her; that it was remarkable had in fact quite counted, at first and always, and for each of them equally, as part of their inspiration and their support. There were plenty of singular things they were NOT enamoured of—flights of brilliancy, of audacity, of originality, that, speaking at least for the dear man and herself, were not at all in their line; but they liked to think they had given their life this unusual extension and this liberal form, which many families, many couples, and still more many pairs of couples, would not have found workable. That last truth had been distinctly brought home to them by the bright testimony, the quite explicit envy, of most of their friends, who had remarked to them again and again that they must, on all the showing, to keep on such terms, be people of the highest amiability—equally including in the praise, of course, Amerigo and Charlotte. It had given them pleasure—as how should it not?—to find themselves shed such a glamour; it had certainly, that is, given pleasure to her father and herself, both of them distinguishably of a nature so slow to presume that they would scarce have been sure of their triumph without this pretty reflection of it. It was thus that their felicity had fructified; so it was that the ivory tower, visible and admirable doubtless, from any point of the social field, had risen stage by stage. Maggie's actual reluctance to ask herself with proportionate sharpness why she had ceased to take comfort in the sight of it represented accordingly a lapse from that ideal consistency on which her moral comfort almost at any time depended. To remain consistent she had always been capable of cutting down more or less her prior term.

Moving for the first time in her life as in the darkening shadow of a false position, she reflected that she should either not have ceased to be right—that is, to be confident—or have recognised that she was wrong; though she tried to deal with herself, for a space, only as a silken-coated spaniel who has scrambled out of a pond and who rattles the water from his ears. Her shake of her head, again and again, as she went, was much of that order, and she had the resource, to which, save for the rude equivalent of his generalising bark, the spaniel would have been a stranger, of humming to herself hard as a sign that nothing had happened to her. She had not, so to speak, fallen in; she had had no accident and had not got wet; this at any rate was her pretension until after she began a little to wonder if she mightn't, with or without exposure, have taken cold. She could at all events remember no time at which she had felt so excited, and certainly none—which was another special point—that so brought with it as well the necessity for concealing excitement. This birth of a new eagerness became a high pastime, in her view, precisely by reason of the ingenuity required for keeping the thing born out of sight. The ingenuity was thus a private and absorbing exercise, in the light of which, might I so far multiply my metaphors, I should compare her to the frightened but clinging young mother of an unlawful child. The idea that had possession of her would be, by our new analogy, the proof of her misadventure, but likewise, all the while, only another sign of a relation that was more to her than anything on earth. She had lived long enough to make out for herself that any deep-seated passion has its pangs as well as its joys, and that we are made by its aches and its anxieties most richly conscious of it. She had never doubted of the force of the feeling that bound her to her husband; but to become aware, almost suddenly, that it had begun to vibrate with a violence that had some of the effect of a strain would, rightly looked at, after all but show her she was, like thousands of women, every day, acting up to the full privilege of passion. Why in the world shouldn't she, with every right—if, on consideration, she saw no good reason against it? The best reason against it would have been the possibility of some consequence disagreeable or inconvenient to others— especially to such others as had never incommoded her by the egotism of THEIR passions; but if once that danger were duly guarded against the fulness of one's measure amounted to no more than the equal use of one's faculties or the proper playing of one's part. It had come to the Princess, obscurely at first, but little by little more conceivably, that her faculties had not for a good while been concomitantly used; the case resembled in a manner that of her once-loved dancing, a matter of remembered steps that had grown vague from her ceasing to go to balls. She would go to balls again—that seemed, freely, even crudely, stated, the remedy; she would take out of the deep receptacles in which she had laid them away the various ornaments congruous with the greater occasions, and of which her store, she liked to think, was none of the smallest. She would have been easily to be figured for us at this occupation; dipping, at off moments and quiet hours, in snatched visits and by draughty candle-light, into her rich collections and seeing her jewels again a little shyly, but all unmistakably, glow. That in fact may pass as the very picture of her semi-smothered agitation, of the diversion she to some extent successfully found in referring her crisis, so far as was possible, to the mere working of her own needs.

It must be added, however, that she would have been at a loss to determine—and certainly at first—to which order, that of self-control or that of large expression, the step she had taken the afternoon of her husband's return from Matcham with his companion properly belonged. For it had been a step, distinctly, on Maggie's part, her deciding to do something, just then and there, which would strike Amerigo as unusual, and this even though her departure from custom had merely consisted in her so arranging that he wouldn't find her, as he would definitely expect to do, in Eaton Square. He would have, strangely enough, as might seem to him, to come back home for it, and there get the impression of her rather pointedly, or at least all impatiently and independently, awaiting him. These were small variations and mild manoeuvres, but they went accompanied on Maggie's part, as we have mentioned, with an infinite sense of intention. Her watching by his fireside for her husband's return from an absence might superficially have presented itself as the most natural act in the world, and the only one, into the bargain, on which he would positively have reckoned. It fell by this circumstance into the order of plain matters, and yet the very aspect by which it was, in the event, handed over to her brooding fancy was the fact that she had done with it all she had designed. She had put her thought to the proof, and the proof had shown its edge; this was what was before her, that she was no longer playing with blunt and idle tools, with weapons that didn't cut. There passed across her vision ten times a day the gleam of a bare blade, and at this it was that she most shut her eyes, most knew the impulse to cheat herself with motion and sound. She had merely driven, on a certain Wednesday, to Portland Place, instead of remaining in Eaton Square, and she privately repeated it again and again—there had appeared beforehand no reason why she should have seen the mantle of history flung, by a single sharp sweep, over so commonplace a deed. That, all the same, was what had happened; it had been bitten into her mind, all in an hour, that nothing she had ever done would hereafter, in some way yet to be determined, so count for her—perhaps not even what she had done in accepting, in their old golden Rome, Amerigo's proposal of marriage. And yet, by her little crouching posture there, that of a timid tigress, she had meant nothing recklessly ultimate, nothing clumsily fundamental; so that she called it names, the invidious, the grotesque attitude, holding it up to her own ridicule, reducing so far as she could the portee of what had followed it. She had but wanted to get nearer—nearer to something indeed that she couldn't, that she wouldn't, even to herself, describe; and the degree of this achieved nearness was what had been in advance incalculable. Her actual multiplication of distractions and suppressions, whatever it did for her, failed to prevent her living over again any chosen minute—for she could choose them, she could fix them—of the freshness of relation produced by her having administered to her husband the first surprise to which she had ever treated him. It had been a poor thing, but it had been all her own, and the whole passage was backwardly there, a great picture hung on the wall of her daily life, for her to make what she would of.

It fell, for retrospect, into a succession of moments that were WATCHABLE still; almost in the manner of the different things done during a scene on the stage, some scene so acted as to have left a great impression on the tenant of one of the stalls. Several of these moments stood out beyond the others, and those she could feel again most, count again like the firm pearls on a string, had belonged more particularly to the lapse of time before dinner—dinner which had been so late, quite at nine o'clock, that evening, thanks to the final lateness of Amerigo's own advent. These were parts of the experience—though in fact there had been a good many of them—between which her impression could continue sharply to discriminate. Before the subsequent passages, much later on, it was to be said, the flame of memory turned to an equalising glow, that of a lamp in some side-chapel in which incense was thick. The great moment, at any rate, for conscious repossession, was doubtless the first: the strange little timed silence which she had fully gauged, on the spot, as altogether beyond her own intention, but which—for just how long? should she ever really know for just how long?—she could do nothing to break. She was in the smaller drawing-room, in which she always "sat," and she had, by calculation, dressed for dinner on finally coming in. It was a wonder how many things she had calculated in respect to this small incident—a matter for the importance of which she had so quite indefinite a measure. He would be late—he would be very late; that was the one certainty that seemed to look her in the face. There was still also the possibility that if he drove with Charlotte straight to Eaton Square he might think it best to remain there even on learning she had come away. She had left no message for him on any such chance; this was another of her small shades of decision, though the effect of it might be to keep him still longer absent. He might suppose she would already have dined; he might stay, with all he would have to tell, just on purpose to be nice to her father. She had known him to stretch the point, to these beautiful ends, far beyond that; he had more than once stretched it to the sacrifice of the opportunity of dressing.

If she herself had now avoided any such sacrifice, and had made herself, during the time at her disposal, quite inordinately fresh and quite positively smart, this had probably added, while she waited and waited, to that very tension of spirit in which she was afterwards to find the image of her having crouched. She did her best, quite intensely, by herself, to banish any such appearance; she couldn't help it if she couldn't read her pale novel—ah, that, par exemple, was beyond her! but she could at least sit by the lamp with the book, sit there with her newest frock, worn for the first time, sticking out, all round her, quite stiff and grand; even perhaps a little too stiff and too grand for a familiar and domestic frock, yet marked none the less, this time, she ventured to hope, by incontestable intrinsic merit. She had glanced repeatedly at the clock, but she had refused herself the weak indulgence of walking up and down, though the act of doing so, she knew, would make her feel, on the polished floor, with the rustle and the "hang," still more beautifully bedecked. The difficulty was that it would also make her feel herself still more sharply in a state; which was exactly what she proposed not to do. The only drops of her anxiety had been when her thought strayed complacently, with her eyes, to the front of her gown, which was in a manner a refuge, a beguilement, especially when she was able to fix it long enough to wonder if it would at last really satisfy Charlotte. She had ever been, in respect to her clothes, rather timorous and uncertain; for the last year, above all, she had lived in the light of Charlotte's possible and rather inscrutable judgment of them. Charlotte's own were simply the most charming and interesting that any woman had ever put on; there was a kind of poetic justice in her being at last able, in this particular, thanks to means, thanks quite to omnipotence, freely to exercise her genius. But Maggie would have described herself as, in these connections, constantly and intimately "torn"; conscious on one side of the impossibility of copying her companion and conscious on the other of the impossibility of sounding her, independently, to the bottom. Yes, it was one of the things she should go down to her grave without having known—how Charlotte, after all had been said, really thought her stepdaughter looked under any supposedly ingenious personal experiment. She had always been lovely about the stepdaughter's material braveries—had done, for her, the very best with them; but there had ever fitfully danced at the back of Maggie's head the suspicion that these expressions were mercies, not judgments, embodying no absolute, but only a relative, frankness. Hadn't Charlotte, with so perfect a critical vision, if the truth were known, given her up as hopeless—hopeless by a serious standard, and thereby invented for her a different and inferior one, in which, as the only thing to be done, she patiently and soothingly abetted her? Hadn't she, in other words, assented in secret despair, perhaps even in secret irritation, to her being ridiculous?—so that the best now possible was to wonder, once in a great while, whether one mightn't give her the surprise of something a little less out of the true note than usual. Something of this kind was the question that Maggie, while the absentees still delayed, asked of the appearance she was endeavouring to present; but with the result, repeatedly again, that it only went and lost itself in the thick air that had begun more and more to hang, for our young woman, over her accumulations of the unanswered. They were THERE, these accumulations; they were like a roomful of confused objects, never as yet "sorted," which for some time now she had been passing and re-passing, along the corridor of her life. She passed it when she could without opening the door; then, on occasion, she turned the key to throw in a fresh contribution. So it was that she had been getting things out of the way. They rejoined the rest of the confusion; it was as if they found their place, by some instinct of affinity, in the heap. They knew, in short, where to go; and when she, at present, by a mental act, once more pushed the door open, she had practically a sense of method and experience. What she should never know about Charlotte's thought— she tossed THAT in. It would find itself in company, and she might at last have been standing there long enough to see it fall into its corner. The sight moreover would doubtless have made her stare, had her attention been more free—the sight of the mass of vain things, congruous, incongruous, that awaited every addition. It made her in fact, with a vague gasp, turn away, and what had further determined this was the final sharp extinction of the inward scene by the outward. The quite different door had opened and her husband was there.

It had been as strange as she could consent, afterwards, to think it; it had been, essentially, what had made the abrupt bend in her life: he had come back, had followed her from the other house, VISIBLY uncertain—this was written in the face he for the first minute showed her. It had been written only for those seconds, and it had appeared to go, quickly, after they began to talk; but while it lasted it had been written large, and, though she didn't quite know what she had expected of him, she felt she hadn't expected the least shade of embarrassment. What had made the embarrassment—she called it embarrassment so as to be able to assure herself she put it at the very worst—what had made the particular look was his thus distinguishably wishing to see how he should find her. Why FIRST—that had, later on, kept coming to her; the question dangled there as if it were the key to everything. With the sense of it on the spot, she had felt, overwhelmingly, that she was significant, that so she must instantly strike him, and that this had a kind of violence beyond what she had intended. It was in fact even at the moment not absent from her view that he might easily have made an abject fool of her—at least for the time. She had indeed, for just ten seconds, been afraid of some such turn: the uncertainty in his face had become so, the next thing, an uncertainty in the very air. Three words of impatience the least bit loud, some outbreak of "What in the world are you 'up to', and what do you mean?" any note of that sort would instantly have brought her low—and this all the more that heaven knew she hadn't in any manner designed to be high. It was such a trifle, her small breach with custom, or at any rate with his natural presumption, that all magnitude of wonder had already had, before one could deprecate the shadow of it, the effect of a complication. It had made for him some difference that she couldn't measure, this meeting him at home and alone instead of elsewhere and with others, and back and back it kept coming to her that the blankness he showed her before he was able to SEE might, should she choose to insist on it, have a meaning—have, as who should say, an historic value—beyond the importance of momentary expressions in general. She had naturally had on the spot no ready notion of what he might want to see; it was enough for a ready notion, not to speak of a beating heart, that he DID see, that he saw his wife in her own drawing-room at the hour when she would most properly be there. He hadn't in any way challenged her, it was true, and, after those instants during which she now believed him to have been harbouring the impression of something unusually prepared and pointed in her attitude and array, he had advanced upon her smiling and smiling, and thus, without hesitation at the last, had taken her into his arms. The hesitation had been at the first, and she at present saw that he had surmounted it without her help. She had given him no help; for if, on the one hand, she couldn't speak for hesitation, so on the other—and especially as he didn't ask her—she couldn't explain why she was agitated. She had known it all the while down to her toes, known it in his presence with fresh intensity, and if he had uttered but a question it would have pressed in her the spring of recklessness. It had been strange that the most natural thing of all to say to him should have had that appearance; but she was more than ever conscious that any appearance she had would come round, more or less straight, to her father, whose life was now so quiet, on the basis accepted for it, that any alteration of his consciousness even in the possible sense of enlivenment, would make their precious equilibrium waver. THAT was at the bottom of her mind, that their equilibrium was everything, and that it was practically precarious, a matter of a hair's breadth for the loss of the balance. It was the equilibrium, or at all events her conscious fear about it, that had brought her heart into her mouth; and the same fear was, on either side, in the silent look she and Amerigo had exchanged. The happy balance that demanded this amount of consideration was truly thus, as by its own confession, a delicate matter; but that her husband had also HIS habit of anxiety and his general caution only brought them, after all, more closely together. It would have been most beautifully, therefore, in the name of the equilibrium, and in that of her joy at their feeling so exactly the same about it, that she might have spoken if she had permitted the truth on the subject of her behaviour to ring out—on the subject of that poor little behaviour which was for the moment so very limited a case of eccentricity.

"'Why, why' have I made this evening such a point of our not all dining together? Well, because I've all day been so wanting you alone that I finally couldn't bear it, and that there didn't seem any great reason why I should try to. THAT came to me—funny as it may at first sound, with all the things we've so wonderfully got into the way of bearing for each other. You've seemed these last days—I don't know what: more absent than ever before, too absent for us merely to go on so. It's all very well, and I perfectly see how beautiful it is, all round; but there comes a day when something snaps, when the full cup, filled to the very brim, begins to flow over. That's what has happened to my need of you—the cup, all day, has been too full to carry. So here I am with it, spilling it over you—and just for the reason that is the reason of my life. After all, I've scarcely to explain that I'm as much in love with you now as the first hour; except that there are some hours—which I know when they come, because they almost frighten me—that show me I'm even more so. They come of themselves—and, ah, they've been coming! After all, after all—!" Some such words as those were what DIDN'T ring out, yet it was as if even the unuttered sound had been quenched here in its own quaver. It was where utterance would have broken down by its very weight if he had let it get so far. Without that extremity, at the end of a minute, he had taken in what he needed to take—that his wife was TESTIFYING, that she adored and missed and desired him. "After all, after all," since she put it so, she was right. That was what he had to respond to; that was what, from the moment that, as has been said, he "saw," he had to treat as the most pertinent thing possible. He held her close and long, in expression of their personal reunion—this, obviously, was one way of doing so. He rubbed her cheek, tenderly, and with a deep vague murmur, against her face, that side of her face she was not pressing to his breast. That was, not less obviously, another way, and there were ways enough, in short, for his extemporised ease, for the good humour she was afterwards to find herself thinking of as his infinite tact. This last was partly, no doubt, because the question of tact might be felt as having come up at the end of a quarter of an hour during which he had liberally talked and she had genially questioned. He had told her of his day, the happy thought of his roundabout journey with Charlotte, all their cathedral-hunting adventure, and how it had turned out rather more of an affair than they expected. The moral of it was, at any rate, that he was tired, verily, and must have a bath and dress—to which end she would kindly excuse him for the shortest time possible. She was to remember afterwards something that had passed between them on this—how he had looked, for her, during an instant, at the door, before going out, how he had met her asking him, in hesitation first, then quickly in decision, whether she couldn't help him by going up with him. He had perhaps also for a moment hesitated, but he had declined her offer, and she was to preserve, as I say, the memory of the smile with which he had opined that at that rate they wouldn't dine till ten o'clock and that she should go straighter and faster alone. Such things, as I say, were to come back to her—they played, through her full after-sense, like lights on the whole impression; the subsequent parts of the experience were not to have blurred their distinctness. One of these subsequent parts, the first, had been the not inconsiderable length, to her later and more analytic consciousness, of this second wait for her husband's reappearance. She might certainly, with the best will in the world, had she gone up with him, have been more in his way than not, since people could really, almost always, hurry better without help than with it. Still, she could actually hardly have made him take more time than he struck her taking, though it must indeed be added that there was now in this much-thinking little person's state of mind no mere crudity of impatience. Something had happened, rapidly, with the beautiful sight of him and with the drop of her fear of having annoyed him by making him go to and fro. Subsidence of the fearsome, for Maggie's spirit, was always, at first, positive emergence of the sweet, and it was long since anything had been so sweet to her as the particular quality suddenly given by her present emotion to the sense of possession.

XXVI

Amerigo was away from her again, as she sat there, as she walked there without him—for she had, with the difference of his presence in the house, ceased to keep herself from moving about; but the hour was filled nevertheless with the effect of his nearness, and above all with the effect, strange in an intimacy so established, of an almost renewed vision of the facts of his aspect. She had seen him last but five days since, yet he had stood there before her as if restored from some far country, some long voyage, some combination of dangers or fatigues. This unquenchable variety in his appeal to her interest, what did it mean but that—reduced to the flatness of mere statement—she was married, by good fortune, to an altogether dazzling person? That was an old, old story, but the truth of it shone out to her like the beauty of some family picture, some mellow portrait of an ancestor, that she might have been looking at, almost in surprise, after a long intermission. The dazzling person was upstairs and she was down, and there were moreover the other facts of the selection and decision that this demonstration of her own had required, and of the constant care that the equilibrium involved; but she had, all the same, never felt so absorbingly married, so abjectly conscious of a master of her fate. He could do what he would with her; in fact what was actually happening was that he was actually doing it. "What he would," what he REALLY would—only that quantity itself escaped perhaps, in the brightness of the high harmony, familiar naming and discussing. It was enough of a recognition for her that, whatever the thing he might desire, he would always absolutely bring it off. She knew at this moment, without a question, with the fullest surrender, how he had brought off, in her, by scarce more than a single allusion, a perfect flutter of tenderness. If he had come back tired, tired from his long day, the exertion had been, literally, in her service and her father's. They two had sat at home at peace, the Principino between them, the complications of life kept down, the bores sifted out, the large ease of the home preserved, because of the way the others held the field and braved the weather. Amerigo never complained—any more than, for that matter, Charlotte did; but she seemed to see to-night as she had never yet quite done that their business of social representation, conceived as they conceived it, beyond any conception of her own, and conscientiously carried out, was an affair of living always in harness. She remembered Fanny Assingham's old judgment, that friend's description of her father and herself as not living at all, as not knowing what to do or what might be done for them; and there came back to her with it an echo of the long talk they had had together, one September day at Fawns, under the trees, when she put before him this dictum of Fanny's.

That occasion might have counted for them—she had already often made the reflection—as the first step in an existence more intelligently arranged. It had been an hour from which the chain of causes and consequences was definitely traceable—so many things, and at the head of the list her father's marriage, having appeared to her to flow from Charlotte's visit to Fawns, and that event itself having flowed from the memorable talk. But what perhaps most came out in the light of these concatenations was that it had been, for all the world, as if Charlotte had been "had in," as the servants always said of extra help, because they had thus suffered it to be pointed out to them that if their family coach lumbered and stuck the fault was in its lacking its complement of wheels. Having but three, as they might say, it had wanted another, and what had Charlotte done from the first but begin to act, on the spot, and ever so smoothly and beautifully, as a fourth? Nothing had been, immediately, more manifest than the greater grace of the movement of the vehicle—as to which, for the completeness of her image, Maggie was now supremely to feel how every strain had been lightened for herself. So far as SHE was one of the wheels she had but to keep in her place; since the work was done for her she felt no weight, and it wasn't too much to acknowledge that she had scarce to turn round. She had a long pause before the fire during which she might have been fixing with intensity her projected vision, have been conscious even of its taking an absurd, fantastic shape. She might have been watching the family coach pass and noting that, somehow, Amerigo and Charlotte were pulling it while she and her father were not so much as pushing. They were seated inside together, dandling the Principino and holding him up to the windows, to see and be seen, like an infant positively royal; so that the exertion was ALL with the others. Maggie found in this image a repeated challenge; again and yet again she paused before the fire: after which, each time, in the manner of one for whom a strong light has suddenly broken, she gave herself to livelier movement. She had seen herself at last, in the picture she was studying, suddenly jump from the coach; whereupon, frankly, with the wonder of the sight, her eyes opened wider and her heart stood still for a moment. She looked at the person so acting as if this person were somebody else, waiting with intensity to see what would follow. The person had taken a decision—which was evidently because an impulse long gathering had at last felt a sharpest pressure. Only how was the decision to be applied?—what, in particular, would the figure in the picture do? She looked about her, from the middle of the room, under the force of this question, as if THERE, exactly, were the field of action involved. Then, as the door opened again, she recognised, whatever the action, the form, at any rate, of a first opportunity. Her husband had reappeared—he stood before her refreshed, almost radiant, quite reassuring. Dressed, anointed, fragrant, ready, above all, for his dinner, he smiled at her over the end of their delay. It was as if her opportunity had depended on his look—and now she saw that it was good. There was still, for the instant, something in suspense, but it passed more quickly than on his previous entrance. He was already holding out his arms. It was, for hours and hours, later on, as if she had somehow been lifted aloft, were floated and carried on some warm high tide beneath which stumbling blocks had sunk out of sight. This came from her being again, for the time, in the enjoyment of confidence, from her knowing, as she believed, what to do. All the next day, and all the next, she appeared to herself to know it. She had a plan, and she rejoiced in her plan: this consisted of the light that, suddenly breaking into her restless reverie, had marked the climax of that vigil. It had come to her as a question—"What if I've abandoned THEM, you know? What if I've accepted too passively the funny form of our life?" There would be a process of her own by which she might do differently in respect to Amerigo and Charlotte—a process quite independent of any process of theirs. Such a solution had but to rise before her to affect her, to charm her, with its simplicity, an advantageous simplicity she had been stupid, for so long, not to have been struck by; and the simplicity meanwhile seemed proved by the success that had already begun to attend her. She had only had herself to do something to see how immediately it answered. This consciousness of its having answered with her husband was the uplifting, sustaining wave. He had "met" her—she so put it to herself; met her with an effect of generosity and of gaiety, in especial, on his coming back to her ready for dinner, which she wore in her breast as the token of an escape for them both from something not quite definite, but clearly, much less good. Even at that moment, in fact, her plan had begun to work; she had been, when he brightly reappeared, in the act of plucking it out of the heart of her earnestness—plucking it, in the garden of thought, as if it had been some full-blown flower that she could present to him on the spot. Well, it was the flower of participation, and as that, then and there, she held it out to him, putting straightway into execution the idea, so needlessly, so absurdly obscured, of her SHARING with him, whatever the enjoyment, the interest, the experience might be—and sharing also, for that matter, with Charlotte.

She had thrown herself, at dinner, into every feature of the recent adventure of the companions, letting him see, without reserve, that she wished to hear everything about it, and making Charlotte in particular, Charlotte's judgment of Matcham, Charlotte's aspect, her success there, her effect traceably produced, her clothes inimitably worn, her cleverness gracefully displayed, her social utility, in fine, brilliantly exemplified, the subject of endless inquiry. Maggie's inquiry was most empathetic, moreover, for the whole happy thought of the cathedral-hunt, which she was so glad they had entertained, and as to the pleasant results of which, down to the cold beef and bread-and-cheese, the queer old smell and the dirty table-cloth at the inn, Amerigo was good-humouredly responsive. He had looked at her across the table, more than once, as if touched by the humility of this welcome offered to impressions at second-hand, the amusements, the large freedoms only of others—as if recognising in it something fairly exquisite; and at the end, while they were alone, before she had rung for a servant, he had renewed again his condonation of the little irregularity, such as it was, on which she had ventured. They had risen together to come upstairs; he had been talking at the last about some of the people, at the very last of all about Lady Castledean and Mr. Blint; after which she had once more broken ground on the matter of the "type" of Gloucester. It brought her, as he came round the table to join her, yet another of his kind conscious stares, one of the looks, visibly beguiled, but at the same time not invisibly puzzled, with which he had already shown his sense of this charming grace of her curiosity. It was as if he might for a moment be going to say:—"You needn't PRETEND, dearest, quite so hard, needn't think it necessary to care quite so much!"—it was as if he stood there before her with some such easy intelligence, some such intimate reassurance, on his lips. Her answer would have been all ready—that she wasn't in the least pretending; and she looked up at him, while he took her hand, with the maintenance, the real persistence, of her lucid little plan in her eyes. She wanted him to understand from that very moment that she was going to be WITH him again, quite with them, together, as she doubtless hadn't been since the "funny" changes—that was really all one could call them—into which they had each, as for the sake of the others, too easily and too obligingly slipped. They had taken too much for granted that their life together required, as people in London said, a special "form"—which was very well so long as the form was kept only for the outside world and was made no more of among themselves than the pretty mould of an iced pudding, or something of that sort, into which, to help yourself, you didn't hesitate to break with the spoon. So much as that she would, with an opening, have allowed herself furthermore to observe; she wanted him to understand how her scheme embraced Charlotte too; so that if he had but uttered the acknowledgment she judged him on the point of making—the acknowledgment of his catching at her brave little idea for their case—she would have found herself, as distinctly, voluble almost to eloquence.

What befell, however, was that even while she thus waited she felt herself present at a process taking place rather deeper within him than the occasion, on the whole, appeared to require—a process of weighing something in the balance, of considering, deciding, dismissing. He had guessed that she was there with an idea, there in fact by reason of her idea; only this, oddly enough, was what at the last stayed her words. She was helped to these perceptions by his now looking at her still harder than he had yet done—which really brought it to the turn of a hair, for her, that she didn't make sure his notion of her idea was the right one. It was the turn of a hair, because he had possession of her hands and was bending toward her, ever so kindly, as if to see, to understand, more, or possibly give more—she didn't know which; and that had the effect of simply putting her, as she would have said, in his power. She gave up, let her idea go, let everything go; her one consciousness was that he was taking her again into his arms. It was not till afterwards that she discriminated as to this; felt how the act operated with him instead of the words he hadn't uttered—operated, in his view, as probably better than any words, as always better, in fact, at any time, than anything. Her acceptance of it, her response to it, inevitable, foredoomed, came back to her, later on, as a virtual assent to the assumption he had thus made that there was really nothing such a demonstration didn't anticipate and didn't dispose of, and that the spring acting within herself moreover might well have been, beyond any other, the impulse legitimately to provoke it. It made, for any issue, the third time since his return that he had drawn her to his breast; and at present, holding her to his side as they left the room, he kept her close for their moving into the hall and across it, kept her for their slow return together to the apartments above. He had been right, overwhelmingly right, as to the felicity of his tenderness and the degree of her sensibility, but even while she felt these things sweep all others away she tasted of a sort of terror of the weakness they produced in her. It was still, for her, that she had positively something to do, and that she mustn't be weak for this, must much rather be strong. For many hours after, none the less, she remained weak—if weak it was; though holding fast indeed to the theory of her success, since her agitated overture had been, after all, so unmistakably met.

She recovered soon enough on the whole, the sense that this left her Charlotte always to deal with—Charlotte who, at any rate, however SHE might meet overtures, must meet them, at the worst, more or less differently. Of that inevitability, of such other ranges of response as were open to Charlotte, Maggie took the measure in approaching her, on the morrow of her return from Matcham, with the same show of desire to hear all her story. She wanted the whole picture from her, as she had wanted it from her companion, and, promptly, in Eaton Square, whither, without the Prince, she repaired, almost ostentatiously, for the purpose, this purpose only, she brought her repeatedly back to the subject, both in her husband's presence and during several scraps of independent colloquy. Before her father, instinctively, Maggie took the ground that his wish for interesting echoes would be not less than her own—allowing, that is, for everything his wife would already have had to tell him, for such passages, between them, as might have occurred since the evening before. Joining them after luncheon, reaching them, in her desire to proceed with the application of her idea, before they had quitted the breakfast-room, the scene of their mid-day meal, she referred, in her parent's presence, to what she might have lost by delay, and expressed the hope that there would be an anecdote or two left for her to pick up. Charlotte was dressed to go out, and her husband, it appeared, rather positively prepared not to; he had left the table, but was seated near the fire with two or three of the morning papers and the residuum of the second and third posts on a stand beside him—more even than the usual extravagance, as Maggie's glance made out, of circulars, catalogues, advertisements, announcements of sales, foreign envelopes and foreign handwritings that were as unmistakable as foreign clothes. Charlotte, at the window, looking into the side-street that abutted on the Square, might have been watching for their visitor's advent before withdrawing; and in the light, strange and coloured, like that of a painted picture, which fixed the impression for her, objects took on values not hitherto so fully shown. It was the effect of her quickened sensibility; she knew herself again in presence of a problem, in need of a solution for which she must intensely work: that consciousness, lately born in her, had been taught the evening before to accept a temporary lapse, but had quickly enough again, with her getting out of her own house and her walking across half the town—for she had come from Portland Place on foot—found breath still in its lungs.

It exhaled this breath in a sigh, faint and unheard; her tribute, while she stood there before speaking, to realities looming through the golden mist that had already begun to be scattered. The conditions facing her had yielded, for the time, to the golden mist—had considerably melted away; but there they were again, definite, and it was for the next quarter of an hour as if she could have counted them one by one on her fingers. Sharp to her above all was the renewed attestation of her father's comprehensive acceptances, which she had so long regarded as of the same quality with her own, but which, so distinctly now, she should have the complication of being obliged to deal with separately. They had not yet struck her as absolutely extraordinary—which had made for her lumping them with her own, since her view of her own had but so lately begun to change; though it instantly stood out for her that there was really no new judgment of them she should be able to show without attracting in some degree his attention, without perhaps exciting his surprise and making thereby, for the situation she shared with him, some difference. She was reminded and warned by the concrete image; and for a minute Charlotte's face, immediately presented to her, affected her as searching her own to see the reminder tell. She had not less promptly kissed her stepmother, and had then bent over her father, from behind, and laid her cheek upon him; little amenities tantamount heretofore to an easy change of guard—Charlotte's own frequent, though always cheerful, term of comparison for this process of transfer. Maggie figured thus as the relieving sentry, and so smoothly did use and custom work for them that her mate might even, on this occasion, after acceptance of the pass-word, have departed without irrelevant and, in strictness, unsoldierly gossip. This was not, none the less, what happened; inasmuch as if our young woman had been floated over her first impulse to break the existing charm at a stroke, it yet took her but an instant to sound, at any risk, the note she had been privately practising. If she had practised it the day before, at dinner, on Amerigo, she knew but the better how to begin for it with Mrs. Verver, and it immensely helped her, for that matter, to be at once to speak of the Prince as having done more to quicken than to soothe her curiosity. Frankly and gaily she had come to ask—to ask what, in their unusually prolonged campaign, the two had achieved. She had got out of her husband, she admitted, what she could, but husbands were never the persons who answered such questions ideally. He had only made her more curious, and she had arrived early, this way, in order to miss as little as possible of Charlotte's story.

"Wives, papa," she said; "are always much better reporters—though I grant," she added for Charlotte, "that fathers are not much better than husbands. He never," she smiled, "tells me more than a tenth of what you tell him; so I hope you haven't told him everything yet, since in that case I shall probably have lost the best part of it." Maggie went, she went—she felt herself going; she reminded herself of an actress who had been studying a part and rehearsing it, but who suddenly, on the stage, before the footlights, had begun to improvise, to speak lines not in the text. It was this very sense of the stage and the footlights that kept her up, made her rise higher: just as it was the sense of action that logically involved some platform—action quite positively for the first time in her life, or, counting in the previous afternoon, for the second. The platform remained for three or four days thus sensibly under her feet, and she had all the while, with it, the inspiration of quite remarkably, of quite heroically improvising. Preparation and practice had come but a short way; her part opened out, and she invented from moment to moment what to say and to do. She had but one rule of art—to keep within bounds and not lose her head; certainly she might see for a week how far that would take her. She said to herself, in her excitement, that it was perfectly simple: to bring about a difference, touch by touch, without letting either of the three, and least of all her father, so much as suspect her hand. If they should suspect they would want a reason, and the humiliating truth was that she wasn't ready with a reason—not, that is, with what she would have called a reasonable one. She thought of herself, instinctively, beautifully, as having dealt, all her life, at her father's side and by his example, only in reasonable reasons; and what she would really have been most ashamed of would be to produce for HIM, in this line, some inferior substitute. Unless she were in a position to plead, definitely, that she was jealous she should be in no position to plead, decently, that she was dissatisfied. This latter condition would be a necessary implication of the former; without the former behind it it would HAVE to fall to the ground. So had the case, wonderfully, been arranged for her; there was a card she could play, but there was only one, and to play it would be to end the game. She felt herself—as at the small square green table, between the tall old silver candlesticks and the neatly arranged counters—her father's playmate and partner; and what it constantly came back to, in her mind, was that for her to ask a question, to raise a doubt, to reflect in any degree on the play of the others, would be to break the charm. The charm she had to call it, since it kept her companion so constantly engaged, so perpetually seated and so contentedly occupied. To say anything at all would be, in fine, to have to say WHY she was jealous; and she could, in her private hours, but stare long, with suffused eyes, at that impossibility.

By the end of a week, the week that had begun, especially, with her morning hour, in Eaton Square, between her father and his wife, her consciousness of being beautifully treated had become again verily greater than her consciousness of anything else; and I must add, moreover, that she at last found herself rather oddly wondering what else, as a consciousness, could have been quite so overwhelming. Charlotte's response to the experiment of being more with her OUGHT, as she very well knew, to have stamped the experiment with the feeling of success; so that if the success itself seemed a boon less substantial than the original image of it, it enjoyed thereby a certain analogy with our young woman's aftertaste of Amerigo's own determined demonstrations. Maggie was to have retained, for that matter, more than one aftertaste, and if I have spoken of the impressions fixed in her as soon as she had, so insidiously, taken the field, a definite note must be made of her perception, during those moments, of Charlotte's prompt uncertainty. She had shown, no doubt—she couldn't not have shown—that she had arrived with an idea; quite exactly as she had shown her husband, the night before, that she was awaiting him with a sentiment. This analogy in the two situations was to keep up for her the remembrance of a kinship of expression in the two faces in respect to which all she as yet professed to herself was that she had affected them, or at any rate the sensibility each of them so admirably covered, in the same way. To make the comparison at all was, for Maggie, to return to it often, to brood upon it, to extract from it the last dregs of its interest—to play with it, in short, nervously, vaguely, incessantly, as she might have played with a medallion containing on either side a cherished little portrait and suspended round her neck by a gold chain of a firm fineness that no effort would ever snap. The miniatures were back to back, but she saw them forever face to face, and when she looked from one to the other she found in Charlotte's eyes the gleam of the momentary "What does she really want?" that had come and gone for her in the Prince's. So again, she saw the other light, the light touched into a glow both in Portland Place and in Eaton Square, as soon as she had betrayed that she wanted no harm—wanted no greater harm of Charlotte, that is, than to take in that she meant to go out with her. She had been present at that process as personally as she might have been present at some other domestic incident—the hanging of a new picture, say, or the fitting of the Principino with his first little trousers.

She remained present, accordingly, all the week, so charmingly and systematically did Mrs. Verver now welcome her company. Charlotte had but wanted the hint, and what was it but the hint, after all, that, during the so subdued but so ineffaceable passage in the breakfast-room, she had seen her take? It had been taken moreover not with resignation, not with qualifications or reserves, however bland; it had been taken with avidity, with gratitude, with a grace of gentleness that supplanted explanations. The very liberality of this accommodation might indeed have appeared in the event to give its own account of the matter—as if it had fairly written the Princess down as a person of variations and had accordingly conformed but to a rule of tact in accepting these caprices for law. The caprice actually prevailing happened to be that the advent of one of the ladies anywhere should, till the fit had changed, become the sign, unfailingly, of the advent of the other; and it was emblazoned, in rich colour, on the bright face of this period, that Mrs. Verver only wished to know, on any occasion, what was expected of her, only held herself there for instructions, in order even to better them if possible. The two young women, while the passage lasted, became again very much the companions of other days, the days of Charlotte's prolonged visits to the admiring and bountiful Maggie, the days when equality of condition for them had been all the result of the latter's native vagueness about her own advantages. The earlier elements flushed into life again, the frequency, the intimacy, the high pitch of accompanying expression—appreciation, endearment, confidence; the rarer charm produced in each by this active contribution to the felicity of the other: all enhanced, furthermore—enhanced or qualified, who should say which?—by a new note of diplomacy, almost of anxiety, just sensible on Charlotte's part in particular; of intensity of observance, in the matter of appeal and response, in the matter of making sure the Princess might be disposed or gratified, that resembled an attempt to play again, with more refinement, at disparity of relation. Charlotte's attitude had, in short, its moments of flowering into pretty excesses of civility, self-effacements in the presence of others, sudden little formalisms of suggestion and recognition, that might have represented her sense of the duty of not "losing sight" of a social distinction. This impression came out most for Maggie when, in their easier intervals, they had only themselves to regard, and when her companion's inveteracy of never passing first, of not sitting till she was seated, of not interrupting till she appeared to give leave, of not forgetting, too, familiarly, that in addition to being important she was also sensitive, had the effect of throwing over their intercourse a kind of silver tissue of decorum. It hung there above them like a canopy of state, a reminder that though the lady-in-waiting was an established favourite, safe in her position, a little queen, however, good-natured, was always a little queen and might, with small warning, remember it.

And yet another of these concomitants of feverish success, all the while, was the perception that in another quarter too things were being made easy. Charlotte's alacrity in meeting her had, in one sense, operated slightly overmuch as an intervention: it had begun to reabsorb her at the very hour of her husband's showing her that, to be all there, as the phrase was, he likewise only required—as one of the other phrases was too—the straight tip. She had heard him talk about the straight tip, in his moods of amusement at English slang, in his remarkable displays of assimilative power, power worthy of better causes and higher inspirations; and he had taken it from her, at need, in a way that, certainly, in the first glow of relief, had made her brief interval seem large. Then, however, immediately, and even though superficially, there had declared itself a readjustment of relations to which she was, once more, practically a little sacrificed. "I must do everything," she had said, "without letting papa see what I do—at least till it's done!" but she scarce knew how she proposed, even for the next few days, to blind or beguile this participant in her life. What had in fact promptly enough happened, she presently recognised, was that if her stepmother had beautifully taken possession of her, and if she had virtually been rather snatched again thereby from her husband's side, so, on the other hand, this had, with as little delay, entailed some very charming assistance for her in Eaton Square. When she went home with Charlotte, from whatever happy demonstration, for the benefit of the world in which they supposed themselves to live, that there was no smallest reason why their closer association shouldn't be public and acclaimed—at these times she regularly found that Amerigo had come either to sit with his father-in-law in the absence of the ladies, or to make, on his side, precisely some such display of the easy working of the family life as would represent the equivalent of her excursions with Charlotte. Under this particular impression it was that everything in Maggie most melted and went to pieces—every thing, that is, that belonged to her disposition to challenge the perfection of their common state. It divided them again, that was true, this particular turn of the tide—cut them up afresh into pairs and parties; quite as if a sense for the equilibrium was what, between them all, had most power of insistence; quite as if Amerigo himself were all the while, at bottom, equally thinking of it and minding it. But, as against that, he was making her father not miss her, and he could have rendered neither of them a more excellent service. He was acting in short on a cue, the cue given him by observation; it had been enough for him to see the shade of change in her behaviour; his instinct for relations, the most exquisite conceivable, prompted him immediately to meet and match the difference, to play somehow into its hands. That was what it was, she renewedly felt, to have married a man who was, sublimely, a gentleman; so that, in spite of her not wanting to translate ALL their delicacies into the grossness of discussion, she yet found again and again, in Portland Place, moments for saying: "If I didn't love you, you know, for yourself, I should still love you for HIM." He looked at her, after such speeches, as Charlotte looked, in Eaton Square, when she called HER attention to his benevolence: through the dimness of the almost musing smile that took account of her extravagance, harmless though it might be, as a tendency to reckon with. "But my poor child," Charlotte might under this pressure have been on the point of replying, "that's the way nice people ARE, all round—so that why should one be surprised about it? We're all nice together—as why shouldn't we be? If we hadn't been we wouldn't have gone far—and I consider that we've gone very far indeed. Why should you 'take on' as if you weren't a perfect dear yourself, capable of all the sweetest things?—as if you hadn't in fact grown up in an atmosphere, the atmosphere of all the good things that I recognised, even of old, as soon as I came near you, and that you've allowed me now, between you, to make so blessedly my own." Mrs. Verver might in fact have but just failed to make another point, a point charmingly natural to her as a grateful and irreproachable wife. "It isn't a bit wonderful, I may also remind you, that your husband should find, when opportunity permits, worse things to do than to go about with mine. I happen, love, to appreciate my husband—I happen perfectly to understand that his acquaintance should be cultivated and his company enjoyed."

Some such happily-provoked remarks as these, from Charlotte, at the other house, had been in the air, but we have seen how there was also in the air, for our young woman, as an emanation from the same source, a distilled difference of which the very principle was to keep down objections and retorts. That impression came back—it had its hours of doing so; and it may interest us on the ground of its having prompted in Maggie a final reflection, a reflection out of the heart of which a light flashed for her like a great flower grown in a night. As soon as this light had spread a little it produced in some quarters a surprising distinctness, made her of a sudden ask herself why there should have been even for three days the least obscurity. The perfection of her success, decidedly, was like some strange shore to which she had been noiselessly ferried and where, with a start, she found herself quaking at the thought that the boat might have put off again and left her. The word for it, the word that flashed the light, was that they were TREATING her, that they were proceeding with her—and, for that matter, with her father—by a plan that was the exact counterpart of her own. It was not from her that they took their cue, but—and this was what in particular made her sit up—from each other; and with a depth of unanimity, an exact coincidence of inspiration that, when once her attention had begun to fix it, struck her as staring out at her in recovered identities of behaviour, expression and tone. They had a view of her situation, and of the possible forms her own consciousness of it might take—a view determined by the change of attitude they had had, ever so subtly, to recognise in her on their return from Matcham. They had had to read into this small and all-but-suppressed variation a mute comment—on they didn't quite know what; and it now arched over the Princess's head like a vault of bold span that important communication between them on the subject couldn't have failed of being immediate. This new perception bristled for her, as we have said, with odd intimations, but questions unanswered played in and out of it as well—the question, for instance, of why such promptitude of harmony SHOULD have been important. Ah, when she began to recover, piece by piece, the process became lively; she might have been picking small shining diamonds out of the sweepings of her ordered house. She bent, in this pursuit, over her dust-bin; she challenged to the last grain the refuse of her innocent economy. Then it was that the dismissed vision of Amerigo, that evening, in arrest at the door of her salottino while her eyes, from her placed chair, took him in—then it was that this immense little memory gave out its full power. Since the question was of doors, she had afterwards, she now saw, shut it out; she had responsibly shut him in, as we have understood, shut in there with her sentient self, only the fact of his reappearance and the plenitude of his presence. These things had been testimony, after all, to supersede any other, for on the spot, even while she looked, the warmly-washing wave had travelled far up the strand. She had subsequently lived, for hours she couldn't count, under the dizzying, smothering welter positively in submarine depths where everything came to her through walls of emerald and mother-of-pearl; though indeed she had got her head above them, for breath, when face to face with Charlotte again, on the morrow, in Eaton Square. Meanwhile, none the less, as was so apparent, the prior, the prime impression had remained, in the manner of a spying servant, on the other side of the barred threshold; a witness availing himself, in time, of the lightest pretext to re-enter. It was as if he had found this pretext in her observed necessity of comparing—comparing the obvious common elements in her husband's and her stepmother's ways of now "taking" her. With or without her witness, at any rate, she was led by comparison to a sense of the quantity of earnest intention and, operating so harmoniously, between her companions; and it was in the mitigated midnight of these approximations that she had made out the promise of her dawn.

It was a worked-out scheme for their not wounding her, for their behaving to her quite nobly; to which each had, in some winning way, induced the other to contribute, and which therefore, so far as that went, proved that she had become with them a subject of intimate study. Quickly, quickly, on a certain alarm taken, eagerly and anxiously, before they SHOULD, without knowing it, wound her, they had signalled from house to house their clever idea, the idea by which, for all these days, her own idea had been profiting. They had built her in with their purpose—which was why, above her, a vault seemed more heavily to arch; so that she sat there, in the solid chamber of her helplessness, as in a bath of benevolence artfully prepared for her, over the brim of which she could but just manage to see by stretching her neck. Baths of benevolence were very well, but, at least, unless one were a patient of some sort, a nervous eccentric or a lost child, one was usually not so immersed save by one's request. It wasn't in the least what she had requested. She had flapped her little wings as a symbol of desired flight, not merely as a plea for a more gilded cage and an extra allowance of lumps of sugar. Above all she hadn't complained, not by the quaver of a syllable—so what wound in particular had she shown her fear of receiving? What wound HAD she received—as to which she had exchanged the least word with them? If she had ever whined or moped they might have had some reason; but she hadn't, she was sure, done that went, proved that she had become with them a subject of intimate study, in strong language—if she had been, from beginning to end, anything but pliable and mild. It all came back, in consequence, to some required process of their own, a process operating, quite positively, as a precaution and a policy. They had got her into the bath and, for consistency with themselves—which was with each other—must keep her there. In that condition she wouldn't interfere with the policy, which was established, which was arranged. Her thought, over this, arrived at a great intensity—had indeed its pauses and timidities, but always to take afterwards a further and lighter spring. The ground was well-nigh covered by the time she had made out her husband and his colleague as directly interested in preventing her freedom of movement. Policy or no policy, it was they themselves who were arranged. She must be kept in position so as not to DISarrange them. It fitted immensely together, the whole thing, as soon as she could give them a motive; for, strangely as it had by this time begun to appear to herself, she had hitherto not imagined them sustained by an ideal distinguishably different from her own. Of course they were arranged—all four arranged; but what had the basis of their life been, precisely, but that they were arranged together? Amerigo and Charlotte were arranged together, but she—to confine the matter only to herself—was arranged apart. It rushed over her, the full sense of all this, with quite another rush from that of the breaking wave of ten days before; and as her father himself seemed not to meet the vaguely-clutching hand with which, during the first shock of complete perception, she tried to steady herself, she felt very much alone.

XXVII

There had been, from far back—that is from the Christmas time on—a plan that the parent and the child should "do something lovely" together, and they had recurred to it on occasion, nursed it and brought it up theoretically, though without as yet quite allowing it to put its feet to the ground. The most it had done was to try a few steps on the drawing-room carpet, with much attendance, on either side, much holding up and guarding, much anticipation, in fine, of awkwardness or accident. Their companions, by the same token, had constantly assisted at the performance, following the experiment with sympathy and gaiety, and never so full of applause, Maggie now made out for herself, as when the infant project had kicked its little legs most wildly—kicked them, for all the world, across the Channel and half the Continent, kicked them over the Pyrenees and innocently crowed out some rich Spanish name. She asked herself at present if it had been a "real" belief that they were but wanting, for some such adventure, to snatch their moment; whether either had at any instant seen it as workable, save in the form of a toy to dangle before the other, that they should take flight, without wife or husband, for one more look, "before they died," at the Madrid pictures as well as for a drop of further weak delay in respect to three or four possible prizes, privately offered, rarities of the first water, responsibly reported on and profusely photographed, still patiently awaiting their noiseless arrival in retreats to which the clue had not otherwise been given away. The vision dallied with during the duskier days in Eaton Square had stretched to the span of three or four weeks of springtime for the total adventure, three or four weeks in the very spirit, after all, of their regular life, as their regular life had been persisting; full of shared mornings, afternoons, evenings, walks, drives, "looks-in," at old places, on vague chances; full also, in especial, of that purchased social ease, the sense of the comfort and credit of their house, which had essentially the perfection of something paid for, but which "came," on the whole, so cheap that it might have been felt as costing—as costing the parent and child—nothing. It was for Maggie to wonder, at present, if she had been sincere about their going, to ask herself whether she would have stuck to their plan even if nothing had happened.

Her view of the impossibility of sticking to it now may give us the measure of her sense that everything had happened. A difference had been made in her relation to each of her companions, and what it compelled her to say to herself was that to behave as she might have behaved before would be to act, for Amerigo and Charlotte, with the highest hypocrisy. She saw in these days that a journey abroad with her father would, more than anything else, have amounted, on his part and her own, to a last expression of an ecstasy of confidence, and that the charm of the idea, in fact, had been in some such sublimity. Day after day she put off the moment of "speaking," as she inwardly and very comprehensively called it—speaking, that is, to her father; and all the more that she was ridden by a strange suspense as to his himself breaking silence. She gave him time, gave him, during several days, that morning, that noon, that night, and the next and the next and the next; even made up her mind that if he stood off longer it would be proof conclusive that he too wasn't at peace. They would then have been, all successfully, throwing dust in each other's eyes; and it would be at last as if they must turn away their faces, since the silver mist that protected them had begun to grow sensibly thin. Finally, at the end of April, she decided that if he should say nothing for another period of twenty-four hours she must take it as showing that they were, in her private phraseology, lost; so little possible sincerity could there be in pretending to care for a journey to Spain at the approach of a summer that already promised to be hot. Such a proposal, on his lips, such an extravagance of optimism, would be HIS way of being consistent—for that he didn't really want to move, or to move further, at the worst, than back to Fawns again, could only signify that he wasn't, at heart, contented. What he wanted, at any rate, and what he didn't want were, in the event, put to the proof for Maggie just in time to give her a fresh wind. She had been dining, with her husband, in Eaton Square, on the occasion of hospitality offered by Mr. and Mrs. Verver to Lord and Lady Castledean. The propriety of some demonstration of this sort had been for many days before our group, the question reduced to the mere issue of which of the two houses should first take the field. The issue had been easily settled—in the manner of every issue referred in any degree to Amerigo and Charlotte: the initiative obviously belonged to Mrs. Verver, who had gone to Matcham while Maggie had stayed away, and the evening in Eaton Square might have passed for a demonstration all the more personal that the dinner had been planned on "intimate" lines. Six other guests only, in addition to the host and the hostess of Matcham, made up the company, and each of these persons had for Maggie the interest of an attested connection with the Easter revels at that visionary house. Their common memory of an occasion that had clearly left behind it an ineffaceable charm—this air of beatific reference, less subdued in the others than in Amerigo and Charlotte, lent them, together, an inscrutable comradeship against which the young woman's imagination broke in a small vain wave.

It wasn't that she wished she had been of the remembered party and possessed herself of its secrets; for she didn't care about its secrets—she could concern herself at present, absolutely, with no secret but her own. What occurred was simply that she became aware, at a stroke, of the quantity of further nourishment required by her own, and of the amount of it she might somehow extract from these people; whereby she rose, of a sudden, to the desire to possess and use them, even to the extent of braving, of fairly defying, of directly exploiting, of possibly quite enjoying, under cover of an evil duplicity, the felt element of curiosity with which they regarded her. Once she was conscious of the flitting wing of this last impression—the perception, irresistible, that she was something for their queer experience, just as they were something for hers—there was no limit to her conceived design of not letting them escape. She went and went, again, to-night, after her start was taken; went, positively, as she had felt herself going, three weeks before, on the morning when the vision of her father and his wife awaiting her together in the breakfast-room had been so determinant. In this other scene it was Lady Castledean who was determinant, who kindled the light, or at all events the heat, and who acted on the nerves; Lady Castledean whom she knew she, so oddly, didn't like, in spite of reasons upon reasons, the biggest diamonds on the yellowest hair, the longest lashes on the prettiest, falsest eyes, the oldest lace on the most violet velvet, the rightest manner on the wrongest assumption. Her ladyship's assumption was that she kept, at every moment of her life, every advantage—it made her beautifully soft, very nearly generous; so she didn't distinguish the little protuberant eyes of smaller social insects, often endowed with such a range, from the other decorative spots on their bodies and wings. Maggie had liked, in London, and in the world at large, so many more people than she had thought it right to fear, right even to so much as judge, that it positively quickened her fever to have to recognise, in this case, such a lapse of all the sequences. It was only that a charming clever woman wondered about her—that is wondered about her as Amerigo's wife, and wondered, moreover, with the intention of kindness and the spontaneity, almost, of surprise.

The point of view—that one—was what she read in their free contemplation, in that of the whole eight; there was something in Amerigo to be explained, and she was passed about, all tenderly and expertly, like a dressed doll held, in the right manner, by its firmly-stuffed middle, for the account she could give. She might have been made to give it by pressure of her stomach; she might have been expected to articulate, with a rare imitation of nature, "Oh yes, I'm HERE all the while; I'm also in my way a solid little fact and I cost originally a great deal of money: cost, that is, my father, for my outfit, and let in my husband for an amount of pains—toward my training—that money would scarce represent." Well, she WOULD meet them in some such way, and she translated her idea into action, after dinner, before they dispersed, by engaging them all, unconventionally, almost violently, to dine with her in Portland Place, just as they were, if they didn't mind the same party, which was the party she wanted. Oh she was going, she was going—she could feel it afresh; it was a good deal as if she had sneezed ten times or had suddenly burst into a comic song. There were breaks in the connection, as there would be hitches in the process; she didn't wholly see, yet, what they would do for her, nor quite how, herself, she should handle them; but she was dancing up and down, beneath her propriety, with the thought that she had at least begun something—she so fairly liked to feel that she was a point for convergence of wonder. It wasn't after all, either, that THEIR wonder so much signified—that of the cornered six, whom she glimmered before her that she might still live to drive about like a flock of sheep: the intensity of her consciousness, its sharpest savour, was in the theory of her having diverted, having, as they said, captured the attention of Amerigo and Charlotte, at neither of whom, all the while, did she so much as once look. She had pitched them in with the six, for that matter, so far as they themselves were concerned; they had dropped, for the succession of minutes, out of contact with their function—had, in short, startled and impressed, abandoned their post. "They're paralysed, they're paralysed!" she commented, deep within; so much it helped her own apprehension to hang together that they should suddenly lose their bearings.

Her grasp of appearances was thus out of proportion to her view of causes; but it came to her then and there that if she could only get the facts of appearance straight, only jam them down into their place, the reasons lurking behind them, kept uncertain, for the eyes, by their wavering and shifting, wouldn't perhaps be able to help showing. It wasn't of course that the Prince and Mrs. Verver marvelled at her being civil to their friends; it was rather, precisely, that civil was just what she wasn't: she had so departed from any such custom of delicate approach—approach by the permitted note, the suggested "if," the accepted vagueness—as would enable the people in question to put her off if they wished. And the profit of her plan, the effect of the violence she was willing to let it go for, was exactly in their BEING the people in question, people she had seemed to be rather shy of before and for whom she suddenly opened her mouth so wide. Later on, we may add, with the ground soon covered by her agitated but resolute step, it was to cease to matter what people they were or weren't; but meanwhile the particular sense of them that she had taken home to-night had done her the service of seeming to break the ice where that formation was thickest. Still more unexpectedly, the service might have been the same for her father; inasmuch as, immediately, when everyone had gone, he did exactly what she had been waiting for and despairing of—and did it, as he did everything, with a simplicity that left any purpose of sounding him deeper, of drawing him out further, of going, in his own frequent phrase, "behind" what he said, nothing whatever to do. He brought it out straight, made it bravely and beautifully irrelevant, save for the plea of what they should lose by breaking the charm: "I guess we won't go down there after all, will we, Mag?—just when it's getting so pleasant here." That was all, with nothing to lead up to it; but it was done for her at a stroke, and done, not less, more rather, for Amerigo and Charlotte, on whom the immediate effect, as she secretly, as she almost breathlessly measured it, was prodigious. Everything now so fitted for her to everything else that she could feel the effect as prodigious even while sticking to her policy of giving the pair no look. There were thus some five wonderful minutes during which they loomed, to her sightless eyes, on either side of her, larger than they had ever loomed before, larger than life, larger than thought, larger than any danger or any safety. There was thus a space of time, in fine, fairly vertiginous for her, during which she took no more account of them than if they were not in the room.

She had never, never treated them in any such way—not even just now, when she had plied her art upon the Matcham band; her present manner was an intenser exclusion, and the air was charged with their silence while she talked with her other companion as if she had nothing but him to consider. He had given her the note amazingly, by his allusion to the pleasantness—that of such an occasion as his successful dinner—which might figure as their bribe for renouncing; so that it was all as if they were speaking selfishly, counting on a repetition of just such extensions of experience. Maggie achieved accordingly an act of unprecedented energy, threw herself into her father's presence as by the absolute consistency with which she held his eyes; saying to herself, at the same time that she smiled and talked and inaugurated her system, "What does he mean by it? That's the question—what does he mean?" but studying again all the signs in him that recent anxiety had made familiar and counting the stricken minutes on the part of the others. It was in their silence that the others loomed, as she felt; she had had no measure, she afterwards knew, of this duration, but it drew out and out—really to what would have been called in simpler conditions awkwardness—as if she herself were stretching the cord. Ten minutes later, however, in the homeward carriage, to which her husband, cutting delay short, had proceeded at the first announcement, ten minutes later she was to stretch it almost to breaking. The Prince had permitted her to linger much less, before his move to the door, than they usually lingered at the gossiping close of such evenings; which she, all responsive, took for a sign of his impatience to modify for her the odd effect of his not having, and of Charlotte's not having, instantly acclaimed the issue of the question debated, or more exactly, settled, before them. He had had time to become aware of this possible impression in her, and his virtually urging her into the carriage was connected with his feeling that he must take action on the new ground. A certain ambiguity in her would absolutely have tormented him; but he had already found something to soothe and correct—as to which she had, on her side, a shrewd notion of what it would be. She was herself, for that matter, prepared, and she was, of a truth, as she took her seat in the brougham, amazed at her preparation. It allowed her scarce an interval; she brought it straight out.

"I was certain that was what father would say if I should leave him alone. I HAVE been leaving him alone, and you see the effect. He hates now to move—he likes too much to be with us. But if you see the effect"—she felt herself magnificently keeping it up—"perhaps you don't see the cause. The cause, my dear, is too lovely."

Her husband, on taking his place beside her, had, during a minute or two, for her watching sense, neither said nor done anything; he had been, for that sense, as if thinking, waiting, deciding: yet it was still before he spoke that he, as she felt it to be, definitely acted. He put his arm round her and drew her close—indulged in the demonstration, the long, firm embrace by his single arm, the infinite pressure of her whole person to his own, that such opportunities had so often suggested and prescribed. Held, accordingly, and, as she could but too intimately feel, exquisitely solicited, she had said the thing she was intending and desiring to say, and as to which she felt, even more than she felt anything else, that whatever he might do she mustn't be irresponsible. Yes, she was in his exerted grasp, and she knew what that was; but she was at the same time in the grasp of her conceived responsibility, and the extraordinary thing was that, of the two intensities, the second was presently to become the sharper. He took his time for it meanwhile, but he met her speech after a fashion.

"The cause of your father's deciding not to go?"

"Yes, and of my having wanted to let it act for him quietly—I mean without my insistence." She had, in her compressed state, another pause, and it made her feel as if she were immensely resisting. Strange enough was this sense for her, and altogether new, the sense of possessing, by miraculous help, some advantage that, absolutely then and there, in the carriage, as they rolled, she might either give up or keep. Strange, inexpressibly strange—so distinctly she saw that if she did give it up she should somehow give up everything for ever. And what her husband's grasp really meant, as her very bones registered, was that she SHOULD give it up: it was exactly for this that he had resorted to unfailing magic. He KNEW HOW to resort to it—he could be, on occasion, as she had lately more than ever learned, so munificent a lover: all of which was, precisely, a part of the character she had never ceased to regard in him as princely, a part of his large and beautiful ease, his genius for charm, for intercourse, for expression, for life. She should have but to lay her head back on his shoulder with a certain movement to make it definite for him that she didn't resist. To this, as they went, every throb of her consciousness prompted her—every throb, that is, but one, the throb of her deeper need to know where she "really" was. By the time she had uttered the rest of her idea, therefore, she was still keeping her head and intending to keep it; though she was also staring out of the carriage-window with eyes into which the tears of suffered pain had risen, indistinguishable, perhaps, happily, in the dusk. She was making an effort that horribly hurt her, and, as she couldn't cry out, her eyes swam in her silence. With them, all the same, through the square opening beside her, through the grey panorama of the London night, she achieved the feat of not losing sight of what she wanted; and her lips helped and protected her by being able to be gay. "It's not to leave YOU, my dear—for that he'll give up anything; just as he would go off anywhere, I think, you know, if you would go with him. I mean you and he alone," Maggie pursued with her gaze out of her window.

For which Amerigo's answer again took him a moment. "Ah, the dear old boy! You would like me to propose him something—?"

"Well, if you think you could bear it."

"And leave," the Prince asked, "you and Charlotte alone?"

"Why not?" Maggie had also to wait a minute, but when she spoke it came clear. "Why shouldn't Charlotte be just one of MY reasons—my not liking to leave her? She has always been so good, so perfect, to me—but never so wonderfully as just now. We have somehow been more together—thinking, for the time, almost only of each other; it has been quite as in old days." And she proceeded consummately, for she felt it as consummate: "It's as if we had been missing each other, had got a little apart—though going on so side by side. But the good moments, if one only waits for them," she hastened to add, "come round of themselves. Moreover you've seen for yourself, since you've made it up so to father; feeling, for yourself, in your beautiful way, every difference, every air that blows; not having to be told or pushed, only being perfect to live with, through your habit of kindness and your exquisite instincts. But of course you've seen, all the while, that both he and I have deeply felt how you've managed; managed that he hasn't been too much alone and that I, on my side, haven't appeared, to—what you might call—neglect him. This is always," she continued, "what I can never bless you enough for; of all the good things you've done for me you've never done anything better." She went on explaining as for the pleasure of explaining—even though knowing he must recognise, as a part of his easy way too, her description of his large liberality. "Your taking the child down yourself, those days, and your coming, each time, to bring him away—nothing in the world, nothing you could have invented, would have kept father more under the charm. Besides, you know how you've always suited him, and how you've always so beautifully let it seem to him that he suits you. Only it has been, these last weeks, as if you wished—just in order to please him—to remind him of it afresh. So there it is," she wound up; "it's your doing. You've produced your effect—that of his wanting not to be, even for a month or two, where you're not. He doesn't want to bother or bore you—THAT, I think, you know, he never has done; and if you'll only give me time I'll come round again to making it my care, as always, that he shan't. But he can't bear you out of his sight."

She had kept it up and up, filling it out, crowding it in; and all, really, without difficulty, for it was, every word of it, thanks to a long evolution of feeling, what she had been primed to the brim with. She made the picture, forced it upon him, hung it before him; remembering, happily, how he had gone so far, one day, supported by the Principino, as to propose the Zoo in Eaton Square, to carry with him there, on the spot, under this pleasant inspiration, both his elder and his younger companion, with the latter of whom he had taken the tone that they were introducing Granddaddy, Granddaddy nervous and rather funking it, to lions and tigers more or less at large. Touch by touch she thus dropped into her husband's silence the truth about his good nature and his good manners; and it was this demonstration of his virtue, precisely, that added to the strangeness, even for herself, of her failing as yet to yield to him. It would be a question but of the most trivial act of surrender, the vibration of a nerve, the mere movement of a muscle; but the act grew important between them just through her doing perceptibly nothing, nothing but talk in the very tone that would naturally have swept her into tenderness. She knew more and more—every lapsing minute taught her—how he might by a single rightness make her cease to watch him; that rightness, a million miles removed from the queer actual, falling so short, which would consist of his breaking out to her divinely, indulgently, with the last happy inconsequence. "Come away with me, somewhere, YOU—and then we needn't think, we needn't even talk, of anything, of anyone else:" five words like that would answer her, would break her utterly down. But they were the only ones that would so serve. She waited for them, and there was a supreme instant when, by the testimony of all the rest of him, she seemed to feel them in his heart and on his lips; only they didn't sound, and as that made her wait again so it made her more intensely watch. This in turn showed her that he too watched and waited, and how much he had expected something that he now felt wouldn't come. Yes, it wouldn't come if he didn't answer her, if he but said the wrong things instead of the right. If he could say the right everything would come—it hung by a hair that everything might crystallise for their recovered happiness at his touch. This possibility glowed at her, however, for fifty seconds, only then to turn cold, and as it fell away from her she felt the chill of reality and knew again, all but pressed to his heart and with his breath upon her cheek, the slim rigour of her attitude, a rigour beyond that of her natural being. They had silences, at last, that were almost crudities of mutual resistance—silences that persisted through his felt effort to treat her recurrence to the part he had lately played, to interpret all the sweetness of her so talking to him, as a manner of making love to him. Ah, it was no such manner, heaven knew, for Maggie; she could make love, if this had been in question, better than that! On top of which it came to her presently to say, keeping in with what she had already spoken: "Except of course that, for the question of going off somewhere, he'd go readily, quite delightedly, with you. I verily believe he'd like to have you for a while to himself."

"Do you mean he thinks of proposing it?" the Prince after a moment sounded.

"Oh no—he doesn't ask, as you must so often have seen. But I believe he'd go 'like a shot,' as you say, if you were to suggest it."

It had the air, she knew, of a kind of condition made, and she had asked herself while she spoke if it wouldn't cause his arm to let her go. The fact that it didn't suggested to her that she had made him, of a sudden, still more intensely think, think with such concentration that he could do but one thing at once. And it was precisely as if the concentration had the next moment been proved in him. He took a turn inconsistent with the superficial impression—a jump that made light of their approach to gravity and represented for her the need in him to gain time. That she made out, was his drawback—that the warning from her had come to him, and had come to Charlotte, after all, too suddenly. That they were in face of it rearranging, that they had to rearrange, was all before her again; yet to do as they would like they must enjoy a snatch, longer or shorter, of recovered independence. Amerigo, for the instant, was but doing as he didn't like, and it was as if she were watching his effort without disguise. "What's your father's idea, this year, then, about Fawns? Will he go at Whitsuntide, and will he then stay on?"

Maggie went through the form of thought. "He will really do, I imagine, as he has, in so many ways, so often done before; do whatever may seem most agreeable to yourself. And there's of course always Charlotte to be considered. Only their going early to Fawns, if they do go," she said, "needn't in the least entail your and my going."

"Ah," Amerigo echoed, "it needn't in the least entail your and my going?"

"We can do as we like. What they may do needn't trouble us, since they're by good fortune perfectly happy together."

"Oh," the Prince returned, "your father's never so happy as with you near him to enjoy his being so."

"Well, I may enjoy it," said Maggie, "but I'm not the cause of it."

"You're the cause," her husband declared, "of the greater part of everything that's good among us." But she received this tribute in silence, and the next moment he pursued: "If Mrs. Verver has arrears of time with you to make up, as you say, she'll scarcely do it—or you scarcely will—by our cutting, your and my cutting, too loose."

"I see what you mean," Maggie mused.

He let her for a little to give her attention to it; after which, "Shall I just quite, of a sudden," he asked, "propose him a journey?"

Maggie hesitated, but she brought forth the fruit of reflection. "It would have the merit that Charlotte then would be with me—with me, I mean, so much more. Also that I shouldn't, by choosing such a time for going away, seem unconscious and ungrateful, seem not to respond, seem in fact rather to wish to shake her off. I should respond, on the contrary, very markedly—by being here alone with her for a month."

"And would you like to be here alone with her for a month?"

"I could do with it beautifully. Or we might even," she said quite gaily, "go together down to Fawns."

"You could be so very content without me?" the Prince presently inquired.

"Yes, my own dear—if you could be content for a while with father. That would keep me up. I might, for the time," she went on, "go to stay there with Charlotte; or, better still, she might come to Portland Place."

"Oho!" said the Prince with cheerful vagueness.

"I should feel, you see," she continued, "that the two of us were showing the same sort of kindness."

Amerigo thought. "The two of us? Charlotte and I?"

Maggie again hesitated. "You and I, darling."

"I see, I see"—he promptly took it in. "And what reason shall I give—give, I mean, your father?"

"For asking him to go off? Why, the very simplest—if you conscientiously can. The desire," said Maggie, "to be agreeable to him. Just that only."

Something in this reply made her husband again reflect. "'Conscientiously?' Why shouldn't I conscientiously? It wouldn't, by your own contention," he developed, "represent any surprise for him. I must strike him sufficiently as, at the worst, the last person in the world to wish to do anything to hurt him."

Ah, there it was again, for Maggie—the note already sounded, the note of the felt need of not working harm! Why this precautionary view, she asked herself afresh, when her father had complained, at the very least, as little as herself? With their stillness together so perfect, what had suggested so, around them, the attitude of sparing them? Her inner vision fixed it once more, this attitude, saw it, in the others, as vivid and concrete, extended it straight from her companion to Charlotte. Before she was well aware, accordingly, she had echoed in this intensity of thought Amerigo's last words. "You're the last person in the world to wish to do anything to hurt him."

She heard herself, heard her tone, after she had spoken, and heard it the more that, for a minute after, she felt her husband's eyes on her face, very close, too close for her to see him. He was looking at her because he was struck, and looking hard—though his answer, when it came, was straight enough. "Why, isn't that just what we have been talking about—that I've affected you as fairly studying his comfort and his pleasure? He might show his sense of it," the Prince went on, "by proposing to ME an excursion."

"And you would go with him?" Maggie immediately asked.

He hung fire but an instant. "Per Dio!"

She also had her pause, but she broke it—since gaiety was in the air—with an intense smile. "You can say that safely, because the proposal's one that, of his own motion, he won't make."

She couldn't have narrated afterwards—and in fact was at a loss to tell herself—by what transition, what rather marked abruptness of change in their personal relation, their drive came to its end with a kind of interval established, almost confessed to, between them. She felt it in the tone with which he repeated, after her, "'Safely'—?"

"Safely as regards being thrown with him perhaps after all, in such a case, too long. He's a person to think you might easily feel yourself to be. So it won't," Maggie said, "come from father. He's too modest."

Their eyes continued to meet on it, from corner to corner of the brougham. "Oh your modesty, between you—!" But he still smiled for it. "So that unless I insist—?"

"We shall simply go on as we are."

"Well, we're going on beautifully," he answered—though by no means with the effect it would have had if their mute transaction, that of attempted capture and achieved escape, had not taken place. As Maggie said nothing, none the less, to gainsay his remark, it was open to him to find himself the next moment conscious of still another idea. "I wonder if it would do. I mean for me to break in."

"'To break in'—?"

"Between your father and his wife. But there would be a way," he said—"we can make Charlotte ask him." And then as Maggie herself now wondered, echoing it again: "We can suggest to her to suggest to him that he shall let me take him off."

"Oh!" said Maggie.

"Then if he asks her why I so suddenly break out she'll be able to tell him the reason."

They were stopping, and the footman, who had alighted, had rung at the house-door. "That you think it would be so charming?"

"That I think it would be so charming. That we've persuaded HER will be convincing."

"I see," Maggie went on while the footman came back to let them out. "I see," she said again; though she felt a little disconcerted. What she really saw, of a sudden, was that her stepmother might report her as above all concerned for the proposal, and this brought her back her need that her father shouldn't think her concerned in any degree for anything. She alighted the next instant with a slight sense of defeat; her husband, to let her out, had passed before her, and, a little in advance, he awaited her on the edge of the low terrace, a step high, that preceded their open entrance, on either side of which one of their servants stood. The sense of a life tremendously ordered and fixed rose before her, and there was something in Amerigo's very face, while his eyes again met her own through the dusky lamplight, that was like a conscious reminder of it. He had answered her, just before, distinctly, and it appeared to leave her nothing to say. It was almost as if, having planned for the last word, she saw him himself enjoying it. It was almost as if—in the strangest way in the world—he were paying her back, by the production of a small pang, that of a new uneasiness, for the way she had slipped from him during their drive.

XXVIII

Maggie's new uneasiness might have had time to drop, inasmuch as she not only was conscious, during several days that followed, of no fresh indication for it to feed on, but was even struck, in quite another way, with an augmentation of the symptoms of that difference she had taken it into her head to work for. She recognised by the end of a week that if she had been in a manner caught up her father had been not less so—with the effect of her husband's and his wife's closing in, together, round them, and of their all having suddenly begun, as a party of four, to lead a life gregarious, and from that reason almost hilarious, so far as the easy sound of it went, as never before. It might have been an accident and a mere coincidence—so at least she said to herself at first; but a dozen chances that furthered the whole appearance had risen to the surface, pleasant pretexts, oh certainly pleasant, as pleasant as Amerigo in particular could make them, for associated undertakings, quite for shared adventures, for its always turning out, amusingly, that they wanted to do very much the same thing at the same time and in the same way. Funny all this was, to some extent, in the light of the fact that the father and daughter, for so long, had expressed so few positive desires; yet it would be sufficiently natural that if Amerigo and Charlotte HAD at last got a little tired of each other's company they should find their relief not so much in sinking to the rather low level of their companions as in wishing to pull the latter into the train in which they so constantly moved. "We're in the train," Maggie mutely reflected after the dinner in Eaton Square with Lady Castledean; "we've suddenly waked up in it and found ourselves rushing along, very much as if we had been put in during sleep—shoved, like a pair of labelled boxes, into the van. And since I wanted to 'go' I'm certainly going," she might have added; "I'm moving without trouble—they're doing it all for us: it's wonderful how they understand and how perfectly it succeeds." For that was the thing she had most immediately to acknowledge: it seemed as easy for them to make a quartette as it had formerly so long appeared for them to make a pair of couples—this latter being thus a discovery too absurdly belated. The only point at which, day after day, the success appeared at all qualified was represented, as might have been said, by her irresistible impulse to give her father a clutch when the train indulged in one of its occasional lurches. Then—there was no denying it—his eyes and her own met; so that they were themselves doing active violence, as against the others, to that very spirit of union, or at least to that very achievement of change, which she had taken the field to invoke.

The maximum of change was reached, no doubt, the day the Matcham party dined in Portland Place; the day, really perhaps, of Maggie's maximum of social glory, in the sense of its showing for her own occasion, her very own, with every one else extravagantly rallying and falling in, absolutely conspiring to make her its heroine. It was as if her father himself, always with more initiative as a guest than as a host, had dabbled too in the conspiracy; and the impression was not diminished by the presence of the Assinghams, likewise very much caught-up, now, after something of a lull, by the side-wind of all the rest of the motion, and giving our young woman, so far at least as Fanny was concerned, the sense of some special intention of encouragement and applause. Fanny, who had not been present at the other dinner, thanks to a preference entertained and expressed by Charlotte, made a splendid show at this one, in new orange-coloured velvet with multiplied turquoises, and with a confidence, furthermore, as different as possible, her hostess inferred, from her too-marked betrayal of a belittled state at Matcham. Maggie was not indifferent to her own opportunity to redress this balance—which seemed, for the hour, part of a general rectification; she liked making out for herself that on the high level of Portland Place, a spot exempt, on all sorts of grounds, from jealous jurisdictions, her friend could feel as "good" as any one, and could in fact at moments almost appear to take the lead in recognition and celebration, so far as the evening might conduce to intensify the lustre of the little Princess. Mrs. Assingham produced on her the impression of giving her constantly her cue for this; and it was in truth partly by her help, intelligently, quite gratefully accepted, that the little Princess, in Maggie, was drawn out and emphasised. She couldn't definitely have said how it happened, but she felt herself, for the first time in her career, living up to the public and popular notion of such a personage, as it pressed upon her from all round; rather wondering, inwardly too, while she did so, at that strange mixture in things through which the popular notion could be evidenced for her by such supposedly great ones of the earth as the Castledeans and their kind. Fanny Assingham might really have been there, at all events, like one of the assistants in the ring at the circus, to keep up the pace of the sleek revolving animal on whose back the lady in short spangled skirts should brilliantly caper and posture. That was all, doubtless Maggie had forgotten, had neglected, had declined, to be the little Princess on anything like the scale open to her; but now that the collective hand had been held out to her with such alacrity, so that she might skip up into the light, even, as seemed to her modest mind, with such a show of pink stocking and such an abbreviation of white petticoat, she could strike herself as perceiving, under arched eyebrows, where her mistake had been. She had invited for the later hours, after her dinner, a fresh contingent, the whole list of her apparent London acquaintance—which was again a thing in the manner of little princesses for whom the princely art was a matter of course. That was what she was learning to do, to fill out as a matter of course her appointed, her expected, her imposed character; and, though there were latent considerations that somewhat interfered with the lesson, she was having to-night an inordinate quantity of practice, none of it so successful as when, quite wittingly, she directed it at Lady Castledean, who was reduced by it at last to an unprecedented state of passivity. The perception of this high result caused Mrs. Assingham fairly to flush with responsive joy; she glittered at her young friend, from moment to moment, quite feverishly; it was positively as if her young friend had, in some marvellous, sudden, supersubtle way, become a source of succour to herself, become beautifully, divinely retributive. The intensity of the taste of these registered phenomena was in fact that somehow, by a process and through a connexion not again to be traced, she so practised, at the same time, on Amerigo and Charlotte—with only the drawback, her constant check and second-thought, that she concomitantly practised perhaps still more on her father.

This last was a danger indeed that, for much of the ensuing time, had its hours of strange beguilement—those at which her sense for precautions so suffered itself to lapse that she felt her communion with him more intimate than any other. It COULDN'T but pass between them that something singular was happening—so much as this she again and again said to herself; whereby the comfort of it was there, after all, to be noted, just as much as the possible peril, and she could think of the couple they formed together as groping, with sealed lips, but with mutual looks that had never been so tender, for some freedom, some fiction, some figured bravery, under which they might safely talk of it. The moment was to come—and it finally came with an effect as penetrating as the sound that follows the pressure of an electric button—when she read the least helpful of meanings into the agitation she had created. The merely specious description of their case would have been that, after being for a long time, as a family, delightfully, uninterruptedly happy, they had still had a new felicity to discover; a felicity for which, blessedly, her father's appetite and her own, in particular, had been kept fresh and grateful. This livelier march of their intercourse as a whole was the thing that occasionally determined in him the clutching instinct we have glanced at; very much as if he had said to her, in default of her breaking silence first: "Everything is remarkably pleasant, isn't it?—but WHERE, for it, after all, are we? up in a balloon and whirling through space, or down in the depths of the earth, in the glimmering passages of a gold-mine?" The equilibrium, the precious condition, lasted in spite of rearrangement; there had been a fresh distribution of the different weights, but the balance persisted and triumphed: all of which was just the reason why she was forbidden, face to face with the companion of her adventure, the experiment of a test. If they balanced they balanced—she had to take that; it deprived her of every pretext for arriving, by however covert a process, at what he thought.

But she had her hours, thus, of feeling supremely linked to him by the rigour of their law, and when it came over her that, all the while, the wish, on his side, to spare her might be what most worked with him, this very fact of their seeming to have nothing "inward" really to talk about wrapped him up for her in a kind of sweetness that was wanting, as a consecration, even in her yearning for her husband. She was powerless, however, was only more utterly hushed, when the interrupting flash came, when she would have been all ready to say to him, "Yes, this is by every appearance the best time we've had yet; but don't you see, all the same, how they must be working together for it, and how my very success, my success in shifting our beautiful harmony to a new basis, comes round to being their success, above all; their cleverness, their amiability, their power to hold out, their complete possession, in short, of our life?" For how could she say as much as that without saying a great deal more? without saying "They'll do everything in the world that suits us, save only one thing—prescribe a line for us that will make them separate." How could she so much as imagine herself even faintly murmuring that without putting into his mouth the very words that would have made her quail? "Separate, my dear? Do you want them to separate? Then you want US to—you and me? For how can the one separation take place without the other?" That was the question that, in spirit, she had heard him ask—with its dread train, moreover, of involved and connected inquiries. Their own separation, his and hers, was of course perfectly thinkable, but only on the basis of the sharpest of reasons. Well, the sharpest, the very sharpest, would be that they could no longer afford, as it were, he to let his wife, she to let her husband, "run" them in such compact formation. And say they accepted this account of their situation as a practical finality, acting upon it and proceeding to a division, would no sombre ghosts of the smothered past, on either side, show, across the widening strait, pale unappeased faces, or raise, in the very passage, deprecating, denouncing hands?

Meanwhile, however such things might be, she was to have occasion to say to herself that there might be but a deeper treachery in recoveries and reassurances. She was to feel alone again, as she had felt at the issue of her high tension during their return from meeting the Castledeans in Eaton Square. The evening in question had left her with a larger alarm, but then a lull had come—the alarm, after all, was yet to be confirmed. There came an hour, inevitably, when she knew, with a chill, what she had feared and why; it had taken, this hour, a month to arrive, but to find it before her was thoroughly to recognise it, for it showed her sharply what Amerigo had meant in alluding to a particular use that they might make, for their reaffirmed harmony and prosperity, of Charlotte. The more she thought, at present, of the tone he had employed to express their enjoyment of this resource, the more it came back to her as the product of a conscious art of dealing with her. He had been conscious, at the moment, of many things—conscious even, not a little, of desiring; and thereby of needing, to see what she would do in a given case. The given case would be that of her being to a certain extent, as she might fairly make it out, MENACED—horrible as it was to impute to him any intention represented by such a word. Why it was that to speak of making her stepmother intervene, as they might call it, in a question that seemed, just then and there, quite peculiarly their own business—why it was that a turn so familiar and so easy should, at the worst, strike her as charged with the spirit of a threat, was an oddity disconnected, for her, temporarily, from its grounds, the adventure of an imagination within her that possibly had lost its way. That, precisely, was doubtless why she had learned to wait, as the weeks passed by, with a fair, or rather indeed with an excessive, imitation of resumed serenity. There had been no prompt sequel to the Prince's equivocal light, and that made for patience; yet she was none the less to have to admit, after delay, that the bread he had cast on the waters had come home, and that she should thus be justified of her old apprehension. The consequence of this, in turn, was a renewed pang in presence of his remembered ingenuity. To be ingenious with HER—what DIDN'T, what mightn't that mean, when she had so absolutely never, at any point of contact with him, put him, by as much as the value of a penny, to the expense of sparing, doubting, fearing her, of having in any way whatever to reckon with her? The ingenuity had been in his simply speaking of their use of Charlotte as if it were common to them in an equal degree, and his triumph, on the occasion, had been just in the simplicity. She couldn't—and he knew it—say what was true: "Oh, you 'use' her, and I use her, if you will, yes; but we use her ever so differently and separately—not at all in the same way or degree. There's nobody we really use together but ourselves, don't you see?—by which I mean that where our interests are the same I can so beautifully, so exquisitely serve you for everything, and you can so beautifully, so exquisitely serve me. The only person either of us needs is the other of us; so why, as a matter of course, in such a case as this, drag in Charlotte?"

She couldn't so challenge him, because it would have been—and there she was paralysed—the NOTE. It would have translated itself on the spot, for his ear, into jealousy; and, from reverberation to repercussion, would have reached her father's exactly in the form of a cry piercing the stillness of peaceful sleep. It had been for many days almost as difficult for her to catch a quiet twenty minutes with her father as it had formerly been easy; there had been in fact, of old—the time, so strangely, seemed already far away—an inevitability in her longer passages with him, a sort of domesticated beauty in the calculability, round about them, of everything. But at present Charlotte was almost always there when Amerigo brought her to Eaton Square, where Amerigo was constantly bringing her; and Amerigo was almost always there when Charlotte brought her husband to Portland Place, where Charlotte was constantly bringing HIM. The fractions of occasions, the chance minutes that put them face to face had, as yet, of late, contrived to count but little, between them, either for the sense of opportunity or for that of exposure; inasmuch as the lifelong rhythm of their intercourse made against all cursory handling of deep things. They had never availed themselves of any given quarter-of-an-hour to gossip about fundamentals; they moved slowly through large still spaces; they could be silent together, at any time, beautifully, with much more comfort than hurriedly expressive. It appeared indeed to have become true that their common appeal measured itself, for vividness, just by this economy of sound; they might have been talking "at" each other when they talked with their companions, but these latter, assuredly, were not in any direter way to gain light on the current phase of their relation. Such were some of the reasons for which Maggie suspected fundamentals, as I have called them, to be rising, by a new movement, to the surface—suspected it one morning late in May, when her father presented himself in Portland Place alone. He had his pretext—of that she was fully aware: the Principino, two days before, had shown signs, happily not persistent, of a feverish cold and had notoriously been obliged to spend the interval at home. This was ground, ample ground, for punctual inquiry; but what it wasn't ground for, she quickly found herself reflecting, was his having managed, in the interest of his visit, to dispense so unwontedly—as their life had recently come to be arranged—with his wife's attendance. It had so happened that she herself was, for the hour, exempt from her husband's, and it will at once be seen that the hour had a quality all its own when I note that, remembering how the Prince had looked in to say he was going out, the Princess whimsically wondered if their respective sposi mightn't frankly be meeting, whimsically hoped indeed they were temporarily so disposed of. Strange was her need, at moments, to think of them as not attaching an excessive importance to their repudiation of the general practice that had rested only a few weeks before on such a consecrated rightness. Repudiations, surely, were not in the air—they had none of them come to that; for wasn't she at this minute testifying directly against them by her own behaviour? When she should confess to fear of being alone with her father, to fear of what he might then—ah, with such a slow, painful motion as she had a horror of!—say to her, THEN would be time enough for Amerigo and Charlotte to confess to not liking to appear to foregather.

She had this morning a wonderful consciousness both of dreading a particular question from him and of being able to check, yes even to disconcert, magnificently, by her apparent manner of receiving it, any restless imagination he might have about its importance. The day, bright and soft, had the breath of summer; it made them talk, to begin with, of Fawns, of the way Fawns invited—Maggie aware, the while, that in thus regarding, with him, the sweetness of its invitation to one couple just as much as to another, her humbugging smile grew very nearly convulsive. That was it, and there was relief truly, of a sort, in taking it in: she was humbugging him already, by absolute necessity, as she had never, never done in her life—doing it up to the full height of what she had allowed for. The necessity, in the great dimly-shining room where, declining, for his reasons, to sit down, he moved about in Amerigo's very footsteps, the necessity affected her as pressing upon her with the very force of the charm itself; of the old pleasantries, between them, so candidly playing up there again; of the positive flatness of their tenderness, a surface all for familiar use, quite as if generalised from the long succession of tapestried sofas, sweetly faded, on which his theory of contentment had sat, through unmeasured pauses, beside her own. She KNEW, from this instant, knew in advance and as well as anything would ever teach her, that she must never intermit for a solitary second her so highly undertaking to prove that there was nothing the matter with her. She saw, of a sudden, everything she might say or do in the light of that undertaking, established connections from it with any number of remote matters, struck herself, for instance, as acting all in its interest when she proposed their going out, in the exercise of their freedom and in homage to the season, for a turn in the Regent's Park. This resort was close at hand, at the top of Portland Place, and the Principino, beautifully better, had already proceeded there under high attendance: all of which considerations were defensive for Maggie, all of which became, to her mind, part of the business of cultivating continuity.

Upstairs, while she left him to put on something to go out in, the thought of his waiting below for her, in possession of the empty house, brought with it, sharply if briefly, one of her abrupt arrests of consistency, the brush of a vain imagination almost paralysing her, often, for the minute, before her glass—the vivid look, in other words, of the particular difference his marriage had made. The particular difference seemed at such instants the loss, more than anything else, of their old freedom, their never having had to think, where they were together concerned, of any one, of anything but each other. It hadn't been HER marriage that did it; that had never, for three seconds, suggested to either of them that they must act diplomatically, must reckon with another presence—no, not even with her husband's. She groaned to herself, while the vain imagination lasted, "WHY did he marry? ah, why DID he?" and then it came up to her more than ever that nothing could have been more beautiful than the way in which, till Charlotte came so much more closely into their life, Amerigo hadn't interfered. What she had gone on owing him for this mounted up again, to her eyes, like a column of figures—or call it even, if one would, a house of cards; it was her father's wonderful act that had tipped the house down and made the sum wrong. With all of which, immediately after her question, her "Why did he, why did he?" rushed back, inevitably, the confounding, the overwhelming wave of the knowledge of his reason. "He did it for ME, he did it for me," she moaned, "he did it, exactly, that our freedom—meaning, beloved man, simply and solely mine—should be greater instead of less; he did it, divinely, to liberate me so far as possible from caring what became of him." She found time upstairs, even in her haste, as she had repeatedly found time before, to let the wonderments involved in these recognitions flash at her with their customary effect of making her blink: the question in especial of whether she might find her solution in acting, herself, in the spirit of what he had done, in forcing her "care" really to grow as much less as he had tried to make it. Thus she felt the whole weight of their case drop afresh upon her shoulders, was confronted, unmistakably, with the prime source of her haunted state. It all came from her not having been able not to mind—not to mind what became of him; not having been able, without anxiety, to let him go his way and take his risk and lead his life. She had made anxiety her stupid little idol; and absolutely now, while she stuck a long pin, a trifle fallaciously, into her hat—she had, with an approach to irritation, told her maid, a new woman, whom she had lately found herself thinking of as abysmal, that she didn't want her—she tried to focus the possibility of some understanding between them in consequence of which he should cut loose.

Very near indeed it looked, any such possibility! that consciousness, too, had taken its turn by the time she was ready; all the vibration, all the emotion of this present passage being, precisely, in the very sweetness of their lapse back into the conditions of the simpler time, into a queer resemblance between the aspect and the feeling of the moment and those of numberless other moments that were sufficiently far away. She had been quick in her preparation, in spite of the flow of the tide that sometimes took away her breath; but a pause, once more, was still left for her to make, a pause, at the top of the stairs, before she came down to him, in the span of which she asked herself if it weren't thinkable, from the perfectly practical point of view, that she should simply sacrifice him. She didn't go into the detail of what sacrificing him would mean—she didn't need to; so distinct was it, in one of her restless lights, that there he was awaiting her, that she should find him walking up and down the drawing-room in the warm, fragrant air to which the open windows and the abundant flowers contributed; slowly and vaguely moving there and looking very slight and young and, superficially, almost as much like her child, putting it a little freely, as like her parent; with the appearance about him, above all, of having perhaps arrived just on purpose to SAY it to her, himself, in so many words: "Sacrifice me, my own love; do sacrifice me, do sacrifice me!" Should she want to, should she insist on it, she might verily hear him bleating it at her, all conscious and all accommodating, like some precious, spotless, exceptionally intelligent lamb. The positive effect of the intensity of this figure, however, was to make her shake it away in her resumed descent; and after she had rejoined him, after she had picked him up, she was to know the full pang of the thought that her impossibility was MADE, absolutely, by his consciousness, by the lucidity of his intention: this she felt while she smiled there for him, again, all hypocritically; while she drew on fair, fresh gloves; while she interrupted the process first to give his necktie a slightly smarter twist and then to make up to him for her hidden madness by rubbing her nose into his cheek according to the tradition of their frankest levity.

From the instant she should be able to convict him of intending, every issue would be closed and her hypocrisy would have to redouble. The only way to sacrifice him would be to do so without his dreaming what it might be for. She kissed him, she arranged his cravat, she dropped remarks, she guided him out, she held his arm, not to be led, but to lead him, and taking it to her by much the same intimate pressure she had always used, when a little girl, to mark the inseparability of her doll—she did all these things so that he should sufficiently fail to dream of what they might be for.

XXIX

There was nothing to show that her effort in any degree fell short till they got well into the Park and he struck her as giving, unexpectedly, the go-by to any serious search for the Principino. The way they sat down awhile in the sun was a sign of that; his dropping with her into the first pair of sequestered chairs they came across and waiting a little, after they were placed, as if now at last she might bring out, as between them, something more specific. It made her but feel the more sharply how the specific, in almost any direction, was utterly forbidden her—how the use of it would be, for all the world, like undoing the leash of a dog eager to follow up a scent. It would come out, the specific, where the dog would come out; would run to earth, somehow, the truth—for she was believing herself in relation to the truth!—at which she mustn't so much as indirectly point. Such, at any rate, was the fashion in which her passionate prudence played over possibilities of danger, reading symptoms and betrayals into everything she looked at, and yet having to make it evident, while she recognised them, that she didn't wince. There were moments between them, in their chairs, when he might have been watching her guard herself and trying to think of something new that would trip her up. There were pauses during which, with her affection as sweet and still as the sunshine, she might yet, as at some hard game, over a table, for money, have been defying him to fasten upon her the least little complication of consciousness. She was positively proud, afterwards, of the great style in which she had kept this up; later on, at the hour's end, when they had retraced their steps to find Amerigo and Charlotte awaiting them at the house, she was able to say to herself that, truly, she had put her plan through; even though once more setting herself the difficult task of making their relation, every minute of the time, not fall below the standard of that other hour, in the treasured past, which hung there behind them like a framed picture in a museum, a high watermark for the history of their old fortune; the summer evening, in the park at Fawns, when, side by side under the trees just as now, they had let their happy confidence lull them with its most golden tone. There had been the possibility of a trap for her, at present, in the very question of their taking up anew that residence; wherefore she had not been the first to sound it, in spite of the impression from him of his holding off to see what she would do. She was saying to herself in secret: "CAN we again, in this form, migrate there? Can I, for myself, undertake it? face all the intenser keeping-up and stretching-out, indefinitely, impossibly, that our conditions in the country, as we've established and accepted them, would stand for?" She had positively lost herself in this inward doubt—so much she was subsequently to remember; but remembering then too that her companion, though perceptibly perhaps as if not to be eager, had broken the ice very much as he had broken it in Eaton Square after the banquet to the Castledeans.

Her mind had taken a long excursion, wandered far into the vision of what a summer at Fawns, with Amerigo and Charlotte still more eminently in presence against that higher sky, would bring forth. Wasn't her father meanwhile only pretending to talk of it? just as she was, in a manner, pretending to listen? He got off it, finally, at all events, for the transition it couldn't well help thrusting out at him; it had amounted exactly to an arrest of her private excursion by the sense that he had begun to IMITATE—oh, as never yet!—the ancient tone of gold. It had verily come from him at last, the question of whether she thought it would be very good—but very good indeed—that he should leave England for a series of weeks, on some pretext, with the Prince. Then it had been that she was to know her husband's "menace" hadn't really dropped, since she was face to face with the effect of it. Ah, the effect of it had occupied all the rest of their walk, had stayed out with them and come home with them, besides making it impossible that they shouldn't presently feign to recollect how rejoining the child had been their original purpose. Maggie's uneffaced note was that it had, at the end of five minutes more, driven them to that endeavour as to a refuge, and caused them afterwards to rejoice, as well, that the boy's irrepressibly importunate company, in due course secured and enjoyed, with the extension imparted by his governess, a person expectant of consideration, constituted a cover for any awkwardness. For that was what it had all come to, that the dear man had spoken to her to TRY her—quite as he had been spoken to himself by Charlotte, with the same fine idea. The Princess took it in, on the spot, firmly grasping it; she heard them together, her father and his wife, dealing with the queer case. "The Prince tells me that Maggie has a plan for your taking some foreign journey with him, and, as he likes to do everything she wants, he has suggested my speaking to you for it as the thing most likely to make you consent. So I do speak—see?—being always so eager myself, as you know, to meet Maggie's wishes. I speak, but without quite understanding, this time, what she has in her head. Why SHOULD she, of a sudden, at this particular moment, desire to ship you off together and to remain here alone with me? The compliment's all to me, I admit, and you must decide quite as you like. The Prince is quite ready, evidently, to do his part—but you'll have it out with him. That is you'll have it out with HER." Something of that kind was what, in her mind's ear, Maggie heard—and this, after his waiting for her to appeal to him directly, was her father's invitation to her to have it out. Well, as she could say to herself all the rest of the day, that was what they did while they continued to sit there in their penny chairs, that was what they HAD done as much as they would now ever, ever, have out anything. The measure of this, at least, had been given, that each would fight to the last for the protection, for the perversion, of any real anxiety. She had confessed, instantly, with her humbugging grin, not flinching by a hair, meeting his eyes as mildly as he met hers, she had confessed to her fancy that they might both, he and his son-in-law, have welcomed such an escapade, since they had both been so long so furiously domestic. She had almost cocked her hat under the inspiration of this opportunity to hint how a couple of spirited young men, reacting from confinement and sallying forth arm-in-arm, might encounter the agreeable in forms that would strike them for the time at least as novel. She had felt for fifty seconds, with her eyes, all so sweetly and falsely, in her companion's, horribly vulgar; yet without minding it either—such luck should she have if to be nothing worse than vulgar would see her through. "And I thought Amerigo might like it better," she had said, "than wandering off alone."

"Do you mean that he won't go unless I take him?"

She had considered here, and never in her life had she considered so promptly and so intently. If she really put it that way, her husband, challenged, might belie the statement; so that what would that do but make her father wonder, make him perhaps ask straight out, why she was exerting pressure? She couldn't of course afford to be suspected for an instant of exerting pressure; which was why she was obliged only to make answer: "Wouldn't that be just what you must have out with HIM?"

"Decidedly—if he makes me the proposal. But he hasn't made it yet."

Oh, once more, how she was to feel she had smirked! "Perhaps he's too shy!"

"Because you're so sure he so really wants my company?"

"I think he has thought you might like it."

"Well, I should—!" But with this he looked away from her, and she held her breath to hear him either ask if she wished him to address the question to Amerigo straight, or inquire if she should be greatly disappointed by his letting it drop. What had "settled" her, as she was privately to call it, was that he had done neither of these things, and had thereby markedly stood off from the risk involved in trying to draw out her reason. To attenuate, on the other hand, this appearance, and quite as if to fill out the too large receptacle made, so musingly, by his abstention, he had himself presently given her a reason—had positively spared her the effort of asking whether he judged Charlotte not to have approved. He had taken everything on himself—THAT was what had settled her. She had had to wait very little more to feel, with this, how much he was taking. The point he made was his lack of any eagerness to put time and space, on any such scale, between himself and his wife. He wasn't so unhappy with her—far from it, and Maggie was to hold that he had grinned back, paternally, through his rather shielding glasses, in easy emphasis of this—as to be able to hint that he required the relief of absence. Therefore, unless it was for the Prince himself—!

"Oh, I don't think it would have been for Amerigo himself. Amerigo and I," Maggie had said, "perfectly rub on together."

"Well then, there we are."

"I see"—and she had again, with sublime blandness, assented. "There we are."

"Charlotte and I too," her father had gaily proceeded, "perfectly rub on together." And then he had appeared for a little to be making time. "To put it only so," he had mildly and happily added—"to put it only so!" He had spoken as if he might easily put it much better, yet as if the humour of contented understatement fairly sufficed for the occasion. He had played then, either all consciously or all unconsciously, into Charlotte's hands; and the effect of this was to render trebly oppressive Maggie's conviction of Charlotte's plan. She had done what she wanted, his wife had—which was also what Amerigo had made her do. She had kept her test, Maggie's test, from becoming possible, and had applied instead a test of her own. It was exactly as if she had known that her stepdaughter would be afraid to be summoned to say, under the least approach to cross-examination, why any change was desirable; and it was, for our young woman herself, still more prodigiously, as if her father had been capable of calculations to match, of judging it important he shouldn't be brought to demand of her what was the matter with her. Why otherwise, with such an opportunity, hadn't he demanded it? Always from calculation—that was why, that was why. He was terrified of the retort he might have invoked: "What, my dear, if you come to that, is the matter with YOU?" When, a minute later on, he had followed up his last note by a touch or two designed still further to conjure away the ghost of the anomalous, at that climax verily she would have had to be dumb to the question. "There seems a kind of charm, doesn't there? on our life—and quite as if, just lately, it had got itself somehow renewed, had waked up refreshed. A kind of wicked selfish prosperity perhaps, as if we had grabbed everything, fixed everything, down to the last lovely object for the last glass case of the last corner, left over, of my old show. That's the only take-off, that it has made us perhaps lazy, a wee bit languid—lying like gods together, all careless of mankind."

"Do you consider that we're languid?"—that form of rejoinder she had jumped at for the sake of its pretty lightness. "Do you consider that we are careless of mankind?—living as we do in the biggest crowd in the world, and running about always pursued and pursuing."

It had made him think indeed a little longer than she had meant; but he came up again, as she might have said, smiling. "Well, I don't know. We get nothing but the fun, do we?"

"No," she had hastened to declare; "we certainly get nothing but the fun."

"We do it all," he had remarked, "so beautifully."

"We do it all so beautifully." She hadn't denied this for a moment. "I see what you mean."

"Well, I mean too," he had gone on, "that we haven't, no doubt, enough, the sense of difficulty."

"Enough? Enough for what?"

"Enough not to be selfish."

"I don't think YOU are selfish," she had returned—and had managed not to wail it.

"I don't say that it's me particularly—or that it's you or Charlotte or Amerigo. But we're selfish together—we move as a selfish mass. You see we want always the same thing," he had gone on—"and that holds us, that binds us, together. We want each other," he had further explained; "only wanting it, each time, FOR each other. That's what I call the happy spell; but it's also, a little, possibly, the immorality."

"The immorality'?" she had pleasantly echoed.

"Well, we're tremendously moral for ourselves—that is for each other; and I won't pretend that I know exactly at whose particular personal expense you and I, for instance, are happy. What it comes to, I daresay, is that there's something haunting—as if it were a bit uncanny—in such a consciousness of our general comfort and privilege. Unless indeed," he had rambled on, "it's only I to whom, fantastically, it says so much. That's all I mean, at any rate—that it's sort of soothing; as if we were sitting about on divans, with pigtails, smoking opium and seeing visions. 'Let us then be up and doing'—what is it Longfellow says? That seems sometimes to ring out; like the police breaking in—into our opium den—to give us a shake. But the beauty of it is, at the same time, that we ARE doing; we're doing, that is, after all, what we went in for. We're working it, our life, our chance, whatever you may call it, as we saw it, as we felt it, from the first. We HAVE worked it, and what more can you do than that? It's a good deal for me," he had wound up, "to have made Charlotte so happy—to have so perfectly contented her. YOU, from a good way back, were a matter of course—I mean your being all right; so that I needn't mind your knowing that my great interest, since then, has rather inevitably been in making sure of the same success, very much to your advantage as well, for Charlotte. If we've worked our life, our idea really, as I say—if at any rate I can sit here and say that I've worked my share of it—it has not been what you may call least by our having put Charlotte so at her ease. THAT has been soothing, all round; that has curled up as the biggest of the blue fumes, or whatever they are, of the opium. Don't you see what a cropper we would have come if she hadn't settled down as she has?" And he had concluded by turning to Maggie as for something she mightn't really have thought of. "You, darling, in that case, I verily believe, would have been the one to hate it most."

"To hate it—?" Maggie had wondered.

"To hate our having, with our tremendous intentions, not brought it off. And I daresay I should have hated it for you even more than for myself."

"That's not unlikely perhaps when it was for me, after all, that you did it."

He had hesitated, but only a moment. "I never told you so."

"Well, Charlotte herself soon enough told me."

"But I never told HER," her father had answered.

"Are you very sure?" she had presently asked.

"Well, I like to think how thoroughly I was taken with her, and how right I was, and how fortunate, to have that for my basis. I told her all the good I thought of her."

"Then that," Maggie had returned, "was precisely part of the good. I mean it was precisely part of it that she could so beautifully understand."

"Yes—understand everything."

"Everything—and in particular your reasons. Her telling me—that showed me how she had understood."

They were face to face again now, and she saw she had made his colour rise; it was as if he were still finding in her eyes the concrete image, the enacted scene, of her passage with Charlotte, which he was now hearing of for the first time and as to which it would have been natural he should question her further. His forbearance to do so would but mark, precisely, the complication of his fears. "What she does like," he finally said, "is the way it has succeeded."

"Your marriage?"

"Yes—my whole idea. The way I've been justified. That's the joy I give her. If for HER, either, it had failed—!" That, however, was not worth talking about; he had broken off. "You think then you could now risk Fawns?"

"Risk' it?"

"Well, morally—from the point of view I was talking of; that of our sinking deeper into sloth. Our selfishness, somehow, seems at its biggest down there."

Maggie had allowed him the amusement of her not taking this up. "Is Charlotte," she had simply asked, "really ready?"

"Oh, if you and I and Amerigo are. Whenever one corners Charlotte," he had developed more at his ease, "one finds that she only wants to know what we want. Which is what we got her for!"

"What we got her for—exactly!" And so, for a little, even though with a certain effect of oddity in their more or less successful ease, they left it; left it till Maggie made the remark that it was all the same wonderful her stepmother should be willing, before the season was out, to exchange so much company for so much comparative solitude.

"Ah," he had then made answer, "that's because her idea, I think, this time, is that we shall have more people, more than we've hitherto had, in the country. Don't you remember that THAT, originally, was what we were to get her for?"

"Oh yes—to give us a life." Maggie had gone through the form of recalling this, and the light of their ancient candour, shining from so far back, had seemed to bring out some things so strangely that, with the sharpness of the vision, she had risen to her feet. "Well, with a 'life' Fawns will certainly do." He had remained in his place while she looked over his head; the picture, in her vision, had suddenly swarmed. The vibration was that of one of the lurches of the mystic train in which, with her companion, she was travelling; but she was having to steady herself, this time, before meeting his eyes. She had measured indeed the full difference between the move to Fawns because each of them now knew the others wanted it and the pairing-off, for a journey, of her husband and her father, which nobody knew that either wanted. "More company" at Fawns would be effectually enough the key in which her husband and her stepmother were at work; there was truly no question but that she and her father must accept any array of visitors. No one could try to marry him now. What he had just said was a direct plea for that, and what was the plea itself but an act of submission to Charlotte? He had, from his chair, been noting her look, but he had, the next minute, also risen, and then it was they had reminded each other of their having come out for the boy. Their junction with him and with his companion successfully effected, the four had moved home more slowly, and still more vaguely; yet with a vagueness that permitted of Maggie's reverting an instant to the larger issue.

"If we have people in the country then, as you were saying, do you know for whom my first fancy would be? You may be amused, but it would be for the Castledeans."

"I see. But why should I be amused?"

"Well, I mean I am myself. I don't think I like her—and yet I like to see her: which, as Amerigo says, is 'rum.'"

"But don't you feel she's very handsome?" her father inquired.

"Yes, but it isn't for that."

"Then what is it for?"

"Simply that she may be THERE—just there before us. It's as if she may have a value—as if something may come of her. I don't in the least know what, and she rather irritates me meanwhile. I don't even know, I admit, why—but if we see her often enough I may find out."

"Does it matter so very much?" her companion had asked while they moved together.

She had hesitated. "You mean because you do rather like her?"

He on his side too had waited a little, but then he had taken it from her. "Yes, I guess I do rather like her."

Which she accepted for the first case she could recall of their not being affected by a person in the same way. It came back therefore to his pretending; but she had gone far enough, and to add to her appearance of levity she further observed that, though they were so far from a novelty, she should also immediately desire, at Fawns, the presence of the Assinghams. That put everything on a basis independent of explanations; yet it was extraordinary, at the same time, how much, once in the country again with the others, she was going, as they used to say at home, to need the presence of the good Fanny. It was the strangest thing in the world, but it was as if Mrs. Assingham might in a manner mitigate the intensity of her consciousness of Charlotte. It was as if the two would balance, one against the other; as if it came round again in that fashion to her idea of the equilibrium. It would be like putting this friend into her scale to make weight—into the scale with her father and herself. Amerigo and Charlotte would be in the other; therefore it would take the three of them to keep that one straight. And as this played, all duskily, in her mind it had received from her father, with a sound of suddenness, a luminous contribution. "Ah, rather! DO let's have the Assinghams."

"It would be to have them," she had said, "as we used so much to have them. For a good long stay, in the old way and on the old terms: 'as regular boarders' Fanny used to call it. That is if they'll come."

"As regular boarders, on the old terms—that's what I should like too. But I guess they'll come," her companion had added in a tone into which she had read meanings. The main meaning was that he felt he was going to require them quite as much as she was. His recognition of the new terms as different from the old, what was that, practically, but a confession that something had happened, and a perception that, interested in the situation she had helped to create, Mrs. Assingham would be, by so much as this, concerned in its inevitable development? It amounted to an intimation, off his guard, that he should be thankful for some one to turn to. If she had wished covertly to sound him he had now, in short, quite given himself away, and if she had, even at the start, needed anything MORE to settle her, here assuredly was enough. He had hold of his small grandchild as they retraced their steps, swinging the boy's hand and not bored, as he never was, by his always bristling, like a fat little porcupine, with shrill interrogation-points—so that, secretly, while they went, she had wondered again if the equilibrium mightn't have been more real, mightn't above all have demanded less strange a study, had it only been on the books that Charlotte should give him a Principino of his own. She had repossessed herself now of his other arm, only this time she was drawing him back, gently, helplessly back, to what they had tried, for the hour, to get away from—just as he was consciously drawing the child, and as high Miss Bogle on her left, representing the duties of home, was complacently drawing HER. The duties of home, when the house in Portland Place reappeared, showed, even from a distance, as vividly there before them. Amerigo and Charlotte had come in—that is Amerigo had, Charlotte, rather, having come out—and the pair were perched together in the balcony, bare-headed, she divested of her jacket, her mantle, or whatever, but crowned with a brilliant brave hat, responsive to the balmy day, which Maggie immediately "spotted" as new, as insuperably original, as worn, in characteristic generous harmony, for the first time; all, evidently, to watch for the return of the absent, to be there to take them over again as punctually as possible. They were gay, they were amused, in the pleasant morning; they leaned across the rail and called down their greeting, lighting up the front of the great black house with an expression that quite broke the monotony, that might almost have shocked the decency, of Portland Place. The group on the pavement stared up as at the peopled battlements of a castle; even Miss Bogle, who carried her head most aloft, gaped a little, through the interval of space, as toward truly superior beings. There could scarce have been so much of the open mouth since the dingy waits, on Christmas Eve, had so lamentably chanted for pennies—the time when Amerigo, insatiable for English customs, had come out, with a gasped "Santissima Vergine!" to marvel at the depositaries of this tradition and purchase a reprieve. Maggie's individual gape was inevitably again for the thought of how the pair would be at work.

XXX

She had not again, for weeks, had Mrs. Assingham so effectually in presence as on the afternoon of that lady's return from the Easter party at Matcham; but the intermission was made up as soon as the date of the migration to Fawns—that of the more or less simultaneous adjournment of the two houses—began to be discussed. It had struck her, promptly, that this renewal, with an old friend, of the old terms she had talked of with her father, was the one opening, for her spirit, that wouldn't too much advertise or betray her. Even her father, who had always, as he would have said, "believed in" their ancient ally, wouldn't necessarily suspect her of invoking Fanny's aid toward any special inquiry—and least of all if Fanny would only act as Fanny so easily might. Maggie's measure of Fanny's ease would have been agitating to Mrs. Assingham had it been all at once revealed to her—as, for that matter, it was soon destined to become even on a comparatively graduated showing. Our young woman's idea, in particular, was that her safety, her escape from being herself suspected of suspicion, would proceed from this friend's power to cover, to protect and, as might be, even showily to represent her—represent, that is, her relation to the form of the life they were all actually leading. This would doubtless be, as people said, a large order; but that Mrs. Assingham existed, substantially, or could somehow be made prevailingly to exist, for her private benefit, was the finest flower Maggie had plucked from among the suggestions sown, like abundant seed, on the occasion of the entertainment offered in Portland Place to the Matcham company. Mrs. Assingham, that night, rebounding from dejection, had bristled with bravery and sympathy; she had then absolutely, she had perhaps recklessly, for herself, betrayed the deeper and darker consciousness—an impression it would now be late for her inconsistently to attempt to undo. It was with a wonderful air of giving out all these truths that the Princess at present approached her again; making doubtless at first a sufficient scruple of letting her know what in especial she asked of her, yet not a bit ashamed, as she in fact quite expressly declared, of Fanny's discerned foreboding of the strange uses she might perhaps have for her. Quite from the first, really, Maggie said extraordinary things to her, such as "You can help me, you know, my dear, when nobody else can;" such as "I almost wish, upon my word, that you had something the matter with you, that you had lost your health, or your money, or your reputation (forgive me, love!) so that I might be with you as much as I want, or keep you with ME, without exciting comment, without exciting any other remark than that such kindnesses are 'like' me." We have each our own way of making up for our unselfishness, and Maggie, who had no small self at all as against her husband or her father and only a weak and uncertain one as against her stepmother, would verily, at this crisis, have seen Mrs. Assingham's personal life or liberty sacrificed without a pang.

The attitude that the appetite in question maintained in her was to draw peculiar support moreover from the current aspects and agitations of her victim. This personage struck her, in truth, as ready for almost anything; as not perhaps effusively protesting, yet as wanting with a restlessness of her own to know what she wanted. And in the long run—which was none so long either—there was to be no difficulty, as happened, about that. It was as if, for all the world, Maggie had let her see that she held her, that she made her, fairly responsible for something; not, to begin with, dotting all the i's nor hooking together all the links, but treating her, without insistence, rather with caressing confidence, as there to see and to know, to advise and to assist. The theory, visibly, had patched itself together for her that the dear woman had somehow, from the early time, had a hand in ALL their fortunes, so that there was no turn of their common relations and affairs that couldn't be traced back in some degree to her original affectionate interest. On this affectionate interest the good lady's young friend now built, before her eyes—very much as a wise, or even as a mischievous, child, playing on the floor, might pile up blocks, skilfully and dizzily, with an eye on the face of a covertly-watching elder.

When the blocks tumbled down they but acted after the nature of blocks; yet the hour would come for their rising so high that the structure would have to be noticed and admired. Mrs. Assingham's appearance of unreservedly giving herself involved meanwhile, on her own side, no separate recognitions: her face of almost anxious attention was directed altogether to her young friend's so vivid felicity; it suggested that she took for granted, at the most, certain vague recent enhancements of that state. If the Princess now, more than before, was going and going, she was prompt to publish that she beheld her go, that she had always known she WOULD, sooner or later, and that any appeal for participation must more or less contain and invite the note of triumph. There was a blankness in her blandness, assuredly, and very nearly an extravagance in her generalising gaiety; a precipitation of cheer particularly marked whenever they met again after short separations: meetings during the first flush of which Maggie sometimes felt reminded of other looks in other faces; of two strangely unobliterated impressions above all, the physiognomic light that had played out in her husband at the shock—she had come at last to talk to herself of the "shock"—of his first vision of her on his return from Matcham and Gloucester, and the wonder of Charlotte's beautiful bold wavering gaze when, the next morning in Eaton Square, this old friend had turned from the window to begin to deal with her.

If she had dared to think of it so crudely she would have said that Fanny was afraid of her, afraid of something she might say or do, even as, for their few brief seconds, Amerigo and Charlotte had been—which made, exactly, an expressive element common to the three. The difference however was that this look had in the dear woman its oddity of a constant renewal, whereas it had never for the least little instant again peeped out of the others. Other looks, other lights, radiant and steady, with the others, had taken its place, reaching a climax so short a time ago, that morning of the appearance of the pair on the balcony of her house to overlook what she had been doing with her father; when their general interested brightness and beauty, attuned to the outbreak of summer, had seemed to shed down warmth and welcome and the promise of protection. They were conjoined not to do anything to startle her—and now at last so completely that, with experience and practice, they had almost ceased to fear their liability. Mrs. Assingham, on the other hand, deprecating such an accident not less, had yet less assurance, as having less control. The high pitch of her cheer, accordingly, the tentative, adventurous expressions, of the would-be smiling order, that preceded her approach even like a squad of skirmishers, or whatever they were called, moving ahead of the baggage train—these things had at the end of a fortnight brought a dozen times to our young woman's lips a challenge that had the cunning to await its right occasion, but of the relief of which, as a demonstration, she meanwhile felt no little need. "You've such a dread of my possibly complaining to you that you keep pealing all the bells to drown my voice; but don't cry out, my dear, till you're hurt—and above all ask yourself how I can be so wicked as to complain. What in the name of all that's fantastic can you dream that I have to complain OF?" Such inquiries the Princess temporarily succeeded in repressing, and she did so, in a measure, by the aid of her wondering if this ambiguity with which her friend affected her wouldn't be at present a good deal like the ambiguity with which she herself must frequently affect her father. She wondered how she should enjoy, on HIS part, such a take-up as she but just succeeded, from day to day, in sparing Mrs. Assingham, and that made for her trying to be as easy with this associate as Mr. Verver, blessed man, all indulgent but all inscrutable, was with his daughter. She had extracted from her, none the less, a vow in respect to the time that, if the Colonel might be depended on, they would spend at Fawns; and nothing came home to her more, in this connection, or inspired her with a more intimate interest, than her sense of absolutely seeing her interlocutress forbear to observe that Charlotte's view of a long visit, even from such allies, was there to be reckoned with.

Fanny stood off from that proposition as visibly to the Princess, and as consciously to herself, as she might have backed away from the edge of a chasm into which she feared to slip; a truth that contributed again to keep before our young woman her own constant danger of advertising her subtle processes. That Charlotte should have begun to be restrictive about the Assinghams—which she had never, and for a hundred obviously good reasons, been before—this in itself was a fact of the highest value for Maggie, and of a value enhanced by the silence in which Fanny herself so much too unmistakably dressed it. What gave it quite thrillingly its price was exactly the circumstance that it thus opposed her to her stepmother more actively—if she was to back up her friends for holding out—than she had ever yet been opposed; though of course with the involved result of the fine chance given Mrs. Verver to ask her husband for explanations. Ah, from the moment she should be definitely CAUGHT in opposition there would be naturally no saying how much Charlotte's opportunities might multiply! What would become of her father, she hauntedly asked, if his wife, on the one side, should begin to press him to call his daughter to order, and the force of old habit—to put it only at that—should dispose him, not less effectively, to believe in this young person at any price? There she was, all round, imprisoned in the circle of the reasons it was impossible she should give—certainly give HIM. The house in the country was his house, and thereby was Charlotte's; it was her own and Amerigo's only so far as its proper master and mistress should profusely place it at their disposal. Maggie felt of course that she saw no limit to her father's profusion, but this couldn't be even at the best the case with Charlotte's, whom it would never be decent, when all was said, to reduce to fighting for her preferences. There were hours, truly, when the Princess saw herself as not unarmed for battle if battle might only take place without spectators.

This last advantage for her, was, however, too sadly out of the question; her sole strength lay in her being able to see that if Charlotte wouldn't "want" the Assinghams it would be because that sentiment too would have motives and grounds. She had all the while command of one way of meeting any objection, any complaint, on his wife's part, reported to her by her father; it would be open to her to retort to his possible "What are your reasons, my dear?" by a lucidly-produced "What are hers, love, please?—isn't that what we had better know? Mayn't her reasons be a dislike, beautifully founded, of the presence, and thereby of the observation, of persons who perhaps know about her things it's inconvenient to her they should know?" That hideous card she might in mere idle play—being by this time, at her still swifter private pace, intimately familiar with all the fingered pasteboard in her pack. But she could play it only on the forbidden issue of sacrificing him; the issue so forbidden that it involved even a horror of finding out if he would really have consented to be sacrificed. What she must do she must do by keeping her hands off him; and nothing meanwhile, as we see, had less in common with that scruple than such a merciless manipulation of their yielding beneficiaries as her spirit so boldly revelled in. She saw herself, in this connexion, without detachment—saw others alone with intensity; otherwise she might have been struck, fairly have been amused, by her free assignment of the pachydermatous quality. If SHE could face the awkwardness of the persistence of her friends at Fawns in spite of Charlotte, she somehow looked to them for an inspiration of courage that would improve upon her own. They were in short not only themselves to find a plausibility and an audacity, but were somehow by the way to pick up these forms for her, Maggie, as well. And she felt indeed that she was giving them scant time longer when, one afternoon in Portland Place, she broke out with an irrelevance that was merely superficial.

"What awfulness, in heaven's name, is there between them? What do you believe, what do you KNOW?"

Oh, if she went by faces her visitor's sudden whiteness, at this, might have carried her far! Fanny Assingham turned pale for it, but there was something in such an appearance, in the look it put into the eyes, that renewed Maggie's conviction of what this companion had been expecting. She had been watching it come, come from afar, and now that it was there, after all, and the first convulsion over, they would doubtless soon find themselves in a more real relation. It was there because of the Sunday luncheon they had partaken of alone together; it was there, as strangely as one would, because of the bad weather, the cold perverse June rain, that was making the day wrong; it was there because it stood for the whole sum of the perplexities and duplicities among which our young woman felt herself lately to have picked her steps; it was there because Amerigo and Charlotte were again paying together alone a "week end" visit which it had been Maggie's plan infernally to promote—just to see if, this time, they really would; it was there because she had kept Fanny, on her side, from paying one she would manifestly have been glad to pay, and had made her come instead, stupidly, vacantly, boringly, to luncheon: all in the spirit of celebrating the fact that the Prince and Mrs. Verver had thus put it into her own power to describe them exactly as they were. It had abruptly occurred, in truth, that Maggie required the preliminary help of determining HOW they were; though, on the other hand, before her guest had answered her question everything in the hour and the place, everything in all the conditions, affected her as crying it out. Her guest's stare of ignorance, above all—that of itself at first cried it out. "'Between them?' What do you mean?"

"Anything there shouldn't be, there shouldn't have BEEN—all this time. Do you believe there is—or what's your idea?"

Fanny's idea was clearly, to begin with, that her young friend had taken her breath away; but she looked at her very straight and very hard. "Do you speak from a suspicion of your own?"

"I speak, at last, from a torment. Forgive me if it comes out. I've been thinking for months and months, and I've no one to turn to, no one to help me to make things out; no impression but my own, don't you see? to go by."

"You've been thinking for months and months?" Mrs. Assingham took it in. "But WHAT then, dear Maggie, have you been thinking?"

"Well, horrible things—like a little beast that I perhaps am. That there may be something—something wrong and dreadful, something they cover up."

The elder woman's colour had begun to come back; she was able, though with a visible effort, to face the question less amazedly. "You imagine, poor child, that the wretches are in love? Is that it?"

But Maggie for a minute only stared back at her. "Help me to find out WHAT I imagine. I don't know—I've nothing but my perpetual anxiety. Have you any?—do you see what I mean? If you'll tell me truly, that at least, one way or the other, will do something for me."

Fanny's look had taken a peculiar gravity—a fulness with which it seemed to shine. "Is what it comes to that you're jealous of Charlotte?"

"Do you mean whether I hate her?"—and Maggie thought. "No; not on account of father."

"Ah," Mrs. Assingham returned, "that isn't what one would suppose. What I ask is if you're jealous on account of your husband."

"Well," said Maggie presently, "perhaps that may be all. If I'm unhappy I'm jealous; it must come to the same thing; and with you, at least, I'm not afraid of the word. If I'm jealous, don't you see? I'm tormented," she went on—"and all the more if I'm helpless. And if I'm both helpless AND tormented I stuff my pocket-handkerchief into my mouth, I keep it there, for the most part, night and day, so as not to be heard too indecently moaning. Only now, with you, at last, I can't keep it longer; I've pulled it out, and here I am fairly screaming at you. They're away," she wound up, "so they can't hear; and I'm, by a miracle of arrangement, not at luncheon with father at home. I live in the midst of miracles of arrangement, half of which I admit, are my own; I go about on tiptoe, I watch for every sound, I feel every breath, and yet I try all the while to seem as smooth as old satin dyed rose-colour. Have you ever thought of me," she asked, "as really feeling as I do?"

Her companion, conspicuously, required to be clear. "Jealous, unhappy, tormented—? No," said Mrs. Assingham; "but at the same time—and though you may laugh at me for it!—I'm bound to confess that I've never been so awfully sure of what I may call knowing you. Here you are indeed, as you say—such a deep little person! I've never imagined your existence poisoned, and, since you wish to know if I consider that it need be, I've not the least difficulty in speaking on the spot. Nothing, decidedly, strikes me as more unnecessary."

For a minute after this they remained face to face; Maggie had sprung up while her friend sat enthroned, and, after moving to and fro in her intensity, now paused to receive the light she had invoked. It had accumulated, considerably, by this time, round Mrs. Assingham's ample presence, and it made, even to our young woman's own sense, a medium in which she could at last take a deeper breath. "I've affected you, these months—and these last weeks in especial—as quiet and natural and easy?"

But it was a question that took, not imperceptibly, some answering. "You've never affected me, from the first hour I beheld you, as anything but—in a way all your own—absolutely good and sweet and beautiful. In a way, as I say," Mrs. Assingham almost caressingly repeated, "just all your very own—nobody else's at all. I've never thought of you but as OUTSIDE of ugly things, so ignorant of any falsity or cruelty or vulgarity as never to have to be touched by them or to touch them. I've never mixed you up with them; there would have been time enough for that if they had seemed to be near you. But they haven't—if that's what you want to know."

"You've only believed me contented then because you've believed me stupid?"

Mrs. Assingham had a free smile, now, for the length of this stride, dissimulated though it might be in a graceful little frisk. "If I had believed you stupid I shouldn't have thought you interesting, and if I hadn't thought you interesting I shouldn't have noted whether I 'knew' you, as I've called it, or not. What I've always been conscious of is your having concealed about you somewhere no small amount of character; quite as much in fact," Fanny smiled, "as one could suppose a person of your size able to carry. The only thing was," she explained, "that thanks to your never calling one's attention to it, I hadn't made out much more about it, and should have been vague, above all, as to WHERE you carried it or kept it. Somewhere UNDER, I should simply have said—like that little silver cross you once showed me, blest by the Holy Father, that you always wear, out of sight, next your skin. That relic I've had a glimpse of"—with which she continued to invoke the privilege of humour. "But the precious little innermost, say this time little golden, personal nature of you—blest by a greater power, I think, even than the Pope—that you've never consentingly shown me. I'm not sure you've ever consentingly shown it to anyone. You've been in general too modest."

Maggie, trying to follow, almost achieved a little fold of her forehead. "I strike you as modest to-day—modest when I stand here and scream at you?"

"Oh, your screaming, I've granted you, is something new. I must fit it on somewhere. The question is, however," Mrs. Assingham further proceeded, "of what the deuce I can fit it on TO. Do you mean," she asked, "to the fact of our friends' being, from yesterday to to-morrow, at a place where they may more or less irresponsibly meet?" She spoke with the air of putting it as badly for them as possible. "Are you thinking of their being there alone—of their having consented to be?" And then as she had waited without result for her companion to say: "But isn't it true that—after you had this time again, at the eleventh hour, said YOU wouldn't—they would really much rather not have gone?"

"Yes—they would certainly much rather not have gone. But I wanted them to go."

"Then, my dear child, what in the world is the matter?"

"I wanted to see if they WOULD. And they've had to," Maggie added. "It was the only thing."

Her friend appeared to wonder. "From the moment you and your father backed out?"

"Oh, I don't mean go for those people; I mean go for us. For father and me," Maggie went on. "Because now they know."

"They 'know'?" Fanny Assingham quavered.

"That I've been for some time past taking more notice. Notice of the queer things in our life."

Maggie saw her companion for an instant on the point of asking her what these queer things might be; but Mrs. Assingham had the next minute brushed by that ambiguous opening and taken, as she evidently felt, a better one. "And is it for that you did it? I mean gave up the visit."

"It's for that I did it. To leave them to themselves—as they less and less want, or at any rate less and less venture to appear to want, to be left. As they had for so long arranged things," the Princess went on, "you see they sometimes have to be." And then, as if baffled by the lucidity of this, Mrs. Assingham for a little said nothing: "Now do you think I'm modest?"

With time, however; Fanny could brilliantly think anything that would serve. "I think you're wrong. That, my dear, is my answer to your question. It demands assuredly the straightest I can make. I see no 'awfulness'—I suspect none. I'm deeply distressed," she added, "that you should do anything else." It drew again from Maggie a long look. "You've never even imagined anything?"

"Ah, God forbid!—for it's exactly as a woman of imagination that I speak. There's no moment of my life at which I'm not imagining something; and it's thanks to that, darling," Mrs. Assingham pursued, "that I figure the sincerity with which your husband, whom you see as viciously occupied with your stepmother, is interested, is tenderly interested, in his admirable, adorable wife." She paused a minute as to give her friend the full benefit of this—as to Maggie's measure of which, however, no sign came; and then, poor woman, haplessly, she crowned her effort.—"He wouldn't hurt a hair of your head."

It had produced in Maggie, at once, and apparently in the intended form of a smile, the most extraordinary expression. "Ah, there it is!"

But her guest had already gone on. "And I'm absolutely certain that Charlotte wouldn't either."

It kept the Princess, with her strange grimace, standing there. "No—Charlotte wouldn't either. That's how they've had again to go off together. They've been afraid not to—lest it should disturb me, aggravate me, somehow work upon me. As I insisted that they must, that we couldn't all fail—though father and Charlotte hadn't really accepted; as I did this they had to yield to the fear that their showing as afraid to move together would count for them as the greater danger: which would be the danger, you see, of my feeling myself wronged. Their least danger, they know, is in going on with all the things that I've seemed to accept and that I've given no indication, at any moment, of not accepting. Everything that has come up for them has come up, in an extraordinary manner, without my having by a sound or a sign given myself away—so that it's all as wonderful as you may conceive. They move at any rate among the dangers I speak of—between that of their doing too much and that of their not having any longer the confidence, or the nerve, or whatever you may call it, to do enough." Her tone, by this time, might have shown a strangeness to match her smile; which was still more marked as she wound up. "And that's how I make them do what I like!"

It had an effect on Mrs. Assingham, who rose with the deliberation that, from point to point, marked the widening of her grasp. "My dear child, you're amazing."

"Amazing—?"

"You're terrible."

Maggie thoughtfully shook her head. "No; I'm not terrible, and you don't think me so. I do strike you as surprising, no doubt—but surprisingly mild. Because—don't you see?—I AM mild. I can bear anything."

"Oh, 'bear'!" Mrs. Assingham fluted.

"For love," said the Princess.

Fanny hesitated. "Of your father?"

"For love," Maggie repeated.

It kept her friend watching. "Of your husband?"

"For love," Maggie said again.

It was, for the moment, as if the distinctness of this might have determined in her companion a choice between two or three highly different alternatives. Mrs. Assingham's rejoinder, at all events—however much or however little it was a choice—was presently a triumph. "Speaking with this love of your own then, have you undertaken to convey to me that you believe your husband and your father's wife to be in act and in fact lovers of each other?" And then as the Princess didn't at first answer: "Do you call such an allegation as that 'mild'?"

"Oh, I'm not pretending to be mild to you. But I've told you, and moreover you must have seen for yourself, how much so I've been to them."

Mrs. Assingham, more brightly again, bridled. "Is that what you call it when you make them, for terror as you say, do as you like?"

"Ah, there wouldn't be any terror for them if they had nothing to hide."

Mrs. Assingham faced her—quite steady now. "Are you really conscious, love, of what you're saying?"

"I'm saying that I'm bewildered and tormented, and that I've no one but you to speak to. I've thought, I've in fact been sure, that you've seen for yourself how much this is the case. It's why I've believed you would meet me half way."

"Half way to what? To denouncing," Fanny asked, "two persons, friends of years, whom I've always immensely admired and liked, and against whom I haven't the shadow of a charge to make?"

Maggie looked at her with wide eyes. "I had much rather you should denounce me than denounce them. Denounce me, denounce me," she said, "if you can see your way." It was exactly what she appeared to have argued out with herself. "If, conscientiously, you can denounce me; if, conscientiously, you can revile me; if, conscientiously, you can put me in my place for a low-minded little pig—!"

"Well?" said Mrs. Assingham, consideringly, as she paused for emphasis.

"I think I shall be saved."

Her friend took it, for a minute, however, by carrying thoughtful eyes, eyes verily portentous, over her head. "You say you've no one to speak to, and you make a point of your having so disguised your feelings—not having, as you call it, given yourself away. Have you then never seen it not only as your right, but as your bounden duty, worked up to such a pitch, to speak to your husband?"

"I've spoken to him," said Maggie.

Mrs. Assingham stared. "Ah, then it isn't true that you've made no sign."

Maggie had a silence. "I've made no trouble. I've made no scene. I've taken no stand. I've neither reproached nor accused him. You'll say there's a way in all that of being nasty enough."

"Oh!" dropped from Fanny as if she couldn't help it.

"But I don't think—strangely enough—that he regards me as nasty. I think that at bottom—for that IS," said the Princess, "the strangeness—he's sorry for me. Yes, I think that, deep within, he pities me."

Her companion wondered. "For the state you've let yourself get into?"

"For not being happy when I've so much to make me so."

"You've everything," said Mrs. Assingham with alacrity. Yet she remained for an instant embarrassed as to a further advance. "I don't understand, however, how, if you've done nothing—"

An impatience from Maggie had checked her. "I've not done absolutely 'nothing.'"

"But what then—?"

"Well," she went on after a minute, "he knows what I've done."

It produced on Mrs. Assingham's part, her whole tone and manner exquisitely aiding, a hush not less prolonged, and the very duration of which inevitably gave it something of the character of an equal recognition. "And what then has HE done?"

Maggie took again a minute. "He has been splendid."

"'Splendid'? Then what more do you want?"

"Ah, what you see!" said Maggie. "Not to be afraid."

It made her guest again hang fire. "Not to be afraid really to speak?"

"Not to be afraid NOT to speak."

Mrs. Assingham considered further. "You can't even to Charlotte?" But as, at this, after a look at her, Maggie turned off with a movement of suppressed despair, she checked herself and might have been watching her, for all the difficulty and the pity of it, vaguely moving to the window and the view of the hill street. It was almost as if she had had to give up, from failure of responsive wit in her friend—the last failure she had feared—the hope of the particular relief she had been working for. Mrs. Assingham resumed the next instant, however, in the very tone that seemed most to promise her she should have to give up nothing. "I see, I see; you would have in that case too many things to consider." It brought the Princess round again, proving itself thus the note of comprehension she wished most to clutch at. "Don't be afraid."

Maggie took it where she stood—which she was soon able to signify. "Thank-you."

It very properly encouraged her counsellor. "What your idea imputes is a criminal intrigue carried on, from day to day, amid perfect trust and sympathy, not only under your eyes, but under your father's. That's an idea it's impossible for me for a. moment to entertain."

"Ah, there you are then! It's exactly what I wanted from you."

"You're welcome to it!" Mrs. Assingham breathed.

"You never HAVE entertained it?" Maggie pursued.

"Never for an instant," said Fanny with her head very high.

Maggie took it again, yet again as wanting more. "Pardon my being so horrid. But by all you hold sacred?"

Mrs. Assingham faced her. "Ah, my dear, upon my positive word as an honest woman."

"Thank-you then," said the Princess.

So they remained a little; after which, "But do you believe it, love?" Fanny inquired.

"I believe YOU."

"Well, as I've faith in THEM, it comes to the same thing."

Maggie, at this last, appeared for a moment to think again; but she embraced the proposition. "The same thing."

"Then you're no longer unhappy?" her guest urged, coming more gaily toward her.

"I doubtless shan't be a great while."

But it was now Mrs. Assingham's turn to want more. "I've convinced you it's impossible?"

She had held out her arms, and Maggie, after a moment, meeting her, threw herself into them with a sound that had its oddity as a sign of relief. "Impossible, impossible," she emphatically, more than emphatically, replied; yet the next minute she had burst into tears over the impossibility, and a few seconds later, pressing, clinging, sobbing, had even caused them to flow, audibly, sympathetically and perversely, from her friend.

XXXI

The understanding appeared to have come to be that the Colonel and his wife were to present themselves toward the middle of July for the "good long visit" at Fawns on which Maggie had obtained from her father that he should genially insist; as well as that the couple from Eaton Square should welcome there earlier in the month, and less than a week after their own arrival, the advent of the couple from Portland Place. "Oh, we shall give you time to breathe!" Fanny remarked, in reference to the general prospect, with a gaiety that announced itself as heedless of criticism, to each member of the party in turn; sustaining and bracing herself by her emphasis, pushed even to an amiable cynicism, of the confident view of these punctualities of the Assinghams. The ground she could best occupy, to her sense, was that of her being moved, as in this connexion she had always been moved, by the admitted grossness of her avidity, the way the hospitality of the Ververs met her convenience and ministered to her ease, destitute as the Colonel had kept her, from the first, of any rustic retreat, any leafy bower of her own, any fixed base for the stale season now at hand. She had explained at home, she had repeatedly reexplained, the terms of her dilemma, the real difficulty of her, or—as she now put it—of their position. When the pair could do nothing else, in Cadogan Place, they could still talk of marvellous little Maggie, and of the charm, the sinister charm, of their having to hold their breath to watch her; a topic the momentous midnight discussion at which we have been present was so far from having exhausted. It came up, irrepressibly, at all private hours; they had planted it there between them, and it grew, from day to day, in a manner to make their own sense of responsibility almost yield to their sense of fascination. Mrs. Assingham declared at such moments that in the interest of this admirable young thing—to whom, she also declared, she had quite "come over"—she was ready to pass with all the world else, even with the Prince himself, the object, inconsequently, as well, of her continued, her explicitly shameless appreciation, for a vulgar, indelicate, pestilential woman, showing her true character in an abandoned old age. The Colonel's confessed attention had been enlisted, we have seen, as never yet, under pressure from his wife, by any guaranteed imbroglio; but this, she could assure him she perfectly knew, was not a bit because he was sorry for her, or touched by what she had let herself in for, but because, when once they had been opened, he couldn't keep his eyes from resting complacently, resting almost intelligently, on the Princess. If he was in love with HER now, however, so much the better; it would help them both not to wince at what they would have to do for her. Mrs. Assingham had come back to that, whenever he groaned or grunted; she had at no beguiled moment—since Maggie's little march WAS positively beguiling—let him lose sight of the grim necessity awaiting them. "We shall have, as I've again and again told you, to lie for her—to lie till we're black in the face."

"To lie 'for' her?" The Colonel often, at these hours, as from a vague vision of old chivalry in a new form, wandered into apparent lapses from lucidity.

"To lie TO her, up and down, and in and out—it comes to the same thing. It will consist just as much of lying to the others too: to the Prince about one's belief in HIM; to Charlotte about one's belief in HER; to Mr. Verver, dear sweet man, about one's belief in everyone. So we've work cut out—with the biggest lie, on top of all, being that we LIKE to be there for such a purpose. We hate it unspeakably—I'm more ready to be a coward before it, to let the whole thing, to let everyone, selfishly and pusillanimously slide, than before any social duty, any felt human call, that has ever forced me to be decent. I speak at least for myself. For you," she had added, "as I've given you so perfect an opportunity to fall in love with Maggie, you'll doubtless find your account in being so much nearer to her."

"And what do you make," the Colonel could, at this, always imperturbably enough ask, "of the account you yourself will find in being so much nearer to the Prince; of your confirmed, if not exasperated, infatuation with whom—to say nothing of my weak good-nature about it—you give such a pretty picture?"

To the picture in question she had been always, in fact, able contemplatively to return. "The difficulty of my enjoyment of that is, don't you see? that I'm making, in my loyalty to Maggie, a sad hash of his affection for me."

"You find means to call it then, this whitewashing of his crime, being 'loyal' to Maggie?"

"Oh, about that particular crime there is always much to say. It is always more interesting to us than any other crime; it has at least that for it. But of course I call everything I have in mind at all being loyal to Maggie. Being loyal to her is, more than anything else, helping her with her father—which is what she most wants and needs."

The Colonel had had it before, but he could apparently never have too much of it. "Helping her 'with' him—?"

"Helping her against him then. Against what we've already so fully talked of—its having to be recognised between them that he doubts. That's where my part is so plain—to see her through, to see her through to the end." Exaltation, for the moment, always lighted Mrs. Assingham's reference to this plainness; yet she at the same time seldom failed, the next instant, to qualify her view of it. "When I talk of my obligation as clear I mean that it's absolute; for just HOW, from day to day and through thick and thin, to keep the thing up is, I grant you, another matter. There's one way, luckily, nevertheless, in which I'm strong. I can perfectly count on her."

The Colonel seldom failed here, as from the insidious growth of an excitement, to wonder, to encourage. "Not to see you're lying?"

"To stick to me fast, whatever she sees. If I stick to her—that is to my own poor struggling way, under providence, of watching over them ALL—she'll stand by me to the death. She won't give me away. For, you know, she easily can."

This, regularly, was the most lurid turn of their road; but Bob Assingham, with each journey, met it as for the first time. "Easily?"

"She can utterly dishonour me with her father. She can let him know that I was aware, at the time of his marriage—as I had been aware at the time of her own—of the relations that had pre-existed between his wife and her husband."

"And how can she do so if, up to this minute, by your own statement, she is herself in ignorance of your knowledge?"

It was a question that Mrs. Assingham had ever, for dealing with, a manner to which repeated practice had given almost a grand effect; very much as if she were invited by it to say that about this, exactly, she proposed to do her best lying. But she said, and with full lucidity, something quite other: it could give itself a little the air, still, of a triumph over his coarseness. "By acting, immediately with the blind resentment with which, in her place, ninety-nine women out of a hundred would act; and by so making Mr. Verver, in turn, act with the same natural passion, the passion of ninety-nine men out of a hundred. They've only to agree about me," the poor lady said; "they've only to feel at one over it, feel bitterly practised upon, cheated and injured; they've only to denounce me to each other as false and infamous, for me to be quite irretrievably dished. Of course it's I who have been, and who continue to be, cheated—cheated by the Prince and Charlotte; but they're not obliged to give me the benefit of that, or to give either of us the benefit of anything. They'll be within their rights to lump us all together as a false, cruel, conspiring crew, and, if they can find the right facts to support them, get rid of us root and branch."

This, on each occasion, put the matter so at the worst that repetition even scarce controlled the hot flush with which she was compelled to see the parts of the whole history, all its ugly consistency and its temporary gloss, hang together. She enjoyed, invariably, the sense of making her danger present, of making it real, to her husband, and of his almost turning pale, when their eyes met, at this possibility of their compromised state and their shared discredit. The beauty was that, as under a touch of one of the ivory notes at the left of the keyboard, he sounded out with the short sharpness of the dear fond stupid uneasy man. "Conspiring—so far as YOU were concerned—to what end?"

"Why, to the obvious end of getting the Prince a wife—at Maggie's expense. And then to that of getting Charlotte a husband at Mr. Verver's."

"Of rendering friendly services, yes—which have produced, as it turns out, complications. But from the moment you didn't do it FOR the complications, why shouldn't you have rendered them?"

It was extraordinary for her, always, in this connexion, how, with time given him, he fell to speaking better for her than she could, in the presence of her clear-cut image of the "worst," speak for herself. Troubled as she was she thus never wholly failed of her amusement by the way. "Oh, isn't what I may have meddled 'for'—so far as it can be proved I did meddle—open to interpretation; by which I mean to Mr. Verver's and Maggie's? Mayn't they see my motive, in the light of that appreciation, as the wish to be decidedly more friendly to the others than to the victimised father and daughter?" She positively liked to keep it up. "Mayn't they see my motive as the determination to serve the Prince, in any case, and at any price, first; to 'place' him comfortably; in other words to find him his fill of money? Mayn't it have all the air for them of a really equivocal, sinister bargain between us—something quite unholy and louche?"

It produced in the poor Colonel, infallibly, the echo. "'Louche,' love—?"

"Why, haven't you said as much yourself?—haven't you put your finger on that awful possibility?" She had a way now, with her felicities, that made him enjoy being reminded of them. "In speaking of your having always had such a 'mash'—?"

"Such a mash, precisely, for the man I was to help to put so splendidly at his ease. A motherly mash an impartial look at it would show it only as likely to have been—but we're not talking, of course, about impartial looks. We're talking of good innocent people deeply worked upon by a horrid discovery, and going much further, in their view of the lurid, as such people almost always do, than those who have been wider awake, all round, from the first. What I was to have got from my friend, in such a view, in exchange for what I had been able to do for him—well, that would have been an equivalent, of a kind best known to myself, for me shrewdly to consider." And she easily lost herself, each time, in the anxious satisfaction of filling out the picture. "It would have been seen, it would have been heard of, before, the case of the woman a man doesn't want, or of whom he's tired, or for whom he has no use but SUCH uses, and who is capable, in her infatuation, in her passion, of promoting his interests with other women rather than lose sight of him, lose touch of him, cease to have to do with him at all. Cela s'est vu, my dear; and stranger things still—as I needn't tell YOU! Very good then," she wound up; "there is a perfectly possible conception of the behaviour of your sweet wife; since, as I say, there's no imagination so lively, once it's started, as that of really agitated lambs. Lions are nothing to them, for lions are sophisticated, are blases, are brought up, from the first, to prowling and mauling. It does give us, you'll admit, something to think about. My relief is luckily, however, in what I finally do think."

He was well enough aware, by this time, of what she finally did think; but he was not without a sense, again, also for his amusement by the way. It would have made him, for a spectator of these passages between the pair, resemble not a little the artless child who hears his favourite story told for the twentieth time and enjoys it exactly because he knows what is next to happen. "What of course will pull them up, if they turn out to have less imagination than you assume, is the profit you can have found in furthering Mrs. Verver's marriage. You weren't at least in love with Charlotte."

"Oh," Mrs. Assingham, at this, always brought out, "my hand in that is easily accounted for by my desire to be agreeable to HIM."

"To Mr. Verver?"

"To the Prince—by preventing her in that way from taking, as he was in danger of seeing her do, some husband with whom he wouldn't be able to open, to keep open, so large an account as with his father-in-law. I've brought her near him, kept her within his reach, as she could never have remained either as a single woman or as the wife of a different man."

"Kept her, on that sweet construction, to be his mistress?"

"Kept her, on that sweet construction, to be his mistress." She brought it out grandly—it had always so, for her own ear as well as, visibly, for her husband's, its effect. "The facilities in the case, thanks to the particular conditions, being so quite ideal."

"Down even to the facility of your minding everything so little—from your own point of view—as to have supplied him with the enjoyment of TWO beautiful women."

"Down even to THAT—to the monstrosity of my folly. But not," Mrs. Assingham added, "'two' of anything. One beautiful woman—and one beautiful fortune. That's what a creature of pure virtue exposes herself to when she suffers her pure virtue, suffers her sympathy, her disinterestedness, her exquisite sense for the lives of others, to carry her too far. Voila."

"I see. It's the way the Ververs have you."

"It's the way the Ververs 'have' me. It's in other words the way they would be able to make such a show to each other of having me—if Maggie weren't so divine."

"She lets you off?" He never failed to insist on all this to the very end; which was how he had become so versed in what she finally thought.

"She lets me off. So that now, horrified and contrite at what I've done, I may work to help her out. And Mr. Verver," she was fond of adding, "lets me off too."

"Then you do believe he knows?"

It determined in her always, there, with a significant pause, a deep immersion in her thought. "I believe he would let me off if he did know—so that I might work to help HIM out. Or rather, really," she went on, "that I might work to help Maggie. That would be his motive, that would be his condition, in forgiving me; just as hers, for me, in fact, her motive and her condition, are my acting to spare her father. But it's with Maggie only that I'm directly concerned; nothing, ever—not a breath, not a look, I'll guarantee—shall I have, whatever happens, from Mr. Verver himself. So it is, therefore, that I shall probably, by the closest possible shave, escape the penalty of my crimes."

"You mean being held responsible."

"I mean being held responsible. My advantage will be that Maggie's such a trump."

"Such a trump that, as you say, she'll stick to you."

"Stick to me, on our understanding—stick to me. For our understanding's signed and sealed." And to brood over it again was ever, for Mrs. Assingham, to break out again with exaltation. "It's a grand, high compact. She has solemnly promised."

"But in words—?"

"Oh yes, in words enough—since it's a matter of words. To keep up HER lie so long as I keep up mine."

"And what do you call 'her' lie?"

"Why, the pretence that she believes me. Believes they're innocent."

"She positively believes then they're guilty? She has arrived at that, she's really content with it, in the absence of proof?" It was here, each time, that Fanny Assingham most faltered; but always at last to get the matter, for her own sense, and with a long sigh, sufficiently straight. "It isn't a question of belief or of proof, absent or present; it's inevitably, with her, a question of natural perception, of insurmountable feeling. She irresistibly knows that there's something between them. But she hasn't 'arrived' at it, as you say, at all; that's exactly what she hasn't done, what she so steadily and intensely refuses to do. She stands off and off, so as not to arrive; she keeps out to sea and away from the rocks, and what she most wants of me is to keep at a safe distance with her—as I, for my own skin, only ask not to come nearer." After which, invariably, she let him have it all. "So far from wanting proof—which she must get, in a manner, by my siding with her—she wants DISproof, as against herself, and has appealed to me, so extraordinarily, to side against her. It's really magnificent, when you come to think of it, the spirit of her appeal. If I'll but cover them up brazenly enough, the others, so as to show, round and about them, as happy as a bird, she on her side will do what she can. If I'll keep them quiet, in a word, it will enable her to gain time—time as against any idea of her father's—and so, somehow, come out. If I'll take care of Charlotte, in particular, she'll take care of the Prince; and it's beautiful and wonderful, really pathetic and exquisite, to see what she feels that time may do for her."

"Ah, but what does she call, poor little thing, 'time'?"

"Well, this summer at Fawns, to begin with. She can live as yet, of course, but from hand to mouth; but she has worked it out for herself, I think, that the very danger of Fawns, superficially looked at, may practically amount to a greater protection. THERE the lovers—if they ARE lovers!—will have to mind. They'll feel it for themselves, unless things are too utterly far gone with them."

"And things are NOT too utterly far gone with them?"

She had inevitably, poor woman, her hesitation for this, but she put down her answer as, for the purchase of some absolutely indispensable article, she would have put down her last shilling. "No."

It made him always grin at her. "Is THAT a lie?"

"Do you think you're worth lying to? If it weren't the truth, for me," she added, "I wouldn't have accepted for Fawns. I CAN, I believe, keep the wretches quiet."

"But how—at the worst?"

"Oh, 'the worst'—don't talk about the worst! I can keep them quiet at the best, I seem to feel, simply by our being there. It will work, from week to week, of itself. You'll see."

He was willing enough to see, but he desired to provide—! "Yet if it doesn't work?"

"Ah, that's talking about the worst!"

Well, it might be; but what were they doing, from morning to night, at this crisis, but talk? "Who'll keep the others?"

"The others—?"

"Who'll keep THEM quiet? If your couple have had a life together, they can't have had it completely without witnesses, without the help of persons, however few, who must have some knowledge, some idea about them. They've had to meet, secretly, protectedly, they've had to arrange; for if they haven't met, and haven't arranged, and haven't thereby, in some quarter or other, had to give themselves away, why are we piling it up so? Therefore if there's evidence, up and down London—"

"There must be people in possession of it? Ah, it isn't all," she always remembered, "up and down London. Some of it must connect them—I mean," she musingly added, "it naturally WOULD—with other places; with who knows what strange adventures, opportunities, dissimulations? But whatever there may have been, it will also all have been buried on the spot. Oh, they've known HOW—too beautifully! But nothing, all the same, is likely to find its way to Maggie of itself."

"Because every one who may have anything to tell, you hold, will have been so squared?" And then inveterately, before she could say—he enjoyed so much coming to this: "What will have squared Lady Castledean?"

"The consciousness"—she had never lost her promptness—"of having no stones to throw at any one else's windows. She has enough to do to guard her own glass. That was what she was doing," Fanny said, "that last morning at Matcham when all of us went off and she kept the Prince and Charlotte over. She helped them simply that she might herself be helped—if it wasn't perhaps, rather, with her ridiculous Mr. Blint, that HE might be. They put in together, therefore, of course, that day; they got it clear—and quite under her eyes; inasmuch as they didn't become traceable again, as we know, till late in the evening." On this historic circumstance Mrs. Assingham was always ready afresh to brood; but she was no less ready, after her brooding, devoutly to add "Only we know nothing whatever else—for which all our stars be thanked!"

The Colonel's gratitude was apt to be less marked. "What did they do for themselves, all the same, from the moment they got that free hand to the moment (long after dinner-time, haven't you told me?) of their turning up at their respective homes?"

"Well, it's none of your business!"

"I don't speak of it as mine, but it's only too much theirs. People are always traceable, in England, when tracings are required. Something, sooner or later, happens; somebody, sooner or later, breaks the holy calm. Murder will out."

"Murder will—but this isn't murder. Quite the contrary perhaps! I verily believe," she had her moments of adding, "that, for the amusement of the row, you would prefer an explosion."

This, however, was a remark he seldom noticed; he wound up, for the most part, after a long, contemplative smoke, with a transition from which no exposed futility in it had succeeded in weaning him. "What I can't for my life make out is your idea of the old boy."

"Charlotte's too inconceivably funny husband? I HAVE no idea."

"I beg your pardon—you've just shown it. You never speak of him but as too inconceivably funny."

"Well, he is," she always confessed. "That is he may be, for all I know, too inconceivably great. But that's not an idea. It represents only my weak necessity of feeling that he's beyond me—which isn't an idea either. You see he MAY be stupid too."

"Precisely—there you are."

"Yet on the other hand," she always went on, "he MAY be sublime: sublimer even than Maggie herself. He may in fact have already been. But we shall never know." With which her tone betrayed perhaps a shade of soreness for the single exemption she didn't yearningly welcome. "THAT I can see."

"Oh, I say—!" It came to affect the Colonel himself with a sense of privation.

"I'm not sure, even, that Charlotte will."

"Oh, my dear, what Charlotte doesn't know—!"

But she brooded and brooded. "I'm not sure even that the Prince will." It seemed privation, in short, for them all. "They'll be mystified, confounded, tormented. But they won't know—and all their possible putting their heads together won't make them. That," said Fanny Assingham, "will be their punishment." And she ended, ever, when she had come so far, at the same pitch. "It will probably also—if I get off with so little—be mine."

"And what," her husband liked to ask, "will be mine?"

"Nothing—you're not worthy of any. One's punishment is in what one feels, and what will make ours effective is that we SHALL feel." She was splendid with her "ours"; she flared up with this prophecy. "It will be Maggie herself who will mete it out."

"Maggie—?"

"SHE'LL know—about her father; everything. Everything," she repeated. On the vision of which, each time, Mrs. Assingham, as with the presentiment of an odd despair, turned away from it. "But she'll never tell us."

XXXII

If Maggie had not so firmly made up her mind never to say, either to her good friend or to any one else, more than she meant about her father, she might have found herself betrayed into some such overflow during the week spent in London with her husband after the others had adjourned to Fawns for the summer. This was because of the odd element of the unnatural imparted to the so simple fact of their brief separation by the assumptions resident in their course of life hitherto. She was used, herself, certainly, by this time, to dealing with odd elements; but she dropped, instantly, even from such peace as she had patched up, when it was a question of feeling that her unpenetrated parent might be alone with them. She thought of him as alone with them when she thought of him as alone with Charlotte—and this, strangely enough, even while fixing her sense to the full on his wife's power of preserving, quite of enhancing, every felicitous appearance. Charlotte had done that—under immeasurably fewer difficulties indeed—during the numerous months of their hymeneal absence from England, the period prior to that wonderful reunion of the couples, in the interest of the larger play of all the virtues of each, which was now bearing, for Mrs. Verver's stepdaughter at least, such remarkable fruit. It was the present so much briefer interval, in a situation, possibly in a relation, so changed—it was the new terms of her problem that would now tax Charlotte's art. The Princess could pull herself up, repeatedly, by remembering that the real "relation" between her father and his wife was a thing that she knew nothing about and that, in strictness, was none of her business; but she none the less failed to keep quiet, as she would have called it, before the projected image of their ostensibly happy isolation. Nothing could have had less of the quality of quietude than a certain queer wish that fitfully flickered up in her, a wish that usurped, perversely, the place of a much more natural one. If Charlotte, while she was about it, could only have been WORSE!—that idea Maggie fell to invoking instead of the idea that she might desirably have been better. For, exceedingly odd as it was to feel in such ways, she believed she mightn't have worried so much if she didn't somehow make her stepmother out, under the beautiful trees and among the dear old gardens, as lavish of fifty kinds of confidence and twenty kinds, at least, of gentleness. Gentleness and confidence were certainly the right thing, as from a charming woman to her husband, but the fine tissue of reassurance woven by this lady's hands and flung over her companion as a light, muffling veil, formed precisely a wrought transparency through which she felt her father's eyes continually rest on herself. The reach of his gaze came to her straighter from a distance; it showed him as still more conscious, down there alone, of the suspected, the felt elaboration of the process of their not alarming or hurting him. She had herself now, for weeks and weeks, and all unwinkingly, traced the extension of this pious effort; but her perfect success in giving no sign—she did herself THAT credit—would have been an achievement quite wasted if Mrs. Verver should make with him those mistakes of proportion, one set of them too abruptly, too incoherently designed to correct another set, that she had made with his daughter. However, if she HAD been worse, poor woman, who should say that her husband would, to a certainty, have been better?

One groped noiselessly among such questions, and it was actually not even definite for the Princess that her own Amerigo, left alone with her in town, had arrived at the golden mean of non-precautionary gallantry which would tend, by his calculation, to brush private criticism from its last perching-place. The truth was, in this connection, that she had different sorts of terrors, and there were hours when it came to her that these days were a prolonged repetition of that night-drive, of weeks before, from the other house to their own, when he had tried to charm her, by his sovereign personal power, into some collapse that would commit her to a repudiation of consistency. She was never alone with him, it was to be said, without her having sooner or later to ask herself what had already become of her consistency; yet, at the same time, so long as she breathed no charge, she kept hold of a remnant of appearance that could save her from attack. Attack, real attack, from him, as he would conduct it was what she above all dreaded; she was so far from sure that under that experience she mightn't drop into some depth of weakness, mightn't show him some shortest way with her that he would know how to use again. Therefore, since she had given him, as yet, no moment's pretext for pretending to her that she had either lost faith or suffered by a feather's weight in happiness, she left him, it was easy to reason, with an immense advantage for all waiting and all tension. She wished him, for the present, to "make up" to her for nothing. Who could say to what making-up might lead, into what consenting or pretending or destroying blindness it might plunge her? She loved him too helplessly, still, to dare to open the door, by an inch, to his treating her as if either of them had wronged the other. Something or somebody—and who, at this, which of them all?—would inevitably, would in the gust of momentary selfishness, be sacrificed to that; whereas what she intelligently needed was to know where she was going. Knowledge, knowledge, was a fascination as well as a fear; and a part, precisely, of the strangeness of this juncture was the way her apprehension that he would break out to her with some merely general profession was mixed with her dire need to forgive him, to reassure him, to respond to him, on no ground that she didn't fully measure. To do these things it must be clear to her what they were FOR; but to act in that light was, by the same effect, to learn, horribly, what the other things had been. He might tell her only what he wanted, only what would work upon her by the beauty of his appeal; and the result of the direct appeal of ANY beauty in him would be her helpless submission to his terms. All her temporary safety, her hand-to-mouth success, accordingly, was in his neither perceiving nor divining this, thanks to such means as she could take to prevent him; take, literally from hour to hour, during these days of more unbroken exposure. From hour to hour she fairly expected some sign of his having decided on a jump. "Ah yes, it HAS been as you think; I've strayed away, I've fancied myself free, given myself in other quantities, with larger generosities, because I thought you were different—different from what I now see. But it was only, only, because I didn't know—and you must admit that you gave me scarce reason enough. Reason enough, I mean, to keep clear of my mistake; to which I confess, for which I'll do exquisite penance, which you can help me now, I too beautifully feel, to get completely over."

That was what, while she watched herself, she potentially heard him bring out; and while she carried to an end another day, another sequence and yet another of their hours together, without his producing it, she felt herself occupied with him beyond even the intensity of surrender. She was keeping her head, for a reason, for a cause; and the labour of this detachment, with the labour of her keeping the pitch of it down, held them together in the steel hoop of an intimacy compared with which artless passion would have been but a beating of the air. Her greatest danger, or at least her greatest motive for care, was the obsession of the thought that, if he actually did suspect, the fruit of his attention to her couldn't help being a sense of the growth of her importance. Taking the measure, with him, as she had taken it with her father, of the prescribed reach of her hypocrisy, she saw how it would have to stretch even to her seeking to prove that she was NOT, all the same, important. A single touch from him—oh, she should know it in case of its coming!—any brush of his hand, of his lips, of his voice, inspired by recognition of her probable interest as distinct from pity for her virtual gloom, would hand her over to him bound hand and foot. Therefore to be free, to be free to act, other than abjectly, for her father, she must conceal from him the validity that, like a microscopic insect pushing a grain of sand, she was taking on even for herself. She could keep it up with a change in sight, but she couldn't keep it up forever; so that, really, one extraordinary effect of their week of untempered confrontation, which bristled with new marks, was to make her reach out, in thought, to their customary companions and calculate the kind of relief that rejoining them would bring. She was learning, almost from minute to minute, to be a mistress of shades since, always, when there were possibilities enough of intimacy, there were also, by that fact, in intercourse, possibilities of iridescence; but she was working against an adversary who was a master of shades too, and on whom, if she didn't look out, she should presently have imposed a consciousness of the nature of their struggle. To feel him in fact, to think of his feeling himself, her adversary in things of this fineness—to see him at all, in short, brave a name that would represent him as in opposition— was already to be nearly reduced to a visible smothering of her cry of alarm. Should he guess they were having, in their so occult manner, a HIGH fight, and that it was she, all the while, in her supposed stupidity, who had made it high and was keeping it high—in the event of his doing this before they could leave town she should verily be lost.

The possible respite for her at Fawns would come from the fact that observation, in him, there, would inevitably find some of its directness diverted. This would be the case if only because the remarkable strain of her father's placidity might be thought of as likely to claim some larger part of his attention. Besides which there would be always Charlotte herself to draw him off. Charlotte would help him again, doubtless, to study anything, right or left, that might be symptomatic; but Maggie could see that this very fact might perhaps contribute, in its degree, to protect the secret of her own fermentation. It is not even incredible that she may have discovered the gleam of a comfort that was to broaden in the conceivable effect on the Prince's spirit, on his nerves, on his finer irritability, of some of the very airs and aspects, the light graces themselves, of Mrs. Verver's too perfect competence. What it would most come to, after all, she said to herself, was a renewal for him of the privilege of watching that lady watch her. Very well, then: with the elements after all so mixed in him, how long would he go on enjoying mere spectatorship of that act? For she had by this time made up her mind that in Charlotte's company he deferred to Charlotte's easier art of mounting guard. Wouldn't he get tired—to put it only at that—of seeing her always on the rampart, erect and elegant, with her lace-flounced parasol now folded and now shouldered, march to and fro against a gold-coloured east or west? Maggie had gone far, truly for a view of the question of this particular reaction, and she was not incapable of pulling herself up with the rebuke that she counted her chickens before they were hatched. How sure she should have to be of so many things before she might thus find a weariness in Amerigo's expression and a logic in his weariness!

One of her dissimulated arts for meeting their tension, meanwhile, was to interweave Mrs. Assingham as plausibly as possible with the undulations of their surface, to bring it about that she should join them, of an afternoon, when they drove together or if they went to look at things—looking at things being almost as much a feature of their life as if they were bazaar-opening royalties. Then there were such combinations, later in the day, as her attendance on them, and the Colonel's as well, for such whimsical matters as visits to the opera no matter who was singing, and sudden outbreaks of curiosity about the British drama. The good couple from Cadogan Place could always unprotestingly dine with them and "go on" afterwards to such publicities as the Princess cultivated the boldness of now perversely preferring. It may be said of her that, during these passages, she plucked her sensations by the way, detached, nervously, the small wild blossoms of her dim forest, so that she could smile over them at least with the spacious appearance, for her companions, for her husband above all, of bravely, of altogether frivolously, going a-maying. She had her intense, her smothered excitements, some of which were almost inspirations; she had in particular the extravagant, positively at moments the amused, sense of using her friend to the topmost notch, accompanied with the high luxury of not having to explain. Never, no never, should she have to explain to Fanny Assingham again—who, poor woman, on her own side, would be charged, it might be forever, with that privilege of the higher ingenuity. She put it all off on Fanny, and the dear thing herself might henceforth appraise the quantity. More and more magnificent now in her blameless egoism, Maggie asked no questions of her, and thus only signified the greatness of the opportunity she gave her. She didn't care for what devotions, what dinners of their own the Assinghams might have been "booked"; that was a detail, and she could think without wincing of the ruptures and rearrangements to which her service condemned them. It all fell in beautifully, moreover; so that, as hard, at this time, in spite of her fever, as a little pointed diamond, the Princess showed something of the glitter of consciously possessing the constructive, the creative hand. She had but to have the fancy of presenting herself, of presenting her husband, in a certain high and convenient manner, to make it natural they should go about with their gentleman and their lady. To what else but this, exactly, had Charlotte, during so many weeks of the earlier season, worked her up?—herself assuming and discharging, so far as might be, the character and office of one of those revolving subordinate presences that float in the wake of greatness.

The precedent was therefore established, and the group normally constituted. Mrs. Assingham, meanwhile, at table, on the stairs, in the carriage or the opera-box, might—with her constant overflow of expression, for that matter, and its singularly resident character where men in especial were concerned—look across at Amerigo in whatever sense she liked: it was not of that Maggie proposed to be afraid. She might warn him, she might rebuke him, she might reassure him, she might—if it were impossible not to—absolutely make love to him; even this was open to her, as a matter simply between them, if it would help her to answer for the impeccability he had guaranteed. And Maggie desired in fact only to strike her as acknowledging the efficacy of her aid when she mentioned to her one evening a small project for the morrow, privately entertained—the idea, irresistible, intense, of going to pay, at the Museum, a visit to Mr. Crichton. Mr. Crichton, as Mrs. Assingham could easily remember, was the most accomplished and obliging of public functionaries, whom every one knew and who knew every one—who had from the first, in particular, lent himself freely, and for the love of art and history, to becoming one of the steadier lights of Mr. Verver's adventurous path. The custodian of one of the richest departments of the great national collection of precious things, he could feel for the sincere private collector and urge him on his way even when condemned to be present at his capture of trophies sacrificed by the country to parliamentary thrift. He carried his amiability to the point of saying that, since London, under pettifogging views, had to miss, from time to time, its rarest opportunities, he was almost consoled to see such lost causes invariably wander at last, one by one, with the tormenting tinkle of their silver bells, into the wondrous, the already famous fold beyond the Mississippi. There was a charm in his "almosts" that was not to be resisted, especially after Mr. Verver and Maggie had grown sure—or almost, again—of enjoying the monopoly of them; and on this basis of envy changed to sympathy by the more familiar view of the father and the daughter, Mr. Crichton had at both houses, though especially in Eaton Square, learned to fill out the responsive and suggestive character. It was at his invitation, Fanny well recalled, that Maggie, one day, long before, and under her own attendance precisely, had, for the glory of the name she bore, paid a visit to one of the ampler shrines of the supreme exhibitory temple, an alcove of shelves charged with the gold-and-brown, gold-and-ivory, of old Italian bindings and consecrated to the records of the Prince's race. It had been an impression that penetrated, that remained; yet Maggie had sighed, ever so prettily, at its having to be so superficial. She was to go back some day, to dive deeper, to linger and taste; in spite of which, however, Mrs. Assingham could not recollect perceiving that the visit had been repeated. This second occasion had given way, for a long time, in her happy life, to other occasions—all testifying, in their degree, to the quality of her husband's blood, its rich mixture and its many remarkable references; after which, no doubt, the charming piety involved had grown, on still further grounds, bewildered and faint.

It now appeared, none the less, that some renewed conversation with Mr. Crichton had breathed on the faintness revivingly, and Maggie mentioned her purpose as a conception of her very own, to the success of which she designed to devote her morning. Visits of gracious ladies, under his protection, lighted up rosily, for this perhaps most flower-loving and honey-sipping member of the great Bloomsbury hive, its packed passages and cells; and though not sworn of the province toward which his friend had found herself, according to her appeal to him, yearning again, nothing was easier for him than to put her in relation with the presiding urbanities. So it had been settled, Maggie said to Mrs. Assingham, and she was to dispense with Amerigo's company. Fanny was to remember later on that she had at first taken this last fact for one of the finer notes of her young woman's detachment, imagined she must be going alone because of the shade of irony that, in these ambiguous days, her husband's personal presence might be felt to confer, practically, on any tribute to his transmitted significance. Then as, the next moment, she felt it clear that so much plotted freedom was virtually a refinement of reflection, an impulse to commemorate afresh whatever might still survive of pride and hope, her sense of ambiguity happily fell and she congratulated her companion on having anything so exquisite to do and on being so exquisitely in the humour to do it. After the occasion had come and gone she was confirmed in her optimism; she made out, in the evening, that the hour spent among the projected lights, the annals and illustrations, the parchments and portraits, the emblazoned volumes and the murmured commentary, had been for the Princess enlarging and inspiring. Maggie had said to her some days before, very sweetly but very firmly, "Invite us to dine, please, for Friday, and have any one you like or can—it doesn't in the least matter whom;" and the pair in Cadogan Place had bent to this mandate with a docility not in the least ruffled by all that it took for granted.

It provided for an evening—this had been Maggie's view; and she lived up to her view, in her friend's eyes, by treating the occasion, more or less explicitly, as new and strange. The good Assinghams had feasted in fact at the two other boards on a scale so disproportionate to the scant solicitations of their own that it was easy to make a joke of seeing how they fed at home, how they met, themselves, the question of giving to eat. Maggie dined with them, in short, and arrived at making her husband appear to dine, much in the manner of a pair of young sovereigns who have, in the frolic humour of the golden years of reigns, proposed themselves to a pair of faithfully-serving subjects. She showed an interest in their arrangements, an inquiring tenderness almost for their economies; so that her hostess not unnaturally, as they might have said, put it all down—the tone and the freedom of which she set the example—to the effect wrought in her afresh by one of the lessons learned, in the morning, at the altar of the past. Hadn't she picked it up, from an anecdote or two offered again to her attention, that there were, for princesses of such a line, more ways than one of being a heroine? Maggie's way to-night was to surprise them all, truly, by the extravagance of her affability. She was doubtless not positively boisterous; yet, though Mrs. Assingham, as a bland critic, had never doubted her being graceful, she had never seen her put so much of it into being what might have been called assertive. It was all a tune to which Fanny's heart could privately palpitate: her guest was happy, happy as a consequence of something that had occurred, but she was making the Prince not lose a ripple of her laugh, though not perhaps always enabling him to find it absolutely not foolish. Foolish, in public, beyond a certain point, he was scarce the man to brook his wife's being thought to be; so that there hovered before their friend the possibility of some subsequent scene between them, in the carriage or at home, of slightly sarcastic inquiry, of promptly invited explanation; a scene that, according as Maggie should play her part in it, might or might not precipitate developments. What made these appearances practically thrilling, meanwhile, was this mystery—a mystery, it was clear, to Amerigo himself—of the incident or the influence that had so peculiarly determined them.

The lady of Cadogan Place was to read deeper, however, within three days, and the page was turned for her on the eve of her young confidant's leaving London. The awaited migration to Fawns was to take place on the morrow, and it was known meanwhile to Mrs. Assingham that their party of four were to dine that night, at the American Embassy, with another and a larger party; so that the elder woman had a sense of surprise on receiving from the younger, under date of six o'clock, a telegram requesting her immediate attendance. "Please come to me at once; dress early, if necessary, so that we shall have time: the carriage, ordered for us, will take you back first." Mrs. Assingham, on quick deliberation, dressed, though not perhaps with full lucidity, and by seven o'clock was in Portland Place, where her friend, "upstairs" and described to her on her arrival as herself engaged in dressing, instantly received her. She knew on the spot, poor Fanny, as she was afterwards to declare to the Colonel, that her feared crisis had popped up as at the touch of a spring, that her impossible hour was before her. Her impossible hour was the hour of its coming out that she had known of old so much more than she had ever said; and she had often put it to herself, in apprehension, she tried to think even in preparation, that she should recognise the approach of her doom by a consciousness akin to that of the blowing open of a window on some night of the highest wind and the lowest thermometer. It would be all in vain to have crouched so long by the fire; the glass would have been smashed, though the icy air would fill the place. If the air in Maggie's room then, on her going up, was not, as yet, quite the polar blast she had expected, it was distinctly, none the less, such an atmosphere as they had not hitherto breathed together. The Princess, she perceived, was completely dressed—that business was over; it added indeed to the effect of her importantly awaiting the assistance she had summoned, of her showing a deck cleared, so to speak, for action. Her maid had already left her, and she presented herself, in the large, clear room, where everything was admirable, but where nothing was out of place, as, for the first time in her life rather "bedizened." Was it that she had put on too many things, overcharged herself with jewels, wore in particular more of them than usual, and bigger ones, in her hair?—a question her visitor presently answered by attributing this appearance largely to the bright red spot, red as some monstrous ruby, that burned in either of her cheeks. These two items of her aspect had, promptly enough, their own light for Mrs. Assingham, who made out by it that nothing more pathetic could be imagined than the refuge and disguise her agitation had instinctively asked of the arts of dress, multiplied to extravagance, almost to incoherence. She had had, visibly, her idea—that of not betraying herself by inattentions into which she had never yet fallen, and she stood there circled about and furnished forth, as always, in a manner that testified to her perfect little personal processes. It had ever been her sign that she was, for all occasions, FOUND ready, without loose ends or exposed accessories or unremoved superfluities; a suggestion of the swept and garnished, in her whole splendid, yet thereby more or less encumbered and embroidered setting, that reflected her small still passion for order and symmetry, for objects with their backs to the walls, and spoke even of some probable reference, in her American blood, to dusting and polishing New England grandmothers. If her apartment was "princely," in the clearness of the lingering day, she looked as if she had been carried there prepared, all attired and decorated, like some holy image in a procession, and left, precisely, to show what wonder she could work under pressure. Her friend felt—how could she not?—as the truly pious priest might feel when confronted, behind the altar, before the festa, with his miraculous Madonna. Such an occasion would be grave, in general, with all the gravity of what he might look for. But the gravity to-night would be of the rarest; what he might look for would depend so on what he could give.

XXXIII

"Something very strange has happened, and I think you ought to know it."

Maggie spoke this indeed without extravagance, yet with the effect of making her guest measure anew the force of her appeal. It was their definite understanding: whatever Fanny knew Fanny's faith would provide for. And she knew, accordingly, at the end of five minutes, what the extraordinary, in the late occurrence, had consisted of, and how it had all come of Maggie's achieved hour, under Mr. Crichton's protection, at the Museum. He had desired, Mr. Crichton, with characteristic kindness, after the wonderful show, after offered luncheon at his incorporated lodge hard by, to see her safely home; especially on his noting, in attending her to the great steps, that she had dismissed her carriage; which she had done, really, just for the harmless amusement of taking her way alone. She had known she should find herself, as the consequence of such an hour, in a sort of exalted state, under the influence of which a walk through the London streets would be exactly what would suit her best; an independent ramble, impressed, excited, contented, with nothing to mind and nobody to talk to, and shop-windows in plenty to look at if she liked: a low taste, of the essence, it was to be supposed, of her nature, that she had of late, for so many reasons, been unable to gratify. She had taken her leave, with her thanks—she knew her way quite enough; it being also sufficiently the case that she had even a shy hope of not going too straight. To wander a little wild was what would truly amuse her; so that, keeping clear of Oxford Street and cultivating an impression as of parts she didn't know, she had ended with what she had more or less been fancying, an encounter with three or four shops—an old bookseller's, an old printmonger's, a couple of places with dim antiquities in the window—that were not as so many of the other shops, those in Sloane Street, say; a hollow parade which had long since ceased to beguile. There had remained with her moreover an allusion of Charlotte's, of some months before—seed dropped into her imagination in the form of a casual speech about there being in Bloomsbury such "funny little fascinating" places and even sometimes such unexpected finds. There could perhaps have been no stronger mark than this sense of well-nigh romantic opportunity—no livelier sign of the impression made on her, and always so long retained, so watchfully nursed, by any observation of Charlotte's, however lightly thrown off. And then she had felt, somehow, more at her ease than for months and months before; she didn't know why, but her time at the Museum, oddly, had done it; it was as if she hadn't come into so many noble and beautiful associations, nor secured them also for her boy, secured them even for her father, only to see them turn to vanity and doubt, turn possibly to something still worse. "I believed in him again as much as ever, and I felt how I believed in him," she said with bright, fixed eyes; "I felt it in the streets as I walked along, and it was as if that helped me and lifted me up, my being off by myself there, not having, for the moment, to wonder and watch; having, on the contrary, almost nothing on my mind."

It was so much as if everything would come out right that she had fallen to thinking of her father's birthday, had given herself this as a reason for trying what she could pick up for it. They would keep it at Fawns, where they had kept it before—since it would be the twenty-first of the month; and she mightn't have another chance of making sure of something to offer him. There was always the impossibility, of course, of finding him anything, the least bit "good," that he wouldn't already, long ago, in his rummagings, have seen himself—and only not to think a quarter good enough; this, however, was an old story, and one could not have had any fun with him but for his sweet theory that the individual gift, the friendship's offering, was, by a rigorous law of nature, a foredoomed aberration, and that the more it was so the more it showed, and the more one cherished it for showing, how friendly it had been. The infirmity of art was the candour of affection, the grossness of pedigree the refinement of sympathy; the ugliest objects, in fact, as a general thing, were the bravest, the tenderest mementos, and, as such, figured in glass cases apart, worthy doubtless of the home, but not worthy of the temple—dedicated to the grimacing, not to the clear-faced, gods. She herself, naturally, through the past years, had come to be much represented in those receptacles; against the thick, locked panes of which she still liked to flatten her nose, finding in its place, each time, everything she had on successive anniversaries tried to believe he might pretend, at her suggestion, to be put off with, or at least think curious. She was now ready to try it again: they had always, with his pleasure in her pretence and her pleasure in his, with the funny betrayal of the sacrifice to domestic manners on either side, played the game so happily. To this end, on her way home, she had loitered everywhere; quite too deludedly among the old books and the old prints, which had yielded nothing to her purpose, but with a strange inconsequence in one of the other shops, that of a small antiquarian, a queer little foreign man, who had shown her a number of things, shown her finally something that, struck with it as rather a rarity and thinking it would, compared to some of her ventures, quite superlatively do, she had bought—bought really, when it came to that, for a price. "It appears now it won't do at all," said Maggie, "something has happened since that puts it quite out of the question. I had only my day of satisfaction in it, but I feel, at the same time, as I keep it here before me, that I wouldn't have missed it for the world."

She had talked, from the first of her friend's entrances coherently enough, even with a small quaver that overstated her calm; but she held her breath every few seconds, as if for deliberation and to prove she didn't pant—all of which marked for Fanny the depth of her commotion: her reference to her thought about her father, about her chance to pick up something that might divert him, her mention, in fine, of his fortitude under presents, having meanwhile, naturally, it should be said, much less an amplitude of insistence on the speaker's lips than a power to produce on the part of the listener herself the prompt response and full comprehension of memory and sympathy, of old amused observation. The picture was filled out by the latter's fond fancy. But Maggie was at any rate under arms; she knew what she was doing and had already her plan—a plan for making, for allowing, as yet, "no difference"; in accordance with which she would still dine out, and not with red eyes, nor convulsed features, nor neglected items of appearance, nor anything that would raise a question. Yet there was some knowledge that, exactly to this support of her not breaking down, she desired, she required, possession of; and, with the sinister rise and fall of lightning unaccompanied by thunder, it played before Mrs. Assingham's eyes that she herself should have, at whatever risk or whatever cost, to supply her with the stuff of her need. All our friend's instinct was to hold off from this till she should see what the ground would bear; she would take no step nearer unless INTELLIGIBLY to meet her, and, awkward though it might be to hover there only pale and distorted, with mere imbecilities of vagueness, there was a quality of bald help in the fact of not as yet guessing what such an ominous start could lead to. She caught, however, after a second's thought, at the Princess's allusion to her lost reassurance.

"You mean you were so at your ease on Monday—the night you dined with us?"

"I was very happy then," said Maggie.

"Yes—we thought you so gay and so brilliant." Fanny felt it feeble, but she went on. "We were so glad you were happy."

Maggie stood a moment, at first only looking at her. "You thought me all right, eh?"

"Surely, dearest; we thought you all right."

"Well, I daresay it was natural; but in point of fact I never was more wrong in my life. For, all the while, if you please, this was brewing."

Mrs. Assingham indulged, as nearly as possible to luxury, her vagueness. "'This'—?"

"THAT!" replied the Princess, whose eyes, her companion now saw, had turned to an object on the chimney-piece of the room, of which, among so many precious objects—the Ververs, wherever they might be, always revelled peculiarly in matchless old mantel ornaments—her visitor had not taken heed.

"Do you mean the gilt cup?"

"I mean the gilt cup."

The piece now recognised by Fanny as new to her own vision was a capacious bowl, of old-looking, rather strikingly yellow gold, mounted, by a short stem, on an ample foot, which held a central position above the fire-place, where, to allow it the better to show, a clearance had been made of other objects, notably of the Louis-Seize clock that accompanied the candelabra. This latter trophy ticked at present on the marble slab of a commode that exactly matched it in splendour and style. Mrs. Assingham took it, the bowl, as a fine thing; but the question was obviously not of its intrinsic value, and she kept off from it, admiring it at a distance. "But what has that to do—?"

"It has everything. You'll see." With which again, however, for the moment, Maggie attached to her strange wide eyes. "He knew her before—before I had ever seen him."

"'He' knew—?" But Fanny, while she cast about her for the links she missed, could only echo it.

"Amerigo knew Charlotte—more than I ever dreamed."

Fanny felt then it was stare for stare. "But surely you always knew they had met."

"I didn't understand. I knew too little. Don't you see what I mean?" the Princess asked.

Mrs. Assingham wondered, during these instants, how much she even now knew; it had taken a minute to perceive how gently she was speaking. With that perception of its being no challenge of wrath, no heat of the deceived soul, but only a free exposure of the completeness of past ignorance, inviting derision even if it must, the elder woman felt, first, a strange, barely credible relief: she drew in, as if it had been the warm summer scent of a flower, the sweet certainty of not meeting, any way she should turn, any consequence of judgment. She shouldn't be judged—save by herself; which was her own wretched business. The next moment, however, at all events, she blushed, within, for her immediate cowardice: she had thought of herself, thought of "getting off," before so much as thinking—that is of pitifully seeing—that she was in presence of an appeal that was ALL an appeal, that utterly accepted its necessity. "In a general way, dear child, yes. But not—a—in connexion with what you've been telling me."

"They were intimate, you see. Intimate," said the Princess.

Fanny continued to face her, taking from her excited eyes this history, so dim and faint for all her anxious emphasis, of the far-away other time. "There's always the question of what one considers—!"

"What one considers intimate? Well, I know what I consider intimate now. Too intimate," said Maggie, "to let me know anything about it."

It was quiet—yes; but not too quiet for Fanny Assingham's capacity to wince. "Only compatible with letting ME, you mean?" She asked it after a pause, but turning again to the new ornament of the chimney and wondering, even while she took relief from it, at this gap in her experience. "But here are things, my dear, of which my ignorance is perfect."

"They went about together—they're known to have done it. And I don't mean only before—I mean after."

"After?" said Fanny Assingham.

"Before we were married—yes; but after we were engaged."

"Ah, I've known nothing about that!" And she said it with a braver assurance—clutching, with comfort, at something that was apparently new to her.

"That bowl," Maggie went on, "is, so strangely—too strangely, almost, to believe at this time of day—the proof. They were together all the while—up to the very eve of our marriage. Don't you remember how just before that she came back, so unexpectedly, from America?"

The question had for Mrs. Assingham—and whether all consciously or not—the oddest pathos of simplicity. "Oh yes, dear, of course I remember how she came back from America—and how she stayed with US, and what view one had of it."

Maggie's eyes still, all the time, pressed and penetrated; so that, during a moment, just here, she might have given the little flare, have made the little pounce, of asking what then "one's" view had been. To the small flash of this eruption Fanny stood, for her minute, wittingly exposed; but she saw it as quickly cease to threaten—quite saw the Princess, even though in all her pain, refuse, in the interest of their strange and exalted bargain, to take advantage of the opportunity for planting the stab of reproach, the opportunity thus coming all of itself. She saw her—or she believed she saw her—look at her chance for straight denunciation, look at it and then pass it by; and she felt herself, with this fact, hushed well-nigh to awe at the lucid higher intention that no distress could confound and that no discovery—since it was, however obscurely, a case of "discovery"—could make less needful. These seconds were brief—they rapidly passed; but they lasted long enough to renew our friend's sense of her own extraordinary undertaking, the function again imposed on her, the answerability again drilled into her, by this intensity of intimation. She was reminded of the terms on which she was let off—her quantity of release having made its sufficient show in that recall of her relation to Charlotte's old reappearance; and deep within the whole impression glowed—ah, so inspiringly when it came to that! her steady view, clear from the first, of the beauty of her companion's motive. It was like a fresh sacrifice for a larger conquest "Only see me through now, do it in the face of this and in spite of it, and I leave you a hand of which the freedom isn't to be said!" The aggravation of fear—or call it, apparently, of knowledge—had jumped straight into its place as an aggravation above all for her father; the effect of this being but to quicken to passion her reasons for making his protectedness, or in other words the forms of his ignorance, still the law of her attitude and the key to her solution. She kept as tight hold of these reasons and these forms, in her confirmed horror, as the rider of a plunging horse grasps his seat with his knees; and she might absolutely have been putting it to her guest that she believed she could stay on if they should only "meet" nothing more. Though ignorant still of what she had definitely met Fanny yearned, within, over her spirit; and so, no word about it said, passed, through mere pitying eyes, a vow to walk ahead and, at crossroads, with a lantern for the darkness and wavings away for unadvised traffic, look out for alarms. There was accordingly no wait in Maggie's reply. "They spent together hours—spent at least a morning—the certainty of which has come back to me now, but that I didn't dream of it at the time. That cup there has turned witness—by the most wonderful of chances. That's why, since it has been here, I've stood it out for my husband to see; put it where it would meet him, almost immediately, if he should come into the room. I've wanted it to meet him," she went on, "and I've wanted him to meet it, and to be myself present at the meeting. But that hasn't taken place as yet; often as he has lately been in the way of coming to see me here—yes, in particular lately—he hasn't showed to-day." It was with her managed quietness, more and more, that she talked—an achieved coherence that helped her, evidently, to hear and to watch herself; there was support, and thereby an awful harmony, but which meant a further guidance, in the facts she could add together. "It's quite as if he had an instinct—something that has warned him off or made him uneasy. He doesn't quite know, naturally, what has happened, but guesses, with his beautiful cleverness, that something has, and isn't in a hurry to be confronted with it. So, in his vague fear, he keeps off."

"But being meanwhile in the house—?"

"I've no idea—not having seen him to-day, by exception, since before luncheon. He spoke to me then," the Princess freely explained, "of a ballot, of great importance, at a club—for somebody, some personal friend, I think, who's coming up and is supposed to be in danger. To make an effort for him he thought he had better lunch there. You see the efforts he can make"—for which Maggie found a smile that went to her friend's heart. "He's in so many ways the kindest of men. But it was hours ago."

Mrs. Assingham thought. "The more danger then of his coming in and finding me here. I don't know, you see, what you now consider that you've ascertained; nor anything of the connexion with it of that object that you declare so damning." Her eyes rested on this odd acquisition and then quitted it, went back to it and again turned from it: it was inscrutable in its rather stupid elegance, and yet, from the moment one had thus appraised it, vivid and definite in its domination of the scene. Fanny could no more overlook it now than she could have overlooked a lighted Christmas-tree; but nervously and all in vain she dipped into her mind for some floating reminiscence of it. At the same time that this attempt left her blank she understood a good deal, she even not a little shared the Prince's mystic apprehension. The golden bowl put on, under consideration, a sturdy, a conscious perversity; as a "document," somehow, it was ugly, though it might have a decorative grace. "His finding me here in presence of it might be more flagrantly disagreeable—for all of us—than you intend or than would necessarily help us. And I must take time, truly, to understand what it means."

"You're safe, as far as that goes," Maggie returned; "you may take it from me that he won't come in; and that I shall only find him below, waiting for me, when I go down to take the carriage."

Fanny Assingham took it from her, took it and more. "We're to sit together at the Ambassador's then—or at least you two are—with this new complication thrust up before you, all unexplained; and to look at each other with faces that pretend, for the ghastly hour, not to be seeing it?"

Maggie looked at HER with a face that might have been the one she was preparing. "'Unexplained,' my dear? Quite the contrary—explained: fully, intensely, admirably explained, with nothing really to add. My own love"—she kept it up—"I don't want anything more. I've plenty to go upon and to do with, as it is."

Fanny Assingham stood there in her comparative darkness, with her links, verily, still missing; but the most acceptable effect of this was, singularly, as yet, a cold fear of getting nearer the fact. "But when you come home—? I mean he'll come up with you again. Won't he see it then?"

On which Maggie gave her, after an instant's visible thought, the strangest of slow headshakes. "I don't know. Perhaps he'll never see it—if it only stands there waiting for him. He may never again," said the Princess, "come into this room."

Fanny more deeply wondered, "Never again? Oh—!"

"Yes, it may be. How do I know? With THIS!" she quietly went on. She had not looked again at the incriminating piece, but there was a marvel to her friend in the way the little word representing it seemed to express and include for her the whole of her situation. "Then you intend not to speak to him—?"

Maggie waited. "To 'speak'—?"

"Well, about your having it and about what you consider that it represents."

"Oh, I don't know that I shall speak—if he doesn't. But his keeping away from me because of that—what will that be but to speak? He can't say or do more. It won't be for me to speak," Maggie added in a different tone, one of the tones that had already so penetrated her guest. "It will be for me to listen."

Mrs. Assingham turned it over. "Then it all depends on that object that you regard, for your reasons, as evidence?"

"I think I may say that I depend on it. I can't," said Maggie, "treat it as nothing now."

Mrs. Assingham, at this, went closer to the cup on the chimney—quite liking to feel that she did so, moreover, without going closer to her companion's vision. She looked at the precious thing—if precious it was—found herself in fact eyeing it as if, by her dim solicitation, to draw its secret from it rather than suffer the imposition of Maggie's knowledge. It was brave and rich and firm, with its bold deep hollow; and, without this queer torment about it, would, thanks to her love of plenty of yellow, figure to her as an enviable ornament, a possession really desirable. She didn't touch it, but if after a minute she turned away from it the reason was, rather oddly and suddenly, in her fear of doing so. "Then it all depends on the bowl? I mean your future does? For that's what it comes to, I judge."

"What it comes to," Maggie presently returned, "is what that thing has put me, so almost miraculously, in the way of learning: how far they had originally gone together. If there was so much between them before, there can't—with all the other appearances—not be a great deal more now." And she went on and on; she steadily made her points. "If such things were already then between them they make all the difference for possible doubt of what may have been between them since. If there had been nothing before there might be explanations. But it makes to-day too much to explain. I mean to explain away," she said.

Fanny Assingham was there to explain away—of this she was duly conscious; for that at least had been true up to now. In the light, however, of Maggie's demonstration the quantity, even without her taking as yet a more exact measure, might well seem larger than ever. Besides which, with or without exactness, the effect of each successive minute in the place was to put her more in presence of what Maggie herself saw. Maggie herself saw the truth, and that was really, while they remained there together, enough for Mrs. Assingham's relation to it. There was a force in the Princess's mere manner about it that made the detail of what she knew a matter of minor importance. Fanny had in fact something like a momentary shame over her own need of asking for this detail. "I don't pretend to repudiate," she said after a little, "my own impressions of the different times I suppose you speak of; any more," she added, "than I can forget what difficulties and, as it constantly seemed to me, what dangers, every course of action—whatever I should decide upon—made for me. I tried, I tried hard, to act for the best. And, you know," she next pursued, while, at the sound of her own statement, a slow courage and even a faint warmth of conviction came back to her—"and, you know, I believe it's what I shall turn out to have done."

This produced a minute during which their interchange, though quickened and deepened, was that of silence only, and the long, charged look; all of which found virtual consecration when Maggie at last spoke. "I'm sure you tried to act for the best."

It kept Fanny Assingham again a minute in silence. "I never thought, dearest, you weren't an angel."

Not, however, that this alone was much help! "It was up to the very eve, you see," the Princess went on—"up to within two or three days of our marriage. That, THAT, you know—!" And she broke down for strangely smiling.

"Yes, as I say, it was while she was with me. But I didn't know it. That is," said Fanny Assingham, "I didn't know of anything in particular." It sounded weak—that she felt; but she had really her point to make. "What I mean is that I don't know, for knowledge, now, anything I didn't then. That's how I am." She still, however, floundered. "I mean it's how I WAS."

"But don't they, how you were and how you are," Maggie asked, "come practically to the same thing?" The elder woman's words had struck her own ear as in the tone, now mistimed, of their recent, but all too factitious understanding, arrived at in hours when, as there was nothing susceptible of proof, there was nothing definitely to disprove. The situation had changed by—well, by whatever there was, by the outbreak of the definite; and this could keep Maggie at least firm. She was firm enough as she pursued. "It was ON the whole thing that Amerigo married me." With which her eyes had their turn again at her damnatory piece. "And it was on that—it was on that! But they came back to her visitor. "And it was on it all that father married HER."

Her visitor took it as might be. "They both married—ah, that you must believe!—with the highest intentions."

"Father did certainly!" And then, at the renewal of this consciousness, it all rolled over her. "Ah, to thrust such things on us, to do them here between us and with us, day after day, and in return, in return—! To do it to HIM—to him, to him!"

Fanny hesitated. "You mean it's for him you most suffer?" And then as the Princess, after a look, but turned away, moving about the room—which made the question somehow seem a blunder—"I ask," she continued, "because I think everything, everything we now speak of, may be for him, really may be MADE for him, quite as if it hadn't been."

But Maggie had, the next moment faced about as if without hearing her. "Father did it for ME—did it all and only for me."

Mrs. Assingham, with a certain promptness, threw up her head; but she faltered again before she spoke. "Well—!"

It was only an intended word, but Maggie showed after an instant that it had reached her. "Do you mean that that's the reason, that that's A reason—?"

Fanny at first, however, feeling the response in this, didn't say all she meant; she said for the moment something else instead. "He did it for you—largely at least for you. And it was for you that I did, in my smaller, interested way—well, what I could do. For I could do something," she continued; "I thought I saw your interest as he himself saw it. And I thought I saw Charlotte's. I believed in her."

"And I believed in her," said Maggie.

Mrs. Assingham waited again; but she presently pushed on. "She believed then in herself."

"Ah?" Maggie murmured.

Something exquisite, faintly eager, in the prompt simplicity of it, supported her friend further. "And the Prince believed. His belief was real. Just as he believed in himself."

Maggie spent a minute in taking it from her. "He believed in himself?"

"Just as I too believed in him. For I absolutely did, Maggie." To which Fanny then added: "And I believe in him yet. I mean," she subjoined—"well, I mean I DO."

Maggie again took it from her; after which she was again, restlessly, set afloat. Then when this had come to an end: "And do you believe in Charlotte yet?"

Mrs. Assingham had a demur that she felt she could now afford. "We'll talk of Charlotte some other day. They both, at any rate, thought themselves safe at the time."

"Then why did they keep from me everything I might have known?"

Her friend bent upon her the mildest eyes. "Why did I myself keep it from you?"

"Oh, you weren't, for honour, obliged."

"Dearest Maggie," the poor woman broke out on this, "you ARE divine!"

"They pretended to love me," the Princess went on. "And they pretended to love HIM."

"And pray what was there that I didn't pretend?"

"Not, at any rate, to care for me as you cared for Amerigo and for Charlotte. They were much more interesting—it was perfectly natural. How couldn't you like Amerigo?" Maggie continued.

Mrs. Assingham gave it up. "How couldn't I, how couldn't I?" Then, with a fine freedom, she went all her way. "How CAN'T I, how can't I?"

It fixed afresh Maggie's wide eyes on her. "I see—I see. Well, it's beautiful for you to be able to. And of course," she added, "you wanted to help Charlotte."

"Yes"—Fanny considered it—"I wanted to help Charlotte. But I wanted also, you see, to help you—by not digging up a past that I believed, with so much on top of it, solidly buried. I wanted, as I still want," she richly declared, "to help every one."

It set Maggie once more in movement—movement which, however, spent itself again with a quick emphasis. "Then it's a good deal my fault—if everything really began so well?"

Fanny Assingham met it as she could. "You've been only too perfect. You've thought only too much."

But the Princess had already caught at the words. "Yes—I've thought only too much!" Yet she appeared to continue, for the minute, full of that fault. She had it in fact, by this prompted thought, all before her. "Of him, dear man, of HIM—!"

Her friend, able to take in thus directly her vision of her father, watched her with a new suspense. THAT way might safety lie—it was like a wider chink of light. "He believed—with a beauty!—in Charlotte."

"Yes, and it was I who had made him believe. I didn't mean to, at the time, so much; for I had no idea then of what was coming. But I did it, I did it!" the Princess declared.

"With a beauty—ah, with a beauty, you too!" Mrs. Assingham insisted.

Maggie, however, was seeing for herself—it was another matter, "The thing was that he made her think it would be so possible."

Fanny again hesitated. "The Prince made her think—?"

Maggie stared—she had meant her father. But her vision seemed to spread. "They both made her think. She wouldn't have thought without them."

"Yet Amerigo's good faith," Mrs. Assingham insisted, "was perfect. And there was nothing, all the more," she added, "against your father's."

The remark, however, kept Maggie for a moment still. "Nothing perhaps but his knowing that she knew."

"'Knew'?"

"That he was doing it, so much, for me. To what extent," she suddenly asked of her friend, "do you think he was aware that she knew?"

"Ah, who can say what passes between people in such a relation? The only thing one can be sure of is that he was generous." And Mrs. Assingham conclusively smiled. "He doubtless knew as much as was right for himself."

"As much, that is, as was right for her."

"Yes then—as was right for her. The point is," Fanny declared, "that, whatever his knowledge, it made, all the way it went, for his good faith."

Maggie continued to gaze, and her friend now fairly waited on her successive movements. "Isn't the point, very considerably, that his good faith must have been his faith in her taking almost as much interest in me as he himself took?"

Fanny Assingham thought. "He recognised, he adopted, your long friendship. But he founded on it no selfishness."

"No," said Maggie with still deeper consideration: "he counted her selfishness out almost as he counted his own."

"So you may say."

"Very well," Maggie went on; "if he had none of his own, he invited her, may have expected her, on her side, to have as little. And she may only since have found that out."

Mrs. Assingham looked blank. "Since—?"

"And he may have become aware," Maggie pursued, "that she has found it out. That she has taken the measure, since their marriage," she explained, "of how much he had asked of her—more, say, than she had understood at the time. He may have made out at last how such a demand was, in the long run, to affect her."

"He may have done many things," Mrs. Assingham responded; "but there's one thing he certainly won't have done. He'll never have shown that he expected of her a quarter as much as she must have understood he was to give."

"I've often wondered," Maggie mused, "what Charlotte really understood. But it's one of the things she has never told me."

"Then as it's one of the things she has never told me either, we shall probably never know it; and we may regard it as none of our business. There are many things," said Mrs. Assingham, "that we shall never know."

Maggie took it in with a long reflection. "Never."

"But there are others," her friend went on, "that stare us in the face and that—under whatever difficulty you may feel you labour—may now be enough for us. Your father has been extraordinary."

It had been as if Maggie were feeling her way; but she rallied to this with a rush. "Extraordinary."

"Magnificent," said Fanny Assingham.

Her companion held tight to it. "Magnificent."

"Then he'll do for himself whatever there may be to do. What he undertook for you he'll do to the end. He didn't undertake it to break down; in what—quiet, patient, exquisite as he is—did he ever break down? He had never in his life proposed to himself to have failed, and he won't have done it on this occasion."

"Ah, this occasion!"—and Maggie's wail showed her, of a sudden, thrown back on it. "Am I in the least sure that, with everything, he even knows what it is? And yet am I in the least sure he doesn't?"

"If he doesn't then, so much the better. Leave him alone."

"Do you mean give him up?"

"Leave HER," Fanny Assingham went on. "Leave her TO him."

Maggie looked at her darkly. "Do you mean leave him to HER? After this?"

"After everything. Aren't they, for that matter, intimately together now?"

"'Intimately'—? How do I know?"

But Fanny kept it up. "Aren't you and your husband—in spite of everything?"

Maggie's eyes still further, if possible, dilated. "It remains to be seen!"

"If you're not then, where's your faith?"

"In my husband—?"

Mrs. Assingham but for an instant hesitated. "In your father. It all comes back to that. Rest on it."

"On his ignorance?"

Fanny met it again. "On whatever he may offer you. TAKE that."

"Take it—?" Maggie stared.

Mrs. Assingham held up her head. "And be grateful." On which, for a minute, she let the Princess face her. "Do you see?"

"I see," said Maggie at last.

"Then there you are." But Maggie had turned away, moving to the window, as if still to keep something in her face from sight. She stood there with her eyes on the street while Mrs. Assingham's reverted to that complicating object on the chimney as to which her condition, so oddly even to herself, was that both of recurrent wonder and recurrent protest. She went over it, looked at it afresh and yielded now to her impulse to feel it in her hands. She laid them on it, lifting it up, and was surprised, thus, with the weight of it—she had seldom handled so much massive gold. That effect itself somehow prompted her to further freedom and presently to saying: "I don't believe in this, you know."

It brought Maggie round to her. "Don't believe in it? You will when I tell you."

"Ah, tell me nothing! I won't have it," said Mrs. Assingham. She kept the cup in her hand, held it there in a manner that gave Maggie's attention to her, she saw the next moment, a quality of excited suspense. This suggested to her, oddly, that she had, with the liberty she was taking, an air of intention, and the impression betrayed by her companion's eyes grew more distinct in a word of warning. "It's of value, but its value's impaired, I've learned, by a crack."

"A crack?—in the gold—?"

"It isn't gold." With which, somewhat strangely, Maggie smiled.

"That's the point."

"What is it then?"

"It's glass—and cracked, under the gilt, as I say, at that."

"Glass?—of this weight?"

"Well," said Maggie, "it's crystal—and was once, I suppose, precious. But what," she then asked, "do you mean to do with it?" She had come away from her window, one of the three by which the wide room, enjoying an advantageous "back," commanded the western sky and caught a glimpse of the evening flush; while Mrs. Assingham, possessed of the bowl, and possessed too of this indication of a flaw, approached another for the benefit of the slowly-fading light. Here, thumbing the singular piece, weighing it, turning it over, and growing suddenly more conscious, above all, of an irresistible impulse, she presently spoke again. "A crack? Then your whole idea has a crack."

Maggie, by this time at some distance from her, waited a moment. "If you mean by my idea the knowledge that has come to me THAT—"

But Fanny, with decision, had already taken her up. "There's only one knowledge that concerns us—one fact with which we can have anything to do."

"Which one, then?"

"The fact that your husband has never, never, never—!" But the very gravity of this statement, while she raised her eyes to her friend across the room, made her for an instant hang fire.

"Well, never what?"

"Never been half so interested in you as now. But don't you, my dear, really feel it?"

Maggie considered. "Oh, I think what I've told you helps me to feel it. His having to-day given up even his forms; his keeping away from me; his not having come." And she shook her head as against all easy glosses. "It is because of that, you know."

"Well then, if it's because of this—!" And Fanny Assingham, who had been casting about her and whose inspiration decidedly had come, raised the cup in her two hands, raised it positively above her head, and from under it, solemnly, smiled at the Princess as a signal of intention. So for an instant, full of her thought and of her act, she held the precious vessel, and then, with due note taken of the margin of the polished floor, bare, fine and hard in the embrasure of her window, she dashed it boldly to the ground, where she had the thrill of seeing it, with the violence of the crash, lie shattered. She had flushed with the force of her effort, as Maggie had flushed with wonder at the sight, and this high reflection in their faces was all that passed between them for a minute more. After which, "Whatever you meant by it—and I don't want to know NOW—has ceased to exist," Mrs. Assingham said.

"And what in the world, my dear, did you mean by it?"—that sound, as at the touch of a spring, rang out as the first effect of Fanny's speech. It broke upon the two women's absorption with a sharpness almost equal to the smash of the crystal, for the door of the room had been opened by the Prince without their taking heed. He had apparently had time, moreover, to catch the conclusion of Fanny's act; his eyes attached themselves, through the large space allowing just there, as happened, a free view, to the shining fragments at this lady's feet. His question had been addressed to his wife, but he moved his eyes immediately afterwards to those of her visitor, whose own then held them in a manner of which neither party had been capable, doubtless, for mute penetration, since the hour spent by him in Cadogan Place on the eve of his marriage and the afternoon of Charlotte's reappearance. Something now again became possible for these communicants, under the intensity of their pressure, something that took up that tale and that might have been a redemption of pledges then exchanged. This rapid play of suppressed appeal and disguised response lasted indeed long enough for more results than one—long enough for Mrs. Assingham to measure the feat of quick self-recovery, possibly therefore of recognition still more immediate, accompanying Amerigo's vision and estimate of the evidence with which she had been—so admirably, she felt as she looked at him—inspired to deal. She looked at him and looked at him—there were so many things she wanted, on the spot, to say. But Maggie was looking too—and was moreover looking at them both; so that these things, for the elder woman, quickly enough reduced themselves to one. She met his question—not too late, since, in their silence, it had remained in the air. Gathering herself to go, leaving the golden bowl split into three pieces on the ground, she simply referred him to his wife. She should see them later, they would all meet soon again; and meanwhile, as to what Maggie had meant—she said, in her turn, from the door—why, Maggie herself was doubtless by this time ready to tell him.

XXXIV

Left with her husband, Maggie, however, for the time, said nothing; she only felt, on the spot, a strong, sharp wish not to see his face again till he should have had a minute to arrange it. She had seen it enough for her temporary clearness and her next movement—seen it as it showed during the stare of surprise that followed his entrance. Then it was that she knew how hugely expert she had been made, for judging it quickly, by that vision of it, indelibly registered for reference, that had flashed a light into her troubled soul the night of his late return from Matcham. The expression worn by it at that juncture, for however few instants, had given her a sense of its possibilities, one of the most relevant of which might have been playing up for her, before the consummation of Fanny Assingham's retreat, just long enough to be recognised. What she had recognised in it was HIS recognition, the result of his having been forced, by the flush of their visitor's attitude and the unextinguished report of her words, to take account of the flagrant signs of the accident, of the incident, on which he had unexpectedly dropped. He had, not unnaturally, failed to see this occurrence represented by the three fragments of an object apparently valuable which lay there on the floor and which, even across the width of the room, his kept interval, reminded him, unmistakably though confusedly, of something known, some other unforgotten image. That was a mere shock, that was a pain—as if Fanny's violence had been a violence redoubled and acting beyond its intention, a violence calling up the hot blood as a blow across the mouth might have called it. Maggie knew as she turned away from him that she didn't want his pain; what she wanted was her own simple certainty—not the red mark of conviction flaming there in his beauty. If she could have gone on with bandaged eyes she would have liked that best; if it were a question of saying what she now, apparently, should have to, and of taking from him what he would say, any blindness that might wrap it would be the nearest approach to a boon.

She went in silence to where her friend—never, in intention, visibly, so much her friend as at that moment—had braced herself to so amazing an energy, and there, under Amerigo's eyes, she picked up the shining pieces. Bedizened and jewelled, in her rustling finery, she paid, with humility of attitude, this prompt tribute to order—only to find, however, that she could carry but two of the fragments at once. She brought them over to the chimney-piece, to the conspicuous place occupied by the cup before Fanny's appropriation of it, and, after laying them carefully down, went back for what remained, the solid detached foot. With this she returned to the mantel-shelf, placing it with deliberation in the centre and then, for a minute, occupying herself as with the attempt to fit the other morsels together. The split, determined by the latent crack, was so sharp and so neat that if there had been anything to hold them the bowl might still, quite beautifully, a few steps away, have passed for uninjured. But, as there was, naturally, nothing to hold them but Maggie's hands, during the few moments the latter were so employed, she could only lay the almost equal parts of the vessel carefully beside their pedestal and leave them thus before her husband's eyes. She had proceeded without words, but quite as if with a sought effect-in spite of which it had all seemed to her to take a far longer time than anything she had ever so quickly accomplished. Amerigo said nothing either-though it was true that his silence had the gloss of the warning she doubtless appeared to admonish him to take: it was as if her manner hushed him to the proper observation of what she was doing. He should have no doubt of it whatever: she*knew* and her broken bowl was proof that she knew-yet the least part of her desire was to make him waste words. He would have to think-this she knew even better still; and all she was for the present concerned with was that he should be aware. She had taken him for aware all day, or at least for obscurely and instinctively anxious-as to that she had just committed herself to Fanny Assingham; but what she had been wrong about was the effect of his anxiety. His fear of staying away, as a marked symptom, had at least proved greater than his fear of coming in ; he had come in even at the risk of bringing it with him-and, ah, what more did she require now than her sense, established within the first minute or two, that he had brought it, however he might be steadying himself against dangers of betrayal by some wrong word, and that it was shut in there between them, the successive moments throbbing under it the while as the pulse of fever throbs under the doctor's thumb? Maggie's sense, in fine, in his presence, was that though the bowl had been broken, her reason hadn't; the reason for which she had made up her mind, the reason for which she had summoned her friend, the reason for which she had prepared the place for her husband's eyes; it was all one reason, and, as her intense little clutch held the matter, what had happened by Fanny's act and by his apprehension of it had not in the least happened to *her* but absolutely and directly to himself, as he must proceed to take in. There it was that her wish for time interposed-time for Amerigo's use, not for hers, since she, for ever so long now, for hours and hours as they seemed, had been living with eternity; with which she would continue to live. She wanted to say to him, " Take it, take it, take all you need of it ; arrange yourself so as to suffer least, or to be, at any rate, least distorted and disfigured Only *see* see that *I* see, and make up your mind, on this new basis, at your convenience. Wait-it won't be long-till you can confer again with Charlotte, for you'll do it much better then-more easily to both of us. Above all don't show me, till you've got it well under, the dreadful blur, the ravage of suspense and embarrassment, produced, and produced by my doing, in your personal serenity, your incomparable superiority." After she had squared again her little objects on the chimney, she was within an ace, in fact, of turning on him with that appeal; besides its being lucid for her, all the while, that the occasion was passing, that they were dining out, that he wasn't dressed, and that, though she herself was, she was yet, in all probability, so horribly red in the face and so awry, in many ways, with agitation, that in view of the Ambassador's company, of possible comments and constructions, she should need, before her glass, some restoration of appearances.

Amerigo, meanwhile, after all, could clearly make the most of her having enjoined on him to wait—suggested it by the positive pomp of her dealings with the smashed cup; to wait, that is, till she should pronounce as Mrs. Assingham had promised for her. This delay, again, certainly tested her presence of mind—though that strain was not what presently made her speak. Keep her eyes, for the time, from her husband's as she might, she soon found herself much more drivingly conscious of the strain on his own wit. There was even a minute, when her back was turned to him, during which she knew once more the strangeness of her desire to spare him, a strangeness that had already, fifty times, brushed her, in the depth of her trouble, as with the wild wing of some bird of the air who might blindly have swooped for an instant into the shaft of a well, darkening there by his momentary flutter the far-off round of sky. It was extraordinary, this quality in the taste of her wrong which made her completed sense of it seem rather to soften than to harden and it was the more extraordinary the more she had to recognise it; for what it came to was that seeing herself finally sure, knowing everything, having the fact, in all its abomination, so utterly before her that there was nothing else to add—what it came to was that, merely by being WITH him there in silence, she felt, within her, the sudden split between conviction and action. They had begun to cease, on the spot, surprisingly, to be connected; conviction, that is, budged no inch, only planting its feet the more firmly in the soil—but action began to hover like some lighter and larger, but easier form, excited by its very power to keep above ground. It would be free, it would be independent, it would go in—wouldn't it?—for some prodigious and superior adventure of its own. What would condemn it, so to speak, to the responsibility of freedom—this glimmered on Maggie even now—was the possibility, richer with every lapsing moment, that her husband would have, on the whole question, a new need of her, a need which was in fact being born between them in these very seconds. It struck her truly as so new that he would have felt hitherto none to compare with it at all; would indeed, absolutely, by this circumstance, be REALLY needing her for the first one in their whole connection. No, he had used her, had even exceedingly enjoyed her, before this; but there had been no precedent for that character of a proved necessity to him which she was rapidly taking on. The immense advantage of this particular clue, moreover, was that she should have now to arrange, alter, to falsify nothing; should have to be but consistently simple and straight. She asked herself, with concentration, while her back was still presented, what would be the very ideal of that method; after which, the next instant, it had all come to her and she had turned round upon him for the application. "Fanny Assingham broke it—knowing it had a crack and that it would go if she used sufficient force. She thought, when I had told her, that that would be the best thing to do with it—thought so from her own point of view. That hadn't been at all my idea, but she acted before I understood. I had, on the contrary," she explained, "put it here, in full view, exactly that you might see."

He stood with his hands in his pockets; he had carried his eyes to the fragments on the chimney-piece, and she could already distinguish the element of relief, absolutely of succour, in his acceptance from her of the opportunity to consider the fruits of their friend's violence—every added inch of reflection and delay having the advantage, from this point on, of counting for him double. It had operated within her now to the last intensity, her glimpse of the precious truth that by her helping him, helping him to help himself, as it were, she should help him to help HER. Hadn't she fairly got into his labyrinth with him?—wasn't she indeed in the very act of placing herself there, for him, at its centre and core, whence, on that definite orientation and by an instinct all her own, she might securely guide him out of it? She offered him thus, assuredly, a kind of support that was not to have been imagined in advance, and that moreover required—ah most truly!—some close looking at before it could be believed in and pronounced void of treachery. "Yes, look, look," she seemed to see him hear her say even while her sounded words were other—"look, look, both at the truth that still survives in that smashed evidence and at the even more remarkable appearance that I'm not such a fool as you supposed me. Look at the possibility that, since I AM different, there may still be something in it for you—if you're capable of working with me to get that out. Consider of course, as you must, the question of what you may have to surrender, on your side, what price you may have to pay, whom you may have to pay WITH, to set this advantage free; but take in, at any rate, that there is something for you if you don't too blindly spoil your chance for it." He went no nearer the damnatory pieces, but he eyed them, from where he stood, with a degree of recognition just visibly less to be dissimulated; all of which represented for her a certain traceable process. And her uttered words, meanwhile, were different enough from those he might have inserted between the lines of her already-spoken. "It's the golden bowl, you know, that you saw at the little antiquario's in Bloomsbury, so long ago—when you went there with Charlotte, when you spent those hours with her, unknown to me, a day or two before our marriage. It was shown you both, but you didn't take it; you left it for me, and I came upon it, extraordinarily, through happening to go into the same shop on Monday last; in walking home, in prowling about to pick up some small old thing for father's birthday, after my visit to the Museum, my appointment there with Mr. Crichton, of which I told you. It was shown me, and I was struck with it and took it—knowing nothing about it at the time. What I now know I've learned since—I learned this afternoon, a couple of hours ago; receiving from it naturally a great impression. So there it is—in its three pieces. You can handle them—don't be afraid—if you want to make sure the thing is the thing you and Charlotte saw together. Its having come apart makes an unfortunate difference for its beauty, its artistic value, but none for anything else. Its other value is just the same—I mean that of its having given me so much of the truth about you. I don't therefore so much care what becomes of it now—unless perhaps you may yourself, when you come to think, have some good use for it. In that case," Maggie wound up, "we can easily take the pieces with us to Fawns."

It was wonderful how she felt, by the time she had seen herself through this narrow pass, that she had really achieved something—that she was emerging a little, in fine, with the prospect less contracted. She had done for him, that is, what her instinct enjoined; had laid a basis not merely momentary on which he could meet her. When, by the turn of his head, he did finally meet her, this was the last thing that glimmered out of his look; but it came into sight, none the less, as a perception of his distress and almost as a question of his eyes; so that, for still another minute, before he committed himself, there occurred between them a kind of unprecedented moral exchange over which her superior lucidity presided. It was not, however, that when he did commit himself the show was promptly portentous. "But what in the world has Fanny Assingham had to do with it?"

She could verily, out of all her smothered soreness, almost have smiled: his question so affected her as giving the whole thing up to her. But it left her only to go the straighter. "She has had to do with it that I immediately sent for her and that she immediately came. She was the first person I wanted to see—because I knew she would know. Know more about what I had learned, I mean, than I could make out for myself. I made out as much as I could for myself—that I also wanted to have done; but it didn't, in spite of everything, take me very far, and she has really been a help. Not so much as she would like to be—not so much as, poor dear, she just now tried to be; yet she has done her very best for you—never forget that!—and has kept me along immeasurably better than I should have been able to come without her. She has gained me time; and that, these three months, don't you see? has been everything."

She had said "Don't you see?" on purpose, and was to feel the next moment that it had acted. "These three months'?" the Prince asked.

"Counting from the night you came home so late from Matcham. Counting from the hours you spent with Charlotte at Gloucester; your visit to the cathedral—which you won't have forgotten describing to me in so much detail. For that was the beginning of my being sure. Before it I had been sufficiently in doubt. Sure," Maggie developed, "of your having, and of your having for a long time had, TWO relations with Charlotte."

He stared, a little at sea, as he took it up. "Two—?"

Something in the tone of it gave it a sense, or an ambiguity, almost foolish—leaving Maggie to feel, as in a flash, how such a consequence, a foredoomed infelicity, partaking of the ridiculous even in one of the cleverest, might be of the very essence of the penalty of wrong-doing. "Oh, you may have had fifty—had the same relation with her fifty times! It's of the number of KINDS of relation with her that I speak—a number that doesn't matter, really, so long as there wasn't only one kind, as father and I supposed. One kind," she went on, "was there before us; we took that fully for granted, as you saw, and accepted it. We never thought of there being another, kept out of our sight. But after the evening I speak of I knew there was something else. As I say, I had, before that, my idea—which you never dreamed I had. From the moment I speak of it had more to go upon, and you became yourselves, you and she, vaguely, yet uneasily, conscious of the difference. But it's within these last hours that I've most seen where we are; and as I've been in communication with Fanny Assingham about my doubts, so I wanted to let her know my certainty—with the determination of which, however, you must understand, she has had nothing to do. She defends you," Maggie remarked.

He had given her all his attention, and with this impression for her, again, that he was, in essence, fairly reaching out to her for time—time, only time—she could sufficiently imagine, and to whatever strangeness, that he absolutely liked her to talk, even at the cost of his losing almost everything else by it. It was still, for a minute, as if he waited for something worse; wanted everything that was in her to come out, any definite fact, anything more precisely nameable, so that he too—as was his right—should know where he was. What stirred in him above all, while he followed in her face the clear train of her speech, must have been the impulse to take up something she put before him that he was yet afraid directly to touch. He wanted to make free with it, but had to keep his hands off—for reasons he had already made out; and the discomfort of his privation yearned at her out of his eyes with an announcing gleam of the fever, the none too tolerable chill, of specific recognition. She affected him as speaking more or less for her father as well, and his eyes might have been trying to hypnotise her into giving him the answer without his asking the question. "Had HE his idea, and has he now, with you, anything more?"—those were the words he had to hold himself from not speaking and that she would as yet, certainly, do nothing to make easy. She felt with her sharpest thrill how he was straitened and tied, and with the miserable pity of it her present conscious purpose of keeping him so could none the less perfectly accord. To name her father, on any such basis of anxiety, of compunction, would be to do the impossible thing, to do neither more nor less than give Charlotte away. Visibly, palpably, traceably, he stood off from this, moved back from it as from an open chasm now suddenly perceived, but which had been, between the two, with so much, so strangely much, quite uncalculated. Verily it towered before her, this history of their confidence. They had built strong and piled high—based as it was on such appearances—their conviction that, thanks to her native complacencies of so many sorts, she would always, quite to the end and through and through, take them as nobly sparing her. Amerigo was at any rate having the sensation of a particular ugliness to avoid, a particular difficulty to count with, that practically found him as unprepared as if he had been, like his wife, an abjectly simple person. And she meanwhile, however abjectly simple, was further discerning, for herself, that, whatever he might have to take from her—she being, on her side, beautifully free—he would absolutely not be able, for any qualifying purpose, to name Charlotte either. As his father-in-law's wife Mrs. Verver rose between them there, for the time, in august and prohibitive form; to protect her, defend her, explain about her, was, at the least, to bring her into the question—which would be by the same stroke to bring her husband. But this was exactly the door Maggie wouldn't open to him; on all of which she was the next moment asking herself if, thus warned and embarrassed, he were not fairly writhing in his pain. He writhed, on that hypothesis, some seconds more, for it was not till then that he had chosen between what he could and what he couldn't.

"You're apparently drawing immense conclusions from very small matters. Won't you perhaps feel, in fairness, that you're striking out, triumphing, or whatever I may call it, rather too easily—feel it when I perfectly admit that your smashed cup there does come back to me? I frankly confess, now, to the occasion, and to having wished not to speak of it to you at the time. We took two or three hours together, by arrangement; it WAS on the eve of my marriage—at the moment you say. But that put it on the eve of yours too, my dear—which was directly the point. It was desired to find for you, at the eleventh hour, some small wedding-present—a hunt, for something worth giving you, and yet possible from other points of view as well, in which it seemed I could be of use. You were naturally not to be told—precisely because it was all

FOR you. We went forth together and we looked; we rummaged about and, as I remember we called it, we prowled; then it was that, as I freely recognise, we came across that crystal cup—which I'm bound to say, upon my honour, I think it rather a pity Fanny Assingham, from whatever good motive, should have treated so." He had kept his hands in his pockets; he turned his eyes again, but more complacently now, to the ruins of the precious vessel; and Maggie could feel him exhale into the achieved quietness of his explanation a long, deep breath of comparative relief. Behind everything, beneath everything, it was somehow a comfort to him at last to be talking with her—and he seemed to be proving to himself that he COULD talk. "It was at a little shop in Bloomsbury—I think I could go to the place now. The man understood Italian, I remember; he wanted awfully to work off his bowl. But I didn't believe in it, and we didn't take it."

Maggie had listened with an interest that wore all the expression of candour. "Oh, you left it for me. But what did you take?"

He looked at her; first as if he were trying to remember, then as if he might have been trying to forget. "Nothing, I think—at that place."

"What did you take then at any other? What did you get me—since that was your aim and end—for a wedding-gift?"

The Prince continued very nobly to bethink himself. "Didn't we get you anything?"

Maggie waited a little; she had for some time, now, kept her eyes on him steadily; but they wandered, at this, to the fragments on her chimney. "Yes; it comes round, after all, to your having got me the bowl. I myself was to come upon it, the other day, by so wonderful a chance; was to find it in the same place and to have it pressed upon me by the same little man, who does, as you say, understand Italian. I did 'believe in it,' you see—must have believed in it somehow instinctively; for I took it as soon as I saw it. Though I didn't know at all then," she added, "what I was taking WITH it."

The Prince paid her for an instant, visibly, the deference of trying to imagine what this might have been. "I agree with you that the coincidence is extraordinary—the sort of thing that happens mainly in novels and plays. But I don't see, you must let me say, the importance or the connexion—"

"Of my having made the purchase where you failed of it?" She had quickly taken him up; but she had, with her eyes on him once more, another drop into the order of her thoughts, to which, through whatever he might say, she was still adhering. "It's not my having gone into the place, at the end of four years, that makes the strangeness of the coincidence; for don't such chances as that, in London, easily occur? The strangeness," she lucidly said, "is in what my purchase was to represent to me after I had got it home; which value came," she explained, "from the wonder of my having found such a friend."

"'Such a friend'?" As a wonder, assuredly, her husband could but take it.

"As the little man in the shop. He did for me more than he knew—I owe it to him. He took an interest in me," Maggie said; "and, taking that interest, he recalled your visit, he remembered you and spoke of you to me."

On which the Prince passed the comment of a sceptical smile. "Ah but, my dear, if extraordinary things come from people's taking an interest in you—"

"My life in that case," she asked, "must be very agitated? Well, he liked me, I mean—very particularly. It's only so I can account for my afterwards hearing from him—and in fact he gave me that to-day," she pursued, "he gave me it frankly as his reason."

"To-day?" the Prince inquiringly echoed.

But she was singularly able—it had been marvellously "given" her, she afterwards said to herself—to abide, for her light, for her clue, by her own order.

"I inspired him with sympathy—there you are! But the miracle is that he should have a sympathy to offer that could be of use to me. That was really the oddity of my chance," the Princess proceeded—"that I should have been moved, in my ignorance, to go precisely to him."

He saw her so keep her course that it was as if he could, at the best, but stand aside to watch her and let her pass; he only made a vague demonstration that was like an ineffective gesture. "I'm sorry to say any ill of your friends, and the thing was a long time ago; besides which there was nothing to make me recur to it. But I remember the man's striking me as a decided little beast."

She gave a slow headshake—as if, no, after consideration, not THAT way were an issue. "I can only think of him as kind, for he had nothing to gain. He had in fact only to lose. It was what he came to tell me—that he had asked me too high a price, more than the object was really worth. There was a particular reason, which he hadn't mentioned, and which had made him consider and repent. He wrote for leave to see me again—wrote in such terms that I saw him here this afternoon."

"Here?"—it made the Prince look about him.

"Downstairs—in the little red room. While he was waiting he looked at the few photographs that stand about there and recognised two of them. Though it was so long ago, he remembered the visit made him by the lady and the gentleman, and that gave him his connexion. It gave me mine, for he remembered everything and told me everything. You see you too had produced your effect; only, unlike you, he had thought of it again—he HAD recurred to it. He told me of your having wished to make each other presents—but of that's not having come off. The lady was greatly taken with the piece I had bought of him, but you had your reason against receiving it from her, and you had been right. He would think that of you more than ever now," Maggie went on; "he would see how wisely you had guessed the flaw and how easily the bowl could be broken. I had bought it myself, you see, for a present—he knew I was doing that. This was what had worked in him—especially after the price I had paid."

Her story had dropped an instant; she still brought it out in small waves of energy, each of which spent its force; so that she had an opportunity to speak before this force was renewed. But the quaint thing was what he now said. "And what, pray, WAS the price?"

She paused again a little. "It was high, certainly—for those fragments. I think I feel, as I look at them there, rather ashamed to say."

The Prince then again looked at them; he might have been growing used to the sight. "But shall you at least get your money back?"

"Oh, I'm far from wanting it back—I feel so that I'm getting its worth." With which, before he could reply, she had a quick transition. "The great fact about the day we're talking of seems to me to have been, quite remarkably, that no present was then made me. If your undertaking had been for that, that was not at least what came of it."

"You received then nothing at all?" The Prince looked vague and grave, almost retrospectively concerned.

"Nothing but an apology for empty hands and empty pockets; which was made me—as if it mattered a mite!—ever so frankly, ever so beautifully and touchingly."

This Amerigo heard with interest, yet not with confusion. "Ah, of course you couldn't have minded!" Distinctly, as she went on, he was getting the better of the mere awkwardness of his arrest; quite as if making out that he need SUFFER arrest from her now—before they should go forth to show themselves in the world together—in no greater quantity than an occasion ill-chosen at the best for a scene might decently make room for. He looked at his watch; their engagement, all the while, remained before him. "But I don't make out, you see, what case against me you rest—"

"On everything I'm telling you? Why, the whole case—the case of your having for so long so successfully deceived me. The idea of your finding something for me—charming as that would have been—was what had least to do with your taking a morning together at that moment. What had really to do with it," said Maggie, "was that you had to: you couldn't not, from the moment you were again face to face. And the reason of that was that there had been so much between you before—before I came between you at all."

Her husband had been for these last moments moving about under her eyes; but at this, as to check any show of impatience, he again stood still. "You've never been more sacred to me than you were at that hour—unless perhaps you've become so at this one."

The assurance of his speech, she could note, quite held up its head in him; his eyes met her own so, for the declaration, that it was as if something cold and momentarily unimaginable breathed upon her, from afar off, out of his strange consistency. She kept her direction still, however, under that. "Oh, the thing I've known best of all is that you've never wanted, together, to offend us. You've wanted quite intensely not to, and the precautions you've had to take for it have been for a long time one of the strongest of my impressions. That, I think," she added, "is the way I've best known."

"Known?" he repeated after a moment.

"Known. Known that you were older friends, and so much more intimate ones, than I had any reason to suppose when we married. Known there were things that hadn't been told me—and that gave their meaning, little by little, to other things that were before me."

"Would they have made a difference, in the matter of our marriage," the Prince presently asked, "if you HAD known them?"

She took her time to think. "I grant you not—in the matter of OURS." And then as he again fixed her with his hard yearning, which he couldn't keep down: "The question is so much bigger than that. You see how much what I know makes of it for me." That was what acted on him, this iteration of her knowledge, into the question of the validity, of the various bearings of which, he couldn't on the spot trust himself to pretend, in any high way, to go. What her claim, as she made it, represented for him—that he couldn't help betraying, if only as a consequence of the effect of the word itself, her repeated distinct "know, know," on his nerves. She was capable of being sorry for his nerves at a time when he should need them for dining out, pompously, rather responsibly, without his heart in it; yet she was not to let that prevent her using, with all economy, so precious a chance for supreme clearness. "I didn't force this upon you, you must recollect, and it probably wouldn't have happened for you if you hadn't come in."

"Ah," said the Prince, "I was liable to come in, you know."

"I didn't think you were this evening."

"And why not?"

"Well," she answered, "you have many liabilities—of different sorts." With which she recalled what she had said to Fanny Assingham. "And then you're so deep."

It produced in his features, in spite of his control of them, one of those quick plays of expression, the shade of a grimace, that testified as nothing else did to his race. "It's you, cara, who are deep."

Which, after an instant, she had accepted from him; she could so feel at last that it was true. "Then I shall have need of it all."

"But what would you have done," he was by this time asking, "if I HADN'T come in?"

"I don't know." She had hesitated. "What would you?"

"Oh; I oh—that isn't the question. I depend upon you. I go on. You would have spoken to-morrow?"

"I think I would have waited."

"And for what?" he asked.

"To see what difference it would make for myself. My possession at last, I mean, of real knowledge."

"Oh!" said the Prince.

"My only point now, at any rate," she went on, "is the difference, as I say, that it may make for YOU. Your knowing was—from the moment you did come in—all I had in view." And she sounded it again—he should have it once more. "Your knowing that I've ceased—"

"That you've ceased—?" With her pause, in fact, she had fairly made him press her for it.

"Why, to be as I was. NOT to know."

It was once more then, after a little, that he had had to stand receptive; yet the singular effect of this was that there was still something of the same sort he was made to want. He had another hesitation, but at last this odd quantity showed. "Then does any one else know?"

It was as near as he could come to naming her father, and she kept him at that distance. "Any one—?"

"Any one, I mean, but Fanny Assingham."

"I should have supposed you had had by this time particular means of learning. I don't see," she said, "why you ask me."

Then, after an instant—and only after an instant, as she saw—he made out what she meant; and it gave her, all strangely enough, the still further light that Charlotte, for herself, knew as little as he had known. The vision loomed, in this light, it fairly glared, for the few seconds—the vision of the two others alone together at Fawns, and Charlotte, as one of them, having gropingly to go on, always not knowing and not knowing! The picture flushed at the same time with all its essential colour—that of the so possible identity of her father's motive and principle with her own. HE was "deep," as Amerigo called it, so that no vibration of the still air should reach his daughter; just as she had earned that description by making and by, for that matter, intending still to make, her care for his serenity, or at any rate for the firm outer shell of his dignity, all marvellous enamel, her paramount law. More strangely even than anything else, her husband seemed to speak now but to help her in this. "I know nothing but what you tell me."

"Then I've told you all I intended. Find out the rest—!"

"Find it out—?" He waited.

She stood before him a moment—it took that time to go on. Depth upon depth of her situation, as she met his face, surged and sank within her; but with the effect somehow, once more, that they rather lifted her than let her drop. She had her feet somewhere, through it all—it was her companion, absolutely, who was at sea. And she kept her feet; she pressed them to what was beneath her. She went over to the bell beside the chimney and gave a ring that he could but take as a summons for her maid. It stopped everything for the present; it was an intimation to him to go and dress. But she had to insist. "Find out for yourself!"

PART FIFTH

XXXV

After the little party was again constituted at Fawns—which had taken, for completeness, some ten days—Maggie naturally felt herself still more possessed, in spirit, of everything that had last happened in London. There was a phrase that came back to her from old American years: she was having, by that idiom, the time of her life—she knew it by the perpetual throb of this sense of possession, which was almost too violent either to recognise or to hide. It was as if she had come out—that was her most general consciousness; out of a dark tunnel, a dense wood, or even simply a smoky room, and had thereby, at least, for going on, the advantage of air in her lungs. It was as if she were somehow at last gathering in the fruits of patience; she had either been really more patient than she had known at the time, or had been so for longer: the change brought about by itself as great a difference of view as the shift of an inch in the position of a telescope. It was her telescope in fact that had gained in range—just as her danger lay in her exposing herself to the observation by the more charmed, and therefore the more reckless, use of this optical resource. Not under any provocation to produce it in public was her unremitted rule; but the difficulties of duplicity had not shrunk, while the need of it had doubled. Humbugging, which she had so practised with her father, had been a comparatively simple matter on the basis of mere doubt; but the ground to be covered was now greatly larger, and she felt not unlike some young woman of the theatre who, engaged for a minor part in the play and having mastered her cues with anxious effort, should find herself suddenly promoted to leading lady and expected either to appear in every act of the five. She had made much to her husband, that last night, of her "knowing"; but it was exactly this quantity she now knew that, from the moment she could only dissimulate it, added to her responsibility and made of the latter all a mere question of having something precious and precarious in charge. There was no one to help her with it—not even Fanny Assingham now; this good friend's presence having become, inevitably, with that climax of their last interview in Portland Place, a severely simplified function. She had her use, oh yes, a thousand times; but it could only consist henceforth in her quite conspicuously touching at no point whatever—assuredly, at least with Maggie—the matter they had discussed. She was there, inordinately, as a value, but as a value only for the clear negation of everything. She was their general sign, precisely, of unimpaired beatitude—and she was to live up to that somewhat arduous character, poor thing, as she might. She might privately lapse from it, if she must, with Amerigo or with Charlotte—only not, of course, ever, so much as for the wink of an eye, with the master of the house. Such lapses would be her own affair, which Maggie at present could take no thought of. She treated her young friend meanwhile, it was to be said, to no betrayal of such wavering; so that from the moment of her alighting at the door with the Colonel everything went on between them at concert pitch. What had she done, that last evening in Maggie's room, but bring the husband and wife more together than, as would seem, they had ever been? Therefore what indiscretion should she not show by attempting to go behind the grand appearance of her success?—which would be to court a doubt of her beneficent work. She knew accordingly nothing but harmony and diffused, restlessly, nothing but peace—an extravagant, expressive, aggressive peace, not incongruous, after all, with the solid calm of the place; a kind of helmetted, trident-shaking pax Britannica.

The peace, it must be added, had become, as the days elapsed, a peace quite generally animated and peopled—thanks to that fact of the presence of "company" in which Maggie's ability to preserve an appearance had learned, from so far back, to find its best resource. It was not inconspicuous, it was in fact striking, that this resource, just now, seemed to meet in the highest degree every one's need: quite as if every one were, by the multiplication of human objects in the scene, by the creation, by the confusion, of fictive issues, hopeful of escaping somebody else's notice. It had reached the point, in truth, that the collective bosom might have been taken to heave with the knowledge of the descent upon adjacent shores, for a short period, of Mrs. Rance and the Lutches, still united, and still so divided, for conquest: the sense of the party showed at least, oddly enough, as favourable to the fancy of the quaint turn that some near "week-end" might derive from their reappearance. This measured for Maggie the ground they had all travelled together since that unforgotten afternoon of the none so distant year, that determinant September Sunday when, sitting with her father in the park, as in commemoration of the climax both of their old order and of their old danger, she had proposed to him that they should "call in" Charlotte,—call her in as a specialist might be summoned to an invalid's chair. Wasn't it a sign of something rather portentous, their being ready to be beholden, as for a diversion, to the once despised Kitty and Dotty? That had already had its application, in truth, to her invocation of the Castledeans and several other members, again, of the historic Matcham week, made before she left town, and made, always consistently, with an idea—since she was never henceforth to approach these people without an idea, and since that lurid element of their intercourse grew and grew for her with each occasion. The flame with which it burned afresh during these particular days, the way it held up the torch to anything, to everything, that MIGHT have occurred as the climax of revels springing from traditions so vivified—this by itself justified her private motive and reconsecrated her diplomacy. She had already produced by the aid of these people something of the effect she sought—that of being "good" for whatever her companions were good for, and of not asking either of them to give up anyone or anything for her sake. There was moreover, frankly, a sharpness of point in it that she enjoyed; it gave an accent to the truth she wished to illustrate—the truth that the surface of her recent life, thick-sown with the flower of earnest endeavour, with every form of the unruffled and the undoubting, suffered no symptom anywhere to peep out. It was as if, under her pressure, neither party could get rid of the complicity, as it might be figured, of the other; as if, in a word, she saw Amerigo and Charlotte committed, for fear of betrayals on their own side, to a kind of wan consistency on the subject of Lady Castledean's "set," and this latter group, by the same stroke, compelled to assist at attestations the extent and bearing of which they rather failed to grasp and which left them indeed, in spite of hereditary high spirits, a trifle bewildered and even a trifle scared.

They made, none the less, at Fawns, for number, for movement, for sound—they played their parts during a crisis that must have hovered for them, in the long passages of the old house, after the fashion of the established ghost, felt, through the dark hours as a constant possibility, rather than have menaced them in the form of a daylight bore, one of the perceived outsiders who are liable to be met in the drawing-room or to be sat next to at dinner. If the Princess, moreover, had failed of her occult use for so much of the machinery of diversion, she would still have had a sense not other than sympathetic for the advantage now extracted from it by Fanny Assingham's bruised philosophy. This good friend's relation to it was actually the revanche, she sufficiently indicated, of her obscured lustre at Matcham, where she had known her way about so much less than most of the others. She knew it at Fawns, through the pathless wild of the right tone, positively better than any one, Maggie could note for her; and her revenge had the magnanimity of a brave pointing out of it to every one else, a wonderful irresistible, conscious, almost compassionate patronage. Here was a house, she triumphantly caused it to be noted, in which she so bristled with values that some of them might serve, by her amused willingness to share, for such of the temporarily vague, among her fellow-guests, such of the dimly disconcerted, as had lost the key to their own. It may have been partly through the effect of this especial strain of community with her old friend that Maggie found herself, one evening, moved to take up again their dropped directness of reference. They had remained downstairs together late; the other women of the party had filed, singly or in couples, up the "grand" staircase on which, from the equally grand hall, these retreats and advances could always be pleasantly observed; the men had apparently taken their way to the smoking-room; while the Princess, in possession thus of a rare reach of view, had lingered as if to enjoy it. Then she saw that Mrs. Assingham was remaining a little—and as for the appreciation of her enjoyment; upon which they stood looking at each other across the cleared prospect until the elder woman, only vaguely expressive and tentative now, came nearer. It was like the act of asking if there were anything she could yet do, and that question was answered by her immediately feeling, on this closer view, as she had felt when presenting herself in Portland Place after Maggie's last sharp summons. Their understanding was taken up by these new snatched moments where that occasion had left it.

"He has never told her that I know. Of that I'm at last satisfied." And then as Mrs. Assingham opened wide eyes: "I've been in the dark since we came down, not understanding what he has been doing or intending—not making out what can have passed between them. But within a day or two I've begun to suspect, and this evening, for reasons—oh, too many to tell you!—I've been sure, since it explains. NOTHING has passed between them—that's what has happened. It explains," the Princess repeated with energy; "it explains, it explains!" She spoke in a manner that her auditor was afterwards to describe to the Colonel, oddly enough, as that of the quietest excitement; she had turned back to the chimney-place, where, in honour of a damp day and a chill night, the piled logs had turned to flame and sunk to embers; and the evident intensity of her vision for the fact she imparted made Fanny Assingham wait upon her words. It explained, this striking fact, more indeed than her companion, though conscious of fairly gaping with good-will, could swallow at once. The Princess, however, as for indulgence and confidence, quickly filled up the measure. "He hasn't let her know that I know—and, clearly, doesn't mean to. He has made up his mind; he'll say nothing about it. Therefore, as she's quite unable to arrive at the knowledge by herself, she has no idea how much I'm really in possession. She believes," said Maggie, "and, so far as her own conviction goes, she knows, that I'm not in possession of anything. And that, somehow, for my own help seems to me immense."

"Immense, my dear!" Mrs. Assingham applausively murmured, though not quite, even as yet, seeing all the way. "He's keeping quiet then on purpose?"

"On purpose." Maggie's lighted eyes, at least, looked further than they had ever looked. "He'll NEVER tell her now."

Fanny wondered; she cast about her; most of all she admired her little friend, in whom this announcement was evidently animated by an heroic lucidity. She stood there, in her full uniform, like some small erect commander of a siege, an anxious captain who has suddenly got news, replete with importance for him, of agitation, of division within the place. This importance breathed upon her comrade. "So you're all right?"

"Oh, ALL right's a good deal to say. But I seem at least to see, as I haven't before, where I am with it."

Fanny bountifully brooded; there was a point left vague. "And you have it from him?—your husband himself has told you?"

"Told' me—?"

"Why, what you speak of. It isn't of an assurance received from him then that you do speak?"

At which Maggie had continued to stare. "Dear me, no. Do you suppose I've asked him for an assurance?"

"Ah, you haven't?" Her companion smiled. "That's what I supposed you MIGHT mean. Then, darling, what HAVE you—?"

"Asked him for? I've asked him for nothing."

But this, in turn, made Fanny stare. "Then nothing, that evening of the Embassy dinner, passed between you?"

"On the contrary, everything passed."

"Everything—?"

"Everything. I told him what I knew—and I told him how I knew it."

Mrs. Assingham waited. "And that was all?"

"Wasn't it quite enough?"

"Oh, love," she bridled, "that's for you to have judged!"

"Then I HAVE judged," said Maggie—"I did judge. I made sure he understood—then I let him alone."

Mrs. Assingham wondered. "But he didn't explain—?"

"Explain? Thank God, no!" Maggie threw back her head as with horror at the thought, then the next moment added: "And I didn't, either."

The decency of pride in it shed a cold little light—yet as from heights at the base of which her companion rather panted. "But if he neither denies nor confesses—?"

"He does what's a thousand times better—he lets it alone. He does," Maggie went on, "as he would do; as I see now that I was sure he would. He lets me alone."

Fanny Assingham turned it over. "Then how do you know so where, as you say, you 'are'?"

"Why, just BY that. I put him in possession of the difference; the difference made, about me, by the fact that I hadn't been, after all—though with a wonderful chance, I admitted, helping me—too stupid to have arrived at knowledge. He had to see that I'm changed for him—quite changed from the idea of me that he had so long been going on with. It became a question then of his really taking in the change—and what I now see is that he is doing so."

Fanny followed as she could. "Which he shows by letting you, as you say, alone?"

Maggie looked at her a minute. "And by letting her."

Mrs. Assingham did what she might to embrace it—checked a little, however, by a thought that was the nearest approach she could have, in this almost too large air, to an inspiration. "Ah, but does Charlotte let HIM?"

"Oh, that's another affair—with which I've practically nothing to do. I dare say, however, she doesn't." And the Princess had a more distant gaze for the image evoked by the question. "I don't in fact well see how she CAN. But the point for me is that he understands."

"Yes," Fanny Assingham cooed, "understands—?"

"Well, what I want. I want a happiness without a hole in it big enough for you to poke your finger."

"A brilliant, perfect surface—to begin with at least. I see."

"The golden bowl—as it WAS to have been." And Maggie dwelt musingly on this obscured figure. "The bowl with all our happiness in it. The bowl without the crack."

For Mrs. Assingham too the image had its force, and the precious object shone before her again, reconstituted, plausible, presentable. But wasn't there still a piece missing? "Yet if he lets you alone and you only let him—?"

"Mayn't our doing so, you mean, be noticed?—mayn't it give us away? Well, we hope not—we try not—we take such care. We alone know what's between us—we and you; and haven't you precisely been struck, since you've been here, with our making so good a show?"

Her friend hesitated. "To your father?"

But it made her hesitate too; she wouldn't speak of her father directly. "To everyone. To her—now that you understand."

It held poor Fanny again in wonder. "To Charlotte—yes: if there's so much beneath it, for you, and if it's all such a plan. That makes it hang together it makes YOU hang together." She fairly exhaled her admiration. "You're like nobody else—you're extraordinary."

Maggie met it with appreciation, but with a reserve. "No, I'm not extraordinary—but I AM, for every one, quiet."

"Well, that's just what is extraordinary. 'Quiet' is more than *I* am, and you leave me far behind." With which, again, for an instant, Mrs. Assingham frankly brooded. "'Now that I understand,' you say—but there's one thing I don't understand." And the next minute, while her companion waited, she had mentioned it. "How can Charlotte, after all, not have pressed him, not have attacked him about it? How can she not have asked him—asked him on his honour, I mean—if you know?"

"How can she 'not'? Why, of course," said the Princess limpidly, "she MUST!"

"Well then—?"

"Well then, you think, he must have told her? Why, exactly what I mean," said Maggie, "is that he will have done nothing of the sort; will, as I say, have maintained the contrary."

Fanny Assingham weighed it. "Under her direct appeal for the truth?"

"Under her direct appeal for the truth."

"Her appeal to his honour?"

"Her appeal to his honour. That's my point."

Fanny Assingham braved it. "For the truth as from him to her?"

"From him to any one."

Mrs. Assingham's face lighted. "He'll simply, he'll insistently have lied?"

Maggie brought it out roundly. "He'll simply, he'll insistently have lied."

It held again her companion, who next, however, with a single movement, throwing herself on her neck, overflowed. "Oh, if you knew how you help me!"

Maggie had liked her to understand, so far as this was possible; but had not been slow to see afterwards how the possibility was limited, when one came to think, by mysteries she was not to sound. This inability in her was indeed not remarkable, inasmuch as the Princess herself, as we have seen, was only now in a position to boast of touching bottom. Maggie lived, inwardly, in a consciousness that she could but partly open even to so good a friend, and her own visitation of the fuller expanse of which was, for that matter, still going on. They had been duskier still, however, these recesses of her imagination—that, no doubt, was what might at present be said for them. She had looked into them, on the eve of her leaving town, almost without penetration: she had made out in those hours, and also, of a truth, during the days which immediately followed, little more than the strangeness of a relation having for its chief mark—whether to be prolonged or not—the absence of any "intimate" result of the crisis she had invited her husband to recognise. They had dealt with this crisis again, face to face, very briefly, the morning after the scene in her room—but with the odd consequence of her having appeared merely to leave it on his hands. He had received it from her as he might have received a bunch of keys or a list of commissions—attentive to her instructions about them, but only putting them, for the time, very carefully and safely, into his pocket. The instructions had seemed, from day to day, to make so little difference for his behaviour—that is for his speech or his silence; to produce, as yet, so little of the fruit of action. He had taken from her, on the spot, in a word, before going to dress for dinner, all she then had to give—after which, on the morrow, he had asked her for more, a good deal as if she might have renewed her supply during the night; but he had had at his command for this latter purpose an air of extraordinary detachment and discretion, an air amounting really to an appeal which, if she could have brought herself to describe it vulgarly, she would have described as cool, just as he himself would have described it in any one else as "cheeky"; a suggestion that she should trust him on the particular ground since she didn't on the general. Neither his speech nor his silence struck her as signifying more, or less, under this pressure, than they had seemed to signify for weeks past; yet if her sense hadn't been absolutely closed to the possibility in him of any thought of wounding her, she might have taken his undisturbed manner, the perfection of his appearance of having recovered himself, for one of those intentions of high impertinence by the aid of which great people, les grands seigneurs, persons of her husband's class and type, always know how to re-establish a violated order.

It was her one purely good fortune that she could feel thus sure impertinence—to HER at any rate—was not among the arts on which he proposed to throw himself; for though he had, in so almost mystifying a manner, replied to nothing, denied nothing, explained nothing, apologised for nothing, he had somehow conveyed to her that this was not because of any determination to treat her case as not "worth" it. There had been consideration, on both occasions, in the way he had listened to her—even though at the same time there had been extreme reserve; a reserve indeed, it was also to be remembered, qualified by the fact that, on their second and shorter interview, in Portland Place, and quite at the end of this passage, she had imagined him positively proposing to her a temporary accommodation. It had been but the matter of something in the depths of the eyes he had finally fixed upon her, and she had found in it, the more she kept it before her, the tacitly-offered sketch of a working arrangement. "Leave me my reserve; don't question it—it's all I have, just now, don't you see? so that, if you'll make me the concession of letting me alone with it for as long a time as I require, I promise you something or other, grown under cover of it, even though I don't yet quite make out what, as a return for your patience." She had turned away from him with some such unspoken words as that in her ear, and indeed she had to represent to herself that she had spiritually heard them, had to listen to them still again, to explain her particular patience in face of his particular failure. He hadn't so much as pretended to meet for an instant the question raised by her of her accepted ignorance of the point in time, the period before their own marriage, from which his intimacy with Charlotte dated. As an ignorance in which he and Charlotte had been personally interested—and to the pitch of consummately protecting, for years, each other's interest—as a condition so imposed upon her the fact of its having ceased might have made it, on the spot, the first article of his defence. He had vouchsafed it, however, nothing better than his longest stare of postponed consideration. That tribute he had coldly paid it, and Maggie might herself have been stupefied, truly, had she not had something to hold on by, at her own present ability, even provisional, to make terms with a chapter of history into which she could but a week before not have dipped without a mortal chill. At the rate at which she was living she was getting used hour by hour to these extensions of view; and when she asked herself, at Fawns, to what single observation of her own, in London, the Prince had an affirmation to oppose, she but just failed to focus the small strained wife of the moments in question as some panting dancer of a difficult step who had capered, before the footlights of an empty theatre, to a spectator lounging in a box.

Her best comprehension of Amerigo's success in not committing himself was in her recall, meanwhile, of the inquiries he had made of her on their only return to the subject, and which he had in fact explicitly provoked their return in order to make. He had had it over with her again, the so distinctly remarkable incident of her interview at home with the little Bloomsbury shopman. This anecdote, for him, had, not altogether surprisingly, required some straighter telling, and the Prince's attitude in presence of it had represented once more his nearest approach to a cross-examination. The difficulty in respect to the little man had been for the question of his motive—his motive in writing, first, in the spirit of retraction, to a lady with whom he had made a most advantageous bargain, and in then coming to see her so that his apology should be personal. Maggie had felt her explanation weak; but there were the facts, and she could give no other. Left alone, after the transaction, with the knowledge that her visitor designed the object bought of him as a birthday-gift to her father—for Maggie confessed freely to having chattered to him almost as to a friend—the vendor of the golden bowl had acted on a scruple rare enough in vendors of any class, and almost unprecedented in the thrifty children of Israel. He hadn't liked what he had done, and what he had above all made such a "good thing" of having done; at the thought of his purchaser's good faith and charming presence, opposed to that flaw in her acquestion which would make it, verily, as an offering to a loved parent, a thing of sinister meaning and evil effect, he had known conscientious, he had known superstitious visitings, had given way to a whim all the more remarkable to his own commercial mind, no doubt, from its never having troubled him in other connexions. She had recognised the oddity of her adventure and left it to show for what it was. She had not been unconscious, on the other hand, that if it hadn't touched Amerigo so nearly he would have found in it matter for some amused reflection. He had uttered an extraordinary sound, something between a laugh and a howl, on her saying, as she had made a point of doing: "Oh, most certainly, he TOLD me his reason was because he 'liked' me"—though she remained in doubt of whether that inarticulate comment had been provoked most by the familiarities she had offered or by those that, so pictured, she had had to endure. That the partner of her bargain had yearned to see her again, that he had plainly jumped at a pretext for it, this also she had frankly expressed herself to the Prince as having, in no snubbing, no scandalised, but rather in a positively appreciative and indebted spirit, not delayed to make out. He had wished, ever so seriously, to return her a part of her money, and she had wholly declined to receive it; and then he had uttered his hope that she had not, at all events, already devoted the crystal cup to the beautiful purpose she had, so kindly and so fortunately, named to him. It wasn't a thing for a present to a person she was fond of, for she wouldn't wish to give a present that would bring ill luck. That had come to him—so that he couldn't rest, and he should feel better now that he had told her. His having led her to act in ignorance was what he should have been ashamed of; and, if she would pardon, gracious lady as she was, all the liberties he had taken, she might make of the bowl any use in life but that one.

It was after this that the most extraordinary incident of all, of course, had occurred—his pointing to the two photographs with the remark that those were persons he knew, and that, more wonderful still, he had made acquaintance with them, years before, precisely over the same article. The lady, on that occasion, had taken up the fancy of presenting it to the gentleman, and the gentleman, guessing and dodging ever so cleverly, had declared that he wouldn't for the world receive an object under such suspicion. He himself, the little man had confessed, wouldn't have minded—about THEM; but he had never forgotten either their talk or their faces, the impression altogether made by them, and, if she really wished to know, now, what had perhaps most moved him, it was the thought that she should ignorantly have gone in for a thing not good enough for other buyers. He had been immensely struck—that was another point—with this accident of their turning out, after so long, friends of hers too: they had disappeared, and this was the only light he had ever had upon them. He had flushed up, quite red, with his recognition, with all his responsibility—had declared that the connexion must have had, mysteriously, something to do with the impulse he had obeyed. And Maggie had made, to her husband, while he again stood before her, no secret of the shock, for herself, so suddenly and violently received. She had done her best, even while taking it full in the face, not to give herself away; but she wouldn't answer—no, she wouldn't—for what she might, in her agitation, have made her informant think. He might think what he would—there had been three or four minutes during which, while she asked him question upon question, she had doubtless too little cared. And he had spoken, for his remembrance, as fully as she could have wished; he had spoken, oh, delightedly, for the "terms" on which his other visitors had appeared to be with each other, and in fact for that conviction of the nature and degree of their intimacy under which, in spite of precautions, they hadn't been able to help leaving him. He had observed and judged and not forgotten; he had been sure they were great people, but no, ah no, distinctly, hadn't "liked" them as he liked the Signora Principessa. Certainly—she had created no vagueness about that—he had been in possession of her name and address, for sending her both her cup and her account. But the others he had only, always, wondered about—he had been sure they would never come back. And as to the time of their visit, he could place it, positively, to a day—by reason of a transaction of importance, recorded in his books, that had occurred but a few hours later. He had left her, in short, definitely rejoicing that he had been able to make up to her for not having been quite "square" over their little business by rendering her, so unexpectedly, the service of this information. His joy, moreover, was—as much as Amerigo would!—a matter of the personal interest with which his kindness, gentleness, grace, her charming presence and easy humanity and familiarity, had inspired him. All of which, while, in thought, Maggie went over it again and again—oh, over any imputable rashness of her own immediate passion and pain, as well as over the rest of the straight little story she had, after all, to tell—might very conceivably make a long sum for the Prince to puzzle out.

There were meanwhile, after the Castledeans and those invited to meet them had gone, and before Mrs. Rance and the Lutches had come, three or four days during which she was to learn the full extent of her need not to be penetrable; and then it was indeed that she felt all the force, and threw herself upon all the help, of the facts she had confided, several nights earlier, to Fanny Assingham. She had known it in advance, had warned herself of it while the house was full: Charlotte had designs upon her of a nature best known to herself, and was only waiting for the better opportunity of their finding themselves less companioned. This consciousness had been exactly at the bottom of Maggie's wish to multiply their spectators; there were moments for her, positively, moments of planned postponement, of evasion scarcely less disguised than studied, during which she turned over with anxiety the different ways—there being two or three possible ones—in which her young stepmother might, at need, seek to work upon her. Amerigo's not having "told" her of his passage with his wife gave, for Maggie, altogether a new aspect to Charlotte's consciousness and condition—an aspect with which, for apprehension, for wonder, and even, at moments, inconsequently enough, for something like compassion, the Princess had now to reckon. She asked herself—for she was capable of that—what he had MEANT by keeping the sharer of his guilt in the dark about a matter touching her otherwise so nearly; what he had meant, that is, for this unmistakably mystified personage herself. Maggie could imagine what he had meant for her—all sorts of thinkable things, whether things of mere "form" or things of sincerity, things of pity or things of prudence: he had meant, for instance, in all probability, primarily, to conjure away any such appearance of a changed relation between the two women as his father-in-law might notice and follow up. It would have been open to him however, given the pitch of their intimacy, to avert this danger by some more conceivable course with Charlotte; since an earnest warning, in fact, the full freedom of alarm, that of his insisting to her on the peril of suspicion incurred, and on the importance accordingly of outward peace at any price, would have been the course really most conceivable. Instead of warning and advising he had reassured and deceived her; so that our young woman, who had been, from far back, by the habit, if her nature, as much on her guard against sacrificing others as if she felt the great trap of life mainly to be set for one's doing so, now found herself attaching her fancy to that side of the situation of the exposed pair which involved, for themselves at least, the sacrifice of the least fortunate.

She never, at present, thought of what Amerigo might be intending, without the reflection, by the same stroke, that, whatever this quantity, he was leaving still more to her own ingenuity. He was helping her, when the thing came to the test, only by the polished, possibly almost too polished surface his manner to his wife wore for an admiring world; and that, surely, was entitled to scarcely more than the praise of negative diplomacy. He was keeping his manner right, as she had related to Mrs. Assingham; the case would have been beyond calculation, truly, if, on top of everything, he had allowed it to go wrong. She had hours of exaltation indeed when the meaning of all this pressed in upon her as a tacit vow from him to abide without question by whatever she should be able to achieve or think fit to prescribe. Then it was that, even while holding her breath for the awe of it, she truly felt almost able enough for anything. It was as if she had passed, in a time incredibly short, from being nothing for him to being all; it was as if, rightly noted, every turn of his head, every tone of his voice, in these days, might mean that there was but one way in which a proud man reduced to abjection could hold himself. During those of Maggie's vigils in which that view loomed largest, the image of her husband that it thus presented to her gave out a beauty for the revelation of which she struck herself as paying, if anything, all too little. To make sure of it—to make sure of the beauty shining out of the humility, and of the humility lurking in all the pride of his presence—she would have gone the length of paying more yet, of paying with difficulties and anxieties compared to which those actually before her might have been as superficial as headaches or rainy days.

The point at which these exaltations dropped, however, was the point at which it was apt to come over her that if her complications had been greater the question of paying would have been limited still less to the liabilities of her own pocket. The complications were verily great enough, whether for ingenuities or sublimities, so long as she had to come back to it so often that Charlotte, all the while, could only be struggling with secrets sharper than her own. It was odd how that certainty again and again determined and coloured her wonderments of detail; the question, for instance, of HOW Amerigo, in snatched opportunities of conference, put the haunted creature off with false explanations, met her particular challenges and evaded—if that was what he did do!—her particular demands. Even the conviction that Charlotte was but awaiting some chance really to test her trouble upon her lover's wife left Maggie's sense meanwhile open as to the sight of gilt wires and bruised wings, the spacious but suspended cage, the home of eternal unrest, of pacings, beatings, shakings, all so vain, into which the baffled consciousness helplessly resolved itself. The cage was the deluded condition, and Maggie, as having known delusion—rather!—understood the nature of cages. She walked round Charlotte's—cautiously and in a very wide circle; and when, inevitably, they had to communicate she felt herself, comparatively, outside, on the breast of nature, and saw her companion's face as that of a prisoner looking through bars. So it was that through bars, bars richly gilt, but firmly, though discreetly, planted, Charlotte finally struck her as making a grim attempt; from which, at first, the Princess drew back as instinctively as if the door of the cage had suddenly been opened from within.

XXXVI

They had been alone that evening—alone as a party of six, and four of them, after dinner, under suggestion not to be resisted, sat down to "bridge" in the smoking-room. They had passed together to that apartment, on rising from table, Charlotte and Mrs. Assingham alike indulgent, always, to tobacco, and in fact practising an emulation which, as Fanny said, would, for herself, had the Colonel not issued an interdict based on the fear of her stealing his cigars, have stopped only at the short pipe. Here cards had with inevitable promptness asserted their rule, the game forming itself, as had often happened before, of Mr. Verver with Mrs. Assingham for partner and of the Prince with Mrs. Verver. The Colonel, who had then asked of Maggie license to relieve his mind of a couple of letters for the earliest post out on the morrow, was addressing himself to this task at the other end of the room, and the Princess herself had welcomed the comparatively hushed hour—for the bridge-players were serious and silent—much in the mood of a tired actress who has the good fortune to be "off," while her mates are on, almost long enough for a nap on the property sofa in the wing. Maggie's nap, had she been able to snatch forty winks, would have been of the spirit rather than of the sense; yet as she subsided, near a lamp, with the last salmon-coloured French periodical, she was to fail, for refreshment, even of that sip of independence.

There was no question for her, as she found, of closing her eyes and getting away; they strayed back to life, in the stillness, over the top of her Review; she could lend herself to none of those refinements of the higher criticism with which its pages bristled; she was there, where her companions were, there again and more than ever there; it was as if, of a sudden, they had been made, in their personal intensity and their rare complexity of relation, freshly importunate to her. It was the first evening there had been no one else. Mrs. Rance and the Lutches were due the next day; but meanwhile the facts of the situation were upright for her round the green cloth and the silver flambeaux; the fact of her father's wife's lover facing his mistress; the fact of her father sitting, all unsounded and unblinking, between them; the fact of Charlotte keeping it up, keeping up everything, across the table, with her husband beside her; the fact of Fanny Assingham, wonderful creature, placed opposite to the three and knowing more about each, probably, when one came to think, than either of them knew of either. Erect above all for her was the sharp-edged fact of the relation of the whole group, individually and collectively, to herself—herself so speciously eliminated for the hour, but presumably more present to the attention of each than the next card to be played.

Yes, under that imputation, to her sense, they sat—the imputation of wondering, beneath and behind all their apparently straight play, if she weren't really watching them from her corner and consciously, as might be said, holding them in her hand. She was asking herself at last how they could bear it—for, though cards were as nought to her and she could follow no move, so that she was always, on such occasions, out of the party, they struck her as conforming alike, in the matter of gravity and propriety, to the stiff standard of the house. Her father, she knew, was a high adept, one of the greatest—she had been ever, in her stupidity, his small, his sole despair; Amerigo excelled easily, as he understood and practised every art that could beguile large leisure; Mrs. Assingham and Charlotte, moreover, were accounted as "good" as members of a sex incapable of the nobler consistency could be. Therefore, evidently, they were not, all so up to their usual form, merely passing it off, whether for her or for themselves; and the amount of enjoyed, or at least achieved, security represented by so complete a conquest of appearances was what acted on her nerves, precisely, with a kind of provocative force. She found herself, for five minutes, thrilling with the idea of the prodigious effect that, just as she sat there near them, she had at her command; with the sense that if she were but different—oh, ever so different!—all this high decorum would hang by a hair. There reigned for her, absolutely, during these vertiginous moments, that fascination of the monstrous, that temptation of the horribly possible, which we so often trace by its breaking out suddenly, lest it should go further, in unexplained retreats and reactions.

After it had been thus vividly before her for a little that, springing up under her wrong and making them all start, stare and turn pale, she might sound out their doom in a single sentence, a sentence easy to choose among several of the lurid—after she had faced that blinding light and felt it turn to blackness, she rose from her place, laying aside her magazine, and moved slowly round the room, passing near the card-players and pausing an instant behind the chairs in turn. Silent and discreet, she bent a vague mild face upon them, as if to signify that, little as she followed their doings, she wished them well; and she took from each, across the table, in the common solemnity, an upward recognition which she was to carry away with her on her moving out to the terrace, a few minutes later. Her father and her husband, Mrs. Assingham and Charlotte, had done nothing but meet her eyes; yet the difference in these demonstrations made each a separate passage—which was all the more wonderful since, with the secret behind every face, they had alike tried to look at her THROUGH it and in denial of it.

It all left her, as she wandered off, with the strangest of impressions—the sense, forced upon her as never yet, of an appeal, a positive confidence, from the four pairs of eyes, that was deeper than any negation, and that seemed to speak, on the part of each, of some relation to be contrived by her, a relation with herself, which would spare the individual the danger, the actual present strain, of the relation with the others. They thus tacitly put it upon her to be disposed of, the whole complexity of their peril, and she promptly saw why because she was there, and there just as she was, to lift it off them and take it; to charge herself with it as the scapegoat of old, of whom she had once seen a terrible picture, had been charged with the sins of the people and had gone forth into the desert to sink under his burden and die. That indeed wasn't THEIR design and their interest, that she should sink under hers; it wouldn't be their feeling that she should do anything but live, live on somehow for their benefit, and even as much as possible in their company, to keep proving to them that they had truly escaped and that she was still there to simplify. This idea of her simplifying, and of their combined struggle, dim as yet but steadily growing, toward the perception of her adopting it from them, clung to her while she hovered on the terrace, where the summer night was so soft that she scarce needed the light shawl she had picked up. Several of the long windows of the occupied rooms stood open to it, and the light came out in vague shafts and fell upon the old smooth stones. The hour was moonless and starless and the air heavy and still—which was why, in her evening dress, she need fear no chill and could get away, in the outer darkness, from that provocation of opportunity which had assaulted her, within, on her sofa, as a beast might have leaped at her throat.

Nothing in fact was stranger than the way in which, when she had remained there a little, her companions, watched by her through one of the windows, actually struck her as almost consciously and gratefully safer. They might have been—really charming as they showed in the beautiful room, and Charlotte certainly, as always, magnificently handsome and supremely distinguished—they might have been figures rehearsing some play of which she herself was the author; they might even, for the happy appearance they continued to present, have been such figures as would, by the strong note of character in each, fill any author with the certitude of success, especially of their own histrionic. They might in short have represented any mystery they would; the point being predominantly that the key to the mystery, the key that could wind and unwind it without a snap of the spring, was there in her pocket—or rather, no doubt, clasped at this crisis in her hand and pressed, as she walked back and forth, to her breast. She walked to the end and far out of the light; she returned and saw the others still where she had left them; she passed round the house and looked into the drawing-room, lighted also, but empty now, and seeming to speak the more, in its own voice, of all the possibilities she controlled. Spacious and splendid, like a stage again awaiting a drama, it was a scene she might people, by the press of her spring, either with serenities and dignities and decencies, or with terrors and shames and ruins, things as ugly as those formless fragments of her golden bowl she was trying so hard to pick up.

She continued to walk and continued to pause; she stopped afresh for the look into the smoking-room, and by this time—it was as if the recognition had of itself arrested her—she saw as in a picture, with the temptation she had fled from quite extinct, why it was she had been able to give herself so little, from the first, to the vulgar heat of her wrong. She might fairly, as she watched them, have missed it as a lost thing; have yearned for it, for the straight vindictive view, the rights of resentment, the rages of jealousy, the protests of passion, as for something she had been cheated of not least: a range of feelings which for many women would have meant so much, but which for HER husband's wife, for HER father's daughter, figured nothing nearer to experience than a wild eastern caravan, looming into view with crude colours in the sun, fierce pipes in the air, high spears against the sky, all a thrill, a natural joy to mingle with, but turning off short before it reached her and plunging into other defiles. She saw at all events why horror itself had almost failed her; the horror that, foreshadowed in advance, would, by her thought, have made everything that was unaccustomed in her cry out with pain; the horror of finding evil seated, all at its ease, where she had only dreamed of good; the horror of the thing HIDEOUSLY behind, behind so much trusted, so much pretended, nobleness, cleverness, tenderness. It was the first sharp falsity she had known in her life, to touch at all, or be touched by; it had met her like some bad-faced stranger surprised in one of the thick-carpeted corridors of a house of quiet on a Sunday afternoon; and yet, yes, amazingly, she had been able to look at terror and disgust only to know that she must put away from her the bitter-sweet of their freshness. The sight, from the window, of the group so constituted, TOLD her why, told her how, named to her, as with hard lips, named straight AT her, so that she must take it full in the face, that other possible relation to the whole fact which alone would bear upon her irresistibly. It was extraordinary: they positively brought home to her that to feel about them in any of the immediate, inevitable, assuaging ways, the ways usually open to innocence outraged and generosity betrayed, would have been to give them up, and that giving them up was, marvellously, not to be thought of. She had never, from the first hour of her state of acquired conviction, given them up so little as now; though she was, no doubt, as the consequence of a step taken a few minutes later, to invoke the conception of doing that, if might be, even less. She had resumed her walk—stopping here and there, while she rested on the cool smooth stone balustrade, to draw it out; in the course of which, after a little, she passed again the lights of the empty drawing-room and paused again for what she saw and felt there.

It was not at once, however, that this became quite concrete; that was the effect of her presently making out that Charlotte was in the room, launched and erect there, in the middle, and looking about her; that she had evidently just come round to it, from her card-table, by one of the passages—with the expectation, to all appearance, of joining her stepdaughter. She had pulled up at seeing the great room empty—Maggie not having passed out, on leaving the group, in a manner to be observed. So definite a quest of her, with the bridge-party interrupted or altered for it, was an impression that fairly assailed the Princess, and to which something of attitude and aspect, the air of arrested pursuit and purpose, in Charlotte, together with the suggestion of her next vague movements, quickly added its meaning. This meaning was that she had decided, that she had been infinitely conscious of Maggie's presence before, that she knew that she would at last find her alone, and that she wanted her, for some reason, enough to have presumably called on Bob Assingham for aid. He had taken her chair and let her go, and the arrangement was for Maggie a signal proof of her earnestness; of the energy, in fact, that, though superficially commonplace in a situation in which people weren't supposed to be watching each other, was what affected our young woman, on the spot, as a breaking of bars. The splendid shining supple creature was out of the cage, was at large; and the question now almost grotesquely rose of whether she mightn't by some art, just where she was and before she could go further, be hemmed in and secured. It would have been for a moment, in this case, a matter of quickly closing the windows and giving the alarm—with poor Maggie's sense that, though she couldn't know what she wanted of her, it was enough for trepidation that, at these firm hands, anything should be to say nothing of the sequel of a flight taken again along the terrace, even under the shame of the confessed feebleness of such evasions on the part of an outraged wife. It was to this feebleness, none the less, that the outraged wife had presently resorted; the most that could be said for her being, as she felt while she finally stopped short, at a distance, that she could at any rate resist her abjection sufficiently not to sneak into the house by another way and safely reach her room. She had literally caught herself in the act of dodging and ducking, and it told her there, vividly, in a single word, what she had all along been most afraid of.

She had been afraid of the particular passage with Charlotte that would determine her father's wife to take him into her confidence as she couldn't possibly as yet have done, to lay before him a statement of her wrong, to lay before him the infamy of what she was apparently suspected of. This, should she have made up her mind to do it, would rest on a calculation the thought of which evoked, strangely, other possibilities and visions. It would show her as sufficiently believing in her grasp of her husband to be able to assure herself that, with his daughter thrown on the defensive, with Maggie's cause and Maggie's word, in fine, against her own, it wasn't Maggie's that would most certainly carry the day. Such a glimpse of her conceivable idea, which would be founded on reasons all her own, reasons of experience and assurance, impenetrable to others, but intimately familiar to herself—such a glimpse opened out wide as soon as it had come into view; for if so much as this was still firm ground between the elder pair, if the beauty of appearances had been so consistently preserved, it was only the golden bowl as Maggie herself knew it that had been broken. The breakage stood not for any wrought discomposure among the triumphant three—it stood merely for the dire deformity of her attitude toward them. She was unable at the minute, of course, fully to measure the difference thus involved for her, and it remained inevitably an agitating image, the way it might be held over her that if she didn't, of her own prudence, satisfy Charlotte as to the reference, in her mocking spirit, of so much of the unuttered and unutterable, of the constantly and unmistakably implied, her father would be invited without further ceremony to recommend her to do so. But ANY confidence, ANY latent operating insolence, that Mrs. Verver should, thanks to her large native resources, continue to be possessed of and to hold in reserve, glimmered suddenly as a possible working light and seemed to offer, for meeting her, a new basis and something like a new system. Maggie felt, truly, a rare contraction of the heart on making out, the next instant, what the new system would probably have to be—and she had practically done that before perceiving that the thing she feared had already taken place. Charlotte, extending her search, appeared now to define herself vaguely in the distance; of this, after an instant, the Princess was sure, though the darkness was thick, for the projected clearness of the smoking-room windows had presently contributed its help.

Her friend came slowly into that circle—having also, for herself, by this time, not indistinguishably discovered that Maggie was on the terrace. Maggie, from the end, saw her stop before one of the windows to look at the group within, and then saw her come nearer and pause again, still with a considerable length of the place between them.

Yes, Charlotte had seen she was watching her from afar, and had stopped now to put her further attention to the test. Her face was fixed on her, through the night; she was the creature who had escaped by force from her cage, yet there was in her whole motion assuredly, even as so dimly discerned, a kind of portentous intelligent stillness. She had escaped with an intention, but with an intention the more definite that it could so accord with quiet measures. The two women, at all events, only hovered there, for these first minutes, face to face over their interval and exchanging no sign; the intensity of their mutual look might have pierced the night, and Maggie was at last to start with the scared sense of having thus yielded to doubt, to dread, to hesitation, for a time that, with no other proof needed, would have completely given her away. How long had she stood staring?—a single minute or five? Long enough, in any case, to have felt herself absolutely take from her visitor something that the latter threw upon her, irresistibly, by this effect of silence, by this effect of waiting and watching, by this effect, unmistakably, of timing her indecision and her fear. If then, scared and hanging back, she had, as was so evident, sacrificed all past pretences, it would have been with the instant knowledge of an immense advantage gained that Charlotte finally saw her come on. Maggie came on with her heart in her hands; she came on with the definite prevision, throbbing like the tick of a watch, of a doom impossibly sharp and hard, but to which, after looking at it with her eyes wide open, she had none the less bowed her head. By the time she was at her companion's side, for that matter, by the time Charlotte had, without a motion, without a word, simply let her approach and stand there, her head was already on the block, so that the consciousness that everything had now gone blurred all perception of whether or no the axe had fallen. Oh, the "advantage," it was perfectly enough, in truth, with Mrs. Verver; for what was Maggie's own sense but that of having been thrown over on her back, with her neck, from the first, half broken and her helpless face staring up? That position only could account for the positive grimace of weakness and pain produced there by Charlotte's dignity.

"I've come to join you—I thought you would be here."

"Oh yes, I'm here," Maggie heard herself return a little flatly. "It's too close in-doors."

"Very—but close even here." Charlotte was still and grave—she had even uttered her remark about the temperature with an expressive weight that verged upon solemnity; so that Maggie, reduced to looking vaguely about at the sky, could only feel her not fail of her purpose. "The air's heavy as if with thunder—I think there'll be a storm." She made the suggestion to carry off an awkwardness—which was a part, always, of her companion's gain; but the awkwardness didn't diminish in the silence that followed. Charlotte had said nothing in reply; her brow was dark as with a fixed expression, and her high elegance, her handsome head and long, straight neck testified, through the dusk, to their inveterate completeness and noble erectness. It was as if what she had come out to do had already begun, and when, as a consequence, Maggie had said helplessly, "Don't you want something? won't you have my shawl?" everything might have crumbled away in the comparative poverty of the tribute. Mrs. Verver's rejection of it had the brevity of a sign that they hadn't closed in for idle words, just as her dim, serious face, uninterruptedly presented until they moved again, might have represented the success with which she watched all her message penetrate. They presently went back the way she had come, but she stopped Maggie again within range of the smoking-room window and made her stand where the party at cards would be before her. Side by side, for three minutes, they fixed this picture of quiet harmonies, the positive charm of it and, as might have been said, the full significance—which, as was now brought home to Maggie, could be no more, after all, than a matter of interpretation, differing always for a different interpreter. As she herself had hovered in sight of it a quarter-of-an-hour before, it would have been a thing for her to show Charlotte—to show in righteous irony, in reproach too stern for anything but silence. But now it was she who was being shown it, and shown it by Charlotte, and she saw quickly enough that, as Charlotte showed it, so she must at present submissively seem to take it.

The others were absorbed and unconscious, either silent over their game or dropping remarks unheard on the terrace; and it was to her father's quiet face, discernibly expressive of nothing that was in his daughter's mind, that our young woman's attention was most directly given. His wife and his daughter were both closely watching him, and to which of them, could he have been notified of this, would he have felt it most important to destroy—for HIS clutch at the equilibrium—any germ of uneasiness? Not yet, since his marriage, had Maggie so sharply and so formidably known her old possession of him as a thing divided and contested. She was looking at him by Charlotte's leave and under Charlotte's direction; quite in fact as if the particular way she should look at him were prescribed to her; quite, even, as if she had been defied to look at him in any other. It came home to her too that the challenge wasn't, as might be said, in his interest and for his protection, but, pressingly, insistently, in Charlotte's, for that of HER security at any price. She might verily, by this dumb demonstration, have been naming to Maggie the price, naming it as a question for Maggie herself, a sum of money that she, properly, was to find. She must remain safe and Maggie must pay—what she was to pay with being her own affair.

Straighter than ever, thus, the Princess again felt it all put upon her, and there was a minute, just a supreme instant, during which there burned in her a wild wish that her father would only look up. It throbbed for these seconds as a yearning appeal to him—she would chance it, that is, if he would but just raise his eyes and catch hers, across the larger space, standing in the outer dark together. Then he might be affected by the sight, taking them as they were; he might make some sign—she scarce knew what—that would save her; save her from being the one, this way, to pay all. He might somehow show a preference— distinguishing between them; might, out of pity for her, signal to her that this extremity of her effort for him was more than he asked. That represented Maggie's one little lapse from consistency—the sole small deflection in the whole course of her scheme. It had come to nothing the next minute, for the dear man's eyes had never moved, and Charlotte's hand, promptly passed into her arm, had already, had very firmly drawn her on—quite, for that matter, as from some sudden, some equal perception on her part too of the more ways than one in which their impression could appeal. They retraced their steps along the rest of the terrace, turning the corner of the house, and presently came abreast of the other windows, those of the pompous drawing-room, still lighted and still empty. Here Charlotte again paused, and it was again as if she were pointing out what Maggie had observed for herself, the very look the place had of being vivid in its stillness, of having, with all its great objects as ordered and balanced as for a formal reception, been appointed for some high transaction, some real affair of state. In presence of this opportunity she faced her companion once more; she traced in her the effect of everything she had already communicated; she signified, with the same success, that the terrace and the sullen night would bear too meagre witness to the completion of her idea. Soon enough then, within the room, under the old lustres of Venice and the eyes of the several great portraits, more or less contemporary with these, that awaited on the walls of Fawns their final far migration—soon enough Maggie found herself staring, and at first all too gaspingly, at the grand total to which each separate demand Mrs. Verver had hitherto made upon her, however she had made it, now amounted.

"I've been wanting—and longer than you'd perhaps believe—to put a question to you for which no opportunity has seemed to me yet quite so good as this. It would have been easier perhaps if you had struck me as in the least disposed ever to give me one. I have to take it now, you see, as I find it." They stood in the centre of the immense room, and Maggie could feel that the scene of life her imagination had made of it twenty minutes before was by this time sufficiently peopled. These few straight words filled it to its uttermost reaches, and nothing was more absent from her consciousness, either, of the part she was called upon to play in it. Charlotte had marched straight in, dragging her rich train; she rose there beautiful and free, with her whole aspect and action attuned to the firmness of her speech. Maggie had kept the shawl she had taken out with her, and, clutching it tight in her nervousness, drew it round her as if huddling in it for shelter, covering herself with it for humility. She

254

looked out as from under an improvised hood—the sole headgear of some poor woman at somebody's proud door; she waited even like the poor woman; she met her friend's eyes with recognitions she couldn't suppress. She might sound it as she could—"What question then?"—everything in her, from head to foot, crowded it upon Charlotte that she knew. She knew too well—that she was showing; so that successful vagueness, to save some scrap of her dignity from the imminence of her defeat, was already a lost cause, and the one thing left was if possible, at any cost, even that of stupid inconsequence, to try to look as if she weren't afraid. If she could but appear at all not afraid she might appear a little not ashamed—that is not ashamed to be afraid, which was the kind of shame that could be fastened on her, it being fear all the while that moved her. Her challenge, at any rate, her wonder, her terror—the blank, blurred surface, whatever it was that she presented became a mixture that ceased to signify; for to the accumulated advantage by which Charlotte was at present sustained her next words themselves had little to add.

"Have you any ground of complaint of me? Is there any wrong you consider I've done you? I feel at last that I've a right to ask you." Their eyes had to meet on it, and to meet long; Maggie's avoided at least the disgrace of looking away. "What makes you want to ask it?"

"My natural desire to know. You've done that, for so long, little justice." Maggie waited a moment. "For so long? You mean you've thought—?"

"I mean, my dear, that I've seen. I've seen, week after week, that YOU seemed to be thinking—of something that perplexed or worried you. Is it anything for which I'm in any degree responsible?" Maggie summoned all her powers. "What in the world SHOULD it be?"

"Ah, that's not for me to imagine, and I should be very sorry to have to try to say! I'm aware of no point whatever at which I may have failed you," said Charlotte; "nor of any at which I may have failed any one in whom I can suppose you sufficiently interested to care. If I've been guilty of some fault I've committed it all unconsciously, and am only anxious to hear from you honestly about it. But if I've been mistaken as to what I speak of—the difference, more and more marked, as I've thought, in all your manner to me—why, obviously, so much the better. No form of correction received from you could give me greater satisfaction."

She spoke, it struck her companion, with rising, with extraordinary ease; as if hearing herself say it all, besides seeing the way it was listened to, helped her from point to point. She saw the way she was right—that this WAS the tone for her to try to say! the thing as to which she was probably feeling that she had in advance, in her delays and uncertainties, much exaggerated the difficulty. The difficulty was small, and it grew smaller as her adversary continued to shrink; she was not only doing as she wanted, but had by this time effectively done it and hung it up. All of which but deepened Maggie's sense of the sharp and simple need, now, of seeing her through to the end. "'If' you've been mistaken, you say?"—and the Princess but barely faltered. "You HAVE been mistaken."

Charlotte looked at her splendidly hard. "You're perfectly sure it's ALL my mistake?"

"All I can say is that you've received a false impression."

"Ah then—so much the better! From the moment I HAD received it I knew I must sooner or later speak of it—for that, you see, is, systematically, my way. And now," Charlotte added, "you make me glad I've spoken. I thank you very much."

It was strange how for Maggie too, with this, the difficulty seemed to sink. Her companion's acceptance of her denial was like a general pledge not to keep things any worse for her than they essentially had to be; it positively helped her to build up her falsehood—to which, accordingly, she contributed another block. "I've affected you evidently—quite accidentally—in some way of which I've been all unaware. I've NOT felt at any time that you've wronged me."

"How could I come within a mile," Charlotte inquired, "of such a possibility?"

Maggie, with her eyes on her more easily now, made no attempt to say; she said, after a little, something more to the present point. "I accuse you—I accuse you of nothing."

"Ah, that's lucky!"

Charlotte had brought this out with the richness, almost, of gaiety; and Maggie, to go on, had to think, with her own intensity, of Amerigo—to think how he, on his side, had had to go through with his lie to her, how it was for his wife he had done so, and how his doing so had given her the clue and set her the example. He must have had his own difficulty about it, and she was not, after all, falling below him. It was in fact as if, thanks to her hovering image of him confronted with this admirable creature even as she was confronted, there glowed upon her from afar, yet straight and strong, a deep explanatory light which covered the last inch of the ground. He had given her something to conform to, and she hadn't unintelligently turned on him, "gone back on" him, as he would have said, by not conforming. They were together thus, he and she, close, close together—whereas Charlotte, though rising there radiantly before her, was really off in some darkness of space that would steep her in solitude and harass her with care. The heart of the Princess swelled, accordingly, even in her abasement; she had kept in tune with the right, and something, certainly, something that might be like a rare flower snatched from an impossible ledge, would, and possibly soon, come of it for her. The right, the right—yes, it took this extraordinary form of her humbugging, as she had called it, to the end. It was only a question of not, by a hair's breadth, deflecting into the truth. So, supremely, was she braced. "You must take it from me that your anxiety rests quite on a misconception. You must take it from me that I've never at any moment fancied I could suffer by you." And, marvellously, she kept it up—not only kept it up, but improved on it. "You must take it from me that I've never thought of you but as beautiful, wonderful and good. Which is all, I think, that you can possibly ask."

Charlotte held her a moment longer: she needed—not then to have appeared only tactless—the last word. "It's much more, my dear, than I dreamed of asking. I only wanted your denial."

"Well then, you have it."

"Upon your honour?"

"Upon my honour."

And she made a point even, our young woman, of not turning away. Her grip of her shawl had loosened—she had let it fall behind her; but she stood there for anything more and till the weight should be lifted. With which she saw soon enough what more was to come. She saw it in Charlotte's face, and felt it make between them, in the air, a chill that completed the coldness of their conscious perjury. "Will you kiss me on it then?"

She couldn't say yes, but she didn't say no; what availed her still, however, was to measure, in her passivity, how much too far Charlotte had come to retreat. But there was something different also, something for which, while her cheek received the prodigious kiss, she had her opportunity—the sight of the others, who, having risen from their cards to join the absent members of their party, had reached the open door at the end of the room and stopped short, evidently, in presence of the demonstration that awaited them. Her husband and her father were in front, and Charlotte's embrace of her—which wasn't to be distinguished, for them, either, she felt, from her embrace of Charlotte—took on with their arrival a high publicity.

XXXVII

Her father had asked her, three days later, in an interval of calm, how she was affected, in the light of their reappearance and of their now perhaps richer fruition, by Dotty and Kitty, and by the once formidable Mrs. Rance; and the consequence of this inquiry had been, for the pair, just such another stroll together, away from the rest of the party and off into the park, as had asserted its need to them on the occasion of the previous visit of these anciently more agitating friends—that of their long talk, on a sequestered bench beneath one of the great trees, when the particular question had come up for them the then purblind discussion of which, at their enjoyed leisure, Maggie had formed the habit of regarding as the "first beginning" of their present situation. The whirligig of time had thus brought round for them again, on their finding themselves face to face while the others were gathering for tea on the terrace, the same odd impulse quietly to "slope"—so Adam Verver himself, as they went, familiarly expressed it—that had acted, in its way, of old; acted for the distant autumn afternoon and for the sharpness of their since so outlived crisis. It might have been funny to them now that the presence of Mrs. Rance and the Lutches—and with symptoms, too, at that time less developed—had once, for their anxiety and their prudence, constituted a crisis; it might have been funny that these ladies could ever have figured, to their imagination, as a symbol of dangers vivid enough to precipitate the need of a remedy. This amount of entertainment and assistance they were indeed disposed to extract from their actual impressions; they had been finding it, for months past, by Maggie's view, a resource and a relief to talk, with an approach to intensity, when they met, of all the people they weren't really thinking of and didn't really care about, the people with whom their existence had begun almost to swarm; and they closed in at present round the spectres of their past, as they permitted themselves to describe the three ladies, with a better imitation of enjoying their theme than they had been able to achieve, certainly, during the stay, for instance, of the Castledeans. The Castledeans were a new joke, comparatively, and they had had—always to Maggie's view— to teach themselves the way of it; whereas the Detroit, the Providence party, rebounding so from Providence, from Detroit, was an old and ample one, of which the most could be made and as to which a humorous insistence could be guarded.

Sharp and sudden, moreover, this afternoon, had been their well-nigh confessed desire just to rest together, a little, as from some strain long felt but never named; to rest, as who should say, shoulder to shoulder and hand in hand, each pair of eyes so yearningly—and indeed what could it be but so wearily?—closed as to render the collapse safe from detection by the other pair. It was positively as if, in short, the inward felicity of their being once more, perhaps only for half-an-hour, simply daughter and father had glimmered out for them, and they had picked up again on their old bench, conscious that the party on the terrace, augmented, as in the past, by neighbours, would do beautifully without them, it was wonderfully like their having got together into some boat and paddled off from the shore where husbands and wives, luxuriant complications, made the air too tropical. In the boat they were father and daughter, and poor Dotty and Kitty supplied abundantly, for their situation, the oars or the sail. Why, into the bargain, for that matter—this came to Maggie—couldn't they always live, so far as they lived together, in a boat? She felt in her face, with the question, the breath of a possibility that soothed her; they needed only KNOW each other, henceforth, in the unmarried relation. That other sweet evening, in the same place, he had been as unmarried as possible—which had kept down, so to speak, the quantity of change in their state. Well then, that other sweet evening was what the present sweet evening would resemble; with the quite calculable effect of an exquisite inward refreshment. They HAD, after all, whatever happened, always and ever each other; each other—that was the hidden treasure and the saving truth—to do exactly what they would with: a provision full of possibilities. Who could tell, as yet, what, thanks to it, they wouldn't have done before the end?

They had meanwhile been tracing together, in the golden air that, toward six o'clock of a July afternoon, hung about the massed Kentish woods, several features of the social evolution of her old playmates, still beckoned on, it would seem, by unattainable ideals, still falling back, beyond the sea, to their native seats, for renewals of the moral, financial, conversational—one scarce knew what to call it—outfit, and again and for ever reappearing like a tribe of Wandering Jewesses. Our couple had finally exhausted, however, the study of these annals, and Maggie was to take up, after a drop, a different matter, or one at least with which the immediate connection was not at first apparent. "Were you amused at me just now—when I wondered what other people could wish to struggle for? Did you think me," she asked with some earnestness—"well, fatuous?"

"'Fatuous'?"—he seemed at a loss.

"I mean sublime in OUR happiness—as if looking down from a height. Or, rather, sublime in our general position—that's what I mean." She spoke as from the habit of her anxious conscience something that disposed her frequently to assure herself, for her human commerce, of the state of the "books" of the spirit. "Because I don't at all want," she explained, "to be blinded, or made 'sniffy,' by any sense of a social situation." Her father listened to this declaration as if the precautions of her general mercy could still, as they betrayed themselves, have surprises for him—to say nothing of a charm of delicacy and beauty; he might have been wishing to see how far she could go and where she would, all touchingly to him, arrive. But she waited a little—as if made nervous, precisely, by feeling him depend too much on what she said. They were avoiding the serious, standing off, anxiously, from the real, and they fell, again and again, as if to disguise their precaution itself, into the tone of the time that came back to them from their other talk, when they had shared together this same refuge. "Don't you remember," she went on, "how, when they were here before, I broke it to you that I wasn't so very sure we, ourselves, had the thing itself?"

He did his best to do so. "Had, you mean a social situation?"

"Yes—after Fanny Assingham had first broken it to me that, at the rate we were going, we should never have one."

"Which was what put us on Charlotte?" Oh yes, they had had it over quite often enough for him easily to remember.

Maggie had another pause—taking it from him that he now could both affirm and admit without wincing that they had been, at their critical moment, "put on" Charlotte. It was as if this recognition had been threshed out between them as fundamental to the honest view of their success. "Well," she continued, "I recall how I felt, about Kitty and Dotty, that even if we had already then been more 'placed,' or whatever you may call what we are now, it still wouldn't have been an excuse for wondering why others couldn't obligingly leave me more exalted by having, themselves, smaller ideas. For those," she said, "were the feelings we used to have."

"Oh yes," he responded philosophically—"I remember the feelings we used to have."

Maggie appeared to wish to plead for them a little, in tender retrospect—as if they had been also respectable. "It was bad enough, I thought, to have no sympathy in your heart when you HAD a position. But it was worse to be sublime about it—as I was so afraid, as I'm in fact still afraid of being—when it wasn't even there to support one." And she put forth again the earnestness she might have been taking herself as having outlived; became for it—which was doubtless too often even now her danger—almost sententious. "One must always, whether or no, have some imagination of the states of others—of what they may feel deprived of. However," she added, "Kitty and Dotty couldn't imagine we were deprived of anything. And now, and now—!" But she stopped as for indulgence to their wonder and envy.

"And now they see, still more, that we can have got everything, and kept everything, and yet not be proud."

"No, we're not proud," she answered after a moment. "I'm not sure that we're quite proud enough." Yet she changed the next instant that subject too. She could only do so, however, by harking back—as if it had been a fascination. She might have been wishing, under this renewed, this still more suggestive visitation, to keep him with her for remounting the stream of time and dipping again, for the softness of the water, into the contracted basin of the past. "We talked about it—we talked about it; you don't remember so well as I. You too didn't know—and it was beautiful of you; like Kitty and Dotty you too thought we had a position, and were surprised when *I* thought we ought to have told them we weren't doing for them what they supposed. In fact," Maggie pursued, "we're not doing it now. We're not, you see, really introducing them. I mean not to the people they want."

"Then what do you call the people with whom they're now having tea?"

It made her quite spring round. "That's just what you asked me the other time—one of the days there was somebody. And I told you I didn't call anybody anything."

"I remember—that such people, the people we made so welcome, didn't 'count'; that Fanny Assingham knew they didn't." She had awakened, his daughter, the echo; and on the bench there, as before, he nodded his head amusedly, he kept nervously shaking his foot. "Yes, they were only good enough—the people who came—for US. I remember," he said again: "that was the way it all happened."

"That was the way—that was the way. And you asked me," Maggie added, "if I didn't think we ought to tell them. Tell Mrs. Rance, in particular, I mean, that we had been entertaining her up to then under false pretences."

"Precisely—but you said she wouldn't have understood."

"To which you replied that in that case you were like her. YOU didn't understand."

"No, no—but I remember how, about our having, in our benighted innocence, no position, you quite crushed me with your explanation."

"Well then," said Maggie with every appearance of delight, "I'll crush you again. I told you that you by yourself had one—there was no doubt of that. You were different from me—you had the same one you always had."

"And THEN I asked you," her father concurred, "why in that case you hadn't the same."

"Then indeed you did." He had brought her face round to him before, and this held it, covering him with its kindled brightness, the result of the attested truth of their being able thus, in talk, to live again together. "What I replied was that I had lost my position by my marriage. THAT one—I know how I saw it—would never come back. I had done something TO it—I didn't quite know what; given it away, somehow, and yet not, as then appeared, really got my return. I had been assured—always by dear Fanny—that I COULD get it, only I must wake up. So I was trying, you see, to wake up—trying very hard."

"Yes—and to a certain extent you succeeded; as also in waking me. But you made much," he said, "of your difficulty." To which he added: "It's the only case I remember, Mag, of you ever making ANYTHING of a difficulty."

She kept her eyes on him a moment. "That I was so happy as I was?"

"That you were so happy as you were."

"Well, you admitted"—Maggie kept it up—"that that was a good difficulty. You confessed that our life did seem to be beautiful."

He thought a moment. "Yes—I may very well have confessed it, for so it did seem to me." But he guarded himself with his dim, his easier smile. "What do you want to put on me now?"

"Only that we used to wonder—that we were wondering then—if our life wasn't perhaps a little selfish." This also for a time, much at his leisure, Adam Verver retrospectively fixed. "Because Fanny Assingham thought so?"

"Oh no; she never thought, she couldn't think, if she would, anything of that sort. She only thinks people are sometimes fools," Maggie developed; "she doesn't seem to think so much about their being wrong—wrong, that is, in the sense of being wicked. She doesn't," the Princess further adventured, "quite so much mind their being wicked."

"I see—I see." And yet it might have been for his daughter that he didn't so very vividly see. "Then she only thought US fools?"

"Oh no—I don't say that. I'm speaking of our being selfish."

"And that comes under the head of the wickedness Fanny condones?"

"Oh, I don't say she CONDONES—!" A scruple in Maggie raised its crest. "Besides, I'm speaking of what was."

Her father showed, however, after a little, that he had not been reached by this discrimination; his thoughts were resting for the moment where they had settled. "Look here, Mag," he said reflectively—"I ain't selfish. I'll be blowed if I'm selfish."

Well, Maggie, if he WOULD talk of that, could also pronounce. "Then, father, *I* am."

"Oh shucks!" said Adam Verver, to whom the vernacular, in moments of deepest sincerity, could thus come back. "I'll believe it," he presently added, "when Amerigo complains of you."

"Ah, it's just he who's my selfishness. I'm selfish, so to speak, FOR him. I mean," she continued, "that he's my motive—in everything."

Well, her father could, from experience, fancy what she meant. "But hasn't a girl a right to be selfish about her husband?"

"What I DON'T mean," she observed without answering, "is that I'm jealous of him. But that's his merit—it's not mine."

Her father again seemed amused at her. "You COULD be—otherwise?"

"Oh, how can I talk," she asked, "of otherwise? It ISN'T, luckily for me, otherwise. If everything were different"—she further presented her thought—"of course everything WOULD be." And then again, as if that were but half: "My idea is this, that you only love a little you're naturally not jealous—or are only jealous also a little, so that it doesn't matter. But when you love in a deeper and intenser way, then you are, in the same proportion, jealous; your jealousy has intensity and, no doubt, ferocity. When, however, you love in the most abysmal and unutterable way of all—why then you're beyond everything, and nothing can pull you down."

Mr. Verver listened as if he had nothing, on these high lines, to oppose. "And that's the way YOU love?"

For a minute she failed to speak, but at last she answered: "It wasn't to talk about that. I do FEEL, however, beyond everything—and as a consequence of that, I dare say," she added with a turn to gaiety, "seem often not to know quite WHERE I am."

The mere fine pulse of passion in it, the suggestion as of a creature consciously floating and shining in a warm summer sea, some element of dazzling sapphire and silver, a creature cradled upon depths, buoyant among dangers, in which fear or folly, or sinking otherwise than in play, was impossible—something of all this might have been making once more present to him, with his discreet, his half shy assent to it, her probable enjoyment of a rapture that he, in his day, had presumably convinced no great number of persons either of his giving or of his receiving. He sat awhile as if he knew himself hushed, almost admonished, and not for the first time; yet it was an effect that might have brought before him rather what she had gained than what he had missed.

Besides, who but himself really knew what he, after all, hadn't, or even had, gained? The beauty of her condition was keeping him, at any rate, as he might feel, in sight of the sea, where, though his personal dips were over, the whole thing could shine at him, and the air and the plash and the play become for him too a sensation. That couldn't be fixed upon him as missing; since if it wasn't personally floating, if it wasn't even sitting in the sand, it could yet pass very well for breathing the bliss, in a communicated irresistible way—for tasting the balm. It could pass, further, for knowing—for knowing that without him nothing might have been: which would have been missing least of all.

"I guess I've never been jealous," he finally remarked. And it said more to her, he had occasion next to perceive, than he was intending; for it made her, as by the pressure of a spring, give him a look that seemed to tell of things she couldn't speak.

But she at last tried for one of them. "Oh, it's you, father, who are what I call beyond everything. Nothing can pull YOU down."

He returned the look as with the sociability of their easy communion, though inevitably throwing in this time a shade of solemnity. He might have been seeing things to say, and others, whether of a type presumptuous or not, doubtless better kept back. So he settled on the merely obvious. "Well then, we make a pair. We're all right."

"Oh, we're all right!" A declaration launched not only with all her discriminating emphasis, but confirmed by her rising with decision and standing there as if the object of their small excursion required accordingly no further pursuit. At this juncture, however—with the act of their crossing the bar, to get, as might be, into port—there occurred the only approach to a betrayal of their having had to beat against the wind. Her father kept his place, and it was as if she had got over first and were pausing for her consort to follow. If they were all right; they were all right; yet he seemed to hesitate and wait for some word beyond. His eyes met her own, suggestively, and it was only after she had contented herself with simply smiling at him, smiling ever so fixedly, that he spoke, for the remaining importance of it, from the bench; where he leaned back, raising his face to her, his legs thrust out a trifle wearily and his hands grasping either side of the seat. They had beaten against the wind, and she was still fresh; they had beaten against the wind, and he, as at the best the more battered vessel, perhaps just vaguely drooped. But the effect of their silence was that she appeared to beckon him on, and he might have been fairly alongside of her when, at the end of another minute, he found their word. "The only thing is that, as for ever putting up again with your pretending that you're selfish—!"

At this she helped him out with it. "You won't take it from me?"

"I won't take it from you."

"Well, of course you won't, for that's your way. It doesn't matter, and it only proves—! But it doesn't matter, either, what it proves. I'm at this very moment," she declared, "frozen stiff with selfishness."

He faced her awhile longer in the same way; it was, strangely, as if, by this sudden arrest, by their having, in their acceptance of the unsaid, or at least their reference to it, practically given up pretending—it was as if they were "in" for it, for something they had been ineffably avoiding, but the dread of which was itself, in a manner, a seduction, just as any confession of the dread was by so much an allusion. Then she seemed to see him let himself go. "When a person's of the nature you speak of there are always other persons to suffer. But you've just been describing to me what you'd take, if you had once a good chance, from your husband."

"Oh, I'm not talking about my husband!"

"Then whom, ARE you talking about?"

Both the retort and the rejoinder had come quicker than anything previously exchanged, and they were followed, on Maggie's part, by a momentary drop. But she was not to fall away, and while her companion kept his eyes on her, while she wondered if he weren't expecting her to name his wife then, with high hypocrisy, as paying for his daughter's bliss, she produced something that she felt to be much better. "I'm talking about YOU."

"Do you mean I've been your victim?"

"Of course you've been my victim. What have you done, ever done, that hasn't been FOR me?"

"Many things; more than I can tell you—things you've only to think of for yourself. What do you make of all that I've done for myself?"

"'Yourself?—'" She brightened out with derision.

"What do you make of what I've done for American City?"

It took her but a moment to say. "I'm not talking of you as a public character—I'm talking of you on your personal side."

"Well, American City—if 'personalities' can do it—has given me a pretty personal side. What do you make," he went on, "of what I've done for my reputation?"

"Your reputation THERE? You've given it up to them, the awful people, for less than nothing; you've given it up to them to tear to pieces, to make their horrible vulgar jokes against you with."

"Ah, my dear, I don't care for their horrible vulgar jokes," Adam Verver almost artlessly urged.

"Then there, exactly, you are!" she triumphed. "Everything that touches you, everything that surrounds you, goes on—by your splendid indifference and your incredible permission—at your expense."

Just as he had been sitting he looked at her for an instant longer; then he slowly rose, while his hands stole into his pockets, and stood there before her. "Of course, my dear, YOU go on at my expense: it has never been my idea," he smiled, "that you should work for your living. I wouldn't have liked to see it." With which, for a little again, they remained face to face. "Say therefore I HAVE had the feelings of a father. How have they made me a victim?"

"Because I sacrifice you."

"But to what in the world?"

At this it hung before her that she should have had as never yet her opportunity to say, and it held her for a minute as in a vise, her impression of her now, with his strained smile, which touched her to deepest depths, sounding her in his secret unrest. This was the moment, in the whole process of their mutual vigilance, in which it decidedly most hung by a hair that their thin wall might be pierced by the lightest wrong touch. It shook between them, this transparency, with their very breath; it was an exquisite tissue, but stretched on a frame, and would give way the next instant if either so much as breathed too hard. She held her breath, for she knew by his eyes, the light at the heart of which he couldn't blind, that he was, by his intention, making sure—sure whether or no her certainty was like his. The intensity of his dependence on it at that moment—this itself was what absolutely convinced her so that, as if perched up before him on her vertiginous point and in the very glare of his observation, she balanced for thirty seconds, she almost rocked: she might have been for the time, in all her conscious person, the very form of the equilibrium they were, in their different ways, equally trying to save. And they were saving it—yes, they were, or at least she was: that was still the workable issue, she could say, as she felt her dizziness drop. She held herself hard; the thing was to be done, once for all, by her acting, now, where she stood. So much was crowded into so short a space that she knew already she was keeping her head. She had kept it by the warning of his eyes; she shouldn't lose it again; she knew how and why, and if she had turned cold this was precisely what helped her. He had said to himself "She'll break down and name Amerigo; she'll say it's to him she's sacrificing me; and its by what that will give me—with so many other things too—that my suspicion will be clinched." He was watching her lips, spying for the symptoms of the sound; whereby these symptoms had only to fail and he would have got nothing that she didn't measure out to him as she gave it. She had presently in fact so recovered herself that she seemed to know she could more easily have made him name his wife than he have made her name her husband. It was there before her that if she should so much as force him just NOT consciously to avoid saying "Charlotte, Charlotte" he would have given himself away. But to be sure of this was enough for her, and she saw more clearly with each lapsing instant what they were both doing. He was doing what he had steadily been coming to; he was practically OFFERING himself, pressing himself upon her, as a sacrifice—he had read his way so into her best possibility; and where had she already, for weeks and days past, planted her feet if not on her acceptance of the offer? Cold indeed, colder and colder she turned, as she felt herself suffer this close personal vision of his attitude still not to make her weaken. That was her very certitude, the intensity of his pressure; for if something dreadful hadn't happened there wouldn't, for either of them, be these dreadful things to do. She had meanwhile, as well, the immense advantage that she could have named Charlotte without exposing herself—as, for that matter, she was the next minute showing him.

"Why, I sacrifice you, simply, to everything and to every one. I take the consequences of your marriage as perfectly natural."

He threw back his head a little, settling with one hand his eyeglass. "What do you call, my dear, the consequences?"

"Your life as your marriage has made it."

"Well, hasn't it made it exactly what we wanted?" She just hesitated, then felt herself steady—oh, beyond what she had dreamed. "Exactly what *I* wanted—yes."

His eyes, through his straightened glasses, were still on hers, and he might, with his intenser fixed smile, have been knowing she was, for herself, rightly inspired. "What do you make then of what I wanted?"

"I don't make anything, any more than of what you've got. That's exactly the point. I don't put myself out to do so—I never have; I take from you all I can get, all you've provided for me, and I leave you to make of your own side of the matter what you can. There you are—the rest is your own affair. I don't even pretend to concern myself—!"

"To concern yourself—?" He watched her as she faintly faltered, looking about her now so as not to keep always meeting his face.

"With what may have REALLY become of you. It's as if we had agreed from the first not to go into that—such an arrangement being of course charming for ME. You can't say, you know, that I haven't stuck to it."

He didn't say so then—even with the opportunity given him of her stopping once more to catch her breath. He said instead: "Oh, my dear—oh, oh!"

But it made no difference, know as she might what a past—still so recent and yet so distant—it alluded to; she repeated her denial, warning him off, on her side, from spoiling the truth of her contention. "I never went into anything, and you see I don't; I've continued to adore you—but what's that, from a decent daughter to such a father? what but a question of convenient arrangement, our having two houses, three houses, instead of one (you would have arranged for fifty if I had wished!) and my making it easy for you to see the child? You don't claim, I suppose, that my natural course, once you had set up for yourself, would have been to ship you back to American City?"

These were direct inquiries, they quite rang out, in the soft, wooded air; so that Adam Verver, for a minute, appeared to meet them with reflection. She saw reflection, however, quickly enough show him what to do with them. "Do you know, Mag, what you make me wish when you talk that way?" And he waited again, while she further got from him the sense of something that had been behind, deeply in the shade, coming cautiously to the front and just feeling its way before presenting itself. "You regularly make me wish that I had shipped back to American City. When you go on as you do—" But he really had to hold himself to say it.

"Well, when I go on—?"

"Why, you make me quite want to ship back myself. You make me quite feel as if American City would be the best place for us."

It made her all too finely vibrate. "For 'us'—?"

"For me and Charlotte. Do you know that if we should ship, it would serve you quite right?" With which he smiled—oh he smiled! "And if you say much more we WILL ship."

Ah, then it was that the cup of her conviction, full to the brim, overflowed at a touch! THERE was his idea, the clearness of which for an instant almost dazzled her. It was a blur of light, in the midst of which she saw Charlotte like some object marked, by contrast, in blackness, saw her waver in the field of vision, saw her removed, transported, doomed. And he had named Charlotte, named her again, and she had MADE him—which was all she had needed more: it was as if she had held a blank letter to the fire and the writing had come out still larger than she hoped. The recognition of it took her some seconds, but she might when she spoke have been folding up these precious lines and restoring them to her pocket. "Well, I shall be as much as ever then the cause of what you do. I haven't the least doubt of your being up to that if you should think I might get anything out of it; even the little pleasure," she laughed, "of having said, as you call it, 'more.' Let my enjoyment of this therefore, at any price, continue to represent for you what *I* call sacrificing you."

She had drawn a long breath; she had made him do it ALL for her, and had lighted the way to it without his naming her husband. That silence had been as distinct as the sharp, the inevitable sound, and something now, in him, followed it up, a sudden air as of confessing at last fully to where she was and of begging the particular question. "Don't you think then I can take care of myself?"

"Ah, it's exactly what I've gone upon. If it wasn't for that—!"

But she broke off, and they remained only another moment face to face. "I'll let you know, my dear, the day *I* feel you've begun to sacrifice me."

"'Begun'?" she extravagantly echoed.

"Well, it will be, for me, the day you've ceased to believe in me."

With which, his glasses still fixed on her, his hands in his pockets, his hat pushed back, his legs a little apart, he seemed to plant or to square himself for a kind of assurance it had occurred to him he might as well treat her to, in default of other things, before they changed their subject. It had the effect, for her, of a reminder—a reminder of all he was, of all he had done, of all, above and beyond his being her perfect little father, she might take him as representing, take him as having, quite eminently, in the eyes of two hemispheres, been capable of, and as therefore wishing, not—was it?—illegitimately, to call her attention to. The "successful," beneficent person, the beautiful, bountiful, original, dauntlessly wilful great citizen, the consummate collector and infallible high authority he had been and still was—these things struck her, on the spot, as making up for him, in a wonderful way, a character she must take into account in dealing with him either for pity or for envy. He positively, under the impression, seemed to loom larger than life for her, so that she saw him during these moments in a light of recognition which had had its brightness for her at many an hour of the past, but which had never been so intense and so almost admonitory. His very quietness was part of it now, as always part of everything, of his success, of his originality, of his modesty, of his exquisite public perversity, his inscrutable, incalculable energy; and this quality perhaps it might be—all the more too as the result, for the present occasion, of an admirable, traceable effort—that placed him in her eyes as no precious a work of art probably had ever been placed in his own. There was a long moment, absolutely, during which her impression rose and rose, even as that of the typical charmed gazer, in the still museum, before the named and dated object, the pride of the catalogue, that time has polished and consecrated. Extraordinary, in particular, was the number of the different ways in which he thus affected her as showing. He was strong—that was the great thing. He was sure—sure for himself, always, whatever his idea: the expression of that in him had somehow never appeared more identical with his proved taste for the rare and the true. But what stood out beyond everything was that he was always, marvellously, young—which couldn't but crown, at this juncture, his whole appeal to her imagination. Before she knew it she was lifted aloft by the consciousness that he was simply a great and deep and high little man, and that to love him with tenderness was not to be distinguished, a whit, from loving him with pride. It came to her, all strangely, as a sudden, an immense relief. The sense that he wasn't a failure, and could never be, purged their predicament of every meanness—made it as if they had really emerged, in their transmuted union, to smile almost without pain. It was like a new confidence, and after another instant she knew even still better why. Wasn't it because now, also, on his side, he was thinking of her as his daughter, was TRYING her, during these mute seconds, as the child of his blood? Oh then, if she wasn't with her little conscious passion, the child of any weakness, what was she but strong enough too? It swelled in her, fairly; it raised her higher, higher: she wasn't in that case a failure either—hadn't been, but the contrary; his strength was her strength, her pride was his, and they were decent and competent together. This was all in the answer she finally made him.

"I believe in you more than any one."

"Than any one at all?"

She hesitated, for all it might mean; but there was—oh a thousand times!—no doubt of it. "Than any one at all." She kept nothing of it back now, met his eyes over it, let him have the whole of it; after which she went on: "And that's the way, I think, you believe in me."

He looked at her a minute longer, but his tone at last was right. "About the way—yes."

"Well then—?" She spoke as for the end and for other matters—for anything, everything, else there might be. They would never return to it.

"Well then—!" His hands came out, and while her own took them he drew her to his breast and held her. He held her hard and kept her long, and she let herself go; but it was an embrace that, august and almost stern, produced, for all its intimacy, no revulsion and broke into no inconsequence of tears.

XXXVIII

Maggie was to feel, after this passage, how they had both been helped through it by the influence of that accident of her having been caught, a few nights before, in the familiar embrace of her father's wife. His return to the saloon had chanced to coincide exactly with this demonstration, missed moreover neither by her husband nor by the Assinghams, who, their card-party suspended, had quitted the billiard-room with him. She had been conscious enough at the time of what such an impression, received by the others, might, in that extended state, do for her case; and none the less that, as no one had appeared to wish to be the first to make a remark about it, it had taken on perceptibly the special shade of consecration conferred by unanimities of silence. The effect, she might have considered, had been almost awkward—the promptitude of her separation from Charlotte, as if they had been discovered in some absurdity, on her becoming aware of spectators. The spectators, on the other hand—that was the appearance—mightn't have supposed them, in the existing relation, addicted to mutual endearments; and yet, hesitating with a fine scruple between sympathy and hilarity, must have felt that almost any spoken or laughed comment could be kept from sounding vulgar only by sounding, beyond any permitted measure, intelligent. They had evidently looked, the two young wives, like a pair of women "making up" effusively, as women were supposed to do, especially when approved fools, after a broil; but taking note of the reconciliation would imply, on her father's part, on Amerigo's, and on Fanny Assingham's, some proportionate vision of the grounds of their difference. There had been something, there had been but too much, in the incident, for each observer; yet there was nothing any one could have said without seeming essentially to say: "See, see, the dear things—their quarrel's blissfully over!" "Our quarrel? What quarrel?" the dear things themselves would necessarily, in that case, have demanded; and the wits of the others would thus have been called upon for some agility of exercise. No one had been equal to the flight of producing, off-hand, a fictive reason for any estrangement—to take, that is, the place of the true, which had so long, for the finer sensibility, pervaded the air; and every one, accordingly, not to be inconveniently challenged, was pretending, immediately after, to have remarked nothing that any one else hadn't.

Maggie's own measure had remained, all the same, full of the reflection caught from the total inference; which had acted, virtually, by enabling every one present—and oh Charlotte not least!—to draw a long breath. The message of the little scene had been different for each, but it had been this, markedly, all round, that it reinforced—reinforced even immensely—the general effort, carried on from week to week and of late distinctly more successful, to look and talk and move as if nothing in life were the matter. Supremely, however, while this glass was held up to her, had Maggie's sense turned to the quality of the success constituted, on the spot, for Charlotte. Most of all, if she was guessing how her father must have secretly started, how her husband must have secretly wondered, how Fanny Assingham must have secretly, in a flash, seen daylight for herself—most of all had she tasted, by communication, of the high profit involved for her companion. She FELT, in all her pulses, Charlotte feel it, and how publicity had been required, absolutely, to crown her own abasement. It was the added touch, and now nothing was wanting—which, to do her stepmother justice, Mrs. Verver had appeared but to desire, from that evening, to show, with the last vividness, that she recognised. Maggie lived over again the minutes in question—had found herself repeatedly doing so; to the degree that the whole evening hung together, to her aftersense, as a thing appointed by some occult power that had dealt with her, that had for instance—animated the four with just the right restlessness too, had decreed and directed and exactly timed it in them, making their game of bridge—however abysmal a face it had worn for her—give way, precisely, to their common unavowed impulse to find out, to emulate Charlotte's impatience; a preoccupation, this latter, attached detectedly to the member of the party who was roaming in her queerness and was, for all their simulated blindness, not roaming unnoted.

If Mrs. Verver meanwhile, then, had struck her as determined in a certain direction by the last felicity into which that night had flowered, our young woman was yet not to fail of appreciating the truth that she had not been put at ease, after all, with absolute permanence. Maggie had seen her, unmistakably, desire to rise to the occasion and be magnificent—seen her decide that the right way for this would be to prove that the reassurance she had extorted there, under the high, cool lustre of the saloon, a twinkle of crystal and silver, had not only poured oil upon the troubled waters of their question, but had fairly drenched their whole intercourse with that lubricant. She had exceeded the limit of discretion in this insistence on her capacity to repay in proportion a service she acknowledged as handsome. "Why handsome?" Maggie would have been free to ask; since if she had been veracious the service assuredly would not have been huge. It would in that case have come up vividly, and for each of them alike, that the truth, on the Princess's lips, presented no difficulty. If the latter's mood, in fact, could have turned itself at all to private gaiety it might have failed to resist the diversion of seeing so clever a creature so beguiled. Charlotte's theory of a generous manner was manifestly to express that her stepdaughter's word, wiping out, as she might have said, everything, had restored them to the serenity of a relation without a cloud. It had been, in short, in this light, ideally conclusive, so that no ghost of anything it referred to could ever walk again. What was the ecstasy of that, however, but in itself a trifle compromising?—as truly, within the week, Maggie had occasion to suspect her friend of beginning, and rather abruptly, to remember. Convinced as she was of the example already given her by her husband, and in relation to which her profession of trust in his mistress had been an act of conformity exquisitely calculated, her imagination yet sought in the hidden play of his influence the explanation of any change of surface, any difference of expression or intention. There had been, through life, as we know, few quarters in which the Princess's fancy could let itself loose; but it shook off restraint when it plunged into the figured void of the detail of that relation. This was a realm it could people with images—again and again with fresh ones; they swarmed there like the strange combinations that lurked in the woods at twilight; they loomed into the definite and faded into the vague, their main present sign for her being, however, that they were always, that they were duskily, agitated. Her earlier vision of a state of bliss made insecure by the very intensity of the bliss—this had dropped from her; she had ceased to see, as she lost herself, the pair of operatic, of high Wagnerian lovers (she found, deep within her, these comparisons) interlocked in their wood of enchantment, a green glade as romantic as one's dream of an old German forest. The picture was veiled, on the contrary, with the dimness of trouble; behind which she felt, indistinguishable, the procession of forms that had lost, all so pitifully, their precious confidence. Therefore, though there was in these days, for her, with Amerigo, little enough even of the imitation, from day to day, of unembarrassed references—as she had foreseen, for that matter, from the first, that there would be—her active conception of his accessibility to their companion's own private and unextinguished right to break ground was not much less active than before. So it was that her inner sense, in spite of everything, represented him as still pulling wires and controlling currents, or rather indeed as muffling the whole possibility, keeping it down and down, leading his accomplice continually on to some new turn of the road. As regards herself Maggie had become more conscious from week to week of his ingenuities of intention to make up to her for their forfeiture, in so dire a degree, of any reality of frankness—a privation that had left on his lips perhaps a little of the same thirst with which she fairly felt her own distorted, the torment of the lost pilgrim who listens in desert sands for the possible, the impossible, plash of water. It was just this hampered state in him, none the less, that she kept before her when she wished most to find grounds of dignity for the hard little passion which nothing he had done could smother. There were hours enough, lonely hours, in which she let dignity go; then there were others when, clinging with her winged concentration to some deep cell of her heart, she stored away her hived tenderness as if she had gathered it all from flowers. He was meanwhile not the easier to bear for this aspect under which Charlotte was presented as depending on him for guidance, taking it from him even in doses of bitterness, and yet lost with him in devious depths. Nothing was thus more sharply to be inferred than that he had promptly enough warned her, on hearing from her of the precious assurance received from his wife, that she must take care her satisfaction didn't betray something of her danger. Maggie had a day of still waiting, after allowing him time to learn how unreservedly she had lied for him—of waiting as for the light of she scarce knew what slow-shining reflection of this knowledge in his personal attitude. What retarded evolution, she asked herself in these hours, mightn't poor Charlotte all unwittingly have precipitated? She was thus poor Charlotte again for Maggie even while Maggie's own head was bowed, and the reason for this kept coming back to our young woman in the conception of what would secretly have passed. She saw her, face to face with the Prince, take from him the chill of his stiffest admonition, with the possibilities of deeper difficulty that it represented for each. She heard her ask, irritated and sombre, what tone, in God's name—since her bravery didn't suit him—she was then to adopt; and, by way of a fantastic flight of divination, she heard Amerigo reply, in a voice of which every fine note, familiar and admirable, came home to her, that one must really manage such prudences a little for one's self. It was positive in the Princess that, for this, she breathed Charlotte's cold air—turned away from him in it with her, turned with her, in growing compassion, this way and that, hovered behind her while she felt her ask herself where then she should rest. Marvellous the manner in which, under such imaginations, Maggie thus circled and lingered—quite as if she were, materially, following her unseen, counting every step she helplessly wasted, noting every hindrance that brought her to a pause.

A few days of this, accordingly, had wrought a change in that apprehension of the instant beatitude of triumph—of triumph magnanimous and serene—with which the upshot of the night-scene on the terrace had condemned our young woman to make terms. She had had, as we know, her vision of the gilt bars bent, of the door of the cage forced open from within and the creature imprisoned roaming at large—a movement, on the creature's part, that was to have even, for the short interval, its impressive beauty, but of which the limit, and in yet another direction, had loomed straight into view during her last talk under the great trees with her father. It was when she saw his wife's face ruefully attached to the quarter to which, in the course of their session, he had so significantly addressed his own—it was then that Maggie could watch for its turning pale, it was then she seemed to know what she had meant by thinking of her, in she shadow of his most ominous reference, as "doomed." If, as I say, her attention now, day after day, so circled and hovered, it found itself arrested for certain passages during which she absolutely looked with Charlotte's grave eyes. What she unfailingly made out through them was the figure of a little quiet gentleman who mostly wore, as he moved, alone, across the field of vision, a straw hat, a white waistcoat and a blue necktie, keeping a cigar in his teeth and his hands in his pockets, and who, oftener than not, presented a somewhat meditative back while he slowly measured the perspectives of the park and broodingly counted (it might have appeared) his steps. There were hours of intensity, for a week or two, when it was for all the world as if she had guardedly tracked her stepmother, in the great house, from room to room and from window to window, only to see her, here and there and everywhere, TRY her uneasy outlook, question her issue and her fate. Something, unmistakably, had come up for her that had never come up before; it represented a new complication and had begotten a new anxiety—things, these, that she carried about with her done up in the napkin of her lover's accepted rebuke, while she vainly hunted for some corner where she might put them safely down. The disguised solemnity, the prolonged futility of her search might have been grotesque to a more ironic eye; but Maggie's provision of irony, which we have taken for naturally small, had never been so scant as now, and there were moments while she watched with her, thus unseen, when the mere effect of being near her was to feel her own heart in her throat, was to be almost moved to saying to her: "Hold on tight, my poor dear—without TOO MUCH terror—and it will all come out somehow."

Even to that indeed, she could reflect, Charlotte might have replied that it was easy to say; even to that no great meaning could attach so long as the little meditative man in the straw hat kept coming into view with his indescribable air of weaving his spell, weaving it off there by himself. In whatever quarter of the horizon the appearances were scanned he was to be noticed as absorbed in this occupation; and Maggie was to become aware of two or three extraordinary occasions of receiving from him the hint that he measured the impression he produced. It was not really till after their recent long talk in the park that she knew how deeply, how quite exhaustively, they had then communicated—so that they were to remain together, for the time, in consequence, quite in the form of a couple of sociable drinkers who sit back from the table over which they have been resting their elbows, over which they have emptied to the last drop their respective charged cups. The cups were still there on the table, but turned upside down; and nothing was left for the companions but to confirm by placid silences the fact that the wine had been good. They had parted, positively, as if, on either side, primed with it—primed for whatever was to be; and everything between them, as the month waned, added its touch of truth to this similitude. Nothing, truly, WAS at present between them save that they were looking at each other in infinite trust; it fairly wanted no more words, and when they met, during the deep summer days, met even without witnesses, when they kissed at morning and evening, or on any of the other occasions of contact that they had always so freely celebrated, a pair of birds of the upper air could scarce have appeared less to invite each other to sit down and worry afresh. So it was that in the house itself, where more of his waiting treasures than ever were provisionally ranged, she sometimes only looked at him—from end to end of the great gallery, the pride of the house, for instance—as if, in one of the halls of a museum, she had been an earnest young woman with a Baedeker and he a vague gentleman to whom even Baedekers were unknown. He had ever, of course, had his way of walking about to review his possessions and verify their condition; but this was a pastime to which he now struck her as almost extravagantly addicted, and when she passed near him and he turned to give her a smile she caught—or so she fancied—the greater depth of his small, perpetual hum of contemplation. It was as if he were singing to himself, sotto voce, as he went—and it was also, on occasion, quite ineffably, as if Charlotte, hovering, watching, listening, on her side too, kept sufficiently within earshot to make it out as song, and yet, for some reason connected with the very manner of it, stood off and didn't dare.

One of the attentions she had from immediately after her marriage most freely paid him was that of her interest in his rarities, her appreciation of his taste, her native passion for beautiful objects and her grateful desire not to miss anything he could teach her about them.

Maggie had in due course seen her begin to "work" this fortunately natural source of sympathy for all it was worth. She took possession of the mound throughout its extent; she abounded, to odd excess, one might have remarked, in the assumption of its being for her, with her husband, ALL the ground, the finest, clearest air and most breathable medium common to them. It had been given to Maggie to wonder if she didn't, in these intensities of approbation, too much shut him up to his province; but this was a complaint he had never made his daughter, and Charlotte must at least have had for her that, thanks to her admirable instinct, her range of perception marching with her own and never falling behind, she had probably not so much as once treated him to a rasping mistake or a revealing stupidity. Maggie, wonderfully, in the summer days, felt it forced upon her that that was one way, after all, of being a genial wife; and it was never so much forced upon her as at these odd moments of her encountering the sposi, as Amerigo called them, under the coved ceilings of Fawns while, so together, yet at the same time so separate, they were making their daily round. Charlotte hung behind, with emphasised attention; she stopped when her husband stopped, but at the distance of a case or two, or of whatever other succession of objects; and the likeness of their connection would not have been wrongly figured if he had been thought of as holding in one of his pocketed hands the end of a long silken halter looped round her beautiful neck. He didn't twitch it, yet it was there; he didn't drag her, but she came; and those indications that I have described the Princess as finding extraordinary in him were two or three mute facial intimations which his wife's presence didn't prevent his addressing his daughter—nor prevent his daughter, as she passed, it was doubtless to be added, from flushing a little at the receipt of. They amounted perhaps only to a wordless, wordless smile, but the smile was the soft shake of the twisted silken rope, and Maggie's translation of it, held in her breast till she got well away, came out only, as if it might have been overheard, when some door was closed behind her. "Yes, you see—I lead her now by the neck, I lead her to her doom, and she doesn't so much as know what it is, though she has a fear in her heart which, if you had the chances to apply your ear there that I, as a husband, have, you would hear thump and thump and thump. She thinks it MAY be, her doom, the awful place over there—awful for HER; but she's afraid to ask, don't you see? just as she's afraid of not asking; just as she's afraid of so many other things that she sees multiplied round her now as portents and betrayals. She'll know, however—when she does know."

Charlotte's one opportunity, meanwhile, for the air of confidence she had formerly worn so well and that agreed so with her firm and charming type, was the presence of visitors, never, as the season advanced, wholly intermitted—rather, in fact, so constant, with all the people who turned up for luncheon or for tea and to see the house, now replete, now famous, that Maggie grew to think again of this large element of "company" as of a kind of renewed water-supply for the tank in which, like a party of panting gold-fish, they kept afloat. It helped them, unmistakably, with each other, weakening the emphasis of so many of the silences of which their intimate intercourse would otherwise have consisted. Beautiful and wonderful for her, even, at times, was the effect of these interventions—their effect above all in bringing home to each the possible heroism of perfunctory things. They learned fairly to live in the perfunctory; they remained in it as many hours of the day as might be; it took on finally the likeness of some spacious central chamber in a haunted house, a great overarched and overglazed rotunda, where gaiety might reign, but the doors of which opened into sinister circular passages. Here they turned up for each other, as they said, with the blank faces that denied any uneasiness felt in the approach; here they closed numerous doors carefully behind them—all save the door that connected the place, as by a straight tented corridor, with the outer world, and, encouraging thus the irruption of society, imitated the aperture through which the bedizened performers of the circus are poured into the ring. The great part Mrs. Verver had socially played came luckily, Maggie could make out, to her assistance; she had "personal friends"—Charlotte's personal friends had ever been, in London, at the two houses, one of the most convenient pleasantries—who actually tempered, at this crisis, her aspect of isolation; and it wouldn't have been hard to guess that her best moments were those in which she suffered no fear of becoming a bore to restrain her appeal to their curiosity. Their curiosity might be vague, but their clever hostess was distinct, and she marched them about, sparing them nothing, as if she counted, each day, on a harvest of small crowns. Maggie met her again, in the gallery, at the oddest hours, with the party she was entertaining; heard her draw out the lesson, insist upon the interest, snub, even, the particular presumption and smile for the general bewilderment—inevitable features, these latter, of almost any occasion—in a manner that made our young woman, herself incurably dazzled, marvel afresh at the mystery by which a creature who could be in some connexions so earnestly right could be in others so perversely wrong. When her father, vaguely circulating, was attended by his wife, it was always Charlotte who seemed to bring up the rear; but he hung in the background when she did cicerone, and it was then perhaps that, moving mildly and modestly to and fro on the skirts of the exhibition, his appearance of having put her spell was, for the initiated conscience, least to be resisted. Brilliant women turned to him in vague emotion, but his response scarce committed him more than if he had been the person employed to see that, after the invading wave was spent, the cabinets were all locked and the symmetries all restored.

There was a morning when, during the hour before luncheon and shortly after the arrival of a neighbourly contingent—neighbourly from ten miles off—whom Mrs. Verver had taken in charge, Maggie paused on the threshold of the gallery through which she had been about to pass, faltered there for the very impression of his face as it met her from an opposite door. Charlotte, half-way down the vista, held together, as if by something almost austere in the grace of her authority, the semi-scared (now that they were there!) knot of her visitors, who, since they had announced themselves by telegram as yearning to inquire and admire, saw themselves restricted to this consistency. Her voice, high and clear and a little hard, reached her husband and her step-daughter while she thus placed beyond doubt her cheerful submission to duty. Her words, addressed to the largest publicity, rang for some minutes through the place, every one as quiet to listen as if it had been a church sermon with tapers and she were taking her part in some hymn of praise. Fanny Assingham looked rapt in devotion—Fanny Assingham who forsook this other friend as little as she forsook either her host or the Princess or the Prince or the Principino; she supported her, in slow revolutions, in murmurous attestations of presence, at all such times, and Maggie, advancing after a first hesitation, was not to fail of noting her solemn, inscrutable attitude, her eyes attentively lifted, so that while escape being provoked to betray an impression. She betrayed one, however, as Maggie approached, dropping her gaze to the latter's level long enough to seem to adventure, marvellously, on a mute appeal. "You understand, don't you, that if she didn't do this there would be no knowing what she might do?" This light Mrs. Assingham richly launched while her younger friend, unresistingly moved, became uncertain again, and then, not too much to show it—or, rather, positively to conceal it, and to conceal something more as well—turned short round to one of the windows and awkwardly, pointlessly waited. "The largest of the three pieces has the rare peculiarity that the garlands, looped round it, which, as you see, are the finest possible vieux Saxe, are not of the same origin or period, or even, wonderful as they are, of a taste quite so perfect. They have been put on at a later time, by a process of which there are very few examples, and none so important as this, which is really quite unique—so that, though the whole thing is a little baroque, its value as a specimen is, I believe, almost inestimable."

So the high voice quavered, aiming truly at effects far over the heads of gaping neighbours; so the speaker, piling it up, sticking at nothing, as less interested judges might have said, seemed to justify the faith with which she was honoured. Maggie meanwhile, at the window, knew the strangest thing to be happening: she had turned suddenly to crying, or was at least on the point of it—the lighted square before her all blurred and dim. The high voice went on; its quaver was doubtless for conscious ears only, but there were verily thirty seconds during which it sounded, for our young woman, like the shriek of a soul in pain. Kept up a minute longer it would break and collapse—so that Maggie felt herself, the next thing, turn with a start to her father. "Can't she be stopped? Hasn't she done it ENOUGH?"—some such question as that she let herself ask him to suppose in her. Then it was that, across half the gallery—for he had not moved from where she had first seen him—he struck her as confessing, with strange tears in his own eyes, to sharp identity of emotion. "Poor thing, poor thing"—it reached straight— "ISN'T she, for one's credit, on the swagger?" After which, as, held thus together they had still another strained minute, the shame, the pity, the better knowledge, the smothered protest, the divined anguish even, so overcame him that, blushing to his eyes, he turned short away. The affair but of a few muffled moments, this snatched communion yet lifted Maggie as on air—so much, for deep guesses on her own side too, it gave her to think of. There was, honestly, an awful mixture in things, and it was not closed to her aftersense of such passages—we have already indeed, in other cases, seen it open—that the deepest depth of all, in a perceived penalty, was that you couldn't be sure some of your compunctions and contortions wouldn't show for ridiculous. Amerigo, that morning, for instance, had been as absent as he at this juncture appeared to desire he should mainly be noted as being; he had gone to London for the day and the night—a necessity that now frequently rose for him and that he had more than once suffered to operate during the presence of guests, successions of pretty women, the theory of his fond interest in whom had been publicly cultivated. It had never occurred to his wife to pronounce him ingenuous, but there came at last a high dim August dawn when she couldn't sleep and when, creeping restlessly about and breathing at her window the coolness of wooded acres, she found the faint flush of the east march with the perception of that other almost equal prodigy. It rosily coloured her vision that—even such as he was, yes—her husband could on occasion sin by excess of candour. He wouldn't otherwise have given as his reason for going up to Portland Place in the August days that he was arranging books there. He had bought a great many of late, and he had had others, a large number, sent from Rome—wonders of old print in which her father had been interested. But when her imagination tracked him to the dusty town, to the house where drawn blinds and pale shrouds, where a caretaker and a kitchenmaid were alone in possession, it wasn't to see him, in his shirtsleeves, unpacking battered boxes.

She saw him, in truth, less easily beguiled—saw him wander, in the closed dusky rooms, from place to place, or else, for long periods, recline on deep sofas and stare before him through the smoke of ceaseless cigarettes. She made him out as liking better than anything in the world just now to be alone with his thoughts. Being herself connected with his thoughts, she continued to believe, more than she had ever been, it was thereby a good deal as if he were alone with HER. She made him out as resting so from that constant strain of the perfunctory to which he was exposed at Fawns; and she was accessible to the impression of the almost beggared aspect of this alternative. It was like his doing penance in sordid ways—being sent to prison or being kept without money; it wouldn't have taken much to make her think of him as really kept without food. He might have broken away, might easily have started to travel; he had a right—thought wonderful Maggie now—to so many more freedoms than he took! His secret was of course that at Fawns he all the while winced, was all the while in presences in respect to which he had thrown himself back, with a hard pressure, on whatever mysteries of pride, whatever inward springs familiar to the man of the world, he could keep from snapping. Maggie, for some reason, had that morning, while she watched the sunrise, taken an extraordinary measure of the ground on which he would have HAD to snatch at pretexts for absence. It all came to her there—he got off to escape from a sound. The sound was in her own ears still—that of Charlotte's high coerced quaver before the cabinets in the hushed gallery; the voice by which she herself had been pierced the day before as by that of a creature in anguish and by which, while she sought refuge at the blurred window, the tears had been forced into her eyes. Her comprehension soared so high that the wonder for her became really his not feeling the need of wider intervals and thicker walls. Before THAT admiration she also meditated; consider as she might now, she kept reading not less into what he omitted than into what he performed a beauty of intention that touched her fairly the more by being obscure. It was like hanging over a garden in the dark; nothing was to be made of the confusion of growing things, but one felt they were folded flowers, and their vague sweetness made the whole air their medium. He had to bear, but he wasn't at least a coward; he would wait on the spot for the issue of what he had done on the spot. She sank to her knees with her arm on the ledge of her window-seat, where she blinded her eyes from the full glare of seeing that his idea could only be to wait, whatever might come, at her side. It was to her buried face that she thus, for a long time, felt him draw nearest; though after a while, when the strange wail of the gallery began to repeat its inevitable echo, she was conscious of how that brought out his pale hard grimace.

XXXIX

The resemblance had not been present to her on first coming out into the hot, still brightness of the Sunday afternoon—only the second Sunday, of all the summer, when the party of six, the party of seven including the Principino, had practically been without accessions or invasions; but within sight of Charlotte, seated far away, very much where she had expected to find her, the Princess fell to wondering if her friend wouldn't be affected quite as she herself had been, that night on the terrace, under Mrs. Verver's perceptive pursuit. The relation, to-day, had turned itself round; Charlotte was seeing her come, through patches of lingering noon, quite as she had watched Charlotte menace her through the starless dark; and there was a moment, that of her waiting a little as they thus met across the distance, when the interval was bridged by a recognition not less soundless, and to all appearance not less charged with strange meanings, than that of the other occasion. The point, however, was that they had changed places; Maggie had from her window, seen her stepmother leave the house—at so unlikely an hour, three o'clock of a canicular August, for a ramble in garden or grove—and had thereupon felt her impulse determined with the same sharpness that had made the spring of her companion's three weeks before. It was the hottest day of the season, and the shaded siesta, for people all at their ease, would certainly rather have been prescribed; but our young woman had perhaps not yet felt it so fully brought home that such refinements of repose, among them, constituted the empty chair at the feast. This was the more distinct as the feast, literally, in the great bedimmed dining-room, the cool, ceremonious semblance of luncheon, had just been taking place without Mrs. Verver. She had been represented but by the plea of a bad headache, not reported to the rest of the company by her husband, but offered directly to Mr. Verver himself, on their having assembled, by her maid, deputed for the effect and solemnly producing it.

Maggie had sat down, with the others, to viands artfully iced, to the slow circulation of precious tinkling jugs, to marked reserves of reference in many directions—poor Fanny Assingham herself scarce thrusting her nose out of the padded hollow into which she had withdrawn. A consensus of languor, which might almost have been taken for a community of dread, ruled the scene—relieved only by the fitful experiments of Father Mitchell, good holy, hungry man, a trusted and overworked London friend and adviser, who had taken, for a week or two, the light neighbouring service, local rites flourishing under Maggie's munificence, and was enjoying, as a convenience, all the bounties of the house. HE conversed undiscouraged, Father Mitchell—conversed mainly with the indefinite, wandering smile of the entertainers, and the Princess's power to feel him on the whole a blessing for these occasions was not impaired by what was awkward in her consciousness of having, from the first of her trouble, really found her way without his guidance. She asked herself at times if he suspected how more than subtly, how perversely, she had dispensed with him, and she balanced between visions of all he must privately have guessed and certitudes that he had guessed nothing whatever. He might nevertheless have been so urbanely filling up gaps, at present, for the very reason that his instinct, sharper than the expression of his face, had sufficiently served him—made him aware of the thin ice, figuratively speaking, and of prolongations of tension, round about him, mostly foreign to the circles in which he was akin to virtue. Some day in some happier season, she would confess to him that she hadn't confessed, though taking so much on her conscience; but just now she was carrying in her weak, stiffened hand a glass filled to the brim, as to which she had recorded a vow that no drop should overflow. She feared the very breath of a better wisdom, the jostle of the higher light, the breath of heavenly help itself; and, in addition, however that might be, she drew breath this afternoon, as never yet, in an element heavy to oppression.

Something grave had happened, somehow and somewhere, and she had, God knew, her choice of suppositions: her heart stood still when she wondered above all if the cord mightn't at last have snapped between her husband and her father. She shut her eyes for dismay at the possibility of such a passage—there moved before them the procession of ugly forms it might have taken. "Find out for yourself!" she had thrown to Amerigo, for her last word, on the question of who else "knew," that night of the breaking of the Bowl; and she flattered herself that she hadn't since then helped him, in her clear consistency, by an inch. It was what she had given him, all these weeks, to be busy with, and she had again and again lain awake for the obsession of this sense of his uncertainty ruthlessly and endlessly playing with his dignity. She had handed him over to an ignorance that couldn't even try to become indifferent and that yet wouldn't project itself, either, into the cleared air of conviction. In proportion as he was generous it had bitten into his spirit, and more than once she had said to herself that to break the spell she had cast upon him and that the polished old ivory of her father's inattackable surface made so absolute, he would suddenly commit some mistake or some violence, smash some windowpane for air, fail even of one of his blest inveteracies of taste. In that way, fatally, he would have put himself in the wrong— blighting by a single base step the perfection of his outward show.

These shadows rose and fell for her while Father Mitchell prattled; with other shadows as well, those that hung over Charlotte herself, those that marked her as a prey to equal suspicions—to the idea, in particular, of a change, such a change as she didn't dare to face, in the relations of the two men. Or there were yet other possibilities, as it seemed to Maggie; there were always too many, and all of them things of evil when one's nerves had at last done for one all that nerves could do; had left one in a darkness of prowling dangers that was like the predicament of the night-watcher in a beast-haunted land who has no more means for a fire. She might, with such nerves, have supposed almost anything of any one; anything, almost, of poor Bob Assingham, condemned to eternal observances and solemnly appreciating her father's wine; anything, verily, yes, of the good priest, as he finally sat back with fat folded hands and twiddled his thumbs on his stomach. The good priest looked hard at the decanters, at the different dishes of dessert—he eyed them, half-obliquely, as if THEY might have met him to-day, for conversation, better than any one present. But the Princess had her fancy at last about that too; she was in the midst of a passage, before she knew it, between Father Mitchell and Charlotte—some approach he would have attempted with her, that very morning perhaps, to the circumstance of an apparent detachment, recently noted in her, from any practice of devotion. He would have drawn from this, say, his artless inference—taken it for a sign of some smothered inward trouble and pointed, naturally, the moral that the way out of such straits was not through neglect of the grand remedy. He had possibly prescribed contrition—he had at any rate quickened in her the beat of that false repose to which our young woman's own act had devoted her at her all so deluded instance. The falsity of it had laid traps compared to which the imputation of treachery even accepted might have seemed a path of roses. The acceptance, strangely, would have left her nothing to do—she could have remained, had she liked, all insolently passive; whereas the failure to proceed against her, as it might have been called, left her everything, and all the more that it was wrapped so in confidence. She had to confirm, day after day, the rightness of her cause and the justice and felicity of her exemption—so that wouldn't there have been, fairly, in any explicit concern of Father Mitchell's, depths of practical derision of her success?

The question was provisionally answered, at all events, by the time the party at luncheon had begun to disperse—with Maggie's version of Mrs. Verver sharp to the point of representing her pretext for absence as a positive flight from derision. She met the good priest's eyes before they separated, and priests were really, at the worst, so to speak, such wonderful people that she believed him for an instant on the verge of saying to her, in abysmal softness: "Go to Mrs. Verver, my child—YOU go: you'll find that you can help her." This didn't come, however; nothing came but the renewed twiddle of thumbs over the satisfied stomach and the full flush, the comical candour, of reference to the hand employed at Fawns for mayonnaise of salmon. Nothing came but the receding backs of each of the others—her father's slightly bent shoulders, in especial, which seemed to weave his spell, by the force of habit, not less patiently than if his wife had been present. Her husband indeed was present to feel anything there might be to feel—which was perhaps exactly why this personage was moved promptly to emulate so definite an example of "sloping." He had his occupations—books to arrange perhaps even at Fawns; the idea of the siesta, moreover, in all the conditions, had no need to be loudly invoked. Maggie, was, in the event, left alone for a minute with Mrs. Assingham, who, after waiting for safety, appeared to have at heart to make a demonstration. The stage of "talking over" had long passed for them; when they communicated now it was on quite ultimate facts; but Fanny desired to testify to the existence, on her part, of an attention that nothing escaped. She was like the kind lady who, happening to linger at the circus while the rest of the spectators pour grossly through the exits, falls in with the overworked little trapezist girl— the acrobatic support presumably of embarrassed and exacting parents—and gives her, as an obscure and meritorious artist, assurance of benevolent interest. What was clearest, always, in our young woman's imaginings, was the sense of being herself left, for any occasion, in the breach. She was essentially there to bear the burden, in the last resort, of surrounding omissions and evasions, and it was eminently to that office she had been to-day abandoned—with this one alleviation, as appeared, of Mrs. Assingham's keeping up with her. Mrs. Assingham suggested that she too was still on the ramparts—though her gallantry proved indeed after a moment to consist not a little of her curiosity. She had looked about and seen their companions beyond earshot.

"Don't you really want us to go—?"

Maggie found a faint smile. "Do you really want to—?"

It made her friend colour. "Well then—no. But we WOULD, you know, at a look from you. We'd pack up and be off—as a sacrifice."

"Ah, make no sacrifice," said Maggie. "See me through."

"That's it—that's all I want. I should be too base—! Besides," Fanny went on, "you're too splendid."

"Splendid?"

"Splendid. Also, you know, you ARE all but 'through.' You've done it," said Mrs. Assingham. But Maggie only half took it from her.

"What does it strike you that I've done?"

"What you wanted. They're going."

Maggie continued to look at her. "Is that what I wanted?"

"Oh, it wasn't for you to say. That was his business."

"My father's?" Maggie asked after an hesitation.

"Your father's. He has chosen—and now she knows. She sees it all before her—and she can't speak, or resist, or move a little finger. That's what's the matter with HER," said Fanny Assingham.

It made a picture, somehow, for the Princess, as they stood there—the picture that the words of others, whatever they might be, always made for her, even when her vision was already charged, better than any words of her own. She saw, round about her, through the chinks of the shutters, the hard glare of nature—saw Charlotte, somewhere in it, virtually at bay, and yet denied the last grace of any protecting truth. She saw her off somewhere all unaided, pale in her silence and taking in her fate. "Has she told you?" she then asked.

Her companion smiled superior. "I don't need to be told—either! I see something, thank God, every day." And then as Maggie might appear to be wondering what, for instance: "I see the long miles of ocean and the dreadful great country, State after State—which have never seemed to me so big or so terrible. I see THEM at last, day by day and step by step, at the far end—and I see them never come back. But NEVER—simply. I see the extraordinary 'interesting' place—which I've never been to, you know, and you have—and the exact degree in which she will be expected to be interested."

"She WILL be," Maggie presently replied. "Expected?"

"Interested."

For a little, after this, their eyes met on it; at the end of which Fanny said: "She'll be—yes—what she'll HAVE to be. And it will be—won't it? for ever and ever." She spoke as abounding in her friend's sense, but it made Maggie still only look at her.

These were large words and large visions—all the more that now, really, they spread and spread. In the midst of them, however, Mrs. Assingham had soon enough continued. "When I talk of 'knowing,' indeed, I don't mean it as you would have a right to do. You know because you see—and I don't see HIM. I don't make him out," she almost crudely confessed.

Maggie again hesitated. "You mean you don't make out Amerigo?"

But Fanny shook her head, and it was quite as if, as an appeal to one's intelligence, the making out of Amerigo had, in spite of everything, long been superseded. Then Maggie measured the reach of her allusion, and how what she next said gave her meaning a richness. No other name was to be spoken, and Mrs. Assingham had taken that, without delay, from her eyes—with a discretion, still, that fell short but by an inch. "You know how he feels."

Maggie at this then slowly matched her headshake. "I know nothing."

"You know how YOU feel."

But again she denied it. "I know nothing. If I did—!"

"Well, if you did?" Fanny asked as she faltered.

She had had enough, however. "I should die," she said as she turned away.

She went to her room, through the quiet house; she roamed there a moment, picking up, pointlessly, a different fan, and then took her way to the shaded apartments in which, at this hour, the Principino would be enjoying his nap. She passed through the first empty room, the day nursery, and paused at an open door. The inner room, large, dim and cool, was equally calm; her boy's ample, antique, historical, royal crib, consecrated, reputedly, by the guarded rest of heirs-apparent, and a gift, early in his career, from his grandfather, ruled the scene from the centre, in the stillness of which she could almost hear the child's soft breathing. The prime protector of his dreams was installed beside him; her father sat there with as little motion—with head thrown back and supported, with eyes apparently closed, with the fine foot that was so apt to betray nervousness at peace upon the other knee, with the unfathomable heart folded in the constant flawless freshness of the white waistcoat that could always receive in its armholes the firm prehensile thumbs. Mrs. Noble had majestically melted, and the whole place signed her temporary abdication; yet the actual situation was regular, and Maggie lingered but to look. She looked over her fan, the top of which was pressed against her face, long enough to wonder if her father really slept or if, aware of her, he only kept consciously quiet. Did his eyes truly fix her between lids partly open, and was she to take this—his forebearance from any question—only as a sign again that everything was left to her? She at all events, for a minute, watched his immobility—then, as if once more renewing her total submission, returned, without a sound, to her own quarters.

A strange impulse was sharp in her, but it was not, for her part, the desire to shift the weight. She could as little have slept as she could have slept that morning, days before, when she had watched the first dawn from her window. Turned to the east, this side of her room was now in shade, with the two wings of the casement folded back and the charm she always found in her seemingly perched position—as if her outlook, from above the high terraces, was that of some castle-tower mounted on a rock. When she stood there she hung over, over the gardens and the woods—all of which drowsed below her, at this hour, in the immensity of light. The miles of shade looked hot, the banks of flowers looked dim; the peacocks on the balustrades let their tails hang limp and the smaller birds lurked among the leaves. Nothing therefore would have appeared to stir in the brilliant void if Maggie, at the moment she was about to turn away, had not caught sight of a moving spot, a clear green sunshade in the act of descending a flight of steps. It passed down from the terrace, receding, at a distance, from sight, and carried, naturally, so as to conceal the head and back of its bearer; but Maggie had quickly recognised the white dress and the particular motion of this adventurer—had taken in that Charlotte, of all people, had chosen the glare of noon for an exploration of the gardens, and that she could be betaking herself only to some unvisited quarter deep in them, or beyond them, that she had already marked as a superior refuge. The Princess kept her for a few minutes in sight, watched her long enough to feel her, by the mere betrayal of her pace and direction, driven in a kind of flight, and then understood, for herself, why the act of sitting still had become impossible to either of them. There came to her, confusedly, some echo of an ancient fable—some vision of Io goaded by the gadfly or of Ariadne roaming the lone sea-strand. It brought with it all the sense of her own intention and desire; she too might have been, for the hour, some far-off harassed heroine—only with a part to play for which she knew, exactly, no inspiring precedent. She knew but that, all the while—all the while of her sitting there among the others without her—she had wanted to go straight to this detached member of the party and make somehow, for her support, the last demonstration. A pretext was all that was needful, and Maggie after another instant had found one. She had caught a glimpse, before Mrs. Verver disappeared, of her carrying a book—made out, half lost in the folds of her white dress, the dark cover of a volume that was to explain her purpose in case of her being met with surprise, and the mate of which, precisely, now lay on Maggie's table. The book was an old novel that the Princess had a couple of days before mentioned having brought down from Portland Place in the charming original form of its three volumes. Charlotte had hailed, with a specious glitter of interest, the opportunity to read it, and our young woman had, thereupon, on the morrow, directed her maid to carry it to Mrs. Verver's apartments. She was afterwards to observe that this messenger, unintelligent or inadvertent, had removed but one of the volumes, which happened not to be the first. Still possessed, accordingly, of the first while Charlotte, going out, fantastically, at such an hour, to cultivate romance in an arbour, was helplessly armed with the second, Maggie prepared on the spot to sally forth with succour. The right volume, was all she required—in addition, that is, to the bravery of her general idea. She passed again through the house, unchallenged, and emerged upon the terrace, which she followed, hugging the shade, with that consciousness of turning the tables on her friend which we have already noted. But so far as she went, after descending into the open and beginning to explore the grounds, Mrs. Verver had gone still further—with the increase of the oddity, moreover, of her having exchanged the protection of her room for these exposed and shining spaces. It was not, fortunately, however, at last, that by persisting in pursuit one didn't arrive at regions of admirable shade: this was the asylum, presumably, that the poor wandering woman had had in view—several wide alleys, in particular, of great length, densely overarched with the climbing rose and the honeysuckle and converging, in separate green vistas, at a sort of umbrageous temple, an ancient rotunda, pillared and statued, niched and roofed, yet with its uncorrected antiquity, like that of everything else at Fawns, conscious hitherto of no violence from the present and no menace from the future. Charlotte had paused there, in her frenzy, or what ever it was to be called; the place was a conceivable retreat, and she was staring before her, from the seat to which she appeared to have sunk, all unwittingly, as Maggie stopped at the beginning of one of the perspectives.

It was a repetition more than ever then of the evening on the terrace; the distance was too great to assure her she had been immediately seen, but the Princess waited, with her intention, as Charlotte on the other occasion had waited—allowing, oh allowing, for the difference of the intention! Maggie was full of the sense of THAT—so full that it made her impatient; whereupon she moved forward a little, placing herself in range of the eyes that had been looking off elsewhere, but that she had suddenly called to recognition. Charlotte had evidently not dreamed of being followed, and instinctively, with her pale stare, she stiffened herself for protest. Maggie could make that out—as well as, further, however, that her second impression of her friend's approach had an instant effect on her attitude. The Princess came nearer, gravely and in silence, but fairly paused again, to give her time for whatever she would. Whatever she would, whatever she could, was what Maggie wanted—wanting above all to make it as easy for her as the case permitted. That was not what Charlotte had wanted the other night, but this never mattered—the great thing was to allow her, was fairly to produce in her, the sense of highly choosing. At first, clearly, she had been frightened; she had not been pursued, it had quickly struck her, without some design on the part of her pursuer, and what might she not be thinking of in addition but the way she had, when herself the pursuer, made her stepdaughter take in her spirit and her purpose? It had sunk into Maggie at the time, that hard insistence, and Mrs. Verver had felt it and seen it and heard it sink; which wonderful remembrance of pressure successfully applied had naturally, till now, remained with her. But her stare was like a projected fear that the buried treasure, so dishonestly come by, for which her companion's still countenance, at the hour and afterwards, had consented to serve as the deep soil, might have worked up again to the surface, to be thrown back upon her hands. Yes, it was positive that during one of these minutes the Princess had the vision of her particular alarm. "It's her lie, it's her lie that has mortally disagreed with her; she can keep down no longer her rebellion at it, and she has come to retract it, to disown it and denounce it—to give me full in my face the truth instead." This, for a concentrated instant, Maggie felt her helplessly gasp—but only to let it bring home the indignity, the pity of her state. She herself could but tentatively hover, place in view the book she carried, look as little dangerous, look as abjectly mild, as possible; remind herself really of people she had read about in stories of the wild west, people who threw up their hands, on certain occasions, as a sign they weren't carrying revolvers. She could almost have smiled at last, troubled as she yet knew herself, to show how richly she was harmless; she held up her volume, which was so weak a weapon, and while she continued, for consideration, to keep her distance, she explained with as quenched a quaver as possible. "I saw you come out—saw you from my window, and couldn't bear to think you should find yourself here without the beginning of your book. THIS is the beginning; you've got the wrong volume, and I've brought you out the right."

She remained after she had spoken; it was like holding a parley with a possible adversary, and her intense, her exalted little smile asked for formal leave. "May I come nearer now?" she seemed to say—as to which, however, the next minute, she saw Charlotte's reply lose itself in a strange process, a thing of several sharp stages, which she could stand there and trace. The dread, after a minute, had dropped from her face; though, discernibly enough, she still couldn't believe in her having, in so strange a fashion, been deliberately made up to. If she had been made up to, at least, it was with an idea—the idea that had struck her at first as necessarily disagreeable. That it wasn't, insistently wasn't, this shone from Maggie with a force finally not to be resisted; and on that perception, on the immense relief so constituted, everything had by the end of three minutes extraordinarily changed. Maggie had come out to her, really, because she knew her doomed, doomed to a separation that was like a knife in her heart; and in the very sight of her uncontrollable, her blinded physical quest of a peace not to be grasped, something of Mrs. Assingham's picture of her as thrown, for a grim future, beyond the great sea and the great continent had at first found fulfilment. She had got away, in this fashion—burning behind her, almost, the ships of disguise—to let her horror of what was before her play up without witnesses; and even after Maggie's approach had presented an innocent front it was still not to be mistaken that she bristled with the signs of her extremity. It was not to be said for them, either, that they wore draped at this hour in any of her usual graces; unveiled and all but unashamed, they were tragic to the Princess in spite of the dissimulation that, with the return of comparative confidence, was so promptly to operate. How tragic, in essence, the very change made vivid, the instant stiffening of the spring of pride—this for possible defence if not for possible aggression. Pride indeed, the next moment, had become the mantle caught up for protection and perversity; she flung it round her as a denial of any loss of her freedom. To be doomed was, in her situation, to have extravagantly incurred a doom, so that to confess to wretchedness was, by the same stroke, to confess to falsity. She wouldn't confess, she didn't—a thousand times no; she only cast about her, and quite frankly and fiercely, for something else that would give colour to her having burst her bonds. Her eyes expanded, her bosom heaved as she invoked it, and the effect upon Maggie was verily to wish she could only help her to it. She presently got up—which seemed to mean "Oh, stay if you like!" and when she had moved about awhile at random, looking away, looking at anything, at everything but her visitor; when she had spoken of the temperature and declared that she revelled in it; when she had uttered her thanks for the book, which, a little incoherently, with her second volume, she perhaps found less clever than she expected; when she had let Maggie approach sufficiently closer to lay, untouched, the tribute in question on a bench and take up obligingly its superfluous mate: when she had done these things she sat down in another place, more or less visibly in possession of her part. Our young woman was to have passed, in all her adventure, no stranger moments; for she not only now saw her companion fairly agree to take her then for the poor little person she was finding it so easy to appear, but fell, in a secret, responsive ecstasy, to wondering if there were not some supreme abjection with which she might be inspired. Vague, but increasingly brighter, this possibility glimmered on her. It at last hung there adequately plain to Charlotte that she had presented herself once more to (as they said) grovel; and that, truly, made the stage large. It had absolutely, within the time, taken on the dazzling merit of being large for each of them alike.

"I'm glad to see you alone—there's something I've been wanting to say to you. I'm tired," said Mrs. Verver, "I'm tired—!"

"Tired—?" It had dropped the next thing; it couldn't all come at once; but Maggie had already guessed what it was, and the flush of recognition was in her face.

"Tired of this life—the one we've been leading. You like it, I know, but I've dreamed another dream." She held up her head now; her lighted eyes more triumphantly rested; she was finding, she was following her way. Maggie, by the same influence, sat in sight of it; there was something she was SAVING, some quantity of which she herself was judge; and it was for a long moment, even with the sacrifice the Princess had come to make, a good deal like watching her, from the solid shore, plunge into uncertain, into possibly treacherous depths. "I see something else," she went on; "I've an idea that greatly appeals to me—I've had it for a long time. It has come over me that we're wrong. Our real life isn't here."

Maggie held her breath. "'Ours'—?"

"My husband's and mine. I'm not speaking for you."

"Oh!" said Maggie, only praying not to be, not even to appear, stupid.

"I'm speaking for ourselves. I'm speaking," Charlotte brought out, "for HIM."

"I see. For my father."

"For your father. For whom else?" They looked at each other hard now, but Maggie's face took refuge in the intensity of her interest. She was not at all even so stupid as to treat her companion's question as requiring an answer; a discretion that her controlled stillness had after an instant justified. "I must risk your thinking me selfish—for of course you know what it involves. Let me admit it—I AM selfish. I place my husband first."

"Well," said Maggie smiling and smiling, "since that's where I place mine—!"

"You mean you'll have no quarrel with me? So much the better then; for," Charlotte went on with a higher and higher flight, "my plan is completely formed."

Maggie waited—her glimmer had deepened; her chance somehow was at hand. The only danger was her spoiling it; she felt herself skirting an abyss. "What then, may I ask IS your plan?"

It hung fire but ten seconds; it came out sharp. "To take him home—to his real position. And not to wait."

"Do you mean—a—this season?"

"I mean immediately. And—I may as well tell you now—I mean for my own time. I want," Charlotte said, "to have him at last a little to myself; I want, strange as it may seem to you"—and she gave it all its weight "to KEEP the man I've married. And to do so, I see, I must act."

Maggie, with the effort still to follow the right line, felt herself colour to the eyes. "Immediately?" she thoughtfully echoed.

"As soon as we can get off. The removal of everything is, after all, but a detail. That can always be done; with money, as he spends it, everything can. What I ask for," Charlotte declared, "is the definite break. And I wish it now." With which her head, like her voice rose higher. "Oh," she added, "I know my difficulty!"

Far down below the level of attention, in she could scarce have said what sacred depths, Maggie's inspiration had come, and it had trembled the next moment into sound. "Do you mean I'M your difficulty?"

"You and he together—since it's always with you that I've had to see him. But it's a difficulty that I'm facing, if you wish to know; that I've already faced; that I propose to myself to surmount. The struggle with it—none too pleasant—hasn't been for me, as you may imagine, in itself charming; I've felt it in it at times, if I must tell you all, too great and too strange, an ugliness. Yet I believe it may succeed."

She had risen, with this, Mrs. Verver, and had moved, for the emphasis of it, a few steps away; while Maggie, motionless at first, but sat and looked at her. "You want to take my father FROM me?"

The sharp, successful, almost primitive wail in it made Charlotte turn, and this movement attested for the Princess the felicity of her deceit. Something in her throbbed as it had throbbed the night she stood in the drawing-room and denied that she had suffered. She was ready to lie again if her companion would but give her the opening. Then she should know she had done all. Charlotte looked at her hard, as if to compare her face with her note of resentment; and Maggie, feeling this, met it with the signs of an impression that might pass for the impression of defeat. "I want really to possess him," said Mrs. Verver. "I happen also to feel that he's worth it."

Maggie rose as if to receive her. "Oh—worth it!" she wonderfully threw off.

The tone, she instantly saw, again had its effect: Charlotte flamed aloft—might truly have been believing in her passionate parade. "You've thought YOU'VE known what he's worth?"

"Indeed then, my dear, I believe I have—as I believe I still do."

She had given it, Maggie, straight back, and again it had not missed. Charlotte, for another moment, only looked at her; then broke into the words—Maggie had known they would come—of which she had pressed the spring. "How I see that you loathed our marriage!"

"Do you ASK me?" Maggie after an instant demanded.

Charlotte had looked about her, picked up the parasol she had laid on a bench, possessed herself mechanically of one of the volumes of the relegated novel and then, more consciously, flung it down again: she was in presence, visibly, of her last word. She opened her sunshade with a click; she twirled it on her shoulder in her pride. "'Ask' you? Do I need? How I see," she broke out, "that you've worked against me!"

"Oh, oh, oh!" the Princess exclaimed.

Her companion, leaving her, had reached one of the archways, but on this turned round with a flare. "You haven't worked against me?"

Maggie took it and for a moment kept it; held it, with closed eyes, as if it had been some captured fluttering bird pressed by both hands to her breast. Then she opened her eyes to speak. "What does it matter—if I've failed?"

"You recognise then that you've failed?" asked Charlotte from the threshold.

Maggie waited; she looked, as her companion had done a moment before, at the two books on the seat; she put them together and laid them down; then she made up her mind. "I've failed!" she sounded out before Charlotte, having given her time, walked away. She watched her, splendid and erect, float down the long vista; then she sank upon a seat. Yes, she had done all.

PART SIXTH.

The Alps (1834) by Adalbert Stifter (1805–1868)

XL

"I'll do anything you like," she said to her husband on one of the last days of the month, "if our being here, this way at this time, seems to you too absurd, or too uncomfortable, or too impossible. We'll either take leave of them now, without waiting—or we'll come back in time, three days before they start. I'll go abroad with you, if you but say the word; to Switzerland, the Tyrol, the Italian Alps, to whichever of your old high places you would like most to see again—those beautiful ones that used to do you good after Rome and that you so often told me about."

Where they were, in the conditions that prompted this offer, and where it might indeed appear ridiculous that, with the stale London September close at hand, they should content themselves with remaining, was where the desert of Portland Place looked blank as it had never looked, and where a drowsy cabman, scanning the horizon for a fare, could sink to oblivion of the risks of immobility. But Amerigo was of the odd opinion, day after day, that their situation couldn't be bettered; and he even went at no moment through the form of replying that, should their ordeal strike her as exceeding their patience, any step they might take would be for her own relief. This was, no doubt, partly because he stood out so wonderfully, to the end, against admitting, by a weak word at least, that any element of their existence WAS, or ever had been, an ordeal; no trap of circumstance, no lapse of "form," no accident of irritation, had landed him in that inconsequence. His wife might verily have suggested that he was consequent—consequent with the admirable appearance he had from the first so undertaken, and so continued, to present—rather too rigidly at HER expense; only, as it happened, she was not the little person to do anything of the sort, and the strange tacit compact actually in operation between them might have been founded on an intelligent comparison, a definite collation positively, of the kinds of patience proper to each. She was seeing him through—he had engaged to come out at the right end if he WOULD see him: this understanding, tacitly renewed from week to week, had fairly received, with the procession of the weeks, the consecration of time; but it scarce needed to be insisted on that she was seeing him on HIS terms, not all on hers, or that, in other words, she must allow him his unexplained and uncharted, his one practicably workable way. If that way, by one of the intimate felicities the liability to which was so far from having even yet completely fallen from him, happened handsomely to show him as more bored than boring (with advantages of his own freely to surrender, but none to be persuadedly indebted to others for,) what did such a false face of the matter represent but the fact itself that she was pledged? If she had questioned or challenged or interfered—if she had reserved herself that right—she wouldn't have been pledged; whereas there were still, and evidently would be yet a while, long, tense stretches during which their case might have been hanging, for every eye, on her possible, her impossible defection. She must keep it up to the last, mustn't absent herself for three minutes from her post: only on those lines, assuredly, would she show herself as with him and not against him.

It was extraordinary how scant a series of signs she had invited him to make of being, of truly having been at any time, "with" his wife: that reflection she was not exempt from as they now, in their suspense, supremely waited—a reflection under the brush of which she recognised her having had, in respect to him as well, to "do all," to go the whole way over, to move, indefatigably, while he stood as fixed in his place as some statue of one of his forefathers. The meaning of it would seem to be, she reasoned in sequestered hours, that he HAD a place, and that this was an attribute somehow indefeasible, unquenchable, which laid upon others—from the moment they definitely wanted anything of him— the necessity of taking more of the steps that he could, of circling round him, of remembering for his benefit the famous relation of the mountain to Mahomet. It was strange, if one had gone into it, but such a place as Amerigo's was like something made for him beforehand by innumerable facts, facts largely of the sort known as historical, made by ancestors, examples, traditions, habits; while Maggie's own had come to show simply as that improvised "post"—a post of the kind spoken of as advanced—with which she was to have found herself connected in the fashion of a settler or a trader in a new country; in the likeness even of some Indian squaw with a papoose on her back and barbarous bead-work to sell. Maggie's own, in short, would have been sought in vain in the most rudimentary map of the social relations as such. The only geography marking it would be doubtless that of the fundamental passions. The "end" that the Prince was at all events holding out for was represented to expectation by his father-in-law's announced departure for America with Mrs. Verver; just as that prospective event had originally figured as advising, for discretion, the flight of the younger couple, to say nothing of the withdrawal of whatever other importunate company, before the great upheaval of Fawns. This residence was to be peopled for a month by porters, packers and hammerers, at whose operations it had become peculiarly public—public that is for Portland Place—that Charlotte was to preside in force; operations the quite awful appointed scale and style of which had at no moment loomed so large to Maggie's mind as one day when the dear Assinghams swam back into her ken besprinkled with sawdust and looking as pale as if they had seen Samson pull down the temple. They had seen at least what she was not seeing, rich dim things under the impression of which they had retired; she having eyes at present but for the clock by which she timed her husband, or for the glass—the image perhaps would be truer—in which she reflected to her as HE timed the pair in the country. The accession of their friends from Cadogan Place contributed to all their intermissions, at any rate, a certain effect of resonance; an effect especially marked by the upshot of a prompt exchange of inquiries between Mrs. Assingham and the Princess. It was noted, on the occasion of that anxious lady's last approach to her young friend at Fawns, that her sympathy had ventured, after much accepted privation, again to become inquisitive, and it had perhaps never so yielded to that need as on this question of the present odd "line" of the distinguished eccentrics.

"You mean to say really that you're going to stick here?" And then before Maggie could answer: "What on earth will you do with your evenings?"

Maggie waited a moment—Maggie could still tentatively smile. "When people learn we're here—and of course the papers will be full of it!—they'll flock back in their hundreds, from wherever they are, to catch us. You see you and the Colonel have yourselves done it. As for our evenings, they won't, I dare say, be particularly different from anything else that's ours. They won't be different from our mornings or our afternoons—except perhaps that you two dears will sometimes help us to get through them. I've offered to go anywhere," she added; "to take a house if he will. But THIS—just this and nothing else—is Amerigo's idea. He gave it yesterday" she went on, "a name that, as he said, described and fitted it. So you see"—and the Princess indulged again in her smile that didn't play, but that only, as might have been said, worked—"so you see there's a method in our madness."

It drew Mrs. Assingham's wonder. "And what then is the name?"

"'The reduction to its simplest expression of what we ARE doing'—that's what he called it. Therefore as we're doing nothing, we're doing it in the most aggravated way—which is the way he desires." With which Maggie further said: "Of course I understand."

"So do I!" her visitor after a moment breathed. "You've had to vacate the house—that was inevitable. But at least here he doesn't funk."

Our young woman accepted the expression. "He doesn't funk."

It only, however, half contented Fanny, who thoughtfully raised her eyebrows. "He's prodigious; but what is there—as you've 'fixed' it—TO dodge? Unless," she pursued, "it's her getting near him; it's—if you'll pardon my vulgarity—her getting AT him. That," she suggested, "may count with him."

But it found the Princess prepared. "She can get near him here. She can get 'at' him. She can come up."

"CAN she?" Fanny Assingham questioned.

"CAN'T she?" Maggie returned.

Their eyes, for a minute, intimately met on it; after which the elder woman said: "I mean for seeing him alone."

"So do I," said the Princess.

At which Fanny, for her reasons, couldn't help smiling. "Oh, if it's for THAT he's staying—!"

"He's staying—I've made it out—to take anything that comes or calls upon him. To take," Maggie went on, "even that." Then she put it as she had at last put it to herself. "He's staying for high decency."

"Decency?" Mrs. Assingham gravely echoed.

"Decency. If she SHOULD try—!"

"Well—?" Mrs. Assingham urged.

"Well, I hope—!"

"Hope he'll see her?"

Maggie hesitated, however; she made no direct reply. "It's useless hoping," she presently said. "She won't. But he ought to." Her friend's expression of a moment before, which had been apologised for as vulgar, prolonged its sharpness to her ear—that of an electric bell under continued pressure. Stated so simply, what was it but dreadful, truly, that the feasibility of Charlotte's "getting at" the man who for so long had loved her should now be in question? Strangest of all things, doubtless, this care of Maggie's as to what might make for it or make against it; stranger still her fairly lapsing at moments into a vague calculation of the conceivability, on her own part, with her husband, of some direct sounding of the subject. Would it be too monstrous, her suddenly breaking out to him as in alarm at the lapse of the weeks: "Wouldn't it really seem that you're bound in honour to do something for her, privately, before they go?" Maggie was capable of weighing the risk of this adventure for her own spirit, capable of sinking to intense little absences, even while conversing, as now, with the person who had most of her confidence, during which she followed up the possibilities. It was true that Mrs. Assingham could at such times somewhat restore the balance—by not wholly failing to guess her thought. Her thought, however, just at present, had more than one face—had a series that it successively presented. These were indeed the possibilities involved in the adventure of her concerning herself for the quantity of compensation that Mrs. Verver might still look to. There was always the possibility that she WAS, after all, sufficiently to get at him—there was in fact that of her having again and again done so. Against this stood nothing but Fanny Assingham's apparent belief in her privation—more mercilessly imposed, or more hopelessly felt, in the actual relation of the parties; over and beyond everything that, from more than three months back, of course, had fostered in the Princess a like conviction. These assumptions might certainly be baseless—inasmuch as there were hours and hours of Amerigo's time that there was no habit, no pretence of his accounting for; inasmuch too as Charlotte, inevitably, had had more than once, to the undisguised knowledge of the pair in Portland Place, been obliged to come up to Eaton Square, whence so many of her personal possessions were in course of removal. She didn't come to Portland Place—didn't even come to ask for luncheon on two separate occasions when it reached the consciousness of the household there that she was spending the day in London. Maggie hated, she scorned, to compare hours and appearances, to weigh the idea of whether there hadn't been moments, during these days, when an assignation, in easy conditions, a snatched interview, in an air the season had so cleared of prying eyes, mightn't perfectly work. But the very reason of this was partly that, haunted with the vision of the poor woman carrying off with such bravery as she found to her hand the secret of her not being appeased, she was conscious of scant room for any alternative image. The alternative image would have been that the secret covered up was the secret of appeasement somehow obtained, somehow extorted and cherished; and the difference between the two kinds of hiding was too great to permit of a mistake. Charlotte was hiding neither pride nor joy—she was hiding humiliation; and here it was that the Princess's passion, so powerless for vindictive flights, most inveterately bruised its tenderness against the hard glass of her question.

Behind the glass lurked the WHOLE history of the relation she had so fairly flattened her nose against it to penetrate—the glass Mrs. Verver might, at this stage, have been frantically tapping, from within, by way of supreme, irrepressible entreaty. Maggie had said to herself complacently, after that last passage with her stepmother in the garden of Fawns, that there was nothing left for her to do and that she could thereupon fold her hands. But why wasn't it still left to push further and, from the point of view of personal pride, grovel lower?—why wasn't it still left to offer herself as the bearer of a message reporting to him their friend's anguish and convincing him of her need?

She could thus have translated Mrs. Verver's tap against the glass, as I have called it, into fifty forms; could perhaps have translated it most into the form of a reminder that would pierce deep. "You don't know what it is to have been loved and broken with. You haven't been broken with, because in your RELATION what can there have been, worth speaking of, to break? Ours was everything a relation could be, filled to the brim with the wine of consciousness; and if it was to have no meaning, no better meaning than that such a creature as you could breathe upon it, at your hour, for blight, why was I myself dealt with all for deception? why condemned after a couple of short years to find the golden flame—oh, the golden flame!—a mere handful of black ashes?" Our young woman so yielded, at moments, to what was insidious in these foredoomed ingenuities of her pity, that for minutes together, sometimes, the weight of a new duty seemed to rest upon her—the duty of speaking before separation should constitute its chasm, of pleading for some benefit that might be carried away into exile like the last saved object of price of the emigre, the jewel wrapped in a piece of old silk and negotiable some day in the market of misery.

This imagined service to the woman who could no longer help herself was one of the traps set for Maggie's spirit at every turn of the road; the click of which, catching and holding the divine faculty fast, was followed inevitably by a flutter, by a struggle of wings and even, as we may say, by a scattering of fine feathers. For they promptly enough felt, these yearnings of thought and excursions of sympathy, the concussion that couldn't bring them down—the arrest produced by the so remarkably distinct figure that, at Fawns, for the previous weeks, was constantly crossing, in its regular revolution, the further more of any watched perspective. Whoever knew, or whoever didn't, whether or to what extent Charlotte, with natural business in Eaton Square, had shuffled other opportunities under that cloak, it was all matter for the kind of quiet ponderation the little man who so kept his wandering way had made his own. It was part of the very inveteracy of his straw hat and his white waistcoat, of the trick of his hands in his pockets, of the detachment of the attention he fixed on his slow steps from behind his secure pince-nez. The thing that never failed now as an item in the picture was that gleam of the silken noose, his wife's immaterial tether, so marked to Maggie's sense during her last month in the country. Mrs. Verver's straight neck had certainly not slipped it; nor had the other end of the long cord—oh, quite conveniently long!—disengaged its smaller loop from the hooked thumb that, with his fingers closed upon it, her husband kept out of sight. To have recognised, for all its tenuity, the play of this gathered lasso might inevitably be to wonder with what magic it was twisted, to what tension subjected, but could never be to doubt either of its adequacy to its office or of its perfect durability. These reminded states for the Princess were in fact states of renewed gaping. So many things her father knew that she even yet didn't!

All this, at present, with Mrs. Assingham, passed through her in quick vibrations. She had expressed, while the revolution of her thought was incomplete, the idea of what Amerigo "ought," on his side, in the premises, to be capable of, and then had felt her companion's answering stare. But she insisted on what she had meant. "He ought to wish to see her—and I mean in some protected and independent way, as he used to—in case of her being herself able to manage it. That," said Maggie with the courage of her conviction, "he ought to be ready, he ought to be happy, he ought to feel himself sworn—little as it is for the end of such a history!—to take from her. It's as if he wished to get off without taking anything."

Mrs. Assingham deferentially mused. "But for what purpose is it your idea that they should again so intimately meet?"

"For any purpose they like. That's THEIR affair."

Fanny Assingham sharply laughed, then irrepressibly fell back to her constant position. "You're splendid—perfectly splendid." To which, as the Princess, shaking an impatient head, wouldn't have it again at all, she subjoined: "Or if you're not it's because you're so sure. I mean sure of HIM."

"Ah, I'm exactly NOT sure of him. If I were sure of him I shouldn't doubt—!" But Maggie cast about her.

"Doubt what?" Fanny pressed as she waited.

"Well, that he must feel how much less than she pays—and how that ought to keep her present to him."

This, in its turn, after an instant, Mrs. Assingham could meet with a smile. "Trust him, my dear, to keep her present! But trust him also to keep himself absent. Leave him his own way."

"I'll leave him everything," said Maggie. "Only—you know it's my nature—I THINK."

"It's your nature to think too much," Fanny Assingham a trifle coarsely risked.

This but quickened, however, in the Princess the act she reprobated. "That may be. But if I hadn't thought—!"

"You wouldn't, you mean, have been where you are?"

"Yes, because they, on their side, thought of everything BUT that. They thought of everything but that I might think."

"Or even," her friend too superficially concurred, "that your father might!"

As to this, at all events, Maggie discriminated. "No, that wouldn't have prevented them; for they knew that his first care would be not to make me do so. As it is," Maggie added, "that has had to become his last."

Fanny Assingham took it in deeper—for what it immediately made her give out louder. "HE'S splendid then." She sounded it almost aggressively; it was what she was reduced to—she had positively to place it.

"Ah, that as much as you please!"

Maggie said this and left it, but the tone of it had the next moment determined in her friend a fresh reaction. "You think, both of you, so abysmally and yet so quietly. But it's what will have saved you."

"Oh," Maggie returned, "it's what—from the moment they discovered we could think at all—will have saved THEM. For they're the ones who are saved," she went on. "We're the ones who are lost."

"Lost—?"

"Lost to each other—father and I." And then as her friend appeared to demur, "Oh yes," Maggie quite lucidly declared, "lost to each other much more, really, than Amerigo and Charlotte are; since for them it's just, it's right, it's deserved, while for us it's only sad and strange and not caused by our fault. But I don't know," she went on, "why I talk about myself, for it's on father it really comes. I let him go," said Maggie.

"You let him, but you don't make him."

"I take it from him," she answered.

"But what else can you do?"

"I take it from him," the Princess repeated. "I do what I knew from the first I SHOULD do. I get off by giving him up."

"But if he gives you?" Mrs. Assingham presumed to object. "Doesn't it moreover then," she asked, "complete the very purpose with which he married—that of making you and leaving you more free?"

Maggie looked at her long. "Yes—I help him to do that."

Mrs. Assingham hesitated, but at last her bravery flared. "Why not call it then frankly his complete success?"

"Well," said Maggie, "that's all that's left me to do."

"It's a success," her friend ingeniously developed, "with which you've simply not interfered." And as if to show that she spoke without levity Mrs. Assingham went further. "He has made it a success for THEM—!"

"Ah, there you are!" Maggie responsively mused. "Yes," she said the next moment, "that's why Amerigo stays."

"Let alone it's why Charlotte goes." that Mrs. Assingham, and emboldened, smiled "So he knows—?"

But Maggie hung back. "Amerigo—?" After which, however, she blushed—to her companion's recognition.

"Your father. He knows what YOU know? I mean," Fanny faltered—"well, how much does he know?" Maggie's silence and Maggie's eyes had in fact arrested the push of the question—which, for a decent consistency, she couldn't yet quite abandon. "What I should rather say is does he know how much?" She found it still awkward. "How much, I mean, they did. How far"—she touched it up—"they went."

Maggie had waited, but only with a question. "Do you think he does?"

"Know at least something? Oh, about him I can't think. He's beyond me," said Fanny Assingham.

"Then do you yourself know?"

"How much—?"

"How much."

"How far—?"

"How far."

Fanny had appeared to wish to make sure, but there was something she remembered—remembered in time and even with a smile. "I've told you before that I know absolutely nothing."

"Well—that's what I know," said the Princess.

Her friend again hesitated. "Then nobody knows—? I mean," Mrs. Assingham explained, "how much your father does."

Oh, Maggie showed that she understood. "Nobody."

"Not—a little—Charlotte?"

"A little?" the Princess echoed. "To know anything would be, for her, to know enough."

"And she doesn't know anything?"

"If she did," Maggie answered, "Amerigo would."

"And that's just it—that he doesn't?"

"That's just it," said the Princess profoundly.

On which Mrs. Assingham reflected. "Then how is Charlotte so held?"

"Just by that."

"By her ignorance?"

"By her ignorance." Fanny wondered. "A torment—?"

"A torment," said Maggie with tears in her eyes.

Her companion a moment watched them. "But the Prince then—?"

"How is HE held?" Maggie asked.

"How is HE held?"

"Oh, I can't tell you that!" And the Princess again broke off.

XLI

A telegram, in Charlotte's name, arrived early—"We shall come and ask you for tea at five, if convenient to you. Am wiring for the Assinghams to lunch." This document, into which meanings were to be read, Maggie promptly placed before her husband, adding the remark that her father and his wife, who would have come up the previous night or that morning, had evidently gone to an hotel. The Prince was in his "own" room, where he often sat now alone; half-a-dozen open newspapers, the "Figaro" notably, as well as the "Times," were scattered about him; but, with a cigar in his teeth and a visible cloud on his brow, he appeared actually to be engaged in walking to and fro. Never yet, on thus approaching him—for she had done it of late, under one necessity or another, several times—had a particular impression so greeted her; supremely strong, for some reason, as he turned quickly round on her entrance. The reason was partly the look in his face—a suffusion like the flush of fever, which brought back to her Fanny Assingham's charge, recently uttered under that roof, of her "thinking" too impenetrably. The word had remained with her and made her think still more; so that, at first, as she stood there, she felt responsible for provoking on her part an irritation of suspense at which she had not aimed. She had been going about him these three months, she perfectly knew, with a maintained idea—of which she had never spoken to him; but what had at last happened was that his way of looking at her, on occasion, seemed a perception of the presence not of one idea, but of fifty, variously prepared for uses with which she somehow must reckon. She knew herself suddenly, almost strangely, glad to be coming to him, at this hour, with nothing more abstract than a telegram; but even after she had stepped into his prison under her pretext, while her eyes took in his face and then embraced the four walls that enclosed his restlessness, she recognised the virtual identity of his condition with that aspect of Charlotte's situation for which, early in the summer and in all the amplitude of a great residence, she had found, with so little seeking, the similitude of the locked cage. He struck her as caged, the man who couldn't now without an instant effect on her sensibility give an instinctive push to the door she had not completely closed behind her. He had been turning twenty ways, for impatiences all his own, and when she was once shut in with him it was yet again as if she had come to him in his more than monastic cell to offer him light or food. There was a difference none the less, between his captivity and Charlotte's—the difference, as it might be, of his lurking there by his own act and his own choice; the admission of which had indeed virtually been in his starting, on her entrance, as if even this were in its degree an interference. That was what betrayed for her, practically, his fear of her fifty ideas, and what had begun, after a minute, to make her wish to repudiate or explain. It was more wonderful than she could have told; it was for all the world as if she was succeeding with him beyond her intention. She had, for these instants, the sense that he exaggerated, that the imputation of purpose had fairly risen too high in him. She had begun, a year ago, by asking herself how she could make him think more of her; but what was it, after all, he was thinking now? He kept his eyes on her telegram; he read it more than once, easy as it was, in spite of its conveyed deprecation, to understand; during which she found herself almost awestruck with yearning, almost on the point of marking somehow what she had marked in the garden at Fawns with Charlotte—that she had truly come unarmed. She didn't bristle with intentions—she scarce knew, as he at this juncture affected her, what had become of the only intention she had come with. She had nothing but her old idea, the old one he knew; she hadn't the ghost of another. Presently in fact, when four or five minutes had elapsed, it was as if she positively, hadn't so much even as that one. He gave her back her paper, asking with it if there were anything in particular she wished him to do.

She stood there with her eyes on him, doubling the telegram together as if it had been a precious thing and yet all the while holding her breath. Of a sudden, somehow, and quite as by the action of their merely having between them these few written words, an extraordinary fact came up. He was with her as if he were hers, hers in a degree and on a scale, with an intensity and an intimacy, that were a new and a strange quantity, that were like the irruption of a tide loosening them where they had stuck and making them feel they floated. What was it that, with the rush of this, just kept her from putting out her hands to him, from catching at him as, in the other time, with the superficial impetus he and Charlotte had privately conspired to impart, she had so often, her breath failing her, known the impulse to catch at her father? She did, however, just yet, nothing inconsequent—though she couldn't immediately have said what saved her; and by the time she had neatly folded her telegram she was doing something merely needful. "I wanted you simply to know—so that you mayn't by accident miss them. For it's the last," said Maggie.

"The last?"

"I take it as their good-bye." And she smiled as she could always smile. "They come in state—to take formal leave. They do everything that's proper. Tomorrow," she said, "they go to Southampton."

"If they do everything that's proper," the Prince presently asked, "why don't they at least come to dine?"

She hesitated, yet she lightly enough provided her answer. "That we must certainly ask them. It will be easy for you. But of course they're immensely taken—!"

He wondered. "So immensely taken that they can't—that your father can't—give you his last evening in England?"

This, for Maggie, was more difficult to meet; yet she was still not without her stop-gap. "That may be what they'll propose—that we shall go somewhere together, the four of us, for a celebration—except that, to round it thoroughly off, we ought also to have Fanny and the Colonel. They don't WANT them at tea, she quite sufficiently expresses; they polish them off, poor dears, they get rid of them, beforehand. They want only us together; and if they cut us down to tea," she continued, "as they cut Fanny and the Colonel down to luncheon, perhaps it's for the fancy, after all, of their keeping their last night in London for each other."

She said these things as they came to her; she was unable to keep them back, even though, as she heard herself, she might have been throwing everything to the winds. But wasn't that the right way—for sharing his last day of captivity with the man one adored? It was every moment more and more for her as if she were waiting with him in his prison—waiting with some gleam of remembrance of how noble captives in the French Revolution, the darkness of the Terror, used to make a feast, or a high discourse, of their last poor resources. If she had broken with everything now, every observance of all the past months, she must simply then take it so—take it that what she had worked for was too near, at last, to let him keep her head. She might have been losing her head verily in her husband's eyes—since he didn't know, all the while, that the sudden freedom of her words was but the diverted intensity of her disposition personally to seize him. He didn't know, either, that this was her manner—now she was with him—of beguiling audaciously the supremacy of suspense. For the people of the French Revolution, assuredly, there wasn't suspense; the scaffold, for those she was thinking of, was certain—whereas what Charlotte's telegram announced was, short of some incalculable error, clear liberation. Just the point, however, was in its being clearer to herself than to him; her clearnesses, clearances—those she had so all but abjectly laboured for—threatened to crowd upon her in the form of one of the clusters of angelic heads, the peopled shafts of light beating down through iron bars, that regale, on occasion, precisely, the fevered vision of those who are in chains. She was going to know, she felt, later on—was going to know with compunction, doubtless, on the very morrow, how thumpingly her heart had beaten at this foretaste of their being left together: she should judge at leisure the surrender she was making to the consciousness of complications about to be bodily lifted. She should judge at leisure even that avidity for an issue which was making so little of any complication but the unextinguished presence of the others; and indeed that she was already simplifying so much more than her husband came out for her next in the face with which she listened. He might certainly well be puzzled, in respect to his father-in-law and Mrs. Verver, by her glance at their possible preference for a concentrated evening. "But it isn't—is it?" he asked—"as if they were leaving each other?"

"Oh no; it isn't as if they were leaving each other. They're only bringing to a close—without knowing when it may open again—a time that has been, naturally, awfully interesting to them." Yes, she could talk so of their "time"—she was somehow sustained; she was sustained even to affirm more intensely her present possession of her ground. "They have their reasons—many things to think of; how can one tell? But there's always, also, the chance of his proposing to me that we shall have our last hours together; I mean that he and I shall. He may wish to take me off to dine with him somewhere alone—and to do it in memory of old days. I mean," the Princess went on, "the real old days; before my grand husband was invented and, much more, before his grand wife was: the wonderful times of his first great interest in what he has since done, his first great plans and opportunities, discoveries and bargains. The way we've sat together late, ever so late, in foreign restaurants, which he used to like; the way that, in every city in Europe, we've stayed on and on, with our elbows on the table and most of the lights put out, to talk over things he had that day seen or heard of or made his offer for, the things he had secured or refused or lost! There were places he took me to—you wouldn't believe!—for often he could only have left me with servants. If he should carry me off with him to-night, for old sake's sake, to the Earl's Court Exhibition, it will be a little—just a very, very little—like our young adventures." After which while Amerigo watched her, and in fact quite because of it, she had an inspiration, to which she presently yielded. If he was wondering what she would say next she had found exactly the thing. "In that case he will leave you Charlotte to take care of in our absence. You'll have to carry her off somewhere for your last evening; unless you may prefer to spend it with her here. I shall then see that you dine, that you have everything, quite beautifully. You'll be able to do as you like."

She couldn't have been sure beforehand, and had really not been; but the most immediate result of this speech was his letting her see that he took it for no cheap extravagance either of irony or of oblivion. Nothing in the world, of a truth, had ever been so sweet to her, as his look of trying to be serious enough to make no mistake about it. She troubled him—which hadn't been at all her purpose; she mystified him—which she couldn't help and, comparatively, didn't mind; then it came over her that he had, after all, a simplicity, very considerable, on which she had never dared to presume. It was a discovery—not like the other discovery she had once made, but giving out a freshness; and she recognised again in the light of it the number of the ideas of which he thought her capable. They were all, apparently, queer for him, but she had at least, with the lapse of the months, created the perception that there might be something in them; whereby he stared there, beautiful and sombre, at what she was at present providing him with. There was something of his own in his mind, to which, she was sure, he referred everything for a measure and a meaning; he had never let go of it, from the evening, weeks before, when, in her room, after his encounter with the Bloomsbury cup, she had planted it there by flinging it at him, on the question of her father's view of him, her determined "Find out for yourself!" She had been aware, during the months, that he had been trying to find out, and had been seeking, above all, to avoid the appearance of any evasions of such a form of knowledge as might reach him, with violence or with a penetration more insidious, from any other source. Nothing, however, had reached him; nothing he could at all conveniently reckon with had disengaged itself for him even from the announcement, sufficiently sudden, of the final secession of their companions. Charlotte was in pain, Charlotte was in torment, but he himself had given her reason enough for that; and, in respect to the rest of the whole matter of her obligation to follow her husband, that personage and she, Maggie, had so shuffled away every link between consequence and cause, that the intention remained, like some famous poetic line in a dead language, subject to varieties of interpretation. What renewed the obscurity was her strange image of their common offer to him, her father's and her own, of an opportunity to separate from Mrs. Verver with the due amount of form—and all the more that he was, in so pathetic a way, unable to treat himself to a quarrel with it on the score of taste. Taste, in him, as a touchstone, was now all at sea; for who could say but that one of her fifty ideas, or perhaps forty-nine of them, wouldn't be, exactly, that taste by itself, the taste he had always conformed to, had no importance whatever? If meanwhile, at all events, he felt her as serious, this made the greater reason for her profiting by it as she perhaps might never be able to profit again. She was invoking that reflection at the very moment he brought out, in reply to her last words, a remark which, though perfectly relevant and perfectly just, affected her at first as a high oddity. "They're doing the wisest thing, you know. For if they were ever to go—!" And he looked down at her over his cigar.

If they were ever to go, in short, it was high time, with her father's age, Charlotte's need of initiation, and the general magnitude of the job of their getting settled and seasoned, their learning to "live into" their queer future—it was high time that they should take up their courage. This was eminent sense, but it didn't arrest the Princess, who, the next moment, had found a form for her challenge. "But shan't you then so much as miss her a little? She's wonderful and beautiful, and I feel somehow as if she were dying. Not really, not physically," Maggie went on—"she's so far, naturally, splendid as she is, from having done with life. But dying for us—for you and me; and making us feel it by the very fact of there being so much of her left."

The Prince smoked hard a minute. "As you say, she's splendid, but there is—there always will be—much of her left. Only, as you also say, for others."

"And yet I think," the Princess returned, "that it isn't as if we had wholly done with her. How can we not always think of her? It's as if her unhappiness had been necessary to us—as if we had needed her, at her own cost, to build us up and start us."

He took it in with consideration, but he met it with a lucid inquiry. "Why do you speak of the unhappiness of your father's wife?"

They exchanged a long look—the time that it took her to find her reply. "Because not to—!"

"Well, not to—?"

"Would make me have to speak of him. And I can't," said Maggie, "speak of him."

"You 'can't'—?"

"I can't." She said it as for definite notice, not to be repeated. "There are too many things," she nevertheless added. "He's too great."

The Prince looked at his cigar-tip, and then as he put back the weed: "Too great for whom?" Upon which she hesitated, "Not, my dear, too great for you," he declared. "For me—oh, as much as you like."

"Too great for me is what I mean. I know why I think it," Maggie said. "That's enough."

He looked at her yet again as if she but fanned his wonder; he was on the very point, he judged, of asking her why she thought it. But her own eyes maintained their warning, and at the end of a minute he had uttered other words. "What's of importance is that you're his daughter. That at least we've got. And I suppose that, if I may say nothing else, I may say at least that I value it."

"Oh yes, you may say that you value it. I myself make the most of it."

This again she took in, letting it presently put forth for him a striking connection. "She ought to have known you. That's what's present to me. She ought to have understood you better."

"Better than you did?"

"Yes," he gravely maintained, "better than I did. And she didn't really know you at all. She doesn't know you now."

"Ah, yes she does!" said Maggie.

But he shook his head—he knew what he meant. "She not only doesn't understand you more than I, she understands you ever so much less. Though even I—!"

"Well, even you?" Maggie pressed as he paused. "Even I, even I even yet—!" Again he paused and the silence held them.

But Maggie at last broke it. "If Charlotte doesn't understand me, it is that I've prevented her. I've chosen to deceive her and to lie to her."

The Prince kept his eyes on her. "I know what you've chosen to do. But I've chosen to do the same."

"Yes," said Maggie after an instant—"my choice was made when I had guessed yours. But you mean," she asked, "that she understands YOU?"

"It presents small difficulty!"

"Are you so sure?" Maggie went on.

"Sure enough. But it doesn't matter." He waited an instant; then looking up through the fumes of his smoke, "She's stupid," he abruptly opined.

"O—oh!" Maggie protested in a long wail.

It had made him in fact quickly change colour. "What I mean is that she's not, as you pronounce her, unhappy." And he recovered, with this, all his logic. "Why is she unhappy if she doesn't know?"

"Doesn't know—?" She tried to make his logic difficult.

"Doesn't know that YOU know."

It came from him in such a way that she was conscious, instantly, of three or four things to answer. But what she said first was: "Do you think that's all it need take?" And before he could reply, "She knows, she knows!" Maggie proclaimed.

"Well then, what?"

But she threw back her head, she turned impatiently away from him. "Oh, I needn't tell you! She knows enough. Besides," she went on, "she doesn't believe us."

It made the Prince stare a little. "Ah, she asks too much!" That drew, however, from his wife another moan of objection, which determined in him a judgment. "She won't let you take her for unhappy."

"Oh, I know better than any one else what she won't let me take her for!"

"Very well," said Amerigo, "you'll see."

"I shall see wonders, I know. I've already seen them, and I'm prepared for them." Maggie recalled—she had memories enough. "It's terrible"—her memories prompted her to speak. "I see it ALWAYS terrible for women."

The Prince looked down in his gravity. "Everything's terrible, cara, in the heart of man. She's making her life," he said. "She'll make it."

His wife turned back upon him; she had wandered to a table, vaguely setting objects straight. "A little by the way then too, while she's about it, she's making ours." At this he raised his eyes, which met her own, and she held him while she delivered herself of some thing that had been with her these last minutes.

"You spoke just now of Charlotte's not having learned from you that I 'know.' Am I to take from you then that you accept and recognise my knowledge?"

He did the inquiry all the honours—visibly weighed its importance and weighed his response. "You think I might have been showing you that a little more handsomely?"

"It isn't a question of any beauty," said Maggie; "it's only a question of the quantity of truth."

"Oh, the quantity of truth!" the Prince richly, though ambiguously, murmured.

"That's a thing by itself, yes. But there are also such things, all the same, as questions of good faith."

"Of course there are!" the Prince hastened to reply. After which he brought up more slowly: "If ever a man, since the beginning of time, acted in good faith!" But he dropped it, offering it simply for that.

For that then, when it had had time somewhat to settle, like some handful of gold-dust thrown into the air—for that then Maggie showed herself, as deeply and strangely taking it. "I see." And she even wished this form to be as complete as she could make it. "I see."

The completeness, clearly, after an instant, had struck him as divine. "Ah, my dear, my dear, my dear—!" It was all he could say.

She wasn't talking, however, at large. "You've kept up for so long a silence—!"

"Yes, yes, I know what I've kept up. But will you do," he asked, "still one thing more for me?"

It was as if, for an instant, with her new exposure, it had made her turn pale. "Is there even one thing left?"

"Ah, my dear, my dear, my dear!"—it had pressed again in him the fine spring of the unspeakable. There was nothing, however, that the Princess herself couldn't say. "I'll do anything, if you'll tell me what."

"Then wait." And his raised Italian hand, with its play of admonitory fingers, had never made gesture more expressive. His voice itself dropped to a tone—! "Wait," he repeated. "Wait."

She understood, but it was as if she wished to have it from him. "Till they've been here, you mean?"

"Yes, till they've gone. Till they're away."

She kept it up. "Till they've left the country?" She had her eyes on him for clearness; these were the conditions of a promise—so that he put the promise, practically, into his response. "Till we've ceased to see them—for as long as God may grant! Till we're really alone."

"Oh, if it's only that—!" When she had drawn from him thus then, as she could feel, the thick breath of the definite—which was the intimate, the immediate, the familiar, as she hadn't had them for so long—she turned away again, she put her hand on the knob of the door. But her hand rested at first without a grasp; she had another effort to make, the effort of leaving him, of which everything that had just passed between them, his presence, irresistible, overcharged with it, doubled the difficulty. There was something—she couldn't have told what; it was as if, shut in together, they had come too far—too far for where they were; so that the mere act of her quitting him was like the attempt to recover the lost and gone. She had taken in with her something that, within the ten minutes, and especially within the last three or four, had slipped away from her—which it was vain now, wasn't it? to try to appear to clutch or to pick up. That consciousness in fact had a pang, and she balanced, intensely, for the lingering moment, almost with a terror of her endless power of surrender. He had only to press, really, for her to yield inch by inch, and she fairly knew at present, while she looked at him through her cloud, that the confession of this precious secret sat there for him to pluck. The sensation, for the few seconds, was extraordinary; her weakness, her desire, so long as she was yet not saving herself, flowered in her face like a light or a darkness. She sought for some word that would cover this up; she reverted to the question of tea, speaking as if they shouldn't meet sooner. "Then about five. I count on you."

On him too, however, something had descended; as to which this exactly gave him his chance. "Ah, but I shall see you—! No?" he said, coming nearer.

She had, with her hand still on the knob, her back against the door, so that her retreat, under his approach must be less than a step, and yet she couldn't for her life, with the other hand, have pushed him away. He was so near now that she could touch him, taste him, smell him, kiss him, hold him; he almost pressed upon her, and the warmth of his face—frowning, smiling, she mightn't know which; only beautiful and strange—was bent upon her with the largeness with which objects loom in dreams. She closed her eyes to it, and so the next instant, against her purpose, she had put out her hand, which had met his own and which he held. Then it was that, from behind her closed eyes, the right word came. "Wait!" It was the word of his own distress and entreaty, the word for both of them, all they had left, their plank now on the great sea. Their hands were locked, and thus she said it again. "Wait. Wait." She kept her eyes shut, but her hand, she knew, helped her meaning—which after a minute she was aware of his own had absorbed. He let her go—he turned away with this message, and when she saw him again his back was presented, as he had left her, and his face staring out of the window. She had saved herself and she got off.

XLII

Later on, in the afternoon, before the others arrived, the form of their reunion was at least remarkable: they might, in their great eastward drawing-room, have been comparing notes or nerves in apprehension of some stiff official visit. Maggie's mind, in its restlessness, even played a little with the prospect; the high cool room, with its afternoon shade, with its old tapestries uncovered, with the perfect polish of its wide floor reflecting the bowls of gathered flowers and the silver and linen of the prepared tea-table, drew from her a remark in which this whole effect was mirrored, as well as something else in the Prince's movement while he slowly paced and turned. "We're distinctly bourgeois!" she a trifle grimly threw off, as an echo of their old community; though to a spectator sufficiently detached they might have been quite the privileged pair they were reputed, granted only they were taken as awaiting the visit of Royalty. They might have been ready, on the word passed up in advance, to repair together to the foot of the staircase—the Prince somewhat in front, advancing indeed to the open doors and even going down, for all his princedom, to meet, on the stopping of the chariot, the august emergence. The time was stale, it was to be admitted, for incidents of magnitude; the September hush was in full possession, at the end of the dull day, and a couple of the long windows stood open to the balcony that overhung the desolation—the balcony from which Maggie, in the springtime, had seen Amerigo and Charlotte look down together at the hour of her return from the Regent's Park, near by, with her father, the Principino and Miss Bogle. Amerigo now again, in his punctual impatience, went out a couple of times and stood there; after which, as to report that nothing was in sight, he returned to the room with frankly nothing else to do. The Princess pretended to read; he looked at her as he passed; there hovered in her own sense the thought of other occasions when she had cheated appearances of agitation with a book. At last she felt him standing before her, and then she raised her eyes.

"Do you remember how, this morning, when you told me of this event, I asked you if there were anything particular you wished me to do? You spoke of my being at home, but that was a matter of course. You spoke of something else," he went on, while she sat with her book on her knee and her raised eyes; "something that makes me almost wish it may happen. You spoke," he said, "of the possibility of my seeing her alone. Do you know, if that comes," he asked, "the use I shall make of it?" And then as she waited: "The use is all before me."

"Ah, it's your own business now!" said his wife. But it had made her rise.

"I shall make it my own," he answered. "I shall tell her I lied to her."

"Ah no!" she returned.

"And I shall tell her you did."

She shook her head again. "Oh, still less!"

With which therefore they stood at difference, he with his head erect and his happy idea perched, in its eagerness, on his crest. "And how then is she to know?"

"She isn't to know."

"She's only still to think you don't—?"

"And therefore that I'm always a fool? She may think," said Maggie, "what she likes."

"Think it without my protest—?"

The Princess made a movement. "What business is it of yours?"

"Isn't it my right to correct her—?"

Maggie let his question ring—ring long enough for him to hear it himself; only then she took it up. "'Correct' her?"—and it was her own now that really rang. "Aren't you rather forgetting who she is?" After which, while he quite stared for it, as it was the very first clear majesty he had known her to use, she flung down her book and raised a warning hand. "The carriage. Come!"

The "Come!" had matched, for lucid firmness, the rest of her speech, and, when they were below, in the hall, there was a "Go!" for him, through the open doors and between the ranged servants, that matched even that. He received Royalty, bareheaded, therefore, in the persons of Mr. and Mrs. Verver, as it alighted on the pavement, and Maggie was at the threshold to welcome it to her house. Later on, upstairs again, she even herself felt still more the force of the limit of which she had just reminded him; at tea, in Charlotte's affirmed presence—as Charlotte affirmed it—she drew a long breath of richer relief. It was the strangest, once more, of all impressions; but what she most felt, for the half-hour, was that Mr. and Mrs. Verver were making the occasion easy. They were somehow conjoined in it, conjoined for a present effect as Maggie had absolutely never yet seen them; and there occurred, before long, a moment in which Amerigo's look met her own in recognitions that she couldn't suppress. The question of the amount of correction to which Charlotte had laid herself open rose and hovered, for the instant, only to sink, conspicuously, by its own weight; so high a pitch she seemed to give to the unconsciousness of questions, so resplendent a show of serenity she succeeded in making. The shade of the official, in her beauty and security, never for a moment dropped; it was a cool, high refuge, like the deep, arched recess of some coloured and gilded image, in which she sat and smiled and waited, drank her tea, referred to her husband and remembered her mission. Her mission had quite taken form—it was but another name for the interest of her great opportunity—that of representing the arts and the graces to a people languishing, afar off, in ignorance. Maggie had sufficiently intimated to the Prince, ten minutes before, that she needed no showing as to what their friend wouldn't consent to be taken for; but the difficulty now indeed was to choose, for explicit tribute of admiration, between the varieties of her nobler aspects. She carried it off, to put the matter coarsely, with a taste and a discretion that held our young woman's attention, for the first quarter-of-an-hour, to the very point of diverting it from the attitude of her overshadowed, her almost superseded companion. But Adam Verver profited indeed at this time, even with his daughter, by his so marked peculiarity of seeming on no occasion to have an attitude; and so long as they were in the room together she felt him still simply weave his web and play out his long fine cord, knew herself in presence of this tacit process very much as she had known herself at Fawns. He had a way, the dear man, wherever he was, of moving about the room, noiselessly, to see what it might contain; and his manner of now resorting to this habit, acquainted as he already was with the objects in view, expressed with a certain sharpness the intention of leaving his wife to her devices. It did even more than this; it signified, to the apprehension of the Princess, from the moment she more directly took thought of him, almost a special view of these devices, as actually exhibited in their rarity, with an independent, a settled appreciation of their general handsome adequacy, which scarcely required the accompaniment of his faint contemplative hum.

Charlotte throned, as who should say, between her hostess and her host, the whole scene having crystallised, as soon as she took her place, to the right quiet lustre; the harmony was not less sustained for being superficial, and the only approach to a break in it was while Amerigo remained standing long enough to let his father-in-law, vaguely wondering, to appeal to him, invite or address him, and then, in default of any such word, selected for presentation to the other visitor a plate of petits fours. Maggie watched her husband—if it now could be called watching—offer this refreshment; she noted the consummate way—for "consummate" was the term she privately applied—in which Charlotte cleared her acceptance, cleared her impersonal smile, of any betrayal, any slightest value, of consciousness; and then felt the slow surge of a vision that, at the end of another minute or two, had floated her across the room to where her father stood looking at a picture, an early Florentine sacred subject, that he had given her on her marriage. He might have been, in silence, taking his last leave of it; it was a work for which he entertained, she knew, an unqualified esteem. The tenderness represented for her by his sacrifice of such a treasure had become, to her sense, a part of the whole infusion, of the immortal expression; the beauty of his sentiment looked out at her, always, from the beauty of the rest, as if the frame made positively a window for his spiritual face: she might have said to herself, at this moment, that in leaving the thing behind him, held as in her clasping arms, he was doing the most possible toward leaving her a part of his palpable self. She put her hand over his shoulder, and their eyes were held again, together, by the abiding felicity; they smiled in emulation, vaguely, as if speech failed them through their having passed too far; she would have begun to wonder the next minute if it were reserved to them, for the last stage, to find their contact, like that of old friends reunited too much on the theory of the unchanged, subject to shy lapses.

"It's all right, eh?"

"Oh, my dear—rather!"

He had applied the question to the great fact of the picture, as she had spoken for the picture in reply, but it was as if their words for an instant afterwards symbolised another truth, so that they looked about at everything else to give them this extension. She had passed her arm into his, and the other objects in the room, the other pictures, the sofas, the chairs, the tables, the cabinets, the "important" pieces, supreme in their way, stood out, round them, consciously, for recognition and applause. Their eyes moved together from piece to piece, taking in the whole nobleness—quite as if for him to measure the wisdom of old ideas. The two noble persons seated, in conversation, at tea, fell thus into the splendid effect and the general harmony: Mrs. Verver and the Prince fairly "placed" themselves, however unwittingly, as high expressions of the kind of human furniture required, esthetically, by such a scene. The fusion of their presence with the decorative elements, their contribution to the triumph of selection, was complete and admirable; though, to a lingering view, a view more penetrating than the occasion really demanded, they also might have figured as concrete attestations of a rare power of purchase. There was much indeed in the tone in which Adam Verver spoke again, and who shall say where his thought stopped? "Le compte y est. You've got some good things."

Maggie met it afresh—"Ah, don't they look well?" Their companions, at the sound of this, gave them, in a spacious intermission of slow talk, an attention, all of gravity, that was like an ampler submission to the general duty of magnificence; sitting as still, to be thus appraised, as a pair of effigies of the contemporary great on one of the platforms of Madame Tussaud. "I'm so glad—for your last look."

With which, after Maggie—quite in the air—had said it, the note was struck indeed; the note of that strange accepted finality of relation, as from couple to couple, which almost escaped an awkwardness only by not attempting a gloss. Yes, this was the wonder, that the occasion defied insistence precisely because of the vast quantities with which it dealt—so that separation was on a scale beyond any compass of parting. To do such an hour justice would have been in some degree to question its grounds—which was why they remained, in fine, the four of them, in the upper air, united in the firmest abstention from pressure. There was no point, visibly, at which, face to face, either Amerigo or Charlotte had pressed; and how little she herself was in danger of doing so Maggie scarce needed to remember. That her father wouldn't, by the tip of a toe—of that she was equally conscious: the only thing was that, since he didn't, she could but hold her breath for what he would do instead. When, at the end of three minutes more, he said, with an effect of suddenness, "Well, Mag—and the Principino?" it was quite as if that were, by contrast, the hard, the truer voice.

She glanced at the clock. "I 'ordered' him for half-past five—which hasn't yet struck. Trust him, my dear, not to fail you!"

"Oh, I don't want HIM to fail me!" was Mr. Verver's reply; yet uttered in so explicitly jocose a relation to the possibilities of failure that even when, just afterwards, he wandered in his impatience to one of the long windows and passed out to the balcony, she asked herself but for a few seconds if reality, should she follow him, would overtake or meet her there. She followed him of necessity—it came, absolutely, so near to his inviting her, by stepping off into temporary detachment, to give the others something of the chance that she and her husband had so fantastically discussed. Beside him then, while they hung over the great dull place, clear and almost coloured now, coloured with the odd, sad, pictured, "old-fashioned" look that empty London streets take on in waning afternoons of the summer's end, she felt once more how impossible such a passage would have been to them, how it would have torn them to pieces, if they had so much as suffered its suppressed relations to peep out of their eyes. This danger would doubtless indeed have been more to be reckoned with if the instinct of each—she could certainly at least answer for her own—had not so successfully acted to trump up other apparent connexions for it, connexions as to which they could pretend to be frank.

"You mustn't stay on here, you know," Adam Verver said as a result of his unobstructed outlook. "Fawns is all there for you, of course—to the end of my tenure. But Fawns so dismantled," he added with mild ruefulness, "Fawns with half its contents, and half its best things, removed, won't seem to you, I'm afraid, particularly lively."

"No," Maggie answered, "we should miss its best things. Its best things, my dear, have certainly been removed. To be back there," she went on, "to be back there—!" And she paused for the force of her idea.

"Oh, to be back there without anything good—!" But she didn't hesitate now; she brought her idea forth. "To be back there without Charlotte is more than I think would do." And as she smiled at him with it, so she saw him the next instant take it—take it in a way that helped her smile to pass all for an allusion to what she didn't and couldn't say. This quantity was too clear—that she couldn't at such an hour be pretending to name to him what it was, as he would have said, "going to be," at Fawns or anywhere else, to want for HIM. That was now—and in a manner exaltedly, sublimely—out of their compass and their question; so that what was she doing, while they waited for the Principino, while they left the others together and their tension just sensibly threatened, what was she doing but just offer a bold but substantial substitute? Nothing was stranger moreover, under the action of Charlotte's presence, than the fact of a felt sincerity in her words. She felt her sincerity absolutely sound—she gave it for all it might mean. "Because Charlotte, dear, you know," she said, "is incomparable." It took thirty seconds, but she was to know when these were over that she had pronounced one of the happiest words of her life. They had turned from the view of the street; they leaned together against the balcony rail, with the room largely in sight from where they stood, but with the Prince and Mrs. Verver out of range. Nothing he could try, she immediately saw, was to keep his eyes from lighting; not even his taking out his cigarette-case and saying before he said anything else: "May I smoke?" She met it, for encouragement, with her "My dear!" again, and then, while he struck his match, she had just another minute to be nervous—a minute that she made use of, however, not in the least to falter, but to reiterate with a high ring, a ring that might, for all she cared, reach the pair inside: "Father, father—Charlotte's great!"

It was not till after he had begun to smoke that he looked at her. "Charlotte's great."

They could close upon it—such a basis as they might immediately feel it make; and so they stood together over it, quite gratefully, each recording to the other's eyes that it was firm under their feet. They had even thus a renewed wait, as for proof of it; much as if he were letting her see, while the minutes lapsed for their concealed companions, that this was finally just why—but just WHY! "You see," he presently added, "how right I was. Right, I mean, to do it for you."

"Ah, rather!" she murmured with her smile. And then, as to be herself ideally right: "I don't see what you would have done without her."

"The point was," he returned quietly, "that I didn't see what you were to do. Yet it was a risk."

"It was a risk," said Maggie—"but I believed in it. At least for myself!" she smiled.

"Well NOW," he smoked, "we see."

"We see."

"I know her better."

"You know her best."

"Oh, but naturally!" On which, as the warranted truth of it hung in the air—the truth warranted, as who should say, exactly by the present opportunity to pronounce, this opportunity created and accepted—she found herself lost, though with a finer thrill than she had perhaps yet known, in the vision of all he might mean. The sense of it in her rose higher, rose with each moment that he invited her thus to see him linger; and when, after a little more, he had said, smoking again and looking up, with head thrown back and hands spread on the balcony rail, at the grey, gaunt front of the house, "She's beautiful, beautiful!" her sensibility reported to her the shade of a new note. It was all she might have wished, for it was, with a kind of speaking competence, the note of possession and control; and yet it conveyed to her as nothing till now had done the reality of their parting. They were parting, in the light of it, absolutely on Charlotte's VALUE—the value that was filling the room out of which they had stepped as if to give it play, and with which the Prince, on his side, was perhaps making larger acquaintance. If Maggie had desired, at so late an hour, some last conclusive comfortable category to place him in for dismissal, she might have found it here in its all coming back to his ability to rest upon high values. Somehow, when all was said, and with the memory of her gifts, her variety, her power, so much remained of Charlotte's! What else had she herself meant three minutes before by speaking of her as great? Great for the world that was before her—that he proposed she should be: she was not to be wasted in the application of his plan. Maggie held to this then—that she wasn't to be wasted. To let his daughter know it he had sought this brief privacy. What a blessing, accordingly, that she could speak her joy in it! His face, meanwhile, at all events, was turned to her, and as she met his eyes again her joy went straight. "It's success, father."

"It's success. And even this," he added as the Principino, appearing alone, deep within, piped across an instant greeting—"even this isn't altogether failure!"

They went in to receive the boy, upon whose introduction to the room by Miss Bogle Charlotte and the Prince got up—seemingly with an impressiveness that had caused Miss Bogle not to give further effect to her own entrance. She had retired, but the Principino's presence, by itself, sufficiently broke the tension—the subsidence of which, in the great room, ten minutes later, gave to the air something of the quality produced by the cessation of a sustained rattle. Stillness, when the Prince and Princess returned from attending the visitors to their carriage, might have been said to be not so much restored as created; so that whatever next took place in it was foredoomed to remarkable salience. That would have been the case even with so natural, though so futile, a movement as Maggie's going out to the balcony again to follow with her eyes her father's departure. The carriage was out of sight—it had taken her too long solemnly to reascend, and she looked awhile only at the great grey space, on which, as on the room still more, the shadow of dusk had fallen. Here, at first, her husband had not rejoined her; he had come up with the boy, who, clutching his hand, abounded, as usual, in remarks worthy of the family archives; but the two appeared then to have proceeded to report to Miss Bogle. It meant something for the Princess that her husband had thus got their son out of the way, not bringing him back to his mother; but everything now, as she vaguely moved about, struck her as meaning so much that the unheard chorus swelled. Yet THIS above all—her just being there as she was and waiting for him to come in, their freedom to be together there always—was the meaning most disengaged: she stood in the cool twilight and took in, all about her, where it lurked, her reason for what she had done. She knew at last really why—and how she had been inspired and guided, how she had been persistently able, how, to her soul, all the while, it had been for the sake of this end. Here it was, then, the moment, the golden fruit that had shone from afar; only, what were these things, in the fact, for the hand and for the lips, when tested, when tasted—what were they as a reward? Closer than she had ever been to the measure of her course and the full face of her act, she had an instant of the terror that, when there has been suspense, always precedes, on the part of the creature to be paid, the certification of the amount. Amerigo knew it, the amount; he still held it, and the delay in his return, making her heart beat too fast to go on, was like a sudden blinding light on a wild speculation. She had thrown the dice, but his hand was over her cast.

He opened the door, however, at last—he hadn't been away ten minutes; and then, with her sight of him renewed to intensity, she seemed to have a view of the number. His presence alone, as he paused to look at her, somehow made it the highest, and even before he had spoken she had begun to be paid in full. With that consciousness, in fact, an extraordinary thing occurred; the assurance of her safety so making her terror drop that already, within the minute, it had been changed to concern for his own anxiety, for everything that was deep in his being and everything that was fair in his face. So far as seeing that she was "paid" went, he might have been holding out the money-bag for her to come and take it. But what instantly rose, for her, between the act and her acceptance was the sense that she must strike him as waiting for a confession. This, in turn, charged her with a new horror: if that was her proper payment she would go without money. His acknowledgment hung there, too monstrously, at the expense of Charlotte, before whose mastery of the greater style she had just been standing dazzled. All she now knew, accordingly, was that she should be ashamed to listen to the uttered word; all, that is, but that she might dispose of it on the spot forever.

"Isn't she too splendid?" she simply said, offering it to explain and to finish.

"Oh, splendid!" With which he came over to her.

"That's our help, you see," she added—to point further her moral.

It kept him before her therefore, taking in—or trying to—what she so wonderfully gave. He tried, too clearly, to please her—to meet her in her own way; but with the result only that, close to her, her face kept before him, his hands holding her shoulders, his whole act enclosing her, he presently echoed: "See"? I see nothing but you." And the truth of it had, with this force, after a moment, so strangely lighted his eyes that, as for pity and dread of them, she buried her own in his breast.

The End

The Outcry

BOOK FIRST

I

Staircase at the mansion by Joseph-Maria Charlemagne-Baudet (1824-1870)

"NO, my lord," Banks had replied, "no stranger has yet arrived. But I'll see if any one has come in—or who has." As he spoke, however, he observed Lady Sandgate's approach to the hall by the entrance giving upon the great terrace, and addressed her on her passing the threshold. "Lord John, my lady." With which, his duty majestically performed, he retired to the quarter—that of the main access to the spacious centre of the house—from which he had ushered the visitor.

This personage, facing Lady Sandgate as she paused there a moment framed by the large doorway to the outer expanses, the small pinkish paper of a folded telegram in her hand, had partly before him, as an immediate effect, the high wide interior, still breathing the quiet air and the fair pannelled security of the couple of hushed and stored centuries, in which certain of the reputed treasures of Dedborough Place beautifully disposed themselves; and then, through ample apertures and beyond the stately stone outworks of the great seated and supported house—uplifting terrace, balanced, balustraded steps and containing basins where splash and spray were at rest—all the rich composed extension of garden and lawn and park. An ancient, an assured elegance seemed to reign; pictures and preserved "pieces," cabinets and tapestries, spoke, each for itself, of fine selection and high distinction; while the originals of the old portraits, in more or less deserved salience, hung over the happy scene as the sworn members of a great guild might have sat, on the beautiful April day, at one of their annual feasts.

Such was the setting confirmed by generous time, but the handsome woman of considerably more than forty whose entrance had all but coincided with that of Lord John either belonged, for the eye, to no such complacent company or enjoyed a relation to it in which the odd twists and turns of history must have been more frequent than any dull avenue or easy sequence. Lady Sandgate was shiningly modern, and perhaps at no point more so than by the effect of her express repudiation of a mundane future certain to be more and more offensive to women of real quality and of formed taste. Clearly, at any rate, in her hands, the clue to the antique confidence had lost itself, and repose, however founded, had given way to curiosity—that is to speculation—however disguised. She might have consented, or even attained, to being but gracefully stupid, but she would presumably have confessed, if put on her trial for restlessness or for intelligence, that she *was*, after all, almost clever enough to be vulgar. Unmistakably, moreover, she had still, with her fine stature, her disciplined figure, her cherished complexion, her bright important hair, her kind bold eyes and her large constant smile, the degree of beauty that might pretend to put every other question by.

Lord John addressed her as with a significant manner that he might have had—that of a lack of need, or even of interest, for any explanation about herself: it would have been clear that he was apt to discriminate with sharpness among possible claims on his attention. "I luckily find you at least, Lady Sandgate—they tell me Theign's off somewhere."

She replied as with the general habit, on her side, of bland reassurance; it mostly had easier consequences—for herself—than the perhaps more showy creation of alarm. "Only off in the park—open to-day for a school-feast from Dedborough, as you may have made out from the avenue; giving good advice, at the top of his lungs, to four hundred and fifty children."

It was such a scene, and such an aspect of the personage so accounted for, as Lord John could easily take in, and his recognition familiarly smiled. "Oh he's so great on such occasions that I'm sorry to be missing it."

"I've *had* to miss it," Lady Sandgate sighed—"that is to miss the peroration. I've just left them, but he had even then been going on for twenty minutes, and I dare say that if you care to take a look you'll find him, poor dear victim of duty, still *at* it."

"I'll warrant—for, as I often tell him, he makes the idea of one's duty an awful thing to his friends by the extravagance with which he always overdoes it." And the image itself appeared in some degree to prompt this particular edified friend to look at his watch and consider. "I should like to come in for the grand *finale*, but I rattled over in a great measure to meet a party, as he calls himself—and calls, if you please, even me!—who's motoring down by appointment and whom I think I should be here to receive; as well as a little, I confess, in the hope of a glimpse of Lady Grace: if you can perhaps imagine *that!*"

"I can imagine it perfectly," said Lady Sandgate, whom evidently no perceptions of that general order ever cost a strain. "It quite sticks out of you, and every one moreover has for some time past been waiting to see. But you haven't then," she added, "come from town?"

"No, I'm for three days at Chanter with my mother; whom, as she kindly lent me her car, I should have rather liked to bring."

Lady Sandgate left the unsaid, in this connection, languish no longer than was decent. "But whom you doubtless had to leave, by her preference, just settling down to bridge."

"Oh, to sit down would imply that my mother at some moment of the day gets up——!"

"Which the Duchess never does?"—Lady Sand-gate only asked to be allowed to show how she saw it. "She fights to the last, invincible; gathering in the spoils and only routing her friends?" She abounded genially in her privileged vision. "Ah yes—we know something of that!"

Lord John, who was a young man of a rambling but not of an idle eye, fixed her an instant with a surprise that was yet not steeped in compassion. "You too then?"

She wouldn't, however, too meanly narrow it down. "Well, in this house generally; where I'm so often made welcome, you see, and where——"

"Where," he broke in at once, "your jolly good footing quite sticks out of *you*, perhaps you'll let me say!"

She clearly didn't mind his seeing her ask herself how she should deal with so much rather juvenile intelligence; and indeed she could only decide to deal quite simply. "You can't say more than I feel—and am proud to feel!—as being of comfort when they're worried."

This but fed the light flame of his easy perception—which lighted for him, if she would, all the facts equally. "And they're worried now, you imply, because my terrible mother is capable of heavy gains and of making a great noise if she isn't paid? I ought to mind speaking of that truth," he went on as with a practised glance in the direction of delicacy; "but I think I should like you to know that I myself am not a bit ignorant of why it has made such an impression here."

Lady Sandgate forestalled his knowledge. "Because poor Kitty Imber—who should either never touch a card or else learn to suffer in silence, as I've had to, goodness knows!—has thrown herself, with her impossible big debt, upon her father? whom she thinks herself entitled to 'look to' even more as a lovely young widow with a good jointure than she formerly did as the mere most beautiful daughter at home."

She had put the picture a shade interrogatively, but this was as nothing to the note of free inquiry in Lord John's reply. "You mean that our lovely young widows—to say nothing of lovely young wives—ought by this time to have made out, in predicaments, how to turn round?"

His temporary hostess, even with his eyes on her, appeared to decide after a moment not wholly to disown his thought. But she smiled for it. "Well, in that set——!"

"My mother's set?" However, if she could smile he could laugh. "I'm much obliged!"

"Oh," she qualified, "I don't criticise her Grace; but the ways and traditions and tone of this house——"

"Make it"—he took her sense straight from her—"the house in England where one feels most the false note of a dishevelled and bankrupt elder daughter breaking in with a list of her gaming debts—to say nothing of others!—and wishing to have at least those wiped out in the interest of her reputation? Exactly so," he went on before she could meet it with a diplomatic ambiguity; "and just that, I assure you, is a large part of the reason I like to come here—since I personally don't come with any such associations."

"Not the association of bankruptcy—no; as you represent the payee!"

The young man appeared to regard this imputation for a moment almost as a liberty taken. "How do you know so well, Lady Sandgate, what I represent?"

She bethought herself—but briefly and bravely. "Well, don't you represent, by your own admission, certain fond aspirations? Don't you represent the belief—very natural, I grant—that more than *one* perverse and extravagant flower will be unlikely on such a fine healthy old stem; and, consistently with that, the hope of arranging with our admirable host here that he shall lend a helpful hand to your commending yourself to dear Grace?"

Lord John might, in the light of these words, have felt any latent infirmity in such a pretension exposed; but as he stood there facing his chances he would have struck a spectator as resting firmly enough on some felt residuum of advantage: whether this were cleverness or luck, the strength of his backing or that of his sincerity. Even with the young woman to whom our friends' reference thus broadened still a vague quantity for us, you would have taken his sincerity as quite possible—and this despite an odd element in him that you might have described as a certain delicacy of brutality. This younger son of a noble matron recognised even by himself as terrible enjoyed in no immediate or aggressive manner any imputable private heritage or privilege of arrogance. He would on the contrary have irradiated fineness if his lustre hadn't been a little prematurely dimmed. Active yet insubstantial, he was slight and short and a trifle too punctually, though not yet quite lamentably, bald. Delicacy was in the arch of his eyebrow, the finish of his facial line, the economy of "treatment" by which his negative nose had been enabled to look important and his meagre mouth to smile its spareness away.

He had pleasant but hard little eyes—they glittered, handsomely, without promise—and a neatness, a coolness and an ease, a clear instinct for making point take, on his behalf, the place of weight and immunity that of capacity, which represented somehow the art of living at a high pitch and yet at a low cost. There was that in his satisfied air which still suggested sharp wants—and this was withal the ambiguity; for the temper of these appetites or views was certainly, you would have concluded, not such as always to sacrifice to form. If he really, for instance, wanted Lady Grace, the passion or the sense of his interest in it would scarce have been considerably irritable.

"May I ask what you mean," he inquired of Lady Sandgate, "by the question of my 'arranging'?"

"I mean that you're the very clever son of a very clever mother."

"Oh, I'm less clever than you think," he replied—"if you really think it of me at all; and mamma's a good sight cleverer!"

"Than I think?" Lady Sandgate echoed. "Why, she's the person in all our world I would gladly most resemble—for her general ability to put what she wants through." But she at once added: "That is if—!" pausing on it with a smile.

"If what then?"

"Well, if I could be absolutely certain to have all in her kinds of cleverness without exception—and to have them," said Lady Sandgate, "to the very end."

He definitely, he almost contemptuously declined to follow her. "The very end of what?"

She took her choice as amid all the wonderful directions there might be, and then seemed both to risk and to reserve something. "Say of her so wonderfully successful *general* career."

It doubtless, however, warranted him in appearing to cut insinuations short. "When you're as clever as she you'll be as good." To which he subjoined: "You don't begin to have the opportunity of knowing how good she is." This pronouncement, to whatever comparative obscurity it might appear to relegate her, his interlocutress had to take—he was so prompt with a more explicit challenge. "What is it exactly that you suppose yourself to know?"

Lady Sandgate had after a moment, in her supreme good humour, decided to take everything. "I always proceed on the assumption that I know everything, because that makes people tell me."

"It wouldn't make we," he quite rang out, "if I didn't want to! But as it happens," he allowed, "there's a question it would be convenient to me to put to you. You must be, with your charming unconventional relation with him, extremely in Theign's confidence."

She waited a little as for more. "Is that your question—*whether* I am?"

"No, but if you are you'll the better answer it"

She had no objection then to answering it beautifully. "We're the best friends in the world; he has been really my providence, as a lone woman with almost nobody and nothing of her own, and I feel my footing here, as so frequent and yet so discreet a visitor, simply perfect But I'm happy to say that—for my pleasure when I'm really curious—this doesn't close to me the sweet resource of occasionally guessing things."

"Then I hope you've ground for believing that if I go the right way about it he's likely to listen to me."

Lady Sandgate measured her ground—which scarce seemed extensive. "The person he most listens to just now—and in fact at any time, as you must have seen for yourself—is that arch-tormentor, or at least beautiful wheedler, his elder daughter."

"Lady Imber's *here?*" Lord John alertly asked.

"She arrived last night and—as we've other visitors—seems to have set up a side-show in the garden."

"Then she'll 'draw' of course immensely, as she always does. But her sister won't be in that case with her," the young man supposed.

"Because Grace feels herself naturally an independent show? So she well may," said Lady Sandgate, "but I must tell you that when I last noticed them sure Kitty was in the very act of leading her away."

Lord John figured it a moment. "Lady Imber"—he ironically enlarged the figure—"*can* lead people away."

"Oh, dear Grace," his companion returned, "happens fortunately to be firm!"

This seemed to strike him for a moment as equivocal. "Not against *me,* however—you don't mean? You don't think she has a beastly prejudice——?"

"Surely you can judge about it; as knowing best what may—or what mayn't—have happened between you."

"Well, I try to judge"—and such candour as was possible to Lord John seemed to sit for a moment on his brow. "But I'm in fear of seeing her too much as I want to see her."

There was an appeal in it that Lady Sandgate might have been moved to meet "Are you absolutely in earnest about her?"

"Of course I am—why shouldn't I be? But," he said with impatience, "I want help."

"Very well then, that's what Lady Imber's giving you." And as it appeared to take him time to read into these words their full sense, she produced others, and so far did help him—though the effort was in a degree that of her exhibiting with some complacency her own unassisted control of stray signs and shy lights. "By telling her, by bringing it home to her, that if she'll make up her mind to accept you the Duchess will do the handsome thing. Handsome, I mean, by *her.*"

Lord John, appropriating for his convenience the truth in this, yet regarded it as open to a becoming, an improving touch from himself. "Well, and by *me.*" To which he added with more of a challenge in it: "But you really know what my mother will do?"

"By my system," Lady Sandgate smiled, "you see I've guessed. What your mother will do is what brought you over!"

"Well, it's that," he allowed—"and something else."

"Something else?" she derisively echoed. "I should think 'that,' for an ardent lover, would have been enough."

"Ah, but it's all one Job! I mean it's one idea," he hastened to explain—"if you think Lady Imber's really acting on her."

"Mightn't you go and see?"

"I would in a moment if I hadn't to look out for another matter too." And he renewed his attention to his watch. "I mean getting straight at my American, the party I just mentioned——"

But she had already taken him up. "You too have an American and a 'party,' and yours also motors down——?"

"Mr. Breckenridge Bender." Lord John named him with a shade of elation.

She gaped at the fuller light "You *know* my Breckenridge?—who I hoped was coming for me!"

Lord John as freely, but more gaily, wondered. "Had he told you so?"

She held out, opened, the telegram she had kept folded in her hand since her entrance. "He has sent me that—which, delivered to me ten minutes ago out there, has brought me in to receive him."

The young man read out this missive. "'Failing to find you in Bruton Street, start in pursuit and hope to overtake you about four.'" It did involve an ambiguity. "Why, he has been engaged these three days to coincide with myself, and not to fail of him has been part of my business."

Lady Sandgate, in her demonstrative way, appealed to the general rich scene. "Then why does he say it's me he's pursuing?"

He seemed to recognise promptly enough in her the sense of a menaced monopoly. "My dear lady, he's pursuing expensive works of art."

"By which you imply that I'm one?" She might have been wound up by her disappointment to almost any irony.

"I imply—or rather I affirm—that every handsome woman is! But what he arranged with me about," Lord John explained, "was that he should see the Dedborough pictures in general and the great Sir Joshua in particular—of which he had heard so much and to which I've been thus glad to assist him."

This news, however, with its lively interest, but deepened the listener's mystification. "Then why—this whole week that I've been in the house—hasn't our good friend here mentioned to me his coming?"

"Because our good friend here has had no reason"—Lord John could treat it now as simple enough. "Good as he is in all ways, he's so best of all about showing the house and its contents that I haven't even thought necessary to write him that I'm introducing Breckenridge."

"I should have been happy to introduce him," Lady Sandgate just quavered—"if I had at all known he wanted it."

Her companion weighed the difference between them and appeared to pronounce it a trifle he didn't care a fig for. "I surrender you that privilege then—of presenting him to his host—if I've seemed to you to snatch it from you." To which Lord John added, as with liberality unrestricted, "But I've been taking him about to see what's worth while—as only last week to Lady Lappington's Longhi."

This revelation, though so casual in its form, fairly drew from Lady Sandgate, as she took it in, an interrogative wail. "Her Longhi?"

"Why, don't you know her great Venetian family group, the What-do-you-call-'ems?—seven full-length figures, each one a gem, for which he paid her her price before he left the house."

She could but make it more richly resound—almost stricken, lost in her wistful thought: "Seven full-length figures? Her price?"

"Eight thousand—slap down. Bender knows," said Lord John, "what he wants."

"And does he want only"—her wonder grew and grew—

"What-do-you-call-'ems'?"

"He most usually wants what he can't have." Lord John made scarce more of it than that. "But, awfully hard up as I fancy her, Lady Lappington went at him."

It determined in his friend a boldly critical attitude. "How horrible—at the rate things are leaving us!" But this was far from the end of her interest. "And is that the way he pays?"

"Before he leaves the house?" Lord John lived it amusedly over. "Well, she took care of that."

"How incredibly vulgar!" It all had, however, for Lady Sandgate, still other connections—which might have attenuated Lady Lappington's case, though she didn't glance at this. "He makes the most scandalous eyes—the ruffian!—at my great-grandmother." And then as richly to enlighten any blankness: "My tremendous Lawrence, don't you know?—in her wedding-dress, down to her knees; with such extraordinarily speaking eyes, such lovely arms and hands, such wonderful flesh-tints: universally considered the masterpiece of the artist."

Lord John seemed to look a moment not so much at the image evoked, in which he wasn't interested, as at certain possibilities lurking behind it. "And are you going to sell the masterpiece of the artist?"

She held her head high. "I've indignantly refused—for all his pressing me so hard."

"Yet that's what he nevertheless pursues you to-day to keep up?"

The question had a little the ring of those of which the occupant of a witness-box is mostly the subject, but Lady Sandgate was so far as this went an imperturbable witness. "I need hardly fear it perhaps if—in the light of what you tell me of your arrangement with him—his pursuit becomes, where I am concerned, a figure of speech."

"Oh," Lord John returned, "he kills two birds with one stone—he sees both Sir Joshua and you."

This version of the case had its effect, for the moment, on his fair associate. "Does he want to buy their pride and glory?"

The young man, however, struck on his own side, became at first but the bright reflector of her thought. "Is that wonder for sale?"

She closed her eyes as with the shudder of hearing such words. "Not, surely, by any monstrous chance! Fancy dear, proud Theign——!"

"I can't fancy him—no!" And Lord John appeared to renounce the effort. "But a cat may look at a king and a sharp funny Yankee at anything."

These things might be, Lady Sandgate's face and gesture apparently signified; but another question diverted her. "You're clearly a wonderful showman, but do you mind my asking you whether you're on such an occasion a—well, a closely interested one?"

"'Interested'?" he echoed; though it wasn't to gain time, he showed, for he would in that case have taken more. "To the extent, you mean, of my little percentage?" And then as in silence she but kept a slightly grim smile on him: "Why do you ask if—with your high delicacy about your great-grandmother—you've nothing to place?"

It took her a minute to say, while her fine eye only rolled; but when she spoke that organ boldly rested and the truth vividly appeared. "I ask because people like you, Lord John, strike me as dangerous to the—how shall I name it?—the common weal; and because of my general strong feeling that we don't want any more of our national treasures (for I regard my great-grandmother as national) to be scattered about the world."

"There's much in this country and age," he replied in an off-hand manner, "to be said about that," The present, however, was not the time to say it all; so he said something else instead, accompanying it with a smile that signified sufficiency. "To my friends, I need scarcely remark to you, I'm all the friend."

She had meanwhile seen the butler reappear by the door that opened to the terrace, and though the high, bleak, impersonal approach of this functionary was ever, and more and more at every step, a process to defy interpretation, long practice evidently now enabled her to suggest, as she turned again to her fellow-visitor a reading of it. "It's the friend then clearly who's wanted in the park."

She might, by the way Banks looked at her, have snatched from his hand a missive addressed to another; though while he addressed himself to her companion he allowed for her indecorum sufficiently to take it up where she had left it. "By her ladyship, my lord, who sends to hope you'll join them below the terrace."

"Ah, Grace hopes," said Lady Sandgate for the young man's encouragement. "There you are!"

Lord John took up the motor-cap he had lain down on coming in. "I rush to Lady Grace, but don't demoralise Bender!" And he went forth to the terrace and the gardens.

Banks looked about as for some further exercise of his high function. "Will you have tea, my lady?"

This appeared to strike her as premature. "Oh, thanks—when they all come in."

"They'll scarcely *all*, my lady"—he indicated respectfully that he knew what he was talking about. "There's tea in her ladyship's tent; but," he qualified, "it has also been ordered for the saloon."

"Ah then," she said cheerfully, "Mr. Bender will be glad—!" And she became, with this, aware of the approach of another visitor. Banks considered, up and down, the gentleman ushered in, at the left, by the footman who had received him at the main entrance to the house. "Here he must be, my lady." With which he retired to the spacious opposite quarter, where he vanished, while the footman, his own office performed, retreated as he had come, and Lady Sandgate, all hospitality, received the many-sided author of her specious telegram, of Lord John's irritating confidence and of Lady Lappington's massive cheque.

II

Drawing room (c. 1840) by Thomas Leeson the Elder Rowbotham (1782-1853)

Having greeted him with an explicitly gracious welcome and both hands out, she had at once gone on: "You'll of course have tea?—in the saloon."

But his mechanism seemed of the type that has to expand and revolve before sounding. "Why; the very first thing?"

She only desired, as her laugh showed, to accommodate. "Ah, have it the last if you like!"

"You see your English teas—!" he pleaded as he looked about him, so immediately and frankly interested in the place and its contents that his friend could only have taken this for the very glance with which he must have swept Lady Lappington's inferior scene.

"They're too much for you?"

"Well, they're too many. I think I've had two or three on the road—at any rate my man did. I like to do business before—" But his sequence dropped as his eye caught some object across the wealth of space.

She divertedly picked it up. "Before tea, Mr. Bender?"

"Before everything, Lady Sandgate." He was immensely genial, but a queer, quaint, rough-edged distinctness somehow kept it safe—for himself.

"Then you've *come* to do business?" Her appeal and her emphasis melted as into a caress—which, however, spent itself on his large high person as he consented, with less of demonstration but more of attention, to look down upon her. She could therefore but reinforce it by an intenser note. "To tell me you *will* treat?"

Mr. Bender had six feet of stature and an air as of having received benefits at the hands of fortune. Substantial, powerful, easy, he shone as with a glorious cleanness, a supplied and equipped and appointed sanity and security; aids to action that might have figured a pair of very ample wings—wide pinions for the present conveniently folded, but that he would certainly on occasion agitate for great efforts and spread for great flights. These things would have made him quite an admirable, even a worshipful, image of full-blown life and character, had not the affirmation and the emphasis halted in one important particular. Fortune, felicity, nature, the perverse or interfering old fairy at his cradle-side—whatever the ministering power might have been—had simply overlooked and neglected his vast wholly-shaven face, which thus showed not so much for perfunctorily scamped as for not treated, as for neither formed nor fondled nor finished, at all. Nothing seemed to have been done for it but what the razor and the sponge, the tooth-brush and the looking-glass could officiously do; it had in short resisted any possibly finer attrition at the hands of fifty years of offered experience. It had developed on the lines, if lines they could be called, of the mere scoured and polished and initialled "mug" rather than to any effect of a composed physiognomy; though we must at the same time add that its wearer carried this featureless disk as with the warranted confidence that might have attended a warning headlight or a glaring motor-lamp. The object, however one named it, showed you at least where he was, and most often that he was straight upon you. It was fearlessly and resistingly across the path of his advance that Lady Sandgate had thrown herself, and indeed with such success that he soon connected her demonstration with a particular motive. "For your grandmother, Lady Sandgate?" he then returned.

"For my grandmother's *mother*, Mr. Bender—the most beautiful woman of her time and the greatest of all Lawrences, no matter whose; as you quite acknowledged, you know, in our talk in Bruton Street."

Mr. Bender bethought himself further—yet drawing it out; as if the familiar fact of his being "made up to" had never had such special softness and warmth of pressure. "Do you want very, *very* much——?"

She had already caught him up. "'Very, very much' for her? Well, Mr. Bender," she smilingly replied, "I think I should like her full value."

"I mean"—he kindly discriminated—"do you want so badly to work her off?"

"It would be an intense convenience to me—so much so that your telegram made me at once fondly hope you'd be arriving to conclude."

Such measure of response as he had good-naturedly given her was the mere frayed edge of a mastering detachment, the copious, impatient range elsewhere of his true attention. Somehow, however, he still seemed kind even while, turning his back upon her, he moved off to look at one of the several, the famous Dedborough pictures—stray specimens, by every presumption, lost a little in the whole bright bigness. "'Conclude'?" he echoed as he approached a significantly small canvas. "You ladies want to get there before the road's so much as laid or the country's safe! Do you know what this *here* is?" he at once went on.

"Oh, you can't have *that!*" she cried as with full authority—"and you must really understand that you can't have everything. You mustn't expect to ravage Dedborough."

He had his nose meanwhile close to the picture. "I guess it's a bogus Cuyp—but I know Lord Theign *has* things. He won't do business?"

"He's not in the least, and can never be, in my tight place," Lady Sandgate replied; "but he's as proud as he's kind, dear man, and as solid as he's proud; so that if you came down under a different impression—!" Well, she could only exhale the folly of his error with an unction that represented, whatever he might think of it, all her competence to answer for their host.

He scarce thought of it enough, on any side, however, to be diverted from prior dispositions. "I came on an understanding that I should find my friend Lord John, and that Lord Theign would, on his introduction, kindly let me look round. But being before lunch in Bruton Street I knocked at your door——"

"For another look," she quickly interposed, "at my Lawrence?"

"For another look at *you*, Lady Sandgate—your great-grandmother wasn't required. Informed you were here, and struck with the coincidence of my being myself presently due," he went on, "I despatched you my wire, on coming away, just to keep up your spirits."

"You *don't* keep them up, you depress them to anguish," she almost passionately protested, "when you don't tell me you'll treat!"

He paused in his preoccupation, his perambulation, conscious evidently of no reluctance that was worth a scene with so charming and so hungry a woman. "Well, if it's a question of your otherwise suffering torments, may I have another interview with the old lady?"

"Dear Mr. Bender, she's in the flower of her youth; she only yearns for interviews, and you may have," Lady Sandgate earnestly declared, "as many as you like."

"Oh, you must be there to protect me!"

"Then as soon as I return——!"

"Well,"—it clearly cost him little to say—"I'll come right round."

She joyously registered the vow. "Only meanwhile then, please, never a word!"

"Never a word, certainly. But where all this time," Mr. Bender asked, "is Lord John?"

Lady Sandgate, as he spoke, found her eyes meeting those of a young woman who, presenting herself from without, stood framed in the doorway to the terrace; a slight fair grave young woman, of middle, stature and simply dressed, whose brow showed clear even under the heavy shade of a large hat surmounted with big black bows and feathers. Her eyes had vaguely questioned those of her elder, who at once replied to the gentleman forming the subject of their inquiry: "Lady Grace must know." At this the young woman came forward, and Lady Sandgate introduced the visitor. "My dear Grace, this is Mr. Breckenridge Bender."

The younger daughter of the house might have arrived in preoccupation, but she had urbanity to spare. "Of whom Lord John has told me," she returned, "and whom I'm glad to see. Lord John," she explained to his waiting friend, "is detained a moment in the park, open to-day to a big Temperance school-feast, where our party is mostly gathered; so that if you care to go out—!" She gave him in fine his choice.

But this was clearly a thing that, in the conditions, Mr. Bender wasn't the man to take precipitately; though his big useful smile disguised his prudence. "Are there any pictures in the park?"

Lady Grace's facial response represented less humour perhaps, but more play. "We find our park itself rather a picture."

Mr. Bender's own levity at any rate persisted. "With a big Temperance school-feast?"

"Mr. Bender's a great judge of pictures," Lady Sandgate said as to forestall any impression of excessive freedom.

"Will there be more tea?" he pursued, almost presuming on this.

It showed Lady Grace for comparatively candid and literal. "Oh, there'll be plenty of tea."

This appeared to determine Mr. Bender. "Well, Lady Grace, I'm after pictures, but I take them 'neat.' May I go right round here?"

"Perhaps, love," Lady Sandgate at once said, "you'll let me show him."

"A moment, dear"—Lady Grace gently demurred. "Do go round," she conformably added to Mr. Bender; "take your ease and your time. Everything's open and visible, and, with our whole company dispersed, you'll have the place to yourself."

He rose, in his genial mass, to the opportunity. "I'll be in clover—sure!" But present to him was the richest corner of the pasture, which he could fluently enough name. "And I'll find 'The Beautiful Duchess of Waterbridge'?"

She indicated, off to the right, where a stately perspective opened, the quarter of the saloon to which we have seen Mr. Banks retire. "At the very end of *those* rooms."

He had wide eyes for the vista. "About thirty in a row, hey?" And he was already off. "I'll work right through!"

III

Ladies gathered (1894) by Jozsef Rippl-Ronai (1861-1927)

Left with her friend, Lady Grace had a prompt question. "Lord John warned me he was 'funny'—but you already know him?"

There might have been a sense of embarrassment in the way in which, as to gain time, Lady Sandgate pointed, instead of answering, to the small picture pronounced upon by Mr. Bender. "He thinks your little Cuyp a fraud."

"That one?" Lady Grace could but stare. "The wretch!" However, she made, without alarm, no more of it; she returned to her previous question. "You've met him before?"

"Just a little—in town. Being 'after pictures'" Lady Sandgate explained, "he has been after my great-grandmother."

"She," said Lady Grace with amusement, "must have found him funny! But he can clearly take care of himself, while Kitty takes care of Lord John, and while you, if you'll be so good, go back to support father—in the hour of his triumph: which he wants you so much to witness that he complains of your desertion and goes so far as to speak of you as sneaking away."

Lady Sandgate, with a slight flush, turned it over. "I delight in his triumph, and whatever I do is at least above board; but if it's a question of support, aren't you yourself failing him quite as much?"

This had, however, no effect on the girl's confidence. "Ah, my dear, I'm not at all the same thing, and as I'm the person in the world he least misses—" Well, such a fact spoke for itself.

"You've been free to return and wait for Lord John?"—that was the sense in which the elder woman appeared to prefer to understand it as speaking.

The tone of it, none the less, led her companion immediately, though very quietly, to correct her. "I've not come back to wait for Lord John."

"Then he hasn't told you—if you've talked—with what idea he has come?"

Lady Grace had for a further correction the same shade of detachment. "Kitty has told me—what it suits her to pretend to suppose."

"And Kitty's pretensions and suppositions always go with what happens—at the moment, among all her wonderful happenings—to suit her?"

Lady Grace let that question answer itself—she took the case up further on. "What I can't make out is why this *should* so suit her!"

"And what *I* can't!" said Lady Sandgate without gross honesty and turning away after having watched the girl a moment. She nevertheless presently faced her again to follow this speculation up. "Do you like him enough to risk the chance of Kitty's being for once right?"

Lady Grace gave it a thought—with which she moved away. "I don't know how much I like him!"

"Nor how little!" cried her friend, who evidently found amusement in the tone of it. "And you're not disposed to take the time to find out? He's at least better than the others."

"The 'others'?"—Lady Grace was blank for them.

"The others of his set."

"Oh, his set! That wouldn't be difficult—by what I imagine of some of them. But he means well enough," the girl added; "he's very charming and does me great honour."

It determined in her companion, about to leave her, another brief arrest. "Then may I tell your father?"

This in turn brought about in Lady Grace an immediate drop of the subject. "Tell my father, please, that I'm expecting Mr. Crimble; of whom I've spoken to him even if he doesn't remember, and who bicycles this afternoon ten miles over from where he's staying—with some people we don't know—to look at the pictures, about which he's awfully keen."

Lady Sandgate took it in. "Ah, like Mr. Bender?"

"No, not at all, I think, like Mr. Bender."

This appeared to move in the elder woman some deeper thought "May I ask then—if one's to meet him—who he is?"

"Oh, father knows—or ought to—that I sat next him, in London, a month ago, at dinner, and that he then told me he was working, tooth and nail, at what he called the wonderful modern science of Connoisseurship—which is upsetting, as perhaps you're not aware, all the old-fashioned canons of art-criticism, everything we've stupidly thought right and held dear; that he was to spend Easter in these parts, and that he should like greatly to be allowed some day to come over and make acquaintance with our things. I told him," Lady Grace wound up, "that nothing would be easier; a note from him arrived before dinner——"

Lady Sandgate jumped the rest "And it's for him you've come in."

"It's for him I've come in," the girl assented with serenity.

"Very good—though he sounds most detrimental! But will you first just tell me *this*—whether when you sent in ten minutes ago for Lord John to come out to you it was wholly of your own movement?" And she followed it up as her young friend appeared to hesitate. "Was it because you knew why he had arrived?"

The young friend hesitated still. "'Why '?"

"So particularly to speak to you."

"Since he was expected and mightn't know where I was," Lady Grace said after an instant, "I wanted naturally to be civil to him."

"And had he time there to tell you," Lady Sand-gate asked, "how very civil he wants to be to you?"

"No, only to tell me that his friend—who's off there—was coming; for Kitty at once appropriated him and was still in possession when I came away." Then, as deciding at last on perfect frankness, Lady Grace went on: "If you want to know, I sent for news of him because Kitty insisted on my doing so; saying, so very oddly and quite in her own way, that she herself didn't wish to 'appear in it.' She had done nothing but say to me for an hour, rather worryingly, what you've just said—that it's me he's what, like Mr. Bender, she calls 'after'; but as soon as he appeared she pounced on him, and I left him—I assure you quite resignedly—in her hands."

"She wants"—it was easy for Lady Sandgate to remark—"to talk of you to him."

"I don't know *what* she wants," the girl replied as with rather a tired patience; "Kitty wants so many things at once. She always wants money, in quantities, to begin with—and all to throw so horribly away; so that whenever I see her 'in' so very deep with any one I always imagine her appealing for some new tip as to how it's to be come by."

"Kitty's an abyss, I grant you, and with my disinterested devotion to your father—in requital of all his kindness to me since Lord Sandgate's death and since your mother's—I can never be too grateful to you, my dear, for your being so different a creature. But what is she going to gain financially," Lady Sand-gate pursued with a strong emphasis on her adverb, "by working up our friend's confidence in your listening to him—if you *are* to listen?"

"I haven't in the least engaged to listen," said Lady Grace—"it will depend on the music he makes!" But she added with light cynicism: "Perhaps she's to gain a commission!"

"On his fairly getting you?" And then as the girl assented by silence: "Is he in a position to pay her one?" Lady Sandgate asked.

"I dare say the Duchess is!"

"But do you see the Duchess *producing* money—with all that Kitty, as we're not ignorant, owes her? Hundreds and hundreds and hundreds!"—Lady Sandgate piled them up.

Her young friend's gesture checked it. "Ah, don't tell me how many—it's too sad and too ugly and too wrong!" To which, however, Lady Grace added: "But perhaps that will be just her way!" And then as her companion seemed for the moment not quite to follow: "By letting Kitty off her debt."

"You mean that Kitty goes free if Lord John wins your promise?"

"Kitty goes free."

"She has her creditor's release?"

"For every shilling."

"And if he only fails?"

"Why then of course," said now quite lucid Lady Grace, "she throws herself more than ever on poor father."

"Poor father indeed!"—Lady Sandgate richly sighed it

It appeared even to create in the younger woman a sense of excess. "Yes—but he after all and in spite of everything adores her."

"To the point, you mean"—for Lady Sandgate could clearly but wonder—"of really sacrificing you?"

The weight of Lady Grace's charming deep eyes on her face made her pause while, at some length, she gave back this look and the interchange determined in the girl a grave appeal. "You think I *should* be sacrificed if I married him?"

Lady Sandgate replied, though with an equal emphasis, indirectly. "*Could* you marry him?"

Lady Grace waited a moment "Do you mean for Kitty?"

"For himself even—if they should convince you, among them, that he cares for you."

Lady Grace had another delay. "Well, he's his awful mother's son."

"Yes—but you wouldn't marry his mother."

"No—but I should only be the more uncomfortably and intimately conscious of her."

"Even when," Lady Sandgate optimistically put it, "she so markedly likes you?"

This determined in the girl a fine impatience. "She doesn't 'like' me, she only *wants* me—which is a very different thing; wants me for my father's so particularly beautiful position, and my mother's so supremely great people, and for everything we have been and have done, and still are and still have: except of course poor not-at-all-model Kitty."

To this luminous account of the matter Lady Sand-gate turned as to a genial sun-burst. "I see indeed—for the general immaculate connection."

The words had no note of irony, but Lady Grace, in her great seriousness, glanced with deprecation at the possibility. "Well, we *haven't* had false notes. We've scarcely even had bad moments."

"Yes, you've been beatific!"—Lady Sandgate enviously, quite ruefully, felt it. But any further treatment of the question was checked by the re-entrance of the footman—a demonstration explained by the concomitant appearance of a young man in eyeglasses and with the ends of his trousers clipped together as for cycling. "This must be your friend," she had only time to say to the daughter of the house; with which, alert and reminded of how she was awaited elsewhere, she retreated before her companion's visitor, who had come in with his guide from the vestibule. She passed away to the terrace and the gardens, Mr. Hugh Crimble's announced name ringing in her ears—to some effect that we are as yet not qualified to discern.

IV

Lady Grace had turned to meet Mr. Hugh Crimble, whose pleasure in at once finding her lighted his keen countenance and broke into easy words. "So awfully kind of you—in the midst of the great doings I noticed—to have found a beautiful minute for me."

"I left the great doings, which are almost over, to every one's relief, I think," the girl returned, "so that your precious time shouldn't be taken to hunt for me."

It was clearly for him, on this bright answer, as if her white hand were holding out the perfect flower of felicity. "You came in from your revels on purpose—with the same charity you showed me from that first moment?" They stood smiling at each other as in an exchange of sympathy already confessed—and even as if finding that their relation had grown during the lapse of contact; she recognising the effect of what they had originally felt as bravely as he might name it. What the fine, slightly long oval of her essentially quiet face—quiet in spite of certain vague depths of reference to forces of the strong high order, forces involved and implanted, yet also rather spent in the process—kept in range from under her redundant black hat was the strength of expression, the directness of communication, that her guest appeared to borrow from the unframed and unattached nippers unceasingly perched, by their mere ground-glass rims, as she remembered, on the bony bridge of his indescribably authoritative (since it was at the same time decidedly inquisitive) young nose. She must, however, also have embraced in this contemplation, she must more or less again have interpreted, his main physiognomic mark, the degree to which his clean jaw was underhung and his lower lip protruded; a lapse of regularity made evident by a suppression of beard and moustache as complete as that practised by Mr. Bender—though without the appearance consequent in the latter's case, that of the flagrantly vain appeal in the countenance for some other exhibition of a history, of a process of production, than this so superficial one. With the interested and interesting girl sufficiently under our attention while we thus try to evoke her, we may even make out some wonder in her as to why the so perceptibly protrusive lower lip of this acquaintance in an hour or two should positively have contributed to his being handsome instead of much more logically interfering with it. We might in fact in such a case even have followed her into another and no less refined a speculation—the question of whether the surest seat of his good looks mightn't after all be his high, fair, if somewhat narrow, forehead, crowned with short crisp brown hair and which, after a fashion of its own, predominated without overhanging. He spoke after they had stood just face to face almost long enough for awkwardness. "I haven't forgotten one item of your kindness to me on that rather bleak occasion."

"Bleak do you call it?" she laughed. "Why I found it, rather, tropical—'lush.' My neighbour on the other side wanted to talk to me of the White City."

"Then you made it doubtless bleak for *him*, let us say. *I* couldn't let you alone, I remember, about *this*—it was like a shipwrecked signal to a sail on the horizon." "This" obviously meant for the young man exactly what surrounded him; he had begun, like Mr. Bender, to be conscious of a thick solicitation of the eye—and much more than he, doubtless, of a tug at the imagination; and he broke—characteristically, you would have been sure—into a great free gaiety of recognition.

"Oh, we've nothing particular in the hall," Lady Grace amiably objected.

"Nothing, I see, but Claudes and Cuyps! I'm an ogre," he said—"before a new and rare feast!"

She happily took up his figure. "Then won't you begin—as a first course—with tea after your ride? If the other, that is—for there has been an ogre before you—has left any."

"Some tea, with pleasure"—he looked all his longing; "though when you talk of a fellow-feaster I should have supposed that, on such a day as this especially, you'd find yourselves running a continuous *table d'hôte*."

"Ah, we can't work sports in our gallery and saloon—the banging or whacking and shoving amusements that are all most people care for; unless, perhaps," Lady Grace went on, "your own peculiar one, as I understand you, of playing football with the old benighted traditions and attributions everywhere meet: in fact I think you said the old idiotic superstitions."

Hugh Crimble went more than half-way to meet this description of his fondest activity; he indeed even beckoned it on. "The names and stories and styles—the so often vain legend, not to be too invidious—of author or subject or school?" But he had a drop, no less, as from the sense of a cause sometimes lost. "Ah, that's a game at which we *all* can play!"

"Though scarcely," Lady Grace suggested, "at which we all can score."

The words appeared indeed to take meaning from his growing impression of the place and its charm—of the number of objects, treasures of art, that pressed for appreciation of their importance. "Certainly," he said, "no one can ever have scored much on sacred spots of *this* order—which express so the grand impunity of their pride, their claims, their assurance!"

"We've had great luck," she granted—"as I've just been reminded; but ever since those terrible things you told me in town—about the tremendous tricks of the whirligig of time and the aesthetic fools' paradise in which so many of us live—I've gone about with my heart in my mouth. Who knows that while I talk Mr. Bender mayn't be pulling us to pieces?"

Hugh Crimble had a shudder of remembrance. "Mr. Bender?"

"The rich American who's going round."

It gave him a sharper shock. "The wretch who bagged Lady Lappington's Longhi?"

Lady Grace showed surprise. "Is he a wretch?"

Her visitor but asked to be extravagant. "Rather—the scoundrel. He offered his infernal eight thousand down."

"Oh, I thought you meant he had played some trick!"

"I wish he had—he could then have been collared."

"Well," Lady Grace peacefully smiled, "it's no use his offering *us* eight thousand—or eighteen or even eighty!"

Hugh Crimble stared as at the odd superfluity of this reassurance, almost crude on exquisite lips and contradicting an imputation no one would have indecently made. "Gracious goodness, I hope not! The man surely doesn't *suppose* you'd traffic."

She might, while she still smiled at him, have been fairly enjoying the friendly horror she produced. "I don't quite know what he supposes. But people *have* trafficked; people do; people are trafficking all round."

"Ah," Hugh Crimble cried, "that's what deprives me of my rest and, as a lover of our vast and beneficent art-wealth, poisons my waking hours. That art-wealth is at the mercy of a leak there appears no means of stopping." She had tapped a spring in him, clearly, and the consequent flood might almost at any moment become copious. "Precious things are going out of our distracted country at a quicker rate than the very quickest—a century and more ago—of their ever coming in."

She was sharply struck, but was also unmistakably a person in whom stirred thought soon found connections and relations. "Well, I suppose our art-wealth came in—save for those awkward Elgin Marbles!—mainly by purchase too, didn't it? We ourselves largely took it away from somewhere, didn't we? We didn't *grow* it all."

"We grew some of the loveliest flowers—and on the whole to-day the most exposed." He had been pulled up but for an instant. "Great Gainsboroughs and Sir Joshuas and Romneys and Sargents, great Turners and Constables and old Cromes and Brabazons, form, you'll recognise, a vast garden in themselves. What have we ever for instance more successfully grown than your splendid 'Duchess of Waterbridge'?"

The girl showed herself ready at once to recognise under his eloquence anything he would. "Yes—it's our Sir Joshua, I believe, that Mr. Bender has proclaimed himself particularly 'after.'"

It brought a cloud to her friend's face. "Then he'll be capable of anything."

"Of anything, no doubt, but of making my father capable—! And you haven't at any rate," she said, "so much as seen the picture."

"I beg your pardon—I saw it at the Guildhall three years ago; and am almost afraid of getting again, with a fresh sense of its beauty, a livelier sense of its danger."

Lady Grace, however, was so far from fear that she could even afford pity. "Poor baffled Mr. Bender!"

"Oh, rich and confident Mr. Bender!" Crimble cried. "Once given his money, his confidence is a horrid engine in itself—there's the rub! I dare say"—the young man saw it all—"he has brought his poisonous cheque."

She gave it her less exasperated wonder. "One has heard of that, but only in the case of some particularly pushing dealer."

"And Mr. Bender, to do him justice, isn't a particularly pushing dealer?"

"No," Lady Grace judiciously returned; "I think he's not a dealer at all, but just what you a moment ago spoke of yourself as being." He gave a glance at his possibly wild recent past. "A fond true lover?"

"As we *all* were in our lucky time—when we rum-aged Italy and Spain."

He appeared to recognise this complication—of Bender's voracious integrity; but only to push it away. "Well, I don't know whether the best lovers are, or ever were, the best buyers—but I feel to-day that they're the best keepers."

The breath of his emphasis blew, as her eyes showed, on the girl's dimmer fire. "It's as if it were suddenly in the air that you've brought us some light or some help—that you may do something really good for us."

"Do you mean 'mark down,' as they say at the shops, all your greatest claims?"

His chord of sensibility had trembled all gratefully into derision, and not to seem to swagger he had put his possible virtue at its lowest. This she beautifully showed that she beautifully saw. "I dare say that if you did even that we should have to take it from you."

"Then it may very well be," he laughed back, "the reason why I feel, under my delightful, wonderful impression, a bit anxious and nervous and afraid."

"That shows," she returned, "that you suspect us of horrors hiding from justice, and that your natural kindness yet shrinks from handing us over!"

Well, clearly, she might put it as she liked—it all came back to his being more charmed. "Heaven knows I've wanted a chance at you, but what should you say if, having then at last just taken you in in your so apparent perfection, I should feel it the better part of valour simply to mount my 'bike' again and spin away?"

"I should be sure that at the end of the avenue you'd turn right round and come back. You'd think again of Mr. Bender."

"Whom I don't, however, you see—if he's prowling off there—in the least want to meet." Crimble made the point with gaiety. "I don't know what I mightn't do to him—and yet it's not of my temptation to violence, after all, that I'm most afraid. It's of the brutal mistake of one's breaking—with one's priggish, precious modernity and one's possibly futile discriminations—into a *general* situation or composition, as we say, so serene and sound and right. What should one do here, out of respect for that felicity, but hold one's breath and walk on tip-toe? The very celebrations and consecrations, as you tell me, instinctively stay outside. I saw that all," the young man went on with more weight in his ardour, "I saw it, while we talked in London, as your natural setting and your native air—and now ten minutes on the spot have made it sink into my spirit. You're a case, all together, of enchanted harmony, of perfect equilibrium—there's nothing to be done or said."

His friend listened to this eloquence with her eyes lowered, then raising them to meet, with a vague insistence, his own; after which something she had seen there appeared to determine in her another motion. She indicated the small landscape that Mr. Bender had, by Lady Sandgate's report, rapidly studied and denounced. "For what do you take that little picture?"

Hugh Crimble went over and looked. "Why, don't you know? It's a jolly little Vandermeer of Delft."

"It's not a base imitation?"

He looked again, but appeared at a loss. "An imitation of Vandermeer?"

"Mr. Bender thinks of Cuyp."

It made the young man ring out: "Then Mr. Bender's doubly dangerous!"

"Singly is enough!" Lady Grace laughed. "But you see you *have* to speak."

"Oh, to *him*, rather, after that—if you'll just take me to him."

"Yes then," she said; but even while she spoke Lord John, who had returned, by the terrace, from his quarter of an hour passed with Lady Imber, was there practically between them; a fact that she had to notice for her other visitor, to whom she was hastily reduced to naming him.

His lordship eagerly made the most of this tribute of her attention, which had reached his ear; he treated it—her "Oh Lord John!"—as a direct greeting. "Ah Lady Grace! I came back particularly to find you."

She could but explain her predicament. "I was taking Mr. Crimble to see the pictures." And then more pointedly, as her manner had been virtually an introduction of that gentleman, an introduction which Lord John's mere noncommittal stare was as little as possible a response to: "Mr. Crimble's one of the quite new connoisseurs."

"Oh, I'm at the very lowest round of the ladder. But I aspire!" Hugh laughed.

"You'll mount!" said Lady Grace with friendly confidence.

He took it again with gay deprecation. "Ah, if by that time there's anything left here to mount *on!*"

"Let us hope there will be at least what Mr. Bender, poor man, won't have been able to carry off." To which Lady Grace added, as to strike a helpful spark from the personage who had just joined them, but who had the air of wishing to preserve his detachment: "It's to Lord John that we owe Mr. Bender's acquaintance."

Hugh looked at the gentleman to whom they were so indebted. "Then do you happen to know, sir, what your friend means to *do* with his spoil?"

The question got itself but dryly treated, as if it might be a commercially calculating or interested one. "Oh, not sell it again."

"Then ship it to New York?" the inquirer pursued, defining himself somehow as not snubbed and, from this point, not snubbable.

That appearance failed none the less to deprive Lord John of a betrayed relish for being able to displease Lady Grace's odd guest by large assent. "As fast as ever he can—and you can land things there *now,* can't you? in three or four days."

"I dare say. But can't he be induced to have a little mercy?" Hugh sturdily pursued.

Lord John pushed out his lips. "A 'little'? How much do you want?"

"Well, one wants to be able somehow to stay his hand."

"I doubt if you can any more stay Mr. Bender's hand than you can empty his purse."

"Ah, the Despoilers!" said Crimble with strong expression. "But it's *we,*" he added, "who are base."

"'Base'?"—and Lord John's surprise was apparently genuine.

"To want only to 'do business,' I mean, with our treasures, with our glories."

Hugh's words exhaled such a sense of peril as to draw at once Lady Grace. "Ah, but if we're above that *here,* as you know————!"

He stood smilingly corrected and contrite. "Of course I know—but you must forgive me if I have it on the brain. And show me first of all, won't you? the Moretto of Brescia."

"You know then about the Moretto of Brescia?"

"Why, didn't you tell me yourself?" It went on between them for the moment quite as if there had been no Lord John.

"Probably, yes," she recalled; "so how I must have swaggered!" After which she turned to the other visitor with a kindness strained clear of urgency. "Will you also come?"

He confessed to a difficulty—which his whole face begged her also to take account of. "I hoped you'd be at leisure—for something I've so at heart!"

This had its effect; she took a rapid decision and turned persuasively to Crimble—for whom, in like manner, there must have been something in *her* face. "Let Mr. Bender himself then show you. And there are things in the library too."

"Oh yes, there are things in the library." Lord John, happy in his gained advantage and addressing Hugh from the strong ground of an initiation already complete, quite sped him on the way.

Hugh clearly made no attempt to veil the penetration with which he was moved to look from one of these counsellors to the other, though with a ready "Thank-you!" for Lady Grace he the next instant started in pursuit of Mr. Bender.

<h2 style="text-align:center">V</h2>

"Your friend seems remarkably hot!" Lord John remarked to his young hostess as soon as they had been left together.

"He has cycled twenty miles. And indeed," she smiled, "he does appear to care for what he cares for!"

Her companion then, during a moment's silence, might have been noting the emphasis of her assent. "Have you known him long?"

"No—not long."

"Nor seen him often?"

"Only once—till now."

"Oh!" said Lord John with another pause. But he soon proceeded. "Let us leave him then to cool! I haven't cycled twenty miles, but I've motored forty very much in the hope of *this,* Lady Grace—the chance of being able to assure you that I too care very much for what I care for." To which he added on an easier note, as to carry off a slight awkwardness while she only waited: "You certainly mustn't let yourself—between us all—be worked to death."

"Oh, such days as this—I" She made light enough of her burden.

"They don't come often to *me* at least, Lady Grace! I hadn't grasped in advance the scale of your fête," he went on; "but since I've the great luck to find you alone—!" He paused for breath, however, before the full sequence.

She helped him out as through common kindness, but it was a trifle colourless. "Alone or in company, Lord John, I'm always very glad to see you."

"Then that assurance helps me to wonder if you don't perhaps gently guess what it is I want to say." This time indeed she left him to his wonder, so that he had to support himself. "I've tried, all considerately—these three months—to let you see for yourself how I feel. I feel very strongly, Lady Grace; so that at last"—and his impatient sincerity took after another instant the jump—"well, I regularly worship you. You're my absolute ideal. I think of you the whole time."

She measured out consideration as if it had been a yard of pretty ribbon. "Are you sure you *know* me enough?"

"I think I know a perfect woman when I see one!" Nothing now at least could have been more prompt, and while a decent pity for such a mistake showed in her smile he followed it up. "Isn't what you rather mean that you haven't cared sufficiently to know *me?* If so, that can be little by little mended, Lady Grace." He was in fact altogether gallant about it. "I'm aware of the limits of what I have to show or to offer, but I defy you to find a limit to my possible devotion."

She deferred to that, but taking it in a lower key. "I believe you'd be very good to me."

"Well, isn't *that* something to start with?"—he fairly pounced on it. "I'll do any blest thing in life you like, I'll accept any condition you impose, if you'll only tell me you see your way."

"Shouldn't I have a little more first to see yours?" she asked. "When you say you'll do anything in life I like, isn't there anything you yourself want strongly enough to do?"

He cast a stare about on the suggestions of the scene. "Anything that will make money, you mean?"

"Make money or make reputation—or even just make the time pass."

"Oh, what I have to look to in the way of a career?" If that was her meaning he could show after an instant that he didn't fear it. "Well, your father, dear delightful man, has been so good as to give me to understand that he backs me for a decent deserving creature; and I've noticed, as you doubtless yourself have, that when Lord Theign backs a fellow——!"

He left the obvious moral for her to take up—which she did, but all interrogatively. "The fellow at once comes in for something awfully good?"

"I don't in the least mind your laughing at me," Lord John returned, "for when I put him the question of the lift he'd give me by speaking to you first he bade me simply remember the complete personal liberty in which he leaves you, and yet which doesn't come—take my word!" said the young man sagely—"from his being at all indifferent."

"No," she answered—"father isn't indifferent. But father's 'great'"

"Great indeed!"—her friend took it as with full comprehension. This appeared not to prevent, however, a second and more anxious thought. "Too great for *you?*"

"Well, he makes me feel—even as his daughter—my extreme comparative smallness."

It was easy, Lord John indicated, to see what she meant "He's a *grand seigneur*, and a serious one—that's what he is: the very type and model of it, down to the ground. So you can imagine," the young man said, "what he makes me feel—most of all when he's so awfully good-natured to me. His being as 'great' as you say and yet backing me—such as I am!—doesn't *that* strike you as a good note for me, the best you could possibly require? For he really *would* like what I propose to you."

She might have been noting, while she thought, that he had risen to ingenuity, to fineness, on the wings of his argument; under the effect of which her reply had the air of a concession. "Yes—he would like it."

"Then he *has* spoken to you?" her suitor eagerly asked.

"He hasn't needed—he has ways of letting one know."

"Yes, yes, he has ways; all his own—like everything else he has. He's wonderful."

She fully agreed. "He's wonderful."

The tone of it appeared somehow to shorten at once for Lord John the rest of his approach to a conclusion. "So you do see your way?"

"Ah—!" she said with a quick sad shrinkage.

"I mean," her visitor hastened to explain, "if he does put it to you as the very best idea he has for you. When he does that—as I believe him ready to do—will you really and fairly listen to him? I'm certain, honestly, that when you know me better—!" His confidence in short donned a bravery.

"I've been feeling this quarter of an hour," the girl returned, "that I do know you better."

"Then isn't that all I want?—unless indeed I ought perhaps to ask rather if it isn't all *you* do! At any rate," said Lord John, "I may see you again here?"

She waited a moment. "You must have patience with me."

"I *am* having it But *after* your father's appeal."

"Well," she said, "that must come first."

"Then you won't dodge it?"

She looked at him straight "I don't dodge, Lord John."

He admired the manner of it "You look awfully handsome as you say so—and you see what *that* does to me." As to attentuate a little the freedom of which he went on: "May I fondly hope that if Lady Imber too should wish to put in another word for me——?"

"Will I listen to her?"—it brought Lady Grace straight down. "No, Lord John, let me tell you at once that I'll do nothing of the sort Kitty's quite another affair, and I never listen to her a bit more than I can help."

Lord John appeared to feel, on this, that he mustn't too easily, in honour, abandon a person who had presented herself to him as an ally. "Ah, you strike me as a little hard on her. Your father himself—in his looser moments!—takes pleasure in what she says."

Our young woman's eyes, as they rested on him after this remark, had no mercy for its extreme feebleness. "If you mean that she's the most reckless rattle one knows, and that she never looks so beautiful as when she's at her worst, and that, always clever for where she makes out her interest, she has learnt to 'get round' him till he only sees through her eyes—if you mean *that* I understand you perfectly. But even if you think me horrid for reflecting so on my nearest and dearest, it's not on the side on which he has most confidence in his elder daughter that his youngest is moved to have most confidence in *him.*"

Lord John stared as if she had shaken some odd bright fluttering object in his face; but then recovering himself: "He hasn't perhaps an absolutely boundless confidence—"

"In any one in the world but himself?"—she had taken him straight up. "He hasn't indeed, and that's what we must come to; so that even if he likes you as much as you doubtless very justly feel, it won't be because you are right about your being nice, but because *he* is!"

"You mean that if I were wrong about it he would still insist that he isn't't?"

Lady Grace was indeed sure. "Absolutely—if he had begun so! He began so with Kitty—that is with allowing her everything."

Lord John appeared struck. "Yes—and he still allows her two thousand."

"I'm glad to hear it—she has never told me how much!" the girl undisguisedly smiled.

"Then perhaps I oughtn't't!"—he glowed with the light of contrition.

"Well, you can't help it now," his companion remarked with amusement.

"You mean that he ought to allow *you* as much?" Lord John inquired. "I'm sure you're right, and that he will," he continued quite as in good faith; "but I want you to understand that I don't care in the least what it may be!"

The subject of his suit took the longest look at him she had taken yet. "You're very good to say so!"

If this was ironic the touch fell short, thanks to his perception that they had practically just ceased to be alone. They were in presence of a third figure, who had arrived from the terrace, but whose approach to them was not so immediate as to deprive Lord John of time for another question. "Will you let *him* tell you, at all events, how good he thinks me?—and then let me come back and have it from you again?"

Lady Grace's answer to this was to turn, as he drew nearer, to the person by whom they were now joined. "Lord John desires you should tell me, father, how good you think him."

"'Good,' my dear?—good for what?" said Lord Theign a trifle absurdly, but looking from one of them to the other.

"I feel I must ask *him* to tell you."

"Then I shall give him a chance—as I should particularly like you to go back and deal with those overwhelming children."

"Ah, they don't overwhelm *you*, father!"—the girl put it with some point.

"If you mean to say I overwhelmed *them*, I dare say I did," he replied—"from my view of that vast collective gape of six hundred painfully plain and perfectly expressionless faces. But that was only for the time: I pumped advice—oh *such* advice!—and they held the large bucket as still as my pet pointer, when I scratch him, holds his back. The bucket, under the stream—"

290

"Was bound to overflow?" Lady Grace suggested.

"Well, the strong recoil of the wave of intelligence has been not unnaturally followed by the formidable break. You must really," Lord Theign insisted, "go and deal with it."

His daughter's smile, for all this, was perceptibly cold. "You work people up, father, and then leave others to let them down."

"The two things," he promptly replied, "require different natures." To which he simply added, as with the habit of authority, though not of harshness, "Go!"

It was absolute and she yielded; only pausing an instant to look as with a certain gathered meaning from one of the men to the other. Faintly and resignedly sighing she passed away to the terrace and disappeared.

"The nature that *can* let you down—I rather like it, you know!" Lord John threw off. Which, for an airy elegance in them, were perhaps just slightly rash words—his companion gave him so sharp a look as the two were left together.

VI

Face to face with his visitor the master of Dedborough betrayed the impression his daughter appeared to have given him. "She didn't want to go?" And then before Lord John could reply: "What the deuce is the matter with her?"

Lord John took his time. "I think perhaps a little Mr. Crimble."

"And who the deuce is a little Mr. Crimble?"

"A young man who was just with her—and whom she appears to have invited."

"Where is he then?" Lord Theign demanded.

"Off there among the pictures—which he seems partly to have come for."

"Oh!"—it made his lordship easier. "Then he's all right—on such a day."

His companion could none the less just wonder. "Hadn't Lady Grace told you?"

"That he was coming? Not that I remember." But Lord Theign, perceptibly preoccupied, made nothing of this. "We've had other fish to fry, and you know the freedom I allow her."

His friend had a vivid gesture. "My dear man, I only ask to profit by it!" With which there might well have been in Lord John's face a light of comment on the pretension in such a quarter to allow freedom.

Yet it was a pretension that Lord Theign sustained—as to show himself far from all bourgeois narrowness. "She has her friends by the score—at this time of day." There was clearly a claim here also—to *know* the time of day. "But in the matter of friends where, by the way, is your own—of whom I've but just heard?"

"Oh, off there among the pictures too; so they'll have met and taken care of each other." Accounting for this inquirer would be clearly the least of Lord John's difficulties. "I mustn't appear to Bender to have failed him; but I must at once let you know, before I join him, that, seizing my opportunity, I have just very definitely, in fact very pressingly, spoken to Lady Grace. It hasn't been perhaps," he continued, "quite the pick of a chance; but that seemed never to come, and if I'm not too fondly mistaken, at any rate, she listened to me without abhorrence. Only I've led her to expect—for our case—that you'll be so good, without loss of time, as to say the clinching word to her yourself."

"Without loss, you mean, of—a—my daughter's time?" Lord Theign, confessedly and amiably interested, had accepted these intimations—yet with the very blandness that was not accessible to hustling and was never forgetful of its standing privilege of criticism. He had come in from his public duty, a few minutes before, somewhat flushed and blown; but that had presently dropped—to the effect, we should have guessed, of his appearing to Lord John at least as cool as the occasion required. His appearance, we ourselves certainly should have felt, was in all respects charming—with the great note of it the beautiful restless, almost suspicious, challenge to you, on the part of deep and mixed things in him, his pride and his shyness, his conscience, his taste and his temper, to deny that he was admirably simple. Obviously, at this rate, he had a passion for simplicity—simplicity, above all, of relation with you, and would show you, with the last subtlety of displeasure, his impatience of your attempting anything more with himself. With such an ideal of decent ease he would, confound you, "sink" a hundred other attributes—or the recognition at least and the formulation of them—that you might abjectly have taken for granted in him: just to show you that in a beastly vulgar age you had, and small wonder, a beastly vulgar imagination. He sank thus, surely, in defiance of insistent vulgarity, half his consciousness of his advantages, flattering himself that mere facility and amiability, a true effective, a positively ideal suppression of reference in any one to anything that might complicate, alone floated above. This would be quite his religion, you might infer—to cause his hands to ignore in whatever contact any opportunity, however convenient, for an unfair pull. Which habit it was that must have produced in him a sort of ripe and radiant fairness; if it be allowed us, that is, to figure in so shining an air a nobleman of fifty-three, of an undecided rather than a certified frame or outline, of a head thinly though neatly covered and not measureably massive, of an almost trivial freshness, of a face marked but by a fine inwrought line or two and lighted by a merely charming expression. You might somehow have traced back the whole character so presented to an ideal privately invoked—that of his establishing in the formal garden of his suffered greatness such easy seats and short perspectives, such winding paths and natural-looking waters, as would mercifully break up the scale. You would perhaps indeed have reflected at the same time that the thought of so much mercy was almost more than anything else the thought of a great option and a great margin—in fine of fifty alternatives. Which remarks of ours, however, leave his lordship with his last immediate question on his hands.

"Well, yes—*that*, of course, in all propriety," his companion has meanwhile replied to it. "But I was thinking a little, you understand, of the importance of our own time."

Divinably Lord Theign put himself out less, as we may say, for the comparatively matter-of-course haunters of his garden than for interlopers even but slightly accredited. He seemed thus not at all to strain to "understand" in this particular connection—it would be his familiarly amusing friend Lord John, clearly, who must do most of the work for him. "'Our own' in the sense of yours and mine?"

"Of yours and mine and Lady Imber's, yes—and a good bit, last not least, in that of my watching and waiting mother's." This struck no prompt spark of apprehension from his listener, so that Lord John went on: "The last thing she did this morning was to remind me, with her fine old frankness, that she would like to learn without more delay where, on the whole question, she *is*, don't you know? What she put to me"—the younger man felt his ground a little, but proceeded further—"what she put to me, with her rather grand way of looking *all* questions straight in the face, you see, was: Do we or don't we, decidedly, take up practically her very handsome offer—'very handsome' being, I mean, what *she* calls it; though it strikes even me too, you know, as rather decent."

Lord Theign at this point resigned himself to know. "Kitty has of course rubbed into me how decent she herself finds it. She hurls herself again on me—successfully!—for everything, and it suits her down to the ground. She pays her beastly debt—that is, I mean to say," and he took himself up, though it was scarce more than perfunctory, "discharges her obligations—by her sister's fair hand; not to mention a few other trifles for which I naturally provide."

Lord John, a little unexpectedly to himself on the defensive, was yet but briefly at a loss. "Of course we take into account, don't we? not only the fact of my mother's desire (intended, I assure you, to be most flattering) that Lady Grace shall enter our family with all honours, but her expressed readiness to facilitate the thing by an understanding over and above——"

"Over and above Kitty's release from her damnable payment?"—Lord Theign reached out to what his guest had left rather in the air. "Of course we take *everything* into account—or I shouldn't, my dear fellow, be discussing with you at all a business one or two of whose aspects so little appeal to me: especially as there's nothing, you easily conceive, that a daughter of mine can come in for by entering even your family, or any other (as a family) that she wouldn't be quite as sure of by just staying in her own. The Duchess's idea, at any rate, if I've followed you, is that if Grace does accept you she settles on you twelve thousand; with the condition—"

Lord John was already all there. "Definitely, yes, of your settling the equivalent on Lady Grace."

"And what do you call the equivalent of twelve thousand?"

"Why, tacked on to a value so great and so charming as Lady Grace herself, I dare say such a sum as nine or ten would serve."

"And where the mischief, if you please, at this highly inconvenient time, am I to pick up nine or ten thousand?"

Lord John declined, with a smiling, a fairly irritating eye for his friend's general resources, to consider that question seriously. "Surely you can have no difficulty whatever—!"

"Why not?—when you can see for yourself that I've had this year to let poor dear old Hill Street! Do you call it the moment for me to have *liked* to see myself all but cajoled into planking down even such a matter as the very much lower figure of Kitty's horrid incubus?"

"Ah, but the inducement and the *quid pro quo*," Lord John brightly indicated, "are here much greater! In the case you speak of you will only have removed the incubus—which, I grant you, she must and you must feel as horrid. In this other you pacify Lady Imber *and* marry Lady Grace: marry her to a man who has set his heart on her and of whom she has just expressed—to himself—a very kind and very high opinion."

"She has expressed a very high opinion of you?"—Lord Theign scarce glowed with credulity.

But the younger man held his ground. "She has told me she thoroughly likes me and that—though a fellow feels an ass repeating such things—she thinks me perfectly charming."

"A tremendous creature, eh, all round? Then," said Lord Theign, "what does she want more?"

"She very possibly wants nothing—but I'm to that beastly degree, you see," his visitor patiently explained, "in the cleft stick of my fearfully positive mother's wants. Those are her 'terms,' and I don't mind saying that they're most disagreeable to me—I quite hate 'em: there! Only I think it makes a jolly difference that I wouldn't touch 'em with a long pole if my personal feeling—in respect to Lady Grace—wasn't so immensely enlisted."

"I assure you I'd chuck 'em out of window, my boy, if I didn't believe you'd be really good to her," Lord Theign returned with the properest spirit.

It only encouraged his companion. "You *will* just tell her then, now and here, how good you honestly believe I shall be?"

This appeal required a moment—a longer look at him. "You truly hold that that friendly guarantee, backed by my parental weight, will do your job?"

"That's the conviction I entertain."

Lord Theign thought again. "Well, even if your conviction's just, that still doesn't tell me into which of my very empty pockets it will be of the least use for me to fumble."

"Oh," Lord John laughed, "when a man has such a tremendous assortment of breeches—!" He pulled up, however, as, in his motion, his eye caught the great vista of the open rooms. "If it's a question of pockets—and what's *in* 'em—here precisely is my man!" This personage had come back from his tour of observation and was now, on the threshold of the hall, exhibited to Lord Theign as well. Lord John's welcome was warm. "I've had awfully to fail you, Mr. Bender, but I was on the point of joining you. Let me, however, still better, introduce you to our host."

VII

Mr. Bender indeed, formidably advancing, scarce had use for this assistance. "Happy to meet you—especially in your beautiful home, Lord Theign." To which he added while the master of Dedborough stood good-humouredly passive to his approach: "I've been round, by your kind permission and the light of nature, and haven't required support; though if I had there's a gentleman there who seemed prepared to allow me any amount." Mr. Bender, out of his abundance, evoked as by a suggestive hand this contributory figure. "A young, spare, nervous gentleman with eye-glasses—I guess he's an author. A friend of yours too?" he asked of Lord John.

The answer was prompt and emphatic. "No, the gentleman is no friend at all of mine, Mr. Bender."

"A friend of my daughter's," Lord Theign easily explained. "I hope they're looking after him."

"Oh, they took care he had tea and bread and butter to any extent; and were so good as to move something," Mr. Bender conscientiously added, "so that he could get up on a chair and see straight into the Moretto."

This was a touch, however, that appeared to affect Lord John unfavourably. "Up on a chair? I say!"

Mr. Bender took another view. "Why, I got right up myself—a little more and I'd almost have begun to paw it! He got me quite interested"—the proprietor of the picture would perhaps care to know—"in that Moretto." And it was on these lines that Mr. Bender continued to advance. "I take it that your biggest value, however, Lord Theign, is your splendid Sir Joshua. Our friend there has a great deal to say about that too—but it didn't lead to our moving any more furniture." On which he paused as to enjoy, with a show of his fine teeth, his host's reassurance. "It *has* yet, my impression of that picture, sir, led to something else. Are you prepared, Lord Theign, to entertain a proposition?"

Lord Theign met Mr. Bender's eyes while this inquirer left these few portentous words to speak for themselves. "To the effect that I part to you with 'The Beautiful Duchess of Waterbridge'? No, Mr. Bender, such a proposition would leave me intensely cold."

Lord John had meanwhile had a more headlong cry. "My dear Bender, I *envy* you!"

"I guess you don't envy me," his friend serenely replied, "as much as I envy Lord Theign." And then while Mr. Bender and the latter continued to face each other searchingly and firmly: "What I allude to is an overture of a strong and simple stamp—such as perhaps would shed a softer light on the difficulties raised by association and attachment. I've had some experience of first shocks, and I'd be glad to meet you as man to man."

Mr. Bender was, quite clearly, all genial and all sincere; he intended no irony and used, consciously, no great freedom. Lord Theign, not less evidently, saw this, and it permitted him amusement. "As rich man to poor man is how I'm to understand it? For me to meet *you*," he added, "I should have to be tempted—and I'm not even temptable. So there we are," he blandly smiled.

His blandness appeared even for a moment to set an example to Lord John. "'The Beautiful Duchess of Waterbridge,' Mr. Bender, is a golden apple of one of those great family trees of which respectable people don't lop off the branches whose venerable shade, in this garish and denuded age, they so much enjoy."

Mr. Bender looked at him as if he had cut some irrelevant caper. "Then if they don't sell their ancestors where in the world are all the ancestors bought?"

"Doesn't it for the moment sufficiently answer your question," Lord Theign asked, "that they're definitely not bought at Dedborough?"

"Why," said Mr. Bender with a wealthy patience, "you talk as if it were my interest to be *reasonable*—which shows how little you understand. I'd be ashamed—with the lovely ideas I have—if I didn't make you kick." And his sturdy smile for it all fairly proclaimed his faith. "Well, I guess I can wait."

This again in turn visibly affected Lord John: marking the moment from which he, in spite of his cultivated levity, allowed an intenser and more sustained look to keep straying toward their host. "Mr. Bender's bound to *have* something!"

It was even as if after a minute Lord Theign had been reached by his friend's mute pressure. "'Something'?"

"Something, Mr. Bender?" Lord John insisted.

It made their visitor rather sharply fix him. "Why, have *you* an interest, Lord John?"

This personage, though undisturbed by the challenge, if such it was, referred it to Lord Theign. "Do you authorise me to speak—a little—as if I have an interest?"

Lord Theign gave the appeal—and the speaker—a certain attention, and then appeared rather sharply to turn away from them. "My dear fellow, you may amuse yourself at my expense as you like!"

"Oh, I don't mean at your expense," Lord John laughed—"I mean at Mr. Bender's!"

"Well, go ahead, Lord John," said that gentleman, always easy, but always too, as you would have felt, aware of everything—"go ahead, but don't sweetly hope to create me in any desire that doesn't already exist in the germ. The attempt has often been made, over here—has in fact been organised on a considerable scale; but I guess I've got some peculiarity, for it doesn't seem as if the thing could be done. If the germ is there, on the other hand," Mr. Bender conceded, "it develops independently of all encouragement."

Lord John communicated again as in a particular sense with Lord Theign. "He thinks I really mean to *offer* him something!"

Lord Theign, who seemed to wish to advertise a degree of detachment from the issue, or from any other such, strolled off, in his restlessness, toward the door that opened to the terrace, only stopping on his way to light a cigarette from a matchbox on a small table. It was but after doing so that he made the remark: "Ah, Mr. Bender may easily be too much for you!"

"That makes me the more sorry, sir," said his visitor, "not to have been enough for *you!*"

"I risk it, at any rate," Lord John went on—"I put you, Bender, the question of whether you wouldn't Move,' as you say, to acquire that Moretto."

Mr. Bender's large face had a commensurate gaze. "As I say? I haven't said anything of the sort!"

"But you do 'love' you know," Lord John slightly overgrimaced.

"I don't when I don't want to. I'm different from most people—I can love or not as I like. The trouble with that Moretto," Mr. Bender continued, "is that it ain't what I'm after."

His "after" had somehow, for the ear, the vividness of a sharp whack on the resisting surface of things, and was concerned doubtless in Lord John's speaking again across to their host. "The worst he can do for me, you see, is to refuse it."

Lord Theign, who practically had his back turned and was fairly dandling about in his impatience, tossed out to the terrace the cigarette he had but just lighted. Yet he faced round to reply: "It's the very first time in the history of this house (a long one, Mr. Bender) that a picture, or anything else in it, has been offered——!"

It was not imperceptible that even if he hadn't dropped Mr. Bender mightn't have been markedly impressed. "Then it must be the very first time such an offer has failed."

"Oh, it isn't that we in the least press it!" Lord Theign quite naturally laughed.

"Ah, I beg your pardon—I press it very hard!" And Lord John, as taking from his face and manner a cue for further humorous license, went so far as to emulate, though sympathetically enough, their companion's native form. "You don't mean to say you don't feel the interest of that Moretto?"

Mr. Bender, quietly confident, took his time to reply. "Well, if you had seen me up on that chair you'd have thought I did."

"Then you must have stepped down from the chair properly impressed."

"I stepped down quite impressed with that young man."

"Mr. Crimble?"—it came after an instant to Lord John. "With *his* opinion, really? Then I hope he's aware of the picture's value."

"You had better ask him," Mr. Bender observed.

"Oh, we don't depend here on the Mr. Crimbles!" Lord John returned.

Mr. Bender took a longer look at him. "Are you aware of the value yourself?"

His friend resorted again, as for the amusement of the thing, to their entertainer. "Am I aware of the value of the Moretto?"

Lord Theign, who had meanwhile lighted another cigarette, appeared, a bit extravagantly smoking, to wish to put an end to his effect of hovering aloof.

"That question needn't trouble us—when I see how much Mr. Bender himself knows about it."

"Well, Lord Theign, I only know what that young man puts it at." And then as the others waited, "Ten thousand," said Mr. Bender.

"Ten thousand?" The owner of the work showed no emotion.

"Well," said Lord John again in Mr. Bender's style, "what's the matter with ten thousand?"

The subject of his gay tribute considered. "There's nothing the matter with ten thousand."

"Then," Lord Theign asked, "is there anything the matter with the picture?"

"Yes, sir—I guess there is."

It gave an upward push to his lordship's eyebrows. "But what in the world——?"

"Well, that's just the question!"

The eyebrows continued to rise. "Does he pretend there's a question of whether it *is* a Moretto?"

"That's what he was up there trying to find out."

"But if the value's, according to himself, ten thousand——?"

"Why, of course," said Mr. Bender, "it's a fine work anyway."

"Then," Lord Theign brought good-naturedly out, "what's the matter with *you*, Mr. Bender?"

That gentleman was perfectly clear. "The matter with me, Lord Theign, is that I've no use for a ten thousand picture."

"'No use?'"—the expression had an oddity. "But what's it your idea to do with such things?"

"I mean," Mr. Bender explained, "that a picture of that rank is not what I'm after."

"The figure," said his noble host—speaking thus, under pressure, commercially—"is beyond what you see your way to?"

But Lord John had jumped at the truth. "The matter with Mr. Bender is that he sees his way much further."

"Further?" their companion echoed.

"The matter with Mr. Bender is that he wants to give millions."

Lord Theign sounded this abyss with a smile. "Well, there would be no difficulty about *that*, I think!"

"Ah," said his guest, "you know the basis, sir, on which I'm ready to pay."

"On the basis then of the Sir Joshua," Lord John inquired, "how far would you go?"

Mr. Bender indicated by a gesture that on a question reduced to a moiety by its conditional form he could give but semi-satisfaction. "Well, I'd go all the way."

"He wants, you see," Lord John elucidated, "an *ideally* expensive thing."

Lord Theign appeared to decide after a moment to enter into the pleasant spirit of this; which he did by addressing his younger friend. "Then why shouldn't I make even the Moretto as expensive as he desires?"

"Because you can't do violence to *that* master's natural modesty," Mr. Bender declared before Lord John had time to speak. And conscious at this moment of the reappearance of his fellow-explorer, he at once supplied a further light. "I guess this gentleman at any rate can tell you."

<h2 style="text-align:center">VIII</h2>

Hugh Crimble had come back from his voyage of discovery, and it was visible as he stood there flushed and quite radiant that he had caught in his approach Lord Theign's last inquiry and Mr. Bender's reply to it. You would have imputed to him on the spot the lively possession of a new idea, the sustaining sense of a message important enough to justify his irruption. He looked from one to the other of the three men, scattered a little by the sight of him, but attached eyes of recognition then to Lord Theign's, whom he remained an instant longer communicatively smiling at. After which, as you might have gathered, he all confidently plunged, taking up the talk where the others had left it. "I should say, Lord Theign, if you'll allow me, in regard to what you appear to have been discussing, that it depends a good deal on just that question—of what your Moretto, at any rate, may be presumed or proved to 'be.' Let me thank you," he cheerfully went on, "for your kind leave to go over your treasures."

The personage he so addressed was, as we know, nothing if not generally affable; yet if that was just then apparent it was through a shade of coolness for the slightly heated familiarity of so plain, or at least so free, a young man in eye-glasses, now for the first time definitely apprehended. "Oh, I've scarcely 'treasures'—but I've some things of interest."

Hugh, however, entering the opulent circle, as it were, clearly took account of no breath of a chill. "I think possible, my lord, that you've a great treasure—if you've really so high a rarity as a splendid Manto-vano."

"A 'Mantovano'?" You wouldn't have been sure that his lordship didn't pronounce the word for the first time in his life.

"There have been supposed to be only *seven* real examples about the world; so that if by an extraordinary chance you find yourself the possessor of a magnificent eighth——"

But Lord John had already broken in. "Why, there you *are*, Mr. Bender!"

"Oh, Mr. Bender, with whom I've made acquaintance," Hugh returned, "was there as it began to work in me—"

"That your Moretto, Lord Theign"—Mr. Bender took their informant up—"isn't, after all, a Moretto at all." And he continued amusedly to Hugh: "It began to work in you, sir, like very strong drink!"

"Do I understand you to suggest," Lord Theign asked of the startling young man, "that my precious picture isn't genuine?"

Well, Hugh knew exactly what he suggested. "As a picture, Lord Theign, as a great portrait, one of the most genuine things in Europe. But it strikes me as probable that from far back—for reasons!—there has been a wrong attribution; that the work has been, in other words, traditionally, obstinately miscalled. It has passed for a Moretto, and at first I quite took it for one; but I suddenly, as I looked and looked and saw and saw, began to doubt, and now I know *why* I doubted."

Lord Theign had during this speech kept his eyes on the ground; but he raised them to Mr. Crimble's almost palpitating presence for the remark: "I'm bound to say that I hope you've some very good grounds!"

"I've three or four, Lord Theign; they seem to me of the best—as yet. They made me wonder and wonder—and then light splendidly broke."

His lordship didn't stint his attention. "Reflected, you mean, from *other* Mantovanos—that I don't know?"

"I mean from those I know myself," said Hugh; "and I mean from fine analogies with one in particular."

"Analogies that in all these years, these centuries, have so remarkably not been noticed?"

"Well," Hugh competently explained, "they're a sort of thing the very sense of, the value and meaning of, are a highly modern—in fact a quite recent growth."

Lord John at this professed with cordiality that he at least quite understood. "Oh, we know a lot more about our pictures and things than ever our ancestors did!"

"Well, I guess it's enough for *me*," Mr. Bender contributed, "that your ancestors knew enough to get 'em!"

"Ah, that doesn't go so far," cried Hugh, "unless we ourselves know enough to keep 'em!"

The words appeared to quicken in a manner Lord Theign's view of the speaker. "Were *your* ancestors, Mr. Crimble, great collectors?"

Arrested, it might be, in his general assurance, Hugh wondered and smiled. "Mine—collectors? Oh, I'm afraid I haven't any—to speak of. Only it has seemed to me for a long time," he added, "that on that head we should all feel together."

Lord Theign looked for a moment as if these were rather large presumptions; then he put them in their place a little curtly. "It's one thing to keep our possessions for ourselves—it's another to keep them for other people."

"Well," Hugh good-humouredly returned, "I'm perhaps not so absolutely sure of myself, if you press me, as that I sha'n't be glad of a higher and wiser opinion—I mean than my own. It would be awfully interesting, if you'll allow me to say so, to have the judgment of one or two of the great men."

"You're not yourself, Mr. Crimble, one of the great men?" his host asked with tempered irony.

"Well, I guess he's going to be, anyhow," Mr. Bender cordially struck in; "and this remarkable exhibition of intelligence may just let him loose on the world, mayn't it?"

"Thank you, Mr. Bender!"—and Hugh obviously tried to look neither elated nor snubbed. "I've too much still to learn, but I'm learning every day, and I shall have learnt immensely this afternoon."

"Pretty well at my expense, however," Lord Theign laughed, "if you demolish a name we've held for generations so dear."

"You may have held the name dear, my lord," his young critic answered; "but my whole point is that, if I'm right, you've held the picture itself cheap."

"Because a Mantovano," said Lord John, "is so much greater a value?"

Hugh met his eyes a moment "Are you talking of values pecuniary?"

"What values are *not* pecuniary?"

Hugh might, during his hesitation, have been imagined to stand off a little from the question. "Well, some things have in a higher degree that one, and some have the associational or the factitious, and some the clear artistic."

"And some," Mr. Bender opined, "have them *all*—in the highest degree. But what you mean," he went on, "is that a Mantovano would come higher under the hammer than a Moretto?"

"Why, sir," the young man returned, "there aren't any, as I've just stated, *to* 'come.' I account—or I easily can—for every one of the very small number."

"Then do you consider that you account for this one?"

"I believe I shall if you'll give me time."

"Oh, time!" Mr. Bender impatiently sighed. "But we'll give you all we've got—only I guess it isn't much." And he appeared freely to invite their companions to join in this estimate. They listened to him, however, they watched him, for the moment, but in silence, and with the next he had gone on: "How much higher—if your idea is correct about it—would Lord Theign's picture come?"

Hugh turned to that nobleman. "Does Mr. Bender mean come to *him*, my lord?"

Lord Theign looked again hard at Hugh, and then harder than he had done yet at his other invader. "I don't know *what* Mr. Bender means!" With which he turned off.

"Well, I guess I mean that it would come higher to me than to any one! But how *much* higher?" the American continued to Hugh. "How much higher to *you?*"

"Oh, I can size *that*. How much higher as a Mantovano?"

Unmistakably—for us at least—our young man was gaining time; he had the instinct of circumspection and delay. "To any one?"

"To any one."

"Than as a Moretto?" Hugh continued.

It even acted on Lord John's nerves. "That's what we're talking about—really!"

But Hugh still took his ease; as if, with his eyes first on Bender and then on Lord Theign, whose back was practically presented, he were covertly studying signs. "Well," he presently said, "in view of the very great interest combined with the very great rarity, more than—ah more than can be estimated off-hand."

It made Lord Theign turn round. "But a fine Moretto has a very great rarity and a very great interest."

"Yes—but not on the whole the same amount of either."

"No, not on the whole the same amount of either!"—Mr. Bender judiciously echoed it. "But how," he freely pursued, "are you going to find out?"

"Have I your permission, Lord Theign," Hugh brightly asked, "to attempt to find out?"

The question produced on his lordship's part a visible, a natural anxiety. "What would it be your idea then to *do* with my property?"

"Nothing at all here—it could all be done, I think, at Verona. What besets, what quite haunts me," Hugh explained, "is the vivid image of a Mantovano—one of the glories of the short list—in a private collection in that place. The conviction grows in me that the two portraits must be of the same original. In fact I'll bet my head," the young man quite ardently wound up, "that the wonderful subject of the Verona picture, a very great person clearly, is none other than the very great person of yours."

Lord Theign had listened with interest. "Mayn't he be that and yet from another hand?"

"It isn't another hand"—oh Hugh was quite positive. "It's the hand of the very same painter."

"How can you prove it's the same?"

"Only by the most intimate internal evidence, I admit—and evidence that of course has to be estimated."

"Then who," Lord Theign asked, "is to estimate it?"

"Well,"—Hugh was all ready—"will you let Pap-pendick, one of the first authorities in Europe, a good friend of mine, in fact more or less my master, and who is generally to be found at Brussels? I happen to know he knows your picture—he once spoke to me of it; and he'll go and look again at the Verona one, he'll go and judge our issue, if I apply to him, in the light of certain new tips that I shall be able to give him."

Lord Theign appeared to wonder. "If you 'apply' to him?"

"Like a shot, I believe, if I ask it of him—as a service."

"A service to *you?* He'll be very obliging," his lordship smiled.

"Well, I've obliged *him!*" Hugh readily retorted.

"The obligation will be to we"—Lord Theign spoke more formally.

"Well, the satisfaction," said Hugh, "will be to all of us. The things Pappendick has seen he intensely, ineffaceably keeps in mind, to every detail; so that he'll tell me—as no one else really can—if the Verona man is *your* man."

"But then," asked Mr. Bender, "we've got to believe anyway what he says?"

"The market," said Lord John with emphasis, "would have to believe it—that's the point."

"Oh," Hugh returned lightly, "the market will have nothing to do with it, I hope; but I think you'll feel when he has spoken that you really know where you are."

Mr. Bender couldn't doubt of that. "Oh, if he gives us a bigger thing we won't complain. Only, how long will it take him to get there? I want him to start right away."

"Well, as I'm sure he'll be deeply interested——"

"We *may*"—Mr. Bender took it straight up—"get news next week?"

Hugh addressed his reply to Lord Theign; it was already a little too much as if he and the American between them were snatching the case from that possessor's hands. "The day I hear from Pappendick you shall have a full report. And," he conscientiously added, "if I'm proved to have been unfortunately wrong——!"

His lordship easily pointed the moral. "You'll have caused me some inconvenience."

"Of course I shall," the young man unreservedly agreed—"like a wanton meddling ass!" His candour, his freedom had decidedly a note of their own. "But my conviction, after those moments with your picture, was too strong for me not to speak—and, since you allow it, I face the danger and risk the test."

"I allow it of course in the form of business." This produced in Hugh a certain blankness. "'Business'?" "If I consent to the inquiry I pay for the inquiry." Hugh demurred. "Even if I turn out mistaken?" "You make me in any event your proper charge." The young man thought again, and then as for vague accommodation: "Oh, my charge won't be high!"

"Ah," Mr. Bender protested, "it ought to be handsome if the thing's marked *up*!" After which he looked at his watch. "But I guess I've got to go, Lord Theign, though your lovely old Duchess—for it's to *her* I've lost my heart—does cry out for me again."

"You'll find her then still there," Lord John observed with emphasis, but with his eyes for the time on Lord Theign; "and if you want another look at her I'll presently come and take one too."

"I'll order your car to the garden-front," Lord Theign added to this; "you'll reach it from the saloon, but I'll see you again first."

Mr. Bender glared as with the round full force of his pair of motor lamps. "Well, if you're ready to talk about anything, I am. Good-bye, Mr. Crimble."

"Good-bye, Mr. Bender." But Hugh, addressing their host while his fellow-guest returned to the saloon, broke into the familiarity of confidence. "As if you *could* be ready to 'talk'!"

This produced on the part of the others present a mute exchange that could only have denoted surprise at all the irrepressible young outsider thus projected upon them took for granted. "I've an idea," said Lord John to his friend, "that you're quite ready to talk with *me*."

Hugh then, with his appetite so richly quickened, could but rejoice. "Lady Grace spoke to me of things in the library."

"You'll find it *that* way"—Lord Theign gave the indication.

"Thanks," said Hugh elatedly, and hastened away.

Lord John, when he had gone, found relief in a quick comment. "Very sharp, no doubt—but he wants taking down."

The master of Dedborough wouldn't have put it so crudely, but the young expert did bring certain things home. "The people my daughters, in the exercise of a wild freedom, do pick up——!"

"Well, don't you see that all you've got to do—on the question we're dealing with—is to claim your very own wild freedom? Surely I'm right in feeling you," Lord John further remarked, "to have jumped at once to my idea that Bender is heaven-sent—and at what they call the psychologic moment, don't they?—to point that moral. Why look anywhere else for a sum of money that—smaller or greater—you can find with perfect ease in that extraordinarily bulging pocket?"

Lord Theign, slowly pacing the hall again, threw up his hands. "Ah, with 'perfect ease' can scarcely be said!"

"Why not?—when he absolutely thrusts his dirty dollars down your throat."

"Oh, I'm not talking of ease to *him*," Lord Theign returned—"I'm talking of ease to myself. I shall have to make a sacrifice."

"Why not then—for so great a convenience—gallantly make it?"

"Ah, my dear chap, if you want me to sell my Sir Joshua——!"

But the horror in the words said enough, and Lord John felt its chill. "I don't make a point of that—God forbid! But there are other things to which the objection wouldn't apply."

"You see how it applies—in the case of the Moret-to—for *him*. A mere Moretto," said Lord Theign, "is too cheap—for a Yankee 'on the spend.'"

"Then the Mantovano wouldn't be."

"It remains to be proved that it *is* a Mantovano."

"Well," said Lord John, "go into it."

"Hanged if I won't!" his friend broke out after a moment. "It *would* suit me. I mean"—the explanation came after a brief intensity of thought—"the possible size of his cheque would."

"Oh," said Lord John gaily, "I guess there's no limit to the possible size of his cheque!"

"Yes, it would suit me, it would suit me!" the elder man, standing there, audibly mused. But his air changed and a lighter question came up to him as he saw his daughter reappear at the door from the terrace. "Well, the infant horde?" he immediately put to her.

Lady Grace came in, dutifully accounting for them. "They've marched off—in a huge procession."

"Thank goodness! And our friends?"

"All playing tennis," she said—"save those who are sitting it out." To which she added, as to explain her return: "Mr. Crimble has gone?"

Lord John took upon him to say. "He's in the library, to which you addressed him—making discoveries."

"Not then, I hope," she smiled, "to our disadvantage!"

"To your very great honour and glory." Lord John clearly valued the effect he might produce. "Your Moretto of Brescia—do you know what it really and splendidly is?" And then as the girl, in her surprise, but wondered: "A Mantovano, neither more nor less. Ever so much more swagger."

"A Mantovano?" Lady Grace echoed. "Why, how tremendously jolly!"

Her father was struck. "Do you know the artist—of whom I had never heard?"

"Yes, something of the little that *is* known." And she rejoiced as her knowledge came to her. "He's a tremendous swell, because, great as he was, there are but seven proved examples——"

"With this of yours," Lord John broke in, "there are eight."

"Then why haven't I known about him?" Lord Theign put it as if so many other people were guilty for this.

His daughter was the first to plead for the vague body. "Why, I suppose in order that you should have exactly this pleasure, father."

"Oh, pleasures not desired are like acquaintances not sought—they rather bore one!" Lord Theign sighed. With which he moved away from her.

Her eyes followed him an instant—then she smiled at their guest. "Is he bored at having the higher prize—if you're sure it *is* the higher?"

"Mr. Crimble is sure—because if he isn't," Lord John added, "he's a wretch."

"Well," she returned, "as he's certainly not a wretch it must be true. And fancy," she exclaimed further, though as more particularly for herself, "our having suddenly incurred this immense debt to him!"

"Oh, I shall pay Mr. Crimble!" said her father, who had turned round.

The whole question appeared to have provoked in Lord John a rise of spirits and a flush of humour. "Don't you let him stick it on."

His host, however, bethinking himself, checked him. "Go *you* to Mr. Bender straight!"

Lord John saw the point. "Yes—till he leaves. But I shall find you here, shan't I?" he asked with all earnestness of Lady Grace.

She had an hesitation, but after a look at her father she assented. "I'll wait for you."

"Then *à tantôt!*" It made him show for happy as, waving his hand at her, he proceeded to seek Mr. Bender in presence of the object that most excited that gentleman's appetite—to say nothing of the effect involved on Lord John's own.

IX

Lord Theign, when he had gone, revolved—it might have been nervously—about the place a little, but soon broke ground. "He'll have told you, I understand, that I've promised to speak to you for him. But I understand also that he has found something to say for himself."

"Yes, we talked—a while since," the girl said. "At least he did."

"Then if you listened I hope you listened with a good grace."

"Oh, he speaks very well—and I've never disliked him."

It pulled her father up. "Is that *all*—when I think so much of him?"

She seemed to say that she had, to her own mind, been liberal and gone far; but she waited a little. "Do you think very, *very* much?"

"Surely I've made my good opinion clear to you!"

Again she had a pause. "Oh yes, I've seen you like him and believe in him—and I've found him pleasant and clever."

"He has never had," Lord Theign more or less ingeniously explained, "what I call a real show." But the character under discussion could after all be summed up without searching analysis. "I consider nevertheless that there's plenty in him."

It was a moderate claim, to which Lady Grace might assent. "He strikes me as naturally quick and—well, nice. But I agree with you than he hasn't had a chance."

"Then if you can see your way by sympathy and confidence to help him to one I dare say you'll find your reward."

For a third time she considered, as if a certain curtness in her companion's manner rather hindered, in such a question, than helped. Didn't he simplify too much, you would have felt her ask, and wasn't his visible wish for brevity of debate a sign of his uncomfortable and indeed rather irritated sense of his not making a figure in it? "Do you desire it very particularly?" was, however, all she at last brought out.

"I should like it exceedingly—if you act from conviction. Then of course only; but of one thing I'm myself convinced—of what he thinks of yourself and feels for you."

"Then would you mind my waiting a little?" she asked. "I mean to be absolutely sure of myself." After which, on his delaying to agree, she added frankly, as to help her case: "Upon my word, father, I should like to do what would please you."

But it determined in him a sharper impatience. "Ah, what would please *me!* Don't put it off on 'me'! Judge absolutely for yourself"—he slightly took himself up—"in the light of my having consented to do for him what I always *hate* to do: deviate from my normal practice of never intermeddling. If I've deviated now you can judge. But to do so all round, of course, take—in reason!—your time."

"May I ask then," she said, "for still a little more?"

He looked for this, verily, as if it was not in reason. "You know," he then returned, "what he'll feel that a sign of."

"Well, I'll tell him what I mean."

"Then I'll send him to you."

He glanced at his watch and was going, but after a "Thanks, father," she had stopped him. "There's one thing more." An embarrassment showed in her manner, but at the cost of some effect of earnest abruptness she surmounted it. "What does your American—Mr. Bender—want?"

Lord Theign plainly felt the challenge. "'My' American? He's none of mine!"

"Well then Lord John's."

"He's none of his either—more, I mean, than any one else's. He's every one's American, literally—to all appearance; and I've not to tell *you*, surely, with the freedom of your own visitors, how people stalk in and out here."

"No, father—certainly," she said. "You're splendidly generous."

His eyes seemed rather sharply to ask her then how he could improve on that; but he added as if it were enough: "What the man must by this time want more than anything else is his car."

"Not then anything of ours?" she still insisted.

"Of 'ours'?" he echoed with a frown. "Are you afraid he has an eye to something of *yours?*"

"Why, if we've a new treasure—which we certainly have if we possess a Mantovano—haven't we all, even I, an immense interest in it?" And before he could answer, "Is *that* exposed?" she asked.

Lord Theign, a little unready, cast about his storied halls; any illusion to the "exposure" of the objects they so solidly sheltered was obviously unpleasant to him. But then it was as if he found at a stroke both his own reassurance and his daughter's. "How can there be a question of it when he only wants Sir Joshuas?"

"He wants ours?" the girl gasped.

"At absolutely any price."

"But you're not," she cried, "discussing it?"

He hesitated as between chiding and contenting her—then he handsomely chose. "My dear child, for what do you take me?" With which he impatiently started, through the long and stately perspective, for the saloon.

She sank into a chair when he had gone; she sat there some moments in a visible tension of thought, her hands clasped in her lap and her dropped eyes fixed and unperceiving; but she sprang up as Hugh Crimble, in search of her, again stood before her. He presented himself as with winged sandals.

"What luck to find you! I must take my spin back."

"You've seen everything as you wished?"

"Oh," he smiled, "I've seen wonders."

She showed her pleasure. "Yes, we've got some things."

"So Mr. Bender says!" he laughed. "You've got five or six—"

"Only five or six?" she cried in bright alarm.

"'Only'?" he continued to laugh. "Why, that's enormous, five or six things of the first importance! But I think I ought to mention to you," he added, "a most barefaced 'Rubens' there in the library."

"It isn't a Rubens?"

"No more than I'm a Ruskin."

"Then you'll brand us—expose us for it?"

"No, I'll let you off—I'll be quiet if you're good, if you go straight. I'll only hold it *in terrorem*. One can't be sure in these dreadful days—that's always to remember; so that if you're not good I'll come down on you with it. But to balance against that threat," he went on, "I've made the very grandest find. At least I believe I have!"

She was all there for this news. "Of the Manto-vano—hidden in the other thing?"

Hugh wondered—almost as if she had been before him. "You don't mean to say *you've* had the idea of that?"

"No, but my father has told me."

"And is your father," he eagerly asked, "really gratified?"

With her conscious eyes on him—her eyes could clearly be very conscious about her father—she considered a moment. "He always prefers old associations and appearances to new; but I'm sure he'll resign himself if you see your way to a certainty."

"Well, it will be a question of the weight of expert opinion that I shall invoke. But I'm not afraid," he resolutely said, "and I shall make the thing, from its splendid rarity, the crown and flower of your glory."

Her serious face shone at him with a charmed gratitude. "It's awfully beautiful then your having come to us so. It's awfully beautiful your having brought us this way, in a flash—as dropping out of a chariot of fire—more light and what you apparently feel with myself as more honour."

"Ah, the beauty's in your having yourself done it!" he returned. He gave way to the positive joy of it. "If I've brought the 'light' and the rest—that's to say the very useful information—who in the world was it brought *me?*"

She had a gesture of protest "You'd have come in some other way."

"I'm not so sure! I'm beastly shy—little as I may seem to show it: save in great causes, when I'm horridly bold and hideously offensive. Now at any rate I only know what *has* been." She turned off for it, moving away from him as with a sense of mingled things that made for unrest; and he had the next moment grown graver under the impression. "But does anything in it all," he asked, "trouble you?"

She faced about across the wider space, and there was a different note in what she brought out. "I don't know what forces me so to *tell* you things."

"'Tell' me?" he stared. "Why, you've told me nothing more monstrous than that I've been welcome!"

"Well, however that may be, what did you mean just now by the chance of our not 'going straight'? When you said you'd expose our bad—or is it our false?—Rubens in the event of a certain danger."

"Oh, in the event of your ever being bribed"—he laughed again as with relief. And then as her face seemed to challenge the word: "Why, to let anything—of your best!—ever leave Dedborough. By which I mean really of course leave the country." She turned again on this, and something in her air made him wonder. "I hope you don't feel there *is* such a danger? I understood from you half an hour ago that it was unthinkable."

"Well, it *was*, to me, half an hour ago," she said as she came nearer. "But if it has since come up?"

"'If it has! But *has* it? In the form of that monster? What Mr. Bender wants is the great Duchess," he recalled.

"And my father won't sell *her*? No, he won't sell the great Duchess—there I feel safe. But he greatly needs a certain sum of money—or he thinks he does—and I've just had a talk with him."

"In which he has told you that?"

"He has told me nothing," Lady Grace said—"or else told me quite other things. But the more I think of them the more it comes to me that he feels urged or tempted—"

"To despoil and denude these walls?" Hugh broke in, looking about in his sharper apprehension.

"Yes, to satisfy, to save my sister. *Now* do you think our state so ideal?" she asked—but without elation for her hint of triumph.

He had no answer for this save "Ah, but you terribly interest me. May I ask what's the matter with your sister?"

Oh, she wanted to go on straight now! "The matter is—in the first place—that she's too dazzlingly, dreadfully beautiful."

"More beautiful than you?" his sincerity easily risked.

"Millions of times." Sad, almost sombre, she hadn't a shade of coquetry. "Kitty has debts—great heaped-up gaming debts."

"But to such amounts?"

"Incredible amounts it appears. And mountains of others too. She throws herself all on our father."

"And he *has* to pay them? There's no one else?" Hugh asked.

She waited as if he might answer himself, and then as he apparently didn't, "He's only afraid there *may* be some else—that's how she makes him do it," she said. And "Now do you think," she pursued, "that I don't tell you things?"

He turned them over in his young perception and pity, the things she told him. "Oh, oh, oh!" And then, in the great place, while as, just spent by the effort of her disclosure, she moved from him again, he took them all in. "That's the situation that, as you say, may force his hand."

"It absolutely, I feel, does force it." And the renewal of her appeal brought her round. "Isn't it too lovely?"

His frank disgust answered. "It's too damnable!"

"And it's you," she quite terribly smiled, "who—by the 'irony of fate'!—have given him help."

He smote his head in the light of it. "By the Mantovano?"

"By the possible Mantovano—as a substitute for the impossible Sir Joshua. You've made him aware of a value."

"Ah, but the value's to be fixed!"

"Then Mr. Bender will fix it!"

"Oh, but—as he himself would say—I'll fix Mr. Bender!" Hugh declared. "And he won't buy a pig in a poke."

This cleared the air while they looked at each other; yet she had already asked: "What in the world can you do, and how in the world can you do it?"

Well, he was too excited for decision. "I don't quite see now, but give me time." And he took out his watch as already to measure it. "Oughtn't I before I go to say a word to Lord Theign?"

"Is it your idea to become a lion in his path?"

"Well, say a cub—as that's what I'm afraid he'll call me! But I think I should speak to him."

She drew a conclusion momentarily dark. "He'll have to learn in that case that I've told you of my fear."

"And is there any good reason why he shouldn't?"

She kept her eyes on him and the darkness seemed to clear. "No!" she at last replied, and, having gone to touch an electric bell, was with him again. "But I think I'm rather sorry for you."

"Does that represent a reason why I should be so for you?"

For a little she said nothing; but after that: "None whatever!"

"Then is the sister of whom you speak Lady Imber?"

Lady Grace, at this, raised her hand in caution: the butler had arrived, with due gravity, in answer to her ring; to whom she made known her desire. "Please say to his lordship—in the saloon or wherever—that Mr. Crimble must go." When Banks had departed, however, accepting the responsibility of this mission, she answered her friend's question. "The sister of whom I speak is Lady Imber."

"She loses then so heavily at bridge?"

"She loses more than she wins."

Hugh gazed as with interest at these oddities of the great. "And yet she still plays?"

"What else, in her set, should she do?"

This he was quite unable to say; but he could after a moment's exhibition of the extent to which he was out of it put a question instead. "So *you're* not in her set?"

"I'm not in her set."

"Then decidedly," he said, "I don't want to save her. I only want—"

He was going on, but she broke in: "I know what you want!"

He kept his eyes on her till he had made sure—and this deep exchange between them had a beauty. "So you're now *with* me?"

"I'm now *with* you!"

"Then," said Hugh, "shake hands on it"

He offered her his hand, she took it, and their grasp became, as you would have seen in their fine young faces, a pledge in which they stood a minute locked. Lord Theign came upon them from the saloon in the midst of the process; on which they separated as with an air of its having consisted but of Hugh's leave-taking. With some such form of mere civility, at any rate, he appeared, by the manner in which he addressed himself to Hugh, to have supposed them occupied.

"I'm sorry my daughter can't keep you; but I must at least thank you for your interesting view of my picture."

Hugh indulged in a brief and mute, though very grave, acknowledgment of this expression; presently speaking, however, as on a resolve taken with a sense of possibly awkward consequences: "May I—before you're sure of your indebtedness—put you rather a straight question, Lord Theign?" It sounded doubtless, and of a sudden, a little portentous—as was in fact testified to by his lordship's quick stiff stare, full of wonder at so free a note. But Hugh had the courage of his undertaking. "If I contribute in ny modest degree to establishing the true authorship of the work you speak of, may I have from you an assurance that my success isn't to serve as a basis for any peril—or possibility—of its leaving the country?"

Lord Theign was visibly astonished, but had also, independently of this, turned a shade pale. "You ask of me an 'assurance'?"

Hugh had now, with his firmness and his strained smile, quite the look of having counted the cost of his step. "I'm afraid I *must*, you see."

It pressed at once in his host the spring of a very grand manner. "And pray by what right here do you do anything of the sort?"

"By the right of a person from whom you, on your side, are accepting a service."

Hugh had clearly determined in his opponent a rise of what is called spirit. "A service that you half an hour ago thrust on me, sir—and with which you may take it from me that I'm already quite prepared to dispense."

"I'm sorry to appear indiscreet," our young man returned; "I'm sorry to have upset you in any way. But I can't overcome my anxiety—"

Lord Theign took the words from his lips. "And you therefore invite me—at the end of half an hour in this house!—to account to you for my personal intentions and my private affairs and make over my freedom to your hands?"

Hugh stood there with his eyes on the black and white pavement that stretched about him—the great loz-enged marble floor that might have figured that ground of his own vision which he had made up his mind to "stand." "I can only see the matter as I see it, and I should be ashamed not to have seized any chance to appeal to you." Whatever difficulty he had had shyly to face didn't exist for him now. "I entreat you to think again, to think *well*, before you deprive us of such a source of just envy."

"And you regard your entreaty as helped," Lord Theign asked, "by the beautiful threat you are so good as to attach to it?" Then as his monitor, arrested, exchanged a searching look with Lady Grace, who, showing in her face all the pain of the business, stood off at the distance to which a woman instinctively retreats when a scene turns to violence as precipitately as this one appeared to strike her as having turned: "I ask you that not less than I should like to know whom you speak of as 'deprived' of property that happens—for reasons that I don't suppose you also quarrel with!—to be mine."

"Well, I know nothing about threats, Lord Theign," Hugh said, "but I speak of *all* of us—of all the people of England; who would deeply deplore such an act of alienation, and whom, for the interest they bear you, I beseech you mercifully to consider."

"The interest they bear me?"—the master of Dedborough fairly bristled with wonder. "Pray how the devil do they show it?"

"I think they show it in all sorts of ways"—and Hugh's critical smile, at almost any moment hovering, played over the question in a manner seeming to convey that he meant many things.

"Understand then, please," said Lord Theign with every inch of his authority, "that they'll show it best by minding their own business while I very particularly mind mine."

"You simply do, in other words," Hugh explicitly concluded, "what happens to be convenient to you."

"In very distinct preference to what happens to be convenient to *you!* So that I need no longer detain you," Lord Theign added with the last dryness and as if to wind up their brief and thankless connection.

The young man took his dismissal, being able to do no less, while, unsatisfied and unhappy, he looked about mechanically for the cycling-cap he had laid down somewhere in the hall on his arrival. "I apologise, my lord, if I seem to you to have ill repaid your hospitality. But," he went on with his uncommended cheer, "my interest in your picture remains."

Lady Grace, who had stopped and strayed and stopped again as a mere watchful witness, drew nearer hereupon, breaking her silence for the first time. "And please let me say, father, that mine also grows and grows."

It was obvious that this parent, surprised and disconcerted by her tone, judged her contribution superfluous. "I'm happy to hear it, Grace—but yours is another affair."

"I think on the contrary that it's quite the same one," she returned—"since it's on my hint to him that Mr. Crimble has said to you what he has." The resolution she had gathered while she awaited her chance sat in her charming eyes, which met, as she spoke, the straighter paternal glare. "I let him know that I supposed you to think of profiting by the importance of Mr. Bender's visit."

"Then you might have spared, my dear, your—I suppose and hope well-meant—interpretation of my mind." Lord Theign showed himself at this point master of the beautiful art of righting himself as without having been in the wrong. "Mr. Bender's visit will terminate—as soon as he has released Lord John—without my having profited in the smallest particular."

Hugh meanwhile evidently but wanted to speak for his friend. "It was Lady Grace's anxious inference, she will doubtless let me say for her, that my idea about the Moretto would add to your power—well," he pushed on not without awkwardness, "of 'realising' advantageously on such a prospective rise."

Lord Theign glanced at him as for positively the last time, but spoke to Lady Grace. "Understand then, please, that, as I detach myself from any association with this gentleman's ideas—whether about the Moretto or about anything else—his further application of them ceases from this moment to concern us."

The girl's rejoinder was to address herself directly to Hugh, across their companion. "Will you make your inquiry for *me* then?"

The light again kindled in him. "With all the pleasure in life!" He had found his cap and, taking them together, bowed to the two, for departure, with high emphasis of form. Then he marched off in the direction from which he had entered.

Lord Theign scarce waited for his disappearance to turn in wrath to Lady Grace. "I denounce the indecency, wretched child, of your public defiance of me!"

They were separated by a wide interval now, and though at her distance she met his reproof so unshrinkingly as perhaps to justify the terms into which it had broken, she became aware of a reason for his not following it up. She pronounced in quick warning "Lord John!"—for their friend, released from among the pictures, was rejoining them, was already there.

He spoke straight to his host on coming into sight. "Bender's at last off, but"—he indicated the direction of the garden front—"you may still find him, out yonder, prolonging the agony with Lady Sand-gate."

Lord Theign remained a moment, and the heat of his resentment remained. He looked with a divided discretion, the pain of his indecision, from his daughter's suitor and his approved candidate to that contumacious young woman and back again; then choosing his course in silence he had a gesture of almost desperate indifference and passed quickly out by the door to the terrace.

It had left Lord John gaping. "What on earth's the matter with your father?"

"What on earth indeed?" Lady Grace unaidingly asked. "Is he discussing with that awful man?"

"Old Bender? Do you think him so awful?" Lord John showed surprise—which might indeed have passed for harmless amusement; but he shook everything off in view of a nearer interest. He quite waved old Bender away. "My dear girl, what do *we* care—?"

"I care immensely, I assure you," she interrupted, "and I ask of you, please, to tell me!"

Her perversity, coming straight and which he had so little expected, threw him back so that he looked at her with sombre eyes. "Ah, it's not for such a matter I'm here, Lady Grace—I'm here with that fond question of my own." And then as she turned away, leaving him with a vehement motion of protest: "I've come for your kind answer—the answer your father instructed me to count on."

"I've no kind answer to give you!"—she raised forbidding hands. "I entreat you to leave me alone."

There was so high a spirit and so strong a force in it that he stared as if stricken by violence. "In God's name then what has happened—when you almost gave me your word?"

"What has happened is that I've found it impossible to listen to you." And she moved as if fleeing she scarce knew whither before him.

He had already hastened around another way, however, as to meet her in her quick circuit of the hall. "That's all you've got to say to me after what has passed between us?"

He had stopped her thus, but she had also stopped him, and her passionate denial set him a limit. "I've got to say—sorry as I am—that if you*must* have an answer it's this: that never, Lord John, never, can there be anything more between us." And her gesture cleared her path, permitting her to achieve her flight. "Never, no, never," she repeated as she went—"never, never, never!" She got off by the door at which she had been aiming to some retreat of her own, while aghast and defeated, left to make the best of it, he sank after a moment into a chair and remained quite pitiably staring before him, appealing to the great blank splendour.

BOOK SECOND

I

Orchestra at the opera (c. 1870) by Edgar Degas (1834-1917)

LADY SANDGATE, on a morning late in May, entered her drawing-room by the door that opened at the right of that charming retreat as a person coming in faced Bruton Street; and she met there at this moment Mr. Gotch, her butler, who had just appeared in the much wider doorway forming opposite the Bruton Street windows an apartment not less ample, lighted from the back of the house and having its independent connection with the upper floors and the lower. She showed surprise at not immediately finding the visitor to whom she had been called.

"But Mr. Crimble———?"

"Here he is, my lady." And he made way for that gentleman, who emerged from the back room; Gotch observing the propriety of a prompt withdrawal.

"I went in for a minute, with your servant's permission," Hugh explained, "to see your famous Lawrence—which is splendid; he was so good as to arrange the light." The young man's dress was of a form less relaxed than on the occasion of his visit to Dedborough; yet the soft felt hat that he rather restlessly crumpled as he talked marked the limit of his sacrifice to vain appearances.

Lady Sandgate was at once interested in the punctuality of his reported act. "Gotch thinks as much of my grandmother as I do—and even seems to have ended by taking her for his very own."

"One sees, unmistakably, from her beauty, that you at any rate are of her line," Hugh allowed himself, not without confidence, the amusement of replying; "and I must make sure of another look at her when I've a good deal more time."

His hostess heard him as with a lapse of hope. "You hadn't then come *for* the poor dear?" And then as he obviously hadn't, but for something quite else: "I thought, from so prompt an interest, that she might be coveted—!" It dropped with a yearning sigh.

"You imagined me sent by some prowling collector?" Hugh asked. "Ah, I shall never do their work—unless to betray them: *that* I shouldn't in the least mind!—and I'm here, frankly, at this early hour, to ask your consent to my seeing Lady Grace a moment on a particular business, if she can kindly give me time."

"You've known then of her being with me?"

"I've known of her coming to you straight on leaving Dedborough," he explained; "of her wishing not to go to her sister's, and of Lord Theign's having proceeded, as they say, or being on the point of proceeding, to some foreign part."

"And you've learnt it from having seen her—these three or four weeks?"

"I've met her—but just barely—two or three times: at a 'private view' at the opera, in the lobby, and that sort of thing. But she hasn't told you?"

Lady Sandgate neither affirmed nor denied; she only turned on him her thick lustre. "I wanted to see how much *you'd* tell." She waited even as for more, but this not coming she helped herself. "Once again at dinner?"

"Yes, but alas not near her!"

"Once then at a private view?—when, with the squash they usually are, you might have been very near her indeed!"

The young man, his hilarity quickened, took but a moment for the truth. "Yes—it *was* a squash!"

"And once," his hostess pursued, "in the lobby of the opera?"

"After 'Tristan'—yes; but with some awful grand people I didn't know."

She recognised; she estimated the grandeur. "Oh, the Pennimans are nobody! But now," she asked, "you've come, you say, on 'business'?"

"Very important, please—which accounts for the hour I've ventured and the appearance I present."

"I don't ask you too much to 'account,'" Lady Sandgate kindly said; "but I can't not wonder if she hasn't told you what things have happened."

He cast about. "She has had no chance to tell me anything—beyond the fact of her being here."

"Without the reason?"

"'The reason'?" he echoed.

She gave it up, going straighter. "She's with me then as an old firm friend. Under my care and protection."

"I see"—he took it, with more penetration than enthusiasm, as a hint in respect to himself. "She puts you on your guard."

Lady Sandgate expressed it more graciously. "She puts me on my honour—or at least her father does."

"As to her seeing *me*"

"As to *my* seeing at least—what may happen to her."

"Because—you say—things *have* happened?"

His companion fairly sounded him. "You've only talked—when you've met—of 'art'?"

"Well," he smiled, "'art is long'!"

"Then I hope it may see you through! But you should know first that Lord Theign is presently due—"

"*Here*, back already from abroad?"—he was all alert.

"He has not yet gone—he comes up this morning to start."

"And stops here on his way?"

"To take the *train de luxe* this afternoon to his annual Salsomaggiore. But with so little time to spare," she went on reassuringly, "that, to simplify—as he wired me an hour ago from Dedborough—he has given rendezvous here to Mr. Bender, who is particularly to wait for him."

"And who may therefore arrive at any moment?"

She looked at her bracelet watch. "Scarcely before noon. So you'll just have your chance—"

"Thank the powers then!"—Hugh grasped at it. "I shall have it best if you'll be so good as to tell me first—well," he faltered, "what it is that, to my great disquiet, you've further alluded to; what it is that has occurred."

Lady Sandgate took her time, but her good-nature and other sentiments pronounced. "Haven't you at least guessed that she has fallen under her father's extreme reprobation?"

"Yes, so much as that—that she must have greatly annoyed him—I have been supposing. But isn't it by her having asked me to act for her? I mean about the Mantovano—which I *have* done."

Lady Sandgate wondered. "You've 'acted'?"

"It's what I've come to tell her at last—and I'm all impatience."

"I see, I see"—she had caught a clue. "He hated that—yes; but you haven't really made out," she put to him, "the *other* effect of your hour at Dedborough?" She recognised, however, while she spoke, that his divination had failed, and she didn't trouble him to confess it. "Directly you had gone she 'turned down' Lord John. Declined, I mean, the offer of his hand in marriage."

Hugh was clearly as much mystified as anything else. "He proposed there—?"

"He had spoken, that day, *before*—before your talk with Lord Theign, who had every confidence in her accepting him. But you came, Mr. Crimble, you went; and when her suitor reappeared, just after you *had* gone, for his answer—"

"She wouldn't have him?" Hugh asked with a precipitation of interest.

But Lady Sandgate could humour almost any curiosity. "She wouldn't look at him."

He bethought himself. "But had she said she would?"

"So her father indignantly considers."

"That's the *ground* of his indignation?"

"He had his reasons for counting on her, and it has determined a painful crisis."

Hugh Crimble turned this over—feeling apparently for something he didn't find. "I'm sorry to hear such things, but where's the connection with me?"

"Ah, you know best yourself, and if you don't see any—-!" In that case, Lady Sandgate's motion implied, she washed her hands of it.

Hugh had for a moment the air of a young man treated to the sweet chance to guess a conundrum—which he gave up. "I really don't see any, Lady Sandgate. But," he a little inconsistently said, "I'm greatly obliged to you for telling me."

"Don't mention it!—though I think it *is* good of me," she smiled, "on so short an acquaintance." To which she added more gravely: "I leave you the situation—but I'm willing to let you know that I'm all on Grace's side."

"So am I, *rather!*—please let me frankly say."

He clearly refreshed, he even almost charmed her. "It's the very least you can say!—though I'm not sure whether you say it as the simplest or as the very subtlest of men. But in case you don't know as I do how little the particular candidate I've named——"

"Had a right or a claim to succeed with her?" he broke in—all quick intelligence here at least. "No, I don't perhaps know as well as you do—but I think I know as well as I just yet require."

"There you are then! And if you did prevent," his hostess maturely pursued, "what wouldn't have been—well, good or nice, I'm quite on your side too."

Our young man seemed to feel the shade of ambiguity, but he reached at a meaning. "You're with me in my plea for our defending at any cost of effort or ingenuity—"

"The precious picture Lord Theign exposes?"—she took his presumed sense faster than he had taken hers. But she hung fire a moment with her reply to it. "Well, will you keep the secret of everything I've said or say?"

Henry James

"To the death, to the stake, Lady Sandgate!"

"Then," she momentously returned, "I only want, too, to make Bender impossible. If you ask me," she pursued, "how I arrange that with my deep loyalty to Lord Theign——"

"I don't ask you anything of the sort," he interrupted—"I wouldn't ask you for the world; and my own bright plan for achieving the *coup* you mention——"

"You'll have time, at the most," she said, consulting afresh her bracelet watch, "to explain to Lady Grace." She reached an electric bell, which she touched—facing then her visitor again with an abrupt and slightly embarrassed change of tone. "You do think *my* great portrait splendid?"

He had strayed far from it and all too languidly came back. "Your Lawrence there? As I said, magnificent."

But the butler had come in, interrupting, straight from the lobby; of whom she made her request. "Let her ladyship know—Mr. Crimble."

Gotch looked hard at Hugh and the crumpled hat—almost as if having an option. But he resigned himself to repeating, with a distinctness that scarce fell short of the invidious, "Mr. Crimble," and departed on his errand.

Lady Sandgate's fair flush of diplomacy had meanwhile not faded. "Couldn't you, with your immense cleverness and power, get the Government to do something?"

"About your picture?" Hugh betrayed on this head a graceless detachment. "You too then want to sell?"

Oh she righted herself. "Never to a private party!"

"Mr. Bender's not after it?" he asked—though scarce lighting his reluctant interest with a forced smile.

"Most intensely after it. But never," cried the proprietress, "to a bloated alien!"

"Then I applaud your patriotism. Only why not," he asked, "carrying that magnanimity a little further, set us all an example as splendid as the object itself?"

"Give it you for nothing?" She threw up shocked hands. "Because I'm an aged female pauper and can't make *every* sacrifice."

Hugh pretended—none too convincingly—to think. "Will you let them have it very cheap?"

"Yes—for less than such a bribe as Bender's."

"Ah," he said expressively, "that might be, and still——!"

"Well," she had a flare of fond confidence. "I'll find out what he'll offer—if you'll on your side do what you can—and then ask them a third less." And she followed it up—as if suddenly conceiving him a prig. "See here, Mr. Crimble, I've been—and this very first time I—charming to you."

"You have indeed," he returned; "but you throw back on it a lurid light if it has all been for *that!*"

"It has been—well, to keep things as I want them; and if I've given you precious information mightn't you on your side—"

"Estimate its value in cash?"—Hugh sharply took her up. "Ah, Lady Sandgate, I *am* in your debt, but if you really bargain for your precious information I'd rather we assume that I haven't enjoyed it."

She made him, however, in reply, a sign for silence; she had heard Lady Grace enter the other room from the back landing, and, reaching the nearer door, she disposed of the question with high gay bravery. "I won't bargain with the Treasury!"—she had passed out by the time Lady Grace arrived.

303

II

Paris market (1881) by Victor Gabriel Gilbert (1847-1935)

As Hugh recognised in this friend's entrance and face the light of welcome he went, full of his subject, straight to their main affair. "I haven't been able to wait, I've wanted so much to tell you—I mean how I've just come back from Brussels, where I saw Pappen-dick, who was free and ready, by the happiest chance, to start for Verona, which he must have reached some time yesterday."

The girl's responsive interest fairly broke into rapture. "Ah, the dear sweet thing!"

"Yes, he's a brick—but the question now hangs in the balance. Allowing him time to have got into relation with the picture, I've begun to expect his wire, which will probably come to my club; but my fidget, while I wait, has driven me"—he threw out and dropped his arms in expression of his soft surrender—"well, just to do *this*: to come to you here, in my fever, at an unnatural hour and uninvited, and at least let you know I've 'acted.'"

"Oh, but I simply rejoice," Lady Grace declared, "to be acting *with* you."

"Then if you are, if you are," the young man cried, "why everything's beautiful and right!"

"It's all I care for and think of now," she went on in her bright devotion, "and I've only wondered and hoped!"

Well, Hugh found for it all a rapid, abundant lucidity. "He was away from home at first, and I had to wait—but I crossed last week, found him and settled incoming home by Paris, where I had a grand four days' jaw with the fellows there and saw *their* great specimen of our master: all of which has given him time."

"And now his time's up?" the girl eagerly asked.

"It *must* be—and we shall see." But Hugh postponed that question to a matter of more moment still. "The thing is that at last I'm able to tell you how I feel the trouble I've brought you."

It made her, quickly colouring, rest grave eyes on him. "What do you know—when I haven't told you—about my 'trouble'?"

"Can't I have guessed, with a ray of intelligence?"—he had his answer ready. "You've sought asylum with this good friend from the effects of your father's resentment."

"'Sought asylum' is perhaps excessive," Lady Grace returned—"though it wasn't pleasant with him after that hour, no," she allowed. "And I couldn't go, you see, to Kitty."

"No indeed, you couldn't go to Kitty." He smiled at her hard as he added: "I should have liked to see you go to Kitty! Therefore exactly is it that I've set you adrift—that I've darkened and poisoned your days. You're paying with your comfort, with your peace, for having joined so gallantly in my grand remonstrance."

She shook her head, turning from him, but then turned back again—as if accepting, as if even relieved by, this version of the prime cause of her state. "Why do you talk of it as 'paying'—if it's all to come back to my *being* paid? I mean by your blest success—if you really do what you want."

"I have your word for it," he searchingly said, "that our really pulling it off together will make up to you——?"

"I should be ashamed if it didn't, for everything!"—she took the question from his mouth. "I believe in such a cause exactly as you do—and found a lesson, at Dedborough, in your frankness and your faith."

"Then you'll help me no end," he said all simply and sincerely.

"You've helped *me* already"—that she gave him straight back. And on it they stayed a moment, their strenuous faces more intensely communing.

"You're very wonderful—for a girl!" Hugh brought out.

"One *has* to be a girl, naturally, to be a daughter of one's house," she laughed; "and that's all I am of ours—but a true and a right and a straight one."

He glowed with his admiration. "You're splendid!"

That might be or not, her light shrug intimated; she gave it, at any rate, the go-by and more exactly stated her case. "I see our situation."

"So do I, Lady Grace!" he cried with the strongest emphasis. "And your father only doesn't."

"Yes," she said for intelligent correction—"he sees it, there's nothing in life he sees so much. But unfortunately he sees it all wrong."

Hugh seized her point of view as if there had been nothing of her that he wouldn't have seized. "He sees it all wrong then! My appeal the other day he took as a rude protest. And any protest——"

"Any protest," she quickly and fully agreed, "he takes as an offence, yes. It's his theory that he still has rights," she smiled, "though he *is* a miserable peer."

"How should he not have rights," said Hugh, "when he has really everything on earth?"

"Ah, he doesn't even *know* that—he takes it so much for granted." And she sought, though as rather sadly and despairingly, to explain. "He lives all in his own world."

"He lives all in his own, yes; but he does business all in ours—quite as much as the people who come up to the city in the Tube." With which Hugh had a still sharper recall of the stiff actual. "And he must be here to do business to-day."

"You know," Lady Grace asked, "that he's to meet Mr. Bender?"

"Lady Sandgate kindly warned me, and," her companion saw as he glanced at the clock on the chimney, "I've only ten minutes, at best. The 'Journal' won't have been good for him," he added—"you doubtless have seen the 'Journal'?"

"No"—she was vague. "We live by the 'Morning Post.'"

"That's why our friend here didn't speak then," Hugh said with a better light—"which, out of a dim consideration for her, I didn't do, either. But they've a leader this morning about Lady Lappington and her Longhi, and on Bender and his hauls, and on the certainty—if we don't do something energetic—of more and more Benders to come: such a conquering horde as invaded the old civilisation, only armed now with huge cheque-books instead of with spears and battle-axes. They refer to the rumour current—as too horrific to believe—of Lord Theign's putting up his Moretto; with the question of how properly to qualify any such sad purpose in him should the further report prove true of a new and momentous opinion about the picture entertained by several eminent authorities."

"Of whom," said the girl, intensely attached to this recital, "you're of course seen as not the least."

"Of whom, of course, Lady Grace, I'm as yet—however I'm 'seen'—the whole collection. But we've time"—he rested on that "The fat, if you'll allow me the expression, is on the fire—which, as I see the matter, is where this particular fat *should* be."

"Is the article, then," his companion appealed, "very severe?"

"I prefer to call it very enlightened and very intelligent—and the great thing is that it immensely 'marks,' as they say. It will have made a big public difference—from this day; though it's of course aimed not so much at persons as at conditions; which it calls upon us all somehow to tackle."

"Exactly"—she was full of the saving vision; "but as the conditions are directly embodied in persons——"

"Oh, of course it here and there bells the cat; which means that it bells three or four."

"Yes," she richly brooded—"Lady Lappington *is* a cat!"

"She will have been 'belled,' at any rate, with your father," Hugh amusedly went on, "to the certainty of a row; and a row can only be good for us—I mean for *us* in particular." Yet he had to bethink himself. "The case depends a good deal of course on how your father *takes* such a resounding rap."

"Oh, I know how he'll take it!"—her perception went all the way.

"In the very highest and properest spirit?"

"Well, you'll see." She was as brave as she was clear. "Or at least I shall!"

Struck with all this in her he renewed his homage. "You *are*, yes, splendid!"

"I even," she laughed, "surprise myself."

But he was already back at his calculations. "How early do the papers get to you?"

"At Dedborough? Oh, quite for breakfast—which isn't, however, very early."

"Then that's what has caused his wire to Bender."

"But how will such talk strike *him*?" the girl asked.

Hugh meanwhile, visibly, had not only followed his train of thought, he had let it lead him to certainty. "It will have moved Mr. Bender to absolute rapture."

"Rather," Lady Grace wondered, "than have put him off?"

"It will have put him prodigiously *on*! Mr. Bender—as he said to me at Dedborough of his noble host there," Hugh pursued—"is 'a very nice man; but he's a product of the world of advertisment, and advertisement is all he sees and aims at. He lives in it as a saint in glory or a fish in water."

She took it from him as half doubting. "But mayn't advertisement, in so special a case, turn, on the whole, against him?"

Hugh shook a negative forefinger with an expression he might have caught from foreign comrades. "He rides the biggest whirlwind—he has got it saddled and bitted."

She faced the image, but cast about "Then where does our success come in?"

"In our making the beast, all the same, bolt with him and throw him." And Hugh further pointed the moral. "If in such proceedings all he knows is publicity the thing is to give him publicity, and it's only a question of giving him enough. By the time he has enough for himself, you see, he'll have too much for every one else—so that we shall 'up' in a body and slay him."

The girl's eyebrows, in her wondering face, rose to a question. "But if he has meanwhile got the picture?"

"We'll slay him before he gets it!" He revelled in the breadth of his view. "Our own policy must be to *organise* to that end the inevitable outcry. Organise Bender himself—organise him to scandal." Hugh had already even pity to spare for their victim. "He won't know it from a boom."

Though carried along, however, Lady Grace could still measure. "But that will be only if he wants and decides for the picture."

"We must make him then want and decide for it—decide, that is, for 'ours.' To save it we must work him up—he'll in that case want it so indecently much. Then *we* shall have to want it more!"

"Well," she anxiously felt it her duty to remind him, "you can take a horse to water——!"

"Oh, trust me to make him drink!"

There appeared a note in this that convinced her. "It's you, Mr. Crimble, who are 'splendid'!"

"Well, I shall be—with my jolly wire!" And all on that scent again, "May I come back to you from the club with Pappendick's news?" he asked.

"Why, rather, of course, come back!"

"Only not," he debated, "till your father has left."

Lady Grace considered too, but sharply decided. "Come when you *have* it. But tell me first," she added, "one thing." She hung fire a little while he waited, but she brought it out. "Was it you who got the 'Journal' to speak?"

"Ah, one scarcely 'gets' the 'Journal'!"

"Who then gave them their 'tip'?"

"About the Mantovano and its peril?" Well, he took a moment—but only not to say; in addition to which the butler had reappeared, entering from the lobby. "I'll tell you," he laughed, "when I come back!"

Gotch had his manner of announcement while the visitor was mounting the stairs. "Mr. Breckenridge Bender!"

"Ah then I go," said Lady Grace at once.

"I'll stay three minutes." Hugh turned with her, alertly, to the easier issue, signalling hope and cheer from that threshold as he watched her disappear; after which he faced about with as brave a smile and as ready for immediate action as if she had there within kissed her hand to him. Mr. Bender emerged at the same instant, Gotch withdrawing and closing the door behind him; and the former personage, recognising his young friend, threw up his hands for friendly pleasure.

III

Art collector (1901) by Ilya Repin (1844-1930)

"Ah, Mr. Crimble," he cordially inquired, "you've come with your great news?"

Hugh caught the allusion, it would have seemed, but after a moment. "News of the Moretto? No, Mr. Bender, I haven't news *yet*." But he added as with high candour for the visitor's motion of disappointment: "I think I warned you, you know, that it would take three or four weeks."

"Well, in *my* country," Mr. Bender returned with disgust, "it would take three or four minutes! Can't you make 'em step more lively?"

"I'm expecting, sir," said Hugh good-humouredly, "a report from hour to hour."

"Then will you let me have it right off?"

Hugh indulged in a pause; after which very frankly: "Ah, it's scarcely for you, Mr. Bender, that I'm acting!"

The great collector was but briefly checked. "Well, can't you just act for Art?"

"Oh, you're doing that yourself so powerfully," Hugh laughed, "that I think I had best leave it to you!"

His friend looked at him as some inspector on circuit might look at a new improvement. "Don't you want to go round acting *with* me?"

"Go 'on tour,' as it were? Oh, frankly, Mr. Bender," Hugh said, "if I had any weight——!"

"You'd add it to your end of the beam? Why, what have I done that *you* should go back on me—after working me up so down there? The worst I've done," Mr. Bender continued, "is to refuse that Moretto."

"Has it deplorably been *offered* you?" our young man cried, unmistakably and sincerely affected. After which he went on, as his fellow-visitor only eyed him hard, not, on second thoughts, giving the owner of the great work away: "Then why are you—as if you were a banished Romeo—so keen for news from Verona?" To this odd mixture of business and literature Mr. Bender made no reply, contenting himself with but a large vague blandness that wore in him somehow the mark of tested utility; so that Hugh put him another question: "Aren't you here, sir, on the chance of the Mantovano?"

"I'm here," he then imperturbably said, "because Lord Theign has wired me to meet him. Ain't you here for that yourself?"

Hugh betrayed for a moment his enjoyment of a "big" choice of answers. "Dear, no! I've but been in, by Lady Sandgate's leave, to see that grand Lawrence."

"Ah yes, she's very kind about it—one does go 'in.'" After which Mr. Bender had, even in the atmosphere of his danger, a throb of curiosity. "Is any one *after* that grand Lawrence?"

"Oh, I hope not," Hugh laughed, "unless you again dreadfully are: wonderful thing as it is and so just in its right place there."

"You call it," Mr. Bender impartially inquired, "a *very* wonderful thing?"

"Well, as a Lawrence, it has quite bowled me over"—Hugh spoke as for the strictly aesthetic awkwardness of that. "But you know I take my pictures hard." He gave a punch to his hat, pressed for time in this connection as he was glad truly to appear to his friend. "I must make my little*rapport*." Yet before it he did seek briefly to explain. "We're a band of young men who care—and we watch the great things. Also—for I must give you the real truth about myself—we watch the great people."

"Well, I guess I'm used to being watched—if that's the worst you can do." To which Mr. Bender added in his homely way: "But you know, Mr. Crimble, what I'm *really* after."

Hugh's strategy on this would again have peeped out for us. "The man in this morning's 'Journal' appears at least to have discovered."

"Yes, the man in this morning's 'Journal' has discovered three or four weeks—as it appears to take you here for everything—after my beginning to talk. Why, they knew I was talking *that* time ago on the other side."

"Oh, they know things in the States," Hugh cheerfully agreed, "so independently of their happening! But you must have talked loud."

"Well, I haven't so much talked as raved," Mr. Bender conceded—"for I'm afraid that when I do want a thing I rave till I get it. You heard me at Ded-borough, and your enterprising daily press has at last caught the echo."

"Then they'll make up for lost time! But have you done it," Hugh asked, "to prepare an alibi?"

"An alibi?"

"By 'raving,' as you say, the saddle on the wrong horse. I don't think you at all believe you'll get the Sir Joshua—but meanwhile we shall have cleared up the question of the Moretto."

Mr. Bender, imperturbable, didn't speak till he had done justice to this picture of his subtlety. "Then, why on earth do you want to boom the Moretto?"

"You ask that," said Hugh, "because it's the boomed thing that's most in peril."

"Well, it's the big, the bigger, the biggest things, and if you drag their value to the light why shouldn't we want to grab them and carry them off—the same as all of *you* originally did?"

"Ah, not quite the same," Hugh smiled—"that I *will* say for you!"

"Yes, you stick it on now—you *have* got an eye for the rise in values. But I grant you your unearned increment, and you ought to be mighty glad that, to such a time, I'll pay it you."

Our young man kept, during a moment's thought, his eyes on his companion, and then resumed with all intensity and candour: "You may easily, Mr. Bender, be too much for me—as you appear too much for far greater people. But may I ask you, very earnestly, for your word on *this*, as to any case in which that happens—that when precious things, things we are to lose here, *are* knocked down to you, you'll let us at least take leave of them, let us have a sight of them in London, before they're borne off?"

Mr. Bender's big face fell almost with a crash. "Hand them over, you mean, to the sandwich men on Bond Street?"

"To one or other of the placard and poster men—I don't insist on the inserted human slice! Let the great values, as a compensation to us, be on view for three or four weeks."

"You ask me," Mr. Bender returned, "for a *general* assurance to that effect?"

"Well, a particular one—so it be particular enough," Hugh said—"will do just for now. Let me put in my plea for the issue—well, of the value that's actually in the scales."

"The Mantovano-Moretto?"

"The Moretto-Mantovano!"

Mr. Bender carnivorously smiled. "Hadn't we better know which it is first?"

Hugh had a motion of practical indifference for this. "The public interest—playing so straight on the question—may help to settle it. By which I mean that it will profit enormously—the question of probability, of identity itself will—by the discussion it will create. The discussion will promote certainty——"

"And certainty," Mr. Bender massively mused, "will kick up a row."

"*Of course* it will kick up a row!"—Hugh thoroughly guaranteed that. "You'll be, for the month, the best-abused man in England—if you venture to remain here at all; except, naturally, poor Lord Theign."

"Whom it won't be my interest, at the same time, to worry into backing down."

"But whom it will be exceedingly *mine* to practise on"—and Hugh laughed as at the fun before them—"if I may entertain the sweet hope of success. The only thing is—from my point of view," he went on—"that backing down before what he will call vulgar clamour isn't in the least in his traditions, nothing less so; and that if there should be really too much of it for his taste or his nerves he'll set his handsome face as a stone and never budge an inch. But at least again what I appeal to you for will have taken place—the picture will have been seen by a lot of people who'll care."

"It will have been seen," Mr. Bender amended—"on the mere contingency of my acquisition of it—only if its present owner consents."

"'Consents'?" Hugh almost derisively echoed; "why, he'll propose it himself, he'll insist on it, he'll put it through, once he's angry enough—as angry, I mean, as almost any public criticism of a personal act of his will be sure to make him; and I'm afraid the striking criticism, or at least animadversion, of this morning, will have blown on his flame of bravado."

Inevitably a student of character, Mr. Bender rose to the occasion. "Yes, I guess he's pretty mad."

"They've imputed to him"—Hugh but wanted to abound in that sense—"an intention of which after all he isn't guilty."

"So that"—his listener glowed with interested optimism—"if they don't look out, if they impute it to him again, I guess he'll just go and be guilty!"

Hugh might at this moment have shown to an initiated eye as fairly elated by the sense of producing something of the effect he had hoped. "You entertain the fond vision of lashing them up to that mistake, oh fisher in troubled waters?" And then with a finer art, as his companion, expansively bright but crudely acute, eyed him in turn as if to sound *him*: "The strongest thing in such a type—one does make out— is his resentment of a liberty taken; and the most natural furthermore is quite that he should feel almost anything you do take uninvited from the groaning board of his banquet of life to *be* such a liberty."

Mr. Bender participated thus at his perceptive ease in the exposed aristocratic illusion. "Yes, I guess he has always lived as he likes, the way those of you who have got things fixed for them *do*, over here; and to have to quit it on account of unpleasant remark—"

But he gave up thoughtfully trying to express what this must be; reduced to the mere synthetic interjection "My!"

"That's it, Mr. Bender," Hugh said for the consecration of such a moral; "he won't quit it without a hard struggle."

Mr. Bender hereupon at last gave himself quite gaily away as to his high calculation of impunity. "Well, I guess he won't struggle too hard for me to hold on to him if I *want* to!"

"In the thick of the conflict then, however that may be," Hugh returned, "don't forget what I've urged on you—the claim of our desolate country."

But his friend had an answer to this. "My natural interest, Mr. Crimble—considering what I do for it—is in the claim of ours. But I wish you were on my side!"

"Not so much," Hugh hungrily and truthfully laughed, "as I wish you were on mine!" Decidedly, none the less, he had to go. "Good-bye—for another look here!"

He reached the doorway of the second room, where, however, his companion, freshly alert at this, stayed him by a gesture. "How much is she really worth?"

"'She'?" Hugh, staring a moment, was miles at sea. "Lady Sandgate?"

"Her great-grandmother."

A responsible answer was prevented—the butler was again with them; he had opened wide the other door and he named to Mr. Bender the personage under his convoy. "Lord John!"

Hugh caught this from the inner threshold, and it gave him his escape. "Oh, ask *that* friend!" With which he sought the further passage to the staircase and street, while Lord John arrived in charge of Mr. Gotch, who, having remarked to the two occupants of the front drawing-room that her ladyship would come, left them together.

IV

"Then Theign's not yet here!" Lord John had to resign himself as he greeted his American ally. "But he told me I should find you."

"He has kept me waiting," that gentleman returned—"but what's the matter with him anyway?"

"The matter with him"—Lord John treated such ignorance as irritating—"must of course be this beastly thing in the 'Journal.'"

Mr. Bender proclaimed, on the other hand, his incapacity to seize such connections. "What's the matter with the beastly thing?"

"Why, aren't you aware that the stiffest bit of it is a regular dig at you?"

"If you call *that* a regular dig you can't have had much experience of the Papers. I've known them to dig much deeper."

"I've had *no* experience of such horrid attacks, thank goodness; but do you mean to say," asked Lord John with the surprise of his own delicacy, "that you don't unpleasantly feel it?"

"Feel it where, my dear sir?"

"Why, God bless me, such impertinence, everywhere!"

"All over me at once?"—Mr. Bender took refuge in easy humour. "Well, I'm a large man—so when I want to feel so much I look out for something good. But what, if he suffers from the blot on his ermine—ain't that what you wear?—does our friend propose to do about it?"

Lord John had a demur, which was immediately followed by the apprehension of support in his uncertainty. Lady Sandgate was before them, having reached them through the other room, and to her he at once referred the question. "What *will* Theign propose, do you think, Lady Sandgate, to do about it?"

She breathed both her hospitality and her vagueness. "To 'do'——?"

"Don't you know about the thing in the 'Journal'—awfully offensive all round?"

"There'd be even a little pinch for *you* in it," Mr. Bender said to her—"if you were bent on fitting the shoe!"

Well, she met it all as gaily as was compatible with a firm look at her elder guest while she took her place with them. "Oh, the shoes of such monsters as that are much too big for poor *me!*" But she was more specific for Lord John. "I know only what Grace has just told me; but since it's a question of footgear dear Theign will certainly—what you may call—take his stand!"

Lord John welcomed this assurance. "If I know him he'll take it splendidly!"

Mr. Bender's attention was genial, though rather more detached. "And what—while he's about it—will he take it particularly *on?*"

"Oh, we've plenty of things, thank heaven," said Lady Sandgate, "for a man in Theign's position to hold fast by!"

Lord John freely confirmed it. "Scores and scores—rather! And I will say for us that, with the rotten way things seem going, the fact may soon become a real convenience."

Mr. Bender seemed struck—and not unsympathetic. "I see that your system would be rather a fraud if you hadn't pretty well fixed *that!*"

Lady Sandgate spoke as one at present none the less substantially warned and convinced. "It doesn't, however, alter the fact that we've thus in our ears the first growl of an outcry."

"Ah," Lord John concurred, "we've unmistakably the first growl of an outcry!"

Mr. Bender's judgment on the matter paused at sight of Lord Theign, introduced and announced, as Lord John spoke, by Gotch; but with the result of his addressing directly the person so presenting himself. "Why, they tell me that what this means, Lord Theign, is the first growl of an outcry!"

The appearance of the most eminent figure in the group might have been held in itself to testify to some such truth; in the sense at least that a certain conscious radiance, a gathered light of battle in his lordship's aspect would have been explained by his having taken the full measure—an inner success with which he glowed—of some high provocation. He was flushed, but he bore it as the ensign of his house; he was so admirably, vividly dressed, for the morning hour and for his journey, that he shone as with the armour of a knight; and the whole effect of him, from head to foot, with every jerk of his unconcern and every flash of his ease, was to call attention to his being utterly unshaken and knowing perfectly what he was about. It was at this happy pitch that he replied to the prime upsetter of his peace.

"I'm afraid I don't know what anything means to *you*, Mr. Bender—but it's exactly to find out that I've asked you, with our friend John, kindly to meet me here. For a very brief conference, dear lady, by your good leave," he went on to Lady Sandgate; "at which I'm only too pleased that you yourself should assist. The 'first growl' of any outcry, I may mention to you all, affects me no more than the last will——!"

"So I'm delighted to gather"—Lady Sandgate took him straight up—"that you don't let go your inestimable Cure."

He at first quite stared superior—"'Let go'?"—but then treated it with a lighter touch. "Upon my honour I might, you know—that dose of the daily press has made me feel so fit! I arrive at any rate," he pursued to the others and in particular to Mr. Bender, "I arrive with my decision taken—which I've thought may perhaps interest you. If that tuppeny rot *is* an attempt at an outcry I simply nip it in the bud."

Lord John rejoicingly approved. "Absolutely the only way—with the least self-respect—to treat it!"

Lady Sandgate, on the other hand, sounded a sceptical note. "But are you sure it's so easy, Theign, to hush up a *real* noise?"

"It ain't what I'd call a real one, Lady Sandgate," Mr. Bender said; "you can generally distinguish a real one from the squeak of two or three mice! But granted mice do affect you, Lord Theign, it will interest me to hear what sort of a trap—by what you say—you propose to set for them."

"You must allow me to measure, myself, Mr. Bender," his lordship replied, "the importance of a gross freedom publicly used with my absolutely personal proceedings and affairs; to the cause and origin of any definite report of which—in such circles!—I'm afraid I rather wonder if you yourself can't give me a clue."

It took Mr. Bender a minute to do justice to these stately remarks. "You rather wonder if I've talked of how I feel about your detaining in your hands my Beautiful Duchess——?"

"Oh, if you've already published her as 'yours'—with your *power* of publication!" Lord Theign coldly laughed,—"of course I trace the connection!"

Mr. Benders acceptance of responsibility clearly cost him no shade of a pang. "Why, I haven't for quite a while talked of a blessed other thing—and I'm capable of growing more profane over my *not* getting her than I guess any one would dare to be if I did."

"Well, you'll certainly not 'get' her, Mr. Bender," Lady Sandgate, as for reasons of her own, bravely trumpeted; "and even if there were a chance of it don't you see that your way wouldn't be publicly to abuse our noble friend?"

Mr. Bender but beamed, in reply, upon that personage. "Oh, I guess our noble friend knows I *have* to talk big about big things. You understand, sir, the scream of the eagle!"

"I'll forgive you," Lord Theign civilly returned, "all the big talk you like if you'll now understand *me*. My retort to that hireling pack shall be at once to dispose of a picture."

Mr. Bender rather failed to follow. "But that's what you wanted to do before."

"Pardon me," said his lordship—"I make a difference. It's what you wanted me to do."

The mystification, however, continued. "And you were *not*—as you seemed then—willing?"

Lord Theign waived cross-questions. "Well, I'm willing *now*—that's all that need concern us. Only, once more and for the last time," he added with all authority, "you can't have our Duchess!"

"You can't have our Duchess!"—and Lord John, as before the altar of patriotism, wrapped it in sacrificial sighs.

"You can't have our Duchess!" Lady Sandgate repeated, but with a grace that took the sting from her triumph. And she seemed still all sweet sociability as she added: "I wish he'd tell you too, you dreadful rich thing, that you can't have anything at all!"

Lord Theign, however, in the interest of harmony, deprecated that rigour. "Ah, what then would become of my happy retort?"

"And what—as it *is*," Mr. Bender asked—"becomes of my unhappy grievance?"

"Wouldn't a really great capture make up to you for that?"

"Well, I take more interest in what I want than in what I have—and it depends, don't you see, on how you measure the size."

Lord John had at once in this connection a bright idea. "Shouldn't you like to go back there and take the measure yourself?"

Mr. Bender considered him as through narrowed eyelids. "Look again at that tottering Moretto?"

"Well, its size—as you say—isn't in *any* light a negligible quantity."

"You mean that—big as it is—it hasn't yet stopped growing?"

The question, however, as he immediately showed, resided in what Lord Theign himself meant "It's more to the purpose," he said to Mr. Bender, "that I should mention to you the leading feature, or in other words the very essence, of my plan of campaign—which is to put the picture at once on view." He marked his idea with a broad but elegant gesture. "On view as a thing definitely disposed of."

"I say, I say, I say!" cried Lord John, moved by this bold stroke to high admiration.

Lady Sandgate's approval was more qualified. "But on view, dear Theign, how?"

"With one of those pushing people in Bond Street." And then as for the crushing climax of his policy: "As a Mantovano pure and simple."

"But my dear man," she quavered, "if it *isn't* one?"

Mr. Bender at once anticipated; the wind had suddenly risen for him and he let out sail. "Lady Sand-gate, it's going, by all that's—well, interesting, to *be* one!"

Lord Theign took him up with pleasure. "You seize me? We *treat* it as one!"

Lord John eagerly borrowed the emphasis. "We *treat* it as one!"

Mr. Bender meanwhile fed with an opened appetite on the thought—he even gave it back larger. "As the long-lost Number Eight!"

Lord Theign happily seized *him*. "That will be it—to a charm!"

"It will make them," Mr. Bender asked, "madder than anything?"

His patron—if not his client—put it more nobly. "It will markedly affirm my attitude."

"Which in turn the more markedly create discussion."

"It may create all it will!"

"Well, if *you* don't mind it, *I* don't!" Mr. Bender concluded. But though bathed in this high serenity he was all for the rapid application of it elsewhere. "You'll put the thing on view right off?"

"As soon as the proper arrangement——"

"You put off your journey to *make* it?" Lady Sand-gate at once broke in.

Lord Theign bethought himself—with the effect of a gracious confidence in the others. "Not if these friends will act."

"Oh, I guess we'll *act!*" Mr. Bender declared.

"Ah, *won't* we though!" Lord John re-echoed.

"You understand then I have an interest?" Mr. Bender went on to Lord Theign.

His lordship's irony met it. "I accept that complication—which so much simplifies!"

"And yet also have a liberty?"

"Where else would be those you've taken? The point is," said Lord Theign, "that *I* have a show."

It settled Mr. Bender. "Then I'll *fix* your show." He snatched up his hat. "Lord John, come right round!"

Lord John had of himself reached the door, which he opened to let the whirlwind tremendously figured by his friend pass out first. Taking leave of the others he gave it even his applause. "The fellow can do anything anywhere!" And he hastily followed.

V

Lady Sandgate, left alone with Lord Theign, drew the line at their companion's enthusiasm. "That may be true of Mr. Bender—for it's dreadful how he bears one down. But I simply find him a terror."

"Well," said her friend, who seemed disposed not to fatigue the question, "I dare say a terror will help me." He had other business to which he at once gave himself. "And now, if you please, for that girl."

"I'll send her to you," she replied, "if you can't stay to luncheon."

"I've three or four things to do," he pleaded, "and I lunch with Kitty at one."

She submitted in that case—but disappointedly. "With Berkeley Square then you've time. But I confess I don't quite grasp the so odd inspiration that you've set those men to carry out."

He showed surprise and regret, but even greater decision. "Then it needn't trouble you, dear—it's enough that I myself go straight."

"Are you so very convinced it's straight?"—she wouldn't be a bore to him, but she couldn't not be a blessing.

"What in the world else is it," he asked, "when, having good reasons, one acts on 'em?"

"You must have an immense array," she sighed, "to fly so in the face of Opinion!"

"'Opinion'?" he commented—"I fly in its face? Why, the vulgar thing, as I'm taking my quiet walk, flies in mine! I give it a whack with my umbrella and send it about its business." To which he added with more reproach: "It's enough to have been dished by Grace—without *your* falling away!"

Sadly and sweetly she defended herself. "It's only my great affection—and all that these years have been for us: *they* it is that make me wish you weren't so proud."

"I've a perfect sense, my dear, of what these years have been for us—a very charming matter. But 'proud' is it you find me of the daughter who does her best to ruin me, or of the one who does her best to humiliate me?"

Lady Sandgate, not undiscernibly, took her choice of ignoring the point of this. "Your surrenders to Kitty are your own affair—but are you sure you can really bear to see Grace?"

"I seem expected indeed to bear much," he said with more and more of his parental bitterness, "but I don't know that I'm yet in a funk before my child. Doesn't she *want* to see me, with any contrition, after the trick she has played me?" And then as his companion's answer failed: "In spite of which trick you suggest that I should leave the country with no sign of her explaining—?"

His hostess raised her head. "She does want to see you, I know; but you must recall the sequel to that bad hour at Dedborough—when it was you who declined to see *her*."

"Before she left the house with you, the next day, for this?"—he was entirely reminiscent. "What I recall is that even if I had condoned—that evening—her deception of *me* in my folly, I still loathed, for my friend's sake, her practical joke on poor John."

Lady Sandgate indulged in the shrug conciliatory. "It was your very complaint that your own appeal to her *became* an appeal from herself."

"Yes," he returned, so well he remembered, "she was about as civil to me then—picking a quarrel with me on such a trumped-up ground!—as that devil of a fellow in the newspaper; the taste of whose elegant remarks, for that matter, she must now altogether enjoy!"

His good friend showily balanced and might have been about to reply with weight; but what she in fact brought out was only: "I see you're right about it: I must let her speak for herself."

"That I shall greatly prefer to her speaking—as she did so extraordinarily, out of the blue, at Dedborough, upon my honour—for the wonderful friends she picks up: the picture-man introduced by her (what was his name?) who regularly 'cheeked' me, as I suppose he'd call it, in my own house, and whom I hope, by the way, that under this roof she's not able to be quite so thick with!"

If Lady Sandgate winced at that vain dream she managed not to betray it, and she had, in any embarrassment on this matter, the support, as we know, of her own tried policy. "She leads her life under this roof very much as under yours; and she's not of an age, remember, for me to pretend either to watch her movements or to control her contacts." Leaving him however thus to perform his pleasure the charming woman had before she went an abrupt change of tone. "Whatever your relations with others, dear friend, don't forget that *I'm* still here."

Lord Theign accepted the reminder, though, the circumstances being such, it scarce moved him to ecstasy. "That you're here, thank heaven, is of course a comfort—or would be if you understood."

"Ah," she submissively sighed, "if I don't always 'understand' a spirit so much higher than mine and a situation so much more complicated, certainly, I at least always defer, I at least always—well, what can I say but worship?" And then as he remained not other than finely passive, "The old altar, Theign," she went on—"and a spark of the old fire!"

He had not looked at her on this—it was as if he shrank, with his preoccupations, from a tender passage; but he let her take his left hand. "So I feel!" he was, however, kind enough to answer.

"Do feel!" she returned with much concentration. She raised the hand to her pressed lips, dropped it and with a rich "Good-bye!" reached the threshold of the other room.

"May I smoke?" he asked before she had disappeared.

"Dear, yes!"

He had meanwhile taken out his cigarette case and was looking about for a match. But something else occurred to him. "You must come to Victoria."

"Rather!" she said with intensity; and with that she passed away.

VI

Left alone he had a moment's meditation where he stood; it found issue in an articulate "Poor dear thing!"—an exclamation marked at once with patience and impatience, with resignation and ridicule. After which, waiting for his daughter, Lord Theign slowly and absently roamed, finding matches at last and lighting his cigarette—all with an air of concern that had settled on him more heavily from the moment of his finding himself alone. His luxury of gloom—if gloom it was—dropped, however, on his taking heed of Lady Grace, who, arriving on the scene through the other room, had had just time to stand and watch him in silence.

"Oh!" he jerked out at sight of her—which she had to content herself with as a parental greeting after separation, his next words doing little to qualify its dryness. "I take it for granted that you know I'm within a couple of hours of leaving England under a necessity of health." And then as drawing nearer, she signified without speaking her possession of this fact: "I've thought accordingly that before I go I should—on this first possible occasion since that odious occurrence at Dedborough—like to leave you a little more food for meditation, in my absence, on the painfully false position in which you there placed me." He carried himself restlessly even perhaps with a shade of awkwardness, to which her stillness was a contrast; she just waited, wholly passive—possibly indeed a trifle portentous. "If you had plotted and planned it in advance," he none the less firmly pursued, "if you had acted from some uncanny or malignant motive, you couldn't have arranged more perfectly to incommode, to disconcert and, to all intents and purposes, make light of me and insult me." Even before this charge she made no sign; with her eyes now attached to the ground she let him proceed. "I had practically guaranteed to our excellent, our charming friend, your favourable view of his appeal—which you yourself too, remember, had left him in so little doubt of!—so that, having by your performance so egregiously failed him, I have the pleasure of their coming down on me for explanations, for compensations, and for God knows what besides."

Lady Grace, looking at last, left him in no doubt of the rigour of her attention. "I'm sorry indeed, father, to have done you any wrong; but may I ask whom, in such a connection, you refer to as 'they'?"

"'They'?" he echoed in the manner of a man who has had handed back to his more careful eye, across the counter, some questionable coin that he has tried to pass. "Why, your own sister to begin with—whose interest in what may make for your happiness I suppose you decently recognise; and his people, one and all, the delightful old Duchess in particular, who only wanted to be charming to you, and who are as good people, and as pleasant and as clever, damn it, when all's said and done, as any others that are likely to come your way." It clearly did his lordship good to work out thus his case, which grew more and more coherent to him and glowed with irresistible colour. "Letting alone gallant John himself, most amiable of men, about whose merits and whose claims you appear to have pretended to agree with me just that you might, when he presumed, poor chap, ardently to urge them, deal him with the more cruel effect that calculated blow on the mouth!"

It was clear that in the girl's great gravity embarrassment had no share. "They so come down on you I understand then, father, that you're obliged to come down on *me?*"

"Assuredly—for some better satisfaction than your just moping here without a sign!"

"But a sign of what, father?" she asked—as helpless as a lone islander scanning the horizon for a sail.

"Of your appreciating, of your in some degree dutifully considering, the predicament into which you've put me!"

"Hasn't it occurred to you in the least that you've rather put *me* into one?"

He threw back his head as from exasperated nerves. "I put you certainly in the predicament of your receiving by my care a handsome settlement in life—which all the elements that would make for your enjoying it had every appearance of successfully commending to you." The perfect readiness of which on his lips had, like a higher wave, the virtue of lifting and dropping him to still more tangible ground. "And if I understand you aright as wishing to know whether I apologise for that zeal, why you take a most preposterous view of our relation as father and daughter."

"You understand me no better than I fear I understand you," Lady Grace returned, "if what you expect of me is really to take back my words to Lord John." And then as he didn't answer, while their breach gaped like a jostled wound, "Have you seriously come to propose—and from *him* again," she added—"that I shall reconsider my resolute act and lend myself to your beautiful arrangement?"

It had so the sound of unmixed ridicule that he could only, for his dignity, not give way to passion. "I've come, above all, for *this,* I may say, Grace: to remind you of whom you're addressing when you jibe at me, and to make of you assuredly a plain demand—exactly as to whether you judged us to have actively *incurred* your treatment of our unhappy friend, to have brought it upon us, he and I, by my refusal to discuss with you at such a crisis the question of my disposition of a particular item of my property. I've only to look at you, for that matter," Lord Theign continued—always with a finer point and a higher consistency as his rehearsal of his wrongs broadened—"to have my inquiry, as it seems to me, eloquently answered. You flounced away from poor John, you took, as he tells me, 'his head off,' just to repay me for what you chose to regard as my snub on the score of your challenging my entertainment of a possible purchaser; a rebuke launched at me, practically, in the presence of a most inferior person, a stranger and an intruder, from whom you had all the air of taking your cue for naming me the great condition on which you'd gratify my hope. Am I to understand, in other words,"—and his lordship mounted to a climax—"that you sent us about our business because I failed to gratify *your* hope: that of my knocking under to your sudden monstrous pretension to lay down the law for my choice of ways and means of raising, to my best convenience, a considerable sum of money? You'll be so good as to understand, once for all, that I recognise there no right of interference from any quarter—and also to let that knowledge govern your behaviour in my absence."

Lady Grace had thus for some minutes waited on his words—waited even as almost with anxiety for the safe conduct he might look to from some of the more extravagant of them. But he at least felt at the end—if it was an end—all he owed them; so that there was nothing for her but to accept as achieved his dreadful felicity. "You're very angry with me, and I hope you won't feel me simply 'aggravating' if I say that, thinking everything over, I've done my best to allow for that. But I *can* answer your question if I do answer it by saying that my discovery of your possible sacrifice of one of our most beautiful things didn't predispose me to decide in favour of a person—however 'backed' by you—for whose benefit the sacrifice was to take place. Frankly," the girl pushed on, "I did quite hate, for the moment, everything that might make for such a mistake; and took the darkest view, let me also confess, of every one, without exception, connected with it I interceded with you, earnestly, for our precious picture, and you wouldn't on any terms *have* my intercession. On top of that Lord John blundered in, without timeliness or tact—and I'm afraid that, as I hadn't been the least in love with him even before, he did have to take the consequence."

Lord Theign, with an elated swing of his person, greeted this as all he could possibly want. "You recognise then that your reception of him was purely vindictive!"—the meaning of which is that unless my conduct of my private interests, of which you know nothing whatever, happens to square with your superior wisdom you'll put me under boycott all round! While you chatter about mistakes and blunders, and about our charming friend's lack of the discretion of which you yourself set so grand an example, what account have you to offer of the scene you made me there before that fellow—your confederate, as he had all the air of being!—by giving it me with such effrontery that, if I had eminently done with him after his remarkable display, you at least were but the more determined to see him keep it up?"

The girl's justification, clearly, was very present to her, and not less obviously the truth that to make it strong she must, avoiding every side-issue, keep it very simple, "The only account I can give you, I think, is that I could but speak at such a moment as I felt, and that I felt—well, how can I say how deeply? If you can really bear to know, I feel so still I care in fact more than ever that we shouldn't do such things. I care, if you like, to indiscretion—I care, if you like, to offence, to arrogance, to folly. But even as my last word to you before you leave England on the conclusion of such a step, I'm ready to cry out to you that you oughtn't, you oughtn't, you oughtn't!"

Her father, with wonder-moved, elevated brows and high commanding hand, checked her as in an act really of violence—save that, like an inflamed young priestess, she had already, in essence, delivered her message. "Hallo, hallo, hallo, my distracted daughter—no 'crying out,' if you please!" After which, while arrested but unabashed, she still kept her lighted eyes on him, he gave back her conscious stare for a minute, inwardly and rapidly turning things over, making connections, taking, as after some long and lamentable lapse of observation, a new strange measure of her: all to the upshot of his then speaking with a difference of tone, a recognition of still more of the odious than he had supposed, so that the case might really call for some coolness. "You keep bad company, Grace—it pays the devil with your sense of proportion. If you make this row when I sell a picture, what will be left to you when I forge a cheque?"

"If you had arrived at the necessity of forging a cheque," she answered, "I should then resign myself to that of your selling a picture."

"But not short of that!"

"Not short of that. Not one of ours."

"But I couldn't," said his lordship with his best and coldest amusement, "sell one of somebody else's!"

She was, however, not disconcerted. "Other people do other things—they appear to have done them, and to be doing them, all about us. But *we* have been so decently different—always and ever. We've never done anything disloyal."

"'Disloyal'?"—he was more largely amazed and even interested now.

Lady Grace stuck to her word. "That's what it seems to *me!*"

"It seems to you"—and his sarcasm here was easy—"more disloyal to sell a picture than to buy one? Because we didn't paint 'em all ourselves, you know!"

She threw up impatient hands. "I don't ask you either to paint or to buy——!"

"Oh, *that's* a mercy!" he interrupted, riding his irony hard; "and I'm glad to hear you at least let me off *such* efforts! However, if it strikes you as gracefully filial to apply to your father's conduct so invidious a word," he went on less scathingly, "you must take from him, in your turn, his quite other view of what makes disloyalty—understanding distinctly, by the same token, that he enjoins on you not to give an odious illustration of it, while he's away, by discussing and deploring with any *one* of your extraordinary friends any aspect or feature whatever of his walk and conversation. That—pressed as I am for time," he went on with a glance at his watch while she remained silent—"is the main sense of what I have to say to you; so that I count on your perfect conformity. When you have told me that I *may* so count"—and casting about for his hat he espied it and went to take it up—"I shall most cordially bid you good-bye."

His daughter looked as if she had been for some time expecting the law thus imposed upon her—had been seeing where he must come out; but in spite of this preparation she made him wait for his reply in such tension as he had himself created. "To Kitty I've practically said nothing—and she herself can tell you why: I've in fact scarcely seen her this fortnight. Putting aside then Amy Sandgate, the only person to whom I've spoken—of your 'sacrifice,' as I suppose you'll let me call it?—is Mr. Hugh Crimble, whom you talk of as my 'confederate' at Dedborough."

Lord Theign recovered the name with relief. "Mr. Hugh Crimble—that's it!—whom you so amazingly caused to be present, and apparently invited to be active, at a business that so little concerned him."

"He certainly took upon himself to be interested, as I had hoped he would. But it was because I had taken upon *my* self—"

"To act, yes," Lord Theign broke in, "with the grossest want of delicacy! Well, it's from that exactly that you'll now forbear; and 'interested' as he may be—for which I'm deucedly obliged to him!—you'll not speak to Mr. Crimble again."

"Never again?"—the girl put it as for full certitude.

"Never of the question that I thus exclude. You may chatter your fill," said his lordship curtly, "about any others."

"Why, the particular question you forbid," Grace returned with great force, but as if saying something very reasonable—"that question is *the* question we care about: it's our very ground of conversation."

"Then," her father decreed, "your conversation will please to *dispense* with a ground; or you'll perhaps, better still—if that's the only way!—dispense with your conversation."

Lady Grace took a moment as if to examine this more closely. "You require of me not to communicate with Mr. Crimble at all?"

"Most assuredly I require it—since it's to that you insist on reducing me." He didn't look reduced, the master of Dedborough, as he spoke—which was doubtless precisely because he held his head so high to affirm what he suffered. "Is it so essential to your comfort," he demanded, "to hear him, or to make him, abuse me?"

"'Abusing' you, father dear, has nothing whatever to do with it!"—his daughter had fairly lapsed, with a despairing gesture, to the tenderness involved in her compassion for his perversity. "We look at the thing in a much larger way," she pursued, not heeding that she drew from him a sound of scorn for her "larger." "It's of our Treasure itself we talk—and of what can be *done* in such cases; though with a close application, I admit, to the case that you embody."

"Ah," Lord Theign asked as with absurd curiosity, "I embody a case?"

"Wonderfully, father—as you do everything; and it's the fact of its being exceptional," she explained, "that makes it so difficult to deal with."

His lordship had a gape for it. "'To deal with'? You're undertaking to 'deal' with me?"

She smiled more frankly now, as for a rift in the gloom. "Well, how can we help it if you *will* be a case?" And then as her tone but visibly darkened his wonder: "What we've set our hearts on is saving the picture."

"What you've set your hearts on, in other words, is working straight against me?"

But she persisted without heat. "What we've set our hearts on is working for England."

"And pray who in the world's 'England,'" he cried in his stupefaction, "unless I am?"

"Dear, dear father," she pleaded, "that's all we *want* you to be! I mean"—she didn't fear firmly to force it home—"in the real, the right, the grand sense; the sense that, you see, is so intensely ours."

"'Ours'?"—he couldn't but again throw back her word at her. "Isn't it, damn you, just *in* ours—?"

"No, no," she interrupted—"not in *ours!*" She smiled at him still, though it was strained, as if he really ought to perceive.

But he glared as at a senseless juggle. "What and who the devil are you talking about? What are 'we,' the whole blest lot of us, pray, but the best and most English thing in the country: people walking—and riding!—straight; doing, disinterestedly, most of the difficult and all the thankless jobs; minding their own business, above all, and expecting others to mind theirs?" So he let her "have" the stout sound truth, as it were—and so the direct force of it clearly might, by his view, have made her reel. "You and I, my lady, and your two decent brothers, God be thanked for them, and mine into the bargain, and all the rest, the jolly lot of us, take us together—make us numerous enough without any foreign aid or mixture: if that's what I understand you to mean!"

"You don't understand me at all—evidently; and above all I see you don't want to!" she had the bravery to add, "By 'our' sense of what's due to the nation in such a case I mean Mr. Crimble's and mine—and nobody's else at all; since, as I tell you, it's only with him I've talked."

It gave him then, every inch of him showed, the full, the grotesque measure of the scandal he faced. "So that 'you and Mr. Crimble' represent the standard, for me, in your opinion, of the proprieties and duties of our house?"

Well, she was too earnest—as she clearly wished to let him see—to mind his perversion of it. "I express to you the way we feel."

"It's most striking to hear, certainly, what you express"—he had positively to laugh for it; "and you speak of him, with your insufferable 'we,' as if you were presenting him as your—God knows what! You've enjoyed a large exchange of ideas, I gather, to have arrived at such unanimity." And then, as if to fall into no trap he might somehow be laying for her, she dropped all eagerness and rebutted nothing: "You must see a great deal of your fellow-critic not to be able to speak of yourself without him!"

"Yes, we're fellow-critics, father"—she accepted this opening. "I perfectly adopt your term." But it took her a minute to go further. "I saw Mr. Crim-ble here half an hour ago."

"Saw him 'here'?" Lord Theign amazedly asked. "He *comes* to you here—and Amy Sandgate has been silent?"

"It wasn't her business to tell you—since, you see, she could leave it to me. And I quite expect," Lady Grace then produced, "that he'll come again."

It brought down with a bang all her father's authority. "Then I simply exact of you that you don't see him."

The pause of which she paid it the deference was charged like a brimming cup. "Is that what you *really* meant by your condition just now—that when I do see him I shall not speak to him?"

"What I 'really meant' is what I really mean—that you bow to the law I lay upon you and drop the man altogether."

"Have nothing to do with him at all?"

"Have nothing to do with him at all."

"In fact"—she took it in—"give him wholly up."

He had an impatient gesture. "You sound as if I asked you to give up a fortune!" And then, though she had phrased his idea without consternation—verily as if it had been in the balance for her—he might have been moved by something that gathered in her eyes. "You're so wrapped up in him that the precious sacrifice is like *that* sort of thing?"

Lady Grace took her time—but showed, as her eyes continued to hold him, what *had* gathered. "I like Mr. Crimble exceedingly, father—I think him clever, intelligent, good; I want what he wants—I want it, I think, really, as much; and I don't at all deny that he has helped to make me so want it. But that doesn't matter. I'll wholly cease to see him, I'll give him up forever, if—if—!" She faltered, however, she hung fire with a smile that anxiously, intensely appealed. Then she began and stopped again, "If—if—!" while her father caught her up with irritation.

"'If,' my lady? If *what*, please?"

"If you'll withdraw the offer of our picture to Mr. Bender—and never make another to any one else!"

He stood staring as at the size of it—then translated it into his own terms. "If I'll obligingly announce to the world that I've made an ass of myself you'll kindly forbear from our united effort—the charming pair of you—to show me up for one?"

Lady Grace, as if consciously not caring or attempting to answer this, simply gave the first flare of his criticism time to drop. It wasn't till a minute passed that she said: "You don't agree to my compromise?"

Ah, the question but fatally sharpened at a stroke the stiffness of his spirit. "Good God, I'm to 'compromise' on top of everything?—I'm to let you browbeat me, haggle and bargain with me, over a thing that I'm entitled to settle with you as things have ever *been* settled among us, by uttering to you my last parental word?"

"You don't care enough then for what you name?"—she took it up as scarce heeding now what he said.

"For putting an end to your odious commerce—? I give you the measure, on the contrary," said Lord Theign, "of how much I care: as you give me, very strangely indeed, it strikes me, that of what it costs you—!" But his other words were lost in the hard long look at her from which he broke off in turn as for disgust.

It was with an effect of decently shielding herself—the unuttered meaning came so straight—that she substituted words of her own. "Of what it costs me to redeem the picture?"

"To lose your tenth-rate friend"—he spoke without scruple now.

She instantly broke into ardent deprecation, pleading at once and warning. "Father, father, oh—! You hold the thing in your hands."

He pulled up before her again as to thrust the responsibility straight back. "My orders then are so much rubbish to you?"

Lady Grace held her ground, and they remained face to face in opposition and accusation, neither making the other the sign of peace. But the girl at least *had*, held out the olive-branch, while Lord Theign had but reaffirmed his will. It was for her acceptance of this that he searched her, her last word not having yet come. Before it had done so, however, the door from the lobby opened and Mr. Gotch had regained their presence. This appeared to determine in Lady Grace a view of the importance of delay, which she signified to her companion in a "Well—I must think!" For the butler positively resounded, and Hugh was there.

"Mr. Crimble!" Mr. Gotch proclaimed—with the further extravagance of projecting the visitor straight upon his lordship.

VII

Our young man showed another face than the face his friend had lately seen him carry off, and he now turned it distressfully from that source of inspiration to Lord Theign, who was flagrantly, even from this first moment, no such source at all, and then from his noble adversary back again, under pressure of difficulty and effort, to Lady Grace, whom he directly addressed. "Here I am again, you see—and I've got my news, worse luck!" But his manner to her father was the next instant more brisk. "I learned you were here, my lord; but as the case is important I told them it was all right and came up. I've been to my club," he added for the girl, "and found the tiresome thing—!" But he broke down breathless.

"And it isn't good?" she cried with the highest concern.

Ruefully, yet not abjectly, he confessed, "Not so good as I hoped. For I assure you, my lord, I counted—"

"It's the report from Pappendick about the picture at Verona," Lady Grace interruptingly explained.

Hugh took it up, but, as we should well have seen, under embarrassment dismally deeper; the ugly particular defeat he had to announce showing thus, in his thought, for a more awkward force than any reviving possibilities that he might have begun to balance against them. "The man I told *you* about also," he said to his formidable patron; "whom I went to Brussels to talk with and who, most kindly, has gone for us to Verona. He has been able to get straight at *their* Mantovano, but the brute horribly wires me that he doesn't quite see the thing; see, I mean"—and he gathered his two hearers together now in his overflow of chagrin, conscious, with his break of the ice, more exclusively of that—"my vivid vital point, the absolute screaming identity of the two persons represented. I still hold," he persuasively went on, "that our man is their man, but Pappendick decides that he isn't—and as Pappendick has so *much* to be reckoned with of course I'm awfully abashed."

Lord Theign had remained what he had begun by being, immeasurably and inaccessibly detached—only with his curiosity more moved than he could help and as, on second thought, to see what sort of a still more offensive fool the heated youth would really make of himself. "Yes—you seem indeed remarkably abashed!"

Hugh clearly was thrown again, by the cold "cut" of this, colder than any mere social ignoring, upon a sense of the damnably poor figure he did offer; so that, while he straightened himself and kept a mastery of his manner and a control of his reply, we should yet have felt his cheek tingle. "I backed my own judgment strongly, I know—and I've got my snub. But I don't in the least knock under."

"Only the first authority in Europe doesn't care, I suppose, whether you do or not!"

"He isn't *the* first authority in Europe, thank God," the young man returned—"though he is, I admit, one of the three or four first. And I mean to appeal—I've another shot in my locker," he went on with his rather painfully forced smile to Lady Grace. "I had already written, you see, to dear old Bardi."

"Bardi of Milan?"—she recognised, it was admirably manifest, the appeal of his directness to her generosity, awkward as their predicament was also for her herself, and spoke to him as she might have spoken without her father's presence.

It would have shown for beautiful, on the spot, had there been any one to perceive it, that he devoutly recorded her intelligence. "You know of him?—how delightful of you! For the Italians, I now feel," he quickly explained, "he must have *most* the instinct—and it has come over me since that he'd have been more our man. Besides of course his so knowing the Verona picture."

She had fairly hung on his lips. "But does he know ours?"

"No—not ours yet. That is"—he consciously and quickly took himself up—"not yours! But as Pap-pendick went to Verona for us I've asked Bardi to do us the great favour to come here—if Lord Theign will be so good," he said, bethinking himself with a turn, "as to let him examine the Moretto." He faced again to the personage he mentioned, who, simply standing off and watching, in concentrated interest as well as detachment, this interview of his cool daughter and her still cooler guest, had plainly "elected," as it were, to give them rope to hang themselves. Staring very hard at Hugh he met his appeal, but in a silence clearly calculated; against which, however, the young man, bearing up, made such head as he could. He offered his next word, that is, equally to the two companions. "It's not at all impossible—for such curious effects have been!—that the Dedborough picture seen *after* the Verona will point a different moral from the Verona seen after the Dedborough."

"And so awfully *long* after—wasn't it?" Lady Grace asked.

"Awfully long after—it was years ago that Pappen-dick, being in this country for such purposes, was kindly admitted to your house when none of you were there, or at least visible."

"Oh of course we don't see *every one!*"—she heroically kept it up.

"You don't see every one," Hugh bravely laughed, "and that makes it all the more charming that you did, and that you still do, see me. I shall really get Bardi," he pursued, "to go again to Verona——"

"The last thing before coming here?"—she guessed before he could say it; and still she sustained it, so that he could shine at her for assent. "How happy they should like so to work for you!"

"Ah, we're a band of brothers," he returned—"'we few, we happy few'—from country to country"; to which he added, gaining more ease for an eye at Lord Theign: "though we do have our little rubs and disputes, like Pappendick and me now. The thing, you see, is the ripping *interest* of it all; since," he developed and explained, for his elder friend's benefit, with pertinacious cheer and an assurance superficially at least recovered, "when we're really 'hit' over a case we'll do almost anything in life."

Lady Grace, recklessly throbbing in the breath of it all, immediately appropriated what her father let alone. "It must be so lovely to *feel* so hit!"

"It does spoil one," Hugh laughed, "for milder joys. Of course what I have to consider is the chance—putting it at the *merest* chance—of Bardi's own wet blanket! But that's again so very small—though," he pulled up with a drop to the comparative dismal, which he offered as an almost familiar tribute to Lord Theign, "you'll retort upon me naturally that I promised you the possibility of Pappendick's veto would be: all on the poor dear old basis, you'll claim, of the wish father to the thought. Well, I do wish to be right as much as I believe I am. Only give me time!" he sublimely insisted.

"How can we prevent your using it?" Lady Grace again interrupted; "or the fact either that if the worst comes to the worst—"

"The thing"—he at once pursued—"will always be at the least the greatest of Morettos? Ah," he cried so cheerily that there was still a freedom in it toward any it might concern, "the worst sha'n't come to the worst, be the best to the best: my conviction of which it is that supports me in the deep regret I have to express"—and he faced Lord Theign again—"for any inconvenience I may have caused you by my abortive undertaking. That, I vow here before Lady Grace, I will yet more than make up!"

Lord Theign, after the longest but the blankest contemplation of him, broke hereupon, for the first time, that attitude of completely sustained and separate silence which he had yet made compatible with his air of having deeply noted every element of the scene—so that it was of this full view his participation had effectively consisted, "I haven't the least idea, sir, what you're talking about!" And he squarely turned his back, strolling toward the other room, the threshold of which he the next moment had passed, remaining scantily within, however, and in sight of the others, not to say of ourselves; even though averted and ostensibly lost in some scrutiny that might have had for its object the great enshrined Lawrence.

There ensued upon his words and movement a vivid mute passage, the richest of commentaries, between his companions; who, deeply divided by the width of the ample room, followed him with their eyes and then used for their own interchange these organs of remark, eloquent now over Hugh's unmistakable dismissal at short order, on which obviously he must at once act. Lady Grace's young arms conveyed to him by a despairing contrite motion of surrender that she had done for him all she could do in his presence and that, however sharply doubtful the result, he was to leave the rest to herself. They communicated thus, the strenuous pair, for their full moment, without speaking; only with the prolonged, the charged give and take of their gaze and, it might well have been imagined, of their passion. Hugh had for an instant a show of hesitation—of the arrested impulse, while he kept her father within range, to launch at that personage before going some final remonstrance. It was the girl's raised hand and gesture of warning that waved away for him such a mistake; he decided, under her pressure, and after a last searching and answering look at her reached the door and let himself out. The stillness was then prolonged a minute by the further wait of the two others, Lord Theign where he had been standing and his daughter on the spot from which she had not moved. It presently ended in his lordship's turn about as if inferring by the silence that the intruder had withdrawn.

"Is that young man your lover?" he said as he drew again near.

Lady Grace waited a little, but spoke as quietly as if she had been prepared. "Has the question a bearing on the promise you a short time ago demanded of me?"

"It has a bearing on the so extraordinary appearance of your intimacy with him!"

"You mean that if he *should* be—what you ask me about—your exaction would then be modified?"

"My request that you break it short off? That request would, on the contrary," Lord Theign pronounced, "rest on an immense new ground. Therefore I insist on your telling me the truth."

"Won't the truth be before you, father, if you'll *think* a moment—without extravagance?" After which, while, as stiffly as ever—and it probably seemed to her impatience as stupidly—he didn't rise to it, she went on: "If I *offered* you not again to see him, does that make for you the appearance—?"

"If you offered it, you mean, on your condition—my promising not to sell? I promised," said Lord Theign, "absolutely nothing at all!"

She took him up with all expression. "So I promised as little! But that I should have been able to say what I did sufficiently meets your curiosity."

She might, wronged as she held herself, have felt him stupid not to see *how* wronged; but he was in any case acute for an evasion. "You risked your offer for the great equivalent over which you've so wildly worked yourself up."

"Yes, I've worked myself—that, I grant you and don't blush for! But hardly so much as to renounce my 'lover'—if," she prodigiously smiled, "I were so fortunate as to have one!"

"You renounced poor John mightily easily—whom you were so fortunate as to have!"

Her brows rose as high as his own had ever done. "Do you call Lord John my lover?"

"He was your suitor most assuredly," Lord Theign inimitably said, though without looking at her; "and as strikingly encouraged as he was respectfully ardent!"

"Encouraged by *you*, dear father, beyond doubt!"

"Encouraged—er—by every one: because you were (yes, you *were!*) encouraging. And what I ask of you now is a word of common candour as to whether you didn't, on your honour, turn him off because of your just then so stimulated views on the person who has been with us."

Grace replied but after an instant, as moved by more things than she could say—moved above all, in her trouble and her pity for him, by other things than harshness: "Oh father, father, father——!"

He searched her through all the compassion of her cry, but appeared to give way to her sincerity. "Well then if I *have* your denial I take it as answering my whole question—in a manner that satisfies me. If there's nothing, on your word, of that sort between you, you can all the more drop him."

"But you said a moment ago that I should all the more in the other case—that of there *being* something!"

He brushed away her logic-chopping. "If you're so keen then for past remarks I take up your own words—I accept your own terms for your putting an end to Mr. Crimble." To which, while, turning pale, she said nothing, he added: "You recognise that you profess yourself ready——"

"Not again to see him," she now answered, "if you tell me the picture's safe? Yes, I recognise that I *was* ready—as well as how scornfully little you then were!"

"Never mind what I then was—the question's of what I actually am, since I close with you on it The picture's therefore as safe as you please," Lord Theign pursued, "if you'll do what you just now engaged to."

"I engaged to do nothing," she replied after a pause; and the face she turned to him had grown suddenly tragic. "I've no word to take back, for none passed between us; but I *won't* do what I mentioned and what you at once laughed at Because," she finished, "the case is different."

"Different?" he almost shouted—"*how*, different?"

She didn't look at him for it, but she was none the less strongly distinct "He has *been* here—and that has done it He knows," she admirably emphasised.

"Knows what I think of him, no doubt—for a brazen young prevaricator! But what else?"

She still kept her eyes on a far-off point. "What he will have seen—I feel we're too good friends."

"Then your denial of it's false," her father fairly thundered—"and you *are* infatuated!"

It made her the more quiet. "I like him very much."

"So that your row about the picture," he demanded with passion, "has been all a blind?" And then as her quietness still held her: "And his a blind as much—to help him to get *at* you?"

She looked at him again now. "He must speak for himself. I've said what I mean."

"But what the devil *do* you mean?" Lord Theign, taking in the hour, had reached the door as in supremely baffled conclusion and with a sense of time lamentably lost.

Their eyes met upon it all dreadfully across the wide space, and, hurried and incommoded as she saw him, she yet made him still stand a minute. Then she let everything go. "Do what you like with the picture!"

He jerked up his arm and guarding hand as before a levelled blow at his face, and with the other hand flung open the door, having done with her now and immediately lost to sight. Left alone she stood a moment looking before her; then with a vague advance, held apparently by a quickly growing sense of the implication of her act, reached a table where she remained a little, deep afresh in thought—only the next thing to fall into a chair close to it and there, with her elbows on it, yield to the impulse of covering her flushed face with her hands.

BOOK THIRD

I

Railway station by William frith (1819-1909)

HUGH CRIMBLE waited again in the Bruton Street drawing-room—this time at the afternoon hour; he restlessly shifted his place, looked at things about him without seeing them; all he saw, all he outwardly studied, was his own face and figure as he stopped an instant before a long glass suspended between two windows. Just as he turned from that brief and perhaps not wholly gratified inspection Lady Grace—that he had sent up his name to whom was immediately apparent—presented herself at the entrance from the other room. These young persons had hereupon no instant exchange of words; their exchange was mute—they but paused where they were; while the silence of each evidently tested the other for full confidence. A measure of this comfort came first, it would have appeared, to Hugh; though he then at once asked for confirmation of it.

"Am I right, Lady Grace, am I right?—to have *come*, I mean, after so many days of not hearing, not knowing, and perhaps, all too stupidly, not trying." And he went on as, still with her eyes on him, she didn't speak; though, only, we should have guessed, from her stress of emotion. "Even if I'm wrong, let me tell you, I don't care—simply because, whatever new difficulty I may have brought about for you here a fortnight ago, there's something that to-day adds to my doubt and my fear too great a pang, and that has made me feel I can scarce bear the suspense of them as they are."

The girl came nearer, and if her grave face expressed a pity it yet declined a dread. "Of what suspense do you speak? Your still being without the other opinion—?"

"Ah, that worries me, yes; and all the more, at this hour, as I say, that—" He dropped it, however: "I'll tell you in a moment! My *real* torment, all the while, has been not to know, from day to day, what situation, what complication that last scene of ours with your father here has let you in for; and yet at the same time—having no sign nor sound from you!—to see the importance of not making anything possibly worse by approaching you again, however discreetly. I've been in the dark," he pursued, "and feeling that I must leave *you* there; so that now—just brutally turning up once more under personal need and at any cost—I don't know whether I most want or most fear what I may learn from you."

Lady Grace, listening and watching, appeared to choose between different ways of meeting this appeal; she had a pacifying, postponing gesture, marked with a beautiful authority, a sign of the value for her of what she gave precedence to and which waved off everything else. "Have you had—first of all—any news yet of Bardi?"

"That I have is what has driven me straight *at* you again—since I've shown you before how I turn to you at a crisis. He has come as I hoped and like a regular good 'un," Hugh was able to state; "I've just met him at the station, but I pick him up again, at his hotel in Clifford Street, at five. He stopped, on his way from Dover this morning, to my extreme exasperation, to 'sample' Canterbury, and I leave him to a bath and a change and tea. Then swooping down I whirl him round to Bond Street, where his very first apprehension of the thing (an apprehension, oh I guarantee you, so quick and clean and fine and wise) will be the flash-light projected—well," said the young man, to wind up handsomely, but briefly and reasonably, "over the whole field of our question."

She panted with comprehension. "That of the two portraits being but the one sitter!"

"That of the two portraits being but the one sitter. With everything so to the good, more and more, that bangs in, up to the head, the golden nail of authenticity, and"—he quite glowed through his gloom for it—"we take our stand in glory on the last Mantovano in the world."

It was a presumption his friend visibly yearned for—but over which, too, with her eyes away from him, she still distinguished the shadow of a cloud. "That is if the flash-light comes!"

"That is if it comes indeed, confound it!"—he had to enlarge a little under the recall of past experience. "So now, at any rate, you see my tension!"

She looked at him again as with a vision too full for a waste of words. "While you on your side of course keep well in view Mr. Bender's."

"Yes, while I keep well in view Mr. Bender's; though he doesn't know, you see, of Bardi's being at hand."

"Still," said the girl, always all lucid for the case, "if the 'flash-light' does presently break——!"

"It will first take him in the eye?" Hugh had jumped to her idea, but he adopted it only to provide: "It might if he didn't now wear goggles, so to say!—clapped on him too hard by Pappendick's so damnably perverse opinion." With which, however, he quickly bethought himself. "Ah, these wretched days, you haven't known of Pappendick's personal visit. After that wire from Verona I wired him back defiance—"

"And that brought him?" she cried.

"To do the honest thing, yes—I *will* say for him: to renew, for full assurance, his early memory of our picture."

She hung upon it. "But only to stick then to what he had telegraphed?"

"To declare that for *him*, lackaday! our thing's a pure Moretto—and to declare as much, moreover, with all the weight of his authority, to Bender himself, who of course made a point of seeing him."

"So that Bender"—she followed and wondered—"is, as a consequence, wholly off?"

It made her friend's humour play up in his acute-ness. "Bender, Lady Grace, is, by the law of his being, never 'wholly' off—or on!—anything. He lives, like the moon, in mid-air, shedding his silver light on earth; never quite gone, yet never *all* there—save for inappreciable moments. He*would* be in eclipse as a peril, I grant," Hugh went on—"if the question had struck him as really closed. But luckily the blessed Press—which is a pure heavenly joy and now quite immense on it—keeps it open as wide as Piccadilly."

"Which makes, however," Lady Grace discriminated, "for the danger of a grab."

"Ah, but all the more for the shame of a surrender! Of course I admit that when it's a question of a life spent, like his, in waiting, acquisitively, for the cat to jump, the only thing for one, at a given moment, as against that signal, is to be found one's self by the animal in the line of its trajectory. That's exactly," he laughed, "where we are!"

She cast about as intelligently to note the place. "Your great idea, you mean, *has* so worked—with the uproar truly as loud as it has seemed to come to us here?"

"All beyond my wildest hope," Hugh returned; "since the sight of the picture, flocked to every day by thousands, so beautifully *tells*. That we must at any cost keep it, that the nation must, and hang on to it tight, is the cry that fills the air—to the tune of ten letters a day in the Papers, with every three days a gorgeous leader; to say nothing of more and more passionate talk all over the place, some of it awfully wild, but all of it wind in our sails."

"I suppose it was that wind then that blew me round there to see the thing in its new light," Lady Grace said. "But I couldn't stay—for tears!"

"Ah," Hugh insisted on his side for comfort, "we'll crow loudest yet! And don't meanwhile, just *don't*, those splendid strange eyes of the fellow seem consciously to plead? The women, bless them, adore him, cling to him, and there's talk of a 'Ladies' League of Protest'—all of which keeps up the pitch."

"Poor Amy and I are a ladies' league," the girl joylessly joked—"as we now take in the 'Journal' regardless of expense."

"Oh then you practically *have* it all—since," Hugh, added after a brief hesitation, "I suppose Lord Theign himself doesn't languish uninformed."

"At far-off Salsomaggiore—by the papers? No doubt indeed he isn't spared even the worst," said Lady Grace—"and no doubt too it's a drag on his cure."

Her companion seemed struck with her lack of assurance. "Then you don't—if I may ask—hear from him?"

"I? Never a word."

"He doesn't write?" Hugh allowed himself to insist.

"He doesn't write. And I don't write either."

"And Lady Sandgate?" Hugh once more ventured.

"Doesn't *she* write?"

"Doesn't *she* hear?" said the young man, treating the other form of the question as a shade evasive.

"I've asked her not to tell me," his friend replied—"that is if he simply holds out."

"So that as she doesn't tell you"—Hugh made clear for the inference—"he of course does hold out." To which he added almost accusingly while his eyes searched her: "But your case is really bad."

She confessed to it after a moment, but as if vaguely enjoying it. "My case is really bad."

He had a vividness of impatience and contrition. "And it's I who—all too blunderingly!—have made it so?"

"I've made it so myself," she said with a high head-shake, "and you, on the contrary—!" But here she checked her emphasis.

"Ah, I've so *wanted*, through our horrid silence, to help you!" And he pressed to get more at the truth. "You've so quite fatally displeased him?"

"To the last point—as I tell you. But it's not to that I refer," she explained; "it's to the ground of complaint I've given *you*." And then as this but left him blank, "It's time—it was at once time—that you should know," she pursued; "and yet if it's hard for me to speak, as you see, it was impossible for me to write. But there it is." She made her sad and beautiful effort. "The last thing before he left us I let the picture go." 197

"You mean—?" But he could only wonder—till, however, it glimmered upon him. "You gave up your protest?"

"I gave up my protest. I told him that—so far as I'm concerned!—he might do as he liked."

Her poor friend turned pale at the sharp little shock of it; but if his face thus showed the pang of too great a surprise he yet wreathed the convulsion in a gay grimace. "You leave me to struggle alone?"

"I leave you to struggle alone."

He took it in bewilderingly, but tried again, even to the heroic, for optimism. "Ah well, you decided, I suppose, on some new personal ground."

"Yes; a reason came up, a reason I hadn't to that extent looked for and which of a sudden—quickly, before he went—I *had* somehow to deal with. So to give him my word in the dismal sense I mention was my only way to meet the strain." She paused; Hugh waited for something further, and "I gave him my word I wouldn't help you," she wound up.

He turned it over. "To *act* in the matter—I see."

"To act in the matter"—she went through with it—"after the high stand I had taken."

Still he studied it. "I see—I see. It's between you and your father."

"It's between him and me—yes. An engagement not again to trouble him."

Hugh, from his face, might have feared a still greater complication; so he made, as he would probably have said, a jolly lot of this. "Ah, that was nice of you. And natural. *That's* all right!"

"No"—she spoke from a deeper depth—"it's altogether wrong. For whatever happens I must now accept it."

"Well, say you must"—he really declined not to treat it almost as rather a "lark"—"if we can at least go on talking."

"Ah, we *can* at least go on talking!" she perversely sighed. "I can say anything I like so long as I don't say it to *him*" she almost wailed. But she added with more firmness: "I can still hope—and I can still pray."

He set free again with a joyous gesture all his confidence. "Well, what more *could* you do, anyhow? So isn't that enough?"

It took her a moment to say, and even then she didn't. "Is it enough for *you*, Mr. Crimble?"

"What *is* enough for me"—he could for his part readily name it—"is the harm done you at our last meeting by my irruption; so that if you got his consent to see me——!"

"I didn't get his consent!"—she had turned away from the searching eyes, but she faced them again to rectify: "I see you against his express command."

"Ah then thank God I came!"—it was like a bland breath on a *feu de joie*: he flamed so much higher.

"Thank God you've come, yes—for my deplorable exposure." And to justify her name for it before he could protest, "I *offered* him here not to see you," she rigorously explained.

"'Offered him?'"—Hugh did drop for it. "Not to see me—ever again?"

She didn't falter. "Never again."

Ah then he understood. "But he wouldn't let that serve——?"

"Not for the price I put on it."

"His yielding on the picture?"

"His yielding on the picture."

Hugh lingered before it all. "Your proposal wasn't 'good enough'?"

"It wasn't good enough."

"I see," he repeated—"I see." But he was in that light again mystified. "Then why are you therefore not free?"

"Because—just after—you came back, and I *did* see you again!"

Ah, it was all present. "You found you were too sorry for me?"

"I found I was too sorry for you—as he himself found I was."

Hugh had got hold of it now. "And *that*, you mean, he couldn't stomach?"

"So little that when you had gone (and *how* you had to go you remember) he at once proposed, rather than that I should deceive you in a way so different from his own——"

"To do all we want of him?"

"To do all I did at least."

"And it was *then*," he took in, "that you wouldn't deal?"

"Well"—try though she might to keep the colour out, it all came straighter and straighter now—"those moments had brought you home to me as they had also brought *him*; making such a difference, I felt, for what he veered round to agree to."

"The difference"—Hugh wanted it so adorably definite—"that you didn't see your way to accepting——?"

"No, not to accepting the condition he named."

"Which was that he'd keep the picture for you if you'd treat me as too 'low'——?"

"If I'd treat you," said Lady Grace with her eyes on his fine young face, "as impossible."

He kept her eyes—he clearly liked so to make her repeat it. "And not even for the sake of the picture—?" After he had given her time, however, her silence, with her beautiful look in it, seemed to admonish him not to force her for his pleasure; as if what she had already told him didn't make him throb enough for the wonder of it. He *had* it, and let her see by his high flush how he made it his own—while, the next thing, as it was but part of her avowal, the rest of that illumination called for a different intelligence. "Your father's reprobation of me personally is on the ground that you're all such great people?"

She spared him the invidious answer to this as, a moment before, his eagerness had spared her reserve; she flung over the "ground" that his question laid bare the light veil of an evasion, "'Great people,' I've learned to see, mustn't—to remain great—do what my father's doing."

"It's indeed on the theory of their not so behaving," Hugh returned, "that we see them—all the inferior rest of us—in the grand glamour of their greatness!"

If he had spoken to meet her admirable frankness half-way, that beauty in her almost brushed him aside to make at a single step the rest of the journey. "You won't see them in it for long—if they don't now, under such tests and with such opportunities, begin to take care."

This had given him, at a stroke, he clearly felt, all freedom for the closer criticism. "Lord Theign perhaps recognises some such canny truth, but 'takes care,' with the least trouble to himself and the finest short cut—does it, if you'll let me say so, rather on the cheap—by finding 'the likes' of me, as his daughter's trusted friend, out of the question."

"Well, you won't mind that, will you?" Lady Grace asked, "if he finds his daughter herself, in any such relation to you, quite as much so."

"Different enough, from position to position and person to person," he brightly brooded, "is the view that gets itself *most* comfortably taken of the implications of Honour!"

"Yes," the girl returned; "my father, in the act of despoiling us all, all who are interested, without apparently the least unpleasant consciousness, keeps the balance showily even, to his mostly so fine, so delicate sense, by suddenly discovering that he's scandalised at my caring for your friendship."

Hugh looked at her, on this, as with the gladness verily of possession promised and only waiting—or as if from that moment forth he had her assurance of everything that most concerned him and that might most inspire. "Well, isn't the moral of it all simply that what his perversity of pride, as we can only hold it, will have most done for us is to bring us—and to keep us—blessedly together?"

She seemed for a moment to question his "simply." "Do you regard us as so much 'together' when you remember where, in spite of everything, I've put myself?"

"By telling him to do what he likes?" he recalled without embarrassment. "Oh, that wasn't in spite of 'everything'—it was only in spite of the Manto-vano."

"'Only'?" she flushed—"when I've given the picture up?"

"Ah," Hugh cried, "I don't care a hang for the picture!" And then as she let him, closer, close to her with this, possess himself of her hands: "We both only care, don't we, that we're given to each other thus? We both only care, don't we, that nothing can keep us apart?"

"Oh, if you've forgiven me—!" she sighed into his fond face.

"Why, since you gave the thing up *for* me," he pleadingly laughed, "it isn't as if you had given *me* up——!"

"For anything, anything? Ah never, never!" she breathed.

"Then why aren't we all right?"

"Well, if you will——!"

"Oh for ever and ever and ever!"—and with this ardent cry of his devotion his arms closed in their strength and she was clasped to his breast and to his lips.

The next moment, however, she had checked him with the warning "Amy Sandgate!"—as if she had heard their hostess enter the other room. Lady Sand-gate was in fact almost already upon them—their disjunction had scarce been effected and she had reached the nearer threshold. They had at once put the widest space possible between them—a little of the flurry of which transaction agitated doubtless their clutch at composure. They gave back a shade awkwardly and consciously, on one side and the other, the speculative though gracious attention she for a few moments made them and their recent intimate relation the subject of; from all of which indeed Lady Grace sought and found cover in a prompt and responsible address to Hugh. "Mustn't you go without more delay to Clifford Street?"

He came back to it all alert "At once!" He had recovered his hat and reached the other door, whence he gesticulated farewell to the elder lady. "Please pardon me"—and he disappeared.

Lady Sandgate hereupon stood for a little silently confronted with the girl. "Have you freedom of mind for the fact that your father's suddenly at hand?"

"He has come back?"—Lady Grace was sharply struck.

"He arrives this afternoon and appears to go straight to Kitty—according to a wire that I find downstairs on coming back late from my luncheon. He has returned with a rush—as," said his correspondent in the elation of triumph, "I was *sure* he would!"

Her young friend was more at sea. "Brought back, you mean, by the outcry—even though he so hates it?"

But she was more and more all lucidity—save in so far as she was now almost all authority. "Ah, hating still more to seem afraid, he has come back to face the music!"

Lady Grace, turning away as in vague despair for the manner in which the music might affect him, yet wheeled about again, after thought, to a positive recognition and even to quite an inconsequent pride. "Yes—that's dear old father!"

And what is Lady Sandgate moreover but mistress now of the subject? "At the point the row has reached he couldn't stand it another day; so he has thrown up his cure and—lest we should oppose him!—not even announced his start."

"Well," her companion returned, "now that I've *done* it all I shall never oppose him again!"

Lady Sandgate appeared to show herself as still under the impression she might have received on entering. "He'll only oppose *you!*"

"If he does," said Lady Grace, "we're at present two to bear it."

"Heaven save us then"—the elder woman was quick, was even cordial, for the sense of this—"your good friend *is* clever!"

Lady Grace honoured the remark. "Mr. Crim-ble's remarkably clever."

"And you've arranged——?"

"We haven't arranged—but we've understood. So that, dear Amy, if *you* understand—!" Lady Grace paused, for Gotch had come in from the hall.

"His lordship has arrived?" his mistress immediately put to him.

"No, my lady, but Lord John has—to know if he's expected *here*, and in that case, by your ladyship's leave, to come up."

Her ladyship turned to the girl. "May Lord John—as we do await your father—come up?"

"As suits *you*, please!"

"He may come up," said Lady Sandgate to Gotch. "His lordship's expected." She had a pause till they were alone again, when she went on to her companion: "You asked me just now if I understood. Well—I do understand!"

Lady Grace, with Gotch's withdrawal, which left the door open, had reached the passage to the other room. "Then you'll excuse me!"—she made her escape.

II

Gallery scene (c.1880) by Alexandre Brun (1853-1941)

Lord John, reannounced the next instant from the nearest quarter and quite waiving salutations, left no doubt of the high pitch of his eagerness and tension as soon as the door had closed behind him. "What on earth then do you suppose he has come back to *do*——?" To which he added while his hostess's gesture impatiently disclaimed conjecture: "Because when a fellow really finds himself the centre of a cyclone——!"

"Isn't it just at the centre," she interrupted, "that you keep remarkably still, and only in the suburbs that you feel the rage? I count on dear Theign's doing nothing in the least foolish—!"

"Ah, but he can't have chucked everything for nothing," Lord John sharply returned; "and wherever you place him in the rumpus he can't not meet somehow, hang it, such an assault on his character as a great nobleman and good citizen."

"It's his luck to have become with the public of the newspapers the scapegoat-in-chief: for the sins, so-called, of a lot of people!" Lady Sandgate inconclusively sighed.

"Yes," Lord John concluded for her, "the mercenary millions on whose traffic in their trumpery values—when they're so lucky as to have any!—*this* isn't a patch!"

"Oh, there are cases *and* cases: situations and responsibilities so intensely differ!"—that appeared on the whole, for her ladyship, the moral to be gathered.

"Of course everything differs, all round, from everything," Lord John went on; "and who in the world knows anything of his own case but the victim of circumstances exposing himself, for the highest and purest motives, to be literally torn to pieces?"

"Well," said Lady Sandgate as, in her strained suspense, she freshly consulted her bracelet watch, "I hope he isn't already torn—if you tell me you've been to Kitty's."

"Oh, he was all right so far: he had arrived and gone out again," the young man explained, "as Lady Imber hadn't been at home."

"Ah cool Kitty!" his hostess sighed again—but diverted, as she spoke, by the reappearance of her butler, this time positively preceding Lord Theign, whom she met, when he presently stood before her, his garb of travel exchanged for consummate afternoon dress, with yearning tenderness and compassionate curiosity. "At last, dearest friend—what a joy! But with Kitty not at home to receive you?"

That young woman's parent made light of it for the indulged creature's sake. "Oh I knew my Kitty! I dressed and I find her at five-thirty." To which he added as he only took in further, without expression, Lord John: "But Bender, who came there before my arrival—he hasn't tried for me here?"

It was a point on which Lord John himself could at least be expressive. "I met him at the club at luncheon; he had had your letter—but for which chance, my dear man, I should have known nothing. You'll see him all right at this house; but I'm glad, if I may say so, Theign," the speaker pursued with some emphasis—"I'm glad, you know, to get hold of you first."

Lord Theign seemed about to ask for the meaning of this remark, but his other companion's apprehension had already overflowed. "You haven't come back, have you—to whatever it may be!—for *trouble* of any sort with Breckenridge?"

His lordship transferred his penetration to this fair friend, "Have you become so intensely absorbed—these remarkable days!—in 'Breckenridge'?"

She felt the shadow, you would have seen, of his claimed right, or at least privilege, of search—yet easily, after an instant, emerged clear. "I've thought and dreamt but of *you*—suspicious man!—in proportion as the clamour has spread; and Mr. Bender meanwhile, if you want to know, hasn't been near me once!"

Lord John came in a manner, and however unconsciously, to her aid. "You'd have seen, if he had been, what's the matter with him, I think—and what perhaps Theign has seen from his own letter: since," he went on to his fellow-visitor, "I understood him a week ago to have been much taken up with writing you."

Lord Theign received this without comment, only again with an air of expertly sounding the speaker; after which he gave himself afresh for a moment to Lady Sandgate. "I've not come home for any clamour, as you surely know me well enough to believe; or to notice for a minute the cheapest insolence and aggression—which frankly scarce reached me out there; or which, so far as it did, I was daily washed clean of by those blest waters. I returned on Mr. Bender's letter," he then vouchsafed to Lord John—"three extraordinarily vulgar pages about the egregious Pap-pendick!"

"About his having suddenly turned up in person, yes, and, as Breckenridge says, marked the picture down?"—the young man was clearly all-knowing. "That *has* of course weighed on Bender—being confirmed apparently, on the whole, by the drift of public opinion."

Lord Theign took, on this, with a frank show of reaction from some of his friend's terms, a sharp turn off; he even ironically indicated the babbler or at least the blunderer in question to Lady Sandgate. "He too has known me so long, and he comes here to talk to me of 'the drift of public opinion'!" After which he quite charged at his vain informant. "Am I to tell you again that I snap my fingers at the drift of public opinion?—which is but another name for the chatter of all the fools one doesn't know, in addition to all those (and plenty of 'em!) one damnably does."

Lady Sandgate, by a turn of the hand, dropped oil from her golden cruse. "Ah, you did *that*, in your own grand way, before you went abroad!"

"I don't speak of the matter, my dear man, in the light of its effect on *you*," Lord John importantly explained—"but in the light of its effect on Bender; who so consumedly wants the picture, if he *is* to have it, to be a Mantovano, but seems unable to get it taken at last for anything but the fine old Moretto that of course it has always been."

Lord Theign, in growing disgust at the whole beastly complication, betrayed more and more the odd pitch of the temper that had abruptly restored him with such incalculable weight to the scene of action. "Well, isn't a fine old Moretto good enough for him; confound him?"

It pulled up not a little Lord John, who yet made his point. "A fine old Moretto, you know, was exactly what he declined at Dedborough—for its comparative, strictly comparative, insignificance; and he only thought of the picture when the wind began to rise for the enormous rarity—"

"That that mendacious young cad who has bamboozled Grace," Lord Theign broke in, "tried to befool us, for his beggarly reasons, into claiming for it?"

Lady Sandgate renewed her mild influence. "Ah, the knowing people haven't had their last word—the possible Mantovano isn't exploded *yet!*" Her noble friend, however, declined the offered spell. "I've had enough of the knowing people—the knowing people are serpents! My picture's to take or to leave—and it's what I've come back, if you please, John, to say to your man to his face."

This declaration had a report as sharp and almost as multiplied as the successive cracks of a discharged revolver; yet when the light smoke cleared Lady Sand-gate at least was still left standing and smiling. "Yes, why in mercy's name can't he choose *which?*—and why does he write him, dreadful Breckenridge, such tiresome argumentative letters?"

Lord John took up her idea as with the air of something that had been working in him rather vehemently, though under due caution too, as a consequence of this exchange, during which he had apprehensively watched his elder. "I don't think I quite see *how*, my dear Theign, the poor chap's letter was so offensive."

In that case his dear Theign could tell him. "Because it was a tissue of expressions that may pass current—over counters and in awful newspapers—in *his* extraordinary world or country, but that I decline to take time to puzzle out here."

"If he didn't make himself understood," Lord John took leave to laugh, "it must indeed have been an unusual production for Bender."

"Oh, I often, with the wild beauty, if you will, of so many of his turns, haven't a notion," Lady Sandgate confessed with an equal gaiety, "of what he's talking about."

"I think I never miss his weird sense," her younger guest again loyally contended—"and in fact as a general thing I rather like it!"

"I happen to like nothing that I don't enjoy," Lord Theign rejoined with some asperity—"and so far as I do follow the fellow he assumes on my part an interest in his expenditure of purchase-money that I neither feel nor pretend to. He doesn't want—by what I spell out—the picture he refused at Dedborough; he may possibly want—if one reads it so—the picture on view in Bond Street; and he yet appears to make, with great emphasis, the stupid ambiguous point that these two 'articles' (the greatest of Morettos an 'article'!) haven't been 'by now' proved different: as if I engaged with him that I myself would so prove them!"

Lord John indulged in a pause—but also in a suggestion. "He must allude to your hoping—when you allowed us to place the picture with Mackintosh—that it would show to all London in the most precious light conceivable."

"Well, if it hasn't so shown"—and Lord Theign stared as if mystified—"what in the world's the meaning of this preposterous racket?"

"The racket is largely," his young friend explained, "the vociferation of the people who contradict each other about it."

On which their hostess sought to enliven the gravity of the question. "Some—yes—shouting on the housetops that's a Mantovano of the Mantovanos, and others shrieking back at them that they're donkeys if not criminals."

"He may take it for whatever he likes," said Lord Theign, heedless of these contributions, "he may father it on Michael Angelo himself if he'll but clear round and let me alone!"

"What he'd *like* to take it for," Lord John at this point saw his way to remark, "is something in the nature of a Hundred Thousand."

"A Hundred Thousand?" cried his astonished friend.

"Quite, I dare say, a Hundred Thousand"—the young man enjoyed clearly handling even by the lips so round a sum.

Lady Sandgate disclaimed however with agility any appearance of having gaped. "Why, haven't you yet realised, Theign, that those are the American figures?"

His lordship looked at her fixedly and then did the same by Lord John, after which he waited a little. "I've nothing to do with the American figures—which seem to me, if you press me, you know, quite intolerably vulgar."

"Well, I'd be as vulgar as anybody for a Hundred Thousand!" Lady Sandgate hastened to proclaim.

"Didn't he let us know at Dedborough," Lord John asked of the master of that seat, "that he had no use, as he said, for lower values?"

"I've heard him remark myself," said their companion, rising to the monstrous memory, "that he wouldn't take a cheap picture—even though a 'handsome' one—as a present."

"And does he call the thing round the corner a cheap picture?" the proprietor of the work demanded.

Lord John threw up his arms with a grin of impatience. "All he wants to do, don't you see? is to prevent your *making* it one!"

Lord Theign glared at this imputation to him of a low ductility. "I offered the thing, as it was, at an estimate worthy of it—and of *me*."

"My dear reckless friend," his young adviser protested, "you named no figure *at all* when it came to the point——!"

"It *didn't* come to the point! Nothing came to the point but that I put a Moretto on view; as a thing, yes, perfectly"—Lord Theign accepted the reminding gesture—"on which a rich American had an eye and in which he had, so to speak, an interest. That was what I wanted, and so we left it—parting each of us ready but neither of us bound."

"Ah, Mr. Bender's bound, as he'd say," Lady Sand-gate interposed—"'bound' to make you swallow the enormous luscious plum that your appetite so morbidly rejects!"

"My appetite, as morbid as you like"—her old friend had shrewdly turned on her—"is my own affair, and if the fellow must deal in enormities I warn him to carry them elsewhere!"

Lord John, plainly, by this time, was quite exasperated at the absurdity of him. "But how can't you see that it's only a plum, as she says, for a plum and an eye for an eye—since the picture itself, with this huge ventilation, is now quite a different affair?"

"How the deuce a different affair when just what the man himself confesses is that, in spite of all the chatter of the prigs and pedants, there's no really established ground for treating it as anything but the same?" On which, as having so unanswerably spoken, Lord Theign shook himself free again, in his high petulance, and moved restlessly to where the passage to the other room appeared to offer his nerves an issue; all moreover to the effect of suggesting to us that something still other than what he had said might meanwhile work in him behind and beneath that quantity. The spectators of his trouble watched him, for the time, in uncertainty and with a mute but associated comment on the perversity and oddity he had so suddenly developed; Lord John giving a shrug of almost bored despair and Lady Sandgate signalling caution and tact for their action by a finger flourished to her lips, and in fact at once proceeding to apply these arts. The subject of her attention had still remained as in worried thought; he had even mechanically taken up a book from a table—which he then, after an absent glance at it, tossed down.

"You're so detached from reality, you adorable dreamer," she began—"and unless you stick to *that* you might as well have done nothing. What you call the pedantry and priggishness and all the rest of it is exactly what poor Breckenridge asked almost on his knees, wonderful man, to be*allowed* to pay you for; since even if the meddlers and chatterers haven't settled anything for those who know—though which of the elect themselves after all *does* seem to know?—it's a great service rendered him to have started such a hare to run!"

Lord John took freedom to throw off very much the same idea. "Certainly his connection with the whole question and agitation makes no end for his glory."

It didn't, that remark, bring their friend back to him, but it at least made his indifference flash with derision. "His 'glory'—Mr. Bender's glory? Why, they quite universally loathe him—judging by the stuff they print!"

"Oh, here—as a corrupter of our morals and a promoter of our decay, even though so many are flat on their faces to him—yes! But it's another affair over there where the eagle screams like a thousand steam-whistles and the newspapers flap like the leaves of the forest: *there* he'll be, if you'll only let him, the biggest thing going; since sound, in that air, seems to mean size, and size to be all that counts. If he said of the thing, as you recognise," Lord John went on, "'It's going to be a Mantovano,' why you can bet your life that it *is*—that it has *got* to be some kind of a one."

His fellow-guest, at this, drew nearer again, irritated, you would have been sure, by the unconscious infelicity of the pair—worked up to something quite openly wilful and passionate. "No kind of a furious flaunting one, under *my* patronage, that I can prevent, my boy! The Dedborough picture in the market—owing to horrid little circumstances that regard myself alone—is the Dedborough picture at a decent, sufficient, civilised Dedborough price, and nothing else whatever; which I beg you will take as my last word on the subject."

Lord John, trying whether he *could* take it, momentarily mingled his hushed state with that of their hostess, to whom he addressed a helpless look; after which, however, he appeared to find that he could only reassert himself. "May I nevertheless reply that I think you'll not be able to prevent *anything?*—since the discussed object will completely escape your control in New York!"

"And almost any discussed object"—Lady Sand-gate rose to the occasion also—"is in New York, by what one hears, easily *worth* a Hundred Thousand!"

Lord Theign looked from one of them to the other. "I sell the man a Hundred Thousand worth of swagger and advertisement; and of fraudulent swagger and objectionable advertisement at that?"

"Well"—Lord John was but briefly baffled—"when the picture's his you can't help its doing what it can and what it will for him anywhere!"

"Then it isn't his yet," the elder man retorted—"and I promise you never will be if he has *sent* you to me with his big drum!"

Lady Sandgate turned sadly on this to her associate in patience, as if the case were now really beyond them. "Yes, how indeed can it ever*become* his if Theign simply won't let him pay for it?"

Her question was unanswerable. "It's the first time in all my life I've known a man feel insulted, in such a piece of business, by happening *not* to be, in the usual way, more or less swindled!"

"Theign is unable to take it in," her ladyship explained, "that—as I've heard it said of all these money-monsters of the new type—Bender simply can't *afford* not to be cited and celebrated as the biggest buyer who ever lived."

"Ah, cited and celebrated at my *expense*—say it at once and have it over, that I may enjoy what you all want to do to me!"

"The dear man's inimitable—at his 'expense'!" It was more than Lord John could bear as he fairly flung himself off in his derisive impotence and addressed his wail to Lady Sandgate.

"Yes, at my expense is exactly what I mean," Lord Theign asseverated—"at the expense of my modest claim to regulate my behaviour by my own standards. There you perfectly *are* about the man, and it's precisely what I say—that he's to hustle and harry me *because* he's a money-monster: which I never for a moment dreamed of, please understand, when I let you, John, thrust him at me as a pecuniary resource at Dedborough. I didn't put my property on view that *he* might blow about it———!"

"No, if you like it," Lady Sandgate returned; "but you certainly didn't so arrange"—she seemed to think her point somehow would help—"that you might blow about it yourself!"

"Nobody wants to 'blow,'" Lord John more stoutly interposed, "either hot or cold, I take it; but I really don't see the harm of Bender's liking to be known for the scale of his transactions—actual or merely imputed even, if you will; since that scale is really so magnificent."

Lady Sandgate half accepted, half qualified this plea. "The only question perhaps is why he doesn't try for some precious work that somebody—less delicious than dear Theign—*can* be persuaded on bended knees to accept a hundred thousand for."

"'Try' for one?"—her younger visitor took it up while her elder more attentively watched him. "That was exactly what he did try for when he pressed you so hard in vain for the great Sir Joshua."

"Oh well, he mustn't come back to *that*—must he, Theign?" her ladyship cooed.

That personage failed to reply, so that Lord John went on, unconscious apparently of the still more suspicious study to which he exposed himself. "Besides which there *are* no things of that magnitude knocking about, don't you know?—they've *got* to be worked up first if they're to reach the grand publicity of the Figure! Would you mind," he continued to his noble monitor, "an agreement on some such basis as *this*?—that you shall resign yourself to the biggest equivalent you'll squeamishly consent to take, if it's at the same time the smallest he'll squeamishly consent to offer; but that, that done, you shall leave him free——"

Lady Sandgate took it up straight, rounding it off, as their companion only waited. "Leave him free to talk about the sum offered and the sum taken as practically one and the same?"

"Ah, you know," Lord John discriminated, "he doesn't 'talk' so much himself—there's really nothing blatant or crude about poor Bender. It's the rate at which—by the very way he's 'fixed': an awful way indeed, I grant you!—a perfect army of reporter-wretches, close at his heels, are always talking for him and of him."

Lord Theign spoke hereupon at last with the air as of an impulse that had been slowly gathering force. "*You* talk for him, my dear chap, pretty well. You urge his case, my honour, quite as if you were assured of a commission on the job—on a fine ascending scale! Has he put you up to that proposition, eh? *Do* you get a handsome percentage and *are* you to make a good thing of it?"

The young man coloured under this stinging pleasantry—whether from a good conscience affronted or from a bad one made worse; but he otherwise showed a bold front, only bending his eyes a moment on his watch. "As he's to come to you himself—and I don't know why the mischief he doesn't come!—he will answer you that graceful question."

"Will he answer it," Lord Theign asked, "with the veracity that the suggestion you've just made on his behalf represents him as so beautifully adhering to?" On which he again quite fiercely turned his back and recovered his detachment, the others giving way behind him to a blanker dismay.

Lord John, in spite of this however, pumped up a tone. "I don't see why you should speak as if I were urging some abomination."

"Then I'll tell you why!"—and Lord Theign was upon him again for the purpose. "Because I had rather give the cursed thing away outright and for good and all than that it should hang out there another day in the interest of such equivocations!"

Lady Sandgate's dismay yielded to her wonder, and her wonder apparently in turn to her amusement. "'Give it away,' my dear friend, to a man who only longs to smother you in gold?"

Her dear friend, however, had lost patience with her levity. "Give it away—just for a luxury of protest and a stoppage of chatter—to some cause as unlike as possible that of Mr. Bender's power of sound and his splendid reputation: to the Public, to the Authorities, to the Thingumbob, to the Nation!"

Lady Sandgate broke into horror while Lord John stood sombre and stupefied. "Ah, my dear creature, you've flights of extravagance——!"

"One thing's very certain," Lord Theign quite heedlessly pursued—"that the thought of my property on view there does give intolerably on my nerves, more and more every minute that I'm conscious of it; so that, hang it, if one thinks of it, why shouldn't I, for my relief, do again, damme, *what I like?*—that is bang the door in their faces, have the show immediately stopped?" He turned with the attraction of this idea from one of his listeners to the other. "It's *my* show—it isn't Bender's, surely!—and I can do just as I choose with it."

"Ah, but isn't that the very point?"—and Lady Sandgate put it to Lord John. "Isn't it Bender's show much more than his?"

Her invoked authority, however, in answer to this, made but a motion of disappointment and disgust at so much rank folly—while Lord Theign, on the other hand, followed up his happy thought. "Then if it's Bender's show, or if he claims it is, there's all the more reason!" And it took his lordship's inspiration no longer to flower. "See here, John—do this: go right round there this moment, please, and tell them from me to shut straight down!"

"'Shut straight down'?" the young man abhorrently echoed.

"Stop it *to-night*—wind it up and end it: see?" The more the entertainer of that vision held it there the more charm it clearly took on for him. "Have the picture removed from view and the incident closed."

"You seriously ask *that* of me!" poor Lord John quavered.

"Why in the world shouldn't I? It's a jolly lot less than you asked of me a month ago at Dedborough."

"What then am I to say to them?" Lord John spoke but after a long moment, during which he had only looked hard and—an observer might even then have felt—ominously at his taskmaster.

That personage replied as if wholly to have done with the matter. "Say anything that comes into your clever head. I don't really see that there's anything else *for* you!" Lady Sandgate sighed to the messenger, who gave no sign save of positive stiffness.

The latter seemed still to weigh his displeasing obligation; then he eyed his friend significantly—almost portentously. "Those are absolutely your sentiments?"

"Those are absolutely my sentiments"—and Lord Theign brought this out as with the force of a physical push.

"Very well then!" But the young man, indulging in a final, a fairly sinister, study of such a dealer in the arbitrary, made sure of the extent, whatever it was, of his own wrong. "Not one more day?"

Lord Theign only waved him away. "Not one more hour!"

He paused at the door, this reluctant spokesman, as if for some supreme protest; but after another prolonged and decisive engagement with the two pairs of eyes that waited, though differently, on his performance, he clapped on his hat as in the rage of his resentment and departed on his mission.

III

"He can't bear to do it, poor man!" Lady Sandgate ruefully remarked to her remaining guest after Lord John had, under extreme pressure, dashed out to Bond Street.

"I dare say not!"—Lord Theign, flushed with the felicity of self-expression, made little of that. "But he goes too far, you see, and it clears the air—pouah! Now therefore"—and he glanced at the clock—"I must go to Kitty."

"Kitty—with what Kitty wants," Lady Sandgate opined—"won't thank you for *that!*"

"She never thanks me for anything"—and the fact of his resignation clearly added here to his bitterness. "So it's no great loss!"

"Won't you at any rate," his hostess asked, "wait for Bender?"

His lordship cast it to the winds. "What have I to do with him now?"

"Why surely if he'll accept your own price—!"

Lord Theign thought—he wondered; and then as if fairly amused at himself: "Hanged if I know what *is* my own price!" After which he went for his hat. "But there's one thing," he remembered as he came back with it: "where's my too, *too* unnatural daughter?"

"If you mean Grace and really want her I'll send and find out."

"Not now"—he bethought himself. "But does she *see* that chatterbox?"

"Mr. Crimble? Yes, she sees him."

He kept his eyes on her. "Then how far has it gone?"

Lady Sandgate overcame an embarrassment. "Well, not even yet, I think, so far as they'd like."

"They'd 'like'—heaven save the mark!—to marry?"

"I suspect them of it. What line, if it should come to that," she asked, "would you then take?"

He was perfectly prompt. "The line that for Grace it's simply ignoble."

The force of her deprecation of such language was qualified by tact. "Ah, darling, as dreadful as *that?*"

He could but view the possibility with dark resentment. "It lets us so down—from what we've always been and done; so down, down, down that I'm amazed you don't feel it!"

"Oh, I feel there's still plenty to keep you up!" she soothingly laughed.

He seemed to consider this vague amount—which he apparently judged, however, not so vast as to provide for the whole yearning of his nature. "Well, my dear," he thus more blandly professed, "I shall need all the extra *agrément* that your affection can supply."

If nothing could have been, on this, richer response, nothing could at the same time have bee more pleasing than her modesty. "Ah, my affectionate Theign, is, as I think you know, a fountain always in flood; but in any more worldly element than that—as you've ever seen for yourself—a poor strand with my own sad affairs, a broken reed; not 'great' as they used so finely to call it! You *are*—with the natural sense of greatness and, for supreme support, the instinctive grand man doing and taking things."

He sighed, none the less, he groaned, with his thoughts of trouble, for the strain he foresaw on these resolutions. "If you mean that I hold up my head, on higher grounds, I grant that I always have. But how much longer possible when my children commit such vulgarities? Why in the name of goodness are such children? What the devil has got into them, and is it really the case that when Grace offers as a proof of her license and a specimen of her taste a son-in-law as you tell me I'm in danger of helplessly to swallow the dose?"

"Do you find Mr. Crimble," Lady Sandgate as if there might really be something to say, "so utterly out of the question?"

"I found him on the two occasions I went away in the last degree offensive and outrageous; but even if he charged one and one's poor dear decent old defences with less rabid a fury everything about him would forbid *that* kind of relation."

What kind of relation, if any, Hugh's deficiencies might still render thinkable Lord Theign was kept from going on to mention by the voice of Mr. Gotch, who had thrown open the door to the not altogether assured sound of "Mr. Breckenridge Bender." The guest in possession gave a cry of impatience, but Lady Sandgate said "Coming up?"

"If his lordship will see him."

"Oh, he's beyond his time," his lordship pronounced—"I can't see him now!"

"Ah, but *mustn't* you—and mayn't *I* then?" She waited, however, for no response to signify to her servant "Let him come," and her companion could but exhale a groan of reluctant accommodation as if he wondered at the point she made of it. It enlightened him indeed perhaps a little that she went on while Gotch did her bidding. "Does the kind of relation you'd be condemned to with Mr. Crimble let you down, down, down, as you say, more than the relation you've been having with Mr. Bender?"

Lord Theign had for it the most uninforming of stares. "Do you mean don't I hate 'em equally both?"

She cut his further reply short, however, by a "Hush!" of warning—Mr. Bender was there and his introducer had left them.

Lord Theign, full of his purpose of departure, sacrificed thereupon little to ceremony. "I've had a moment, to my regret, to give you, Mr. Bender, and if you've been unavoidably detained, as you great bustling people are so apt to be, it will perhaps still be soon enough for your comfort to hear from me that I've just given order to close our exhibition. From the present hour on, sir"—he put it with the firmness required to settle the futility of an appeal.

Mr. Bender's large surprise lost itself, however, promptly enough, in Mr. Bender's larger ease. "Why, do you really mean it, Lord Theign?—removing already from view a work that gives innocent gratification to thousands?"

"Well," said his lordship curtly, "if thousands have seen it I've done what I wanted, and if they've been gratified I'm content—and invite *you* to be."

Mr. Bender showed more keenness for this richer implication. "In other words it's I who may remove the picture?"

"Well—if you'll take it on my estimate."

"But what, Lord Theign, all this time," Mr. Bender almost pathetically pleaded, "*is* your estimate?"

The parting guest had another pause, which prolonged itself, after he had reached the door, in a deep solicitation of their hostess's conscious eyes. This brief passage apparently inspired his answer. "Lady Sandgate will tell you." The door closed behind him.

The charming woman smiled then at her other friend, whose comprehensive presence appeared now to demand of her some account of these strange proceedings. "He means that your own valuation is much too shockingly high."

"But how can I know *how* much unless I find out what he'll take?" The great collector's spirit had, in spite of its volume, clearly not reached its limit of expansion. "Is he crazily waiting for the thing to be proved *not* what Mr. Crimble claims?"

"No, he's waiting for nothing—since he holds that claim demolished by Pappendick's tremendous negative, which you wrote to tell him of."

Vast, undeveloped and suddenly grave, Mr. Bender's countenance showed like a barren tract under a black cloud. "I wrote to *report*, fair and square, on Pap-pendick, but to tell him I'd take the picture just the same, negative and all."

"Ah, but take it in that way not for what it is but for what it isn't."

"We know nothing about what it 'isn't,'" said Mr. Bender, "after all that has happened—we've only learned a little better every day what it is."

"You mean," his companion asked, "the biggest bone of artistic contention——?"

"Yes,"—he took it from her—"the biggest that has been thrown into the arena for quite a while. I guess I can do with it for *that*."

Lady Sandgate, on this, after a moment, renewed her personal advance; it was as if she had now made sure of the soundness of her main bridge. "Well, if it's the biggest bone I won't touch it; I'll leave it to be mauled by my betters. But since his lordship has asked me to name a price, dear Mr. Bender, I'll name one—and as you prefer big prices I'll try to make it suit you. Only it won't be for the portrait of a person nobody is agreed about. The whole world is agreed, you know, about my great-grandmother."

"Oh, shucks, Lady Sandgate!"—and her visitor turned from her with the hunch of overcharged shoulders.

But she apparently felt that she held him, or at least that even if such a conviction might be fatuous she must now put it to the touch.

"You've been delivered into my hands—too charmingly; and you won't really pretend that you don't recognise that and in fact rather like it."

He faced about to her again as to a case of coolness unparalleled—though indeed with a quick lapse of real interest in the question of whether he had been artfully practised upon; an indifference to bad debts or peculation like that of some huge hotel or other business involving a margin for waste. He could afford, he could work waste too, clearly—and what was it, that term, you might have felt him ask, but a mean measure, anyway? quite as the "artful," opposed to his larger game, would be the hiding and pouncing of children at play. "Do I gather that those uncanny words of his were just meant to put me off?" he inquired. And then as she but boldly and smilingly shrugged, repudiating responsibility, "Look here, Lady Sandgate, ain't you honestly going to help me?" he pursued.

This engaged her sincerity without affecting her gaiety. "Mr. Bender, Mr. Bender, I'll help you if you'll help *me!*"

"You'll really get me something from him to go on with?"

"I'll get you something from him to go on with."

"That's all I ask—to get *that*. Then I can move the way I want. But without it I'm held up."

"You shall have it," she replied, "if I in turn may look to *you* for a trifle on account."

"Well," he dryly gloomed at her, "what do you call a trifle?"

"I mean"—she waited but an instant—"what you would feel as one."

"That won't do. You haven't the least idea, Lady Sandgate," he earnestly said, "*how* I feel at these foolish times. I've never got used to them yet."

"Ah, don't you understand," she pressed, "that if I give you an advantage I'm completely at your mercy?"

"Well, what mercy," he groaned, "do you deserve?"

She waited a little, brightly composed—then she indicated her inner shrine, the whereabouts of her precious picture. "Go and look at her again and you'll see."

His protest was large, but so, after a moment, was his compliance—his heavy advance upon the other room, from just within the doorway of which the great Lawrence was serenely visible. Mr. Bender gave it his eyes once more—though after the fashion verily of a man for whom it had now no freshness of a glamour, no shade of a secret; then he came back to his hostess. "Do you call giving me an advantage squeezing me by your sweet modesty for less than I may possibly bear?"

"How can I say fairer," she returned, "than that, with my backing about the other picture, which I've passed you my word for, thrown in, I'll resign myself to whatever you may be disposed—characteristically!—to give for this one."

"If it's a question of resignation," said Mr. Bender, "you mean of course what I may be disposed—characteristically!—*not* to give."

She played on him for an instant all her radiance. "Yes then, you dear sharp rich thing!"

"And you take in, I assume," he pursued, "that I'm just going to lean on you, for what I want, with the full weight of a determined man."

"Well," she laughed, "I promise you I'll thoroughly obey the direction of your pressure."

"All right then!" And he stopped before her, in his unrest, monumentally pledged, yet still more massively immeasurable. "How'll you have it?"

She bristled as with all the possible beautiful choices; then she shed her selection as a heaving fruit-tree might have dropped some round ripeness. It was for her friend to pick up his plum and his privilege. "Will you write a cheque?"

"Yes, if you want it right away." To which, however, he added, clapping vainly a breast-pocket: "But my cheque-book's down in my car."

"At the door?" She scarce required his assent to touch a bell. "I can easily send for it." And she threw off while they waited: "It's so sweet your 'flying round' with your cheque-book!"

He put it with promptitude another way. "It flies round pretty well with *Mr*——!"

"Mr. Bender's cheque-book—in his car," she went on to Gotch, who had answered her summons.

The owner of the interesting object further instructed him: "You'll find in the pocket a large red morocco case."

"Very good, sir," said Gotch—but with another word for his mistress. "Lord John would like to know—"

"Lord John's there?" she interrupted.

Gotch turned to the open door. "Here he is, my lady."

She accommodated herself at once, under Mr. Bender's eye, to the complication involved in his lordship's presence. "It's he who went round to Bond Street."

Mr. Bender stared, but saw the connection. "To stop the show?" And then as the young man was already there: "You've stopped the show?"

"It's 'on' more than ever!" Lord John responded while Gotch retired: a hurried, flurried, breathless Lord John, strikingly different from the backward messenger she had lately seen despatched. "But Theign should be here!"—he addressed her excitedly. "I announce you a call from the Prince."

"The Prince?"—she gasped as for the burden of the honour. "He follows you?"

Mr. Bender, with an eagerness and a candour there was no mistaking, recognised on behalf of his ampler action a world of associational advantage and auspicious possibility. "Is the Prince *after* the thing?"

Lord John remained, in spite of this challenge, conscious of nothing but his message. "He was there with Mackintosh—to see and admire the picture; which he thinks, by the way, a Mantovano pure and simple!—and did me the honour to remember me. When he heard me report to Mackintosh in his presence the sentiments expressed to me here by our noble friend and of which, embarrassed though I doubtless was," the young man pursued to Lady Sandgate, "I gave as clear an account as I could, he was so delighted with it that he declared they mustn't think then of taking the thing off, but must on the contrary keep putting it forward for all it's worth, and he would come round and congratulate and thank Theign and explain him his reasons."

Their hostess cast about for a sign. "Why Theign is at Kitty's, worse luck! The Prince calls on him *here?*"

"He calls, you see, on *you,* my lady—at five-forty-five; and graciously desired me so to put it you."

"He's very kind, but"—she took in her condition—"I'm not even *dressed!*"

"You'll have time"—the young man was a comfort—"while I rush to Berkeley Square. And pardon me, Bender—though it's so near—if I just bag your car."

"That's, that's it, take his car!"—Lady Sandgate almost swept him away.

"You may use my car all right," Mr. Bender contributed—"but what I want to know is what the man's *after*."

"The man? what man?" his friend scarce paused to ask.

"The Prince then—if you allow he *is* a man! Is he after my picture?"

Lord John vividly disclaimed authority. "If you'll wait, my dear fellow, you'll see."

"Oh why should he 'wait'?" burst from their cautious companion—only to be caught up, however, in the next breath, so swift her gracious revolution. "Wait, wait indeed, Mr. Bender—I won't give you up for any Prince!" With which she appealed again to Lord John. "He wants to 'congratulate'?"

"On Theign's decision, as I've told you—which I announced to Mackintosh, by Theign's extraordinary order, under his Highness's nose, and which his Highness, by the same token, took up like a shot."

Her face, as she bethought herself, was convulsed as by some quick perception of what her informant must have done and what therefore the Prince's interest rested on; all, however, to the effect, given their actual company, of her at once dodging and covering that issue. "The decision to remove the picture?"

Lord John also observed a discretion. "He wouldn't hear of such a thing—says it must stay stock still. So there you are!"

This determined in Mr. Bender a not unnatural, in fact quite a clamorous, series of questions. "But *where* are we, and what has the Prince to do with Lord Theign's decision when that's all *I'm* here for? What in thunder *is* Lord Theign's decision—what was his 'extraordinary order'?"

Lord John, too long detained and his hand now on the door, put off this solicitor as he had already been put off. "Lady Sandgate, *you* tell him! I rush!"

Mr. Bender saw him vanish, but all to a greater bewilderment. "What the h—— then (I beg your pardon!) is he talking about, and what 'sentiments' did he report round there that Lord Theign had been expressing?"

His hostess faced it not otherwise than if she had resolved not to recognise the subject of his curiosity—for fear of other recognitions. "They put everything on *me*, my dear man—but I haven't the least idea."

He looked at her askance. "Then why does the fellow say you have?"

Much at a loss for the moment, she yet found her way. "Because the fellow's so agog that he doesn't know *what* he says!" In addition to which she was relieved by the reappearance of Gotch, who bore on a salver the object he had been sent for and to which he duly called attention.

"The large red morocco case."

Lady Sandgate fairly jumped at it. "Your blessed cheque-book. Lay it on my desk," she said to Gotch, though waiting till he had departed again before she resumed to her visitor: "Mightn't we conclude before he comes?"

"The Prince?" Mr. Bender's imagination had strayed from the ground to which she sought to lead it back, and it but vaguely retraced its steps. "Will *he* want your great-grandmother?"

"Well, he may when he sees her!" Lady Sandgate laughed. "And Theign, when he comes, will give you on his own question, I feel sure, every information. Shall I fish it out for you?" she encouragingly asked, beside him by her secretary-desk, at which he had arrived under her persuasive guidance and where she sought solidly to establish him, opening out the gilded crimson case for his employ, so that he had but to help himself. "What enormous cheques! *You* can never draw one for two-pound-ten!"

"That's exactly what you deserve I *should* do!" He remained after this solemnly still, however, like some high-priest circled with ceremonies; in consonance with which, the next moment, both her hands held out to him the open and immaculate page of the oblong series much as they might have presented a royal infant at the christening-font.

He failed, in his preoccupation, to receive it; so she placed it before him on the table, coming away with a brave gay "Well, I leave it to you!" She had not, restlessly revolving, kept her discreet distance for many minutes before she found herself almost face to face with the recurrent Gotch, upright at the door with a fresh announcement.

"Mr. Crimble, please—for Lady Grace."

"Mr. Crimble *again*?"—she took it discomposedly.

It reached Mr. Bender at the secretary, but to a different effect. "Mr. Crimble? Why he's just the man I want to see!"

Gotch, turning to the lobby, had only to make way for him. "Here he is, my lady."

"Then tell her ladyship."

"She has come down," said Gotch while Hugh arrived and his companion withdrew, and while Lady Grace, reaching the scene from the other quarter, emerged in bright equipment—in her hat, scarf and gloves.

IV

Zephyr by Rinaldo Mantovano (active 1527-1539)

These young persons were thus at once confronted across the room, and the girl explained her preparation. "I was listening hard—for your knock and your voice."

"Then know that, thank God, it's all right!"—Hugh was breathless, jubilant, radiant.

"A Mantovano?" she delightedly cried.

"A Mantovano!" he proudly gave back.

"A Mantovano!"—it carried even Lady Sandgate away.

"A Mantovano—a sure thing?" Mr. Bender jumped up from his business, all gaping attention to Hugh.

"I've just left our blest Bardi," said that young man—"who hasn't the shadow of a doubt and is delighted to publish it everywhere."

"Will he publish it right here to *me?*" Mr. Bender hungrily asked.

"Well," Hugh smiled, "you can try him."

"But try him how, where?" The great collector, straining to instant action, cast about for his hat "Where *is* he, hey?"

"Don't you wish I'd tell you?" Hugh, in his personal elation, almost cynically answered.

"Won't you wait for the Prince?" Lady Sandgate had meanwhile asked of her friend; but had turned more inspectingly to Lady Grace before he could reply. "My dear child—though you're lovely!—are you sure you're ready for him?"

"For the Prince!"—the girl was vague. "Is he coming?"

"At five-forty-five." With which she consulted her bracelet watch, but only at once to wail for alarm. "Ah, it *is* that, and I'm not dressed!" She hurried off through the other room.

Mr. Bender, quite accepting her retreat, addressed himself again unabashed to Hugh: "It's your blest Bardi I want first—I'll take the Prince after."

The young man clearly could afford indulgence now. "Then I left him at Long's Hotel."

"Why, right near! I'll come back." And Mr. Bender's flight was on the wings of optimism.

But it all gave Hugh a quick question for Lady Grace. "Why does the Prince come, and what in the world's happening?"

"My father has suddenly returned—it may have to do with that."

The shadow of his surprise darkened visibly to that of his fear. "Mayn't it be more than anything else to give you and me his final curse?"

"I don't know—and I think I don't care. I don't care," she said, "so long as you're right and as the greatest light of all declares you are."

"He *is* the greatest"—Hugh was vividly of that opinion now: "I could see it as soon as I got there with him, the charming creature! There, *before*the holy thing, and with the place, by good luck, for those great moments, practically to ourselves—without Macintosh to take in what was happening or any one else at all to speak of—it was but a matter of ten minutes: he had come, he had seen, and *I* had conquered."

"Naturally you had!"—the girl hung on him for it; "and what was happening beyond everything else was that for your original dear divination, one of the divinations of genius—with every creature all these ages so stupid—you were being baptized on the spot a great man."

"Well, he did let poor Pappendick have it at least-he doesn't think *he's* one: that that eminent judge couldn't, even with such a leg up, rise to my level or seize my point. And if you really want to know," Hugh went on in his gladness, "what for *us* has most particularly and preciously taken place, it is that in his opinion, for my career—"

"Your reputation," she cried, "blazes out and your fortune's made?"

He did a happy violence to his modesty. "Well, Bardi adores intelligence and takes off his hat to me."

"Then you need take off yours to nobody!"—such was Lady Grace's proud opinion. "But I should like to take off mine to *him*," she added; "which I seem to have put on—to get out and away with you—expressly for that."

Hugh, as he looked her over, took it up in bliss. "Ah, we'll go forth together to him then—thanks to your happy, splendid impulse!—and you'll back him gorgeously up in the good he thinks of me."

His friend yet had on this a sombre second thought. "The only thing is that our awful American——!"

But he warned her with a raised hand. "Not to speak of our awful Briton!"

For the door had opened from the lobby, admitting Lord Theign, unattended, who, at sight of his daughter and her companion, pulled up and held them a minute in reprehensive view—all at least till Hugh undauntedly, indeed quite cheerfully, greeted him.

"Since you find me again in your path, my lord, it's because I've a small, but precious document to deliver you, if you'll allow me to do so; which I feel it important myself to place in your hand." He drew from his breast a pocket-book and extracted thence a small unsealed envelope; retaining the latter a trifle helplessly in his hand while Lord Theign only opposed to this demonstration an unmitigated blankness. He went none the less bravely on. "I mentioned to you the last time we somewhat infelicitously met that I intended to appeal to another and probably more closely qualified artistic authority on the subject of your so-called Moretto; and I in fact saw the picture half an hour ago with Bardi of Milan, who, there in presence of it, did absolute, did ideal justice, as I had hoped, to the claim I've been making. I then went with him to his hotel, close at hand, where he dashed me off this brief and rapid, but quite conclusive, Declaration, which, if you'll be so good as to read it, will enable you perhaps to join us in regarding the vexed question as settled."

His lordship, having faced this speech without a sign, rested on the speaker a somewhat more confessed intelligence, then looked hard at the offered note and hard at the floor—all to avert himself actively afterward and, with his head a good deal elevated, add to his distance, as it were, from every one and everything so indelicately thrust on his attention. This movement had an ambiguous makeshift air, yet his companions, under the impression of it, exchanged a hopeless look. His daughter none the less lifted her voice. "If you won't take what he has for you from Mr. Crimble, father, will you take it from me?" And then as after some apparent debate he appeared to decide to heed her, "It may be so long again," she said, "before you've a chance to do a thing I ask."

"The chance will depend on yourself!" he returned with high dry emphasis. But he held out his hand for the note Hugh had given her and with which she approached him; and though face to face they seemed more separated than brought near by this contact without commerce. She turned away on one side when he had taken the missive, as Hugh had turned away on the other; Lord Theign drew forth the contents of the envelope and broodingly and inexpressively read the few lines; after which, as having done justice to their sense, he thrust the paper forth again till his daughter became aware and received it. He restored it to her friend while her father dandled off anew, but coming round this time, almost as by a circuit of the room, and meeting Hugh, who took advantage of it to repeat by a frank gesture his offer of Bardi's attestation. Lord Theign passed with the young man on this a couple of mute minutes of the same order as those he had passed with Lady Grace in the same connection; their eyes dealt deeply with their eyes—but to the effect of his lordship's accepting the gift, which after another minute he had slipped into his breast-pocket. It was not till then that he brought out a curt but resonant "Thank you!" While the others awaited his further pleasure he again bethought himself—then he addressed Lady Grace. "I must let Mr. Bender know——"

"Mr. Bender," Hugh interposed, "does know. He's at the present moment with the author of that note at Long's Hotel."

"Then I must now write him"—and his lordship, while he spoke and from where he stood, looked in refined disconnectedness out of the window.

"Will you write *there?*"—and his daughter indicated Lady Sandgate's desk, at which we have seen Mr. Bender so importantly seated.

Lord Theign had a start at her again speaking to him; but he bent his view on the convenience awaiting him and then, as to have done with so tiresome a matter, took advantage of it. He went and placed himself, and had reached for paper and a pen when, struck apparently with the display of some incongruous object, he uttered a sharp "Hallo!"

"You don't find things?" Lady Grace asked—as remote from him in one quarter of the room as Hugh was in another.

"On the contrary!" he oddly replied. But plainly suppressing any further surprise he committed a few words to paper and put them into an envelope, which he addressed and brought away.

"If you like," said Hugh urbanely, "I'll carry him that myself."

"But how do you know what it consists of?"

"I don't know. But I risk it."

His lordship weighed the proposition in a high impersonal manner—he even nervously weighed his letter, shaking it with one hand upon the finger-tips of the other; after which, as finally to acquit himself of any measurable obligation, he allowed Hugh, by a surrender of the interesting object, to redeem his offer of service. "Then you'll learn," he simply said.

"And may *I* learn?" asked Lady Grace.

"You?" The tone made so light of her that it was barely interrogative.

"May I go *with* him?"

Her father looked at the question as at some cup of supreme bitterness—a nasty and now quite regular dose with which his lips were familiar, but before which their first movement was always tightly to close. "*With* me, my lord," said Hugh at last, thoroughly determined they should open and intensifying the emphasis.

He had his effect, and Lord Theign's answer, addressed to Lady Grace, made indifference very comprehensive. "You may do what ever you dreadfully like!"

At this then the girl, with an air that seemed to present her choice as absolutely taken, reached the door which Hugh had come across to open for her.

Here she paused as for another, a last look at her father, and her expression seemed to say to him unaidedly that, much as she would have preferred to proceed to her act without this gross disorder, she could yet find inspiration too in the very difficulty and the old faiths themselves that he left her to struggle with. All this made for depth and beauty in her serious young face—as it had indeed a force that, not indistinguishably, after an instant, his lordship lost any wish for longer exposure to. His shift of his attitude before she went out was fairly an evasion; if the extent of the levity of one of his daughter's made him afraid, what might have been his present strange sense but a fear of the other from the extent of her gravity? Lady Grace passes from us at any rate in her laced and pearled and plumed slimness and her pale concentration—

leaving her friend a moment, however, with his hand on the door.

"You thanked me just now for Bardi's opinion after all," Hugh said with a smile; "and it seems to me that—after all as well—I've grounds for thanking you!" On which he left his benefactor alone.

"Tit for tat!" There broke from Lord Theign, in his solitude, with the young man out of earshot, that vague ironic comment; which only served his turn, none the less, till, bethinking himself, he had gone back to the piece of furniture used for his late scribble and come away from it again the next minute delicately holding a fair slip that we naturally recognise as Mr. Bender's forgotten cheque. This apparently surprising value he now studied at his ease and to the point of its even drawing from him an articulate "What in damnation—?" His speculation dropped before the return of his hostess, whose approach through the other room fell upon his ear and whom he awaited after a quick thrust of the cheque into his waistcoat.

Lady Sandgate appeared now in due—that is in the most happily adjusted—splendour; she had changed her dress for something smarter and more appropriate to the entertainment of Princes, "Tea will be downstairs," she said. "But you're alone?"

"I've just parted," her friend replied, "with Grace and Mr. Crimble."

"'Parted' with them?"—the ambiguity struck her.

"Well, they've gone out together to flaunt their monstrous connection!"

"You speak," she laughed, "as if it were too gross—I They're surely coming back?"

"Back to you, if you like—but not to me."

"Ah, what are you and I," she tenderly argued, "but one and the same quantity? And though you may not as yet absolutely rejoice in—well, whatever they're doing," she cheerfully added, "you'll get beautifully used to it."

"That's just what I'm afraid of—what such horrid matters make of one!"

"At the worst then, you see"—she maintained her optimism—"the recipient of royal attentions!"

"Oh," said her companion, whom his honour seemed to leave comparatively cold, "it's simply as if the gracious Personage were coming to condole!"

Impatient of the lapse of time, in any case, she assured herself again of the hour. "Well, if he only does come!"

"John—the wretch!" Lord Theign returned—"will take care of that: he has nailed him and will bring him."

"What was it then," his friend found occasion in the particular tone of this reference to demand, "what was it that, when you sent him off, John spoke of you in Bond Street as specifically intending?"

Oh he saw it now all lucidly—if not rather luridly—and thereby the more tragically. "He described me in his nasty rage as consistently—well, heroic!"

"His rage"—she pieced it sympathetically out—"at your destroying his cherished credit with Bender?"

Lord Theign was more and more possessed of this view of the manner of it. "I had come between him and some profit that he doesn't confess to, but that made him viciously and vindictively serve me up there, as he caught the chance, to the Prince—and the People!"

She cast about, in her intimate interest, as for some closer conception of it. "By saying that you had remarked here that you offered the People the picture—?"

"As a sacrifice—yes!—to morbid, though respectable scruples." To which he sharply added, as if struck with her easy grasp of the scene: "But I hope you've nothing to call a memory for any such extravagance?"

Lady Sandgate waited—then boldly took her line. "None whatever! You had reacted against Bender—but you hadn't gone so far as *that!*"

He had it now all vividly before him. "I had reacted—like a gentleman; but it didn't thereby follow that I acted—or spoke—like a demagogue; and my mind's a complete blank on the subject of my having done so."

"So that there only flushes through your conscience," she suggested, "the fact that he has forced your hand?"

Fevered with the sore sense of it his lordship wiped his brow. "He has played me, for spite, his damned impertinent trick!"

She found but after a minute—for it wasn't easy—the right word, or the least wrong, for the situation. "Well, even if he did so diabolically commit you, you still don't want—do you?—to back out?"

Resenting the suggestion, which restored all his nobler form, Lord Theign fairly drew himself up. "When did I ever in all my life back out?"

"Never, never in all your life of course!"—she dashed a bucketful at the flare. "And the picture after all——!"

"The picture after all"—he took her up in cold grim gallant despair—"has just been pronounced definitely priceless." And then to meet her gaping ignorance: "By Mr. Crimble's latest and apparently greatest adviser, who strongly stamps it a Mantovano and whose practical affidavit I now possess."

Poor Lady Sandgate gaped but the more—she wondered and yearned. "Definitely priceless?"

"Definitely priceless." After which he took from its place of lurking, considerably unfolding it, the goodly slip he had removed from her blotting-book. "Worth even more therefore than what Bender so blatantly offers."

Her attention fell with interest, from the distance at which she stood, on this confirmatory document, her recognition of which was not immediate. "And is that the affidavit?"

"This is a cheque to your order, my lady, for ten thousand pounds."

"Ten thousand?"—she echoed it with a shout.

"Drawn by some hand unknown," he went on quietly.

"Unknown?"—again, in her muffled joy, she let it sound out.

"Which I found there at your desk a moment ago, and thought best, in your interest, to rescue from accident or neglect; even though it be, save for the single stroke of a name begun," he wound up with his look like a playing searchlight, "unhappily unsigned."

"Unsigned?"—the exhibition of her design, of her defeat, kept shaking her. "Then it isn't good—?"

"It's a Barmecide feast, my dear!"—he had still, her kind friend, his note of grimness and also his penetration of eye. "But who is it writes you colossal cheques?"

"And then leaves them lying about?" Her case was so bad that you would have seen how she felt she must *do* something—something quite splendid. She recovered herself, she faced the situation with all her bright bravery of expression and aspect; conscious, you might have guessed, that she had never more strikingly embodied, on such lines, the elegant, the beautiful and the true. "Why, who can it have been but poor Breckenridge too?"

"'Breckenridge'—?" Lord Theign had *his* smart echoes. "What in the world does he owe you money for?"

It took her but an instant more—she performed the great repudiation quite as she might be prepared to sweep, in the Presence impending, her grandest curtsey. "*Not,* you sweet suspicious thing, for my great-grandmother!" And then as his glare didn't fade: "Bender makes my life a burden—for the love of my precious Lawrence."

"Which you're weakly letting him grab?"—nothing could have been finer with this than Lord Theign's reprobation unless it had been his surprise.

She shook her head as in bland compassion for such an idea. "It isn't a payment, you goose—it's a bribe! I've withstood him, these trying weeks, as a rock the tempest; but he wrote that and left it there, the fiend, to tempt me—to corrupt me!"

"Without putting his name?"—her companion again turned over the cheque.

She bethought herself, clearly with all her genius, as to this anomaly, and the light of reality broke. "He must have been interrupted in the artful act—he sprang up with such a bound at Mr. Crimble's news. At once then—for his interest in it—he hurried off, leaving the cheque forgotten and unfinished." She smiled more intensely, her eyes attached, as from fascination, to the morsel of paper still handled by her friend. "But of course on his next visit he'll *add* his great signature."

"The devil he will!"—and Lord Theign, with the highest spirit, tore the crisp token into several pieces, which fluttered, as worthless now as pure snowflakes, to the floor.

"Ay, ay, ay!"—it drew from her a wail of which the character, for its sharp inconsequence, was yet comic.

This renewed his stare at her. "Do *you* want to back out? I mean from your noble stand."

As quickly, however, she had saved herself. "I'd rather do even what you're doing—offer my treasure to the Thingumbob!"

He was touched by this even to sympathy. "Will you then *join* me in setting the example of a great donation———?"

"To the What-do-you-call-it?" she extravagantly smiled.

"I call it," he said with dignity, "the 'National Gallery.'"

She closed her eyes as with a failure of breath. "Ah my dear friend—!"

"It would convince me," he went on, insistent and persuasive.

"Of the sincerity of my affection?"—she drew nearer to him.

"It would comfort me"—he was satisfied with his own expression. Yet in a moment, when she had come all rustlingly and fragrantly close, "It would captivate me," he handsomely added.

"It would captivate you?" It was for *her*, we should have seen, to be satisfied with his expression; and, with our more informed observation of all it was a question of her giving up, she would have struck us as subtly bargaining.

He gallantly amplified. "It would peculiarly—by which I mean it would so naturally—unite us!"

Well, that was all she wanted. "Then for a complete union with you—of fact as well as of fond fancy!" she smiled—"there's nothing, even to my one ewe lamb, I'm not ready to surrender."

"Ah, we don't surrender," he urged—"we enjoy!"

"Yes," she understood: "with the glory of our grand gift thrown in."

"We quite swagger," he gravely observed—"though even swaggering would after this be dull without you."

"Oh, I'll *swagger* with you!" she cried as if it quite settled and made up for everything; and then impatiently, as she beheld Lord John, whom the door had burst open to admit: "The Prince?"

"The Prince!"—the young man launched it as a call to arms.

They had fallen apart on the irruption, the pair discovered, but she flashed straight at her lover: "Then we can swagger now!"

Lord Theign had reached the open door. "I meet him below."

Demurring, debating, however, she stayed him a moment. "But oughtn't I—in my own house?"

His lordship caught her meaning. "You mean he may think—?" But he as easily pronounced. "He shall think the Truth!" And with a kiss of his hand to her he was gone.

Lord John, who had gazed in some wonder at these demonstrations, was quickly about to follow, but she checked him with an authority she had never before used and which was clearly the next moment to prove irresistible. "Lord John, be so good as to stop." Looking about at the condition of a room on the point of receiving so august a character, she observed on the floor the fragments of the torn cheque, to which she sharply pointed. "And please pick up that litter!"

The End.